The Works

of

Nathaniel Hawthorne

One Volume Edition

BLACK'S READERS SERVICE

ROSLYN, NEW YORK

Contents

THE SCARLET LETTER

CHAPTER I

THE PRISON-DOOR

A THRONG of bearded men, in sad-colored garments, and gray, steeple-crowned hats, intermixed with women, some wearing hoods, and others bare-headed, was assembled in front of a wooden edifice, the door of which was heavily timbered with oak, and studded with iron spikes.

The founders of a new colony, whatever Utopia of human virtue and happiness they might originally project, have invariably recognized it among their earliest practical necessities to allot a portion of the virgin soil as a cemetery, and another portion as the site of a prison. In accordance with this rule, it may safely be assumed that the forefathers of Boston had built the first prison-house somewhere in the vicinity of Cornhill, almost as seasonably as they marked out the first burial-ground, on Isaac Johnson's lot, and round about his grave, which subsequently became the nucleus of all the congregated sepulchres in the old church-yard of King's Chapel. Certain it is, that, some fifteen or twenty years after the settlement of the town, the wooden jail was already marked with weather-stains and other indications of age, which gave a yet darker aspect to its beetle-browed and gloomy front. The rust on the ponderous iron-work of its oaken door looked more antique

than anything else in the New World. Like all that pertains to crime, it seemed never to have known a youthful era. Before this ugly edifice, and between it and the wheel-track of the street, was a grass-plot, much overgrown with burdock, pig-weed, apple-peru, and such unsightly vegetation, which evidently found something congenial in the soil that had so early borne the black flower of civilized society, a prison. But, on one side of the portal, and rooted almost at the threshold, was a wild rose-bush, covered, in this month of June, with its delicate gems, which might be imagined to offer their fragrance and fragile beauty to the prisoner as he went in, and to the condemned criminal as he came forth to his doom, in token that the deep heart of Nature could pity and be kind to him.

This rose-bush, by a strange chance, has been kept alive in history; but whether it had merely survived out of the stern old wilderness, so long after the fall of the gigantic pines and oaks that originally overshadowed it,—or whether, as there is fair authority for believing, it had sprung up under the footsteps of the sainted Ann Hutchinson, as she entered the prison-door,—we shall not take upon us to determine. Finding it so directly on the threshold of our narrative, which is now about to issue from that inauspicious portal, we could hardly do otherwise than pluck one of its flowers, and present it to the reader. It may serve, let us hope, to symbolize some sweet mor: blossom, that may be found along th track, or relieve the darkening clos of a tale of human frailty and sorrov

CHAPTER II

THE MARKET-PLACE

THE grass-plot before the jail, in Prison-lane, on a certain summer morning, not less than two centuries ago, was occupied by a pretty large number of the inhabitants of Boston; all with their eyes intently fastened on the iron-clamped oaken door. Amongst any other population, or at a later period in the history of New England, the grim rigidity that petrified the bearded physiognomies of these good people would have augured some awful business in hand. It could have betokened nothing short of the anticipated execution of some noted culprit, on whom the sentence of a legal tribunal had but confirmed the verdict of public sentiment. But, in that early severity of the Puritan character, an inference of this kind could not so indubitably be drawn. It might be that a sluggish bond-servant, or an undutiful child, whom his parents had given over to the civil authority, was to be corrected at the whipping-post. It might be, that an Antinomian, a Quaker, or other heterodox religionist, was to be scourged out of the town, or an idle and vagrant Indian, whom the white man's fire-water had made riotous about the streets, was to be driven with stripes into the shadow of the forest. It might be, too, that a

witch, like old Mistress Hibbins, th bitter-tempered widow of the magis trate, was to die upon the gallows. I either case, there was very much th same solemnity of demeanor on th part of the spectators; as befitted people amongst whom religion and la\ were almost identical, and in whos character both were so thoroughly inter fused, that the mildest and the severes acts of public discipline were alike mad venerable and awful. Meagre, indeed and cold, was the sympathy that transgressor might look for, from suc bystanders, at the scaffold. On the othe hand, a penalty which, in our day: would infer a degree of mocking in famy and ridicule, might then be in vested with almost as stern a dignit as the punishment of death itself.

It was a circumstance to be noted on the summer morning when our stor begins its course, that the women, o whom there were several in the crowd appeared to take a peculiar interest i whatever penal infliction might be ex pected to ensue. The age had not s much refinement, that any sense of im propriety restrained the wearers of pe ticoat and farthingale from steppin forth into the public ways, and wedg ing their not unsubstantial persons, i ccasion were, into the throng nearest o the scaffold at an execution. Morally, s well as materially, there was a coarser bre in those wives and maidens of ld English birth and breeding, than in heir fair descendants, separated from 1em by a series of six or seven generations; for, throughout that chain of ncestry, every successive mother has ansmitted to her child a fainter bloom, more delicate and briefer beauty, and slighter physical frame, if not a character of less force and solidity, than er own. The women who were now anding about the prison-door stood ithin less than half a century of the eriod when the man-like Elizabeth had een the not altogether unsuitable representative of the sex. They were her ountrywomen; and the beef and ale f their native land, with a moral diet ot a whit more refined, entered largely to their composition. The bright morng sun, therefore, shone on broad oulders and well-developed busts, and n round and ruddy cheeks, that had pened in the far-off island, and had ardly yet grown paler or thinner in e atmosphere of New England. There as, moreover, a boldness and rotuny of speech among these matrons, most of them seemed to be, that ould startle us at the present day, hether in respect to its purport or its olume of tone.

"Goodwives," said a hard-featured ame of fifty, "I'll tell ye a piece of y mind. It would be greatly for e public behoof, if we women, being mature age and church-members in od repute, should have the handling such malefactresses as this Hester rynne. What think ye, gossips? If e hussy stood up for judgment be-

fore us five, that are now here in a knot together, would she come off with such a sentence as the worshipful magistrates have awarded? Marry, I trow not!"

"People say," said another, "that the Reverend Master Dimmesdale, her godly pastor, takes it very grievously to heart that such a scandal should have come upon his congregation."

"The magistrates are God-fearing gentlemen, but merciful overmuch,— that is a truth," added a third autumnal matron. "At the very least, they should have put the brand of a hot iron on Hester Prynne's forehead. Madam Hester would have winced at that, I warrant me. But she, the naughty baggage,—little will she care what they put upon the bodice of her gown! Why, look you, she may cover it with a brooch, or such like heathenish adornment, and so walk the streets as brave as ever!"

"Ah, but," interposed, more softly, a young wife, holding a child by the hand, "let her cover the mark as she will, the pang of it will be always in her heart."

"What do we talk of marks and brands, whether on the bodice of her gown, or the flesh of her forehead?" cried another female, the ugliest as well as the most pitiless of these self-constituted judges. "This woman has brought shame upon us all, and ought to die. Is there not law for it? Truly there is, both in the Scripture and the statute-book. Then let the magistrates, who have made it of no effect, thank themselves if their own wives and daughters go astray!"

"Mercy on us, goodwife," exclaimed a man in the crowd, "is there no virtue in woman, save what springs from a wholesome fear of the gallows? That is the hardest word yet! Hush, now, gossips! for the lock is turning in the prison door, and here comes Mistress Prynne herself."

The door of the jail being flung open from within, there appeared, in the first place, like a black shadow emerging into sunshine, the grim and grisly presence of the town-beadle, with a sword by his side, and his staff of office in his hand. This personage prefigured and represented in his aspect the whole dismal severity of the Puritanic code of law, which it was his business to administer in its final and closest application to the offender. Stretching forth the official staff in his left hand, he laid his right upon the shoulder of a young woman, whom he thus drew forward; until, on the threshold of the prison-door, she repelled him, by an action marked with natural dignity and force of character, and stepped into the open air, as if by her own free will. She bore in her arms a child, a baby of some three months old, who winked and turned aside its little face from the too vivid light of day; because its existence, heretofore, had brought it acquainted only with the gray twilight of a dungeon, or other darksome apartment of the prison.

When the young woman—the mother of this child—stood fully revealed before the crowd, it seemed to be her first impulse to clasp the infant closely to her bosom; not so much by an impulse of motherly affection, as that she might thereby conceal a certain token, which was wrought or fastened into her dress. In a moment, however, wisely judging that one token of her shame would but poorly serve to hide another, she took the baby on her arm, and, with a burning blush, and yet a haughty smile, and a glance that would not be abashed, looked around at her townspeople and neighbors. On the breast of her gown, in fine red cloth, surrounded with an elaborate embroidery and fantastic flourishes of gold thread, appeared the letter A. It was so artistically done, and with so much fertility and gorgeous luxuriance of fancy, that it had all the effect of a last and fitting decoration to the apparel which she wore; and which was of a splendor in accordance with the taste of the age, but greatly beyond what was allowed by the sumptuary regulations of the colony.

The young woman was tall, with a figure of perfect elegance on a large scale. She had dark and abundant hair, so glossy that it threw off the sunshine with a gleam, and a face which, besides being beautiful from regularity of feature and richness of complexion, had the impressiveness belonging to a marked brow and deep black eyes. She was lady-like, too, after the manner of the feminine gentility of those days; characterized by a certain state and dignity, rather than by the delicate, evanescent, and indescribable grace, which is now recognized as its indication. And never had Hester Prynne appeared more lady-like, in the antique interpretation of the term, than as she issued from the prison. Those who had before known her, and had expected to behold her dimmed and obscured by a disastrous cloud, were astonished, and even startled, to perceive how her beauty shone out, and made a halo of the misfortune and ignominy in which she was

veloped. It may be true, that, to a
nsitive observer, there was something
xquisitely painful in it. Her attire,
hich, indeed, she had wrought for the
ccasion, in prison, and had modelled
uch after her own fancy, seemed to
xpress the attitude of her spirit, the
esperate recklessness of her mood, by
s wild and picturesque peculiarity. But
e point which drew all eyes, and, as
were, transfigured the wearer,—so
at both men and women, who had
en familiarly acquainted with Hester
rynne, were now impressed as if they
held her for the first time,—was that
CARLET LETTER, so fantastically em-
roidered and illuminated upon her
osom. It had the effect of a spell,
king her out of the ordinary relations
ith humanity, and enclosing her in a
here by herself.

"She hath good skill at her needle,
at's certain," remarked one of her fe-
ale spectators; "but did ever a
oman, before this brazen hussy, con-
ive such a way of showing it! Why,
ossips, what is it but to laugh in the
ces of our godly magistrates, and
ake a pride out of what they, worthy
ntlemen, meant for a punishment?"

"It were well," muttered the most
on-visaged of the old dames, "if we
ripped Madam Hester's rich gown off
er dainty shoulders; and as for the
d letter, which she hath stitched so
riously, I'll bestow a rag of mine own
eumatic flannel, to make a fitter one!"

"O, peace, neighbors, peace!" whis-
ered their youngest companion; "do
ot let her hear you! Not a stitch in
at embroidered letter, but she has felt
in her heart."

The grim beadle now made a gesture
ith his staff.

"Make way, good people, make way,
in the King's name!" cried he. "Open
a passage; and, I promise ye, Mistress
Prynne shall be set where man, woman
and child, may have a fair sight of
her brave apparel, from this time till
an hour past meridian. A blessing on
the righteous Colony of the Massachusetts, where iniquity is dragged out into
the sunshine! Come along, Madam
Hester, and show your scarlet letter in
the market-place!"

A lane was forthwith opened through
the crowd of spectators. Preceded by
the beadle, and attended by an irregular
procession of stern-browed men and unkindly visaged women, Hester Prynne
set forth towards the place appointed
for her punishment. A crowd of eager
and curious school-boys, understanding
little of the matter in hand, except that
it gave them a half-holiday, ran before
her progress, turning their heads continually to stare into her face, and at
the winking baby in her arms, and at
the ignominious letter on her breast.
It was no great distance, in those days,
from the prison-door to the market-
place. Measured by the prisoner's experience, however, it might be reckoned
a journey of some length; for, haughty
as her demeanor was, she perchance
underwent an agony from every footstep of those that thronged to see her,
as if her heart had been flung into the
street for them all to spurn and trample
upon. In our nature, however, there is
a provision, alike marvellous and merciful, that the sufferer should never know
the intensity of what he endures by its
present torture, but chiefly by the pang
that rankles after it. With almost a
serene deportment, therefore, Hester
Prynne passed through this portion of

her ordeal, and came to a sort of scaffold, at the western extremity of the market-place. It stood nearly beneath the eaves of Boston's earliest church, and appeared to be a fixture there.

In fact, this scaffold constituted a portion of a penal machine, which now, for two or three generations past, has been merely historical and traditionary among us, but was held, in the old time, to be as effectual an agent, in the promotion of good citizenship, as ever was the guillotine among the terrorists of France. It was, in short, the platform of the pillory; and above it rose the framework of that instrument of discipline, so fashioned as to confine the human head in its tight grasp, and thus hold it up to the public gaze. The very ideal of ignominy was embodied and made manifest in this contrivance of wood and iron. There can be no outrage, methinks, against our common nature,—whatever be the delinquencies of the individual,—no outrage more flagrant than to forbid the culprit to hide his face for shame; as it was the essence of this punishment to do. In Hester Prynne's instance, however, as not unfrequently in other cases, her sentence bore, that she should stand a certain time upon the platform, but without undergoing that gripe about the neck and confinement of the head, the proneness to which was the most devilish characteristic of this ugly engine. Knowing well her part, she ascended a flight of wooden steps, and was thus displayed to the surrounding multitude, at about the height of a man's shoulders above the street.

Had there been a Papist among the crowd of Puritans, he might have seen in this beautiful woman, so picturesque in her attire and mien, and with the infant at her bosom, an object to remind him of the image of Divine Maternity, which so many illustrious painters have vied with one another to represent something which should remind him, indeed, but only by contrast, of that sacred image of sinless motherhood whose infant was to redeem the world. Here, there was the taint of deepest sin in the most sacred quality of human life, working such effect, that the world was only the darker for this woman's beauty, and the more lost for the infant that she had borne.

The scene was not without a mixture of awe, such as must always invest the spectacle of guilt and shame in a fellow-creature, before society shall have grown corrupt enough to smile, instead of shuddering, at it. The witnesses of Hester Prynne's disgrace had not yet passed beyond their simplicity. They were stern enough to look upon her death, had that been the sentence, without a murmur at its severity, but had none of the heartlessness of another social state, which would find only a theme for jest in an exhibition like the present. Even had there been a disposition to turn the matter into ridicule, it must have been repressed and overpowered by the solemn presence of men no less dignified than the Governor, and several of his counsellors, a judge, a general, and the ministers of the town; all of whom sat or stood in a balcony of the meeting-house, looking down upon the platform. When such personages could constitute a part of the spectacle, without risking the majesty or reverence of rank and office, it was safely to be inferred that the infliction of a legal sentence would have a arnest and effectual meaning. Accordingly, the crowd was sombre and grave. The unhappy culprit sustained herself as best a woman might, under the heavy weight of a thousand unrelenting eyes, all fastened upon her, and concentrated at her bosom. It was almost intolerable to be borne. Of an impulsive and passionate nature, she had fortified herself to encounter the stings and venomous stabs of public contumely, wreaking itself in every variety of insult; but there was a quality so much more terrible in the solemn mood of the popular mind, that she longed rather to behold all those rigid countenances contorted with scornful merriment, and herself the object. Had a roar of laughter burst from the multitude,—each man, each woman, each little shrill-voiced child, contributing their individual parts,—Hester Prynne might have repaid them all with a bitter and disdainful smile. But, under the leaden infliction which it was her doom to endure, she felt, at moments, as if she must needs shriek out with the full power of her lungs, and cast herself from the scaffold down upon the ground, or else go mad at once.

Yet there were intervals when the whole scene, in which she was the most conspicuous object, seemed to vanish from her eyes, or, at least, glimmered indistinctly before them, like a mass of imperfectly shaped and spectral images. Her mind, and especially her memory, was preternaturally active, and kept bringing up other scenes than this roughly hewn street of a little town, on the edge of the Western wilderness; other faces than were lowering upon her from beneath the brims of those steeple-crowned hats. Reminiscences, the most trifling and immaterial, passages of infancy and school-days, sports, childish quarrels, and the little domestic traits of her maiden years, came swarming back upon her, intermingled with recollections of whatever was gravest in her subsequent life; one picture precisely as vivid as another; as if all were of similar importance, or all alike a play. Possibly, it was an instinctive device of her spirit, to relieve itself, by the exhibition of these phantasmagoric forms, from the cruel weight and hardness of the reality.

Be that as it might, the scaffold of the pillory was a point of view that revealed to Hester Prynne the entire track along which she had been treading, since her happy infancy. Standing on that miserable eminence, she saw again her native village, in Old England, and her paternal home; a decayed house of gray stone, with a poverty-stricken aspect, but retaining a half-obliterated shield of arms over the portal, in token of antique gentility. She saw her father's face, with its bald brow, and reverend white beard, that flowed over the old-fashioned Elizabethan ruff; her mother's, too, with the look of heedful and anxious love which it always wore in her remembrance, and which, even since her death, had so often laid the impediment of a gentle remonstrance in her daughter's pathway. She saw her own face, glowing with girlish beauty, and illuminating all the interior of the dusky mirror in which she had been wont to gaze at it. There she beheld another countenance, of a man well stricken in years, a pale, thin, scholar-like visage, with eyes dim and bleared by the lamp-light that had served them to pore over many ponderous books. Yet those same bleared optics had a strange, penetrating power, when it was their owner's purpose to read the human soul. This figure of the study and the cloister, as Hester Prynne's womanly fancy failed not to recall, was slightly deformed, with the left shoulder a trifle higher than the right. Next rose before her, in memory's picture-gallery, the intricate and narrow thoroughfares, the tall, gray houses, the huge cathedrals, and the public edifices, ancient in date and quaint in architecture, of a Continental city; where a new life had awaited her, still in connection with the misshapen scholar; a new life, but feeding itself on time-worn materials, like a tuft of green moss on a crumbling wall. Lastly, in lieu of these shifting scenes, came back the rude marke place of the Puritan settlement, wit all the townspeople assembled an levelling their stern regards at Heste Prynne,—yes, at herself,—who stoo on the scaffold of the pillory, an infar on her arm, and the letter A, in scarle fantastically embroidered with gol thread, upon her bosom!

Could it be true? She clutched th child so fiercely to her breast, that sent forth a cry; she turned her eye downward at the scarlet letter, and eve touched it with her finger, to assur herself that the infant and the sham were real. Yes!—these were her real ties,—all else had vanished!

CHAPTER III

THE RECOGNITION

FROM this intense consciousness of being the object of severe and universal observation, the wearer of the scarlet letter was at length relieved, by discerning, on the outskirts of the crowd, a figure which irresistibly took possession of her thoughts. An Indian, in his native garb, was standing there; but the red men were not so infrequent visitors of the English settlements, that one of them would have attracted any notice from Hester Prynne, at such a time; much less would he have excluded all other objects and ideas from her mind. By the Indian's side, and evidently sustaining a companionship with him, stood a white man, clad in a strange disarray of civilized and savage costume.

He was small in stature, with a fur rowed visage, which, as yet, coul hardly be termed aged. There was remarkable intelligence in his feature as of a person who had so cultivate his mental part that it could not fail t mould the physical to itself, and be come manifest by unmistakable token. Although, by a seemingly careless ar rangement of his heterogeneous garb he had endeavored to conceal or abat the peculiarity, it was sufficiently evi dent to Hester Prynne, that one of thi man's shoulders rose higher than th other. Again, at the first instant of per ceiving that thin visage, and the sligh deformity of the figure, she pressed he nfant to her bosom, with so convulsive a force that the poor babe uttered another cry of pain. But the mother did not seem to hear it.

At his arrival in the market-place, and some time before she saw him, the stranger had bent his eyes on Hester Prynne. It was carelessly, at first, like a man chiefly accustomed to look inward, and to whom external matters are of little value and import, unless they bear relation to something within his mind. Very soon, however, his look became keen and penetrative. A writhing horror twisted itself across his features, like a snake gliding swiftly over them, and making one little pause, with all its wreathed intervolutions in open sight. His face darkened with some powerful emotion, which, nevertheless, he so instantaneously controlled by an effort of his will, that, save at a single moment, its expression might have passed for calmness. After a brief space, the convulsion grew almost imperceptible, and finally subsided into the depths of his nature. When he found the eyes of Hester Prynne fastened on his own, and saw that she appeared to recognize him, he slowly and calmly raised his finger, made a gesture with it in the air, and laid it on his lips.

Then, touching the shoulder of a townsman who stood next to him, he addressed him, in a formal and courteous manner.

"I pray you, good Sir," said he, "who is this woman?—and wherefore is she here set up to public shame?"

"You must needs be a stranger in this region, friend," answered the townsman, looking curiously at the questioner and his savage companion, "else you would surely have heard of Mistress Hester Prynne, and her evil doings. She hath raised a great scandal, I promise you, in godly Master Dimmesdale's church."

"You say truly," replied the other. "I am a stranger, and have been a wanderer, sorely against my will. I have met with grievous mishaps by sea and land, and have been long held in bonds among the heathen-folk, to the southward; and am now brought hither by this Indian, to be redeemed out of my captivity. Will it please you, therefore, to tell me of Hester Prynne's,—have I her name rightly?—of this woman's offences, and what has brought her to yonder scaffold?"

"Truly, friend; and methinks it must gladden your heart, after your troubles and sojourn in the wilderness," said the townsman, "to find yourself, at length, in a land where iniquity is searched out, and punished in the sight of rulers and people; as here in our godly New England. Yonder woman, Sir, you must know, was the wife of a certain learned man, English by birth, but who had long dwelt in Amsterdam, whence, some good time agone, he was minded to cross over and cast in his lot with us of the Massachusetts. To this purpose, he sent his wife before him, remaining himself to look after some necessary affairs. Marry, good Sir, in some two years, or less, that the woman has been a dweller here in Boston, no tidings have come of this learned gentleman, Master Prynne; and his young wife, look you, being left to her own misguidance—"

"Ah!—aha!—I conceive you," said the stranger, with a bitter smile. "So learned a man as you speak of should have learned this too in his books. And who, by your favor, Sir, may be the father of yonder babe—it is some three or four months old, I should judge—which Mistress Prynne is holding in her arms?"

"Of a truth, friend, that matter remaineth a riddle; and the Daniel who shall expound it is yet a-wanting," answered the townsman. "Madam Hester absolutely refuseth to speak, and the magistrates have laid their heads together in vain. Peradventure the guilty one stands looking on at this sad spectacle, unknown of man, and forgetting that God sees him."

"The learned man," observed the stranger, with another smile, "should come himself, to look into the mystery."

"It behooves him well, if he be still in life," responded the townsman. "Now, good Sir, our Massachusetts magistracy, bethinking themselves that this woman is youthful and fair, and doubtless was strongly tempted to her fall;—and that, moreover, as is most likely, her husband may be at the bottom of the sea;—they have not been bold to put in force the extremity of our righteous law against her. The penalty thereof is death. But in their great mercy and tenderness of heart, they have doomed Mistress Prynne to stand only a space of three hours on the platform of the pillory, and then and thereafter, for the remainder of her natural life, to wear a mark of shame upon her bosom."

"A wise sentence!" remarked the stranger, gravely bowing his head. "Thus she will be a living sermon against sin, until the ignominious letter be engraved upon her tomb-stone. It irks me, nevertheless, that the partner of her iniquity should not, at least,

stand on the scaffold by her side. But he will be known!—he will be known! —he will be known!"

He bowed courteously to the communicative townsman, and, whispering a few words to his Indian attendant, they both made their way through the crowd.

While this passed, Hester Prynne had been standing on her pedestal, still with a fixed gaze towards the stranger; so fixed a gaze, that, at moments of intense absorption, all other objects in the visible world seemed to vanish, leaving only him and her. Such an interview, perhaps, would have been more terrible than even to meet him as she now did, with the hot, midday sun burning down upon her face, and lighting up its shame; with the scarlet token of infamy on her breast; with the sin-born infant in her arms; with a whole people, drawn forth as to a festival, staring at the features that should have been seen only in the quiet gleam of the fireside, in the happy shadow of a home, or beneath a matronly veil, at church. Dreadful as it was, she was conscious of a shelter in the presence of these thousand witnesses. It was better to stand thus, with so many betwixt him and her, than to greet him, face to face, they two alone. She fled for refuge, as it were, to the public exposure, and dreaded the moment when its protection should be withdrawn from her. Involved in these thoughts, she scarcely heard a voice behind her, until it had repeated her name more than once, in a loud and solemn tone, audible to the whole multitude.

"Hearken unto me, Hester Prynne!" said the voice.

It has already been noticed, that di-

ectly over the platform on which Hes-
er Prynne stood was a kind of balcony,
r open gallery, appended to the meet-
ng-house. It was the place whence
proclamations were wont to be made,
midst an assemblage of the magis-
racy, with all the ceremonial that at-
ended such public observances in those
ays. Here, to witness the scene which
ve are describing, sat Governor Bel-
ngham himself, with four sergeants
bout his chair, bearing halberds, as a
uard of honor. He wore a dark feather
1 his hat, a border of embroidery on
is cloak, and a black velvet tunic be-
eath; a gentleman advanced in years,
vith a hard experience written in his
rrinkles. He was not ill fitted to be the
ead and representative of a commu-
ity, which owed its origin and prog-
ess, and its present state of develop-
nent, not to the impulses of youth, but
o the stern and tempered energies of
nanhood, and the sombre sagacity of
ge; accomplishing so much, precisely
ecause it imagined and hoped so little.
The other eminent characters, by whom
ne chief ruler was surrounded, were
istinguished by a dignity of mien, be-
onging to a period when the forms of
uthority were felt to possess the
acredness of Divine institutions. They
vere, doubtless, good men, just, and
age. But, out of the whole human fam-
y, it would not have been easy to
elect the same number of wise and
irtuous persons, who should be less
apable of sitting in judgment on an
rring woman's heart, and disentangling
s mesh of good and evil, than the
ages of rigid aspect towards whom
lester Prynne now turned her face.
he seemed conscious, indeed, that
rhatever sympathy she might expect

lay in the larger and warmer heart of
the multitude; for, as she lifted her
eyes towards the balcony, the unhappy
woman grew pale and trembled.

The voice which had called her attention was that of the reverend and
famous John Wilson, the eldest clergyman of Boston, a great scholar, like
most of his contemporaries in the profession, and withal a man of kind and
genial spirit. This last attribute, however, had been less carefully developed
than his intellectual gifts, and was, in
truth, rather a matter of shame than
self-congratulation with him. There he
stood, with a border of grizzled locks
beneath his skull-cap; while his gray
eyes, accustomed to the shaded light
of his study, were winking, like those
of Hester's infant, in the unadulterated
sunshine. He looked like the darkly engraved portraits which we see prefixed
to old volumes of sermons; and had no
more right than one of those portraits
would have, to step forth, as he now
did, and meddle with a question of
human guilt, passion and anguish.

"Hester Prynne," said the clergyman,
"I have striven with my young brother
here, under whose preaching of the
word you have been privileged to sit,"
—here Mr. Wilson laid his hand on
the shoulder of a pale young man beside him,—"I have sought, I say, to
persuade this godly youth, that he
should deal with you, here in the face
of Heaven, and before these wise and
upright rulers, and in hearing of all the
people, as touching the vileness and
blackness of your sin. Knowing your
natural temper better than I, he could
the better judge what arguments to
use, whether of tenderness or terror,
such as might prevail over your hard-

ness and obstinacy; insomuch that you should no longer hide the name of him who tempted you to this grievous fall. But he opposes to me, (with a young man's over-softness, albeit wise beyond his years,) that it were wronging the very nature of woman to force her to lay open her heart's secrets in such broad daylight, and in presence of so great a multitude. Truly, as I sought to convince him, the shame lay in the commission of the sin, and not in the showing of it forth. What say you to it, once again, brother Dimmesdale? Must it be thou, or I, that shall deal with this poor sinner's soul?"

There was a murmur among the dignified and reverend occupants of the balcony; and Governor Bellingham gave expression to its purport, speaking in an authoritative voice, although tempered with respect towards the youthful clergyman whom he addressed.

"Good Master Dimmesdale," said he, "the responsibility of this woman's soul lies greatly with you. It behooves you, therefore, to exhort her to repentance, and to confession, as a proof and consequence thereof."

The directness of this appeal drew the eyes of the whole crowd upon the Reverend Mr. Dimmesdale; a young clergyman, who had come from one of the great English universities, bringing all the learning of the age into our wild forest-land. His eloquence and religious fervor had already given the earnest of high eminence in his profession. He was a person of very striking aspect, with a white, lofty, and impending brow, large, brown, melancholy eyes, and a mouth which, unless when he forcibly compressed it, was apt to be tremulous, expressing both nervous sensibility and

a vast power of self-restraint. Notwith standing his high native gifts an scholar-like attainments, there was a air about this young minister,—an ap prehensive, a startled, a half-frightene look,—as of a being who felt himsel quite astray and at a loss in the path way of human existence, and could onl be at ease in some seclusion of his own Therefore, so far as his duties woul permit, he trod in the shadowy by-paths and thus kept himself simple and child like; coming forth, when occasion wa with a freshness, and fragrance, an dewy purity of thought, which, as man people said, affected them like th speech of an angel.

Such was the young man whom th Reverend Mr. Wilson and the Gover nor had introduced so openly to th public notice, bidding him speak, in th hearing of all men, to that mystery o a woman's soul, so sacred even in it pollution. The trying nature of his posi tion drove the blood from his cheek and made his lips tremulous.

"Speak to the woman, my brother, said Mr. Wilson. "It is of moment t her soul, and therefore, as the worship ful Governor says, momentous to thin own, in whose charge hers is. Exhort he to confess the truth!"

The Reverend Mr. Dimmesdale ben his head, in silent prayer, as it seemec and then came forward.

"Hester Prynne," said he, leanin over the balcony, and looking dow steadfastly into her eyes, "thou heares what this good man says, and seest th accountability under which I labor. I thou feelest it to be for thy soul's peace and that thy earthly punishment wi thereby be made more effectual to sa vation, I charge thee to speak out th

me of thy fellow-sinner and fellow-
sufferer! Be not silent from any mis-
ken pity and tenderness for him; for,
lieve me, Hester, though he were to
ep down from a high place, and stand
ere beside thee, on thy pedestal of
ame, yet better were it so, than to
de a guilty heart through life. What
n thy silence do for him, except it
mpt him—yea, compel him, as it were
-to add hypocrisy to sin? Heaven hath
anted thee an open ignominy, that
ereby thou mayest work out an open
iumph over the evil within thee, and
e sorrow without. Take heed how thou
eniest to him—who, perchance, hath
ot the courage to grasp it for himself
-the bitter, but wholesome, cup that
now presented to thy lips!"

The young pastor's voice was trem-
ously sweet, rich, deep, and broken.
he feeling that it so evidently mani-
ested, rather than the direct purport
f the words, caused it to vibrate within
ll hearts, and brought the listeners into
ne accord of sympathy. Even the poor
aby, at Hester's bosom, was affected
y the same influence; for it directed
s hitherto vacant gaze towards Mr.
Dimmesdale, and held up its little arms,
ith a half pleased, half plaintive murmur. So powerful seemed the minister's
ppeal, that the people could not be-
eve but that Hester Prynne would
peak out the guilty name; or else that
ne guilty one himself, in whatever high
or lowly place he stood, would be drawn
orth by an inward and inevitable neces-
ty, and compelled to ascend the scaf-
old.

Hester shook her head.

"Woman, transgress not beyond the
mits of Heaven's mercy!" cried the
Reverend Mr. Wilson, more harshly

than before. "That little babe hath been
gifted with a voice, to second and confirm the counsel which thou hast heard.
Speak out the name! That, and thy repentance, may avail to take the scarlet
letter off thy breast."

"Never!" replied Hester Prynne,
looking, not at Mr. Wilson, but into
the deep and troubled eyes of the
younger clergyman. "It is too deeply
branded. Ye cannot take it off. And
would that I might endure his agony,
as well as mine!"

"Speak, woman!" said another voice,
coldly and sternly, proceeding from the
crowd about the scaffold. "Speak; and
give your child a father!"

"I will not speak!" answered Hester,
turning pale as death, but responding to
this voice, which she too surely recognized. "And my child must seek a
heavenly Father; she shall never know
an earthly one!"

"She will not speak!" murmured Mr.
Dimmesdale, who, leaning over the balcony, with his hand upon his heart, had
awaited the result of his appeal. He now
drew back, with a long respiration.
"Wondrous strength and generosity of a
woman's heart! She will not speak!"

Discerning the impracticable state of
the poor culprit's mind, the elder clergyman, who had carefully prepared himself for the occasion, addressed to the
multitude a discourse on sin, in all its
branches, but with continual reference
to the ignominious letter. So forcibly
did he dwell upon this symbol, for the
hour or more during which his periods
were rolling over the people's heads,
that it assumed new terrors in their imagination, and seemed to derive its scarlet hue from the flames of the infernal
pit. Hester Prynne, meanwhile, kept her

place upon the pedestal of shame, with glazed eyes, and an air of weary indifference. She had borne, that morning, all that nature could endure; and as her temperament was not of the order that escapes from too intense suffering by a swoon, her spirit could only shelter itself beneath a stony crust of insensibility, while the faculties of animal life remained entire. In this state, the voice of the preacher thundered remorselessly, but unavailingly, upon her ears. The infant, during the latter po tion of her ordeal, pierced the air wi its wailings and screams; she strove hush it, mechanically, but seeme scarcely to sympathize with its troubl With the same hard demeanor, she w led back to prison, and vanished fro the public gaze within its iron-clampe portal. It was whispered, by those wl peered after her, that the scarlet lett threw a lurid gleam along the dark pa sage-way of the interior.

CHAPTER IV

THE INTERVIEW

AFTER her return to the prison, Hester Prynne was found to be in a state of nervous excitement that demanded constant watchfulness, lest she should perpetrate violence on herself, or do some half-frenzied mischief to the poor babe. As night approached, it proving impossible to quell her insubordination by rebuke or threats of punishment, Master Brackett, the jailer, thought fit to introduce a physician. He described him as a man of skill in all Christian modes of physical science, and likewise familiar with whatever the savage people could teach, in respect to medicinal herbs and roots that grew in the forest. To say the truth, there was much need of professional assistance, not merely for Hester herself, but still more urgently for the child; who, drawing its sustenance from the maternal bosom, seemed to have drank in with it all the turmoil, the anguish and despair, which pervaded the mother's system. It now writhed in convulsions of pain, and wa a forcible type, in its little frame, the moral agony which Hester Prynr had borne throughout the day.

Closely following the jailer into th dismal apartment, appeared that ind vidual, of singular aspect, whose pre ence in the crowd had been of such dee interest to the wearer of the scarlet le ter. He was lodged in the prison, not a suspected of any offence, but as th most convenient and suitable mode c disposing of him, until the magistrate should have conferred with the India sagamores respecting his ransom. H name was announced as Roger Chilling worth. The jailer, after ushering hi into the room, remained a momen marvelling at the comparative quiet tha followed his entrance; for Heste Prynne had immediately become as sti as death, although the child continue to moan.

"Prithee, friend, leave me alone wit

y patient," said the practitioner.
Trust me, good jailer, you shall briefly
ave peace in your house; and, I prom-
e you, Mistress Prynne shall hereafter
e more amenable to just authority than
ou may have found her heretofore."

"Nay, if your worship can accom-
ish that," answered Master Brackett,
I shall own you for a man of skill ined! Verily, the woman hath been like
possessed one; and there lacks little,
at I should take in hand to drive
atan out of her with stripes."

The stranger had entered the room
ith the characteristic quietude of the
rofession to which he announced him-
lf as belonging. Nor did his demeanor
ange, when the withdrawal of the
rison-keeper left him face to face with
he woman, whose absorbed notice of
m, in the crowd, had intimated so
ose a relation between himself and
er. His first care was given to the
aild; whose cries, indeed, as she lay
rithing on the trundle-bed, made it of
eremptory necessity to postpone all
her business to the task of soothing
er. He examined the infant carefully,
d then proceeded to unclasp a leathern
ase, which he took from beneath his
ess. It appeared to contain medical
reparations, one of which he mingled
ith a cup of water.

"My old studies in alchemy," ob-
erved he, "and my sojourn, for above
year past, among a people well versed
the kindly properties of simples, have
ade a better physician of me than
any that claim the medical degree.
Iere, woman! The child is yours,—
he is none of mine,—neither will she
ecognize my voice or aspect as a
ather's. Administer this draught, there-
ore, with thine own hand."

Hester repelled the offered medicine,
at the same time gazing with strongly
marked apprehension into his face.

"Wouldst thou avenge thyself on the
innocent babe?" whispered she.

"Foolish woman!" responded the
physician, half coldly, half soothingly.
"What should ail me, to harm this mis-
begotten and miserable babe? The
medicine is potent for good; and were
it my child,—yea, mine own, as well
as thine!—I could do no better for it."

As she still hesitated, being, in fact,
in no reasonable state of mind, he took
the infant in his arms, and himself administered the draught. It soon proved
its efficacy, and redeemed the leech's
pledge. The moans of the little patient
subsided; its convulsive tossings gradually ceased; and, in a few moments,
as is the custom of young children after
relief from pain, it sank into a profound and dewy slumber. The physician, as he had a fair right to be termed,
next bestowed his attention on the
mother. With calm and intent scrutiny,
he felt her pulse, looked into her eyes,
—a gaze that made her heart shrink
and shudder, because so familiar, and
yet so strange and cold, and, finally,
satisfied with his investigation, proceeded to mingle another draught.

"I know not Lethe nor Nepenthe,"
remarked he; "but I have learned many
new secrets in the wilderness, and here
is one of them,—a recipe that an Indian
taught me, in requital of some lessons
of my own, that were as old as Para-
celsus. Drink it! It may be less soothing
than a sinless conscience. That I cannot
give thee. But it will calm the swell and
heaving of thy passion, like oil thrown
on the waves of a tempestuous sea."

He presented the cup to Hester, who

received it with a slow, earnest look into his face; not precisely a look of fear, yet full of doubt and questioning, as to what his purposes might be. She looked also at her slumbering child.

"I have thought of death," said she, —"have wished for it,—would even have prayed for it, were it fit that such as I should pray for anything. Yet, if death be in this cup, I bid thee think again, ere thou beholdest me quaff it. See! It is even now at my lips."

"Drink, then," replied he, still with the same cold composure. "Dost thou know me so little, Hester Prynne? Are my purposes wont to be so shallow? Even if I imagine a scheme of vengeance, what could I do better for my object than to let thee live,—than to give thee medicines against all harm and peril of life,—so that this burning shame may still blaze upon thy bosom?" As he spoke, he laid his long forefinger on the scarlet letter, which forthwith seemed to scorch into Hester's breast, as if it had been red-hot. He noticed her involuntary gesture, and smiled. "Live, therefore, and bear about thy doom with thee, in the eyes of men and women,—in the eyes of him whom thou didst call thy husband,—in the eyes of yonder child! And, that thou mayest live, take off this draught."

Without further expostulation or delay, Hester Prynne drained the cup, and, at the motion of the man of skill, seated herself on the bed where the child was sleeping; while he drew the only chair which the room afforded, and took his own seat beside her. She could not but tremble at these preparations; for she felt that—having now done all that humanity, or principle, or, if so it were, a refined cruelty, impelled him

to do, for the relief of physical suffering—he was next to treat with her as the man whom she had most deeply and irreparably injured.

"Hester," said he, "I ask not wherefore, nor how, thou hast fallen into the pit, or say, rather, thou hast ascended to the pedestal of infamy, on which I found thee. The reason is not far to seek. It was my folly, and thy weakness. I,—a man of thought,—the bookworm of great libraries,—a man already in decay, having given my best years to feed the hungry dream of knowledge —what had I to do with youth and beauty like thine own! Misshapen from my birth-hour, how could I delude myself with the idea that intellectual gifts might veil physical deformity in a young girl's fantasy! Men call me wise. If sages were ever wise in their own behoof, I might have foreseen all this. I might have known that, as I came out of the vast and dismal forest, and entered this settlement of Christian men, the very first object to meet my eyes would be thyself, Hester Prynne, standing up, a statue of ignominy, before the people. Nay, from the moment when we came down the old church steps together, a married pair, I might have beheld the bale-fire of that scarlet letter blazing at the end of our path!"

"Thou knowest," said Hester,—for, depressed as she was, she could not endure this last quiet stab at the token of her shame,—"thou knowest that I was frank with thee. I felt no love, nor feigned any."

"True," replied he. "It was my folly, I have said it. But, up to that epoch of my life, I had lived in vain. The world had been so cheerless! My heart was a habitation large enough for many guests,

ıt lonely and chill, and without a
ousehold fire. I longed to kindle one!
 seemed not so wild a dream,—old as
was, and sombre as I was, and mis-
ıapen as I was,—that the simple bliss,
ɥich is scattered far and wide, for
ɪ mankind to gather up, might yet be
ine. And so, Hester, I drew thee into
y heart, into its innermost chamber,
ɪd sought to warm thee by the warmth
ɥich thy presence made there!"

"I have greatly wronged thee," mur-
ured Hester.

"We have wronged each other," an-
ʋered he. "Mine was the first wrong,
ɥen I betrayed thy budding youth into
false and unnatural relation with my
ɔcay. Therefore, as a man who has
ɔt thought and philosophized in vain,
seek no vengeance, plot no evil against
ɪee. Between thee and me, the scale
ɪngs fairly balanced. But, Hester, the
an lives who has wronged us both!
ɥo is he?"

"Ask me not!" replied Hester Prynne,
ɔking firmly into his face. "That thou
ɪalt never know!"

"Never, sayest thou?" rejoined he,
ith a smile of dark and self-relying
ɪtelligence. "Never know him! Be-
ɛve me, Hester, there are few things,
-whether in the outward world, or, to
certain depth, in the invisible sphere
Ꮜ thought,—few things hidden from
ɪe man who devotes himself earnestly
ɪd unreservedly to the solution of a
ɪystery. Thou mayest cover up thy
ɔcret from the prying multitude. Thou
ɪayest conceal it, too, from the minis-
ɪrs and magistrates, even as thou didst
ɪis day, when they sought to wrench
ɪe name out of thy heart, and give thee
partner on thy pedestal. But, as for
ɛ, I come to the inquest with other

senses than they possess. I shall seek
this man, as I have sought truth in
books; as I have sought gold in alchemy. There is a sympathy that will
make me conscious of him. I shall see
him tremble. I shall feel myself shudder, suddenly and unawares. Sooner or
later, he must needs be mine!"

The eyes of the wrinkled scholar
glowed so intensely upon her, that Hester Prynne clasped her hands over her
heart, dreading lest he should read the
secret there at once.

"Thou wilt not reveal his name? Not
the less he is mine," resumed he, with
a look of confidence, as if destiny were
at one with him. "He bears no letter of
infamy wrought into his garment, as
thou dost; but I shall read it on his
heart. Yet fear not for him! Think not
that I shall interfere with Heaven's
own method of retribution, or, to my
own loss, betray him to the gripe of
human law. Neither do thou imagine
that I shall contrive aught against his
life; no, nor against his fame, if, as I
judge, he be a man of fair repute. Let
him live! Let him hide himself in outward honor, if he may! Not the less he
shall be mine!"

"Thy acts are like mercy," said Hester, bewildered and appalled. "But thy
words interpret thee as a terror!"

"One thing, thou that wast my wife,
I would enjoin upon thee," continued
the scholar. "Thou hast kept the secret
of thy paramour. Keep, likewise, mine!
There are none in this land that know
me. Breathe not, to any human soul,
that thou didst ever call me husband!
Here, on this wild outskirt of the earth,
I shall pitch my tent; for, elsewhere a
wanderer, and isolated from human interests, I find here a woman, a man,

a child, amongst whom and myself there exist the closest ligaments. No matter whether of love or hate; no matter whether of right or wrong! Thou and thine, Hester Prynne, belong to me. My home is where thou art, and where he is. But betray me not!"

"Wherefore dost thou desire it?" inquired Hester, shrinking, she hardly knew why, from this secret bond. "Why not announce thyself openly, and cast me off at once?"

"It may be," he replied, "because I will not encounter the dishonor that besmirches the husband of a faithless woman. It may be for other reasons. Enough, it is my purpose to live and die unknown. Let, therefore, thy husband be to the world as one already dead, and of whom no tidings shall ever come. Recognize me not, by word, by sign, by look! Breathe not the secret, above all, to the man thou wottest of. Shouldst thou fail me in this, beware!

His fame, his position, his life, will be in my hands. Beware!"

"I will keep thy secret, as I have his," said Hester.

"Swear it!" rejoined he.

And she took the oath.

"And now, Mistress Prynne," said old Roger Chillingworth, as he was her after to be named, "I leave thee alone, alone with thy infant, and the scarlet letter! How is it, Hester? Doth thy sentence bind thee to wear the token thy sleep? Art thou not afraid of night mares and hideous dreams?"

"Why dost thou smile so at me," inquired Hester, troubled at the expression of his eyes. "Art thou like the Black Man that haunts the forest round about us? Hast thou enticed me into a bond that will prove the ruin of my soul?"

"Not thy soul," he answered, with another smile. "No, not thine!"

CHAPTER V

HESTER AT HER NEEDLE

HESTER PRYNNE'S term of confinement was now at an end. Her prison-door was thrown open, and she came forth into the sunshine, which, falling on all alike, seemed, to her sick and morbid heart, as if meant for no other purpose than to reveal the scarlet letter on her breast. Perhaps there was a more real torture in her first unattended footsteps from the threshold of the prison, than even in the procession and spectacle that have been described,

where she was made the common infamy, at which all mankind was summoned to point its finger. Then, she was supported by an unnatural tension of the nerves, and by all the combative energy of her character, which enabled her to convert the scene into a kind of lurid triumph. It was, moreover, a separate and insulated event, to occur but once in her lifetime, and to meet which, therefore, reckless of economy, she might call up the vital strength that

uld have sufficed for many quiet
ars. The very law that condemned her
-a giant of stern features, but with
gor to support, as well as to annihi-
.e, in his iron arm—had held her up,
rough the terrible ordeal of her
nominy. But now, with this unat-
nded walk from her prison-door, be-
n the daily custom; and she must
her sustain and carry it forward by
e ordinary resources of her nature,
sink beneath it. She could no longer
orrow from the future to help her
rough the present grief. To-morrow
ould bring its own trial with it; so
ould the next day, and so would the
ext; each its own trial, and yet the
ery same that was now so unutterably
ievous to be borne. The days of the
r-off future would toil onward, still
ith the same burden for her to take
, and bear along with her, but never
fling down; for the accumulating
ays, and added years, would pile up
eir misery upon the heap of shame.
hroughout them all, giving up her in-
viduality, she would become the gen-
al symbol at which the preacher and
oralist might point, and in which they
ight vivify and embody their images
' woman's frailty and sinful passion.
hus the young and pure would be
ught to look at her, with the scarlet
tter flaming on her breast,—at her,
e child of honorable parents,—at her,
e mother of a babe, that would here-
'ter be a woman,—at her, who had
ace been innocent,—as the figure, the
ody, the reality of sin. And over her
ave, the infamy that she must carry
ither would be her only monument.
It may seem marvellous, that, with
e world before her,—kept by no re-
rictive clause of her condemnation

within the limits of the Puritan settlement, so remote and so obscure,—free
to return to her birth-place, or to any
other European land, and there hide
her character and identity under a new
exterior, as completely as if emerging
into another state of being,—and having also the passes of the dark, inscrutable forest open to her, where the
wildness of her nature might assimilate itself with a people whose customs
and life were alien from the law that
had condemned her,—it may seem marvellous, that this woman should still
call that place her home, where, and
where only, she must needs be the type
of shame. But there is a fatality, a
feeling so irresistible and inevitable that
it has the force of doom, which almost
invariably compels human beings to
linger around and haunt, ghost-like, the
spot where some great and marked
event has given the color to their lifetime; and still the more irresistibly, the
darker the tinge that saddens it. Her
sin, her ignominy, were the roots which
she had struck into the soil. It was as
if a new birth, with stronger assimi-
lations than the first, had converted the
forest-land, still so uncongenial to every
other pilgrim and wanderer, into Hester
Prynne's wild and dreary, but life-long
home. All other scenes of earth—even
that village of rural England, where
happy infancy and stainless maiden-
hood seemed yet to be in her mother's
keeping, like garments put off long ago
—were foreign to her, in comparison.
The chain that bound her here was of
iron links, and galling to her inmost
soul, but could never be broken.

It might be, too,—doubtless it was
so, although she hid the secret from
herself, and grew pale whenever it

struggled out of her heart, like a serpent from its hole,—it might be that another feeling kept her within the scene and pathway that had been so fatal. There dwelt, there trode the feet of one with whom she deemed herself connected in a union, that, unrecognized on earth, would bring them together before the bar of final judgment, and make that their marriage-altar, for a joint futurity of endless retribution. Over and over again, the tempter of souls had thrust this idea upon Hester's contemplation, and laughed at the passionate and desperate joy with which she seized, and then strove to cast it from her. She barely looked the idea in the face, and hastened to bar it in its dungeon. What she compelled herself to believe,—what, finally, she reasoned upon, as her motive for continuing a resident of New England,—was half a truth, and half a self-delusion. Here, she said to herself, had been the scene of her guilt, and here should be the scene of her earthly punishment; and so, perchance, the torture of her daily shame would at length purge her soul, and work out another purity than that which she had lost; more saint-like, because the result of martyrdom.

Hester Prynne, therefore, did not flee. On the outskirts of the town, within the verge of the peninsula, but not in close vicinity to any other habitation, there was a small thatched cottage. It had been built by an earlier settler, and abandoned, because the soil about it was too sterile for cultivation, while its comparative remoteness put it out of the sphere of that social activity which already marked the habits of the emigrants. It stood on the shore, looking across a basin of the sea at the forest-covered hills, towards the wes A clump of scrubby trees, such as alor grew on the peninsula, did not so muc conceal the cottage from view, as seer to denote that here was some obje which would fain have been, or at lea ought to be, concealed. In this littl lonesome dwelling, with some slende means that she possessed, and by th license of the magistrates, who still kep an inquisitorial watch over her, Heste established herself, with her infar child. A mystic shadow of suspicio immediately attached itself to the spo Children, too young to comprehen wherefore this woman should be shu out from the sphere of human charitie would creep nigh enough to behold he plying her needle at the cottage-wir dow, or standing in the doorway, c laboring in her little garden, or comin forth along the pathway that led towr ward; and, discerning the scarlet lette on her breast, would scamper off wit a strange, contagious fear.

Lonely as was Hester's situation, an without a friend on earth who dared t show himself, she, however, incurred n risk of want. She possessed an art tha sufficed, even in a land that afforde comparatively little scope for its exe cise, to supply food for her thrivin infant and herself. It was the art— then, as now, almost the only one withi a woman's grasp—of needle-work. Sh bore on her breast, in the curiously em broidered letter, a specimen of her deli cate and imaginative skill, of which th dames of a court might gladly hav availed themselves, to add the riche and more spiritual adornment of huma ingenuity to their fabrics of silk an gold. Here, indeed, in the sable sim plicity that generally characterized th ritanic modes of dress, there might an infrequent call for the finer pro-ctions of her handiwork. Yet the taste the age, demanding whatever was borate in compositions of this kind, d not fail to extend its influence over r stern progenitors, who had cast be-nd them so many fashions which it ght seem harder to dispense with. blic ceremonies, such as ordinations, e installation of magistrates, and all at could give majesty to the forms in nich a new government manifested it-lf to the people, were, as a matter of licy, marked by a stately and well-nducted ceremonial, and a sombre, but t a studied magnificence. Deep ruffs, infully wrought bands, and gorgeously nbroidered gloves, were all deemed cessary to the official state of men suming the reins of power; and were adily allowed to individuals dignified rank or wealth, even while sumptuary ws forbade these and similar extrava-nces to the plebeian order. In the ray of funerals, too,—whether for the parel of the dead body, or to typify, manifold emblematic devices of ble cloth and snowy lawn, the sorrow the survivors,—there was a frequent d characteristic demand for such bor as Hester Prynne could supply. aby-linen—for babies then wore robes state—afforded still another possi-lity of toil and emolument.

By degrees, nor very slowly, her ndiwork became what would now be rmed the fashion. Whether from com-iseration for a woman of so miser-le a destiny; or from the morbid riosity that gives a fictitious value en to common or worthless things; or y whatever other intangible circum-ance was then, as now, sufficient to

bestow, on some persons, what others might seek in vain; or because Hester really filled a gap which must other-wise have remained vacant; it is cer-tain that she had ready and fairly requited employment for as many hours as she saw fit to occupy with her needle. Vanity, it may be, chose to mortify it-self, by putting on, for ceremonials of pomp and state, the garments that had been wrought by her sinful hands. Her needle-work was seen on the ruff of the Governor; military men wore it on their scarfs, and the minister on his band; it decked the baby's little cap; it was shut up, to be mildewed and moulder away, in the coffins of the dead. But it is not recorded that, in a single instance, her skill was called in aid to embroider the white veil which was to cover the pure blushes of a bride. The exception indicated the ever relentless vigor with which society frowned upon her sin.

Hester sought not to acquire any-thing beyond a subsistence, of the plain-est and most ascetic description, for herself, and a simple abundance for her child. Her own dress was of the coarsest materials and the most sombre hue; with only that one ornament,—the scar-let letter,—which it was her doom to wear. The child's attire, on the other hand, was distinguished by a fanciful, or, we might rather say, a fantastic in-genuity, which served, indeed, to heighten the airy charm that early be-gan to develop itself in the little girl, but which appeared to have also a deeper meaning. We may speak further of it hereafter. Except for that small expenditure in the decoration of her in-fant, Hester bestowed all her superflu-ous means in charity, on wretches less miserable than herself, and who not unfrequently insulted the hand that fed them. Much of the time, which she might readily have applied to the better efforts of her art, she employed in making coarse garments for the poor. It is probable that there was an idea of penance in this mode of occupation, and that she offered up a real sacrifice of enjoyment, in devoting so many hours to such rude handiwork. She had in her nature a rich, voluptuous, Oriental characteristic,—a taste for the gorgeously beautiful, which, save in the exquisite productions of her needle, found nothing else, in all the possibilities of her life, to exercise itself upon. Women derive a pleasure, incomprehensible to the other sex, from the delicate toil of the needle. To Hester Prynne it might have been a mode of expressing, and therefore soothing, the passion of her life. Like all other joys, she rejected it as sin. This morbid meddling of conscience with an immaterial matter betokened, it is to be feared, no genuine and steadfast penitence, but something doubtful, something that might be deeply wrong, beneath.

In this manner, Hester Prynne came to have a part to perform in the world. With her native energy of character, and rare capacity, it could not entirely cast her off, although it had set a mark upon her, more intolerable to a woman's heart than that which branded the brow of Cain. In all her intercourse with society, however, there was nothing that made her feel as if she belonged to it. Every gesture, every word, and even the silence of those with whom she came in contact, implied, and often expressed, that she was banished, and as much alone as if she inhabited another sphere, or communicated with the common nature by other organs and senses than the rest of human kind. She stood apart from moral interests, yet close beside them, like a ghost that revisits the familiar fireside, and can no longer make itself seen or felt; no more smile with the household joy, nor mourn with the kindred sorrow; or, should it succeed in manifesting its forbidden sympathy, awakening only terror and horrible repugnance. These emotions, in fact, and its bitterest scorn besides, seemed to be the sole portion that she retained in the universal heart. It was not an age of delicacy; and her position, although she understood it well, and was in little danger of forgetting it, was often brought before her vivid self-perception, like a new anguish, by the rudest touch upon the tenderest spot. The poor, as we have already said, whom she sought out to be the objects of her bounty, often reviled the hand that was stretched forth to succor them. Dames of elevated rank, likewise, whose doors she entered in the way of her occupation, were accustomed to distil drops of bitterness into her heart; sometimes through that alchemy of quiet malice, by which women can concoct a subtile poison from ordinary trifles; and sometimes, also, by a coarser expression, that fell upon the sufferer's defenceless breast like a rough blow upon an ulcerated wound. Hester had schooled herself long and well; she never responded to these attacks, save by a flush of crimson that rose irrepressibly over her pale cheek, and again subsided into the depths of her bosom. She was patient,—a martyr, indeed,— but she forebore to pray for

enemies; lest, in spite of her for-
ing aspirations, the words of the
essing should stubbornly twist them-
ves into a curse.

Continually, and in a thousand other
ys, did she feel the innumerable
robs of anguish that had been so
nningly contrived for her by the un-
ing, the ever-active sentence of the
uritan tribunal. Clergymen paused in
e street to address words of ex-
rtation, that brought a crowd, with
mingled grin and frown, around the
or, sinful woman. If she entered a
urch, trusting to share the Sabbath
ile of the Universal Father, it was
ten her mishap to find herself the
xt of the discourse. She grew to
ve a dread of children; for they had
bibed from their parents a vague idea
something horrible in this dreary
man, gliding silently through the
wn, with never any companion but
e only child. Therefore, first allowing
r to pass, they pursued her at a dis-
nce with shrill cries, and the utterance
a word that had no distinct purport
their own minds, but was none the
ss terrible to her, as proceeding from
ps that babbled it unconsciously. It
emed to argue so wide a diffusion of
r shame, that all nature knew of it;
could have caused her no deeper
ng, had the leaves of the trees whis-
red the dark story among themselves,
had the summer breeze murmured
out it—had the wintry blast shrieked
aloud! Another peculiar torture was
lt in the gaze of a new eye. When
rangers looked curiously at the scar-
t letter,—and none ever failed to
so,—they branded it afresh into Hes-
r's soul; so that, oftentimes, she could
arcely refrain, yet always did refrain,

from covering the symbol with her
hand. But then, again, an accustomed
eye had likewise its own anguish to
inflict. Its cool stare of familiarity was
intolerable. From first to last, in short,
Hester Prynne had always this dreadful
agony in feeling a human eye upon the
token; the spot never grew callous; it
seemed, on the contrary, to grow more
sensitive with daily torture.

But sometimes, once in many days,
or perchance in many months, she felt
an eye—a human eye—upon the ignominious brand, that seemed to give a
momentary relief, as if half of her
agony were shared. The next instant,
back it all rushed again, with still a
deeper throb of pain; for, in that brief
interval, she had sinned anew. Had Hester sinned alone?

Her imagination was somewhat affected, and, had she been of a softer
moral and intellectual fibre, would have
been still more so, by the strange and
solitary anguish of her life. Walking to
and fro, with those lonely footsteps, in
the little world with which she was
outwardly connected, it now and then
appeared to Hester,—if altogether
fancy, it was nevertheless too potent to
be resisted,—she felt or fancied, then,
that the scarlet letter had endowed her
with a new sense. She shuddered to
believe, yet could not help believing,
that it gave her a sympathetic knowledge of the hidden sin in other hearts.
She was terror-stricken by the revelations that were thus made. What were
they? Could they be other than the
insidious whispers of the bad angel,
who would fain have persuaded the
struggling woman, as yet only half his
victim, that the outward guise of purity
was but a lie, and that, if truth were

everywhere to be shown, a scarlet letter would blaze forth on many a bosom besides Hester Prynne's? Or, must she receive those intimations—so obscure, yet so distinct—as truth? In all her miserable experience, there was nothing else so awful and so loathsome as this sense. It perplexed, as well as shocked her, by the irreverent inopportuneness of the occasions that brought it into vivid action. Sometimes the red infamy upon her breast would give a sympathetic throb, as she passed near a venerable minister or magistrate, the model of piety and justice, to whom that age of antique reverence looked up, as to a mortal man in fellowship with angels. "What evil thing is at hand?" would Hester say to herself. Lifting her reluctant eyes, there would be nothing human within the scope of view, save the form of this earthly saint! Again, a mystic sisterhood would contumaciously assert itself, as she met the sanctified frown of some matron, who, according to the rumor of all tongues, had kept cold snow within her bosom throughout life. That unsunned snow in the matron's bosom, and the burning shame on Hester Prynne's, what had the two in common? Or, once more, the electric thrill would give her warning,—"Behold, Hester, here is a companion!"—and, looking up, she wou detect the eyes of a young maid glancing at the scarlet letter, shyly a aside, and quickly averted, with a fai chill crimson in her cheeks; as if h purity were somewhat sullied by th momentary glance. O Fiend, whose tal man was that fatal symbol, woul thou leave nothing, whether in you or age, for this poor sinner to rever —such loss of faith is ever one of t saddest results of sin. Be it accept as a proof that all was not corru in this poor victim of her own frail and man's hard law, that Hester Pryn yet struggled to believe that no fello mortal was guilty like herself.

The vulgar, who, in those dreary c times, were always contributing a gr tesque horror to what interested the imaginations, had a story about t scarlet letter which we might readi work up into a terrific legend. Th averred, that the symbol was not me scarlet cloth, tinged in an earthly dy pot, but was red-hot with infernal fir and could be seen glowing all aligh whenever Hester Prynne walked abro in the night-time. And we must nee say, it seared Hester's bosom so deepl that perhaps there was more truth the rumor than our modern increduli may be inclined to admit.

CHAPTER VI

PEARL

WE have as yet hardly spoken of the infant; that little creature, whose innocent life had sprung, by the inscrutable decree of Providence, a lovely and im mortal flower, out of the rank luxur ance of a guilty passion. How strang

seemed to the sad woman, as she
watched the growth, and the beauty
that became every day more brilliant,
and the intelligence that threw its quiv-
ing sunshine over the tiny features
this child! Her Pearl!—For so had
ester called her; not as a name ex-
essive of her aspect, which had noth-
g of the calm, white, unimpassioned
stre that would be indicated by the
mparison. But she named the infant
Pearl," as being of great price,—pur-
ased with all she had,—her mother's
ly treasure! How strange, indeed!
an had marked this woman's sin by
scarlet letter, which had such potent
d disastrous efficacy that no human
mpathy could reach her, save it were
ful like herself. God, as a direct con-
quence of the sin which man thus
nished, had given her a lovely child,
ose place was on that same dis-
nored bosom, to connect her parent
rever with the race and descent of
ortals, and to be finally a blessed
ul in heaven! Yet these thoughts af-
cted Hester Prynne less with hope
an apprehension. She knew that her
ed had been evil; she could have
faith, therefore, that its result would
good. Day after day, she looked
arfully into the child's expanding na-
re; ever dreading to detect some dark
d wild peculiarity, that should corre-
ond with the guiltiness to which she
ved her being.

Certainly, there was no physical de-
ct. By its perfect shape, its vigor,
d its natural dexterity in the use of
l its untried limbs, the infant was
orthy to have been brought forth in
den; worthy to have been left there,
be the plaything of the angels, after
e world's first parents were driven

out. The child had a native grace which
does not invariably coëxist with fault-
less beauty; its attire, however simple,
always impressed the beholder as if
it were the very garb that precisely
became it best. But little Pearl was
not clad in rustic weeds. Her mother,
with a morbid purpose that may be
better understood hereafter, had bought
the richest tissues that could be pro-
cured, and allowed her imaginative faculty its full play in the arrangement
and decoration of the dresses which the
child wore, before the public eye. So
magnificent was the small figure, when
thus arrayed, and such was the splendor of Pearl's own proper beauty, shining through the gorgeous robes which
might have extinguished a paler loveliness, that there was an absolute circle
of radiance around her, on the darksome
cottage floor. And yet a russet gown,
torn and soiled with the child's rude
play, made a picture of her just as
perfect. Pearl's aspect was imbued with
a spell of infinite variety; in this one
child there were many children, comprehending the full scope between the
wild-flower prettiness of a peasant-baby,
and the pomp, in little, of an infant
princess. Throughout all, however, there
was a trait of passion, a certain depth
of hue, which she never lost; and if,
in any of her changes, she had grown
fainter or paler, she would have ceased
to be herself;—it would have been no
longer Pearl!

This outward mutability indicated,
and did not more than fairly express,
the various properties of her inner life.
Her nature appeared to possess depth,
too, as well as variety; but—or else
Hester's fears deceived her—it lacked
reference and adaptation to the world

into which she was born. The child could not be made amenable to rules. In giving her existence, a great law had been broken; and the result was a being whose elements were perhaps beautiful and brilliant, but all in disorder; or with an order peculiar to themselves, amidst which the point of variety and arrangement was difficult or impossible to be discovered. Hester could only account for the child's character—and even then most vaguely and imperfectly—by recalling what she herself had been, during that momentous period while Pearl was imbibing her soul from the spiritual world, and her bodily frame from its material of earth. The mother's impassioned state had been the medium through which were transmitted to the unborn infant the rays of its moral life; and, however white and clear originally, they had taken the deep stains of crimson and gold, the fiery lustre, the black shadow, and the untempered light, of the intervening substance. Above all, the warfare of Hester's spirit, at that epoch, was perpetuated in Pearl. She could recognize her wild, desperate, defiant mood, the flightiness of her temper, and even some of the very cloud-shapes of gloom and despondency that had brooded in her heart. They were now illuminated by the morning radiance of a young child's disposition, but, later in the day of earthly existence, might be prolific of the storm and whirlwind.

The discipline of the family, in those days, was of a far more rigid kind than now. The frown, the harsh rebuke, the frequent application of the rod, enjoined by Scriptural authority, were used, not merely in the way of punishment for actual offences, but as a wholesome regi-

men for the growth and promotion all childish virtues. Hester Pryn nevertheless, the lonely mother of t one child, ran little risk of erring the side of undue severity. Mindf however, of her own errors and m fortunes, she early sought to impose tender, but strict control over the fant immortality that was committed her charge. But the task was beyond skill. After testing both smiles a frowns, and proving that neither mo of treatment possessed any calcula influence, Hester was ultimately co pelled to stand aside, and permit t child to be swayed by her own i pulses. Physical compulsion or restra was effectual, of course, while it last As to any other kind of discipli whether addressed to her mind or hea little Pearl might or might not be wit its reach, in accordance with the capr that ruled the moment. Her moth while Pearl was yet an infant, grew quainted with a certain peculiar lo that warned her when it would be lak thrown away to insist, persuade, plead. It was a look so intelligent, inexplicable, so perverse, sometimes malicious, but generally accompanied a wild flow of spirits, that Hester co not help questioning, at such momen whether Pearl was a human child. S seemed rather an airy sprite, whi after playing its fantastic sports a little while upon the cottage-flo would flit away with a mocking sm Whenever that look appeared in wild, bright, deeply black eyes, it vested her with a strange remoten and intangibility; it was as if she w hovering in the air and might vani like a glimmering light, that comes know not whence, and goes we kn

t whither. Beholding it, Hester was
nstrained to rush towards the child,
to pursue the little elf in the flight
.ich she invariably began,—to snatch
r to her bosom, with a close pressure
d earnest kisses,—not so much from
erflowing love, as to assure herself
at Pearl was flesh and blood, and not
erly delusive. But Pearl's laugh, when
e was caught, though full of merri-
nt and music, made her mother more
ubtful than before.

Heart-smitten at this bewildering and
ffling spell, that so often came be-
een herself and her sole treasure,
om she had bought so dear, and who
s all her world, Hester sometimes
rst into passionate tears. Then, per-
ps,—for there was no foreseeing how
might affect her,—Pearl would frown,
d clench her little fist, and harden
r small features into a stern, unsym-
thizing look of discontent. Not sel-
m, she would laugh anew, and louder
an before, like a thing incapable and
intelligent of human sorrow. Or—
t this more rarely happened—she
uld be convulsed with a rage of grief,
d sob out her love for her mother,
broken words, and seem intent on
oving that she had a heart, by break-
g it. Yet Hester was hardly safe in
nfiding herself to that gusty tender-
ss; it passed, as suddenly as it came.
ooding over all these matters, the
ther felt like one who has evoked
spirit, but, by some irregularity in the
ocess of conjuration, has failed to win
e master-word that should control this
w and incomprehensible intelligence.
r only real comfort was when the
ild lay in the placidity of sleep. Then
e was sure of her, and tasted hours
quiet, sad, delicious happiness; until

—perhaps with that perverse expression
glimmering from beneath her opening
lids—little Pearl awoke!

How soon—with what strange rapidity, indeed!—did Pearl arrive at an age
that was capable of social intercourse,
beyond the mother's ever-ready smile
and nonsense-words! And then what a
happiness would it have been, could
Hester Prynne have heard her clear,
bird-like voice mingling with the uproar
of other childish voices, and have distinguished and unravelled her own darling's tones, amid all the entangled outcry of a group of sportive children!
But this could never be. Pearl was a
born outcast of the infantile world. An
imp of evil, emblem and product of
sin, she had no right among christened
infants. Nothing was more remarkable
than the instinct, as it seemed, with
which the child comprehended her loneliness; the destiny that had drawn an
inviolable circle round about her; the
whole peculiarity, in short, of her position in respect to other children. Never,
since her release from prison, had Hester met the public gaze without her.
In all her walks about the town, Pearl,
too, was there; first as the babe in
arms, and afterwards as the little girl,
small companion of her mother, holding
a forefinger with her whole grasp, and
tripping along at the rate of three or
four footsteps to one of Hester's. She
saw the children of the settlement, on
the grassy margin of the street, or at
the domestic thresholds, disporting
themselves in such grim fashion as the
Puritanic nurture would permit; playing at going to church, perchance; or
at scourging Quakers; or taking scalps
in a sham-fight with the Indians; or
scaring one another with freaks of imi-

tative witchcraft. Pearl saw, and gazed intently, but never sought to make acquaintance. If spoken to, she would not speak again. If the children gathered about her, as they sometimes did, Pearl would grow positively terrible in her puny wrath, snatching up stones to fling at them, with shrill, incoherent exclamations, that made her mother tremble, because they had so much the sound of a witch's anathemas in some unknown tongue.

The truth was, that the little Puritans, being of the most intolerant brood that ever lived, had got a vague idea of something outlandish, unearthly, or at variance with ordinary fashions, in the mother and child; and therefore scorned them in their hearts, and not unfrequently reviled them with their tongues. Pearl felt the sentiment, and requited it with the bitterest hatred that can 'be supposed to rankle in a childish bosom. These outbreaks of a fierce temper had a kind of value, and even comfort, for her mother; because there was at least an intelligible earnestness in the mood, instead of the fitful caprice that so often thwarted her in the child's manifestations. It appalled her, nevertheless, to discern here, again, a shadowy reflection of the evil that had existed in herself. All this enmity and passion had Pearl inherited, by inalienable right, out of Hester's heart. Mother and daughter stood together in the same circle of seclusion from human society; and in the nature of the child seemed to be perpetuated those unquiet elements that had distracted Hester Prynne before Pearl's birth, but had since begun to be soothed away by the softening influences of maternity.

At home, within and around her mother's cottage, Pearl wanted not wide and various circle of acquaintan The spell of life went forth from l ever creative spirit, and communicat itself to a thousand objects, as a tor kindles a flame wherever it may applied. The unlikeliest materials,— stick, a bunch of rags, a flower,—we the puppets of Pearl's witchcraft, ar without undergoing any outward chan; became spiritually adapted to whatev drama occupied the stage of her inn world. Her one baby-voice served multitude of imaginary personages, c and young, to talk withal. The pine-tre aged, black and solemn, and flingi groans and other melancholy utte ances on the breeze, needed little tra formation to figure as Puritan elder the ugliest weeds of the garden we their children, whom Pearl smote do and uprooted, most unmercifully. It w wonderful, the vast variety of forr into which she threw her intellect, wi no continuity, indeed, but darting and dancing, always in a state of p ternatural activity,—soon sinking dov as if exhausted by so rapid and feveri a tide of life,—and succeeded by oth shapes of a similar wild energy. It w like nothing so much as the phanta magoric play of the northern lights. the mere exercise of the fancy, howeve and the sportiveness of a growing mir there might be little more than w observable in other children of brig faculties; except as Pearl, in the dear of human playmates, was thrown mc upon the visionary throng which s created. The singularity lay in the in tile feelings with which the child g garded all these offspring of her ov heart and mind. She never created friend, but seemed always to be sow;

roadcast the dragon's teeth, whence
rung a harvest of armed enemies,
gainst whom she rushed to battle. It
as inexpressibly sad—then what depth
f sorrow to a mother, who felt in her
wn heart the cause!—to observe, in
ne so young, this constant recognition
f an adverse world, and so fierce a
aining of the energies that were to
ake good her cause, in the contest
at must ensue.

Gazing at Pearl, Hester Prynne often
ropped her work upon her knees, and
ied out with an agony which she would
in have hidden, but which made ut-
rance for itself, betwixt speech and
groan,—"O Father in Heaven,—if
hou art still my Father,—what is this
ing which I have brought into the
orld!" And Pearl, overhearing the
aculation, or aware through some
ore subtile channel, of those throbs
anguish, would turn her vivid and
autiful little face upon her mother,
ile with sprite-like intelligence, and
sume her play.

One peculiarity of the child's deport-
ent remains yet to be told. The very
st thing which she had noticed, in
r life, was—what?—not the mother's
ile, responding to it, as other babies
, by that faint, embryo smile of the
tle mouth, remembered so doubtfully
terwards, and with such fond discus-
n whether it were indeed a smile. By
means! But the first object of which
arl seemed to become aware was—
all we say it?—the scarlet letter on
ster's bosom! One day, as her mother
oped over the cradle, the infant's
es had been caught by the glimmering
the gold embroidery about the let-
r; and, putting up her little hand, she
sped at it, smiling, not doubtfully,

but with a decided gleam, that gave
her face the look of a much older
child. Then, gasping for breath, did
Hester Prynne clutch the fatal token,
instinctively endeavoring to tear it
away; so infinite was the torture inflicted by the intelligent touch of Pearl's
baby-hand. Again, as if her mother's
agonized gesture were meant only to
make sport for her, did little Pearl
look into her eyes, and smile! From that
epoch, except when the child was asleep,
Hester had never felt a moment's safety; not a moment's calm enjoyment of
her. Weeks, it is true, would sometimes
elapse, during which Pearl's gaze might
never once be fixed upon the scarlet
letter; but then, again, it would come
at unawares, like the stroke of sudden
death, and always with that peculiar
smile, and odd expression of the eyes.

Once, this freakish, elvish cast came
into the child's eyes, while Hester was
looking at her own image in them, as
mothers are fond of doing; and, suddenly,—for women in solitude, and with
troubled hearts, are pestered with unaccountable delusions,—she fancied that
she beheld, not her own miniature portrait, but another face, in the small
black mirror of Pearl's eye. It was a
face, fiend-like, full of smiling malice,
yet bearing the semblance of features
that she had known full well, though
seldom with a smile, and never with
malice in them. It was as if an evil
spirit possessed the child, and had just
then peeped forth in mockery. Many
a time afterwards had Hester been tortured, though less vividly, by the same
illusion.

In the afternoon of a certain summer's day, after Pearl grew big enough
to run about, she amused herself with

gathering handfuls of wild-flowers, and flinging them, one by one, at her mother's bosom; dancing up and down, like a little elf, whenever she hit the scarlet letter. Hester's first motion had been to cover her bosom with her clasped hands. But, whether from pride or resignation, or a feeling that her penance might best be wrought out by this unutterable pain, she resisted the impulse, and sat erect, pale as death, looking sadly into little Pearl's wild eyes. Still came the battery of flowers, almost invariably hitting the mark, and covering the mother's breast with hurts for which she could find no balm in this world, nor knew how to seek it in another. At last, her shot being all expended, the child stood still and gazed at Hester, with that little, laughing image of a fiend peeping out—or, whether it peeped or no, her mother so imagined it—from the unsearchable abyss of her black eyes.

"Child, what art thou?" cried the mother.

"O, I am your little Pearl!" answered the child.

But, while she said it, Pearl laughed, and began to dance up and down, with the humorsome gesticulation of a little imp, whose next freak might be to fly up the chimney.

"Art thou my child, in very truth?" asked Hester.

Nor did she put the question altogether idly, but, for the moment, with a portion of genuine earnestness; for, such was Pearl's wonderful intelligence, that her mother half doubted whether she were not acquainted with the secret spell of her existence, and might not now reveal herself.

"Yes; I am little Pearl!" repeated the child, continuing her antics.

"Thou are not my child! Thou a no Pearl of mine!" said the mothe half playfully; for it was often t case that a sportive impulse came ov her, in the midst of her deepest suffe ing. "Tell me, then, what thou art, a who sent thee hither?"

"Tell me, mother!" said the chi seriously, coming up to Hester, a pressing herself close to her knees. "I thou tell me!"

"Thy Heavenly Father sent thee answered Hester Prynne.

But she said it with a hesitation th did not escape the acuteness of t child. Whether moved only by her or nary freakishness, or because an e spirit prompted her, she put up h small forefinger, and touched the scar letter.

"He did not send me!" cried s positively. "I have no Heavenly Fa er!"

"Hush, Pearl, hush! Thou must r talk so!" answered the mother, su pressing a groan. "He sent us all in this world. He sent even me, t mother. Then, much more, thee! if not, thou strange and elfish chi whence didst thou come?"

"Tell me! Tell me!" repeated Pea no longer seriously, but laughing, a capering about the floor. "It is th that must tell me!"

But Hester could not resolve query, being herself in a dismal lal rinth of doubt. She remembered— twixt a smile and a shudder—the t of the neighboring townspeople; w seeking vainly elsewhere for the chi paternity, and observing some of odd attributes, had given out that p little Pearl was a demon offspring; s

, ever since old Catholic times, had casionally been seen on earth, through e agency of their mother's sin, and promote some foul and wicked pur-se. Luther, according to the scandal of his monkish enemies, was a brat of that hellish breed; nor was Pearl the only child to whom this inauspicious origin was assigned, among the New England Puritans.

CHAPTER VII

THE GOVERNOR'S HALL

HESTER PRYNNE went, one day, to e mansion of Governor Bellingham, th a pair of gloves, which she had nged and embroidered to his order, d which were to be worn on some eat occasion of state; for, though the ances of a popular election had caused s former ruler to descend a step or o from the highest rank, he still d an honorable and influential place iong the colonial magistracy.

Another and far more important rea- n than the delivery of a pair of em- oidered gloves impelled Hester, at s time, to seek an interview with personage of so much power and ivity in the affairs of the settlement. had reached her ears, that there was design on the part of some of the ding inhabitants, cherishing the more id order of principles in religion and vernment, to deprive her of her child. the supposition that Pearl, as al- dy hinted, was of demon origin, these d people not unreasonably argued t a Christian interest in the moth- s soul required them to remove such stumbling-block from her path. If child, on the other hand, were really able of moral and religious growth, d possessed the elements of ultimate

salvation, then, surely, it would enjoy all the fairer prospect of these advantages, by being transferred to wiser and better guardianship than Hester Prynne's. Among those who promoted the design, Governor Bellingham was said to be one of the most busy. It may appear singular, and, indeed, not a little ludicrous, that an affair of this kind, which, in later days, would have been referred to no higher jurisdiction than that of the selectmen of the town, should then have been a question publicly discussed, and on which statesmen of eminence took sides. At that epoch of pristine simplicity, however, matters of even slighter public interest, and of far less intrinsic weight, than the welfare of Hester and her child, were strangely mixed up with the deliberations of legislators and acts of state. The period was hardly, if at all, earlier than that of our story, when a dispute concerning the right of property in a pig, not only caused a fierce and bitter contest in the legislative body of the colony, but resulted in an important modification of the framework itself of the legislature.

Full of concern, therefore,—but so conscious of her own right that it seemed scarcely an unequal match between the public, on the one side, and a lonely woman, backed by the sympathies of nature, on the other,—Hester Prynne set forth from her solitary cottage. Little Pearl, of course, was her companion. She was now of an age to run lightly along by her mother's side, and, constantly in motion, from morn till sunset, could have accomplished a much longer journey than that before her. Often, nevertheless, more from caprice than necessity, she demanded to be taken up in arms; but was soon as imperious to be set down again, and frisked onward before Hester on the grassy pathway, with many a harmless trip and tumble. We have spoken of Pearl's rich and luxuriant beauty; a beauty that shone with deep and vivid tints; a bright complexion, eyes possessing intensity both of depth and glow, and hair already of a deep, glossy brown, and which, in after years, would be nearly akin to black. There was fire in her and throughout her; she seemed the unpremeditated offshoot of a passionate moment. Her mother, in contriving the child's garb, had allowed the gorgeous tendencies of her imagination their full play; arraying her in a crimson velvet tunic, of peculiar cut, abundantly embroidered with fantasies and flourishes of gold thread. So much strength of coloring, which must have given a wan and pallid aspect to cheeks of a fainter bloom, was admirably adapted to Pearl's beauty, and made her the very brightest little jet of flame that ever danced upon the earth.

But it was a remarkable attribute of this garb, and, indeed, of the child's whole appearance, that it irresistibly and inevitably reminded the beholder of the token which Hester Prynne wa doomed to wear upon her bosom. was the scarlet letter in another form the scarlet letter endowed with lif The mother herself—as if the red i nominy were so deeply scorched in her brain that all her conceptions a sumed its form—had carefully wroug out the similitude; lavishing many hou of morbid ingenuity, to create an ana ogy between the object of her affe tion and the emblem of her guilt a torture. But, in truth, Pearl was t one, as well as the other; and on in consequence of that identity h Hester contrived so perfectly to repr sent the scarlet letter in her appearanc

As the two wayfarers came with the precincts of the town, the childr of the Puritans looked up from the play,—or what passed for play wi those sombre little urchins,—and spa gravely one to another:—

"Behold, verily, there is the wom of the scarlet letter; and, of a trut moreover, there is the likeness of t scarlet letter running along by her sid Come, therefore, and let us fling m at them!"

But Pearl, who was a dauntless chi after frowning, stamping her foot, a shaking her little hand with a varie of threatening gestures, suddenly ma a rush at the knot of her enemies, a put them all to flight. She resemble in her fierce pursuit of them, an infa pestilence,—the scarlet fever, or so such half-fledged angel of judgment, whose mission was to punish the si of the rising generation. She scream and shouted, too, with a terrific volu of sound, which, doubtless, caused t hearts of the fugitives to quake wi in them. The victory accomplishe

earl returned quietly to her mother,
nd looked up, smiling, into her face.

Without further adventure, they
eached the dwelling of Governor Bel-
ngham. This was a large wooden house,
uilt in a fashion of which there are
pecimens still extant in the streets of
ur elder towns; now moss-grown,
umbling to decay, and melancholy at
eart with the many sorrowful or joy-
ul occurrences, remembered or forgot-
en, that have happened, and passed
way, within their dusky chambers.
hen, however, there was the freshness
the passing year on its exterior, and
e cheerfulness, gleaming forth from
e sunny windows, of a human habi-
tion, into which death had never en-
red. It had, indeed, a very cheery
pect; the walls being overspread with
kind of stucco, in which fragments
broken glass were plentifully inter-
ixed; so that, when the sunshine fell
lant-wise over the front of the edi-
ce, it glittered and sparkled as if
amonds had been flung against it by
e double handful. The brilliancy might
ve befitted Aladdin's palace, rather
an the mansion of a grave old Puri-
n ruler. It was further decorated with
range and seemingly cabalistic figures
d diagrams, suitable to the quaint
ste of the age, which had been drawn
the stucco when newly laid on, and
d now grown hard and durable, for
e admiration of after times.

Pearl, looking at this bright wonder
a house, began to caper and dance,
d imperatively required that the
ole breadth of sunshine should be
ripped off its front, and given her to
ay with.

"No, my little Pearl!" said her
other. "Thou must gather thine own

sunshine. I have none to give thee!"

They approached the door; which
was of an arched form, and flanked
on each side by a narrow tower or
projection of the edifice, in both of
which were lattice-windows, with
wooden shutters to close over them at
need. Lifting the iron hammer that
hung at the portal, Hester Prynne gave
a summons, which was answered by
one of the Governor's bond-servants; a
free-born Englishman, but now a seven
years' slave. During that term he was
to be the property of his master, and
as much a commodity of bargain and
sale as an ox, or a joint-stool. The
serf wore the blue coat, which was the
customary garb of serving-men at that
period, and long before, in the old hereditary halls of England.

"Is the worshipful Governor Bellingham within?" inquired Hester.

"Yea, forsooth," replied the bond-
servant, staring with wide-open eyes at
the scarlet letter, which, being a new-
comer in the country, he had never
before seen. "Yea, his honorable worship is within. But he hath a godly
minister or two with him, and likewise
a leech. Ye may not see his worship
now."

"Nevertheless, I will enter," answered Hester Prynne; and the bond-
servant, perhaps judging from the decision of her air, and the glittering
symbol in her bosom, that she was a
great lady in the land, offered no opposition.

So the mother and little Pearl were
admitted into the hall of entrance. With
many variations, suggested by the nature of his building-materials, diversity
of climate, and a different mode of
social life, Governor Bellingham had

planned his new habitation after the residences of gentlemen of fair estate in his native land. Here, then, was a wide and reasonably lofty hall, extending through the whole depth of the house, and forming a medium of general communication, more or less directly, with all the other apartments. At one extremity, this spacious room was lighted by the windows of the two towers, which formed a small recess on either side of the portal. At the other end, though partly muffled by a curtain, it was more powerfully illuminated by one of those embowed hall-windows which we read of in old books, and which was provided with a deep and cushioned seat. Here, on the cushion, lay a folio tome, probably of the Chronicles of England, or other such substantial literature; even as, in our own days, we scatter gilded volumes on the centre-table, to be turned over by the casual guest. The furniture of the hall consisted of some ponderous chairs, the backs of which were elaborately carved with wreaths of oaken flowers; and likewise a table in the same taste; the whole being of the Elizabethan age, or perhaps earlier, and heirlooms, transferred hither from the Governor's paternal home. On the table —in token that the sentiment of old English hospitality had not been left behind—stood a large pewter tankard, at the bottom of which, had Hester or Pearl peeped into it, they might have seen the frothy remnant of a recent draught of ale.

On the wall hung a row of portraits, representing the forefathers of the Bellingham lineage, some with armor on their breasts, and others with stately ruffs and robes of peace. All were char-

acterized by the sternness and severi which old portraits so invariably put on as if they were the ghosts, rather tha the pictures, of departed worthies, an were gazing with harsh and intolera criticism at the pursuits and enjoymen of living men.

At about the centre of the oaken pa els, that lined the hall, was suspende a suit of mail, not, like the picture an ancestral relic, but of the mo modern date; for it had been man factured by a skilful armorer in Lo don, the same year in which Govern Bellingham came over to New En land. There was a steel headpiece, cuirass, a gorget, and greaves, with pair of gauntlets and a sword hangi beneath; all, and especially the helm and breastplate, so highly burnished to glow with white radiance, and sca ter an illumination everywhere abo upon the floor. This bright panoply w not meant for mere idle show, but ha been worn by the Governor on many solemn muster and training field, an had glittered, moreover, at the head a regiment in the Pequod war. F though bred a lawyer, and accustom to speak of Bacon, Coke, Noye, a Finch, as his professional associates, t exigences of this new country had tran formed Governor Bellingham into soldier, as well as a statesman and rul

Little Pearl—who was as great pleased with the gleaming armor as s had been with the glittering frontispie of the house—spent some time looki into the polished mirror of the brea plate.

"Mother," cried she, "I see you he Look! Look!"

Hester looked, by way of humori the child; and she saw that, owing

e peculiar effect of this convex mir-
r, the scarlet letter was represented
exaggerated and gigantic proportions;
as to be greatly the most prominent
ature of her appearance. In truth, she
emed absolutely hidden behind it.
earl pointed upward, also, at a similar
cture in the headpiece; smiling at her
other, with the elfish intelligence that
as so familiar an expression on her
nall physiognomy. That look of
ughty merriment was likewise re-
ected in the mirror, with so much
readth and intensity of effect, that it
ade Hester Prynne feel as if it could
ot be the image of her own child, but
an imp who was seeking to mould
self into Pearl's shape.

"Come along, Pearl," said she, draw-
g her away. "Come and look into this
ir garden. It may be, we shall see
wers there; more beautiful ones than
e find in the woods."

Pearl, accordingly, ran to the bow-
ndow, at the further end of the hall,
d looked along the vista of a garden-
lk, carpeted with closely shaven grass,
d bordered with some rude and im-
ature attempt at shrubbery. But the
oprietor appeared already to have re-
quished, as hopeless, the effort to per-
tuate on this side of the Atlantic,
a hard soil and amid the close struggle
r subsistence, the native English taste
r ornamental gardening. Cabbages

grew in plain sight; and a pumpkin-vine,
rooted at some distance, had run across
the intervening space, and deposited one
of its gigantic products directly beneath
the hall-window; as if to warn the Governor that this great lump of vegetable
gold was as rich an ornament as New
England earth would offer him. There
were a few rose-bushes, however, and
a number of apple-trees, probably the
descendants of those planted by the
Reverend Mr. Blackstone, the first settler of the peninsula; that half mytho-
logical personage, who rides through our
early annals, seated on the back of a
bull.

Pearl, seeing the rose-bushes, began
to cry for a red rose, and would not
be pacified.

"Hush, child, hush!" said her mother,
earnestly. "Do not cry, dear little Pearl!
I hear voices in the garden. The Governor is coming, and gentlemen along
with him!"

In fact, adown the vista of the garden
avenue, a number of persons were seen
approaching towards the house. Pearl,
in utter scorn of her mother's attempt
to quiet her, gave an eldritch scream,
and then became silent; not from any
notion of obedience, but because the
quick and mobile curiosity of her disposition was excited by the appearance
of these new personages.

CHAPTER VIII

THE ELF-CHILD AND THE MINISTER

GOVERNOR BELLINGHAM, in a loose gown and easy cap,—such as elderly gentlemen loved to endue themselves with, in their domestic privacy,—walked foremost, and appeared to be showing off his estate, and expatiating on his projected improvements. The wide circumference of an elaborate ruff, beneath his gray beard, in the antiquated fashion of King James' reign, caused his head to look not a little like that of John the Baptist in a charger. The impression made by his aspect, so rigid and severe, and frost-bitten with more than autumnal age, was hardly in keeping with the appliances of worldly enjoyment wherewith he had evidently done his utmost to surround himself. But it is an error to suppose that our grave forefathers—though accustomed to speak and think of human existence as a state merely of trial and warfare, and though unfeignedly prepared to sacrifice goods and life at the behest of duty—made it a matter of conscience to reject such means of comfort, or even luxury, as lay fairly within their grasp. This creed was never taught, for instance, by the venerable pastor, John Wilson, whose beard, white as a snow-drift, was seen over Governor Bellingham's shoulder; while its wearer suggested that pears and peaches might yet be naturalized in the New England climate, and that purple grapes might possibly be compelled to flourish, against the sunny garden-wall. The old clergyman, nurtured at the rich bosom of the English Church, had a long-established and legitimate taste for a good and comfortable things; and however stern he might show himself i the pulpit, or in his public reproof of such transgressions as that of Hest Prynne, still, the genial benevolence of his private life had won him warmer affection than was accorded to any of his professional contemporaries.

Behind the Governor and Mr. Wilsc came two other guests; one, the Reverend Arthur Dimmesdale, whom the reader may remember, as having take a brief and reluctant part in the scen of Hester Prynne's disgrace; and, close companionship with him, o Roger Chillingworth, a person of gre skill in physic, who, for two or thre years past, had been settled in the tow It was understood that this learned ma was the physician as well as friend the young minister, whose health ha severely suffered, of late, by his to unreserved self-sacrifice to the labo and duties of the pastoral relation.

The Governor, in advance of his vis tors, ascended one or two steps, an throwing open the leaves of the gre hall window, found himself close to litt Pearl. The shadow of the curtain f on Hester Prynne, and partially co cealed her.

"What have we here?" said Govern Bellingham, looking with surprise the scarlet little figure before him. profess, I have never seen the like, sin my days of vanity, in old King Jame time, when I was wont to esteem it high favor to be admitted to a cou mask! There used to be a swarm of these small apparitions, in holiday time; and we called them children of the Lord of Misrule. But how gat such a guest into my hall?"

"Ay, indeed!" cried good old Mr. Wilson. "What little bird of scarlet plumage may this be? Methinks I have seen just such figures, when the sun has been shining through a richly painted window, and tracing out the golden and crimson images across the floor. But that was in the old land. Prithee, young one, who art thou, and what has ailed thy mother to bedizen thee in this strange fashion? Art thou a Christian child,—ha? Dost know thy catechism? Or art thou one of those naughty elfs or fairies, whom we thought to have left behind us, with other relics of Papistry, in merry old England?"

"I am mother's child," answered the scarlet vision, "and my name is Pearl!"

"Pearl?—Ruby, rather!—or Coral!— or Red Rose, at the very least, judging from thy hue!" responded the old minister, putting forth his hand in a vain attempt to pat little Pearl on the cheek. "But where is this mother of thine? Ah! I see," he added; and, turning to Governor Bellingham, whispered, "This is the selfsame child of whom we have held speech together; and behold here the unhappy woman, Hester Prynne, her mother!"

"Sayest thou so?" cried the Governor. "Nay, we might have judged that such a child's mother must needs be a scarlet woman, and a worthy type of her of Babylon! But she comes at a good time; and we will look into this matter forthwith."

Governor Bellingham stepped through the window into the hall, followed by his three guests.

"Hester Prynne," said he, fixing his naturally stern regard on the wearer of the scarlet letter, "there has been much question concerning thee, of late. The point hath been weightily discussed, whether we, that are of authority and influence, do well discharge our consciences by trusting an immortal soul, such as there is in yonder child, to the guidance of one who hath stumbled and fallen, amid the pitfalls of this world. Speak thou, the child's own mother! Were it not, thinkest thou, for thy little one's temporal and eternal welfare, that she be taken out of thy charge, and clad soberly, and disciplined strictly, and instructed in the truths of heaven and earth? What canst thou do for the child, in this kind?"

"I can teach my little Pearl what I have learned from this!" answered Hester Prynne, laying her finger on the red token.

"Woman, it is thy badge of shame!" replied the stern magistrate. "It is because of the stain which that letter indicates, that we would transfer thy child to other hands."

"Nevertheless," said the mother, calmly, though growing more pale, "this badge hath taught me,—it daily teaches me,—it is teaching me at this moment, —lessons whereof my child may be the wiser and better, albeit they can profit nothing to myself."

"We will judge warily," said Bellingham, "and look well what we are about to do. Good Master Wilson, I pray you, examine this Pearl,—since that is her name,—and see whether she hath had such Christian nurture as befits a child of her age."

The old minister seated himself in an

arm-chair, and made an effort to draw Pearl betwixt his knees. But the child, unaccustomed to the touch of familiarity of any but her mother, escaped through the open window, and stood on the upper step, looking like a wild tropical bird, of rich plumage, ready to take flight into the upper air. Mr. Wilson, not a little astonished at this outbreak,—for he was a grandfatherly sort of personage, and usually a vast favorite with children,—essayed, however, to proceed with the examination.

"Pearl," said he, with great solemnity, "thou must take heed to instruction, that so, in due season, thou mayest wear in thy bosom the pearl of great price. Canst thou tell me, my child, who made thee?"

Now Pearl knew well enough who made her; for Hester Prynne, the daughter of a pious home, very soon after her talk with the child about her Heavenly Father, had begun to inform her of those truths which the human spirit, at whatever stage of immaturity, imbibes with such eager interest. Pearl, therefore, so large were the attainments of her three years' lifetime, could have borne a fair examination in the New England Primer, or the first column of the Westminster Catechisms, although unacquainted with the outward form of either of those celebrated works. But that perversity, which all children have more or less of, and of which little Pearl had a ten-fold portion, now, at the most inopportune moment, took thorough possession of her, and closed her lips, or impelled her to speak words amiss. After putting her finger in her mouth, with many ungracious refusals to answer good Mr. Wilson's question, the child finally announced that she

had not been made at all, but had been plucked by her mother off the bush of wild roses that grew by the prison door.

This fantasy was probably suggested by the near proximity of the Governor's red roses, as Pearl stood outside of the window; together with her recollection of the prison rose-bush, which she had passed in coming hither.

Old Roger Chillingworth, with a smile on his face, whispered something in the young clergyman's ear. Hester Prynne looked at the man of skill, and even then, with her fate hanging in the balance, was startled to perceive what a change had come over his features,—how much uglier they were,—how his dark complexion seemed to have grown duskier, and his figure more misshapen —since the days when she had familiarly known him. She met his eyes for an instant, but was immediately constrained to give all her attention to the scene now going forward.

"This is awful!" cried the Governor, slowly recovering from the astonishment into which Pearl's response had thrown him. "Here is a child of three years old, and she cannot tell who made her! Without question, she is equally in the dark as to her soul, its present depravity, and future destiny! Methinks, gentlemen, we need inquire no further."

Hester caught hold of Pearl, and drew her forcibly into her arms, confronting the old Puritan magistrate with almost a fierce expression. Alone in the world, cast off by it, and with this sole treasure to keep her heart alive, she felt that she possessed indefeasible rights against the world, and was ready to defend them to the death.

"God gave me the child!" cried she,

He gave her in requital of all things lse, which ye had taken from me. She my happiness!—she is my torture, one the less! Pearl keeps me here in fe! Pearl punishes me too! See ye not, 1e is the scarlet letter, only capable f being loved, and so endowed with million-fold the power of retribution or my sin? Ye shall not take her! I ill die first!"

"My poor woman," said the not unind old minister, "the child shall be ell cared for!—far better than thou anst do it."

"God gave her into my keeping," reeated Hester Prynne, raising her voice lmost to a shrick. "I will not give her p!"—And here, by a sudden impulse, 1e turned to the young clergyman, Mr. •immesdale, at whom, up to this moent, she had seemed hardly so much s once to direct her eyes.—"Speak 1ou for me!" cried she. "Thou wast ly pastor, and hadst charge of my 1ul, and knowest me better than these 1en can. I will not lose the child! peak for me! Thou knowest,—for 1ou hast sympathies which these men ck!—thou knowest what is in my 2art, and what are a mother's rights, 1d how much the stronger they are, 1en that mother has but her child 1d the scarlet letter! Look thou to ! I will not lose the child! Look to !"

At this wild and singular appeal, hich indicated that Hester Prynne's tuation had provoked her to little less 1an madness, the young minister at 1ce came forward, pale, and holding s hand over his heart, as was his 1stom whenever his peculiarly nervous 1mperament was thrown into agitation. 2 looked now more careworn and ema-

ciated than as we described him at the scene of Hester's public ignomy; and whether it were his failing health, or whatever the cause might be, his large dark eyes had a world of pain in their troubled and melancholy depth.

"There is truth in what she says," began the minister, with a voice sweet, tremulous, but powerful, insomuch that the hall reëchoed, and the hollow armor rang with it,—"truth in what Hester says, and in the feeling which inspires her! God gave her the child, and gave her, too, an instinctive knowledge of its nature and requirements,—both seemingly so peculiar,—which no other mortal being can possess. And, moreover, is there not a quality of awful sacredness in the relation between this mother and this child?"

"Ay!—how is that, good Master Dimmesdale?" interrupted the Governor. "Make that plain, I pray you."

"It must be even so," resumed the minister. "For, if we deem it otherwise, do we not thereby say that the Heavenly Father, the Creator of all flesh, hath lightly recognized a deed of sin, and made of no account the distinction between unhallowed lust and holy love? This child of its father's guilt and its mother's shame hath come from the hand of God, to work in many ways upon her heart, who pleads so earnestly, and with such bitterness of spirit, the right to keep her. It was meant for a blessing; for the one blessing of her life! It was meant, doubtless, as the mother herself hath told us, for a retribution too; a torture to be felt at many an unthought-of moment; a pang, a sting, an ever-recurring agony, in the midst of a troubled joy! Hath she not expressed this thought in the garb of the poor child, so forcibly reminding us of that red symbol which sears her bosom?"

"Well said, again!" cried good Mr. Wilson. "I feared the woman had no better thought than to make a mountebank of her child!"

"O, not so!—not so!" continued Mr. Dimmesdale. "She recognizes, believe me, the solemn miracle which God hath wrought, in the existence of that child. And may she feel, too,—what, methinks, is the very truth,—that this boon was meant, above all things else, to keep the mother's soul alive, and to preserve her from blacker depths of sin into which Satan might else have sought to plunge her! Therefore it is good for this poor, sinful woman that she hath an infant immortality, a being capable of eternal joy or sorrow, confided to her care,—to be trained up by her to righteousness,—to remind her, at every moment, of her fall,—but yet to teach her, as it were by the Creator's sacred pledge, that, if she bring the child to heaven, the child also will bring its parent thither! Herein is the sinful mother happier than the sinful father. For Hester Prynne's sake, then, and no less for the poor child's sake, let us leave them as Providence hath seen fit to place them!"

"You speak, my friend, with a strange earnestness," said old Roger Chillingworth, smiling at him.

"And there is a weighty import in what my young brother hath spoken," added the Reverend Mr. Wilson. "What say you, worshipful Master Bellingham? Hath he not pleaded well for the poor woman?"

"Indeed hath he," answered the magistrate, "and hath adduced such argu-ments, that we will even leave th matter as it now stands; so long, a least, as there shall be no further scar dal in the woman. Care must be ha nevertheless, to put the child to du and stated examination in the cate chism, at thy hands or Master Dim mesdale's. Moreover, at a proper sea son, the tithing-men must take heed tha she go both to school and to meeting.

The young minister, on ceasing t speak, had withdrawn a few steps fro the group, and stood with his face pa tially concealed in the heavy folds c the window-curtain; while the shado of his figure, which the sunlight ca upon the floor, was tremulous with th vehemence of his appeal. Pearl, tha wild and flighty little elf, stole soft towards him, and taking his hand i the grasp of both her own, laid her chee against it; a caress so tender, and with so unobtrusive, that her mother, wh was looking on, asked herself,—"Is tha my Pearl?" Yet she knew that ther was love in the child's heart, althoug it mostly revealed itself in passion, an hardly twice in her lifetime had bee softened by such gentleness as now. Th minister,—for, save the long-sought re gards of woman, nothing is sweeter tha these marks of childish preference, ac corded spontaneously by a spiritual in stinct, and therefore seeming to impl in us something truly worthy to b loved,—the minister looked round, lai his hand on the child's head, hesitate an instant, and then kissed her brow Little Pearl's unwonted mood of senti ment lasted no longer; she laughed an went capering down the hall, so airil that old Mr. Wilson raised a questio whether even her tiptoes touched th floor.

"The little baggage hath witchcraft in er, I profess," said he to Mr. Dimmesale. "She needs no old woman's broom-ick to fly withal!"

"A strange child!" remarked old .oger Chillingworth. "It is easy to see ıe mother's part in her. Would it be eyond a philosopher's research, think e, gentlemen, to analyze that child's ature, and, from its make and mould, ɔ give a shrewd guess at the father?"

"Nay; it would be sinful, in such a uestion, to follow the clew of pro-ıne philosophy," said Mr. Wilson. Better to fast and pray upon it; and ill better, it may be, to leave the ıystery as we find it, unless Providence ɔveal it of its own accord. Thereby, very good Christian man hath a title ɔ show a father's kindness towards ıe poor, deserted babe."

The affair being so satisfactorily con-luded, Hester Prynne, with Pearl, de-arted from the house. As they de-cended the steps, it is averred that the attice of a chamber-window was thrown pen, and forth into the sunny day was hrust the face of Mistress Hibbins, ;overnor Bellingham's bitter-tempered ister, and the same who, a few years later, was executed as a witch.

"Hist, hist!" said she, while her ill-omened physiognomy seemed to cast a shadow over the cheerful newness of the house. "Wilt thou go with us to-night? There will be a merry company in the forest; and I well-nigh promised the Black Man that comely Hester Prynne should make one."

"Make my excuse to him, so please you!" answered Hester, with a triumphant smile. "I must tarry at home, and keep watch over my little Pearl. Had they taken her from me, I would willingly have gone with thee into the forest, and signed my name in the Black Man's book too, and that with mine own blood!"

"We shall have thee there anon!" said the witch-lady, frowning as she drew back her head.

But here—if we suppose this interview betwixt Mistress Hibbins and Hester Prynne to be authentic, and not a parable—was already an illustration of the young minister's argument against sundering the relation of a fallen mother to the offspring of her frailty. Even thus early had the child saved her from Satan's snare.

CHAPTER IX

THE LEECH

UNDER the appellation of Roger Chil-ngworth, the reader will remember, ɤas hidden another name, which its ɔrmer wearer had resolved should never ıore be spoken. It has been related, .ow, in the crowd that witnessed Hes-ter Prynne's ignominious exposure, stood a man, elderly, travel-worn, who, just emerging from the perilous wilderness, beheld the woman, in whom he hoped to find embodied the warmth and cheerfulness of home, set up as a type of sin before the people. Her matronly frame was trodden under all men's feet. Infamy was babbling around her in the public market-place. For her kindred, should the tidings ever reach them, and for the companions of her unspotted life, there remained nothing but the contagion of her dishonor; which would not fail to be distributed in strict accordance and proportion with the intimacy and sacredness of their previous relationship. Then why—since the choice was with himself—should the individual, whose connection with the fallen woman had been the most intimate and sacred of them all, come forward· to vindicate his claim to an inheritance so little desirable? He resolved not to be pilloried beside her on her pedestal of shame. Unknown to all but Hester Prynne, and possessing the lock and key of her silence, he chose to withdraw his name from the roll of mankind, and, as regarded his former ties and interest, to vanish out of life as completely as if he indeed lay at the bottom of the ocean, whither rumor had long ago consigned him. This purpose once effected, new interests would immediately spring up, and likewise a new purpose; dark, it is true, if not guilty, but of force enough to engage the full strength of his faculties.

In pursuance of this resolve, he took up his residence in the Puritan town, as Roger Chillingworth, without other introduction than the learning and intelligence of which he possessed more than a common measure. As his studies, at a previous period of his life, had made him extensively acquainted with the medical science of the day, it was as a physician that he presented himself, and as such was cordially received.

Skillful men, of the medical and chirurgical profession, were of rare occurrence in the colony. They seldom, it would appear, partook of the religious zeal that brought other emigrants across the Atlantic. In their researches into the human frame, it may be that the higher and more subtile faculties of such men were materialized, and that they lost the spiritual view of existence amid the intricacies of that wondrous mechanism, which seemed to involve art enough to comprise all of life within itself. At all events, the health of the good town of Boston, so far as medicine had aught to do with it, had hitherto lain in the guardianship of an aged deacon and apothecary, whose piety and godly deportment were stronger testimonials in his favor than any that he could have produced in the shape of a diploma. The only surgeon was one who combined the occasional exercise of that noble art with the daily and habitual flourish of a razor. To such a professional body Roger Chillingworth was a brilliant acquisition. He soon manifested his familiarity with the ponderous and imposing machinery of antique physic; in which every remedy contained a multitude of far-fetched and heterogeneous ingredients, as elaborately compounded as if the proposed result had been the Elixir of Life. In his Indian captivity, moreover, he had gained much knowledge of the properties of native herbs and roots; nor did he conceal from his patients, that these simple medicines, Nature's boon to the untutored savage, had quite as large a share of his own confidence as the European pharmacopœia, which so many learned doctors had spent centuries in elaborating.

This learned stranger was exemplary, s regarded, at least, the outward forms f a religious life, and, early after his rrival, had chosen for his spiritual uide the Reverend Mr. Dimmesdale. 'he young divine, whose scholar-like nown still lived in Oxford, was condered by his more fervent admirers s little less than a heavenly-ordained postle, destined, should he live and bor for the ordinary term of life, to o as great deeds for the now feeble Iew England Church, as the early 'athers had achieved for the infancy f the Christian faith. About this peiod, however, the health of Mr. Dimiesdale had evidently begun to fail. y those best acquainted with his habs, the paleness of the young minister's heek was accounted for by his too arnest devotion to study, his scrupuus fulfilment of parochial duty, and, iore than all, by the fasts and vigils f which he made a frequent practice, i order to keep the grossness of this arthly state from clogging and obscurig his spiritual lamp. Some declared, iat, if Mr. Dimmesdale were really oing to die, it was cause enough, that he world was not worthy to be any nger trodden by his feet. He himself, n the other hand, with characteristic umility, avowed his belief, that, if 'rovidence should see fit to remove im, it would be because of his own nworthiness to perform its humblest iission here on earth. With all this diference of opinion as to the cause of is decline, there could be no question f the fact. His form grew emaciated; is voice, though still rich and sweet, ad a certain melancholy prophecy of ecay in it; he was often observed, on ny slight alarm or other sudden acci

dent, to put his hand over his heart, with first a flush and then a paleness, indicative of pain.

Such was the young clergyman's condition, and so imminent the prospect that his dawning light would be extinguished, all untimely, when Roger Chillingworth made his advent to the town. His first entry on the scene, few people could tell whence, dropping down, as it were, out of the sky, or starting from the nether earth, had an aspect of mystery, which was easily heightened to the miraculous. He was now known to be a man of skill; it was observed that he gathered herbs, and the blossoms of wild-flowers, and dug up roots, and plucked off twigs from the forest-trees, like one acquainted with hidden virtues in what was valueless to common eyes. He was heard to speak of Sir Kenelm Digby, and other famous men,—whose scientific attainments were esteemed hardly less than supernatural, —as having been his correspondents or associates. Why, with such rank in the learned world, had he come hither? What could he, whose sphere was in great cities, be seeking in the wilderness? In answer to this query a rumor gained ground,—and, however absurd, was entertained by some very sensible people,—that Heaven had wrought an absolute miracle, by transporting an eminent Doctor of Physic, from a German university, bodily through the air, and setting him down at the door of Mr. Dimmesdale's study! Individuals of wiser faith, indeed, who knew that Heaven promotes its purposes without aiming at the stage-effect of what is called miraculous interposition, were inclined to see a providential hand in Roger Chillingworth's so opportune arrival.

This idea was countenanced by the strong interest which the physician ever manifested in the young clergyman; he attached himself to him as a parishioner, and sought to win a friendly regard and confidence from his naturally reserved sensibility. He expressed great alarm at his pastor's state of health, but was anxious to attempt the cure, and, if early undertaken, seemed not despondent of a favorable result. The elders, the deacons, the motherly dames, and the young and fair maidens, of Mr. Dimmesdale's flock, were alike importunate that he should make trial of the physician's frankly offered skill. Mr. Dimmesdale gently repelled their entreaties.

"I need no medicine," said he.

But how could the young minister say so, when, with every successive Sabbath, his cheek was paler and thinner, and his voice more tremulous than before,—when it had now become a constant habit, rather than a casual gesture, to press his hand over his heart? Was he weary of his labors? Did he wish to die? These questions were solemnly propounded to Mr. Dimmesdale by the elder ministers of Boston and the deacons of his church, who, to use their own phrase, "dealt with him" on the sin of rejecting the aid which Providence so manifestly held out. He listened in silence, and finally promised to confer with the physician.

"Were it God's will," said the Reverend Mr. Dimmesdale, when, in fulfilment of this pledge, he requested old Roger Chillingworth's professional advice, "I could be well content, that my labors, and my sorrows, and my sins, and my pains, should shortly end with

me, and what is earthly of them be buried in my grave, and the spiritual go with me to my eternal state, rather than that you should put your skill to the proof in my behalf."

"Ah," replied Roger Chillingworth with that quietness which, whether imposed or natural, marked all his deportment, "it is thus that a young clergyman is apt to speak. Youthful men, not having taken a deep root, give up their hold of life so easily And saintly men, who walk with God on earth, would fain be away, to walk with Him on the golden pavements of the New Jerusalem."

"Nay," rejoined the young minister, putting his hand to his heart, with a flush of pain flitting over his brow, "were I worthier to walk there, I could be better content to toil here."

"Good men ever interpret themselve too meanly," said the physician.

In this manner, the mysterious old Roger Chillingworth became the medical adviser of the Reverend Mr. Dimmesdale. As not only the disease interested the physician, but he was strongly moved to look into the character and qualities of the patient, these two men so different in age, came gradually to spend much time together. For the sake of the minister's health, and to enable the leech to gather plants with healing balm in them, they took long walks on the sea-shore, or in the forest; mingling various talk with the plash and murmur of the waves, and the solemn wind anthem among the tree-tops. Often, likewise, one was the guest of the other in his place of study and retirement There was a fascination for the minister in the company of the man of science in whom he recognized an intellectual

ivation of no moderate depth or
pe; together with a range and free-
n of ideas, that he would have
ily looked for among the members
his own profession. In truth, he was
rtled, if not shocked, to find this
ibute in the physician. Mr. Dimmes-
e was a true priest, a true religionist,
h the reverential sentiment largely
eloped, and an order of mind that
elled itself powerfully along the
ck of a creed, and wore its pas-
e continually deeper with the lapse
time. In no state of society would
have been what is called a man of
eral views; it would always be es-
tial to his peace to feel the pressure
a faith about his, supporting, while
confined him within its iron frame-
rk. Not the less, however, though
h a tremulous enjoyment, did he
the occasional relief of looking
the universe through the medium of
ther kind of intellect than those with
ich he habitually held converse. It
s as if a window were thrown open,
nitting a freer atmosphere into the
se and stifled study, where his life
s wasting itself away, amid lamp-
t, or obstructed day-beams, and the
sty fragrance, be it sensual or moral,
t exhales from books. But the air
s too fresh and chill to be long
athed with comfort. So the minister,
the physician with him, withdrew
in within the limits of what their
irch defined as orthodox.

Thus Roger Chillingworth scrutinized
patient carefully, both as he saw
n in his ordinary life, keeping an
ustomed pathway in the range of
ughts familiar to him, and as he
peared when thrown amidst other
ral scenery, the novelty of which

might call out something new to the
surface of his character. He deemed it
essential, it would seem, to know the
man, before attempting to do him good.
Wherever there is a heart and an intellect, the diseases of the physical
frame are tinged with the peculiarities
of these. In Arthur Dimmesdale,
thought and imagination were so active,
and sensibility so intense, that the
bodily infirmity would be likely to have
its groundwork there. So Roger Chillingworth—the man of skill, the kind
and friendly physician—strove to go
deep into his patient's bosom, delving
among his principles, prying into his
recollections, and probing everything
with a cautious touch, like a treasure-
seeker in a dark cavern. Few secrets
can escape an investigator, who has opportunity and license to undertake such
a quest, and skill to follow it up. A man
burdened with a secret should especially avoid the intimacy of his physician. If the latter possess native sagacity, and a nameless something more,—
let us call it intuition; if he show no
intrusive egotism, nor disagreeably
prominent characteristics of his own;
if he have the power, which must be
born with him, to bring his mind into
such affinity with his patient's, that
this last shall unawares have spoken
what he imagines himself only to have
thought; if such revelations be received
without tumult, and acknowledged not
so often by an uttered sympathy as by
silence, an inarticulate breath, and here
and there a word, to indicate that all
is understood; if to these qualifications
of a confidant he joined the advantages
afforded by his recognized character as
a physician;—then, at some inevitable
moment, will the soul of the sufferer

be dissolved, and flow forth in a dark, but transparent stream, bringing all its mysteries into the daylight.

Roger Chillingworth possessed all, or most, of the attributes above enu-merated. Nevertheless, time went on; a kind of intimacy, as we have said, grew up between these two cultivated minds, which had as wide a field as the whole sphere of human thought and study, to meet upon; they discussed every topic of ethics and religion, of public affairs, and private character; they talked much, on both sides, of matters that seemed personal to themselves; and yet no secret, such as the physician fancied must exist there, ever stole out of the minister's consciousness into his com-panion's ear. The latter had his sus-picions, indeed, that even the nature of Mr. Dimmesdale's bodily disease had never fairly been revealed to him. It was a strange reserve! After a time, at a hint from Roger Chillingworth, the friends of Mr. Dimmesdale effected an arrangement by which the two were lodged in the same house; so that every ebb and flow of the minister's life-tide might pass under the eye of his anxious and attached physician. There was much joy throughout the town when this greatly desirable object was attained. It was held to be the best possible meas-ure for the young clergyman's welfare; unless, indeed, as often urged by such as felt authorized to do so, he had se-lected some one of the many bloom-ing damsels, spiritually devoted to him, to become his devoted wife. This latter step, however, there was no present prospect that Arthur Dimmesdale would be prevailed upon to take; he rejected all suggestions of the kind, as if priestly celibacy were one of his articles of

church-discipline. Doomed by his ow choice, therefore, as Mr. Dimmesda so evidently was, to eat his unsavo morsel always at another's board, an endure the life-long chill which must his lot who seeks to warm himself on at another's fireside, it truly seem that his sagacious, experienced, benev lent old physician, with his concord paternal and reverential love for tl young pastor, was the very man, of mankind, to be constantly within rea of his voice.

The new abode of the two frien was with a pious widow, of good soci rank, who dwelt in a house coverin pretty nearly the site on which the ve erable structure of King's Chapel h since been built. It had the grave-yar originally Isaac Johnson's homefield, one side, and so was well adapted call up serious reflections, suited their respective employments, in bo minister and man of physic. T motherly care of the good widow a signed to Mr. Dimmesdale a fro apartment, with a sunny exposure, an heavy window-curtains, to create noontide shadow, when desirable. T walls were hung round with tapestr said to be from the Gobelin looms, an at all events, representing the Scri tural story of David and Bathsheba, ar Nathan the Prophet, in colors still u faded, but which made the fair woma of the scene almost as grimly pictu esque as the woe-denouncing seer. Her the pale clergyman piled up his librar rich with parchment-bound folios the Fathers, and the lore of Rabb and monkish erudition, of which tl Protestant divines, even while the vilified and decried that class of write were yet constrained often to av

emselves. On the other side of the
use, old Roger Chillingworth ar-
nged his study and laboratory; not
ch as a modern man of science would
ckon even tolerably complete, but
ovided with a distilling apparatus, and
e means of compounding drugs and
emicals, which the practised alchemist
ew well how to turn to purpose. With
ch commodiousness of situation, these
o learned persons sat themselves
wn, each in his own domain, yet
miliarly passing from one apartment
the other, and bestowing a mutual
d not incurious inspection into one
other's business.

And the Reverend Arthur Dimmes-
le's best discerning friends, as we
ve intimated, very reasonably im-
ined that the hand of Providence had
ne all this, for the purpose—besought
so many public, and domestic, and
cret prayers—of restoring the young
nister to health. But—it must now be
d—another portion of the commun-
r had latterly begun to take its own
ew of the relation betwixt Mr. Dim-
esdale and the mysterious old physi-
an. When an uninstructed multitude
tempts to see with its eyes, it is ex-
edingly apt to be deceived. When,
wever, it forms its judgment, as it
ually does, on the intuitions of its
eat and warm heart, the conclusions
us attained are often so profound and
unerring, as to possess the character
truths supernaturally revealed. The
ople, in the case of which we speak,
uld justify its prejudice against Roger
illingworth by no fact or argument
rthy of serious refutation. There was
aged handicraftsman, it is true, who
d been a citizen of London at the
riod of Sir Thomas Overbury's mur-

der, now some thirty years agone; he
testified to having seen the physician,
under some other name, which the narrator of the story had now forgotten,
in company with Doctor Forman, the
famous old conjurer, who was impli-
cated in the affair of Overbury. Two
or three individuals hinted, that the
man of skill, during his Indian captivity, had enlarged his medical attainments by joining in the incantations of
the savage priests; who were uni-
versally acknowledged to be powerful
enchanters, often performing seemingly
miraculous °cures by their skill in the
black art. A large number—and many
of these were persons of such sober
sense and practical observation that
their opinions would have been valuable, in other matters—affirmed that
Roger Chillingworth's aspect had undergone a remarkable change while he
had dwelt in town, and especially since
his abode with Mr. Dimmesdale. At
first, his expression had been calm,
meditative, scholar-like. Now, there was
something ugly and evil in his face,
which they had not previously noticed,
and which grew still the more obvious
to sight, the oftener they looked upon
him. According to the vulgar idea, the
fire in his laboratory had been brought
from the lower regions, and was fed
with infernal fuel; and so, as might be
expected, his visage was getting sooty
with the smoke.

To sum up the matter, it .grew to
be a widely diffused opinion, that the
Reverend Arthur Dimmesdale, like
many other personages of especial sanctity, in all ages of the Christian world
was haunted either by Satan himself,
or Satan's emissary, in the guise of old
Roger Chillingworth. This diabolical

agent had the Divine permission, for a season, to burrow into the clergyman's intimacy, and plot against his soul. No sensible man, it was confessed, could doubt on which side the victory would turn. The people looked, with an unshaken hope, to see the minister come forth out of the conflict, transfigured with the glory which he would unques-tionably win. Meanwhile, neverthele[ss] it was sad to think of the percha[nce] mortal agony through which he m[ust] struggle towards his triumph.

Alas! to judge from the glo[om] and terror in the depths of the p[oor] minister's eyes, the battle was [a] sore one, and the victory anything [but] secure.

CHAPTER X

THE LEECH AND HIS PATIENT

OLD Roger Chillingworth, throughout life, had been calm in temperament, kindly, though not of warm affections, but ever, and in all his relations with the world, a pure and upright man. He had begun an investigation, as he imagined, with the severe and equal integrity of a judge, desirous only of truth, even as if the question involved no more than the air-drawn lines and figures of a geometrical problem, instead of human passions, and wrongs inflicted on himself. But, as he proceeded, a terrible fascination, a kind of fierce, though still calm, necessity seized the old man within its gripe, and never set him free again, until he had done all its bidding. He now dug into the poor clergyman's heart, like a miner searching for gold; or, rather, like a sexton delving into a grave, possibly in quest of a jewel that had been buried on the dead man's bosom, but likely to find nothing save mortality and corruption. Alas for his own soul, if these were what he sought!

Sometimes, a light glimmered out of the physician's eyes, burning blue a[nd] ominous, like the reflection of a f[ur]-nace, or, let us say, like one of th[ose] gleams of ghastly fire that darted fr[om] Bunyan's awful doorway in the hill-si[de] and quivered on the pilgrim's face. [The] soil where this dark miner was work[ing] had perchance shown indications th[at] encouraged him.

"This man," said he, at one such m[o]-ment, to himself, "pure as they de[em] him,—all spiritual as he seems,—ha[s] inherited a strong animal nature fr[om] his father or his mother: Let us dig [a] little further in the direction of t[his] vein!"

Then, after long search into the m[in]-ister's dim interior, and turning ov[er] many precious materials, in the sha[pe] of high aspirations for the welfare [of] his race, warm love of souls, pure sen[ti]-ments, natural piety, strengthened [by] thought and study, and illuminated [by] revelation,—all of which invaluable g[old] was perhaps no better than rubbish [to] the seeker,—he would turn back, d[is]-couraged, and begin his quest towar[ds]

ther point. He groped along as
lthily, with as cautious a tread, and
wary an outlook, as a thief entering
hamber where a man lies only half
ep,—or, it may be, broad awake,—
h the purpose to steal the very treas-
which this man guards as the apple
his eye. In spite of his premeditated
efulness, the floor would now and
n creak; his garments would rustle;
shadow of his presence, in a for-
den proximity, would be thrown
oss his victim. In other words, Mr.
nmesdale, whose sensibility of nerve
en produced the effect of spiritual
uition, would become vaguely aware
t something inimical to his peace had
ust itself into relation with him. But
Roger Chillingworth, too, had per-
tions that were almost intuitive; and
en the minister threw his startled
s towards him, there the physician
; his kind, watchful, sympathizing,
never intrusive friend.

Yet Mr. Dimmesdale would perhaps
ve seen this individual's character
re perfectly, if a certain morbidness,
which sick hearts are liable, had not
dered him suspicious of all mankind.
usting no man as his friend, he could
recognize his enemy when the latter
ually appeared. He therefore still
t up a familiar intercourse with him,
ly receiving the old physician in his
dy; or visiting the laboratory, and,
recreation's sake, watching the proc-
es by which weeds were converted
o drugs of potency.

One day, leaning his forehead on his
nd, and his elbow on the sill of the
en window, that looked towards the
ave-yard, he talked with Roger Chill-
worth, while the old man was exam-
ng a bundle of unsightly plants.

"Where," asked he, with a look
askance at them,—for it was the clergyman's peculiarity that he seldom, now-
adays, looked straightforth at any object, whether human or inanimate—
"where, my kind doctor, did you gather
those herbs, with such a dark, flabby
leaf?"

"Even in the grave-yard here at
hand," answered the physician, continuing his employment. "They are new
to me. I found them growing on a grave,
which bore no tomb-stone, nor other
memorial of the dead man, save these
ugly weeds, that have taken upon themselves to keep him in remembrance.
They grew out of his heart, and typify,
it may be, some hideous secret that was
buried with him, and which he had done
better to confess during his lifetime."

"Perchance," said Mr. Dimmesdale,
"he earnestly desired it, but could not."

"And wherefore?" rejoined the physician. "Wherefore not; since all the
powers of nature call so earnestly for
the confession of sin, that these black
weeds have sprung up out of a buried
heart, to make manifest an unspoken
crime?"

"That, good Sir, is but a fantasy of
yours," replied the minister. "There can
be, if I forebode aright, no power, short
of the Divine mercy, to disclose,
whether by uttered words or by type
or emblem, the secrets that may be
buried with a human heart. The heart,
making itself guilty of such secrets,
must perforce hold them, until the day
when all hidden things shall be revealed.
Nor have I so read or interpreted Holy
Writ, as to understand that the disclosure of human thoughts and deeds,
then to be made, is intended as a part
of the retribution. That, surely, were a

shallow view of it. No; these revelations, unless I greatly err, are meant merely to promote the intellectual satisfaction of all intelligent beings, who will stand waiting, on that day, to see the dark problem of this life made plain. A knowledge of men's hearts will be needful to the completest solution of that problem. And I conceive, moreover, that the hearts holding such miserable secrets as you speak of will yield them up, at that last day, not with reluctance, but. with a joy unutterable."

"Then why not reveal them here?" asked Roger Chillingworth, glancing quietly aside at the minister. "Why should not the guilty ones sooner avail themselves of this unutterable solace?"

"They mostly do," said the clergyman, griping hard at his breast, as if afflicted with an importunate throb of pain. "Many, many a poor soul hath given its confidence to me, not only on the death-bed, but while strong in life, and fair in reputation. And ever, after such an outpouring, O, what a relief have I witnessed in those sinful brethren! even as in one who at last draws free air, after long stifling with his own polluted breath. How can it be otherwise? Why should a wretched man, guilty, we will say, of murder, prefer to keep the dead corpse buried in his own heart, rather than fling it forth at once, and let the universe take care of it!"

"Yet some men bury their secrets thus," observed the calm physician.

"True; there are such men," answered Mr. Dimmesdale. "But, not to suggest more obvious reasons, it may be that they are kept silent by the very constitution of their nature. Or,—can we not suppose it?—guilty as they

may be, retaining, nevertheless, a z for God's glory and man's welfare, th shrink from displaying themselves bla and filthy in the view of men; becau thenceforward, no good can be achiev by them; no evil of the past be deemed by better service. So, to th own unutterable torment, they go abo among their fellow-creatures, looki pure as new-fallen snow; while th hearts are all speckled and spotted wi iniquity of which they cannot rid the selves."

"These men deceive themselves," sa Roger Chillingworth, with somewh more emphasis than usual, and maki a slight gesture with his forefing "They fear to take up the shame th rightfully belongs to them. Their lo for man, their zeal for God's service, these holy impulses may or may n coëxist in their hearts with the evil i mates to which their guilt has unbarr the door, and which must needs prop gate a hellish breed. within them. B if they seek to glorify God, let the not lift heavenward their uncle hands! If they would serve their f low-men, let 'them do it by maki manifest the power and reality of co science, in constraining them to pe tential self-abasement! Wouldst th have me to believe, O wise and pio friend, that a false show can be bett —can be more for God's glory, or' mar welfare—than God's own truth? Tru me, such men deceive themselves!"

"It may be so," said the young clerg man, indifferently, as waiving a d cussion that he considered irrelevant unseasonable. He had a ready facult indeed, of escaping from any topic th agitated his too sensitive and nervo temperament.—"But, now, I would a

my well-skilled physician, whether,
good soothe, he deems me to have
fited by his kindly care of this weak
me of mine?"

Before Roger Chillingworth could
wer, they heard the clear, wild
ghter of a young child's voice, pro-
ding from the adjacent burial-
und. Looking instinctively from the
en window,—for it was summer-time,
the minister beheld Hester Prynne
l little Pearl passing along the foot-
h that traversed the enclosure. Pearl
ked as beautiful as the day, but was
one of those moods of perverse
rriment which, whenever they oc-
rred, seemed to remove her entirely
t of the sphere of sympathy or human
ntact. She now skipped irreverently
m one grave to another; until, com-
g to the broad, flat, armorial tomb-
ne of a departed worthy,—perhaps
Isaac Johnson himself,—she began
dance upon it. In reply to her
ther's command and entreaty that
e would behave more decorously, lit-
Pearl paused to gather the prickly
rrs from a tall burdock which grew
side the tomb. Taking a handful of
ese, she arranged them along the lines
the scarlet letter that decorated the
aternal bosom, to which the burrs,
their nature was, tenaciously adhered.
ester did not pluck them off.

Roger Chillingworth had by this time
proached the window, and smiled
mly down.

"There is no law, nor reverence for
thority, no regard for human ordi-
nces or opinions, right or wrong,
ixed up with that child's composi-
n," remarked he, as much to himself
to his companion. "I saw her, the
her day, bespatter the Governor himself with water, at the cattle-trough in
Spring-lane. What, in Heaven's name,
is she? Is the imp altogether evil? Hath
she affections? Hath she any discover-
able principle of being?"

"None,—save the freedom of a
broken law," answered Mr. Dimmesdale, in a quiet way, as if he had been
discussing the point within himself.
"Whether capable of good, I know not."

The child probably overheard their
voices; for, looking up to the window,
with a bright, but naughty smile of
mirth and intelligence, she threw one
of the prickly burrs at the Reverend
Mr. Dimmesdale. The sensitive clergyman shrank, with nervous dread, from
the light missile. Detecting his emotion,
Pearl clapped her little hands, in the
most extravagant ecstasy. Hester
Prynne, likewise, had involuntarily
looked up; and all these four persons,
old and young, regarded one another
in silence, till the child laughed aloud,
and shouted,—"Come away, mother!
Come away, or yonder old Black Man
will catch you! He hath got hold of
the minister already. Come away,
mother, or he will catch you! But he
cannot catch little Pearl!"

So she drew her mother away, skipping, dancing, and frisking fantastically,
among the hillocks of the dead people,
like a creature that had nothing in common with a bygone and buried generation, nor owned herself akin to it. It
was as if she had been made afresh,
out of new elements, and must perforce
be permitted to live her own life, and
be a law unto herself, without her eccentricities being reckoned to her for a
crime.

"There goes a woman," resumed
Roger Chillingworth, after a pause,

"who, be her demerits what they may, hath none of that mystery of hidden sinfulness which you deem so grievous to be borne. Is Hester Prynne the less miserable, think you, for that scarlet letter on her breast?"

"I do verily believe it," answered the clergyman. "Nevertheless, I cannot answer for her. There was a look of pain in her face, which I would gladly have been spared the sight of. But still, methinks, it must needs be better for the sufferer to be free to show his pain, as this poor woman Hester is, than to cover it all up in his heart."

There was another pause; and the physician began anew to examine and arrange the plants which he had gathered.

"You inquired of me, a little time agone," said he, at length, "my judgment as touching your health."

"I did," answered the clergyman, "and would gladly learn it. Speak frankly, I pray you, be it for life or death."

"Freely, then, and plainly," said the physician, still busy with his plants, but keeping a wary eye on Mr. Dimmesdale, "the disorder is a strange one; not so much in itself, nor as outwardly manifested,—in so far, at least, as the symptoms have been laid open to my observation. Looking daily at you, my good Sir, and watching the tokens of your aspect, now for months gone by, I should deem you a man sore sick, it may be, yet not so sick but that an instructed and watchful physician might well hope to cure you. But—I know not what to say—the disease is what I seem to know, yet know it not."

"You speak in riddles, learned Sir," said the pale minister, glancing aside out of the window.

"Then, to speak more plainly," continued the physician, "and I crave pardon, Sir,—should it seem to require pardon,—for this needful plainness of my speech. Let me ask,—as your friend —as one having charge, under Providence, of your life and physical well-being,—hath all the operation of this disorder been fairly laid open and recounted to me?"

"How can you question it?" asked the minister. "Surely, it were child's play, to call in a physician, and then hide the sore!"

"You would tell me, then, that I know all?" said Roger Chillingworth, deliberately, and fixing an eye, bright with intense and concentrated intelligence, on the minister's face. "Be it so! But, again! He to whom only the outward and physical evil is laid open, knoweth, oftentimes, but half the evil which he is called upon to cure. A bodily disease, which we look upon as whole and entire within itself, may, after all, be but a symptom of some ailment in the spiritual part. Your pardon, once again, good Sir, if my speech give the shadow of offence. You, Sir, of all men whom I have known, are he whose body is the closest conjoined, and imbued and identified, so to speak, with the spirit whereof it is the instrument."

"Then I need ask no further," said the clergyman, somewhat hastily rising from his chair. "You deal not, I take it, in medicine for the soul!"

"Thus, a sickness," continued Roger Chillingworth, going on, in an unaltered tone, without heeding the interruption —but standing up, and confronting the emaciated and white-cheeked minister with his low, dark, and misshapen

—"a sickness, a sore place, if we
y so call it, in your spirit hath im-
diately its appropriate manifestation
our bodily frame. Would you, there-
e, that your physician heal the bodily
? How may this be, unless you first
open to him the wound or trouble
your soul?"

No!—not to thee!—not to an
thly physician!" cried Mr. Dimmes-
e, passionately, and turning his eyes,
and bright, with a kind of fierce-
s, on old Roger Chillingworth. "Not
thee! But, if it be the soul's disease,
n do I commit myself to the one
ysician of the soul! He, if it stand
h his good pleasure, can cure; or
can kill! Let him do with me as, in
justice and wisdom, he shall see
d. But who art thou, that meddlest
this matter?—that dares thrust him-
between the sufferer and his God?"
With a frantic gesture, he rushed out
the room.

"It is as well to have made this
p," said Roger Chillingworth to him-
, looking after the minister, with a
ve smile. "There is nothing lost. We
ll be friends again anon. But see,
w, how passion takes hold upon this
n, and hurrieth him out of himself!
with one passion, so with another!
hath done a wild thing ere now, this
us Master Dimmesdale, in the hot
sion of his heart!"

It proved not difficult to reëstablish
intimacy of the two companions,
the same footing and in the same
gree as heretofore. The young clergy-
n, after a few hours of privacy, was
sible that the disorder of his nerves
d hurried him into an unseemly out-
ak of temper, which there had been
thing in the physician's words to ex-

cuse or palliate. He marvelled, indeed,
at the violence with which he had thrust
back the kind old man, when merely
proffering the advice which it was his
duty to bestow, and which the minister
himself had expressly sought. With
these remorseful feelings, he lost no
time in making the amplest apologies,
and besought his friend still to continue
the care, which, if not successful in restoring him to health, had, in all probability, been the means of prolonging
his feeble existence to that hour. Roger
Chillingworth readily assented, and
went on with his medical supervision
of the minister; doing his best for him,
in all good faith, but always quitting
the patient's apartment, at the close of
a professional interview, with a mysterious and puzzled smile upon his lips.
This expression was invisible in Mr.
Dimmesdale's presence, but grew
strongly evident as the physician
crossed the threshold.

"A rare case!" he muttered. "I must
needs look deeper into it. A strange
sympathy betwixt soul and body! Were
it only for the art's sake, I must search
this matter to the bottom!"

It came to pass, not long after the
scene above recorded, that the Reverend
Mr. Dimmesdale, at noon-day, and entirely unawares, fell into a deep, deep
slumber, sitting in his chair, with a
large black-letter volume open before
him on the table. It must have been a
work of vast ability in the somniferous
school of literature. The profound depth
of the minister's repose was the more
remarkable, inasmuch as he was one of
those persons whose sleep, ordinarily,
is as light, as fitful, and as easily scared
away, as a small bird hopping on a
twig. To such an unwonted remoteness,

however, had his spirit now withdrawn into itself, that he stirred not in his chair, when old Roger Chillingworth, without any extraordinary precaution, came into the room. The physician advanced directly in front of his patient, laid his hand upon his bosom, and thrust aside the vestment, that, hitherto, had always covered it even from the professional eye.

Then, indeed, Mr. Dimmesdale shuddered, and slightly stirred.

After a brief pause, the physician turned away.

But, with what a wild look of wonder, joy, and horror! With what a ghastly rapture, as it were, too mighty to be expressed only by the eye a features, and therefore bursting fo through the whole ugliness of his figu and making itself even riotously ma fest by the extravagant gestures w which he threw up his arms towa the ceiling, and stamped his foot up the floor! Had a man seen old Ro Chillingworth, at that moment of ecstasy, he would have had no need ask how Satan comports himself, wh a precious human soul is lost to heav and won into his kingdom.

But what distinguished the phy cian's ecstasy from Satan's was the tr of wonder in it!

CHAPTER XI

THE INTERIOR OF A HEART

AFTER the incident last described, the intercourse between the clergyman and the physician, though externally the same, was really of another character than it had previously been. The intellect of Roger Chillingworth had now a sufficiently plain path before it. It was not, indeed, precisely that which he had laid out for himself to tread. Calm, gentle, passionless, as he appeared, there was yet, we fear, a quiet depth of malice, hitherto latent, but active now, in this unfortunate old man, which led him to imagine a more intimate revenge than any mortal had ever wreaked upon an enemy. To make himself the one trusted friend, to whom should be confided all the fear, the remorse, the agony, the ineffectual repentance, the backward rush of sinful thoughts, pelled in vain! All that guilty sorro hidden from the world, whose gre heart would have pitied and forgiv to be revealed to him, the Pitiless, him, the Unforgiving! All that da treasure to be lavished on the very m. to whom nothing else could so ad quately pay the debt of vengeance!

The clergyman's shy and sensitive serve had balked this scheme. Rog Chillingworth, however, was inclined be hardly, if at all, less satisfied w the aspect of affairs, which Provider —using the avenger and his victim f its own purposes, and, perchance, pa doning, where it seemed most to puni —had substituted for his black devic A revelation, he could almost say, h

n granted to him. It mattered little,
his object, whether celestial, or
m what other region. By its aid, in
the subsequent relations betwixt him
l Mr. Dimmesdale, not merely the
ernal presence, but the very inmost
l, of the latter, seemed to be brought
before his eyes, so that he could see
l comprehend its every movement.
became, thenceforth, not a specta-
only, but a chief actor, in the poor
nister's interior world. He could play
on him as he chose. Would he arouse
n with a throb of agony? The victim
s forever on the rack; it needed only
know the spring that controlled the
gine;—and the physician knew it
ll! Would he startle him with sudden
r? As at the waving of a magician's
nd, uprose a grisly phantom,—uprose
housand phantoms,—in many shapes,
death, or more awful shame, all
cking round about the clergyman, and
inting with their fingers at his breast!
All this was accomplished with a
btlety so perfect, that the minister,
ugh he had constantly a dim per-
otion of some evil influence watching
er him, could never gain a knowledge
its actual nature. True, he looked
ubtfully, fearfully,—even, at times,
th horror and the bitterness of hatred,
at the deformed figure of the old
ysician. His gestures, his gait, his
zzled beard, his slightest and most
different acts, the very fashion of
garments, were odious in the clergy-
n's sight; a token implicitly to be
ied on, of a deeper antipathy in the
east of the latter than he was willing
acknowledge to himself. For, as it
s impossible to assign a reason for
ch distrust and abhorrence, so Mr.
mmesdale, conscious that the poison

of one morbid spot was infecting his
heart's entire substance, attributed all
his presentiments to no other cause. He
took himself to task for his bad sympathies in reference to Roger Chillingworth, disregarded the lesson that he
should have drawn from them, and did
his best to root them out. Unable to
accomplish this, he nevertheless, as a
matter of principle, continued his
habits of social familiarity with the old
man, and thus gave him constant opportunities for perfecting the purpose
to which—poor, forlorn creature that
he was, and more wretched than his
victim—the avenger had devoted himself.

While thus suffering under bodily disease, and gnawed and tortured by some
black trouble of the soul, and given
over to the machinations of his deadliest
enemy, the Reverend Mr. Dimmesdale
had achieved a brilliant popularity in
his sacred office. He won it, indeed, in
great part, by his sorrows. His intellectual gifts, his moral perceptions, his
power of experiencing and communicating emotion, were kept in a state of
preternatural activity by the prick and
anguish of his daily life. His fame,
though still on its upward slope, already
overshadowed the soberer reputations
of his fellow-clergymen, eminent as several of them were. There were scholars
among them, who had spent more years
in acquiring abstruse lore, connected
with the divine profession, than Mr.
Dimmesdale had lived; and who might
well, therefore, be more profoundly
versed in such solid and valuable attainments than their youthful brother.
There were men, too, of a sturdier texture of mind than his, and endowed
with a far greater share of shrewd,

hard, iron, or granite understanding; which, duly mingled with a fair proportion of doctrinal ingredient, constitutes a highly respectable, efficacious, and unamiable variety of the clerical species. There were others, again, true saintly fathers, whose faculties had been elaborated by weary toil among their books, and by patient thought, and etherealized, moreover, by spiritual communications with the better world, into which their purity of life had almost introduced these holy personages, with their garments of mortality still clinging to them. All that they lacked was the gift that descended upon the chosen disciples at Pentecost, in tongues of flame; symbolizing, it would seem, not the power of speech in foreign, and unknown languages, but that of addressing the whole human brotherhood in the heart's native language. These fathers, otherwise so apostolic, lacked Heaven's last and rarest attestation of their office, the Tongue of Flame. They would have vainly sought —had they ever dreamed of seeking— to express the highest truths through the humblest medium of familiar words and images. Their voices came down, afar and indistinctly, from the upper heights where they habitually dwelt.

Not improbably, it was to this latter class of men that Mr. Dimmesdale, by many of his traits of character, naturally belonged. To the high mountain-peaks of faith and sanctity he would have climbed, had not the tendency been thwarted by the burden, whatever it might be, of crime or anguish, beneath which it was his doom to totter. It kept him down, on a level with the lowest; him, the man of ethereal attributes, whose voice the angels might

else have listened to and answered! this very burden it was, that gave sympathies so intimate with the sir brotherhood of mankind; so that heart vibrated in unison with theirs, received their pain into itself, and s its own throb of pain through a th sand other hearts, in gushes of sad, p suasive eloquence. Oftenest persuas but sometimes terrible! The peo knew not the power that moved th thus. They deemed the young cler man a miracle of holiness. They fanc him the mouthpiece of Heaven's m sages of wisdom, and rebuke, and lo In their eyes, the very ground on wh he trod was sanctified. The virgins his church grew pale around him, tims of a passion so imbued with ligious sentiment that they imagined to be all religion, and brought it oper in their white bosoms, as their most ceptable sacrifice before the altar. aged members of his flock, behold Mr. Dimmesdale's frame so feel while they were themselves so rug in their infirmity, believed that would go heavenward before them, enjoined it upon their children, t their old bones should be buried cl to their young pastor's holy grave. A all this time, perchance, when poor Dimmesdale was thinking of his gra he questioned with himself whether grass would ever grow on it, because accursed thing must there be buried!

It is inconceivable, the agony w which this public veneration tortu him! It was his genuine impulse adore the truth, and to reckon all thi shadow-like, and utterly devoid weight or value, that had not its div essence as the life within their li Then, what was he?—a substance?—

dimmest of all shadows? He longed
speak out, from his own pulpit, at
full height of his voice, and tell
people what he was. "I, whom you
old in these black garments of the
esthood,—I, who ascend the sacred
k, and turn my pale face heaven-
rd, taking upon myself to hold com-
nion, in your behalf, with the Most
gh Omniscience,—I, in whose daily
you discern the sanctity of Enoch,
, whose footsteps, as you suppose,
ve a gleam along my earthly track,
ereby the pilgrims that shall come
er me may be guided to the regions
the blest,—I, who have laid the hand
baptism upon your children,—I, who
ve breathed the parting prayer on
ir dying friends, to whom the Amen
nded faintly from a world which
y had quitted,—I, your pastor, whom
so reverence and trust, am utterly
ollution and a lie!"

More than once, Mr. Dimmesdale
d gone into the pulpit, with a purse never to come down its steps,
il he should have spoken words like
above. More than once, he had
ared his throat, and drawn in the
g, deep, and tremulous breath, which,
en sent forth again, would come bur-
ed with the black secret of his soul.
re than once—nay, more than a hun-
d times—he had actually spoken!
oken! But how? He had told his
rers that he was altogether vile, a
er companion of the vilest, the worst
sinners, an abomination, a thing of
imaginable iniquity; and that the
ly wonder was, that they did not see
wretched body shrivelled up before
ir eyes, by the burning wrath of the
mighty! Could there be plainer
ech than this? Would not the peo-

ple start up in their seats, by a simultaneous impulse, and tear him down
out of the pulpit which he defiled? Not
so, indeed! They heard it all, and did
but reverence him the more. They little
guessed what deadly purport lurked in
those self-condemning words. "The
godly youth!" said they among themselves. "The saint on earth! Alas, if
he discern such sinfulness in his own
white soul, what horrid spectacle would
he behold in thine or mine!" The minister well knew—subtle, but remorseful
hypocrite that he was!—the light in
which his vague confession would be
viewed. He had striven to put a cheat
upon himself by making the avowal of
a guilty conscience, but had gained only
one other sin, and a self-acknowledged
shame, without the momentary relief
of being self-deceived. He had spoken
the very truth, and transformed it into
the veriest falsehood. And yet, by the
constitution of his nature, he loved the
truth, and loathed the lie, as few men
ever did. Therefore, above all things
else, he loathed his miserable self!

His inward trouble drove him to practices more in accordance with the old,
corrupted faith of Rome, than with
the better light of the church in which
he had been born and bred. In Mr.
Dimmesdale's secret closet, under lock
and key, there was a bloody scourge.
Oftentimes, this Protestant and Puritan divine had plied it on his own shoulders; laughing bitterly at himself the
while, and smiting so much the more
pitilessly because of that bitter laugh.
It was his custom, too, as it has been
that of many other pious Puritans, to
fast,—not, however, like them, in order
to purify the body and render it the
fitter medium of celestial illumination,

but rigorously, and until his knees trembled beneath him, as an act of penance. He kept vigils, likewise, night after night, sometimes in utter darkness; sometimes with a glimmering lamp; and sometimes viewing his own face in a looking-glass, by the most powerful light which he could throw upon it. He thus typified the constant introspection wherewith he tortured, but could not purify, himself. In these lengthened vigils, his brain often reeled, and visions seemed to flit before him; perhaps seen doubtfully, and by a faint light of their own, in the remote dimness of the chamber, or more vividly, and close beside him, within the looking-glass. Now it was a herd of diabolic shapes, that grinned and mocked at the pale minister, and beckoned him away with them; now a group of shining angels, who flew upward heavily, as sorrow-laden, but grew more ethereal as they rose. Now came the dead friends of his youth, and his white-bearded father, with a saint-like frown, and his mother, turning her face away as she passed by. Ghost of a mother,—thinnest fantasy of a mother,—methinks she might yet have thrown a pitying glance towards her son! And now, through the chamber which these spectral thoughts had made so ghastly, glided Hester Prynne, leading along little Pearl, in her scarlet garb, and pointing her forefinger, first at the scarlet letter on her bosom, and then at the clergyman's own breast.

None of these visions ever quite deluded him. At any moment, by an effort of his will, he could discern substance through their misty lack of substance and convince himself that they were not solid in their nature, like yonder table of carved oak, or that big, square leathern-bound and brazen-clasped volume of divinity. But, for all that, they were, in one sense, the truest and most substantial things which the poor minister now dealt with. It is the unspeakable misery of a life so false as his, that it steals the pith and substance out of whatever realities there are around, and which were meant by Heaven to be the spirit's joy and nutriment. To the untrue man, the whole universe is false,—it is impalpable,—it shrinks to nothing within his grasp. And he himself, in so far as he shows himself in a false light, becomes a shadow, or, indeed, ceases to exist. The only truth that continued to give Mr. Dimmesdale a real existence on this earth, was the anguish in his inmost soul, and the undissembled expression of it in his aspect. Had he once found power to smile, and wear a face of gayety, there would have been no such man!

On one of those ugly nights, which we have faintly hinted at, but forbore to picture forth, the minister started from his chair. A new thought had struck him. There might be a moment's peace in it. Attiring himself with much care as if it had been for public worship, and precisely in the same manner, he stole softly down the staircase, undid the door, and issued forth.

CHAPTER XII

THE MINISTER'S VIGIL

ⱲALKING in the shadow of a dream,
it were, and perhaps actually under
influence of a species of somnam-
ism, Mr. Dimmesdale reached the
t, where, now so long since, Hester
ⱲⱤnne had lived through her first hours
public ignominy. The same platform
scaffold, black and weather-stained
h the storm or sunshine of seven
g years, and foot-worn, too, with
tread of many culprits who had
ce ascended it, remained standing be-
th the balcony of the meeting-house.
e minister went up the steps.
t was an obscure night of early May.
unvaried pall of cloud muffled the
ole expanse of sky from zenith to
rizon. If the same multitude which
l stood as eye-witnesses while Hester
ⱲⱤnne sustained her punishment could
v have been summoned forth, they
uld have discerned no face above the
tform, nor hardly the outline of a
nan shape, in the dark gray of the
ⱡnight. But the town was all asleep.
ere was no peril of discovery. The
nister might stand there, if it so
ased him, until morning should red-
ⱼn in the east, without other risk
ⱡn that the dank and chill night-air
uld creep into his frame, and stiffen
joints with rheumatism, and clog
throat with catarrh and cough;
ⱥreby defrauding the expectant audi-
ⱡe of to-morrow's prayer and sermon.
 eye could see him, save that ever-
ⱡkeful one which had seen him in his
ⱡset, wielding the bloody scourge.
ⱥy, then, had he come hither? Was

it but the mockery of penitence? A
mockery, indeed, but in which his soul
trifled with itself! A mockery at which
angels blushed and wept, while fiends rejoiced, with jeering laughter! He had
been driven hither by the impulse of that
Remorse which dogged him everywhere,
and whose own sister and closely linked
companion was that Cowardice which
invariably drew him back, with her
tremulous gripe, just when the other
impulse had hurried him to the verge of
a disclosure. Poor, miserable man! what
right had infirmity like his to burden
itself with crime? Crime is for the iron-
nerved, who have their choice either to
endure it, or, if it press too hard, to
exert their fierce and savage strength for
a good purpose, and fling it off at once!
This feeble and most sensitive of spirits
could do neither, yet continually did one
thing or another, which intertwined, in
the same inextricable knot, the agony of
heaven-defying guilt and vain repentance.

And thus, while standing on the scaffold, in this vain show of expiation, Mr.
Dimmesdale was overcome with a great
horror of mind, as if the universe were
gazing at a scarlet token on his naked
breast, right over his heart. On that
spot, in very truth, there was, and there
had long been, the gnawing and poisonous tooth of bodily pain. Without any
effort of his will, or power to restrain
himself, he shrieked aloud; an outcry
that went pealing through the night,
and was beaten back from one house
to another, and reverberated from the

hills in the background; as if a company of devils, detecting so much misery and terror in it, had made a plaything of the sound, and were bandying it to and fro.

"It is done!" muttered the minister, covering his face with his hands. "The whole town will awake, and hurry forth, and find me here!"

But it was not so. The shriek had perhaps sounded with a far greater power, to his own startled ears, than it actually possessed. The town did not awake, or, if it did, the drowsy slumberers mistook the cry either for something frightful in a dream, or for the noise of witches; whose voices, at that period, were often heard to pass over the settlements or lonely cottages, as they rode with Satan through the air. The clergyman, therefore, hearing no symptoms of disturbance, uncovered his eyes and looked about him. At one of the chamber-windows of Governor Bellingham's mansion, which stood at some distance, on the line of another street, he beheld the appearance of the old magistrate himself, with a lamp in his hand, a white night-cap on his head, and a long white gown enveloping his figure. He looked like a ghost, evoked unseasonably from the grave. The cry had evidently startled him. At another window of the same house, moreover, appeared old Mistress Hibbins, the Governor's sister, also with a lamp, which, even thus far off, revealed the expression of her sour and discontented face. She thrust forth her head from the lattice, and looked anxiously upward. Beyond the shadow of a doubt, this venerable witch-lady had heard Mr. Dimmesdale's outcry, and interpreted it, with its multitudinous echoes and reverberations, as the clamor of the fie and night-hags, with whom she was known to make excursions into forest.

Detecting the gleam of Governor lingham's lamp the old lady qui extinguished her own, and vanis Possibly, she went up among the clo The minister saw nothing further her motions. The magistrate, afte wary observation of the darkness— which, nevertheless, he could see little further than he might into a r stone—retired from the window.

The minister grew comparati calm. His eyes, however, were s greeted by a little, glimmering li which, at first a long way off, was proaching up the street. It threw gleam of recognition on here a p and there a garden-fence, and her latticed window-pane, and there a pu with its full trough of water, and h again, an arched door of oak, with iron knocker, and a rough log for door-step. The Reverend Mr. Dimm dale noted all these minute particul even while firmly convinced that doom of his existence was stealing ward, in the footsteps which he r heard; and that the gleam of the l tern would fall upon him, in a moments more, and reveal his lo hidden secret. As the light grew nea he beheld, within its illuminated cir his brother clergyman,—or, to sp more accurately, his professional fat as well as highly valued friend,— Reverend Mr. Wilson; who, as Dimmesdale now conjectured, had b praying at the bedside of some dy man. And so he had. The good minister came freshly from the dea chamber of Governor Winthrop, v

d passed from earth to heaven within
t very hour. And now, surrounded,
e the saint-like personages of olden
1es, with a radiant halo, that glorified
m amid this gloomy night of sin,—
if the departed Governor had left
n an inheritance of his glory, or as
he had caught upon himself the dis-
t shine of the celestial city, while
king thither-ward to see the trium-
ant pilgrim pass within its gates,—
w, in short, good Father Wilson was
ving homeward, aiding his footsteps
h a lighted lantern! The glimmer
this luminary suggested the above
iceits to Mr. Dimmesdale, who
iled,—nay, almost laughed at them,
1nd then wondered if he were going
d.

As the Reverend Mr. Wilson passed
side the scaffold, closely muffling his
neva cloak about him with one arm,
I holding the lantern before his breast
h the other, the minister could hard-
restrain himself from speaking.

'A good evening to you, venerable
ther Wilson! Come up hither, I pray
1, and pass a pleasant hour with me!"
3ood heavens! Had Mr. Dimmesdale
ually spoken? For one instant, he
ieved that these words had passed
lips. But they were uttered only
hin his imagination. The venerable
ther Wilson continued to step slowly
ward, looking carefully at the muddy
hway before his feet, and never once
ning his head towards the guilty
tform. When the light of the glim-
ring lantern had faded quite away,
 minister discovered, by the faint-
ss which came over him, that the
t few moments had been a crisis of
rible anxiety; although his mind had
de an involuntary effort to relieve itself by a kind of lurid playfulness.

Shortly afterwards, the like grisly
sense of the humorous again stole in
among the solemn phantoms of his
thought. He felt his limbs growing stiff
with the unaccustomed chilliness of the
night, and doubted whether he should
be able to descend the steps of the
scaffold. Morning would break, and find
him there. The neighborhood would begin to rouse itself. The earliest riser,
coming forth in the dim twilight, would
perceive a vaguely defined figure aloft
on the place of shame; and, half crazed
betwixt alarm and curiosity, would go,
knocking from door to door, summoning
all the people to behold the ghost—
as he needs must think it—of some
defunct transgressor. A dusky tumult
would flap its wings from one house to
another. Then—the morning light still
waxing stronger—old patriarchs would
rise up in great haste, each in his flannel gown, and matronly dames, without
pausing to put off their night-gear. The
whole tribe of decorous personages, who
had never heretofore been seen with
a single hair of their heads awry would
start into public view, with the disorder of a nightmare in their aspects.
Old Governor Bellingham would come
grimly forth, with his King James' ruff
fastened askew; and Mistress Hibbins,
with some twigs of the forest clinging
to her skirts, and looking sourer than
ever, as having hardly got a wink of
sleep after her night ride; and good
Father Wilson, too, after spending half
the night at a death-bed, and liking ill
to be disturbed, thus early, out of his
dreams about the glorified saints. Hither,
likewise, would come the elders and
deacons of Mr. Dimmesdale's church,
and the young virgins who so idolized

their minister, and had made a shrine for him in their white bosoms; which now, by the by, in their hurry and confusion, they would scantly have given themselves time to cover with their kerchiefs. All people, in a word, would come stumbling over their thresholds, and turning up their amazed and horror-stricken visages around the scaffold. Whom would they discern there, with the red eastern light upon his brow? Whom, but the Reverend Arthur Dimmesdale, half frozen to death, overwhelmed with shame, and standing where Hester Prynne had stood!

Carried away by the grotesque horror of this picture, the minister, unawares, and to his own infinite alarm, burst into a great peal of laughter. It was immediately responded to by a light, airy, childish laugh, in which a thrill of the heart,—but he knew not whether of exquisite pain, or pleasure as acute, —he recognized the tones of little Pearl.

"Pearl! Little Pearl!" cried he, after a moment's pause; then, suppressing his voice,—"Hester! Hester Prynne! Are you there?"

"Yes; it is Hester Prynne!" she replied, in a tone of surprise; and the minister heard her footsteps approaching from the sidewalk, along which she had been passing. "It is I, and my little Pearl."

"Whence come you, Hester?" asked the minister. "What sent you hither?"

"I have been watching at a death-bed," answered Hester Prynne;—"at Governor Winthrop's death-bed, and have taken his measure for a robe, and am now going homeward to my dwelling."

"Come up hither, Hester, thou and little Pearl," said the Reverend Mr. Dimmesdale. "Ye have both been he before, but I was not with you. Co up hither once again, and we will sta all three together!"

She silently ascended the steps, a stood on the platform, holding lit Pearl by the hand. The minister felt the child's other hand, and took it. T moment that he did so, there came wh seemed a tumultuous rush of new li other life than his own, pouring l a torrent into his heart, and hurry through all his veins, as if the mot and the child were communicating th vital warmth to his half-torpid syste The three formed an electric chain.

"Minister!" whispered little Pearl

"What wouldst thou say, chil asked Mr. Dimmesdale.

"Wilt thou stand here with mot and me, to-morrow noon-tide?" inqui Pearl.

"Nay; not so, my little Pearl," swered the minister; for, with the n energy of the moment, all the dread public exposure, that had so long b the anguish of his life, had retur upon him; and he was already trembl at the conjunction in which—with strange joy, nevertheless—he now fou himself. "Not so, my child. I shall, deed, stand with thy mother and t one other day, but not to-morrow."

Pearl laughed, and attempted to p away her hand. But the minister h it fast.

"A moment longer, my child!" s he.

"But wilt thou promise," asked Pe "to take my hand, and mother's ha to-morrow noontide?"

"Not then, Pearl," said the minis "but another time."

'And what other time?" persisted the
ld.

'At the great judgment day," whis-
ed the minister,—and, strangely
ough, the sense that he was a profes-
nal teacher of the truth impelled him
answer the child so. "Then, and there,
ore the judgment-seat, thy mother,
l thou, and I, must stand together.
t the daylight of this world shall not
our meeting!"

Pearl laughed again.

But before Mr. Dimmesdale had done
aking, a light gleamed far and wide
er all the muffled sky. It was doubt-
s caused by one of those meteors,
ich the night-watcher may so often
serve burning out to waste, in the
ant regions of the atmosphere. So
werful was its radiance, that it thor-
ghly illuminated the dense medium of
ud betwixt the sky and earth. The
at vault brightened, like the dome
an immense lamp. It showed the
niliar scene of the street, with the
tinctness of mid-day, but also with
e awfulness that is always imparted
familiar objects by an unaccustomed
nt. The wooden houses, with their
ting stories and quaint gable-peaks;
e doorsteps and thresholds, with the
ly grass springing up about them; the
den-plots, black with freshly turned
th; the wheel-track, little worn, and,
en in the market-place, margined with
en on either side;—all were visible,
t with a singularity of aspect that
med to give another moral interpre-
ion to the things of this world than
y had ever borne before. And there
od the minister, with his hand over
heart; and Hester Prynne, with the
broidered letter glimmering on her
som; and little Pearl, herself a sym-

bol, and the connecting link between
those two. They stood in the noon of
that strange and solemn splendor, as
if it were the light that is to reveal
all secrets, and the daybreak that shall
unite all who belong to one another.

There was witchcraft in little Pearl's
eyes; and her face, as she glanced upward at the minister, wore that naughty
smile which made its expression frequently so elvish. She withdrew her
hand from Mr. Dimmesdale's, and
pointed across the street. But he clasped
both his hands over his breast, and cast
his eyes towards the zenith.

Nothing was more common, in those
days, than to interpret all meteoric appearances, and other natural phenomena,
that occurred with less regularity than
the rise and set of sun and moon, as
so many revelations from a supernatural
source. Thus, a blazing spear, a sword
of flame, a bow, or a sheaf of arrows,
seen in the midnight sky, prefigured Indian warfare. Pestilence was known to
have been foreboded by a shower of
crimson light. We doubt whether any
marked event, for good or evil, ever
befell New England, from its settlement down to Revolutionary times, of
which the inhabitants had not been
previously warned by some spectacle of
this nature. Not seldom, it had been
seen by multitudes. Oftener, however,
its credibility rested on the faith of
some lonely eye-witness, who beheld
the wonder through the colored, magnifying, and distorting medium of his
imagination, and shaped it more distinctly in his after-thought. It was, indeed,
a majestic idea, that the destiny of
nations should be revealed, in these
awful hieroglyphics, on the cope of
heaven. A scroll so wide might not be

deemed too expansive for Providence to write a people's doom upon. The belief was a favorite one with our forefathers, as betokening that their infant commonwealth was under a celestial guardianship of peculiar intimacy and strictness. But what shall we say, when an individual discovers a revelation, addressed to himself alone, on the same vast sheet of record! In such a case, it could only be the symptom of a highly disordered mental state, when a man, rendered morbidly self-contemplative by long, intense, and secret pain, had extended his egotism over the whole expanse of nature, until the firmament itself should appear no more than a fitting page for his soul's history and fate!

We impute it, therefore, solely to the disease in his own eye and heart, that the minister, looking upward to the zenith, beheld there the appearance of an immense letter,—the letter A,—marked out in lines of dull red light. Not but the meteor may have shown itself at that point, burning duskily through a veil of cloud; but with no such shape as his guilty imagination gave it; or, at least, with so little definiteness, that another's guilt might have seen another symbol in it.

There was a singular circumstance that characterized Mr. Dimmesdale's psychological state, at this moment. All the time that he gazed upward to the zenith, he was, nevertheless, perfectly aware that little Pearl was pointing her finger towards old Roger Chillingworth, who stood at no great distance from the scaffold. The minister appeared to see him, with the same glance that discerned the miraculous letter. To his features, as to all other objects, the mete-oric light imparted a new expressio or it might well be that the physici was not careful then, as at all oth times, to hide the malevolence wi which he looked upon his victim. C tainly, if the meteor kindled up t sky, and disclosed the earth, with awfulness that admonished Hest Prynne and the clergyman of the d of judgment, then might Roger Chillin worth have passed with them for t arch-fiend, standing there with a sm and scowl, to claim his own. So viv was the expression, or so intense t minister's perception of it, that seemed still to remain painted on t darkness, after the meteor had vanishe with an effect as if the street and things else were at once annihilated.

"Who is that man, Hester?" gasp Mr. Dimmesdale, overcome with terr "I shiver at him! Dost thou know t man? I hate him, Hester!"

She remembered her oath, and w silent.

"I tell thee, my soul shivers at him muttered the minister again. "Who he? Who is he? Canst thou do nothi for me? I have a nameless horror of t man!"

"Minister," said little Pearl, "I c tell thee who he is!"

"Quickly, then, child!" said the mi ister, bending his ear close to her li "Quickly!—and as low as thou car whisper."

Pearl mumbled something into h ear, that sounded, indeed, like hum language, but was only such gibberi as children may be heard amusing the selves with, by the hour together. all events, if it involved any secr information in regard to old Roger Ch lingworth, it was in a tongue unknov the erudite clergyman, and did but crease the bewilderment of his mind. ae elvish child then laughed aloud.

"Dost thou mock me now?" said the inister.

"Thou wast not bold!—thou wast not ae!"—answered the child. "Thou ouldst not promise to take my hand, d mother's hand, to-morrow noon-le!"

"Worthy Sir," answered the physi-an, who had now advanced to the ot of the platform. "Pious Master mmesdale! can this be you? Well, ell, indeed! We men of study, whose ads are in our books, have need to straitly looked after! We dream in r waking moments, and walk in our ep. Come, good Sir, and my dear end, I pray you, let me lead you me!"

"How knewest thou that I was here?" ked the minister, fearfully.

"Verily, and in good faith," answered oger Chillingworth, "I knew nothing the matter. I had spent the better rt of the night at the bedside of the orshipful Governor Winthrop, doing aat my poor skill might to give him se. He going home to a better world, likewise, was on my way homeward, aen this strange light shone out. Come th me, I beseech you, Reverend Sir; e you will be poorly able to do Sab-th duty to-morrow. Aha! see now, w they trouble the brain,—these oks!—these books! You should study s, good Sir, and take a little pastime; these night-whimsies will grow upon u."

"I will go home with you," said Mr. mmesdale.

With a chill despondency, like one awaking, all nerveless, from an ugly dream, he yielded himself to the physician, and was led away.

The next day, however, being the Sabbath, he preached a discourse which was held to be the richest and most powerful, and the most replete with heavenly influences, that had ever proceeded from his lips. Souls, it is said, more souls than one, were brought to the truth by the efficacy of that sermon, and vowed within themselves to cherish a holy gratitude towards Mr. Dimmesdale throughout the long hereafter. But, as he came down the pulpit steps, the gray-bearded sexton met him, holding up a black glove, which the minister recognized as his own.

"It was found," said the sexton, "this morning, on the scaffold where evildoers are set up to public shame. Satan dropped it there, I take it, intending a scurrilous jest against your reverence. But, indeed, he was blind and foolish, as he ever and always is. A pure hand needs no glove to cover it!"

"Thank you, my good friend," said the minister, gravely, but startled at heart; for, so confused was his remembrance, that he had almost brought himself to look at the events of the past night as visionary. "Yes, it seems to be my glove, indeed!"

"And, since Satan saw fit to steal it, your reverence must needs handle him without gloves, henceforward," remarked the old sexton, grimly smiling. "But did your reverence hear of the portent that was seen last night?—a great red letter in the sky,—the letter A, which we interpret to stand for Angel. For, as our good Governor Winthrop was made an angel this past night, it was doubtless held fit that there should be some notice thereof!"

"No," answered the minister, "I h not heard of it."

CHAPTER XIII

ANOTHER VIEW OF HESTER

In her late singular interview with Mr. Dimmesdale, Hester Prynne was shocked at the condition to which she found the clergyman reduced. His nerve seemed absolutely destroyed. His moral force was abased into more than childish weakness. It grovelled helpless on the ground, even while his intellectual faculties retained their pristine strength, or had perhaps acquired a morbid energy, which disease only could have given them. With her knowledge of a train of circumstances hidden from all others, she could readily infer that, besides that legitimate action of his own conscience, a terrible machinery had been brought to bear, and was still operating, on Mr. Dimmesdale's well-being and repose. Knowing what this poor, fallen man had once been, her whole soul was moved by the shuddering terror with which he had appealed to her, —the outcast woman,—for support against his instinctively discovered enemy. She decided, moreover, that he had a right to her utmost aid. Little accustomed, in her long seclusion from society, to measure her ideas of right and wrong by any standard external to herself, Hester saw—or seemed to see—that there lay a responsibility upon her, in reference to the clergyman, which she owed to no other, nor to the whole world besides. The links that united her to the rest of human ki —links of flowers, or silk, or gold, whatever the material—had all be broken. Here was the iron link of m tual crime, which neither he nor s could break. Like all other ties, brought along with it its obligatio

Hester Prynne did not now occu precisely the same position in wh we beheld her during the earlier perio of her ignominy. Years had come a gone. Pearl was now seven years o Her mother, with the scarlet letter her breast, glittering in its fantas embroidery, had long been a famil object to the townspeople. As is apt be the case when a person stands in any prominence before the commu ity, and, at the same time, interfe neither with public nor individual int ests and convenience, a species of g eral regard had ultimately grown in reference to Hester Prynne. It is the credit of human nature, that, cept where its selfishness is brou into play, it loves more readily th it hates. Hatred, by a gradual and qu process, will even be transformed love, unless the change be impeded a continually new irritation of the or inal feeling of hostility. In this mat of Hester Prynne, there was neitl irritation nor irksomeness. She ne battled with the public, but submitt

complainingly, to its worst usage;
made no claim upon it, in requital
what she suffered; she did not weigh
on its sympathies. Then, also, the
meless purity of her life during all
se years in which she had been set
rt to infamy, was reckoned largely
her favor. With nothing now to lose,
the sight of mankind, and with no
pe, and seemingly no wish, of gaining
ything, it could only be a genuine
ard for virtue that had brought back
poor wanderer to its path.

It was perceived, too, that while Hes-
never put forward even the hum-
st title to share in the world's privi-
es,—further than to breathe the com-
n air, and earn daily bread for little
arl and herself by the faithful labor
her hands,—she was quick to ac-
owledge her sisterhood with the race
man, whenever benefits were to be
nferred. None so ready as she to give
er little substance to every demand of
verty; even though the bitter-hearted
uper threw back a gibe in requital
the food brought regularly to his
or, or the garments wrought for him
the fingers that could have embroid-
d a monarch's robe. None so self-
voted as Hester, when pestilence
lked through the town. In all sea-
s of calamity, indeed, whether gen-
l or of individuals, the outcast of
ciety at once found her place. She
me, not as a guest, but as a rightful
nate, into the household that was
rkened by trouble; as if its gloomy
ilight were a medium in which she
s entitled to hold intercourse with
r fellow-creatures. There glimmered
embroidered letter, with comfort in
unearthly ray. Elsewhere the token
sin, it was the taper of the sick-

chamber. It had even thrown its gleam,
in the sufferer's hard extremity, across
the verge of time. It had shown him
where to set his foot, while the light
of earth was fast becoming dim, and ere
the light of futurity could reach him.
In such emergencies, Hester's nature
showed itself warm and rich; a well-
spring of human tenderness, unfailing to
every real demand and inexhaustible by
the largest. Her breast, with its badge
of shame, was but the softer pillow
for the head that needed one. She was
self-ordained a Sister of Mercy; or, we
may rather say, the world's heavy hand
had so ordained her, when neither the
world nor she looked forward to this
result. The letter was the symbol of
her calling. Such helpfulness was found
in her,—so much power to do, and
power to sympathize,—that many people refused to interpret the scarlet A
by its original signification. They said
that it meant Able; so strong was
Hester Prynne, with a woman's strength.

It was only the darkened house that
could contain her. When sunshine came
again, she was not there. Her shadow
had faded across the threshold. The
helpful inmate had departed, without
one backward glance to gather up the
meed of gratitude, if any were in the
hearts of those whom she had served
so zealously. Meeting them in the street,
she never raised her head to receive
their greeting. If they were resolute to
accost her, she laid her finger on the
scarlet letter, and passed on. This might
be pride, but was so like humility, that
it produced all the softening influence
of the latter quality on the public mind.
The public is despotic in its temper;
it is capable of denying common justice, when too strenuously demanded as

a right; but quite as frequently it awards more than justice, when the appeal is made, as despots love to have it made, entirely to its generosity. Interpreting Hester Prynne's deportment as an appeal of this nature, society was inclined to show its former victim a more benign countenance than she cared to be favored with, or, perchance, than she deserved.

The rulers, and the wise and learned men of the community, were longer in acknowledging the influence of Hester's good qualities than the people. The prejudices which they shared in common with the latter were fortified in themselves by an iron framework of reasoning, that made it a far tougher labor to expel them. Day by day, nevertheless, their sour and rigid wrinkles were relaxing into something which, in the due course of years, might grow to be an expression of almost benevolence. Thus it was with the men of rank, on whom their eminent position imposed the guardianship of the public morals. Individuals in private life, meanwhile, had quite forgiven Hester Prynne for her frailty; nay, more, they had begun to look upon the scarlet letter as the token, not of that one sin, for which she had borne so long and dreary a penance, but of her many good deeds since. "Do you see that woman with the embroidered badge?" they would say to strangers. "It is our Hester,—the town's own Hester,—who is so kind to the poor, so helpful to the sick, so comfortable to the afflicted!" Then, it is true, the propensity of human nature to tell the very worst of itself, when embodied in the person of another, would constrain them to whisper the black scandal of bygone years.

It was none the less a fact, howev that, in the eyes of the very men w spoke thus, the scarlet letter had t effect of the cross on a nun's boso It imparted to the wearer a kind sacredness, which enabled her to wa securely amid all peril. Had she fal among thieves, it would have kept h safe. It was reported, and believed many, that an Indian had drawn arrow against the badge, and that t missile struck, but fell harmless to t ground.

The effect of the symbol—or, rath of the position in respect to socie that was indicated by it—on the mi of Hester Prynne herself, was power and peculiar. All the light and grace foliage of her character had been wit ered up by this red-hot brand, and h long ago fallen away, leaving a bare a harsh outline, which might have be repulsive, had she possessed friends companions to be repelled by it. Ev the attractiveness of her person b undergone a similar change. It might partly owing to the studied austerity her dress, and partly to the lack demonstration in her manners. It was sad transformation, too, that her ri and luxuriant hair had either been c off, or was so completely hidden by cap, that not a shining lock of it ev once gushed into the sunshine. It w due in part to all these causes, but st more to something else, that the seemed to be no longer anything Hester's face for Love to dwell upo nothing in Hester's form, though m jestic and statue-like, that Passion wou ever dream of clasping in its embrac nothing in Hester's bosom, to make ever again the pillow of Affection. Sor attribute had departed from her, t

rmanence of which had been essential
keep her a woman. Such is frequently
e fate, and such the stern develop-
ent, of the feminine character and
rson, when the woman has encoun-
red, and lived through, an experience
peculiar severity. If she be all tender-
ss, she will die. If she survive, the
iderness will either be crushed out
her, or—and the outward semblance
the same—crushed so deeply into her
art that it can never show itself more.
ie latter is perhaps the truest theory.
e who has once been woman, and
ised to be so, might at any moment
come a woman again, if there were
ly the magic touch to effect the trans-
iration. We shall see whether Hes-
Prynne were ever afterwards so
iched, and so transfigured.

Much of the marble coldness of Hes-
's impression was to be attributed
the circumstance, that her life had
ned, in a great measure, from pas-
n and feeling, to thought. Standing
ne in the world,—alone, as to any
pendence on society, and with little
arl to be guided and protected,—
ne, and hopeless of retrieving her
sition, even had she not scorned to
isider it desirable,—she cast away the
gments of a broken chain. The
rld's law was no law for her mind.
was an age in which the human in-
lect, newly emancipated, had taken a
re active and a wider range than
many centuries before. Men of the
ord had overthrown nobles and kings.
n bolder than these had overthrown
I rearranged—not actually, but with-
the sphere of theory, which was their
st real abode—the whole system of
ient prejudice, wherewith was linked
ich of ancient principle. Hester

Prynne imbibed this spirit. She assumed
a freedom of speculation, then common enough on the other side of the
Atlantic, but which our forefathers,
had they known it, would have held
to be a deadlier crime than that stigmatized by the scarlet letter. In her
lonesome cottage, by the seashore,
thoughts visited her, such as dared to
enter no other dwelling in New England; shadowy guests, that would have
been as perilous as demons to their
entertainer, could they have been seen
so much as knocking at her door.

It is remarkable, that persons who
speculate the most boldly often conform
with the most perfect quietude to the
external regulations of society. The
thought suffices them, without investing
itself in the flesh and blood of action.
So it seemed to be with Hester. Yet,
had little Pearl never come to her from
the spiritual world, it might have been
far otherwise. Then, she might have
come down to us in history, hand in
hand with Ann Hutchinson, as the
foundress of a religious sect. She might,
in one of her phases, have been a
prophetess. She might, and not improbably would, have suffered death from
the stern tribunals of the period, for
attempting to undermine the foundations of the Puritan establishment. But,
in the education of her child, the
mother's enthusiasm of thought had
something to wreak itself upon. Providence, in the person of this little girl,
had assigned to Hester's charge the
germ and blossom of womanhood, to be
cherished and developed amid a host
of difficulties. Everything was against
her. The world was hostile. The child's
own nature had something wrong in it,
which continually betokened that she

had been born amiss,—the effluence of her mother's lawless passion,—and often impelled Hester to ask, in bitterness of heart, whether it were for ill or good that the poor little creature had been born at all.

Indeed, the same dark question often rose into her mind, with reference to the whole race of womanhood. Was existence worth accepting, even to the happiest among them? As concerned her own individual existence, she had long ago decided in the negative, and dismissed the point as settled. A tendency to speculation, though it may keep woman quiet, as it does man, yet makes her sad. She discerns, it may be, such a hopeless task before her. As a first step, the whole system of society is to be torn down, and built up anew. Then, the very nature of the opposite sex, or its long hereditary habit, which has become like nature, is to be essentially modified, before woman can be allowed to assume what seems a fair and suitable position. Finally, all other difficulties being obviated, woman cannot take advantage of these preliminary reforms, until she herself shall have undergone a still mightier change; in which, perhaps, the ethereal essence, wherein she has her truest life, will be found to have evaporated. A woman never overcomes these problems by any exercise of thought. They are not to be solved, or only in one way. If her heart chance to come uppermost, they vanish. Thus, Hester Prynne, whose heart had lost its regular and healthy throb, wandered without a clew in the dark labyrinth of mind; now turned aside by an insurmountable precipice; now starting back from a deep chasm. There was wild and ghastly scenery all

around her, and a home and comf[e] nowhere. At times, a fearful dou[bt] strove to possess her soul, whether [it] were not better to send Pearl at on[ce] to heaven, and go herself to such f[u]turity as Eternal Justice should p[ro]vide.

The scarlet letter had not done [its] office.

Now, however, her interview with t[he] Reverend Mr. Dimmesdale, on the nig[ht] of his vigil, had given her a new the[me] of reflection, and held up to her [an] object that appeared worthy of a[ny] exertion and sacrifice for its atta[in]ment. She had witnessed the inte[nse] misery beneath which the minis[ter] struggled, or, to speak more accurate[ly,] had ceased to struggle. She saw th[at] he stood on the verge of lunacy, if [he] had not already stepped across it. [It] was impossible to doubt, that, wh[at]ever painful efficacy there might be [in] the secret sting of remorse, a deadl[y] venom had been infused into it [by] the hand that proffered relief. A sec[ret] enemy had been continually by his si[de,] under the semblance of a friend a[nd] helper, and had availed himself of [the] opportunities thus afforded for tamp[er]ing with the delicate springs of M[r.] Dimmesdale's nature. Hester could [not] but ask herself, whether there had [not] originally been a defect of truth, co[ur]age and loyalty, on her own part, [in] allowing the minister to be thrown i[nto] a position where so much evil was [to] be foreboded, and nothing auspicious [to] be hoped. Her only justification lay [in] the fact, that she had been able [to] discern no method of rescuing him fr[om] a blacker ruin than had overwhelm[ed] herself, except by acquiescing in Ro[ger] Chillingworth's scheme of disguise. [U]

r that impulse, she had made her
oice, and had chosen, as it now ap-
ared, the more wretched alternative
the two. She determined to redeem
r error, so far as it might yet be
ssible. Strengthened by years of hard
d solemn trial, she felt herself no
ger so inadequate to cope with Roger
iillingworth as on that night, abased
sin, and half maddened by the ig-
miny that was still new, when they
d talked together in the prison-
amber. She had climbed her way,
ice then, to a higher point. The old
n, on the other hand, had brought

himself nearer to her level, or perhaps
below it, by the revenge which he had
stooped for.

In fine, Hester Prynne resolved to
meet her former husband, and do what
might be in her power for the rescue
of the victim on whom he had so evidently set his gripe. The occasion was
not long to seek. One afternoon, walking with Pearl in a retired part of the
peninsula, she beheld the old physician,
with a basket on one arm, and a staff
in the other hand, stooping along the
ground, in quest of roots and herbs
to concoct his medicines withal.

CHAPTER XIV

HESTER AND THE PHYSICIAN

HESTER bade little Pearl run down
the margin of the water, and play
th the shells and tangled seaweed, un-
she should have talked awhile with
nder gatherer of herbs. So the child
w away like a bird, and, making bare
r small white feet, went pattering
ng the moist margin of the sea. Here
d there she came to a full stop, and
eped curiously into a pool, left by the
iring tide as a mirror for Pearl to
e her face in. Forth peeped at her, out
the pool, with dark, glistening curls
und her head, and an elf-smile in
r eyes, the image of a little maid,
om Pearl, having no other playmate,
vited to take her hand, and run a
ce with her. But the visionary little
iid, on her part, beckoned likewise,
if to say,—"This is a better place!
me thou into the pool!" And Pearl,

stepping in, mid-leg deep, beheld her
own white feet at the bottom; while,
out of a still lower depth, came the
gleam of a kind of fragmentary smile,
floating to and fro in the agitated water.

Meanwhile, her mother had accosted
the physician.

"I would speak a word with you,"
said she,—"a word that concerns us
much."

"Aha! and is it Mistress Hester that
has a word for old Roger Chillingworth?" answered he, raising himself
from his stooping posture. "With all
my heart! Why, Mistress, I hear good
tidings of you, on all hands! No longer
ago than yester-eve, a magistrate, a wise
and godly man, was discoursing of your
affairs, Mistress Hester, and whispered
me that there had been question concerning you in the council. It was de-

bated whether or no, with safety to the common weal, yonder scarlet letter might be taken off your bosom. On my life, Hester, I made my entreaty to the worshipful magistrate that it might be done forthwith!"

"It lies not in the pleasure of the magistrates to take off this badge," calmly replied Hester. "Were I worthy to be quit of it, it would fall away of its own nature, or be transformed into something that should speak a different purport."

"Nay, then, wear it, if it suit you better," rejoined he. "A woman must needs follow her own fancy, touching the adornment of her person. The letter is gayly embroidered, and shows right bravely on your bosom!"

All this while, Hester had been looking steadily at the old man, and was shocked, as well as wonder-smitten, to discern what a change had been wrought upon him within the past seven years. It was not so much that he had grown older; for though the traces of advancing life were visible, he bore his age well, and seemed to retain a wiry vigor and alertness. But the former aspect of an intellectual and studious man, calm and quiet, which was what she best remembered in him, had altogether vanished, and been succeeded by an eager, searching, almost fierce, yet carefully guarded look. It seemed to be his wish and purpose to mask this expression with a smile; but the latter played him false, and flickered over his visage so derisively, that the spectator could see his blackness all the better for it. Ever and anon, too, there came a glare of red light out of his eyes; as if the old man's soul were on fire, and kept on smouldering duskily within

his breast, until, by some casual pu of passion, it was blown into a mome tary flame. This he repressed, as spee ily as possible, and strove to look if nothing of the kind had happened.

In a word, old Roger Chillingwor was a striking evidence of a man's fa ulty of transforming himself into devil, if he will only, for a reasonab space of time, undertake a devil's o fice. This unhappy person had effect such a transformation, by devoting hir self, for seven years, to the consta analysis of a heart full of torture, ar deriving his enjoyment thence, and ad ing fuel to those fiery tortures whi he analyzed and gloated over.

The scarlet letter burned on Hest Prynne's bosom. Here was another rui the responsibility of which came part home to her.

"What see you in my face," ask the physician, "that you look at it earnestly?"

"Something that would make r weep, if there were any tears bitt enough for it," answered she. "But it pass! It is of yonder miserable ma that I would speak."

"And what of him?" cried Rog Chillingworth, eagerly, as if he lov the topic, and were glad of an oppo tunity to discuss it with the only pe son of whom he could make a confidar "Not to hide the truth, Mistress He ter, my thoughts happen just now be busy with the gentleman. So spe freely; and I will make answer."

"When we last spake together," sa Hester, "now seven years ago, it w your pleasure to extort a promise secrecy, as touching the former relati betwixt yourself and me. As the li and good fame of yonder man we

your hands, there seemed no choice
me, save to be silent, in accordance
ith your behest. Yet it was not with-
it heavy misgivings that I thus bound
yself; for, having cast off all duty
wards other human beings, there re-
ained a duty towards him; and some-
ing whispered me that I was betraying
, in pledging myself to keep your
unsel. Since that day, no man is so
ar to him as you. You tread behind
s every footstep. You are beside him,
eeping and waking. You search his
oughts. You burrow and rankle in his
art! Your clutch is on his life, and
u cause him to die daily a living
ath; and still he knows you not. In
rmitting this, I have surely acted a
lse part by the only man to whom the
wer was left me to be true!"

"What choice had you?" asked Roger
hillingworth. "My finger, pointed at
is man, would have hurled him from
s pulpit into a dungeon,—thence, per-
venture, to the gallows!"

"It had been better so!" said Hes-
r Prynne.

"What evil have I done the man?"
ked Roger Chillingworth again. "I
ll thee, Hester Prynne, the richest fee
at ever physician earned from mon-
ch could not have bought such care

I have wasted on this miserable
iest! But for my aid, his life would
ve burned away in torments, within
e first two years, after the perpetra-
n of his crime and thine. For, Hes-
r, his spirit lacked the strength that
uld have borne up, as thine has, be-
ath a burden like thy scarlet letter.

I could reveal a goodly secret! But
ough! What art can do, I have ex-
usted on him. That he now breathes,
d creeps about on earth, is owing

all to me!"

"Better he had died at once!" said
Hester Prynne.

"Yea, woman, thou sayest truly!"
cried old Roger Chillingworth, letting
the lurid fire of his heart blaze out
before her eyes. "Better had he died
at once! Never did mortal suffer what
this man has suffered. And all, all, in
the sight of his worst enemy! He has
been conscious of me. He has felt an
influence dwelling always upon him like
a curse. He knew, by some spiritual
sense,—for the Creator never made another being so sensitive as this,—he
knew that no friendly hand was pulling
at his heart-strings, and that an eye
was looking curiously into him, which
sought only evil, and found it. But he
knew not that the eye and hand were
mine! With the superstition common to
his brotherhood, he fancied himself
given over to a fiend, to be tortured
with frightful dreams, and desperate
thoughts, the sting of remorse, and
despair of pardon; as a foretaste of
what awaits him beyond the grave. But
it was the constant shadow of my
presence!—the closest propinquity of
the man whom he had most vilely
wronged!—and who had grown to exist
only by this perpetual poison of the
direst revenge! Yea, indeed!—he did
not err!—there was a fiend at his elbow! A mortal man, with once a human
heart, has become a fiend for his especial torment!"

The unfortunate physician, while uttering these words, lifted his hands with
a look of horror, as if he had beheld
some frightful shape, which he could
not recognize, usurping the place of his
own image in a glass. It was one of
those moments—which sometimes occur

only at the interval of years—when a man's moral aspect is faithfully revealed to his mind's eye. Not improbably, he had never before viewed himself as he did now.

"Hast thou not tortured him enough?" said Hester, noticing the old man's look. "Has he not paid thee all?"

"No!—no!—He has but increased the debt!" answered the physician; and as he proceeded, his manner lost its fiercer characteristics, and subsided into gloom. "Dost thou remember me, Hester, as I was nine years agone? Even then, I was in the autumn of my days, nor was it the early autumn. But all my life had been made up of earnest, studious, thoughtful, quiet years, bestowed faithfully for the increase of mine own knowledge, and faithfully, too, though this latter object was but casual to the other,—faithfully for the advancement of human welfare. No life had been more peaceful and innocent than mine; few lives so rich with benefits conferred. Dost thou remember me? Was I not, though you might deem me cold, nevertheless a man thoughtful for others, craving little for himself,—kind, true, just, and of constant, if not warm affections? Was I not all this?"

"All this, and more," said Hester.

"And what am I now?" demanded he, looking into her face, and permitting the whole evil within him to be written on his features. "I have already told thee what I am! A fiend! Who made me so?"

"It was myself!" cried Hester, shuddering. "It was I, not less than he. Why hast thou not avenged thyself on me?"

"I have left thee to the scarlet letter," replied Roger Chillingworth. "If

that have not avenged me, I can no more!"

He laid his finger on it, with a smi

"It has avenged thee!" answered H ter Prynne.

"I judged no less," said the phy cian. "And now, what wouldst thou w me touching this man?"

"I must reveal the secret," answer Hester, firmly. "He must discern th in thy true character. What may the result, I know not. But this lo debt of confidence, due from me him, whose bane and ruin I have bee shall at length be paid. So far as co cerns the overthrow or preservation his fair fame and his earthly sta and perchance his life, he is in t hands. Nor do I,—whom the scar letter has disciplined to truth, thou it be the truth of red-hot iron, enteri into the living soul,—nor do I percei such advantage in his living any long a life of ghastly emptiness, that I sh stoop to implore thy mercy. Do w him as thou wilt! There is no go for him,—no good for me,—no go for thee! There is no good for lit Pearl! There is no path to guide out of this dismal maze!"

"Woman, I could well-nigh p thee!" said Roger Chillingworth, una to restrain a thrill of admiration to for there was a quality almost majes in the despair which she express "Thou hadst great elements. Peradv ture, hadst thou met earlier with better love than mine, this evil k not been. I pity thee, for the good t has been wasted in thy nature!"

"And I thee," answered Hes Prynne, "for the hatred that has tra formed a wise and just man to a fie Wilt thou yet purge it out of thee, a

once more human? If not for his
ke, then doubly for thine own! For-
ve, and leave his further retribution
the Power that claims it! I said,
t now, that there could be no good
ent for him, or thee, or me, who are
re wandering together in this gloomy
aze of evil, and stumbling, at every
ep, over the guilt wherewith we have
rewn our path. It is not so! There
ght be good for thee, and thee alone,
ace thou hast been deeply wronged,
d hast it at thy will to pardon. Wilt
ou give up that only privilege? Wilt
ou reject that priceless benefit?"

"Peace, Hester, Peace!" replied the
d man, with gloomy sternness. "It is
t granted me to pardon. I have no

such power as thou tellest me of. My
old faith, long forgotten, comes back
to me, and explains all that we do, and
all we suffer. By thy first step awry,
thou didst plant the germ of evil; but
since that moment, it has all been a
dark necessity. Ye that have wronged
me are not sinful, save in a kind of
typical illusion; neither am I fiend-like,
who have snatched a fiend's office from
his hands. It is our fate. Let the black
flower blossom as it may! Now go thy
ways, and deal as thou wilt with yonder
man."

He waved his hand, and betook himself again to his employment of gathering herbs.

CHAPTER XV

HESTER AND PEARL

So Roger Chillingworth—a deformed
d figure, with a face that haunted
en's memories longer than they liked
took leave of Hester Prynne, and
ent stooping away along the earth. He
thered here and there an herb, or
ubbed up a root, and put it into
e basket on his arm. His gray beard
most touched the ground, as he crept
ward. Hester gazed after him a little
ile, looking with a half fantastic curi-
ity to see whether the tender grass
early spring would not be blighted
neath him, and show the wavering
ack of his footsteps, sere and brown,
ross its cheerful verdure. She won-
red what sort of herbs they were,
ich the old man was so sedulous to

gather. Would not the earth, quickened
to an evil purpose by the sympathy of
his eye, greet him with poisonous shrubs,
of species hitherto unknown, that would
start up under his fingers? Or might it
suffice him, that every wholesome
growth should be converted into something deleterious and malignant at his
touch? Did the sun, which shone so
brightly everywhere else, really fall
upon him? Or was there, as it rather
seemed, a circle of ominous shadow
moving along with his deformity, which-
ever way he turned himself? And
whither was he now going? Would he
not suddenly sink into the earth, leaving a barren and blasted spot, where,
in due course of time, would be seen

deadly nightshade, dogwood, henbane, and whatever else of vegetable wickedness the climate could produce, all flourishing with hideous luxuriance? Or would he spread bat's wings and flee away, looking so much the uglier, the higher he rose towards heaven?

"Be it sin or no," said Hester Prynne, bitterly, as she still gazed after him, "I hate the man!"

She upbraided herself for the sentiment, but could not overcome or lessen it. Attempting to do so, she thought of those long-past days, in a distant land, when he used to emerge at eventide from the seclusion of his study, and sit down in the fire-light of their home, and in the light of her nuptial smile. He needed to bask himself in that smile, he said, in order that the chill of so many lonely hours among his books might be taken off the scholar's heart. Such scenes had once appeared not otherwise than happy, but now, as viewed through the dismal medium of her subsequent life, they classed themselves among her ugliest remembrances. She marvelled how such scenes could have been! She marvelled how she could ever have been wrought upon to marry him! She deemed it a crime most to be repented of, that she had ever endured, and reciprocated, the lukewarm grasp of his hand, and had suffered the smile of her lips and eyes to mingle and melt into his own. And it seemed a fouler offence committed by Roger Chillingworth, than any which had since been done him, that, in the time when her heart knew no better, he had persuaded her to fancy herself happy by his side.

"Yes, I hate him!" repeated Hester, more bitterly than before. "He betrayed me! He has done me worse wrong than I did him!"

Let men tremble to win the hand woman, unless they win along with the utmost passion of her heart! E it may be their miserable fortune, it was Roger Chillingworth's, when sor mightier touch than their own may ha awakened all her sensibilities, to be proached even for the calm content, t marble image of happiness, which th will have imposed upon her as the war reality. But Hester ought long ago have done with this injustice. What d it betoken? Had seven long years, und the torture of the scarlet letter, flicted so much of misery, and wroug out no repentance?

The emotions of that brief spa while she stood gazing after the crook figure of old Roger Chillingworth, thr a dark light on Hester's state of mir revealing much that she might n otherwise have acknowledged to he self.

He being gone, she summoned ba her child.

"Pearl! Little Pearl! Where a you?"

Pearl, whose activity of spirit new flagged, had been at no loss for amus ment while her mother talked with t old gatherer of herbs. At first, as ready told, she had flirted fancifu with her own image in a pool of wat beckoning the phantom forth, and— it declined to venture—seeking a pa sage for herself into its sphere of i palpable earth and unattainable sk Soon finding, however, that either s or the image was unreal, she turn elsewhere for better pastime. She ma little boats out of birch-bark, a freighted them with snail-shells, and se out more ventures on the mighty de

n any merchant in New England;
the larger part of them foundered
r the shore. She seized a live horse-
e by the tail, and made prize of
eral five-fingers, and laid out a jelly-
a to melt in the warm sun. Then she
k up the white foam, that streaked
line of the advancing tide, and
ew it upon the breeze, scampering
er it, with winged footsteps, to catch
great snow-flakes ere they fell. Per-
ving a flock of beach-birds, that fed
l fluttered along the shore, the
ghty child picked up her apron full
pebbles, and, creeping from rock to
k after these small sea-fowl, dis-
yed remarkable dexterity in pelting
m. One little gray bird, with a white
ast, Pearl was almost sure, had been
by a pebble, and fluttered away with
roken wing. But then the elf-child
hed, and gave up her sport; because
grieved her to have done harm to
ittle being that was as wild as the
-breeze, or as wild as Pearl herself.
Her final employment was to gather
-weed, of various kinds, and make
self a scarf, or mantle, and a head-
ss, and thus assume the aspect of a
le mermaid. She inherited her moth-
s gift for devising drapery and cos-
ne. As the last touch to her mer-
id's garb, Pearl took some eel-grass,
l imitated, as best she could, on her
n bosom, the decoration with which
was so familiar on her mother's.
letter,—the letter A,—but freshly
en, instead of scarlet! The child bent
chin upon her breast, and contem-
ted this device with strange interest;
n as if the one only thing for which
had been sent into the world was
make out its hidden import.
"I wonder if mother will ask me what

it means?" thought Pearl.

Just then, she heard her mother's
voice, and flitting along as lightly as
one of the little sea-birds, appeared before Hester Prynne, dancing, laughing,
and pointing her finger to the ornament
upon her bosom.

"My little Pearl," said Hester, after
a moment's silence, "the green letter,
and on thy childish bosom, has no purport. But dost thou know, my child,
what this letter means which thy mother
is doomed to wear?"

"Yes, mother," said the child. "It
is the great letter A. Thou hast taught
me in the horn-book."

Hester looked steadily into her little
face; but, though there was that singular expression which she had so often
remarked in her black eyes, she could
not satisfy herself whether Pearl really
attached any meaning to the symbol.
She felt a morbid desire to ascertain
the point.

"Dost thou know, child, wherefore
thy mother wears this letter?"

"Truly do I!" answered Pearl, looking brightly into her mother's face. "It
is for the same reason that the minister keeps his hand over his heart!"

"And what reason is that?" asked
Hester, half smiling at the absurd incongruity of the child's observation;
but, on second thoughts, turning pale.
"What has the letter to do with any
heart, save mine?"

"Nay, mother, I have told all I
know," said Pearl, more seriously than
she was wont to speak. "Ask yonder
old man whom thou hast been talking
with! It may be he can tell. But in
good earnest now, mother dear, what
does this scarlet letter mean?—and why
dost thou wear it on thy bosom?—and

why does the minister keep his hand over his heart?"

She took her mother's hand in both her own, and gazed into her eyes with an earnestness that was seldom seen in her wild and capricious character. The thought occurred to Hester, that the child might really be seeking to approach her with child-like confidence, and doing what she could, and as intelligently as she knew how, to establish a meeting-point of sympathy. It showed Pearl in an unwonted aspect. Heretofore, the mother, while loving her child with the intensity of a sole affection, had schooled herself to hope for little other return than the waywardness of an April breeze; which spends its time in airy sport, and has its gusts of inexplicable passion, and is petulant in its best of moods, and chills oftener than caresses you, when you take it to your bosom; in requital of which misdemeanors, it will sometimes, of its own vague purpose, kiss your cheek with a kind of doubtful tenderness, and play gently with your hair, and then begone about its other idle business, leaving a dreamy pleasure at your heart. And this, moreover, was a mother's estimate of the child's disposition. Any other observer might have seen few but unamiable traits, and have given them a far darker coloring. But now the idea came strongly into Hester's mind, that Pearl, with her remarkable precocity and acuteness, might already have approached the age when she could be made a friend, and intrusted with as much of her mother's sorrows as could be imparted, without irreverence either to the parent or the child. In the little chaos of Pearl's character, there might be seen emerging—and could have been,

from the very first—the steadfast pr ciples of an unflinching courage,— uncontrollable will,—a sturdy pri which might be disciplined into s respect,—and a bitter scorn of ma things, which, when examined, might found to have the taint of falsehood them. She possessed affections, t though hitherto acrid and disagreeal as are the richest flavors of unr fruit. With all these sterling attribut thought Hester, the evil which she herited from her mother must be gr indeed, if a noble woman do not gr out of this elfish child.

Pearl's inevitable tendency to ho about the enigma of the scarlet let seemed an innate quality of her bei From the earliest epoch of her consci life, she had entered upon this as appointed mission. Hester had of fancied that Providence had a des of justice and retribution, in endow the child with this marked propensi but never, until now, had she bethou herself to ask, whether, linked with t design, there might not likewise be purpose of mercy and beneficence. little Pearl were entertained with fa and trust, as a spirit messenger no than an earthly child, might it not her errand to soothe away the sorr that lay cold in her mother's hea and converted it into a tomb—and help her to overcome the passion, o so wild, and even yet neither dead asleep, but only imprisoned within same tomb-like heart?

Such were some of the thoughts t now stirred in Hester's mind, with much vivacity of impression as if t had actually been whispered into ear. And there was little Pearl, all t while, holding her mother's hand in b own, and turning her face upward, ile she put these searching questions ce, and again, and still a third time. 'What does the letter mean, mother? nd why dost thou wear it?—and y does the minister keep his hand er his heart?"

'What shall I say?" thought Hester herself. "No! If this be the price the child's sympathy, I cannot pay

Then she spoke aloud.

'Silly Pearl," said she, "what ques- ns are these? There are many things this world that a child must not about. What know I of the min- er's heart? And as for the scarlet ter, I wear it for the sake of its gold ead."

In all the seven bygone years, Hester ynne had never before been false to symbol on her bosom. It may be t it was the talisman of a stern and ere, but yet a guardian spirit, who w forsook her; as recognizing that, spite of his strict watch over her rt, some new evil had crept into

it, or some old one had never been expelled. As for little Pearl, the earnest- ness soon passed out of her face.

But the child did not see fit to let the matter drop. Two or three times, as her mother and she went homeward, and as often at supper-time, and while Hester was putting her to bed, and once after she seemed to be fairly asleep, Pearl looked up, with mischief gleaming in her black eyes.

"Mother," said she, "what does the scarlet letter mean?"

And the next morning, the first in- dication the child gave of being awake was by propping up her head from the pillow, and making that other inquiry, which she had so unaccountably con- nected with her investigations about the scarlet letter:—

"Mother!—Mother!—Why does the minister keep his hand over his heart?"

"Hold thy tongue, naughty child!" answered her mother, with an asperity that she had never permitted to herself before. "Do not tease me; else I shall shut thee into the dark closet!"

CHAPTER XVI

A FOREST WALK

HESTER PRYNNE remained constant in r resolve to make known to Mr. Dim- esdale, at whatever risk of present in or ulterior consequences, the true aracter of the man who had crept o his intimacy. For several days, how- er, she vainly sought an opportunity addressing him in some of the medi- ive walks which she knew him to be

in the habit of taking, along the shores of the peninsula, or on the wooded hills of the neighboring country. There would have been no scandal, indeed, nor peril to the holy whiteness of the clergy- man's good fame, had she visited him in his own study; where many a peni- tent, ere now, had confessed sins of perhaps as deep a dye as the one betokened by the scarlet letter. But, partly that she dreaded the secret or undisguised interference of old Roger Chillingworth, and partly that her conscious heart imputed suspicion where none could have been felt, and partly that both the minister and she would need the whole wide world to breathe in, while they talked together,—for all these reasons, Hester never thought of meeting him in any narrower privacy than beneath the open sky.

At last, while attending in a sick-chamber, whither the Reverend Mr. Dimmesdale had been summoned to make a prayer, she learnt that he had gone, the day before, to visit the Apostle Eliot, among his Indian converts. He would probably return, by a certain hour, in the afternoon of the morrow. Betimes, therefore, the next day, Hester took little Pearl,—who was necessarily the companion of all her mother's expeditions, however inconvenient her presence,—and set forth.

The road, after the two wayfarers had crossed from the peninsula to the mainland, was no other than a foot-path. It straggled onward into the mystery of the primeval forest. This hemmed it in so narrowly, and stood so black and dense on either side, and disclosed such imperfect glimpses of the sky above, that, to Hester's mind, it imaged not amiss the moral wilderness in which she had so long been wandering. The day was chill and sombre. Overhead was a gay expanse of cloud, slightly stirred, however, by a breeze; so that a gleam of flickering sunshine might now and then be seen at its solitary play along the path. This flitting cheerfulness was always at the further extremity of some long vista through the forest. The sportive s light—feebly sportive, at best, in predominant pensiveness of the day scene—withdrew itself as they ca nigh, and left the spots where it danced the drearier, because they hoped to find them bright.

"Mother," said little Pearl, "the s shine does not love you. It runs av and hides itself, because it is afraid something on your bosom. Now, s There it is, playing, a good way Stand you here, and let me run a catch it. I am but a child. It will flee from me; for I wear nothing my bosom yet!"

"Nor ever will, my child, I hop said Hester.

"And why not, mother?" asked Pe stopping short, just at the beginn of her race. "Will not it come of own accord, when I am a won grown?"

"Run away, child," answered mother, "and catch the sunshine! will soon be gone."

Pearl set forth, at a great pace, a as Hester smiled to perceive, did ac ally catch the sunshine, and stood lau ing in the midst of it, all brighten by its splendor, and scintillating w the vivacity excited by rapid moti The light lingered about the lon child, as if glad of such a playm until her mother had drawn almost n enough to step into the magic cir too.

"It will go now," said Pearl, shak her head.

"See!" answered Hester, smil "Now I can stretch out my hand, grasp some of it."

As she attempted to do so, the s shine vanished; or, to judge from

ght expression that was dancing on
rl's features, her mother could have
cied that the child had absorbed it
» herself, and would give it forth
in, with a gleam about her path,
they should plunge into some gloom-
shade. There was no other attribute
: so much impressed her with a sense
new and untransmitted vigor in
rl's nature, as this never-failing vi-
ity of spirits; she had not the dis-
: of sadness, which almost all chil-
n, in these latter days, inherit, with
scrofula, from the troubles of their
estors. Perhaps this too was a dis-
:, and but the reflex of the wild en-
y with which Hester had fought
inst her sorrows, before Pearl's
h. It was certainly a doubtful charm,
arting a hard, metallic lustre to the
d's character. She wanted—what
e people want throughout life—a
f that should deeply touch her, and
s humanize and make her capable
ympathy. But there was time enough
for little Pearl.

Come, my child!" said Hester, look-
about her from the spot where Pearl
stood still in the sunshine. "We will
down a little way within the wood,
rest ourselves."

I am not aweary, mother," replied
little girl. "But you may sit down, if
will tell me a story meanwhile."

A story, child!" said Hester. "And
ut what?"

O, a story about the Black Man,"
wered Pearl, taking hold of her
ther's gown, and looking up half
estly, half mischievously, into her
. "How he haunts this forest, and
ies a book with him,—a big, heavy
k, with iron clasps; and how this
y Black Man offers his book and

an iron pen to everybody that meets
him here among the trees; and they are
to write their names with their own
blood. And then he sets his mark on
their bosoms! Didst thou ever meet
the Black Man, mother?"

"And who told you this story, Pearl?"
asked her mother, recognizing a common superstition of the period.

"It was the old dame in the chimney-
corner, at the house where you watched
last night," said the child. "But she
fancied me asleep while she was talking
of it. She said that a thousand and a
thousand people had met him here, and
had written in his book, and have his
mark on them. And that ugly-tempered
lady, old Mistress Hibbins, was one.
And, mother, the old dame said that
this scarlet letter was the Black Man's
mark on thee, and that it glows like
a red flame when thou meetest him at
midnight, here in the dark wood. Is it
true, mother? And dost thou go to
meet him in the night-time?"

"Didst thou ever awake, and find thy
mother gone?" asked Hester.

"Not that I remember," said the
child. "If thou fearest to leave me in
our cottage, thou mightest take me
along with thee. I would very gladly
go! But, mother, tell me now! Is there
such a Black Man? And didst thou ever
meet him? And is this his mark?"

"Wilt thou let me be at peace, if I
once tell thee?" asked her mother.

"Yes, if thou tellest me all," answered
Pearl.

"Once in my life I met the Black
Man!" said her mother. "This scarlet
letter is his mark!"

Thus conversing, they entered sufficiently deep into the wood to secure
themselves from the observation of any

casual passenger along the forest track. Here they sat down on a luxuriant heap of moss; which, at some epoch of the preceding century, had been a gigantic pine, with its roots and trunk in the darksome shade, and its head aloft in the upper atmosphere. It was a little dell where they had seated themselves, with a leaf-strewn bank rising gently on either side, and a brook flowing through the midst, over a bed of fallen and drowned leaves. The trees impending over it had flung down great branches, from time to time, which choked up the current, and compelled it to form eddies and black depths at some points; while, in its swifter and livelier passages, there appeared a channel-way of pebbles, and brown, sparkling sand. Letting the eyes follow along the course of the stream, they could catch the reflected light from its water, at some short distance within the forest, but soon lost all traces of it amid the bewilderment of tree-trunks and underbrush, and here and there a huge rock covered over with gray lichens. All these giant trees and boulders of granite seemed intent on making a mystery of the course of this small brook; fearing, perhaps, that, with its never-ceasing loquacity, it should whisper tales out of the heart of the old forest whence it flowed, or mirror its revelations on the smooth surface of a pool. Continually, indeed, as it stole onward, the streamlet kept up a babble, kind, quiet, soothing, but melancholy, like the voice of a young child that was spending its infancy without playfulness, and knew not how to be merry among sad acquaintance and events of sombre hue.

"O brook! O foolish and tiresome little brook!" cried Pearl, after listening awhile to its talk. "Why art thou sad? Pluck up a spirit, and do not all the time sighing and murmuring

But the brook, in the course of little lifetime among the forest-tre had gone through so solemn an ex rience that it could not help talk about it, and seemed to have noth else to say. Pearl resembled the bro inasmuch as the current of her l gushed from a well-spring as mysterio and had flowed through scenes sh owed as heavily with gloom. But, unl the little stream, she danced and sp kled, and prattled airily along course.

"What does this sad little brook s mother?" inquired she.

"If thou hadst a sorrow of th own, the brook might tell thee of i answered her mother, "even as it telling me of mine! But now, Pe I hear a foot-step along the path, a the noise of one putting aside branches. I would have thee betake t self to play, and leave me to speak w him that comes yonder."

"Is it the Black Man?" asked Pe

"Wilt thou go and play, child?" peated her mother. "But do not st far into the wood. And take heed t thou come at my first call."

"Yes, mother," answered Pearl. " if it be the Black Man, wilt thou let me stay a moment, and look at h with his big book under his arm?"

"Go, silly child!" said her moth impatiently. "It is no Black Man! T canst see him now, through the tr It is the minister!"

"And so it is!" said the child. "A mother, he has his hand over his hea Is it because, when the minister wr his name in the book, the Black M

his mark in that place? But why
s he not wear it outside his bosom,
thou dost, mother?"

"Go now, child, and thou shalt tease
as thou wilt another time," cried
ster Prynne. "But do not stray far.
ep where thou canst hear the babble
the brook."

The child went singing away, fol-
ving up the current of the brook,
l striving to mingle a more light-
ne cadence with its melancholy voice.
t the little stream would not be com-
ted, and still kept telling its unin-
igible secret of some very mourn-
 mystery that had happened—or
king a prophetic lamentation about
 nething that was yet to happen—
hin the verge of the dismal forest.

Pearl, who had enough of shadow
her own little life, chose to break
all acquaintance with this repining
 ok. She set herself, therefore, to
hering violets and wood-anemones,
l some scarlet columbines that she
 nd growing in the crevices of a high
 k.

Vhen her elf-child had departed, Hes-
Prynne made a step or two towards
track that led through the forest, but
 l remained under the deep shadow

of the trees. She beheld the minister
advancing along the path, entirely alone,
and leaning on a staff which he had
cut by the way-side. He looked haggard and feeble, and betrayed a nerveless despondency in his air, which had
never so remarkably characterized him
in his walks about the settlement, nor
in any other situation where he deemed
himself liable to notice. Here it was
wofully visible, in this intense seclusion
of the forest, which of itself would
have been a heavy trial to the spirits.
There was a listlessness in his gait;
as if he saw no reason for taking one
step further, nor felt any desire to
do so, but would have been glad, could
he be glad of anything, to fling himself
down at the root of the nearest tree,
and lie there passive, forevermore. The
leaves might bestrew him, and the soil
gradually accumulate and form a little
hillock over his frame, no matter
whether there were life in it or no.
Death was too definite an object to
be wished for, or avoided.

To Hester's eye, the Reverend Mr.
Dimmesdale exhibited no symptom of
positive and vivacious suffering, except
that, as little Pearl had remarked, he
kept his hand over his heart.

CHAPTER XVII

THE PASTOR AND HIS PARISHIONER

Slowly as the minister walked, he
l almost gone by, before Hester
ynne could gather voice enough to
ract his observation. At length, she
 ceeded.

"Arthur Dimmesdale!" she said, faintly at first; then louder, but hoarsely.
"Arthur Dimmesdale!"

"Who speaks?" answered the minister.

Gathering himself quickly up, he stood more erect, like a man taken by surprise in a mood to which he was reluctant to have witnesses. Throwing his eyes anxiously in the direction of the voice, he indistinctly beheld a form under the trees, clad in garments so sombre, and so little relieved from the gray twilight into which the clouded sky and the heavy foliage had darkened the noontide, that he knew not whether it were a woman or a shadow. It may be, that his pathway through life was haunted thus, by a spectre that had stolen out from among his thoughts.

He made a step nigher, and discovered the scarlet letter.

"Hester! Hester Prynne!" said he. "Is it thou? Art thou in life?"

"Even so!" she answered. "In such life as has been mine these seven years past! And thou, Arthur Dimmesdale, dost thou yet live?"

It was no wonder that they thus questioned one another's actual and bodily existence, and even doubted of their own. So strangely did they meet, in the dim wood, that it was like the first encounter, in the world beyond the grave, of two spirits who had been intimately connected in their former life, but now stood coldly shuddering, in mutual dread; as not yet familiar with their state, nor wonted to the companionship of disembodied beings. Each a ghost, and awe-stricken at the other ghost! They were awe-stricken likewise at themselves; because the crisis flung back to them their consciousness, and revealed to each heart its history and experience, as life never does, except at such breathless epochs. The soul beheld its features in the mirror of the passing moment. It was

with fear, and tremulously, and, as were, by a slow, reluctant necessity, t Arthur Dimmesdale put forth his ha chill as death, and touched the c hand of Hester Prynne. The grasp, c as it was, took away what was drear in the interview. They now felt the selves, at least, inhabitants of the sa sphere.

Without a word more spoken neither he nor she assuming the gu ance, but with an unexpressed conse —they glided back into the shadow the woods, whence Hester had emerg and sat down on the heap of m where she and Pearl had before b sitting. When they found voice to spe it was, at first, only to utter rema and inquiries such as any two acquai ances might have made, about gloomy sky, the threatening storm, a next, the health of each. Thus they w onward, not boldly, but step by st into the themes that were brood deepest in their hearts. So long estran by fate and circumstances, they nee something slight and casual to run fore, and throw open the doors of int course, so that their real thoughts mi be led across the threshold.

After a while, the minister fixed eyes on Hester Prynne's.

"Hester," said he, "hast thou fou peace?"

She smiled drearily, looking do upon her bosom.

"Hast thou?" she asked.

"None!—nothing but despair!" answered. "What else could I look being what I am, and leading suc life as mine? Were I an atheist, man devoid of conscience,—a wre with coarse and brutal instincts, might have found peace, long ere n

y, I never should have lost it! But,
matters stand with my soul, what-
r of good capacity there originally
in me, all of God's gifts that were
choicest have become the ministers
spiritual torment. Hester, I am most
erable!"

The people reverence thee," said
ter. "And surely thou workest good
ng them! Dost this bring thee no
fort?"

More misery, Hester!—only the
e misery!" answered the clergyman,
a a bitter smile. "As concerns the
d which I may appear to do, I have
faith in it. It must needs be a
sion. What can a ruined soul, like
e, effect towards the redemption of
er souls?—or a polluted soul, to-
ds their purification? And as for
people's reverence, would that it
e turned to scorn and hatred! Canst
i deem it, Hester, a consolation, that
ust stand up in my pulpit, and meet
many eyes turned upward to my
e, as if the light of heaven were
ning from it!—must see my flock
gry for the truth, and listening to
words as if a tongue of Pentecost
e speaking!—and then look inward,
discern the black reality of what
idolize? I have laughed, in bitter-
and agony of heart, at the con-
t between what I seem and what
m! And Satan laughs at it!"

You wrong yourself in this," said
ter, gently. "You have deeply and
ly repented. Your sin is left be-
d you, in the days long past. Your
ent life is not less holy, in very
h, than it seems in people's eyes.
there no reality in the penitence
s sealed and witnessed by good
ks? And wherefore should it not

bring you peace?"

"No, Hester, no!" replied the clergyman. "There is no substance in it! It
is cold and dead, and can do nothing
for me! Of penance, I have had enough!
Of penitence, there has been none! Else,
I should long ago have thrown off these
garments of mock holiness, and have
shown myself to mankind as they will
see me at the judgment-seat. Happy
are you, Hester, that wear the scarlet
letter openly upon your bosom! Mine
burns in secret! Thou little knowest
what a relief it is, after the torment
of a seven years' cheat, to look into an
eye that recognizes me for what I am!
Had I one friend,—or were it my worst
enemy!—to whom, when sickened with
the praises of all other men, I could
daily betake myself, and be known as
the vilest of all sinners, methinks my
soul might keep itself alive thereby.
Even thus much of truth would save
me! But now, it is all falsehood!—all
emptiness!—all death!"

Hester Prynne looked into his face,
but hesitated to speak. Yet, uttering his
long-restrained emotions so vehemently
as he did, his words here offered her
the very point of circumstances in which
to interpose what she came to say. She
conquered her fears, and spoke.

"Such a friend as thou hast even
now wished for," said she, "with whom
to weep over thy sin, thou hast in me,
the partner of it!"—Again she hesitated, but brought out the words with
an effort.—"Thou hast long had such
an enemy, and dwellest with him, under
the same roof."

The minister started to his feet, gasping for breath, and clutching at his
heart, as if he would have torn it out
of his bosom.

"Ha! What sayest thou!" cried he. "An enemy! And under mine own roof! What mean you?"

Hester Prynne was now fully sensible of the deep injury for which she was responsible to this unhappy man, in permitting him to lie for so many years, or, indeed, for a single moment, at the mercy of one whose purposes could not be other than malevolent. The very contiguity of his enemy, beneath whatever mask the latter might conceal himself, was enough to disturb the magnetic sphere of a being so sensitive as Arthur Dimmesdale. There had been a period when Hester was less alive to this consideration; or, perhaps, in the misanthropy of her own trouble, she left the minister to bear what she might picture to herself as a more tolerable doom. But of late, since the night of his vigil, all her sympathies towards him had been both softened and invigorated. She now read his heart more accurately. She doubted not, that the continual presence of Roger Chillingworth,—the secret poison of his malignity, infecting all the air about him,—and his authorized interference, as a physician, with the minister's physical and spiritual infirmities,—that these bad opportunities had been turned to a cruel purpose. By means of them, the sufferer's conscience had been kept in an irritated state, the tendency of which was, not to cure by wholesome pain, but to disorganize and corrupt his spiritual being. Its result, on earth, could hardly fail to be insanity, and hereafter, that eternal alienation from the Good and True, of which madness is perhaps the earthly type.

Such was the ruin to which she had brought the man, once,—nay, why should we not speak it?—still so p[as]sionately loved! Hester felt that [the] sacrifice of the clergyman's good na[me] and death itself, as she had already t[old] Roger Chillingworth, would have b[een] infinitely preferable to the alternat[ive] which she had taken upon herself [to] choose. And now, rather than have h[ad] this grievous wrong to confess, [she] would gladly have lain down on [the] forest-leaves, and died there, at Art[hur] Dimmesdale's feet.

"O Arthur," cried she, "forgive [me!] In all things else, I have striven to [be] true! Truth was the one virtue wh[ich] I might have held fast, and did h[old] fast, through all extremity; save w[hen] thy good,—thy life,—thy fame,—w[ere] put in question! Then I consented t[o a] deception. But a lie is never good, e[ven] though death threaten on the other si[de!] Dost thou not see what I would s[ay?] That old man!—the physician!—[he] whom they call Roger Chillingworth[—] he was my husband!"

The minister looked at her, for [an] instant, with all that violence of p[as]sion, which—intermixed, in more sha[pes] than one, with his higher, purer, so[fter] qualities,—was, in fact, the portion [of] him which the Devil claimed, [and] through which he sought to win [the] rest. Never was there a blacker o[r] fiercer frown than Hester now enco[un]tered. For the brief space that it las[ted,] it was a dark transfiguration. But [his] character had been so much enfee[bled] by suffering, that even its lower ener[gies] were incapable of more than a tem[po]rary struggle. He sank down on [the] ground, and buried his face in [his] hands.

"I might have known it," murm[ured] he. "I did know it! Was not the se[cret]

l me, in the natural recoil of my
rt, at the first sight of him, and as
en as I have seen him since? Why
I not understand? O Hester Prynne,
u little, little knowest all the horror
this thing! And the shame!—the in-
icacy!—the horrible ugliness of this
osure of a sick and guilty heart to
very eye that would gloat over it!
man, woman, thou art accountable
this! I cannot forgive thee!"

Thou shalt forgive me!" cried Hes-
flinging herself on the fallen leaves
ide him. "Let God punish! Thou
lt forgive!"

Vith sudden and desperate tender-
s, she threw her arms around him,
pressed his head against her bosom;
e caring though his cheek rested
the scarlet letter. He would have
ased himself, but strove in vain to
so. Hester would not set him free,
he should look her sternly in the
e. All the world had frowned on
,—for seven long years had it
wned upon this lonely woman,—and
she bore it all, nor ever once turned
ly her firm, sad eyes. Heaven, like-
e, had frowned upon her, and she
not died. But the frown of this
e, weak, sinful, and sorrow-stricken
n was what Hester could not bear,
live!

Wilt thou yet forgive me?" she re-
ted, over and over again. "Wilt
u not frown? Wilt thou forgive?"

I do forgive you, Hester," replied
minister, at length, with a deep
erance, out of an abyss of sadness,
no anger. "I freely forgive you
v. May God forgive us both! We
not, Hester, the worst sinners in
world. There is one worse than
n the polluted priest! That old man's

revenge has been blacker than my sin.
He has violated, in cold blood, the
sanctity of a human heart. Thou and
I, Hester, never did so!"

"Never, never!" whispered she.
"What we did had a consecration of its
own. We felt it so! We said so to
each other! Hast thou forgotten it?"

"Hush, Hester!" said Arthur Dimmesdale, rising from the ground. "No; I
have not forgotten!"

They sat down again, side by side,
and hand clasped in hand, on the mossy
trunk of the fallen tree. Life had never
brought them a gloomier hour; it was
the point whither their pathway had
so long been tending, and darkening
ever, as it stole along;—and yet it
enclosed a charm that made them
linger upon it, and claim another, and
another, and, after all, another moment.
The forest was obscure around them,
and creaked with a blast that was passing through it. The boughs were tossing heavily above their heads; while
one solemn old tree groaned dolefully
to another, as if telling the sad story
of the pair that sat beneath, or constrained to forebode evil to come.

And yet they lingered. How dreary
looked the forest-track that led backward to the settlement, where Hester
Prynne must take up again the burden
of her ignominy, and the minister the
hollow mockery of his good name! So
they lingered an instant longer. No
golden light had ever been so precious
as the gloom of this dark forest. Here,
seen only by his eyes, the scarlet letter need not burn into the bosom of
the fallen woman! Here, seen only by
her eyes, Arthur Dimmesdale, false to
God and man, might be, for one moment, true!

He started at a thought that suddenly occurred to him.

"Hester," cried he, "here is a new horror! Roger Chillingworth knows your purpose to reveal his true character. Will he continue, then, to keep our secret? What will now be the course of his revenge?"

"There is a strange secrecy in his nature," replied Hester, thoughtfully; "and it has grown upon him by the hidden practices of his revenge. I deem it not likely that he will betray the secret. He will doubtless seek other means of satiating his dark passion."

"And I!—how am I to live longer, breathing the same air with this deadly enemy?" exclaimed Arthur Dimmesdale, shrinking within himself, and pressing his hand nervously against his heart, —a gesture that had grown involuntary with him. "Think for me, Hester! Thou art strong. Resolve for me!"

"Thou must dwell no longer with this man," said Hester, slowly and firmly. "Thy heart must be no longer under his evil eye!"

"It were far worse than death!" replied the minister. "But how to avoid it? What choice remains to me? Shall I lie down again on these withered leaves, where I cast myself when thou didst tell me what he was? Must I sink down there, and die at once?"

"Alas, what a ruin has befallen thee!" said Hester, with the tears gushing into her eyes. "Wilt thou die for very weakness? There is no other cause!"

"The judgment of God is on me," answered the conscience-stricken priest. "It is too mighty for me to struggle with!"

"Heaven would show mercy," rejoined Hester, "hadst thou but the strength to take advantage of it."

"Be thou strong for me!" answer he. "Advise me what to do."

"Is the world, then, so narrow?" claimed Hester Prynne, fixing her eyes on the minister's, and instinct exercising a magnetic power over a sp so shattered and subdued that it c hardly hold itself erect. "Doth the verse lie within the compass of yo town, which only a little time ago but a leaf-strewn desert, as lonel this around us? Whither leads yo forest track? Backward to the se ment, thou sayest! Yes; but onw too! Deeper it goes, and deeper, the wilderness, less plainly to be at every step; until, some few m hence, the yellow leaves will show vestige of the white man's tread. T thou art free! So brief a journey w bring thee from a world where thou been most wretched, to one where mayest still be happy! Is there shade enough in all this boundless est to hide thy heart from the of Roger Chillingworth?"

"Yes, Hester; but only under fallen leaves!" replied the minister, a sad smile.

"Then there is the broad pathwa the sea!" continued Hester. "It bro thee hither. If thou so choose, it bear thee back again. In our na land, whether in some remote village or in vast London,—or, su in Germany, in France, in plea Italy,—thou wouldst be beyond power and knowledge! And what thou to do with all these iron men, their opinions? They have kept better part in bondage too long ready!"

"It cannot be!" answered the

, listening as if he were called
to realize a dream. "I am power-
to go! Wretched and sinful as I
I have had no other thought than
rag on my earthly existence in the
re where Providence hath placed
Lost as my own soul is, I would
do what I may for other human
! I dare not quit my post, though
unfaithful sentinel, whose sure re-
is death and dishonor, when his
ry watch shall come to an end!"

hou art crushed under this seven
s' weight of misery," replied Hes-
fervently resolved to buoy him up
her own energy. "But thou shalt
it all behind thee! It shall not
er thy steps, as thou treadest along
forest-path; neither shalt thou
ht the ship with it, if thou prefer
oss the sea. Leave this wreck and
here where it hath happened.
dle no more with it! Begin all
! Hast thou exhausted possibility
e failure of this one trial? Not
The future is yet full of trial and
ss. There is happiness to be en-
d! There is good to be done! Ex-
ge this false life of thine for a
one. Be, if thy spirit summon thee
uch a mission, the teacher and
tle of the red men. Or,—as is more

thy nature,—be a scholar and a sage
among the wisest and the most renowned of the cultivated world. Preach!
Write! Act! Do anything, save to lie
down and die! Give up this name of
Arthur Dimmesdale, and make thyself
another, and a high one, such as thou
canst wear without fear or shame. Why
shouldst thou tarry so much as one
other day in the torments that have so
gnawed into thy life!—that have made
thee feeble to will and to do!—that will
leave thee powerless even to repent! Up,
and away!"

"O Hester!" cried Arthur Dimmesdale, in whose eyes a fitful light, kindled
by her enthusiasm, flashed up and died
away, "thou tellest of running a race
to a man whose knees are tottering
beneath him! I must die here! There is
not the strength or courage left me to
venture into the wide, strange, difficult
world, alone!"

It was the last expression of the
despondency of a broken spirit. He
lacked energy to grasp the better fortune that seemed within his reach.

He repeated the word.

"Alone, Hester!"

"Thou shalt not go alone!" answered
she, in a deep whisper.

Then, all was spoken!

CHAPTER XVIII

A FLOOD OF SUNSHINE

THUR DIMMESDALE gazed into Hes-
face with a look in which hope
joy shone out, indeed, but with
betwixt them, and a kind of hor-

ror at her boldness, who had spoken
what he vaguely hinted at, but dared
not speak.

But Hester Prynne, with a mind of

native courage and activity, and for so long a period not merely estranged, but outlawed, from society, had habituated herself to such latitude of speculation as was altogether foreign to the clergyman. She had wandered, without rule or guidance, in a moral wilderness; as vast, as intricate and shadowy, as the untamed forest, amid the gloom of which they were now holding a colloquy that was to decide their fate. Her intellect and heart had their home, as it were, in desert places, where she roamed as freely as the wild Indian in his woods. For years past she had looked from this estranged point of view at human institutions, and whatever priests or legislators had established; criticising all with hardly more reverence than the Indian would feel for the clerical band, the judicial robe, the pillory, the gallows, the fireside, or the church. The tendency of her fate and fortunes had been to set her free. The scarlet letter was her passport into regions where other women dared not tread. Shame, Despair, Solitude! These had been her teachers,— stern and wild ones,—and they had made her strong, but taught her much amiss.

The minister, on the other hand, had never gone through an experience calculated to lead him beyond the scope of generally received laws; although, in a single instance, he had so fearfully transgressed one of the most sacred of them. But this had been a sin of passion, not of principle, nor even purpose. Since that wretched epoch, he had watched, with morbid zeal and minuteness, not his acts,—for those it was easy to arrange,—but each breath of emotion, and his every thought. At the head of the social system, as the clergy men of that day stood, he was on the more trammelled by its regulatic its principles, and even its prejudi As a priest, the framework of his or inevitably hemmed him in. As a m who had once sinned, but who k his conscience all alive and painfu sensitive by the fretting of an unhea wound, he might have been suppo safer within the line of virtue than he had never sinned at all.

Thus, we seem to see that, as garded Hester Prynne, the whole se years of outlaw and ignominy had b little other than a preparation for very hour. But Arthur Dimmesda Were such a man once more to f what plea could be urged in extenuat of his crime? None; unless it a him somewhat, that he was broken do by long and exquisite suffering; t his mind was darkened and confu by the very remorse which harro it; that, between fleeing as an avow criminal, and remaining as a hypocr conscience might find it hard to st the balance; that it was human to av the peril of death and infamy, and inscrutable machinations of an enen that, finally, to this poor pilgrim, his dreary and desert path, faint, s miserable, there appeared a glimpse human affection and sympathy, a life, and a true one, in exchange the heavy doom which he was expiating. And be the stern and truth spoken, that the breach wl guilt has once made into the hur soul is never, in this mortal state, paired. It may be watched and guard so that the enemy shall not force way again into the citadel, and m even, in his subsequent assaults, se

ie other avenue, in preference to
t where he had formerly succeeded.
. there is still the ruined wall, and,
r it, the stealthy tread of the foe
t would win over again his unfor-
ten triumph.

'he struggle, if there were one, need
be described. Let it suffice, that the
'gyman resolved to flee, and not
ie.

If, in all these past seven years,"
ught he, "I could recall one instant
peace or hope, I would yet endure,
the sake of that earnest of Heaven's
cy. But now,—since I am irrevoca-
doomed,—wherefore should I not
tch the solace allowed to the con-
ined culprit before his execution?
if this be the path to a better life,
Hester would persuade me, I surely
e up no fairer prospect by pursuing
Neither can I any longer live without
companionship; so powerful is she
ustain,—so tender to soothe! O Thou
whom I dare not lift mine eyes,
Thou yet pardon me!"

Thou wilt go!" said Hester, calmly,
ie met her glance.

he decision once made, a glow of
nge enjoyment threw its flickering
htness over the trouble of his breast.
vas the exhilarating effect—upon a
oner just escaped from the dungeon
is own heart—of breathing the wild,
atmosphere of an unredeemed, un-
stianized, lawless region. His spirit
, as it were, with a bound, and
ined a nearer prospect of the sky,
a throughout all the misery which
kept him grovelling on the earth.
. deeply religious temperament, there
inevitably a tinge of the devotional
lis mood.

Do I feel joy again?" cried he,
wondering at himself. "Methought the
germ of it was dead in me! O Hester,
thou art my better angel! I seem to
have flung myself—sick, sin-stained, and
sorrow-blackened—down upon these forest-leaves, and to have risen up all
made anew, and with new powers to
glorify Him that hath been merciful!
This is already the better life! Why
did we not find it sooner?"

"Let us not look back," answered
Hester Prynne. "The past is gone!
Wherefore should we linger upon it
now? See! With this symbol, I undo
it all, and make it as it had never
been!"

So speaking, she undid the clasp that
fastened the scarlet letter, and, taking
it from her bosom, threw it to a distance among the withered leaves. The
mystic token alighted on the hither
verge of the stream. With a hand's
breadth further flight it would have
fallen into the water, and have given
the little brook another woe to carry
onward, besides the unintelligible tale
which it still kept murmuring about.
But there lay the embroidered letter,
glittering like a lost jewel, which some
ill-fated wanderer might pick up, and
thenceforth be haunted by strange phantoms of guilt, sinkings of the heart, and
unaccountable misfortune.

The stigma gone, Hester heaved a
long, deep sigh, in which the burden
of shame and anguish departed from
her spirit. O exquisite relief! She had
not known the weight, until she felt
the freedom! By another impulse, she
took off the formal cap that confined
her hair; and down it fell upon her
shoulders, dark and rich, with at once
a shadow and a light in its abundance,
and imparting the charm of softness

to her features. There played around her mouth, and beamed out of her eyes, a radiant and tender smile, that seemed gushing from the very heart of womanhood. A crimson flush was glowing on her cheek, that had been long so pale. Her sex, her youth, and the whole richness of her beauty, came back from what men call the irrevocable past, and clustered themselves, with her maiden hope, and a happiness before unknown, within the magic circle of this hour. And, as if the gloom of the earth and sky had been but the effluence of these two mortal hearts, it vanished with their sorrow. All at once, as with a sudden smile of heaven, forth burst the sunshine, pouring a very flood into the obscure forest, gladdening each green leaf, transmuting the yellow fallen ones to gold, and gleaming adown the gray trunks of the solemn trees. The objects that had made a shadow hitherto, embodied the brightness now. The course of the little brook might be traced by its merry gleam afar into the wood's heart of mystery, which had become a mystery of joy.

Such was the sympathy of Nature —that wild, heathen Nature of the forest, never subjugated by human law, nor illumined by higher truth—with the bliss of these two spirits! Love, whether newly born, or aroused from a death-like slumber, must always create a sunshine, filling the heart so full of radiance, that it overflows upon the outward world. Had the forest still kept its gloom, it would have been bright in Hester's eyes, and bright in Arthur Dimmesdale's.

Hester looked at him with the thrill of another joy.

"Thou must know Pearl!" said she.

"Our little Pearl! Thou hast seen —yes, I know it!—but thou wilt her now with other eyes. She i strange child! I hardly comprehend l But thou wilt love her dearly, as I and wilt advise me how to deal ▼ her."

"Dost thou think the child will glad to know me?" asked the mini somewhat uneasily. "I have long shr from children, because they often s a distrust,—a backwardness to be fa iar with me. I have even been af of little Pearl!"

"Ah, that was sad!" answered mother. "But she will love thee de: and thou her. She is not far off. I call her! Pearl! Pearl!"

"I see the child," observed the ▼ ister. "Yonder she is, standing i streak of sunshine, a good way off the other side of the brook. So ▼ thinkest the child will love me?"

Hester smiled, and again callec Pearl, who was visible, at some tance, as the minister had descr her, like a bright-apparelled vision a sunbeam, which fell down upon through an arch of boughs. The quivered to and fro, making her fi dim or distinct,—now like a real c now like a child's spirit,—as the s dor went and came again. She h her mother's voice, and approa slowly through the forest.

Pearl had not found the hour wearisomely, while her mother sat ing with the clergyman. The great I forest—stern as it showed itself to t who brought the guilt and trouble the world into its bosom—became playmate of the lonely infant, as as it knew how. Sombre as it it put on the kindest of its m

elcome her. It offered her the par-
e-berries, the growth of the preced-
autumn but ripening only in the
g, and now red as drops of blood
the withered leaves. These Pearl
ered, and was pleased with their
flavor. The small denizens of the
erness hardly took pains to move
of her path. A partridge, indeed,
a brood of ten behind her, ran
ard threateningly, but soon repented
er fierceness, and clucked to her
g ones not to be afraid. A pigeon,
e on a low branch, allowed Pearl
ome beneath, and uttered a sound
uch of greeting as alarm. A squir-
from the lofty depths of his domes-
ree, chattered either in anger or
iment,—for a squirrel is such a
eric and humorous little personage,
it is hard to distinguish between
oods,—so he chattered at the child,
flung down a nut upon her head.
as a last year's nut, and already
ved by his sharp tooth. A fox,
led from his sleep by her light
tep on the leaves, looked inquisi-
y at Pearl, as doubting whether it
better to steal off, or renew his

nap on the same spot. A wolf, it is
said,—but here the tale has surely
lapsed into the improbable,—came up,
and smelt of Pearl's robe, and offered
his savage head to be patted by her
hand. The truth seems to be, however,
that the mother-forest, and these wild
things which it nourished, all recognized a kindred wildness in the human
child.

And she was gentler here than in
the grassy-margined streets of the settlement, or in her mother's cottage. The
flowers appeared to know it; and one
and another whispered as she passed,
"Adorn thyself with me, thou beautiful
child, adorn thyself with me!"—and,
to please them, Pearl gathered the violets, and anemones, and columbines, and
some twigs of the freshest green, which
the old trees held down before her eyes.
With these she decorated her hair, and
her young waist, and became a nymph-
child, or an infant dryad, or whatever
else was in closest sympathy with the
antique wood. In such guise had Pearl
adorned herself, when she heard her
mother's voice, and came slowly back.

Slowly; for she saw the clergyman!

CHAPTER XIX

THE CHILD AT THE BROOK-SIDE

HOU wilt love her dearly," repeated
er Prynne, as she and the minister
vatching little Pearl. "Dost thou not
: her beautiful? And see with what
ral skill she has made those simple
ers adorn her! Had she gathered
ls, and diamonds, and rubies, in

the wood, they could not have become
her better. She is a splendid child! But
I know whose brow she has!"

"Dost thou know, Hester," said
Arthur Dimmesdale, with an unquiet
smile, "that this dear child, tripping
about always at thy side, hath caused

me many an alarm? Methought—O Hester, what a thought is that, and how terrible to dread it!—that my own features were partly repeated in her face, and so strikingly that the world might see them! But she is mostly thine!"

"No, no! Not mostly!" answered the mother, with a tender smile. "A little longer, and thou needest not to be afraid to trace whose child she is. But how strangely beautiful she looks, with those wild flowers in her hair! It is as if one of the fairies, whom we left in our dear old England, had decked her out to meet us."

It was with a feeling which neither of them had ever before experienced, that they sat and watched Pearl's slow advance. In her was visible the tie that united them. She had been offered to the world, these seven years past, as the living hieroglyphic, in which was revealed the secret they so darkly sought to hide,—all written in this symbol,—all plainly manifest,—had there been a prophet or magician skilled to read the character of flame! And Pearl was the oneness of their being. Be the foregone evil what it might, how could they doubt that their earthly lives and future destinies were conjoined, when they beheld at once the material union, and the spiritual idea, in whom they met, and were to dwell immortally together? Thoughts like these—and perhaps other thoughts, which they did not acknowledge or define—threw an awe about the child, as she came onward.

"Let her see nothing strange—no passion nor eagerness—in thy way of accosting her," whispered Hester. "Our Pearl is a fitful and fantastic little elf, sometimes. Especially, she is seldom tol-

erant of emotion, when she does fully comprehend the why and wh fore. But the child hath strong af tions! She loves me, and will thee!"

"Thou canst not think," said the ister, glancing aside at Hester Pry "how my heart dreads this interv and yearns for it! But, in truth, a already told thee, children are not re ily won to be familiar with me. T will not climb my knee, nor prattl my ear, nor answer to my smile; stand apart, and eye me strangely. E little babes, when I take them in arms, weep bitterly. Yet Pearl, twic her little lifetime, hath been kind me! The first time,—thou knowes well! The last was when thou l her with thee to the house of yo stern old Governor."

"And thou didst plead so bravel her behalf and mine!" answered mother. "I remember it; and so little Pearl. Fear nothing! She may strange and shy at first, but will learn to love thee!"

By this time Pearl had reached margin of the brook, and stood on further side, gazing silently at He and the clergyman, who still sat gether on the mossy tree-trunk, wa to receive her. Just where she paused, the brook chanced to for pool, so smooth and quiet that it flected a perfect image of her figure with all the brilliant pictures ness of her beauty, in its adornmen flowers and wreathed foliage, but r refined and spiritualized than the rea This image, so nearly identical the living Pearl, seemed to commun somewhat of its own shadowy and tangible quality to the child hersel

strange, the way in which Pearl
d, looking so steadfastly at them
ugh the dim medium of the forest-
m; herself, meanwhile, all glorified
a ray of sunshine, that was ated thitherward as by a certain sym-
y. In the brook beneath stood an-
r child,—another and the same,—
likewise its ray of golden light.
er felt herself, in some indistinct
tantalizing manner, estranged from
l; as if the child, in her lonely
le through the forest, had strayed
of the sphere in which she and her
er dwelt together, and was now
y seeking to return to it.

ere was both truth and error in
impression, the child and mother
estranged, but through Hester's
, not Pearl's. Since the latter
led from her side, another inmate
been admitted within the circle of
mother's feelings, and so modified
aspect of them all, that Pearl, the
ning wanderer, could not find her
ed place, and hardly knew where
was.

have a strange fancy," observed
sensitive minister, "that this brook
e boundary between two worlds,
that thou canst never meet thy
l again. Or is she an elfish spirit,
as the legends of our childhood
nt us, is forbidden to cross a run-
stream? Pray hasten her; for this
y has already imparted a tremor
my nerves."

ome, dearest child!" said Hester,
uragingly, and stretching out both
arms. "How slow thou art! When
thou been so sluggish before now?
is a friend of mine, who must
ay friend also. Thou wilt have twice
much love, henceforward, as thy

mother alone could give thee! Leap
across the brook, and come to us. Thou
canst leap like a young deer!"

Pearl, without responding in any manner to these honey-sweet expressions,
remained on the other side of the brook.
Now she fixed her bright, wild eyes
on her mother, now on the minister,
and now included them both in the same
glance; as if to detect and explain to
herself the relation which they bore to
one another. For some unaccountable
reason, as Arthur Dimmesdale felt the
child's eyes upon himself, his hand—
with that gesture so habitual as to have
become involuntary—stole over his
heart. At length, assuming a singular air
of authority, Pearl stretched out her
hand, with the small forefinger extended,
and pointing evidently towards her
mother's breast. And beneath, in the
mirror of the brook, there was the
flower-girdled and sunny image of little
Pearl, pointing her small forefinger too.

"Thou strange child, why dost thou
not come to me?" exclaimed Hester.

Pearl still pointed with her forefinger;
and a frown gathered on her brow; the
more impressive from the childish, the
almost baby-like aspect of the features
that conveyed it. As her mother still
kept beckoning to her, and arraying her
face in a holiday suit of unaccustomed
smiles, the child stamped her foot with
a yet more imperious look and gesture.
In the brook, again, was the fantastic
beauty of the image, with its reflected
frown, its pointed finger, and imperious
gesture, giving emphasis to the aspect
of little Pearl.

"Hasten, Pearl; or I shall be angry
with thee!" cried Hester Prynne, who,
however inured to such behavior on the
elf-child's part at other seasons, was

naturally anxious for a more seemly deportment now. "Leap across the brook, naughty child, and run hither! Else I must come to thee!"

But Pearl, not a whit startled at her mother's threats, any more than mollified by her entreaties, now suddenly burst into a fit of passion, gesticulating violently, and throwing her small figure into the most extravagant contortions. She accompanied this wild outbreak with piercing shrieks, which the woods reverberated on all sides; so that, alone as she was in her childish and unreasonable wrath, it seemed as if a hidden multitude were lending her their sympathy and encouragement. Seen in the brook, once more, was the shadowy wrath of Pearl's image, crowned and girdled with flowers, but stamping its foot, wildly gesticulating, and, in the midst of all, still pointing its small forefinger at Hester's bosom!

"I see what ails the child," whispered Hester to the clergyman, and turning pale in spite of a strong effort to conceal her trouble and annoyance. "Children will not abide any, the slightest, change in the accustomed aspect of things that are daily before their eyes. Pearl misses something which she has always seen me wear!"

"I pray you," answered the minister, "if thou hast any means of pacifying the child, do it forthwith! Save it were the cankered wrath of an old witch, like Mistress Hibbins," added he, attempting to smile, "I know nothing that I would not sooner encounter than this passion in a child. In Pearl's young beauty, as in the wrinkled witch, it has a preternatural effect. Pacify her, if thou lovest me!"

Hester turned again towards Pearl,

with a crimson blush upon her ch[...] a conscious glance aside at the cl[...] man, and then a heavy sigh; w[...] even before she had time to speak[...] blush yielded to a deadly pallor.

"Pearl," said she, sadly, "look d[...] at thy feet! There!—before thee!— the hither side of the brook!"

The child turned her eyes to the p[...] indicated; and there lay the scarlet[...] ter, so close upon the margin of[...] stream, that the gold embroidery[...] reflected in it.

"Bring it hither," said Hester.

"Come thou and take it up!" [an]swered Pearl.

"Was ever such a child!" obse[rved] Hester, aside to the minister. "O, I [have] much to tell thee about her! Bu[t in] very truth, she is right as regards to[his] hateful token. I must bear its to[rture] yet a little longer,—only a few [days] longer,—until we shall have left [this] region, and look back hither as [a] land which we have dreamed of. [The] forest cannot hide it! The mid-o[cean] shall take it from my hand, and sw[allow] it up forever!"

With these words, she advance[d to] the margin of the brook, took up[the] scarlet letter, and fastened it [again] into her bosom. Hopefully, but a [mo]ment ago, as Hester had spoke[n of] drowning it in the deep sea, there [was] a sense of inevitable doom upon [her,] as she thus received back this d[eadly] symbol from the hand of fate. She [had] flung it into infinite space!—she [had] drawn an hour's free breath!—and [here] again was the scarlet misery, glitt[ering] on the old spot! So it ever is, wh[ether] thus typified or no, that an evil [deed] invests itself with the characte[r of] doom. Hester next gathered up[...]

ry tresses of her hair, and confined
n beneath her cap. As if there were
ithering spell in the sad letter, her
ity, the warmth and richness of her
manhood, departed, like fading sun-
e; and a gray shadow seemed to
across her.

Then the dreary change was wrought,
extended her hand to Pearl.

Dost thou know thy mother now,
d?" asked she, reproachfully, but
a a subdued tone. "Wilt thou come
ss the brook, and own thy mother,
that she has her shame upon her,
ow that she is sad?"

Yes; now I will!" answered the
d, bounding across the brook, and
ping Hester in her arms. "Now thou
my mother indeed! And I am thy
e Pearl!"

a a mood of tenderness that was not
l with her, she drew down her moth-
head, and kissed her brow and
a her cheeks. But then—by a kind of
ssity that always impelled this child
alloy whatever comfort she might
ce to give with a throb of anguish
earl put up her mouth, and kissed
scarlet letter too!

That was not kind!" said Hester.
en thou hast shown me a little
, thou mockest me!"

Why doth the minister sit yonder?"
d Pearl.

He waits to welcome thee," replied
mother. "Come thou, and entreat
blessing! He loves thee, my little
l, and loves thy mother too. Wilt
not love him? Come! he longs to
t thee!"

Doth he love us?" said Pearl, look-
up, with acute intelligence, into her
her's face. "Will he go back with
us, hand in hand, we three together,
into the town?"

"Not now, dear child," answered
Hester. "But in days to come he will
walk hand in hand with us. We will
have a home and fireside of our own;
and thou shalt sit upon his knee; and
he will teach thee many things, and
love thee dearly. Thou wilt love him;
wilt thou not?"

"And will he always keep his hand
over his heart?" inquired Pearl.

"Foolish child, what a question is
that!" exclaimed her mother. "Come
and ask his blessing!"

But, whether influenced by the jealousy that seems instinctive with every
petted child towards a dangerous rival,
or from whatever caprice of her freakish nature, Pearl would show no favor
to the clergyman. It was only by an
exertion of force that her mother
brought her up to him, hanging back,
and manifesting her reluctance by odd
grimaces; of which, ever since her babyhood, she had possessed a singular variety, and could transform her mobile
physiognomy into a series of different
aspects, with a new mischief in them,
each and all. The minister—painfully
embarrassed, but hoping that a kiss
might prove a talisman to admit him
into the child's kindlier regards—bent
forward, and impressed one on her brow.
Hereupon, Pearl broke away from her
mother, and, running to the brook,
stooped over it, and bathed her forehead, until the unwelcome kiss was
quite washed off, and diffused through
a long lapse of the gliding water. She
then remained apart, silently watching
Hester and the clergyman; while they
talked together, and made such arrange-

ments as were suggested by their new position, and the purposes soon to be filled.

And now this fateful interview had come to a close. The dell was to be left a solitude among its dark, old trees, which, with their multitudinous tongues, would whisper long of what had passed there, and no mortal be wiser. And the melancholy brook w⊘ add this other tale to the mystery ⊘ which its little heart was already o⊘ burdened, and whereof it still kept a murmuring babble, with not a ⊘ more cheerfulness of tone than for ⊘ heretofore.

CHAPTER XX

THE MINISTER IN A MAZE

As the minister departed, in advance of Hester Prynne and little Pearl, he threw a backward glance; half expecting that he should discover only some faintly traced features or outline of the mother and the child, slowly fading into the twilight of the woods. So great a vicissitude in his life could not at once be received as real. But there was Hester, clad in her gray robe, still standing beside the tree-trunk, which some blast had overthrown a long antiquity ago, and which time had ever since been covering with moss, so that these two fated ones, with earth's heaviest burden on them, might there sit down together, and find a single hour's rest and solace. And there was Pearl, too, lightly dancing from the margin of the brook,—now that the intrusive third person was gone,—and taking her old place by her mother's side. So the minister had not fallen asleep, and dreamed!

In order to free his mind from this indistinctness and duplicity of impression, which vexed it with a strange disquietude, he recalled and more thoroughly defined the plans which Hester and himself had sketched for their parture. It had been determined betw them, that the Old World, with crowds and cities, offered them a r eligible shelter and concealment the wilds of New England, or all A⊘ ica, with its alternatives of an In wigwam, or the few settlements of E peans, scattered thinly along the board. Not to speak of the clergyn health, so inadequate to sustain the h ships of a forest life, his native g his culture, and his entire developm would secure him a home only in midst of civilization and refinement higher the state, the more delic⊘ adapted to it the man. In further of this choice, it so happened th⊘ ship lay in the harbor; one of t questionable cruisers, frequent at day, which, without being absol⊘ outlaws of the deep, yet roamed its surface with a remarkable irres⊘ sibility of character. This vessel ha⊘ cently arrived from the Spanish M and, within three days' time, would for Bristol. Hester Prynne—whose cation, as a self-enlisted Sister of C

had brought her acquainted with
captain and crew—could take upon
self to secure the passage of two in-
dduals and a child, with all the se-
cy which circumstances rendered
re than desirable.

'he minister had inquired of Hester,
h no little interest, the precise time
which the vessel might be expected
depart. It would probably be on the
rth day from the present. "That is
st fortunate!" he had then said to
self. Now, why the Reverend Mr.
amesdale considered it so very for-
ate, we hesitate to reveal. Neverthe-
,—to hold nothing back from the
ler,—it was because, on the third
from the present, he was to preach
Election Sermon; and, as such an
asion formed an honorable epoch
the life of a New England clergy-
a, he could not have chanced upon
ore suitable mode and time of ter-
ating his professional career. "At
t, they shall say of me," thought
exemplary man, "that I leave no
lic duty unperformed, nor ill per-
ned!" Sad, indeed, that an intro-
ction so profound and acute as this
r minister's should be so miserably
ived! We have had, and may still
e, worse things to tell of him; but
e, we apprehend, so pitiably weak;
evidence, at once so slight and ir-
agable, of a subtle disease, that had
y since begun to eat into the real
stance of his character. No man,
any considerable period, can wear
face to himself, and another to the
titude, without finally getting be-
lered as to which may be the true.
he excitement of Mr. Dimmesdale's
ings, as he returned from his inter-
v with Hester, lent him unaccus-

tomed physical energy, and hurried him
townward at a rapid pace. The pathway among the woods seemed wilder,
more uncouth with its rude natural ob-
stacles, and less trodden by the foot
of man, than he remembered it on his
outward journey. But he leaped across
the plashy places, thrust himself through
the clinging underbrush, climbed the
ascent, plunged into the hollow, and
overcame, in short, all the difficulties
of the track, with an unweariable activity that astonished him. He could not
but recall how feebly, and with what
frequent pauses for breath, he had
toiled over the same ground, only two
days before. As he drew near the town,
he took an impression of change from
the series of familiar objects that presented themselves. It seemed not yesterday, not one, nor two, but many
days, or even years ago, since he had
quitted them. There, indeed, was each
former trace of the street, as he remembered it, and all the peculiarities
of the houses, with the due multitude
of gable-peaks, and a weather-cock at
every point where his memory suggested one. Not the less, however, came
this importunately obtrusive sense of
change. The same was true as regarded
the acquaintances whom he met, and
all the well-known shapes of human life,
about the little town. They looked
neither older nor younger now; the
beards of the aged were no whiter, nor
could the creeping babe of yesterday
walk on his feet to-day; it was impossible to describe in what respect they
differed from the individuals on whom
he had so recently bestowed a parting
glance; and yet the minister's deepest
sense seemed to inform him of their
mutability. A similar impression struck

him most remarkably, as he passed under the walls of his own church. The edifice had so very strange, and yet so familiar, an aspect, that Mr. Dimmesdale's mind vibrated between two ideas; either that he had seen it only in a dream hitherto, or that he was merely dreaming about it now.

This phenomenon, in the various shapes which it assumed, indicated no external change, but so sudden and important a change in the spectator of the familiar scene, that the intervening space of a single day had operated on his consciousness like the lapse of years. The minister's own will, and Hester's will, and the fate that grew between them, had wrought this transformation. It was the same town as heretofore; but the same minister returned not from the forest. He might have said to the friends who greeted him,—"I am not the man for whom you take me! I left him yonder in the forest, withdrawn into a secret dell, by a mossy tree-trunk, and near a melancholy brook! Go, seek your minister, and see if his emaciated figure, his thin cheek, his white, heavy, pain-wrinkled brow, be not flung down there, like a cast-off garment!" His friends, no doubt, would still have insisted with him,—"Thou art thyself the man!"—but the error would have been their own, not his.

Before Mr. Dimmesdale reached home, his inner man gave him other evidences of a revolution in the sphere of thought and feeling. In truth, nothing short of a total change of dynasty and moral code, in that interior kingdom, was adequate to account for the impulses now communicated to the unfortunate and startled minister. At every step he was incited to do some strange,

wild, wicked thing or other, wit[h] sense that it would be at once invo[lun]tary and intentional; in spite of [him]self, yet growing out of a profou[nder] self than that which opposed the [im]pulse. For instance, he met one of [his] own deacons. The good old man [ad]dressed him with the paternal a[ffec]tion and patriarchal privilege, which [his] venerable age, his upright and holy c[har]acter, and his station in the Chu[rch] entitled him to use; and, conjoined [with] this, the deep, almost worshipping [re]spect, which the minister's professi[on] and private claims alike deman[d.] Never was there a more beautiful [ex]ample of how the majesty of age [and] wisdom may comport with the obeis[ance] and respect enjoined upon it, as f[rom] a lower social rank, and inferior o[rder] of endowment, towards a higher. N[ow,] during a conversation of some tw[o or] three moments between the Rever[end] Mr. Dimmesdale and this excellent [and] hoary-bearded deacon, it was only [by] the most careful self-control that [the] former could refrain from uttering [cer]tain blasphemous suggestions that [rose] into his mind, respecting the comm[un]ion-supper. He absolutely trembled [and] turned pale as ashes, lest his ton[gue] should wag itself, in utterance of t[hese] horrible matters, and plead his [own] consent for so doing, without his ha[ving] fairly given it. And, even with this [ter]ror in his heart, he could hardly a[void] laughing, to imagine how the sanct[ified] old patriarchal deacon would have [been] petrified by his minister's impiety!

Again, another incident of the s[ame] nature. Hurrying along the street, [the] Reverend Mr. Dimmesdale encount[ered] the eldest female member of his chu[rch,] a most pious and exemplary old da[me,]

r, widowed, lonely, and with a heart
ull of reminiscences about her dead
band and children, and her dead
nds of long ago, as a burial-ground
ull of storied gravestones. Yet all
, which would else have been such
vy sorrow, was made almost a sol-
joy to her devout old soul, by
gious consolations and the truths of
pture, wherewith she had fed her-
continually for more than thirty
rs. And, since Mr. Dimmesdale had
n her in charge, the good gran-
's chief earthly comfort—which, un-
it had been likewise a heavenly
fort, could have been none at all
as to meet her pastor, whether cas-
y, or of set purpose, and be re-
hed with a word of warm, fragrant,
ven-breathing Gospel truth, from his
ved lips, into her dulled, but rap-
usly attentive ear. But, on this
sion, up to the moment of putting
lips to the old woman's ear, Mr.
mesdale, as the great enemy of
s would have it, could recall no
of Scripture, nor aught else, except
ief, pithy, and, as it then appeared
im, unanswerable argument against
immortality of the human soul.
instilment thereof into her mind
ld probably have caused this aged
r to drop down dead, at once, as
he effect of an intensely poisonous
sion. What he really did whisper,
minister could never afterwards rec-
t. There was, perhaps, a fortunate
rder in his utterance, which failed
npart any distinct idea to the good
w's comprehension, or which Provi-
e interpreted after a method of its
. Assuredly, as the minister looked
, he beheld an expression of divine
itude and ecstasy that seemed like

the shine of the celestial city on her
face, so wrinkled and ashy pale.

Again, a third instance. After parting from the old church-member, he
met the youngest sister of them all. It
was a maiden newly won—and won by
the Reverend Mr. Dimmesdale's own
sermon, on the Sabbath after his vigil
—to barter the transitory pleasures of
the world for the heavenly hope, that
was to assume brighter substance as life
grew dark around her, and which would
gild the utter gloom with final glory.
She was fair and pure as a lily that
had bloomed in Paradise. The minister
knew well that he was himself enshrined
within the stainless sanctity of her
heart, which hung its snowy curtains
about his image, imparting to religion
the warmth of love, and to love a
religious purity. Satan, that afternoon,
had surely led the poor young girl
away from her mother's side, and thrown
her into the pathway of this sorely
tempted, or—shall we not rather say?
—this lost and desperate man. As she
drew nigh, the arch-fiend whispered him
to condense into small compass and drop
into her tender bosom a germ of evil
that would be sure to blossom darkly
soon, and bear black fruit betimes. Such
was his sense of power over this virgin
soul, trusting him as she did, that the
minister felt potent to blight all the
field of innocence with but one wicked
look, and develop all its opposite with
but a word. So—with a mightier struggle
than he had yet sustained—he held his
Geneva cloak before his face, and hurried onward, making no sign of recognition, and leaving the young sister to
digest his rudeness as she might. She
ransacked her conscience,—which was
full of harmless little matters, like her

pocket or her work-bag,—and took herself to task, poor thing! for a thousand imaginary faults; and went about her household duties with swollen eyelids the next morning.

Before the minister had time to celebrate his victory over this last temptation, he was conscious of another impulse, more ludicrous, and almost as horrible. It was,—we blush to tell it,—it was to stop short in the road, and teach some very wicked words to a knot of little Puritan children who were playing there, and had but just begun to talk. Denying himself this freak, as unworthy of his cloth, he met a drunken seaman, one of the ship's crew from the Spanish Main. And, here, since he had so valiantly forborne all other wickedness, poor Mr. Dimmesdale longed, at least, to shake hands with the tarry blackguard, and recreate himself with a few improper jests, such as dissolute sailors so abound with, and a volley of good, round, solid, satisfactory, and heaven-defying oaths! It was not so much a better principle, as partly his natural good taste, and still more his buckramed habit of clerical decorum, that carried him safely through the latter crisis.

"What is it that haunts and tempts me thus?" cried the minister to himself, at length, pausing in the street, and striking his hand against his forehead. "Am I mad? or am I given over utterly to the fiend? Did I make a contract with him in the forest, and sign it with my blood? And does he now summon me to its fulfilment, by suggesting the performance of every wickedness which his most foul imagination can conceive?"

At the moment when the Reverend Mr. Dimmesdale thus communed w[ith] himself, and struck his forehead w[ith] his hand, old Mistress Hibbins, the [re]puted witch-lady, is said to have b[een] passing by. She made a very gr[and] appearance; having on a high he[ad]-dress, a rich gown of velvet, and a [ruff] done up with the famous yellow star[ch,] of which Ann Turner, her espe[cial] friend, had taught her the secret, bef[ore] this last good lady had been han[ged] for Sir Thomas Overbury's murd[er.] Whether the witch had read the m[in]ister's thoughts, or no, she came t[o a] full stop, looked shrewdly into his fa[ce,] smiled craftily, and—though little gi[ven] to converse with clergymen—bega[n] conversation.

"So, reverend Sir, you have mad[e a] visit into the forest," observed [the] witch-lady, nodding her high head d[ark] at him. "The next time, I pray you[,] allow me only a fair warning, an[d I] shall be proud to bear you compa[ny.] Without taking overmuch upon mys[elf,] my good word will go far towards ga[in]ing any strange gentleman a fair [re]ception from yonder potentate you w[ot] of!"

"I profess, madam," answered [the] clergyman, with a grave obeisance, s[uch] as the lady's rank demanded, and [his] own good-breeding made imperative[,] "I profess, on my conscience and ch[ar]acter, that I am utterly bewildered [as] touching the purport of your wor[ds.] I went not into the forest to see[k a] potentate; neither do I, at any fut[ure] time, design a visit thither, with [a] view to gaining the favor of such p[er]sonage. My one sufficient object was [to] greet that pious friend of mine, [the] Apostle Eliot, and rejoice with h[im] over the many precious souls he h[as] n from heathendom!"

'Ha, ha, ha!" cackled the old witch-
y, still nodding her high head-dress
the minister. "Well, well, we must
·ds talk thus in the daytime! You
ry it off like an old hand! But at
·night, and in the forest, we shall
·e other talk together!"

she passed on with her aged stateli-
s, but often turning back her head
 smiling at him, like one willing to
ognize a secret intimacy of connec-
1.

Have I then sold myself," thought
 minister, "to the fiend whom, if
1 say true, this yellow-starched and
veted old hag has chosen for her
1ce and master!"

The wretched minister! He had made
·argain very like it! Tempted by a
am of happiness, he had yielded him-
, with deliberate choice, as he had
er done before, to what he knew
 deadly sin. And the infectious poi-
of that sin had been thus rapidly
used throughout his moral system.
had stupefied all blessed impulses,
 awakened into vivid life the whole
therhood of bad ones. Scorn, bitter-
s, unprovoked malignity, gratuitous
ire of ill, ridicule of whatever was
d and holy, all awoke, to tempt, even
le they frightened him. And his en-
nter with old Mistress Hibbins, if
were a real incident, did but show
 sympathy and fellowship with
ked mortals, and the world of per-
:ed spirits.

Ie had, by this time, reached his
·lling, on the edge of the burial-
und, and, hastening up the stairs, took
ige in his study. The minister was
I to have reached this shelter, with-
first betraying himself to the world

by any of those strange and wicked
eccentricities to which he had been continually impelled while passing through
the streets. He entered the accustomed
room, and looked around him on its
books, its windows, its fireplace, and
the tapestried comfort of the walls,
with the same perception of strangeness
that had haunted him throughout his
walk from the forest-dell into the town,
and thitherward. Here he had studied
and written; here, gone through fast
and vigil, and come forth half alive;
here, striven to pray; here, borne a hundred thousand agonies! There was the
Bible, in its rich old Hebrew, with
Moses and the Prophets speaking to
him, and God's voice through all! There,
on the table, with the inky pen beside
it, was an unfinished sermon, with a
sentence broken in the midst, where
his thoughts had ceased to gush out
upon the page, two days before. He
knew that it was himself, the thin and
white-cheeked minister, who had done
and suffered these things, and written
thus far into the Election Sermon! But
he seemed to stand apart, and eye this
former self with' scornful, pitying, but
half-envious curiosity. That self was
gone. Another man had returned out
of the forest; a wiser one; with a knowledge of hidden mysteries which the simplicity of the former never could have
reached. A bitter kind of knowledge
that!

While occupied with these reflections,
a knock came at the door of the study,
and the minister said, "Come in!"—not
wholly devoid of an idea that he might
behold an evil spirit. And so he did!
It was old Roger Chillingworth that
entered. The minister stood, white and
speechless, with one hand on the He-

brew Scriptures, and the other spread upon his breast.

"Welcome home, reverend Sir," said the physician. "And how found you that godly man, the Apostle Eliot? But methinks, dear Sir, you look pale; as if the travel through the wilderness had been too sore for you. Will not my aid be requisite to put you in heart and strength to preach your Election Sermon?"

"Nay, I think not so," rejoined the Reverend Mr. Dimmesdale. "My journey, and the sight of the holy Apostle yonder, and the free air which I have breathed, have done me good, after so long confinement in my study. I think to need no more of your drugs, my kind physician, good though they be, and administered by a friendly hand."

All this time, Roger Chillingworth was looking at the minister with the grave and intent regard of a physician towards his patient. But, in spite of his outward show, the latter was almost convinced of the old man's knowledge, or, at least, his confident suspicion, with respect to his own interview with Hester Prynne. The physician knew then, that, in the minister's regard, he was no longer a trusted friend, but his bitterest enemy. So much being known, it would appear natural that a part of it should be expressed. It is singular, however, how long a time often passes before words embody things; and with what security two persons, who choose to avoid a certain subject, may approach its very verge, and retire without disturbing it. Thus, the minister felt no apprehension that Roger Chillingworth would touch, in express words, upon the real position which they sustained towards one another. Yet did the physi-

cian, in his dark way, creep frightfu near the secret.

"Were it not better," said he, "t you use my poor skill to-night? Vei dear Sir, we must take pains to m you strong and vigorous for this casion of the Election discourse. ' people look for great things from y apprehending that another year r come about, and find their pa gone."

"Yea, to another world," replied minister, with pious resignation. "Hea grant it be a better one; for, in g sooth, I hardly think to tarry with flock through the flitting seasons another year! But, touching your m cine, kind Sir, in my present frame body, I need it not."

"I joy to hear it," answered the p sician. "It may be that my remec so long administered in vain, begin to take due effect. Happy man wer and well deserving of New Engla gratitude, could I achieve this cure!

"I thank you from my heart, n watchful friend," said the Reverend Dimmesdale, with a solemn smile. thank you, and can but requite y good deeds with my prayers."

"A good man's prayers are gol recompense!" rejoined old Roger C lingworth, as he took his leave. "\ they are the current gold coin of New Jerusalem, with the King's mint-mark on them!"

Left alone, the minister summone servant of the house, and reque food, which, being set before him ate with ravenous appetite. Then, f ing the already written pages of Election Sermon into the fire, he fo with began another, which he wrote such an impulsive flow of thought otion, that he fancied himself in- red; and only wondered that Heaven uld see fit to transmit the grand and emn music of its oracles through so ıl an organ-pipe as he. However, leav- that mystery to solve itself, or go ,olved forever, he drove his task on- rd, with earnest haste and ecstasy. us the night fled away, as if it were a winged steed, and he careering on it; morning came, and peeped, blushing, through the curtains; and at last sunrise threw a golden beam into the study, and laid it right across the minister's be- dazzled eyes. There he was, with the pen still between his fingers, and a vast, immeasurable tract of written space be- hind him!

CHAPTER XXI

THE NEW ENGLAND HOLIDAY

ΒETIMES in the morning of the day which the new Governor was to re- ⱱe his office at the hands of the ple, Hester Prynne and little Pearl ɪe into the market-place. It was al- dy thronged with the craftsmen and er plebeian inhabitants of the town, :onsiderable numbers; among whom, wise, were many rough figures, whose ɪe of deer-skins marked them as be- ɜing to some of the forest settle- ıts, which surrounded the little me- ɔolis of the colony.

)n this public holiday, as on all other ısions, for seven years past, Hester clad in a garment of coarse gray h. Not more by its hue than by ɪe indescribable peculiarity in its ʌion, it had the effect of making her ɛ personally out of sight and outline; le, again, the scarlet letter brought back from this twilight indistinct- s, and revealed her under the moral ɛct of its own illumination. Her face, long familiar to the townspeople, wed the marble quietude which they ɛ accustomed to behold there. It was like a mask; or, rather, like the frozen calmness of a dead woman's fea- tures; owing this dreary resemblance to the fact that Hester was actually dead, in respect to any claim of sym- pathy, and had departed out of the world with which she still seemed to mingle.

It might be, on this one day, that there was an expression unseen before, nor, indeed, vivid enough to be detected now; unless some preternaturally gifted observer should have first read the heart, and have afterwards sought a corresponding development in the coun- tenance and mien. Such a spiritual seer might have conceived, that, after sus- taining the gaze of the multitude through seven miserable years as a necessity, a penance, and something which it was a stern religion to endure, she now, for one last time more, encountered it freely and voluntarily, in order to convert what had so long been agony into a kind of triumph. "Look your last on the scarlet letter and its wearer!"—the peo- ple's victim and life-long bond-slave, as they fancied her, might say to them. "Yet a little while, and she will be beyond your reach! A few hours longer, and the deep, mysterious ocean will quench and hide forever the symbol which ye have caused to burn upon her bosom!" Nor were it an inconsistency too improbable to be assigned to human nature, should we suppose a feeling of regret in Hester's mind, at the moment when she was about to win her freedom from the pain which had been thus deeply incorporated with her being. Might there not be an irresistible desire to quaff a last, long, breathless draught of the cup of wormwood and aloes, with which nearly all her years of womanhood had been perpetually flavored? The wine of life, henceforth to be presented to her lips, must be indeed rich, delicious, and exhilarating, in its chased and golden beaker; or else leave an inevitable and weary languor, after the lees of bitterness wherewith she had been drugged, as with a cordial of intensest potency.

Pearl was decked out with airy gayety, It would have been impossible to guess that this bright and sunny apparition owed its existence to the shape of gloomy gray; or that a fancy, at once so gorgeous and so delicate as must have been requisite to contrive the child's apparel, was the same that had achieved a task perhaps more difficult, in imparting so distinct a peculiarity to Hester's simple robe. The dress, so proper was it to little Pearl, seemed an effluence, or inevitable development and outward manifestation of her character, no more to be separated from her than the many hued brilliancy from a butterfly's wing, or the painted glory from the leaf of a bright flower. As

with these, so with the child; her g was all of one idea with her nat On this eventful day, moreover, th was a certain singular inquietude excitement in her mood, resembl nothing so much as the shimmer o diamond, that sparkles and flashes v the varied throbbings of the breast which it is displayed. Children h always a sympathy in the agitations those connected with them; alwa especially, a sense of any trouble impending revolution, of whatever ki in domestic circumstances; and the fore Pearl, who was the gem on mother's unquiet bosom, betrayed, the very dance of her spirits, the ex tions which none could detect in marble passiveness of Hester's brow

This effervescence made her flit v a bird-like movement, rather than w by her mother's side. She broke c tinually into shouts of a wild, inarti late, and sometimes piercing mu When they reached the market-pla she became still more restless, on p ceiving the stir and bustle that en ened the spot; for it was usually m like the broad and lonesome green fore a village meeting-house, than centre of a town's business.

"Why, what is this, mother?" c she. "Wherefore have all the pe left their work to-day? Is it a p day for the whole world? See, ther the blacksmith! He has washed sooty face, and put on his Sabbathclothes, and looks as if he would gla be merry, if any kind body would c teach him how! And there is Ma Brackett, the old jailer, nodding smiling at me. Why does he do mother?"

"He remembers thee a little ba

child," answered Hester.

"He should not nod and smile at me,
all that,—the black, grim, ugly-eyed
man!" said Pearl. "He may nod at
me, if he will; for thou art clad in
gray, and wearest the scarlet letter.
But see, mother, how many faces of
strange people, and Indians among them,
and sailors! What have they all come
to do, here in the market-place?"

"They wait to see the procession
pass," said Hester. "For the Governor
and the magistrates are to go by, and
the ministers, and all the great people
and good people, with the music and
the soldiers marching before them."

"And will the minister be there?"
asked Pearl. "And will he hold out both
his hands to me, as when thou ledst me
to him from the brook-side?"

"He will be there, child," answered
her mother. "But he will not greet thee
to-day; nor must thou greet him."

"What a strange, sad man is he!" said
the child, as if speaking partly to herself. "In the dark night-time he calls
us to him, and holds thy hand and mine,
as when we stood with him on the
scaffold yonder! And in the deep forest,
where only the old trees can hear, and
a strip of sky see it, he talks with
thee, sitting on a heap of moss! And
he kisses my forehead, too, so that the
little brook would hardly wash it off!
But here, in the sunny day, and among
all the people, he knows us not; nor
must we know him! A strange, sad
man is he, with his hand always over
his heart!"

"Be quiet, Pearl! Thou understandest
not these things," said her mother.
"Think not now of the minister, but
look about thee, and see how cheery
everybody's face to-day. The chil-

dren have come from their schools, and
the grown people from their workshops,
and their fields, on purpose to be happy.
For, to-day, a new man is beginning to
rule over them; and so—as has been
the custom of mankind ever since a
nation was first gathered—they make
merry and rejoice; as if a good and
golden year were at length to pass over
the poor old world!"

It was as Hester said, in regard to
the unwonted jollity that brightened the
faces of the people. Into this festal
season of the year—as it already was,
and continued to be during the greater
part of two centuries—the Puritans compressed whatever mirth and public joy
they deemed allowable to human infirmity; thereby so far dispelling the customary cloud, that, for the space of
a single holiday, they appeared scarcely
more grave than most other communities at a period of general affliction.

But we perhaps exaggerate the gray
or sable tinge, which undoubtedly characterized the mood and manners of the
age. The persons now in the market-
place of Boston had not been born to
an inheritance of Puritanic gloom. They
were native Englishmen, whose fathers
had lived in the sunny richness of the
Elizabethan epoch; a time when the
life of England, viewed as one great
mass, would appear to have been as
stately, magnificent, and joyous, as the
world has ever witnessed. Had they
followed their hereditary taste, the New
England settlers would have illustrated
all events of public importance by bonfires, banquets, pageantries, and processions. Nor would it have been impracticable, in the observance of majestic ceremonies, to combine mirthful recreation
with solemnity, and give, as it were, a

grotesque and brilliant embroidery to the great robe of state, which a nation, at such festivals, puts on. There was some shadow of an attempt of this kind in the mode of celebrating the day on which the political year of the colony commenced. The dim reflection of a remembered splendor, a colorless and manifold diluted repetition of what they had beheld in proud old London, —we will not say at a royal coronation, but at a Lord Mayor's show,—might be traced in the customs which our forefathers instituted, with reference to the annual installation of magistrates. The fathers and founders of the commonwealth—the statesman, the priest, and the soldier—deemed it a duty then to assume the outward state and majesty, which, in accordance with antique style, was looked upon as the proper garb of public or social eminence. All came forth, to move in procession before the people's eye, and thus impart a needed dignity to the simple framework of a government so newly constructed.

Then, too, the people were countenanced, if not encouraged, in relaxing the severe and close application to their various modes of rugged industry, which, at all other times, seemed of the same piece and material with their religion. Here, it is true, were none of the appliances which popular merriment would so readily have found in the England of Elizabeth's time, or that of James;—no rude shows of a theatrical kind; no minstrel, with his harp and legendary ballad, nor gleeman, with an ape dancing to his music; no juggler, with his tricks of mimic witchcraft; no Merry Andrew, to stir up the multitude with jests, perhaps hundreds of years old, but still effective, by th appeals to the very broadest sour of mirthful sympathy. All such prof sors of the several branches of jocu ity would have been sternly repress not only by the rigid discipline of l but by the general sentiment wh gives law its vitality. Not the l however, the great, honest face of people smiled, grimly, perhaps, widely too. Nor were sports wanti such as the colonists had witness and shared in, long ago, at the coun fairs and on the village-greens of E land; and which it was thought v to keep alive on this new soil, the sake of the courage and manlin that were essential in them. Wrestli matches, in the different fashions Cornwall and Devonshire, were s here and there about the market-pla in one corner, there was a friendly b at quarterstaff; and—what attrac most interest of all—on the platform the pillory, already so noted in our pa two masters of defence were comme ing an exhibition with the buckler broadsword. But, much to the dis pointment of the crowd, this latter b iness was broken off by the interp tion of the town beadle, who had idea of permitting the majesty of law to be violated by such an ab of one of its consecrated places.

It may not be too much to affi on the whole, (the people being the the first stages of joyless deportm and the offspring of sires who known how to be merry, in their da that they would compare favorably point of holiday keeping, with t descendants, even at so long an in val as ourselves. Their immediate terity, the generation next to the e

igrants, wore the blackest shade of
ritanism, and so darkened the na-
nal visage with it, that all the sub-
quent years have not sufficed to clear
up. We have yet to learn again the
gotten art of gayety.

The picture of human life in the
arket-place, though its general tint
s the sad gray, brown, or black of
e English emigrants, was yet enliv-
ed by some diversity of hue. A party
Indians—in their savage finery of
riously embroidered deer-skin robes;
mpum-belts, red and yellow ochre,
d feathers, and armed with the bow
d arrow and stone-headed spear—
od apart, with countenances of in-
xible gravity, beyond what even the
ritan aspect could attain. Nor, wild
were these painted barbarians, were
ey the wildest feature of the scene.
is distinction could more justly be
imed by some mariners,—a part of
e crew of the vessel from the Span-
Main,—who had come ashore to
e the humors of Election Day. They
re rough-looking desperadoes, with
n-blackened faces, and an immensity
beard; their wide, short trousers were
nfined about the waist by belts, often
asped with a rough plate of gold, and
staining always a long knife, and, in
me instances, a sword. From beneath
eir broad-brimmed hats of palm-leaf,
eamed eyes which, even in good na-
re and merriment, had a kind of
imal ferocity. They transgressed, with-
t fear or scruple, the rules of behavior
at were binding on all others; smok-
g tobacco under the beadle's very
se, although each whiff would have
st a townsman a shilling; and quaff-
g, at their pleasure, draughts of wine
aqua-vitæ from pocket-flasks, which

they freely tendered to the gaping crowd
around them. It remarkably characterized the incomplete morality of the age,
rigid as we call it, that a license was
allowed the seafaring class, not merely
for their freaks on shore, but for far
more desperate deeds on their proper
element. The sailor of that day would
go near to be arraigned as a pirate
in our own. There could be little doubt,
for instance, that this very ship's crew,
though no unfavorable specimens of the
nautical brotherhood, had been guilty,
as we should phrase it, of depredations
on the Spanish commerce, such as
would have perilled all their necks in
a modern court of justice.

But the sea, in those old times,
heaved, swelled and foamed very much
at its own will, or subject only to the
tempestuous wind, with hardly any attempts at regulation by human law. The
buccaneer on the wave might relinquish
his calling, and become at once, if he
chose, a man of probity and piety on
land; nor, even in the full career of
his reckless life, was he regarded as
a personage with whom it was dis-
reputable to traffic, or casually associate.
Thus, the Puritan elders, in their black
cloaks, starched bands, and steeple-
crowned hats, smiled not unbenignantly
at the clamor and rude deportment of
these jolly seafaring men; and it excited
neither surprise nor animadversion,
when so reputable a citizen as old Roger
Chillingworth, the physician, was seen
to enter the market-place, in close and
familiar talk with the commander of
the questionable vessel.

The latter was by far the most showy
and gallant figure, so far as apparel
went, anywhere to be seen among the
multitude. He wore a profusion of rib-

bons on his garment, and gold lace on his hat, which was also encircled by a gold chain, and surmounted with a feather. There was a sword at his side, and a sword-cut on his forehead, which, by the arrangement of his hair, he seemed anxious rather to display than hide. A landsman could hardly have worn this garb and shown this face, and worn and shown them both with such a galliard air, without undergoing stern question before a magistrate, and probably incurring fine or imprisonment, or perhaps an exhibition in the stocks. As regarded the shipmaster, however, all was looked upon as pertaining to the character, as to a fish his glistening scales.

After parting from the physician, the commander of the Bristol ship strolled idly through the market-place; until, happening to approach the spot where Hester Prynne was standing, he appeared to recognize, and did not hesitate to address her. As was usually the case wherever Hester stood, a small vacant area—a sort of magic circle—had formed itself about her, into which, though the people were elbowing one another at a little distance, none ventured, or felt disposed to intrude. It was a forcible type of the moral solitude in which the scarlet letter enveloped its fated wearer; partly by her own reserve, and partly by the instinctive, though no longer so unkindly, withdrawal of her fellow-creatures. Now, if never before, it answered a good purpose, by enabling Hester and the seaman to speak together without risk of being overheard; and so changed was Hester Prynne's repute before the

public, that the matron in town m[ost] eminent for rigid morality could [not] have held such intercourse with [less] result of scandal than herself.

"So, mistress," said the mariner, [I] must bid the steward make ready [one] more berth than you bargained f[or]! No fear of scurvy or ship-fever, [this] voyage! What with the ship's surg[eon] and this other doctor, our only dan[ger] will be from drug or pill; more[over], token, as there is a lot of apothecar[y] stuff aboard, which I traded for w[ith] a Spanish vessel."

"What mean you?" inquired Hes[ter], startled more than she permitted to [ap]pear. "Have you another passenger?"

"Why, know you not," cried the sh[ip]master, "that this physician here—C[hil]lingworth, he calls himself—is min[ded] to try my cabin-fare with you? Ay, ay, you must have known it; for he t[old] me he is of your party, and a cl[ose] friend to the gentleman you spoke [of] —he that is in peril from these sour [old] Puritan rulers!"

"They know each other well, indee[d]," replied Hester, with a mien of calmn[ess], though in the utmost consternati[on]. "They have dwelt together."

Nothing further passed between the mariner and Hester Prynne. But, [at] that instant, she beheld old Roger C[hil]lingworth himself, standing in the [re]motest corner of the market-place, a[nd] smiling on her; a smile which—acr[oss] the wide and bustling square, a[nd] through all the talk and laughter, a[nd] various thoughts, moods, and intere[sts] of the crowd,—conveyed secret a[nd] fearful meaning.

CHAPTER XXII

THE PROCESSION

ƷEFORE Hester Prynne could call to-
her her thoughts, and consider what
s practicable to be done in this new
l startling aspect of affairs, the sound
military music was heard approach-
along a contiguous street. It denoted
advance of the procession of magis-
tes and citizens, on its way towards
meeting-house; where, in compliance
h a custom thus early established,
l ever since observed, the Reverend
. Dimmesdale was to deliver an Elec-
n Sermon.

Soon the head of the procession
wed itself, with a slow and stately
rch, turning a corner, and making
way across the market-place. First
ne the music. It comprised a variety
instruments, perhaps imperfectly
pted to one another, and played with
great skill; but yet attaining the
at object for which the harmony of
m and clarion addresses itself to the
ltitude,—that of imparting a higher
l more heroic air to the scene of
that passes before the eye. Little
rl at first clapped her hands, but
n lost, for an instant, the restless
ation that had kept her in a con-
ual effervescence throughout the
rning; she gazed silently, and seemed
be borne upward, like a floating sea-
d, on the long heaves and swells of
nd. But she was brought back to her
mer mood by the shimmer of the
shine on the weapons and bright
or of the military company, which
owed after the music, and formed
honorary escort of the procession.

This body of soldiery—which still sustains a corporate existence, and marches
down from past ages with an ancient
and honorable fame—was composed of
no mercenary materials. Its ranks were
filled with gentlemen, who felt the stir-
rings of martial impulse, and sought to
establish a kind of College of Arms,
where, as in an association of Knights
Templars, they might learn the science,
and, so far as peaceful exercise would
teach them, the practices of war. The
high estimation then placed upon the
military character might be seen in the
lofty port of each individual member
of the company. Some of them, indeed,
by their services in the Low Countries
and on other fields of European warfare, had fairly won their title to assume the name and pomp of soldiership.
The entire array, moreover, clad in
burnished steel, and with plumage nodding over their bright morions, had
a brilliancy of effect which no modern
display can aspire to equal.

And yet the men of civil eminence,
who came immediately behind the military escort, were better worth a thoughtful observer's eye. Even in outward
demeanor, they showed a stamp of
majesty that made the warrior's haughty
stride look vulgar, if not absurd. It
was an age when what we call talent
had far less consideration than now, but
the massive materials which produce
stability and dignity of character a great
deal more. The people possessed, by
hereditary right, the quality of reverence; which, in their descendants, if it

survive at all, exists in smaller proportion, and with a vastly diminished force, in the selection and estimate of public men. The change may be for good or ill, and is partly, perhaps, for both. In that old day, the English settler on these rude shores—having left king, nobles, and all degrees of awful rank behind, while still the faculty and necessity of reverence were strong in him—bestowed it on the white hair and venerable brow of age; on long-tried integrity; on solid wisdom and sad-colored experience; on endowments of that grave and weighty order which gives the idea of permanence, and comes under the general definition of respectability. These primitive statesmen, therefore,—Bradstreet, Endicott, Dudley, Bellingham, and their compeers,—who were elevated to power by the early choice of the people, seem to have been not often brilliant, but distinguished by a ponderous sobriety, rather than activity of intellect. They had fortitude and self-reliance, and, in time of difficulty or peril, stood up for the welfare of the state like a line of cliffs against a tempestuous tide. The traits of character here indicated were well represented in the square cast of countenance and large physical development of the new colonial magistrates. So far as a demeanor of natural authority was concerned, the mother country need not have been ashamed to see these foremost men of an actual democracy adopted into the House of Peers, or made the Privy Council of the sovereign.

Next in order to the magistrates came the young and eminently distinguished divine, from whose lips the religious discourse of the anniversary was expected.

His was the profession, at that era, which intellectual ability displayed self far more than in political life; —leaving a higher motive out of t question—it offered inducements pow ful enough, in the almost worshippi respect of the community, to win t most aspiring ambition into its servi Even political power—as in the ca of Increase Mather—was within t grasp of a successful priest.

It was the observation of those w beheld him now, that never, since M Dimmesdale first set his foot on t New England shore, had he exhibit such energy as was seen in the g and air with which he kept his pa in the procession. There was no feeb ness of step, as at other times; frame was not bent; nor did his ha rest ominously upon his heart. Yet, the clergyman were rightly viewed, strength seemed not of the body. might be spiritual, and imparted to h by angelic ministrations. It might the exhilaration of that potent cordi which is distilled only in the furna glow of earnest and long-continu thought. Or, perchance, his sensiti temperament was invigorated by t loud and piercing music, that swell heavenward, and uplifted him on ascending wave. Nevertheless, so a stracted was his look, it might be qu tioned whether Mr. Dimmesdale ev heard the music. There was his bod moving onward, and with an unacc tomed force. But where was his min Far and deep in its own region, bus ing itself, with preternatural activit to marshal a procession of state thoughts that were soon to issue thenc and so he saw nothing, heard not ing, knew nothing, of what was arou n; but the spiritual element took up e feeble frame, and carried it along, conscious of the burden, and convert- g it to spirit like itself. Men of un- mmon intellect, who have grown mor- d, possess this occasional power of ghty effort, into which they throw e life of many days, and then are eless for as many more.

Hester Prynne, gazing steadfastly at e clergyman, felt a dreary influence me over her, but wherefore or whence e knew not; unless that he seemed remote from her own sphere, and terly beyond her reach. One glance of cognition, she had imagined, must eds pass between them. She thought the dim forest, with its little dell solitude, and love, and anguish, and mossy tree-trunk, where, sitting hand hand, they had mingled their sad d passionate talk with the melancholy rmur of the brook. How deeply had ey known each other then! And was s the man? She hardly knew him w! He, moving proudly past, envel- ed, as it were, in the rich music, th the procession of majestic and nerable fathers; he, so unattainable his worldly position, and still more in that far vista of his unsympathiz- ; thoughts, through which she now held him! Her spirit sank with the a that all must have been a de- ion, and that, vividly as she had amed it, there could be no real bond wixt the clergyman and herself. And s much of woman was there in Hes- , that she could scarcely forgive him, least of all now, when the heavy tstep of their approaching Fate might heard, nearer, nearer, nearer!—for ing able so completely to withdraw nself from their mutual world; while

she groped darkly, and stretched forth her cold hands, and found him not.

Pearl either saw and responded to her mother's feelings, or herself felt the remoteness and intangibility that had fallen around the minister. While the procession passed, the child was uneasy, fluttering up and down, like a bird on the point of taking flight. When the whole had gone by, she looked up into Hester's face.

"Mother," said she, "was that the same minister that kissed me by the brook?"

"Hold thy peace, dear little Pearl!" whispered her mother. "We must not always talk in the market-place of what happens to us in the forest."

"I could not be sure that it was he; so strange he looked," continued the child. "Else I would have run to him, and bid him kiss me now, before all the people; even as he did yonder among the dark old trees. What would the minister have said, mother? Would he have clapped his hand over his heart, and scowled on me, and bid me be- gone?"

"What should he say, Pearl," an- swered Hester, "save that it was no time to kiss, and that kisses are not to be given in the market-place? Well for thee, foolish child, that thou didst not speak to him!"

Another shade of the same sentiment, in reference to Mr. Dimmesdale, was expressed by a person whose eccentrici- ties—or insanity, as we should term it —led her to do what few of the towns- people would have ventured on; to be- gin a conversation with the wearer of the scarlet letter, in public. It was Mis- tress Hibbins, who, arrayed in great magnificence, with a triple ruff, a broidered stomacher, a gown of rich velvet, and a gold-headed cane, had come forth to see the procession. As this ancient lady had the renown (which subsequently cost her no less a price than her life) of being a principal actor in all the works of necromancy that were continually going forward, the crowd gave way before her, and seemed to fear the touch of her garment, as if it carried the plague among its gorgeous folds. Seen in conjunction with Hester Prynne,—kindly as so many now felt towards the latter,—the dread inspired by Mistress Hibbins was doubled, and caused a general movement from that part of the market-place in which the two women stood.

"Now, what mortal imagination could conceive it!" whispered the old lady, confidentially, to Hester. "Yonder divine man! That saint on earth, as the people uphold him to be, and as—I must needs say—he really looks! Who, now, that saw him pass in the procession, would think how little while it is since he went forth out of his study,—chewing a Hebrew text of Scripture in his mouth, I warrant,—to take an airing in the forest! Aha! we know what that means, Hester Prynne! But, truly, forsooth, I find it hard to believe him the same man. Many a church-member saw I, walking behind the music, that has danced in the same measure with me, when Somebody was fiddler, and, it might be, an Indian powwow or a Lapland wizard changing hands with us! That is but a trifle, when a woman knows the world. But this minister! Couldst thou surely tell, Hester, whether he was the same man that encountered thee on the forest-path?"

"Madam, I know not of what you speak," answered Hester Prynne, fe[e]ing Mistress Hibbins to be of infi[rm] mind; yet strangely startled and a[we]stricken by the confidence with wh[ich] she affirmed a personal connection [be]tween so many persons (herself amo[ng] them) and the Evil One. "It is not [for] me to talk lightly of a learned and pi[ous] minister of the Word, like the Rev[er]end Mr. Dimmesdale!"

"Fie, woman, fie!" cried the old la[dy,] shaking her finger at Hester. "D[ost] thou think I have been to the for[est] so many times, and have yet no s[kill] to judge who else has been there? Y[ea,] though no leaf of the wild garlan[d] which they wore while they danced, [be] left in their hair! I know thee, Hest[er,] for I behold the token. We may [all] see it in the sunshine; and it glo[ws] like a red flame in the dark. Thou we[ar]est it openly; so there need be no qu[es]tion about that. But this minister! [Let] me tell thee, in thine ear! When [the] Black Man sees one of his own serva[nts,] signed and sealed, so shy of owning the bond as is the Reverend Mr. Di[m]mesdale, he hath a way of order[ing] matters so that the mark shall be [dis]closed in open daylight to the eyes [of] all the world! What is it that [the] minister seeks to hide, with his ha[nd] always over his heart? Ha, Hes[ter] Prynne!"

"What is it, good Mistress Hibbin[s?"] eagerly asked little Pearl. "Hast th[ou] seen it?"

"No matter, darling!" responded M[is]tress Hibbins, making Pearl a profou[nd] reverence. "Thou thyself wilt see [it,] one time or another. They say, ch[ild,] thou art of the lineage of the Pri[nce] of the Air! Wilt thou ride with [me] some fine night, to see thy fath[er?]

n thou shalt know wherefore the
ister keeps his hand over his heart!"
Laughing so shrilling that all the mar-
-place could hear her, the weird old
tlewoman took her departure.

y this time the preliminary prayer
been offered in the meeting-house,
the accents of the Reverend Mr.
nmesdale were heard commencing
discourse. An irresistible feeling kept
ster near the spot. As the sacred edi-
was too much thronged to admit
ther auditor, she took up her posi-
a close beside the scaffold of the
ory. It was in sufficient proximity
bring the whole sermon to her ears,
he shape of an indistinct, but varied,
rmur and flow of the minister's very
uliar voice.

his vocal organ was in itself a rich
owment; insomuch that a listener,
prehending nothing of the language
which the preacher spoke, might still
e been swayed to and fro by the
re tone and cadence. Like all other
sic, it breathed passion and pathos,
emotions high or tender, in a tongue
ive to the human heart, wherever
cated. Muffled as the sound was by
passage through the church-walls,
ster Prynne listened with such intent-
s, and sympathized so intimately,
t the sermon had throughout a mean-
for her, entirely apart from its in-
inguishable words. These, perhaps,
more distinctly heard, might have
n only a grosser medium, and have
ged the spiritual sense. Now she
ght the low undertone, as of the
d sinking down to repose itself; then
ended with it, as it rose through
gressive gradations of sweetness
power, until its volume seemed to
elop her with an atmosphere of

awe and solemn grandeur. And yet, majestic as the voice sometimes became,
there was forever in it an essential
character of plaintiveness. A loud or
low expression of anguish,—the whisper, or the shriek, as it might be conceived, of suffering humanity, that
touched a sensibility in every bosom!
At times this deep strain of pathos was
all that could be heard, and scarcely
heard, sighing amid a desolate silence.
But even when the minister's voice grew
high and commanding,—when it gushed
irrepressibly upward,—when it assumed
its utmost breadth and power, so over-
filling the church as to burst its way
through the solid walls, and diffuse itself in the open air,—still, if the auditor
listened intently, and for the purpose,
he could detect the same cry of pain.
What was it? The complaint of a human
heart, sorrow-laden, perchance guilty,
telling its secret, whether of guilt or
sorrow, to the great heart of mankind;
beseeching its sympathy or forgiveness,
—at every moment,—in each accent,—
and never in vain! It was this profound
and continual undertone that gave the
clergyman his most appropriate power.

During all this time, Hester stood,
statue-like, at the foot of the scaffold.
If the minister's voice had not kept her
there, there would nevertheless have
been an inevitable magnetism in that
spot, whence she dated the first hour
of her life of ignominy. There was a
sense within her,—too ill-defined to be
made a thought, but weighing heavily
on her mind,—that her whole orb of
life, both before and after, was connected with this spot, as with the one
point that gave it unity.

Little Pearl, meanwhile, had quitted
her mother's side, and was playing at

her own will about the market-place. She made the sombre crowd cheerful by her erratic and glistening ray; even as a bird of bright plumage illuminates a whole tree of dusky foliage, by darting to and fro, half seen and half concealed amid the twilight of the clustering leaves. She had an undulating, but, oftentimes, a sharp and irregular movement. It indicated the restless vivacity of her spirit, which to-day was doubly indefatigable in its tiptoe dance, because it was played upon and vibrated with her mother's disquietude. Whenever Pearl saw anything to excite her ever active and wandering curiosity, she flew thitherward, and, as we might say, seized upon that man or thing as her own property, so far as she desired it; but without yielding the minutest degree of control over her motions in requital. The Puritans looked on, and, if they smiled, were none the less inclined to pronounce the child a demon offspring, from the indescribable charm of beauty and eccentricity that shone through her little figure, and sparkled with its activity. She ran and looked the wild Indian in the face; and he grew conscious of a nature wilder than his own. Thence, with native audacity, but still with a reserve as characteristic, she flew into the midst of a group of mariners, the swarthy-cheeked wild men of the ocean, as the Indians were of the land; and they gazed wonderingly and admiringly at Pearl, as if a flake of the sea-foam had taken the shape of a little maid, and were gifted with a soul of the sea-fire, that flashes beneath the prow in the night-time.

One of these seafaring men—the shipmaster, indeed, who had spoken to Hester Prynne—was so smitten with Pearl's

aspect, that he attempted to lay ha[nd] upon her, with purpose to snatch a ki[ss]. Finding it as impossible to touch [her] as to catch a humming-bird in the a[ir], he took from his hat the gold ch[ain] that was twisted about it, and thr[ew] it to the child. Pearl immediately twi[ned] it around her neck and waist, with su[ch] happy skill, that, once seen there, [it] became a part of her, and it was di[ffi]cult to imagine her without it.

"Thy mother is yonder woman w[ith] the scarlet letter," said the seam[an]. "Wilt thou carry her a message fr[om] me?"

"If the message pleases me, I wi[ll]," answered Pearl.

"Then tell her," rejoined he, "th[at] I spake again with the black-a-visag[ed,] hump-shouldered old doctor, and he [en]gages to bring his friend, the gentlem[an] she wots of, aboard with him. So [let] thy mother take no thought, save [for] herself and thee. Wilt thou tell her th[is,] thou witch-baby?"

"Mistress Hibbins says my father [is] the Prince of the Air!" cried Pea[rl] with a naughty smile. "If thou call[est] me that ill name, I shall tell him [on] thee; and he will chase thy ship w[ith] a tempest!"

Pursuing a zigzag course across t[he] market-place, the child returned to h[er] mother, and communicated what t[he] mariner had said. Hester's strong, ca[lm,] steadfastly enduring spirit almost sa[nk] at last, on beholding this dark and gr[im] countenance of an inevitable doo[m,] which—at the moment when a passa[ge] seemed to open for the minister a[nd] herself out of their labyrinth of mise[ry] —showed itself, with an unrelenti[ng] smile, right in the midst of their pa[th.]

With her mind harassed by the t[er]

le perplexity in which the shipmaster's
elligence involved her, she was also
bjected to another trial. There were
ny people present, from the country
and about, who had often heard of
: scarlet letter, and to whom it had
en made terrific by a hundred false
exaggerated rumors, but who had
ver beheld it with their own bodily
:s. These, after exhausting other
des of amusement, now thronged
out Hester Prynne with rude and
orish intrusiveness. Unscrupulous as
was, however, it could not bring them
arer than a circuit of several yards.
that distance they accordingly stood,
ed there by the centrifugal force of
: repugnance which the mystic sym-
l inspired. The whole gang of sailors,
ewise, observing the press of spec-
ors, and learning the purport of the
rlet letter, came and thrust their sun-
rnt and desperado-looking faces into
: ring. Even the Indians were affected
a sort of cold shadow of the white
n's curiosity, and, gliding through the
wd, fastened their snake-like black
s on Hester's bosom; conceiving, per-
os, that the wearer of this brilliantly
broidered badge must needs be a
rsonage of high dignity among her
ople. Lastly the inhabitants of the
wn (their own interest in this worn-

out subject languidly reviving itself
by sympathy with what they saw others
feel) lounged idly to the same quarter,
and tormented Hester Prynne, perhaps
more than all the rest, with their cool,
well-acquainted gaze at her familiar
shame. Hester saw and recognized the
self-same faces of that group of matrons, who had awaited her forthcoming
from the prison-door, seven years ago;
all save one, the youngest and only
compassionate among them, whose bur-
ial-robe she had since made. At the final
hour, when she was so soon to fling
aside the burning letter, it had strangely
become the centre of more remark and
excitement, and was thus made to sear
her breast more painfully, than at any
time since the first day she put it on.

While Hester stood in that magic
circle of ignominy, where the cunning
cruelty of her sentence seemed to have
fixed her forever, the admirable preacher
was looking down from the sacred pulpit upon an audience, whose very inmost spirits had yielded to his control.
The sainted minister in the church!
The woman of the scarlet letter in the
market-place! What imagination would
have been irreverent enough to surmise
that the same scorching stigma was on
them both!

CHAPTER XXIII

THE REVELATION OF THE SCARLET LETTER

THE eloquent voice, on which the
uls of the listening audience had been
rne aloft as on the swelling waves

of the sea, at length came to a pause.
There was a momentary silence, profound as what should follow the utter-

ance of oracles. Then ensued a murmur and half-hushed tumult; as if the auditors, released from the high spell that had transported them into the region of another's mind, were returning into themselves, with all their awe and wonder still heavy on them. In a moment more, the crowd began to gush forth from the doors of the church. Now that there was an end, they needed other breath, more fit to support the gross and earthly life into which they relapsed, than that atmosphere which the preacher had converted into words of flame, and had burdened with the rich fragrance of his thought.

In the open air their rapture broke into speech. The street and the market-place absolutely babbled, from side to side, with applause of the minister. His hearers could not rest until they had told one another of what each knew better than he could tell or hear. According to their united testimony, never had man spoken in so wise, so high, and so holy a spirit, as he that spake this day; nor had inspiration ever breathed through mortal lips more evidently than it did through his. Its influence could be seen, as it were, descending upon him, and possessing him, and continually lifting him out of the written discourse that lay before him, and filling him with ideas that must have been as marvellous to himself as to his audience. His subject, it appeared, had been the relation between the Deity and the communities of mankind, with a special reference to the New England which they were here planting in the wilderness. And, as he drew towards the close, a spirit as of prophecy had come upon him, constraining him to its purpose as mightily as the old prophets

of Israel were constrained; only w this difference, that, whereas the Jew seers had denounced judgments and r on their country, it was his mission foretell a high and glorious destiny the newly gathered people of the Lc But, throughout it all, and through whole discourse, there had been a c tain deep, sad undertone of path which could not be interpreted oth wise than as the natural regret of soon to pass away. Yes; their minis whom they so loved—and who so lo them all, that he could not depart he enward without a sigh—had the fe boding of untimely death upon him, a would soon leave them in their tea This idea of his transitory stay on ea gave the last emphasis to the eff which the preacher had produced; was as if an angel, in his passage to skies, had shaken his bright wings o the people for an instant,—at once shadow and a splendor,—and had sl down a shower of golden truths up them.

Thus, there had come to the Rev end Mr. Dimmesdale—as to most m in their various spheres, though seld recognized until they see it far beh them—an epoch of life more brilli and full of triumph than any previ one, or than any which could hereaf be. He stood, at this moment, on very proudest eminence of superior to which the gifts of intellect, rich lc prevailing eloquence, and a reputat of whitest sanctity, could exalt a cler man in New England's earliest da when the professional character was itself a lofty pedestal. Such was position which the minister occupied, he bowed his head forward on the cu ions of the pulpit, at the close of

eotion Sermon. Meanwhile Hester
ynne was standing beside the scaffold
the pillory, with the scarlet letter
ll burning on her breast!

Now was heard again the clangor of
: music, and the measured tramp of
: military escort, issuing from the
irch-door. The procession was to be
rshalled thence to the town-hall,
ere a solemn banquet would complete
: ceremonies of the day.

Once more, therefore, the train of
ierable and majestic fathers was seen
ving through a broad pathway of
: people, who drew back reverently,
either side, as the Governor and
gistrates, the old and wise men, the
ly ministers, and all that were emi-
it and renowned, advanced into the
dst of them. When they were fairly
the market-place, their presence was
eted by a shout. This—though doubt-
s it might acquire additional force
l volume from the childlike loyalty
ich the age awarded to its rulers—
s felt to be an irrepressible outburst
enthusiasm kindled in the auditors
that high strain of eloquence which
s yet reverberating in their ears. Each
t the impulse in himself, and, in the
ne breath, caught it from his neigh-
-. Within the church, it had hardly
n kept down; beneath the sky, it
led upward to the zenith. There were
nan beings enough, and enough of
hly wrought and symphonious feel-
, to produce that more impressive
ind than the organ tones of the blast,
the thunder, or the roar of the sea;
n that mighty swell of many voices,
nded into one great voice by the
versal impulse which makes likewise
: vast heart out of the many. Never,
m the soil of New England, had gone

up such a shout! Never, on New England soil, had stood the man so honored
by his mortal brethren as the preacher!

How fared it with him then? Were
there not the brilliant particles of a
halo in the air about his head? So
etherealized by spirit as he was, and
so apotheosized by worshipping admirers, did his footsteps, in the procession,
really tread upon the dust of earth?

As the ranks of military men and
civil fathers moved onward, all eyes
were turned towards the point where
the minister was seen to approach
among them. The shout died into a
murmur, as one portion of the crowd
after another obtained a glimpse of him.
How feeble and pale he looked, amid
all his triumph! The energy—or say,
rather, the inspiration which had held
him up, until he should have delivered
the sacred message that brought its own
strength along with it from heaven—
was withdrawn, now that it had so faithfully performed its office. The glow,
which they had just before beheld burning on his cheek, was extinguished, like
a flame that sinks down hopelessly
among the late-decaying embers. It
seemed hardly the face of a man alive,
with such a deathlike hue; it was hardly
a man with life in him, that tottered on
his path so nervelessly, yet tottered, and
did not fall!

One of his clerical brethren,—it was
the venerable John Wilson,—observing
the state in which Mr. Dimmesdale was
left by the retiring wave of intellect
and sensibility, stepped forward hastily
to offer his support. The minister tremulously, but decidedly, repelled the old
man's arm. He still walked onward, if
that movement could be so described,
which rather resembled the wavering

effort of an infant, with its mother's arms in view, outstretched to tempt him forward. And now, almost imperceptible as were the latter steps of his progress, he had come opposite the well-remembered and weather-darkened scaffold, where, long since, with all that dreary lapse of time between, Hester Prynne had encountered the world's ignominious stare. There stood Hester, holding little Pearl by the hand! And there was the scarlet letter on her breast! The minister here made a pause; although the music still played the stately and rejoicing march to which the procession moved. It summoned him onward,—onward to the festival!—but here he made a pause.

Bellingham, for the last few moments, had kept an anxious eye upon him. He now left his own place in the procession, and advanced to give assistance; judging, from Mr. Dimmesdale's aspect, that he must otherwise inevitably fall. But there was something in the latter's expression that warned back the magistrate, although a man not readily obeying the vague intimations that pass from one spirit to another. The crowd, meanwhile, looked on with awe and wonder. This earthly faintness was, in their view, only another phase of the minister's celestial strength; nor would it have seemed a miracle too high to be wrought for one so holy, had he ascended before their eyes, waxing dimmer and brighter, and fading at last into the light of heaven!

He turned towards the scaffold, and stretched forth his arms.

"Hester," said he, "come hither! Come, my little Pearl!"

It was a ghastly look with which he regarded them; but there was something

at once tender and strangely triumph[a] in it. The child, with the bird-like m[o]tion which was one of her character[is]tics, flew to him, and clasped her ar[m] about his knees. Hester Prynne—slow[ly] as if impelled by inevitable fate, a[nd] against her strongest will—likewise dr[ew] near, but paused before she reach[ed] him. At this instant, old Roger Ch[il]lingworth thrust himself through [the] crowd,—or, perhaps, so dark, disturb[ed] and evil, was his look, he rose up [out] of some nether region,—to snatch ba[ck] his victim from what he sought to d[o] Be that as it might, the old man rush[ed] forward, and caught the minister [by] the arm.

"Madman, hold! what is your p[ur]pose?" whispered he. "Wave back th[at] woman! Cast off this child! All sh[all] be well! Do not blacken your fam[e] and perish in dishonor! I can yet sa[ve] you! Would you bring infamy on yo[ur] sacred profession?"

"Ha, tempter! Methinks thou art t[oo] late!" answered the minister, encount[er]ing his eye, fearfully, but firmly. "T[hy] power is not what it was! With Go[d's] help, I shall escape thee now!"

He again extended his hand to t[he] woman of the scarlet letter.

"Hester Prynne," cried he, with [a] piercing earnestness, "in the name [of] Him, so terrible and so merciful, w[ho] gives me grace, at this last mome[nt] to do what—for my own heavy s[in] and miserable agony—I withheld mys[elf] from doing seven years ago, come hith[er] now, and twine thy strength about m[e] Thy strength, Hester; but let it [be] guided by the will which God ha[s] granted me! This wretched and wrong[ed] old man is opposing it with all [his] might!—with all his own might, a[nd]

fiend's! Come, Hester, come! Sup-
t me up yonder scaffold!"

The crowd was in a tumult. The men
rank and dignity, who stood more
nediately around the clergyman, were
taken by surprise, and so perplexed
to the purport of what they saw,
mable to receive the explanation
ich most readily presented itself, or
imagine any other,—that they reined silent and inactive spectators of
judgment which Providence seemed
ut to work. They beheld the min-
r, leaning on Hester's shoulder, and
ported by her arm around him, ap-
ach the scaffold, and ascend its
os; while still the little hand of the
-born child was clasped in his. Old
ger Chillingworth followed, as one
mately connected with the drama of
lt and sorrow in which they had all
n actors, and well entitled, therefore,
be present, at its closing scene.

'Hadst thou sought the whole earth
r," said he, looking darkly at the
rgyman, "there was no one place
secret,—no high place nor lowly
ce, where thou couldst have escaped
,—save on this very scaffold!"

'Thanks be to Him who hath led
hither!" answered the minister.

Yet he trembled, and turned to Hes-
with an expression of doubt and
ciety in his eyes, not the less evi-
tly betrayed, that there was a feeble
ile upon his lips.

'Is not this better," murmured he,
an what we dreamed of in the for-
?"

'I know not! I know not!" she hur-
dly replied. "Better? Yea; so we may
h die, and little Pearl die with us!"

'For thee and Pearl, be it as God
ll order," said the minister; "and

God is merciful! Let me now do the
will which he hath made plain before
my sight. For, Hester, I am a dying
man. So let me make haste to take my
shame upon me!"

Partly supported by Hester Prynne,
and holding one hand of little Pearl's,
the Reverend Mr. Dimmesdale turned
to the dignified and venerable rulers;
to the holy ministers, who were his
brethren; to the people, whose great
heart was thoroughly appalled, yet overflowing with tearful sympathy, as knowing that some deep life-matter—which,
if full of sin, was full of anguish and
repentance likewise—was now to be laid
open to them. The sun, but little past
its meridian, shone down upon the
clergyman, and gave a distinctness to
his figure, as he stood out from all the
earth, to put in his plea of guilty at
the bar of Eternal Justice.

"People of New England!" cried he,
with a voice that rose over them, high,
solemn, and majestic,—yet had always
a tremor through it, and sometimes a
shriek, struggling up out of a fathom-
less depth of remorse and woe,—"ye,
that have loved me!—ye, that have
deemed me holy!—behold me here, the
one sinner of the world! At last!—at
last!—I stand upon the spot where,
seven years since, I should have stood;
here, with this woman, whose arm, more
than the little strength wherewith I have
crept hitherward, sustains me, at this
dreadful moment, from grovelling down
upon my face! Lo, the scarlet letter
which Hester wears! Ye have all shuddered at it! Wherever her walk hath
been, — wherever, so miserably burdened,
she may have hoped to find repose,—
it hath cast a lurid gleam of awe and
horrible repugnance round about her.

But there stood one in the midst of you, at whose brand of sin and infamy ye have not shuddered!"

It seemed, at this point, as if the minister must leave the remainder of his secret undisclosed. But he fought back the bodily weakness,—and, still more, the faintness of heart,—that was striving for the mastery with him. He threw off all resistance, and stepped passionately forward a pace before the woman and the child.

"It was on him!" he continued, with a kind of fierceness; so determined was he to speak out the whole. "God's eye beheld it! The angels were forever pointing at it! The Devil knew it well, and fretted it continually with the touch of his burning finger! But he hid it cunningly from men, and walked among you with the mien of a spirit, mournful, because so pure in a sinful world! —and sad, because he missed his heavenly kindred! Now, at the death-hour, he stands up before you! He bids you look again at Hester's scarlet letter! He tells you, that, with all its mysterious horror, it is but the shadow of what he bears on his own breast, and that even this, his own red stigma, is no more than the type of what has seared his inmost heart! Stand any here that question God's judgment on a sinner? Behold! Behold a dreadful witness of it!"

With a convulsive motion, he tore away the ministerial band from before his breast. It was revealed! But it were irreverent to describe that revelation. For an instant, the gaze of the horror-stricken multitude was concentred on the ghastly miracle; while the minister stood, with a flush of triumph in his face, as one who, in the crisis of acutest pain, had won a victory. Then, down he

sank upon the scaffold! Hester pa[r] raised him, and supported his h[e] against her bosom. Old Roger Chilli[ng] worth knelt down beside him, with blank, dull countenance, out of wh[ich] the life seemed to have departed.

"Thou hast escaped me!" he repea[ted] more than once. "Thou hast escap[ed] me!"

"May God forgive thee!" said [the] minister. "Thou, too, hast dee[ply] sinned!"

He withdrew his dying eyes from [the] old man, and fixed them on the wom[an] and the child.

"My little Pearl," said he, feebly[—] and there was a sweet and gentle sm[ile] over his face, as of a spirit sink[ing] into deep repose; nay, now that [the] burden was removed, it seemed alm[ost] as if he would be sportive with [the] child,—"dear little Pearl, wilt thou k[iss] me now? Thou wouldst not, yon[der] in the forest! But now thou wilt?"

Pearl kissed his lips. A spell [was] broken. The great scene of grief, [in] which the wild infant bore a part, [had] developed all her sympathies; and [as] her tears fell upon her father's che[ek,] they were the pledge that she wo[uld] grow up amid human joy and sorr[ow,] nor forever do battle with the wo[rld,] but be a woman in it. Towards [her] mother, too, Pearl's errand as a mess[en]ger of anguish was all fulfilled.

"Hester," said the clergyman, "fa[re]well!"

"Shall we not meet again?" wh[is]pered she, bending her face down cl[ose] to his. "Shall we not spend our [im]mortal life together? Surely, surely, [we] have ransomed one another, with [all] this woe! Thou lookest far into etern[ity] with those bright dying eyes! T[ell] me what thou seest?"

Hush, Hester, hush!" said he, with
nulous solemnity. "The law we
ke!—the sin here so awfully re-
led!—let these alone be in thy
ughts! I fear! I fear! It may be,
, when we forgot our God,—when
violated our reverence each for the
er's soul,—it was thenceforth vain
nope that we could meet hereafter,
n everlasting and pure reunion. God
ws; and he is merciful! He hath
ved his mercy, most of all, in my
ctions. By giving me this burning
ure to bear upon my breast! By
sending yonder dark and terrible old
man, to keep the torture always at red-
heat! By bringing me hither, to die
this death of triumphant ignominy before the people! Had either of these
agonies been wanting, I had been lost
forever! Praised be his name! His will
be done! Farewell!"

That final word came forth with the
minister's expiring breath. The multitude, silent till then, broke out in a
strange, deep voice of awe and wonder,
which could not as yet find utterance,
save in this murmur that rolled so
heavily after the departed spirit.

CHAPTER XXIV

CONCLUSION

AFTER many days, when time sufficed
the people to arrange their thoughts
reference to the foregoing scene, there
more than one account of what
been witnessed on the scaffold.
Most of the spectators testified to
ing seen, on the breast of the un-
py minister, a SCARLET LETTER—the
y semblance of that worn by Hester
nne—imprinted in the flesh. As re-
led its origin, there were various
lanations, all of which must neces-
ly have been conjectural. Some af-
ed that the Reverend Mr. Dimmes-
, on the very day when Hester
nne first wore her ignominious
ge, had begun a course of penance,
which he afterwards, in so many
le methods, followed out,—by ining a hideous torture on himself.
ers contended that the stigma had
not been produced until a long time
subsequent, when old Roger Chillingworth, being a potent necromancer, had
caused it to appear, through the agency
of magic and poisonous drugs. Others,
again,—and those best able to appreciate the minister's peculiar sensibility,
and the wonderful operation of his spirit
upon the body,—whispered their belief,
that the awful symbol was the effect
of the ever active tooth of remorse,
gnawing from the inmost heart outwardly, and at last manifesting Heaven's
dreadful judgment by the visible presence of the letter. The reader may
choose among these theories. We have
thrown all the light we could acquire
upon the portent, and would gladly,
now that it has done its office, erase
its deep print out of our own brain;
where long meditation has fixed it in

very undesirable distinctness.

It is singular, nevertheless, that certain persons, who were spectators of the whole scene, and professed never once to have removed their eyes from the Reverend Mr. Dimmesdale, denied that there was any mark whatever on his breast, more than on a new-born infant's. Neither, by their report, had his dying words acknowledged, nor even remotely implied, any, the slightest connection, on his part, with the guilt for which Hester Prynne had so long worn the scarlet letter. According to these highly respectable witnesses, the minister, conscious that he was dying,— conscious, also, that the reverence of the multitude placed him already among saints and angels,—had desired, by yielding up his breath in the arms of that fallen woman, to express to the world how utterly nugatory is the choicest of man's own righteousness. After exhausting life in his efforts for mankind's spiritual good, he had made the manner of his death a parable, in order to impress on his admirers the mighty and mournful lesson, that, in the view of Infinite Purity, we are sinners all alike. It was to teach them, that the holiest among us has but attained so far above his fellows as to discern more clearly the Mercy which looks down, and repudiate more utterly the phantom of human merit, which would look aspiringly upward. Without disputing a truth so momentous, we must be allowed to consider this version of Mr. Dimmesdale's story as only an instance of that stubborn fidelity with which a man's friends—and especially a clergyman's —will sometimes uphold his character, when proofs, clear as the mid-day sunshine on the scarlet letter, establish him

a false and sin-stained creature of dust.

The authority which we have chi followed,—a manuscript of old d. drawn up from the verbal testim of individuals, some of whom known Hester Prynne, while others heard the tale from contemporary nesses,—fully confirms the view ta in the foregoing pages. Among m morals which press upon us from poor minister's miserable experience, put only this into a sentence:— true! Be true! Be true! Show fre to the world, if not your worst, some trait whereby the worst may inferred!"

Nothing was more remarkable t the change which took place, alm immediately after Mr. Dimmesda death, in the appearance and demea of the old man known as Roger C lingworth. All his strength and ene —all his vital and intellectual forc seemed at once to desert him; ir much that he positively withered shrivelled away, and almost vanis from mortal sight, like an uprooted w that lies wilting in the sun. This happy man had made the very princ of his life to consist in the pursuit systematic·exercise of revenge; when, by its completest triumph consummation, that evil principle left with no further material to s port it, when, in short, there was more Devil's work on earth for him do, it only remained for the unhum ized mortal to betake himself whit his Master would find him tasks eno and pay him his wages duly. But, all these shadowy beings, so long near acquaintances.—as well Ro Chillingworth as his companions,—

d fain be merciful. It is a curious
ct of observation and inquiry,
her hatred and love be not the
thing at bottom. Each, in its ut-
development, supposes a high de-
of intimacy and heart-knowledge;
renders one individual dependent
he food of his affections and spir-
life upon another; each leaves the
onate lover, or the no less paste hater, forlorn and desolate by
withdrawal of his subject. Philo-
cally considered, therefore, the two
ons seem essentially the same, ex-
that one happens to be seen in a
ial radiance, and the other in a
and lurid glow. In the spiritual
, the old physician and the min-
—mutual victims as they have been
y, unawares, have found their
y stock of hatred and antipathy
muted into golden love.

ving this discussion apart, we have
tter of business to communicate
e reader. At old Roger Chilling-
's decease, (which took place
the year,) and by his last will
estament, of which Governor Bel-
m and the Reverend Mr. Wilson
executors, he bequeathed a very
derable amount of property, both
and in England, to little Pearl, the
ter of Hester Prynne.

Pearl—the elf-child,—the demon
ing, as some people, up to that
, persisted in considering her,—
e the richest heiress of her day,
New World. Not improbably, this
nstance wrought a very material
e in the public estimation; and,
e mother and child remained here,
Pearl, at a marriageable period of
night have mingled her wild blood
the lineage of the devoutest Puri-

tan among them all. But, in no long
time after the physician's death, the
wearer of the scarlet letter disappeared,
and Pearl along with her. For many
years, though a vague report would now
and then find its way across the sea,—
like a shapeless piece of driftwood tost
ashore, with the initials of a name upon
it,—yet no tidings of them unquestionably authentic were received. The story
of the scarlet letter grew into a legend.
Its spell, however, was still potent, and
kept the scaffold awful where the poor
minister had died, and likewise the cottage by the sea-shore, where Hester
Prynne had dwelt. Near this latter spot,
one afternoon, some children were at
play, when they beheld a tall woman,
in a gray robe, approach the cottage-
door. In all those years it had never
once been opened; but either she unlocked it, or the decaying wood and iron
yielded to her hand, or she glided
shadowlike through these impediments,
—and, at all events, went in.

On the threshold she paused,—turned
partly round,—for, perchance, the idea
of entering all alone, and all so changed,
the home of so intense a former life,
was more dreary and desolate than even
she could bear. But her hesitation was
only for an instant, though long enough
to display a scarlet letter on her breast.

And Hester Prynne had returned, and
taken up her long-forsaken shame! But
where was little Pearl? If still alive, she
must now have been in the flush and
bloom of early womanhood. None knew
—nor ever learned, with the fulness of
perfect certainty—whether the elf-child
had gone thus untimely to a maiden
grave; or whether her wild, rich nature
had been softened and subdued, and
made capable of a woman's gentle hap-

piness. But, through the remainder of
Hester's life, there were indications that
the recluse of the scarlet letter was the
object of love and interest with some
inhabitant of another land. Letters
came, with armorial seals upon them,
though of bearings unknown to English
heraldry. In the cottage there were articles of comfort and luxury, such as
Hester never cared to use, but which
only wealth could have purchased, and
affection have imagined for her. There
were trifles, too, little ornaments, beautiful tokens of a continual remembrance,
that must have been wrought by delicate fingers, at the impulse of a fond
heart. And, once, Hester was seen em-
broidering a baby garment, with such
a lavish richness of golden fancy as
would have raised a public tumult, had
any infant, thus apparelled, been shown
to our sober-hued community.

In fine, the gossips of that day believed,—and Mr. Surveyor Pue, who
made investigations a century later, believed,—and one of his recent successors in office, moreover, faithfully believes,—that Pearl was not only alive,
but married, and happy, and mindful
of her mother; and that she would most
joyfully have entertained that sad and
lonely mother at her fireside.

But there was a more real life for
Hester Prynne, here, in New England,
than in that unknown region where
Pearl had found a home. Here had been
her sin; here, her sorrow; and here
was yet to be her penitence. She had
returned, therefore, and resumed,—of
her own free will, for not the sternest
magistrate of that iron period would
have imposed it,—resumed the symbol
of which we have related so dark a
tale. Never afterwards did it quit her

bosom. But, in the lapse of the
some, thoughtful, and self-devoted
that made up Hester's life, the sc
letter ceased to be a stigma which
tracted the world's scorn and bitter
and became a type of something t
sorrowed over, and looked upon
awe, yet with reverence too. And
Hester Prynne had no selfish ends,
lived in any measure for her own p
and enjoyment, people brought all
sorrows and perplexities, and beso
her counsel, as one who had herself
through a mighty trouble. Women,
especially,—in the continually recu
trials of wounded, wasted, wronged,
placed, or erring and sinful passic
or with the dreary burden of a
unyielded, because unvalued and
sought,—came to Hester's cottage
manding why they were so wretched
what the remedy! Hester comforted
counselled them, as best she might.
assured them, too, of her firm b
that, at some brighter period, when
world should have grown ripe fo
in Heaven's own time, a new
would be revealed, in order to esta
the whole relation between man
woman on a surer ground of m
happiness. Earlier in life, Hester
vainly imagined that she herself m
be the destined prophetess, but had
since recognized the impossibility
any mission of divine and myste
truth should be confided to a w
stained with sin, bowed down
shame, or even burdened with a
long sorrow. The angel and apost
the coming revelation must be a wo
indeed, but lofty, pure, and beaut
and wise, moreover, not through d
grief, but the ethereal medium of
and showing how sacred love sh

us happy, by the truest test of
successful to such an end!

said Hester Prynne, and glanced
sad eyes downward at the scarlet
. And, after many, many years, a
grave was delved, near an old and
en one, in that burial-ground beside
King's Chapel has since been
It was near that old and sunken
, yet with a space between, as if
dust of the two sleepers had no
to mingle. Yet one tombstone
d for both. All around, there were
ments carved with armorial bear-

ings; and on this simple slab of slate
—as the curious investigator may still
discern, and perplex himself with the
purport—there appeared the semblance
of an engraved escutcheon. It bore a
device, a herald's wording of which
might serve for a motto and brief
description of our now concluded legend;
so sombre is it, and relieved only by
one ever-glowing point of light gloomier
than the shadow:—

"ON A FIELD, SABLE, THE LETTER A,
GULES."

TWICE-TOLD TALES

THE GRAY CHAMPION

ERE was once a time when New
nd groaned under the actual pres-
of heavier wrongs than those threat-
ones which brought on the Revo-
. James II., the bigoted successor
arles the Voluptuous, had annulled
harters of all the colonies, and
a harsh and unprincipled soldier
e away our liberties and endanger
eligion. The Administration of Sir
nd Andros lacked scarcely a single
cteristic of tyranny: a Governor
Council, holding office from the
, and wholly independent of the
ry; laws made and taxes levied
ut concurrence of the people, im-
te or by their representatives; the
of private citizens violated, and
itles of all landed property devoid; the voice of complaint
d by restrictions on the press; and,
, disaffection overawed by the
and of mercenary troops that ever
hed on our free soil. For two
our ancestors were kept in sullen
ission, by that filial love which
nvariably secured their allegiance
mother country, whether its head
ed to be a Parliament, Protector,
opish Monarch. Till these evil
, however, such allegiance had been
y nominal, and the colonists had
themselves, enjoying far more
om than is even yet the privilege
e native subjects of Great Britain.
length a rumor reached our shores

that the Prince of Orange had ventured
on an enterprise, the success of which
would be the triumph of civil and religious rights and the salvation of New
England. It was but a doubtful whisper;
it might be false, or the attempt might
fail; and, in either case, the man that
stirred against King James would lose
his head. Still the intelligence produced
a marked effect. The people smiled mys-
teriously in the streets, and threw bold
glances at their oppressors; while, far
and wide, there was a subdued and
silent agitation, as if the slightest signal would rouse the whole land from
its sluggish despondency. Aware of their
danger, the rulers resolved to avert it
by an imposing display of strength, and
perhaps to confirm their despotism by
yet harsher measures. One afternoon
in April, 1689, Sir Edmund Andros and
his favorite councillors, being warm
with wine, assembled the redcoats of
the Governor's Guard, and made their
appearance in the streets of Boston.
The sun was near setting when the
march commenced.

The roll of the drum, at that unquiet crisis, seemed to go through the
streets, less as the martial music of
the soldiers, than as a muster call to
the inhabitants themselves. A multitude,
by various avenues, assembled in King
Street, which was destined to be the
scene, nearly a century afterwards, of
another encounter between the troops

of Britain, and a people struggling against her tyranny. Though more than sixty years had elapsed, since the Pilgrims came, this crowd of their descendants still showed the strong and sombre features of their character, perhaps more strikingly in such a stern emergency than on happier occasions. There were the sober garb, the general severity of mien, the gloomy but undismayed expression, the scriptural forms of speech, and the confidence in Heaven's blessing on a righteous cause, which would have marked a band of the original Puritans, when threatened by some peril of the wilderness. Indeed, it was not yet time for the old spirit to be extinct; since there were men in the street, that day, who had worshipped there beneath the trees, before a house was reared to the God for whom they had become exiles. Old soldiers of the Parliament were here, too, smiling grimly at the thought, that their aged arms might strike another blow against the house of Stuart. Here, also, were the veterans of King Philip's war, who had burned villages and slaughtered young and old, with pious fierceness, while the godly souls throughout the land were helping them with prayer. Several ministers were scattered among the crowd which, unlike all other mobs, regarded them with such reverence, as if there were sanctity in their very garments. These holy men exerted their influence to quiet the people, but not to disperse them. Meantime, the purpose of the Governor, in disturbing the peace of the town, at a period when the slightest commotion might throw the country into a ferment, was almost the universal subject of inquiry, and variously explained.

"Satan will strike his master-s[t] presently," cried some, "because knoweth that his time is short. Al godly pastors are to be dragge prison! We shall see them at a S[t] field fire in King Street!"

Hereupon the people of each p[t] gathered closer round their min[t] who looked calmly upwards and sumed a more apostolic dignity, as befitted a candidate for the hi[g] honor of his profession, the crow[n] martyrdom. It was actually fancie that period, that New England n[t] have a John Rogers of her own, to the place of that worthy in the Pr[i]

"The Pope of Rome has given o[t] for a new St. Batholomew!" others. "We are to be massacred, and male child!"

Neither was this rumor wholly credited, although the wiser class lieved the Governor's object some less atrocious. His predecessor u[t] the old charter, Bradstreet, a vene[r] companion of the first settlers, known to be in town. There grounds for conjecturing, that Sir mund Andros intended, at once, to s[t] terror, by a parade of military f[t] and to confound the opposite fac[t] by possessing himself of their chi[t]

"Stand firm for the old charter [t] ernor!" shouted the crowd, seizing the idea. "The good old Governor B[t] street!"

While this cry was at the loudest people were surprised by the well-kn[own] figure of Governor Bradstreet him[self] a patriarch of nearly ninety, who peared on the elevated steps of a [t] and, with characteristic mildness, sought them to submit to the constit[t] authorities.

My children," concluded this venle person, "do nothing rashly. Cry
aloud, but pray for the welfare of
England, and expect patiently what
Lord will do in this matter!"

ne event was soon to be decided.
his time, the roll of the drum had
approaching through Cornhill,
er and deeper, till with reverbera-
s from house to house, and the
lar tramp of martial footsteps, it
t into the street. A double rank
oldiers made their appearance, oc-
ing the whole breadth of the pas-
, with shouldered matchlocks, and
ches burning, so as to present a
of fires in the dusk. Their steady
ch was like the progress of a ma-
e, that would roll irresistibly over
ything in its way. Next, moving
ly, with a confused clatter of hoofs
the pavement, rode a party of
nted gentlemen, the central figure
g Sir Edmund Andros, elderly, but
and soldier-like. Those around him
his favorite councillors, and the
rest foes of New England. At his
hand rode Edward Randolph, our
-enemy, that "blasted wretch," as
on Mather calls him, who achieved
lownfall of our ancient government,
was followed with a sensible curse,
ugh life and to his grave. On the
r side was Bullivant, scattering jests
mockery as he rode along. Dudley
e behind, with a down-cast look,
ding, as well he might, to meet
indignant gaze of the people, who
ld him, their only countryman by
, among the oppressors of his na-
land. The captain of a frigate in
harbor, and two or three civil of-
s under the Crown, were also there.
the figure which most attracted the

public eye, and stirred up the deepest
feeling, was the Episcopal clergyman
of King's Chapel, riding haughtily among
the magistrates in his priestly vestments,
the fitting representative of prelacy and
persecution, the union of church and
state, and all those abominations which
had driven the Puritans to the wilderness. Another guard of soldiers, in
double rank, brought up the rear.

The whole scene was a picture of the
condition of New England, and its
moral, the deformity of any government that does not grow out of the
nature of things and the character of
the people. On one side the religious
multitude, with their sad visages and
dark attire, and on the other, the group
of despotic rulers, with the high church-
man in the midst, and here and there
a crucifix at their bosoms, all magnifi-
cently clad, flushed with wine, proud
of unjust authority, and scoffing at the
universal groan. And the mercenary
soldiers, waiting but the word to deluge
the street with blood, showed the only
means by which obedience could be secured.

"O Lord of Hosts," cried a voice
among the crowd, "provide a Champion
for thy people!"

This ejaculation was loudly uttered,
and served as a herald's cry, to introduce a remarkable personage. The crowd
had rolled back, and were now huddled
together nearly at the extremity of the
street, while the soldiers had advanced
no more than a third of its length.
The intervening space was empty,—a
paved solitude, between lofty edifices,
which threw almost a twilight shadow
over it. Suddenly, there was seen the
figure of an ancient man, who seemed
to have emerged from among the people,

and was walking by himself along the centre of the street, to confront the armed band. He wore the old Puritan dress, a dark cloak and a steeple-crowned hat, in the fashion of at least fifty years before, with a heavy sword upon his thigh, but a staff in his hand to assist the tremulous gait of age.

When at some distance from the multitude, the old man turned slowly round, displaying a face of antique majesty, rendered doubly venerable by the hoary beard that descended on his breast. He made a gesture at once of encouragement and warning, then turned again, and resumed his way.

"Who is this gray patriarch?" asked the young men of their sires.

"Who is this venerable brother?" asked the old men among themselves.

But none could make reply. The fathers of the people, those of fourscore years and upwards, were disturbed, deeming it strange that they should forget one of such evident authority, whom they must have known in their early days, the associate of Winthrop, and all the old councillors, giving laws, and making prayers, and leading them against the savage. The elderly men ought to have remembered him, too, with locks as gray in their youth, as their own were now. And the young! How could he have passed so utterly from their memories,—that hoary sire, the relic of long-departed times, whose awful benediction had surely been bestowed on their uncovered heads, in childhood?

"Whence did he come? What is his purpose? Who can this old man be?" whispered the wondering crowd.

Meanwhile, the venerable stranger, staff in hand, was pursuing his solitary walk along the centre of the s[...]

As he drew near the advancing sol[...] and as the roll of their drum [...] full upon his ear, the old man r[...] himself to a loftier mien, while [...] decrepitude of age seemed to fall [...] his shoulders, leaving him in gray [...] unbroken dignity. Now, he marche[...] ward with a warrior's step, keeping [...] to the military music. Thus the [...] form advanced on one side, and [...] whole parade of soldiers and magist[...] on the other, till, when scarcely tw[...] yards remained between, the old [...] grasped his staff by the middle, [...] held it before him like a leader's [...] cheon.

"Stand!" cried he.

The eye, the face, and attitud[...] command; the solemn, yet warlike [...] of that voice, fit either to rule a [...] in the battle-field or be raised to [...] in prayer, were irresistible. At the [...] man's word and outstretched arm [...] roll of the drum was hushed at [...] and the advancing line stood sti[...] tremulous enthusiasm seized upon [...] multitude. That stately form, con[...] ing the leader and the saint, so [...] so dimly seen, in such an ancient [...] could only belong to some old cham[...] of the righteous cause, whom the [...] pressor's drum had summoned from [...] grave. They raised a shout of awe [...] exaltation, and looked for the del[...] ance of New England.

The Governor, and the gentleme[...] his party, perceiving themselves bro[...] to an unexpected stand, rode ha[...] forward, as if they would have pr[...] their snorting and affrighted horses [...] against the hoary apparition. He, [...] ever, blenched not a step, but gla[...] his severe eye round the group, w[...]

encompassed him, at last bent it
ㅤly on Sir Edmund Andros. One
ㅤd have thought that the dark old
ㅤwas chief ruler there, and that
ㅤGovernor and Council, with sol-
ㅤs at their back, representing the
ㅤle power and authority of the
ㅤwn, had no alternative but obedi-
ㅤ.

ㅤVhat does this old fellow here?"
ㅤl Edward Randolph, fiercely. "On,
ㅤEdmund! Bid the soldiers forward,
ㅤgive the dotard the same choice
ㅤyou give all his countrymen,—to
ㅤd aside or be trampled on!"

ㅤVay, nay, let us show respect to
ㅤgood grandsire," said Bullivant,
ㅤhing. "See you not, he is some
ㅤround-headed dignitary, who hath
ㅤasleep these thirty years, and knows
ㅤing of the change of times? Doubt-
ㅤhe thinks to put us down with a
ㅤlamation in Old Noll's name!"

ㅤAre you mad, old man?" demanded
ㅤEdmund Andros, in loud and harsh
ㅤs. "How dare you stay the march
ㅤKing James's Governor?"

ㅤhave stayed the march of a King
ㅤself, ere now," replied the gray fig-
ㅤwith stern composure. "I am here,
ㅤGovernor, because the cry of an
ㅤessed people hath disturbed me in
ㅤsecret place; and beseeching this
ㅤr earnestly of the Lord, it was
ㅤhsafed me to appear once again on
ㅤ1, in the good old cause of his
ㅤs. And what speak ye of James?
ㅤe is no longer a Popish tyrant on
ㅤthrone of England, and by to-
ㅤow noon, his name shall be a by-
ㅤl in this very street, where ye would
ㅤe it a word of terror. Back, thou
ㅤwast a Governor, back! With this
ㅤt thy power is ended,—to-morrow,

the prison!—back, lest I foretell the
scaffold!"

The people had been drawing nearer
and nearer, and drinking in the words
of their champion, who spoke in accents
long disused, like one unaccustomed to
converse, except with the dead of many
years ago. But his voice stirred their
souls. They confronted the soldiers, not
wholly without arms, and ready to
convert the very stones of the street
into deadly weapons. Sir Edmund Andros looked at the old man; then he
cast his hard and cruel eye over the
multitude, and beheld them burning with
that lurid wrath, so difficult to kindle
or to quench; and again he fixed his
gaze on the aged form, which stood
obscurely in an open space, where
neither friend nor foe had thrust himself. What were his thoughts, he uttered no word which might discover.
But whether the oppressor were overawed by the Gray Champion's look, or
perceived his peril in the threatening
attitude of the people, it is certain that
he gave back, and ordered his soldiers
to commence a slow and guarded retreat. Before another sunset, the Governor, and all that rode so proudly
with him, were prisoners, and long ere
it was known that James had abdicated,
King William was proclaimed throughout New England.

But where was the Gray Champion?
Some reported that, when the troops
had gone from King Street, and the
people were thronging tumultuously in
their rear, Bradstreet, the aged Governor, was seen to embrace a form more
aged than his own. Others soberly affirmed, that while they marvelled at
the venerable grandeur of his aspect,
the old man had faded from their eyes,

melting slowly into the hues of twilight, till, where he stood, there was an empty space. But all agreed that the hoary shape was gone. The men of that generation watched for his reappearance, in sunshine and in twilight, but never saw him more, nor knew when his funeral passed, nor where his gravestone was.

And who was the Gray Champion? Perhaps his name might be found in the records of that stern Court of Justice which passed a sentence, too mighty for the age, but glorious in all after times for its humbling lesson to the monarch and its high example to the subject. I have heard that, whenever the descendants of the Puritans are to show the spirit of their sires, the old man appears again. When eighty years had passed, he walked once more in King Street. Five years later, in twilight of an April morning, he s on the green, beside the meeting-ho at Lexington, where now the ob of granite, with a slab of slate in commemorates the first fallen of Revolution. And when our fathers toiling at the breastwork on Bun Hill, all through that night the warrior walked his rounds. Long, may it be, ere he comes again! hour is one of darkness and adve and peril. But should domestic tyra oppress us, or the invader's step po our soil, still may the Gray Cham come; for he is the type of New land's hereditary spirit; and his s owy march, on the eve of danger, ever be the pledge that New Engla sons will vindicate their ancestry.

SUNDAY AT HOME

EVERY Sabbath morning in the summer time, I thrust back the curtain to watch the sunrise stealing down a steeple, which stands opposite my chamber window. First, the weathercock begins to flash; then, a fainter lustre gives the spire an airy aspect; next it encroaches on the tower, and causes the index of the dial to glisten like gold, as it points to the gilded figure of the hour. Now, the loftiest window gleams, and now the lower. The carved framework of the portal is marked strongly out. At length the morning glory, in its descent from heaven, comes down the stone steps, one by one; and there stands the steeple, glowing with fresh radiance, while the shades of twi still hide themselves among the n of the adjacent buildings. Meth though the same sun brightens it e fair morning, yet the steeple h peculiar robe of brightness for the bath.

By dwelling near a church, a pe soon contracts an attachment for edifice. We naturally personify it, conceive its massy walls, and its emptiness, to be instinct with a and meditative and somewhat m choly spirit. But the steeple stands most in our thoughts as well as lo It impresses us as a giant, wi mind comprehensive and discrimin

igh to care for the great and small
:erns of all the town. Hourly, while
)eaks a moral to the few that think,
minds thousands of busy individuals
:heir separate and most secret af-
;. It is the steeple, too, that flings
»ad the hurried and irregular ac-
s of general alarm; neither have
1ess and festivity found a better
:rance than by its tongue; and when
dead are slowly passing to their
», the steeple has a melancholy voice
id them welcome. Yet, in spite of
connection with human interests,
: a moral loneliness on week days
ds round about its stately height!
1s no kindred with the houses above
h it towers; it looks down into
narrow thoroughfare, the lonelier,
use the crowd are elbowing their
1ge at its base. A glance at the
' of the church deepens this im-
sion. Within, by the light of dis-
windows, amid refracted shadows,
iiscern the vacant pews and empty
ries, the silent organ, the voiceless
t, and the clock, which tells to
1de how time is passing. Time,—
e man lives not,—what is it but
ity? And in the church, we might
ose, are garnered up, throughout
veek, all thoughts and feelings that
reference to eternity, until the
day comes round again to let them
. Might not, then, its more ap-
riate site be in the outskirts of
own, with space for old trees to
around it, and throw their solemn
)ws over a quiet green? We will
nore of this hereafter.
t on the Sabbath I watch the
st sunshine, and fancy that a holier
iness marks the day when there
be no buzz of voices on the ex-

change, nor traffic in the shops, nor
crowd, nor business, anywhere but at
church. Many have fancied so. For my
own part, whether I see it scattered
down among tangled woods, or beaming broad across the fields, or hemmed
in between brick buildings, or tracing
out the figure of the casement on my
chamber floor, still I recognize the Sabbath sunshine. And ever let me recognize it! Some illusions, and this among
them, are the shadows of great truths.
Doubts may flit around me, or seem
to close their evil wings, and settle
down; but, so long as I imagine that
the earth is hallowed and the light of
heaven retains its sanctity on the Sabbath,—while that blessed sunshine lives
within me,—never can my soul have
lost the instinct of its faith. If it have
gone astray, it will return again.

I love to spend such pleasant Sabbaths, from morning till night, behind
the curtain of my open window. Are
they spent amiss? Every spot, so near
the church as to be visited by the
circling shadow of the steeple, should
be deemed consecrated ground, to-day.
With stronger truth be it said, that a
devout heart may consecrate a den of
thieves, as an evil one may convert
a temple to the same. My heart, perhaps, has not such holy, nor, I would
fain trust, such impious potency. It
must suffice, that, though my form be
absent, my inner man goes constantly
to church, while many, whose bodily
presence fills the accustomed seats, have
left their souls at home. But I am there,
even before my friend, the sexton. At
length, he comes,—a man of kindly,
but sombre aspect, in dark gray clothes,
and hair of the same mixture,—he comes
and applies his key to the wide portal.

Now, my thoughts may go in among the dusty pews, or ascend the pulpit without sacrilege, but soon come forth again to enjoy the music of the bell. How glad, yet solemn too! All the steeples in town are talking together, aloft in the sunny air, and rejoicing among themselves, while their spires point heavenward. Meantime, here are the children assembling to the Sabbath school, which is kept somewhere within the church. Often, while looking at the arched portal I have been gladdened by the sight of a score of these little girls and boys, in pink, blue, yellow, and crimson frocks, bursting suddenly forth into the sunshine, like a swarm of gay butterflies that had been shut up in the solemn gloom. Or I might compare them to cherubs, haunting that holy place.

About a quarter of an hour before the second ringing of the bell, individuals of the congregation begin to appear. The earliest is invariably an old woman in black, whose bent frame and rounded shoulders are evidently laden with some heavy affliction, which she is eager to rest upon the altar. Would that the Sabbath came twice as often, for the sake of that sorrowful old soul! There is an elderly man, also, who arrives in good season, and leans against the corner of the tower, just within the line of its shadow, looking downward with a darksome brow. I sometimes fancy that the old woman is the happier of the two. After these, others drop in singly, and by twos and threes, either disappearing through the doorway, or taking their stand in its vicinity. At last, and always with an unexpected sensation, the bell turns in the steeple overhead, and throws out an irregular

clangor, jarring the tower to its f dation. As if there were magic in sound, the sidewalks of the street, up and down along, are immedi thronged with two long lines of pe all converging hitherward, and strear into the church. Perhaps the fa roar of a coach draws nearer,—a de thunder by its contrast with the rounding stillness,—until it sets c the wealthy worshippers at the pc among their humblest brethren. Be that entrance, in theory at least, t are no distinctions of earthly r nor, indeed, by the goodly apparel w is flaunting in the sun, would there s to be such, on the hither side. T pretty girls! Why will they disturb pious meditations! Of all days in week, they should strive to look fascinating on the Sabbath, instea heightening their mortal loveliness if to rival the blessed angels, and our thoughts from heaven. Were I minister himself, I must needs One girl is white muslin from the upwards, and black silk downward her slippers; a second, blushes topknot to shoetie, one universal let; another shines of a pervading low, as if she had made a garmen the sunshine. The greater part, how have adopted a milder cheerfulnes hue. Their veils, especially when wind raises them, give a lightnes the general effect, and make them pear like airy phantoms, as they up the steps, and vanish into the so doorway. Nearly all—though it is strange that I should know it— white stockings, white as snow, neat slippers, laced crosswise with ribbon, pretty high above the ar A white stocking is infinitely mor ve than a black one.

ere comes the clergyman, slow and
nn, in severe simplicity, needing
lack-silk gown to denote his office.
aspect claims my reverence, but
ot win my love. Were I to picture
. Peter, keeping fast the gate of
ven, and frowning more stern than
ul, on the wretched applicants, that
should be my study. By middle
or sooner, the creed has generally
ght upon the heart, or been at-
ered by it. As the minister passes
the church, the bell holds its iron
ue, and all the low murmur of the
regation dies away. The gray sex-
ooks up and down the street, and
at my window curtain, where,
ugh the small peephole, I half fancy
he has caught my eye. Now, every
er has gone in, and the street lies
p in the quiet sun, while a feeling
neliness comes over me, and brings
an uneasy sense of neglected privi-
and duties. O, I ought to have
to church! The bustle of the rising
regation reaches my ears. They are
ling up to pray. Could I bring my
into unison with those who are
ng in yonder church, and lift it
enward, with a fervor of supplica-
but no distinct request, would not
be the safest kind of prayer? "Lord,
down upon me in mercy!" With
sentiment gushing from my soul,
t I not leave all the rest to Him?
rk! the hymn. This, at least, is
rtion of the service which I can
better than if I sat within the
, where the full choir, and the
ive melody of the organ would
with a weight upon me. At this
nce, it thrills through my frame,
plays upon my heart-strings, with

a pleasure both of the sense and spirit.
Heaven be praised, I know nothing of
music, as a science; and the most elaborate harmonies, if they please me,
please as simply as a nurse's lullaby.
The strain has ceased, but prolongs
itself in my mind, with fanciful echoes,
till I start from my reverie, and find
that the sermon has commenced. It is
my misfortune seldom to fructify, in a
regular way, by any but printed sermons. The first strong idea which the
preacher utters gives birth to a train
of thought, and leads me onward, step
by step, quite out of hearing of the
good man's voice, unless he be indeed
a son of thunder. At my open window,
catching now and then a sentence of the
"parson's saw," I am as well situated
as at the foot of the pulpit stairs. The
broken and scattered fragments of this
one discourse will be the texts of many
sermons, preached by those colleague
pastors,—colleagues, but often disput-
ants,—my Mind and Heart. The former
pretends to be a scholar, and perplexes
me with doctrinal points; the latter
takes me on the score of feeling; and
both, like several other preachers, spend
their strength to very little purpose. I,
their sole auditor, cannot always understand them.

Suppose that a few hours have passed,
and behold me still behind my curtain,
just before the close of the afternoon
service. The hour-hand on the dial has
passed beyond four o'clock. The declining sun is hidden behind the steeple,
and throws its shadow straight across
the street, so that my chamber is darkened as with a cloud. Around the church
door all is solitude, and an impenetrable
obscurity beyond the threshold. A commotion is heard. The seats are slammed

down, and the pew-doors thrown back, —a multitude of feet are trampling along the unseen aisles,—and the congregation burst suddenly through the portal. Foremost, scampers a rabble of boys, behind whom moves a dense and dark phalanx of grown men, and lastly, a crowd of females, with young children, and a few scattered husbands. This instantaneous outbreak of life into loneliness is one of the pleasantest scenes of the day. Some of the good people are rubbing their eyes, thereby intimating that they have been wrapped, as it were, in a sort of holy trance by the fervor of their devotion. There is a young man, a third-rate coxcomb, whose first care is always to flourish a white handkerchief, and brush the seat of a tight pair of black-silk pantaloons, which shine as if varnished. They must have been made of the stuff called "everlasting," or perhaps of the same piece as Christian's garments in the Pilgrim's Progress, for he put them on two summers ago, and has not yet worn the gloss off. I have taken a great liking to those black-silk pantaloons. But, now, with nods and greetings among friends, each matron takes her husband's arm, and paces gravely homeward, while the girls also flutter away, after arranging sunset walks with their favored bachelors. The Sabbath eve is the eve of love. At length, the whole congregation is dispersed. No; here, with faces as glossy as black satin, come two sable ladies and a sable gentleman, and close in their rear the minister, who softens his severe visage, and bestows a kind word on each. Poor souls! To them the most captivating picture of

bliss in heaven is,—"There we shal white!"

All is solitude again. But, hark broken warbling of voices, and r attuning its grandeur to their sw ness, a stately peal of the organ. are the choristers? Let me dream the angels, who came down f Heaven, this blessed morn, to b themselves with the worship of the t good, are playing and singing their f well to the earth. On the wings of rich melody they were borne upwar

This, gentle reader, is merely a fl of poetry. A few of the singing and singing women had lingered hind their fellows, and raised t voices fitfully, and blew a careless upon the organ. Yet it lifted my higher than all their former str They are gone,—the sons and daugh of music,—and the gray sexton is closing the portal. For six days there will be no face of man in pews and aisles and galleries, no voice in the pulpit, nor music in choir. Was it worth while to rear massive edifice to be a desert in heart of the town, and populous for a few hours of each seventh O, but the church is a symbol of ligion. May its site, which was secrated on the day when the first was felled, be kept holy forever, a of solitude and peace, amid the tro and vanity of our week-day w There is a moral, and a religion even in the silent walls. And may steeple still point heavenward, an decked with the hallowed sunshin the Sabbath morn!

THE WEDDING KNELL

HERE is a certain church in the of New York, which I have always rded with peculiar interest, on account of a marriage there solemnized, er very singular circumstances, in grandmother's girlhood. That venle lady chanced to be a spectator the scene, and ever after made it favorite narrative. Whether the edinow standing on the same site be identical one to which she referred, n not antiquarian enough to know; would it be worth while to correct elf, perhaps, of an agreeable error, reading the date of its erection on tablet over the door. It is a stately ch, surrounded by an enclosure of loveliest green, within which appear , pillars, obelisks, and other forms monumental marble, the tributes of ate affection, or more splendid meials of historic dust. With such a e, though the tumult of the city beneath its tower, one would be ng to connect some legendary inst.

he marriage might be considered as esult of an early engagement, though e had been two intermediate weds on the lady's part, and forty s of celibacy on that of the gentle. At sixty-five, Mr. Ellenwood was y, but not quite a secluded man; sh, like all men who brood over own hearts, yet manifesting, on occasions, a vein of generous sennt; a scholar, throughout life, gh always an indolent one, because studies had no definite object, either ublic advantage or personal amn; a gentleman, high bred and fastidiously delicate, yet sometimes requiring a considerable relaxation, in his behalf, of the common rules of society. In truth, there were so many anomalies in his character, and though shrinking with diseased sensibility from public notice, it had been his fatality so often to become the topic of the day, by some wild eccentricity of conduct, that people searched his lineage for an hereditary taint of insanity. But there was no need of this. His caprices had their origin in a mind that lacked the support of an engrossing purpose, and in feelings that preyed upon themselves, for want of other food. If he were mad, it was the consequence, and not the cause, of an aimless and abortive life.

The widow was as complete a contrast to her third bridegroom, in everything but age, as can well be conceived. Compelled to relinquish her first engagement, she had been united to a man of twice her own years, to whom she became an exemplary wife, and by whose death she was left in possession of a splendid fortune. A Southern gentleman, considerably younger than herself, succeeded to her hand, and carried her to Charleston, where, after many uncomfortable years, she found herself again a widow. It would have been singular, if any uncommon delicacy of feeling had survived through such a life as Mrs. Dabney's; it could not but be crushed and killed by her early disappointment, the cold duty of her first marriage, the dislocation of the heart's principles consequent on a second union, and the unkindness of her Southern husband, which had inevitably driven her to connect the idea of his death with that of her comfort. To be brief, she was that wisest, but unloveliest variety of woman, a philosopher, bearing troubles of the heart with equanimity, dispensing with all that should have been her happiness, and making the best of what remained. Sage in most matters, the widow was perhaps the more amiable, for the one frailty that made her ridiculous. Being childless, she could not remain beautiful by proxy, in the person of a daughter; she therefore refused to grow old and ugly, on any consideration; she struggled with Time, and held fast her roses in spite of him, till the venerable thief appeared to have relinquished the spoil, as not worth the trouble of acquiring it.

The approaching marriage of this woman of the world with such an unworldly man as Mr. Ellenwood was announced soon after Mrs. Dabney's return to her native city. Superficial observers, and deeper ones, seemed to concur in supposing that the lady must have borne no inactive part in arranging the affair; there were considerations of expediency, which she would be far more likely to appreciate than Mr. Ellenwood; and there was just the specious phantom of sentiment and romance, in this late union of two early lovers, which sometimes makes a fool of a woman, who has lost her true feelings among the accidents of life. All the wonder was, how the gentleman, with his lack of worldly wisdom, and agonizing consciousness of ridicule, could have been induced to take a measure at once so prudent and so laughable. But while people talked, the wedding-day arrived. The ceremony was to be solemnized according to the Episcopalian forms,

and in open church, with a degree publicity that attracted many spe tors, who occupied the front seats the galleries, and the pews near altar and along the broad aisle. It been arranged, or possibly it was custom of the day, that the pa should proceed separately to church some accident, the bridegroom wa little less punctual than the widow her bridal attendants; with whose rival, after this tedious, but neces preface, the action of our tale may said to commence.

The clumsy wheels of several fashioned coaches were heard, and gentlemen and ladies composing bridal party came through the ch door, with the sudden and glads effect of a burst of sunshine. The w group, except the principal figure, made up of youth and gayety. As streamed up the broad aisle, while pews and pillars seemed to brighte either side, their steps were as buo as if they mistook the church f ball-room, and were ready to d hand in hand to the altar. So bril was the spectacle, that few took n of a singular phenomenon that marked its entrance. At the mo when the bride's foot touched threshold, the bell swung heavily i tower above her, and sent forth its est knell. The vibrations died away returned, with prolonged solemnit she entered the body of the churc

"Good heavens! what an omen," pered a young lady to her lover.

"On my honor," replied the ge man, "I believe the bell has the taste to toll of its own accord. has she to do with weddings? If dearest Julia, were approaching the

bell would ring out its merriest
ıl. It has only a funeral knell for
r."

The bride, and most of her company,
d been too much occupied with the
stle of entrance to hear the first bod-
; stroke of the bell, or at least to
lect on the singularity of such a wel-
me to the altar. They therefore con-
,ued to advance with undiminished
yety. The gorgeous dresses of the
ıe, the crimson velvet coats, the gold-
ed hats, the hoop petticoats, the silk,
.in, brocade, and embroidery, the
ckles, canes, and swords, all displayed
the best advantage on persons suited
such finery, made the group appear
re like a bright-colored picture than
ything real. But by what perversity
taste had the artist represented his
incipal figure as so wrinkled and de-
yed, while yet he had decked her
t in the brightest splendor of attire,
if the loveliest maiden had suddenly
thered into age and become a moral
the beautiful around her! On the
ent, however, and had glittered along
out a third of the aisle, when another
roke of the bell seemed to fill the
urch with a visible gloom, dimming
d obscuring the bright pageant till it
one forth again as from a mist.

This time the party wavered, stopped,
d huddled closer together, while a
ght scream was heard from some of
e ladies, and a confused whispering
10ng the gentlemen. Thus tossing to
d fro, they might have been fancifully
mpared to a splendid bunch of flow-
s suddenly shaken by a puff of wind,
hich threatened to scatter the leaves
an old, brown, withered rose, on the
me stalk with two dewy buds; such
ing the emblem of the widow between

her fair young bridemaids. But her
heroism was admirable. She had started
with an irrepressible shudder, as if the
stroke of the bell had fallen directly
on her heart; then, recovering herself,
while her attendants were yet in dismay,
she took the lead, and paced calmly up
the aisle. The bell continued to swing,
strike, and vibrate with the same doleful regularity as when a corpse is on
its way to the tomb.

"My young friends here have their
nerves a little shaken," said the widow,
with a smile, to the clergyman at the
altar. "But so many weddings have been
ushered in with the merriest peal of
the bells, and yet turned out unhappily,
that I shall hope for better fortune un
der such different auspices."

"Madam," answered the rector, in
great perplexity, "this strange occurrence brings to my mind a marriage
sermon of the famous Bishop Taylor,
wherein he mingles so many thoughts
of mortality and future woe, that, to
speak somewhat after his own rich style,
he seems to hang the bridal chamber
in black, and cut the wedding garment
out of a coffin pall. And it has been
the custom of divers nations to infuse
something of sadness into their marriage ceremonies; so to keep death in
mind while contracting that engagement
which is life's chiefest business. Thus
we may draw a sad but profitable moral
from this funeral knell."

But, though the clergyman might
have given his moral even a keener
point, he did not fail to despatch an
attendant to inquire into the mystery,
and stop those sounds so dismally appropriate to such a marriage. A brief
space elapsed, during which the silence
was broken only by whispers and a few

suppressed titterings among the wedding party and the spectators, who, after
the first shock, were disposed to draw
an ill-natured merriment from the affair. The young have less charity for
aged follies than the old for those
of youth. The widow's glance was observed to wander for an instant towards a window of the church, as if
searching for the time-worn marble that
she had dedicated to her first husband;
then her eyelids dropped over their
faded orbs, and her thoughts were
drawn irresistibly to another grave. Two
buried men, with a voice at her ear,
and a cry afar off, were calling her to
lie down beside them. Perhaps, with
momentary truth of feeling, she thought
how much happier had been her fate
if, after years of bliss, the bell were
now tolling for her funeral, and she
were followed to the grave by the old
affection of her earliest lover, long her
husband. But why had she returned to
him, when their cold hearts shrank
from each other's embrace?

Still the death bell tolled so mournfully that the sunshine seemed to fade
in the air. A whisper, communicated
from those who stood nearest the windows, now spread through the church;
a hearse, with a train of several coaches,
was creeping along the street, conveying some dead man to the churchyard,
while the bride awaited a living one at
the altar. Immediately after, the footsteps of the bridegroom and his friends
were heard at the door. The widow
looked down the aisle, and clinched the
arm of one of her bridemaids in her
bony hand with such unconscious violence that the fair girl trembled.

"You frighten me, my dear madam!"
cried she. "For Heaven's sake, what is

the matter?"

"Nothing, my dear, nothing," s[a]
the widow; then whispering close
her ear,—"There is a foolish fancy t[h]
I cannot get rid of. I am expecting [my]
bridegroom to come into the chu[rch]
with my first two husbands for groo[ms]
men!"

"Look, look!" screamed the brid[e]
maid. "What is here? The funeral!"

As she spoke, a dark procession pac[ed]
into the church. First came an old m[an]
and woman, like chief mourners at [a]
funeral, attired from head to foot [in]
the deepest black, all but their p[ale]
features and hoary hair; he leaning [on]
a staff, and supporting her decre[pit]
form with his nerveless arm. Behi[nd]
appeared another, and another pair,
aged, as black, and mournful as t[he]
first. As they drew near, the wid[ow]
recognized in every face some trait [of]
former friends, long forgotten, but n[ow]
returning, as if from their old grav[es]
to warn her to prepare a shroud; [or]
with purpose almost as unwelcome,
exhibit their wrinkles and infirmity, a[nd]
claim her as their companion by t[he]
tokens of her own decay. Many a mer[ry]
night had she danced with them, [in]
youth. And now, in joyless age, she f[elt]
that some withered partner should [re]
quest her hand, and all unite, in a dan[ce]
of death, to the music of the funer[al]
bell.

While these aged mourners we[re]
passing up the aisle, it was observ[ed]
that, from pew to pew, the spectato[rs]
shuddered with irrepressible awe,
some object, hitherto concealed by t[he]
intervening figures, came full in sig[ht]
Many turned away their faces; othe[rs]
kept a fixed and rigid stare; and [a]
young girl giggled hysterically, a[nd]

nted with the laughter on her lips.
hen the spectral procession ap-
oached the altar, each couple sepa-
ted, and slowly diverged, till in the
ntre appeared a form that had been
rthily ushered in with all this gloomy
mp, the death knell, and the funeral.
was the bridegroom in his shroud!

No garb but that of the grave could
ve befitted such a deathlike aspect;
e eyes, indeed, had the wild gleam of
sepulchral lamp; all else was fixed in
e stern calmness which old men wear
the coffin. The corpse stood motion-
ss, but addressed the widow in ac-
nts that seemed to melt into the clang
the bell, which fell heavily on the air
ile he spoke.

"Come, my bride!" said those pale
s, "the hearse is ready. The sexton
nds waiting for us at the door of the
mb. Let us be married; and then to
r coffins!"

How shall the widow's horror be
presented? It gave her the ghastliness
a dead man's bride. Her youthful
iends stood apart, shuddering at the
ourners, the shrouded bridegroom, and
rself; the whole scene expressed, by
e strongest imagery, the vain struggle
the gilded vanities of this world,
en opposed to age, infirmity, sorrow,
d death. The awe-stricken silence was
st broken by the clergyman.

"Mr. Ellenwood," said he sooth-
gly, yet with somewhat of authori.y,
ou are not well. Your mind has been
itated by the unusual circumstances
which you are placed. The ceremony
ust be deferred. As an old friend, let
e entreat you to return home."

"Home! yes; but not without my
ide," answered he, in the same hollow
cents. "You deem this mockery; per-

haps madness. Had I bedizened my aged
and broken frame with scarlet and embroidery,—had I forced my withered
lips to smile at my dead heart,—that
might have been mockery, or madness.
But now, let young and old declare,
which of us has come hither without a
wedding garment,—the bridegroom or
the bride!"

He stepped forward at a ghostly pace,
and stood beside the widow, contrasting
the awful simplicity of his shroud with
the glare and glitter in which she had
arrayed herself for this unhappy scene.
None that beheld them could deny the
terrible strength of the moral which his
disordered intellect had contrived to
draw.

"Cruel! cruel!" groaned the heart-
stricken bride.

"Cruel!" repeated he; then losing his
death-like composure in a wild bitterness,—"Heaven judge, which of us has
been cruel to the other! In youth, you
deprived me of my happiness, my hopes,
my aims; you took away all the substance of my life, and made it a dream,
without reality enough even to grieve
at,—with only a pervading gloom,
through which I walked wearily and
cared not whither. But after forty years,
when I have built my tomb, and would
not give up the thought of resting there,
—no, not for such a life as we once
pictured,—you call me to the altar. At
your summons I am here. But other
husbands have enjoyed your youth,
your beauty, your warmth of heart, and
all that could be termed your life. What
is there for me but your decay and
death? And therefore I have bidden
these funeral friends, and bespoken the
sexton's deepest knell, and am come, in
my shroud, to wed you, as with a

burial service, that we may join our hands at the door of the sepulchre, and enter it together."

It was not frenzy; it was not merely the drunkenness of strong emotion, in a heart unused to it, that now wrought upon the bride. The stern lesson of the day had done its work; her worldliness was gone. She seized the bridegroom's hand.

"Yes!" cried she. "Let us wed, even at the door of the sepulchre! My life is gone in vanity and emptiness. But at its close, there is one true feeling. It has made me what I was in youth; it makes me worthy of you. Time is no more for both of us. Let us wed for eternity!"

With a long and deep regard, the bridegroom looked into her eyes, while a tear was gathering in his own. How strange that gush of human feeling from the frozen bosom of a corpse! He wiped away the tear even with his shroud.

"Beloved of my youth," said he, "I have been wild. The despair of my whole lifetime had returned at once, and maddened me. Forgive; and be forgiven. Yes; it is evening with us now; and we have realized none of our morning dreams of happiness. But let us join our hands before the altar, as lovers whom adverse circumstances have separated through life, yet who meet again as they are leaving it, and find their earthly affection changed into something holy as religion. And what is Time, to the married of Eternity?"

Amid the tears of many, and a swell of exalted sentiment, in those who felt aright, was solemnized the union of two immortal souls. The train of withered mourners, the hoary bridegroom in his shroud, the pale features of the aged bride, and the death bell tolling through the whole, till its deep voice overpowered the marriage words, all marked the funeral of earthly hope. But as the ceremony proceeded, the organ, as if stirred by the sympathies of this impressive scene, poured forth an anthem, first mingling with the dismal knell, then rising to a loftier strain, till the soul looked down upon its woe. And when the awful rite was finished, and with cold hand in cold hand, the Married of Eternity withdrew, the organ's peal of solemn triumph drowned the Wedding Knell.

THE MINISTER'S BLACK VEIL

A PARABLE *

THE sexton stood in the porch of Milford meeting-house, pulling busily at the bell-rope. The old people of the village came stooping along the street. Children with bright faces tripped merrily beside their parents, or mimicked a graver gait, in the conscious dignity of their Sunday clothes. Spruce bachelors looked sidelong at the pretty maidens, and fancied that the Sabbath sunshine made them prettier than on week days. When

* Another clergyman in New England, Mr. Joseph Moody, of York, Maine, who died about eighty years since, made himself remarkable by the same eccentricity that is here related of the Reverend Mr. Hooper. In his case, however, the symbol had a different import. In early life he had accidentally killed a beloved friend; and from that day till the hour of his own death he hid his face from men.

throng had mostly streamed into
porch, the sexton began to toll the
l, keeping his eye on the Reverend
. Hooper's door. The first glimpse
the clergyman's figure was the signal
the bell to cease its summons.

'But what has good Parson Hooper
upon his face?" cried the sexton in
onishment.

All within hearing immediately turned
out, and beheld the semblance of Mr.
ooper, pacing slowly his meditative
y towards the meeting-house. With
e accord they started, expressing more
nder than if some strange minister
re coming to dust the cushions of
. Hooper's pulpit.

"Are you sure it is our parson?" in-
red Goodman Gray of the sexton.

"Of a certainty it is good Mr.
ooper," replied the sexton. "He was
have exchanged pulpits with Parson
ute, of Westbury; but Parson Shute
it to excuse himself yesterday, being
preach a funeral sermon."

The cause of so much amazement
y appear sufficiently slight. Mr.
ooper, a gentlemanly person, of about
irty, though still a bachelor, was
essed with due clerical neatness, as if
careful wife had starched his band,
d brushed the weekly dust from his
nday's garb. There was but one thing
narkable in his appearance. Swathed
out his forehead, and hanging down
er his face so low as to be shaken by
s breath, Mr. Hooper had on a black
il. On a nearer view, it seemed to con-
t of two folds of crape, which en-
ely concealed his features, except the
outh and chin, but probably did not
ercept his sight, further than to give
darkened aspect to all living and in-
imate things. With this gloomy shade

before him, good Mr. Hooper walked
onward, at a slow and quiet pace, stooping somewhat, and looking on the
ground, as is customary with abstracted
men, yet nodding kindly to those of his
parishioners who still waited on the
meeting-house steps. But so wonderstruck were they, that his greeting
hardly met with a return.

"I can't really feel as if good Mr.
Hooper's face was behind that piece of
crape," said the sexton.

"I don't like it," muttered an old
woman, as she hobbled into the meeting-house. "He has changed himself into
something awful, only by hiding his
face."

"Our parson has gone mad!" cried
Goodman Gray, following him across
the threshold.

A rumor of some unaccountable phenomenon had preceded Mr. Hooper into
the meeting-house, and set all the congregation astir. Few could refrain from
twisting their heads towards the door;
many stood upright, and turned directly
about; while several little boys clambered upon the seats, and came down
again with a terrible racket. There was
a general bustle, a rustling of the
women's gowns and shuffling of the
men's feet, greatly at variance with that
hushed repose which should attend the
entrance of the minister. But Mr.
Hooper appeared not to notice the per-
turbation of his people. He entered with
an almost noiseless step, bent his head
mildly to the pews on each side, and
bowed as he passed his oldest parishioner, a white-haired great-grandsire,
who occupied an arm-chair in the centre
of the aisle. It was strange to observe
how slowly this venerable man became
conscious of something singular in the

appearance of his pastor. He seemed not fully to partake of the prevailing wonder, till Mr. Hooper had ascended the stairs, and showed himself in the pulpit, face to face with his congregation, except for the black veil. That mysterious emblem was never once withdrawn. It shook with his measured breath as he gave out the psalm; it threw its obscurity between him and the holy page, as he read the Scriptures; and while he prayed, the veil lay heavily on his uplifted countenance. Did he seek to hide it from the dread Being whom he was addressing?

Such was the effect of this simple piece of crape, that more than one woman of delicate nerves was forced to leave the meeting-house. Yet perhaps the pale-faced congregation was almost as fearful a sight to the minister as his black veil to them.

Mr. Hooper had the reputation of a good preacher, but not an energetic one: he strove to win his people heavenward by mild, persuasive influences, rather than to drive them thither by the thunders of the Word. The sermon which he now delivered was marked by the same characteristics of style and manner as the general series of his pulpit oratory. But there was something, either in the sentiment of the discourse itself, or in the imagination of the auditors, which made it greatly the most powerful effort that they had ever heard from their pastor's lips. It was tinged rather more darkly than usual with the gentle gloom of Mr. Hooper's temperament. The subject had reference to secret sin, and those sad mysteries which we hide from our nearest and dearest, and would fain conceal from our own consciousness, even forgetting that the Omniscient can

detect them. A subtle power was breathed into his words. Each member of the congregation, the most innocent girl, and the man of hardened breast felt as if the preacher had crept upon them, behind his awful veil, and discovered their hoarded iniquity of deed or thought. Many spread their clasped hands on their bosoms. There was nothing terrible in what Mr. Hooper said, at least, no violence; and yet with every tremor of his melancholy voice the hearers quaked. An unsought pathos came hand in hand with awe. So sensible were the audience of some unwonted attribute in their minister, that they longed for a breath of wind to blow aside the veil, almost believing that a stranger's visage would be discovered, though the form, gesture, and voice were those of Mr. Hooper.

At the close of the services, the people hurried out with indecorous confusion, eager to communicate their pent-up amazement, and conscious of lighter spirits the moment they lost sight of the black veil. Some gathered in little circles, huddled closely together, with their mouths all whispering in the centre; some went homeward alone, wrapt in silent meditation; some talked loudly, and profaned the Sabbath day with ostentatious laughter. A few shook their sagacious heads, intimating that they could penetrate the mystery; while one or two affirmed that there was no mystery at all, but only that Mr. Hooper's eyes were so weakened by the midnight lamp as to require a shade. After a brief interval, forth came good Mr. Hooper also, in the rear of his flock. Turning his veiled face from one group to another, he paid due reverence to the hoary heads, saluted the middle aged

h kind dignity, as their friend and
ritual guide, greeted the young with
ngled authority and love, and laid
 hands on the little children's heads
bless them. Such was always his cus-
n on the Sabbath day. Strange and
wildered looks repaid him for his
urtesy. None, as on former occasions,
ired to the honor of walking by their
stor's side. Old Squire Saunders,
ibtless by an accidental lapse of
mory, neglected to invite Mr. Hooper
his table, where the good clergyman
l been wont to bless the food almost
ry Sunday since his settlement. He
urned, therefore, to the parsonage,
l, at the moment of closing the door,
s observed to look back upon the
ople, all of whom had their eyes fixed
on the minister. A sad smile gleamed
ntly from beneath the black veil, and
kered about his mouth, glimmering
he disappeared.

'How strange," said a lady, "that a
ple black veil, such as any woman
ght wear on her bonnet, should be-
ne such a terrible thing on Mr.
ooper's face!"

"Something must surely be amiss with
. Hooper's intellects," observed her
sband, the physician of the village.
ut the strangest part of the affair is
 effect of this vagary, even on a
er-minded man like myself. The
ck veil, though it covers only our
stor's face, throws its influence over
 whole person, and makes him ghost-
 from head to foot. Do you not feel
o?"

'Truly do I," replied the lady; "and
vould not be alone with him for the
rld. I wonder he is not afraid to be
ne with himself!"

"Men sometimes are so," said her
husband.

The afternoon service was attended
with similar circumstances. At its conclusion, the bell tolled for the funeral
of a young lady. The relatives and
friends were assembled in the house,
and the more distant acquaintances
stood about the door, speaking of the
good qualities of the deceased, when
their talk was interrupted by the appearance of Mr. Hooper, still covered
with his black veil. It was now an appropriate emblem. The clergyman
stepped into the room where the corpse
was laid, and bent over the coffin, to
take a last farewell of his deceased
parishioner. As he stooped, the veil hung
straight down from his forehead, so
that, if her eyelids had not been closed
forever, the dead maiden might have
seen his face. Could Mr. Hooper be
fearful of her glance, that he so hastily
caught back the black veil? A person
who watched the interview between the
dead and living, scrupled not to affirm,
that, at the instant when the clergyman's features were disclosed, the corpse
had slightly shuddered, rustling the
shroud and muslin cap, though the countenance retained the composure of
death. A superstitious old woman was
the only witness of this prodigy. From
the coffin Mr. Hooper passed into the
chamber of the mourners, and thence
to the head of the staircase, to make the
funeral prayer. It was a tender and
heart-dissolving prayer, full of sorrow,
yet so imbued with celestial hopes, that
the music of a heavenly harp, swept by
the fingers of the dead, seemed faintly
to be heard among the saddest accents
of the minister. The people trembled,
though they but darkly understood him

when he prayed that they, and himself, and all of mortal race, might be ready, as he trusted this young maiden had been, for the dreadful hour that should snatch the veil from their faces. The bearers went heavily forth, and the mourners followed, saddening all the street, with the dead before them, and Mr. Hooper in his black veil behind.

"Why do you look back?" said one in the procession to his partner.

"I had a fancy," replied she, "that the minister and the maiden's spirit were walking hand in hand."

"And so had I, at the same moment," said the other.

That night, the handsomest couple in Milford village were to be joined in wedlock. Though reckoned a melancholy man, Mr. Hooper had a placid cheerfulness for such occasions, which often excited a sympathetic smile, where livelier merriment would have been thrown away. There was no quality of his disposition which made him more beloved than this. The company at the wedding awaited his arrival with impatience, trusting that the strange awe which had gathered over him throughout the day would now be dispelled. But such was not the result. When Mr. Hooper came, the first thing that their eyes rested on was the same horrible black veil, which had added deeper gloom to the funeral, and could portend nothing but evil to the wedding. Such was its immediate effect on the guests, that a cloud seemed to have rolled duskily from beneath the black crape, and dimmed the light of the candles. The bridal pair stood up before the minister. But the bride's cold fingers quivered in the tremulous hand of the bridegroom, and her deathlike paleness

caused a whisper, that the maiden w[ ] had been buried a few hours before w[ ] come from her grave to be married. [ ] ever another wedding was so dismal[ ] was that famous one where they to[ ] the wedding knell. After performing [ ] ceremony, Mr. Hooper raised a glass [ ] wine to his lips, wishing happiness [ ] the new-married couple, in a strain [ ] mild pleasantry that ought to ha[ ] brightened the features of the gues[ ] like a cheerful gleam from the hear[ ] At that instant, catching a glimpse [ ] his figure in the looking-glass, the bla[ ] veil involved his own spirit in t[ ] horror with which it overwhelmed [ ] others. His frame shuddered,—his l[ ] grew white,—he spilt the untasted wi[ ] upon the carpet,—and rushed forth in[ ] the darkness. For the Earth, too, h[ ] on her Black Veil.

The next day, the whole village [ ] Milford talked of little else than Pars[ ] Hooper's black veil. That, and the my[ ] tery concealed behind it, supplied [ ] topic for discussion between acquai[ ] ances meeting in the street, and go[ ] women gossiping at their open windo[ ] It was the first item of news that t[ ] tavern-keeper told to his guests. T[ ] children babbled of it on their way [ ] school. One imitative little imp cover[ ] his face with an old black handkerchi[ ] thereby so affrighting his playmates th[ ] the panic seized himself, and he we[ ] nigh lost his wits by his own waggery[ ]

It was remarkable that, of all t[ ] busybodies and impertinent people [ ] the parish, not one ventured to put t[ ] plain question to Mr. Hooper, wheref[ ] he did this thing. Hitherto, whenev[ ] there appeared the slightest call for su[ ] interference, he had never lacked a[ ] visers, nor shown himself averse to ided by their judgment. If he erred all, it was by so painful a degree of f-distrust, that even the mildest cen-re would lead him to consider an different action as a crime. Yet, ough so well acquainted with this iable weakness, no individual among parishioners chose to make the black il a subject of friendly remonstrance. ere was a feeling of dread, neither inly confessed nor carefully con-led, which caused each to shift the ponsibility upon another, till at gth it was found expedient to send a putation of the church, in order to al with Mr. Hooper about the mys-y, before it should grow into a scan-. Never did an embassy so ill dis-arge its duties. The minister received m with friendly courtesy, but be-ne silent, after they were seated, ving to his visitors the whole burden introducing their important business. e topic, it might be supposed, was vious enough. There was the black l, swathed round Mr. Hooper's fore-d, and concealing every feature ove his placid mouth, on which, at es, they could perceive the glimmer-; of a melancholy smile. But that ce of crape, to their imagination, med to hang down before his heart, symbol of a fearful secret between and them. Were the veil but cast de, they might speak freely of it, but till then. Thus they sat a consider-e time, speechless, confused, and inking uneasily from Mr. Hooper's , which they felt to be fixed upon m with an invisible glance. Finally, deputies returned abashed to their stituents, pronouncing the matter weighty to be handled, except by a ncil of the churches, if, indeed, it might not require a general synod.

But there was one person in the village, unappalled by the awe with which the black veil had impressed all beside herself. When the deputies returned without an explanation, or even venturing to demand one, she, with the calm energy of her character, determined to chase away the strange cloud that appeared to be settling round Mr. Hooper, every moment more darkly than before. As his plighted wife, it should be her privilege to know what the black veil concealed. At the minister's first visit, therefore, she entered upon the subject, with a direct simplicity, which made the task easier both for him and her. After he had seated himself, she fixed her eyes steadfastly upon the veil, but could discern nothing of the dreadful gloom that had so overawed the multitude: it was but a double fold of crape, hanging down from his forehead to his mouth, and slightly stirring with his breath.

"No," said she aloud, and smiling, "there is nothing terrible in this piece of crape, except that it hides a face which I am always glad to look upon. Come, good sir, let the sun shine from behind the cloud. First lay aside your black veil; then tell me why you put it on."

Mr. Hooper's smile glimmered faintly.

"There is an hour to come," said he, "when all of us shall cast aside our veils. Take it not amiss, beloved friend, if I wear this piece of crape till then."

"Your words are a mystery too," returned the young lady. "Take away the veil from them, at least."

"Elizabeth, I will," said he, "so far as my vow may suffer me. Know, then, this veil is a type and a symbol, and I am bound to wear it ever, both in light and darkness, in solitude and before the gaze of multitudes, and as with stran‑ gers, so with my familiar friends. No mortal eye will see it withdrawn. This dismal shade must separate me from the world: even you, Elizabeth, can never come behind it!"

"What grievous affliction hath be‑ fallen you," she earnestly inquired, "that you should thus darken your eyes for‑ ever?"

"If it be a sign of mourning," re‑ plied Mr. Hooper, "I, perhaps, like most other mortals, have sorrows dark enough to be typified by a black veil."

"But what if the world will not be‑ lieve that it is the type of an innocent sorrow?" urged Elizabeth. "Beloved and respected as you are, there may be whispers, that you hide your face under the consciousness of secret sin. For the sake of your holy office, do away this scandal!"

The color rose into her cheeks as she intimated the nature of the rumors that were already abroad in the village. But Mr. Hooper's mildness did not forsake him. He even smiled again,—that same sad smile, which always appeared like a faint glimmering of light, proceeding from the obscurity beneath the veil.

"If I hide my face for sorrow, there is cause enough," he merely replied; "and if I cover it for secret sin, what mortal might not do the same?"

And with this gentle, but unconquer‑ able obstinacy did he resist all her en‑ treaties. At length Elizabeth sat silent. For a few moments she appeared lost in thought, considering, probably, what new methods might be tried, to with‑ draw her lover from so dark a fantasy, which, if it had no other meaning, was

perhaps a symptom of mental dise Though of a firmer character than own, the tears rolled down her che But, in an instant, as it were, a feeling took the place of sorrow: eyes were fixed insensibly on the b veil, when, like a sudden twilight in air, its terrors fell around her. She ar and stood trembling before him.

"And do you feel it then at las said he, mournfully.

She made no reply, but covered eyes with her hand, and turned to le the room. He rushed forward caught her arm.

"Have patience with me, Elizabet cried he, passionately. "Do not de me, though this veil must be betw us here on earth. Be mine, and herea there shall be no veil over my face, darkness between our souls! It is b mortal veil,—it is not for eternity! you know not how lonely I am, how frightened, to be alone, behind black veil! Do not leave me in miserable obscurity forever!"

"Lift the veil but once, and look in the face," said she.

"Never! It cannot be!" replied Hooper.

"Then, farewell!" said Elizabeth.

She withdrew her arm from his gr and slowly departed, pausing at door, to give one long, shuddering g that seemed almost to penetrate mystery of the black veil. But, e amid his grief, Mr. Hooper smiled think that only a material emblem separated him from happiness, tho the horrors which it shadowed fo must be drawn darkly between fondest of lovers.

From that time no attempts w made to remove Mr. Hooper's bl

l, or, by a direct appeal, to discover secret which it was supposed to e. By persons who claimed a superi- ty to popular prejudice, it was reck- d merely an eccentric whim, such often mingles with the sober actions men otherwise rational, and tinges m all with its own semblance of anity. But with the multitude, good . Hooper was irreparably a bugbear. could not walk the street with any ce of mind, so conscious was he that gentle and timid would turn aside avoid him, and that others would ke it a point of hardihood to throw mselves in his way. The imperti- ce of the latter class compelled him give up his customary walk, at sun- to the burial-ground; for when he ned pensively over the gate, there ld always be faces behind the grave- nes, peeping at his black veil. A fable it the rounds, that the stare of the d people drove him thence. It ved him, to the very depth of his d heart, to observe how the children from his approach, breaking up ir merriest sports, while his melan- ly figure was yet afar off. Their in- ctive dread caused him to feel, more ngly than aught else, that a preter- ural horror was interwoven with the ads of the black crape. In truth, his antipathy to the veil was known be so great, that he never willingly sed before a mirror, nor stooped to k at a still fountain, lest, in its ceful bosom, he should be affrighted himself. This was what gave plausi- y to the whispers, that Mr. per's conscience tortured him for e great crime too horrible to be en- ly concealed, or otherwise than so curely intimated. Thus, from be-

neath the black veil, there rolled a cloud into the sunshine, an ambiguity of sin or sorrow, which enveloped the poor minister, so that love or sympathy could never reach him. It was said, that ghost and fiend consorted with him there. With self-shudderings and out- ward terrors, he walked continually in its shadow, groping darkly within his own soul, or gazing through a medium that saddened the whole world. Even the lawless wind, it was believed, re- spected his dreadful secret, and never blew aside the veil. But still good Mr. Hooper sadly smiled at the pale visages of the worldly throng as he passed by.

Among all its bad influences, the black veil had the one desirable effect, of making its wearer a very efficient clergyman. By the aid of his mysterious emblem—for there was no other appar- ent cause—he became a man of awful power, over souls that were in agony for sin. His converts always regarded him with a dread peculiar to them- selves, affirming, though but figur- atively, that, before he brought them to celestial light, they had been with him behind the black veil. Its gloom, indeed, enabled him to sympathize with all dark affections. Dying sinners cried aloud for Mr. Hooper, and would not yield their breath till he appeared; though ever, as he stooped to whisper consolation, they shuddered at the veiled face so near their own. Such were the terrors of the black veil, even when Death had bared his visage! Strangers came long distances to attend service at his church, with the mere idle purpose of gazing at his figure, because it was forbidden them to behold his face. But many were made to quake ere they departed! Once, during Governor Belcher's administration, Mr. Hooper was appointed to preach the election sermon. Covered with his black veil, he stood before the chief magistrate, the council, and the representatives, and wrought so deep an impression, that the legislative measures of that year were characterized by all the gloom and piety of our earliest ancestral sway.

In this manner Mr. Hooper spent a long life, irreproachable in outward act, yet shrouded in dismal suspicions; kind and loving, though unloved, and dimly feared; a man apart from men, shunned in their health and joy, but ever summoned to their aid in mortal anguish. As years wore on, shedding their snows above his sable veil, he acquired a name throughout the New England churches, and they called him Father Hooper. Nearly all his parishioners, who were of mature age when he was settled, had been borne away by many a funeral: he had one congregation in the church, and a more crowded one in the churchyard; and having wrought so late into the evening, and done his work so well, it was now good Father Hooper's turn to rest.

Several persons were visible by the shaded candlelight in the death-chamber of the old clergyman. Natural connections he had none. But there was the decorously grave, though unmoved physician, seeking only to mitigate the last pangs of the patient whom he could not save. There were the deacons, and other eminently pious members of his church. There, also, was the Reverend Mr. Clark, of Westbury, a young and zealous divine, who had ridden in haste to pray by the bedside of the expiring minister. There was the nurse, no hired handmaiden of death, but one whose calm affection had endured thus lo[ng] in secrecy, in solitude, amid the chill age, and would not perish, even at t[he] dying hour. Who, but Elizabeth! A[nd] there lay the hoary head of good Fath[er] Hooper upon the death pillow, with t[he] black veil still swathed about his bro[w] and reaching down over his face, so th[at] each more difficult gasp of his fai[nt] breath caused it to stir. All through li[fe] that piece of crape had hung betwe[en] him and the world: it had separated hi[m] from cheerful brotherhood and woma[n's] love, and kept him in that saddest of [a]ll prisons, his own heart; and still it l[ay] upon his face, as if to deepen the glo[om] of his darksome chamber, and sha[de] him from the sunshine of eternity.

For some time previous, his mi[nd] had been confused, wavering dou[bt]fully between the past and the prese[nt,] and hovering forward, as it were, [at] intervals, into the indistinctness of t[he] world to come. There had been fever[ish] turns, which tossed him from side [to] side, and wore away what little stren[gth] he had. But in his most convulsi[ve] struggles, and in the wildest vagaries [of] his intellect, when no other thou[ght] retained its sober influence, he s[till] showed an awful solicitude lest [the] black veil should slip aside. Even [if] his bewildered soul could have forg[ot]ten, there was a faithful woman at [his] pillow, who, with averted eyes, wo[uld] have covered that aged face, which s[he] had last beheld in the comeliness [of] manhood. At length the death-strick[en] old man lay quietly in the torpor [of] mental and bodily exhaustion, with [an] imperceptible pulse, and breath t[hat] grew fainter and fainter, except whe[n a] long, deep, and irregular inspirat[ion]

emed to prelude the flight of his
irit.

The minister of Westbury approached
e bedside.

"Venerable Father Hooper," said he,
ne moment of your release is at
nd. Are you ready for the lifting of
e veil, that shuts in time from eter-
y?"

Father Hooper at first replied merely
 a feeble motion of his head; then,
prehensive, perhaps, that his meaning
ght be doubtful, he exerted himself
 speak.

"Yea," said he, in faint accents, "my
il hath a patient weariness until that
.l be lifted."

'And is it fitting," resumed the Rev-
nd Mr. Clark, "that a man so given
 prayer, of such a blameless example,
ly in deed and thought, so far as
rtal judgment may pronounce; is it
.ing that a father in the Church
uld leave a shadow on his memory,
.t may seem to blacken a life so
re? I pray you, my venerable brother,
 not this thing be! Suffer us to
 gladdened by your triumphant as-
:t, as you go to your reward. Before
 veil of eternity be lifted, let me
 t aside this black veil from your
 e!"

And thus speaking, the Reverend Mr.
.rk bent forward to reveal the mys-
y of so many years. But, exerting a
lden energy, that made all the be-
ders stand aghast, Father Hooper
.tched both his hands from beneath
 bedclothes, and pressed them
ongly on the black veil, resolute to
 uggle, if the minister of Westbury
 uld contend with a dying man.

"Never!" cried the veiled clergyman.
n earth, never!"

"Dark old man!" exclaimed the
affrighted minister, "with what horrible
crime upon your soul are you now passing to the judgment?"

Father Hooper's breath heaved; it
rattled in his throat; but, with a mighty
effort, grasping forward with his hands,
he caught hold of life, and held it back
till he should speak. He even raised
himself in bed; and there he sat, shivering with the arms of death around him,
while the black veil hung down, awful,
at that last moment, in the gathered
terrors of a lifetime. And yet the faint,
sad smile, so often there, now seemed to
glimmer from its obscurity, and linger
on Father Hooper's lips.

"Why do you tremble at me alone?"
cried he, turning his veiled face round
the circle of pale spectators. "Tremble
also at each other! Have men avoided
me, and women shown no pity, and
children screamed and fled, only for my
black veil? What, but the mystery
which it obscurely typifies, has made
this piece of crape so awful? When the
friend shows his inmost heart to his
friend; the lover to his best beloved;
when man does not vainly shrink from
the eye of his Creator, loathsomely
treasuring up the secret of his sin; then
deem me a monster, for the symbol
beneath which I have lived, and died!
I look around me, and, lo! on every
visage a Black Veil!"

While his auditors shrank from one
another, in mutual affright, Father
Hooper fell back upon his pillow, a
veiled corpse, with a faint smile lingering on the lips. Still veiled, they laid
him in his coffin, and a veiled corpse
they bore him to the grave. The grass
of many years has sprung up and
withered on that grave, the burial stone

is moss-grown, and good Mr. Hooper's face is dust; but awful is still the thought, that it mouldered beneath Black Veil!

THE MAYPOLE OF MERRY MOUNT

There is an admirable foundation for a philosophic romance, in the curious history of the early settlement of Mount Wollaston, or Merry Mount. In the slight sketch here attempted, the facts, recorded on the grave pages of our New England annalists, have wrought themselves, almost spontaneously, into a sort of allegory. The masques, mummeries, and festive customs described in the text are in accordance with the manners of the age. Authority on these points may be found in Strutt's Book of English Sports and Pastimes.

BRIGHT were the days at Merry Mount, when the Maypole was the banner staff of that gay colony! They who reared it, should their banner be triumphant, were to pour sunshine over New England's rugged hills, and scatter flower-seeds throughout the soil. Jollity and gloom were contending for an empire. Midsummer eve had come, bringing deep verdure to the forest, and roses in her lap, of a more vivid hue than the tender buds of Spring. But May, or her mirthful spirit, dwelt all the year round at Merry Mount, sporting with the summer months, and revelling with Autumn, and basking in the glow of Winter's fireside. Through a world of toil and care she flitted with a dreamlike smile, and came hither to find a home among the lightsome hearts of Merry Mount. Never had the Maypole been so gayly decked as at sunset on midsummer eve. This venerated emblem was a pine-tree, which had preserved the slender grace

of youth, while it equalled the lofti height of the old wood monarchs. Fr its top streamed a silken banner, colo like the rainbow. Down nearly to ground the pole was dressed w birchen boughs, and others of the li liest green, and some with silv leaves, fastened by ribbons that fl tered in fantastic knots of twenty ferent colors, but no sad ones. Gar flowers, and blossoms of the wildern laughed gladly forth amid the verdu so fresh and dewy, that they must h grown by magic on that happy pi tree. Where this green and flow splendor terminated, the shaft of Maypole was stained with the se brilliant hues of the banner at its t On the lowest green bough hung abundant wreath of roses, some t had been gathered in the sunniest sp of the forest, and others, of still ric blush, which the colonists had rea from English seed. O people of Golden Age, the chief of your h bandry was to raise flowers!

But what was the wild throng t stood hand in hand about the Maypc It could not be, that the fauns nymphs, when driven from their cla groves and homes of ancient fable, sought refuge, as all the persecuted in the fresh woods of the West. Th were Gothic monsters, though perh of Grecian ancestry. On the shoulc of a comely youth uprose the head

nching antlers of a stag; a second,
nan in all other points, had the grim
ge of a wolf; a third, still with the
nk and limbs of a mortal man,
wed the beard and horns of a vener-
e he-goat. There was the likeness of
ear erect, brute in all but his hind
s, which were adorned with pink silk
kings. And here again, almost as
ndrous, stood a real bear of the dark
est, lending each of his fore paws to
grasp of a human hand, and as
ly for the dance as any in that circle.
inferior nature rose half way, to
et his companions as they stooped.
er faces wore the similitude of man
woman, but distorted or extravagant,
n red noses pendulous before their
ths, which seemed of awful depth,
stretched from ear to ear in an
nal fit of laughter. Here might be
the Salvage Man, well known in
ldry, hairy as a baboon, and girdled
green leaves. By his side, a nobler
re, but still a counterfeit, appeared
Indian hunter, with feathery crest
wampum belt. Many of this strange
pany wore foolscaps, and had little
s appended to their garments,
ling with a silvery sound, responsive
he inaudible music of their gleesome
its. Some youths and maidens were
soberer garb, yet well maintained
r places in the irregular throng, by
expression of wild revelry upon their
ures. Such were the colonists of
rry Mount, as they stood in the
d smile of sunset, round their ven-
ed Maypole.

ad a wanderer, bewildered in the
ncholy forest, heard their mirth,
stolen a half-affrighted glance, he
ht have fancied them the crew of
us, some already transformed to
brutes, some midway between man and
beast, and the others rioting in the flow
of tipsy jollity that foreran the change.
But a band of Puritans, who watched
the scene, invisible themselves, compared the masks to those devils and
ruined souls with whom their superstition peopled the black wilderness.

Within the ring of monsters appeared
the two airiest forms that had ever
trodden on any more solid footing than
a purple and golden cloud. One was a
youth in glistening apparel, with a scarf
of the rainbow pattern crosswise on his
breast. His right hand held a gilded
staff, the ensign of high dignity among
the revellers, and his left grasped the
slender fingers of a fair maiden not less
gayly decorated than himself. Bright
roses glowed in contrast with the dark
and glossy curls of each, and were scattered round their feet, or had sprung
up spontaneously there. Behind this
lightsome couple, so close to the Maypole that its boughs shaded his jovial
face, stood the figure of an English
priest, canonically dressed, yet decked
with flowers, in heathen fashion, and
wearing a chaplet of the native vine-
leaves. By the riot of his rolling eye,
and the pagan decorations of his holy
garb, he seemed the wildest monster
there, and the very Comus of the crew.

"Votaries of the Maypole," cried the
flower-decked priest, "merrily, all day
long, have the woods echoed to your
mirth. But be this your merriest hour,
my hearts! Lo, here stand the Lord and
Lady of the May, whom I, a clerk of
Oxford, and high-priest of Merry
Mount, am presently to join in holy
matrimony. Up with your nimble spirits,
ye morris dancers, green men, and glee
maidens, bears and wolves, and horned

gentlemen! Come; a chorus now, rich with the old mirth of Merry England, and the wilder glee of this fresh forest; and then a dance, to show the youthful pair what life is made of, and how airily they should go through it! All ye that love the Maypole, lend your voices to the nuptial song of the Lord and Lady of the May!"

This wedlock was more serious than most affairs of Merry Mount, where jest and delusion, trick and fantasy, kept up a continual carnival. The Lord and Lady of the May, though their titles must be laid down at sunset, were really and truly to be partners for the dance of life, beginning the measure that same bright eve. The wreath of roses that hung from the lowest green bough of the Maypole had been twined for them, and would be thrown over both their heads, in symbol of their flowery union. When the priest had spoken, therefore, a riotous uproar burst from the rout of monstrous figures.

"Begin you the stave, reverend Sir," cried they all, "and never did the woods ring to such a merry peal as we of the Maypole shall send up!"

Immediately a prelude of pipe, cithern, and viol, touched with practised minstrelsy, began to play from a neighboring thicket in such a mirthful cadence that the boughs of the Maypole quivered to the sound. But the May Lord, he of the gilded staff, chancing to look into his Lady's eyes, was wonderstruck at the almost pensive glance that met his own.

"Edith, sweet Lady of the May," whispered he, reproachfully, "is yon wreath of roses a garland to hang above our graves, that you look so sad? O Edith, this is our golden time! Tarnish

it not by any pensive shadow of t mind; for it may be that nothing futurity will be brighter than the me remembrance of what is now passing

"That was the very thought that sa dened me! How came it in your min too?" said Edith, in a still lower to than he; for it was high treason to sad at Merry Mount. "Therefore do sigh amid this festive music. And I sides, dear Edgar, I struggle as with dream, and fancy that these shapes our jovial friends are visionary, a their mirth unreal, and that we are true Lord and Lady of the May. Wh is the mystery in my heart?"

Just then, as if a spell had loosen them, down came a little shower withering rose-leaves from the Maypo Alas for the young lovers! No soo had their hearts glowed with real p sion than they were sensible of som thing vague and unsubstantial in th former pleasures, and felt a dreary p sentiment of inevitable change. Fr the moment that they truly loved, th had subjected themselves to earth doom of care and sorrow and troub joy, and had no more a home at Me Mount. That was Edith's mystery. N leave we the priest to marry them, a the maskers to sport round the M pole, till the last sunbeam be withdra from its summit, and the shadows the forest mingle gloomily in the dan Meanwhile, we may discover who th gay people were.

Two hundred years ago, and mo the Old World and its inhabitants came mutually weary of each oth Men voyaged by thousands to West; some to barter glass beads, a such like jewels for the furs of Indian hunter; some to conquer vir

res; and one stern band to pray.
none of these motives had much
ht with the colonists of Merry
nt. Their leaders were men who
sported so long with life that, when
ght and Wisdom came, even these
lcome guests were led astray by
rowd of vanities which they should
put to flight. Erring Thought and
rted Wisdom were made to put on
s and play the fool. The men of
n we speak, after losing the heart's
gayety, imagined a wild philoso-
of pleasure, and came hither to act
heir latest day-dream. They gath-
followers from all that giddy tribe,
e whole life is like the festal days
oberer men. In their train were
rels, not unknown in London
ts; wandering players, whose the-
had been the halls of noblemen;
mers, rope-dancers, and mounte-
, who would long be missed at
s, church ales, and fairs; in a word,
-makers of every sort, such as
ded in that age, but now began to
scountenanced by the rapid growth
ritanism. Light had their footsteps
on land, and as lightly they came
s the sea. Many had been mad-
by their previous troubles into a
espair; others were as madly gay
flush of youth, like the May Lord
is Lady; but whatever might be
quality of their mirth, old and
were gay at Merry Mount. The
deemed themselves happy. The
spirits, if they knew that mirth
ut the counterfeit of happiness,
ollowed the false shadow wilfully,
se at least her garments glittered
est. Sworn triflers of a lifetime,
would not venture among the sober
of life, not even to be truly blest.

All the hereditary pastimes of Old
England were transplanted hither. The
King of Christmas was duly crowned,
and the Lord of Misrule bore potent
sway. On the eve of Saint John they
felled whole acres of the forest to make
bonfires, and danced by the blaze all
night, crowned with garlands, and
throwing flowers into the flame. At harvest time, though their crop was of the
smallest, they made an image with the
sheaves of Indian corn, and wreathed it
with autumnal garlands, and bore it
home triumphantly. But what chiefly
characterized the colonists of Merry
Mount was their veneration for the
Maypole. It has made their true history
a poet's tale. Spring decked the hallowed
emblem with young blossoms and fresh
green boughs; Summer brought roses of
the deepest blush, and the perfected
foliage of the forest; Autumn enriched
it with that red and yellow gorgeousness which converts each wildwood leaf
into a painted flower; and Winter silvered it with sleet and hung it round
with icicles till it flashed in the cold
sunshine, itself a frozen sunbeam. Thus
each alternate season did homage to the
Maypole, and paid it a tribute of its
own richest splendor. Its votaries
danced round it, once, at least, in every
month; sometimes they called it their
religion, or their altar; but always it
was the banner-staff of Merry Mount.

Unfortunately, there were men in the
New World of a sterner faith than these
Maypole worshippers. Not far from
Merry Mount was a settlement of Puritans, most dismal wretches, who said
their prayers before daylight, and then
wrought in the forest or the cornfield
till evening made it prayer time again.
Their weapons were always at hand, to

shoot down the straggling savage. When they met in conclave, it was never to keep up the old English mirth, but to hear sermons three hours long, or to proclaim bounties on the heads of wolves and the scalps of Indians. Their festivals were fast days, and their chief pastime the singing of psalms. Woe to the youth or maiden who did but dream of a dance! The selectman nodded to the constable; and there sat the light-heeled reprobate in the stocks; or if he danced, it was round the whipping-post, which might be termed the Puritan Maypole.

A party of these grim Puritans, toiling through the difficult woods, each with a horseload of iron armor to burden his footsteps, would sometimes draw near the sunny precincts of Merry Mount. There were the silken colonists, sporting round their Maypole; perhaps teaching a bear to dance, or striving to communicate their mirth to the grave Indian; or masquerading in the skins of deer and wolves, which they had hunted for that especial purpose. Often, the whole colony were playing at blindman's bluff, magistrates and all with their eyes bandaged, except a single scapegoat, whom the blinded sinners pursued by the tinkling of the bells at his garments. Once, it is said, they were seen following a flower-decked corpse, with merriment and festive music, to his grave. But did the dead man laugh? In their quietest times, they sang ballads and told tales, for the edification of their pious visitors; or perplexed them with juggling tricks; or grinned at them through horse-collars; and when sport itself grew wearisome, they made game of their own stupidity, and began a yawning match. At the very least of

these enormities, the men of iron s their heads and frowned so darkly, the revellers looked up, imagining a momentary cloud had overcast sunshine, which was to be perp there. On the other hand, the Pur affirmed, that, when a psalm was ing from their place of worship echo which the forest sent them seemed often like the chorus of a catch, closing with a roar of laug Who but the fiend, and his bond-sl the crew of Merry Mount, had disturbed them? In due time, a arose, stern and bitter on one side as serious on the other as anything be among such light spirits as sworn allegiance to the Maypole. future complexion of New Englan involved in this important qu Should the grizzly saints establish jurisdiction over the gay sinners, would their spirits darken all the and make it a land of clouded vi of hard toil, of sermon and psalm ever. But should the banner sta Merry Mount be fortunate, sun would break upon the hills, and fle would beautify the forest, and late terity do homage to the Maypole.

After these authentic passages history, we return to the nuptials Lord and Lady of the May. Alas have delayed too long, and must d our tale too suddenly. As we again at the Maypole, a solitary beam is fading from the summit leaves only a faint, golden tinge, bl with the hues of the rainbow ba Even that dim light is now withd relinquishing the whole domain of Mount to the evening gloom, whic rushed so instantaneously from black surrounding woods. But so

black shadows have rushed forth
man shape.

s, with the setting sun, the last
of mirth had passed from Merry
t. The ring of gay maskers was
dered and broken; the stag lowered
ntlers in dismay; the wolf grew
er than a lamb; the bells of the
s dancers tinkled with tremulous
ht. The Puritans had played a
cteristic part in the Maypole mum-
s. Their darksome figures were
nixed with the wild shapes of their
and made the scene a picture of
oment, when waking thoughts start
mid the scattered fantasies of a
. The leader of the hostile party
in the centre of the circle, while
out of monsters cowered around
like evil spirits in the presence of
ad magician. No fantastic foolery
look him in the face. So stern an
nergy of his aspect, that the whole
visage, frame, and soul, seemed
ght of iron, gifted with life and
ht, yet all of one substance with
eadpiece and breastplate. It was
uritan of Puritans; it was Endicott
lf!

and off, priest of Baal!" said he,
a grim frown, and laying no rever-
and upon the surplice. "I know
Blackstone! * Thou art the man.
couldst not abide the rule even of
own corrupted church, and hast
hither to preach iniquity, and to
example of it in thy life. But now
it be seen that the Lord hath sanc-
this wilderness for his peculiar
e. Woe unto them that would de-

d Governor Endicott speak less posi-
we should suspect a mistake here. The
Mr. Blackstone, though an eccentric, is
own to have been an immoral man. We
doubt his identity with the priest of
Mount.

file it! And first for this flower-decked
abomination, the altar of thy worship!"

And with his keen sword, Endicott
assaulted the hallowed Maypole. Nor
long did it resist his arm. It groaned
with a dismal sound; it showered leaves
and rosebuds upon the remorseless enthusiast; and finally, with all its green
boughs, and ribbons, and flowers, symbolic of departed pleasures, down fell
the banner staff of Merry Mount. As it
sank, tradition says, the evening sky
grew darker, and the woods threw forth
a more sombre shadow.

"There," cried Endicott, looking triumphantly on his work, "there lies the
only Maypole in New England! The
thought is strong within me, that by its
fall is shadowed forth the fate of light
and idle mirthmakers, amongst us
and our posterity. Amen, saith John
Endicott."

"Amen!" echoed his followers.

But the votaries of the Maypole gave
one groan for their idol. At the sound,
the Puritan leader glanced at the crew
of Comus, each a figure of broad mirth,
yet, at this moment, strangely expressive of sorrow and dismay.

"Valiant captain," quoth Peter Palfrey, the Ancient of the band, "what
order shall be taken with the prisoners?"

"I thought not to repent me of cutting
down a Maypole," replied Endicott,
"yet now I could find in my heart to
plant it again, and give each of these
bestial pagans one other dance round
their idol. It would have served rarely
for a whipping-post!"

"But there are pine-trees enow," suggested the lieutenant.

"True, good Ancient," said the leader.
"Wherefore, bind the heathen crew, and
bestow on them a small matter of

stripes apiece, as earnest of our future justice. Set some of the rogues in the stocks to rest themselves, so soon as Providence shall bring us to one of our own well-ordered settlements, where such accommodations may be found. Further penalties, such as branding and cropping of ears, shall be thought of hereafter."

"How many stripes for the priest?" inquired Ancient Palfrey.

"None as yet," answered Endicott, bending his iron frown upon the culprit. "It must be for the Great and General Court to determine, whether stripes and long imprisonment, and other grievous penalty, may atone for his transgressions. Let him look to himself! For such as violate our civil order, it may be permitted us to show mercy. But woe to the wretch that troubleth our religion!"

"And this dancing bear," resumed the officer. "Must he share the stripes of his fellows?"

"Shoot him through the head!" said the energetic Puritan. "I suspect witchcraft in the beast."

"Here be a couple of shining ones," continued Peter Palfrey, pointing his weapon at the Lord and Lady of the May. "They seem to be of high station among these misdoers. Methinks their dignity will not be fitted with less than a double share of stripes."

Endicott rested on his sword, and closely surveyed the dress and aspect of the hapless pair. There they stood, pale, downcast, and apprehensive. Yet there was an air of mutual support, and of pure affection, seeking aid and giving it, that showed them to be man and wife, with the sanction of the priest upon their love. The youth, in the peril of the moment, had dropped his gilded staff, and thrown his arm about the of the May, who leaned against breast, too lightly to burden him with weight enough to express that destinies were linked together, for or evil. They looked first at each and then into the grim captain's There they stood, in the first ho wedlock, while the idle pleasure which their companions were the blems, had given place to the ste care of life, personified by the Puritans. But never had their you beauty seemed so pure and high, as its glow was chastened by adversit

"Youth," said Endicott, "ye sta an evil case, thou and thy maiden Make ready presently; for I am m that ye shall both have a token t member your wedding-day!"

"Stern man," cried the May "how can I move thee? Were the r at hand, I would resist to the Being powerless, I entreat! Do wit as thou wilt, but let Edith go touched!"

"Not so," replied the immiti zealot. "We are not wont to sho idle courtesy to that sex, whicl quireth the stricter discipline. sayest thou, maid? Shall thy bridegroom suffer thy share of penalty besides his own?"

"Be it death," said Edith, "and all on me!"

Truly, as Endicott had said, the lovers stood in a woful case. Thei were triumphant, their friends c and abased, their home desolate benighted wilderness around them a rigorous destiny, in the shape c Puritan leader, their only guide. Y deepening twilight could not alto conceal that the iron man was soft niled at the fair spectacle of early he almost sighed for the inevitable t of early hopes.

'he troubles of life have come ly on this young couple," observed cott. "We will see how they com- themselves under their present , ere we burden them with greater. mong the spoil, there be any gar- s of a more decent fashion, let be put upon this May Lord and Lady, instead of their glistening ies. Look to it, some of you."

nd shall not the youth's hair be ' asked Peter Palfrey, looking with rrence at the love-lock and long y curls of the young man.

'rop it forthwith, and that in the pumpkin-shell fashion," answered captain. "Then bring them along us, but more gently than their fel- There be qualities in the youth n may make him valiant to fight, sober to toil, and pious to pray; n the maiden, that may fit her to ne a mother in our Israel, bringing up babes in better nurture than her own hath been. Nor think ye, young ones, that they are the happiest, even in our lifetime of a moment, who misspend it in dancing round a Maypole!"

And Endicott, the severest Puritan of all who laid the rock foundation of New England, lifted the wreath of roses from the ruin of the Maypole, and threw it, with his own gauntleted hand, over the heads of the Lord and Lady of the May. It was a deed of prophecy. As the moral gloom of the world overpowers all sys- tematic gayety, even so was their home of wild mirth made desolate amid the sad forest. They returned to it no more. But as their flowering garland was wreathed of the brightest roses that had grown there, so in the tie that united them were intertwined all the purest and best of their early joys. They went heavenward, supporting each other along the difficult path which it was their lot to tread, and never wasted one regretful thought on the vanities of Merry Mount.

THE GENTLE BOY

the course of the year 1656, sev- of the people called Quakers, led, as professed, by the inward movement e spirit, made their appearance in England. Their reputation, as rs of mystic and pernicious prin- s, having spread before them, the ans early endeavored to banish, and event the further intrusion of the sect. But the measures by which s intended to purge the land of y, though more than sufficiently vigorous, were entirely unsuccessful. The Quakers, esteeming persecution as a divine call to the post of danger, laid claim to a holy courage, unknown to the Puritans themselves, who had shunned the cross, by providing for the peaceable exercise of their religion in a distant wilderness. Though it was the singular fact, that every nation of the earth re- jected the wandering enthusiasts who practised peace towards all men, the place of greatest uneasiness and peril, and therefore, in their eyes the most eligible, was the province of Massachusetts Bay.

The fines, imprisonments, and stripes, liberally distributed by our pious forefathers; the popular antipathy, so strong that it endured nearly a hundred years after actual persecution had ceased, were attractions as powerful for the Quakers, as peace, honor, and reward would have been for the worldly-minded. Every European vessel brought new cargoes of the sect, eager to testify against the oppression which they hoped to share; and, when shipmasters were restrained by heavy fines from affording them passage, they made long and circuitous journeys through the Indian country, and appeared in the province as if conveyed by a supernatural power. Their enthusiasm, heightened almost to madness by the treatment which they received, produced actions contrary to the rules of decency, as well as of rational religion, and presented a singular contrast to the calm and staid deportment of their sectarian successors of the present day. The command of the spirit, inaudible except to the soul, and not to be controverted on grounds of human wisdom, was made a plea for most indecorous exhibitions, which, abstractedly considered, well deserved the moderate chastisement of the rod. These extravagances, and the persecution which was at once their cause and consequence, continued to increase, till, in the year 1659, the government of Massachusetts Bay indulged two members of the Quaker sect with the crown of martyrdom.

An indelible stain of blood is upon the hands of all who consented to this act, but a large share of the awful re-

sponsibility must rest upon the pe then at the head of the government was a man of narrow mind and perfect education, and his uncompr ing bigotry was made hot and mis vous by violent and hasty passions exerted his influence indecorously unjustifiably to compass the deat the enthusiasts; and his whole con in respect to them, was marke brutal cruelty. The Quakers, whos vengeful feelings were not less dee cause they were inactive, rememb this man and his associates in times. The historian of the sect af that, by the wrath of Heaven, a b fall upon the land in the vicinity o "bloody town" of Boston, so tha wheat would grow there; and he his stand, as it were, among the g of the ancient persecutors, and triu antly recounts the judgments that took them, in old age or at the pa hour. He tells us that they died denly, and violently, and in mad but nothing can exceed the mockery with which he records loathsome disease, and "death rottenness," of the fierce and governor.

*   *   *   *   *

On the evening of the autumn that had witnessed the martyrdo two men of the Quaker persuasi Puritan settler was returning fro metropolis to the neighboring co town in which he resided. The ai cool, the sky clear, and the ling twilight was made brighter by the of a young moon, which had now r reached the verge of the horizon. traveller, a man of middle age, wr in a gray frieze cloak, quickene pace when he reached the outski

own, for a gloomy extent of nearly
miles lay between him and his
e. The low, straw-thatched houses
scattered at considerable intervals
g the road, and the country having
settled but about thirty years, the
s of original forest still bore no
l proportion to the cultivated
nd. The autumn wind wandered
ng the branches, whirling away the
es from all except the pine trees,
noaning as if it lamented the deso-
n of which it was the instrument.
road had penetrated the mass of
ls that lay nearest to the town, and
just emerging into an open space,
. the traveller's ears were saluted
sound more mournful than even
of the wind. It was like the wailing
ome one in distress, and it seemed
oceed from beneath a tall and lone-
-tree, in the centre of a cleared, but
closed and uncultivated field. The
an could not but remember that
was the very spot, which had been
accursed a few hours before, by
execution of the Quakers, whose
es had been thrown together into
hasty grave, beneath the tree on
n they suffered. He struggled, how-
against the superstitious fears
n belonged to the age, and com-
d himself to pause and listen.

'he voice is most likely mortal, nor
I cause to tremble if it be other-
" thought he, straining his eyes
gh the dim moonlight. "Methinks
like the wailing of a child; some
t, it may be, which has strayed
its mother, and chanced upon this
of death. For the ease of mine
conscience, I must search this mat-
ut."

therefore left the path, and walked

somewhat fearfully across the field.
Though now so desolate, its soil was
pressed down and trampled by the thousand footsteps of those who had witnessed the spectacle of that day, all of
whom had now retired, leaving the
dead to their loneliness. The traveller
at length reached the fir-tree, which
from the middle upward was covered
with living branches, although a scaffold
had been erected beneath, and other
preparations made for the work of
death. Under this unhappy tree, which
in after times was believed to drop
poison with its dew, sat the one solitary
mourner for innocent blood. It was a
slender and light clad little boy, who
leaned his face upon a hillock of fresh-
turned and half-frozen earth, and wailed
bitterly, yet in a suppressed tone, as if
his grief might receive the punishment
of crime. The Puritan, whose approach
had been unperceived, laid his hand upon
the child's shoulder, and addressed him
compassionately.

"You have chosen a dreary lodging,
my poor boy, and no wonder that you
weep," said he. "But dry your eyes, and
tell me where your mother dwells. I
promise you if the journey be not too
far, I will leave you in her arms to-
night."

The boy had hushed his wailing at
once, and turned his face upward to the
stranger. It was a pale, bright-eyed
countenance, certainly not more than
six years old, but sorrow, fear, and want
had destroyed much of its infantile expression. The Puritan, seeing the boy's
frightened gaze, and feeling that he
trembled under his hand, endeavored to
reassure him.

"Nay, if I intended to do you harm,
little lad, the readiest way were to leave

you here. What! you do not fear to sit beneath the gallows on a new-made grave, and yet you tremble at a friend's touch. Take heart, child, and tell me what is your name, and where is your home?"

"Friend," replied the little boy, in a sweet, though faltering voice, "they call me Ilbrahim, and my home is here."

The pale, spiritual face, the eyes that seemed to mingle with the moonlight, the sweet, airy voice, and the outlandish name, almost made the Puritan believe that the boy was in truth a being which had sprung up out of the grave on which he sat. But perceiving that the apparition stood the test of a short mental prayer, and remembering that the arm which he had touched was life-like, he adopted a more rational supposition. "The poor child is stricken in his intellect," thought he, "but verily his words are fearful, in a place like this." He then spoke soothingly, intending to humor the boy's fantasy.

"Your home will scarce be comfortable, Ilbrahim, this cold autumn night, and I fear you are ill provided with food. I am hastening to a warm supper and bed, and if you will go with me, you shall share them!"

"I thank thee, friend, but though I be hungry, and shivering with cold, thou wilt not give me food nor lodging," replied the boy, in the quiet tone which despair had taught him, even so young. "My father was of the people whom all men hate. They have laid him under this heap of earth, and here is my home."

The Puritan, who had laid hold of little Ilbrahim's hand, relinquished it as if he were touching a loathsome reptile. But he possessed a compassionate heart, which not even religious prejudice

could harden into stone.

"God forbid that I should leave child to perish, though he comes of accursed sect," said he to himself. we not all spring from an evil root? we not all in darkness till the doth shine upon us? He shall not pe neither in body, nor, if prayer and struction may avail for him, in s He then spoke aloud and kindly Ilbrahim, who had again hid his in the cold earth of the grave. " every door in the land shut against my child, that you have wandere this unhallowed spot?"

"They drove me forth from the p when they took my father thence," the boy, "and I stood afar off, wat the crowd of people, and when were gone I came hither, and found this grave. I knew that my father sleeping here, and I said, This sha my home."

"No, child, no; not while I ha roof over my head or a morsel to with you!" exclaimed the Puritan, w sympathies were now fully ex "Rise up and come with me, and not any harm."

The boy wept afresh, and clung t heap of earth, as if the cold hear neath it were warmer to him than in a living breast. The traveller, ever, continued to entreat him ten and, seeming to acquire some degr confidence, he at length arose. Bu slender limbs tottered with weak his little head grew dizzy, and he l against the tree of death for suppo

"My poor boy, are you so fee said the Puritan. "When did you food last?"

"I ate of bread and water wit father in the prison," replied Ilbra

t they brought him none neither yes-
¡ay nor to-day, saying that he had
·n enough to bear him to his jour-
's end. Trouble not thyself for my
ger, kind friend, for I have lacked
l many times ere now."

he traveller took the child in his
s and wrapped his cloak about him,
e his heart stirred with shame and
·r against the gratuitous cruelty of
instruments in this persecution. In
awakened warmth of his feelings he
lved that, at whatever risk, he would
forsake the poor little defenceless
g whom Heaven had confided to his
. With this determination he left
accursed field and resumed the
eward path from which the wailing
¡e boy had called him. The light and
onless burden scarcely impeded his
ress, and he soon beheld the fire
from the windows of the cottage
h he, a native of a distant clime,
built in the Western wilderness.
as surrounded by a considerable ex-
of cultivated ground, and the dwell-
was situated in the nook of a
l-covered hill, whither it seemed to
crept for protection.

.ook up, child," said the Puritan to
him, whose faint head had sunk
his shoulder, "there is our home."
the word "home" a thrill passed
¡gh the child's frame, but he con-
d silent. A few moments brought
to the cottage door, at which the
r knocked; for at that early period,
¡ savages were wandering every-
e among the settlers, bolt and bar
indispensable to the security of the
ling. The summons was answered
, bond-servant, a coarse-clad and
featured piece of humanity, who,
ascertaining that his master was

the applicant, undid the door, and held
a flaring pine-knot torch to light him in.
Farther back in the passage-way, the
red blaze discovered a matronly woman,
but no little crowd of children came
bounding forth to greet their father's
return. As the Puritan entered he thrust
aside his cloak, and displayed Ilbrahim's
face to the female.

"Dorothy, here is a little outcast
whom Providence hath put into our
hands," observed he. "Be kind to him,
even as if he were of those dear ones
who have departed from us."

"What pale and bright-eyed little boy
is this, Tobias?" she inquired. "Is he
one whom the wilderness folk have
ravished from some Christian mother?"

"No, Dorothy, this poor child is no
captive from the wilderness," he replied.
"The heathen savage would have given
him to eat of his scanty morsel, and
to drink of his birchen cup; but Christian men, alas! had cast him out to die."

Then he told her how he had found
him beneath the gallows, upon his
father's grave; and how his heart had
prompted him, like the speaking of an
inward voice, to take the little outcast
home, and be kind unto him. He acknowledged his resolution to feed and
clothe him as if he were his own child,
and to afford him the instruction which
should counteract the pernicious errors
hitherto instilled into his infant mind.
Dorothy was gifted with even a quicker
tenderness than her husband, and she
approved of all his doings and intentions.

"Have you a mother, dear child?" she
inquired.

The tears burst forth from his full
heart as he attempted to reply; but
Dorothy at length understood that he

had a mother, who, like the rest of her sect, was a persecuted wanderer. She had been taken from the prison a short time before, carried into the uninhabited wilderness, and left to perish there by hunger or wild beasts. This was no uncommon method of disposing of the Quakers, and they were accustomed to boast that the inhabitants of the desert were more hospitable to them than civilized man.

"Fear not, little boy, you shall not need a mother, and a kind one," said Dorothy, when she had gathered this information. "Dry your tears, Ilbrahim, and be my child, as I will be your mother."

The good woman prepared the little bed from which her own children had successively been borne to another resting-place. Before Ilbrahim would consent to occupy it, he knelt down, and as Dorothy listened to his simple and affecting prayer, she marvelled how the parents that had taught it to him could have been judged worthy of death. When the boy had fallen asleep, she bent over his pale and spiritual countenance, pressed a kiss upon his white brow, drew the bed-clothes up about his neck, and went away with a pensive gladness in her heart.

Tobias Pearson was not among the earliest emigrants from the old country. He had remained in England during the first years of the civil war, in which he had borne some share as a cornet of dragoons, under Cromwell. But when the ambitious designs of his leader began to develop themselves, he quitted the army of the Parliament and sought a refuge from the strife, which was no longer holy, among the people of his persuasion in the colony of Massachu-

setts. A more worldly consideration perhaps, an influence in drawing thither; for New England offered vantages to men of unprosperous tunes as well as to dissatisfied relig ists, and Pearson had hitherto foun difficult to provide for a wife and creasing family. To this supposed purity of motive, the more big Puritans were inclined to impute removal by death of all the children whose earthly good the father had overthoughtful. They had left their tive country blooming like roses, like roses they had perished in a for soil. Those expounders of the way Providence, who had thus judged brother, and attributed his dome sorrows to his sin, were not more c table when they saw him and Dor endeavoring to fill up the void in hearts by the adoption of an infan the accursed sect. Nor did they fa communicate their disapprobation Tobias; but the latter, in reply, me pointed at the little, quiet, lovely whose appearance and deportment indeed as powerful arguments as c possibly have been adduced in his favor. Even his beauty, however, his winning manners, sometimes duced an effect ultimately unfavora for the bigots, when the outer sur of their iron hearts had been soft and again grew hard, affirmed tha merely natural cause could have worked upon them.

Their antipathy to the poor in was also increased by the ill succes divers theological discussions, in w it was attempted to convince him o errors of his sect. Ilbrahim, it is was not a skilful controversialist; the feeling of his religion was stro

inct in him, and he could neither be
ced nor driven from the faith which
father had died for. The odium of
stubbornness was shared in a great
sure by the child's protectors, inso-
ch that Tobias and Dorothy very
rtly began to experience a most bit-
species of persecution, in the cold
rds of many a friend whom they had
ed. The common people manifested
r opinions more openly. Pearson was
an of some consideration, being a
esentative to the General Court, and
approved lieutenant in the train-
ds, yet within a week after his adop-
of Ilbrahim, he had been both
ed and hooted. Once, also, when
king through a solitary piece of
ds, he heard a loud voice from some
sible speaker; and it cried, "What
be done to the backslider? Lo! the
rge is knotted for him, even the
of nine cords, and every cord three
s!" These insults irritated Pearson's
er for the moment; they entered
into his heart, and became imper-
ible but powerful workers towards
nd, which his most secret thought
not yet whispered.

*   *   *   *   *   *

the second Sabbath after Ilbrahim
me a member of their family, Pear-
and his wife deemed it proper that
hould appear with them at public
hip. They had anticipated some op-
ion to this measure from the boy,
he prepared himself in silence, and
e appointed hour was clad in the
mourning suit which Dorothy had
ght for him. As the parish was
and during many subsequent years,
ovided with a bell, the signal for
commencement of religious exer-
was the beat of a drum. At the

first sound of that martial call to the
place of holy and quiet thoughts, Tobias
and Dorothy set forth, each holding a
hand of little Ilbrahim, like two parents
linked together by the infant of their
love. On their path through the leafless
woods, they were overtaken by many
persons of their acquaintance, all of
whom avoided them, and passed by on
the other side; but a severer trial
awaited their constancy when they had
descended the hill, and drew near the
pine-built and undecorated house of
prayer. Around the door, from which
the drummer still sent forth his thundering summons, was drawn up a formidable phalanx, including several of
the oldest members of the congregation,
many of the middle aged, and nearly
all the younger males. Pearson found it
difficult to sustain their united and disapproving gaze, but Dorothy, whose
mind was differently circumstanced,
merely drew the boy closer to her, and
faltered not in her approach. As they
entered the door, they overheard the
muttered sentiments of the assemblage,
and when the reviling voices of the little
children smote Ilbrahim's ear, he wept.

The interior aspect of the meeting-
house was rude. The low ceiling, the un-
plastered walls, the naked woodwork,
and the undraperied pulpit, offered
nothing to excite the devotion, which,
without such external aids, often remains latent in the heart. The floor of
the building was occupied by rows of
long, cushionless benches, supplying the
place of pews, and the broad aisle
formed a sexual division, impassable except by children beneath a certain age.

Pearson and Dorothy separated at the
door of the meeting-house, and Ilbrahim, being within the years of infancy

was retained under the care of the latter. The wrinkled beldams involved themselves in their rusty cloaks as he passed by; even the mild-featured maidens seemed to dread contamination; and many a stern old man arose, and turned his repulsive and unheavenly countenance upon the gentle boy, as if the sanctuary were polluted by his presence. He was a sweet infant of the skies, that had strayed away from his home, and all the inhabitants of this miserable world closed up their impure hearts against him, drew back their earth-soiled garments from his touch, and said, "We are holier than thou."

Ilbrahim, seated by the side of his adopted mother, and retaining fast hold of her hand, assumed a grave and decorous demeanor, such as might befit a person of matured taste and understanding, who should find himself in a temple dedicated to some worship which he did not recognize, but felt himself bound to respect. The exercises had not yet commenced, however, when the boy's attention was arrested by an event, apparently of trifling interest. A woman, having her face muffled in a hood, and a cloak drawn completely about her form, advancing slowly up the broad aisle, and took a place upon the foremost bench. Ilbrahim's faint color varied, his nerves fluttered, he was unable to turn his eyes from the muffled female.

When the preliminary prayer and hymn were over, the minister arose, and having turned the hour-glass which stood by the great Bible, commenced his discourse. He was now well-stricken in years, a man of pale, thin countenance, and his gray hairs were closely covered by a black-velvet skullcap. In his

younger days he had practically lear[n]
the meaning of persecution from A[rch]
bishop Laud, and he was not now [dis]
posed to forget the lesson against w[hich]
he had murmured then. Introducing [the]
often discussed subject of the Quak[ers,]
he gave a history of that sect, an[d a]
description of their tenets, in w[hich]
error predominated, and prejudice [dis]
torted the aspect of what was true. [He]
adverted to the recent measures in [the]
province, and cautioned his hearers [in]
weaker parts against calling in ques[tion]
the just severity, which God-fea[ring]
magistrates had at length been c[om]
pelled to exercise. He spoke of [the]
danger of pity, in some cases a c[om]
mendable and Christian virtue, but [not]
applicable to this pernicious sect. [He]
observed that such was their devi[lish]
obstinacy in error, that even the li[ttle]
children, the sucking babes, were ha[rd]
ened and desperate heretics. He affir[med]
that no man, without Heaven's espe[cial]
warrant, should attempt their con[ver]
sion, lest while he lent his hand to d[raw]
them from the slough, he should [him]
self be precipitated into its low[est]
depths.

The sands of the second hour w[ere]
principally in the lower half of the g[lass]
when the sermon concluded. An app[rov]
ing murmur followed, and the cle[rgy]
man, having given out a hymn, took [his]
seat with much self-congratulation, [and]
endeavored to read the effect of [his]
eloquence in the visages of the pe[ople.]
But while voices from all parts of [the]
house were tuning themselves to sin[g, a]
scene occurred, which, though not [un]
unusual at that period in the prov[ince,]
happened to be without preceden[t in]
this parish.

The muffled female, who had hith[erto]

motionless in the front rank of the
ence, now arose, and with slow,
ely, and unwavering step, ascended
pulpit stairs. The quiverings of inent harmony were hushed, and the
he sat in speechless and almost terri-
astonishment, while she undid the
, and stood up in the sacred desk
1 which his maledictions had just
thundered. She then divested her-
of the cloak and hood, and appeared
most singular array. A shapeless
of sackcloth was girded about her
t with a knotted cord; her raven
fell down upon her shoulders, and
lackness was defiled by pale streaks
shes, which she had strown upon
head. Her eyebrows, dark and
ngly defined, added to the deathly
eness of a countenance, which,
ciated with want, and wild with en-
iasm and strange sorrows, retained
race of earlier beauty. This figure
d gazing earnestly on the audience,
there was no sound, nor any move-
t, except a faint shuddering which
y man observed in his neighbor, but
scarcely conscious of in himself. At
h, when her fit of inspiration came,
spoke, for the first few moments, in
w voice, and not invariably distinct
ance. Her discourse gave evidence
n imagination hopelessly entangled
her reason; it was a vague and in-
prehensible rhapsody, which, how-
, seemed to spread its own atmos-
e round the hearer's soul, and to
e his feelings by some influence un-
ected with the words. As she pro-
ed, beautiful but shadowy images
d sometimes be seen, like bright
s moving in a turbid river; or
rong and singularly-shaped idea
d forth, and seized at once on the

understanding or the heart. But the
course of her unearthly eloquence soon
led her to the persecutions of her sect,
and from thence the step was short to
her own peculiar sorrows. She was
naturally a woman of mighty passions,
and hatred and revenge now wrapped
themselves in the garb of piety; the
character of her speech was changed,
her images became distinct though wild,
and her denunciations had an almost
hellish bitterness.

"The Governor and his mighty men,"
she said, "have gathered together, taking counsel among themselves and saying, 'What shall we do unto this people,
—even unto the people that have come
into this land to put our iniquity to the
blush?' And lo! the Devil entereth into
the council-chamber, like a lame man
of low stature and gravely apparelled,
with a dark and twisted countenance,
and a bright, downcast eye. And he
standeth up among the rulers; yea, he
goeth to and fro, whispering to each;
and every man lends his ear, for his
word is 'slay, slay!' But I say unto ye,
Woe to them that slay! Woe to them
that shed the blood of saints! Woe to
them that have slain the husband, and
cast forth the child, the tender infant, to
wander homeless and hungry and cold,
till he die; and have saved the mother
alive, in the cruelty of their tender
mercies! Woe to them in their lifetime,
cursed are they in the delight and pleasure of their hearts! Woe to them in their
death hour, whether it come swiftly
with blood and violence, or after long
and lingering pain! Woe, in the dark
house, in the rottenness of the grave,
when the children's children shall revile
the ashes of the fathers! Woe, woe, woe,
at the judgment, when all the persecuted

and all the slain in this bloody land, and the father, the mother, and the child, shall await them in a day that they cannot escape! Seed of the faith, seed of the faith, yet whose hearts are moving with a power that ye know not, arise, wash your hands of this innocent blood! Life your voices, chosen ones, cry aloud, and call down a woe and a judgment with me!"

Having thus given vent to the flood of malignity which she mistook for inspiration, the speaker was silent. Her voice was succeeded by the hysteric shrieks of several women, but the feelings of the audience generally had not been drawn onward in the current with her own. They remained stupefied, stranded as it were, in the midst of a torrent, which deafened them by its roaring, but might not move them by its violence. The clergyman, who could not hitherto have ejected the usurper of his pulpit otherwise than by bodily force, now addressed her in the tone of just indignation and legitimate authority.

"Get you down, woman, from the holy place which you profane," he said. "Is it to the Lord's house that you come to pour forth the foulness of your heart, and the inspiration of the Devil? Get you down, and remember that the sentence of death is on you; yea, and shall be executed, were it but for this day's work."

"I go, friend, I go, for the voice hath had its utterance," replied she, in a depressed and even mild tone. "I have done my mission unto thee and to thy people. Reward me with stripes, imprisonment, or death, as ye shall be permitted."

The weakness of exhausted passion caused her steps to totter as she scended the pulpit stairs. The people the mean while, were stirring to and on the floor of the house, whispe among themselves, and glancing tow the intruder. Many of them now re nized her as the woman who had saulted the governor with frightful guage, as he passed by the window her prison; they knew, also, that was adjudged to suffer death, and been preserved only by an involun banishment into the wilderness. new outrage, by which she had prove her fate, seemed to render fur lenity impossible; and a gentleman military dress, with a stout man of ferior rank, drew towards the doo the meeting-house, and awaited her proach. Scarcely did her feet press floor, however, when an unexpe scene occurred. In that moment of peril, when every eye frowned death, a little timid boy pressed fo and threw his arms round his mother

"I am here, mother, it is I, and I go with thee to prison," he exclaime

She gazed at him with a doub and almost frightened expression, she knew that the boy had been cast to perish, and she had not hoped to his face again. She feared, perhaps, it was but one of the happy visions, which her excited fancy had often ceived her, in the solitude of the des or in prison. But when she felt his h warm within her own, and heard little eloquence of childish love, she gan to know that she was yet a mot

"Blessed art thou, my son," sobbed. "My heart was withered; dead with thee and with thy father; now it leaps as in the first moment w I pressed thee to my bosom."

he knelt down and embraced him
in and again, while the joy that
ld find no words, expressed itself in
ken accents, like the bubbles gushing
to vanish at the surface of a deep
ntain. The sorrows of past years, and
darker peril that was nigh, cast not
adow on the brightness of that fleet-
moment. Soon, however, the spec-
rs saw a change upon her face, as
consciousness of her sad estate re-
ned, and grief supplied the fount of
s which joy had opened. By the
ds she uttered, it would seem that
indulgence of natural love had given
mind a momentary sense of its
rs, and made her know how far
had strayed from duty, in following
dictates of a wild fanaticism.
In a doleful hour art thou returned
me, poor boy," she said, "for thy
her's path has gone darkening on-
d, till now the end is death. Son,
I have borne thee in my arms when
limbs were tottering, and I have
thee with the food that I was faint-
for; yet I have ill performed a
her's part by thee in life, and now
ave thee no inheritance but woe and
ne. Thou wilt go seeking through
world, and find all hearts closed
nst thee, and their sweet affections
ed to bitterness for my sake. My
l, my child, how many a pang awaits
gentle spirit, and I the cause of all!"
ne hid her face on Ilbrahim's head,
her long, raven hair, discolored with
ashes of her mourning, fell down
t him like a veil. A low and inter-
ed moan was the voice of her
t's anguish, and it did not fail to
e the sympathies of many who mis-
their involuntary virtue for a sin.
s were audible in the female section

of the house, and every man who was
a father drew his hand across his eyes.
Tobias Pearson was agitated and uneasy,
but a certain feeling like the consciousness of guilt oppressed him, so that he
could not go forth and offer himself as
the protector of the child. Dorothy,
however, had watched her husband's
eye. Her mind was free from the influence that had begun to work on his,
and she drew near the Quaker woman,
and addressed her in the hearing of all
the congregation.

"Stranger, trust this boy to me, and
I will be his mother," she said, taking
Ilbrahim's hand. "Providence has sig-
nally marked out my husband to protect
him, and he has fed at our table and
lodged under our roof, now many days,
till our hearts have grown very strongly
unto him. Leave the tender child with
us, and be at ease concerning his welfare."

The Quaker rose from the ground,
but drew the boy closer to her, while
she gazed earnestly in Dorothy's face.
Her mild, but saddened features, and
neat matronly attire, harmonized together, and were like a verse of fireside
poetry. Her very aspect proved that she
was blameless, so far as mortal could
be so, in respect to God and man; while
the enthusiast, in her robe of sackcloth
and girdle of knotted cord, had as evidently violated the duties of the present
life and the future, by fixing her attention wholly on the latter. The two
females, as they held each a hand of
Ilbrahim, formed a practical allegory;
it was rational piety and unbridled
fanaticism, contending for the empire
of a young heart.

"Thou art not of our people," said
the Quaker, mournfully.

"No we are not of your people," replied Dorothy, with mildness, "but we
are Christians, looking upward to the
same Heaven with you. Doubt not that
your boy shall meet you there, if there
be a blessing on our tender and prayer-
ful guidance of him. Thither, I trust, my
own children have gone before me, for
I also have been a mother. I am no
longer so," she added, in a faltering
tone, "and your son will have all my
care."

"But will ye lead him in the path
which his parents have trodden?" demanded the Quaker. "Can ye teach him
the enlightened faith which his father
has died for, and for which I, even I,
am soon to become an unworthy martyr? The boy has been baptized in
blood; will ye keep the mark fresh and
ruddy upon his forehead?"

"I will not deceive you," answered
Dorothy. "If your child become our
child, we must breed him up in the instruction which Heaven has imparted to
us; we must pray for him the prayers
of our own faith; we must do towards
him according to the dictates of our
own consciences, and not of yours. Were
we to act otherwise, we should abuse
your trust, even in complying with your
wishes."

The mother looked down upon her
boy with a troubled countenance, and
then turned her eyes upward to heaven.
She seemed to pray internally, and the
contention of her soul was evident.

"Friend," she said at length to Dorothy, "I doubt not that my son shall
receive all earthly tenderness at thy
hands. Nay, I will believe that even thy
imperfect lights may guide him to a
better world; for surely thou art on
the path thither. But thou hast spoken

of a husband. Doth he stand here am[ong]
this multitude of people? Let him co[me]
forth, for I must know to whom I c[om]
mit this most precious trust."

She turned her face upon the m[ute]
auditors, and after a momentary de[lay]
Tobias Pearson came forth from am[ong]
them. The Quaker saw the dress wh[ich]
marked his military rank, and shook [her]
head; but then she noted the hesita[ting]
air, the eyes that struggled with [his]
own, and were vanquished; the c[olor]
that went and came, and could find [no]
resting-place. As she gazed an unmi[rth]
ful smile spread over her features, [like]
sunshine that grows melancholy in s[ome]
desolate spot. Her lips moved inaudi[bly,]
but at length she spake.

"I hear it, I hear it. The voice spe[ak]
eth within me and saith, 'Leave [thy]
child, Catharine, for his place is h[ere,]
and go hence, for I have other work [for]
thee. Break the bonds of natural a[ffec]
tion, martyr thy love, and know tha[t]
all these things eternal wisdom hath [its]
ends.' I go, friends, I go. Take ye [my]
boy, my precious jewel. I go he[nce,]
trusting that all shall be well, and [that]
even for his infant hands there is a l[abor]
in the vineyard."

She knelt down and whispered [to]
Ilbrahim, who at first struggled [and]
clung to his mother, with sobs and te[ars,]
but remained passive when she
kissed his cheek and arisen from [the]
ground. Having held her hands ove[r his]
head in mental prayer, she was read[y to]
depart.

"Farewell, friends in mine extrem[ity,"]
she said to Pearson and his wife; "[the]
good deed ye have done me is a trea[sure]
laid up in Heaven, to be return[ed a]
thousand-fold hereafter. And far[ewell]
ye, mine enemies, to whom it is

mitted to harm so much as a hair of
head, nor to stay my footsteps even
a moment. The day is coming when
shall call upon me to witness for ye
this one sin uncommitted, and I will
up and answer."

he turned her steps towards the
r, and the men, who had stationed
nselves to guard it, withdrew, and
ered her to pass. A general senti-
t of pity overcame the virulence of
gious hatred. Sanctified by her love
her affliction, she went forth, and
the people gazed after her till she
journeyed up the hill, and was lost
ind its brow. She went, the apostle
er own unquiet heart, to renew the
derings of past years. For her voice
been already heard in many lands
Christendom; and she had pined in
cells of a Catholic Inquisition, be-
she felt the lash, and lay in the
geons of the Puritans. Her mission
extended also to the followers of
Prophet, and from them she had re-
ed the courtesy and kindness which
the contending sects of our purer
gion united to deny her. Her hus-
d and herself had resided many
ths in Turkey, where even the Sul-
s countenance was gracious to them;
hat pagan land, too, was Ilbrahim's
place, and his Oriental name was
ark of gratitude for the good deeds
n unbeliever.

 *   *   *   *   *   *

hen Pearson and his wife had thus
ired all the rights over Ilbrahim
could be delegated, their affection
him became, like the memory of
r native land, or their mild sorrow
the dead, a piece of the immovable
iture of their hearts. The boy, also,
r a week or two of mental disquiet,

began to gratify his protectors by many
inadvertent proofs that he considered
them as parents, and their house as
home. Before the winter snows were
melted, the persecuted infant, the little
wanderer from a remote and heathen
country, seemed native in the New England cottage, and inseparable from the
warmth and security of its hearth.
Under the influence of kind treatment,
and in the consciousness that he was
loved, Ilbrahim's demeanor lost a premature manliness, which had resulted
from his earlier situation; he became
more childlike, and his natural character
displayed itself with freedom. It was in
many respects a beautiful one, yet the
disordered imagination of both his father
and mother had perhaps propagated a
certain unhealthiness in the mind of the
boy. In his general state, Ilbrahim
would derive enjoyment from the most
trifling events, and from every object
about him; he seemed to discover rich
treasures of happiness, by a faculty
analogous to that of the witch hazel,
which points to hidden gold where all
is barren to the eye His airy gayety,
coming to him from a thousand sources,
communicated itself to the family, and
Ilbrahim was like a domesticated sunbeam, brightening moody countenances,
and chasing away the gloom from the
dark corners of the cottage.

On the other hand, as the suscepti-
bility of pleasure is also that of pain,
the exuberant cheerfulness of the boy's
prevailing temper sometimes yielded to
moments of deep depression. His sorrows could not always be followed up to
their original source, but most frequently they appeared to flow, though
Ilbrahim was young to be sad for such
a cause, from wounded love. The flighti-

ness of his mirth rendered him often guilty of offences against the decorum of a Puritan household, and on these occasions he did not invariably escape rebuke. But the slightest word of real bitterness, which he was infallible in distinguishing from pretended anger, seemed to sink into his heart and poison all his enjoyments, till he became sensible that he was entirely forgiven. Of the malice, which generally accompanies a superfluity of sensitiveness, Ilbrahim was altogether destitute; when trodden upon, he would not turn; when wounded, he could but die. His mind was wanting in the stamina for self-support; it was a plant that would twine beautifully round something stronger than itself, but if repulsed or torn away, it had no choice but to wither on the ground. Dorothy's acuteness taught her that severity would crush the spirit of the child, and she nurtured him with the gentle care of one who handles a butterfly. Her husband manifested an equal affection, although it grew daily less productive of familiar caresses.

The feelings of the neighboring people, in regard to the Quaker infant and his protectors, had not undergone a favorable change, in spite of the momentary triumph which the desolate mother had obtained over their sympathies. The scorn and bitterness of which he was the object, were very grievous to Ilbrahim, especially when any circumstance made him sensible that the children, his equals in age, partook of the enmity of their parents. His tender and social nature had already overflowed in attachments to everything about him, and still there was a residue of unappropriated love, which he yearned to bestow upon the little

ones who were taught to hate him. the warm days of spring came on, Ilb ham was accustomed to remain hours, silent and inactive, within he ing of the children's voices at their pl yet, with his usual delicacy of feeli he avoided their notice, and would and hide himself from the smallest dividual among them. Chance, howev at length seemed to open a medium communication between his heart a theirs; it was by means of a boy ab two years older than Ilbrahim, who injured by a fall from a tree in vicinity of Pearson's habitation. As sufferer's own home was at some tance, Dorothy willingly received under her roof and became his ten and careful nurse.

Ilbrahim was the unconscious poss sor of much skill in physiognomy, a it would have deterred him, in ot circumstances, from attempting to m a friend of this boy. The countena of the latter immediately impressed beholder disagreeably, but it requi some examination to discover that cause was a very slight distortion of mouth, and the irregular, broken li and near approach of the eyebro Analogous, perhaps, to these trifling formities, was an almost impercepti twist of every joint, and the une prominence of the breast; forming body, regular in its general outline, faulty in almost all its details. disposition of the boy was sullen reserved, and the village schoolmas stigmatized him as obtuse in intelle although, at a later period of life, evinced ambition and very pecu talents. But whatever might be his sonal or moral irregularities, Ilbrahi heart seized upon, and clung to h

m the moment that he was brought
ınded into the cottage; the child of
secution seemed to compare his own
e with that of the sufferer, and to
l that even different modes of mis-
tune had created a sort of relation-
ɔ between them. Food, rest, and the
sh air, for which he languished, were
lected; he nestled continually by the
lside of the little stranger, and, with
ond jealousy, endeavored to be the
dium of all the cares that were be-
wed upon him. As the boy became
valescent, Ilbrahim contrived games
table to his situation, or amused him
a faculty which he had perhaps
athed in with the air of his barbaric
thplace. It was that of reciting imag-
ry adventures, on the spur of the
ment, and apparently in inexhaustible
cession. His tales were of course
nstrous, disjointed, and without aim;
they were curious on account of a
n of human tenderness, which ran
ough them all, and was like a sweet,
iiliar face, encountered in the midst
wild and unearthly scenery. The
litor paid much attention to these
nances, and sometimes interrupted
m by brief remarks upon the inci-
its, displaying shrewdness above his
rs, mingled with a moral obliquity
ich grated very harshly against Il-
him's instinctive rectitude. Nothing,
vever, could arrest the progress of
latter's affection, and there were
ny proofs that it met with a response
m the dark and stubborn nature on
ich it was lavished. The boy's parents
length removed him, to complete his
e under their own roof.

Ilbrahim did not visit his new friend
er his departure; but he made anx-
s and continual inquiries respecting

him, and informed himself of the day
when he was to reappear among his
playmates. On a pleasant summer afternoon, the children of the neighborhood
had assembled in the little forest-
crowned amphitheatre behind the meeting-house, and the recovering invalid
was there, leaning on a staff. The glee
of a score of untainted bosoms was
heard in light and airy voices, which
danced among the trees like sunshine
become audible; the grown men of this
weary world, as they journeyed by the
spot, marvelled why life, beginning in
such brightness, should proceed in
gloom; and their hearts, or their imaginations, answered them and said, that
the bliss of childhood gushes from its
innocence. But it happened that an unexpected addition was made to the
heavenly little band. It was Ilbrahim,
who came towards the children with a
look of sweet confidence on his fair and
spiritual face, as if, having manifested
his love to one of them, he had no
longer to fear a repulse from their
society. A hush came over their mirth
the moment they beheld him, and they
stood whispering to each other while he
drew nigh; but, all at once, the devil
of their fathers entered into the unbreeched fanatics, and sending up a
fierce, shrill cry, they rushed upon the
poor Quaker child. In an instant, he was
the centre of a brood of baby-fiends,
who lifted sticks against him, pelted him
with stones, and displayed an instinct
of destruction far more loathsome than
the bloodthirstiness of manhood.

The invalid, in the mean while, stood
apart from the tumult, crying out with
a loud voice, "Fear not, Ilbrahim, come
hither and take my hand"; and his
unhappy friend endeavored to obey him.

After watching the victim's struggling approach, with a calm smile and unabashed eye, the foul-hearted little villain lifted his staff, and struck Ilbrahim on the mouth, so forcibly that the blood issued in a stream. The poor child's arms had been raised to guard his head from the storm of blows; but now he dropped them at once. His persecutors beat him down, trampled upon him, dragged him by his long, fair locks, and Ilbrahim was on the point of becoming as veritable a martyr as ever entered bleeding into Heaven. The uproar, however, attracted the notice of a few neighbors, who put themselves to the trouble of rescuing the little heretic, and of conveying him to Pearson's door.

Ilbrahim's bodily harm was severe, but long and careful nursing accomplished his recovery; the injury done to his sensitive spirit was more serious, though not so visible. Its signs were principally of a negative character, and to be discovered only by those who had previously known him. His gait was thenceforth slow, even, and unvaried by the sudden bursts of sprightlier motion, which had once corresponded to his overflowing gladness; his countenance was heavier, and its former play of expression, the dance of sunshine reflected from moving water, was destroyed by the cloud over his existence; his notice was attracted in a far less degree by passing events, and he appeared to find greater difficulty in comprehending what was new to him, than at a happier period. A stranger, founding his judgment upon these circumstances, would have said that the dulness of the child's intellect widely contradicted the promise of his features;

but the secret was in the direction Ilbrahim's thoughts, which were bro ing within him when they should na rally have been wandering abroad. attempt of Dorothy to revive his for sportiveness was the single occasion, which his quiet demeanor yielded a violent display of grief; he burst i passionate weeping, and ran and himself, for his heart had become miserably sore, that even the hand kindness tortured it like fire. Som times, at night, and probably in dreams, he was heard to cry, "Moth Mother!" as if her place, which stranger had supplied while Ilbral was happy, admitted of no substit in his extreme affliction. Perhaps, am the many life-weary wretches then u the earth, there was not one who co bined innocence and misery like poor, broken-hearted infant, so soon victim of his own heavenly nature.

While this melancholy change taken place in Ilbrahim, one of earlier origin and of different charac had come to its perfection in his adop father. The incident with which tale commences found Pearson in a st of religious dulness, yet mentally quieted, and longing for a more fer faith than he possessed. The first eff of his kindness to Ilbrahim was to p duce a softened feeling, and incipi love for the child's whole sect; joined to this, and resulting perh from self-suspicion, was a proud ostentatious contempt of their ten and practical extravagances. In course of much thought, however, the subject struggled irresistibly i his mind, the foolishness of the doct began to be less evident, and the po which had particularly offended his

assumed another aspect, or vanished
irely away. The work within him ap-
red to go on even while he slept,
that which had been a doubt, when
laid down to rest, would often hold
place of a truth, confirmed by some
gotten demonstration, when he re-
ed his thoughts in the morning. But
le he was thus becoming assimilated
the enthusiasts, his contempt, in no
decreasing towards them, grew very
ce against himself; he imagined,
, that every face of his acquaintance
e a sneer, and that every word ad-
ssed to him was a gibe. Such was
state of mind at the period of Il-
him's misfortune; and the emotions
sequent upon that event completed
change, of which the child had been
original instrument.

n the mean time, neither the fierce-
s of the persecutors, nor the infatu-
n of their victims, had decreased.
dungeons were never empty; the
ets of almost every village echoed
y with the lash; the life of a woman,
se mild and Christian spirit no
elty could embitter, had been sacri-
d; and more innocent blood was
to pollute the hands that were so
en raised in prayer. Early after the
toration, the English Quakers repre-
ted to Charles II. that a "vein of
od was open in his dominions"; but
ugh the displeasure of the voluptu-
king was roused, his interference
not prompt. And now the tale must
de forward over many months, leav-
Pearson to encounter ignominy and
fortune; his wife to a firm endur-
e of a thousand sorrows; poor Il-
im to pine and droop like a cankered
bud; his mother to wander on a
taken errand, neglectful of the

holiest trust which can be committed to
a woman.

* * * * * *

A winter evening, a night of storm,
had darkened over Pearson's habitation,
and there were no cheerful faces to
drive the gloom from his broad hearth.
The fire, it is true, sent forth a glowing heat and a ruddy light, and large
logs, dripping with half-melted snow,
lay ready to be cast upon the embers.
But the apartment was saddened in its
aspect by the absence of much of the
homely wealth which had once adorned
it; for the exaction of repeated fines,
and his own neglect of temporal affairs, had greatly impoverished the
owner. And with the furniture of peace,
the implements of war had likewise disappeared; the sword was broken, the
helm and cuirass were cast away forever; the soldier had done with battles,
and might not lift so much as his naked
hand to guard his head. But the Holy
Book remained, and the table on which
it rested was drawn before the fire,
while two of the persecuted sect sought
comfort from its pages.

He who listened, while the other read,
was the master of the house, now emaciated in form, and altered as to the
expression and healthiness of his countenance; for his mind had dwelt too
long among visionary thoughts, and his
body had been worn by imprisonment
and stripes. The hale and weather-
beaten old man, who sat beside him,
had sustained less injury from a far
longer course of the same mode of
life. In person he was tall and dignified, and, which alone would have made
him hateful to the Puritans, his gray
locks fell from beneath the broad-
brimmed hat, and rested on his shoul-

ders. As the old man read the sacred page, the snow drifted against the windows, or eddied in at the crevices of the door, while a blast kept laughing in the chimney, and the blaze leaped fiercely up to seek it. And sometimes, when the wind struck the hill at a certain angle, and swept down by the cottage across the wintry plain, its voice was the most doleful that can be conceived; it came as if the Past were speaking, as if the Dead had contributed each a whisper, as if the Desolation of Ages were breathed in that one lamenting sound.

The Quaker at length closed the book, retaining however his hand between the pages which he had been reading, while he looked steadfastly at Pearson. The attitude and features of the latter might have indicated the endurance of bodily pain; he leaned his forehead on his hands, his teeth were firmly closed, and his frame was tremulous at intervals with a nervous agitation.

"Friend Tobias," inquired the old man, compassionately, "hast thou found no comfort in these many blessed passages of Scripture?"

"Thy voice has fallen on my ear like a sound afar off and indistinct," replied Pearson, without lifting his eyes. "Yea, and when I have hearkened carefully, the words seemed cold and lifeless, and intended for another and a lesser grief than mine. Remove the book," he added, in a tone of sullen bitterness. "I have no part in its consolations, and they do but fret my sorrow the more."

"Nay, feeble brother, be not as one who hath never known the light," said the elder Quaker, earnestly, but with mildness. "Art thou he that wouldst

be content to give all, and endure for conscience' sake; desiring even culiar trials, that thy faith might purified, and thy heart weaned fr worldly desires? And wilt thou s beneath an affliction which happ alike to them that have their port here below, and to them that lay treasure in heaven? Faint not, for burden is yet light."

"It is heavy! It is heavier thar can bear!" exclaimed Pearson, with impatience of a variable spirit. "Fr my youth upward I have been a m marked out for wrath; and year year, yea, day after day, I have dured sorrows, such as others kn not in their lifetime. And now I sp not of the love that has been turn to hatred, the honor to ignominy, ease and plentifulness of all things danger, want, and nakedness. All t I could have borne, and counted mys blessed. But when my heart was de late with many losses I fixed it up the child of a stranger, and he beca dearer to me than all my buried on and now he too must die as if my l were poison. Verily, I am an accur man, and I will lay me down in dust, and lift up my head no more.'

"Thou sinnest, brother, but it is for me to rebuke thee; for I also h had my hours of darkness, wherei have murmured against the cross," s the old Quaker. He continued, perh in the hope of distracting his comp ion's thoughts from his own sorro "Even of late was the light obscu within me, when the men of blood b banished me on pain of death, and constables led me onward from lage to village, towards the wildern A strong and cruel hand was wield knotted cords; they sunk deep into flesh, and thou mightst have tracked ry reel and totter of my footsteps the blood that followed. As we went —"

Have I not borne all this; and have iurmured?" interrupted Pearson, im- iently.

Nay, friend, but hear me," con- ied the other. "As we journeyed on, ht darkened on our path, so that man could see the rage of the per- itors, or the constancy of my en- ance, though Heaven forbid that hould glory therein. The lights be- to glimmer in the cottage win- vs, and I could discern the inmates they gathered in comfort and se- ity, every man with his wife and idren by their own evening hearth. length we came to a tract of fertile d; in the dim light the forest was visible around it; and behold! there a straw-thatched dwelling, which e the very aspect of my home, far r the wild ocean, far in our own gland. Then came bitter thoughts n me; yea, remembrances that were death to my soul. The happiness my early days was painted to me; disquiet of my manhood, the altered h of my declining years. I remem- ed how I had been moved to go th a wanderer, when my daughter, youngest, the dearest of my flock, on her dying bed, and—"

Couldst thou obey the command at h a moment?" exclaimed Pearson, iddering.

Yea, yea," replied the old man, hur- lly. "I was kneeling by her bedside en the voice spoke loud within me; immediately I rose, and took my ff, and gat me gone. O, that it were

permitted me to forget her woful look when I thus withdrew my arm, and left her journeying through the dark valley alone! for her soul was faint, and she had leaned upon my prayers. Now in that night of horror I was assailed by the thought that I had been an erring Christian, and a cruel parent; yea, even my daughter, with her pale, dying features, seemed to stand by me and whisper, 'Father, you are deceived; go home and shelter your gray head.' O Thou, to whom I have looked in my farthest wanderings," con- tinued the Quaker, raising his agitated eyes to Heaven, "inflict not upon the bloodiest of our persecutors the unmiti- gated agony of my soul, when I be- lieved that all I had done and suffered for Thee was at the instigation of a mocking fiend! But I yielded not; I knelt down and wrestled with the tempt- er, while the scourge bit more fiercely into the flesh. My prayer was heard, and I went on in peace and joy towards the wilderness."

The old man, though his fanaticism had generally all the calmness of reason, was deeply moved while reciting this tale; and his unwonted emotion seemed to rebuke and keep down that of his companion. They sat in silence, with their faces to the fire, imagining per- haps, in its red embers, new scenes of persecution yet to be encountered. The snow still drifted hard against the win- dows, and sometimes, as the blaze of the logs had gradually sunk, came down the spacious chimney and hissed upon the hearth. A cautious footstep might now and then be heard in a neighboring apartment, and the sound invariably drew the eyes of both Quakers to the door which led thither. When a fierce and riotous gust of wind had led his thoughts, by a natural association, to homeless travellers on such a night, Pearson resumed the conversation.

"I have wellnigh sunk under my own share of this trial," observed he, sighing heavily; "yet I would that it might be doubled to me, if so the child's mother could be spared. Her wounds have been deep and many, but this will be the sorest of all."

"Fear not for Catharine," replied the old Quaker; "for I know that valiant woman, and have seen how she can bear the cross. A mother's heart, indeed, is strong in her, and may seem to contend mightily with her faith; but soon she will stand up and give thanks that her son has been thus early an accepted sacrifice. The boy hath done his work, and she will feel that he is taken hence in kindness both to him and her. Blessed, blessed are they, that with so little suffering can enter into peace!"

The fitful rush of the wind was now disturbed by a portentous sound; it was a quick and heavy knocking at the outer door. Pearson's wan countenance grew paler, for many a visit of persecution had taught him what to dread; the old man, on the other hand, stood up erect, and his glance was firm as that of the tried soldier, who awaits his enemy.

"The men of blood have come to seek me," he observed, with calmness. "They have heard how I was moved to return from banishment; and now am I to be led to prison, and thence to death. It is an end I have long looked for. I will open unto them, lest they say, 'Lo, he feareth!'"

"Nay, I will present myself before them," said Pearson, with recovered for-

titude. "It may be that they seek [ ] alone, and know not that thou abi[ ] with me."

"Let us go boldly, both one and [ ] other," rejoined his companion. "I[ ] not fitting that thou or I should shrin[ ]

They therefore proceeded through [ ] entry to the door, which they open[ ] bidding the applicant "Come in, in G[ ] name!" A furious blast of wind dr[ ] the storm into their faces, and ex[ ] guished the lamp; they had barely t[ ] to discern a figure, so white from h[ ] to foot with the drifted snow, tha[ ] seemed like Winter's self, come [ ] human shape to seek refuge from [ ] own desolation.

"Enter, friend, and do thy errand[ ] it what it may," said Pearson. "It m[ ] needs be pressing, since thou comest [ ] such a bitter night."

"Peace be with this household," s[ ] the stranger, when they stood on [ ] floor of the inner apartment.

Pearson started, the elder Qua[ ] stirred the slumbering embers of [ ] fire, till they sent up a clear and lo[ ] blaze; it was a female voice that [ ] spoken; it was a female form that sh[ ] out, cold and wintry, in that comf[ ] able light.

"Catharine, blessed woman," [ ] claimed the old man, "art thou c[ ] to this darkened land again? art t[ ] come to bear a valiant testimony a[ ] former years? The scourge hath not [ ] vailed against thee, and from the d[ ] geon hast thou come forth triumph[ ] but strengthen, strengthen now [ ] heart, Catharine, for Heaven will pr[ ] thee yet this once, ere thou go to [ ] reward."

"Rejoice, friends!" she replied. "T[ ] who hast long been of our people, u whom a little child hath led to rejoice! Lo! I come, the messenger glad tidings, for the day of perse-ion is overpast. The heart of the g, even Charles, hath been moved gentleness towards us, and he hath t forth his letters to stay the hands the men of blood. A ship's company our friends hath arrived at yonder 'n, and I also sailed joyfully among m."

As Catharine spoke, her eyes were ming about the room, in search of a for whose sake security was dear her. Pearson made a silent appeal the old man, nor did the latter ink from the painful task assigned .

Sister," he began, in a softened yet fectly calm tone, "thou tellest us of love, manifested in temporal good; now must we speak to thee of that same love, displayed in chastenings. herto, Catharine, thou hast been as journeying in a darksome and diffi-path, and leading an infant by the d; fain wouldst thou have looked venward continually, but still the es of that little child have drawn ae eyes and thy affections to the h. Sister, go on rejoicing, for his ering footsteps shall impede thine no more."

But the unhappy mother was not thus be consoled; she shook like a leaf, turned white as the very snow that g drifted into her hair. The firm man extended his hand and held up, keeping his eye upon hers, as o repress any outbreak of passion.

I am a woman, I am but a woman; He try me above my strength?" Catharine, very quickly, and almost a whisper. "I have been wounded sore; I have suffered much; many things in the body, many in the mind; cruci-fied in myself, and in them that were dearest to me. Surely," added she, with a long shudder, "He hath spared me in this one thing." She broke forth with sudden and irrepressible violence. "Tell me, man of cold heart, what has God done to me? Hath He cast me down, never to rise again? Hath He crushed my very heart in his hand? And thou, to whom I committed my child, how hast thou fulfilled thy trust? Give me back the boy, well, sound, alive, alive; or earth and heaven shall avenge me!"

The agonized shriek of Catharine was answered by the faint, the very faint voice of a child.

On this day it had become evident to Pearson, to his aged guest, and to Dorothy, that Ilbrahim's brief and troubled pilgrimage drew near its close. The two former would willingly have remained by him, to make use of the prayers and pious discourses which they deemed appropriate to the time, and which, if they be impotent as to the departing traveller's reception in the world whither it goes, may at least sus-tain him in bidding adieu to earth. But though Ilbrahim uttered no complaint, he was disturbed by the faces that looked upon him; so that Dorothy's en-treaties, and their own conviction that the child's feet might tread Heaven's pavement and not soil it, had induced the two Quakers to remove. Ilbrahim then closed his eyes and grew calm, and, except for now and then a kind and low word to his nurse, might have been thought to slumber. As nightfall came on, however, and the storm began to rise, something seemed to trouble the repose of the boy's mind, and to render his sense of hearing active and acute. If a passing wind lingered to shake the casement, he strove to turn his head towards it; if the door jarred to and fro upon its hinges, he looked long and anxiously thitherward; if the heavy voice of the old man, as he read the Scriptures, rose but a little higher, the child almost held his dying breath to listen; if a snow-drift swept by the cottage, with a sound like the trailing of a garment, Ilbrahim seemed to watch that some visitant should enter.

But, after a little time, he relinquished whatever secret hope had agitated him, and, with one low, complaining whisper, turned his cheek upon the pillow. He then addressed Dorothy with his usual sweetness, and besought her to draw near him; she did so, and Ilbrahim took her hand in both of his, grasping it with a gentle pressure, as if to assure himself that he retained it. At intervals, and without disturbing the repose of his countenance, a very faint trembling passed over him from head to foot, as if a mild but somewhat cool wind had breathed upon him, and made him shiver. As the boy thus led her by the hand in his quiet progress over the borders of eternity, Dorothy almost imagined that she could discern the near, though dim delightfulness, of the home he was about to reach; she would not have enticed the little wanderer back, though she bemoaned herself that she must leave him and return. But just when Ilbrahim's feet were pressing on the soil of Paradise, he heard a voice behind him, and it recalled him a few, few paces of the weary path which he had travelled. As Dorothy looked upon his features, she perceived that their placid expression

was again disturbed; her own thoug[ht] had been so wrapped in him, that [the] sounds of the storm, and of hum[an] speech, were lost to her; but wh[en] Catharine's shriek pierced through [the] room, the boy strove to raise himsel[f.]

"Friend, she is come! Open u[nto] her!" cried he.

In a moment, his mother was kne[el]ing by the bedside; she drew Ilbra[him] to her bosom, and he nestled there, w[ith] no violence of joy, but contentedly [as] if he were hushing himself to sle[ep.] He looked into her face, and read[ing] its agony, said, with feeble earnestn[ess,] "Mourn not, dearest Mother. I [am] happy now." And with these words, [the] gentle boy was dead.

* * * * * *

The king's mandate to stay the N[ew] England persecutors was effectual [in] preventing further martyrdoms; but [the] colonial authorities, trusting in the [re]moteness of their situation, and p[er]haps in the supposed instability of [the] royal government, shortly renewed th[eir] severities in all other respects. Ca[th]arine's fanaticism had become wil[d] by the sundering of all human ties; a[nd] wherever a scourge was lifted, th[ere] was she to receive the blow; and wh[er]ever a dungeon was unbarred, thit[her] she came to cast herself upon the fl[oor.] But in process of time, a more Ch[ris]tian spirit,—a spirit of forbearan[ce,] though not of cordiality or appro[ba]tion, began to pervade the land in [re]gard to the persecuted sect. And th[en,] when the rigid old Pilgrims eyed [her] rather in pity than in wrath; w[hen] the matrons fed her with the fragm[ents] of their children's food, and offered [her] a lodging on a hard and lowly b[ed] when no little crowd of school-boys

ir sports to cast stones after the
ing enthusiast; then did Catharine
irn to Pearson's dwelling, and made
t her home.

is if Ilbrahim's sweetness yet lined round his ashes; as if his gentle
it came down from Heaven to teach
parent a true religion, her fierce and
dictive nature was softened by the
ie griefs which had once irritated
When the course of years had made
features of the unobtrusive mourner
iiliar in the settlement, she became

a subject of not deep, but general interest; a being on whom the otherwise
superfluous sympathies of all might be
bestowed. Every one spoke of her with
that degree of pity which it is pleasant
to experience; every one was ready to
do her the little kindnesses, which are
not costly, yet manifest good will; and
when at last she died, a long train of
her once bitter persecutors followed
her, with decent sadness and tears that
were not painful, to her place by Ilbrahim's green and sunken grave.

MR. HIGGINBOTHAM'S CATASTROPHE

A YOUNG fellow, a tobacco pedler by
le, was on his way from Morris-
n, where he had dealt largely with
Deacon of the Shaker settlement,
:he village of Parker's Falls, on Sal-
n River. He had a neat little cart,
ited green, with a box of cigars
icted on each side pannel, and an
ian chief, holding a pipe and a
den tobacco-stalk, on the rear. The
ler drove a smart little mare, and
s a young man of excellent charac-
keen at a bargain, but none the
se liked by the Yankees; who, as
iave heard them say, would rather
shaved with a sharp razor than a
i one. Especially was he beloved by
pretty girls along the Connecticut,
ise favor he used to court by pres-
s of the best smoking tobacco in his
:k; knowing well that the country
.es of New England are generally
it performers on pipes. Moreover,
will be seen in the course of my
ry, the pedler was inquisitive, and

something of a tattler, always itching
to hear the news, and anxious to tell it
again.

After an early breakfast at Morristown, the tobacco pedler, whose name
was Dominicus Pike, had travelled seven
miles through a solitary piece of woods,
without speaking a word to anybody
but himself and his little gray mare.
It being nearly seven o'clock, he was
as eager to hold a morning gossip as a
city shopkeeper to read the morning
paper. An opportunity seemed at hand,
when, after lighting a cigar with a sun-
glass, he looked up, and perceived a
man coming over the brow of the hill,
at the foot of which the pedler had
stopped his green cart. Dominicus
watched him as he descended, and noticed that he carried a bundle over his
shoulder on the end of a stick, and
travelled with a weary, yet determined
pace. He did not look as if he had
started in the freshness of the morning, but had footed it all night, and

meant to do the same all day.

"Good morning, mister," said Dominicus, when within speaking distance. "You go a pretty good jog. What's the latest news at Parker's Falls?"

The man pulled the broad brim of a gray hat over his eyes, and answered, rather sullenly, that he did not come from Parker's Falls, which, as being the limit of his own day's journey, the pedler had naturally mentioned in his inquiry.

"Well, then," rejoined Dominicus Pike, "let's have the latest news where you did come from. I'm not particular about Parker's Falls. Any place will answer."

Being thus importuned, the traveller —who was as ill looking a fellow as one would desire to meet, in a solitary piece of woods—appeared to hesitate a little, as if he was either searching his memory for news, or weighing the expediency of telling it. At last mounting on the step of the cart, he whispered in the ear of Dominicus, though he might have shouted aloud, and no other mortal would have heard him.

"I do remember one little trifle of news," said he. "Old Mr. Higginbotham, of Kimballton, was murdered in his orchard, at eight o'clock last night, by an Irishman and a nigger. They strung him up to the branch of a St. Michael's pear-tree, where nobody would find him till the morning."

As soon as this horrible intelligence was communicated, the stranger betook himself to his journey again, with more speed than ever, not even turning his head when Dominicus invited him to smoke a Spanish cigar and relate all the particulars. The pedler whistled to his mare and went up the hill, pondering on the doleful fate of Mr. Higginbotham, whom he had known in way of trade, having sold him ma a bunch of long nines, and a great d of pigtail, lady's twist, and fig tobac He was rather astonished at the rap ity with which the news had spre Kimballton was nearly sixty miles tant in a straight line; the murder been perpetrated only at eight o'clc the preceding night; yet Dominicus heard of it at seven in the morni when, in all probability, poor Mr. H ginbotham's own family had but j discovered his corpse, hanging on St. Michael's pear-tree. The stran on foot must have worn seven-lea boots, to travel at such a rate.

"Ill news flies fast, they say," thou Dominicus Pike; "but this beats r roads. The fellow ought to be hired go express with the President's M sage."

The difficulty was solved, by supp ing that the narrator had made a mista of one day, in the date of the occ rence; so that our friend did not he tate to introduce the story at ev tavern and country store along the ro expending a whole bunch of Span wrappers among at least twenty ho fied audiences. He found himself variably the first bearer of the inte gence, and was so pestered with questi that he could not avoid filling up outline, till it became quite a respe able narrative. He met with one pi of corroborative evidence. Mr. Higg botham was a trader; and a former cl of his, to whom Dominicus related facts, testified that the old gentlen was accustomed to return home thro the orchard, about nightfall, with money and valuable papers of the st

his pocket. The clerk manifested but
[li]le grief at Mr. Higginbotham's catas-
[tro]phe, hinting, what the pedler had
[dis]covered in his own dealings with
[hi]m, that he was a crusty old fellow,
[as] close as a vice. His property would
[des]cend to a pretty niece who was now
[kee]ping school in Kimballton.

[W]hat with telling the news for the
[pub]lic good, and driving bargains for
[his] own, Dominicus was so much de-
[lay]ed on the road, that he chose to
[pu]t up at a tavern, about five miles
[sho]rt of Parker's Falls. After supper,
[lig]hting one of his prime cigars, he
[sea]ted himself in the bar-room, and
[we]nt through the story of the murder,
[wh]ich had grown so fast that it took
[hi]m half an hour to tell. There were
[as] many as twenty people in the room,
[nin]eteen of whom received it all for
[gos]pel. But the twentieth was an elder-
[ly] farmer, who had arrived on horse-
[bac]k a short time before, and was now
[sea]ted in a corner, smoking his pipe.
[Wh]en the story was concluded, he rose
[up] very deliberately, brought his chair
[rig]ht in front of Dominicus, and stared
[hi]m full in the face, puffing out the
[vil]est tobacco smoke the pedler had
[eve]r smelt.

["W]ill you make affidavit," demanded
[he,] in the tone of a country justice
[tak]ing an examination, "that old Squire
[Hig]ginbotham of Kimballton was mur-
[der]ed in his orchard the night before
[las]t, and found hanging on his great
[pea]r-tree yesterday morning?"

["I] tell the story as I heard it, mister,"
[ans]wered Dominicus, dropping his half-
[bur]nt cigar; "I don't say that I saw
[the] thing done. So I can't take my
[oat]h that he was murdered exactly in
[tha]t way."

"But I can take mine," said the farmer, "that if Squire Higginbotham was
murdered night before last, I drank a
glass of bitters with his ghost this morning. Being a neighbor of mine, he called
me into his store, as I was riding by,
and treated me, and then asked me to
do a little business for him on the road.
He didn't seem to know any more about
his own murder than I did."

"Why, then, it can't be a fact!"
exclaimed Dominicus Pike.

"I guess he'd have mentioned, if it
was," said the old farmer; and he removed his chair back to the corner,
leaving Dominicus quite down in the
mouth.

Here was a sad resurrection of old
Mr. Higginbotham! The pedler had no
heart to mingle in the conversation any
more, but comforted himself with a
glass of gin and water, and went to bed,
where, all night long, he dreamed of
hanging on the St. Michael's pear-tree.
To avoid the old farmer, (whom he so
detested, that his suspension would have
pleased him better than Mr. Higginbotham's,) Dominicus rose in the gray of
the morning, put the little mare into the
green cart, and trotted swiftly away towards Parker's Falls. The fresh breeze,
the dewy road, and the pleasant summer dawn revived his spirits, and might
have encouraged him to repeat the old
story, had there been anybody awake
to hear it. But he met neither ox team,
light wagon, chaise, horseman, nor foot
traveller, till, just as he crossed Salmon River, a man came trudging down
to the bridge with a bundle over his
shoulder, on the end of a stick.

"Good morning, mister," said the
pedler, reining in his mare. "If you
come from Kimballton or that neigh-

borhood, may be you can tell me the real fact about this affair of old Mr. Higginbotham. Was the old fellow actually murdered two or three nights ago, by an Irishman and a nigger?"

Dominicus had spoken in too great a hurry to observe, at first, that the stranger himself had a deep tinge of negro blood. On hearing this sudden question, the Ethiopian appeared to change his skin, its yellow hue becoming a ghastly white, while, shaking and stammering, he thus replied:—

"No! no! There was no colored man! It was an Irishman that hanged him last night, at eight o'clock. I came away at seven! His folks can't have looked for him in the orchard yet."

Scarcely had the yellow man spoken when he interrupted himself, and though he seemed weary enough before, continued his journey at a pace which would have kept the pedler's mare on a smart trot. Dominicus stared after him in great perplexity. If the murder had not been committed till Tuesday night, who was the prophet that had foretold it, in all its circumstances, on Tuesday morning? If Mr. Higginbotham's corpse were not yet discovered by his own family, how came the mulatto, at above thirty miles' distance, to know that he was hanging in the orchard, especially as he had left Kimballton before the unfortunate man was hanged at all? These ambiguous circumstances, with the stranger's surprise and terror, made Dominicus think of raising a hue and cry after him, as an accomplice in the murder; since a murder, it seemed, had really been perpetrated.

"But let the poor devil go," thought the pedler. "I don't want his black blood on my head; and hanging the nigger wouldn't unhang Mr. Higginbotham. Unhang the old gentleman! a sin, I know; but I should hate have him come to life a second time and give me the lie!"

With these meditations, Dominicus Pike drove into the street of Parker Falls, which, as everybody knows, as thriving a village as three cotton factories and a slitting-mill can make it. The machinery was not in motion and but a few of the shop-doors barred, when he alighted in the stable yard of the tavern, and made it first business to order the mare four quarts of oats. His second duty, course, was to impart Mr. Higginbotham's catastrophe to the ostler. deemed it advisable, however, not be too positive as to the date of direful fact, and also to be uncertain whether it were perpetrated by an Irishman and a mulatto, or by the son Erin alone. Neither did he profess to late it on his own authority, or that any one person; but mentioned it a report generally diffused.

The story ran through the town like fire among girdled trees, and became much the universal talk, that nobody could tell whence it had originated. Higginbotham was as well known Parker's Falls as any citizen of place, being part owner of the slitting-mill, and a considerable stockholder the cotton-factories. The inhabitants their own prosperity interested in fate. Such was the excitement, that Parker's Falls Gazette anticipated regular day of publication, and came with half a form of blank paper an column of double pica emphasized with capitals, and headed HORRID MURDER OF MR. HIGGINBOTHAM.

ong other dreadful details, the
ted account described the mark of
cord round the dead man's neck,
d stated the number of thousand
lars of which he had been robbed;
re was much pathos also about the
ction of his niece, who had gone
m one fainting fit to another, ever
ce her uncle was found hanging on
St. Michael's pear-tree with his
kets inside out. The village poet like-
e commemorated the young lady's
ef in seventeen stanzas of a ballad.
e selectmen held a meeting, and in
sideration of Mr. Higginbotham's
ms on the town, determined to issue
dbills, offering a reward of five hun-
d dollars for the apprehension of his
rderers, and the recovery of the
en property.

Meanwhile, the whole population of
ker's Falls, consisting of shopkeep-
, mistresses of boarding-houses, fac-
y-girls, millmen, and school-boys,
hed into the street and kept up such
errible loquacity, as more than com-
sated for the silence of the cotton-
chines, which refrained from their
al din out of respect to the deceased.
d Mr. Higginbotham cared about
thumous renown, his untimely ghost
uld have exulted in this tumult. Our
nd Dominicus, in his vanity of
rt, forgot his intended precautions,
mounting on the town-pump an-
nced himself as the bearer of the
hentic intelligence which had caused
wonderful a sensation. He immediate-
became the great man of the mont, and had just begun a new edition
the narrative, with a voice like a
d preacher, when the mail stage
ve into the village street. It had
elled all night, and must have shifted

horses at Kimballton, at three in the
morning.

"Now we shall hear all the particulars," shouted the crowd.

The coach rumbled up to the piazza
of the tavern, followed by a thousand
people; for if any man had been mind-
ing his own business till then, he now
left it at sixes and sevens to hear the
news. The pedler, foremost in the race,
discovered two passengers, both of
whom had been startled from a comfortable nap to find themselves in the
centre of a mob. Every man assailing
them with separate questions, all propounded at once, the couple were struck
speechless, though one was a lawyer
and the other a young lady.

"Mr. Higginbotham! Mr. Higginbotham! Tell us the particulars about
old Mr. Higginbotham!" bawled the
mob. "What is the coroner's verdict?
Are the murderers apprehended? Is Mr.
Higginbotham's niece come out of her
fainting fits? Mr. Higginbotham! Mr.
Higginbotham!!"

The coachman said not a word, except to swear awfully at the ostler for
not bringing him a fresh team of horses.
The lawyer inside had generally his
wits about him even when asleep; the
first thing he did, after learning the
cause of the excitement, was to produce
a large, red pocket-book. Meantime,
Dominicus Pike, being an extremely polite young man, and also suspecting that
a female tongue would tell the story
as glibly as a lawyer's, had handed the
lady out of the coach. She was a fine,
smart girl, now wide awake and bright
as a button, and had such a sweet pretty
mouth, that Dominicus would almost
as lief have heard a love-tale from it
as a tale of murder.

"Gentleman and ladies," said the lawyer, to the shopkeepers, the mill-men, and the factory-girls, "I can assure you that some unaccountable mistake, or, more probably, a wilful falsehood, maliciously contrived to injure Mr. Higginbotham's credit, has excited this singular uproar. We passed through Kimballton at three o'clock this morning, and most certainly should have been informed of the murder, had any been perpetrated. But I have proof nearly as strong as Mr. Higginbotham's own oral testimony, in the negative. Here is a note, relating to a suit of his in the Connecticut courts, which was delivered me from that gentleman himself. I find it dated at ten o'clock last evening."

So saying, the lawyer exhibited the date and signature of the note, which irrefragably proved, either that this perverse. Mr. Higginbotham was alive when he wrote it, or—as some deemed the more probable case, of two doubtful ones—that he was so absorbed in worldly business as to continue to transact it, even after his death. But unexpected evidence was forthcoming. The young lady, after listening to the pedler's explanation, merely seized a moment to smooth her gown and put her curls in order, and then appeared at the tavern door, making a modest signal to be heard.

"Good people," said she, "I am Mr. Higginbotham's niece."

A wondering murmur passed through the crowd, on beholding her so rosy and bright; that same unhappy niece, whom they had supposed, on the authority of the Parker's Falls Gazette, to be lying at death's door in a fainting-fit. But some shrewd fellows had

doubted, all along, whether a yo[u] lady would be quite so desperate at hanging of a rich old uncle.

"You see," continued Miss Higg[in]botham, with a smile, "that this stra[nge] story is quite unfounded as to mys[elf] and I believe I may affirm it to [be] equally so in regard to my dear un[cle] Higginbotham. He has the kindness [to] give me a home in his house, tho[ugh] I contribute to my own support [by] teaching a school. I left Kimball[ton] this morning to spend the vacation [of] commencement week with a frie[nd] about five miles from Parker's F[alls] My generous uncle, when he heard [me] on the stairs, called me to his b[ed] side, and gave me two dollars [and] fifty cents to pay my stage fare, [and] another dollar for my extra expen[ses] He then laid his pocketbook under [his] pillow, shook hands with me, and [ad]vised me to take some biscuit in [my] bag, instead of breakfasting on the r[oad] I feel confident, therefore, that I [left] my beloved relative alive, and t[rust] that I shall find him so on my retu[rn]"

The young lady courtesied at [the] close of her speech, which was so s[en]sible, and well worded, and deliv[ered] with such grace and propriety, [that] everybody thought her fit to be [pre]ceptress of the best academy in [the] State. But a stranger would have s[up]posed that Mr. Higginbotham was [the] object of abhorrence at Parker's F[alls] and that a thanksgiving had been [pro]claimed for his murder; so exces[sive] was the wrath of the inhabitants [on] learning their mistake. The millmen [re]solved to bestow public honors on D[om]inicus Pike, only hesitating whethe[r to] tar and feather him, ride him on a [rail] or refresh him with an ablution at [the]

-pump, on the top of which he
declared himself the bearer of the
The selectmen, by advice of the
er, spoke of prosecuting him for a
emeanor, in circulating unfounded
ts, to the great disturbance of the
e of the commonwealth. Nothing
Dominicus, either from mob law
court of justice, but an eloquent
l made by the young lady in his
f. Addressing a few words of heart-
gratitude to his benefactress, he
ted the green cart and rode out
wn, under a discharge of artillery
the school-boys, who found plenty
munition in the neighboring clay-
and mud-holes. As he turned his
to exchange a farewell glance at
Higginbotham's niece, a ball, of
consistence of hasty-pudding, hit
slap in the mouth, giving him a
grim aspect. His whole person was
spattered with the like filthy mis-
that he had almost a mind to ride
and supplicate for the threatened
on at the town-pump; for, though
neant in kindness, it would now
been a deed of charity.
wever, the sun shone bright on
Dominicus, and the mud, an em-
of all stains of undeserved oppro-
was easily brushed off when dry.
a funny rogue, his heart soon
ed up; nor could he refrain from
rty laugh at the uproar which his
had excited. The handbills of the
men would cause the commitment
the vagabonds in the State; the
raph in the Parker's Falls Gazette
be reprinted from Maine to Flor-
nd perhaps form an item in the
n newspapers, and many a miser
tremble for his money-bags and
n learning the catastrophe of Mr.

Higginbotham. The pedler meditated
with much fervor on the charms of the
young schoolmistress, and swore that
Daniel Webster never spoke nor looked
so like an angel as Miss Higginbotham,
while defending him from the wrathful populace at Parker's Falls.

Dominicus was now on the Kimballton turnpike, having all along determined to visit that place, though business had drawn him out of the most
direct road from Morristown. As he
approached the scene of the supposed
murder, he continued to revolve the circumstances in his mind, and was astonished at the aspect which the whole
case assumed. Had nothing occurred to
corroborate the story of the first traveller, it might now have been considered
as a hoax; but the yellow man was
evidently acquainted either with the
report or the fact; and there was a
mystery in his dismayed and guilty look
on being abruptly questioned. When,
to this singular combination of incidents, it was added that the rumor
tallied exactly with Mr. Higginbotham's
character and habits of life; and that
he had an orchard, and a St. Michael's
pear-tree, near which he always passed
at nightfall; the circumstantial evidence
appeared so strong that Dominicus
doubted whether the autograph produced
by the lawyer, or even the niece's direct
testimony, ought to be equivalent. Making cautious inquiries along the road,
the pedler further learned that Mr.
Higginbotham had in his service an
Irishman of doubtful character, whom
he had hired without a recommendation,
on the score of economy.

"May I be hanged myself," exclaimed
Dominicus Pike, aloud, on reaching the
top of a lonely hill, "if I'll believe old

Higginbotham is unhanged, till I see him with my own eyes, and hear it from his own mouth! And as he's a real shaver, I'll have the minister or some other responsible man for an indorser."

It was growing dusk when he reached the toll-house on Kimballton turnpike, about a quarter of a mile from the village of this name. His little mare was fast bringing him up with a man on horseback, who trotted through the gate a few rods in advance of him, nodded to the toll-gatherer, and kept on towards the village. Dominicus was acquainted with the tollman, and while making change, the usual remarks on the weather passed between them.

"I suppose," said the pedler, throwing back his whiplash, to bring it down like a feather on the mare's flank, "you have not seen anything of old Mr. Higginbotham within a day or two?"

"Yes," answered the toll-gatherer. "He passed the gate just before you drove up, and yonder he rides now, if you can see him through the dusk. He's been to Woodfield this afternoon, attending a sheriff's sale there. The old man generally shakes hands and has a little chat with me; but to-night, he nodded,—as if to say, 'Charge my toll,' —and jogged on; for wherever he goes, he must always be at home by eight o'clock."

"So they tell me," said Dominicus.

"I never saw a man look so yellow and thin as the squire does," continued the toll-gatherer. "Says I to myself, to-night, he's more like a ghost or an old mummy than good flesh and blood."

The pedler strained his eyes through the twilight, and could just discern the horseman now far ahead on the village road. He seemed to recognize the rear

of Mr. Higginbotham; but throug[h] evening shadows, and amid the [dust] from the horse's feet, the figur[e ap-] peared dim and unsubstantial; as [the] shape of the mysterious old man [was] faintly moulded of darkness and [gray] light. Dominicus shivered.

"Mr. Higginbotham has come [back] from the other world, by way o[f] Kimballton turnpike," thought he.

He shook the reins and rode fo[rward,] keeping about the same distance [in] rear of the gray old shadow, ti[ll the] latter was concealed by a bend o[f the] road. On reaching this point, the [ped-] ler no longer saw the man on [horse-] back, but found himself at the he[ad of] the village street, not far from a [num-] ber of stores and two taverns clu[stered] round the meeting-house steeple. [On his] left were a stone wall and a gat[e, the] boundary of a wood-lot, beyond [which] lay an orchard, farther still, a m[own] field, and last of all, a house. [These] were the premises of Mr. Higginb[otham,] whose dwelling stood beside th[e old] highway, but had been left in the [back-] ground by the Kimballton tur[npike.] Dominicus knew the place; and th[e little] mare stopped short by instinct; [for he] was not conscious of tightenin[g the] reins.

"For the soul of me I cann[ot get] by this gate!" said he, tremblin[g. "I] never shall be my own man aga[in, till] I see whether Mr. Higginboth[am is] hanging on the St. Michael's pear-[tree."]

He leaped from the cart, gav[e the] rein a turn round the gate-post[, and] ran along the green path of the [wood-] lot as if Old Nick were chasing h[im.] Just then the village clock tolled [eight,] and as each deep stroke fell, Dom[inicus] gave a fresh bound and flew faste[r.]

e, till, dim in the solitary centre e orchard, he saw the fated pear- One great branch stretched from d contorted trunk across the path, hrew the darkest shadow on that spot. But something seemed to le beneath the branch!

e pedler had never pretended to courage than befits a man of able occupation, nor could he ac- for his valor on this awful emer- . Certain it is, however, that he d forward, prostrated a sturdy man with the butt end of his whip, ound—not indeed hanging on the Michael's pear-tree, but trembling th it, with a halter round his neck old, identical Mr. Higginbotham! r. Higginbotham," said Dominicus, ously, "you're an honest man, and ake your word for it. Have you hanged or not?"

he riddle be not already guessed, words will explain the simple ma-

chinery by which this "coming event" was made to "cast its shadow before." Three men had plotted the robbery and murder of Mr. Higginbotham; two of them, successively, lost courage and fled, each delaying the crime one night by their disappearance; the third was in the act of perpetration, when a cham- pion, blindly obeying the call of fate, like the heroes of old romance, appeared in the person of Dominicus Pike.

It only remains to say, that Mr. Hig- ginbotham took the pedler into high favor, sanctioned his addresses to the pretty schoolmistress, and settled his whole property on their children, allow- ing themselves the interest. In due time, the old gentleman capped the climax of his favors, by dying a Christian death, in bed, since which melancholy event, Dominicus Pike has removed from Kim- ballton, and established a large tobacco manufactory in my native village.

LITTLE ANNIE'S RAMBLE

G-DONG! Ding-dong! Ding-dong! own-crier has rung his bell, at a t corner, and little Annie stands father's door-steps, trying to hear the man with the loud voice is g about. Let me listen too. O, he ing the people that an elephant, , lion, and a royal tiger, and a with horns, and other strange from foreign countries, have come wn, and will receive all visitors choose to wait upon them. Per- ittle Annie would like to go. Yes; can see that the pretty child is

weary of this wide and pleasant street, with the green trees flinging their shade across the quiet sunshine, and the pave- ments and the sidewalks all as clean as if the housemaid had just swept them with her broom. She feels that impulse to go strolling away,—that longing after the mystery of the great world,—which many children feel, and which I felt in my childhood. Little Annie shall take a ramble with me. See! I do but hold out my hand, and, like some bright bird in the sunny air, with her blue silk frock fluttering upwards from her white pantalets, she comes bounding on tiptoe across the street.

Smooth back your brown curls, Annie; and let me tie on your bonnet, and we will set forth! What a strange couple to go on their rambles together! One walks in black attire, with a measured step, and a heavy brow, and his thoughtful eyes bent down, while the gay little girl trips lightly along, as if she were forced to keep hold of my hand, lest her feet should dance away from the earth. Yet there is sympathy between us. If I pride myself on anything, it is because I have a smile that children love; and, on the other hand, there are few grown ladies that could entice me from the side of little Annie; for I delight to let my mind go hand in hand with the mind of a sinless child. So, come, Annie; but if I moralize as we go, do not listen to me; only look about you, and be merry!

Now we turn the corner. Here are hacks with two horses, and stage-coaches with four, thundering to meet each other, and trucks and carts moving at a slower pace, being heavily laden with barrels from the wharves, and here are rattling gigs, which perhaps will be smashed to pieces before our eyes. Hitherward, also, comes a man trundling a wheelbarrow along the pavement. Is not little Annie afraid of such a tumult? No; she does not even shrink closer to my side, but passes on with fearless confidence, a happy child amidst a great throng of grown people, who pay the same reverence to her infancy that they would to extreme old age. Nobody jostles her; all turn aside to make way for little Annie; and what is most singular, she appears conscious of her claim to such respect. Now her

eyes brighten with pleasure! A musician has seated himself on the of yonder church, and pours fort strains to the busy town, a melody has gone astray among the tram footsteps, the buzz of voices, an war of passing wheels. Who heed poor organ-grinder? None but n and little Annie, whose feet beg move in unison with the lively tu: if she were loath that music s be wasted without a dance. But would Annie find a partner? Some the gout in their toes, or the rhe tism in their joints; some are with age; some feeble with dis some are so lean that their bones rattle, and others of such pond size that their agility would crac flagstones; but many, many have l feet, because their hearts are far h than lead. It is a sad thought t have chanced upon. What a compa dancers should we be! For I, too, gentleman of sober footsteps, and fore, little Annie, let us walk se on.

It is a question with me, whethe giddy child, or my sage self, have pleasure in looking at the shop dows. We love the silks of sunny that glow within the darkened pre of the spruce dry goods' men; w pleasantly dazzled by the burnishe ver, and the chased gold, the rin wedlock and the costly love ornar glistening at the window of the : ler; but Annie, more than I, seel a glimpse of her passing figure i dusty looking-glasses at the har stores. All that is bright and ga tracts us both.

Here is a shop to which the re tions of my boyhood, as well as

artialities, give a peculiar magic.
delightful to let the fancy revel
e dainties of a confectioner; those
with such white and flaky paste,
contents being a mystery, whether
mince, with whole plums inter-
d, or piquant apple, delicately rose
red; those cakes, heart-shaped or
d, piled in a lofty pyramid; those
little circlets, sweetly named
s; those dark majestic masses, fit
bridal loaves at the wedding of
eiress, mountains in size, their
its deeply snow-covered with
! Then the mighty treasures of
-plums, white, and crimson, and
w, in large glass vases; and candy
varieties; and those little cockles,
atever they are called, much prized
hildren for their sweetness, and
for the mottoes which they en-
by love-sick maids and bachelors!
y mouth waters, little Annie, and
oth yours; but we will not be
ted, except to an imaginary feast;
us hasten onward, devouring the
of a plum-cake.
re are pleasures, as some people
say, of a more exalted kind, in
vindow of a bookseller. Is Annie
rary lady? Yes; she is deeply read
eter Parley's tomes, and has an
sing love for fairy-tales, though
m met with now-a-days, and she
ubscribe, next year, to the Juvenile
ellany. But, truth to tell, she is
turn away from the printed page,
keep gazing at the pretty pictures,
s the gay-colored ones which make
shop window the continual loiter-
ace of children. What would An-
nink, if in the book which I mean
nd her, on New Year's day, she
d find her sweet little self, bound

up in silk or morocco with gilt edges,
there to remain till she become a woman
grown, with children of her own to
read about their mother's childhood?
That would be very queer.

Little Annie is weary of pictures, and
pulls me onward by the hand, till suddenly we pause at the most wondrous
shop in all the town. O my stars! Is
this a toyshop, or is it fairyland? For
here are gilded chariots, in which the
king and queen of the fairies might
ride side by side, while their courtiers,
on these small horses, should gallop in
triumphal procession before and behind
the royal pair. Here, too, are dishes of
china ware, fit to be the dining set of
those same princely personages, when
they make a regal banquet in the stateliest hall of their palace, full five feet
high, and behold their nobles feasting
adown the long perspective of the table.
Betwixt the king and queen should sit
my little Annie, the prettiest fairy of
them all. Here stands a turbaned turk,
threatening us with his sabre, like an
ugly heathen as he is. And next a
Chinese mandarin, who nods his head
at Annie and myself. Here we may
review a whole army of horse and foot,
in red and blue uniforms, with drums,
fifes, trumpets, and all kinds of noiseless music; they have halted on the
shelf of this window, after their weary
march from Liliput. But what cares
Annie for soldiers? No conquering
queen is she, neither a Semiramis nor
a Catharine; her whole heart is set
upon that doll, who gazes at us with
such a fashionable stare. This is the
little girl's true plaything. Though made
of wood, a doll is a visionary and
ethereal personage, endowed by childish fancy with a peculiar life; the mimic

lady is a heroine of romance, an actor and a sufferer in a thousand shadowy scenes, the chief inhabitant of that wild world with which children ape the real one. Little Annie does not understand what I am saying, but looks wishfully at the proud lady in the window. We will invite her home with us as we return. Meantime, good-by, Dame Doll! A toy yourself, you look forth from your window upon many ladies that are also toys, though they walk and speak, and upon a crowd in pursuit of toys, though they wear grave visages. O, with your never-closing eyes, had you but an intellect to moralize on all that flits before them, what a wise doll would you be! Come, little Annie, we shall find toys enough, go where we may.

Now we elbow our way among the throng again. It is curious, in the most crowded part of a town, to meet with living creatures that had their birthplace in some far solitude, but have acquired a second nature in the wilderness of men. Look up, Annie, at that canary-bird, hanging out of the window in his cage. Poor little fellow! His golden feathers are all tarnished in this smoky sunshine; he would have glistened twice as brightly among the summer islands; but still he has become a citizen in all his tastes and habits, and would not sing half so well without the uproar that drowns his music. What a pity that he does not know how miserable he is! There is a parrot, too, calling out, "Pretty Poll! Pretty Poll!" as we pass by. Foolish bird, to be talking about her prettiness to strangers, especially as she is not a pretty Poll, though gaudily dressed in green and yellow. If she had said "Pretty Annie," there would

have been some sense in it. See gray squirrel, at the door of the shop, whirling round and round so rily within his wire wheel! Being demned to the treadmill, he mal an amusement. Admirable philosop

Here comes a big, rough dog, a tryman's dog in search of his m smelling at everybody's heels, and t ing little Annie's hand with his nose, but hurrying away, thoug would fain have patted him. S to your search, Fidelity! And ther a great yellow cat upon a windo a very corpulent and comfortabl gazing at this transitory world, owl's eyes, and making pithy comn doubtless, or what appear such, t silly beast. O sage puss, make roo me beside you, and we will be a of philosophers!

Here we see something to remi of the town-crier, and his ding bell! Look! look at that great spread out in the air, pictured all with wild beasts, as if they hac together to choose a king, accordi their custom in the days of A But they are choosing neither a nor a president; else we should a most horrible snarling! They come from the deep woods, an wild mountains, and the desert and the polar snows, only t homage to my little Annie. As w ter among them, the great ele makes us a bow, in the best st elephantine courtesy, bending down his mountain bulk, with abased, and leg thrust out behind. returns the salute, much to the fication of the elephant, who is ce the best-bred monster in the ca The lion and the lioness are bus

beef-bones. The royal tiger, the
iful, the untamable, keeps pacing
arrow cage with a haughty step,
ndful of the spectators or recall-
he fierce deeds of his former life,
he was wont to leap forth upon
inferior animals, from the jungles
engal.
re we see the very same wolf—
ot go near him, Annie!—the self-
wolf that devoured little Red Rid-
Hood and her grandmother. In the
cage, a hyena from Egypt, who has
less howled around the pyramids,
a black bear from our own forests,
ellow-prisoners, and most excellent
ls. Are there any two living crea-
who have so few sympathies that
cannot possibly be friends? Here
a great white bear, whom common
vers would call a very stupid beast,
h I perceive him to be only ab-
d in contemplation; he is thinking
s voyages on an iceberg, and of
omfortable home in the vicinity
e north pole, and of the little cubs
a he left rolling in the eternal
s. In fact, he is a bear of senti-
But, O, those unsentimental
eys! the ugly, grinning, aping,
ering, ill-natured, mischievous, and
little brutes. Annie does not love
monkeys. Their ugliness shocks her
instinctive delicacy of taste, and
s her mind unquiet, because it
a wild and dark resemblance to
nity. But here is a little pony,
big enough for Annie to ride, and
d and round he gallops in a circle,
ng time with his trampling hoofs
band of music. And here,—with a
coat and a cocked hat, and a
-whip in his hand,—here comes a
gentleman, small enough to be king

of the fairies, and ugly enough to be
king of the gnomes, and takes a flying
leap into the saddle. Merrily, merrily,
plays the music, and merrily gallops the
pony, and merrily rides the little old
gentleman. Come, Annie, into the street
again; perchance we may see monkeys
on horseback there!

Mercy on us, what a noisy world
we quiet people live in! Did Annie ever
read the Cries of London City? With
what lusty lungs doth yonder man proclaim that his wheelbarrow is full of
lobsters! Here comes another mounted
on a cart, and blowing a hoarse and
dreadful blast from a tin horn, as much
as to say "Fresh fish!" And hark! a
voice on high, like that of a muezzin
from the summit of a mosque, announcing that some chimney-sweeper
has emerged from smoke and soot, and
darksome caverns, into the upper air.
What cares the world for that? But,
well-a-day! we hear a shrill voice of
affliction, the scream of a little child,
rising louder with every repetition of
that smart, sharp, slapping sound, produced by an open hand on tender flesh.
Annie sympathizes, though without experience of such direful woe. Lo! the
town-crier again, with some new secret
for the public ear. Will he tell us of
an auction, or of a lost pocket-book,
or a show of beautiful wax figures, or
of some monstrous beast more horrible
than any in the caravan? I guess the
latter. See how he uplifts the bell in
his right hand, and shakes it slowly
at first, then with a hurried motion, till
the clapper seems to strike both sides
at once, and the sounds are scattered
forth in quick succession, far and near.

Ding-dong! Ding-dong! Ding-dong!

Now he raises his clear, loud voice,

above all the din of the town; it drowns the buzzing talk of many tongues, and draws each man's mind from his own business; it rolls up and down the echoing street, and ascends to the hushed chamber of the sick, and penetrates downward to the cellar-kitchen, where the hot cook turns from the fire to listen. Who, of all that address the public ear, whether in church, or courthouse, or hall of state, has such an attentive audience as the town-crier? What saith the people's orator?

"Strayed from her home, a LITTLE GIRL, of five years old, in a blue silk frock and white pantalets, with brown curling hair and hazel eyes. Whoever will bring her back to her afflicted mother—"

Stop, stop, town-crier! The lost is found. O, my pretty Annie, we forgot to tell your mother of our ramble, and she is in despair, and has sent the town-crier to bellow up and down the streets, affrighting old and young, for the loss of a little girl who has not once let go my hand? Well, let us hasten homeward; and as we go, forget not to thank Heaven, my Annie, that, after wandering a little way into the world, you may return at the first summons, with an untainted and unwearied heart, and be a happy child again. But I have gone too far astray for the town-crier to call me back.

Sweet has been the charm of c hood on my spirit, throughout ramble with little Annie! Say not it has been a waste of precious ments, an idle matter, a babbl childish talk, and a reverie of c ish imaginations, about topics unwe of a grown man's notice. Has it merely this? Not so; not so. The not truly wise who would affirr As the pure breath of children re the life of aged men, so is our n nature revived by their free and si thoughts, their native feeling, their mirth, for little cause or none, grief, soon roused and soon all Their influence on us is at least rec cal with ours on them. When our inf is almost forgotten, and our boy long departed, though it seems bu yesterday; when life settles d down upon us, and we doubt wh to call ourselves young any more, it is good to steal away from society of bearded men, and eve gentler woman, and spend an hou two with children. After drinking those fountains of still fresh exist we shall return into the crowd, do now, to struggle onward and do part in life, perhaps as ferventl ever, but, for a time, with a k and purer heart, and a spirit more l ly wise. All this by thy sweet m dear little Annie!

WAKEFIELD

IN some old magazine or newspaper, I recollect a story, told as truth, of a man—let us call him Wakefield—who

absented himself for a long time his wife. The fact, thus abstrac stated, is not very uncommon, n

out a proper distinction of circum-
ces—to be condemned either as
hty or nonsensical. Howbeit, this,
gh far from the most aggravated,
erhaps the strangest instance, on
rd, of marital delinquency; and
over, as remarkable a freak as may
ound in the whole list of human
ies. The wedded couple lived in
lon. The man, under pretence of go-
journey, took lodgings in the next
t to his own house, and there, un-
l of by his wife or friends, and with-
he shadow of a reason for such self-
hment, dwelt upwards of twenty
. During that period, he beheld his
every day, and frequently the for-
Mrs. Wakefield. And after so great
in his matrimonial felicity—when
death was reckoned certain, his
settled, his name dismissed from
ory, and his wife, long, long ago,
ed to her autumnal widowhood—
tered the door one evening, quietly,
om a day's absence, and became a
g spouse till death.

is outline is all that I remember.
he incident, though of the purest
ality, unexampled and probably
to be repeated, is one, I think,
appeals to the generous sym-
es of mankind. We know, each for
lf, that none of us would perpe-
such a folly, yet feel as if some
might. To my own contemplations,
st, it has often recurred, always
ng wonder, but with a sense that
ory must be true, and a conception
hero's character. Whenever any
ct so forcibly affects the mind,
is well spent in thinking of it. If
ader choose, let him do his own
ation; or if he prefer to ramble
me through the twenty years of

Wakefield's vagary, I bid him welcome;
trusting that there will be a pervading
spirit and a moral, even should we fail
to find them, done up neatly, and condensed into the final sentence. Thought
has always its efficacy, and every striking incident its moral?

What sort of a man was Wakefield?
We are free to shape out our own idea,
and call it by his name. He was now
in the meridian of life; his matrimonial
affections, never violent, were sobered
into a calm, habitual sentiment; of all
husbands, he was likely to be the most
constant, because a certain sluggishness
would keep his heart at rest, wherever
it might be placed. He was intellectual,
but not actively so; his mind occupied
itself in long and lazy musings, that
tended to no purpose, or had not vigor
to attain it; his thoughts were seldom
so energetic as to seize hold of words.
Imagination, in the proper meaning of
the term, made no part of Wakefield's
gifts. With a cold, but not depraved nor
wandering heart, and a mind never
feverish with riotous thoughts, nor perplexed with originality, who could have
anticipated, that our friend would entitle
himself to a foremost place among the
doers of eccentric deeds? Had his acquaintances been asked, who was the
man in London the surest to perform
nothing to-day which should be remembered on the morrow, they would have
thought of Wakefield. Only the wife of
his bosom might have hesitated. She,
without having analyzed his character,
was partly aware of a quiet selfishness,
that had rusted into his inactive mind,—
of a peculiar sort of vanity, the most
uneasy attribute about him,—of a disposition to craft, which had seldom produced more positive effects than the

keeping of petty secrets, hardly worth revealing,—and, lastly, of what she called a little strangeness, sometimes, in the good man. This latter quality is indefinable, and perhaps non-existent.

Let us now imagine Wakefield bidding adieu to his wife. It is the dusk of an October evening. His equipment is a drab great coat, a hat covered with an oilcloth, top boots, an umbrella in one hand and a small portmanteau in the other. He has informed Mrs. Wakefield that he is to take the night coach into the country. She would fain inquire the length of his journey, its object, and the probable time of his return; but, indulgent to his harmless love of mystery, interrogates him only by a look. He tells her not to expect him positively by the return coach, nor to be alarmed should he tarry three or four days; but, at all events, to look for him at supper on Friday evening. Wakefield himself, be it considered, has no suspicion of what is before him. He holds out his hands; she gives her own, and meets his parting kiss, in the matter-of-course way of a ten years' matrimony; and forth goes the middle-aged Mr. Wakefield, almost resolved to perplex his good lady by a whole week's absence. After the door has closed behind him, she perceives it thrust partly open, and a vision of her husband's face, through the aperture, smiling on her, and gone in a moment. For the time, this little incident is dismissed without a thought. But, long afterwards, when she has been more years a widow than a wife, that smile recurs, and flickers across all her reminiscences of Wakefield's visage. In her many musings, she surrounds the original smile with a multitude of fantasies, which make it strange and awful;

as, for instance, if she imagines hi a coffin, that parting look is froze his pale features; or, if she dream him in heaven, still his blessed wears a quiet and crafty smile. Ye its sake, when all others have giver up for dead, she sometimes d whether she is a widow.

But our business is with the hus We must hurry after him, along street, ere he lose his individuality melt into the great mass of Londor It would be vain searching for there. Let us follow close at his therefore, until, after several super turns and doublings, we find him fortably established by the fireside small apartment, previously besp He is in the next street to his own at his journey's end. He can sc: trust his good fortune in havin thither unperceived,—recollecting at one time, he was delayed b throng, in the very focus of a li lantern; and, again, there were foo that seemed to tread behind his distinct from the multitudinous around him; and, anon, he heard a shouting afar, and fancied that it his name. Doubtless, a dozen busy had been watching him, and tol wife the whole affair. Poor Wake Little knowest thou thine own nificance in this great world! No i eye but mine has traced thee. Go c to thy bed, foolish man; and, o morrow, if thou wilt be wise, ge home to good Mrs. Wakefield, ar her the truth. Remove not thyself for a little week, from thy place chaste bosom. Were she, for a moment, to deem thee dead, or l lastingly divided from her, thou w be wofully conscious of a change

wife, forever after. It is perilous
ake a chasm in human affections;
hat they gape so long and wide,—
o quickly close again!

nost repenting of his frolic, or
ever it may be termed, Wakefield
down betimes, and, starting from
first nap, spreads forth his arms
the wide and solitary waste of the
ustomed bed. "No,"—thinks he,
ring the bedclothes about him,—"I
ot sleep alone another night."

the morning, he rises earlier than
, and sets himself to consider what
ally means to do. Such are his
and rambling modes of thought,
e has taken this very singular step,
the consciousness of a purpose, in-
but without being able to define it
ently for his own contemplation.
vagueness of the project, and the
ulsive effort with which he plunges
the execution of it, are equally
cteristic of a feeble-minded man.
field sifts his ideas, however, as
ely as he may, and finds himself
is to know the progress of matters
me,—how his exemplary wife will
e her widowhood of a week; and,
, how the little sphere of creatures
circumstances in which he was a
l object will be affected by his re-
. A morbid vanity, therefore, lies
t the bottom of the affair. But
s he to attain his ends? Not, cer-
, by keeping close in this com-
le lodging, where, though he slept
woke in the next street to his
he is as effectually abroad, as if
age-coach had been whirling him
all night. Yet, should he reappear,
whole project is knocked in the
His poor brains being hopelessly
d with this dilemma, he at length

ventures out, partly resolving to cross
the head of the street, and send one
hasty glance towards his forsaken domi-
cile. Habit—for he is a man of habits—
takes him by the hand, and guides him,
wholly unaware, to his own door, where,
just at the critical moment, he is
aroused by the scraping of his foot
upon the step. Wakefield! whither are
you going?

At that instant, his fate was turning
on the pivot. Little dreaming of the
doom to which his first backward step
devotes him, he hurries away, breathless
with agitation hitherto unfelt, and
hardly dares turn his head, at the distant corner. Can it be, that nobody
caught sight of him? Will not the whole
household—the decent Mrs. Wakefield,
the smart maid-servant, and the dirty
little footboy—raise a hue and cry,
through London streets, in pursuit of
their fugitive lord and master? Wonderful escape! He gathers courage to pause
and look homeward, but is perplexed
with a sense of change about the
familiar edifice, such as affects us all,
when, after a separation of months or
years, we again see some hill or lake,
or work of art, with which we were
friends, of old. In ordinary cases, this
indescribable impression is caused by
the comparison and contrast between
our imperfect reminiscences and the
reality. In Wakefield, the magic of a
single night has wrought a similar transformation, because, in that brief period,
a great moral change has been effected.
But this is a secret from himself. Before
leaving the spot, he catches a far and
momentary glimpse of his wife, passing
athwart the front window, with her face
turned towards the head of the street.
The crafty nincompoop takes to his

heels, scared with the idea, that, among a thousand such atoms of mortality, her eye must have detected him. Right glad is his heart, though his brain be somewhat dizzy, when he finds himself by the coal-fire of his lodgings.

So much for the commencement of this long whimwham. After the initial conception, and the stirring up of the man's sluggish temperament to put it in practice, the whole matter evolves itself in a natural train. We may suppose him, as the result of deep deliberation, buying a new wig, of reddish hair, and selecting sundry garments, in a fashion unlike his customary suit of brown, from a Jew's old-clothes bag. It is accomplished. Wakefield is another man. The new system being now established, a retrograde movement to the old would be almost as difficult as the step that placed him in his unparalleled position. Furthermore, he is rendered obstinate by a sulkiness, occasionally incident to his temper, and brought on, at present, by the inadequate sensation which he conceives to have been produced in the bosom of Mrs. Wakefield. He will not go back until she be frightened half to death. Well; twice or thrice has she passed before his sight, each time with a heavier step, a paler cheek, and more anxious brow; and in the third week of his nonappearance, he detects a portent of evil entering the house, in the guise of an apothecary. Next day, the knocker is muffled. Towards nightfall comes the chariot of a physician, and deposits its big-wigged and solemn burden at Wakefield's door, whence, after a quarter of an hour's visit, he emerges, perchance the herald of a funeral. Dear woman! Will she die? By this time

Wakefield is excited to something energy of feeling, but still lingers from his wife's bedside, pleading his conscience, that she must no disturbed at such a juncture. If a else restrains him, he does not kno In the course of a few weeks gradually recovers; the crisis is her heart is sad, perhaps, but quiet; let him return soon or late, it will be feverish for him again. Such glimmer through the mist of Wakef mind, and render him indistinctly scious that an almost impassable divides his hired apartment fro former home. "It is but in the street!" he sometimes says. Fool! it another world. Hitherto, he has p his return from one particular da another; henceforward, he leaves precise time undetermined. Not morrow,—probably next week,—p soon. Poor man! The dead have n as much chance of revisiting earthly homes as the self-ban Wakefield.

Would that I had a folio to writ stead of an article of a dozen p Then might I exemplify how a fluence, beyond our control, lay strong hand on every deed whic do, and weaves its consequences in iron tissue of necessity. Wakefie spell-bound. We must leave him, fo years or so, to haunt around his h without once crossing the threshol to be faithful to his wife, with a affection of which his heart is ca while he is slowly fading out of Long since, it must be remarked, h lost the perception of singularity conduct.

Now for a scene! Amid the t of a London street, we distingu

now waxing elderly, with few
cteristics to attract careless ob-
rs, yet bearing, in his whole aspect,
andwriting of no common fate, for
as have the skill to read it. He
agre; his low and narrow forehead
eply wrinkled; his eyes, small and
less, sometimes wander apprehen-
y about him, but oftener seem to
inward. He bends his head, and
s with an indescribable obliquity
it, as if unwilling to display his full
to the world. Watch him, long
h to see what we have described,
ou will allow, that circumstances,
ich often produce remarkable men
nature's ordinary handiwork,—
produced one such here. Next,
g him to sidle along the footwalk,
our eyes in the opposite direction,
a portly female, considerably in
ane of life, with a prayer-book in
hand, is proceeding to yonder
h. She has the placid mien of
d widowhood. Her regrets have
died away, or have become so
ial to her heart, that they would
orly exchanged for joy. Just as
lean man and well-conditioned
n are passing, a slight obstruction
s, and brings these two figures
ly in contact. Their hands touch;
ressure of the crowd forces her
against his shoulder; they stand;
to face, staring into each other's
After a ten years' separation, thus
field meets his wife!

throng eddies away, and carries
asunder. The sober widow, resum-
r former pace, proceeds to church,
auses in the portal, and throws a
xed glance along the street. She
in, however, opening her prayer-
as she goes. And the man! with so

wild a face, that busy and selfish London
stands to gaze after him, he hurries to
his lodgings, bolts the door, and throws
himself upon the bed. The latent feelings of years break out; his feeble mind
acquires a brief energy from their
strength; all the miserable strangeness
of his life is revealed to him at a glance:
and he cries out, passionately, "Wakefield! Wakefield! You are mad!"

Perhaps he was so. The singularity of
his situation must have so moulded him
to himself, that, considered in regard to
his fellow-creatures and the business of
life, he could not be said to possess his
right mind. He had contrived, or rather
he had happened, to dissever himself
from the world,—to vanish,—to give up
his place and privileges with living men,
without being admitted among the dead.
The life of a hermit is nowise parallel
to his. He was in the bustle of the city,
as of old; but the crowd swept by, and
saw him not; he was, we may figuratively say, always beside his wife, and
at his hearth, yet must never feel the
warmth of the one nor the affection of
the other. It was Wakefield's unprecedented fate to retain his original share
of human sympathies, and to be still
involved in human interests, while he
had lost his reciprocal influence on them.
It would be a most curious speculation
to trace out the effect of such circumstances on his heart and intellect, separately, and in unison. Yet, changed as he
was, he would seldom be conscious of
it, but deem himself the same man as
ever; glimpses of the truth, indeed,
would come, but only for the moment;
and still he would keep saying,—"I
shall soon go back!"—nor reflect that
he had been saying so for twenty years.

I conceive, also, that these twenty

years would appear, in the retrospect, scarcely longer than the week to which Wakefield had at first limited his absence. He would look on the affair as no more than an interlude in the main business of his life. When, after a little while more, he should deem it time to re-enter his parlor, his wife would clap her hands for joy, on beholding the middle-aged Mr. Wakefield. Alas, what a mistake! Would Time but await the close of our favorite follies, we should be young men, all of us, and till Doomsday.

One evening, in the twentieth year since he vanished, Wakefield is taking his customary walk towards the dwelling which he still calls his own. It is a gusty night of autumn, with frequent showers, that patter down upon the pavement, and are gone before a man can put up his umbrella. Pausing near the house, Wakefield discerns, through the parlor windows on the second floor, the red glow, and the glimmer and fitful flash of a comfortable fire. On the ceiling appears a grotesque shadow of good Mrs. Wakefield. The cap, the nose and chin, and the broad waist, form an admirable caricature, which dances, moreover, with the up-flickering and down-sinking blaze, almost too merrily for the shade of an elderly widow. At this instant, a shower chances to fall, and is driven, by the unmannerly gust, full into Wakefield's face and bosom. He is quite penetrated with its autumnal chill.

Shall he stand wet and shivering when his own hearth has a good fi warm him, and his own wife will r fetch the gray coat and small-clo which, doubtless, she has kept car in the closet of their bed-chamber? Wakefield is no such fool. He as the steps—heavily!—for twenty have stiffened his legs, since he down,—but he knows it not. Wakefield! Would you go to the home that is left you? Then step your grave! The door opens. A passes in we have a parting glimp his visage, and recognize the c smile, which was the precursor o little joke, that he has ever since playing off at his wife's expense. unmercifully has he quizzed the wo Well, a good night's rest to Wakefi

This happy event—supposing it such—could only have occurred unpremeditated moment. We wi follow our friend across the thres He has left us much food for the a portion of which shall lend its w to a moral, and be shaped into a f Amid the seeming confusion of mysterious world, individuals a: nicely adjusted to a system, and tems to one another, and to a that, by stepping aside for a mo a man exposes himself to a fearfu of losing his place forever. Like field, he may become, as it were Outcast of the Universe.

A RILL FROM THE TOWN-PUMP

(SCENE,—*the corner of two principal*
s. The TOWN-PUMP *talking through*
se)

ON, by the North clock! Noon, by
ast! High noon, too, by these hot
eams, which fall, scarcely aslope,
my head, and almost make the
bubble and smoke in the trough
my nose. Truly, we public char-
s have a tough time of it! And
g all the town officers, chosen at
h meeting, where is he that sus-
for a single year, the burden of
manifold duties as are imposed, in
tuity, upon the Town-Pump? The
of "town treasurer" is rightfully
as guardian of the best treasure
he town has. The overseers of the
ought to make me their chairman,
I provide bountifully for the pau-
without expense to him that pays
I am at the head of the fire de-
ent, and one of the physicians to
oard of health. As a keeper of the
all water-drinkers I will confess me
to the constable. I perform some
duties of the town clerk, by pro-
ting public notices, when they are
d on my front. To speak within
ds, I am the chief person of the
ipality, and exhibit, moreover, an
able pattern to my brother officers,
e cool, steady, upright, downright,
npartial discharge of my business,
he constancy with which I stand
post. Summer or winter, nobody
me in vain; for, all day long, I
n at the busiest corner, just above
arket, stretching out my arms, to

ex and Washington Streets, Salem.

rich and poor alike; and at night, I hold
a lantern over my head, both to show
where I am, and keep people out of
the gutters.

At this sultry noontide I am cup-
bearer to the parched populace, for
whose benefit an iron goblet is chained
to my waist. Like a dram-seller on the
mall, at muster-day, I cry aloud to all
and sundry, in my plainest accents, and
at the very tiptop of my voice. Here
it is, gentlemen! Here is the good
liquor! Walk up, walk up, gentlemen,
walk up, walk up! Here is the superior
stuff! Here is the unadulterated ale of
father Adam,—better than Cognac, Hol-
lands, Jamaica, strong beer, or wine of
any price; here it is, by the hogshead or
the single glass, and not a cent to pay!
Walk up, gentlemen, walk up, and help
yourselves!

It were a pity if all this outcry should
draw no customers. Here they come.
A hot day, gentlemen! Quaff, and away
again, so as to keep yourselves in a nice
cool sweat. You, my friend, will need
another cupful, to wash the dust out of
your throat, if it be as thick there as
it is on your cowhide shoes. I see that
you have trudged half a score of miles
to-day; and, like a wise man, have passed
by the taverns, and stopped at the running brooks and well-curbs. Otherwise,
betwixt heat without and fire within,
you would have been burned to a cinder,
or melted down to nothing at all, in the
fashion of a jelly-fish. Drink, and make
room for that other fellow, who seeks
my aid to quench the fiery fever of
last night's potations, which he drained
from no cup of mine. Welcome, most

rubicund sir! You and I have been
great strangers, hitherto; nor, to confess
the truth, will my nose be anxious for
a closer intimacy, till the fumes of your
breath be a little less potent. Mercy on
you, man! the water absolutely hisses
down your red-hot gullet, and is converted quite to steam, in the miniature
tophet which you mistake for a stomach.
Fill again, and tell me, on the word of
an honest toper, did you ever, in cellar,
tavern, or any kind of a dram-shop,
spend the price of your children's food
for a swig half so delicious? Now, for
the first time these ten years, you know
the flavor of cold water. Good-by; and,
whenever you are thirsty, remember
that I keep a constant supply, at the old
stand. Who next? O, my little friend,
you are let loose from school, and come
hither to scrub your blooming face, and
drown the memory of certain taps
of the ferule, and other school-boy
troubles, in a draught from the Town-
Pump. Take it, pure as the current of
your young life. Take it, and may your
heart and tongue never be scorched with
a fiercer thirst than now! There, my
dear child, put down the cup, and yield
your place to this elderly gentleman,
who treads so tenderly over the paving-
stones, that I suspect he is afraid of
breaking them. What! he limps by, without so much as thanking me, as if my
hospitable offers were meant only for
people who have no wine-cellars. Well,
well, sir,—no harm done, I hope! Go
draw the cork, tip the decanter; but
when your great toe shall set you
a-roaring, it will be no affair of mine.
If gentlemen love the pleasant titillation
of the gout, it is all one to the Town-
Pump. This thirsty dog, with his red
tongue lolling out, does not scorn my

hospitality, but stands on his hind
and laps eagerly out of the trough.
how lightly he capers away again! J
er, did your worship ever have the g
Are you all satisfied? Then wipe
mouths, my good friends; and, v
my spout has a moment's leisure, I
delight the town with a few histo
reminiscences. In far antiquity, ber
a darksome shadow of venerable bo
a spring bubbled out of the leaf-st
earth, in the very spot where you
behold me, on the sunny pavement.
water was as bright and clear,
deemed as precious, as liquid diam
The Indian sagamores drank of it,
time immemorial, till the fatal d
of the fire-water burst upon the
men, and swept their whole race
from the cold fountains. Endicott
his followers came next, and often
down to drink, dipping their
beards in the spring. The richest
let, then, was of birch bark. Gov
Winthrop, after a journey afoot
Boston, drank here, out of the h
of his hand. The elder Higginson
wet his palm, and laid it on the
of the first town-born child. For
years it was the watering-place, an
it were, the wash-bowl of the vicini
whither all decent folks resorte
purify their visages, and gaze at
afterwards—at least, the pretty ma
did—in the mirror which it made
Sabbath days, whenever a babe w
be baptized, the sexton filled his
here, and placed it on the commu
table of the humble meeting-h
which partly covered the site of y
stately brick one. Thus, one gene
after another was consecrated to H
by its waters, and cast their waxin
waning shadows into its glassy b

d vanished from the earth, as if
ortal life were but a flitting image
a fountain. Finally, the fountain
nished also. Cellars were dug on all
des, and cart-loads of gravel flung
on its source, whence oozed a turbid
ream, forming a mud-puddle, at the
rner of two streets. In the hot months,
en its refreshment was most needed,
e dust flew in clouds over the for-
tten birthplace of the waters, now
eir grave. But, in the course of time,
Town-Pump was sunk into the source
the ancient spring; and when the
st decayed, another took its place,—
d then another, and still another,—
here stand I, gentlemen and ladies,
serve you with my iron goblet. Drink,
d be refreshed! The water is as pure
d cold as that which slaked the thirst
the red sagamore, beneath the aged
ughs, though now the gem of the
lderness is treasured under these hot
ones, where no shadow falls but from
e brick buildings. And be it the moral
my story, that, as this wasted and
g-lost fountain is now known and
ized again, so shall the virtues of cold
ter, too little valued since your
hers' days, be recognized by all.

Your pardon, good people! I must in-
rupt my stream of eloquence, and
out forth a stream of water, to re-
enish the trough for this teamster and
s two yoke of oxen, who have come
om Topsfield, or somewhere along
at way. No part of my business is
easanter than the watering of cattle.
ok! how rapidly they lower the water-
irk on the sides of the trough, till
eir capacious stomachs are moistened
th a gallon or two apiece, and they
n afford time to breathe it in, with
hs of calm enjoyment. Now they roll

their quiet eyes around the brim of their
monstrous drinking-vessel. An ox is your
true toper.

But I perceive, my dear auditors,
that you are impatient for the remainder
of my discourse. Impute it, I beseech
you, to no defect of modesty, if I insist
a little longer on so fruitful a topic as
my own multifarious merits. It is altogether for your good. The better you
think of me, the better men and women
will you find yourselves. I shall say
nothing of my all-important aid on
washing-days; though, on that account
alone, I might call myself the household
god of a hundred families. Far be it
from me also to hint, my respectable
friends, of the show of dirty faces which
you would present without my pains to
keep you clean. Nor will I remind you
how often, when the midnight bells
make you tremble for your combustible
town, you have fled to the Town-Pump,
and found me always at my post, firm,
amid the confusion, and ready to drain
my vital current in your behalf. Neither
is it worth while to lay much stress on
my claims to a medical diploma, as the
physician, whose simple rule of practice
is preferable to all the nauseous lore,
which has found men sick or left them
so, since the days of Hippocrates. Let us
take a broader view of my beneficial
influence on mankind.

No; these are trifles, compared with
the merits which wise men concede to
me—if not in my single self, yet as the
representative of a class—of being the
grand reformer of the age. From my
spout, and such spouts as mine, must
flow the stream, that shall cleanse our
earth of the vast portion of its crime
and anguish, which has gushed from the
fiery fountains of the still. In this

mighty enterprise, the cow shall be my great confederate. Milk and water! The TOWN-PUMP and the Cow! Such is the glorious copartnership that shall tear down the distilleries and brew-houses, uproot the vineyards, shatter the cider-presses, ruin the tea and coffee trade, and finally monopolize the whole business of quenching thirst. Blessed consummation! Then Poverty shall pass away from the land, finding no hovel so wretched, where her squalid form may shelter itself. Then Disease, for lack of other victims, shall gnaw its own heart, and die. Then Sin, if she do not die, shall lose half her strength. Until now, the frenzy of hereditary fever has raged in the human blood, transmitted from sire to son, and rekindled, in every generation, by fresh draughts of liquid flame. When that inward fire shall be extinguished, the heat of passion cannot but grow cool, and war—the drunkenness of nations—perhaps will cease. At least there will be no war of households. The husband and wife, drinking deep of peaceful joy,—a calm bliss of temperate affections,—shall pass hand in hand through life, and lie down, not reluctantly, at its protracted close. To them, the past will be no turmoil of mad dreams, nor the future an eternity of such moments as follows the delirium of the drunkard. Their dead faces shall express what their spirits were, and are to be, by a lingering smile of memory and hope.

Ahem! Dry work, this speechifying; especially to an unpractised orator. I never conceived, till now, what toil the temperance lecturers undergo for my sake. Hereafter they shall have the business to themselves. Do, some kind Christian, pump a stroke or two, just to wet my whistle. Thank you, sir! M dear hearers, when the world shall hav been regenerated, by my instrume tality, you will collect your useless va and liquor-casks into one great pile, ar make a bonfire in honor of the Tow Pump. And when I shall have decaye like my predecessors, then, if you reve my memory, let a marble fountai richly sculptured, take my place upc this spot. Such monuments should I erected everywhere, and inscribed wi the names of the distinguished cham pions of my cause. Now listen; f something very important is to con next.

There are two or three honest frien of mine—and true friends, I know, the are—who, nevertheless, by their fie pugnacity in my behalf, do put me fearful hazard of a broken nose, or ev a total overthrow upon the pavemen and the loss of the treasure which guard. I pray you, gentlemen, let th fault be amended. Is it decent, thi you, to get tipsy with zeal for tempe ance, and take up the honorable cau of the Town-Pump in the style of toper fighting for his brandy-bottle? (can the excellent qualities of cold wat be not otherwise exemplified than l plunging, slapdash, into hot water, ar wofully scalding yourselves and oth people? Trust me they may. In ti moral warfare which you are to wage and, indeed, in the whole conduct your lives—you cannot choose a bett example than myself, who have nev permitted the dust and sultry atmo phere, the turbulence and manifold di quietudes of the world around me, reach that deep, calm well of purit which may be called my soul. A whenever I pour out that soul, it is ol earth's fever or cleanse its stains. One o'clock! Nay, then, if the dinner-ll begins to speak, I may as well hold y peace. Here comes a pretty young rl of my acquaintance, with a large one pitcher for me to fill. May she aw a husband, while drawing her water, as Rachel did of old. Hold out your vessel, my dear! There it is, full to the brim; so now run home, peeping at your sweet image in the pitcher, as you go; and forget not, in a glass of my own liquor, to drink—"SUCCESS TO THE TOWN-PUMP!"

THE GREAT CARBUNCLE *

MYSTERY OF THE WHITE MOUNTAINS

AT nightfall, once, in the olden time, the rugged side of one of the Crystal ills, a party of adventurers were re-shing themselves, after a toilsome and uitless quest for the Great Carbuncle. hey had come thither, not as friends, r partners in the enterprise, but each, ve one youthful pair, impelled by his vn selfish and solitary longing for this ondrous gem. Their feeling of brother-ood, however, was strong enough to duce them to contribute a mutual aid building a rude hut of branches, and ndling a great fire of shattered pines, al had drifted down the headlong cur-nt of the Amonoosuck, on the lower nk of which they were to pass the ght. There was but one of their num-r, perhaps, who had become so es-anged from natural sympathies, by e absorbing spell of the pursuit, as to knowledge no satisfaction at the sight human faces, in the remote and litary region whither they had as-

cended. A vast extent of wilderness lay between them and the nearest settle-ment, while scant a mile above their heads was that black verge, where the hills throw off their shaggy mantle of forest trees, and either robe themselves in clouds or tower naked into the sky. The roar of the Amonoosuck would have been too awful for endurance, if only a solitary man had listened, while the mountain stream talked with the wind.

The adventurers, therefore, exchanged hospitable greetings, and welcomed one another to the hut, where each man was the host, and all were the guests of the whole company. They spread their in-dividual supplies of food on the flat sur-face of a rock, and partook of a general repast; at the close of which, a senti-ment of good fellowship was perceptible among the party, though repressed by the idea that the renewed search for the Great Carbuncle must make them strangers again in the morning. Seven men and one young woman, they warmed themselves together at the fire, which extended its bright wall along the whole front of their wigwam. As they observed the various and contrasted figures that made up the assemblage, each man looking like a caricature of

* The Indian tradition, on which this some-at extravagant tale is founded, is both too d and too beautiful to be adequately wrought in prose. Sullivan, in his History of Maine, itten since the Revolution, remarks that even n the existence of the Great Carbuncle was t entirely discredited.

himself, in the unsteady light that flickered over him, they came mutually to the conclusion, that an odder society had never met, in city or wilderness, on mountain or plain.

The eldest of the group, a tall, lean, weather-beaten man, some sixty years of age, was clad in the skins of wild animals, whose fashion of dress he did well to imitate, since the deer, the wolf, and the bear had long been his most intimate companions. He was one of those ill-fated mortals, such as the Indians told of, whom, in their early youth, the Great Carbuncle smote with a peculiar madness, and became the passionate dream of their existence. All who visited that region knew him as the Seeker, and by no other name. As none could remember when he first took up the search, there went a fable in the valley of the Saco, that for his inordinate lust after the Great Carbuncle he had been condemned to wander among the mountains till the end of time, still with the same feverish hopes at sunrise,—the same despair at eve. Near this miserable Seeker sat a little elderly personage, wearing a high-crowned hat, shaped somewhat like a crucible. He was from beyond the sea, a Doctor Cacaphodel, who had wilted and dried himself into a mummy, by continually stooping over charcoal furnaces and inhaling unwholesome fumes, during his researches in chemistry and alchemy. It was told of him, whether truly or not, that, at the commencement of his studies, he had drained his body of all its richest blood, and wasted it, with other inestimable ingredients, in an unsuccessful experiment,—and had never been a well man since. Another of the adventurers was Master Ichabod Pigsnort, a weighty merchant and selec[t] man of Boston, and an elder of t[he] famous Mr. Norton's church. H[is] enemies had a ridiculous story, th[at] Master Pigsnort was accustomed [to] spend a whole hour, after prayer tim[e], every morning and evening, in wallow[-] ing naked among an immense quanti[ty] of pine-tree shillings, which were t[he] earliest silver coinage of Massachuset[ts]. The fourth whom we shall notice ha[d] no name, that his companions knew [of], and was chiefly distinguished by a sne[er] that always contorted his thin visag[e], and by a prodigious pair of spectacle[s] which were supposed to deform a[nd] discolor the whole face of nature, to th[e] gentleman's perception. The fifth a[d] venturer, likewise lacked a name, whi[ch] was the greater pity, as he appeared [to] be a poet. He was a bright-eyed ma[n], but wofully pined away, which was [no] more than natural, if, as some peop[le] affirmed, his ordinary diet was fo[r] morning mist, and a slice of the dense[st] cloud within his reach, sauced wi[th] moonshine, whenever he could get [it]. Certain it is, that the poetry, whi[ch] flowed from him, had a smack of [all] these dainties. The sixth of the par[ty] was a young man of haughty mien, a[nd] sat somewhat apart from the rest, wea[r] ing his plumed hat loftily among [his] elders, while the fire glittered on t[he] rich embroidery of his dress, a[nd] gleamed intensely on the jewelled po[m] mel of his sword. This was the Lord [de] Vere, who, when at home, was said [to] spend much of his time in the buri[al] vault of his dead progenitors, rumma[g] ing their mouldy coffins in search of [all] the earthly pride and vainglory that w[as] hidden among bones and dust; so th[at], besides his own share, he had the c[redit]

:ted haughtiness of his whole line of
cestry.

Lastly, there was a handsome youth
rustic garb, and by his side, a bloom-
; little person, in whom a delicate
.de of maiden reserve was just melting
o the rich glow of a young wife's
ection. Her name was Hannah, and
r husband's Matthew; two homely
mes, yet well enough adapted to the
nple pair, who seemed strangely out
place among the whimsical fraternity
ose wits had been set agog by the
eat Carbuncle.

Beneath the shelter of one hut, in the
ght blaze of the same fire, sat this
ried group of adventurers, all so intent
on a single object, that, of whatever
e they began to speak, their closing
rds were sure to be illuminated with
: Great Carbuncle. Several related
: circumstances that brought them
ther. One had listened to a traveller's
e of this marvellous stone, in his
n distant country, and had immedi-
ly been seized with such a thirst for
nolding it, as could only be quenched
its intensest lustre. Another, so long
o as when the famous Captain Smith
ited these coasts, had seen it blazing
at sea, and had felt no rest in all
: intervening years, till now that he
ok up the search. A third, being en-
mped on a hunting expedition, full
ty miles south of the White Moun-
ns, awoke at midnight, and beheld
Great Carbuncle gleaming, like a
teor, so that the shadows of the trees
l backward from it. They spoke of
: innumerable attempts which had
en made to reach the spot, and of the
gular fatality which had hitherto
hheld success from all adventurers,
ough it might seem so easy to follow

to its source a light that overpowered
the moon, and almost matched the sun.
It was observable that each smiled
scornfully at the madness of every
other, in anticipating better fortune
than the past, yet nourished a scarcely
hidden conviction, that he would himself be the favored one. As if to allay
their too sanguine hopes, they recurred
to the Indian traditions, that a spirit
kept watch about the gem, and bewildered those who sought it, either by
removing it from peak to peak of the
higher hills, or by calling up a mist from
the enchanted lake over which it hung.
But these tales were deemed unworthy
of credit; all professing to believe, that
the search had been baffled by want
of sagacity or perseverance in the adventurers, or such other causes as might
naturally obstruct the passage to any
given point, among the intricacies of
forest, valley, and mountain.

In a pause of the conversation, the
wearer of the prodigious spectacles
looked around upon the party, making
each individual, in turn, the object of
the sneer which invariably dwelt upon
his countenance.

"So, fellow-pilgrims," said he, "here
we are, seven wise men and one fair
damsel,—who, doubtless, is as wise as
any graybeard of the company: here
we are, I say, all bound on the same
goodly enterprise. Methinks, now, it
were not amiss that each of us declare
what he proposes to do with the Great
Carbuncle, provided he have the good
hap to clutch it. What says our friend
in the bear-skin? How mean you, good
sir, to enjoy the prize which you have
been seeking, the Lord knows how long,
among the Crystal Hills?"

"How enjoy it!" exclaimed the aged

Seeker, bitterly. "I hope for no enjoyment from it,—that folly has past long ago! I keep up the search for this accursed stone, because the vain ambition of my youth has become a fate upon me, in old age. The pursuit alone is my strength,—the energy of my soul,—the warmth of my blood, and the pith and marrow of my bones! Were I to turn my back upon it, I should fall down dead, on the hither side of the Notch, which is the gateway of this mountain region. Yet, not to have my wasted lifetime back again, would I give up my hopes of the Great Carbuncle! Having found it, I shall bear it to a certain cavern that I wot of, and there, grasping it in my arms, lie down and die, and keep it buried with me forever."

"O wretch, regardless of the interests of science!" cried Doctor Cacaphodel, with philosophic indignation. "Thou art not worthy to behold, even from afar off, the lustre of this most precious gem that ever was concocted in the laboratory of Nature. Mine is the sole purpose for which a wise man may desire the possession of the Great Carbuncle. Immediately on obtaining it,—for I have a presentiment, good people, that the prize is reserved to crown my scientific reputation,—I shall return to Europe, and employ my remaining years in reducing it to its first elements. A portion of the stone will I grind to impalpable powder; other parts shall be dissolved in acids, or whatever solvents will act upon so admirable a composition; and the remainder I design to melt in the crucible, or set on fire with the blowpipe. By these various methods I shall gain an accurate analysis, and finally bestow the result of my labors upon the world. in a folio volume."

"Excellent!" quoth the man with t[ ] spectacles. "Nor need you hesita[ ] learned sir, on account of the nece[ ] sary destruction of the gem; since t[ ] perusal of your folio may teach eve[ ] mother's son of us to concoct a Gre[ ] Carbuncle of his own."

"But, verily," said Master Ichab[ ] Pigsnort, "for mine own part I obje[ ] to the making of these counterfeits, being calculated to reduce the marke[ ] able value of the true gem. I tell [ ] frankly, sirs, I have an interest in kee[ ] ing up the price. Here have I quitt[ ] my regular traffic, leaving my warehou[ ] in the care of my clerks, and putti[ ] my credit to great hazard, and, furthe[ ] more, have put myself in peril of dea[ ] or captivity by the accursed heath[ ] savages,—and all this without daring [ ] ask the prayers of the congregation, b[ ] cause the quest for the Great Carbun[ ] is deemed little better than a traf[ ] with the Evil One. Now think ye th[ ] I would have done this grievous wro[ ] to my soul, body, reputation, and esta[ ] without a reasonable chance of profit[ ]

"Not I, pious Master Pigsnort," sa[ ] the man with the spectacles. "I nev[ ] laid such a great folly to thy charge."

"Truly, I hope not," said the me[ ] chant. "Now, as touching this Gre[ ] Carbuncle, I am free to own that I ha[ ] never had a glimpse of it; but be[ ] only the hundredth part so bright [ ] people tell, it will surely outvalue t[ ] Great Mogul's best diamond, which holds at an incalculable sum. Where fore, I am minded to put the Gre[ ] Carbuncle on shipboard, and voya[ ] with it to England, France, Spain, Ita[ ] or unto Heathendom, if Providen[ ] should send me thither, and, in a wo[ ] dispose of the gem to the best bidd[ ]

nong the potentates of the earth, that
may place it among his crown jewels.
any of ye have a wiser plan, let him
pound it."

"That have I, thou sordid man!" ex-
aimed the poet. "Dost thou desire
thing brighter than gold, that thou
uldst transmute all this ethereal lustre
to such dross as thou wallowest in
ready? For myself, hiding the jewel
der my cloak, I shall hie me back
my attic chamber, in one of the
rksome alleys of London. There,
ght and day, will I gaze upon it,—
soul shall drink its radiance,—it
all be diffused throughout my intel-
tual powers, and gleam brightly in
ery line of poesy that I indite. Thus,
ng ages after I am gone, the splen-
r of the Great Carbuncle will blaze
und my name!"

"Well said, Master Poet!" cried he
the spectacles. "Hide it under thy
ak, sayest thou? Why, it will gleam
rough the holes, and make thee look
e a jack-o'lantern!"

"To think!" ejaculated the Lord de
re, rather to himself than his com-
nions, the best of whom he held ut-
ly unworthy of his intercourse,—"to
nk that a fellow in a tattered cloak
uld talk of conveying the Great Car-
ncle to a garret in Grub Street! Have
t I resolved within myself, that the
ole earth contains no fitter ornament
the great hall of my ancestral castle?
ere shall it flame for ages, making
noonday of midnight, glittering on
suits of armor, the banners, and
tcheons that hang around the wall,
d keeping bright the memory of
roes. Wherefore have all other adven-
ers sought the prize in vain, but
t I might win it, and make it a

symbol of the glories of our lofty line?
And never, on the diadem of the White
Mountains did the Great Carbuncle hold
a place half so honored as is reserved
for it in the hall of the De Veres!"

"It is a noble thought," said the
Cynic, with an obsequious sneer. "Yet,
might I presume to say so, the gem
would make a rare sepulchral lamp, and
would display the glories of your lord-
ship's progenitors more truly in the ancestral vault than in the castle hall."

"Nay, forsooth," observed Matthew,
the young rustic, who sat hand in hand
with his bride, "the gentleman has bethought himself of a profitable use for
this bright stone. Hannah here and I
are seeking it for a like purpose."

"How, fellow!" exclaimed his lord-
ship, in surprise. "What castle hall hast
thou to hang it in?"

"No castle," replied Matthew, "but
as neat a cottage as any within sight
of the Crystal Hills. Ye must know,
friends, that Hannah and I, being wedded the last week, have taken up the
search of the Great Carbuncle, because
we shall need its light in the long winter evenings; and it will be such a
pretty thing to show the neighbors when
they visit us. It will shine through the
house, so that we may pick up a pin
in any corner, and will set all the
windows aglowing, as if there were a
great fire of pine-knots in the chimney.
And then how pleasant, when we awake
in the night, to be able to see one
another's faces!"

There was a general smile among the
adventurers at the simplicity of the
young couple's project, in regard to this
wondrous and invaluable stone, with
which the greatest monarch on earth
might have been proud to adorn his

palace. Especially the man with spectacles, who had sneered at all the company in turn, now twisted his visage into such an expression of ill-natured mirth, that Matthew asked him, rather peevishly, what he himself meant to do with the Great Carbuncle.

"The Great Carbuncle!" answered the Cynic, with ineffable scorn. "Why, you blockhead, there is no such thing, in *rerum natura.* I have come three thousand miles, and am resolved to set my foot on every peak of these mountains, and poke my head into every chasm, for the sole purpose of demonstrating to the satisfaction of any man, one whit less an ass than thyself, that the Great Carbuncle is all a humbug!"

Vain and foolish were the motives that had brought most of the adventurers to the Crystal Hills, but none so vain, so foolish, and so impious too, as that of the scoffer with the prodigious spectacles. He was one of those wretched and evil men whose yearnings are downward to the darkness, instead of heavenward, and who, could they but extinguish the lights which God hath kindled for us, would count the midnight gloom their chiefest glory. As the Cynic spoke, several of the party were startled by a gleam of red splendor, that showed the huge shapes of the surrounding mountains, and the rock-bestrewn bed of the turbulent river, with an illumination unlike that of their fire, on the trunks and black boughs of the forest-trees. They listened for the roll of thunder, but heard nothing, and were glad that the tempest came not near them. The stars, those dial-points of heaven, now warned the adventurers to close their eyes on the blazing logs, and open them, in dreams, to the glow of the Great Carbuncle.

The young married couple had tak their lodgings in the farthest corner the wigwam, and were separated fr the rest of the party by a curtain curiously-woven twigs, such as mig have hung, in deep festoons, around t bridal bower of Eve. The modest lit wife had wrought this piece of tapest while the other guests were talking. S and her husband fell asleep with han tenderly clasped, and awoke, from sions of unearthly radiance, to meet t more blessed light of one another's ey They awoke at the same instant, a with one happy smile beaming over th two faces, which grew brighter w their consciousness of the reality of l and love. But no sooner did she rec lect where they were, than the bri peeped through the interstices of t leafy curtain, and saw that the ou room of the hut was deserted.

"Up, dear Matthew!" cried she, haste. "The strange folk are all gor Up, this very minute, or we shall l the Great Carbuncle!"

In truth, so little did these po young people deserve the mighty pr which had lured them thither, that th had slept peacefully all night, and the summits of the hills were glitt ing with sunshine; while the other a venturers had tossed their limbs in verish wakefulness, or dreamed of clin ing precipices, and set off to realize th dreams with the earliest peep of da But Matthew and Hannah, after th calm rest, were as light as two you deer, and merely stopped to say th prayers, and wash themselves in a c pool of the Amonoosuck, and then taste a morsel of food, ere they turr their faces to the mountain-side. It w

sweet emblem of conjugal affection,
they toiled up the difficult ascent,
hering strength from the mutual aid
ich they afforded. After several little
cidents, such as a torn robe, a lost
e, and the entanglement of Han-
's hair in a bough, they reached the
er verge of the forest, and were
v to pursue a more adventurous
rse. The innumerable trunks and
vy foliage of the trees had hither-
shut in their thoughts, which now
ank affrighted from the region of
d, and cloud, and naked rocks, and
olate sunshine, that rose immeasur-
y above them. They gazed back at
obscure wilderness which they had
versed, and longed to be buried again
its depths, rather than trust themes to so vast and visible a solitude.
Shall we go on?" said Matthew,
owing his arm round Hannah's waist,
h to protect her, and to comfort his
rt by drawing her close to it.
But the little bride, simple as she
, had a woman's love of jewels, and
ld not forego the hope of possessing
very brightest in the world, in spite
he perils with which it must be won.
Let us climb a little higher," whis-
d she, yet tremulously, as she
ed her face upward to the lonely

Come, then," said Matthew, muster-
his manly courage, and drawing her
g with him; for she became timid
n the moment that he grew bold.
nd upward, accordingly, went the
rims of the Great Carbuncle, now
ding upon the tops and thickly-
rwoven branches of dwarf pines,
h by the growth of centuries,
igh mossy with age, had barely
hed three feet in altitude. Next,

they came to masses and fragments of
naked rock, heaped confusedly together,
like a cairn reared by giants, in memory
of a giant chief. In this bleak realm
of upper air nothing breathed, nothing
grew; there was no life but what was
concentrated in their two hearts; they
had climbed so high that Nature herself seemed no longer to keep them
company. She lingered beneath them,
within the verge of the forest-trees, and
sent a farewell glance after her children, as they strayed where her own
green footprints had never been. But
soon they were to be hidden from her
eye. Densely and dark the mists began to gather below, casting black spots
of shadow on the vast landscape, and
sailing heavily to one centre, as if the
loftiest mountain-peak had summoned
a council of its kindred clouds. Finally
the vapors welded themselves, as it
were, into a mass, presenting the appearance of a pavement over which the
wanderers might have trodden, but
where they would vainly have sought
an avenue to the blessed earth which
they had lost. And the lovers yearned
to behold that green earth again, more
intensely, alas! than, beneath a clouded
sky, they had ever desired a glimpse
of heaven. They even felt it a relief
to their desolation, when the mists,
creeping gradually up the mountain,
concealed its lonely peak, and thus annihilated, at least for them, the whole
region of visible space. But they drew
closer together, with a fond and melancholy gaze, dreading lest the universal
cloud should snatch them from each
other's sight.

Still, perhaps, they would have been
resolute to climb as far and as high,
between earth and heaven, as they could

find foothold, if Hannah's strength had not begun to fail, and with that her courage also. Her breath grew short. She refused to burden her husband with her weight, but often tottered against his side, and recovered herself each time by a feebler effort. At last she sank down on one of the rocky steps of the acclivity.

"We are lost, dear Matthew," said she, mournfully. "We shall never find our way to the earth again. And O, how happy we might have been in our cottage!"

"Dear heart!—we will yet be happy there," answered Matthew. "Look! In this direction the sunshine penetrates the dismal mist. By its aid I can direct our course to the passage of the Notch. Let us go back, love, and dream no more of the Great Carbuncle!"

"The sun cannot be yonder," said Hannah, with despondence. "By this time it must be noon. If there could ever be any sunshine here, it would come from above our heads."

"But look!" repeated Matthew, in a somewhat altered tone. "It is brightening every moment. If not sunshine, what can it be?"

Nor could the young bride any longer deny that a radiance was breaking through the mist, and changing its dim hue to a dusky red, which continually grew more vivid, as if brilliant particles were interfused with the gloom. Now, also, the cloud began to roll away from the mountain, while, as it heavily withdrew, one object after another started out of its impenetrable obscurity into sight, with precisely the effect of a new creation, before the indistinctness of the old chaos had been completely swallowed up. As the process

went on, they saw the gleaming water close at their feet, and fou[nd] themselves on the very border of [a] mountain lake, deep, bright, clear, a[nd] calmly beautiful, spreading from br[im] to brim of a basin that had be[en] scooped out of the solid rock. [A] ray of glory flashed across its s[mooth] face. The pilgrims looked whence [it] should proceed, but closed their ey[es] with a thrill of awful admiration, [to] exclude the fervid splendor that glow[ed] from the brow of a cliff, impending o[ver] the enchanted lake. For the simple p[air] had reached that lake of mystery, a[nd] found the long-sought shrine of t[he] Great Carbuncle!

They threw their arms around ea[ch] other, and trembled at their own su[c]cess; for as the legends of this w[on]drous gem rushed thick upon their me[m]ory, they felt themselves marked o[ut] by fate,—and the consciousness w[as] fearful. Often, from childhood upwa[rd], they had seen it shining like a dist[ant] star. And now that star was throw[ing] its intensest lustre on their hearts. Th[ey] seemed changed to one another's ey[es] in the red brilliancy that flamed up[on] their cheeks, while it lent the sa[me] fire to the lake, the rocks, and s[ky,] and to the mists which had rol[led] back before its power. But, with th[e] next glance, they beheld an object t[hat] drew their attention even from [the] mighty stone. At the base of the c[liff,] directly beneath the Great Carbun[cle,] appeared the figure of a man, w[ith] his arms extended in the act of clim[b]ing, and his face turned upward, [as] if to drink the full gush of splen[dor.] But he stirred not, no more than [if] changed to marble.

"It is the Seeker," whispered H[annah.]

h, convulsively grasping her husband's
m. "Matthew, he is dead."

"The joy of success has killed him,"
plied Matthew, trembling violently.
Or, perhaps the very light of the Great
arbuncle was death!"

"The Great Carbuncle," cried a pee-
sh voice behind them. "The Great
umbug! If you have found it, prithee
int it out to me."

They turned their heads, and there
as the Cynic, with his prodigious spec-
cles set carefully on his nose, staring
w at the lake, now at the rocks, now
the distant masses of vapor, now
ght at the Great Carbuncle itself, yet
emingly as unconscious of its light,
if all the scattered clouds were con-
nsed about his person. Though its
diance actually threw the shadow of
e unbeliever at his own feet, as he
rned his back upon the glorious jewel,
would not be convinced that there
s the least glimmer there.

"Where is your Great Humbug?" he
peated. "I challenge you to make me
e it!"

"There," said Matthew, incensed at
ch perverse blindness, and turning
e Cynic round towards the illuminated
ff. "Take off those abominable spec-
cles, and you cannot help seeing it!"
Now these colored spectacles prob-
y darkened the Cynic's sight, in at
st as great a degree as the smoked
sses through which people gaze at
eclipse. With resolute bravado, how-
er, he snatched them from his nose,
d fixed a bold stare full upon the
dy blaze of the Great Carbuncle.
t, scarcely had he encountered it,
en, with a deep, shuddering groan,
dropped his head, and pressed both
ds across his miserable eyes. Thence-

forth there was, in very truth, no light
of the Great Carbuncle, nor any other
light on earth, nor light of heaven itself, for the poor Cynic. So long accustomed to view all objects through
a medium that deprived them of every
glimpse of brightness, a single flash of
so glorious a phenomenon, striking upon
his naked vision, had blinded him forever.

"Matthew," said Hannah, clinging to
him, "let us go hence!"

Matthew saw that she was faint, and
kneeling down supported her in his
arms, while he threw some of the thrill-
ingly cold water of the enchanted lake
upon her face and bosom. It revived
her, but could not renovate her courage.

"Yes, dearest!" cried Matthew, pressing her tremulous form to his breast,
—"we will go hence, and return to our
humble cottage. The blessed sunshine,
and the quiet moonlight, shall come
through our window. We will kindle
the cheerful glow of our hearth, at
eventide, and be happy in its light.
But never again will we desire more
light than all the world may share with
us."

"No," said his bride, "for how could
we live by day, or sleep by night in
this awful blaze of the Great Carbuncle!"

Out of the hollow of their hands they
drank each a draught from the lake,
which presented them its waters uncon-
taminated by an earthly lip. Then, lending their guidance to the blinded Cynic,
who uttered not a word, and even stifled
his groans in his own most wretched
heart, they began to descend the mountain. Yet, as they left the shore, till
then untrodden, of the spirit's lake,

they threw a farewell glance towards the cliff, and beheld the vapors gathering in dense volumes, through which the gem burned duskily.

As touching the other pilgrims of the Great Carbuncle, the legend goes on to tell, that the worshipful Master Ichabod Pigsnort soon gave up the quest, as a desperate speculation, and wisely resolved to betake himself again to his warehouse, near the town dock, in Boston. But, as he passed through the Notch of the mountains, a war party of Indians captured our unlucky merchant, and carried him to Montreal, there holding him in bondage, till, by the payment of a heavy ransom, he had wofully subtracted from his hoard of pine-tree shillings. By his long absence, moreover, his affairs had become so disordered, that, for the rest of his life, instead of wallowing in silver, he had seldom a sixpence-worth of copper. Doctor Cacaphodel, the alchemist, returned to his laboratory with a prodigious fragment of granite, which he ground to powder, dissolved in acids, melted in the crucible, and burned with the blowpipe, and published the result of his experiments in one of the heaviest folios of the day. And, for all these purposes, the gem itself could not have answered better than the granite. The poet, by a somewhat similar mistake, made prize of a great piece of ice, which he found in a sunless chasm of the mountains, and swore that it corresponded, in all points, with his idea of the Great Carbuncle. The critics say, that, if his poetry lacked the splendor of the gem, it retained all the coldness of the ice. The Lord de Vere went back to his ancestral hall, where he contented himself with a wax-lighted chandelier, and filled,

in due course of time, another co[f] in the ancestral vault. As the fune[ral] torches gleamed within that dark [re]ceptacle, there was no need of [the] Great Carbuncle to show the vanity [of] earthly pomp.

The Cynic, having cast aside [his] spectacles, wandered about the wo[rld] a miserable object, and was punis[hed] with an agonizing desire of light, [for] the wilful blindness of his former l[ife.] The whole night long, he would [raise] his splendor-blasted orbs to the m[oon] and stars; he turned his face eastwa[rd,] at sunrise, as du'y as a Persian idolat[er;] he made a pilgrimage to Rome, to w[it]ness the magnificent illumination [of] St. Peter's Church; and finally peris[hed] in the great fire of London, into [the] midst of which he had thrust hims[elf,] with the desperate idea of catching [a] feeble ray from the blaze that [was] kindling earth and heaven.

Matthew and his bride spent m[any] peaceful years, and were fond of tel[ling] the legend of the Great Carbuncle. [The] tale, however, towards the close of t[heir] lengthened lives, did not meet with [the] full credence that had been accor[ded] to it by those who remembered [the] ancient lustre of the gem. For it [is] affirmed, that, from the hour when [two] mortals had shown themselves so si[m]wise as to reject a jewel which wo[uld] have dimmed all earthly things, [its] splendor waned. When other pilg[rims] reached the cliff, they found only [an] opaque stone, with particles of m[ica] glittering on its surface. There is [also] a tradition that, as the youthful p[air] departed, the gem was loosened f[rom] the forehead of the cliff, and [fell] into the enchanted lake, and that [at] noontide, the Seeker's form may

seen to bend over its quenchless
am.
Some few believe that this inesti-
ble stone is blazing, as of old, and
that they have caught its radiance,
a flash of summer lightning, far
down the valley of the Saco. And be
it owned, that, many a mile from the
Crystal Hills, I saw a wondrous light
around their summits, and was lured,
by the faith of poesy, to be the latest
pilgrim of the GREAT CARBUNCLE.

THE PROPHETIC PICTURES *

"BUT this painter," cried Walter Lud-
, with animation, "he not only excels
his peculiar art, but possesses vast
uirements in all other learning and
nce. He talks Hebrew with Dr.
ther, and gives lectures in anatomy
Dr. Boylston. In a word, he will
et the best-instructed man among us,
his own ground. Moreover, he is a
ished gentleman,—a citizen of the
ld,—yes, a true cosmopolite; for he
speak like a native of each clime
country on the globe, except our
forests, whither he is now going.
is all this what I most admire in
"

Indeed!" said Elinor, who had lis-
ed with a woman's interest to the
cription of such a man. "Yet this
admirable enough."

Surely it is," replied her lover, "but
less so than his natural gift of adapt-
himself to every variety of char-
r, insomuch that all men—and all
men, too, Elinor—shall find a mirror
hemselves in this wonderful painter.
the greatest wonder is yet to be
."

"Nay, if he have more wonderful attributes than these," said Elinor, laughing, "Boston is a perilous abode for the
poor gentleman. Are you telling me of
a painter, or a wizard?"

"In truth," answered he, "that question might be asked much more seriously than you suppose. They say that
he paints not merely a man's features,
but his mind and heart. He catches the
secret sentiments and passions, and
throws them upon the canvas, like sunshine,—or perhaps, in the portraits of
dark-souled men, like a gleam of infernal fire. It is an awful gift," added
Walter, lowering his voice from its tone
of enthusiasm; "I shall be almost afraid
to sit to him."

"Walter, are you in earnest?" exclaimed Elinor.

"For Heaven's sake, dearest Elinor,
do not let him paint the look which you
now wear," said her lover, smiling,
though rather perplexed. "There: it is
passing away now, but when you spoke,
you seemed frightened to death, and
very sad besides. What were you thinking of?"

"Nothing, nothing," answered Elinor,
hastily. "You paint my face with your
own fantasies. Well, come for me to-
morrow, and we will visit this wonder-

This story was suggested by an anecdote of
rt, related in Dunlap's History of the Arts
Design,—a most entertaining book to the
ral reader, and a deeply interesting one,
should think, to the artist.

ful artist."

But when the young man had departed, it cannot be denied that a remarkable expression was again visible on the fair and youthful face of his mistress. It was a sad and anxious look, little in accordance with what should have been the feelings of a maiden on the eve of wedlock. Yet Walter Ludlow was the chosen of her heart.

"A look!" said Elinor to herself. "No wonder that it startled him, if it expressed what I sometimes feel. I know, by my own experience, how frightful a look may be. But it was all fancy. I thought nothing of it at the time, —I have seen nothing of it since,—I did but dream it."

And she busied herself about the embroidery of a ruff, in which she meant that her portrait should be taken.

The painter, of whom they had been speaking, was not one of those native artists, who, at a later period than this, borrowed their colors from the Indians, and manufactured their pencils of the furs of wild beasts. Perhaps, if he could have revoked his life and prearranged his destiny, he might have chosen to belong to that school without a master, in the hope of being at least original, since there were no works of art to imitate nor rules to follow. But he had been born and educated in Europe. People said, that he had studied the grandeur or beauty of conception, and every touch of the master hand, in all the most famous pictures, in cabinets and galleries, and on the walls of churches, till there was nothing more for his powerful mind to learn. Art could add nothing to its lessons, but Nature might. He had therefore visited a world whither none of his professional brethren had preceded him, to feast h eyes on visible images, that were not and picturesque, yet had never be transferred to canvas. America was t poor to afford other temptations to artist of eminence, though many of t colonial gentry, on the painter's arriv had expressed a wish to transmit th lineaments to posterity by means of h skill. Whenever such proposals we made, he fixed his piercing eyes on t applicant, and seemed to look h through and through. If he beheld or a sleek and comfortable visage, thou there were a gold-laced coat to ado the picture, and golden guineas to p for it, he civilly rejected the task a the reward. But if the face were t index of anything uncommon, thought, sentiment, or experience; or he met a beggar in the street, with white beard and a furrowed brow; or sometimes a child happened to look and smile; he would exhaust all h art on them that he denied to wealth.

Pictorial skill being so rare in t colonies, the painter became an obj of general curiosity. If few or no could appreciate the technical merit his productions, yet there were poi in regard to which the opinion of t crowd was as valuable as the refin judgment of the amateur. He watch the effect that each picture produced such untutored beholders, and deriv profit from their remarks, while th would as soon have thought of instru ing Nature herself as him who seem to rival her. Their admiration, it m be owned, was tinctured with the pre dices of the age and country. So deemed it an offence against the M saic law, and even a presumptu mockery of the Creator, to bring i

istence such lively images of his crea-
res. Others, frightened at the art
iich could raise phantoms at will, and
ep the form of the dead among the
ing, were inclined to consider the
inter as a magician, or perhaps the
nous Black Man of old witch times,
itting mischief in a new guise. These
lish fancies were more than half be-
ved among the mob. Even in superior
cles his character was invested with
vague awe, partly rising like smoke-
eaths from the popular superstitions,
t chiefly caused by the varied knowl-
ge and talents which he made sub-
vient to his profession.

Being on the eve of marriage, Wal-
Ludlow and Elinor were eager to
tain their portraits, as the first of
at, they doubtless hoped, would be
ong series of family pictures. The day
er the conversation above recorded
y visited the painter's rooms. A ser-
t ushered them into an apartment,
ere, though the artist himself was
visble, there were personages whom
y could hardly forbear greeting with
erence. They knew, indeed, that the
ole assembly were but pictures, yet
it impossible to separate the idea
life and intellect from such striking
interfeits. Several of the portraits
e known to them, either as dis-
;uished characters of the day, or
ir private acquaintances. There was
vernor Burnett, looking as if he had
t received an undutiful communica-
1 from the House of Representa-
s, and were inditing a most sharp
ponse. Mr. Cooke hung beside the
er whom he opposed, sturdy, and
ewhat puritanical, as befitted a pop-
r leader. The ancient lady of Sir
liam Phipps eyed them from the

wall, in ruff and farthingale, an imperious old dame, not unsuspected of
witchcraft. John Winslow, then a very
young man, wore the expression of warlike enterprise, which long afterwards
made him a distinguished general. Their
personal friends were recognized at a
glance. In most of the pictures, the
whole mind and character were brought
out on the countenance, and concentrated into a single look, so that, to
speak paradoxically, the originals hardly
resembled themselves so strikingly as
the portraits did.

Among these modern worthies, there
were two old bearded Saints, who had
almost vanished into the darkening canvas. There was also a pale, but unfaded
Madonna, who had perhaps been worshipped in Rome, and now regarded
the lovers with such a mild and holy
look, that they longed to worship too.

"How singular a thought," observed
Walter Ludlow, "that this beautiful
face has been beautiful for above two
hundred years! O, if all beauty would
endure so well! Do you not envy her,
Elinor?"

"If earth were Heaven, I might,"
she replied. "But where all things fade,
how miserable to be the one that could
not fade!"

"This dark old St. Peter has a fierce
and ugly scowl, saint though he be,"
continued Walter. "He troubles me. But
the virgin looks kindly at us."

"Yes; but very sorrowfully, methinks," said Elinor.

The easel stood beneath these three
old pictures, sustaining one that had
been recently commenced. After a little
inspection they began to recognize the
features of their own minister, the Rev.
Dr. Colman, growing into shape and

life, as it were, out of a cloud.

"Kind old man!" exclaimed Elinor. "He gazes at me as if he were about to utter a word of paternal advice."

"And at me," said Walter, "as if he were about to shake his head and rebuke me for some suspected iniquity. But so does the original. I sha'll never feel quite comfortable under his eye till we stand before him to be married."

They now heard a footstep on the floor, and turning, beheld the painter, who had been some moments in the room, and had listened to a few of their remarks. He was a middle-aged man, with a countenance well worthy of his own pencil. Indeed, by the picturesque, though careless arrangement of his rich dress, and, perhaps, because his soul dwelt always among painted shapes, he looked somewhat like a portrait himself. His visitors were sensible of a kindred between the artist and his works, and felt as if one of the pictures had stepped from the canvas to salute them.

Walter Ludlow, who was slightly known to the painter, explained the object of their visit. While he spoke, a sunbeam was falling athwart his figure and Elinor's, with so happy an effect, that they also seemed living pictures of youth and beauty, gladdened by bright fortune. The artist was evidently struck.

"My easel is occupied for several ensuing days, and my stay in Boston must be brief," said he thoughtfully; then, after an observant glance, he added: "but your wishes shall be gratified,. though I disappoint the Chief Justice and Madame Oliver. I must not lose this opportunity, for the sake of painting a few ells of broadcloth a brocade."

The painter expressed a desire introduce both their portraits into picture, and represent them engaged some appropriate action. This p would have delighted the lovers, was necessarily rejected, because large a space of canvas would have b unfit for the room which it was inten to decorate. Two half-length portr. were therefore fixed upon. After t had taken leave, Walter Ludlow as Elinor, with a smile, whether she kn what an influence over their fates painter was about to acquire.

"The old women of Boston affir continued he, "that after he has o got possession of a person's face figure, he may paint him in any act situation whatever,—and the pict will be prophetic. Do you believe it

"Not quite," said Elinor, smil "Yet, if he has such magic, there something so gentle in his manner t I am sure he will use it well."

It was the painter's choice to ceed with both the portraits at same time, assigning as a reason, in mystical language which he someti used, that the faces threw light u each other. Accordingly, he gave a touch to Walter, and now to Eli and the features of one and the o began to start forth so vividly tha appeared as if his triumphant art w actually disengage them from the vas. Amid the rich light and shade, they beheld their phantom se But, though the likeness promise be perfect, they were not quite s fied with the expression; it see more vague than in most of painter's works. He, however, was s

with the prospect of success, and
g much interested in the lovers,
loyed his leisure moments, unknown
hem, in making a crayon sketch of
r two figures. During their sittings
engaged them in conversation, and
led up their faces with characteris-
traits, which, though continually
ing, it was his purpose to combine
fix. At length he announced, that
heir next visit both the portraits
ld be ready for delivery.

f my pencil will but be true to
conception, in the few last touches
h I meditate," observed he, "these
pictures will be my very best per-
ances. Seldom, indeed, has an artist
subjects."

hile speaking he still bent his pene-
ve eye upon them, nor withdrew it
hey had reached the bottom of the
s.

thing, in the whole circle of human
ies takes stronger hold of the imag-
on than this affair of having a
ait painted. Yet why should it be
The looking-glass, the polished
s of the andirons, the mirror-like
t, and all other reflecting surfaces,
nually present us with portraits,
ther ghosts, of ourselves, which
lance at and straightway forget
. But we forget them only because
vanish. It is the idea of duration,
earthly immortality,—that gives
a mysterious interest to our own
aits. Walter and Elinor were not
sible to this feeling, and hastened
e painter's room, punctually at the
nted hour, to meet those pictured
s which were to be their repre-
tives with posterity. The sunshine
d after them into the apartment,
eft it somewhat gloomy as they
closed the door.

Their eyes were immediately attracted to their portraits, which rested
against the farthest wall of the room.
At the first glance, through the dim
light and the distance, seeing themselves
in precisely their natural attitudes, and
with all the air that they recognized so
well, they uttered a simultaneous exclamation of delight.

"There we stand," cried Walter, enthusiastically, "fixed in sunshine forever! No dark passions can gather on
our faces!"

"No," said Elinor, more calmly; "no
dreary change can sadden us."

This was said while they were approaching, and had yet gained only an
imperfect view of the pictures. The
painter, after saluting them, busied himself at a table in completing a crayon
sketch, leaving his visitors to form their
own judgment as to his perfected labors.
At intervals, he sent a glance from beneath his deep eyebrows, watching their
countenances in profile, with his pencil
suspended over the sketch. They had
now stood some moments, each in front
of the other's picture, contemplating it
with entranced attention, but without
uttering a word. At length, Walter
stepped forward,—then back,—viewing
Elinor's portrait in various lights, and
finally spoke.

"Is there not a change?" said he, in
a doubtful and meditative tone. "Yes;
the perception of it grows more vivid
the longer I look. It is certainly the
same picture that I saw yesterday; the
dress,—the features,—all are the same;
and yet something is altered."

"Is, then, the picture less like than
it was yesterday?" inquired the painter,

now drawing near, with irrepressible interest.

"The features are perfect, Elinor," answered Walter; "and, at the first glance, the expression seemed also hers. But I could fancy that the portrait has changed countenance, while I have been looking at it. The eyes are fixed on mine with a strangely sad and anxious expression. Nay, it is grief and terror! Is this like Elinor?"

"Compare the living face with the pictured one," said the painter.

Walter glanced sidelong at his mistress, and started. Motionless and absorbed—fascinated, as it were—in contemplation of Walter's portrait, Elinor's face had assumed precisely the expression of which he had just been complaining. Had she practised for whole hours before a mirror, she could not have caught the look so successfully. Had the picture itself been a mirror, it could not have thrown back her present aspect with stronger and more melancholy truth. She appeared quite unconscious of the dialogue between the artist and her lover.

"Elinor," exclaimed Walter, in amazement, "what change has come over you?"

She did not hear him, nor desist from her fixed gaze, till he seized her hand, and thus attracted her notice; then, with a sudden tremor, she looked from the picture to the face of the original.

"Do you see no change in your portrait?" asked she.

"In mine?—None!" replied Walter, examining it. "But let me see! Yes! there is a slight change,—an improvement, I think, in the picture, though none in the likeness. It has a livelier expression than yesterday, as if some bright thought were flashing from eyes, and about to be uttered from lips. Now that I have caught the it becomes very decided."

While he was intent on these servations, Elinor turned to the pa She regarded him with grief and and felt that he repaid her with pathy and commiseration, though w fore she could but vaguely guess.

"That look!" whispered she, shuddered. "How came it there?"

"Madam," said the painter, taking her hand, and leading her "in both these pictures, I have pa what I saw. The artist—the true —must look beneath the exterior. his gift—his proudest, but often a ancholy one—to see the inmost and, by a power indefinable even to self, to make it glow or darken the canvas, in glances that expres thought and sentiment of years. V that I might convince myself of in the present instance!"

They had now approached the on which were heads in chalk, almost as expressive as ordinary ivied church-towers, thatched cot old thunder-stricken trees, Orienta antique costume, and all such p esque vagaries of an artist's idle ments. Turning them over, with ing carelessness, a crayon sketch o figures was disclosed.

"If I have failed," continued "if your heart does not see itse flected in your own portrait,—i have no secret cause to trust m lineation of the other,—it is nc too late to alter them. I might c the action of these figures too would it influence the event?"

He directed her notice to the s

rill ran through Elinor's frame;
riek was upon her lips; but she
d it, with the self-command that
mes habitual to all who hide
ghts of fear and anguish within
bosoms. Turning from the table,
perceived that Walter had advanced
enough to have seen the sketch,
gh she could not determine whether
d caught his eye.

Ve will not have the pictures al-
," said she, hastily. "If mine is sad,
ill but look the gayer for the con-
"

e it so," answered the painter,
ng. "May your griefs be such fan-
ones, that only your picture may
n for them! For your joys,—may
be true and deep, and paint them-
s upon this lovely face, till it quite
my art!"

ter the marriage of Walter and
r, the pictures formed the two
splendid ornaments of their abode.
hung side by side, separated by
row panel, appearing to eye each
constantly, yet always returning
gaze of the spectator. Travelled
men, who professed a knowledge
ch subjects, reckoned these among
ost admirable specimens of mod-
ortraiture; while common observ-
ompared them with the originals,
e by feature, and were rapturous
aise of the likeness. But, it was
third class—neither travelled con-
urs nor common observers, but
e of natural sensibility—that the
es wrought their strongest effect.
persons might gaze carelessly at
but, becoming interested, would
day after day, and study these
d faces like the pages of a mystic
e. Walter Ludlow's portrait at-

tracted their earliest notice. In the absence of himself and his bride, they
sometimes disputed as to the expression
which the painter had intended to throw
upon the features; all agreeing that
there was a look of earnest import,
though no two explained it alike. There
was less diversity of opinion in regard
to Elinor's picture. They differed indeed, in their attempts to estimate the
nature and depth of the gloom that
dwelt upon her face, but agreed that
it was gloom, and alien from the natural
temperament of their youthful friend.
A certain fanciful person annnounced,
as the result of much scrutiny, that
both these pictures were parts of one
design, and that the melancholy strength
of feeling in Elinor's countenance bore
reference to the more vivid emotion,
or, as he termed it, the wild passion,
in that of Walter. Though unskilled
in the art, he even began a sketch,
in which the action of the two figures
was to correspond with their mutual
expression.

It was whispered among friends, that,
day by day, Elinor's face was assuming a deeper shade of pensiveness, which
threatened soon to render her too true
a counterpart of her melancholy picture. Walter, on the other hand, instead of acquiring the vivid look which
the painter had given him on the canvas, became reserved and downcast,
with no outward flashes of emotion,
however it might be smouldering within. In course of time, Elinor hung a
gorgeous curtain of purple silk, wrought
with flowers, and fringed with heavy
golden tassels, before the pictures, under pretence that the dust would tarnish their hues, or the light dim them.
It was enough. Her visitors felt that

the massive folds of the silk must never be withdrawn, nor the portraits mentioned in her presence.

Time wore on; and the painter came again. He had been far enough to the north to see the silver cascade of the Crystal Hills, and to look over the vast round of cloud and forest, from the summit of New England's loftiest mountain. But he did not profane that scene by the mockery of his art. He had also lain in a canoe on the bosom of Lake George, making his soul the mirror of its loveliness and grandeur, till not a picture in the Vatican was more vivid than his recollection. He had gone with the Indian hunters to Niagara, and there, again, had flung his hopeless pencil down the precipice, feeling that he could as soon paint the roar, as aught else that goes to make up the wondrous cataract. In truth, it was seldom his impulse to copy natural scenery, except as a framework for the delineations of the human form and face, instinct with thought, passion, or suffering. With store of such his adventurous ramble had enriched him: the stern dignity of Indian chiefs; the dusky loveliness of Indian girls; the domestic life of wigwams; the stealthy march; the battle beneath gloomy pine-trees; the frontier fortress with its garrison; the anomaly of the old French partisan, bred in courts, but grown gray in shaggy deserts; such were the scenes and portraits that he had sketched. The glow of perilous moments; flashes of wild feeling; struggles of fierce power, —love, hate, grief, frenzy,—in a word, all the worn-out heart of the old earth had been revealed to him under a new form. His portfolio was filled with graphic illustrations of the volume of

his memory, which genius would tr mute into its own substance, and in with immortality. He felt that the wisdom in his art which he had so so far was found.

But, amid stern or lovely nature the perils of the forest, or its o whelming peacefulness, still there been two phantoms, the companion his way. Like all other men are whom an engrossing purpose wrea itself, he was insulated from the of human kind. He had no aim pleasure, no sympathies, but what ultimately connected with his Though gentle in manner, and up in intent and action, he did not po kindly feelings; his heart was cold living creature could be brought enough to keep him warm. For two beings, however, he had fel its greatest intensity, the sort o terest which always allied him to subjects of his pencil. He had pried their souls with his keenest insight pictured the result upon their fea with his utmost skill, so as bare fall short of that standard whic genius ever reached,—his own s conception. He had caught from duskiness of the future—at least, fancied—a fearful secret, and had scurely revealed it on the portrait much of himself—of his imagin and all other powers—had been lav on the study of Walter and Elinor he almost regarded them as creatio his own, like the thousands with he had peopled the realms of Pi Therefore did they flit through the light of the woods, hover on the of waterfalls, look forth from mirror of the lake, nor melt aw the noontide sun. They haunte

orial fancy, not as mockeries of
nor pale goblins of the dead, but
he guise of portraits, each with the
terable expression which his magic
evoked from the caverns of the
. He could not recross the Atlantic,
he had again beheld the originals
hose airy pictures.

) glorious art!" thus mused the en-
iastic painter, as he trod the street.
ou art the image of the Creator's
The innumerable forms that wan-
in nothingness start into being at
beck. The dead live again. Thou
llest them to their old scenes, and
st their gray shadows the lustre of
tter life, at once earthly and imal. Thou snatchest back the fleet-
moments of History. With thee
e is no Past; for at thy touch all
is great becomes forever present;
illustrious men live through long
in the visible performance of the
deeds which made them what they
O potent Art! as thou bringest the
ly revealed Past to stand in that
w strip of sunlight which we call
, canst thou summon the shrouded
re to meet her there? Have I not
ved it? Am I not thy Prophet?"

us, with a proud yet melancholy
r did he almost cry aloud, as he
d through the toilsome street,
g people that knew not of his rev-
nor could understand nor care
hem. It is not good for man to
sh a solitary ambition. Unless there
ose around him by whose example
ay regulate himself, his thoughts,
es, and hopes will become extrava-
and he the semblance, perhaps the
y, of a madman. Reading other
ns with an acuteness almost pre-
tural, the painter failed to see the
disorder of his own.

"And this should be the house," said
he, looking up and down the front before he knocked. "Heaven help my
brains! That picture! Methinks it will
never vanish. Whether I look at the
windows or the door, there it is framed
within them, painted strongly, and glowing in the richest tints,—the faces of
the portraits,—the figures and action
of the sketch!"

He knocked.

"The Portraits! Are they within?"
inquired he, of the domestic; then recollecting himself,—"your master and
mistress! Are they at home?"

"They are, sir," said the servant,
adding, as he noticed that picturesque
aspect of which the painter could never
divest himself,—"and the Portraits
too!"

The guest was admitted into a parlor,
communicating by a central door with
an interior room of the same size. As
the first apartment was empty, he
passed to the entrance of the second,
within which his eyes were greeted by
those living personages—as well as their
pictured representatives—who had long
been the objects of so singular an interest. He involuntarily paused on the
threshold.

They had not perceived his approach.
Walter and Elinor were standing before the portraits, whence the former
had just flung back the rich and volum-
inous folds of the silken curtain, holding
its golden tassel with one hand, while
the other grasped that of his bride.
The pictures, concealed for months,
gleamed forth again in undiminished
splendor, appearing to throw a sombre
light across the room, rather than to
be disclosed by a borrowed radiance.

That of Elinor had been almost pro-phetic. A pensiveness, and next a gentle sorrow, had successively dwelt upon her countenance, deepening, with the lapse of time, into a quiet anguish. A mixture of affright would now have made it the very expression of the portrait. Walter's face was moody and dull, or animated only by fitful flashes, which left a heav-ier darkness for their momentary illu-mination. He looked from Elinor to her portrait, and thence to his own, in the contemplation of which he finally stood absorbed.

The painter seemed to hear the step of Destiny approaching behind him, on its progress towards its victims. A strange thought darted into his mind. Was not his own the form in which that destiny had embodied itself, and he a chief agent of the coming evil which he had foreshadowed?

Still Walter remained silent before the picture, communing with it, as with his own heart, and abandoning himself to the spell of evil influence that the painter had cast upon the features. Gradually his eyes kindled; while as Elinor watched the increasing wildness of his face, her own assumed a look of terror; and when at last he turned upon her, the resemblance of both to their portraits was complete.

"Our fate is upon us!" howled Wal-ter. "Die!"

Drawing a knife, he sustained he she was sinking to the ground, aimed it at her bosom. In the ac and in the look and attitude of the painter beheld the figures of sketch. The picture, with all its mendous coloring, was finished.

"Hold, madman!" cried he, stern

He had advanced from the door, interposed himself between the wret beings, with the same sense of p to regulate their destiny as to all scene upon the canvas. He stood a magician, controlling the phan which he had evoked.

"What!" muttered Walter Ludlo he relapsed from fierce excitement silent gloom. "Does Fate imped own decree?"

"Wretched lady!" said the pai "Did I not warn you?"

"You did," replied Elinor, calm her terror gave place to the quiet which it had disturbed. "But—I him!"

Is there not a deep moral in tale? Could the result of one, c our deeds, be shadowed forth an before us, some would call it and hurry onward, others be s along by their passionate desires none be turned aside by the Proph Pictures.

DAVID SWAN

A FANTASY

We can be but partially acquainted even with the events which actually in-

fluence our course through life, an final destiny. There are innum other events—if such they ma called—which come close upon u

away without actual results, or
betraying their near approach, by
reflection of any light or shadow
ss our minds. Could we know all
vicissitudes of our fortunes, life
d be too full of hope and fear,
ation or disappointment, to afford
single hour of true serenity. This
may be illustrated by a page from
secret history of David Swan.

e have nothing to do with David
we find him, at the age of twenty,
he high road from his native place
he city of Boston, where his uncle,
all dealer in the grocery line, was
ke him behind the counter. Be it
gh to say, that he was a native
ew Hampshire, born of respectable
ts, and had received an ordinary
ol education, with a classic finish
year at Gilmanton Academy. After
eying on foot, from sunrise till
y noon of a summer's day, his
ness and the increasing heat dened him to sit down in the first
nient shade, and await the coming
the stage-coach. As if planted on
ose for him, there soon appeared
le tuft of maples, with a delightful
s in the midst, and such a fresh
ling spring, that it seemed never
ve sparkled for any wayfarer but
d Swan. Virgin or not, he kissed
h his thirsty lips, and then flung
elf along the brink, pillowing his
upon some skirts and a pair of
loons, tied up in a striped cotton
kerchief. The sunbeams could not
him; the dust did not yet rise
the road, after the heavy rain
sterday; and his grassy lair suited
oung man better than a bed of
The spring murmured drowsily
him; the branches waved dream-

ily across the blue sky overhead; and
a deep sleep, perchance hiding dreams
within its depths, fell upon David Swan.
But we are to relate events which he
did not dream of.

While he lay sound asleep in the
shade, other people were wide awake,
and passed to and fro, afoot, on horseback, and in all sorts of vehicles, along
the sunny road by his bed-chamber.
Some looked neither to the right hand
nor the left, and knew not that he was
there; some merely glanced that way,
without admitting the slumberer among
their busy thoughts; some laughed to
see how soundly he slept; and several,
whose hearts were brimming full of
scorn, ejected their venomous superfluity on David Swan. A middle-aged
widow, when nobody else was near,
thrust her head a little way into the
recess, and vowed that the young fellow
looked charming in his sleep. A temperance lecturer saw him, and wrought
poor David into the texture of his evening's discourse, as an awful instance
of dead drunkenness by the roadside.
But censure, praise, merriment, scorn,
and indifference were all one, or rather
all nothing, to David Swan.

He had slept only a few moments
when a brown carriage, drawn by a
handsome pair of horses, bowled easily
along, and was brought to a standstill
nearly in front of David's resting-
place. A linchpin had fallen out, and
permitted one of the wheels to slide
off. The damage was slight, and occasioned merely a momentary alarm to
an elderly merchant and his wife, who
were returning to Boston in the carriage. While the coachman and a servant were replacing the wheel, the lady
and gentleman sheltered themselves be-

neath the maple trees, and there espied the bubbling fountain and David Swan asleep beside it. Impressed with the awe which the humblest sleeper usually sheds around him, the merchant trod as lightly as the gout would allow; and his spouse took good heed not to rustle her silk gown, lest David should start up, all of a sudden.

"How soundly he sleeps!" whispered the old gentleman. "From what a depth he draws that easy breath! Such sleep as that, brought on without an opiate, would be worth more to me than half my income; for it would suppose health and an untroubled mind."

"And youth, besides," said the lady. "Healthy and quiet age does not sleep thus. Our slumber is no more like his than our wakefulness."

The longer they looked, the more did this elderly couple feel interested in the unknown youth, to whom the wayside and the maple shade were as a secret chamber, with the rich gloom of damask curtains brooding over him. Perceiving that a stray sunbeam glimmered down upon his face, the lady contrived to twist a branch aside, so as to intercept it. And having done this little act of kindness, she began to feel like a mother to him.

"Providence seems to have laid him here," whispered she to her husband, "and to have brought us hither to find him, after our disappointment in our cousin's son. Methinks I can see a likeness to our departed Henry. Shall we waken him?"

"To what purpose?" said the merchant, hesitating. "We know nothing of the youth's character."

"That open countenance!" replied his wife, in the same hushed voice, yet earnestly. "This innocent sleep!"

While these whispers were pass the sleeper's heart did not throb, his breath become agitated, nor his tures betray the least token of inte Yet Fortune was bending over him, ready to let fall a burden of gold. old merchant had lost his only and had no heir to his wealth, ex a distant relative, with whose con he was dissatisfied. In such cases, ple sometimes do stranger things to act the magician, and awaken a y man to splendor who fell aslee poverty.

"Shall we not waken him?" repe the lady, persuasively.

"The coach is ready, sir," said servant, behind.

The old couple started, redde and hurried away, mutually wond that they should ever have drea of doing anything so very ridicu The merchant threw himself bac the carriage, and occupied his with the plan of a magnificent as for unfortunate men of business. M while David Swan enjoyed his nap.

The carriage could not have above a mile or two, when a p young girl came along, with a tri pace, which showed precisely how little heart was dancing in her bo Perhaps it was this merry kind of tion that caused—is there any har saying it?—her garter to slip its Conscious that the silken girth—if it were—was relaxing its hold, turned aside into the shelter of maple trees, and there found a y man asleep by the spring! Blus as red as any rose that she sh have intruded into a gentleman's chamber, and for such a purpose,

was about to make her escape on
oe. But there was peril near the
per. A monster of a bee had been
dering overhead—buzz, buzz, buzz
ow among the leaves, now flashing
ugh the strips of sunshine, and now
in the dark shade, till finally he
eared to be settling on the eyelid
David Swan. The sting of a bee is
etimes deadly. As free-hearted as
was innocent, the girl attacked
intruder with her handkerchief,
shed him soundly, and drove him
n beneath the maple shade. How
et a picture! This good deed accom-
ned, with quickened breath, and a
her blush, she stole a glance at the
thful stranger for whom she had
n battling with a dragon in the air.
He is handsome!" thought she, and
hed redder yet.

ow could it be that no dream of
grew so strong within him, that,
tered by its very strength, it should
asunder, and allow him to per-
the girl among its phantoms? Why,
east, did no smile of welcome
nten upon his face? She was come,
maid whose soul, according to the
and beautiful idea, had been sev-
from his own, and whom, in all
vague but passionate desires, he
ned to meet. Her only could he
with a perfect love,—him only
d she receive into the depths of
heart,—and now her image was
ly blushing in the fountain, by his
should it pass away, its happy
e would never gleam upon his life
.

low sound he sleeps!" murmured
girl.

e departed, but did not trip along
road so lightly as when she came.

Now, this girl's father was a thriving country merchant in the neighborhood, and happened, at that identical time, to be looking out for just
such a young man as David Swan. Had
David formed a wayside acquaintance
with the daughter, he would have became the father's clerk, and all else
in natural succession. So here, again,
had good fortune—the best of fortunes
—stolen so near, that her garments
brushed against him; and he knew nothing of the matter.

The girl was hardly out of sight, when
two men turned aside beneath the maple
shade. Both had dark faces, set off by
cloth caps, which were drawn down
aslant over their brows. Their dresses
were shabby, yet had a certain smart-
ness. These were a couple of rascals,
who got their living by whatever the
Devil sent them; and now, in the in-
terim of other business, had staked the
joint profits of their next piece of vil-
lainy on a game of cards, which was
to have been decided here under the
trees. But finding David asleep by the
spring, one of the rogues whispered to
his fellow,—

"Hist!—Do you see that bundle under
his head?"

The other villain nodded, winked, and
leered.

"I'll bet you a horn of brandy," said
the first, "that the chap has either a
pocket-book, or a snug little hoard of
small change, stowed away amongst his
shirts. And if not there, we shall find
it in his pantaloons pocket."

"But how if he wakes?" said the
other.

His companion thrust aside his waistcoat, pointed to the handle of a dirk,
and nodded.

"So be it!" muttered the second villain.

They approached the unconscious David, and while one pointed the dagger towards his heart, the other began to search the bundle beneath his head. Their two faces, grim, wrinkled, and ghastly with guilt and fear, bent over their victim, looking horrible enough to be mistaken for fiends, should he suddenly awake. Nay, had the villains glanced aside into the spring, even they would hardly have known themselves, as reflected there. But David Swan had never worn a more tranquil aspect, even when asleep on his mother's breast.

"I must take away the bundle," whispered one.

"If he stirs, I'll strike," muttered the other.

But, at this moment, a dog, scenting along the ground, came in beneath the maple trees, and gazed alternately at each of these wicked men, and then at the quiet sleeper. He then lapped out of the fountain.

"Pshaw!" said one villain. "We can do nothing now. The dog's master must be close behind."

"Let's take a drink and be off," said the other.

The man, with the dagger, thrust back the weapon into his bosom, and drew forth a pocket-pistol, but not of that kind which kills by a single discharge. It was a flask of liquor, with a block-tin tumbler screwed upon the mouth. Each drank a comfortable dram, and left the spot, with so many jests, and such laughter at their unaccomplished wickedness, that they might be said to have gone on their way rejoicing. In a few hours, they had forgotten the whole affair, nor once imagined that

the recording angel had written d[own] the crime of murder against their so[uls] in letters as durable as eternity. As [for] David Swan, he still slept quie[tly,] neither conscious of the shadow [of] death when it hung over him, no[r of] the glow of renewed life, when [the] shadow was withdrawn.

He slept, but no longer so quietl[y] at first. An hour's repose had snat[ched] from his elastic frame the weari[ness] with which many hours of toil had [bur]dened it. Now he stirred,—now m[oved] his lips, without a sound,—now ta[lked] in an inward tone, to the noonday s[pec]tres of his dream. But a noise of wh[eels] came rattling louder and louder a[long] the road, until it dashed through [the] dispersing mist of David's slumb[er—] and there was the stage-coach. [He] started up, with all his ideas about [him.]

"Halloo, driver!—Take a passeng[er!"] shouted he.

"Room on top!" answered the dr[iver.]

Up mounted David, and bowled a[way] merrily towards Boston, withou[t so] much as a parting glance at that f[oun]tain of dreamlike vicissitude. He [knew] not that a phantom of Wealth [had] thrown a golden hue upon its wa[ters] —nor that one of Love had si[ghed] softly to their murmur,—nor that [one] of Death had threatened to cri[mson] them with his blood,—all, in the [one] hour since he lay down to sleep. S[leep]ing or waking, we hear not the airy [foot]steps of the strange things that al[most] happen. Does it not argue a su[per]tending Providence, that while vi[sions] and unexpected events thrust t[hem]selves continually athwart our [path,] there should still be regularity en[ough] in mortal life to render foresight [but] partially available?

SIGHTS FROM A STEEPLE

! I have climbed high, and my
rd is small. Here I stand, with
ied knees, earth, indeed, at a dizzy
h below, but heaven far, far beyond
still. O that I could soar up into
very zenith, where man never
thed nor eagle ever flew, and where
ethereal azure melts away from the
and appears only a deepened shade
nothingness! And yet I shiver at
cold and solitary thought. What
ds are gathering in the golden west,
direful intent against the bright-
and the warmth of this summer
noon! They are ponderous air
, black as death, and freighted
the tempest; and at intervals their
der, the signal-guns of that un-
ly squadron, rolls distant along the
of heaven. These nearer heaps of
vapor—methinks I could roll and
upon them the whole day long!
m scattered here and there, for
repose of tired pilgrims through
sky. Perhaps—for who can tell?—
tiful spirits are disporting them-
s there, and will bless my mortal
with the brief appearance of their
locks of golden light, and laugh-
aces, fair and faint as the people
rosy dream. Or, where the float-
mass so imperfectly obstructs the
of the firmament, a slender foot
airy limb, resting too heavily upon
ail support, may be thrust through,
suddenly withdrawn, while longing
follows them in vain. Yonder
is an airy archipelago, where the
ams love to linger in their jour-
gs through space. Every one of
little clouds has been dipped and

steeped in radiance, which the slightest pressure might disengage in silvery
profusion, like water wrung from a sea-
maid's hair. Bright they are as a young
man's visions, and, like them, would
be realized in chillness, obscurity, and
tears. I will look on them no more.

In three parts of the visible circle,
whose centre is this spire, I discern
cultivated fields, villages, white coun-
try-seats, the waving lines of rivulets,
little placid lakes, and here and there a
rising ground, that would fain be termed
a hill. On the fourth side is the sea,
stretching away towards a viewless
boundary, blue and calm, except
where the passing anger of a shadow
flits across its surface, and is
gone. Hitherward, a broad inlet penetrates far into the land; on the
verge of the harbor, formed by its
extremity, is a town; and over it am I,
a watchman, all-heeding and unheeded.
O that the multitude of chimneys could
speak, like those of Madrid, and betray,
in smoky whispers, the secrets of all
who, since their first foundation, have
assembled at the hearths within! O that
the Limping Devil of Le Sage would
perch beside me here, extend his wand
over this contiguity of roofs, uncover
every chamber, and make me familiar
with their inhabitants! The most desirable mode of existence might be that
of a spiritualized Paul Pry, hovering
invisible round man and woman, witnessing their deeds, searching into their
hearts, borrowing brightness from their
felicity, and shade from their sorrow,
and retaining no emotion peculiar to
himself. But none of these things are

possible; and if I would know the interior of brick walls, or the mystery of human bosoms, I can but guess.

Yonder is a fair street, extending north and south. The stately mansions are placed each on its carpet of verdant grass, and a long flight of steps descends from every door to the pavement. Ornamental trees, the broad-leafed horse-chestnut, the elm so lofty and bending, the graceful but infrequent willow, and others whereof I know not the names, grow thrivingly among brick and stone. The oblique rays of the sun are intercepted by these green citizens, and by the houses, so that one side of the street is a shaded and pleasant walk. On its whole extent there is now but a single passenger, advancing from the upper end; and he, unless distance and the medium of a pocket spyglass do him more than justice, is a fine young man of twenty. He saunters slowly forward, slapping his left hand with his folded gloves, bending his eyes upon the pavement, and sometimes raising them to throw a glance before him. Certainly, he has a pensive air. Is he in doubt, or in debt? Is he, if the question be allowable, in love? Does he strive to be melancholy and gentleman-like?—Or, is he merely overcome by the heat? But I bid him farewell, for the present. The door of one of the houses—an aristocratic edifice, with curtains of purple and gold waving from the windows, is now opened, and down the steps come two ladies, swinging their parasols, and lightly arrayed for a summer ramble. Both are young, both are pretty; but methinks the left-hand lass is the fairer of the twain; and, though she be so serious at this moment, I could swear

that there is a treasure of gentle within her. They stand talking a li while upon the steps, and finally ceed up the street. Meantime, as t faces are now turned from me, I look elsewhere.

Upon that wharf, and down the responding street, is a busy contras the quiet scene which I have just ticed. Business evidently has its ce there, and many a man is wasting summer afternoon in labor and anxi in losing riches, or in gaining th when he would be wiser to flee a to some pleasant country village, shaded lake in the forest, or wild cool sea-beach. I see vessels unla at the wharf, and precious merchan strewn upon the ground, abundantl at the bottom of the sea, that ma whence no goods return, and w there is no captain nor supercarge render an account of sales. Here clerks are diligent with their paper pencils, and sailors ply the block tackle that hang over the hold, acc panying their toil with cries, long dr and roughly melodious, till the k and puncheons ascend to upper air a little distance, a group of gentle are assembled round the door of a w house. Grave seniors be they, an would wager—if it were safe, in t times to be responsible for any o that the least eminent among t might vie with old Vicentio, that comparable trafficker of Pisa. I even select the wealthiest of the pany. It is the elderly personage somewhat rusty black, with powd hair, the superfluous whiteness of w is visible upon the cape of his His twenty ships are wafted on s of their many courses by every b

t blows, and his name—I will ven-
e to say, though I know it not—
, familiar sound among the far-sepa-
ed merchants of Europe and the
ies.

3ut I bestow too much of my at-
:ion in this quarter. On looking again
the long and shady walk, I per-
're that the two fair girls have en-
ntered the young man. After a sort
shyness in the recognition, he turns
k with them. Moreover he has sanc-
ed my taste in regard to his com-
ions by placing himself on the inner
: of the pavement, nearest the Venus
whom I—enacting on a steeple top
part of Paris on the top of Ida—
ıdged the golden apple.

n two streets, converging at right
les towards my watchtower, I dis-
uished three different processions.

is a proud array of voluntary sol-
s, in bright uniform, resembling,
n the height whence I look down,
painted veterans that garrison the
lows of a toyshop. And yet, it stirs
heart; their regular advance, their
ding plumes, the sunflash on their
onets and musket-barrels, the roll
heir drums ascending past me, and
fife ever and anon piercing through,
ese things have wakened a war-like
peaceful though I be. Close to their
marches a battalion of school-boys,
ed in crooked and irregular pla-
s, shouldering sticks, thumping a
h and unripe clatter from an instru-
t of tin, and ridiculously aping the
cate manœuvres of the foremost
l. Nevertheless, as slight differences
scarcely perceptible from a church
, one might be tempted to ask,
ich are the boys?"—or rather,
ich the men?" But, leaving these,

let us turn to the third procession,
which, though sadder in outward show,
may excite identical reflections in the
thoughtful mind. It is a funeral. A
hearse, drawn by a black and bony
steed, and covered by a dusty pall; two
or three coaches rumbling over the
stones, their drivers half asleep; a dozen
couple of careless mourners in their
every-day attire; such was not the fashion of our fathers, when they carried
a friend to his grave. There is now no
doleful clang of the bell to proclaim
sorrow to the town. Was the King of
Terrors more awful in those days than
in our own, that wisdom and philosophy
have been able to produce this change?
Not so. Here is a proof that he retains
his proper majesty. The military men
and the military boys, are wheeling
round the corner, and meet the funeral
full in the face. Immediately the drum
is silent, all but the tap that regulates
each simultaneous footfall. The soldiers
yield the path to the dusty hearse and
unpretending train, and the children
quit their ranks, and cluster on the
sidewalks, with timorous and instinctive
curiosity. The mourners enter the
churchyard at the base of the steeple,
and pause by an open grave among the
burial-stones; the lightning glimmers on
them as they lower down the coffin, and
the thunder ·rattles heavily while they
throw the earth upon its lid. Verily, the
shower is near, and I tremble for the
young man and the girls, who have now
disappeared from the long and shady
street.

How various are the situations of the
people covered by the roofs beneath
me, and how diversified are the events
at this moment befalling them! The new
born, the aged, the dying, the strong

in life, and the recent dead, are in the chambers of these many mansions. The full of hope, the happy, the miserable, and the desperate dwell together within the circle of my glance. In some of the houses over which my eyes roam so coldly, guilt is entering into hearts that are still tenanted by a debased and trodden virtue,—guilt is on the very edge of commission, and the impending deed might be averted; guilt is done, and the criminal wonders if it be irrevocable. There are broad thoughts struggling in my mind, and, were I able to give them distinctness, they would make their way in eloquence. Lo! the rain-drops are descending.

The clouds, within a little time, have gathered over all the sky, hanging heavily, as if about to drop in one unbroken mass upon the earth. At intervals, the lightning flashes from their brooding hearts, quivers, disappears, and then comes the thunder, travelling slowly after its twin-born flame. A strong wind has sprung up, howls through the darkened streets, and raises the dust in dense bodies, to rebel against the approaching storm. The disbanded soldiers fly, the funeral has already vanished like its dead, and all people hurry homeward,—all that have a home; while a few lounge by the corners, or trudge on desperately, at their leisure. In a narrow lane, which communicates with the shady street, I discern the rich old merchant, putting himself to the top of his speed, lest the rain should convert his hair-powder to a paste. Unhappy gentleman! By the slow vehemence, and painful moderation wherewith he journeys, it is but too evident that Podagra has left its thrilling tenderness in his great toe. But yonder, at a far more rapid

pace, come three other of my acqu tance,—the two pretty girls and young man, unseasonably interrupte their walk. Their footsteps are ported by the risen dust,—the w lends them its velocity,—they fly three sea-birds driven landward by tempestuous breeze. The ladies w not thus rival Atalanta if they knew that any one were at leisur observe them. Ah! as they hasten ward, laughing in the angry face nature, a sudden catastrophe chanced. At the corner where the row lane enters into the street, come plump against the old merch whose tortoise motion has just bro him to that point. He likes not sweet encounter; the darkness of whole air gathers speedily upon visage, and there is a pause on sides. Finally, he thrusts aside the y with little courtesy, seizes an arm each of the two girls, and plods ward, like a magician with a priz captive fairies. All this is easy t understood. How disconsolate the lover stands! regardless of the rain threatens an exceeding damage to well - fashioned habiliments, till catches a backward glance of mirth f a bright eye, and turns away whatever comfort it conveys.

The old man and his daughters safely housed, and now the storm loose its fury. In every dwelling I ceive the faces of the chambermaic they shut down the windows, exclu the impetuous shower, and shrin away from the quick fiery glare. large drops descend with force the slated roofs, and rise again in sm There is a rush and roar, as of a through the air, and muddy str ble majestically along the pavement, rl their dusky foam into the kennel, disappear beneath iron grates. Thus Arethusa sink. I love not my sta- here aloft, in the midst of the ult which I am powerless to direct quell, with the blue lightning wrin- g on my brow, and the thunder tering its first awful syllables in my I will descend. Yet let me give her glance to the sea, where the n breaks out in long white lines n a broad expanse of blackness, or s up in far distant points, like snowy intain-tops in the eddies of a flood; let me look once more at the green plain, and little hills of the country, over which the giant of the storm is striding in robes· of mist, and at the town, whose obscured and desolate streets might beseem a city of the dead; and turning a single moment to the sky, now gloomy as an author's prospects, I prepare to resume my station on lower earth. But stay! A little speck of azure has widened in the western heavens; the sunbeams find a passage, and go rejoicing through the tempest; and on yonder darkest cloud, born, like hallowed hopes, of the glory of another world, and the trouble and tears of this, brightens forth the Rainbow.

THE HOLLOW OF THE THREE HILLS

those strange old times, when fan- c dreams and madmen's reveries realized among the actual circum- ces of life, two persons met together n appointed hour and place. One a lady, graceful in form and fair eature, though pale and troubled, smitten with an untimely blight in should have been the fullest bloom er years; the other was an ancient meanly-dressed woman, of ill-fa- d aspect, and so withered, shrunken, decrepit, that even the space since began to decay must have exceeded ordinary term of human existence. ne spot where they encountered, no al could observe them. Three little stood near each other, and down he midst of them sunk ·a hollow , almost mathematically circular, or three hundred feet in breadth, of such depth that a stately cedar might but just be visible above the sides. Dwarf pines were numerous upon the hills, and partly fringed the outer verge of the intermediate hollow; within which there was nothing but the brown grass of October, and here and there a tree trunk, that had fallen long ago, and lay mouldering with no green successor from its roots. One of these masses of decaying wood, formerly a majestic oak, rested close beside a pool of green and sluggish water at the bottom of the basin. Such scenes as this (so gray tradition tells) were once the resort of the Power of Evil and his plighted subjects; and here, at midnight or on the dim verge of evening, they were said to stand round the mantling pool, disturbing its putrid waters in the performance of an impious baptismal rite. The chill beauty of an autumnal sunset was now gilding the three hilltops, whence a paler tint stole down their sides into the hollow.

"Here is our pleasant meeting come to pass," said the aged crone, "according as thou hast desired. Say quickly what thou wouldst have of me, for there is but a short hour that we may tarry here."

As the old withered woman spoke, a smile glimmered on her countenance, like lamplight on the wall of a sepulchre. The lady trembled, and cast her eyes upward to the verge of the basin, as if meditating to return with her purpose unaccomplished. But it was not so ordained.

"I am a stranger in this land, as you know," said she at length. "Whence I come it matters not; but I have left those behind me with whom my fate was intimately bound, and from whom I am cut off forever. There is a weight in my bosom that I cannot away with, and I have come hither to inquire of their welfare."

"And who is there by this green pool that can bring thee news from the ends of the earth?" cried the old woman, peering into the lady's face. "Not from my lips mayst thou hear these tidings; yet be thou bold, and the daylight shall not pass away from yonder hill-top, before thy wish be granted."

"I will do your bidding, though I die," replied the lady, desperately.

The old woman seated herself on the trunk of the fallen tree, threw aside the hood that shrouded her gray locks, and beckoned her companion to draw near.

"Kneel down," she said, "and lay your forehead on my knees."

She hesitated a moment, but the anxiety that had long been kindling burned fiercely up within her. As she knelt down, the border of her garment w dipped into the pool; she laid her fo head on the old woman's knees, and latter drew a cloak about the lad face, so that she was in darkness. T she heard the muttered words of pray in the midst of which she started, a would have arisen.

"Let me flee,—let me flee and b myself, that they may not look up me!" she cried. But, with returning r ollection, she hushed herself, and still as death.

For it seemed as if other voice familiar in infancy, and unforgot through many wanderings, and in the vicissitudes of her heart and f tune—were mingling with the accents the prayer. At first the words were fa and indistinct, not rendered so by tance, but rather resembling the pages of a book which we strive read by an imperfect and gradu brightening light. In such a manner the prayer proceeded, did those vo strengthen upon the ear; till at len the petition ended, and the conversa of an aged man, and of a woman bro and decayed like himself, became tinctly audible to the lady as she kn But those strangers appeared not stand in the hollow depth between three hills. Their voices were enc passed and re-echoed by the walls a chamber, the windows of which w rattling in the breeze; the regular vi tion of a clock, the crackling of a and the tinkling of the embers as fell among the ashes, rendered the s almost as vivid as if painted to eye. By a melancholy hearth sat t two old people, the man calmly desp dent, the woman querulous and tea and their words were all of sor

y spoke of a daughter, a wanderer
y knew not where, bearing dishonor
ng with her, and leaving shame and
ction to bring their gray heads to
grave. They alluded also to other
more recent woe, but in the midst
their talk, their voices seemed to
t into the sound of the wind sweep-
mournfully among the autumn
es; and when the lady lifted her
s, there was she kneeling in the hol-
between three hills.

A weary and lonesome time yonder
couple have of it," remarked the old
nan, smiling in the lady's face.
And did you also hear them?" ex-
ned she, a sense of intolerable hu-
ation triumphing over her agony and

.
Tea; and we have yet more to hear,"
ied the old woman. "Wherefore,
r thy face quickly."

gain the withered hag poured forth
monotonous words of a prayer that
not meant to be acceptable in
ven; and soon, in the pauses of her
th, strange murmurings began to
ken, gradually increasing so as to
n and overpower the charm by
h they grew. Shrieks pierced
ugh the obscurity of sound, and were
eeded by the singing of sweet female
es, which in their turn gave way
wild roar of laughter, broken sud-
y by groanings and sobs, forming
ether a ghastly confusion of terror
mourning and mirth. Chains were
ing, fierce and stern voices uttered
ats, and the scourge resounded at
command. All these noises deep-
and became substantial to the lis-
r's ear, till she could distinguish
y soft and dreamy accent of the
songs, that died causelessly into

funeral hymns. She shuddered at the
unprovoked wrath which blazed up like
the spontaneous kindling of flame, and
she grew faint at the fearful merriment,
raging miserably around her. In the
midst of this wild scene, where unbound
passions jostled each other in a drunken
career, there was one solemn voice of
a man, and a manly and melodious voice
it might once have been. He went to
and fro continually, and his feet sounded
upon the floor. In each member of that
frenzied company, whose own burning
thoughts had become their exclusive
world, he sought an auditor for the
story of his individual wrong, and interpreted their laughter and tears as
his reward of scorn or pity. He spoke
of woman's perfidy, of a wife who had
broken her holiest vows, of a home
and heart made desolate. Even as he
went on, the shout, the laugh, the
shriek, the sob, rose up in unison, till
they changed into the hollow, fitful, and
uneven sound of the wind, as it fought
among the pine-trees on those three
lonely hills. The lady looked up, and
there was the withered woman smiling
in her face.

"Couldst thou have thought there
were such merry times in a madhouse?"
inquired the latter.

"True, true," said the lady to herself;
"there is mirth within its walls, but
misery, misery, without."

"Wouldst thou hear more?" demanded the old woman.

"There is one other voice I would
fain listen to again," replied the lady,
faintly.

"Then, lay down thy head speedily
upon my knees, that thou mayst get
thee hence before the hour be passed."

The golden skirts of day were yet

lingering upon the hills, but deep shades obscured the hollow and the pool, as if sombre night were rising thence to overspread the world. Again that evil woman began to weave her spell. Long did it proceed unanswered, till the knolling of a bell stole in among the intervals of her words, like a clang that had travelled far over valley and rising ground, and was just ready to die in the air. The lady shook upon her companion's knees, as she heard that boding sound. Stronger it grew and sadder, and deepened into the tone of a death-bell, knolling dolefully from some ivy-mantled tower, and bearing tidings of mortality and woe to the cottage, to the hall, and to the solitary wayfarer, that all might weep for the doom appointed in turn to them. Then came a measured tread, passing slowly, slowly on, as of mourners with a coffin, their garments trailing on the ground, so that the ear could measure the length of their melancholy array. Before th went the priest, reading the burial se ice, while the leaves of his book w rustling in the breeze. And though voice but his was heard to speak alo still there were revilings and anathem whispered but distinct, from women from men, breathed against the daugh who had wrung the aged hearts of parents,—the wife who had betra the trusting fondness of her husba —the mother who had sinned aga natural affection, and left her child die. The sweeping sound of the fun train faded away like a thin vapor, the wind that just before had seen to shake the coffin pall moaned sa round the verge of the Hollow betw three Hills. But when the old wo stirred the kneeling lady, she lifted her head.

"Here has been a sweet hour's spo said the withered crone, chuckling herself.

THE TOLL-GATHERER'S DAY

A SKETCH OF TRANSITORY LIFE

Methinks, for a person whose instinct bids him rather to pore over the current of life than to plunge into its tumultuous waves, no undesirable retreat were a toll-house beside some thronged thoroughfare of the land. In youth, perhaps, it is good for the observer to run about the earth,—to leave the track of his footsteps far and wide, —to mingle himself with the action of numberless vicissitudes,—and, finally, in some calm solitude, to feed a musing spirit on all that he has seen and But there are natures too indolent too sensitive, to endure the dust, sunshine, or the rain, the turmoil moral and physical elements, to wl all the wayfarers of the world exp themselves. For such a man, how pl ant a miracle, could life be made to its variegated length by the thres of his own hermitage, and the g globe, as it were, perform its revolut and shift its thousand scenes before eyes without whirling him onward ir course. If any mortal be favored v

ot analogous to this, it is the toll-
herer. So, at least, have I often fan-
d, while lounging on a bench at the
r of a small square ediñce, which
nds between shore and shore in the
lst of a long bridge. Beneath the
bers ebbs and flows an arm of the
; while above, like the life-blood
ough a great artery, the travel of
north and east is continually throb-
g. Sitting on the aforesaid bench, I
ise myself with a conception, illus-
ed by numerous pencil-sketches in
air, of the toll-gatherer's day.

n the morning—dim, gray, dewy
imer's morn—the distant roll of pon-
ous wheels begins to mingle with
old friend's slumbers, creaking more
more harshly through the midst of
dream, and gradually replacing it
i realities. Hardly conscious of the
nge from sleep to wakefulness, he
s himself partly clad and throwing
e the toll-gates for the passage of a
rant load of hay. The timbers groan
eath the slow-revolving wheels; one
dy yeoman stalks beside the oxen,
, peering from the summit of the
, by the glimmer of the half-ex-
uished lantern over the toll-house,
een the drowsy visage of his com-
:, who has enjoyed a nap some ten
s long. The toll is paid,—creak,
k again go the wheels, and the huge
now vanishes into the morning mist.
yet, nature is but half awake, and
iliar objects appear visionary. But
der, dashing from the shore with a
ling thunder of the wheels and a
used clatter of hoofs, comes the
er-tiring mail, which has hurried on-
i at the same headlong, restless rate,
hrough the quiet night. The bridge
inds in one continued peal as the

coach rolls on without a pause, merely
affording the toll-gatherer a glimpse
at the sleepy passengers, who now be-
stir their torpid limbs, and snuff a cordial in the briny air. The morn breathes
upon them and blushes, and they forget
how wearily the darkness toiled away.
And behold now the fervid day, in his
bright chariot, glittering aslant over the
waves, now scorning to throw a tribute
of his golden beams on the toll-gatherer's little hermitage. The old man looks
eastward, and (for he is a moralizer)
frames a simile of the stage-coach and
the sun.

While the world is rousing itself, we
may glance slightly at the scene of our
sketch. It sits above the bosom of
the broad flood, a spot not of earth,
but in the midst of waters, which rush
with a murmuring sound among the massive beams beneath. Over the door is
a weather-beaten board, inscribed with
the rates of toll, in letters so nearly
effaced that the gilding of the sunshine
can hardly make them legible. Beneath
the window is a wooden bench, on which
a long succession of weary wayfarers
have reposed themselves. Peeping within doors, we perceive the whitewashed
walls bedecked with sundry lithographic
prints and advertisements of various
import, and the immense showbill of
a wandering caravan. And there sits
our good old toll-gatherer, glorified by
the early sunbeams. He is a man, as
his aspect may announce, of quiet soul,
and thoughtful, shrewd, yet simple
mind, who of the wisdom which the
passing world scatters along the wayside has gathered a reasonable store.

Now the sun smiles upon the landscape, and earth smiles back again upon
the sky. Frequent, now, are the travel-

lers. The toll-gatherer's practised ear can distinguish the weight of every vehicle, the number of its wheels, and how many horses beat the resounding timbers with their iron tramp. Here, in a substantial family chaise, setting forth betimes to take advantage of the dewy road, come a gentleman and his wife, with their rosy-cheeked little girl sitting gladsomely between them. The bottom of the chaise is heaped with multifarious bandboxes, and carpet-bags, and beneath the axle swings a leathern trunk, dusty with yesterday's journey. Next appears a four-wheeled carryall, peopled with a round half-dozen of pretty girls, all drawn by a single horse, and driven by a single gentleman. Luckless wight, doomed, through a whole summer day, to be the butt of mirth and mischief among the frolicsome maidens! Bolt upright in a sulky rides a thin, sour-visaged man, who, as he pays his toll, hands the toll-gatherer a printed card to stick upon the wall. The vinegar-faced traveller proves to be a manufacturer of pickles. Now paces slowly from timber to timber a horseman clad in black, with a meditative brow, as of one who, whithersoever his steed might bear him, would still journey through a mist of brooding thought. He is a country preacher, going to labor at a protracted meeting. The next object passing townward is a butcher's cart, canopied with its arch of snow-white cotton. Behind comes a "sauceman," driving a wagon full of new potatoes, green ears of corn, beets, carrots, turnips, and summer squashes; and next, two wrinkled, withered, witch-looking old gossips, in an antediluvian chaise, drawn by a horse of former generations, and going to peddle out a lot of huckleberries. See

there, a man trundling a wheelbarr load of lobsters. And now a milk-rattles briskly onward, covered v green canvas, and conveying the c tributions of a whole herd of cows large tin canisters. But let all these their toll and pass. Here comes a s tacle that causes the old toll-gath to smile benignantly, as if the travel brought sunshine with them and ished its gladsome influence all along road.

It is a barouche of the newest st the varnished panels of which re the whole moving panorama of the la scape, and show a picture, likewise our friend, with his visage broade so that his meditative smile is tr formed to grotesque merriment. Wit sits a youth, fresh as the summer m and beside him a young lady in w with white gloves upon her sle hands and a white veil flowing d over her face. But methinks her b ing cheek burns through the snowy Another white-robed virgin sits in fr And who are these, on whom, and all that appertains to them, the dus earth seems never to have settled? lovers, whom the priest has bles this blessed morn, and sent them f with one of the bridemaids, on matrimonial tour. Take my blessing ye happy ones! May the sky not fr upon you, nor clouds bedew you their chill and sullen rain! May the sun kindle no fever in your he May your whole life's pilgrimage b blissful as this first day's journey, its close be gladdened with even bri anticipations than those which ha your bridal night!

They pass; and ere the reflectio their joy has faded from his face,

er spectacle throws a melancholy
dow over the spirit of the observ-
man. In a close carriage sits a
;ile figure, muffled carefully, and
nking even from the mild breath of
amer. She leans against a manly
n, and his arm enfolds hers, as if
;uard his treasure from some enemy.
but a few weeks pass, and when
shall strive to embrace that loved
, he will press only desolation to
heart.

nd now has morning gathered up
dewy pearls, and fled away. The sun
s blazing through the sky, and can-
find a cloud to cool his face with.
horses toil sluggishly along the
ge, and heave their glistening sides
hort quick pantings, when the reins
tightened at the toll-house. Glisten,
the faces of the travellers. Their
nents are thickly bestrewn with
; their whiskers and hair look
ry; their throats are choked with
dusty atmosphere which they have
behind them. No air is stirring on
road. Nature dares draw no breath,
she should inhale a stifling cloud
lust. "A hot and dusty day!" cry
poor pilgrims, as they wipe their
imed foreheads, and woo the doubt-
breeze which the river bears along
it. "Awful hot! Dreadful dusty!"
vers the sympathetic toll-gatherer.
y start again, to pass through the
furnace, while he re-enters his
hermitage, and besprinkles it with
il of briny water from the stream
ath. He thinks within himself, that
sun is not so fierce here as else-
re, and that the gentle air does
forget him in these sultry days. Yes,
friend; and a quiet heart will make
g-day temperate. He hears a weary

footstep, and perceives a traveller with
pack and staff, who sits down upon
the hospitable bench, and removes the
hat from his wet brow. The toll-gatherer administers a cup of cold water,
and discovering his guest to be a man
of homely sense, he engages him in
profitable talk, uttering the maxims of
a philosophy which he has found in
his own soul, but knows not how it
came there. And as the wayfarer makes
ready to resume his journey, he tells
him a sovereign remedy for blistered
feet.

Now comes the noontide hour,—of
all the hours, nearest akin to midnight;
for each has its own calmness and repose. Soon, however, the world begins
to turn again upon its axis, and it seems
the busiest epoch of the day; when an
accident impedes the march of sublu-
nary things. The draw being lifted to
permit the passage of a schooner, laden
with wood from the Eastern forests,
she sticks immovably, right athwart the
bridge! Meanwhile, on both sides of
the chasm, a throng of impatient travellers fret and fume. Here are two
sailors in a gig, with the top thrown
back, both puffing cigars, and swearing
all sorts of forecastle oaths; there, in
a smart chaise, a dashingly-dressed
gentleman and lady, he from a tailor's
shopboard, and she from a milliner's
backroom,—the aristocrats of a summer afternoon. And what are the
haughtiest of us, but the ephemeral
aristocrats of a summer's day. Here is
a tin-pedler, whose glittering ware be-
dazzles all beholders, like a travelling
meteor, or opposition sun; and on the
other side a seller of spruce beer, which
brisk liquor is confined in several dozen
of stone bottles. Here comes a party

of ladies on horseback, in green riding-habits, and gentlemen attendant; and there a flock of sheep for the market, pattering over the bridge with a multitudinous clatter of their little hoofs. Here a Frenchman, with a hand-organ on his shoulder; and there an itinerant Swiss jeweller. On this side, heralded by a blast of clarions and bugles, appears a train of wagons, conveying all the wild beasts of a caravan; and on that, a company of summer soldiers, marching from village to village on a festival campaign, attended by the "Brass band." Now look at the scene, and it presents an emblem of the mysterious confusion, the apparently insolvable riddle, in which individuals, or the great world itself, seem often to be involved. What miracle shall set all things right again?

But see! the schooner has thrust her bulky carcass through the chasm; the draw descends; horse and foot pass onward, and leave the bridge vacant from end to end. "And thus," muses the tollgatherer, "have I found it with all stoppages, even though the universe seemed to be at a stand." The sage old man!

Far westward now, the reddening sun throws a broad sheet of splendor acr the flood, and to the eyes of dist boatmen gleams brightly among timbers of the bridge. Strollers co from the town to quaff the freshen breeze. One or two let down long lir and haul up flapping flounders, or c ners, or small cod, or perhaps an Others, and fair girls among them, w the flush of the hot day still on th cheeks, bend over the railing and wa the heaps of seaweed floating upw with the flowing tide. The horses tramp heavily along the bridge, wistfully bethink them of their stab Rest, rest, thou weary world! for morrow's round of toil and pleasure be as wearisome as to-day's has be yet both shall bear thee onward a da march of eternity. Now the old t gatherer looks seaward, and discerns lighthouse kindling on a far island, the stars, too, kindling in the sky, if but a little way beyond; and ming reveries of Heaven with remembran of Earth, the whole procession of m tal travellers, all the dusty pilgrim which he has witnessed, seems lik flitting show of phantoms for thoughtful soul to muse upon.

THE VISION OF THE FOUNTAIN

At fifteen, I became a resident in a country village, more than a hundred miles from home. The morning after my arrival—a September morning, but warm and bright as any in July—I rambled into a wood of oaks, with a few walnut-trees intermixed, forming the closest shade above my head. ground was rocky, uneven, overgr with bushes and clumps of young lings, and traversed only by ca paths. The track, which I chanced follow, led me to a crystal spring, a border of grass, as freshly greer

May morning, and overshadowed by
limb of a great oak. One solitary
beam found its way down, and
ved like a goldfish in the water.
'rom my childhood, I have loved
gaze into a spring. The water filled
circular basin, small but deep, and
round with stones, some of which
e covered with slimy moss, the
ers naked, and of variegated hue,
dish, white and brown. The bottom
covered with coarse sand, which
rkled in the lonely sunbeam, and
ned to illuminate the spring with an
orrowed light. In one spot, the gush
he water violently agitated the sand,
without obscuring the fountain, or
aking the glassiness of its surface.
appeared as if some living creature
e about to emerge—the Naiad of
spring, perhaps—in the shape of a
utiful young woman, with a gown
ilmy water-moss, a belt of rainbow
ps, and a cold, pure, passionless
ntenance. How would the beholder
er, pleasantly, yet fearfully, to see
sitting on one of the stones, pad-
g her white feet in the ripples, and
owing up water, to sparkle in the
! Wherever she laid her hands on
s and flowers, they would immedi-
y be moist as with morning dew.
n would she set about her labors,
a careful housewife, to clear the
ntain of withered leaves, and bits
slimy wood, and old acorns from
oaks above, and grains of corn left
cattle in drinking, till the bright
d, in the bright water, were like a
sury of diamonds. But should the
uder approach too near, he would
only the drops of a summer shower
tening about the spot where he had
n her.

Reclining on the border of grass,
where the dewy goddess should have
been, I bent forward, and a pair of
eyes met mine within the watery mirror. They were the reflection of my
own. I looked again, and lo! another
face, deeper in the fountain than my
own image, more distinct in all the
features, yet faint as thought. The vision had the aspect of a fair young
girl, with locks of paly gold. A mirthful
expression laughed in the eyes and dimpled over the whole shadowy countenance, till it seemed just what a fountain would be, if, while dancing merrily
into the sunshine, it should assume the
shape of a woman. Through the dim
rosiness of the cheeks, I could see the
brown leaves, the slimy twigs, the
acorns, and the sparkling sand. The solitary sunbeam was diffused among the
golden hair, which melted into its faint
brightness, and became a glory round
that head so beautiful.

My description can give no idea how
suddenly the fountain was thus tenanted, and how soon it was left desolate. I breathed; and there was the
face! I held my breath; and it was
gone! Had it passed away, or faded into
nothing? I doubted whether it had ever
been.

My sweet readers, what a dreamy
and delicious hour did I spend, where
that vision found and left me! For a
long time I sat perfectly still, waiting
till it should reappear, and fearful that
the slightest motion, or even the flutter
of my breath, might frighten it away.
Thus have I often started from a pleasant dream, and then kept quiet, in hopes
to wile it back. Deep were my musings,
as to the race and attributes of that
ethereal being. Had I created her? Was

she the daughter of my fancy, akin to those strange shapes which peep under the lids of children's eyes? And did her beauty gladden me, for that one moment, and then die? Or was she a water-nymph within the fountain, or fairy, or woodland goddess, peeping over my shoulder, or the ghost of some forsaken maid, who had drowned herself for love? Or, in good truth, had a lovely girl, with a warm heart, and lips that would bear pressure, stolen softly behind me, and thrown her image into the spring?

I watched and waited, but no vision came again. I departed, but with a spell upon me, which drew me back, that same afternoon, to the haunted spring. There was the water gushing, the sand sparkling, and the sunbeam glittering. There the vision was not, but only a great frog, the hermit of that solitude, who immediately withdrew his speckled snout and made himself invisible, all except a pair of long legs, beneath a stone. Methought he had a devilish look! I could have slain him as an enchanter, who kept the mysterious beauty imprisoned in the fountain.

Sad and heavy, I was returning to the village. Between me and the church-spire rose a little hill, and on its summit a group of trees, insulated from all the rest of the wood, with their own share of radiance hovering on them from the west, and their own solitary shadow falling to the east. The afternoon being far declined, the sunshine was almost pensive, and the shade almost cheerful; glory and gloom were mingled in the placid light; as if the spirits of the Day and Evening had met in friendship under those trees, and

found themselves akin. I was admi the picture, when the shape of a yo girl emerged from behind the clum oaks. My heart knew her; it was Vision; but so distant and ethereal she seem, so unmixed with earth, imbued with the pensive glory of spot where she was standing, that spirit sunk within me, sadder than fore. How could I ever reach her?

While I gazed, a sudden shower c pattering down upon the leaves. I moment the air was full of brightr each rain-drop catching a portion sunlight as it fell, and the whole ge shower appearing like a mist, just stantial enough to bear the burde radiance. A rainbow, vivid as Niaga was painted in the air. Its sout limb came down before the group trees, and enveloped the fair Vision if the hues of Heaven were the garment for her beauty. When the bow vanished, she who had seeme part of it was no longer there. her existence absorbed in nature's liest phenomenon, and did her frame dissolve away in the varied li Yet I would not despair of her ret for, robed in the rainbow, she was emblem of Hope.

Thus did the vision leave me; many a doleful day succeeded to parting moment. By the spring, an the wood, and on the hill, and thr the village; at dewy sunrise, bu noon, and at that magic hour of set, when she had vanished from sight, I sought her, but in vain. W came and went, months rolled a and she appeared not in them. I parted my mystery to none, but dered to and fro, or sat in soli like one that had caught a glimps

.ven, and could take no more joy
earth. I withdrew into an inner
ld, where my thoughts lived and
.thed, and the Vision in the midst
.hem. Without intending it, I be-
.e at once the author and hero of
.mance, conjuring up rivals, imagin-
events, the actions of others and
own, and experiencing every change
.assion, till jealousy and despair had
.t end in bliss. O, had I the burn-
fancy of my early youth, with man-
.l's colder gift, the power of expres-
., your hearts, sweet ladies, should
.er at my tale!

.1 the middle of January, I was sum-
.ed home. The day before my de-
.ure, visiting the spots which had
.l hallowed by the Vision, I found
. the spring had a frozen bosom,
nothing but the snow and a glare
.vinter sunshine, on the hill of the
.bow. "Let me hope," thought I, "or
heart will be as icy as the foun-
., and the whole world as desolate
.his snowy hill." Most of the day
spent in preparing for the journey,
:h was to commence at four o'clock
.next morning. About an hour after
.er, when all was in readiness, I
.ended from my chamber to the sit-
.room, to take leave of the old
.:yman and his family, with whom
.d been an inmate. A gust of wind
. out my lamp as I passed through
.entry.

.:cording to their invariable custom,
.leasant a one when the fire blazes
rfully, the family were sitting in
.parlor, with no other light than
.t came from the hearth. As the
.l clergyman's scanty stipend com-
.:d him to use all sorts of economy,
.foundation of his fires was always

a large heap of tan, or ground bark,
which would smoulder away, from morning till night, with a dull warmth and
no flame. This evening the heap of
tan was newly put on, and surmounted
with three sticks of red oak, full of
moisture, and a few pieces of dry pine,
that had not yet kindled. There was
no light, except the little that came
sullenly from two half-burned brands,
without even glimmering on the andirons. But I knew the position of the
old minister's arm-chair, and also where
his wife sat, with her knitting-work, and
how to avoid his two daughters, one
a stout country lass, and the other a
consumptive girl. Groping through the
gloom, I found my own place next to
that of the son, a learned collegian, who
had come home to keep school in the
village during the winter vacation. I
noticed that there was less room than
usual, to-night, between the collegian's
chair and mine.

As people are always taciturn in the
dark, not a word was said for some time
after my entrance. Nothing broke the
stillness but the regular click of the
matron's knitting-needles. At times, the
fire threw out a brief and dusky gleam,
which twinkled on the old man's glasses,
and hovered doubtfully round our circle,
but was far too faint to portray the
individuals who composed it. Were we
not like ghosts? Dreamy as the scene
was, might it not be a type of the mode
in which departed people, who had
known and loved each other here, would
hold communion in eternity? We were
aware of each other's presence, not by
sight, nor sound, nor touch, but by an
inward consciousness. Would it not be
so among the dead?

The silence was interrupted by the

consumptive daughter addressing a remark to some one in the circle, whom she called Rachel. Her tremulous and decayed accents were answered by a single word, but in a voice that made me start, and bend towards the spot whence it had proceeded. Had I ever heard that sweet, low tone? If not, why did it rouse up so many old recollections, or mockeries of such, the shadows of things familiar, yet unknown, and fill my mind with confused images of her features who had spoken, though buried in the gloom of the parlor? Whom had my heart recognized, that it throbbed so? I listened, to catch her gentle breathing, and strove, by the intensity of my gaze, to picture forth a shape where none was visible.

Suddenly, the dry pine caught; the fire blazed up with a ruddy glow; and where the darkness had been, there was she—the Vision of the Fountain! A spirit of radiance only, she had vanished with the rainbow, and appeared again in the firelight, perhaps to flicker with the blaze, and be gone. Yet her cheek was rosy and lifelike, and her featu in the bright warmth of the room, w even sweeter and tenderer than recollection of them. She knew r The mirthful expression that l laughed in her eyes and dimpled o her countenance, when I beheld faint beauty in the fountain, was lau ing and dimpling there now. One r ment, our glance mingled,—the n down rolled the heap of tan upon kindled wood,—and darkness snatc away that Daughter of the Light, a gave her back to me no more!

Fair ladies, there is nothing more tell. Must the simple mystery be vealed, then, that Rachel was the dau ter of the village squire, and had home for a boarding-school the morn after I arrived, and returned the before my departure? If I transforn her to an angel, it is what every you ful lover does for his mistress. The consists the essence of my story. l slight the change, sweet maids, to m angels of yourselves!

FANCY'S SHOW-BOX

A MORALITY

WHAT is guilt? A stain upon the soul. And it is a point of vast interest whether the soul may contract such stains, in all their depth and flagrancy, from deeds which may have been plotted and resolved upon, but which, physically, have never had existence. Must the fleshly hand and visible frame of man set its seal to the evil designs of the soul, in order to give them t entire validity against the sinner? while none but crimes perpetrated cognizable before an earthly tribu will guilty thoughts—of which gu deeds are no more than shadows— these draw down the full weight o condemning sentence in the supr court of eternity? In the solitude c midnight chamber, or in a desert a from men, or in a church, while

ly is kneeling the soul may pollute
lf even with those crimes which we
accustomed to deem altogether car-
. If this be true, it is a fearful truth.
et us illustrate the subject by an
ginary example. A venerable gentle-
n, one Mr. Smith, who had long been
rded as a pattern of moral excel-
ce, was warming his aged blood with
lass or two of generous wine. His
dren being gone forth about their
ldly business, and his grandchildren
school, he sat alone in a deep, lux-
us arm-chair, with his feet beneath
ichly-carved mahogany table. Some
people have a dread of solitude,
when better company may not be
, rejoice even to hear the quiet
thing of a babe asleep upon the
et. But Mr. Smith, whose silver
was the bright symbol of a life
ained, except by such spots as are
parable from human nature, he had
need of a babe to protect him by
purity, nor of a grown person, to
d between him and his own soul.
ertheless, either Manhood must con-
c with Age, or Womanhood must
he him with gentle cares, or In-
y must sport around his chair, or
thoughts will stray into the misty
on of the past, and the old man be
and sad. Wine will not always
r him. Such might have been the
with Mr. Smith, when, through the
iant medium of his glass of old
leira, he beheld three figures enter-
the room. These were Fancy, who
assumed the garb and aspect of
tinerant showman, with a box of
ures on her back; and Memory, in
likeness of a clerk, with a pen be-
her ear, an inkhorn at her button-
, and a huge manuscript volume

beneath her arm; and lastly, behind the
other two, a person shrouded in a dusky
mantle, which concealed both face and
form. But Mr. Smith had a shrewd
idea that it was Conscience.

How kind of Fancy, Memory, and
Conscience to visit the old gentleman,
just as he was beginning to imagine
that the wine had neither so bright a
sparkle, nor so excellent a flavor, as
when himself and the liquor were less
aged! Through the dim length of the
apartment, where crimson curtains muffled the glare of sunshine, and created
a rich obscurity, the three guests drew
near the silver-haired old man. Memory, with a finger between the leaves
of her huge volume, placed herself at
his right hand. Conscience, with her
face still hidden in the dusky mantle,
took her station on the left, so as
to be next his heart; while Fancy set
down her picture-box upon the table,
with the magnifying glass convenient
to his eye. We can sketch merely the
outlines of two or three out of the
many pictures, which, at the pulling of
a string, successively peopled the box
with the semblances of living scenes.

One was a moonlight picture; in the
background, a lowly dwelling; and in
front, partly shadowed by a tree, yet
besprinkled with flakes of radiance, two
youthful figures, male and female. The
young man stood with folded arms, a
haughty smile upon his lip and a gleam
of triumph in his eye, as he glanced
downward at the kneeling girl. She was
almost prostrate at his feet, evidently
sinking under a weight of shame and
anguish, which hardly allowed her to
lift her clasped hands in supplication.
Her eyes she could not lift. But neither
her agony nor the lovely features on

which it was depicted, nor the slender grace of the form which it convulsed, appeared to soften the obduracy of the young man. He was the personification of triumphant scorn. Now, strange to say, as old Mr. Smith peeped through the magnifying glass, which made the objects start out from the canvas with magical deception, he began to recognize the farmhouse, the tree, and both the figures of the picture. The young man, in times, long past, had often met his gaze within the looking-glass; the girl was the very image of his first love,—his cottage love,—his Martha Burroughs! Mr. Smith was scandalized. "O, vile and slanderous picture!" he exclaims. "When have I triumphed over ruined innocence? Was not Martha wedded, in her teens, to David Tomkins, who won her girlish love and long enjoyed her affection as a wife? And ever since his death she has lived a reputable widow!" Meantime, Memory was turning over the leaves of her volume, rustling them to and fro with uncertain fingers, until, among the earlier pages, she found one which had reference to this picture. She reads it, close to the old gentleman's ear; it is a record merely of sinful thought, which never was embodied in an act; but, while Memory is reading Conscience unveils her face, and strikes a dagger to the heart of Mr. Smith. Though not a death-blow, the torture was extreme.

The exhibition proceeded. One after another, Fancy displayed her pictures, all of which appeared to have been painted by some malicious artist, on purpose to vex Mr. Smith. Not a shadow of proof could have been adduced, in any earthly court, that he

was guilty of the slightest of t[...] sins which were thus made to s[...] him in the face. In one scene t[...] was a table set out, with several [...] tles, and glasses half filled with w[...] which threw back the dull ray of [...] expiring lamp. There had been m[...] and revelry, until the hand of the c[...] stood just at midnight, when mu[...] stepped between the boon compani[...] A young man had fallen on the f[...] and lay stone dead, with a gha[...] wound crushed into his temple, v[...] over him, with a delirium of min[...] rage and horror in his countena[...] stood the youthful likeness of Mr. Sn[...] The murdered youth wore the feat[...] of Edward Spencer! "What does [...] rascal of a painter mean?" cries [...] Smith, provoked beyond all patie[...] "Edward Spencer was my earliest [...] dearest friend, true to me as I to [...] through more than half a cent[...] Neither I, nor any other, ever murd[...] him. Was he not alive within five y[...] and did he not, in token of our [...] friendship, bequeath me his gold-he[...] cane, and a mourning ring?" Again [...] Memory been turning over her vol[...] and fixed at length upon so conf[...] a page, that she surely must have s[...] bled it when she was tipsy. The [...] port was, however, that, while [...] Smith and Edward Spencer were [...] ing their young blood with wine, a c[...] rel had flashed up between them, [...] Mr. Smith, in deadly wrath, had [...] a bottle at Spencer's head. Tru[...] missed its aim, and merely smash[...] looking-glass; and the next mor[...] when the incident was imperfectl[...] membered, they had shaken hands [...] a hearty laugh. Yet, again, while M[...] ory was reading, Conscience unv[...]

face, struck a dagger to the heart
Mr. Smith, and quelled his remon-
nce with her iron frown. The pain
quite excruciating.

ome of the pictures had been painted
a so doubtful a touch, and in colors
faint and pale, that the subjects
d barely be conjectured. A dull,
i-transparent mist had been thrown
' the surface of the canvas, into
ch the figures seemed to vanish,
e the eye sought most earnestly to
hem. But, in every scene, however
ously portrayed, Mr. Smith was in-
ably haunted by his own lineaments,
arious ages, as in a dusty mirror.
r poring several minutes over one
hese blurred and almost indistin-
nable pictures, he began to see that
painter had intended to represent
now in the decline of life, as strip-
the clothes from the backs of
e half-starved children. "Really,
puzzles me!" quoth Mr. Smith,
the irony of conscious rectitude.
ring pardon of the painter, I pro-
ace him a fool, as well as a scandal-
knave. A man of my standing in
world, to be robbing little children
eir clothes! Ridiculous!" But while
poke, Memory had searched her
volume, and found a page, which,
her sad, calm voice, she poured
his ear. It was not altogether in-
cable to the misty scene. It told
Mr. Smith had been grievously
oted by many devilish sophistries,
he ground of a legal quibble, to
nence a lawsuit against three or-
children, joint heirs to a consid-
e estate. Fortunately, before he was
e decided, his claims had turned
nearly as devoid of law as justice.
Memory ceased to read, Conscience

again thrust aside her mantle, and would
have struck her victim with the en-
venomed dagger, only that he struggled,
and clasped his hands before his heart.
Even then, however, he sustained an
ugly gash.

Why should we follow Fancy through
the whole series of those awful pictures?
Painted by an artist of wondrous power,
and terrible acquaintance with the secret soul, they embodied the ghosts of
all the never perpetrated sins that had
glided through the lifetime of Mr.
Smith. And could such beings of cloudy
fantasy, so near akin to nothingness,
give valid evidence against him, at the
day of judgment? Be that the case or
not, there is reason to believe that one
truly penitential tear would have washed
away each hateful picture, and left the
canvas white as snow. But Mr. Smith,
at a prick of Conscience too keen to
be endured, bellowed aloud, with impatient agony, and suddenly discovered
that his three guests were gone. There
he sat alone, a silver-haired and highly
venerated old man, in the rich gloom
of the crimson-curtained room, with no
box of pictures on the table, but only
a decanter of most excellent Madeira.
Yet his heart still seemed to fester
with the venom of the dagger.

Nevertheless, the unfortunate old
gentleman might have argued the matter with Conscience, and alleged many
reasons wherefore she should not smite
him so pitilessly. Were we to take up
his cause, it should be somewhat in
the following fashion: A scheme of
guilt, till it be put in execution, greatly
resembles a train of incidents in a projected tale. The latter, in order to
produce a sense of reality in the reader's mind, must be conceived with such

proportionate strength by the author as to seem, in the glow of fancy, more like truth past, present, or to come, than purely fiction. The prospective sinner, on the other hand, weaves his plot of crime, but seldom or never feels a perfect certainty that it will be executed. There is a dreaminess diffused about his thoughts; in a dream, as it were, he strikes the death-blow into his victim's heart, and starts to find an indelible bloodstain on his hand. Thus a novel-writer, or a dramatist, in creating a villain of romance, and fitting him with evil deeds, and the villain of actual life, in projecting crimes that will be perpetrated, may almost meet each other, half-way between reality and fancy. It is not until the crime is accomplished, that guilt clinches its gripe upon the guilty heart, and claims it for its own. Then, and not before, sin is actually felt and acknowledged, and, if unaccompanied by repentance, grows a thousand-fold more virulent by its self-consciousness. Be it considered, also, that men often over-estimate their capacity for evil. At a distance, while its attendant circumstances do not press upon their notice, and its results are

dimly seen, they can bear to conte plate it. They may take the steps wh lead to crime, impelled by the sa sort of mental action as in work out a mathematical problem, yet powerless with compunction at the f moment. They knew not what d it was that they deemed themselves solved to do. In truth, there is no s thing in man's nature as a settled full resolve, either for good or e except at the very moment of exe tion. Let us hope, therefore, that the dreadful consequences of sin not be incurred, unless the act b set its seal upon the thought.

Yet, with the slight fancy work wh we have framed, some sad and av truths are interwoven. Man must disclaim his brotherhood, even with guiltiest, since, though his hand clean, his heart has surely been pollu by the flitting phantoms of iniquity. must feel, that, when he shall knock the gate of Heaven, no semblance an unspotted life can entitle him entrance there. Penitence must kn and Mercy come from the footstoo the throne, or that golden gate never open!

TWICE-TOLD TALES

DR. HEIDEGGER'S EXPERIMENT

THAT very singular man, old Dr. idegger, once invited four venerable nds to meet him in his study. There e three white-bearded gentlemen, . Medbourne, Colonel Killigrew, and . Gascoigne, and a withered gentle- nan, whose name was the Widow cherly. They were all melancholy creatures, who had been unfortunate life, and whose greatest misfortune was, that they were not long ago heir graves. Mr. Medbourne, in the or of his age, had been a prosperous chant, but had lost his all by a tic speculation, and was now little er than a mendicant. Colonel Killi- v had wasted his best years, and his lth and substance, in the pursuit of ul pleasures, which had given birth a brood of pains, such as the gout, divers other torments of soul and y. Mr. Gascoigne was a ruined poli- n, a man of evil fame, or at least been so, till time had buried him n the knowledge of the present gen- ion, and made him obscure instead nfamous. As for the Widow Wycher- tradition tells us that she was a t beauty in her day; but, for a long e past, she had lived in deep seclu- , on account of certain scandalous ies which had prejudiced the gentry he town against her. It is a circum- ce worth mentioning, that each of e three old gentlemen, Mr. Med- rne, Colonel Killigrew, and Mr. Gascoigne, were early lovers of the Widow Wycherly, and had once been on the point of cutting each other's throats for her sake. And, before proceeding further, I will merely hint that Dr. Heidegger and all his four guests were sometimes thought to be a little beside themselves; as is not unfrequently the case with old people, when worried either by present troubles or woful recollections.

"My dear old friends," said Dr. Heidegger, motioning them to be seated, "I am desirous of your assistance in one of those little experiments with which I amuse myself here in my study."

If all stories were true, Dr. Heidegger's study must have been a very curious place. It was a dim, old-fashioned chamber, festooned with cobwebs and besprinkled with antique dust. Around the walls stood several oaken bookcases, the lower shelves of which were filled with rows of gigantic folios and black-letter quartos, and the upper with little parchment-covered duodecimos. Over the central bookcase was a bronze bust of Hippocrates, with which, according to some authorities, Dr. Heidegger was accustomed to hold consultations in all difficult cases of his practice. In the obscurest corner of the room stood a tall and narrow oaken closet, with its door ajar, within which doubtfully appeared a skeleton. Between two of the bookcases hung a looking-glass, presenting its high and dusty plate within a tarnished gilt frame. Among many wonderful stories related of this mirror, it was fabled that the spirits of all the doctor's deceased patients dwelt within its verge, and would stare him in the face whenever he looked thitherward. The opposite side of the chamber was ornamented with the full-length portrait of a young lady, arrayed in the faded magnificence of silk, satin, and brocade, and with a visage as faded as her dress. Above half a century ago, Dr. Heidegger had been on the point of marriage with this young lady; but, being affected with some slight disorder, she had swallowed one of her lover's prescriptions, and died on the bridal evening. The greatest curiosity of the study remains to be mentioned; it was a ponderous folio volume, bound in black leather, with massive silver clasps. There were no letters on the back, and nobody could tell the title of the book. But it was well known to be a book of magic; and once, when a chambermaid had lifted it merely to brush away the dust, the skeleton had rattled in its closet, the picture of the young lady had stepped one foot upon the floor, and several ghastly faces had peeped forth from the mirror; while the brazen head of Hippocrates frowned, and said—"Forbear!"

Such was Dr. Heidegger's study. On the summer afternoon of our tale, a small round table, as black as ebony, stood in the centre of the room, sustaining a cut-glass vase of beautiful form and elaborate workmanship. The sunshine came through the window, between the heavy festoons of two faded damask curtains, and fell directly across

this vase; so that a mild splendor reflected from it on the ashen vis of the five old people who sat aro Four champagne glasses were also the table.

"My dear old friends," repeated Heidegger, "may I reckon on your in performing an exceedingly cur experiment?"

Now Dr. Heidegger was a strange old gentleman, whose eccenity had become the nucleus for a t sand fantastic stories. Some of t ʿbles, to my shame be it spoken, n possibly be traced back to mine veracious self; and if any passage the present tale should startle the ͬ er's faith, I must be content to the stigma of a fiction-monger.

When the doctor's four guests h him talk of his proposed experin they anticipated nothing more wor ful than the murder of a mouse i ʿair-pump, or the examination of a web by the microscope, or some si nonsense, with which he was consta in the habit of pestering his intim But without waiting for a reply, Heidegger hobbled across the chan and returned with the same pond folio, bound in black leather, v common report affirmed to be a of magic. Undoing the silver clasp opened the volume, and took among its black-letter pages a ros what was once a rose, though nov green leaves and crimson petals assumed one brownish hue, and the cient flower seemed ready to crumb dust in the doctor's hands.

"This rose," said Dr. Heidegger, a sigh, "this same withered and c bling flower, blossomed five and years ago. It was given me by S

d, whose portrait hangs yonder;
I meant to wear it in my bosom
ur wedding. Five and fifty years it
been treasured between the leaves
his old volume. Now, would you
1 it possible that this rose of half a
ury could ever bloom again?"

Nonsense!" said the Widow Wycher-
with a peevish toss of her head.
i might as well ask whether an old
an's wrinkled face could ever bloom
1."

ee!" answered Dr. Heidegger.

c uncovered the vase, and threw
faded rose into the water which it
1ined. At first it lay lightly on the
ice of the fluid, appearing to im-
none of its moisture. Soon, how-
, a singular change began to be
le. The crushed and dried petals
ed, and assumed a deepening tinge
imson, as if the flower were reviv-
from a deathlike slumber; the slen-
stalk and twigs of foliage became
i; and there was the rose of half
ntury, looking as fresh as when
ia Ward had first given it to her
. It was scarcely full blown; for
of its delicate red leaves curled
estly around its moist bosom, with-
hich two or three dew-drops were
ling.

hat is certainly a very pretty de-
on," said the doctor's friends; care-
, however, for they had witnessed
er miracles at a conjurer's show;
how was it effected?"

id you never hear of the 'Foun-
of Youth'?" asked Dr. Heidegger,
ch Ponce de Leon, the Spanish ad-
irer, went in search of two or three
iries ago?"

ut did Ponce de Leon ever find
said the Widow Wycherly.

"No," answered Dr. Heidegger, "for
he never sought it in the right place.
The famous Fountain of Youth, if I
am rightly informed, is situated in the
southern part of the Floridian peninsula, not far from Lake Macaco. Its
source is overshadowed by several gigantic magnolias, which, though numberless centuries old, have been kept
as fresh as violets by the virtues of
this wonderful water. An acquaintance
of mine, knowing my curiosity in such
matters, has sent me what you see in
the vase."

"Ahem!" said Colonel Killigrew, who
believed not a word of the doctor's
story; "and what may be the effect of
this fluid on the human frame?"

"You shall judge for yourself, my
dear colonel," replied Dr. Heidegger;
"and all of you, my respected friends,
are welcome to so much of this admirable fluid as may restore to you the
bloom of youth. For my own part,
having had much trouble in growing
old I am in no hurry to grow young
again. With your permission, therefore,
I will merely watch the progress of
the experiment."

While he spoke, Dr. Heidegger had
been filling the four champagne glasses
with the water of the Fountain of
Youth. It was apparently impregnated
with an effervescent gas, for little bubbles were continually ascending from
the depths of the glasses and bursting
in silvery spray at the surface. As the
liquor diffused a pleasant perfume, the
old people doubted not that it possessed
cordial and comfortable properties; and,
though utter sceptics as to its rejuve-
nescent power, they were inclined to
swallow it at once. But Dr. Heidegger
besought them to stay a moment.

"Before you drink, my respectable old friends," said he, "it would be well that, with the experience of a lifetime to direct you, you should draw up a few general rules for your guidance, in passing a second time through the perils of youth. Think what a sin and shame it would be, if, with your peculiar advantages, you should not become patterns of virtue and wisdom to all the young people of the age!"

The doctor's four venerable friends made him no answer, except by a feeble and tremulous laugh; so very ridiculous was the idea, that, knowing how closely repentance treads behind the steps of error, they should ever go astray again.

"Drink, then," said the doctor, bowing: "I rejoice that I have so well selected the subjects of my experiment."

With palsied hands, they raised the glasses to their lips. The liquor, if it really possessed such virtues as Dr. Heidegger imputed to it, could not have been bestowed on four human beings who needed it more wofully. They looked as if they had never known what youth or pleasure was, but had been the offspring of Nature's dotage, and always the gray, decrepit, sapless, miserable creatures who now sat stooping round the doctor's table, without life enough in their souls or bodies to be animated even by the prospect of growing young again. They drank off the water, and replaced their glasses on the table.

Assuredly there was an almost immediate improvement in the aspect of the party, not unlike what might have been produced by a glass of generous wine, together with a sudden glow of cheerful sunshine, brightening ove their visages at once. There w healthful suffusion on their cheeks stead of the ashen hue that had them look so corpse-like. They at one another, and fancied that magic power had really begun to sn away the deep and sad inscrip which Father Time had been so engraving on their brows. The W Wycherly adjusted her cap, for sh almost like a woman again.

"Give us more of this won water!" cried they, eagerly. "W younger,—but we are still too Quick,—give us more!"

"Patience, patience!" quoth Dr. degger, who sat watching the e ment, with philosophic coolness. have been a long time growing Surely, you might be content to young in half an hour! But the is at your service."

Again he filled their glasses wit liquor of youth, enough of which remained in the vase to turn hal old people in the city to the a their own grandchildren. While the bles were yet sparkling on the the doctor's four guests snatched glasses from the table, and swal the contents at a single gulp. V delusion? even while the draugh passing down their throats, it seen have wrought a change on their systems. Their eyes grew clea bright; a dark shade deepened a their silvery locks; they sat arou table, three gentlemen of middl and a woman hardly beyond her prime.

"My dear widow, you are charr cried Colonel Killigrew, whose ey been fixed upon her face, whi

ows of age were flitting from it
darkness from the crimson day-
.

e fair widow knew, of old, that
nel Killigrew's compliments were
always measured by sober truth;
e started up and ran to the mir-
still dreading that the ugly visage
old woman would meet her gaze.
while, the three gentlemen be-
l in such a manner, as proved that
water of the Fountain of Youth
ssed some intoxicating qualities;
s, indeed, their exhilaration of
s were merely a lightsome dizzi-
caused by the sudden removal of
weight of years. Mr. Gascoigne's
seemed to run on political topics,
whether relating to the past, pres-
or future could not easily be dened, since the same ideas and
es have been in vogue these fifty
Now he rattled forth full-throated
ces about patriotism, national
and the people's right; now he
red some perilous stuff or other, in
and doubtful whisper, so cau-
y that even his own conscience
scarcely catch the secret; and
again, he spoke in measured ac-
and a deeply deferential tone,
a royal ear were listening to his
urned periods. Colonel Killigrew
is time had been trolling forth a
bottle-song, and ringing his glass
nphony with the chorus, while his
wandered toward the buxom figure
Widow Wycherly. On the other
of the table, Mr. Medbourne was
red in a calculation of dollars and
with which was strangely inter-
d a project for supplying the East
with ice, by harnessing a team
ales to the polar icebergs.

As for the Widow Wycherly, she
stood before the mirror courtesying and
simpering to her own image, and greeting it as the friend whom she loved
better than all the world beside. She
thrust her face close to the glass, to
see whether some long-remembered
wrinkle or crow's foot had indeed vanished. She examined whether the snow
had so entirely melted from her hair,
that the venerable cap could be safely
thrown aside. At last, turning briskly
away, she came with a sort of dancing
step to the table.

"My dear old doctor," cried she,
"pray favor me with another glass!"

"Certainly, my dear madam, certainly!" replied the complaisant doctor;
"see! I have already filled the glasses."

There, in fact, stood the four glasses,
brimful of this wonderful water, the
delicate spray of which, as it effervesced
from the surface, resembled the tremulous glitter of diamonds. It was now
so nearly sunset, that the chamber had
grown duskier than ever; but a mild
and moonlike splendor gleamed from
within the vase, and rested alike on the
four guests, and on the doctor's venerable figure. He sat in a high-backed,
elaborately-carved, oaken arm-chair,
with a gray dignity of aspect that might
have well befitted that very Father
Time whose power had never been disputed, save by this fortunate company.
Even while quaffing the third draught of
the Fountain of Youth, they were almost awed by the expression of his
mysterious visage.

But the next moment the exhilarating
gush of young life shot through their
veins. They were now in the happy
prime of youth. Age, with its miserable
train of cares and sorrows and diseases,

was remembered only as the trouble of a dream, from which they had joyously awoke. The fresh gloss of the soul, so early lost, and without which the world's successive scenes had been but a gallery of faded pictures, again threw its enchantment over all their prospects. They felt like new-created beings, in a new-created universe.

"We are young! We are young!" they cried exultingly.

Youth, like the extremity of age, had effaced the strongly-marked characteristics of middle life, and mutually assimilated them all. They were a group of merry youngsters, almost maddened with the exuberant frolicsomeness of their years. The most singular effect of their gayety was an impulse to mock the infirmity and decrepitude of which they had so lately been the victims. They laughed loudly at their old-fashioned attire, the wide-skirted coats and flapped waistcoats of the young men, and the ancient cap and gown of the blooming girl. One limped across the floor, like a gouty grandfather; one set a pair of spectacles astride of his nose, and pretended to pore over the black-letter pages of the book of magic; a third seated himself in an arm-chair, and strove to imitate the venerable dignity of Dr. Heidegger. Then all shouted mirthfully, and leaped about the room. The Widow Wycherly—if so fresh a damsel could be called a widow—tripped up to the doctor's chair, with a mischievous merriment in her rosy face.

"Doctor, you dear old soul," cried she, "get up and dance with me!" And then the four young people laughed louder than ever, to think what a queer figure the poor old doctor would cut.

"Pray excuse me," answered the doc-

tor quietly. "I am old and rheum and my dancing days were over long But either of these gay young gentle will be glad of so pretty a partner."

"Dance with me, Clara," cried Col Killigrew.

"No, no, I will be her partn shouted Mr. Gascoigne.

"She promised me her hand, years ago!" exclaimed Mr. Medbo

They all gathered round her. caught both her hands in his passio grasp,—another threw his arm about waist,—the third buried his hand an the glossy curls that clustered ben the widow's cap. Blushing, pan struggling, chiding, laughing, her v breath fanning each of their face turns, she strove to disengage he yet still remained in their triple brace. Never was there a livelier pi of youthful rivalship, with bewit beauty for the prize. Yet, by a str deception, owing to the duskiness o chamber, and the antique dresses w they still wore, the tall mirror is to have reflected the figures of the old, gray, withered grandsires, ri lously contending for the skinny ness of a shrivelled grandam.

But they were young: their bu passions proved them so. Inflame madness by the coquetry of the widow, who neither granted nor withheld her favors, the three began to interchange threatening gla Still keeping hold of the fair they grappled fiercely at one ano throats. As they struggled to an the table was overturned, and the dashed into a thousand fragments. precious Water of Youth flowed bright stream across the floor, mo ing the wings of a butterfly, w

wn old in the decline of summer, had
ated there to die. The insect fluttered
tly through the chamber, and settled
the snowy head of Dr. Heidegger.
Come, come, gentlemen!—come, Ma-
e Wycherly," exclaimed the doctor,
eally must protest against this riot."

hey stood still, and shivered; for
eemed as if gray Time were calling
a back from their sunny youth, far
n into the chill and darksome vale
ears. They looked at old Dr. Heideg-
who sat in his carved arm-chair
ing the rose of half a century, which
had rescued from among the fragts of the shattered vase. At the
on of his hand the four rioters re-
ed their seats; the more readily, be-
e their violent exertions had wearied
a, youthful though they were.

My poor Sylvia's rose!" ejaculated
Heidegger, holding it in the light
he sunset clouds; "it appears to be
ag again."

nd so it was. Even while the party
: looking at it the flower continued
arivel up, till it became as dry and
le as when the doctor had first
wn it into the vase. He shook off
few drops of moisture which clung
s petals.

love it as well thus as in its dewy
aness," observed he, pressing the
ered rose to his withered lips. While
poke, the butterfly fluttered down
. the doctor's snowy head and fell
a the floor.

is guests shivered again. A strange
aess, whether of the body or spirit
could not tell, was creeping gradu-
over them all. They gazed at one
her, and fancied that each fleeting
aent snatched away a charm, and
a deepening furrow where none had

been before. Was it an illusion? Had
the changes of a lifetime been crowded
into so brief a space, and were they
now four aged people, sitting with their
old friend, Dr. Heidegger?

"Are we grown old again so soon?"
cried they, dolefully.

In truth they had. The Water of
Youth possessed merely a virtue more
transient than that of wine. The delirium which it created had effervesced
away. Yes! they were old again. With
a shuddering impulse that showed her
a woman still, the widow clasped her
skinny hands before her face, and
wished that the coffin-lid were over it
since it could be no longer beautiful.

"Yes, friends, ye are old again," said
Dr. Heidegger; "and lo! the Water of
Youth is all lavished on the ground.
Well—I bemoan it not; for if the fountain gushed at my very doorstep I
would not stoop to bathe my lips in
it,—no, though its delirium were for
years instead of moments. Such is the
lesson ye have taught me!"

But the doctor's four friends had
taught no such lesson to themselves.
They resolved forthwith to make a pilgrimage to Florida, and quaff at morning, noon, and night from the Fountain
of Youth.

Note.—In an English Review, not long since,
I have been accused of plagiarizing the idea
of this story from a chapter in one of the
novels of Alexandre Dumas. There has undoubtedly been a plagiarism on one side or the
other; but as my story was written a good
deal more than twenty years ago, and as the
novel is of considerably more recent date, I
take pleasure in thinking that M. Dumas has
done me the honor to appropriate one of the
fanciful conceptions of my earlier days. He is
heartily welcome to it; nor is it the only instance by many in which the great French
Romancer has exercised the privilege of commanding genius by confiscating the intellectual
property of less famous people to his own use
and behoof.
September, 1860.

LEGENDS OF THE PROVINCE HOUSE

I. HOWE'S MASQUERADE

ONE afternoon last summer, while walking along Washington Street, my eye was attracted by a signboard protruding over a narrow archway, nearly opposite the Old South Church. The sign represented the front of a stately edifice, which was designated as the "OLD PROVINCE HOUSE, kept by Thomas Waite." I was glad to be thus reminded of a purpose, long entertained, of visiting and rambling over the mansion of the old royal governors of Massachusetts; and entering the arched passage, which penetrated through the middle of a brick row of shops, a few steps transported me from the busy heart of modern Boston into a small and secluded court-yard. One side of this space was occupied by the square front of the Province House, three stories high, and surmounted by a cupola, on the top of which a gilded Indian was discernible, with his bow bent and his arrow on the string, as if aiming at the weathercock on the spire of the Old South. The figure has kept this attitude for seventy years or more, ever since good Deacon Drowne, a cunning carver of wood, first stationed him on his long sentinel's watch over the city.

The Province House is constructed of brick, which seems recently to have been overlaid with a coat of light-colored paint. A flight of red freestone steps, fenced in by a balustrade of curiously wrought iron ascends from the court-yard to the spacious porch, over which is a balcony, with an iron balustrade of similar pattern and work-manship to that beneath. These let and figures—16 P. S. 79—are wro into the iron-work of the balcony, probably express the date of the edi with the initials of its founder's na A wide door with double leaves mitted me into the hall or entry, on right of which is the entrance to bar-room.

It was in this apartment, I pres that the ancient governors held levees, with vice-regal pomp, surrou by the military men, the councillors judges, and other officers of the cr while all the loyalty of the prov thronged to do them honor. But room, in its present condition, ca boast even of faded magnificence. panelled wainscot is covered with (paint, and acquires a duskier hue the deep shadow into which the Prov House is thrown by the brick t that shuts it in from Washington S A ray of sunshine never visits apartment any more than the gla the festal torches, which have bee tinguished from the era of the Re tion. The most venerable and mental object is a chimney-piec round with Dutch tiles of blue-fi China, representing scenes from S ture; and, for aught I know, the of Pownall or Bernard may hav beside this fireplace and told her dren the story of each blue tile. in modern style, well replenished decanters, bottles, cigar-boxes, and work bags of lemons, and provided a beer-pump and a soda-fount, ex

g one side of the room. At my
ance, an elderly person was smack-
his lips with a zest which satisfied
that the cellars of the Province
se still hold good liquor, though
otless of other vintages than were
fed by the old governors. After
ing a glass of port sangaree, pre-
d by the skilful hands of Mr.
mas Waite, I besought that worthy
essor and representative of so many
oric personages to conduct me over
r time-honored mansion.

e readily complied; but, to confess
truth, I was forced to draw strenu-
y upon my imagination, in order to
aught that was interesting in a
e which, without its historic as-
ations, would have seemed merely
a tavern as is usually favored by
custom of decent city boarders, and
ashioned country gentlemen. The
abers, which were probably spacious
rmer times, are now cut up by par-
as, and subdivided into little nooks,
affording scanty room for the nar-
bed, and chair, and dressing-table
single lodger. The great staircase,
ver, may be termed, without much
rbole, a feature of grandeur and
ificence. It winds through the
t of the house by flights of broad
, each flight terminating in a square
ng-place, whence the ascent is con-
d towards the cupola. A carved
trade, freshly painted in the lower
es, but growing dingier as we as-
, borders the staircase with its
atly twisted and intertwined pillars,
top to bottom. Up these stairs the
ary boots, or perchance the gouty
s, of many a governor have trodden,
e wearers mounted to the cupola,
a afforded them so wide a view

over their metropolis and the surrounding country. The cupola is an octagon,
with several windows, and a door opening upon the roof. From this station,
as I pleased myself with imagining,
Gage may have beheld his disastrous
victory on Bunker Hill, (unless one of
the tri-mountains intervened,) and Howe
have marked the approaches of Washington's besieging army; although the
buildings since erected in the vicinity,
have shut out almost every object, save
the steeple of the Old South, which
seems almost within arm's length. Descending from the cupola, I paused in
the garret to observe the ponderous
white-oak framework, so much more
massive than the frames of modern
houses, and thereby resembling an antique skeleton. The brick walls, the materials of which were imported from
Holland, and the timbers of the mansion, are still as sound as ever; but the
floors and other interior parts being
greatly decayed, it is contemplated to
gut the whole, and build a new house
within the ancient frame and brick
work. Among other inconveniences of
the present edifice, mine host mentioned
that any jar or motion was apt to shake
down the dust of ages out of the ceiling
of one chamber upon the floor of that
beneath it.

We stepped forth from the great
front window into the balcony, where,
in old times, it was doubtless the custom
of the king's representative to show
himself to a loyal populace, requiting
their huzzas and tossed-up hats with
stately bendings of his dignified person.
In those days, the front of the Province
House looked upon the street; and the
whole site now occupied by the brick
range of stores, as well as the present

courtyard, was laid out in grass plats, overshadowed by trees and bordered by a wrought-iron fence. Now, the old aristocratic edifice hides its time-worn visage behind an upstart modern building; at one of the back windows I observed some pretty tailoresses, sewing, and chatting, and laughing, with now and then a careless glance towards the balcony. Descending thence, we again entered the bar-room, where the elderly gentleman above mentioned, the smack of whose lips had spoken so favorably for Mr. Waite's good liquor, was still lounging in his chair. He seemed to be, if not a lodger, at least a familiar visitor of the house, who might be supposed to have his regular score at the bar, his summer seat at the open window, and his prescriptive corner at the winter's fireside. Being of a sociable aspect, I ventured to address him with a remark, calculated to draw forth his historical reminiscences, if any such were in my mind; and it gratified me to discover, that, between memory and tradition, the old gentleman was really possessed of some very pleasant gossip about the Province House. The portion of his talk which chiefly interested me, was the outline of the following legend. He professed to have received it at one or two removes from an eyewitness; but this derivation, together with the lapse of time, must have afforded opportunities for many variations of the narrative; so that, despairing of literal and absolute truth, I have not scrupled to make such further changes as seemed conducive to the reader's profit and delight.

At one of the entertainments given at the Province House, during the latter part of the siege of Boston, there pa a scene which has never yet been s factorily explained. The officers of British army, and the loyal gentry the province, most of whom were lected within the beleaguered town, been invited to a masked ball; fc was the policy of Sir William How hide the distress and danger of period, and the desperate aspect of siege under an ostentation of festi The spectacle of this evening, if oldest members of the provincial c circle might be believed, was the gay and gorgeous affair that had curred in the annals of the governm The brilliantly-lighted apartments thronged with figures that seemed have stepped from the dark canva historic portraits, or to have flitted f from the magic pages of romance, c least to have flown hither from on the London theatres, without a ch of garments. Steeled knights of the quest, bearded statesmen of Q Elizabeth, and high-ruffled ladies of court, were mingled with character comedy, such as a party-colored M Andrew, jingling his cap and bell Falstaff, almost as provocative of la ter as his prototype; and a Don Qui with a bean-pole for a lance and a p for a shield.

But the broadest merriment was cited by a group of figures ridicule dressed in old regimentals, which see to have been purchased at a mil rag-fair, or pilfered from some re tacle of the cast-off clothes of both French and British armies. Portior their attire had probably been wor the siege of Louisburg, and the coa most recent cut might have been and tattered by sword, ball, or bay

long ago as Wolfe's victory. One of
se worthies—a tall, lank figure,
ndishing a rusty sword of immense
;itude—purported to be no less a
onage than General George Wash-
on; and the other principal officers
he American army, such as Gates,
, Putnam, Schuyler, Ward, and
th, were represented by similar
ecrows. An interview in the mock
ic style, between the rebel warriors
the British commander-in-chief,
received with immense applause,
h came loudest of all from the
lists of the colony. There was one
ae guests, however, who stood apart,
g these antics sternly and scornfully,
ace with a frown and a bitter smile.
was an old man, formerly of high
on and great repute in the province,
who had been a very famous soldier
ais day. Some surprise had been
essed, that a person of Colonel
fe's known whig principles, though
too old to take an active part in
contest, should have remained in
on during the siege, and especially
he should consent to show himself
ae mansion of Sir William Howe.
thither he had come, with a fair
ddaughter under his arm; and
:, amid all the mirth and buffoonery,
d his stern old figure, the best sus-
d character in the masquerade, be-
e so well representing the antique
t of his native land. The other
ts affirmed that Colonel Joliffe's
t puritanical scowl threw a shadow
d about him; although in spite of
ombre influence, their gayety con-
d to blaze higher, like—(an omi-
comparison)—the flickering bril-
y of a lamp which has but a little
e to burn. Eleven strokes, full half

an hour ago, had pealed from the clock
of the Old South, when a rumor was
circulated among the company that
some new spectacle or pageant was
about to be exhibited, which should put
a fitting close to the splendid festivities
of the night.

"What new jest has your Excellency
in hand?" asked the Rev. Mather Byles,
whose Presbyterian scruples had not
kept him from the entertainment.
"Trust me, sir, I have already laughed
more than beseems my cloth, at your
Homeric confabulation with yonder
ragamuffin General of the rebels. One
other such fit of merriment, and I must
throw off my clerical wig and band."

"Not so, good Doctor Byles," answered Sir William Howe; "if mirth
were a crime, you had never gained
your doctorate in divinity. As to this
new foolery, I know no more about it
than yourself; perhaps not so much.
Honestly now, Doctor, have you not
stirred up the sober brains of some of
your countrymen to enact a scene in
our masquerade?"

"Perhaps," slyly remarked the grand-
daughter of Colonel Joliffe, whose high
spirit had been stung by many taunts
against New England,—"perhaps we are
to have a mask of allegorical figures.
Victory, with trophies from Lexington
and Bunker Hill,—Plenty, with her
overflowing horn, to typify the present
abundance in this good town,—and
Glory, with a wreath for his Excellency's brow."

Sir William Howe smiled at words
which he would have answered with one
of his darkest frowns, had they been
uttered by lips that wore a beard. He
was spared the necessity of a retort, by
a singular interruption. A sound of

music was heard without the house, as if proceeding from a full band of military instruments stationed in the street, playing not such a festal strain as was suited to the occasion; but a slow funeral march. The drums appeared to be muffled, and the trumpets poured forth a wailing breath, which at once hushed the merriment of the auditors, filling all with wonder, and some with apprehension. The idea occurred to many, that either the funeral procession of some great personage had halted in front of the Province House, or that a corpse, in a velvet-covered and gorgeously-decorated coffin, was about to be borne from the portal. After listening a moment, Sir William Howe called, in a stern voice, to the leader of the musicians, who had hitherto enlivened the entertainment with gay and lightsome melodies. The man was drum-major to one of the British regiments.

"Dighton," demanded the general, "what means this foolery? Bid your band silence that dead march—or, by my word, they shall have sufficient cause for their lugubrious strains! Silence it, sirrah!"

"Please your honor," answered the drum-major, whose rubicund visage had lost all its color, "the fault is none of mine. I and my band are all here together; and I question whether there be a man of us that could play that march without book. I never heard it but once before, and that was at the funeral of his late Majesty, King George the Second."

"Well, well!" said Sir William Howe, recovering his composure,—"it is the prelude to some masquerading antic. Let it pass."

A figure now presented itself, but among the many fantastic masks were dispersed through the apartm none could tell precisely from wh it came. It was a man in an fashioned dress of black serge, and ing the aspect of a steward, or prin domestic in the household of a n man, or great English landholder. figure advanced to the outer doo the mansion, and throwing both leaves wide open, withdrew a littl one side and looked back towards grand staircase, as if expecting person to descend. At the same the music in the street sounded a and doleful summons. The eyes o William Howe and his guests directed to the staircase, there appe on the uppermost landing-place tha discernible from the bottom, se personages descending towards the The foremost was a man of stern vi wearing a steeple-crowned hat a skullcap beneath it; a dark cloak huge wrinkled boots that came hal up his legs. Under his arm was a r up banner, which seemed to be banner of England, but strangely and torn; he had a sword in his hand, and grasped a Bible in his The next figure was of milder a yet full of dignity, wearing a broac over which descended a beard, a of wrought velvet, and a double hose of black satin. He carried of manuscript in his hand. Close b these two came a young man of striking countenance and dem with deep thought and contemp on his brow, and perhaps a flash thusiasm in his eye. His garb, lik of his predecessors, was of an a fashion, and there was a stain of upon his ruff. In the same group

e were three or four others, all men
dignity and evident command, and
ing themselves like personages who
accustomed to the gaze of the mul-
ie. It was the idea of the beholder,
these figures went to join the mys-
us funeral that had halted in front
ne Province House; yet that sup-
ion seemed to be contradicted by
air of triumph with which they
d their hands, as they crossed the
hold and vanished through the
l.

1 the Devil's name, what is this?"
ered Sir William Howe to a gentle-
beside him; "a procession of the
de judges of King Charles the
yr?"

hese," said Colonel Joliffe, break-
lence almost for the first time that
ng,—"these, if I interpret them
are the Puritan governors—the
of the old, original Democracy of
achusetts. Endicott, with the ban-
rom which he had torn the symbol
bjection, and Winthrop, and Sir
y Vane, and Dudley, Haynes, Bel-
m, and Leverett."

hy had that young man a stain
ood upon his ruff?" asked Miss
.

cause, in after years," answered
grandfather, "he laid down the
head in England upon the block,
e principles of liberty."

ill not your Excellency order out
ard?" whispered Lord Percy, who,
ther British officers, had now ased round the General. "There may
lot under this mummery."

sh! we have nothing to fear,"
ssly replied Sir William Howe.
e can be no worse treason in the
than a jest, and that somewhat

of the dullest. Even were it a sharp and
bitter one, our best policy would be to
laugh it off. See—here come more of
these gentry."

Another group of characters had now
partly descended the staircase. The first
was a venerable and white-bearded
patriarch, who cautiously felt his way
downward with a staff. Treading hastily
behind him, and stretching forth his
gauntleted hand as if to grasp the old
man's shoulder, came a tall, soldier-like
figure, equipped with a plumed cap of
steel, a bright breastplate, and a long
sword, which rattled against the stairs.
Next was seen a stout man, dressed in
rich and courtly attire, but not of courtly
demeanor; his gait had the swinging motion of a seaman's walk; and chancing
to stumble on the staircase, he suddenly
grew wrathful, and was heard to mutter an oath. He was followed by a
noble-looking personage in a curled wig,
such as are represented in the portraits
of Queen Anne's time and earlier; and
the breast of his coat was decorated
with an embroidered star. While advancing to the door, he bowed to the
right hand and to the left, in a very
gracious and insinuating style; but as
he crossed the threshold, unlike the
early Puritan governors, he seemed to
wring his hands with sorrow.

"Prithee, play the part of a chorus,
good Doctor Byles," said Sir William
Howe. "What worthies are these?"

"If it please your Excellency, they
lived somewhat before my day," answered the Doctor; "but doubtless our
friend, the Colonel, has been hand in
glove with them."

"Their living faces I never looked
upon," said Colonel Joliffe, gravely;
"although I have spoken face to face

with many rulers of this land, and shall greet yet another with an old man's blessing ere I die. But we talk of these figures. I take the venerable patriarch to be Bradstreet, the last of the Puritans, who was governor at ninety, or thereabouts. The next is Sir Edmund Andros, a tyrant, as any New England school-boy will tell you; and therefore the people cast him down from his high seat into a dungeon. Then comes Sir William Phipps, shepherd, cooper, sea-captain, and governor,—may many of his countrymen rise as high from as low an origin! Lastly, you saw the gracious Earl of Bellamont, who ruled us under King William."

"But what is the meaning of it all?" asked Lord Percy.

"Now, were I a rebel," said Miss Joliffe, half aloud, "I might fancy that the ghosts of these ancient governors had been summoned to form the funeral procession of royal authority in New England."

Several other figures were now seen at the turn of the staircase. The one in advance had a thoughtful, anxious, and somewhat crafty expression of face; and in spite of his loftiness of manner, which was evidently the result both of an ambitious spirit and of long continuance in high stations, he seemed not incapable of cringing to a greater than himself. A few steps behind came an officer in a scarlet and embroidered uniform, cut in a fashion old enough to have been worn by the Duke of Marlborough. His nose had a rubicund tinge, which, together with the twinkle of his eye, might have marked him as a lover of the wine-cup and good fellowship; notwithstanding which tokens, he appeared ill at ease, and often glanced

around him, as if apprehensive of s[...] secret mischief. Next came a po[...] gentleman, wearing a coat of sha[...] cloth, lined with silken velvet; he [...] sense, shrewdness, and humor in [...] face, and a folio volume under his a[...] but his aspect was that of a man ve[...] and tormented beyond all patience, [...] harassed almost to death. He w[...] hastily down, and was followed b[...] dignified person, dressed in a pu[...] velvet suit, with very rich embroid[...] his demeanor would have posse[...] much stateliness, only that a grievou[...] of the gout compelled him to ho[...] from stair to stair, with contortion[...] face and body. When Doctor B[...] beheld this figure on the staircase [...] shivered as with an ague, but conti[...] to watch him steadfastly, until the g[...] gentleman had reached the thres[...] made a gesture of anguish and des[...] and vanished into the outer gl[...] whither the funeral music summ[...] him.

"Governor Belcher!—my old pat[...] —in his very shape and dress!" ga[...] Doctor Byles. "This is an a[...] mockery!"

"A tedious foolery, rather," sai[...] William Howe, with an air of ind[...] ence. "But who were the three [...] preceded him?"

"Governor Dudley, a cunning [...] tician,—yet his craft once brought [...] to a prison," replied Colonel J[...] "Governor Shute, formerly a Co[...] under Marlborough, and whom [...] people frightened out of the prov[...] and learned Governor Burnet, whor[...] legislature tormented into a m[...] fever."

"Methinks they were miserable [...] these royal governors of Mass[...]

s," observed Miss Joliffe. "Heavens, dim the light grows!"

was certainly a fact that the large p which illuminated the staircase burned dim and duskily: so that eral figures, which passed hastily n the stairs and went forth from porch appeared rather like shadows persons of fleshly substance. Sir iam Howe and his guests stood at doors of the contiguous apartments, ching the progress of this singular ant, with various emotions of anger, empt, or half-acknowledged fear, still with an anxious curiosity. The es which now seemed hastening to the mysterious procession were gnized rather by striking peculiari-of dress, or broad characteristics anner, than by any perceptible re-lance of features to their proto-s. Their faces, indeed, were in-bly kept in deep shadow. But Doc-Byles, and other gentlemen who had been familiar with the successive s of the province, were heard to per the names of Shirley, of Pow-of Sir Francis Bernard, and of the remembered Hutchinson; thereby ssing that the actors, whoever they t be, in this spectral march of rnors, had succeeded in putting on distant portraiture of the real nages. As they vanished from the , still did these shadows toss their into the gloom of night, with a l expression of woe. Following the c representative of Hutchinson a military figure, holding before ace the cocked hat which he had from his powdered head; but his lettes and other insignia of rank those of a general officer; and thing in his mien reminded the

beholders of one who had recently been master of the Province House, and chief of all the land.

"The shape of Gage, as true as in a looking-glass," exclaimed Lord Percy, turning pale.

"No, surely," cried Miss Joliffe, laughing hysterically; "it could not be Gage, or Sir William would have greeted his old comrade in arms! Perhaps he will not suffer the next to pass un-challenged."

"Of that be assured, young lady," answered Sir William Howe, fixing his eyes, with a very marked expression, upon the immovable visage of her grandfather. "I have long enough de-layed to pay the ceremonies of a host to these departing guests. The next that takes his leave shall receive due courtesy."

A wild and dreary burst of music came through the open door. It seemed as if the procession, which had been gradually filling up its ranks, were now about to move, and that this loud peal of the wailing trumpets and roll of the muffled drums were a call to some loiterer to make haste. Many eyes, by an irresistible impulse, were turned upon Sir William Howe, as if it were he whom the dreary music summoned to the funeral of departed power.

"See!—here comes the last!" whis-pered Miss Joliffe, pointing her tremu-lous finger to the staircase.

A figure had come into view as if descending the stairs; although so dusky was the region whence it emerged, some of the spectators fancied that they had seen this human shape suddenly mould-ing itself amid the gloom. Downward the figure came, with a stately and marshal tread, and reaching the lowest stair was observed to be a tall man, booted and wrapped in a military cloak, which was drawn up around the face so as to meet the flapped brim of a laced hat. The features, therefore, were completely hidden. But the British officers deemed that they had seen that military cloak before, and even recognized the frayed embroidery on the collar, as well as the gilded scabbard of a sword which protruded from the folds of the cloak, and glittered in a vivid gleam of light. Apart from these trifling particulars, there were characteristics of gait and bearing which impelled the wondering guests to glance from the shrouded figure to Sir William Howe, as if to satisfy themselves that their host had not suddenly vanished from the midst of them.

With a dark flush of wrath upon his brow, they saw the General draw his sword and advance to meet the figure in the cloak before the latter had stepped one pace upon the floor.

"Villain, unmuffle yourself!" cried he. "You pass no farther!"

The figure, without blenching a hair's breadth from the sword which was pointed at his breast, made a solemn pause and lowered the cape of the cloak from about his face, yet not sufficiently for the spectators to catch a glimpse of it. But Sir William Howe had evidently seen enough. The sternness of his countenance gave place to a look of wild amazement, if not horror, while he recoiled several steps from the figure, and let fall his sword upon the floor. The martial shape again drew the cloak about his features and passed on; but reaching the threshold, with his back towards the spectators, he was seen to stamp his foot and shake his clinched hands in the air. It was afterw affirmed that Sir William Howe had peated that selfsame gesture of and sorrow when, for the last time, as the last royal governor, he pa through the portal of the Prov House.

"Hark!—the procession moves," Miss Joliffe.

The music was dying away along street, and its dismal strains were gled with the knell of midnight the steeple of the Old South. ¬nd the roar of artillery, which annou that the beleaguering army of W ington had intrenched itself upc nearer height than before. As the boom of the cannon smote upor ear, Colonel Joliffe raised himsel the full height of his aged form, smiled sternly on the British Gen

"Would your Excellency inquire ther into the mystery of the page: said he.

"Take care of your gray head," Sir William Howe, fiercely, though a quivering lip. "It has stood too on a traitor's shoulders!"

"You must make haste to chop then," calmly replied the Colonel; a few hours longer and not al power of Sir William Howe, n his master, shall cause one of gray hairs to fall. The empire of ain, in this ancient province, is last gasp to-night;—almost wh speak it is a dead corpse;—and thinks the shadows of the old nors are fit mourners at its fun

With these words Colonel Joliffe on his cloak, and drawing his daughter's arm within his own, r from the last festival that a ruler ever held in the old provir

sachusetts Bay. It was supposed
the Colonel and the young lady
essed some secret intelligence in
rd to the mysterious pageant of
night. However this might be, such
vledge has never become general.
actors in the scene have vanished
deeper obscurity than even that
Indian band who scattered the car-
of the tea-ships on the waves,
gained a place in history, yet left
ames. But superstition among other
ids of this mansion, repeats the
lrous tale, that on the anniversary
: of Britain's discomfiture, the
ts of the ancient governors of Mas-
isetts still glide through the portal
ie Province House. And, last of all,
·s a figure shrouded in a military
:, tossing his clinched hands into
air, and stamping his iron-shod
s upon the broad freestone steps,
a semblance of feverish despair,
without the sound of a foot-
o.

ien the truth-telling accents of the
ly gentleman were hushed, I drew
ig breath and looked round the
, striving, with the best energy of
imagination, to throw a tinge of
ince and historic grandeur over the
ies of the scene. But my nostrils
:d up a scent of cigar-smoke, clouds
hich the narrator had emitted by
of visible emblem, I suppose, of
ebulous obscurity of his tale. More-

over, my gorgeous fantasies were wofully disturbed by the rattling of the
spoon in a tumbler of whiskey-punch,
which Mr. Thomas Waite was mingling
for a customer. Nor did it add to the
picturesque appearance of the panelled
walls, that the slate of the Brookline
stage was suspended against them, instead of the armorial escutcheon of
some far-descended governor. A stage-
driver sat at one of the windows, reading a penny-paper of the day—the
Boston Times—and presenting a figure
which could nowise be brought into
any picture of "Times in Boston" seventy or a hundred years ago. On the
window-seat lay a bundle, neatly done
up in brown paper, the direction of
which I had the idle curiosity to read.
"MISS SUSAN HUGGINS, at the PROV-
INCE HOUSE." A pretty chambermaid,
no doubt. In truth, it is desperately
hard work when we attempt to throw
the spell of hoar antiquity over locali-
ties with which the living world, and the
day that is passing over us, have aught
to do. Yet, as I glanced at the stately
staircase, down which the procession of
the old governors had descended, and
as I emerged through the venerable portal whence their figures had preceded
me, it gladdened me to be conscious
of a thrill of awe. Then diving through
the narrow archway, a few strides transported me into the densest throng of
Washington Street.

II. EDWARD RANDOLPH'S PORTRAIT

THE old legendary guest of the Province House abode in my remembrance from midsummer till January. One idle evening, last winter, confident that he would be found in the snuggest corner of the bar-room, I resolved to pay him another visit, hoping to deserve well of my country, by snatching from oblivion some else unheard-of fact of history. The night was chill and raw, and rendered boisterous by almost a gale of wind, which whistled along Washington Street, causing the gaslights to flare and flicker within the lamps. As I hurried onward my fancy was busy with a comparison between the present aspect of the street and that which it probably wore when the British governors inhabited the mansion whither I was now going. Brick edifices in those times were few, till a succession of destructive fires had swept, and swept again, the wooden dwellings and warehouses from the most populous quarters of the town. The buildings stood insulated and independent, not, as now, merging their separate existences into connected ranges, with a front of tiresome identity,—but each possessing features of its own, as if the owner's individual taste had shaped it,—and the whole presenting a picturesque irregularity, the absence of which is hardly compensated by any beauties of our modern architecture. Such a scene, dimly vanishing from the eye by the ray of here and there a tallow candle, glimmering through the small panes of scattered windows, would form a sombre contrast to the street as I beheld it, with the gaslights blazing from corner to corner, flaming within the shops, throwing a noonday brightness thro the huge plates of glass.

But the black, lowering sky, a turned my eyes upward, wore, do less, the same visage as when it frow upon the ante-Revolutionary New I landers. The wintry blast had the s shriek that was familiar to their e The Old South Church, too, still poi its antique spire into the darkness, was lost between earth and heaven; as I passed, its clock, which had wa so many generations how transitory their lifetime, spoke heavily and the same unregarded moral to my "Only seven o'clock," thought I. ' old friend's legends will scarcely the hours 'twixt this and bedtime.'

Passing through the narrow arc crossed the court-yard, the confined cincts of which were made visible a lantern over the portal of the F ince House. On entering the bar-r I found, as I expected, the old tradi monger seated by a special good of anthracite, compelling clouds smoke from a corpulent cigar. He re nized me with evident pleasure; my rare properties as a patient list invariably make me a favorite elderly gentlemen and ladies of n tive propensities. Drawing a chai the fire, I desired mine host to f us with a glass apiece of whiskey-pu which was speedily prepared, stea hot, with a slice of lemon at the tom, a dark-red stratum of port upon the surface, and a sprinklin nutmeg strewn over all. As we tou our glasses together, my leger end made himself known to me as r. Bela Tiffany; and I rejoiced at e oddity of the name, because it gave image and character a sort of in-iduality in my conception. The old tleman's draught acted as a solvent on his memory, so that it overflowed h tales, traditions, anecdotes of fa-us dead people, and traits of ancient nners, some of which were childish a nurse's lullaby, while others might ve been worth the notice of the grave torian. Nothing impressed me more n a story of a black, mysterious pic-e, which used to hang in one of the mbers of the Province House, direct-above the room where we were now ing. The following is as correct a sion of the fact as the reader would likely to obtain from any other rce, although, assuredly, it has a ge of romance approaching the mar-lous.

n one of the apartments of the vince House there was long pre-ved an ancient picture, the frame of ich was as black as ebony, and the vas itself so dark with age, damp, l smoke, that not a touch of the nter's art could be discerned. Time l thrown an impenetrable veil over and left to tradition, and fable, and jecture to say what had once been re portrayed. During the rule of ny successive governors it had hung, prescriptive and undisputed right, r the mantel-piece of the same cham-; and it still kept its place when utenant-Governor Hutchinson as-ned the administration of the prov-, on the departure of Sir Francis nard.

he Lieutenant-Governor sat, one afternoon, resting his head against the carved back of his stately arm-chair, and gazing up thoughtfully at the void blackness of the picture. It was scarcely a time for such inactive musing, when affairs of the deepest moment required the ruler's decision; for within that very hour Hutchinson had received intelligence of the arrival of a British fleet, bringing three regiments from Halifax to overawe the insubordination of the people. These troops awaited his permission to occupy the fortress of Castle William, and the town itself. Yet, instead of affixing his signature to an official order, there sat the Lieutenant-Governor, so carefully scrutinizing the black waste of canvas, that his demeanor attracted the notice of two young persons who attended him. One, wearing a military dress of buff, was his kinsman, Francis Lincoln, the Provincial Captain of Castle William; the other, who sat on a low stool beside his chair, was Alice Vane, his favorite niece.

She was clad entirely in white, a pale, ethereal creature, who, though a native of New England, had been educated abroad, and seemed not merely a stranger from another clime, but almost a being from another world. For several years, until left an orphan, she had dwelt with her father in sunny Italy, and there had acquired a taste and enthusiasm for sculpture and painting which she found few opportunities of gratifying in the undecorated dwellings of the colonial gentry. It was said that the early productions of her own pencil exhibited no inferior genius, though, perhaps, the rude atmosphere of New England had cramped her hand and dimmed the glowing colors of her fancy. But observing her uncle's stead-fast gaze, which appeared to search through the mist of years to discover the subject of the picture, her curiosity was excited.

"Is it known, my dear uncle," inquired she, "what this old picture once represented? Possibly, could it be made visible, it might prove a masterpiece of some great artist,—else, why has it so long held such a conspicuous place?"

As her uncle, contrary to his usual custom, (for he was as attentive to all the humors and caprices of Alice as if she had been his own best-beloved child,) did not immediately reply, the young Captain of Castle William took that office upon himself.

"This dark old square of canvas, my fair cousin," said he, "has been an heirloom in the Province House from time immemorial. As to the painter, I can tell you nothing; but if half the stories told of it be true, not one of the great Italian masters has ever produced so marvellous a piece of work as that before you."

Captain Lincoln proceeded to relate some of the strange fables and fantasies which, as it was impossible to refute them by ocular demonstration, had grown to be articles of popular belief in reference to this old picture. One of the wildest, and at the same time the best accredited accounts, stated it to be an original and authentic portrait of the Evil One, taken at a witch-meeting near Salem; and that its strong and terrible resemblance had been confirmed by several of the confessing wizards and witches, at their trial, in open court. It was likewise affirmed that a familiar spirit, or demon, abode behind the blackness of the picture, and had shown himself at seaso[ns] of public calamity to more than o[ne] of the royal governors. Shirley, for i[n]stance, had beheld this ominous appa[ri]tion on the eve of General Abercrom[bie's] shameful and bloody defeat und[er] the walls of Ticonderoga. Many of t[he] servants of the Province House h[ad] caught glimpses of a visage frowni[ng] down upon them, at morning or e[ve]ning twilight,—or in the depths of nig[ht] while raking up the fire that glimmer[ed] on the hearth beneath; although, [if] any were bold enough to hold a tor[ch] before the picture, it would appear black and undistinguishable as ever. T[he] oldest inhabitant of Boston recollect[ed] that his father, in whose days the po[r]trait had not wholly faded out of sig[ht] had once looked upon it, but wo[uld] never suffer himself to be question[ed] as to the face which was there rep[re]sented. In connection with such stori[es] it was remarkable that over the t[op] of the frame there were some ragg[ed] remnants of black silk, indicating t[hat] a veil had formerly hung down bef[ore] the picture, until the duskiness of ti[me] had so effectually concealed it. B[ut] after all, it was the most singular p[art] of the affair, that so many of [the] pompous governors of Massachuse[tts] had allowed the obliterated picture [to] remain in the state-chamber of t[he] Province House.

"Some of these fables are really a[w]ful," observed Alice Vane, who h[ad] occasionally shuddered, as well [as] smiled, while her cousin spoke. "[It] would be almost worth while to w[ipe] away the black surface of the canv[as,] since the original picture can hardly [be] so formidable as those which fan[cy] paints instead of it."

"But would it be possible," inquired
r cousin, "to restore this dark pic-
re to its pristine hues?"

"Such arts are known in Italy," said
ice.

The Lieutenant-Governor had roused
mself from his abstracted mood, and
tened with a smile to the conversa-
n of his young relatives. Yet his voice
d something peculiar in its tones,
en he undertook the explanation of
e mystery.

"I am sorry, Alice, to destroy your
ith in the legends of which you are
fond," remarked he; "but my anti-
arian researches have long since made
e acquainted with the subject of this
cture—if picture it can be called—
ich is no more visible, nor ever will
, than the face of the long-buried man
om it once represented. It was the
rtrait of Edward Randolph, the foun-
r of this house, a person famous in
e history of New England."

"Of that Edward Randolph," ex-
imed Captain Lincoln, "who obtained
e repeal of the first provincial charter,
der which our forefathers had en-
ved almost democratic privileges! He
at was styled the arch-enemy of New
gland, and whose memory is still
d in detestation as the destroyer of
r liberties!"

"It was the same Randolph," an-
ered Hutchinson, moving uneasily in
chair. "It was his lot to taste the
terness of popular odium."

"Our annals tell us," continued the
ptain of Castle William, "that the
rse of the people followed this Ran-
lph where he went, and wrought evil
all the subsequent events of his life,
d that its effect was seen likewise
the manner of his death. They say,

too, that the inward misery of that
curse worked itself outward, and was
visible on the wretched man's countenance, making it too horrible to be
looked upon. If so, and if this picture
truly represented his aspect, it was in
mercy that the cloud of blackness has
gathered over it."

"These traditions are folly, to one
who has proved, as I have, how little
of historic truth lies at the bottom,"
said the Lieutenant-Governor. "As regards the life and character of Edward
Randolph, too implicit credence has
been given to Dr. Cotton Mather, who
—I must say it, though some of his
blood runs in my veins—has filled our
early history with old women's tales,
as fanciful and extravagant as those
of Greece or Rome."

"And yet," whispered Alice Vane,
"may not such fables have a moral?
And, methinks, if the visage of this
portrait be so dreadful, it is not without
a cause that it has hung so long in a
chamber of the Province House. When
the rulers feel themselves irresponsible,
it were well that they should be reminded of the awful weight of a
people's curse."

The Lieutenant-Governor started, and
gazed for a moment at his niece, as if
her girlish fantasies had struck upon
some feeling in his own breast, which
all his policy or principles could not
entirely subdue. He knew, indeed, that
Alice, in spite of her foreign education,
retained the native sympathies of a New
England girl.

"Peace, silly child," cried he, at last,
more harshly than he had ever before
addressed the gentle Alice. "The rebuke
of a king is more to be dreaded than
the clamor of a wild, misguided multi-

tude. Captain Lincoln, it is decided. The fortress of Castle William must be occupied by the Royal troops. The two remaining regiments shall be billeted in the town, or encamped upon the Common. It is time, after years of tumult, and almost rebellion, that his majesty's government should have a wall of strength about it."

"Trust, sir,—trust yet a while to the loyalty of the people," said Captain Lincoln; "nor teach them that they can ever be on other terms with British soldiers than those of brotherhood, as when they fought side by side through the French war. Do not convert the streets of your native town into a camp. Think twice before you give up old Castle William, the key of the province, into other keeping than that of true-born New-Englanders."

"Young man, it is decided," repeated Hutchinson, rising from his chair. "A British officer will be in attendance this evening, to receive the necessary instructions for the disposal of the troops. Your presence also will be required. Till then, farewell."

With these words the Lieutenant-Governor hastily left the room, while Alice and her cousin more slowly followed, whispering together, and once pausing to glance back at the mysterious picture. The Captain of Castle William fancied that the girl's air and mien were such as might have belonged to one of those spirits of fable—fairies, or creatures of a more antique mythology—who sometimes mingled their agency with mortal affairs, half in caprice, yet with a sensibility to human weal or woe. As he held the door for her to pass, Alice beckoned to the picture and smiled.

"Come forth, dark and evil Shape[...] cried she. "It is thine hour!"

In the evening, Lieutenant-Gover[...] Hutchinson sat in the same cham[...] where the foregoing scene had occur[...] surrounded by several persons wh[...] various interests had summoned th[...] together. There were the Selectmen [...] Boston, plain, patriarchal fathers of [...] people, excellent representatives of [...] old puritanical founders, whose som[...] strength had stamped so deep an i[...] press upon the New England charact[...] Contrasting with these were one or t[...] members of Council, richly dressed [...] the white wigs, the embroidered wa[...] coats and other magnificence of [...] time, and making a somewhat osten[...] tious display of courtier-like ceremon[...] In attendance, likewise, was a ma[...] of the British army, awaiting the Li[...] tenant-Governor's orders for the la[...] ing of the troops, which still remai[...] on board the transports. The Capt[...] of Castle William stood beside Hutcl[...] son's chair, with folded arms, glanc[...] rather haughtily at the British offi[...] by whom he was soon to be superse[...] in his command. On a table, in [...] centre of the chamber, stood a branc[...] silver candlestick, throwing down [...] glow of half a dozen wax lights u[...] a paper apparently ready for the L[...] tenant-Governor's signature.

Partly shrouded in the volumin[...] folds of one of the window-curta[...] which fell from the ceiling to the fl[...] was seen the white drapery of a la[...] robe. It may appear strange that A[...] Vane should have been there, at s[...] a time; but there was something [...] child-like, so wayward, in her sing[...] character, so apart from ordinary ru[...] that her presence did not surprise [...]

who noticed it. Meantime, the chair-
[m]an of the Selectmen was addressing
the Lieutenant-Governor a long and
[sole]mn protest against the reception of
British troops into the town.

"And if your Honor," concluded this
[exc]ellent, but somewhat prosy old gen-
[tlem]an, "shall see fit to persist in bring-
[ing] these mercenary sworders and mus-
[ket]eers into our quiet streets, not on
[our] heads be the responsibility. Think,
while there is yet time, that if one
[dro]p of blood be shed, that blood shall
[be] an eternal stain upon your Honor's
[mem]ory. You, sir, have written with an
[abl]e pen the deeds of our forefathers.
[The] more to be desired is it, therefore,
[tha]t yourself should deserve honorable
[men]tion, as a true patriot and upright
[rule]r, when your own doings shall be
[writ]ten down in history."

"I am not insensible, my good sir, to
[the] natural desire to stand well in the
[ann]als of my country," replied Hutchin-
[son,] controlling his impatience into cour-
[tesy], "nor know I any better method
[of a]ttaining that end than by withstand-
[ing] the merely temporary spirit of mis-
[chie]f, which, with your pardon, seems
[to h]ave infected elder men than myself.
[Wo]uld you have me wait till the mob
[shal]l sack the Province House, as they
[did] my private mansion? Trust me, sir,
[the] time may come when you will be
[glad] to flee for protection to the King's
[ban]ner, the raising of which is now so
[dist]asteful to you."

"Yes," said the British major, who
[was] impatiently expecting the Lieuten-
[ant-]Governor's orders. "The demagogues
[of t]his Province have raised the Devil,
[and] cannot lay him again. We will ex-
[orci]se him in God's name and the
[Kin]g's."

"If you meddle with the Devil, take
care of his claws!" answered the Captain of Castle William, stirred by the
taunt against his countrymen.

"Craving your pardon, young sir,"
said the venerable Selectman, "let not
an evil spirit enter into your words.
We will strive against the oppressor
with prayer and fasting, as our forefathers would have done. Like them,
moreover, we will submit to whatever
lot a wise Providence may send us,—
always, after our own best exertions
to amend it."

"And there peep forth the Devil's
claws!" muttered Hutchinson, who well
understood the nature of Puritan sub-
mission. "This matter shall be expe-
dited forthwith. When there shall be
a sentinel at every corner, and a court
of guard before the town-house, a loyal
gentleman may venture to walk abroad.
What to me is the outcry of a mob,
in this remote province of the realm?
The King is my master, and England is
my country! Upheld by their armed
strength, I set my foot upon the rabble,
and defy them!"

He snatched a pen, and was about to
affix his signature to the paper that lay
on the table, when the Captain of Castle
William placed his hand upon his shoulder. The freedom of the action, so contrary to the ceremonious respect which
was then considered due to rank and
dignity, awakened general surprise, and
in none more than in the Lieutenant-
Governor himself. Looking angrily up,
he perceived that his young relative was
pointing his finger to the opposite wall.
Hutchinson's eye followed the signal;
and he saw, what had hitherto been un-
observed, that a black silk curtain was
suspended before the mysterious pic-

ture, so as completely to conceal it. His thoughts immediately recurred to the scene of the preceding afternoon; and, in his surprise, confused by indistinct emotions, yet sensible that his niece must have had an agency in this phenomenon, he called loudly upon her.

"Alice!—Come hither, Alice!"

No sooner had he spoken than Alice Vane glided from her station, and pressing one hand across her eyes, with the other snatched away the sable curtain that concealed the portrait. An exclamation of surprise burst from every beholder; but the Lieutenant-Governor's voice had a tone of horror.

"By heaven," said he, in a low, inward murmur, speaking rather to himself than to those around him, "if the spirit of Edward Randolph were to appear among us from the place of torment, he could not wear more of the terrors of hell upon his face!"

"For some wise end," said the aged Selectman, solemnly, "hath Providence scattered away the mist of years that had so long hid this dreadful effigy. Until this hour no living man hath seen what we behold!"

Within the antique frame, which so recently had enclosed a sable waste of canvas, now appeared a visible picture, still dark, indeed, in its hues and shadings, but thrown forward in strong relief. It was a half-length figure of a gentleman in a rich, but very old-fashioned dress of embroidered velvet, with a broad ruff and a beard, and wearing a hat, the brim of which overshadowed his forehead. Beneath this cloud the eyes had a peculiar glare, which was almost lifelike. The whole portrait started so distinctly out of the background, that it had the effect of a person looking down from the w at the astonished and awe-stricken sp tators. The expression of the face, any words can convey an idea of was that of a wretch detected in so hideous guilt, and exposed to the bitt hatred and laughter and withering sco of a vast surrounding multitude. The was the struggle of defiance, beat down and overwhelmed by the crus ing weight of ignominy. The torture the soul had come forth upon his cou tenance. It seemed as if the pictu while hidden behind the cloud of i memorial years, had been all the ti acquiring an intenser depth and da ness of expression, till now it gloom forth again and threw its evil om over the present hour. Such, if the w legend may be credited, was the p trait of Edward Randolph, as he a peared when a people's curse h wrought its influence upon his natur

"'Twould drive me mad,—that aw face!" said Hutchinson, who seemed f cinated by the contemplation of it.

"Be warned, then!" whispered Ali "He trampled on a people's rights. ho'd his punishment,—and avoid a cri like his!"

The Lieutenant-Governor actua trembled for an instant; but, exert his energy—which was not, howev his most characteristic feature— strove to shake off the spell of R dolph's countenance.

"Girl!" cried he, laughing bitterly, he turned to Alice, "have you brou hither your painter's art,—your Ital spirit of intrigue,—your tricks of st effect,—and think to influence the co cils of rulers and the affairs of nati by such shallow contrivances? here!"

"Stay yet awhile," said the Select-
n, as Hutchinson again snatched the
n; "for if ever mortal man received
warning from a tormented soul, your
nor is that man!"

'Away!' answered Hutchinson, fierce-
"Though yonder senseless picture
ed 'Forbear!' it should not move
!"

Casting a scowl of defiance at the
tured face, (which seemed, at that
ment, to intensify the horror of its
erable and wicked look,) he scrawled
the paper, in characters that betok-
d it a deed of desperation, the name
Thomas Hutchinson. Then, it is said,
shuddered, as if that signature had
nted away his salvation.

'It is done," said he; and placed his
d upon his brow.

'May Heaven forgive the deed," said
soft, sad accents of Alice Vane, like
voice of a good spirit flitting away.
When morning came there was a
led whisper through the household,
spreading thence about the town,
t the dark, mysterious picture had
rted from the wall, and spoken face
face with Lieutenant - Governor
chinson. If such a miracle had been
ught, however, no traces of it re-
ned behind; for within the antique
ne nothing could be discerned save
impenetrable cloud which had cov-
d the canvas since the memory of
. If the figure had, indeed, stepped
h, it had fled back, spirit-like, at the
dawn, and hidden itself behind a
ury's obscurity. The truth probably
, that Alice Vane's secret for re-
ing the hues of the picture had
ely effected a temporary renovation.
those who, in that brief interval,
beheld the awful visage of Edward

Randolph desired no second glance, and
ever afterwards trembled at the recollection of the scene, as if an evil spirit
had appeared visibly among them. And
as for Hutchinson, when, far over the
ocean, his dying hour drew on, he
gasped for breath, and complained that
he was choking with the blood of the
Boston Massacre; and Francis Lincoln,
the former Captain of Castle William,
who was standing at his bedside, perceived a likeness in his frenzied look to
that of Edward Randolph. Did his
broken spirit feel, at that dread hour,
the tremendous burden of a People's
curse?

At the conclusion of this miraculous
legend, I inquired of mine host whether
the picture still remained in the chamber over our heads; but Mr. Tiffany
informed me that it had long since been
removed, and was supposed to be hidden in some out-of-the-way corner of
the New England Museum. Perchance
some curious antiquary may light upon
it there, and, with the assistance of Mr.
Howorth, the picture-cleaner, may supply
a not unnecessary proof of the authen-
ticity of the facts here set down. During the progress of the story a storm
had been gathering abroad, and raging
and rattling so loudly in the upper
regions of the Province House, that it
seemed as if all the old governors and
great men were running riot above
stairs, while Mr. Bela Tiffany babbled
of them below. In the course of generations, when many people have lived
and died in an ancient house, the whis-
tling of the wind through its crannies,
and the creaking of its beams and
rafters, become strangely like the
tones of the human voice, or thunder-

ing laughter, or heavy footsteps treading the deserted chambers. It is as if the echoes of half a century were revived. Such were the ghostly sounds that roared and murmured in our ears, when I took leave of the circle rou the fireside of the Province House, a plunging down the door-steps, foug my way homeward against a drifti snow-storm.

III. LADY ELEANORE'S MANTLE

MINE excellent friend, the landlord of the Province House, was pleased, the other evening, to invite Mr. Tiffany and myself to an oyster-supper. This slight mark of respect and gratitude, as he handsomely observed, was far less than the ingenious tale-teller, and I, the humble note-taker of his narratives, had fairly earned, by the public notice which our joint lucubrations had attracted to his establishment. Many a cigar had been smoked within his premises,— many a glass of wine, or more potent aqua vitæ, had been quaffed,—many a dinner had been eaten by curious strangers, who, save for the fortunate conjunction of Mr. Tiffany and me, would never have ventured through that darksome avenue, which gives access to the historic precincts of the Province House. In short, if any credit be due to the courteous assurances of Mr. Thomas Waite, we had brought his forgotten mansion almost as effectually into public view as if we had thrown down the vulgar range of shoe-shops and drygoods stores, which hides its aristocratic front from Washington Street. It may be unadvisable, however, to speak too loudly of the increased custom of the house, lest Mr. Waite should find it difficult to renew the lease on so favorable terms as heretofore.

Being thus welcomed as benefacto neither Mr. Tiffany nor myself felt a scruple in doing full justice to the go things that were set before us. If t feast were less magnificent than th same panelled walls had witnessed a bygone century,—if mine host p sided with somewhat less of state th might have befitted a successor of royal governors,—if the guests ma a less imposing show than the bewigg and powdered and embroidered dig taries, who erst banqueted at the gub natorial table, and now sleep wit their armorial tombs on Copp's Hill, round King's Chapel,—yet never, I m boldly say, did a more comforta little party assemble in the Provin House from Queen Anne's days to Revolution. The occasion was rende more interesting by the presence of venerable personage, whose own act reminiscences went back to the epo of Gage and Howe, and even suppl him with a doubtful anecdote or t of Hutchinson. He was one of t small and now all but extinguisl class, whose attachment to royalty, a to the colonial institutions and custo that were connected with it, had ne yielded to the democratic heresies after times. The young queen of Brit not a more loyal subject in her lm,—perhaps not one who would el before her throne with such reventital love,—as this old grandsire, ose head has whitened beneath the d sway of the Republic, which still, his mellower moments, he terms a rpation. Yet prejudices so obstinate e not made him an ungentle or impracticable companion. If the truth must told, the life of the aged loyalist been of such a scrambling and unled character,—he has had so little ice of friends, and been so often titute of any,—that I doubt whether would refuse a cup of kindness with er Oliver Cromwell or John Hank; to say nothing of any democrat upon the stage. In another paper this series I may perhaps give the ler a closer glimpse of his portrait. ur host, in due season, uncorked a le of Madeira, of such exquisite ume and admirable flavor, that he ly must have discovered it in an ient bin, down deep beneath the pest cellar, where some jolly old er stored away the Governor's icest wine, and forgot to reveal the et on his death-bed. Peace to his nosed ghost, and a libation to his nory! This precious liquor was imd by Mr. Tiffany with peculiar ; and after sipping the third glass, vas his pleasure to give us one of oddest legends which he had yet d from the storehouse where he s such matters. With some suitadornments from my own fancy, an pretty much as follows.

ot long after Colonel Shute had med the government of Massachu-Bay, now nearly a hundred and twenty years ago, a young lady of rank and fortune arrived from England to claim his protection as her guardian. He was her distant relative, but the nearest who had survived the gradual extinction of her family; so that no more eligible shelter could be found for the rich and high-born lady Eleanore Rochcliffe than within the Province House of a Transatlantic colony. The consort of Governor Shute, moreover, had been as a mother to her childhood, and was now anxious to receive her, in the hope that a beautiful young woman would be exposed to infinitely less peril from the primitive society of New England than amid the artifices and corruptions of a court. If either the Governor or his lady had especially consulted their own comfort, they would probably have sought to devolve the responsibility on other hands; since, with some noble and splendid traits of character, Lady Eleanore was remarkable for a harsh, unyielding pride, a haughty consciousness of her hereditary and personal advantages, which made her almost incapable of control. Judging from many traditionary anecdotes, this peculiar temper was hardly less than a monomania; or, if the acts which it inspired were those of a sane person, it seemed due from Providence that pride so sinful should be followed by as severe a retribution. That tinge of the marvellous which is thrown over so many of these half-forgotten legends has probably imparted an additional wildness to the strange story of Lady Eleanore Rochcliffe.

The ship in which she came passenger had arrived at Newport, whence Lady Eleanore was conveyed to Boston in the Governor's coach, attended by a small escort of gentlemen on horseback. The ponderous equipage, with its four black horses, attracted much notice as it rumbled through Cornhill, surrounded by the prancing steeds of half a dozen cavaliers, with swords dangling to their stirrups and pistols at their holsters. Through the large glass windows of the coach, as it rolled along, the people could discern the figure of Lady Eleanore, strangely combining an almost queenly stateliness with the grace and beauty of a maiden in her teens. A singular tale had gone abroad among the ladies of the province, that their fair rival was indebted for much of the irresistible charm of her appearance to a certain article of dress—an embroidered mantle—which had been wrought by the most skilful artist in London, and possessed even magical properties of adornment. On the present occasion, however, she owed nothing to the witchery of dress, being clad in a riding-habit of velvet, which would have appeared stiff and ungraceful on any other form.

The coachman reined in his four black steeds, and the whole cavalcade came to a pause in front of the contorted iron balustrade that fenced the Province House from the public street. It was an awkward coincidence, that the bell of the Old South was just then tolling for a funeral; so that, instead of a gladsome peal with which it was customary to announce the arrival of distinguished strangers, Lady Eleanore Rochcliffe was ushered by a doleful clang, as if calamity had come embodied in her beautiful person.

"A very great disrespect!" exclaimed Captain Langford, an English officer, who had recently brought despatches

to Governor Shute. "The funeral shou have been deferred, lest Lady El nore's spirits be affected by such a d mal welcome."

"With your pardon, sir," replied I Clarke, a physician, and a fam champion of the popular party, "wh ever the heralds may pretend, a de beggar must have precedence of a liv queen. King Death confers high pr ileges."

These remarks were interchang while the speakers waited a pass through the crowd which had gathe on each side of the gateway, leav an open avenue to the portal of Province House. A black slave in ery now leaped from behind the coa and threw open the door; while at same moment Governor Shute scended the flight of steps from mansion to assist Lady Eleanore alighting. But the Governor's sta approach was anticipated in a man that excited general astonishment. pale young man, with his black l all in disorder, rushed from the thr and prostrated himself beside the coa thus offering his person as a foots for Lady Eleanore Rochcliffe to tr upon. She held back an instant; with an expression as if doub whether the young man were worthy bear the weight of her footstep, ra than dissatisfied to receive such ful reverence from a fellow-mortal

"Up, sir," said the Governor, ster at the same time lifting his cane the intruder. "What means the Bed ite by this freak?"

"Nay," answered Lady Eleanore p fully, but with more scorn than in her tone, "your Excellency shall strike him. When men seek onl

trampled upon, it were a pity to
ny them a favor so easily granted,—
d so well deserved!"

Then, though as lightly as a sunbeam
a cloud, she placed her foot upon
: cowering form, and extended her
nd to meet that of the Governor.
ere was a brief interval, during which
dy Eleanore retained this attitude;
l never, surely, was there an apter
blem of aristocracy and hereditary
de, trampling on human sympathies
l the kindred of nature, than these
) figures presented at that moment.
: the spectators were so smitten with
beauty, and so essential did pride
m to the existence of such a crea-
e, that they gave a simultaneous ac-
nation of applause.

Who is this insolent young fellow?"
uired Captain Langford, who still
ained beside Doctor Clarke. "If he
in his senses, his impertinence de-
nds the bastinado. If mad, Lady
anore should be secured from fur-
r inconvenience by his confinement."

His name is Jervase Helwyse," an-
red the Doctor,—"a youth of no
h or fortune, or other advantages,
e the mind and soul that nature gave
.; and being secretary to our colonial
nt in London, it was his misfortune
neet this Lady Eleanore Rochcliffe.
loved her,—and her scorn has driven
mad."

He was mad so to aspire," observed
English officer.

It may be so," said Doctor Clarke,
vning as he spoke. "But I tell you,
I could wellnigh doubt the justice
Heaven above us, if no signal hu-
ation overtake this lady who now
ds so haughtily into yonder man-
. She seeks to place herself above

the sympathies of our common nature,
which envelops all human souls. See if
that nature do not assert its claim over
her in some mode that shall bring her
level with the lowest!"

"Never!" cried Captain Langford,
indignantly,—"neither in life, nor when
they lay her with her ancestors."

Not many days afterwards the Governor gave a ball in honor of Lady
Eleanore Rochcliffe. The principal gentry of the colony received invitations,
which were distributed to their residences, far and near, by messengers on
horseback, bearing missives sealed with
all the formality of official, despatches.
In obedience to the summons, there was
a general gathering of rank, wealth, and
beauty; and the wide door of the Province House had seldom given admittance
to more numerous and honorable guests
than on the evening of Lady Eleanore's
ball. Without much extravagance of
eulogy, the spectacle might even be
termed splendid; for, according to the
fashion of the times, the ladies shone
in rich silks and satins, outspread over
wide-projecting hoops; and the gentlemen glittered in gold embroidery, laid
unsparingly upon the purple, or scarlet, or sky-blue velvet, which was
the material of their coats and
waistcoats. The latter article of dress
was of great importance, since it
enveloped the wearer's body nearly
to the knees, and was perhaps bedizened with the amount of his whole
year's income, in golden flowers and
foliage. The altered taste of the present day,—a taste symbolic of a deep
change in the whole system of society,
—would look upon almost any of those
gorgeous figures as ridiculous; although
that evening the guests sought their re-

flections in the pier-glasses, and rejoiced to catch their own glitter amid the glittering crowd. What a pity that one of the stately mirrors has not preserved a picture of the scene, which, by the very traits that were so transitory, might have taught us much that would be worth knowing and remembering!

Would, at least, that either painter or mirror could convey to us some faint idea of a garment, already noticed in this legend,—the Lady Eleanore's embroidered mantle,—which the gossips whispered was invested with magic properties, so as to lend a new and untried grace to her figure each time that she put it on! Idle fancy as it is, this mysterious mantle has thrown an awe around my image of her, partly from its fabled virtues, and partly because it was the handiwork of a dying woman, and, perchance, owed the fantastic grace of its conception to the delirium of approaching death.

After the ceremonial greetings had been paid, Lady Eleanore Rochcliffe stood apart from the mob of guests, insulating herself within a small and distinguished circle, to whom she accorded a more cordial favor than to the general throng. The waxen torches threw their radiance vividly over the scene, bringing out its brilliant points in strong relief; but she gazed carelessly, and with now and then an expression of weariness or scorn, tempered with such feminine grace, that her auditors scarcely perceived the moral deformity of which it was the utterance. She beheld the spectacle not with vulgar ridicule, as disdaining to be pleased with the provincial mockery of a court festival, but with the deeper scorn of one whose spirit held itself too high to participate in the enjoyment of ot human souls. Whether or no the ollections of those who saw her t evening were influenced by the stra events with which she was subsequer connected, so it was, that her figure e after recurred to them as marked something wild and unnatural; althou at the time, the general whisper of her exceeding beauty, and of indescribable charm which her ma threw around her. Some close obs ers, indeed, detected a feverish f and alternate paleness of countena with a corresponding flow and revul of spirits, and once or twice a pai and helpless betrayal of lassitude, if she were on the point of sinking the ground. Then, with a nervous sh der, she seemed to arouse her energ and threw some bright and playful, half-wicked sarcasm into the conve tion. There was so strange a charac istic in her manners and sentime that it astonished every right-min listener; till looking in her face, a l ing and incomprehensible glance smile perplexed them with doubts l as to her seriousness and sanity. G ually, Lady Eleanore Rochcliffe's ci grew smaller, till only four gentle remained in it. These were Cap Langford, the English officer be mentioned; a Virginian planter, who come to Massachusetts on some p cal errand; a young Episcopal cle man, the grandson of a British and lastly, the private secretary Governor Shute, whose obsequious had won a sort of tolerance from I Eleanore.

At different periods of the eve the liveried servants of the Prov House passed among the guests, l

huge trays of refreshments, and
ench and Spanish wines. Lady Elea-
e Rochcliffe, who refused to wet her
utiful lips even with a bubble of
mpagne, had sunk back into a large
nask chair, apparently overwearied
her with the excitement of the scene
its tedium; and while, for an instant,
was unconscious of voices, laughter,
l music, a young man stole forward,
l knelt down at her feet. He bore
alver in his hand, on which was a
sed silver goblet, filled to the brim
h wine, which he offered as reveren-
ly as to a crowned queen, or rather
a the awful devotion of a priest
ag sacrifice to his idol. Conscious
some one touched her robe, Lady
anore started, and unclosed her eyes
a the pale, wild features and di-
veled hair of Jervase Helwyse.
Why do you haunt me thus?" said
in a languid tone, but with a kind-
feeling than she ordinarily permit-
herself to express. "They tell me
I have done you harm."
Heaven knows if that be so," replied
young man, solemnly. "But, Lady
anore, in requital of that harm, if
l there be, and for your own earthly
heavenly welfare, I pray you to
one sip of this holy wine, and
. to pass the goblet round among
guests. And this shall be a symbol
you have not sought to withdraw
self from the chain of human sym-
ies,—which whoso would shake off
t keep company with fallen angels."
Where has this mad fellow stolen
sacramental vessel?" exclaimed the
copal clergyman.
his question drew the notice of the
ts to the silver cup, which was
gnized as appertaining to the com-

munion plate of the Old South Church;
and, for aught that could be known, it
was brimming over with the consecrated
wine.

"Perhaps it is poisoned," half whispered the Governor's secretary.

"Pour it down the villain's throat!"
cried the Virginian, fiercely.

"Turn him out of the house!" cried
Captain Langford, seizing Jervase Helwyse so roughly by the shoulder that
the sacramental cup was overturned,
and its contents sprinkled upon Lady
Eleanore's mantle. "Whether knave,
fool, or Bedlamite, it is intolerable that
the fellow should go at large."

"Pray, gentlemen, do my poor ad-
mirer no harm," said Lady Eleanore,
with a faint and weary smile. "Take
him out of my sight, if such be your
pleasure; for I can find in my heart
to do nothing but laugh at him,—
whereas, in all decency and conscience,
it would become me to weep for the
mischief I have wrought!"

But while the bystanders were attempting to lead away the unfortunate
young man, he broke from them, and
with a wild, impassioned earnestness,
offered a new and equally strange petition to Lady Eleanore. It was no other
than that she should throw off the
mantel, which, while he pressed the silver cup of wine upon her, she had
drawn more closely around her form,
so as almost to shroud herself within
it.

"Cast it from you!" exclaimed Jervase Helwyse, clasping his hands in an
agony of entreaty. "It may not yet be
too late! Give the accursed garment to
the flames!"

But Lady Eleanore, with a laugh of
scorn, drew the rich folds of the em-

broidered mantle over her head, in such a fashion as to give a completely new aspect to her beautiful face, which— half hidden, half revealed—seemed to belong to some being of mysterious character and purposes.

"Farewell, Jervase Helwyse!" said she. "Keep my image in your remembrance, as you behold it now."

"Alas, lady!" he replied, in a tone no longer wild, but sad as a funeral bell. "We must meet shortly, when your face may wear another aspect, and that shall be the image that must abide within me."

He made no more resistance to the violent efforts of the gentlemen and servants, who almost dragged him out of the apartment, and dismissed him roughly from the iron gate of the Province House. Captain Langford, who had been very active in this affair, was returning to the presence of Lady Eleanore Rochcliffe, when he encountered the physician, Dr. Clarke, with whom he had held some casual talk on the day of her arrival. The Doctor stood apart, separated from Lady Eleanore by the width of the room, but eying her with such keen sagacity, that Captain Langford involuntarily gave him credit for the discovery of some deep secret.

"You appear to be smitten, after all, with the charms of this queenly maiden," said he, hoping thus to draw forth the physician's hidden knowledge.

"God forbid!" answered Doctor Clarke, with a grave smile; "and if you be wise, you will put up the same prayer for yourself. Woe to those who shall be smitten by this beautiful Lady Eleanore! But yonder stands the Governor,—and I have a word or two for

his private ear. Good night!"

He accordingly advanced to Govern Shute, and addressed him in so l a tone that none of the bystande could catch a word of what he sai although the sudden change of his E cellency's hitherto cheerful visage I tokened that the communication co be of no agreeable import. A very f moments afterwards, it was announc to the guests that an unforeseen c cumstance rendered it necessary to [a premature close to the festival.

The ball at the Province House s plied a topic of conversation for colonial metropolis for some days af its occurrence, and might still lon have been the general theme, only t a subject of all-engrossing inter thrust it, for a time, from the pul recollection. This was the appeara of a dreadful epidemic, which, in t age, and long before and afterwa was wont to slay its hundreds and th sands on both sides of the Atlar On the occasion of which we spe it was distinguished by a peculiar v lence, insomuch that it has left its tr —its pit-marks, to use an appropr figure—on the history of the coun the affairs of which were thrown confusion by its ravages. At first, like its ordinary course, the dis seemed to confine itself to the hi circles of society, selecting its vict from among the proud, the well-b and the wealthy, entering unaba into stately chambers, and lying d with the slumberers in silken b Some of the most distinguished gu of the Province House,—even t whom the haughty Lady Eleanore R cliffe had deemed not unworthy of favor,—were stricken by this

urge. It was noticed, with an un-
erous bitterness of feeling, that the
r gentlemen,—the Virginian, the
tish officer, the young clergyman,
l the Governor's secretary,—who had
n her most devoted attendants on
evening of the ball, were the forest on whom the plague-stroke fell.
t the disease, pursuing its onward
gress, soon ceased to be exclusively
prerogative of aristocracy. Its red
nd was no longer conferred, like a
le's star or an order of knighthood.
hreaded its way through the narrow
l crooked streets, and entered the
, mean, darksome dwellings, and
l its hand of death upon the artisans
laboring classes of the town. It
pelled rich and poor to feel themes brethren, then; and stalking to
fro across the Three Hills, with
erceness which made it almost a
pestilence, there was that mighty
queror,—that scourge and horror of
forefathers,—the Small Pox!

e cannot estimate the affright
ch this plague inspired of yore, by
templating it as the fangless mon-
of the present day. We must re-
ber, rather, with what awe we
ched the gigantic footsteps of the
tic cholera, striding from shore to
e of the Atlantic, and marching like
iny upon cities far remote, which
t had already half depopulated.
re is no other fear so horrible and
umanizing, as that which makes man
d to breathe Heaven's vital air,
it be poison, or to grasp the hand
brother or friend, lest the gripe
he pestilence should clutch him.
was the dismay that now followed
ne track of the disease, or ran be-
it throughout the town. Graves

were hastily dug, and the pestilential
relics as hastily covered, because the
dead were enemies of the living, and
strove to draw them headlong, as it
were, into their own dismal pit. The
public councils were suspended, as if
mortal wisdom might relinquish its devices, now that an unearthly usurper
had found his way into the ruler's mansion. Had an enemy's fleet been hovering on the coast, or his armies trampling
on our soil, the people would probably
have committed their defence to that
same direful conqueror who had wrought
their own calamity, and would permit
no interference with his sway. This
conqueror had a symbol of his triumphs.
It was a blood-red flag, that fluttered in
the tainted air over the door of every
dwelling into which the Small Pox had
entered.

Such a banner was long since waving over the portal of the Province
House; for thence, as was proved by
tracking its footsteps back, had all this
dreadful mischief issued. It had been
traced back to a lady's luxurious chamber,—to the proudest of the proud,—
to her that was so delicate, and hardly
owned herself of earthly mould,—to
the haughty one, who took her stand
above human sympathies,—to Lady
Eleanore! There remained no room for
doubt that the contagion had lurked
in that gorgeous mantle which threw so
strange a grace around her at the festival. Its fantastic splendor had been
conceived in the delirious brain of a
woman on her death-bed, and was the
last toil of her stiffening fingers, which
had interwoven fate and misery with
its golden threads. This dark tale, whispered at first, was now bruited far and
wide. The people raved against the

Lady Eleanore, and cried out that her pride and scorn had evoked a fiend, and that, between them both, this monstrous evil had been born. At times their rage and despair took the semblance of grinning mirth; and whenever the red flag of the pestilence was hoisted over another, and yet another door, they clapped their hands and shouted through the street, in bitter mockery: "Behold a new triumph for the Lady Eleanore!"

One day, in the midst of these dismal times, a wild figure approached the portal of the Province House, and, folding his arms, stood contemplating the scarlet banner, which a passing breeze shook fitfully, as if to fling abroad the contagion that it typified. At length, climbing one of the pillars by means of the iron balustrade, he took down the flag, and entered the mansion, waving it above his head. At the foot of the staircase he met the Governor, booted and spurred, with his cloak drawn around him, evidently on the point of setting forth upon a journey.

"Wretched lunatic, what do you seek here?" exclaimed Shute, extending his cane to guard himself from contact. "There is nothing here but Death. Back,—or you will meet him!"

"Death will not touch me, the banner-bearer of the pestilence!" cried Jervase Helwyse, shaking the red flag aloft. "Death, and the Pestilence, who wears the aspect of the Lady Eleanore, will walk through the streets to-night, and I must march before them with this banner!"

"Why do I waste words on the fellow?" muttered the Governor, drawing his cloak across his mouth. "What matters his miserable life, when none of us are sure of twelve hours' breath? On,

fool, to your own destruction!"

He made way for Jervase Helw who immediately ascended the stairc but, on the first landing-place, was rested by the firm grasp of a h upon his shoulder. Looking fiercely with a madman's impulse to stru with and rend asunder his oppon he found himself powerless beneat calm, stern eye, which possessed mysterious property of quelling fr at its height. The person whom he now encountered was the physic Doctor Clarke, the duties of whose profession had led him to the Prov House, where he was an infrequent g in more prosperous times.

"Young man, what is your purpo demanded he.

"I seek the Lady Eleanore," answ Jervase Helwyse, submissively.

"All have fled from her," said physician. "Why do you seek her r I tell you, youth, her nurse fell de stricken on the threshold of that chamber. Know ye not, that never c such a curse to our shores as this lo Lady Eleanore?—that her breath filled the air with poison?—that she shaken pestilence and death upon land from the folds of her accu mantle?"

"Let me look upon her!" rejoinec mad youth, more wildly. "Let me hold her, in her awful beauty, cla the regal garments of the pestile She and Death sit on a throne toge Let me kneel down before them!"

"Poor youth!" said Doctor Cl and, moved by a deep sense of h weakness, a smile of caustic h curled his lip even then. "Wilt still worship the destroyer, and round her image with fantasies the

gnificent the more evil she has
ught? Thus man doth ever to his
nts! Approach, then! Madness, as
ave noted, has that good efficacy,
: it will guard you from contagion,
nd perchance its own cure may be
d in yonder chamber."

scending another flight of stairs, he
w open a door, and signed to Jer-
: Helwyse that he should enter. The
r lunatic, it seems probable, had
ished a delusion that his haughty
ress sat in state, unharmed herself
the pestilential influence which, as
enchantment, she scattered round
it her. He dreamed, no doubt, that
beauty was not dimmed, but bright-
: into superhuman splendor. With
anticipations, he stole reverentially
he door at which the physician
d, but paused upon the threshold,
ig fearfully into the gloom of the
ened chamber.

Where is the Lady Eleanore?"
pered he.

all her," replied the physician.

ady Eleanore!—Princess!—Queen
eath!" cried Jervase Helwyse, ad-
ng three steps into the chamber.
is not here! There, on yonder
, I behold the sparkle of a diamond
i once she wore upon her bosom.
:,"—and he shuddered,—"there
her mantle, on which a dead
in embroidered a spell of dreadful
cy. But where is the Lady Elea-
"

nething stirred within the silken
ns of a canopied bed; and a low
was uttered, which, listening in-
-, Jervase Helwyse began to dis-
sh as a woman's voice, complain-
lefully of thirst. He fancied, even,
ie recognized its tones.

"My throat! — my throat is
scorched!" murmured the voice. "A
drop of water!"

"What thing art thou?" said the
brain-stricken youth, drawing near the
bed and tearing asunder its curtains.
"Whose voice hast thou stolen for thy
murmurs and miserable petitions, as if
Lady Eleanore could be conscious of
mortal infirmity? Fie! Heap of diseased
mortality, why lurkest thou in my lady's
chamber?"

"O Jervase Helwyse," said the voice,
—and as it spoke, the figure contorted
itself, struggling to hide its blasted face,
—"look not now on the woman you
once loved! The curse of Heaven hath
stricken me, because I would not call
man my brother, nor woman sister. I
wrapped myself in PRIDE as in a
MANTLE, and scorned the sympathies
of nature; and therefore has nature
made this wretched body the medium
of a dreadful sympathy. You are
avenged,—they are all avenged,—Nature
is avenged,—for I am Eleanore Rochcliffe!"

The malice of his mental disease,
the bitterness lurking at the bottom of
his heart, mad as he was, for a blighted
and ruined life, and love that had been
paid with cruel scorn, awoke within
the breast of Jervase Helwyse. He shook
his finger at the wretched girl, and the
chamber echoed, the curtains of the
bed were shaken, with his outburst of
insane merriment.

"Another triumph for the Lady Eleanore!" he cried. "All have been her
victims! Who so worthy to be the
final victim as herself?"

Impelled by some new fantasy of
his crazed intellect, he snatched the
fatal mantle, and rushed from the cham-

ber and the house. That night, a procession passed, by torchlight, through the streets, bearing in the midst the figure of a woman, enveloped with a richly-embroidered mantle; while in advance stalked Jervase Helwyse, waving the red flag of the pestilence. Arriving opposite the Province House, the mob burned the effigy, and a strong wind came and swept away the ashes. It was said, that, from that very hour, the pestilence abated, as if its sway had some mysterious connection, from the first plague-stroke to the last, with Lady Eleanore's Mantle. A remarkable uncertainty broods over that unhappy lady's fate. There is a belief, however, that, in a certain chamber of this mansion, a female form may sometimes be duskily discerned, shrinking into the darkest corner, and muffling her face within an embroidered mantle. Supposing the legend true, can this be other than the once proud Lady Eleanore?

Mine host, and the old loyalist, and I, bestowed no little warmth of applause upon this narrative, in which we had all been deeply interested; for the reader can scarcely conceive how unspeakably the effect of such a tale is heightened, when, as in the present case, we may repose confidence in the ve ity of him who tells it. For my part, knowing how scrupulous is Tiffany to settle the foundation of facts, I could not have believed one whit the more faithfully, had professed himself an eyewitness of doings and sufferings of poor I Eleanore. Some sceptics, it is true, m demand documentary evidence, or require him to produce the embroid mantle, forgetting that—Heaven praised!—it was consumed to ashes. now the old loyalist, whose blood warmed by the good cheer, began to in his turn, about the traditions of Province House, and hinted that he, were agreeable, might add a few r niscences to our legendary stock. Tiffany, having no cause to dre rival, immediately besought him to f us with a specimen; my own entrea of course, were urged to the same ef and our venerable guest, well ple to find willing auditors, awaited the return of Mr. Thomas Waite, had been summoned forth to pr accommodations for several new rivals. Perchance the public—but b as its own caprice and ours shall the matter—may read the result i other Tale of the Province Hous

IV. OLD ESTHER DUDLEY

Our host having resumed the chair, he, as well as Mr. Tiffany and myself, expressed much eagerness to be made acquainted with the story to which the loyalist had alluded. That venerable man first of all saw fit to moisten his throat with another glass of wine then, turning his face towards ou fire, looked steadfastly for a few ments into the depths of its ch glow. Finally, he poured forth a fluency of speech. The generous

t he had imbibed, while it warmed
age-chilled blood, likewise took off
chill from his heart and mind, and
e him an energy to think and feel
ch we could hardly have expected
ind beneath the snows of fourscore
ers. His feelings, indeed, appeared
ne more excitable than those of a
nger man; or, at least, the same
ee of feeling manifested itself by
e visible effects, than if his judg-
t and will had possessed the po-
y of meridian life. At the pathetic
ages of his narrative he readily
ed into tears. When a breath of
nation swept across his spirit, the
d flushed his withered visage even
he roots of his white hair; and he
k his clinched fist at the trio of
eful auditors, seeming to fancy
ies in those who felt very kindly
rds the desolate old soul. But ever
anon, sometimes in the midst of
most earnest talk, this ancient per-
intellect would wander vaguely,
g its hold of the matter in hand,
groping for it amid misty shadows.
would he cackle forth a feeble
, and express a doubt whether his
—for by that phrase it pleased our
nt friend to signify his mental
rs—were not getting a little the
e for wear.

der these disadvantages, the old
ist's story required more revision
nder it fit for the public eye than
of the series which have preceded
or should it be concealed, that the
ment and tone of the affair may
undergone some slight, or per-
e more than slight metamorphosis,
transmission to the reader through
nedium of a thoroughgoing demo-
The tale itself is a mere sketch,

with no involution of plot, nor any
great interest of events, yet possessing,
if I have rehearsed it aright, that pensive influence over the mind which
the shadow of the old Province House
flings upon the loiterer in its court-yard.

The hour had come—the hour of defeat and humiliation—when Sir William
Howe was to pass over the threshold of
the Province House, and embark, with
no such triumphal ceremonies as he
once promised himself, on board the
British fleet. He bade his servants and
military attendants go before him, and
lingered a moment in the loneliness of
the mansion, to quell the fierce emotions
that struggled in his bosom as with a
death throb. Preferable, then, would be
have deemed his fate, had a warrior's
death left him a claim to the narrow
territory of a grave within the soil
which the King had given him to defend. With an ominous perception that,
as his departing footsteps echoed adown
the staircase, the sway of Britain was
passing forever from New England, he
smote his clinched hand on his brow,
and cursed the destiny that had flung
the shame of a dismembered empire
upon him.

"Would to God," cried he, hardly re-
pressing his tears of rage, "that the
rebels were even now at the doorstep!
A blood-stain upon the floor should then
bear testimony that the last British
ruler was faithful to his trust."

The tremulous voice of a woman
replied to his exclamation.

"Heaven's cause and the King's are
one," it said. "Go forth, Sir William
Howe, and trust in Heaven to bring
back a royal governor in triumph."

Subduing at once the passion to which

he had yielded only in the faith that it was unwitnessed, Sir William Howe became conscious that an aged woman, leaning on a gold-headed staff, was standing betwixt him and the door. It was old Esther Dudley, who had dwelt almost immemorial years in this mansion, until her presence seemed as inseparable from it as the recollections of its history. She was the daughter of an ancient and once eminent family, which had fallen into poverty and decay, and left its last descendant no resource save the bounty of the King, nor any shelter except within the walls of the Province House. An office in the household, with merely nominal duties, had been assigned to her as a pretext for the payment of a small pension, the greater part of which she expended in adorning herself with an antique magnificence of attire. The claims of Esther Dudley's gentle blood were acknowledged by all the successive governors; and they treated her with the punctilious courtesy which it was her foible to demand, not always with success, from a neglectful world. The only actual share which she assumed in the business of the mansion, was to glide through its passages and public chambers, late at night, to see that the servants had dropped no fire from their flaring torches, nor left embers crackling and blazing on the hearths. Perhaps it was this invariable custom of walking her rounds in the hush of midnight that caused the superstition of the times to invest the old woman with attributes of awe and mystery; fabling that she had entered the portal of the Province House, none knew whence, in the train of the first royal governor, and that it was her fate to dwell there till the

last should have departed. But Sir liam Howe, if he ever heard this leg had forgotten it.

"Mistress Dudley, why are you tering here?" asked he, with some s ity of tone. "It is my pleasure t the last in this mansion of the King

"Not so, if it please your Excelle answered the time-stricken wo "This roof has sheltered me lor will not pass from it until they me to the tomb of my forefat What other shelter is there for Esther Dudley, save the Province H or the grave?"

"Now Heaven forgive me!" sai William Howe to himself. "I was a to leave this wretched old creatu starve or beg. Take this, good Mis Dudley," he added, putting a into her hands. "King George's hea these golden guineas is sterling yet will continue so, I warrant you, should the rebels crown John Hai their king. That purse will buy a ter shelter than the Province Hous now afford."

"While the burden of life re upon me, I will have no other s than this roof," persisted Esther ley, striking her staff upon the with a gesture that expressed immc resolve. "And when your Exce returns in triumph, I will totter the porch to welcome you."

"My poor old friend!" answere British general,—and all his manl martial pride could no longer re a gush of bitter tears. "This is a hour for you and me. The pr which the King intrusted to my is lost. I go hence in misfortune, chance in disgrace,—to return no And you, whose present being is

ited with the past,—who have seen
ernor after governor, in stately
eantry, ascend these steps,—whose
le life has been an observance of
estic ceremonies, and a worship of
King,—how will you endure the
age? Come with us! Bid farewell to
id that has shaken off its allegiance,
live still under a royal government,
lalifax."

Never, never!" said the pertinacious
dame. "Here will I abide; and King
rge shall still have one true subject
is disloyal province."

Beshrew the old fool!" muttered
William Howe, growing impatient
er obstinacy, and ashamed of the
ion into which he had been be-
ed. "She is the very moral of old-
oned prejudice, and could exist no-
e but in this musty edifice. Well,
Mistress Dudley, since you will
s tarry, I give the Province House
large to you. Take this key, and
it safe until myself, or some other
governor, shall demand it of you."
iling bitterly at himself and her,
ok the heavy key of the Province
e, and delivering it into the old
s hands, drew his cloak around
for departure. As the General
ed back at Esther Dudley's antique
:, he deemed her well fitted for
a charge, as being so perfect a
sentative of the decayed past,—
a age gone by, with its manners,
ons, faith, and feelings all fallen
oblivion or scorn,—of what had
been a reality, but was now merely
ion of faded magnificence. Then
7illiam Howe strode forth, smiting
inched hands together, in the fierce
sh of his spirit; and old Esther
:y was left to keep watch in the

lonely Province House, dwelling there
with Memory; and if Hope ever seemed
to flit around her, still it was Memory
in disguise.

The total change of affairs that ensued on the departure of the British
troops did not drive the venerable lady
from her stronghold. There was not,
for many years afterwards, a governor
of Massachusetts; and the magistrates,
who had charge of such matters, saw
no objection to Esther Dudley's residence in the Province House, especially
as they must otherwise have paid a hire-
ling for taking care of the premises,
which with her was a labor of love.
And so they left her the undisturbed
mistress of the old historic edifice. Many
and strange were the fables which the
gossips whispered about her, in all the
chimney-corners of the town. Among
the time-worn articles of furniture that
had been left in the mansion there was
a tall, antique mirror, which was well
worthy of a tale by itself, and perhaps
may hereafter be the theme of one.
The gold of its heavily-wrought frame
was tarnished, and its surface so blurred,
that the old woman's figure, whenever
she paused before it, looked indistinct
and ghost-like. But it was the general
belief that Esther could cause the governors of the overthrown dynasty, with
the beautiful ladies who had once
adorned their festivals, the Indian chiefs
who had come up to the Province House
to hold council or swear allegiance, the
grim Provincial warriors, the severe
clergymen,—in short, all the pageantry
of gone days,—all the figures that ever
swept across the broad plate of glass
in former times,—she could cause the
whole to reappear, and people the inner
world of the mirror with shadows of

old life. Such legends as these, together with the singularity of her isolated existence, her age, and the infirmity that each added winter flung upon her, made Mistress Dudley the object both of fear and pity; and it was partly the result of either sentiment, that, amid all the angry license of the times, neither wrong nor insult ever fell upon her unprotected head. Indeed, there was so much haughtiness in her demeanor towards intruders, among whom she reckoned all persons acting under the new authorities, that it was really an affair of no small nerve to look her in the face. And to do the people justice, stern republicans as they had now become, they were well content that the old gentlewoman, in her hoop petticoat and faded embroidery, should still haunt the palace of ruined pride and overthrown power, the symbol of a departed system, embodying a history in her person. So Esther Dudley dwelt, year after year, in the Province House, still reverencing all that others had flung aside, still faithful to her King, who, so long as the venerable dame yet held her post, might be said to retain one true subject in New England, and one spot of the empire that had been wrested from him.

And did she dwell there in utter loneliness? Rumor said, not so. Whenever her chill and withered heart desired warmth, she was wont to summon a black slave of Governor Shirley's from the blurred mirror, and send him in search of guests who had long ago been familiar in those deserted chambers. Forth went the sable messenger, with the starlight or the moonshine gleaming through him, and did his errand in the burial-ground, knocking at the iron

doors of tombs, or upon the ma slabs that covered them, and whispe to those within, "My mistress, Esther Dudley, bids you to the P₁ ince House at midnight." And pun ally as the clock of the Old South twelve came the shadows of the Oli the Hutchinsons, the Dudleys, all grandees of a bygone generation, gli beneath the portal into the well-kn mansion, where Esther mingled them as if she likewise were a sh Without vouching for the truth of ₁ traditions, it is certain that Mist Dudley sometimes assembled a fev the staunch though crestfallen old t who had lingered in the rebel town ing those days of wrath and tribula Out of a cob-webbed bottle contai liquor that a royal governor might smacked his lips over they qu₁ healths to the King, and babbled tre to the Republic, feeling as if the tecting shadow of the throne were flung around them. But, draining last drops of their liquor, they timorously homeward, and answered again, if the rude mob reviled the the street.

Yet Esther Dudley's most frequent favored guests were the children o town. Towards them she was ₁ stern. A kindly and loving nature, dered elsewhere from its free cc by a thousand rocky prejudices, lavi itself upon these little ones. By b of gingerbread of her own ma stamped with a royal crown, tempted their sunny sportiveness neath the gloomy portal of the Pro House, and would often beguile to spend a whole playday there, si in a circle round the verge of her petticoat, greedily attentive to her

of a dead world. And when these
le boys and girls stole forth again
m the dark mysterious mansion, they
it bewildered, full of old feelings
t graver people had long ago forgot-
, rubbing their eyes at the world
und them, as if they had gone astray
ancient times, and become children
the past. At home, when their par-
s asked where they had loitered
h a weary while, and with whom
y had been at play, the children
ild talk of all the departed worthies
the Province, as far back as Gover-
Belcher, and the haughty dame of
William Phipps. It would seem as
igh they had been sitting on the
es of these famous personages,
m the grave had hidden for half
ntury, and had toyed with the em-
dery of their rich waistcoats, or
ishly pulled the long curls of their
ing wigs. "But Governor Belcher
been dead this many a year," would
mother say to her little boy. "And
you really see him at the Province
se?" "Oh yes, dear mother! yes!"
half-dreaming child would answer.
t when old Esther had done speak-
ibout him, he faded away out of his
r." Thus, without affrighting her
guests, she led them by the hand
the chambers of her own desolate
t, and made childhood's fancy dis-
the ghosts that haunted there.

ving so continually in her own
e of ideas, and never regulating her
l by a proper reference to present
s, Esther Dudley appears to have
n partially crazed. It was found
she had no right sense of the prog-
and true state of the Revolutionary
but held a constant faith that the
es of Britain were victorious on

every field, and destined to be ultimately triumphant. Whenever the town rejoiced for a battle won by Washington,
or Gates, or Morgan, or Greene, the
news, in passing through the door of
the Province House, as through the ivory
gate of dreams, became metamorphosed
into a strange tale of the prowess of
Howe, Clinton, or Cornwallis. Sooner
or later, it was her invincible belief,
the colonies would be prostrate at the
footstool of the King. Sometimes she
seemed to take for granted that such
was already the case. On one occasion,
she startled the town's people by a
brilliant illumination of the Province
House, with candles at every pane of
glass, and a transparency of the King's
initials and a crown of light in the great
balcony window. The figure of the aged
woman, in the most gorgeous of her mildewed velvets and brocades, was seen
passing from casement to casement,
until she paused before the balcony,
and flourished a huge key above her
head. Her wrinkled visage actually
gleamed with triumph, as if the soul
within her were a festal lamp.

"What means this blaze of light?
What does old Esther's joy portend?"
whispered a spectator. "It is frightful
to see her gliding about the chambers,
and rejoicing there without a soul to
bear her company."

"It is as if she were making merry
in a tomb," said another.

"Pshaw! It is no such mystery," observed an old man, after some brief
exercise of memory. "Mistress Dudley
is keeping jubilee for the King of England's birthday."

Then the people laughed aloud, and
would have thrown mud against the
blazing transparency of the King's

crown and initials, only that they pitied
the poor old dame, who was so dismally
triumphant amid the wreck and ruin
of the system to which she appertained.

Oftentimes it was her custom to climb
the weary staircase that wound upward to the cupola, and thence strain
her dimmed eyesight seaward and coun-
tryward, watching for a British fleet,
or for the march of a grand procession,
with the King's banner floating over it.
The passengers in the street below
would discern her anxious visage, and
send up a shout: "When the golden
Indian on the Province House shall
shoot his arrow, and when the cock on
the Old South spire shall crow, then
look for a royal governor again!"—for
this had grown a byword through the
town. And at last, after long, long years,
old Esther Dudley knew, or perchance
she only dreamed, that a royal governor
was on the eve of returning to the
Province House, to receive the heavy
key which Sir William Howe had committed to her charge. Now it was the
fact, that intelligence bearing some
faint analogy to Esther's version of it
was current among the town's people.
She set the mansion in the best order
that her means allowed, and, arraying
herself in silks and tarnished gold, stood
long before the blurred mirror to admire her own magnificence. As she
gazed, the gray and withered lady
moved her ashen lips, murmuring half
aloud, talking to shapes that she saw
within the mirror, to shadows of her
own fantasies, to the household friends
of memory, and bidding them rejoice with her, and come forth to
meet the governor. And while absorbed
in this communion, Mistress Dudley
heard the tramp of many footsteps in

the street, and, looking out at the
dow, beheld what she construed as
royal governor's arrival.

"O happy day! O blessed, ble
hour!" she exclaimed. "Let me but
him welcome within the portal, and
task in the Province House, and
earth is done!"

Then with tottering feet, which
and tremulous joy caused to tread an
she hurried down the grand stair
her silks sweeping and rustling as
went, so that the sound was as if
train of spectral courtiers were thr
ing from the dim mirror. And Es
Dudley fancied, that, as soon as
wide door should be flung open, all
pomp and splendor of bygone ti
would pace majestically into the P
ince House, and the gilded tapestr
the past would be brightened by
sunshine of the present. She turned
key, withdrew it from the lock,
closed the door, and stepped across
threshold. Advancing up the court-
appeared a person of most dign
mien, with tokens, as Esther interpr
them, of gentle blood, high rank,
long-accustomed authority, even in
walk and every gesture. He was ri
dressed, but wore a gouty shoe, w
however, did not lessen the statel
of his gait. Around and behind
were people in plain civic dresses,
two or three war-worn veterans,
dently officers of rank, arrayed
uniform of blue and buff. But E
Dudley, firm in the belief that
fastened its roots about her heart
held only the principal personage,
never doubted that this was the
looked-for governor, to whom she
to surrender up her charge. As h
proached, she involuntarily sank

her knees, and tremblingly held forth
heavy key.

Receive my trust! take it quickly!"
d she; "for methinks Death is striv-
to snatch away my triumph. But
comes too late. Thank Heaven for
blessed hour! God save King
rge!"

That, Madam, is a strange prayer to
offered up at such a moment," re-
d the unknown guest of the Prov-
House, and courteously removing
hat he offered his arm to raise the
woman. "Yet, in reverence for your
hairs and long-kept faith, Heaven
id that any here should say you
Over the realms which still ac-
wledge his sceptre, God save King
rge!"

sther Dudley started to her feet,
hastily clutching back the key,
d with fearful earnestness at the
iger; and dimly and doubtfully, as
uddenly awakened from a dream,
bewildered eyes half recognized his
. Years ago she had known him
ng the gentry of the province. But
ban of the King had fallen upon
How, then, came the doomed vic-
here? Proscribed, excluded from
y, the monarch's most dreaded and
d foe, this New England merchant
stood triumphantly against a king-
's strength; and his foot now trod
humbled Royalty, as he ascended
steps of the Province House, the
le's chosen Governor of Massachu-

Vretch, wretch that I am!" mut-
the old woman, with such a heart-
en expression that the tears gushed
the stranger's eyes. "Have I bid-
a traitor welcome? Come, Death!
quickly!"

"Alas, venerable lady!" said Governor Hancock, lending her his support
with all the reverence that a courtier
would have shown to a queen. "Your
life has been prolonged until the world
has changed around you. You have
treasured up all that time has rendered
worthless,—the principles, feelings, manners, modes of being and acting, which
another generation has flung aside,—
and you are a symbol of the past. And
I, and these around me,—we represent
a new race of men,—living no longer
in the past, scarcely in the present,—
but projecting our lives forward into
the future. Ceasing to model ourselves
on ancestral superstitions, it is our faith
and principle to press onward, onward!
Yet," continued he, turning to his attendants, "let us reverence, for the last
time, the stately and gorgeous prejudices of the tottering Past!"

While the republican governor spoke,
he had continued to support the helpless form of Esther Dudley; her weight
grew heavier against his arm; but at
last, with a sudden effort to free herself, the ancient woman sank down beside one of the pillars of the portal.
The key of the Province House fell
from her grasp, and clanked against the
stone.

"I have been faithful unto death,"
murmured she. "God save the King!"

"She hath done her office!" said Hancock, solemnly. "We will follow her
reverently to the tomb of her ancestors;
and then, my fellow-citizens, onward,
onward! We are no longer children of
the Past!"

As the old loyalist concluded his
narrative, the enthusiasm which had
been fitfully flashing within his sunken

eyes and quivering across his wrinkled visage, faded away, as if all the lingering fire of his soul were extinguished. Just then, too, a lamp upon the mantelpiece threw out a dying gleam, which vanished as speedily as it shot upward, compelling our eyes to grope for one another's features by the dim glow of the hearth. With such a lingering fire, methought, with such a dying dream, had the glory of the ancient system vanished from the Province House, when the spirit of old Esther Dudley took its flight. And now, again, the clock of the Old South threw its voice of ages on the breeze, knolling the hourly knell of the Past, crying out far and wide through the multitudinous city, and filling our ears, as we sat in the dusky chamber, with its reverberating depth of tone. In that same mansion,—in that very chamber,—what a volume of history had been told off into hours by the

same voice that was now trembling the air. Many a governor had he those midnight accents, and longed exchange his stately cares for slumb And as for mine host, and Mr. B Tiffany, and the old loyalist, and we had babbled about dreams of past until we almost fancied that clock was still striking in a bygone c tury. Neither of us would have w dered had a hoop-petticoated phant of Esther Dudley tottered into chamber, walking her rounds in the h of midnight, as of yore, and motio us to quench the fading embers the fire, and leave the historic precin to herself and her kindred shades. as no such vision was vouchsafed retired unbidden, and would advise Tiffany to lay hold of another audi being resolved not to show my in the Province House for a good w hence, if ever.

THE HAUNTED MIND

WHAT a singular moment is the first one, when you have hardly begun to recollect yourself, after starting from midnight slumber! By unclosing your eyes so suddenly, you seem to have surprised the personages of your dream in full convocation round your bed, and catch one broad glance at them before they can flit into obscurity. Or, to vary the metaphor, you find yourself, for a single instant, wide awake in that realm of illusions, whither sleep has been the passport, and behold its ghostly inhabitants and wondrous scenery, with a perception of their strangeness such as you

never attain while the dream is disturbed. The distant sound o church-clock is borne faintly on wind. You question with yourself, seriously, whether it has stolen to waking ear from some gray tower stood within the precincts of dream. While yet in suspense, anc clock flings its heavy clang over slumbering town with so full and tinct a sound, and such a long mu in the neighboring air, that you certain it must proceed from the st at the nearest corner. You count strokes, one—two, and there they c

h a booming sound, like the gather-
of a third stroke within the bell.

f you could choose an hour of wake-
ness out of the whole night, it would
this. Since your sober bedtime, at
ven, you have had rest enough to
e off the pressure of yesterday's
igue; while before you, till the sun
nes from "far Cathay" to brighten
r window, there is almost the space
a summer night; one hour to be
nt in thought, with the mind's eye
shut, and two in pleasant dreams,
two in that strangest of enjoyments,
he forgetfulness alike of joy and
. The moment of rising belongs to
ther period of time, and appears
distant that the plunge out of a
m bed into the frosty air cannot yet
anticipated with dismay. Yesterday
already vanished among the shadows
the past; to-morrow has not yet
rged from the future. You have
nd an intermediate space, where the
ness of life does not intrude; where
passing moment lingers, and bees truly the present; a spot where
er Time, when he thinks nobody
atching him, sits down by the way-
to take breath. O that he would
asleep, and let mortals live on with-
growing older!

itherto you have lain perfectly still,
use the slightest motion would dis-
te the fragments of your slumber.
, being irrevocably awake, you peep
ugh the half-drawn window-curtain,
observe that the glass is ornamented
fanciful devices in frostwork, and
each pane presents something like
ozen dream. There will be time
gh to trace out the analogy, while
ing the summons to breakfast. Seen
ugh the clear portion of the glass,

where the silvery mountain-peaks of the
frost scenery do not ascend, the most
conspicuous object is the steeple; the
white spire of which directs you to the
wintry lustre of the firmament. You
may almost distinguish the figures on
the clock that has just told the hour.
Such a frosty sky, and the snow-covered
roofs, and the long vista of the frozen
street, all white, and the distant water
hardened into rock, might make you
shiver, even under four blankets and
a woolen comforter. Yet look at that
one glorious star! Its beams are dis-
tinguishable from all the rest, and actually cast the shadow of the casement
on the bed with a radiance of deeper
hue than moonlight, though not so accurate an outline.

You sink down and muffle your head
in the clothes, shivering all the while,
but less from bodily chill than the bare
idea of a polar atmosphere. It is too
cold even for the thoughts to venture
abroad. You speculate on the luxury
of wearing out a whole existence in bed,
like an oyster in its shell, content with
the sluggish ecstasy of inaction, and
drowsily conscious of nothing but delicious warmth, such as you now feel
again. Ah! that idea has brought a
hideous one in its train. You think how
the dead are lying in their cold shrouds
and narrow coffins, through the drear
winter of the grave, and cannot persuade your fancy that they neither
shrink nor shiver, when the snow is
drifting over their little hillocks, and
the bitter blast howls against the door
of the tomb. That gloomy thought will
collect a gloomy multitude, and throw
its complexion over your wakeful hour.

In the depths of every heart there is
a tomb and a dungeon, though the lights,

the music, and revelry above may cause us to forget their existence, and the buried ones, or prisoners whom they hide. But sometimes, and oftenest at midnight, these dark receptacles are flung wide open. In an hour like this, when the mind has a passive sensibility, but no active strength; when the imagination is a mirror, imparting vividness to all ideas, without the power of selecting or controlling them; then pray that your griefs may slumber, and the brotherhood of remorse not break their chain. It is too late! A funeral train comes gliding by your bed, in which Passion and Feeling assume bodily shape, and things of the mind become dim spectres to the eye. There is your earliest Sorrow, a pale young mourner, wearing a sister's likeness to first love, sadly beautiful, with a hallowed sweetness in her melancholy features, and grace in the flow of her sable robe. Next appears a shade of ruined loveliness, with dust among her golden hair, and her bright garments all faded and defaced, stealing from your glance with drooping head, as fearful of reproach; she was your fondest Hope, but a delusive one; so call her Disappointment now. A sterner form succeeds, with a brow of wrinkles, a look and gesture of iron authority; there is no name for him unless it be Fatality, an emblem of the evil influence that rules your fortunes; a demon to whom you subjected yourself by some error at the outset of life, and were bound his slave forever, by once obeying him. See! those fiendish lineaments graven on the darkness, the writhed lip of scorn, the mockery of that living eye, the pointed finger, touching the sore place in your heart! Do you remember any act of enormous

folly at which you would blush eve[r] the remotest cavern of the earth? T recognize your Shame.

Pass, wretched band! Well for wakeful one, if, riotously miserabl[e] fiercer tribe do not surround him,— devils of a guilty heart, that holds hell within itself. What if Rem[e] should assume the features of an jured friend? What if the fiend sh[e] come in woman's garments, with a beauty amid sin and desolation, lie down by your side? What if should stand at your bed's foot, in likeness of a corpse, with a bloody s upon the shroud? Sufficient, wit[h] such guilt, is this nightmare of the s this heavy, heavy sinking of the spi[r] this wintry gloom about the heart; indistinct horror of the mind, blen itself with the darkness of the cham

By a desperate effort, you start right, breaking from a sort of consc sleep, and gazing wildly round the as if the fiends were anywhere b[ut] your haunted mind. At the same ment, the slumbering embers on hearth send forth a gleam which p[a] illuminates the whole outer room, flickers through the door of the chamber, but cannot quite dispe[l] obscurity. Your eye searches for w ever may remind you of the living w With eager minuteness, you take of the table near the fireplace, the with an ivory knife between its le[a] the unfolded letter, the hat and fallen glove. Soon the flame vani and with it the whole scene is g though its image remains an insta[nt] your mind's eye, when darkness swallowed the reality. Throughout chamber, there is the same obsc as before, but not the same gloom

your breast. As your head falls back
on the pillow, you think—in a whis-
be it spoken—how pleasant, in these
ht solitudes, would be the rise and
of a softer breathing than your
a, the slight pressure of a tenderer
om, the quiet throb of a purer heart,
arting its peacefulness to your
ubled one, as if the fond sleeper
e involving you in her dream.

Ier influence is over you, though she
e no existence but in that momen-
y image. You sink down in a flow-
spot, on the borders of sleep and
efulness, while your thoughts rise
ore you in pictures, all disconnected,
all assimilated by a pervading glad-
eness and beauty. The wheeling of
eous squadrons, that glitter in the
is succeeded by the merriment of
dren round the door of a school-
se, beneath the glimmering shadow
old trees, at the corner of a rustic
. You stand in the sunny rain of
ummer shower, and wander among
sunny trees of an autumnal wood,
look upward at the brightest of all
bows, over-arching the unbroken
t of snow, on the American side of
ara. Your mind struggles pleasantly
een the dancing radiance round the
th of a young man and his recent

bride, and the twittering flight of birds
in spring about their new-made nest.
You feel the merry bounding of a ship
before the breeze; and watch the tune-
ful feet of rosy girls, as they twine
their last and merriest dance, in a splendid ball-room; and find yourself in the
brilliant circle of a crowded theatre, as
the curtain falls over a light and airy
scene.

With an involuntary start, you seize
hold on consciousness, and prove yourself but half awake, by running a doubtful parallel between human life and the
hour which has now elapsed. In both
you emerge from mystery, pass through
a vicissitude that you can but imperfectly control, and are borne onward
to another mystery. Now comes the
peal of the distant clock, with fainter
and fainter strokes as you plunge farther into the wilderness of sleep. It is
the knell of a temporary death. Your
spirit has departed, and strays like a
free citizen among the people of a shadowy world, beholding strange sights,
yet without wonder or dismay. So calm,
perhaps, will be the final change; so
undisturbed, as if among familiar things,
the entrance of the soul to its eternal
home!

like primitive animal

THE VILLAGE UNCLE

AN IMAGINARY RETROSPECT

OME! another log upon the hearth.
, our little parlor is comfortable,
cially here, where the old man sits
is old arm-chair; but on Thanks-

giving night the blaze should dance
higher up the chimney, and send a
shower of sparks into the outer darkness. Toss on an armful of those dry
oak chips, the last relics of the Mermaid's knee-timbers, the bones of your

namesake, Susan. Higher yet, and clearer be the blaze, till our cottage windows glow the ruddiest in the village, and the light of our household mirth flash far across the bay to Nahant. And now, come, Susan, come, my children, draw your chairs round me, all of you. There is a dimness over your figures! You sit quivering indistinctly with each motion of the blaze, which eddies about you like a flood, so that you all have the look of visions, or people that dwell only in the firelight, and will vanish from existence as completely as your own shadows when the flame shall sink among the embers. Hark! let me listen for the swell of the surf; it should be audible a mile inland on a night like this. Yes; there I catch the sound, but only an uncertain murmur, as if a good way down over the beach; though, by the almanac, it is high tide at eight o'clock, and the billows must now be dashing within thirty yards of our door. Ah! the old man's ears are failing him; and so is his eyesight, and perhaps his mind; else you would not all be so shadowy, in the blaze of his Thanksgiving fire.

How strangely the past is peeping over the shoulders of the present! To judge by my recollections, it is but a few moments since I sat in another room; yonder model of a vessel was not there, nor the old chest of drawers, nor Susan's profile and mine, in that gilt frame; nothing, in short, except this same fire, which glimmered on books, papers, and a picture, and half discovered my solitary figure in a looking-glass. But it was paler than my rugged old self, and younger, too, by almost half a century. Speak to me, Susan; speak, my beloved ones; for the scene

is glimmering on my sight again, a as it brightens you fade away. O should be loath to lose my treas of past happiness, and become o more what I was then,—a hermit the depths of my own mind; sometin yawning over drowsy volumes, and ar a scribbler of wearier trash than w I read; a man who had wandered of the real world and got into shadow, where his troubles, joys, vicissitudes were of such slight s that he hardly knew whether he li or only dreamed of living. Th Heaven, I am an old man now, have done with all such vanities.

Still this dimness of mine eyes! C nearer, Susan, and stand before the f est blaze of the hearth. Now I beh you illuminated from head to foot, your clean cap and decent gown, the dear lock of gray hair across y forehead, and a quiet smile about y mouth, while the eyes alone are c cealed by the red gleam of the fire u your spectacles. There, you made tremble again! When the flame q ered, my sweet Susan, you quive with it, and grew indistinct, as if m ing into the warm light, that my glimpse of you might be as visionar the first was, full many a year since. you remember it? You stood on little bridge over the brook that r across King's Beach into the sea. was twilight; the waves rolling in, wind sweeping by, the crimson clo fading in the west, and the silver m brightening above the hill; and on bridge were you, fluttering in the br like a sea-bird that might skim awa your pleasure. You seemed a daug of the viewless wind, a creature of ocean foam and the crimson light, w

rry life was spent in dancing on the
sts of the billows that threw up their
ray to support your footsteps. As I
w nearer, I fancied you akin to the
e of mermaids, and thought how
asant it would be to dwell with you
ong the quiet coves, in the shadow
the cliffs, and to roam along secluded
ches of the purest sand, and when
northern shores grew bleak, to
nt the islands, green and lonely, far
d summer seas. And yet it glad-
ed me, after all this nonsense, to find
nothing but a pretty young girl,
ly perplexed with the rude behavior
the wind about your petticoats.

hus I did with Susan as with most
er things in my earlier days, dip-
g her image into my mind and color-
it of a thousand fantastic hues, be-
I could see her as she really was.
w, Susan, for a sober picture of our
age! It was a small collection of
llings that seemed to have been
up by the sea, with the rockweed
marine plants that it vomits after
orm, or to have come ashore among
pipe-staves and other lumber which
been washed from the deck of an
tern schooner. There was just space
the narrow and sandy street between
beach in front and a precipitous hill
lifted its rocky forehead in the
, among a waste of juniper-bushes
the wild growth of a broken pas-
. The village was picturesque, in
variety of its edifices, though all
e rude. Here stood a little old hovel,
t, perhaps, of driftwood, there a
of boathouses, and beyond them
wo-story dwelling, of dark and
ther-beaten aspect, the whole inter-
d with one or two snug cottages,
ted white, a sufficiency of pigsties,

and a shoemaker's shop. Two grocery
stores stand opposite each other, in the
centre of the village. These were the
places of resort, at their idle hours, of
a hardy throng of fishermen, in red
baize shirts, oilcloth trousers, and boots
of brown leather covering the whole
leg,—true seven-league boots, but fitter
to wade the ocean than walk the earth.
The wearers seemed amphibious, as if
they did but creep out of salt water
to sun themselves; nor would it have
been wonderful to see their lower limbs
covered with clusters of little shellfish,
such as cling to rocks and old ship-
timber over which the tide ebbs and
flows. When their fleet of boats was
weather-bound, the butchers raised their
price, and the spit was busier than the
frying-pan; for this was a place of fish,
and known as such to all the country
round about; the very air was fishy,
being perfumed with dead sculpins,
hard-heads, and dog-fish, strewn plentifully on the beach. You see, children,
the village is but little changed since
your mother and I were young.

How like a dream it was, when I bent
over a pool of water, one pleasant morning, and saw that the ocean had dashed
its spray over me and made me a fisherman! There were the tarpauling, the
baize shirt, the oilcloth trousers and
seven-league boots, and there my own
features, but so reddened with sunburn
and sea-breezes that methought I had
another face, and on other shoulders
too. The seagulls and the loons, and I,
had now all one trade; we skimmed the
crested waves and sought our prey beneath them, the man with as keen enjoyment as the birds. Always, when
the east grew purple, I launched my
dory, my little flat-bottomed skiff, and

rowed cross-handed to Point Ledge, the Middle Ledge, or, perhaps, beyond Egg Rock; often, too, did I anchor off Dread Ledge, a spot of peril to ships unpiloted; and sometimes spread an adventurous sail and tracked across the bay to South Shore, casting my lines in sight of Scituate. Ere nightfall I hauled my skiff high and dry on the beach, laden with red rock-cod, or the white-bellied ones of deep water; haddock, bearing the black marks of Saint Peter's fingers near the gills; the long-bearded hake, whose liver holds oil enough for a midnight lamp; and now and then a mighty halibut, with a back broad as my boat. In the autumn I tolled and caught those lovely fish, the mackerel. When the wind was high,—when the whale-boats, anchored off the Point, nodded their slender masts at each other, and the dories pitched and tossed in the surf,—when Nahant Beach was thundering three miles off, and the spray broke a hundred feet in air round the distant base of Egg Rock,—when the brimful and boisterous sea threatened to tumble over the street of our village, —then I made a holiday on shore.

Many such a day did I sit snugly in Mr. Bartlett's store, attentive to the yarns of Uncle Parker,—uncle to the whole village, by right of seniority, but of southern blood, with no kindred in New England. His figure is before me now, enthroned upon a mackerel-barrel; a lean old man, of great height, but bent with years, and twisted into an uncouth shape by seven broken limbs; furrowed also, and weather-worn, as if every gale, for the better part of a century, had caught him somewhere on the sea. He looked like a harbinger of tempest; a shipmate of the Flying

Dutchman. After innumerable voya[ges] aboard men-of-war and merchantm[en,] fishing schooners and chebacco bo[ats,] the old salt had become master o[f a] handcart, which he daily trundled ab[out] the vicinity, and sometimes blew [a] fish-horn through the streets of Sal[em.] One of Uncle Parker's eyes had b[een] blown out with gunpowder, and [the] other did but glimmer in its soc[ket.] Turning it upward as he spoke, it [was] his delight to tell of cruises against [the] French, and battles with his own sh[ip]-mates, when he and an antagonist u[sed] to be seated astride of a sailor's ch[est,] each fastened down by a spike-n[ail] through his trousers, and there to f[ight] it out. Sometimes he expatiated on [the] delicious flavor of the hagden, a gre[at] and goose-like fowl, which the sai[lors] catch with hook and line on the Gr[and] Banks. He dwelt with rapture on [an] interminable winter at the Isle [of] Sables, where he had gladdened h[im]-self, amid polar snows, with the [rum] and sugar saved from the wreck o[f a] West India schooner. And wrathf[ully] did he shake his fist as he related h[ow] a party of Cape Cod men had rob[bed] him and his companions of their la[wful] spoil, and sailed away with every [keg] of old Jamaica, leaving him not a d[rop] to drown his sorrow. Villains they w[ere,] and of that wicked brotherhood who [are] said to tie lanterns to horses' tails [to] mislead the mariner along the dange[rous] shores of the Cape.

Even now, I seem to see the gr[oup] of fishermen, with that old salt in [the] midst. One fellow sits on the cou[nter,] a second bestrides an oil barrel, a t[hird] lolls at his length on a parcel of [old] cod-lines, and another has planted [the] tarry seat of his trousers on a hea[p]

t, which will shortly be sprinkled
er a lot of fish. They are a likely set
men. Some have voyaged to the East
lies or the Pacific, and most of them
re sailed in Marblehead schooners to
wfoundland; a few have been no
ther than the Middle Banks, and one
two have always fished along the
re; but, as Uncle Parker used to say,
y have all been christened in salt
er, and know more than men ever
n in the bushes. A curious figure, by
v of contrast, is a fish-dealer from
up country, listening with eyes wide
n to narratives that might startle
bad the sailor. Be it well with you,
brethren! Ye are all gone, some to
r graves ashore, and others to the
ths of ocean; but my faith is strong
: ye are happy; for whenever I be-
l your forms, whether in dream or
on, each departed friend is puffing
long nine, and a mug of the right
k-strap goes round from lip to lip.
ut where was the mermaid in those
ghtful times? At a certain window
the centre of the village appeared
retty display of gingerbread men
horses, picture-books and ballads,
ll fishhooks, pins, needles, sugar-
is, and brass thimbles,—articles on
:h the young fishermen used to ex-
l their money from pure gallantry.
it a picture was Susan behind the
iter! A slender maiden, though the
l of rugged parents, she had the
mest of all waists, brown hair curl-
n her neck, and a complexion rather
, except when the sea-breeze flushed
. few freckles became beauty spots
ath her eyelids. How was it, Susan,
you talked and acted so carelessly,
always for the best, doing whatever
right in your own eyes, and never

once doing wrong in mine, nor shocked a
taste that had been morbidly sensitive
till now? And whence had you that
happiest gift, of brightening every topic
with an unsought gayety, quiet but irresistible, so that even gloomy spirits felt
your sunshine, and did not shrink from
it? Nature wrought the charm. She
made you a frank, simple, kind-hearted,
sensible, and mirthful girl. Obeying nature, you did free things without in-
delicacy, displayed a maiden's thoughts
to every eye, and proved yourself as
innocent as naked Eve.

It was beautiful to observe how her
simple and happy nature mingled itself
with mine. She kindled a domestic fire
within my heart, and took up her dwelling there, even in that chill and lonesome cavern, hung round with glittering
icicles of fancy. She gave me warmth of
feeling, while the influence of my mind
made her contemplative. I taught her
to love the moonlight hour, when the
expanse of the encircled bay was smooth
as a great mirror, and slept in a transparent shadow; while beyond Nahant
the wind rippled the dim ocean into a
dreamy brightness, which grew faint
afar off, without becoming gloomier. I
held her hand and pointed to the long
surf wave, as it rolled calmly on the
beach, in an unbroken line of silver; we
were silent together till its deep and
peaceful murmur had swept by us.
When the Sabbath sun shone down into
the recesses of the cliffs, I led the mermaid thither, and told her that those
huge, gray, shattered rocks, and her
native sea, that raged forever like a
storm against them, and her own slender
beauty, in so stern a scene, were all
combined into a strain of poetry. But
on the Sabbath eve, when her mother

had gone early to bed, and her gentle sister had smiled and left us, as we sat alone by the quiet hearth, with household things around, it was her turn to make me feel that here was a deeper poetry, and that this was the dearest hour of all. Thus went on our wooing, till I had shot wild-fowl enough to feather our bridal bed, and the Daughter of the Sea was mine.

I built a cottage for Susan and myself, and made a gateway in the form of a Gothic arch, by setting up a whale's jaw-bones. We bought a heifer with her first calf, and had a little garden on the hillside, to supply us with potatoes and green sauce for our fish. Our parlor, small and neat, was ornamented with our two profiles in one gilt frame, and with shells and pretty pebbles on the mantel-piece, selected from the sea's treasury of such things, on Nahant Beach. On the desk, beneath the looking-glass, lay the Bible, which I had begun to read aloud at the book of Genesis, and the singing-book that Susan used for her evening psalm. Except the almanac, we had no other literature. All that I heard of books, was when an Indian history or tale of shipwreck was sold by a peddler or wandering subscription man to some one in the village,' and read through its owner's nose to a slumberous auditory. Like my brother fishermen, I grew into the belief that all human erudition was collected in our pedagogue, whose green spectacles and solemn phiz, as he passed to his little school-house, amid a waste of sand, might have gained him a diploma from any college in New England. In truth I dreaded him. When our children were old enough to claim his care, you remember, Susan, how I frowned, though

you were pleased, at this learned m encomiums on their proficiency. I fea to trust them even with the alpha it was the key to a fatal treasure.

But I loved to lead them by t little hands along the beach, and p to nature in the vast and the min the sky, the sea, the green earth, pebbles, and the shells. Then did I course of the mighty works and c tensive goodness of the Deity, with simple wisdom of a man whose n had profited by lonely days upon deep, and his heart by the strong pure affections of his evening h Sometimes my voice lost itself i tremulous depth; for I felt His eye u me as I spoke. Once, while my wife all of us were gazing at ourselves the mirror left by the tide in a ho of the sand, I pointed to the pict heaven below, and bade her obs how religion was strewn everywher our path; since even a casual poo water recalled the idea of that h whither we were travelling, to rest ever with our children. Suddenly image, Susan, and all the little f made up of yours and mine, seeme fade away and vanish around me, l ing a pale visage like my own of fo days within the frame of a large loo glass. Strange illusion!

My life glided on, the past appea to mingle with the present and at the future, till the whole lies befor at a glance. My manhood has long waning with a stanch decay; my e contemporaries, after lives of unbr health, are all at rest, without ha known the weariness of late age; now, with a wrinkled forehead and white hair as badges of my digni have become the patriarch, the Unc village. I love that name; it widens circle of my sympathies; it joins the youthful to my household, in the lred of affection.

ike Uncle Parker, whose rheumatic es were dashed against Egg Rock forty years ago, I am a spinner of ; yarns. Seated on the gunwale of a /, or on the sunny side of a boat-se, where the warmth is grateful to limbs, or by my own hearth, when iend or two are there, I overflow talk, and yet am never tedious. h a broken voice I give utterance to h wisdom. Such, Heaven be praised! e vigor of my faculties, that many rgotten usage, and traditions ancient ny youth, and early adventures of elf or others, hitherto effaced by gs more recent, acquire new dis-ness in my memory. I remember happy days when the haddock were numerous on all the fishing-nds than sculpins in the surf; when deep-water cod swam close in shore, the dogfish, with his poisonous horn, not learned to take the hook. I number every equinoctial storm in h the sea has overwhelmed the t, flooded the cellars of the village, hissed upon our kitchen hearth. I the history of the great whale that landed on Whale Beach, and whose , being now my gate-way, will last ges after my coffin shall have passed ath them. Thence it is an easy dig-on to the halibut, scarcely smaller the whale, which ran out six cod- and hauled my dory to the mouth oston Harbor, before I could touch with the gaff.

melancholy accidents be the theme nversation, I tell how a friend of was taken out of his boat by an enormous shark; and the sad, true tale of a young man on the eve of marriage, who had been nine days missing, when his drowned body floated into the very pathway, on Marblehead Neck, that had often led him to the dwelling of his bride; as if the dripping corpse would have come where the mourner was. With such awful fidelity did that lover return to fulfil his vows! Another favorite story is of a crazy maiden, who conversed with angels and had the gift of prophecy, and whom all the village loved and pitied, though she went from door to door accusing us of sin, exhorting to repentance, and foretelling our destruction by flood or earthquake. If the young men boast their knowledge of the ledges and sunken rocks, I speak of pilots who knew the wind by its scent and the wave by its taste, and could have steered blindfold to any port between Boston and Mount Desert, guided only by the rote of the shore,—the peculiar sound of the surf on each island, beach, and line of rocks along the coast. Thus do I talk, and all my auditors grow wise, while they deem it pastime.

I recollect no happier portion of my life than this, my calm old age. It is like the sunny and sheltered slope of a valley, where, late in the autumn, the grass is greener than in August, and intermixed with golden dandelions, that have not been seen till now since the first warmth of the year. But with me, the verdure and the flowers are not frostbitten in the midst of winter. A playfulness has revisited my mind; a sympathy with the young and gay; an unpainful interest in the business of others; a light and wandering curiosity; arising, perhaps, from the sense that my toil on earth is ended, and the brief hour till bedtime may be spent in play. Still, I have fancied that there is a depth of feeling and reflection, under this superficial levity, peculiar to one who has lived long and is soon to die.

Show me anything that would make an infant smile, and you shall behold a gleam of mirth over the hoary ruin of my visage. I can spend a pleasant hour in the sun, watching the sports of the village children on the edge of the surf; now they chase the retreating wave far down over the wet sand; now it steals softly up to kiss their naked feet; now it comes onward with threatening front, and roars after the laughing crew as they scamper beyond its reach. Why should not an old man be merry too, when the great sea is at play with those little children? I delight, also, to follow in the wake of a pleasure-party of young men and girls, strolling along the beach after an early supper at the Point. Here, with handkerchiefs at nose, they bend over a heap of eel-grass, entangled in which is a dead skate, so oddly accoutred with two legs and a long tail that they mistake him for a drowned animal. A few steps farther the ladies scream, and the gentlemen make ready to protect them against a young shark of the dogfish kind, rolling with a life-like motion in the tide that has thrown him up. Next, they are smit with wonder at the black shells of a wagon-load of live lobsters, packed in rockweed for the country market. And when they reach the fleet of dories, just hauled ashore after the day's fishing, how do I laugh in my sleeve, and sometimes roar outright, at the simplicity of these young folks and the sly humor of the fishermen! In winter, when our village is

thrown into a bustle by the arrival perhaps a score of country dealers, b gaining for frozen fish, to be transpor hundreds of miles, and eaten fresh Vermont or Canada, I am a pleased idle spectator in the throng. For I lau my boat no more.

When the shore was solitary, I h found a pleasure that seemed even exalt my mind, in observing the sp or contentions of two gulls, as t wheeled and hovered about each ot with hoarse screams, one moment f ping on the foam of the wave, and t soaring aloft till their white bos melted into the upper sunshine. In calm of the summer sunset I drag aged limbs, with a little ostentatio activity, because I am so old, up to rocky brow of the hill. There I see white sails of many a vessel outw bound or homeward from afar, and black trail of a vapor behind the eas steamboat; there, too, is the sun, g down, but not in gloom, and there illimitable ocean mingling with the to remind me of eternity.

But sweetest of all is the hour cheerful musing and pleasant talk, comes between the dusk and the lig candle, by my glowing fireside. never, even on the first Thanksgi night, when Susan and I sat alone our hopes, nor the second, whe stranger had been sent to gladden and be the visible image of our affect did I feel such joy as now. All belong to me are here; Death has t none, nor Disease kept them away, Strife divided them from their par or each other; with neither poverty riches to disturb them, nor the m of desires beyond their lot, they kept New England's festival round

riarch's board. For I am a patriarch!
re I sit among my descendants, in
old arm-chair and immemorial cor-
, while the firelight throws an ap-
priate glory round my venerable
ne. Susan! My children! Something
spers me that this happiest hour
st be the final one, and that nothing
ains but to bless you all and depart
h a treasure of recollected joys to
ven. Will you meet me there? Alas!
r figures grow indistinct, fading into
ures on the air, and now to fainter
lines, while the fire is glimmering on
walls of a familiar room, and shows
book that I flung down, and the
et that I left half written, some fifty
rs ago. I lift my eyes to the looking-
s and perceive myself alone, unless
e be the mermaid's features retiring
the depths of the mirror, with a
ler and melancholy smile.

h! one feels a chillness, not bodily,
about the heart, and, moreover, a
foolish dread of looking behind him,
after these pastimes. I can imagine precisely how a magician would sit down
in gloom and terror, after dismissing the
shadows that had personated dead or
distant people, and stripping his cavern
of the unreal splendor which had
changed it to a palace. And now for a
moral to my reverie. Shall it be, that,
since fancy can create so bright a dream
of happiness, it were better to dream
on from youth to age, than to awake
and strive doubtfully for something
real! O, the slight tissue of a dream can
no more preserve us from the stern
reality of misfortune, than a robe of
cobweb could repel the wintry blast.
Be this the moral, then. In chaste and
warm affections, humble wishes, and
honest toil for some useful end, there
is health for the mind, and quiet for the
heart, the prospect of a happy life, and
the fairest hope of Heaven.

THE AMBITIOUS GUEST

NE September night a family had
ered round their hearth, and piled
igh with the driftwood of mountain
ams, the dry cones of the pine, and
splintered ruins of great trees, that
come crashing down the precipice.
the chimney roared the fire, and
htened the room with its broad
e. The faces of the father and
her had a sober gladness; the chil-
laughed; the eldest daughter was
image of Happiness at seventeen;
the aged grandmother, who sat
ting in the warmest place, was the
image of Happiness grown old. They
had found the "herb, heart's-ease," in
the bleakest spot of all New England.
This family were situated in the Notch
of the White Hills, where the wind was
sharp throughout the year, and pitilessly
cold in the winter,—giving their cottage
all its fresh inclemency before it descended on the valley of the Saco. They
dwelt in a cold spot and a dangerous
one; for a mountain towered above
their heads, so steep that the stones
would often rumble down its sides, and
startle them at midnight.

The daughter had just uttered some simple jest that filled them all with mirth, when the wind came through the Notch and seemed to pause before their cottage,—rattling the door, with a sound of wailing and lamentation, before it passed into the valley. For a moment it saddened them, though there was nothing unusual in the tones. But the family were glad again, when they perceived that the latch was lifted by some traveller whose footsteps had been unheard amid the dreary blast which heralded his approach, and wailed as he was entering, and went moaning away from the door.

Though they dwelt in such a solitude, these people held daily converse with the world. The romantic pass of the Notch is a great artery, through which the life-blood of internal commerce is continually throbbing, between Maine on one side, and the Green Mountains and the shores of the St. Lawrence on the other. The stage-coach always drew up before the door of the cottage. The wayfarer, with no companion but his staff, paused here to exchange a word, that the sense of loneliness might not utterly overcome him ere he could pass through the cleft of the mountain, or reach the first house in the valley. And here the teamster, on his way to Portland market, would put up for the night; and, if a bachelor, might sit an hour beyond the usual bedtime, and steal a kiss from the mountain maid at parting. It was one of those primitive taverns where the traveller pays only for food and lodging, but meets with a homely kindness beyond all price. When the footsteps were heard, therefore, between the outer door and the inner one, the whole family rose up,

grandmother, children, and all, as about to welcome some one who longed to them, and whose fate linked with theirs.

The door was opened by a yo man. His face at first wore the me choly expression, almost desponde of one who travels a wild and b road at nightfall and alone, but s brightened up when he saw the ki warmth of his reception. He felt heart spring forward to meet them from the old woman, who wiped a c with her apron, to the little child held out its arms to him. One glance smile placed the stranger on a foo of innocent familiarity with the el daughter.

"Ah, this fire is the right thing!" c he; "especially when there is suc pleasant circle round it. I am quite numbed; for the Notch is just like pipe of a great pair of bellows; it blown a terrible blast in my face the way from Bartlett."

"Then you are going towards mont?" said the master of the h as he helped to take a light knap off the young man's shoulders.

"Yes; to Burlington, and far en beyond," replied he. "I meant to been at Ethan Crawford's to-night; a pedestrian lingers along such a roa this. It is no matter; for, when I this good fire, and all your che faces, I felt as if you had kindl on purpose for me, and were waitin arrival. So I shall sit down among and make myself at home."

The frank-hearted stranger had drawn his chair to the fire, when s thing like a heavy footstep was h without, rushing down the steep si the mountain, as with long and

les, and taking such a leap, in pass-
the cottage, as to strike the opposite
cipice. The family held their breath,
ause they knew the sound, and their
st held his by instinct.

The old mountain has thrown a stone
us, for fear we should forget him,"
the landlord, recovering himself.
e sometimes nods his head, and
atens to come down; but we are old
hbors, and agree together pretty
, upon the whole. Besides, we have
ore place of refuge, hard by, if he
uld be coming in good earnest."

et us now suppose the stranger to
e finished his supper of bear's meat;
by his natural felicity of manner,
ave placed himself on a footing of
dness with the whole family, so that
y talked as freely together as if he
nged to their mountain brood. He
of a proud, yet gentle spirit,—
ghty and reserved among the rich
great; but ever ready to stoop his
d to the lowly cottage door, and be
a brother or a son at the poor man's
ide. In the household of the Notch,
ound warmth and simplicity of feel-
the pervading intelligence of New
land, and a poetry of native growth,
ch they had gathered, when they
e thought of it, from the mountain
s and chasms, and at the very thres-
of their romantic and dangerous
le. He had travelled far and alone;
whole life, indeed, had been a soli-
path; for, with the lofty caution
is nature, he had kept himself apart
a those who might otherwise have
his companions. The family, too,
gh so kind and hospitable, had that
ciousness of unity among themes, and separation from the world
rge, which, in every domestic circle,

should still keep a holy place where no
stranger may intrude. But, this evening,
a prophetic sympathy impelled the refined and educated youth to pour out
his heart before the simple moun-
taineers, and constrained them to answer
him with the same free confidence. And
thus it should have been. Is not the
kindred of a common fate a closer tie
than that of birth?

The secret of the young man's character was a high and abstracted ambition. He could have borne to live an
undistinguished life, but not to be forgotten in the grave. Yearning desire had
been transformed to hope; and hope,
long cherished, had become like certainty, that, obscurely as he journeyed
now, a glory was to beam on all his
pathway,—though not, perhaps, while
he was treading it. But, when posterity
should gaze back into the gloom of what
was now the present, they would trace
the brightness of his footsteps, brightening as meaner glories faded, and confess, that a gifted one had passed from
his cradle to his tomb, with none to
recognize him.

"As yet," cried the stranger,—his
cheek glowing and his eye flashing with
enthusiasm,—"as yet, I have done nothing. Were I to vanish from the earth
to-morrow, none would know so much
of me as you; that a nameless youth
came up, at nightfall, from the valley
of the Saco, and opened his heart to
you in the evening, and passed through
the Notch, by sunrise, and was seen no
more. Not a soul would ask,—'Who was
he?—Whither did the wanderer go?'
But, I cannot die till I have achieved
my destiny. Then, let Death come! I
shall have built my monument!"

There was a continual flow of natural

emotion, gushing forth amid abstracted reverie, which enabled the family to understand this young man's sentiments, though so foreign from their own. With quick sensibility of the ludicrous, he blushed at the ardor into which he had been betrayed.

"You laugh at me," said he, taking the eldest daughter's hand and laughing himself. "You think my ambition as nonsensical as if I were to freeze myself to death on the top of Mount Washington, only that people might spy at me from the country round about. And truly, that would be a noble pedestal for a man's statue!"

"It is better to sit here by this fire," answered the girl, blushing, "and be comfortable and contented, though nobody thinks about us."

"I suppose," said her father, after a fit of musing, "there is something natural in what the young man says; and if my mind had been turned that way, I might have felt just the same. It is strange, wife, how his talk has set my head running on things, that are pretty certain never to come to pass."

"Perhaps they may," observed the wife. "Is the man thinking what he will do when he is a widower?"

"No, no!" cried he, repelling the idea with reproachful kindness. "When I think of your death, Esther, I think of mine, too. But I was wishing we had a good farm in Bartlett, or Bethlehem, or Littleton, or some other township round the White Mountains; but not where they could tumble on our heads. I should want to stand well with my neighbors, and be called Squire, and sent to General Court for a term or two; for a plain, honest man may do as much good there as a lawyer. And when I

should be grown quite an old man, and you an old woman, so as not to be l apart, I might die happy enough in bed, and leave you all crying round A slate gravestone would suit me well as a marble one,—with just name and age, and a verse of a hy and something to let people know I lived an honest man and die Christian."

"There now," exclaimed the stran "it is our nature to desire a monum be it slate, or marble, or a pillar granite, or a glorious memory in universal heart of man."

"We're in a strange way, to-nig said the wife, with tears in her e "They say it's a sign of something, v folks' minds go a wandering so. F to the children!"

They listened accordingly. younger children had been put to in another room, but with an open between, so that they could be h talking busily among themselves. and all seemed to have caught the fection from the fireside circle, and outvying each other, in wild wi and childish projects of what they w do, when they came to be men women. At length, a little boy, ins of addressing his brothers and sis called out to his mother.

"I'll tell you what I wish, moth cried he. "I want you and father, grandma'm, and all of us, and stranger too, to start right away, an and take a drink out of the basi the Flume!"

Nobody could help laughing at child's notion of leaving a warm and dragging them from a cheerful to visit the basin of the Flum brook, which tumbles over the p

e, deep within the Notch. The boy
hardly spoken, when a wagon rattled
ng the road, and stopped a moment
ore the door. It appeared to contain
⬧ or three men, who were cheering
ir hearts with the rough chorus of a
g, which resounded, in broken notes,
ween the cliffs, while the singers
itated whether to continue their
rney, or put up here for the night.
Father," said the girl, "they are call-
you by name."

ut the good man doubted whether
⬧ had really called him, and was un-
ing to show himself too solicitous of
, by inviting people to patronize his
se. He therefore did not hurry to the
r; and the lash being soon applied,
travellers plunged into the Notch,
singing and laughing, though their
ic and mirth came back drearily
1 the heart of the mountain.

There, mother!" cried the boy,
n. "They'd have given us a ride to
Flume."

gain they laughed at the child's per-
cious fancy for a night ramble. But
appened, that a light cloud passed
the daughter's spirit; she looked
ely into the fire, and drew a breath
was almost a sigh. It forced its
, in spite of a little struggle to re-
s it. Then starting and blushing, she
ed quickly round the circle, as if
had caught a glimpse into her
m. The stranger asked what she had
thinking of.

Nothing," answered she, with a
icast smile. "Only I felt lonesome
then."

), I have always had a gift of feel-
what is in other people's hearts,"
he, half seriously. "Shall I tell the
ts of yours? For I know what to

think when a young girl shivers by a
warm hearth, and complains of lone-
someness at her mother's side. Shall I
put these feelings into words?"

"They would not be a girl's feelings
any longer, if they could be put into
words," replied the mountain nymph
laughing, but avoiding his eye.

All this was said apart. Perhaps a
germ of love was springing in their
hearts, so pure that it might blossom in
Paradise, since it could not be matured
on earth; for women worship such
gentle dignity as his; and the proud,
contemplative, yet kindly soul is oftenest captivated by simplicity like hers.
But, while they spoke softly, and he
was watching the happy sadness, the
lightsome shadows, the shy yearnings
of a maiden's nature, the wind, through
the Notch, took a deeper and drearier
sound. It seemed, as the fanciful
stranger said, like the choral strain of
the spirits of the blast, who, in old Indian times, had their dwelling among
these mountains, and made their heights
and recesses a sacred region. There was
a wail along the road as if a funeral
were passing. To chase away the gloom,
the family threw pine-branches on their
fire, till the dry leaves crackled and the
flame arose, discovering once again a
scene of peace and humble happiness.
The light hovered about them fondly,
and caressed them all. There were the
little faces of the children, peeping from
their bed apart, and here the father's
frame of strength, the mother's subdued
and careful mien, the high-browed
youth, the budding girl, and the good
old grandam, still knitting in the warmest place. The aged woman looked up
from her task, and, with fingers ever
busy, was the next to speak.

"Old folks have their notions," said she, "as well as young ones. You've been wishing and planning; and letting your heads run on one thing and another till you've set my mind a wandering too. Now what should an old woman wish for when she can go but a step or two before she comes to her grave? Children, it will haunt me night and day till I tell you.

"What is it, mother?" cried the husband and wife, at once.

Then the old woman, with an air of mystery, which drew the circle closer round the fire, informed them that she had provided her grave-clothes some years before,—a nice linen shroud, a cap with a muslin ruff, and everything of a finer sort than she had worn since her wedding-day. But, this evening, an old superstition had strangely recurred to her. It used to be said, in her younger days, that, if anything were amiss with a corpse, if only the ruff were not smooth, or the cap did not set right, the corpse, in the coffin and beneath the clods, would strive to put up its cold hands and arrange it. The bare thought made her nervous.

"Don't talk so, grandmother!" said the girl, shuddering.

"Now,"—continued the old woman, with singular earnestness, yet smiling strangely at her own folly,—"I want one of you, my children,—when your mother is dressed and in the coffin,—I want one of you to hold a looking-glass over my face. Who knows but I may take a glimpse at myself, and see whether all's right?"

"Old and young, we dream of graves and monuments," murmured the stranger youth. "I wonder how mariners feel when the ship is sinking, and they, un-

known and undistinguished, are to buried together in the ocean,—that and nameless sepulchre?"

For a moment the old wom ghastly conception so engrossed minds of her hearers, that a so abroad in the night, rising like the of a blast, had grown broad, deep, terrible, before the fated group conscious of it. The house, and all in it, trembled; the foundations of earth seemed to be shaken, as if awful sound were the peal of the trump. Young and old exchanged wild glance, and remained an inst pale, affrighted, without utterance power to move. Then the same sh burst simultaneously from all their

"The Slide! The Slide!"

The simplest words must intin but not portray, the unutterable he of the catastrophe. The victims ru from their cottage, and sought re in what they deemed a safer sp where, in contemplation of such emergency, a sort of barrier had reared. Alas! they had quitted security, and fled right into the path of destruction. Down came the w side of the mountain in a catarac ruin. Just before it reached the h the stream broke into two branch shivered not a window there, but whelmed the whole vicinity, blocke the road, and annihilated everythi its dreadful course. Long ere the thu of that great Slide had ceased to among the mountains, the mortal a had been endured, and the victims at peace. Their bodies were never f

The next morning the light s was seen stealing from the co chimney up the mountain side. W the fire was yet smouldering on

th, and the chairs in a circle round
s if the inhabitants had but gone
h to view the devastation of the
e and would shortly return to thank
ven for their miraculous escape. All
left separate tokens, by which those
had known the family were made
hed a tear for each. Who has not
d their name? The story has been
far and wide, and will forever be
gend of these mountains. Poets have
their fate.

here were circumstances which led

some to suppose that a stranger had
been received into the cottage on this
awful night, and had shared the catastrophe of all its inmates. Others denied
that there were sufficient grounds for
such a conjecture. Woe for the high-
souled youth, with his dream of Earthly
Immortality! His name and person
utterly unknown; his history, his way
of life, his plans, a mystery never to
be solved; his death and his existence
equally a doubt! Whose was the agony
of that death-moment?

THE SISTER YEARS

ST night, between eleven and twelve
ck, when the Old Year was leaving
final footprints on the borders of
e's empire, she found herself in pos-
on of a few spare moments, and sat
—of all places in the world—on
steps of our new City Hall. The
ry moonlight showed that she
d weary of body and sad of heart,
many another wayfarer of earth.
garments, having been exposed to
foul weather and rough usage,
in very ill condition; and as the
of her journey had never before
red her to take an instant's rest,
hoes were so worn as to be scarcely
h the mending. But, after trudging
a little distance farther, this poor
Year was destined to enjoy a long
sleep. I forgot to mention, that
she seated herself on the steps she
sited by her side a very capacious
box, in which, as is the custom
g travellers of her sex, she carried
at deal of valuable property. Be-

sides this luggage there was a folio book
under her arm, very much resembling
the annual volume of a newspaper.
Placing this volume across her knees,
and resting her elbows upon it, with
her forehead in her hands, the
weary, bedraggled, world-worn Old Year
heaved a heavy sigh, and appeared to
be taking no very pleasant retrospect
of her past existence.

While she thus awaited the midnight
knell that was to summon her to the
innumerable sisterhood of departed
Years, there came a young maiden
treading lightsomely on tiptoe along the
street, from the direction of the Railroad Depot. She was evidently a
stranger, and perhaps had come to town
by the evening train of cars. There was
a smiling cheerfulness in this fair
maiden's face, which bespoke her fully
confident of a kind reception from the
multitude of people with whom she was
soon to form acquaintance. Her dress
was rather too airy for the season, and

was bedizened with fluttering ribbons and other vanities, which were likely soon to be rent away by the fierce storms, or to fade in the hot sunshine, amid which she was to pursue her changeful course. But still she was a wonderfully pleasant-looking figure, and had so much promise and such an indescribable hopefulness in her aspect that hardly anybody could meet her without anticipating some very desirable thing,—the consummation of some long-sought good,—from her kind offices. A few dismal characters there may be, here and there about the world, who have so often been trifled with by young maidens as promising as she, that they have now ceased to pin any faith upon the skirts of the New Year. But, for my own part, I have great faith in her; and should I live to see fifty more such, still, from each of those successive sisters, I shall reckon upon receiving something that will be worth living for.

The New Year—for this young maiden was no less a personage—carried all her goods and chattels in a basket of no great size or weight, which hung upon her arm. She greeted the disconsolate Old Year with great affection, and sat down beside her on the steps of the City Hall, waiting for the signal to begin her rambles through the world. The two were own sisters, being both granddaughters of Time; and though one looked so much older than the other, it was rather owing to hardships and trouble than to age, since there was but a twelvemonth's difference between them.

"Well, my dear sister," said the New Year, after the first salutations, "you look almost tired to death. What have you been about during your sojourn in this part of Infinite Space?"

"O, I have it all recorded here in Book of Chronicles," answered the Year, in a heavy tone. "There is noth that would amuse you; and you soon get sufficient knowledge of s matters from your own personal exp ence. It is but tiresome reading."

Nevertheless, she turned over leaves of the folio, and glanced at th by the light of the moon, feeling irresistible spell of interest in her biography, although its incidents w remembered without pleasure. volume, though she termed it her B of Chronicles, seemed to be neit more nor less than the Salem Gaz for 1838; in the accuracy of wl journal the sagacious Old Year had much confidence, that she deeme needless to record her history with own pen.

"What have you been doing in political way?" asked the New Yea

"Why, my course here in the Un States," said the Old Year,—"tho perhaps I ought to blush at the fession,—my political course, I n acknowledge, has been rather vac tory, sometimes inclining towards Whigs,—then causing the Adminis tion party to shout for triumph,— now again uplifting what seemed almost prostrate banner of the Opp tion; so that historians will ha know what to make of me, in respect. But the Loco Focos—"

"I do not like these party nicknam interrupted her sister, who seemed markably touchy about some po "Perhaps we shall part in better hu if we avoid any political discussion

"With all my heart," replied the Year, who had already been torme

f to death with squabbles of this
d. "I care not if the names of Whig
Tory, with their interminable brawls
ut Banks and the Sub-Treasury,
olition, Texas, the Florida War, and
iillion of other topics,—which you
learn soon enough for your own
fort,—I care not, I say, if no whis-
of these matters ever reaches my
again. Yet they have occupied so
e a share of my attention, that I
cely know what else to tell you.
re has indeed been a curious sort
war on the Canada border, where
d has streamed in the names of
erty and Patriotism; but it must
ain for some future, perhaps far
ant Year, to tell whether or no those
names have been rightfully ined. Nothing so much depresses me,
ny view of mortal affairs, as to see
energies wasted, and human life
happiness thrown away, for ends
appear oftentimes unwise, and still
ner remain unaccomplished. But the
st people and the best keep a stead-
faith that the progress of Mankind
nward and upward, and that the toil
anguish of the path serve to wear
y the imperfections of the Immortal
rim, and will be felt no more, when
have done their office."

Perhaps," cried the hopeful New
r, "perhaps I shall see that happy
"

doubt whether it be so close at
d," answered the Old Year, gravely
ing. "You will soon grow weary of
ing for that blessed consummation,
will turn for amusement (as has
uently been my own practice) to
affairs of some sober little city, like
of Salem. Here we sit on the steps
he new City Hall, which has been

completed under my administration; and
it would make you laugh to see how the
game of politics, of which the Capitol
at Washington is the great chessboard,
is here played in miniature. Burning
Ambition finds its fuel here; here Patriotism speaks boldly in the people's
behalf, and virtuous Economy demands
retrenchment in the emoluments of a
lamplighter; here the Aldermen range
their senatorial dignity around the
Mayor's chair of state, and the Common
Council feel that they have liberty in
charge. In short, human weakness and
strength, passion and policy, Man's
tendencies, his aims and modes of pursuing them, his individual character, and
his character in the mass, may be
studied almost as well here as on the
theatre of nations; and with this great
advantage, that, be the lesson ever so
disastrous, its Lilliputian scope still
makes the beholder smile."

"Have you done much for the improvement of the City?" asked the New
Year. "Judging from what little I have
seen, it appears to be ancient and time-
worn."

"I have opened the Railroad," said
the elder Year, "and half a dozen times
a day, you will hear the bell (which
once summoned the Monks of a Spanish
Convent to their devotions) announcing
the arrival or departure of the cars. Old
Salem now wears a much livelier expression than when I first beheld her.
Strangers rumble down from Boston by
hundreds at a time. New faces throng
in Essex Street. Railroad hacks and
omnibuses rattle over the pavements.
There is a perceptible increase of
oyster-shops, and other establishments
for the accommodation of a transitory
diurnal multitude. But a more important

change awaits the venerable town. An immense accumulation of musty prejudices will be carried off by the free circulation of society. A peculiarity of character, of which the inhabitants themselves are hardly sensible, will be rubbed down and worn away by the attrition of foreign substances. Much of the result will be good; there will likewise be a few things not so good. Whether for better or worse, there will be a probable diminution of the moral influence of wealth, and the sway of an aristocratic class, which, from an era far beyond my memory, has held firmer dominion here than in any other New England town."

The Old Year having talked away nearly all of her little remaining breath, now closed her Book of Chronicles, and was about to take her departure. But her sister detained her a while longer, by inquiring the contents of the huge bandbox, which she was so painfully lugging along with her.

"These are merely a few trifles," replied the Old Year, "which I have picked up in my rambles, and am going to deposit, in the receptacle of things past and forgotten. We sisterhood of Years never carry anything really valuable out of the world with us. Here are patterns of most of the fashions which I brought into vogue, and which have already lived out their allotted term. You will supply their place, with others equally ephemeral. Here, put up in little China pots, like rouge, is a considerable lot of beautiful women's bloom, which the disconsolate fair ones owe me a bitter grudge for stealing. I have likewise a quantity of men's dark hair, instead of which, I have left gray locks, or none at all. The tears of

widows and other afflicted mortals, have received comfort during the twelve months, are preserved in s dozens of essence bottles, well co and sealed. I have several bundle love-letters, eloquently breathing eternity of burning passion, which ̨ cold and perished, almost before the was dry. Moreover, here is an sortment of many thousand br promises, and other broken ware, very light and packed into little s The heaviest articles in my posses are a large parcel of disappointed h which, a little while ago, were buo enough to have inflated Mr. Lau balloon."

"I have a fine lot of hopes here i basket," remarked the New "They are a sweet-smelling flowe species of rose."

"They soon lose their perfume,' plied the sombre Old Year. "What have you brought to insure a wel from the discontented race of mort

"Why, to say the truth, little or ing else," said her sister, with a sm "save a few new Annuals and Alma and some New Year's gifts for children. But I heartily wish we poor mortals, and mean to do all I for their improvement and happin

"It is a good resolution," rejoine Old Year; "and, by the way, I ha plentiful assortment of good resolut which have now grown so stale musty, that I am ashamed to them any further. Only for fear the City authorities would send stable Mansfield with a warrant me, I should toss them into the s at once. Many other matters go to up the contents of my bandbox; the whole lot would not fetch a

even at an auction of worn-out
iture; and as they are worth noth-
either to you or anybody else, I
not trouble you with a longer
logue."

nd must I also pick up such worth-
luggage in my travels?" asked the
Year.

ost certainly,—and well, if you
no heavier load to bear," replied
other. "And now, my dear sister,
ust bid you farewell, earnestly ad-
g and exhorting you to expect no
tude nor good will from this peev-
unreasonable, inconsiderate, ill-in-
ing, and worse-behaving world.
ever warmly its inhabitants may
to welcome you, yet, do what you
, and lavish on them what means
appiness you please, they will still
omplaining, still craving what it is
in your power to give, still looking
ard to some other Year for the
mplishment of projects which ought
r to have been formed, and which,
iccessful, would only provide new
ciono of discontent. If these ridicu-
people ever seen anything tolerable
ou, it will be after you are gone
ver."

ut I," cried the fresh-hearted New
, "I shall try to leave men wiser
I find them. I will offer them freely
ever good gifts Providence permits
o distribute, and will tell them to
hankful for what they have, and
bly hopeful for more; and surely,
ey are not absolute fools, they will
escend to be happy, and will allow
o be a happy Year. For my happi-
must depend on them."

las for you, then, my poor sister!"
the Old Year, sighing, as she up-
her burden. "We grandchildren of

Time are born to trouble. Happiness,
they say, dwells in the mansions of
Eternity; but we can only lead mortals
thither, step by step, with reluctant
murmurings, and ourselves must perish
on the threshold. But hark! my task is
done."

The clock in the tall steeple of Dr.
Emerson's church struck twelve; there
was a response from Dr. Flint's, in the
opposite quarter of the city; and while
the strokes were yet dropping into the
air, the Old Year either flitted or faded
away,—and not the wisdom and might
of Angels, to say nothing of the remorseful yearnings of the millions who
had used her ill, could have prevailed
with that departed Year to return one
step. But she, in the company of Time
and all her kindred, must hereafter hold
a reckoning with Mankind. So shall it
be, likewise, with the maidenly New
Year, who, as the clock ceased to strike,
arose from the steps of the City Hall
and set out rather timorously on her
earthly course.

"A happy New Year!" cried a watchman, eying her figure very questionably,
but without the least suspicion that he
was addressing the New Year in person.

"Thank you kindly!" said the New
Year; and she gave the watchman
one of the roses of hope from her
basket. "May this flower keep a sweet
smell long after I have bidden you
good-by."

Then she stepped on more briskly
through the silent streets; and such as
were awake at the moment heard her
footfall, and said, "The New Year is
come!" Wherever there was a knot of
midnight roisterers they quaffed her
health. She sighed, however, to perceive
that the air was tainted—as the atmos-

phere of this world must continually be—with the dying breaths of mortals who had lingered just long enough for her to bury them. But there were millions left alive to rejoice at her coming; and so she pursued her way with confidence, strewing emblematic flowers on the doorstep of almost every dwelling, which some persons will gather up and wear in their bosoms, and others will trample under foot. The Carrier can only say further, that, early morning, she filled his basket with Year's Addresses, assuring him that whole City, with our new Mayor, the Aldermen and Common Counci its head, would make a general rus secure copies. Kind Patrons, will you redeem the pledge of the N YEAR?

SNOW-FLAKES

THERE is snow in yonder cold gray sky of the morning!—and, through the partially frosted window-panes, I love to watch the gradual beginning of the storm. A few feathery flakes are scattered widely through the air, and hover downward with uncertain flight, now almost alighting on the earth, now whirled again aloft into remote regions of the atmosphere. These are not the big flakes, heavy with moisture, which melt as they touch the ground, and are portentous of a soaking rain. It is to be, in good earnest, a wintry storm. The two or three people visible on the sidewalks have an aspect of endurance, a blue-nosed, frosty fortitude, which is evidently assumed in anticipation of a comfortless and blustering day. By nightfall, or at least before the sun sheds another glimmering smile upon us, the street and our little garden will be heaped with mountain snow-drifts. The soil, already frozen for weeks past, is prepared to sustain whatever burden may be laid upon it; and, to a Northern eye, the landscape will lose its melancholy bleakness and acquire a beauty of its own, when Mother Earth, like children, shall have put on the fl garb of her winter's wear. The c spirits are slowly weaving her w mantle. As yet, indeed, there is ba a rime like hoarfrost over the br surface of the street; the withered g of the grass plat is still discernible; the slated roofs of the houses do begin to look gray, instead of black the snow that has yet fallen within circumference of my view, wer heaped up together, would hardly e the hillock of a grave. Thus gradu by silent and stealthy influences, great changes wrought. These little s particles, which the storm spirit f by handfuls through the air, will the great earth under their accumul mass, nor permit her to behold her ter sky again for dreary months. likewise, shall lose sight of our mot familiar visage, and must content selves with looking heavenward oftener.

Now, leaving the storm to do his pointed office, let us sit down, pe hand, by our fireside. Gloomy as it

n, there is an influence productive of
erfulness, and favorable to imagina-
thought, in the atmosphere of a
vy day. The native of a southern
ie may woo the muse beneath the
/y shade of summer foliage, reclining
banks of turf, while the sound of
,ing birds and warbling rivulets
nes in with the music of his soul.
ur brief summer, I do not think, but
' exist in the vague enjoyment of a
im. My hour of inspiration—if that
r ever comes—is when the green log
es upon the hearth, and the bright
e, brighter for the gloom of the
nber, rustles high up the chimney,
the coals drop tinkling down among
growing heaps of ashes. When the
ment rattles in the gust, and the
v-flakes or the sleety rain-drops pelt
I against the window-panes, then I
ad out my sheet of paper, with the
iinty that thoughts and fancies will
n forth upon it, like stars at twi-
, or like violets in May,—perhaps
ade as soon. However transitory
' glow, they at least shine amid the
some shadow which the clouds of
outward sky fling through the room.
sed, therefore, and reverently wel-
ed by me, her true-born son, be
England's winter, which makes us,
and all, the nurslings of the storm,
sings a familiar lullaby even in the
est shriek of the December blast.
look we forth again, and see how
i of his task the storm spirit has
.
ow and sure! He has the day, perce the week, before him, and may
his own time to accomplish Na-
s burial in snow. A smooth mantle
ircely yet thrown over the withered
plat, and the dry stalks of an-

nuals still thrust themselves through the
white surface in all parts of the garden.
The leafless rose-bushes stand shivering
in a shallow snow-drift, looking, poor
things! as disconsolate as if they possessed a human consciousness of the
dreary scene. This is a sad time for the
shrubs that do not perish with the summer; they neither live nor die; what
they retain of life seems but the chilling sense of death. Very sad are the
flower-shrubs in midwinter! The roofs
of the houses are now all white, save
where the eddying wind has kept them
bare at the bleak corners. To discern
the real intensity of the storm, we must
fix upon some distant object,—as yonder spire,—and observe how the riotous
gust fights with the descending snow
throughout the intervening space. Sometimes the entire prospect is obscured;
then, again, we have a distinct, but
transient glimpse of the tall steeple,
like a giant's ghost; and now the dense
wreaths sweep between, as if demons
were flinging snow-drifts at each other
in mid-air. Look next into the street,
where we have an amusing parallel to
the combat of those fancied demons in
the upper regions. It is a snow battle
of school-boys. What a pretty satire on
war and military glory might be written,
in the form of a child's story, by describing the snowball fights of two rival
schools, the alternate defeats and victories of each, and the final triumph of
one party, or perhaps of neither! What
pitched battles, worthy to be chanted in
Homeric strains! What storming of for-
tresses, built all of massive snow-blocks!
What feats of individual prowess, and
embodied onsets of martial enthusiasm!
And when some well-contested and decisive victory had put a period to the

war, both armies should unite to build a lofty monument of snow upon the battle-field, and crown it with the victor's statue, hewn of the same frozen marble. In a few days or weeks thereafter, the passer-by would observe a shapeless mound upon the level common; and, unmindful of the famous victory, would ask, "How came it there? Who reared it? And what means it?" The shattered pedestal of many a battle monument has provoked these questions, when none could answer.

Turn we again to the fireside, and sit musing there, lending our ears to the wind, till perhaps it shall seem like an articulate voice, and dictate wild and airy matter for the pen. Would it might inspire me to sketch out the personification of a New England winter! And that idea, if I can seize the snow-wreathed figures that flit before my fancy, shall be the theme of the next page.

How does Winter herald his approach? By the shrieking blast of latter autumn, which is Nature's cry of lamentation, as the destroyer rushes among the shivering groves where she has lingered, and scatters the sear leaves upon the tempest. When that cry is heard, the people wrap themselves in cloaks, and shake their heads disconsolately, saying, "Winter is at hand!" Then the axe of the woodcutter echoes sharp and diligently in the forest, then the coal merchants rejoice, because each shriek of Nature in her agony adds something to the price of coal per ton, —then the peat smoke spreads its aromatic fragrance through the atmosphere. A few days more; and at eventide, the children look out of the window, and dimly perceive the flaunting of a snowy

mantle in the air. It is stern Wint vesture. They crowd around the hea and cling to their mother's gown, press between their father's knees, frightened by the hollow roaring v that bellows adown the wide flue of chimney. It is the voice of Winter; when parents and children hear it, shudder and exclaim, "Winter is co Cold Winter has begun his r already!" Now, throughout New I land, each hearth becomes an a sending up the smoke of a conti sacrifice to the immitigable deity tyrannizes over forest, country side town. Wrapped in his white ma his staff a huge icicle, his beard hair a wind-tossed snow-drift, he tra over the land in the midst of the n ern blast; and woe to the homeless derer whom he finds upon his p There he lies stark and stiff, a hu shape of ice, on the spot where W overtook him. On strides the ty over the rushing rivers and broad I which turn to rock beneath his foots His dreary empire is established around stretches the desolation of Pole. Yet not ungrateful be his England children,—for Winter is sire, though a stern and rough o not ungrateful even for the seve which have nourished our unyie strength of character. And let us t him, too, for the sleigh-rides, ch by the music of merry bells,—fo crackling and rustling hearth, whe ruddy firelight gleams on hardy hood and the blooming cheek of Wo —for all the home enjoyments, an kindred virtues which flourish frozen soil. Not that we grieve, after some seven months of storn bitter frost, Spring, in the guise

ver-crowned virgin, is seen driving
ay the hoary despot, pelting him with
lets by the handful, and strewing
en grass on the path behind him.
en, ere he will give up his empire,
Winter rushes fiercely back and
ds a snow-drift at the shrinking form
Spring; yet, step by step, he is com-
ed to retreat northward, and spends
summer months within the Arctic
le.

uch fantasies, intermixed among
ver toils of mind, have made the
ter's day pass pleasantly. Meanwhile,
storm has raged without abatement,
now, as the brief afternoon de-
es, is tossing denser volumes to and
about the atmosphere. On the win-
-sill there is a layer of snow, reach-
half-way up the lowest pane of
s. The garden is one unbroken bed.
ng the street are two or three spots
uncovered earth, where the gust has
rled away the snow, heaping it else-
re to the fence-tops, or piling huge
ks against the doors of houses. A
ary passenger is seen, now striding
-leg deep across a drift, now scud-
: over the bare ground, while his
k is swollen with the wind. And
the jingling of bells, a sluggish
ad, responsive to the horse's toil-
e progress through the unbroken
ts, announces the passage of a sleigh,
a boy clinging behind, and duck-
his head to escape detection by

the driver. Next comes a sledge, laden
with wood for some unthrifty housekeeper, whom winter has surprised at
a cold hearth. But what dismal equipage
now struggles along the uneven street?
A sable hearse, bestrewn with snow, is
bearing a dead man through the storm
to his frozen bed. O how dreary is a
burial in winter, when the bosom of
Mother Earth has no warmth for her
poor child!

Evening—the early eve of December
—begins to spread its deepening veil
over the comfortless scene; the firelight
gradually brightens, and throws my
flickering shadow upon the walls and
ceiling of the chamber; but still the
storm rages and rattles against the windows. Alas! I shiver, and think it time to
be disconsolate. But, taking a farewell
glance at dead nature in her shroud,
I perceive a flock of snow-birds, skim-
ming lightsomely through the tempest,
and flitting from drift to drift as spor-
tively as swallows in the delightful prime
of summer. Whence come they? Where
do they build their nests, and seek their
food? Why, having airy wings, do they
not follow summer around the earth,
instead of making themselves the playmates of the storm, and fluttering on
the dreary verge of the winter's eve?
I know not whence they come, nor
why; yet my spirit has been cheered
by that wandering flock of snow-birds.

THE SEVEN VAGABONDS

AMBLING on foot in the spring of
life and the summer of the year,
me one afternoon to a point which

gave me the choice of three directions.
Straight before me, the main road extended its dusty length to Boston; on

the left a branch went towards the sea, and would have lengthened my journey a trifle, of twenty or thirty miles; while, by the right-hand path, I might have gone over hills and lakes to Canada, visiting in my way the celebrated town of Stamford. On a level spot of grass, at the foot of the guide-post, appeared an object, which, though locomotive on a different principle, reminded me of Gulliver's portable mansion among the Brobdignags. It was a huge covered wagon, or more properly, a small house on wheels, with a door on one side and a window shaded by green blinds on the other. Two horses, munching provender out of the baskets which muzzled them, were fastened near the vehicle: a delectable sound of music proceeded from the interior; and I immediately conjectured that this was some itinerant show, halting at the confluence of the roads to intercept such idle travellers as myself. A shower had long been climbing up the western sky, and now hung so blackly over my onward path that it was a point of wisdom to seek shelter here.

"Halloo! Who stands guard here? Is the doorkeeper asleep?" cried I, approaching a ladder of two or three steps which was let down from the wagon.

The music ceased at my summons, and there appeared at the door, not the sort of figure that I had mentally assigned to the wandering showman, but a most respectable old personage, whom I was sorry to have addressed in so free a style. He wore a snuff-colored coat and smallclothes, with white-top boots, and exhibited the mild dignity of aspect and manner which may often be noticed in aged schoolmasters, and sometimes in deacons, selectmen, or other poten-

tates of that kind. A small piece of ver was my passport within his pr ises, where I found only one other son, hereafter to be described.

"This is a dull day for busine said the old gentleman, as he ushe me in; "but I merely tarry here to fresh the cattle, being bound for camp-meeting at Stamford."

Perhaps the movable scene of narrative is still peregrinating New I land, and may enable the reader to the accuracy of my description. spectacle—for I will not use the worthy term of puppet-show—consi of a multitude of little people assem on a miniature stage. Among them artisans of every kind, in the attit of their toil, and a group of fair la and gay gentlemen standing ready the dance; a company of foot sol formed a line across the stage, loo stern, grim, and terrible enough make it a pleasant consideration they were but three inches high; conspicuous above the whole was a Merry Andrew, in the pointed cap motley coat of his profession. All inhabitants of this mimic world motionless, like the figures in a pic or like that people who one mo were alive in the midst of their bus and delights, and the next were t formed to statues, preserving an et semblance of labor that was ended, pleasure that could be felt no r Anon, however, the old gentl turned the handle of a barrel o the first note of which produc most enlivening effect upon the fig and awoke them all to their prope cupations and amusements. By the same impulse the tailor plied his ne the blacksmith's hammer desce

n the anvil, and the dancers whirled
y on feathery tiptoes; the company
oldiers broke into platoons, retreated
n the stage, and were succeeded by
:oop of horse, who came prancing
ard with such a sound of trumpets
trampling of hoofs, as might have
tled Don Quixote himself; while an
toper, of inveterate ill habits, up-
d his black bottle and took off a
ty swig. Meantime the Merry An-
w began to caper and turn somersets,
king his sides, nodding his head, and
king his eyes in as lifelike a man-
as if he were ridiculing the nonsense
ill human affairs, and making fun
he whole multitude beneath him.
ength the old magician (for I com-
d the showman to Prospero, enter-
ng his guests with a mask of shad-
paused that I might give utterance
iy wonder.

Vhat an admirable piece of work
iis!" exclaimed I, lifting up my
ls in astonishment.

deed, I liked the spectacle, and was
ed with the old man's gravity as
resided at it, for I had none of
foolish wisdom which reproves
y occupation that is not useful in
world of vanities. If there be a
ity which I possess more perfectly
most men, it is that of throwing
lf mentally into situations foreign
y own, and detecting, with a cheer-
ye, the desirable circumstances of
I could have envied the life of
gray-headed showman, spent as it
been in a course of safe and pleas-
e adventure, in driving his huge
le sometimes through the sands of
Cod, and sometimes over the rough
t roads of the north and east, and
ig now on the green before a vil-

lage meeting-house, and now in a paved
square of the metropolis. How often
must his heart have been gladdened by
the delight of children, as they viewed
these animated figures! or his pride indulged, by haranguing learnedly to
grown men on the mechanical powers
which produced such wonderful effects!
or his gallantry brought into play (for
this is an attribute which such grave
men do not lack) by the visits of
pretty maidens! And then with how
fresh a feeling must he return, at intervals, to his own peculiar home!

"I would I were assured of as happy
a life as his," thought I.

Though the showman's wagon might
have accommodated fifteen or twenty
spectators, it now contained only himself and me, and a third person at whom
I threw a glance on entering. He was
a neat and trim young man of two
or three and twenty; his drab hat, and
green frock-coat with velvet collar, were
smart, though no longer new; while a
pair of green spectacles, that seemed
needless to his brisk little eyes, gave
him something of a scholar-like and
literary air. After allowing me a sufficient time to inspect the puppets, he advanced with a bow, and drew my attention to some books in a corner of
the wagon. These he forthwith began
to extol, with an amazing volubility
of well-sounding words, and an ingenuity of praise that won him my heart,
as being myself one of the most merciful of critics. Indeed, his stock required
some considerable powers of commen-
dation in the salesman; there were several ancient friends of mine, the novels
of those happy days when my affections
wavered between the Scottish Chiefs
and Thomas Thumb; besides a few of

later date, whose merits had not been acknowledged by the public. I was glad to find that dear little venerable volume, the New England Primer, looking as antique as ever, though in its thousandth new edition; a bundle of superannuated gilt picture-books made such a child of me, that, partly for the glittering covers, and partly for the fairy-tales within, I bought the whole; and an assortment of ballads and popular theatrical songs drew largely on my purse. To balance these expenditures, I meddled neither with sermons, nor science, nor morality, though volumes of each were there; nor with a Life of Franklin in the coarsest of paper, but so showily bound that it was emblematical of the Doctor himself, in the court dress which he refused to wear at Paris; nor with Webster's Spelling-Book, nor some of Byron's minor poems, nor half a dozen little Testaments at twenty-five cents each.

Thus far the collection might have been swept from some great bookstore, or picked up at an evening auction-room; but there was one small blue-covered pamphlet, which the pedler handed me with so peculiar an air that I purchased it immediately at his own price; and then, for the first time, the thought struck me, that I had spoken face to face with the veritable author of a printed book. The literary man now evinced a great kindness for me, and I ventured to inquire which way he was travelling.

"O," said he, "I keep company with this old gentleman here, and we are moving now towards the camp-meeting at Stamford."

He then explained to me, that for the present season he had rented a cor-

ner of the wagon as a book-store, wh as he wittily observed, was a true culating Library, since there were parts of the country where it had gone its rounds. I approved of the exceedingly, and began to sum up w in my mind the many uncommon fe ties in the life of a book-pedler, e cially when his character resembled of the individual before me. At a rate was to be reckoned the daily hourly enjoyment of such interview the present, in which he seized u the admiration of a passing stran and made him aware that a man literary taste, and even of lite achievement, was travelling the cou in a showman's wagon. A more valua yet not infrequent triumph, might won in his conversations with s elderly clergyman, long vegetating rocky, woody, watery back settle of New England, who, as he recru his library from the pedler's stoc sermons, would exhort him to se college education and become the scholar in his class. Sweeter and pro yet would be his sensations, when, ing poetry while he sold spelling-bc he should charm the mind, and h touch the heart of a fair country sc mistress, herself an unhonored poe a wearer of blue stockings which but himself took pains to look at. the scene of his completest glory, w be when the wagon had halted for night, and his stock of books was t ferred to some crowded bar-room. would he recommend to the mult ous company, whether traveller the city, or teamster from the hill neighboring squire, or the landlord self, or his loutish hostler, works s to each particular taste and capa

⸱ving, all the while, by acute criticism
⸱ profound remark, that the lore in
books was even exceeded by that
his brain.

Thus happily would he traverse the
⸱d; sometimes a herald before the
⸱rch of Mind; sometimes walking arm
⸱rm with awful Literature; and reap-
⸱ everywhere a harvest of real and
⸱sible popularity, which the secluded
⸱kworms, by whose toil he lived could
⸱er hope for.

If ever I meddle with literature,"
⸱ught I, fixing myself with adaman-
⸱ ⸱resolution, "it shall be as a trav-
⸱ag bookseller."

⸱hough it was still mid-afternoon, the
⸱had now grown dark about us, and
⸱⸱w drops of rain came down upon
⸱ roof of our vehicle, pattering like
⸱ feet of birds that had flown thither
⸱est. A sound of pleasant voices made
⸱isten, and there soon appeared half-
⸱ ⸱ up the ladder the pretty person
⸱ young damsel, whose rosy face was
⸱heerful, that even amid the gloomy
⸱ it seemed as if the sunbeams were
⸱ing under her bonnet. We next saw
⸱dark and handsome features of a
⸱ag man, who, with easier gallantry
⸱ might have been expected in the
⸱t of Yankee-land, was assisting her
⸱the wagon. It became immediately
⸱ent to us, when the two strangers
⸱d within the door, that they were
⸱ profession kindred to those of my
⸱panions; and I was delighted with
⸱more than hospitable, the even pa-
⸱al kindness, of the old showman's
⸱ner, as he welcomed them; while
⸱man of literature hastened to lead
⸱merry-eyed girl to a seat on the
⸱bench.

⸱ou are housed but just in time, my

young friends," said the master of the
wagon. "The sky would have been down
upon you within five minutes."

The young man's reply marked him
as a foreigner, not by any variation
from the idiom and accent of good
English, but because he spoke with more
caution and accuracy, than if perfectly
familiar with the language.

"We knew that a shower was hanging
over us," said he, "and consulted
whether it were best to enter the house
on the top of yonder hill, but seeing
your wagon in the road—"

"We agreed to come hither," interrupted the girl, with a smile, "because
we should be more at home in a wandering house like this."

I, meanwhile, with many a wild and
undetermined fantasy, was narrowly in-
specting these two doves that had flown
into our ark. The young man, tall, agile,
and athletic, wore a mass of black shining curls clustering round a dark and
vivacious countenance, which, if it had
not greater expression, was at least more
active, and attracted readier notice, than
the quiet faces of our countrymen. At
his first appearance, he had been laden
with a neat mahogany box, of about
two feet square, but very light in proportion to its size, which he had immediately unstrapped from his shoulders
and deposited on the floor of the wagon.

The girl had nearly as fair a complexion as our own beauties, and a
brighter one than most of them; the
lightness of her figure, which seemed
calculated to traverse the whole world
without weariness, suited well with the
glowing cheerfulness of her face; and
her gay attire, combining the rainbow
hues of crimson, green, and a deep
orange, was as proper to her lightsome

aspect as if she had been born in it. This gay stranger was appropriately burdened with that mirth-inspiring instrument, the fiddle, which her companion took from her hands, and shortly began the process of tuning. Neither of us—the previous company of the wagon —needed to inquire their trade; for this could be no mystery to frequenters of brigade musters, ordinations, cattleshows, commencements, and other festal meetings in our sober land; and there is a dear friend of mine, who will smile when this page recalls to his memory a chivalrous deed performed by us in rescuing the show-box of such a couple from a mob of great double-fisted countrymen.

"Come," said I to the damsel of gay attire, "shall we visit all the wonders of the world together?"

She understood the metaphor at once; though indeed it would not much have troubled me, if she had assented to the literal meaning of my words. The mahogany box was placed in a proper position, and I peeped in through its small round magnifying window, while the girl sat by my side, and gave short descriptive sketches, as one after another the pictures were unfolded to my view. We visited together, at least our imaginations did, full many a famous city, in the streets of which I had long yearned to tread; once, I remember, we were in the harbor of Barcelona, gazing townwards; next, she bore me through the air to Sicily, and bade me look up at blazing Ætna; then we took wings to Venice, and sat in a gondola beneath the arch of the Rialto; and anon she sat me down among the thronged spectators at the coronation of Napoleon. But there was one scene, its locality she could not

tell, which charmed my attention lor than all those gorgeous palaces churches, because the fancy hau me, that I myself, the preceding s mer, had beheld just such a hun meeting-house, in just such a pine-rounded nook, among our own gr mountains. All these pictures were erably executed, though far inferio the girl's touches of description; was it easy to comprehend, how ir few sentences, and these, as I suppc in a language foreign to her, she trived to present an airy copy of varied scene. When we had trav through the vast extent of the mahog box, I looked into my guide's face.

"Where are you going, my pr maid?" inquired I, in the words o old song.

"Ah," said the gay damsel, might as well ask where the sun wind is going. We are wanderers and there, and everywhere. Wher there is mirth, our merry hearts drawn to it. To-day, indeed, the pe have told us of a great frolic and tival in these parts; so perhaps we be needed at what you call the ca meeting at Stamford."

Then in my happy youth, and v her pleasant voice yet sounded in ears, I sighed; for none but myse thought, should have been her com ion in a life which seemed to re my own wild fancies, cherished through visionary boyhood to that l To these two strangers, the world in its golden age, not that indeed it less dark and sad than ever, but cause its weariness and sorrow ha community with their ethereal na Wherever they might appear in pilgrimage of bliss, Youth would

k their gladness, care-stricken Ma-
ity would rest a moment from its
, and Age, tottering among the
ves, would smile in withered joy for
ir sakes. The lonely cot, the narrow
gloomy street, the sombre shade,
ild catch a passing gleam like that
shining on ourselves, as these bright
its wandered by. Blessed pair, whose
ppy home was throughout all the
h! I looked at my shoulders, and
ight them broad enough to sustain
se pictured towns and mountains;
e, too, was an elastic foot, as tire-
as the wing of the bird of paradise;
e was then an untroubled heart,
would have gone singing on its de-
tful way.

O maiden!" said I aloud, "why did
not come hither alone?"

While the merry girl and myself were
with the showbox, the unceasing
had driven another wayfarer into
wagon. He seemed pretty nearly
the old showman's age, but much
ller, leaner, and more withered than
and less respectably clad in a
hed suit of gray; withal, he had
in, shrewd countenance, and a pair
liminutive gray eyes, which peeped
er too keenly out of their puckered
ets. This old fellow had been joking
the showman, in a manner which
nated previous acquaintance; but
eiving that the damsel and I had
inated our affairs, he drew forth
lded document, and presented it to
As I had anticipated, it proved to
a circular, written in a very fair
legible hand, and signed by several
nguished gentlemen whom I had
r heard of, stating that the bearer
encountered every variety of mis-
ine, and recommending him to the

notice of all charitable people. Previous
disbursements had left me no more than
a five-dollar bill, out of which, however, I offered to make the beggar a
donation, provided he would give me
change for it. The object of my beneficence looked keenly in my face, and
discerned that I had none of that abominable spirit, characteristic though it be
of a full-blooded Yankee, which takes
pleasure in detecting every little harmless piece of knavery.

"Why, perhaps," said the ragged old
mendicant, "if the bank is in good
standing, I can't say but I may have
enough about me to change your bill."

"It is a bill of the Suffolk Bank," said
I, "and better than the specie."

As the beggar had nothing to object,
he now produced a small buff-leather
bag, tied up carefully with a shoestring.
When this was opened, there appeared
a very comfortable treasure of silver
coins, of all sorts and sizes; and I
even fancied that I saw, gleaming among
them, the golden plumage of that rare
bird in our currency, the American
Eagle. In this precious heap was my
bank-note deposited, the rate of exchange being considerably against me.
His wants being thus relieved, the destitute man pulled out of his pocket
an old pack of greasy cards, which had
probably contributed to fill the buff-
leather bag, in more ways than one.

"Come," said he, "I spy a rare fortune in your face, and for twenty-five
cents more, I'll tell you what it is."

I never refuse to take a glimpse into
futurity; so, after shuffling the cards,
and when the fair damsel had cut them,
I dealt a portion to the prophetic beggar. Like others of his profession, before predicting the shadowy events that

were moving on to meet me, he gave proof of his preternatural science, by describing scenes through which I had already passed. Here let me have credit for a sober fact. When the old man had read a page in his book of fate, he bent his keen gray eyes on mine, and proceeded to relate, in all its minute particulars, what was then the most singular event of my life. It was one which I had no purpose to disclose, till the general unfolding of all secrets; nor would it be a much stranger instance of inscrutable knowledge, or fortunate conjecture, if the beggar were to meet me in the street to-day, and repeat, word for word, the page which I have here written. The fortune-teller, after predicting a destiny which time seems loath to make good, put up his cards, secreted his treasure-bag, and began to converse with the other occupants of the wagon.

"Well, old friend," said the showman, "you have not yet told us which way your face is turned this afternoon."

"I am taking a trip northward, this warm weather," replied the conjurer, "across the Connecticut first, and then up through Vermont, and may be into Canada before the fall. But I must stop and see the breaking up of the camp-meeting at Stamford."

I began to think that all the vagrants in New England were converging to the camp-meeting, and had made this wagon their rendezvous by the way. The showman now proposed, that, when the shower was over, they should pursue the road to Stamford together, it being sometimes the policy of these people to form a sort of league or confederacy.

"And the young lady too," observed the gallant bibliopolist, bowing to her

profoundly, "and this foreign gent man, as I understand, are on a jau of pleasure to the same spot. It wo add incalculably to my own enjoyme and I presume to that of my collea and his friend, if they could be preva upon to join our party."

This arrangement met with appro tion on all hands, nor were any of th concerned more sensible of its adv tages than myself, who had no t to be included in it. Having alrea satisfied myself as to the several mo in which the four others attained fe ity, I next set my mind at work to cover what enjoyments were pecu to the old "Straggler," as the people the country would have termed wandering mendicant and prophet. he pretended to familiarity with Devil, so I fancied that he was fi to pursue and take delight in his of life, by possessing some of the m tal and moral characteristics, the lig and more comic ones, of the Devi popular stories. Among them might reckoned a love of deception for own sake, a shrewd eye and keen re for human weakness and ridiculous firmity, and the talent of petty fr Thus to this old man there would pleasure even in the consciousness insupportable to some minds, that whole life was a cheat upon the w and that, so far as he was concer with the public, his little cunning the upper hand of its united wisc Every day would furnish him wi succession of minute and pungent umphs; as when, for instance, his portunity wrung a pittance out of heart of a miser, or when my silly nature transferred a part of my sle purse to his plump leather bag; or

me ostentatious gentleman should
row a coin to the ragged beggar who
is richer than himself; or when,
ough he would not always be so de-
ledly diabolical, his pretended wants
ould make him a sharer in the scanty
ing of real indigence. And then what
  inexhaustible field of enjoyment,
th as enabling him to discern so much
ly and achieve such quantities of
nor mischief, was opened to his sneer-
; spirit by his pretensions to prophetic
owledge.

All this was a sort of happiness which
ould conceive of, though I had little
npathy with it. Perhaps, had I been
n inclined to admit it, I might have
nd that the roving life was more
per to him than to either of his
npanions; for Satan, to whom I had
npared the poor man, has delighted,
r since the time of Job, in "wander-
 up and down upon the earth"; and
eed a crafty disposition, which op-
tes not in deep-laid plans, but in
connected tricks, could not have an
quate scope, unless naturally im-
led to a continual change of scene
l society. My reflections were here
errupted.

"Another visitor!" exclaimed the old
wman.

The door of the wagon had been
sed against the tempest, which was
ring and blustering with prodigious
y and commotion, and beating vio-
ly against our shelter, as if it claimed
 those homeless people for its law-
prey, while we, caring little for the
pleasure of the elements, sat com-
tably talking. There was now an at-
pt to open the door, succeeded by
voice, uttering some strange, unin-
igible gibberish, which my compan-

ions mistook for Greek, and I suspected
to be thieves' Latin. However, the showman stepped forward, and gave admittance to a figure which made me imagine, either that our wagon had rolled
back two hundred years into past ages,
or that the forest and its old inhabitants
had sprung up around us by enchantment.

It was a red Indian, armed with his
bow and arrow. His dress was a sort
of cap, adorned with a single feather
of some wild bird, and a frock of blue
cotton, girded tight about him; on his
breast, like orders of knighthood, hung
a crescent and a circle, and other ornaments of silver; while a small crucifix
betokened that our Father the Pope had
interposed between the Indian and the
Great Spirit, whom he had worshipped
in his simplicity. This son of the wilderness, and pilgrim of the storm, took his
place silently in the midst of us. When
the first surprise was over, I rightly
conjectured him to be one of the Penobscot tribe, parties of which I had often
seen, in their summer excursions down
our Eastern rivers. There they paddle
their birch canoes among the coasting
schooners, and build their wigwam beside some roaring milldam, and drive a
little trade in basket-work where their
fathers hunted deer. Our new visitor
was probably wandering through the
country towards Boston, subsisting on
the careless charity of the people, while
he turned his archery to profitable account by shooting at cents, which were
to be the prize of his successful aim.

The Indian had not long been seated,
ere our merry damsel sought to draw
him into conversation. She, indeed,
seemed all made up of sunshine in the
month of May; for there was nothing

so dark and dismal that her pleasant mind could not cast a glow over it; and the wild man, like a fir-tree in his native forest, soon began to brighten into a sort of sombre cheerfulness. At length, she inquired whether his journey had any particular end or purpose.

"I go shoot at the camp-meeting at Stamford," replied the Indian.

"And here are five more," said the girl, "all aiming at the camp-meeting too. You shall be one of us, for we travel with light hearts; and as for me, I sing merry songs, and tell merry tales; and am full of merry thoughts, and I dance merrily along the road, so that there is never any sadness among them that keep me company. But, O, you would find it very dull indeed to go all the way to Stamford alone!"

My ideas of the aboriginal character led me to fear that the Indian would prefer his own solitary musings to the gay society thus offered him; on the contrary, the girl's proposal met with immediate acceptance, and seemed to animate him with a misty expectation of enjoyment. I now gave myself up to a course of thought which, whether it flowed naturally from this combination of events, or was drawn forth by a wayward fancy, caused my mind to thrill as if I were listening to deep music. I saw mankind, in this weary old age of the world, either enduring a sluggish existence amid the smoke and dust of cities, or, if they breathed a purer air, still lying down at night with no hope but to wear out to-morrow, and all the to-morrows which make up life, among the same dull scenes and in the same wretched toil that had darkened the sunshine of to-day. But there were some, full of the primeval

instinct, who preserved the freshness youth to their latest years by the c tinual excitement of new objects, n pursuits, and new associates; and ca little, though their birthplace mi have been here in New England, if grave should close over them in Cent Asia. Fate was summoning a parliam of these free spirits; unconscious the impulse which directed them t common centre, they had come hit from far and near; and last of appeared the representative of th mighty vagrants who had chased deer during thousands of years, were chasing it now in the Spirit La Wandering down through the waste ages, the woods had vanished arou his path; his arm had lost somew of its strength, his foot of its fleetn his mien of its wild regality, his he and mind of their savage virtue and cultured force; but here, untamable the routine of artificial life, roving along the dusty road, as of old over forest leaves, here was the Indian s

"Well," said the old showman, in midst of my meditations, "here is honest company of us—one, two, th four, five, six—all going to the ca meeting at Stamford. Now, hoping offence, I should like to know wh this young gentleman may be goin

I started. How came I among t wanderers? The free mind that ferred its own folly to another's dom; the open spirit, that found c panions everywhere; above all, restless impulse, that had so o made me wretched in the midst of joyments; these were my claims t of their society.

"My friends!" cried I, stepping the centre of the wagon, "I am g

h you to the camp-meeting at Stam-
d."

'But in what capacity?" asked the
showman, after a moment's silence.
ll of us here can get our bread in
ie creditable way. Every honest man
uld have his livelihood. You, sir, as
ake it, are a mere strolling gentle-
n."

proceeded to inform the company,
t, when Nature gave me a propen-
to their way of life, she had not
me altogether destitute of qualifi-
ons for it; though I could not deny
: my talent was less respectable, and
ht be less profitable than the mean-
of theirs. My design, in short, was
imitate the story-tellers of whom
ntal travellers have told us, and
me an itinerant novelist, reciting
own extemporaneous fictions to such
iences as I could collect.

Either this," said I, "is my voca-
, or I have been born in vain."

he fortune-teller, with a sly wink
he company, proposed to take me
in apprentice to one or the other
his professions, either of which,
oubtedly, would have given full
e to whatever inventive talent I
it possess. The bibliopolist spoke a
words in opposition to my plan,
enced partly, I suspect, by the
usy of authorship, and partly by
apprehension that the *viva voce*
tice would become general among
lists, to the infinite detriment of
book-trade. Dreading a rejection,
licited the interest of the merry
sel.

Iirth," cried I, most aptly appro-
ing the words of L'Allegro, "to
I sue! Mirth, admit me of thy
!"

"Let us indulge the poor youth," said
Mirth, with a kindness which made me
love her dearly, though I was no such
coxcomb as to misinterpret her motives. "I have espied much promise in
him. True, a shadow sometimes flits
across his brow, but the sunshine is
sure to follow in a moment. He is never
guilty of a sad thought, but a merry
one is twin born with it. We will take
him with us; and you shall see that he
will set us all a-laughing before we
reach the camp-meeting at Stamford."

Her voice silenced the scruples of the
rest, and gained me admittance into the
league; according to the terms of which,
without community of goods or profits,
we were to lend each other all the aid,
and avert all the harm, that might be
in our power. This affair settled, a marvellous jollity entered into the whole
tribe of us, manifesting itself charac-
teristically in each individual. The old
showman, sitting down to his barrel-
organ, stirred up the souls of the pygmy
people with one of the quickest tunes in
the music-book; tailors, blacksmiths,
gentlemen, and ladies, all seemed to
share in the spirit of the occasion; and
the Merry Andrew played his part more
facetiously than ever, nodding and winking particularly at me. The young foreigner flourished his fiddle-bow with a
master's hand, and gave an inspiring
echo to the showman's melody. The
bookish man and the merry damsel
started up simultaneously to dance, the
former enacting the double shuffle in a
style which everybody must have witnessed, ere Election week was blotted
out of time; while the girl, setting her
arms akimbo with both hands at her
slim waist, displayed such light rapidity of foot, and harmony of varying

attitude and motion, that I could not conceive how she ever was to stop; imagining, at the moment, that Nature had made her, as the old showman had made his puppets, for no earthly purpose but to dance jigs. The Indian bellowed forth a succession of most hideous outcries, somewhat affrighting us, till we interpreted them as the war song, with which, in imitation of his ancestors, he was prefacing the assault on Stamford. The conjurer, meanwhile, sat demurely in a corner, extracting a sly enjoyment from the whole scene, and, like the facetious Merry Andrew, directing his queer glance particularly at me.

As for myself, with great exhilaration of fancy, I began to arrange and color the incidents of a tale, wherewith I proposed to amuse an audience that very evening; for I saw my associates were a little ashamed of me, and that no time was to be lost in obtaining a public acknowledgment of my abilities.

"Come, fellow-laborers," at last said the old showman, whom we had elected President; "the shower is over, and we must be doing our duty by these poor souls at Stamford."

"We'll come among them in procession, with music and dancing," cried the merry damsel.

Accordingly—for it must be understood that our pilgrimage was to be performed on foot—we sallied joyously out of the wagon, each of us, even the old gentleman in his white-top boots, giving a great skip as we came down the ladder. Above our heads there was such a glory of sunshine and splendor of clouds, and such brightness of verdure below, that, as I modestly remarked at the time, Nature seemed have washed her face, and put on t best of her jewelry and a fresh gre gown, in honor of our confederatic Casting our eyes northward, we beh a horseman approaching leisurely, a splashing through the little puddles the Stamford road. Onward he car sticking up in his saddle with ri perpendicularity, a tall, thin figure rusty black, whom the showman a the conjurer shortly recognized to what his aspect sufficiently indicat a travelling preacher of great fa among the Methodists. What puzz us was the fact, that his face appea turned from, instead of to, the can meeting at Stamford. However, as t new votary of the wandering life d near the little green space, where guide-post and our wagon were situat my six fellow-vagabonds and my rushed forward and surrounded h crying out with united voices:

"What news, what news, from camp-meeting at Stamford?"

The missionary looked down, in prise, at as singular a knot of pec as could have been selected from his heterogeneous auditors. Indeed, c sidering that we might all be classi under the general head of Vagab there was great diversity of chara among the grave old showman, the prophetic beggar, the fiddling forei and his merry damsel, the smart b opolist, the sombre Indian, and my the itinerant novelist, a slender y of eighteen. I even fancied that a s was endeavoring to disturb the gravity of the preacher's mouth.

"Good people," answered he, camp-meeting is broke up."

So saying, the Methodist minister itched his steed, and rode westward. ...r union being thus nullified, by the ...noval of its object, we were sundered once to the four winds of Heaven. ...e fortune-teller, giving a nod to all, ...d a peculiar wink to me, departed his northern tour, chuckling within ...self as he took the Stamford road. ...e old showman and his literary co-...jutor were already tackling their ...ses to the wagon, with a design to ...regrinate southwest along the sea-...st. The foreigner and the merry dam-sel took their laughing leave, and pursued the eastern road, which I had that day trodden; as they passed away, the young man played a lively strain, and the girl's happy spirit broke into a dance: and thus dissolving, as it were, into sunbeams and gay music, that pleasant pair departed from my view. Finally, with a pensive shadow thrown across my mind, yet emulous of the light philosophy of my late companions, I joined myself to the Penobscot Indian and set forth towards the distant city.

THE WHITE OLD MAID

THE moonbeams came through two ...p and narrow windows, and showed ...pacious chamber richly furnished in antique fashion. From one lattice, ...shadow of the diamond panes was ...own upon the floor; the ghostly light, ...ough the other, slept upon a bed, ...ing between the heavy silken cur-...s, and illuminating the face of a ...ng man. But, how quietly the slum-...er lay! how pale his features! and ...y like a shroud the sheet was wound ...ut his frame! Yes; it was a corpse, ...ts burial clothes.

...uddenly the fixed features seemed ...move with dark emotion. Strange ...asy! It was but the shadow of the ...ged curtain, waving betwixt the dead ...e and the moonlight, as the door of ...chamber opened, and a girl stole ...ly to the bedside. Was there de-...on in the moonbeams, or did her ...ure and her eye betray a gleam ...triumph, as she bent over the pale corpse—pale as itself—and pressed her living lips to the cold ones of the dead? As she drew back from that long kiss, her features writhed as if a proud heart were fighting with its anguish. Again it seemed that the features of the corpse had moved, responsive to her own. Still an illusion! The silken curtain had waved a second time betwixt the dead face and the moonlight, as another fair young girl unclosed the door and glided, ghost-like, to the bedside. There the two maidens stood, both beautiful, with the pale beauty of the dead between them. But she who had first entered was proud and stately; and the other, a soft and fragile thing.

"Away!" cried the lofty one. "Thou hadst him living! The dead is mine!"

"Thine!" returned the other, shuddering. "Well hast thou spoken! The dead is thine!"

The proud girl started, and stared into her face, with a ghastly look. But a wild and mournful expression passed across the features of the gentle one; and, weak and helpless, she sank down on the bed, her head pillowed beside that of the corpse, and her hair mingling with his dark locks. A creature of hope and joy, the first draught of sorrow had bewildered her.

"Edith!" cried her rival.

Edith groaned, as with a sudden compression of the heart; and removing her cheek from the dead youth's pillow, she stood upright, fearfully encountering the eyes of the lofty girl.

"Wilt thou betray me?" said the latter, calmly.

"Till the dead bid me speak, I will be silent," answered Edith. "Leave us alone together! Go, and live many years, and then return, and tell me of thy life. He, too, will be here! Then, if thou tellest of sufferings more than death, we will both forgive thee."

"And what shall be the token?" asked the proud girl, as if her heart acknowledged a meaning in these wild words.

"This lock of hair," said Edith, lifting one of the dark, clustering curls that lay heavily on the dead man's brow.

The two maidens joined their hands over the bosom of the corpse, and appointed a day and hour, far, far in time to come, for their next meeting in that chamber. The statelier girl gave one deep look at the motionless countenance, and departed,—yet turned again and trembled, ere she closed the door, almost believing that her dead lover frowned upon her. And Edith, too! Was not her white form fading into the moonlight? Scorning her own weakness, she went forth, and perceived that a negro slave was waiting in the passage,

with a wax light, which he held tween her face and his own, and garded her, as she thought, with an u expression of merriment. Lifting torch on high, the slave lighted down the staircase, and undid the p tal of the mansion. The young cler man of the town had just ascended steps, and bowing to the lady, pas in without a word.

Years, many years rolled on; world seemed new again, so much o was it grown since the night when th pale girls had clasped their hands ac the bosom of the corpse. In the inter a lonely woman had passed from yo to extreme age, and was known by the town as the "Old Maid in the W ing Sheet." A taint of insanity affected her whole life, but so q sad, and gentle, so utterly free f violence, that she was suffered to sue her harmless fantasies, unmole by the world, with whose busines pleasures she had naught to do. dwelt alone, and never came into daylight, except to follow fune Whenever a corpse was borne a the street, in sunshine, rain, or s whether a pompous train, of the and proud, thronged after it, or and humble were the mourners, be them came the lonely woman, in a l white garment, which the people c her shroud. She took no place an the kindred or the friends, but s at the door to hear the funeral pr and walked in the rear of the pro sion, as one whose earthly charg was to haunt the house of mour and be the shadow of affliction, see that the dead were duly bu So long had this been her cus that the inhabitants of the town dee

a part of every funeral, as much
the coffin-pall or the very corpse
lf, and augured ill of the sinner's
tiny, unless the "Old Maid in the
nding Sheet" came gliding, like a
st, behind. Once, it is said, she
ighted a bridal party with her pale
sence, appearing suddenly in the il-
inated hall, just as the priest was
ing a false maid to a wealthy man,
ore her lover had been dead a year.
I was the omen to that marriage!
netimes she stole forth by moon-
t, and visited the graves of vener-
: Integrity, and wedded Love, and
in Innocence, and every spot where
ashes of a kind and faithful heart
e mouldering. Over the hillocks of
se favored dead would she stretch
her arms, with a gesture, as if she
e scattering seeds; and many be-
ed that she brought them from the
len of Paradise; for the graves,
ch she had visited, were green be-
th the snow, and covered with sweet
ers from April to November. Her
sing was better than a holy verse
n the tombstone. Thus wore away
long, sad, peaceful, and fantastic
till few were so old as she, and
people of later generations wondered
the dead had ever been buried, or
rners had endured their grief, with-
the "Old Maid in the Winding
et."

ill, years went on, and still she fol-
ed funerals, and was not yet sumed to her own festival of death. One
rnoon the great street of the town
all alive with business and bustle,
ugh the sun now gilded only the
er half of the church-spire, having
the housetops and loftiest trees in
ow. The scene was cheerful and
animated, in spite of the sombre shade
between the high brick buildings. Here
were pompous merchants, in white wigs
and laced velvet; the bronzed faces of
sea captains; the foreign garb and air
of Spanish creoles; and the disdainful
port of natives of Old England; all contrasted with the rough aspect of one
or two back settlers, negotiating sales
of timber, from forests where axe had
never sounded. Sometimes a lady passed,
swelling roundly forth in an embroidered
petticoat, balancing her steps in high-
heeled shoes, and courtesying, with lofty
grace, to the punctilious obeisances of
the gentlemen. The life of the town
seemed to have its very centre not far
from an old mansion, that stood somewhat back from the pavement, surrounded by neglected grass, with a
strange air of loneliness, rather deepened
than dispelled by the throng so near
it. Its site would have been suitably
occupied by a magnificent Exchange, or
a brick block, lettered all over with
various signs; or the large house itself
might have made a noble tavern, with
the "King's Arms" swinging before it,
and guests in every chamber, instead of
the present solitude. But, owing to some
dispute about the right of inheritance,
the mansion had been long without a
tenant, decaying from year to year, and
throwing the stately gloom of its
shadow over the busiest part of the
town. Such was the scene, and such
the time, when a figure, unlike any that
have been described, was observed at
a distance down the street.

"I espy a strange sail, yonder," remarked a Liverpool captain; "that
woman in the long, white garment!"

The sailor seemed much struck by
the object, as were several others, who,

at the same moment, caught a glimpse of the figure that had attracted his notice. Almost immediately, the various topics of conversation gave place to speculations, in an undertone, on this unwonted occurrence.

"Can there be a funeral so late this afternoon?" inquired some.

They looked for the signs of death at every door,—the sexton, the hearse, the assemblage of black-clad relatives, —all that makes up the woful pomp of funerals. They raised their eyes, also, to the sun-gilt spire of the church, and wondered that no clang proceeded from its bell, which had always tolled till now, when this figure appeared in the light of day. But none had heard that a corpse was to be borne to its home that afternoon, nor was there any token of a funeral, except the apparition of the "Old Maid in the Winding Sheet."

"What may this portend?" asked each man of his neighbor.

All smiled as they put the question, yet with a certain trouble in their eyes, as if pestilence, or some other wide calamity, were prognosticated by the untimely intrusion among the living of one whose presence had always been associated with death and woe. What a comet is to the earth was that sad woman to the town. Still she moved on, while the hum of surprise was hushed at her approach, and the proud and the humble stood aside that her white garment might not wave against them. It was a long, loose robe, of spotless purity. Its wearer appeared very old, pale, emaciated, and feeble, yet glided onward, without the unsteady pace of extreme age. At one point of her course, a little rosy boy burst forth from a door, and ran, with open arms,

towards the ghostly woman, seemi expect a kiss from her bloodless She made a slight pause, fixing he upon him with an expression o earthly sweetness, so that the shivered and stood awestruck, r than affrighted, while the Old passed on. Perhaps her garment have been polluted even by an in touch; perhaps her kiss would been death to the sweet boy wit year.

"She is but a shadow," whis the superstitious. "The child put his arms and could not grasp her r

The wonder was increased when Old Maid passed beneath the por the deserted mansion, ascended moss-covered steps, lifted the knocker, and gave three raps. people could only conjecture that old remembrance, troubling her wildered brain, had impelled the woman hither to visit the friends c youth; all gone from their home, since and forever, unless their g still haunted it,—fit company fo "Old Maid in the Winding Sheet. elderly man approached the steps reverently uncovering his gray essayed to explain the matter.

"None, Madam," said he, "have in this house these fifteen years a —no, not since the death of old Co Fenwicke, whose funeral you ma member to have followed. His being ill agreed among themselves, let the mansion house go to ruin."

The Old Maid looked slowly r with a slight gesture of one hand a finger of the other upon her lip pearing more shadow-like than ev the obscurity of the porch. But she lifted the hammer, and gave

, a single rap. Could it be that a step was now heard coming down staircase of the old mansion, which conceived to have been so long un- nted? Slowly, feebly, yet heavily, the pace of an aged and infirm on, the step approached, more dis- t on every downward stair, till it hed the portal. The bar fell on the le; the door was opened. One up- d glance towards the church-spire, nce the sunshine had just faded, the last that the people saw of "Old Maid in the Winding Sheet." Vho undid the door?" asked many. his question, owing to the depth hadow beneath the porch, no one d satisfactorily answer. Two or e aged men, while protesting against inference, which might be drawn, ned that the person within was a o, and bore a singular resemblance ld Cæsar, formerly a slave in the e, but freed by death some thirty s before.

Ier summons has waked up a ser- of the old family," said one, half usly.

et us wait here," replied another. re guests will knock at the door, . But, the gate of the graveyard ld be thrown open!"

vilight had overspread the town be- the crowd began to separate, or comments on this incident were usted. One after another was wend- his way homeward, when a coach common spectacle in those days— e slowly into the street. It was ld-fashioned equipage, hanging close e ground, with arms on the panels, otman behind, and a grave, corpu- coachman seated high in front,— vhole giving an idea of solemn state and dignity. There was something awful in the heavy rumbling of the wheels. The coach rolled down the street, till, coming to the gateway of the deserted mansion, it drew up, and the footman sprang to the ground.

"Whose grand coach is this?" asked a very inquisitive body.

The footman made no reply, but ascended the steps of the old house, gave three raps with the iron hammer, and returned to open the coach-door. An old man, possessed of the heraldic lore so common in that day, examined the shield of arms on the panel.

"Azure, a lion's head erased, between three flower-de-luces," said he; then whispered the name of the family to whom these bearings belonged. The last inheritor of its honors was recently dead, after a long residence amid the splendor of the British court, where his birth and wealth had given him no mean station. "He left no child," con- tinued the herald, "and these arms, be- ing in a lozenge, betoken that the coach appertains to his widow."

Further disclosures, perhaps, might have been made had not the speaker suddenly been struck dumb by the stern eye of an ancient lady, who thrust forth her head from the coach, preparing to descend. As she emerged the people saw that her dress was magnificent, and her figure dignified, in spite of age and in- firmity,—a stately ruin, but with a look, at once, of pride and wretchedness. Her strong and rigid features had an awe about them unlike that of the white Old Maid, but as of something evil. She passed up the steps, leaning on a gold-headed cane; the door swung open as she ascended,—and the light of a torch glittered on the embroidery of her dress, and gleamed on the pillars of the porch. After a momentary pause,—a glance backwards, and then a desperate effort,—she went in. The decipherer of the coat-of-arms had ventured up the lowest step, and shrinking back immediately, pale and tremulous, affirmed that the torch was held by the very image of old Cæsar.

"But such a hideous grin," added he. "was never seen on the face of mortal man, black or white! It will haunt me till my dying day."

Meantime, the coach had wheeled round, with a prodigious clatter on the pavement, and rumbled up the street disappearing in the twilight, while the ear still tracked its course. Scarcely was it gone when the people began to question whether the coach and attendants, the ancient lady, the spectre of old Cæsar, and the Old Maid herself, were not all a strangely combined delusion, with some dark purport in its mystery. The whole town was astir, so that, instead of dispersing, the crowd continually increased, and stood gazing up at the windows of the mansion, now silvered by the brightening moon. The elders, glad to indulge the narrative propensity of age, told of the long-faded splendor of the family, the entertainments they had given, and the guests, the greatest of the land, and even titled and noble ones from abroad, who had passed beneath that portal. These graphic reminiscences seemed to call up the ghosts of those to whom they referred. So strong was the impression, on some of the more imaginative hearers, that two or three were seized with trembling fits, at one and the same moment, protesting that they had distinctly heard three other raps

of the iron knocker.

"Impossible!" exclaimed others. "The moon shines beneath the porch, shows every part of it, except in narrow shade of that pillar. Ther no one there!"

"Did not the door open?" whisp one of these fanciful persons.

"Didst thou see it, too?" said companion, in a startled tone.

But the general sentiment was posed to the idea, that a third visi had made application at the doo the deserted house. A few, howe adhered to this new marvel, and declared that a red gleam, like tha a torch, had shone through the g front window, as if the negro lighting a guest up the staircase. too, was pronounced a mere fant But, at once, the whole multit started, and each man beheld his terror painted in the faces of all rest.

"What an awful thing is this!" they.

A shriek, too fearfully distinct doubt, had been heard within the n sion, breaking forth suddenly, and ceeded by a deep stillness, as if a h had burst in giving it utterance. people knew not whether to fly f the very sight of the house, or to trembling in, and search out the str mystery. Amid their confusion and fright, they were somewhat reass by the appearance of their clergyr a venerable patriarch, and equall saint, who had taught them and t fathers the way to Heaven for n than the space of an ordinary lifet He was a reverend figure, with l white hair upon his shoulders, a w beard upon his breast, and a back

t over his staff, that he seemed to
looking downward, continually, as
o choose a proper grave for his weary
ne. It was some time before the
d old man, being deaf, and of im-
red intellect, could be made to com-
hend such portions of the affair as
e comprehensible at all. But, when
sessed of the facts, his energies ased unexpected vigor.

Verily," said the old gentleman, "it
be fitting that I enter the mansion
se of the worthy Colonel Fenwicke,
any harm should have befallen that
Christian woman, whom ye call
'Old Maid in the Winding Sheet.' "

ehold, then, the venerable clergy-
ascending the steps of the mansion,
a torch-bearer behind him. It was
elderly man who had spoken to the
Maid, and the same who had after-
ls explained the shield of arms, and
gnized the features of the negro.
their predecessors, they gave three
, with the iron hammer.

ld Cæsar cometh not," observed
priest. "Well I wot he no longer
service in this mansion."

Assuredly, then, it was something
e, in old Cæsar's likeness!" said
ther adventurer.

Be it as God wills," answered the
yman. "See! my strength, though
much decayed, hath sufficed to
this heavy door. Let us enter, and
up the staircase."

re occurred a singular exemplifi-
n of the dreamy state of a very
nan's mind. As they ascended the
flight of stairs, the aged clergyman
ared to move with caution, occa-
lly standing aside, and oftener
ng his head, as it were in salutation,
practising all the gestures of one
who makes his way through a throng.
Reaching the head of the staircase, he
looked around, with sad and solemn
benignity, laid aside his staff, bared his
hoary locks, and was evidently on the
point of commencing a prayer.

"Reverend Sir," said his attendant,
who conceived this a very suitable prelude to their further search, "would it
not be well that the people join with
us in prayer?"

"Welladay!" cried the old clergyman,
staring strangely around him. "Art thou
here with me, and none other? Verily,
past times were present to me, and
I deemed that I was to make a funeral
prayer, as many a time heretofore, from
the head of this staircase. Of a truth,
I saw the shades of many that are gone.
Yea, I have prayed at their burials, one
after another, and the 'Old Maid in
the Winding Sheet' hath seen them to
their graves!"

Being now more thoroughly awake
to their present purpose, he took his
staff, and struck forcibly on the floor,
till there came an echo from each deserted chamber, but no menial, to answer their summons. They therefore
walked along the passage, and again
paused, opposite to the great front window, through which was seen the crowd,
in the shadow and partial moonlight of
the street beneath. On their right hand
was the open door of a chamber, and
a closed one on their left. The clergyman pointed his cane to the carved
oak panel of the latter.

"Within that chamber," observed he,
"a whole lifetime since, did I sit by the
death-bed of a goodly young man, who,
being now at the last gasp—"

Apparently there was some powerful
excitement in the ideas which had now

flashed across his mind. He snatched the torch from his companion's hand, and threw open the door with such sudden violence, that the flame was extinguished, leaving them no other light than the moonbeams, which fell through two windows into the spacious chamber. It was sufficient to discover all that could be known. In a high-backed, oaken arm-chair, upright, with her hands clasped across her breast, and her head thrown back, sat the "Old Maid in the Winding Sheet." The stately dame had fallen on her knees, with her forehead on the holy knees of the Old Maid, one hand upon the floor, and the other pressed convulsively against her heart.

It clutched a lock of hair, once s... now discolored with a greenish m... As the priest and layman advanced... the chamber, the Old Maid's feat... assumed such a semblance of shi... expression, that they trusted to hea... whole mystery explained, by a s... word. But it was only the shado... a tattered curtain, waving betwixt... dead face and the moonlight.

"Both dead!" said the venerable... "Then who shall divulge the se... Methinks it glimmers to and fr... my mind, like the light and sh... across the Old Maid's face. And n... is gone!"

PETER GOLDTHWAITE'S TREASURE

"AND SO, Peter, you won't even consider of the business?" said Mr. John Brown, buttoning his surtout over the snug rotundity of his person, and drawing on his gloves. "You positively refuse to let me have this crazy old house, and the land under and adjoining, at the price named?"

"Neither at that, nor treble the sum," responded the gaunt, grizzled, and threadbare Peter Goldthwaite. "The fact is, Mr. Brown, you must find another site for your brick block, and be content to leave my estate with the present owner. Next summer, I intend to put a splendid new mansion over the cellar of the old house."

"Pho, Peter!" cried Mr. Brown, as he opened the kitchen door; "content yourself with building castles in the air, where house-lots are cheaper than on

earth, to say nothing of the co... bricks and mortar. Such founda... are solid enough for your edi... while this underneath us is just... thing for mine; and so we may... be suited. What say you, again?"

"Precisely what I said before,... Brown," answered Peter Goldth... "And, as for castles in the air,... may not be as magnificent as tha... of architecture, but perhaps as su... tial, Mr. Brown, as the very respe... brick block with dry-goods s... tailors' shops, and banking-rooms... lower floor, and lawyers' offices i... second story, which you are so ar... to substitute."

"And the cost, Peter, eh?" sai... Brown, as he withdrew, in som... of a pet. "That, I suppose, will b... vided for, offhand, by drawing a

3ubble Bank!"

·hn Brown and Peter Goldthwaite
been jointly known to the commer-
world between twenty and thirty
s before, under the firm of Gold-
.ite & Brown; which copartnership,
ever, was speedily dissolved, by the
ral incongruity of its constituent
s. Since that event, John Brown,
exactly the qualities of a thousand
r John Browns, and by just such
ding methods as they used, had
pered wonderfully, and become one
ie wealthiest John Browns on earth.
r Goldthwaite, on the contrary,
· innumerable schemes, which ought
ive collected all the coin and paper
ency of the country into his coffers,
as needy a gentleman as ever wore
tch upon his elbow. The contract
een him and his former partner
be briefly marked: for Brown never
ned upon luck, yet always had it;
: Peter made luck the main condi-
of his projects, and always missed
hile the means held out, his specu-
is had been magnificent, but were
ly confined, of late years, to such
l business as adventures in the
ry. Once, he had gone on a gold-
ering expedition, somewhere to the
1, and ingeniously contrived to
y his pockets more thoroughly than
while others, doubtless, were fill-
heirs with native bullion by the
ful. More recently, he had expended
acy of a thousand or two of dollars
rchasing Mexican scrip, and there-
came the proprietor of a province;
1, however, so far as Peter could
out, was situated where he might
had an empire for the same
y,—in the clouds. From a search
this valuable real estate, Peter re-

turned so gaunt and threadbare, that
on reaching New England, the scare
crows in the cornfields beckoned to him
as he passed by. "They did but flutter
in the wind," quoth Peter Goldthwaite.
No, Peter, they beckoned, for the scare-
crows knew their brother!

At the period of our story his whole
visible income would not have paid the
tax of the old mansion in which we
find him. It was one of those rusty,
moss - grown, many - peaked wooden
houses, which are scattered about the
streets of our elder towns, with a beetle-
browed second story projecting over the
foundation, as if it frowned at the
novelty around it. This old paternal
edifice, needy as he was, and though,
being centrally situated on the principal street of the town, it would have
brought him a handsome sum, the sagacious Peter had his own reasons for
never parting with, either by auction or
private sale. There seemed, indeed, to
be a fatality that connected him with
his birthplace; for, often as he had
stood on the verge of ruin, and standing there even now, he had not yet
taken the step beyond it, which would
have compelled him to surrender the
house to his creditors. So here he dwelt
with bad luck till good should come.

Here, then, in his kitchen, the only
room where a spark of fire took off
the chill of a November evening, poor
Peter Goldthwaite had just been visited
by his rich old partner. At the close
of their interview, Peter, with rather a
mortified look, glanced downwards at
his dress, parts of which appeared as
ancient as the days of Goldthwaite &
Brown. His upper garment was a mixed
surtout, wofully faded, and patched with
newer stuff on each elbow; beneath

this, he wore a threadbare black coat, some of the silk buttons of which had been replaced with others of a different pattern; and lastly, though he lacked not a pair of gray pantaloons, they were very shabby ones, and had been partially turned brown, by the frequent toasting of Peter's shins before a scanty fire. Peter's person was in keeping with his goodly apparel. Gray-headed, hollow-eyed, pale-cheeked, and lean-bodied, he was the perfect picture of a man who had fed on windy schemes and empty hopes, till he could neither live on such unwholesome trash, nor stomach more substantial food. But withal, this Peter Goldthwaite, crack-brained simpleton as, perhaps, he was, might have cut a very brilliant figure in the world, had he employed his imagination in the airy business of poetry, instead of making it a demon of mischief in mercantile pursuits. After all, he was no bad fellow, but as harmless as a child, and as honest and honorable, and as much of the gentleman which nature meant him for, as an irregular life and depressed circumstances will permit any man to be.

As Peter stood on the uneven bricks of his hearth, looking round at the disconsolate old kitchen, his eyes began to kindle with the illumination of an enthusiasm that never long deserted him. He raised his hand, clinched it, and smote it energetically against the smoky panel over the fireplace.

"The time is come!" said he. "With such a treasure at command, it were folly to be a poor man any longer. To-morrow morning I will begin with the garret, nor desist till I have torn the house down!"

Deep in the chimney-corner, like a witch in a dark cavern, sat a little woman, mending one of the two p of stockings wherewith Peter G thwaite kept his toes from being fr bitten. As the feet were ragged all darning, she had cut pieces ou a cast-off flannel petticoat, to make soles. Tabitha Porter was an old m upwards of sixty years of age, fi five of which she had sat in that s chimney-corner, such being the le of time since Peter's grandfather taken her from the almshouse. She no friend but Peter, nor Peter friend but Tabitha; so long as F might have a shelter for his own h Tabitha would know where to sh hers; or, being homeless elsewhere, would take her master by the h and bring him to her native home, almshouse. Should it ever be neces she loved him well enough to feed with her last morsel and clothe with her under petticoat. But Tab was a queer old woman, and, the never infected with Peter's flighti had become so accustomed to his fr and follies, that she viewed them a matters of course. Hearing him thre to tear the house down, she lo quietly up from her work.

"Best leave the kitchen till the Mr. Peter," said she.

"The sooner we have it all down better," said Peter Goldthwaite. "I tired to death of living in this dark, windy, smoky, creaking, groa dismal old house. I shall feel lil younger man, when we get into splendid brick mansion, as, please H en, we shall, by this time next aut You shall have a room on the s side, old Tabby, finished and furni as best may suit your own notion:

'I should like it pretty much such room as this kitchen," answered itha. "It will never be like home me, till the chimney-corner gets as ck with smoke as this; and that 't be these hundred years. How ch do you mean to lay out on the se, Mr. Peter?"

What is that to the purpose?" ex-med Peter, loftily. "Did not my t-granduncle, Peter Goldthwaite, died seventy years ago, and whose nesake I am, leave treasure enough uild twenty such?"

I can't say but he did, Mr. Peter," Tabitha, threading her needle.

abitha well understood that Peter reference to an immense hoard of precious metals, which was said exist somewhere in the cellar or s, or under the floors, or in some cealed closet, or other out-of-the nook of the house. This wealth, rding to tradition, had been ac-ulated by a former Peter Gold-ite, whose character seems to have e a remarkable similitude to that he Peter of our story. Like him he a wild projector, seeking to heap gold by the bushel and the cart-, instead of scraping it together, by coin. Like Peter the second, his projects had almost invariably d, and, but for the magnificent suc-of the final one, would have left with hardly a coat and pair of ches to his gaunt and grizzled per-Reports were various, as to the re of his fortunate speculation; one ating that the ancient Peter had e the gold by alchemy; another, he had conjured it out of people's ets by the black art; and a third, more unaccountable, that the Devil

had given him free access to the old provincial treasury. It was affirmed, however, that some secret impediment had debarred him from the enjoyment of his riches, and that he had a motive for concealing them from his heir, or, at any rate, had died without disclos-ing the place of deposit. The present Peter's father had faith enough in the story to cause the cellar to be dug over. Peter himself chose to consider the legend as an indisputable truth, and, amid his many troubles, had this one consolation, that, should all other re-sources fail, he might build up his for-tunes by tearing his house down. Yet, unless he felt a lurking distrust of the golden tale, it is difficult to account for his permitting the paternal roof to stand so long, since he had never yet seen the moment when his pred-ecessor's treasure would not have found plenty of room in his own strong box. But now was the crisis. Should he delay the search a little longer, the house would pass from the lineal heir, and with it the vast heap of gold, to remain in its burial-place till the ruin of the aged walls should discover it to strangers of a future generation.

"Yes!" cried Peter Goldthwaite, again; "to-morrow I will set about it."

The deeper he looked at the matter, the more certain of success grew Peter. His spirits were naturally so elastic, that even now, in the blasted autumn of his age, he could often compete with the spring-time gayety of other people. Enlivened by his brightening prospects, he began to caper about the kitchen like a hob-goblin, with the queerest antics of his lean limbs, and gesticulations of his starved features. Nay, in the exuber-ance of his feelings, he seized both of

Tabitha's hands, and danced the old lady across the floor, till the oddity of her rheumatic motions set him into a roar of laughter, which was echoed back from the rooms and chambers, as if Peter Goldthwaite were laughing in every one. Finally, he bounded upward, almost out of sight, into the smoke that clouded the roof of the kitchen, and alighting safely on the floor again, endeavored to resume his customary gravity.

"To-morrow, at sunrise," he repeated, taking his lamp, to retire to bed, "I'll see whether this treasure be hid in the wall of the garret."

"And, as we're out of wood, Mr. Peter," said Tabitha, puffing and panting with her late gymnastics, "as fast as you tear the house down, I'll make a fire with the pieces."

Gorgeous, that night, were the dreams of Peter Goldthwaite! At one time, he was turning a ponderous key in an iron door, not unlike the door of a sepulchre, but which, being opened, disclosed a vault, heaped up with gold coin, as plentifully as golden corn in a granary. There were chased goblets, also, and tureens, salvers, dinner-dishes, and dish-covers, of gold, or silver gilt, besides chains and other jewels, incalculably rich, though tarnished with the damps of the vault; for, of all the wealth that was irrevocably lost to man, whether buried in the earth or sunken in the sea, Peter Goldthwaite had found it in this one treasure-place. Anon, he had returned to the old house, as poor as ever, and was received at the door, by the gaunt and grizzled figure of a man, whom he might have mistaken for himself, only that his garments were of a much elder fashion. But the house, with-

out losing its former aspect, had b changed into a palace of the prec metals. The floors, walls, and ceil were of burnished silver; the doors, window-frames, the cornices, the ba trades, and the steps of the stairc of pure gold; and silver, with bottoms, were the chairs, and g standing on silver legs, the high ch of drawers, and silver the bedste with blankets of woven gold, and sh of silver tissue. The house had evide been transmuted by a single touch; it retained all the marks that Pete membered, but in gold or silver, ins of wood; and the initials of his na which, when a boy, he had cut in wooden doorpost, remained as dee the pillar of gold. A happy man w have been Peter Goldthwaite, ex for a certain ocular deception, wh whenever he glanced backward, ca the house to darken from its glitt magnificence into the sordid gloom yesterday.

Up, betimes, rose Peter, seized axe, hammer, and saw, which he placed by his bedside, and hied hin the garret. It was but scantily lig up, as yet, by the frosty fragmen a sunbeam, which began to glin through the almost opaque bull's ey the window. A moralizer might abundant themes for his speculative impracticable wisdom in a garret. T is the limbo of departed fashions, trifles of a day, and whatever was able only to one generation of men which passed to the garret when generation passed to the grave, no safe keeping, but to be out of the Peter saw piles of yellow and m account-books, in parchment co wherein creditors, long dead and bu

written the names of dead and
ed debtors, in ink now so faded,
their moss-grown tombstones were
e legible. He found old moth-eaten
ients all in rags and tatters, or Peter
ld have put them on. Here was a
d and rusty sword, not a sword of
ice, but a gentleman's small French
er, which had never left its scabbard
t lost it. Here were canes of twenty
rent sorts, but no gold-headed ones,
shoe-buckles of various pattern and
erial, but not silver, nor set with
ious stones. Here was a large box
of shoes, with high heels and peaked
Here, on a shelf, were a multitude
hials, half filled with old apothe-
es' stuff, which, when the other half
done its business on Peter's ances-
had been brought hither from the
h chamber. Here—not to give a
er inventory of articles that will
r be put up at auction—was the
ment of a full-length looking-glass,
h, by the dust and dimness of its
ace, made the picture of these old
gs look older than the reality. When
r, not knowing that there was a
or there, caught the faint traces
is own figure, he partly imagined
the former Peter Goldthwaite had
e back either to assist or impede
search for the hidden wealth. And
at moment a strange notion glim-
ed through his brain, that he was
identical Peter who had concealed
gold, and ought to know whereabout
. This, however, he had unaccount-
forgotten.

Vell, Mr. Peter!" cried Tabitha, on
garret stairs. "Have you torn the
e down enough to heat the tea-
e?"

Tot yet, old Tabby," answered

Peter; "but that's soon done—as you
shall see."

With the word in his mouth, he uplifted the axe, and laid about him so
vigorously, that the dust flew, the boards
crashed, and, in a twinkling, the old
woman had an apronful of broken
rubbish.

"We shall get our winter's wood
cheap," quoth Tabitha.

The good work being thus commenced, Peter beat down all before him,
smiting and hewing at the joists and
timbers, unclinching spike-nails, ripping
and tearing away boards, with a tremendous racket, from morning till night.
He took care, however, to leave the outside shell of the house untouched, so
that the neighbors might not suspect
what was going on.

Never, in any of his vagaries, though
each had made him happy while it
lasted, had Peter been happier than now.
Perhaps, after all, there was something
in Peter Goldthwaite's turn of mind,
which brought him an inward recompense for all the external evil that it
caused. If he were poor, ill clad, even
hungry, and exposed, as it were, to be
utterly annihilated by a precipice of
impending ruin, yet only his body remained in these miserable circumstances,
while his aspiring soul enjoyed the sunshine of a bright futurity. It was his
nature to be always young, and the
tendency of his mode of life to keep
him so. Gray hairs were nothing, no,
nor wrinkles, nor infirmity; he might
look old, indeed, and be somewhat disagreeably connected with a gaunt old
figure, much the worse for wear; but
the true, the essential Peter, was a
young man of high hopes, just entering on the world. At the kindling of

each new fire, his burnt-out youth rose afresh from the old embers and ashes. It rose exulting now. Having lived thus long—not too long, but just to the right age—a susceptible bachelor, with warm and tender dreams, he resolved, so soon as the hidden gold should flash to light, to go a-wooing, and win the love of the fairest maid in town. What heart could resist him? Happy Peter Goldthwaite!

Every evening—as Peter had long absented himself from his former lounging-places, at insurance-offices, newsrooms, and bookstores, and as the honor of his company was seldom requested in private circles—he and Tabitha used to sit down sociably by the kitchen hearth. This was always heaped plentifully with the rubbish of his day's labor. As the foundation of the fire, there would be a goodly-sized backlog of red oak, which, after being sheltered from rain or damp above a century, still hissed with the heat, and distilled streams of water from each end, as if the tree had been cut down within a week or two. Next, there were large sticks, sound, black, and heavy, which had lost the principle of decay, and were indestructible except by fire, wherein they glowed like red-hot bars of iron. On this solid basis, Tabitha would rear a lighter structure composed of the splinters of door-panels, ornamented mouldings, and such quick combustibles, which caught like straw, and threw a brilliant blaze high up the spacious flue, making its sooty sides visible almost to the chimney-top. Meantime, the gleam of the old kitchen would be chased out of the cobwebbed corners, and away from the dusky crossbeams overhead, and driven nobody could tell whither, while Peter smiled like a glad-

some man, and Tabitha seemed a ture of comfortable age. All this, course, was but an emblem of the br fortune which the destruction of house would shed upon its occupant

While the dry pine was flaming crackling, like an irregular discharg fairy musketry, Peter sat looking listening, in a pleasant state of ex ment. But, when the brief blaze and roar were succeeded by the dark glow, the substantial heat, and the singing sound, which were to throughout the evening, his humor came talkative. One night, the dredth time, he teased Tabitha to him something new about his gr granduncle.

"You have been sitting in that c ney-corner fifty-five years, old Ta and must have heard many a tradi about him," said Peter. "Did not tell me, that, when you first cam the house, there was an old wo sitting where you sit now, who had housekeeper to the famous Peter C thwaite?"

"So there was, Mr. Peter," answ Tabitha; "and she was near abo hundred years old. She used to say, she and old Peter Goldthwaite had spent a sociable evening by the kit fire,—pretty much as you and I an ing now, Mr. Peter."

"The old fellow must have resem me in more points than one," said F complacently, "or he never would grown so rich. But, methinks, he n have invested the money better tha did—no interest!—nothing but goo curity!—and the house to be torn to come at it! What made him hi so snug, Tabby?"

"Because he could not spend it,"

itha; "for, as often as he went to
ock the chest, the Old Scratch came
ind and caught his arm. The money,
y say, was paid Peter out of his
se; and he wanted Peter to give him
eed of this house and land, which
er swore he would not do."

Just as I swore to John Brown, my
partner," remarked Peter. "But this
ll nonsense, Tabby! I don't believe
story."

Well, it may not be just the truth,"
Tabitha; "for some folks say, that
er did make over the house to the
Scratch; and that's the reason it
always been so unlucky to them
lived in it. And as soon as Peter
given him the deed, the chest flew
, and Peter caught up a handful of
gold. But, lo and behold!—there
nothing in his fist but a parcel of
rags."

Hold your tongue, you silly old
by!" cried Peter in great wrath.
ey were as good golden guineas as
bore the effigies of the king of
and. It seems as if I could recollect
whole circumstance, and how I, or
Peter, or whoever it was, thrust in
hand, or his hand, and drew it out,
f a blaze with gold. Old rags, in-
!"

it it was not an old woman's legend
would discourage Peter Gold-
ite. All night long, he slept among
ant dreams, and awoke at daylight
a joyous throb of the heart, which
are fortunate enough to feel beyond
boyhood. Day after day, he labored
, without wasting a moment, except
eal-times, when Tabitha summoned
to the pork and cabbage, or such
sustenance as she had picked up
rovidence had sent them. Being a

truly pious man, Peter never failed to
ask a blessing; if the food were none of
the best, then so much the more earnestly, as it was more needed;—nor to
return thanks, if the dinner had been
scanty, yet for the good appetite, which
was better than a sick stomach at a
feast. Then did he hurry back to his
toil, and, in a moment, was lost to sight
in a cloud of dust from the old walls,
though sufficiently perceptible to the ear,
by the clatter which he raised in the
midst of it. How enviable is the consciousness of being usefully employed!
Nothing troubled Peter; or nothing but
those phantoms of the mind, which seem
like vague recollections, yet have also
the aspect of presentiments. He often
paused, with his axe uplifted in the
air, and said to himself,—"Peter Goldthwaite, did you never strike this blow
before?"—or, "Peter, what need of tearing the whole house down? Think, a
little while, and you will remember
where the gold is hidden." Days and
weeks passed on, however, without any
remarkable discovery. Sometimes, indeed, a lean gray rat peeped forth at
the lean, gray man, wondering what
devil had got into the old house, which
had always been so peaceable till now.
And, occasionally, Peter sympathized
with the sorrows of a female mouse,
who had brought five or six pretty,
little, soft, and delicate young ones into
the world, just in time to see them
crushed by its ruin. But, as yet, no
treasure!

By this time, Peter, being as determined as Fate, and as diligent as
Time, had made an end with the uppermost regions, and got down to the
second story, where he was busy in one
of the front chambers. It had formerly

been the state bed-chamber, and was honored by tradition as the sleeping apartment of Governor Dudley, and many other eminent guests. The furniture was gone. There were remnants of faded and tattered paper-hangings, but larger spaces of bare wall, ornamented with charcoal-sketches, chiefly of people's heads in profile. These being specimens of Peter's youthful genius, it went more to his heart to obliterate them, than if they had been pictures on a church wall by Michael Angelo. One sketch, however, and that the best one, affected him differently. It represented a ragged man, partly supporting himself on a spade, and bending his lean body over a hole in the earth, with one hand extended to grasp something that he had found. But, close behind him, with a fiendish laugh on his features, appeared a figure with horns, a tufted tail, and a cloven hoof.

"Avaunt, Satan!" cried Peter. "The man shall have his gold!"

Uplifting his axe, he hit the horned gentleman such a blow on the head, as not only demolished him, but the treasure-seeker also, and caused the whole scene to vanish like magic. Moreover, his axe broke quite through the plaster and laths, and discovered a cavity.

"Mercy on us, Mr. Peter, are you quarrelling with the Old Scratch?" said Tabitha, who was seeking some fuel to put under the dinner-pot.

Without answering the old woman, Peter broke down a further space of the wall, and laid open a small closet or cupboard, on one side of the fireplace, about breast high from the ground. It contained nothing but a brass lamp, covered with verdigris, and a dusty piece

of parchment. While Peter inspected latter, Tabitha seized the lamp, and gan to rub it with her apron.

"There is no use in rubbing Tabitha," said Peter. "It is not A din's lamp, though I take it to token of as much luck. Look Tabby!"

Tabitha took the parchment, and it close to her nose, which was sad with a pair of iron-bound specta But no sooner had she begun to p over it, than she burst into a chuc laugh, holding both her hands ag her sides.

"You can't make a fool of the woman!" cried she. "This is your handwriting, Mr. Peter! the sam in the letter you sent me from Mex

"There is certainly a considerabl semblance," said Peter, again exam the parchment. "But you know self, Tabby, that this closet must been plastered up before you cam the house, or I came into the world this is old Peter Goldthwaite's wri these columns of pounds, shillings pence are his figures denoting amount of the treasure; and thi the bottom, is doubtless a referen the place of concealment. But th has either faded or peeled off, so it is absolutely illegible. What a p

"Well, this lamp is as good as That's some comfort," said Tabit

"A lamp!" thought Peter. "Th dicates light on my researches."

For the present, Peter felt mo clined to ponder on this discovery to resume his labors. After Tabith gone down stairs, he stood poring the parchment, at one of the fron dows, which was so obscured wit that the sun could barely throw a ain shadow of the casement across floor. Peter forced it open, and ed out upon the great street of the n, while the sun looked in at his house. The air, though mild, and a warm, thrilled Peter as with a dash vater.

was the first day of the January y. The snow lay deep upon the etops, but was rapidly dissolving millions of water-drops, which kled downwards through the sun-e, with the noise of a summer er beneath the eaves. Along the t, the trodden snow was as hard solid as a pavement of white mar-and had not yet grown moist in the g-like temperature. But, when Peter st forth his head, he saw that the oitants, if not the town, were dy thawed out by this warm day, two or three weeks of winter her. It gladdened him,—a gladness a sigh breathing through it,—to he stream of ladies, gliding along slippery sidewalks, with their red ts set off by quilted hoods, boas, able capes, like roses amidst a new of foliage. The sleigh-bells jingled ad fro continually, sometimes an-cing the arrival of a sleigh from ont, laden with the frozen bodies rkers, or sheep, and perhaps a deer o; sometimes of a regular market with chickens, geese, and turkeys, rising the whole colony of a barn-and sometimes of a farmer and ame, who had come to town partly he ride, partly to go a-shopping, partly for the sale of some eggs utter. This couple rode in an old-ned square sleigh, which had d them twenty winters, and stood y summers in the sun beside their

door. Now, a gentleman and lady skimmed the snow, in an elegant car, shaped somewhat like a cockle-shell. Now, a stage-sleigh, with its cloth curtains thrust aside to admit the sun, dashed rapidly down the street, whirling in and out among the vehicles that obstructed its passage. Now came, round a corner, the similitude of Noah's ark, on runners, being an immense open sleigh, with seats for fifty people, and drawn by a dozen horses. This spacious receptacle was populous with merry maids and merry bachelors, merry girls and boys, and merry old folks, all alive with fun, and grinning to the full width of their mouths. They kept up a buzz of babbling voices and low laughter, and sometimes burst into a deep, joyous shout, which the spectators answered with three cheers, while a gang of roguish boys let drive their snowballs right among the pleasure party. The sleigh passed on, and, when concealed by a bend of the street, was still audible by a distant cry of merriment.

Never had Peter beheld a livelier scene than was constituted by all these accessories: the bright sun; the flashing water-drops; the gleaming snow; the cheerful multitude; the variety of rapid vehicles; and the jingle-jangle of merry bells, which made the heart dance to their music. Nothing dismal was to be seen, except that peaked piece of antiquity, Peter Goldthwaite's house, which might well look sad externally, since such a terrible consumption was preying on its insides. And Peter's gaunt figure, half visible in the projecting second story, was worthy of his house.

"Peter! How goes it, friend Peter?" cried a voice across the street, as Peter was drawing in his head. "Look out here, Peter!"

Peter looked, and saw his old partner, Mr. John Brown, on the opposite sidewalk, portly and comfortable, with his furred cloak thrown open, disclosing a handsome surtout beneath. His voice had directed the attention of the whole town to Peter Goldthwaite's window, and to the dusty scarecrow which appeared at it.

"I say, Peter," cried Mr. Brown again, "what the devil are you about there, that I hear such a racket, whenever I pass by? You are repairing the old house, I suppose,—making a new one of it,—eh?"

"To late for that, I am afraid, Mr. Brown," replied Peter. "If I make it new, it will be new inside and out, from the cellar upwards."

"Had not you better let me take the job?" said Mr. Brown, significantly.

"Not yet," answered Peter, hastily shutting the window; for, ever since he had been in search of the treasure, he hated to have people stare at him.

As he drew back, ashamed of his outward poverty, yet proud of the secret wealth within his grasp, a haughty smile shone out on Peter's visage, with precisely the effect of the dim sunbeams in the squalid chamber. He endeavored to assume such a mien as his ancestor had probably worn, when he gloried in the building of a strong house for a home to many generations of his posterity. But the chamber was very dark to his snow-dazzled eyes, and very dismal, too, in contrast with the living scene that he had just looked upon. His brief glimpse into the street had given him a forcible impression of the manner in which the world kept itself cheerful and prosperous, by social pleasures and

an intercourse of business, while h[e] seclusion, was pursuing an object might possibly be a phantasm, b[ut] method which most people would madness. It is one great advantage gregarious mode of life, that each pe[rson] rectifies his mind by other minds, squares his conduct to that of his n[eigh]bors, so as seldom to be lost in ec tricity. Peter Goldthwaite had exp[osed] himself to this influence, by m[erely] looking out of the window. For a w[hile] he doubted whether there were any den chest of gold, and, in that whether it was so exceedingly wis[e to] tear the house down, only to be vinced of its non-existence.

But this was momentary. Peter, Destroyer, resumed the task which had assigned him, nor faltered a[gain] till it was accomplished. In the c[ourse] of his search, he met with many t[hings] that are usually found in the rui[ns of] an old house, and also with some are not. What seemed most to the pose, was a rusty key, which had thrust into a chink of the wall, w[ith a] wooden label appended to the ha[ndle,] bearing the initials, P. G. Another s[imi]lar discovery was that of a bott[le of] wine, walled up in an old oven. A [tra]dition ran in the family, that P[eter's] grandfather, a jovial officer in th[e old] French war, had set aside many d[ozen] of the precious liquor, for the bene[fit of] topers then unborn. Peter neede[d no] cordial to sustain his hopes, and [there]fore kept the wine to gladden his [suc]cess. Many halfpence did he pic[k up] that had been lost through the [cracks] of the floor, and some few Spanish and the half of a broken sixpence, had doubtless been a love token. was likewise a silver coronation

George the Third. But, old Peter
ldthwaite's strong box fled from one
k corner to another, or otherwise
led the second Peter's clutches, till,
uld he seek much farther, he must
row into the earth.

Ve will not follow him in his trium-
nt progress, step by step. Suffice it,
: Peter worked like a steam-engine,
finished, in that one winter, the
which all the former inhabitants
the house, with the time and the
ients to aid them, had only half done
century. Except the kitchen, every
n and chamber was now gutted.
house was nothing but a shell,—the
irition of a house,—as unreal as the
ted edifices of a theatre. It was like
perfect rind of a great cheese, in
:h a mouse had dwelt and nibbled,
t was a cheese no more. And Peter
the mouse.

'hat Peter had torn down, Tabitha
burned up: for she wisely con-
red that, without a house, they
ild need no wood to warm it;
therefore economy was nonsense.
s the whole house might be said to
: dissolved in smoke, and flown up
ng the clouds, through the great
x flue of the kitchen chimney. It
an admirable parallel to the feat of
man who jumped down his own
it.

a the night between the last day
inter and the first of spring, every
x and cranny had been ransacked,
ot within the precincts of the kit-
. This fated evening was an ugly
A snow-storm had set in some
s before, and was still driven and
d about the atmosphere by a real
cane, which fought against the
e, as if the prince of the air, in per-

son, were putting the final stroke to
Peter's labors. The framework being so
much weakened, and the inward props
removed, it would have been no marvel,
if, in some stronger wrestle of the blast,
the rotten walls of the edifice, and all
the peaked roofs, had come crashing
down upon the owner's head. He, however, was careless of the peril, but as
wild and restless as the night itself, or
as the flame that quivered up the chimney, at each roar of the tempestuous
wind.

"The wine, Tabitha!" he cried. "My
grandfather's rich old wine! We will
drink it now!"

Tabitha arose from her smoke-blackened bench in the chimney-corner, and
placed the bottle before Peter, close
beside the old brass lamp, which had
likewise been the prize of his researches.
Peter held it before his eyes, and looking through the liquid medium, beheld
the kitchen illuminated with a golden
glory, which also enveloped Tabitha,
and gilded her silver hair, and converted
her mean garments into robes of queenly
splendor. It reminded him of his golden
dream.

"Mr. Peter," remarked Tabitha, "must
the wine be drunk before the money is
found?"

"The money *is* found!" exclaimed
Peter, with a sort of fierceness. "The
chest is within my reach. I will not
sleep, till I have turned this key in the
rusty lock. But, first of all, let us
drink!"

There being no corkscrew in the
house, he smote the neck of the bottle
with old Peter Goldthwaite's rusty key,
and decapitated the sealed cork at a
single blow. He then filled two little
china teacups, which Tabitha had

brought from the cupboard. So clear and brilliant was this aged wine, that it shone within the cups, and rendered the sprig of scarlet flowers, at the bottom of each, more distinctly visible than when there had been no wine there. Its rich and delicate perfume wasted itself round the kitchen.

"Drink, Tabitha!" cried Peter. "Blessings on the honest old fellow who set aside this good liquor for you and me! And here's to Peter Goldthwaite's memory!"

"And good cause have we to remember him," quoth Tabitha, as she drank.

How many years, and through what changes of fortune, and various calamity, had that bottle hoarded up its effervescent joy, to be quaffed at last by two such boon companions! A portion of the happiness of a former age had been kept for them, and was now set free, in a crowd of rejoicing visions, to sport amid the storm and desolation of the present time. Until they have finished the bottle, we must turn our eyes elsewhere.

It so chanced, that, on this stormy night, Mr. John Brown found himself ill at ease, in his wire-cushioned armchair, by the glowing grate of anthracite, which heated his handsome parlor. He was naturally a good sort of a man, and kind and pitiful, whenever the misfortunes of others happened to reach his heart through the padded vest of his own prosperity. This evening, he had thought much about his old partner, Peter Goldthwaite, his strange vagaries, and continual ill luck, the poverty of his dwelling at Mr. Brown's last visit, and Peter's crazed and haggard aspect, when he had talked with him at the window.

"Poor fellow!" thought Mr. Brown. "Poor, crack-brained Goldthwaite! For old acquaintance' I ought to have taken care that he comfortable, this rough winter.

These feelings grew so powerful, in spite of the inclement weather resolved to visit Peter Goldthwaite mediately. The strength of the imp was really singular. Every shriek of blast seemed a summons, or would seemed so, had Mr. Brown been ac tomed to hear the echoes of his fancy in the wind. Much amazed at active benevolence, he huddled him in his cloak, muffled his throat and in comforters and handkerchiefs, thus fortified bade defiance to the t est. But the powers of the air had r the best of the battle. Mr. Brown just weathering the corner, by Goldthwaite's house, when the hurri caught him off his feet, tossed him downward into a snow-bank, and ceeded to bury his protuberant par neath fresh drifts. There seemed hope of his reappearance, earlier the next thaw. At the same mon his hat was snatched away, and wh aloft into some far distant re whence no tidings have as yet retu

Nevertheless, Mr. Brown cont to burrow a passage through the s drift, and, with his bare head against the storm, floundered onwa Peter's door. There was such a c ing, and groaning, and rattling, and an ominous shaking throughout crazy edifice, that the loudest rap have been inaudible to those withir therefore entered, without cerem and groped his way to the kitchen

His intrusion, even there, was ticed. Peter and Tabitha stood

r backs to the door, stooping over
arge chest, which, apparently, they
just dragged from a cavity, or con-
ed closet, on the left side of the
nney. By the lamp in the old
aan's hand, Mr. Brown saw that the
t was barred and clamped with iron,
ngthened with iron plates, and
lded with iron nails, so as to be a
receptacle in which the wealth of
century might be hoarded up for
wants of another. Peter Gold-
aite was inserting a key into the

O Tabitha!" cried he, with tremu-
rapture, "how shall I endure the
gence? The gold!—the bright, bright
! Methinks I can remember my last
ce at it, just as the iron-plated lid
down. And ever since, being seventy
s, it has been blazing in secret, and
ering its splendor against this glori-
moment! It will flash upon us like
noonday sun!"

Then shade your eyes, Mr. Peter!"
Tabitha, with somewhat less pa-
e than usual. "But, for mercy's
, do turn the key!"

ad, with a strong effort of both
s, Peter did force the rusty key
igh the intricacies of the rusty lock.

Brown, in the mean time, had
n near, and thrust his eager visage
een those of the other two, at the
nt that Peter threw up the lid. No
en blaze illuminated the kitchen.

What's here?" exclaimed Tabitha,
sting her spectacles, and holding
lamp over the open chest. "Old
r Goldthwaite's hoard of old rags."

retty much so, Tabby," said Mr.
n, lifting a handful of the treasure.
what a ghost of dead and buried
h had Peter Goldthwaite raised,

to scare himself out of his scanty wits
withal! Here was the semblance of an
incalculable sum, enough to purchase
the whole town, and build every street
anew, but which, vast as it was, no sane
man would have given a solid sixpence
for. What then, in sober earnest, were
the delusive treasures of the chest?
Why, here were old provincial bills of
credit, and treasury-notes, and bills of
land banks, and all other bubbles of the
sort, from the first issue, above a century and a half ago, down nearly to the
Revolution. Bills of a thousand pounds
were intermixed with parchment pen-
nies, and worth no more than they.

"And this, then, is old Peter Goldthwaite's treasure!" said John Brown.
"Your namesake, Peter, was something
like yourself; and, when the provincial
currency had depreciated fifty or
seventy-five per cent, he bought it up,
in expectation of a rise. I have heard my
grandfather say, that old Peter gave his
father a mortgage of this very house
and land, to raise cash for his silly
project. But the currency kept sinking,
till nobody would take it as a gift; and
there was old Peter Goldthwaite, like
Peter the second, with thousands in his
strong box, and hardly a coat to his
back. He went mad upon the strength
of it. But, never mind, Peter! It is
just the sort of capital for building
castles in the air."

"The house will be down about our
ears!" cried Tabitha, as the wind shook
it with increasing violence.

"Let it fall!" said Peter, folding his
arms, as he seated himself upon the
chest.

"No, no, my old friend Peter," said
John Brown. "I have house-room for

you and Tabby, and a safe vault for the chest of treasure. To-morrow we will try to come to an agreement about the sale of this old house. Real estate is well up, and I could afford you a pretty handsome price."

"And I," observed Peter Goldthwaite, with reviving spirits, "have a plan for laying out the cash to great advanta[g]

"Why, as to that," muttered J[ohn] Brown to himself, "we must apply the next court for a guardian to t[ake] care of the solid cash; and if P[eter] insists upon speculating, he may d[o so] to his heart's content, with old PE[TER] GOLDTHWAITE'S TREASURE."

TWICE-TOLD TALES

THE SNOW-IMAGE

A CHILDISH MIRACLE

NE afternoon of a cold winter's day,
n the sun shone forth with chilly
htness, after a long storm, two chil-
 asked leave of their mother to run
and play in the new-fallen snow.
 elder child was a little girl, whom,
use she was of a tender and modest
osition, and was thought to be very
 itiful, her parents, and other people
 were familiar with her, used to call
 et. But her brother was known by
 style and title of Peony, on account
 ne ruddiness of his broad and round
 phiz, which made everybody think
 sunshine and great scarlet flowers.
 father of these two children, a cer-
 Mr. Lindsey, it is important to say,
 an excellent but exceedingly matter-
 ct sort of man, a dealer in hard-
 , and was sturdily accustomed to
 what is called the common-sense
 of all matters that came under his
 ideration. With a heart about as
 er as other people's, he had a head
 ird and impenetrable, and therefore,
 aps, as empty, as one of the iron
 which it was part of his business
 ell. The mother's character, on the
 hand, had a strain of poetry in it,
 it of unworldly beauty,—a delicate
 dewy flower, as it were, that had
 ved out of her imaginative youth,
 still kept itself alive amid the
 realities of matrimony and

motherhood.

So, Violet and Peony, as I began with
saying, besought their mother to let
them run out and play in the new snow;
for, though it had looked so dreary and
dismal, drifting downward out of the
gray sky, it had a very cheerful aspect,
now that the sun was shining on it. The
children dwelt in a city, and had no
wider play-place than a little garden
before the house, divided by a white
fence from the street, and with a pear-
tree and two or three plum-trees over-
shadowing it, and some rose-bushes just
in front of the parlor windows. The trees
and shrubs, however, were now leafless,
and their twigs were enveloped in the
light snow, which thus made a kind of
wintry foliage, with here and there a
pendent icicle for the fruit.

"Yes, Violet,—yes, my little Peony,"
said their kind mother, "you may go
out and play in the new snow."

Accordingly, the good lady bundled
up her darlings in woolen jackets and
wadded sacks, and put comforters round
their necks, and a pair of striped gaiters
on each little pair of legs, and worsted
mittens on their hands, and gave them
a kiss apiece, by way of a spell to keep
away Jack Frost. Forth sallied the two
children, with a hop-skip-and-jump, that
carried them at once into the very heart
of a huge snow-drift, whence Violet
emerged like a snow-bunting, while little
Peony floundered out with his round

face in full bloom. Then what a merry time had they! To look at them, frolicking in the wintry garden, you would have thought that the dark and pitiless storm had been sent for no other purpose but to provide a new plaything for Violet and Peony, and that they themselves had been created, as the snow-birds were, to take delight only in the tempest, and in the white mantle which it spread over the earth.

At last, when they had frosted one another all over with handfuls of snow, Violet, after laughing heartily at little Peony's figure, was struck with a new idea.

"You look exactly like a snow-image, Peony," said she, "if your cheeks were not so red. And that puts me in mind! Let us make an image out of snow,— an image of a little girl,—and it shall be our sister, and shall run about and play with us all winter long. Won't it be nice?"

"O yes!" cried Peony, as plainly as he could speak, for he was but a little boy. "That will be nice! And mamma shall see it!"

"Yes," answered Violet, "mamma shall see the new little girl. But she must not make her come into the warm parlor; for, you know, our little snow-sister will not love the warmth."

And forthwith the children began this great business of making a snow-image that should run about; while their mother, who was sitting at the window and overheard some of their talk, could not help smiling at the gravity with which they set about it. They really seemed to imagine that there would be no difficulty whatever in creating a live little girl out of the snow. And, to say the truth, if miracles are ever to be

wrought, it will be by putting our ha[...] to the work in precisely such a sin[...] and undoubting frame of mind as [...] in which Violet and Peony now un[...] took to perform one, without so m[...] as knowing that it was a miracle. [...] thought the mother; and thought, [...] wise, that the new snow, just fa[...] from Heaven, would be excellent [...] terial to make new beings of, if it v[...] not so very cold. She gazed at the [...] dren a moment longer, delighting [...] watch their little figures,—the girl, [...] for her age, graceful and agile, an[...] delicately colored that she looked [...] a cheerful thought more than a phy[...] reality,—while Peony expanded [...] breadth rather than height, and r[...] along on his short and sturdy legs[...] substantial as an elephant, though [...] quite so big. Then the mother resu[...] her work. What it was I forget; [...] she was either trimming a silken bo[...] for Violet, or darning a pair of st[...] ings for little Peony's short legs. A[...] however, and again, and yet o[...] agains, she could not help turning [...] head to the window, to see how [...] children got on with their snow-im[...]

Indeed, it was an exceedingly plea[...] sight, those bright little souls at [...] tasks! Moreover, it was really won[...] ful to observe how knowingly and [...] fully they managed the matter. V[...] assumed the chief direction, and [...] Peony what to do, while, with her [...] delicate fingers, she shaped out all [...] nicer parts of the snow-figure. [...] seemed, in fact, not so much to be [...] by the children, as to grow up u[...] their hands, while they were pla[...] and prattling about it. Their mother [...] quite surprised at this; and the lo[...] she looked, the more and more surp[...]

grew.

"What remarkable children mine
!" thought she, smiling with a
ther's pride; and smiling at herself,
, for being so proud of them. "What
er children could have made any-
ng so like a little girl's figure out of
w, at the first trial? Well;—but now
ust finish Peony's new frock, for
grandfather is coming to-morrow,
I want the little fellow to look
dsome."

o she took up the frock, and was
n as busily at work again with her
dle as the two children with their
w-image. But still, as the needle
elled hither and thither through the
as of the dress, the mother made her
light and happy by listening to the
voices of Violet and Peony. They
talking to one another all the time,
tongues being quite as active as
feet and hands. Except at inter-
she could not distinctly hear what
said, but had merely a sweet im-
sion that they were in a most loving
d, and were enjoying themselves
ly, and that the business of making
snow-image went prosperously on.
and then, however, when Violet
Peony happened to raise their
es, the words were as audible as if
had been spoken in the very parlor
e the mother sat. O, how delight-
those words echoed in her heart,
though they meant nothing so very
or wonderful, after all!

t you must know a mother listens
her heart, much more than with
ars; and thus she is often delighted
the trills of celestial music, when
people can hear nothing of the

eony, Peony!" cried Violet to her
brother, who had gone to another part
of the garden. "bring me some of that
fresh snow, Peony from the very farthest corner, where we have not been
trampling. I want it to shape our little
snow-sister's bosom with. You know
that part must be quite pure, just as it
came out of the sky!"

"Here it is, Violet!" answered Peony,
in his bluff tone,—but a very sweet
tone, too,—as he came floundering
through the half-trodden drifts. "Here
is the snow for her little bosom. O Violet, how beau-ti-ful she begins to look!"

"Yes," said Violet, thoughtfully and
quietly, "our snow-sister does look very
lovely. I did not quite know, Peony,
that we could make such a sweet little
girl as this!"

The mother, as she listened, thought
how fit and delightful an incident it
would be, if fairies, or, still better, if
angel-children were to come from Paradise, and play invisibly with her own
darlings, and help them to make their
snow-image, giving it the features of
celestial babyhood! Violet and Peony
would not be aware of their immortal
playmates,—only they would see that
the image grew very beautiful while
they worked at it, and would think that
they themselves had done it all.

"My little girl and boy deserve such
playmates, if mortal children ever did!"
said the mother to herself; and then she
smiled again at her own motherly pride.

Nevertheless, the idea seized upon her
imagination; and, ever and anon, she
took a glimpse out of the window, half
dreaming that she might see the golden-
haired children of Paradise sporting
with her own golden-haired Violet and
bright-cheeked Peony.

Now, for a few moments, there was

a busy and earnest, but indistinct hum of the two children's voices, as Violet and Peony wrought together with one happy consent. Violet still seemed to be the guiding spirit, while Peony acted rather as a laborer, and brought her the snow from far and near. And yet the little urchin evidently had a proper understanding of the matter, too!

"Peony, Peony!" cried Violet; for her brother was again at the other side of the garden. "Bring me those light wreaths of snow that have rested on the lower branches of the pear-tree. You can clamber on the snow-drift, Peony, and reach them easily. I must have them to make some ringlets for our snow-sister's head!"

"Here they are, Violet!" answered the little boy. "Take care you do not break them. Well done! Well done! How pretty!"

"Does she not look sweetly?" said Violet, with a very satisfied tone; "and now we must have some little shining bits of ice, to make the brightness of her eyes. She is not finished yet. Mamma will see how very beautiful she is; but papa will say, 'Tush! nonsense!— come in out of the cold!' "

"Let us call mamma to look out," said Peony; and then he shouted lustily, "Mamma! mamma!! mamma!!! Look out, and see what a nice 'ittle girl we are making!"

The mother put down her work for an instant, and looked out of the window. But it so happened that the sun—for this was one of the shortest days of the whole year—had sunken so nearly to the edge of the world that his setting shine came obliquely into the lady's eyes. So she was dazzled, you must understand, and could not very distinctly

observe what was in the garden. S however, through all that bright, bli ing dazzle of the sun and the new sn she beheld a small white figure in garden, that seemed to have a wonde deal of human likeness about it. / she saw Violet and Peony,—indeed, looked more at them than at the im —she saw the two children still at wc Peony bringing fresh snow, and Vi applying it to the figure as scientific as a sculptor adds clay to his mc Indistinctly as she discerned the sn child, the mother thought to her that never before was there a sn figure so cunningly made, nor ever s a dear little girl and boy to make i

"They do everything better than o children," said she, very complace: "No wonder they make better sr images!"

She sat down again to her work, made as much haste with it as poss because twilight would soon come, Peony's frock was not yet finished, grandfather was expected, by railr pretty early in the morning. Faster faster, therefore, went her flying fin The children, likewise, kept busil work in the garden, and still the me listened, whenever she could cat word. She was amused to observe their little imaginations had got n up with what they were doing, and carried away by it. They seemed tively to think that the snow-child w run about and play with them.

"What a nice playmate she wi for us, all winter long!" said Viole hope papa will not be afraid of giving us a cold! Shan't you love dearly, Peony?"

"O yes!" cried Peony. "And I hug her, and she shall sit down

me, and drink some of my warm
k!"

'O no, Peony!" answered Violet, with
ve wisdom. "That will not do at all.
rm milk will not be wholesome for
little snow-sister. Little snow-people,
: her, eat nothing but icicles. No,
Peony; we must not give her any-
g warm to drink!"

here was a minute or two of silence;
Peony, whose short legs were never
ry, had gone on a pilgrimage again
he other side of the garden. All of
udden, Violet cried out, loudly and
fully,—

Look here, Peony! Come quickly!
ight has been shining on her cheek
of that rose-colored cloud! and the
r does not go away! Is not that
utiful!"

Yes; it is beau-ti-ful," answered
ny, pronouncing the three syllables
1 deliberate accuracy. "O Violet,
' look at her hair! It is all like
!"

O, certainly," said Violet, with tran-
lity, as if it were very much a mat-
of course. "That color, you know,
es from the golden clouds, that we
up there in the sky. She is almost
hed now. But her lips must be made
' red,—redder than her cheeks. Per-
:, Peony, it will make them red, if
both kiss them!"

ccordingly, the mother heard two
:t little smacks, as if both her chil-
were kissing the snow-image on
rozen mouth. But as this did not
 to make the lips quite red enough,
*t next proposed that the snow-child
ld be invited to kiss Peony's scarlet
k.

.ome, 'ittle snow-sister, kiss me!"
I Peony.

"There! she has kissed you," added
Violet, "and now her lips are very red.
And she blushed a little, too!"

"O, what a cold kiss!" cried Peony.

Just then, there came a breeze of the
pure west wind, sweeping through the
garden and rattling the parlor windows.
It sounded so wintry cold, that the
mother was about to tap on the window-
pane with her thimbled finger, to summon the two children in, when they
both cried out to her with one voice.
The tone was not a tone of surprise,
although they were evidently a good
deal excited; it appeared rather as if
they were very much rejoiced at some
event that had now happened, but
which they had been looking for, and
had reckoned upon all along.

"Mamma! mamma! We have finished
our little snow-sister, and she is running
about the garden with us!"

"What imaginative little beings my
children are!" thought the mother,
putting the last few stitches into Peony's
frock. "And it is strange, too, that they
make me almost as much a child as they
themselves are! I can hardly help believing, now, that the snow-image has
really come to life!"

"Dear mamma!" cried Violet, "pray
look out, and see what a sweet playmate
we have!"

The mother, being thus entreated,
could no longer delay to look forth from
the window. The sun was now gone out
of the sky, leaving, however, a rich inheritance of his brightness among those
purple and golden clouds which make
the sunsets of winter so magnificent.
But there was not the slightest gleam or
dazzle, either on the window or on the
snow; so that the good lady could look
all over the garden, and see everything

and everybody in it. And what do you think she saw there? Violet and Peony, of course, her own two darling children. Ah, but whom or what did she besides? Why, if you will believe me, there was a small figure of a girl, dressed all in white, with rose-tinged cheeks and ringlets of golden hue, playing about the garden with the two children! A stranger though she was, the child seemed to be on as familiar terms with Violet and Peony, and they with her, as if all the three had been playmates during the whole of their little lives. The mother thought to herself that it must certainly be the daughter of one of the neighbors, and that, seeing Violet and Peony in the garden, the child had run across the street to play with them. So this kind lady went to the door, intending to invite the little runaway into her comfortable parlor; for, now that the sunshine was withdrawn, the atmosphere, out of doors, was already growing very cold.

But, after opening the house-door, she stood an instant on the threshold, hesitating whether she ought to ask the child to come in, or whether she should even speak to her. Indeed, she almost doubted whether it were a real child, after all, or only a light wreath of the new-fallen snow, blown hither and thither about the garden by the intensely cold west-wind. There was certainly something very singular in the aspect of the little stranger. Among all the children of the neighborhood, the lady could remember no such face, with its pure white, and delicate rose-color, and the golden ringlets tossing about the forehead and cheeks. And as for her dress, which was entirely of white, and fluttering in the breeze, it was such as

no reasonable woman would put u[ ] a little girl, when sending her out play, in the depth of winter. It m[ ] this kind and careful mother shiver [ ] to look at those small feet, with not[ ] in the world on them except a very [ ] pair of white slippers. Neverthe[ ] airily as she was clad, the child see[ ] to feel not the slightest inconveni[ ] from the cold, but danced so lig[ ] over the snow that the tips of her left hardly a print in its surface; w[ ] Violet could but just keep pace [ ] her, and Peony's short legs compe[ ] him to lag behind.

Once, in the course of their play, [ ] strange child placed herself betw[ ] Violet and Peony, and taking a l[ ] of each, skipped merrily forward, [ ] they along with her. Almost imm[ ] ately, however, Peony pulled away[ ] little fist, and began to rub it as if [ ] fingers were tingling with cold; v[ ] Violet also released herself, though [ ] less abruptness, gravely remarking [ ] it was better not to take hold of ha[ ] The white-robed damsel said not a v[ ] but danced about, just as merrily a[ ] fore. If Violet and Peony did not ch[ ] to play with her, she could make ju[ ] good a playmate of the brisk and [ ] west-wind, which kept blowing he[ ] about the garden, and took such libe[ ] with her, that they seemed to have [ ] friends for a long time. All this v[ ] the mother stood on the threshold, [ ] dering how a little girl could loo[ ] much like a flying snow-drift, or h[ ] snow-drift could look so very li[ ] little girl.

She called Violet, and whispere[ ] her.

"Violet, my darling, what is [ ] child's name?" asked she. "Does sh[ ] r us?"

Why, dearest mamma," answered
let, laughing to think that her mother
not comprehend so very plain an
ir, "this is our little snow-sister,
m we have just been making!"

Yes, dear mamma," cried Peony,
ing to his mother, and looking up
ly into her face. "This is our snow-
ge! Is it not a nice 'ittle child?"

t this instant a flock of snow-birds
e flittering through the air. As was
natural, they avoided Violet and
ny. But—and this looked strange—
flew at once to the white-robed
l, fluttered eagerly about her head,
ted on her shoulders, and seemed
claim her as an old acquaintance.
on her part, was evidently as glad
ee these little birds, old Winter's
dchildren, as they were to see her,
welcomed them by holding out both
hands. Hereupon, they each and all
to alight on her two palms and
small fingers and thumbs, crowding
another off, with an immense flut-
g of their tiny wings. One dear little
nestled tenderly in her bosom; an-
'put its bill to her lips. They were
yous, all the while, and seemed as
in their element, as you may have
them when sporting with a snow-
.

olet and Peony stood laughing at
pretty sight; for they enjoyed the
y time which their new playmate
having with these small-winged
nts almost as much as if they
selves took part in it.

iolet," said her mother, greatly per-
d, "tell me the truth, without any
Who is this little girl?"

Iy darling mamma," answered Vio-
oking seriously into her mother's
face, and apparently surprised that she
should need any further explanation, "I
have told you truly who she is. It is our
little snow-image which Peony and I
have been making. Peony will tell you
so, as well as I."

"Yes, mamma," asseverated Peony,
with much gravity in his crimson little
phiz; "this is 'ittle snow-child. Is not
she a nice one? But, mamma, her hand
is, oh! so very cold!"

While mamma still hesitated what to
think and what to do, the street-gate
was thrown open, and the father of
Violet and Peony appeared, wrapped in
a pilot-cloth sack, with a fur cup drawn
down over his ears, and the thickest
of gloves upon his hands. Mr. Lindsey
was a middle-aged man, with a weary
and yet a happy look in his wind-flushed
and frost-pinched face, as if he had
been busy all the day long, and was glad
to get back to his quiet home. His eyes
brightened at the sight of his wife and
children, although he could not help
uttering a word or two of surprise, at
finding the whole family in the open air,
on so bleak a day and after sunset too.
He soon perceived the little white
stranger, sporting to and fro in the
garden, like a dancing snow-wreath, and
the flock of snow-birds fluttering about
her head.

"Pray, what little girl may that be?"
inquired this very sensible man. "Surely
her mother must be crazy, to let her go
out in such bitter weather as it has been
to-day, with only that flimsy white
gown, and those thin slippers!"

"My dear husband," said his wife, "I
know no more about the little thing
than you do. Some neighbor's child, I
suppose. Our Violet and Peony," she
added, laughing at herself for repeating

so absurd a story, "insist that she is nothing but a snow-image, which they have been busy about in the garden, almost all the afternoon."

As she said this, the mother glanced her eyes toward the spot where the children's snow-image had been made. What was her surprise, on perceiving that there was not the slightest trace of so much labor!—no image at all,—no piled-up heap of snow!—nothing whatever, save the prints of little footsteps around a vacant space!

"This is very strange!" said she.

"What is strange, dear mother?" asked Violet. "Dear father, do not you see how it is? This is our snow-image, which Peony and I have made, because we wanted another playmate. Did not we, Peony?"

"Yes, papa," said crimson Peony. "This be our 'ittle snow-sister. Is she not beau-ti-ful? But she gave me such a cold kiss!"

"Poh, nonsense, children!" cried their good, honest father, who, as we have already intimated, had an exceedingly common-sensible way of looking at matters. "Do not tell me of making live figures out of snow? Come, wife; this little stranger must not stay out in the bleak air a moment longer. We will bring her into the parlor; and you shall give her a supper of warm bread and milk, and make her as comfortable as you can. Meanwhile, I will inquire among the neighbors; or, if necessary, send the city-crier about the streets, to give notice of a lost child."

So saying, this honest and very kind-hearted man was going toward the little white damsel, with the best intentions in the world. But Violet and Peony, each seizing their father by the hand, earn-estly besought him not to make come in.

"Dear father," cried Violet, putt herself before him, "it is true wha have been telling you! This is our li snow-girl, and she cannot live any lon than while she breathes the cold we wind. Do not make her come into hot room!"

"Yes, father," shouted Peony, sta ing his little foot, so mightily was he earnest, "this be nothing but our 'i snow-child! She will not love the fire!"

"Nonsense, children, nonsense, n sense!" cried the father, half ve half laughing at what he conside their foolish obstinacy. "Run into house, this moment! It is too late play any longer, now. I must take of this little girl immediately, or will catch her death-a-cold!"

"Husband! dear husband!" said wife, in a low voice,—for she had l looking narrowly at the snow-child, was more perplexed than ever,—"t is something very singular in all You will think me foolish,—but—b may it not be that some invisible a has been attracted by the simplicity good faith with which our children about their undertaking? May he have spent an hour of his immortalit playing with those dear little souls? so the result is what we call a mir No, no! Do not laugh at me; I see a foolish thought it is!"

"My dear wife," replied the husb laughing heartily, "you are as n a child as Violet and Peony."

And in one sense so she was, fo through life she had kept her heart of childlike simplicity and faith, w was as pure and clear as crystal;

king at all matters through this trans-
ent medium, she sometimes saw
ths so profound, that other people
ghed at them as nonsense and ab-
dity.

But now kind Mr. Lindsey had ened the garden, breaking away from
two children, who still sent their
ill voices after him, beseeching him
et the snow-child stay and enjoy her-
in the cold west-wind. As he ap-
ached, the snow-birds took to flight.
little white damsel, also, fled back-
d, shaking her head, as if to say,
ay, do not touch me!" and roguishly,
t appeared, leading him through the
best of the snow. Once, the good man
mbled, and floundered down upon
face, so that, gathering himself up
in, with the snow sticking to his
gh pilot-cloth sack, he looked as
te and wintry as a snow-image of
largest size. Some of the neighbors,
nwhile, seeing him from their win-
s, wondered what could possess poor
Lindsey to be running about his
len in pursuit of a snow-drift, which
west-wind was driving hither and
her! At length, after a vast deal of
ble, he chased the little stranger
a corner, where she could not possi-
escape him. His wife had been look-
on, and, it being nearly twilight, was
der-struck to observe how the snow-
l gleamed and sparkled, and how
seemed to shed a glow all round
t her; and when driven into the
er, she positively glittered like a
It was a frosty kind of brightness,
like that of an icicle in the moon-
. The wife thought it strange that
Mr. Lindsey should see nothing
arkable in the snow-child's ap-
ance.

"Come, you odd little thing!" cried
the honest man, seizing her by the hand,
"I have caught you at last, and will
make you comfortable in spite of yourself. We will put a nice warm pair of
worsted stockings on your frozen little
feet, and you shall have a good thick
shawl to wrap yourself in. Your poor
white nose, I am afraid, is actually
frost-bitten. But we will make it all
right. Come along in."

And so, with a most benevolent smile
on his sagacious visage, all purple as it
was with the cold, this very well-meaning gentleman took the snow-child by
the hand and led her towards the house.
She followed him, droopingly and reluctant; for all the glow and sparkle was
gone out of her figure; and whereas just
before she had resembled a bright,
frosty, star-gemmed evening, with a
crimson gleam on the cold horizon, she
now looked as dull and languid as a
thaw. As kind Mr. Lindsey led her up
the steps of the door, Violet and Peony
looked into his face,—their eyes full of
tears, which froze before they could run
down their cheeks,—and again entreated
him not to bring their snow-image into
the house.

"Not bring her in!" exclaimed the
kind-hearted man. "Why, you are crazy,
my little Violet!—quite crazy, my small
Peony! She is so cold already, that her
hand has almost frozen mine, in spite
of my thick gloves. Would you have
her freeze to death?"

His wife, as he came up the steps,
had been taking another long, earnest,
almost awe-stricken gaze at the little
white stranger. She hardly knew whether
it was a dream or no; but she could not
help fancying that she saw the delicate
print of Violet's fingers on the child's

neck. It looked just as if, while Violet was shaping out the image, she had given it a gentle pat with her hand, and had neglected to smooth the impression quite away.

"After all, husband," said the mother, recurring to her idea that the angels would be as much delighted to play with Violet and Peony as she herself was,—"after all, she does look strangely like a snow-image! I do believe she is made of snow!"

A puff of the west-wind blew against the snow-child, and again she sparkled like a star.

"Snow!" repeated good Mr. Lindsey, drawing the reluctant guest over his hospitable threshold. "No wonder she looks like snow. She is half frozen, poor little thing! But a good fire will put everything to rights."

Without further talk, and always with the same best intentions, this highly benevolent and common-sensible individual led the little white damsel—drooping, drooping, drooping, more and more—out of the frosty air, and into his comfortable parlor. A Heidenberg stove, filled to the brim with intensely burning anthracite, was sending a bright gleam through the isinglass of its iron door, and causing the vase of water on its top to fume and bubble with excitement. A warm, sultry smell was diffused throughout the room. A thermometer on the wall farthest from the stove stood at eighty degrees. The parlor was hung with red curtains, and covered with a red carpet, and looked just as warm as it felt. The difference betwixt the atmosphere here and the cold, wintry twilight out of doors was like stepping at once from Nova Zembla to the hottest part of India, or from the North Pole

into an oven. O, this was a fine p. for the little white stranger!

The common-sensible man placed snow-child on the hearth-rug, right front of the hissing and fuming sto

"Now she will be comfortable!" c Mr. Lindsey, rubbing his hands looking about him, with the pleasan smile you ever saw. "Make yoursel home, my child."

Sad, sad and drooping looked little white maiden, as she stood on hearth-rug, with the hot blast of stove striking through her like a pe lence. Once, she threw a glance wistf toward the windows, and caugh glimpse, through its red curtains, of snow-covered roofs, and the stars g mering frostily, and all the delicious tensity of the cold night. The bleak w rattled the window-panes, as if it w summoning her to come forth. there stood the snow-child, droor before the hot stove!

But the common-sensible man nothing amiss.

"Come, wife," said he, "let her ha pair of thick stockings and a wo shawl or blanket directly; and tell I to give her some warm supper as as the milk boils. You, Violet Peony, amuse your little friend. Sl out of spirits, you see, at finding he in a strange place. For my part, I go around among the neighbors, find out where she belongs."

The mother, meanwhile, had gon search of the shawl and stockings; her own view of the matter, how subtle and delicate, had given away it always did, to the stubborn terialism of her husband. Without l ing the remonstrances of his two dren, who still kept murmuring

ir little snow-sister did not love the
rmth, good Mr. Lindsey took his de-
ture, shutting the parlor door care-
ly behind him. Turning up the collar
his sack over his ears, he emerged
m the house, and had barely reached
street-gate, when he was recalled
the screams of Violet and Peony,
the rapping of a thimbled finger
inst the parlor window.

'Husband! husband!" cried his wife,
wing her horror-stricken face through
window-panes. "There is no need of
ng for the child's parents!"

We told you so, father!" screamed
let and Peony, as he re-entered the
lor. "You would bring her in; and
our poor—dear—beau-ti-ful little
w-sister is thawed!"

nd their own sweet little faces were
ady dissolved in tears; so that their
ier, seeing what strange things oc-
onally happen in this every-day
ld, felt not a little anxious lest his
dren might be going to thaw too!
he utmost perplexity, he demanded
explanation of his wife. She could
reply, that, being summoned to
parlor by the cries of Violet and
ny, she found no trace of the little
e maiden, unless it were the remains
a heap of snow, which, while she
gazing at it, melted quite away
n the hearth-rug.

And there you see all that is left
!" added she, pointing to a pool of
r, in front of the stove.

Yes, father," said Violet, looking re-
chfully at him, through her tears,
re is all that is left of our dear
e snow-sister!"

Naughty father," cried Peony,
ping his foot, and—I shudder to
—shaking his little fist at the com-

mon-sensible man. "We told you how it
would be. What for did you bring her
in?"

And the Heidenberg stove, through
the isinglass of its door, seemed to glare
at good Mr. Lindsey, like a red-eyed
demon, triumphing in the mischief
which it had done!

This, you will observe, was one of
those rare cases, which yet will occasionally happen, where common-sense
finds itself at fault. The remarkable
story of the snow-image, though to that
sagacious class of people to whom good
Mr. Lindsey belongs it may seem but a
childish affair, is, nevertheless, capable
of being moralized in various methods,
greatly for their edification. One of its
lessons, for instance, might be, that it
behooves men, and especially men of
benevolence, to consider well what they
are about, and, before acting on their
philanthropic purposes, to be quite sure
that they comprehend the nature and
all the relations of the business in hand.
What has been established as an element
of good to one being may prove absolute
mischief to another; even as the warmth
of the parlor was proper enough for
children of flesh and blood, like Violet
and Peony,—though by no means very
wholesome, even for them,—but involved nothing short of annihilation to
the unfortunate snow-image.

But, after all, there is no teaching
anything to wise men of good Mr. Lindsey's stamp. They know everything—
oh, to be sure!—everything that has
been, and everything that is, and everything that, by any future possibility,
can be. And, should some phenomenon
of nature or Providence transcend their
system, they will not recognize it, even
if it come to pass under their very noses.

"Wife," said Mr. Lindsey, after a fit of silence, "see what a quantity of snow the children have brought in on their feet! It has made quite a puddle b before the stove. Pray tell Dora to br some towels and sop it up!"

THE GREAT STONE FACE

ONE afternoon, when the sun was going down, a mother and her little boy sat at the door of their cottage, talking about the Great Stone Face. They had but to lift their eyes, and there it was plainly to be seen, though miles away, with the sunshine brightening all its features.

And what was the Great Stone Face?

Embosomed amongst a family of lofty mountains, there was a valley so spacious that it contained many thousand inhabitants. Some of these good people dwelt in log-huts, with the black forest all around them, on the steep and difficult hillsides. Others had their homes in comfortable farm-houses, and cultivated the rich soil on the gentle slopes or level surfaces of the valley. Others, again, were congregated into populous villages, where some wild, highland rivulet, tumbling down from its birthplace in the upper mountain region, had been caught and tamed by human cunning, and compelled to turn the machinery of cotton-factories. The inhabitants of this valley, in short, were numerous, and of many modes of life. But all of them, grown people and children, had a kind of familiarity with the Great Stone Face, although some possessed the gift of distinguishing this grand natural phenomenon more perfectly than many of their neighbors.

The Great Stone Face, then, was a work of Nature in her mood of maje playfulness, formed on the perpendicu side of a mountain by some imme rocks, which had been thrown toget in such a position as, when viewed a proper distance, precisely to resem the features of the human countenar It seemed as if an enormous giant, o Titan, had sculptured his own liken on the precipice. There was the br arch of the forehead, a hundred feet height; the nose, with its long brid and the vast lips, which, if they co have spoken, would have rolled t thunder accents from one end of valley to the other. True, it is, tha the spectator approached too near, lost the outline of the gigantic vis and could discern only a heap of p derous and gigantic rocks, piled chaotic ruin one upon another. Ret ing his steps, however, the wondr features would again be seen; and farther he withdrew from them, more like a human face, with all original divinity intact, did they app until, as it grew dim in the dista with the clouds and glorified vapo the mountains clustering about it, Great Stone Face seemed positively be alive.

It was a happy lot for childrer grow up to manhood or womanh with the Great Stone Face before t eyes, for all the features were no

l the expression was at once grand
l sweet, as if it were the glow of a
t, warm heart, that embraced all
nkind in its affections, and had room
more. It was an education only to
k at it. According to the belief of
ny people, the valley owed much of
fertility to this benign aspect that
continually beaming over it, illumi-
ing the clouds, and infusing tender-
s into the sunshine.

s we began with saying, a mother
her little boy sat at their cottage
r, gazing at the Great Stone Face,
talking about it. The child's name
Ernest.

Mother," said he, while the Titanic
ge smiled on him, "I wish that it
ld speak, for it looks so very kindly
its voice must needs be pleasant.
were to see a man with such a face,
ould love him dearly."

If an old prophecy should come to
," answered his mother, "we may
a man, some time or other, with
tly such a face as that."

What prophecy do you mean, dear
her?" eagerly inquired Ernest.
ay tell me all about it!"

o his mother told him a story that
own mother had told to her, when
herself was younger than little
est; a story, not of things that were
, but of what was yet to come; a
y, nevertheless, so very old, that
the Indians, who formerly in-
ted this valley, had heard it from
forefathers, to whom, as they
ned, it had been murmured by the
ntain streams, and whispered by
wind among the tree-tops. The pur-
was, that, at some future day, a
l should be born hereabouts, who
destined to become the greatest and

noblest personage of his time, and whose
countenance in manhood should bear an
exact resemblance to the Great Stone
Face. Not a few old-fashioned people,
and young ones likewise, in the ardor
of their hopes, still cherished an enduring faith in this old prophecy. But
others, who had seen more of the world,
had watched and waited till they were
weary, and had beheld no man with such
a face, nor any man that proved to be
much greater or nobler than his neighbors, concluded it to be nothing but an
idle tale. At all events, the great man
of the prophecy had not yet appeared.

"O mother, dear mother!" cried
Ernest, clapping his hands above his
head, "I do hope that I shall live to
see him!"

His mother was an affectionate and
thoughtful woman, and felt that it was
wisest not to discourage the generous
hopes of her little boy. So she only said
to him, "Perhaps you may."

And Ernest never forgot the story
that his mother told him. It was always
in his mind, whenever he looked upon
the Great Stone Face. He spent his
childhood in the log-cottage where he
was born, and was dutiful to his mother,
and helpful to her in many things, assisting her much with his little hands,
and more with his loving heart. In this
manner, from a happy yet often pensive
child, he grew up to be a mild, quiet,
unobtrusive boy, and sun-browned with
labor in the fields, but with more intelligence brightening his aspects than
is seen in many lads who have been
taught at famous schools. Yet Ernest
had had no teacher, save only that the
Great Stone Face became one to him.
When the toil of the day was over, he
would gaze at it for hours, until he be-

gan to imagine that those vast features recognized him, and gave him a smile of kindness and encouragement, responsive to his own look of veneration. We must not take upon us to affirm that this was a mistake, although the Face may have looked no more kindly at Ernest than at all the world besides. But the secret was, that the boy's tender and confiding simplicity discerned what other people could not see; and thus the love, which was meant for all, became his peculiar portion.

About this time, there went a rumor throughout the valley, that the great man, foretold from ages long ago, who was to bear a resemblance to the Great Stone Face, had appeared at last. It seems that, many years before, a young man had migrated from the valley and settled at a distant seaport, where, after getting together a little money, he had set up as a shopkeeper. His name—but I could never learn whether it was his real one, or a nickname that had grown out of his habits and success in life— was Gathergold. Being shrewd and active, and endowed by Providence with that inscrutable faculty which develops itself in what the world calls luck, he became an exceedingly rich merchant, and owner of a whole fleet of bulky-bottomed ships. All the countries of the globe appeared to join hands for the mere purpose of adding heap after heap to the mountainous accumulation of this one man's wealth. The cold regions of the North, almost within the gloom and shadow of the Arctic Circle, sent him their tribute in the shape of furs; hot Africa sifted for him the golden sands of her rivers, and gathered up the ivory tusks of her great elephants out of the forests; the East came bringing him the

rich shawls, and spices, and teas, a the effulgence of diamonds, and gleaming purity of large pearls. ocean, not to be behindhand with earth, yielded up her mighty wha that Mr. Gathergold might sell t oil, and make a profit on it. Be original commodity what it might, was gold within his grasp. It might said of him, as of Midas in the fa that whatever he touched with his fin immediately glistened, and grew yell and was changed at once into ster metal, or, which suited him still bet into piles of coin. And, when Gathergold had become so very that it would have taken him a hund years only to count his wealth, he thought himself of his native valley, resolved to go back thither, and end days where he was born. With this pose in view, he sent a skilful archi to build him such a palace as should fit for a man of his vast wealth live in.

As I have said above, it had alre been rumored in the valley that Gathergold had turned out to be prophetic personage so long and va looked for, and that his visage was perfect and undeniable similitude of Great Stone Face. People were the n ready to believe that this must n be the fact, when they beheld the sp did edifice that rose, as if by ench ment, on the site of his father's weather-beaten farm-house. The exte was of marble, so dazzling white it seemed as though the whole struc might melt away in the sunshine, those humbler ones which Mr. Gat gold, in his young play-days, before fingers were gifted with the touc transmutation, had been accustome

ld of snow. It had a richly orna-
nted portico, supported by tall pillars,
eath which was a lofty door, studded
h silver knobs, and made of a kind
variegated wood that had been
ught from beyond the sea. The win-
vs, from the floor to the ceiling of
h stately apartment, were composed,
pectively, of but one enormous pane
glass, so transparently pure that it
said to be a finer medium than
n the vacant atmosphere. Hardly
body had been permitted to see the
rior of this palace; but it was re-
ted, and with good semblance of
h, to be far more gorgeous than the
side, insomuch that whatever was
or brass in other houses was silver
gold in this; and Mr. Gathergold's
-chamber, especially, made such a
tering appearance that no ordinary
would have been able to close his
there. But, on the other hand, Mr.
hergold was now so inured to wealth,
perhaps he could not have closed
eyes unless where the gleam of it
certain to find its way beneath his
ids.

n due time the mansion was finished;
came the upholsterers, with mag-
cent furniture; then, a whole troop
black and white servants, the har-
ers of Mr. Gathergold, who in his
majestic person, was expected to
ve at sunset. Our friend Ernest,
nwhile, had been deeply stirred by
idea that the great man, the noble
, the man of prophecy, after so
y ages of delay, was at length to be
le manifest to his native valley. He
w, boy as he was, that there were a
sand ways in which Mr. Gathergold,
his vast wealth, might transform
self into an angel of beneficence, and

assume a control over human affairs as
wide and benignant as the smile of the
Great Stone Face. Full of faith and
hope, Ernest doubted not that what the
people said was true, and that now he
was to behold the living likeness of
those wondrous features on the mountain-side. While the boy was still gazing
up the valley, and fancying, as he always
did, that the Great Stone Face returned
his gaze and looked kindly at him, the
rumbling of wheels was heard, approaching swiftly along the winding road.

"Here he comes!" cried a group of
people who were assembled to witness
the arrival. "Here comes the great Mr.
Gathergold!"

A carriage, drawn by four horses,
dashed round the turn of the road.
Within it, thrust partly out of the window, appeared the physiognomy of a
little old man, with a skin as yellow as
if his own Midas-hand had transmuted
it. He had a low forehead, small, sharp
eyes, puckered about with innumerable
wrinkles, and very thin lips, which he
made still thinner by pressing them
forcibly together.

"The very image of the Great Stone
Face!" shouted the people. "Sure
enough, the old prophecy is true; and
here we have the great man come, at
last!"

And, what greatly perplexed Ernest,
they seemed actually to believe that
here was the likeness which they spoke
of. By the roadside there chanced to be
an old beggar-woman and two little
beggar-children, stragglers from some
far-off region, who, as the carriage rolled
onward, held out their hands and lifted
up their doleful voices, most piteously
beseeching charity. A yellow claw—the
very same that had clawed together so

much wealth—poked itself out of the coach-window, and dropped some copper coins upon the ground; so that, though the great man's name seems to have been Gathergold, he might just as suitably have been nicknamed Scatter-copper. Still, nevertheless, with an earnest shout, and evidently with as much good faith as ever, the people bellowed,—

"He is the very image of the Great Stone Face!"

But Ernest turned sadly from the wrinkled shrewdness of that sordid visage, and gazed up the valley, where, amid a gathering mist, gilded by the last sunbeams, he could still distinguish those glorious features which had impressed themselves into his soul. Their aspect cheered him. What did the benign lips seem to say?

"He will come! Fear not, Ernest; the man will come!"

The years went on, and Ernest ceased to be a boy. He had grown to be a young man now. He attracted little notice from the other inhabitants of the valley; for they saw nothing remarkable in his way of life, save that, when the labor of the day was over, he still loved to go apart and gaze and meditate upon the Great Stone Face. According to their idea of the matter, it was a folly, indeed, but pardonable, inasmuch as Ernest was industrious, kind, and neighborly, and neglected no duty for the sake of indulging this idle habit. They knew not that the Great Stone Face had become a teacher to him, and that the sentiment which was expressed in it would enlarge the young man's heart, and fill it with wider and deeper sympathies than other hearts. They knew not that thence

would come a better wisdom than co be learned from books, and a better than could be moulded on the defa example of other human lives. Neit did Ernest know that the thoughts a affections which came to him so na rally, in the fields and at the fires and wherever he communed with h self, were of a higher tone than th which all men shared with him. A sim soul,—simple as when his mother f taught him the old prophecy,—he held the marvellous features beam adown the valley, and still wonde that their human counterpart was long in making his appearance.

By this time poor Mr. Gather was dead and buried; and the od part of the matter was, that his wea which was the body and spirit of existence, had disappeared before death, leaving nothing of him bu living skeleton, covered over wit wrinkled, yellow skin. Since the m ing away of his gold, it had been v generally conceded that there was such striking resemblance, after all, twixt the ignoble features of the ru merchant and that majestic face u the mountain-side. So the people ce to honor him during his lifetime, quietly consigned him to forgetful after his decease. Once in a while is true his memory was brought u connection with the magnificent pa which he had built, and which long ago been turned into a hotel the accommodation of strangers, m tudes of whom came, every summe visit that famous natural curiosity, Great Stone Face. Thus, Mr. Gat gold being discredited and thrown the shade, the man of prophecy yet to come.

t so happened that a native-born son
the valley, many years before, had
sted as a soldier, and, after a great
l of hard fighting, had now become
illustrious commander. Whatever he
y be called in history, he was known
camps and on the battlefield under
nickname of Old Blood-and-Thun-
This war-worn veteran, being now
m with age and wounds, and weary
the turmoil of a military life, and
he roll of the drum and the clangor
the trumpet, that had so long been
ing in his ears, had lately signified
urpose of returning to his native
ey, hoping to find repose where he
embered to have left it. The inhabi-
s, his old neighbors and their grown-
children, were resolved to welcome
renowned warrior with a salute of
on and a public dinner; and all
more enthusiastically, it being af-
ed that now, at last, the likeness
he Great Stone Face had actually
ared. An aide-de-camp of old Blood-
Thunder, travelling through the val-
was said to have been struck with
resemblance. Moreover, the school-
es and early acquaintances of the
ral were ready to testify, on oath,
, to the best of their recollection,
aforesaid general had been exceed-
y like the majestic image, even when
oy, only that the idea had never
rred to them at that period. Great,
efore, was the excitement through-
the valley; and many people, who
never once thought of glancing
he Great Stone Face for years
re, now spent their time in
ng at it, for the sake of knowing
tly how General Blood-and-Thunder
ed.
the day of the great festival,

Ernest, with all the other people of
the valley, left their work, and proceeded to the spot where the sylvan
banquet was prepared. As he approached, the loud voice of the Reverend Doctor Battleblast was heard, beseeching a blessing on the good things
set before them, and on the distinguished friend of peace in whose honor
they were assembled. The tables were
arranged in a cleared space of the
woods, shut in by the surrounding trees,
except where a vista opened eastward,
and afforded a distant view of the
Great Stone Face. Over the general's
chair, which was a relic from the home
of Washington, there was an arch of
verdant boughs, with the laurel pro-
fusely intermixed, and surmounted by
his country's banner, beneath which he
had won his victories. Our friend Ernest raised himself on his tip-toes, in
hopes to get a glimpse of the celebrated guest; but there was a mighty
crowd about the tables anxious to hear
the toasts and speeches, and to catch
any word that might fall from the
general in reply; and a volunteer company, doing duty as a guard, pricked
ruthlessly with their bayonets at any
particularly quiet person among the
throng. So Ernest, being of an unobtrusive character, was thrust quite into
the background, where he could see no
more of Old Blood-and-Thunder's physiognomy than if it had been still blazing
on the battle-field. To console himself,
he turned towards the Great Stone Face,
which, like a faithful and long-remembered friend, looked back and smiled
upon him through the vista of the forest. Meantime, however, he could over-
hear the remarks of various individuals,
who were comparing the features of the

hero with the face on the distant mountain-side.

"'T is the same face, to a hair!" cried one man, cutting a caper for joy.

"Wonderfully like, that's a fact!" responded another.

"Like! why, I call it Old Blood-and-Thunder himself, in a monstrous looking-glass!" cried a third. "And why not? He's the greatest man of this or any other age, beyond a doubt."

And then all three of the speakers gave a great shout, which communicated electricity to the crowd, and called forth a roar from a thousand voices, that went reverberating for miles among the mountains, until you might have supposed that the Great Stone Face had poured its thunder-breath into the cry. All these comments, and this vast enthusiasm, served the more to interest our friend; nor did he think of questioning that now, at length, the mountain-visage had found its human counterpart. It is true, Ernest had imagined that this long-looked-for personage would appear in the character of a man of peace, uttering wisdom, and doing good, and making people happy. But, taking an habitual breadth of view, with all his simplicity, he contended that Providence should choose its own method of blessing mankind, and could conceive that this great end might be effected even by a warrior and a bloody sword, should inscrutable wisdom see fit to order matters so.

"The general! the general!" was now the cry. "Hush! silence! Old Blood-and-Thunder's going to make a speech."

Even so; for, the cloth being removed, the general's health had been drunk amid shouts of applause, and

he now stood upon his feet to th: the company. Ernest saw him. Th he was, over the shoulders of the crow from the two glittering epaulets a embroidered collar upward, beneath arch of green boughs with intertwi: laurel, and the banner drooping as to shade his brow! And there, too, ˅ ible in the same glance, through vista of the forest, appeared the Gr Stone Face! And was there, inde such a resemblance as the crowd 1 testified? Alas, Ernest could not rec nize it! He beheld a war-worn a weather-beaten countenance, full of ergy, and expressive of an iron w but the gentle wisdom, the deep, bro tender sympathies were altogether wa ing in Old Blood-and-Thunder's visa and even if the Great Stone Face 1 assumed his look of stern command, milder traits would still have tempe it.

"This is not the man of prophe: sighed Ernest to himself, as he m his way out of the throng. "And n the world wait longer yet?"

The mists had congregated about distant mountain-side, and there w seen the grand and awful features the Great Stone Face, awful but nignant, as if a mighty angel were ting among the hills, and enrobing h self in a cloud-vesture of gold purple. As he looked, Ernest c hardly believe but that a smile bea over the whole visage, with a radia still brightening, although without tion of the lips. It was probably effect of the western sunshine, mel through the thinly diffused vapors had swept between him and the ob that he gazed at. But—as it alw did—the aspect of his marvellous fr

de Ernest as hopeful as if he had
er hoped in vain.

Fear not, Ernest," said his heart,
n as if the Great Face were whisper-
him,—"fear not, Ernest; he will
e."

lore years sped swiftly and tran-
ly away. Ernest still dwelt in his
ve valley, and was now a man of
dle age. By imperceptible degrees,
ad become known among the people.
v, as heretofore, he labored for his
d, and was the same simple-hearted
a that he had always been. But he
thought and felt so much, he had
n so many of the best hours of
life to unworldly hopes for some
t good to mankind, that it seemed
though he had been talking with
angels, and had imbibed a portion
heir wisdom unawares. It was visible
he calm and well-considered benefi-
e of his daily life, the quiet stream
vhich had made a wide green mar-
all along its course. Not a day
ed by, that the world was not the
er because this man, humble as he
had lived. He never stepped aside
a his own path, yet would always
h a blessing to his neighbor. Al-
t involuntarily, too, he had become
eacher. The pure and high simplic-
of his thought, which, as one of
manifestations, took shape in the
l deeds that dropped silently from
hand, flowed also forth in speech.
uttered truths that wrought upon
moulded the lives of those who
d him. His auditors, it may be,
r suspected that Ernest, their own
nbor and familiar friend, was more
an ordinary man; least of all
Ernest himself suspect it; but, in-
bly as the murmur of a rivulet,

came thoughts out of his mouth that
no other human lips had spoken.

When the people's minds had had
a little time to cool, they were ready
enough to acknowledge their mistake in
imagining a similarity between General
Blood-and-Thunder's truculent physiognomy and the benign visage on the
mountain-side. But now, again, there
were reports and many paragraphs in
the newspapers, affirming that the likeness of the Great Stone Face had appeared upon the broad shoulders of a
certain eminent statesman. He, like Mr.
Gathergold and Old Blood-and-Thunder, was a native of the valley, but
had left it in his early days, and taken
up the trades of law and politics. Instead of the rich man's wealth and the
warrior's sword, he had but a tongue,
and it was mightier than both together.
So wonderfully eloquent was he, that
whatever he might choose to say, his
auditors had no choice but to believe
him; wrong looked like right, and right
like wrong; for when it pleased him
he could make a kind of illuminated fog
with his mere breath, and obscure the
natural daylight with it. His tongue,
indeed, was a magic instrument: sometimes it rumbled like the thunder; sometimes it warbled like the sweetest music.
It was the blast of war,—the song of
peace; and it seemed to have a heart
in it, when there was no such matter.
In good truth he was a wondrous man;
and when his tongue had acquired him
all other imaginable success,—when it
had been heard in halls of state, and in
the courts of princes and potentates,
—after it had made him known all over
the world, even as a voice crying from
shore to shore,—it finally persuaded his
countrymen to select him for the presi-

dency. Before this time,—indeed, as soon as he began to grow celebrated,—his admirers had found out the resemblance between him and the Great Stone Face; and so much were they struck by it, that throughout the country this distinguished gentleman was known by the name of Old Stony Phiz. The phrase was considered as giving a highly favorable aspect to his political prospects; for, as is likewise the case with the Popedom, nobody ever becomes president without taking a name other than his own.

While his friends were doing their best to make him president, Old Stony Phiz, as he was called, set out on a visit to the valley where he was born. Of course, he had no other object than to shake hands with his fellow-citizens, and neither thought nor cared about any effect which his progress through the country might have upon the election. Magnificent preparations were made to receive the illustrious statesman; a cavalcade of horsemen set forth to meet him at the boundary line of the State, and all the people left their business and gathered along the wayside to see him pass. Among these was Ernest. Though more than once disappointed, as we have seen, he had such a hopeful and confiding nature, that he was always ready to believe in whatever seemed beautiful and good. He kept his heart continually open, and thus was sure to catch the blessing from on high, when it should come. So now again, as buoyantly as ever, he went forth to behold the likeness of the Great Stone Face.

The cavalcade came prancing along the road, with a great clattering of hoofs and a mighty cloud of dust, which rose up so dense and high that visage of the mountain-side was c pletely hidden from Ernest's eyes. the great men of the neighborhood v there on horseback: militia officers uniform; the member of Congress; sheriff of the county; the editors newspapers; and many a farmer had mounted his patient steed, his Sunday coat upon his back. It re was a very brilliant spectacle, especi as there were numerous banners fla ing over the cavalcade, on some which were gorgeous portraits of illustrious statesman and the G Stone Face, smiling familiarly at another, like two brothers. If the tures were to be trusted, the mu resemblance, it must be confessed, marvellous. We must not forget to n tion that there was a band of m which made the echoes of the m tains ring and reverberate with loud triumph of its strains; so airy and soul-thrilling melodies b out among all the heights and holl as if every nook of his native va had found a voice, to welcome distinguished guest. But the gran effect was when the far-off moun precipice flung back the music; for the Great Stone Face itself seeme be swelling the triumphant chorus acknowledgment that, at length, man of prophecy was come.

All this while the people were th ing up their hats and shouting, with thusiasm so contagious that the k of Ernest kindled up, and he like threw up his hat, and shouted, as lo as the loudest, "Huzza for the man! Huzza for Old Stony Phiz!" as yet he had not seen him.

"Here he is, now!" cried those

d near Ernest. "There! There! Look
Old Stony Phiz and then at the
Man of the Mountain, and see if
' are not as like as two twin-
hers!"

the midst of all this gallant array
e an open barouche, drawn by four
e horses; and in the barouche, with
massive head uncovered, sat the
trious statesman, Old Stony Phiz
elf.

Confess it," said one of Ernest's
hbors to him, "the Great Stone Face
met its match at last."

ow, it must be owned that, at his
glimpse of the countenance which
bowing and smiling from the
uche, Ernest did fancy that there
a resemblance between it and the
familiar face upon the mountain-
The brow, with its massive depth
loftiness, and all the other features,
ed, were boldly and strongly hewn,
f in emulation of a more than
ic, of a Titanic model. But the sub-
y and stateliness, the grand expres-
of a divine sympathy, that illumi-
d the mountain visage, and ethe-
zed its ponderous granite substance
spirit, might here be sought in vain.
ething had been originally left out,
ad departed. And therefore the
rellously gifted statesman had al-
a weary gloom in the deep caverns
is eyes, as of a child that has out-
n its playthings, or a man of
ty faculties and little aims, whose
with all its high performances,
vague and empty, because no high
ose had endowed it with reality.

ll, Ernest's neighbor was thrusting
lbow into his side, and pressing him
an answer.

onfess! confess! Is not he the very

picture of your Old Man of the Mountain?"

"No!" said Ernest, bluntly, "I see little or no likeness."

"Then so much the worse for the Great Stone Face!" answered his neighbor; and again he set up a shout for Old Stony Phiz.

But Ernest turned away, melancholy, and almost despondent; for this was the saddest of his disappointments, to behold a man who might have fulfilled the prophecy, and had not willed to do so. Meantime, the cavalcade, the banners, the music, and the barouches swept past him, with the vociferous crowd in the rear, leaving the dust to settle down, and the Great Stone Face to be revealed again, with the grandeur that it had worn for untold centuries.

"Lo, here I am, Ernest!" the benign lips seemed to say. "I have waited longer than thou, and am not yet weary. Fear not; the man will come."

The years hurried onward, treading in their haste on one another's heels. And now they began to bring white hairs, and scatter them over the head of Ernest; they made reverend wrinkles across his forehead, and furrows in his cheeks. He was an aged man. But not in vain had he grown old: more than the white hairs on his head were the sage thoughts in his mind; his wrinkles and furrows were inscriptions that Time had graved, and in which he had written legends of wisdom that had been tested by the tenor of a life. And Ernest had ceased to be obscure. Unsought for, undesired, had come the fame which so many seek, and made him known in the great world, beyond the limits of the valley in which he had dwelt so quietly. College professors, and even the active men of cities, came from far to see and converse with Ernest; for the report had gone abroad that this simple husbandman had ideas unlike those of other men, not gained from books, but of a higher tone,— a tranquil and familiar majesty, as if he had been talking with the angels as his daily friends. Whether it were sage, statesman, or philanthropist, Ernest received these visitors with the gentle sincerity that had characterized him from boyhood, and spoke freely with them of whatever came uppermost, or lay deepest in his heart or their own. While they talked together, his face would kindle, unawares, and shine upon them, as with a mild evening light. Pensive with the fulness of such discourse, his guests took leave and went their way; and, passing up the valley, paused to look at the Great Stone Face, imagining that they had seen its likeness in a human countenance, but could not remember where.

While Ernest had been growing up and growing old, a bountiful Providence had granted a new poet to this earth. He, likewise, was a native of the valley, but had spent the greater part of his life at a distance from that romantic region, pouring out his sweet music amid the bustle and din of cities. Often, however, did the mountains which had been familiar to him in his childhood lift their snowy peaks into the clear atmosphere of his poetry. Neither was the Great Stone Face forgotten, for the poet had celebrated it in an ode, which was grand enough to have been uttered by its own majestic lips. This man of genius, we may say, had come down from heaven with wonderful endowments. If he sang of a

mountain, the eyes of all mankind held a mightier grandeur reposing its breast, or soaring to its sum than had before been seen there. his theme were a lovely lake, a ce tial smile had now been thrown c it, to gleam forever on its surf If it were the vast old sea, even deep immensity of its dread bo seemed to swell the higher, as if mo by the emotions of the song. Thus world assumed another and a be aspect from the hour that the blessed it with his happy eyes. Creator had bestowed him, as the best touch to his own handiw Creation was not finished till the came to interpret, and so complet

The effect was no less high and b tiful, when his human brethren were subject of his verse. The man woman, sordid with the common of life, who crossed his daily p and the little child who played ir were glorified if he beheld them in mood of poetic faith. He showed golden links of the great chain intertwined them with an angelic dred; he brought out the hidden t of a celestial birth that made t worthy of such kin. Some, indeed, t were, who thought to show the so ness of their judgment by affirming all the beauty and dignity of the nat world existed only in the poet's fa Let such men speak for themselves, undoubtedly appear to have spawned forth by Nature with a temptuous bitterness; she having tered them up out of her refuse after all the swine were made. As spects all things else, the poet's was the truest truth.

The songs of this poet found

to Ernest. He read them, after
customary toil, seated on the bench
re his cottage door, where, for
a length of time, he had filled
repose with thought, by gazing at
Great Stone Face. And now, as he
stanzas that caused the soul to
within him, he lifted his eyes
he vast countenance beaming on
so benignantly.

) majestic friend," he murmured,
essing the Great Stone Face, "is
this man worthy to resemble thee?"
e Face seemed to smile, but an-
ed not a word.

ow it happened that the poet,
gh he dwelt so far away, had not
heard of Ernest, but had medi-
much upon his character, until
eemed nothing so desirable as to
this man, whose untaught wisdom
ed hand in hand with the noble
icity of his life. One summer morn-
therefore, he took passage by the
ad, and, in the decline of the after-
, alighted from the cars at no
distance from Ernest's cottage.
great hotel, which had formerly
the palace of Mr. Gathergold,
close at hand, but the poet, with
carpet-bag on his arm, inquired at
where Ernest dwelt, and was re-
d to be accepted as his guest.
pproaching the door, he there found
good old man, holding a volume
s hand, which alternately he read,
then, with a finger between the
s, looked lovingly at the Great
e Face.

ood evening," said the poet. "Can
give a traveller a night's lodging?"
Villingly," answered Ernest; and
he added, smiling, "Methinks I
r saw the Great Stone Face look so

hospitably at a stranger."

The poet sat down on the bench beside him, and he and Ernest talked
together. Often had the poet held intercourse with the wittiest and the wisest,
but never before with a man like Ernest, whose thoughts and feelings gushed
up with such a natural freedom, and
who made great truths so familiar by
his simple utterance of them. Angels,
as had been so often said, seemed to
have wrought with him at his labor in
the fields; angels seemed to have sat
with him by the fireside; and, dwelling
with angels as friend with friends, he
had imbibed the sublimity of their
ideas, and imbued it with the sweet
and lowly charm of household words.
So thought the poet. And Ernest, on
the other hand, was moved and agitated by the living images which the
poet flung out of his mind, and which
peopled all the air about the cottage
door with shapes of beauty, both gay
and pensive. The sympathies of these
two men instructed them with a profounder sense than either could have
attained alone. Their minds accorded
into one strain, and made delightful
music which neither of them could have
claimed as all his own, nor distinguished
his own share from the other's. They
led one another, as it were, into a high
pavilion of their thoughts, so remote,
and hitherto so dim, that they had
never entered it before, and so beautiful that they desired to be there always.

As Ernest listened to the poet, he
imagined that the Great Stone Face
was bending forward to listen too. He
gazed earnestly into the poet's glowing
eyes.

"Who are you, my strangely gifted

guest?" he said.

The poet laid his finger on the volume that Ernest had been reading.

"You have read these poems," said he. "You know me, then,—for I wrote them."

Again, and still more earnestly than before, Ernest examined the poet's features; then turned towards the Great Stone Face; then back, with an uncertain aspect, to his guest. But his countenance fell; he shook his head, and sighed.

"Wherefore are you sad?" inquired the poet.

"Because," replied Ernest, "all through life I have awaited the fulfilment of a prophecy; and, when I read these poems, I hoped that it might be fulfilled in you."

"You hoped," answered the poet, faintly smiling, "to find in me the likeness of the Great Stone Face. And you are disappointed, as formerly with Mr. Gathergold, and Old Blood-and-Thunder, and Old Stony Phiz. Yes, Ernest, it is my doom. You must add my name to the illustrious three, and record another failure of your hopes. For—in shame and sadness do I speak it, Ernest —I am not worthy to be typified by yonder benign and majestic image."

"And why?" asked Ernest. He pointed to the volume. "Are not those thoughts divine?"

"They have a strain of the Divinity," replied the poet. "You can hear in them the far-off echo of a heavenly song. But my life, dear Ernest, has not corresponded with my thought. I have had grand dreams, but they have been only dreams, because I have lived—and that, too, by my own choice—among poor and mean realities. Sometimes even—

shall I dare to say it?—I lack f in the grandeur, the beauty, and goodness which my own works are to have made more evident in na and in human life. Why, then, seeker of the good and true, shou thou hope to find me in yonder in of the divine!"

The poet spoke sadly, and his were dim with tears. So, likewise, those of Ernest.

At the hour of sunset, as had been his frequent custom, Ernest to discourse to an assemblage of neighboring inhabitants, in the air. He and the poet, arm in arm, talking together as they went al proceeded to the spot. It was a s nook among the hills, with a precipice behind, the stern front which was relieved by the pleasant age of many creeping plants, that n a tapestry for the naked rock, by h ing their festoons from all its ru angles. At a small elevation above ground, set in a rich framework of dure, there appeared a niche, spac enough to admit a human figure, freedom for such gestures as spont ously accompany earnest thought genuine emotion. Into this natural pit Ernest ascended, and threw a lo familiar kindness around upon his ence. They stood, or sat, or rec upon the grass, as seemed good to with the departing sunshine fa obliquely over them, and minglin subdued cheerfulness with the solem of a grove of ancient trees, beneath amid the boughs of which the g rays were constrained to pass. In other direction was seen the Great S Face, with the same cheer, comb with the same solemnity, in its b aspect.

nest began to speak, giving to the
le of what was in his heart and
. His words had power, because
accorded with his thoughts; and
houghts had reality and depth, be-
they harmonized with the life
h he had always lived. It was not
breath that this preacher uttered;
were the words of life, because a
of good deeds and holy love was
ed into them. Pearls, pure and rich,
been dissolved into this precious
ght. The poet, as he listened, felt
the being and character of Ernest
a nobler strain of poetry than he
ever written. His eyes glistening
tears, he gazed reverentially at
venerable man, and said within him-
that never was there an aspect
orthy of a prophet and a sage as
mild, sweet, thoughtful counte-
e, with the glory of white hair dif-
d about it. At a distance, but dis-
ly to be seen, high up in the golden

light of the setting sun, appeared the
Great Stone Face, with hoary mists
around it, like the white hairs around
the brow of Ernest. Its look of grand
beneficence seemed to embrace the
world.

At that moment, in sympathy with
a thought which he was about to utter,
the face of Ernest assumed a grandeur
of expression, so imbued with benevolence, that the poet, by an irresistible
impulse, threw his arms aloft, and
shouted,—

"Behold! Behold! Ernest is himself
the likeness of the Great Stone Face!"

Then all the people looked, and saw
that what the deep-sighted poet said
was true. The prophecy was fulfilled.
But Ernest, having finished what he
had to say, took the poet's arm, and
walked slowly homeward, still hoping
that some wiser and better man than
himself would by and by appear, bearing a resemblance to the GREAT STONE
FACE.

MAIN-STREET

RESPECTABLE-LOOKING individual
es his bow, and addresses the pub-
in my daily walks along the prin-
street of my native town, it has
occurred to me, that, if its growth
infancy upward, and the vicissi-
of characteristic scenes that have
ed along this thoroughfare during
more than two centuries of its
ence, could be presented to the eye
shifting panorama, it would be an
dingly effective method of illustrat-
he march of time. Acting on this

idea, I have contrived a certain pictorial
exhibition, somewhat in the nature of
a puppet-show, by means of which I
propose to call up the multiform and
many-colored Past before the spectator,
and show him the ghosts of his forefathers, amid a succession of historic
incidents, with no greater trouble than
the turning of a crank. Be pleased,
therefore, my indulgent patrons, to walk
into the show-room, and take your seats
before yonder mysterious curtain. The
little wheels and springs of my machin-

ery have been well oiled; a multitude of puppets are dressed in character, representing all varieties of fashion, from the Puritan cloak and jerkin to the latest Oak Hall coat; the lamps are trimmed, and shall brighten into noontide sunshine, or fade away in moonlight, or muffle their brilliancy in a November cloud, as the nature of the scene may require; and, in short, the exhibition is just ready to commence. Unless something should go wrong,—as, for instance, the misplacing of a picture, whereby the people and events of one ·century might be thrust into the middle of another; or the breaking of a wire, which would bring the course of time to a sudden period, —barring, I say, the casualties to which such a complicated piece of mechanism is liable,—I flatter myself, ladies and gentlemen, that the performance will elicit your generous approbation.

Ting-a-ting-ting! goes the bell; the curtain rises; and we behold—not, indeed, the Main-street—but the track of leaf-strewn forest-land over which its dusty pavement is hereafter to extend.

You perceive, at a glance, that this is the ancient and primitive wood,—the ever-youthful and venerably old,—verdant with new twigs, yet hoary, as it were, with the snowfall of innumerable years, that have accumulated upon its intermingled branches. The white man's axe has never smitten a single tree; his footstep has never crumpled a single one of the withered leaves, which all the autumns since the flood have been harvesting beneath. Yet, see! along through the vista of impending boughs there is already a faintly-traced path, running nearly east and west, as if a

prophecy or foreboding of the fu street had stolen into the heart the solemn old wood. Onward this hardly perceptible track, ascending over a natural swell of l now subsiding gently into a hol traversed here by a little strear which glitters like a snake through gleam of sunshine, and quickly h itself among the underbrush, in its c for the neighboring cove; and imp there by the massy corpse of a g of the forest, which had lived ou incalculable term of life, and been c thrown by mere old age, and lies bu in the new ·vegetation that is bor its decay. What footsteps can worn this half-seen path? Hark! we not hear them now rustling s over the leaves? We discern an In woman, — a majestic and que woman, or else her spectral image not represent her truly,—for th the great Squaw Sachem, whose with that of her sons, extends : Mystic to Agawam. That red chief, stalks by her side, is Wappacowet second husband, the priest and magi whose incantations shall hereafter fright the pale-faced settlers with g phantoms, dancing and shrieking ir woods, at midnight. But greater v be the affright of the Indian n mancer, if, mirrored in the poo water at his feet, he could cat prophetic glimpse of the noonday vels which the white man is des to achieve; if he could see, as dream, the stone-front of the st hall, which will cast its shadow this very spot; if he could be a that the future edifice will conta noble Museum, where, among coun curiosities of earth and sea, a few

arrow-heads shall be treasured up
memorials of a vanished race!
To such forebodings disturb the
aw Sachem and Wappacowet. They
s on, beneath the tangled shade,
ling high talk on matters of state
religion, and imagine, doubtless,
their own system of affairs will
ure forever. Meanwhile, how full of
own proper life is the scene that
around them! The gray squirrel
s up the trees, and rustles among
upper branches. Was not that the
of a deer? And there is the whir
a partridge! Methinks, too, I catch
cruel and stealthy eye of a wolf,
ne draws back into yonder imper-
as density of underbrush. So, there,
d the murmur of boughs, go the
ian queen and the Indian priest;
le the gloom of the broad wilder-
s impends over them, and its sombre
tery invests them as with some-
g preternatural; and only momen-
streaks of quivering sunlight, once
a great while, find their way down,
glimmer among the feathers in
r dusky hair. Can it be that the
nged street of a city will ever pass
this twilight solitude,—over those
heaps of the decaying tree-trunks,
through the swampy places, green
a water-moss, and penetrate that
eless entanglement of great trees,
ch have been uprooted and tossed
ther by a whirlwind? It has been
ilderness from the creation. Must
ot be a wilderness forever?

ere an acidulous-looking gentleman
blue glasses, with bows of Berlin
d, who has taken a seat at the ex-
ity of the front row, begins, at this
y stage of the exhibition, to criticise.
The whole affair is a manifest catch-

penny!" observes he, scarcely under his
breath. "The trees look more like weeds
in a garden than a primitive forest;
the Squaw Sachem and Wappacowet are
stiff in their pasteboard joints; and the
squirrels, the deer, and the wolf move
with all the grace of a child's wooden
monkey, sliding up and down a stick."

"I am obliged to you, sir, for the
candor of your remarks," replies the
showman, with a bow. "Perhaps they
are just. Human art has its limits, and
we must now and then ask a little aid
from the spectator's imagination."

"You will get no such aid from mine,"
responds the critic. "I make it a point
to see things precisely as they are. But
come! go ahead! the stage is waiting!"

The showman proceeds.

Casting our eyes again over the
scene, we perceive that strangers have
found their way into the solitary place.
In more than one spot, among the trees,
an upheaved axe is glittering in the sunshine. Roger Conant, the first settler
in Naumkeag, has built his dwelling,
months ago, on the border of the forest-
path; and at this moment he comes
eastward through the vista of woods,
with his gun over his shoulder, bringing home the choice portions of a deer.
His stalwart figure, clad in a leather
jerkin and breeches of the same, strides
sturdily onward, with such an air of
physical force and energy that we might
almost expect the very trees to stand
aside, and give him room to pass. And
so, indeed, they must; for, humble as
is his name in history, Roger Conant
still is of that class of men who do
not merely find, but make, their place
in the system of human affairs; a man
of thoughtful strength, he has planted
the germ of a city. There stands his

habitation, showing in its rough architecture some features of the Indian wigwam, and some of the log-cabin, and somewhat, too, of the straw-thatched cottage in Old England, where this good yeoman had his birth and breeding. The dwelling is surrounded by a cleared space of a few acres, where Indian corn grows thrivingly among the stumps of the trees; while the dark forest hems it in, and seems to gaze silently and solemnly, as if wondering at the breadth of sunshine which the white man spreads around him. An Indian, half hidden in the dusky shade, is gazing and wondering too.

Within the door of the cottage you discern the wife, with her ruddy English cheek. She is singing, doubtless, a psalm tune, at her household work; or, perhaps she sighs at the remembrance of the cheerful gossip, and all the merry social life, of her native village beyond the vast and melancholy sea. Yet the next moment she laughs, with sympathetic glee, at the sports of her little tribe of children; and soon turns round, with the home-look in her face, as her husband's foot is heard approaching the rough-hewn threshold. How sweet must it be for those who have an Eden in their hearts, like Roger Conant and his wife, to find a new world to project it into, as they have, instead of dwelling among old haunts of men, where so many household fires have been kindled and burnt out, that the very glow of happiness has something dreary in it! Not that this pair are alone in their wild Eden, for here comes Goodwife Massey, the young spouse of Jeffrey Massey, from her home hard by, with an infant at her breast. Dame Conant has another of like age; and it

shall hereafter be one of the disp' points of history which of these babies was the first town-born child

But see! Roger Conant has o neighbors within view. Peter Pal likewise has built himself a house, so has Balch, and Norman, and W bury. Their dwellings, indeed,—suc the ingenious contrivance of this of pictorial mechanism,—seem to arisen, at various points of the s even while we have been lookin, it. The forest-track, trodden and more by the hob-nailed shoe these sturdy and ponderous Eng men, has now a distinctness whi never could have acquired from light tread of a hundred times as r Indian moccasons. It will be a st anon. As we observe it now, it onward from one clearing to ano here plunging into a shadowy stri woods, there open to the sunshine everywhere showing a decided along which human interests have b to hold their career. Over yo swampy spot, two trees have been f and laid side by side, to make a c way. In another place, the axe cleared away a confused intricac fallen trees and clustered boughs, had been tossed together by a hurri So now the little children, just b ning to run alone, may trip along path, and not often stumble ove impediment, unless they stray fr to gather wood-berries beneath trees. And, besides the feet of g people and children, there are the c hoofs of a small herd of cows, seek their subsistence from the grasses, and help to deepen the of the future thoroughfare. Goats browse along it, and nibble at the

t thrust themselves across the way.
seldom, in its more secluded por-
s, where the black shadow of the
est strives to hide the trace of
an footsteps, stalks a gaunt wolf,
the watch for a kid or a young calf;
fixes his hungry gaze on the group
children gathering berries, and can
lly forbear to rush upon them. And
Indians, coming from their distant
wams to view the white man's settle-
at, marvel at the deep track which
makes, and perhaps are saddened by
itting presentiment that this heavy
d will find its way over all the land,
that the wild woods, the wild wolf,
the wild Indian will alike be tram-
beneath it. Even so shall it be.
pavements of the Main-street must
aid over the red man's grave.

ehold! here is a spectacle which
ild be ushered in by the peal of
apets, if Naumkeag had ever yet
d that cheery music, and by the
of cannon, echoing among the
ds. A procession,—for, by its dig-
, as marking an epoch in the history
he street, it deserves that name,—
ocession advances along the path-
The good ship Abigail has arrived
a England, bringing wares and mer-
dise, for the comfort of the inhabi-
s, and traffic with the Indians; bring-
assengers too, and, more important
all, a governor for the new settle-
. Roger Conant and Peter Palfrey,
their companions, have been to
shore to welcome them; and now,
such honor and triumph as their
way of life permits, are escorting
sea-flushed voyagers to their habita-
. At the point where Endicott en-
upon the scene two venerable trees
e their branches high above his

head; thus forming a triumphal arch
of living verdure, beneath which he
pauses, with his wife leaning on his arm,
to catch the first impression of their
new-found home. The old settlers gaze
not less earnestly at him than he at the
hoary woods and the rough surface of
the clearings. They like his bearded
face, under the shadow of the broad-
brimmed and steeple-crowned Puritan
hat;—a visage resolute, grave, and
thoughtful, yet apt to kindle with that
glow of a cheerful spirit by which men
of strong character are enabled to go
joyfully on their proper tasks. His form,
too, as you see it, in a doublet and
hose of sad-colored cloth, is of a manly
make, fit for toil and hardship, and
fit to wield the heavy sword that hangs
from his leathern belt. His aspect is
a better warrant for the ruler's office
than the parchment commission which
he bears, however fortified it may be
with the broad seal of the London council. Peter Palfrey nods to Roger Conant.
"The worshipful Court of Assistants
have done wisely," say they between
themselves. "They have chosen for our
governor a man out of a thousand."
Then they toss up their hats,—they
and all the uncouth figures of their company, most of whom are clad in skins,
inasmuch as their old kersey and linsey-
woolsey garments have been torn and
tattered by many a long month's wear,
—they all toss up their hats, and salute
their new governor and captain with
a hearty English shout of welcome. We
seem to hear it with our own ears, so
perfectly is the action represented in
this life-like, this almost magic picture!

But have you observed the lady who
leans upon the arm of Endicott?—a
rose of beauty from an English garden,

now to be transplanted to a fresher soil. It may be that, long years—centuries, indeed—after this fair flower shall have decayed, other flowers of the same race will appear in the same soil, and gladden other generations with hereditary beauty. Does not the vision haunt us yet? Has not Nature kept the mould unbroken, deeming it a pity that the idea should vanish from mortal sight forever, after only once assuming earthly substance? Do we not recognize in that fair woman's face the model of features which still beam, at happy moments, on what was then the woodland pathway, but has long since grown into a busy street?

"This is too ridiculous!—positively insufferable!" mutters the same critic who had before expressed his disapprobation. "Here is a pasteboard figure, such as a child would cut out of a card with a pair of very dull scissors; and the fellow modestly requests us to see in it the prototype of hereditary beauty!"

"But, sir, you have not the proper point of view," remarks the showman. "You sit altogether too near to get the best effect of my pictorial exhibition. Pray oblige me by removing to this other bench, and I venture to assure you the proper light and shadow will transform the spectacle into quite another thing."

"Pshaw!" replies the critic: "I want no other light and shade. I have already told you that it is my business to see things just as they are."

"I would suggest to the author of this ingenious exhibition," observes a gentlemanly person, who has shown signs of being much interested,—"I would suggest that Anna Gower, the first wife

of Governor Endicott, and who c with him from England, left no terity; and that, consequently, we not be indebted to that honorable for any specimens of feminine loveli now extant among us."

Having nothing to allege against genealogical objection, the show points again to the scene.

During this little interruption, perceive that the Anglo-Saxon en —as the phrase now goes—has bee work in the spectacle before us. many chimneys now send up their sn that it begins to have the aspect village street; although everythin so inartificial and inceptive, tha seems as if one returning wave of wild nature might overwhelm it all. the one edifice which gives the pl of permanence to this bold enter is seen at the central point of the ture. There stands the meeting-h a small structure, low-roofed, wit a spire, and built of rough timber, n hewn, with the sap still in the and here and there a strip of adhering to them. A meaner temple never consecrated to the worship o Deity. With the alternative of kne beneath the awful vault of the fi ment, it is strange that men sh creep into this pent-up nook, and e God's presence there. Such, at one would imagine, might be the fe of these forest-settlers, accustome they had been to stand under the arches of vast cathedrals, and to up their hereditary worship in the ivy-covered churches of rural Eng around which lay the bones of generations of their forefathers. could they dispense with the c altar-work?—how, with the pic lows, where the light of common was hallowed by being transmitted ugh the glorified figures of saints? w, with the lofty roof, imbued, as ust have been, with the prayers had gone upward for centuries?— , with the rich peal of the solemn n, rolling along the aisles, pervading whole church, and sweeping the away on a flood of audible religion? y needed nothing of all this. Their e of worship, like their ceremonial, naked, simple, and severe. But the of a recovered faith burned like a ᵒ within their hearts, enriching ything around them with its radi- ; making of these new walls, and narrow compass, its own cathedral; being, in itself, that spiritual mys- and experience of which sacred tecture, pictured windows, and the n's grand solemnity are remote and rfect symbols. All was well, so as their lamps were freshly kindled ᴉe heavenly flame. After a while, ᵥver, whether in their time or their ren's, these lamps began to burn ᵻ dimly, or with a less genuine e; and then it might be seen how ᵢ cold, and confined was their sys- —how like an iron cage was that ᵻ they called Liberty.

ᵒ much of this. Look again at the re, and observe how the aforesaid ᵒ-Saxon energy is now trampling ᵻ the street, and raising a positive ᵻ of dust beneath its sturdy foot- , For there the carpenters are build- ᵻ new house, the frame of which hewn and fitted in England, of ᵢsh oak, and sent hither on ship- ᵻ; and here a blacksmith makes clang and clatter on his anvil, ᵻng out tools and weapons; and yon-

der a wheelwright, who boasts himself a London workman, regularly bred to his handicraft, is fashioning a set of wagon-wheels, the track of which shall soon be visible. The wild forest is shrinking back; the street has lost the aromatic odor of the pine-trees, and of the sweet-fern that grew beneath them. The tender and modest wild-flowers, those gentle children of savage nature that grew pale beneath the ever-brood- ing shade, have shrunk away and dis-appeared, like stars that vanish in the breadth of light. Gardens are fenced in, and display pumpkin-beds and rows of cabbages and beans; and, though the governor and the minister both view them with a disapproving eye, plants of broad-leaved tobacco, which the cul- tivators are enjoined to use privily, or not at all. No wolf, for a year past, has been heard to bark, or known to range among the dwellings, except that single one, whose grisly head, with a plash of blood beneath it, is now affixed to the portal of the meeting-house. The partridge has ceased to run across the too frequented path. Of all the wild life that used to throng here, only the Indians still come into the settlement, bringing the skins of beaver and otter, bear and elk, which they sell to Endi- cott for the wares of England. And there is little John Massey, the son of Jeffrey Massey and the first-born of Naum- keag, playing beside his father's thresh- old, a child six or seven years old. Which is the better grown infant,— the town or the boy?

The red men have become aware that the street is no longer free to them, save by the sufferance and permission of the settlers. Often, to impress them with an awe of English power, there is a muster and training of the town-forces, and a stately march of the mail-clad band, like this which we now see advancing up the street. There they come, fifty of them, or more; all with their iron breastplates and steel caps well burnished, and glimmering bravely against the sun; their ponderous muskets on their shoulders, their bandoliers about their waists, their lighted matches in their hands, and the drum and fife playing cheerily before them. See! do they not step like martial men? Do they not manœuvre like soldiers who have seen stricken fields? And well they may; for this band is composed of precisely such materials as those with which Cromwell is preparing to beat down the strength of a kingdom; and his famous regiment of Ironsides might be recruited from just such men. In everything, at this period. New England was the essential spirit and flower of that which was about to become uppermost in the mother-country. Many a bold and wise man lost the fame which would have accrued to him in English history by crossing the Atlantic with our forefathers. Many a valiant captain, who might have been foremost at Marston Moor or Naseby, exhausted his martial ardor in the command of a log-built fortress like that which you observe on the gently rising ground at the right of the pathway,—its banner fluttering in the breeze, and the culverins and sakers showing their deadly muzzles over the rampart.

A multitude of people were now thronging to New England: some, because the ancient and ponderous framework of Church and State threatened to tumble down upon their heads;

others, because they despaired of s a downfall. Among those who came Naumkeag were men of history legend, whose feet leave a track brightness along any pathway which t have trodden. You shall behold tl life-like images;—their spectres, if choose so to call them,—passing, countering with a familiar nod, st ping to converse together, praying, b ing weapons, laboring or resting f their labors, in the Main-street. H now, comes Hugh Peters, an earn restless man, walking swiftly, as b impelled by that fiery activity of na which shall hereafter thrust him the conflict of dangerous affairs, m him the chaplain and counsellor Cromwell, and finally bring him t bloody end. He pauses, by the meet house, to exchange a greeting Roger Williams, whose face indic methinks, a gentler spirit, kinder more expansive, than that of Pet yet not less active for what he disc to be the will of God, or the wel of mankind. And look! here is a g for Endicott, coming forth out of forest, through which he has been j neying from Boston, and which its rude branches has caught hold his attire, and has wet his feet its swamps and streams. Still ther something in his mild and vener though not aged presence,—a propr an equilibrium, in Governor Winth nature,—that causes the disarray his costume to be unnoticed, and g us the same impression as if he clad in such grave and rich attir we may suppose him to have in the Council-chamber of the col Is not this characteristic wonder perceptible in our spectral represe of his person? But what dignitary his crossing from the other side to et the governor? A stately personage, a dark velvet cloak, with a hoary rd, and a gold chain across his ast; he has the authoritative port of who has filled the highest civic ion in the first of cities. Of all a in the world, we should least ex- to meet the Lord Mayor of Lon- —as Sir Richard Saltonstall has a, once and again—in a forest- dered settlement of the western wil- less.

arther down the street, we see anuel Downing, a grave and worthy en, with his son George, a stripling has a career before him; his shrewd quick capacity and pliant conscience I not only exalt him high, but se- him from a downfall. Here is her figure, on whose characteristic e and expressive action I will stake credit of my pictorial puppet-show. e you not already detected a quaint, humor in that face,—an eccentricity he manner,—a certain indescribable wardness, all the marks, in short, an original man, unmistakably im- sed, yet kept down by a sense of cal restraint? That is Nathaniel d, the minister of Ipswich, but er remembered as the simple cob- of Agawam. He hammered his sole faithfully, and stitched his upper- er so well, that the shoe is hardly worn out, though thrown aside for e two centuries past. And next, ng these Puritans and Roundheads, observe the very model of a Cava- with the curling lovelock, the fan- cally trimmed beard, the embroid- the ornamented rapier, the gilded er, and all other foppishnesses that

distinguish the wild gallants who rode headlong to their overthrow in the cause of King Charles. This is Morton of Merry Mount, who has come hither to hold a council with Endicott, but will shortly be his prisoner. Yonder pale, decaying figure of a white-robed woman, who glides slowly along the street, is the Lady Arabella, looking for her own grave in the virgin soil. That other female form, who seems to be talking—we might almost say preach- ing or expounding—in the centre of a group of profoundly attentive auditors, is Ann Hutchinson. And here comes Vane—

"But, my dear sir," interrupts the same gentleman who before questioned the showman's genealogical accuracy, "allow me to observe that these histori- cal personages could not possibly have met together in the Main-street. They might, and probably did, all visit our old town, at one time or another, but not simultaneously; and you have fallen into anachronisms that I positively shud- der to think of!"

"The fellow," adds the scarcely civil critic, "has learned a bead-roll of his- toric names, whom he lugs into his pic- torial puppet-show, as he calls it, helter- skelter, without caring whether they were contemporaries or not,—and sets them all by the ears together. But was there ever such a fund of impudence? To hear his running commentary, you would suppose that these miserable slips of painted pasteboard, with hardly the remotest outlines of the human figure, had all the character and expression of Michael Angelo's pictures. Well! go on, sir!"

"Sir, you break the illusion of the

scene," mildly remonstrates the show-man.

"Illusion! What illusion?" rejoins the critic, with a contemptuous snort. "On the word of a gentleman, I see nothing illusive in the wretchedly bedaubed sheet of canvas that forms your back-ground, or in these pasteboard slips that hitch and jerk along the front. The only illusion, permit me to say, is in the puppet-showman's tongue,—and that but a wretched one, into the bargain!"

"We public men," replies the show-man, meekly, "must lay our account, sometimes, to meet an uncandid sever-ity of criticism. But—merely for your own pleasure, sir—let me entreat you to take another point of view. Sit far-ther back, by that young lady, in whose face I have watched the reflection of every changing scene; only oblige me by sitting there; and, take my word for it, the slips of pasteboard shall assume spiritual life, and the bedaubed canvas become an airy and changeable reflex of what it purports to represent."

"I know better," retorts the critic, settling himself in his seat, with sullen but self-complacent immovableness. "And, as for my own pleasure, I shall best consult it by remaining precisely where I am."

The showman bows, and waves his hand; and at the signal, as if time and vicissitude had been awaiting his per-mission to move onward, the mimic street becomes alive again.

Years have rolled over our scene, and converted the forest-track into a dusty thoroughfare, which, being inter-sected with lanes and cross-paths, may fairly be designated as the Main-street. On the ground-sites of many of the log-built sheds, into which the first settlers

crept for shelter, houses of quaint ar-tecture have now risen. These l-edifices are built, as you see, in one erally accordant style, though with s-subordinate variety as keeps the holder's curiosity excited, and ca-each structure, like its owner's chara-to produce its own peculiar impress-Most of them have one huge chim-in the centre, with flues so vast it must have been easy for the wit-to fly out of them, as they were v-to do, when bound on an aerial to the Black Man in the forest. Ar-this great chimney the wooden h-clusters itself, in a whole commu-of gable-ends, each ascending int-own separate peak; the second s-with its lattice-windows, projecting the first; and the door, which is haps arched, provided on the ou-with an iron hammer, wherewith visitor's hand may give a thund-rat-a-tat. The timber framework these houses, as compared with t-of recent date, is like the skeleto-an old giant, beside the frail bon-a modern man of fashion. Man-them, by the vast strength and so-ness of their oaken substance, been preserved through a length of which would have tried the sta-of brick and stone; so that, in al-progressive decay and continual r-struction of the street, down to own days, we shall still behold old edifices occupying their long-a-tomed sites. For instance, on the u-corner of that green lane which hereafter be North-street, we se-Curwen House, newly built, with carpenters still at work on the nailing down the last sheaf of shi-On the lower corner stands an-

lling,—destined, at some period of
existence, to be the abode of an
iccessful alchemist,—which shall
wise survive to our own generation,
  perhaps long outlive it. Thus
ugh the medium of these patriarchal
ces, we have now established a sort
indred and hereditary acquaintance
  the Main-street.

reat as is the transformation pro-
d by a short term of years, each
le day creeps through the Puritan
ement sluggishly enough. It shall
  before your eyes, condensed into
space of a few moments. The gray
  of early morning is slowly diffus-
itself over the scene; and the bell-
, whose office it is to cry the hour
ie street-corners, rings the last peal
i his hand-bell, and goes wearily
ewards, with the owls, the bats,
other creatures of the night. Lat-
are thrust back on their hinges,
i the town were opening its eyes,
ie summer morning. Forth stumbles
till drowsy cow-herd, with his horn;
ing which to his lips, it emits a
wing bray, impossible to be repre-
d in the picture, but which reaches
pricked-up ears of every cow in
settlement, and tells her that the
pasture-hour is come. House after
e awakes, and sends the smoke up
ng from its chimney, like frosty
th from living nostrils; and as
white wreaths of smoke, though
egnated with earthy admixtures,
skyward, so, from each dwelling,
the morning worship—its spiritual
ce bearing up its human imperfec-
—find its way to the Heavenly
er's throne.

ie breakfast-hour being passed, the
itants do not, as usual, go to their

fields or workshops, but remain within
doors; or perhaps walk the street, with
a grave sobriety, yet a disengaged and
unburdened aspect, that belongs neither
to a holiday nor a Sabbath. And, indeed, this passing day is neither, nor
is it a common week-day, although par-
taking of all the three. It is the Thurs-
day Lecture; an institution which New
England has long ago relinquished, and
almost forgotten, yet which it would
have been better to retain, as bearing
relations to both the spiritual and ordinary life, and bringing each acquainted
with the other. The tokens of its observance, however, which here meet
our eyes, are of rather a questionable
cast. It is, in one sense, a day of
public shame; the day on which trans-
gressors, who have made themselves
liable to the minor severities of the
Puritan law, receive their reward of
ignominy. At this very moment, the
constable has bound an idle fellow to
the whipping-post, and is giving him
his deserts with a cat-o'-nine-tails. Ever
since sunrise, Daniel Fairfield has been
standing on the steps of the meeting-
house, with a halter about his neck
which he is condemned to wear visibly
throughout his lifetime; Dorothy Talby
is chained to a post at the corner of
Prison-lane, with the hot sun blazing
on her matronly face, and all for no
other offence than lifting her hand
against her husband; while, through the
bars of that great wooden cage, in the
centre of the scene, we discern either
a human being or a wild beast, or both
in one, whom this public infamy causes
to roar, and gnash his teeth, and shake
the strong oaken bars, as if he would
break forth, and tear in pieces the little
children who have been peeping at him.

Such are the profitable sights that serve the good people to while away the earlier part of lecture-day. Betimes in the forenoon, a traveller—the first traveller that has come hitherward this morning—rides slowly into the street, on his patient steed. He seems a clergyman; and, as he draws near, we recognize the minister of Lynn, who was pre-engaged to lecture here, and has been revolving his discourse as he rode through the hoary wilderness. Behold, now, the whole town thronging into the meeting-house, mostly with such sombre visages that the sunshine becomes little better than a shadow when it falls upon them. There go the Thirteen Men, grim rulers of a grim community! There goes John Massey, the first town-born child, now a youth of twenty, whose eye wanders with peculiar interest towards that buxom damsel who comes up the steps at the same instant. There hobbles Goody Foster, a sour and bitter old beldam, looking as if she went to curse, and not to pray, and whom many of her neighbors suspect of taking an occasional airing on a broomstick. There, too, slinking shamefacedly in, you observe that same poor do-nothing and good-for-nothing whom we saw castigated just now at the whipping-post. Last of all, there goes the tithing-man, lugging in a couple of small boys, whom he has caught at play beneath God's blessed sunshine, in a back lane. What native of Naumkeag, whose recollections go back more than thirty years, does not still shudder at that dark ogre of his infancy, who perhaps had long ceased to have an actual existence, but still lived in his childish belief, in a horrible idea, and in the nurse's threat, as the Tidy Man!

It will be hardly worth our while wait two, or it may be three, turni of the hour-glass, for the conclusion the lecture. Therefore, by my con over light and darkness, I cause dusk, and then the starless night, brood over the street; and summ forth again the bellman, with his lant casting a gleam about his footsteps pace wearily from corner to corner, shout drowsily the hour to drowsy dreaming ears. Happy are we, if nothing else, yet because we did not in those days. In truth, when the novelty and stir of spirit had subsi —when the new settlement, between forest-border and the sea, had bec actually a little town,—its daily must have trudged onward with ha anything to diversify and enliven while also its rigidity could not fai cause miserable distortions of the m nature. Such a life was sinister to intellect, and sinister to the heart; pecially when one generation had queathed its religious gloom, and counterfeit of its religious ardor, to next; for these characteristics, as inevitable, assumed the form both hypocrisy and exaggeration, by b inherited from the example and pre of other human beings, and not fror original and spiritual source. The and grandchildren of the first set were a race of lower and narrower s than their progenitors had been. latter were stern, severe, intolerant, not superstitious, not even fanat and endowed, if any men of that were, with a far-seeing worldly saga But it was impossible for the suc ing race to grow up, in heaven's dom, beneath the discipline which gloomy energy of character had e

hed; nor, it may be, have we even
t thrown off all the unfavorable in-
ences which, among many good ones,
re bequeathed to us by our Puritan
refathers. Let us thank God for hav-
; given us such ancestors; and let
ch successive generation thank him,
t less fervently, for being one step
ther from them in the march of ages.
'What is all this?" cries the critic.
sermon? If so, it is not in the bill."
'Very true," replies the showman;
nd I ask pardon of the audience."

Look now at the street, and observe
trange people entering it. Their gar-
nts are torn and disordered, their
es haggard, their figures emaciated;
they have made their way hither
ough pathless deserts, suffering hun-
and hardship, with no other shelter
n a hollow tree, the lair of a wild
st, or an Indian wigwam. Nor, in
most inhospitable and dangerous of
h lodging-places, was there half the
il that awaits them in this thorough-
e of Christian men, with those secure
ellings and warm hearths on either
e of it, and yonder meeting house as
central object of the scene. These
iderers have received from Heaven
ift that, in all epochs of the world,
brought with it the penalties of
rtal suffering and persecution, scorn,
nity, and death itself;—a gift that,
s terrible to its possessors, has ever
n most hateful to all other men,
ce its very existence seems to threaten
overthrow of whatever else the toil-
e ages have built up;—the gift of a
idea. You can discern it in them,
minating their faces—their whole
ons, indeed, however earthly and
ldish—with a light that inevitably
es through, and makes the startled

community aware that these men are
not as they themselves are,—not brethren nor neighbors of their thought.
Forthwith, it is as if an earthquake
rumbled through the town, making its
vibrations felt at every hearth-stone,
and especially causing the spire of the
meeting-house to totter. The Quakers
have come. We are in peril! See! they
trample upon our wise and well-established laws in the person of our chief
magistrate; for Governor Endicott is
passing, now an aged man, and dignified
with long habits of authority,—and not
one of the irreverent vagabonds has
moved his hat. Did you note the ominous frown of the white-bearded Puritan
governor, as he turned himself about,
and, in his anger, half-uplifted the staff
that has become a needful support to
his old age? Here comes old Mr. Norris,
our venerable minister. Will they doff
their hats, and pay reverence to him?
No: their hats stick fast to their ungracious heads, as if they grew there;
and—impious varlets that they are, and
worse than the heathen Indians!—they
eye our reverend pastor with a peculiar
scorn, distrust, unbelief, and utter denial of his sanctified pretensions, of
which he himself immediately becomes
conscious; the more bitterly conscious,
as he never knew nor dreamed of the
like before.

But look yonder! Can we believe our
eyes? A Quaker woman, clad in sackcloth, and with ashes on her head, has
mounted the steps of the meeting-house.
She addresses the people in a wild, shrill
voice,—wild and shrill it must be, to
suit such a figure,—which makes them
tremble and turn pale, although they
crowd open-mouthed to hear her. She is
bold against established authority; she

denounces the priest and his steeple-house. Many of her hearers are appalled; some weep; and others listen with a rapt attention, as if a living truth had now, for the first time, forced its way through the crust of habit, reached their hearts, and awakened them to life. This matter must be looked to; else we have brought our faith across the seas with us in vain; and it had been better that the old forest were still standing here, waving its tangled boughs, and murmuring to the sky out of its desolate recesses, instead of this goodly street, if such blasphemies be spoken in it.

So thought the old Puritans. What was their mode of action may be partly judged from the spectacles which now pass before your eyes. Joshua Buffum is standing in the pillory. Cassandra Southwick is led to prison. And there a woman,—it is Ann Coleman,—naked from the waist upward, and bound to the tail of a cart, is dragged through the Main-street at the pace of a brisk walk, while the constable follows with a whip of knotted cords. A strong-armed fellow is that constable; and each time that he flourishes his lash in the air, you see a frown wrinkling and twisting his brow, and, at the same instant, a smile upon his lips. He loves his business, faithful officer that he is, and puts his soul into every stroke, zealous to fulfil the injunction of Major Hawthorne's warrant, in the spirit and to the letter. There came down a stroke that has drawn blood! Ten such stripes are to be given in Salem, ten in Boston, and ten in Dedham; and, with those thirty stripes of blood upon her, she is to be driven into the forest. The crimson trail goes wavering along the Main-street; but

Heaven grant that, as the rain of many years has wept upon it, time a time, and washed it all away, so th may have been a dew of mercy, cleanse this cruel blood-stain out of record of the persecutor's life!

Pass on, thou spectral constable, betake thee to thine own place of ment. Meanwhile, by the silent op tion of the mechanism behind scenes, a considerable space of t would seem to have lapsed over street. The older dwellings now b to look weather-beaten, through effect of the many eastern storms have moistened their unpainted shin and clapboards, for not less than f years. Such is the age we would as to the town, judging by the aspec John Massey, the first town-born c whom his neighbors now call Good Massey, and whom we see yonde grave, almost autumnal-looking r with children of his own about him the patriarchs of the settlement, doubt, the Main-street is still but affair of yesterday, hardly more anti even if destined to be more permar than a path shovelled through the s But to the middle-aged and elderly who came hither in childhood or youth, it presents the aspect of a and well-established work, on w they have expended the strength ardor of their life. And the you people, native to the street, w earliest recollections are of cree over the paternal threshold, and r on the grassy margin of the track, at it as one of the perdurable thin our mortal state,—as old as the hil the great pasture, or the headland a harbor's mouth. Their fathers grandsires tell them how, within a

rs past, the forest stood here, with
a lonely track beneath its tangled
de. Vain legend! They cannot make
true and real to their conceptions.
h them, moreover, the Main-street
a street indeed, worthy to hold its
with the thronged and stately ave-
s of cities beyond the sea. The old
itans tell them of the crowds that
ry along Cheapside and Fleet-street
the Strand, and of the rush of
ultuous life at Temple Bar. They
cribe London Bridge, itself a street,
a a row of houses on each side.
y speak of the vast structure of the
ver, and the solemn grandeur of
tminster Abbey. The children listen,
still inquire if the streets of Lon-
are longer and broader than the
before their father's door; if the
ver is bigger than the jail in Prison-
; if the old Abbey will hold a larger
gregation than our meeting-house.
hing impresses them, except their
experience.

seems all a fable, too, that wolves
ever prowled here; and not less
that the Squaw Sachem, and the
amore her son, once ruled over this
on, and treated as sovereign poten-
s with the English settlers, then so
and storm-beaten, now so powerful.
re stand some school-boys, you ob-
e, in a little group around a drunken
an, himself a prince of the Squaw
em's lineage. He brought hither
beaver-skins for sale, and has
dy swallowed the larger portion of
price in deadly draughts of fire-
r. Is there not a touch of pathos
at picture? and does it not go far
rds telling the whole story of the
growth and prosperity of one race,
the fated decay of another?—the

children of the stranger making game
of the great Squaw Sachem's grandson!

But the whole race of red men have
not vanished with that wild princess
and her posterity. This march of soldiers
along the street betokens the breaking
out of King Philip's war; and these
young men, the flower of Essex, are on
their way to defend the villages on the
Connecticut; where, at Bloody Brook,
a terrible blow shall be smitten, and
hardly one of that gallant band be left
alive. And there, at that stately mansion,
with its three peaks in front, and its
two little peaked towers, one on either
side of the door, we see brave Captain
Gardner issuing forth, clad in his embroidered buff-coat, and his plumed cap
upon his head. His trusty sword, in its
steel scabbard, strikes clanking on the
door-step. See how the people throng
to their doors and windows, as the
cavalier rides past, reining his mettled
steed so gallantly, and looking so like
the very soul and emblem of martial
achievement,—destined, too, to meet a
warrior's fate, at the desperate assault
on the fortress of the Narragansetts!

"The mettled steed looks like a pig,"
interrupts the critic, "and Captain Gardner himself like the Devil, though a very
tame one, and on a most diminutive
scale."

"Sir, sir!" cries the persecuted showman, losing all patience,—for, indeed,
he had particularly prided himself on
these figures of Captain Gardner and his
horse,—"I see that there is no hope of
pleasing you. Pray, sir, do me the favor
to take back your money, and withdraw!"

"Not I!" answers the unconscionable
critic. "I am just beginning to get interested in the matter. Come! turn

your crank, and grind out a few more of these fooleries!"

The showman rubs his brow impulsively, whisks the little rod with which he points out the notabilities of the scene,—but, finally, with the inevitable acquiescence of all public servants, resumes his composure, and goes on.

Pass onward, onward, Time! Build up new houses here, and tear down thy works of yesterday, that have already the rusty moss upon them! Summon forth the minister to the abode of the young maiden, and bid him unite her to the joyful bridegroom! Let the youthful parents carry their first-born to the meeting-house, to receive the baptismal rite! Knock at the door, whence the sable line of the funeral is next to issue! Provide other successive generations of men, to trade, talk, quarrel, or walk in friendly intercourse along the street, as their fathers did before them! Do all thy daily and accustomed business, Father Time, in this thoroughfare, which thy footsteps, for so many years, have now made dusty! But here, at last, thou leadest along a procession which, once witnessed, shall appear no more, and be remembered only as a hideous dream of thine, or a frenzy of thy old brain.

"Turn your crank, I say," bellows the remorseless critic, "and grind it out, whatever it be, without further preface!"

The showman deems it best to comply.

Then, here comes the worshipful Captain Curwen, sheriff of Essex, on horseback, at the head of an armed guard, escorting a company of condemned prisoners from the jail to their place of execution on Gallows Hill. The

witches! There is no mistaking ther The witches! As they approach Prison-lane, and turn into the Mai street, let us watch their faces, as if made a part of the pale crowd th presses so eagerly about them, shrinks back with such shudderi dread, leaving an open passage betw a dense throng on either side. Listen what the people say.

There is old George Jacobs, kno hereabouts these sixty years, as a m whom we thought upright in all his w of life, quiet, blameless, a good husba before his pious wife was summon from the evil to come, and a go father to the children whom she l him. Ah! but when that blessed wom went to heaven, George Jacob's he was empty, his hearth lonely, his broken up; his children were marri and betook themselves to habitations their own; and Satan, in his wanderi up and down, beheld this forlorn man, to whom life was a sameness a a weariness, and found the way to ten him. So the miserable sinner was p vailed with to mount into the air, career among the clouds; and he proved to have been present at a wit meeting as far off as Falmouth, on very same night that his next neighb saw him, with his rheumatic stoop, ing in at his own door. There is Jo Willard, too; an honest man we thou him, and so shrewd and active in business, so practical, so intent on eve day affairs, so constant at his little pl of trade, where he bartered Eng goods for Indian corn and all kinds country produce! How could such man find time, or what could put it i his mind, to leave his proper calli and become a wizard? It is a myste less the Black Man tempted him with eat heaps of gold. See that aged uple,—a sad sight, truly,—John Proc-r, and his wife Elizabeth. If there were o old people in all the County of ssex who seemed to have led a true ıristian life, and to be treading hope-lly the little remnant of their earthly th, it was this very pair. Yet have e heard it sworn, to the satisfaction the worshipful Chief-justice Sewell, d all the court and jury, that Proctor d his wife have shown their withered ces at children's bedsides, mocking, ıking mouths, and affrighting the poor tle innocents in the night-time. They, their spectral appearances, have stuck ıs into the afflicted ones, and thrown em into deadly fainting-fits with a ıch, or but a look. And, while we sup-sed the old man to be reading the ble to his old wife,—she meanwhile tting in the chimney-corner,—the r of hoary reprobates have whisked the chimney, both on one broom-ck, and flown away to a witch-com-ınion, far into the depths of the chill, k forest. How foolish! Were it only fear of rheumatic pains in their old es, they had better have stayed at ne. But away they went; and the ghter of their decayed, cackling ces has been heard at midnight, aloft the air. Now, in the sunny noontide, they go tottering to the gallows, it is Devil's turn to laugh.

Behind these two,—who help one an-er along, and seem to be comforting l encouraging each other, in a man-truly pitiful, if it were not a sin to y the old witch and wizard,—behind m comes a woman, with a dark, ud face that has been beautiful, and gure that is still majestic. Do you

know her? It is Martha Carrier, whom the Devil found in a humble cottage, and looked into her discontented heart, and saw pride there, and tempted her with his promise that she should be Queen of Hell. And now, with that lofty demeanor, she is passing to her king-dom, and, by her unquenchable pride, transforms this escort of shame into a triumphal procession, that shall attend her to the gates of her infernal palace, and seat her upon the fiery throne. Within this hour, she shall assume her royal dignity.

Last of the miserable train comes a man clad in black, of small stature and a dark complexion, with a clerical band about his neck. Many a time, in the years gone by, that face has been up-lifted heavenward from the pulpit of the East Meeting-house, when the Rev. Mr. Burroughs seemed to worship God. What!—he? The holy man!—the learned!—the wise! How has the Devil tempted him? His fellow-criminals, for the most part, are obtuse, uncultivated creatures, some of them scarcely half-witted by nature, and others greatly de-cayed in their intellects through age. They were an easy prey for the de-stroyer. Not so with this George Bur-roughs, as we judge by the inward light which glows through his dark counte-nance, and, we might almost say, glorifies his figure, in spite of the soil and hag-gardness of long imprisonment,—in spite of the heavy shadow that must fall on him, while death is walking by his side. What bribe could Satan offer rich enough to tempt and overcome this man? Alas! it may have been in the very strength of his high and searching intellect that the Tempter found the weakness which betrayed him. He yearned for knowledge; he went groping onward into a world of mystery; at first, as the witnesses have sworn, he summoned up the ghosts of his two dead wives, and talked with them of matters beyond the grave; and, when their responses failed to satisfy the intense and sinful craving of his spirit, he called on Satan, and was heard. Yet, —to look at him,—who, that had not known the proof, could believe him guilty? Who would not say, while we see him offering comfort to the weak and aged partners of his horrible crime, —while we hear his ejaculations of prayer, that seem to bubble up out of the depths of his heart, and fly heavenward, unawares,—while we behold a radiance brightening on his features as from the other world, which is but a few steps off,—who would not say, that, over the dusty track of the Main-street, a Christian saint is now going to a martyr's death? May not the Arch Fiend have been too subtle for the court and jury, and betrayed them—laughing in his sleeves the while—into the awful! error of pouring out sanctified blood as an acceptable sacrifice upon God's altar? Ah no! for listen to wise Cotton Mather, who, as he sits there on his horse, speaks comfortably to the perplexed multitude, and tells them that all has been religiously and justly done, and that Satan's power shall this day receive its death-blow in New England.

Heaven grant it be so!—the great scholar must be right; so lead the poor creatures to their death! Do you see that group of children and half-grown girls, and, among them, an old, hag-like Indian woman, Tituba by name? Those are the Afflicted Ones. Behold, at this very instant, a proof of Satan's power

and malice! Mercy Parris, the ministe[r] daughter, has been smitten by a fl[ash] of Martha Carrier's eye, and falls do[wn] in the street, writhing with horri[ble] spasms and foaming at the mouth, l[ike] the possessed one spoken of in Scr[ip]ture. Hurry on the accursed witches [to] the gallows, ere they do more mischi[ef] —ere they fling out their withered ar[ms] and scatter pestilence by handf[uls] among the crowd!—ere, as their pa[rt]ing legacy, they cast a blight over [the] land, so that henceforth it may bear [no] fruit nor blade of grass, and be fit [for] nothing but a sepulchre for their [un]hallowed carcasses! So, on they go; old George Jacobs has stumbled, [by] reason of his infirmity; but Good[man] Proctor and his wife lean on one [an]other, and walk at a reasonably ste[ady] pace, considering their age. Mr. [Bur]roughs seems to administer counse[l to] Martha Carrier, whose face and m[ien,] methinks, are milder and humbler t[han] they were. Among the multitude, m[ean]while, there is horror, fear, and dis[?] trust; and friend looks askance [at] friend, and the husband at his w[ife,] and the wife at him, and even [the] mother at her little child; as if in e[very] creature that God has made they [sus]pected a witch, or dreaded an acc[user.] Never, never again, whether in thi[s or] any other shape, may Universal M[ad]ness riot in the Main-street!

I perceive in your eyes, my indul[gent] spectators, the criticism which you [are] too kind to utter. These scenes, [you] think, are all too sombre. So, ind[eed,] they are; but the blame must res[t on] the sombre spirit of our forefat[hers,] who wove their web of life with ha[rdly] a single thread of rose-color or [gold,] and not on me, who have a tropic[?]

sunshine, and would gladly gild all
 world with it, if I knew where to
 so much. That you may believe
, I will exhibit one of the only class
scenes, so far as my investigation has
ght me, in which our ancestors were
nt to steep their tough old hearts in
e and strong drink, and indulge an
break of grisly jollity.

Iere it comes, out of the same house
nce we saw brave Captain Gardner go
th to the wars. What! A coffin borne
men's shoulders, and six aged gentle-
n as pall-bearers, and a long train of
urners, with black gloves and black
-bands, and everything black, save
hite handkerchief in each mourner's
d, to wipe away his tears withal.
w, my kind patrons, you are angry
h me. You were bidden to a bridal-
ce, and find yourselves walking in
neral procession. Even so; but look
k through all the social customs of
v England, in the first century of her
tence, and read all her traits of
acter; and if you find one occasion,
er than a funeral feast, where jollity
sanctioned by universal practice, I
set fire to my puppet-show without
her word. These are the obsequies
ld Governor Bradstreet, the patri-
 and survivor of the first settlers,
, having intermarried with the
ow Gardner, is now resting from his
rs, at the great age of ninety-four.
white-bearded corpse, which was
spirit's earthly garniture, now lies
eath yonder coffin-lid. Many a cask
le and cider is on tap, and many a
ight of spiced wine and aquavitæ
been quaffed. Else why should the
ers stagger, as they tremulously up-
 the coffin?—and the aged pall-
ers, too, as they strive to walk

solemn'y beside it?—and wherefore do
the mourners tread on one another's
heels?—and why, if we may ask without offence, should the nose of the
Reverend Mr. Noyes, through which he
has just been delivering the funeral discourse, glow like a ruddy coal of fire?
Well, well, old friends! Pass on, with
your burden of mortality, and lay it in
the tomb with jolly hearts. People
should be permitted to enjoy themselves
in their own fashion; every man to his
taste; but New England must have been
a dismal abode for the man of pleasure,
when the only boon-companion was
Death!

Under cover of a mist that has settled
over the scene, a few years flit by, and
escape our notice. As the atmosphere
becomes transparent, we perceive a decrepit grandsire, hobbling along the
street. Do you recognize him? We saw
him, first, as the baby in Goodwife
Massey's arms, when the primeval trees
were flinging their shadow over Roger
Conant's cabin; we have seen him, as
the boy, the youth, the man, bearing
his humble part in all the successive
scenes, and forming the index-figure
whereby to note the age of his coeval
town. And here he is, old Goodman
Massey, taking his last walk,—often
pausing,—often leaning over his staff,—
and calling to mind whose dwelling stood
at such and such a spot, and whose field
or garden occupied the site of those more
recent houses. He can render a reason
for all the bends and deviations of the
thoroughfare, which, in its flexible and
plastic infancy, was made to swerve
aside from a straight line, in order to
visit every settler's door. The Main-
street is still youthful; the coeval man
is in his last age. Soon he will be gone,

a patriarch of fourscore, yet shall retain a sort of infantine life in our local history, as the first town-born child.

Behold here a change, wrought in the twinkling of an eye, like an incident in a tale of magic, even while your observation has been fixed upon the scene. The Main-street has vanished out of sight. In its stead appears a wintry waste of snow, with the sun just peeping over it, cold and bright, and tinging the white expanse with the faintest and most ethereal rose-color. This is the great Snow of 1717, famous for the mountain-drifts in which it buried the whole country. It would seem as if the street, the growth of which we have noted so attentively, following it from its first phase, as an Indian track, until it reached the dignity of sidewalks, were all at once obliterated and resolved into a drearier pathlessness than when the forest covered it. The gigantic swells and billows of the snow have swept over each man's metes and bounds, and annihilated all the visible distinctions of human property. So that now, the traces of former times and hitherto accomplished deeds being done away, mankind should be at liberty to enter on new paths, and guide themselves by other laws than heretofore; if, indeed, the race be not extinct, and it be worth our while to go on with the march of life, over the cold and desolate expanse that lies before us. It may be, however, that matters are not so desperate as they appear. That vast icicle, glittering so cheerlessly in the sunshine, must be the spire of the meeting-house, incrusted with frozen sleet. Those great heaps, too, which we mistook for drifts, are houses, buried up to their eaves, and with their peaked roofs rounded by the

depth of snow upon them. There, no comes a gush of smoke from what judge to be the chimney of the Sl Tavern;—and another—another—a another—from the chimneys of otl dwellings, where fireside comfort, mestic peace, the sports of children, a the quietude of age, are living yet, spite of the frozen crust above them

But it is time to change the sce Its dreary monotony shall not test yo fortitude like one of our actual N England winters, which leaves so la a blank,—so melancholy a death-spot in lives so brief that they ought to all summer-time. Here, at least, I m claim to be ruler of the seasons. turn of the crank shall melt away snow from the Main-street, and sh the trees in their full foliage, and the r bushes in bloom, and a border of gr grass along the sidewalk. There! what! How! The scene will not mc A wire is broken. The street contin buried beneath the snow, and the of Herculaneum and Pompeii has parallel in this catastrophe.

Alas! my kind and gentle audier you know not the extent of your n fortune. The scenes to come were better than the past. The street it would have been more worthy of torial exhibition; the deeds of its habitants, not less so. And how wc your interest have deepened, as, pas out of the cold shadow of antiquity my long and weary course, I sho arrive within the limits of m memory, and, leading you at last the sunshine of the present, should a reflex of the very life that is flit past us! Your own beauty, my townswoman, would have beamed u you out of my scene. Not a gentle

walks the street but should have
ld his own face and figure, his gait,
peculiar swing of his arm, and the
that he put on yesterday. Then,
—and it is what I chiefly regret,—
d expended a vast deal of light and
iancy on a representation of the
t in its whole length, from Buffum's
ner downward, on the night of the
d illumination for General Taylor's
nph. Lastly, I should have given
crank one other turn, and have
ght out the future, showing you
shall walk the Main-street to-morrow, and, perchance, whose funeral shall
pass through it!

But these, like most other human
purposes, lie unaccomplished; and I
have only further to say, that any lady
or gentleman who may feel dissatisfied
with the evening's entertainment shall
receive back the admission fee at the
door.

"Then give me mine," cries the critic,
stretching out his palm. "I said that
your exhibition would prove a humbug,
and so it has turned out. So, hand over
my quarter!"

ETHAN BRAND

APTER FROM AN ABORTIVE ROMANCE

ARTRAM, the lime-burner, a rough,
y-looking man, begrimed with char-
sat watching his kiln, at nightfall,
e his little son played at building
es with the scattered fragments of
ole, when, on the hillside below
a, they heard a roar of laughter,
nirthful, but slow, and even solemn,
a wind shaking the boughs of the
st.

'ather, what is that?" asked the
boy, leaving his play, and pressing
ixt his father's knees.

), some drunken man, I suppose,"
ered the lime-burner; "some merry
w from the bar-room in the village,
dared not laugh loud enough within
s, lest he should blow the roof of
ouse off. So here he is, shaking his
sides at the foot of Graylock."

ut, father," said the child, more
tive than the obtuse, middle-aged

clown, "he does not laugh like a man
that is glad. So the noise frightens me!"

"Don't be a fool, child!" cried his
father, gruffly. "You will never make
a man, I do believe; there is too much
of your mother in you. I have known
the rustling of a leaf startle you. Hark!
Here comes the merry fellow, now. You
shall see that there is no harm in him."

Bartram and his little son, while they
were talking thus, sat watching the same
lime-kiln that had been the scene of
Ethan Brand's solitary and meditative
life, before he began his search for the
Unpardonable Sin. Many years, as we
have seen, had now elapsed since that
portentous night when the IDEA was
first developed. The kiln, however, on
the mountain-side, stood unimpaired,
and was in nothing changed since he had
thrown his dark thoughts into the intense glow of its furnace, and melted
them, as it were, into the one thought
that took possession of his life. It was

a rude, round, tower-like structure, about twenty feet high, heavily built of rough stones, and with a hillock of earth heaped about the larger part of its circumference; so that the blocks and fragments of marble might be drawn by cart-loads, and thrown in at the top. There was an opening at the bottom of the tower, like an oven-mouth, but large enough to admit a man in a stooping posture, and provided with a massive iron door. With the smoke and jets of flame issuing from the chinks and crevices of this door, which seemed to give admittance into the hillside, it resembled nothing so much as the private entrance to the infernal regions, which the shepherds of the Delectable Mountains were accustomed to show to pilgrims.

There are many such lime-kilns in that tract of country, for the purpose of burning the white marble which composes a large part of the substance of the hills. Some of them, built years ago, and long deserted, with weeds growing in the vacant round of the interior, which is open to the sky, and grass and wild-flowers rooting themselves into the chinks of the stones, look already like relics of antiquity, and may yet be overspread with the lichens of centuries to come. Others, where the lime-burner still feeds his daily and night-long fire, afford points of interest to the wanderer among the hills, who seats himself on a log of wood or a fragment of marble, to hold a chat with the solitary man. It is a lonesome, and, when the character is inclined to thought, may be an intensely thoughtful occupation; as it proved in the case of Ethan Brand, who had mused to such strange purpose, in days gone by, while the fire in this very kiln was burning.

The man who now watched the ? was of a different order, and troub himself with no thoughts save the v few that were requisite to his busine At frequent intervals, he flung back clashing weight of the iron door, a turning his face from the insuffera glare, thrust in huge logs of oak, stirred the immense brands with a l pole. Within the furnace were seen curling and riotous flames, and the bu ing marble, almost molten with the tensity of heat; while without, the flection of the fire quivered on the d intricacy of the surrounding forest, showed in the foreground a bright ruddy little picture of the hut, spring beside its door, the athletic coal-begrimed figure of the lime-bur and the half-frightened child, shrink into the protection of his fath shadow. And when again the iron d was closed, then reappeared the ten light of the half-full moon, which va strove to trace out the indistinct sha of the neighboring mountains; and the upper sky, there was a flitting gregation of clouds, still faintly tin with the rosy sunset, though thus down into the valley the sunshine vanished long and long ago.

The little boy now crept still cl to his father, as footsteps were h ascending the hillside, and a hu form thrust aside the bushes that tered beneath the trees.

"Halloo! who is it?" cried the li burner, vexed at his son's timidity, half infected by it. "Come forward, show yourself, like a man, or I'll this chunk of marble at your head!"

"You offer me a rough welcor said a gloomy voice, as the unkn

drew nigh. "Yet I neither claim nor
ire a kinder one, even at my own
side."

'o obtain a distincter view, Bartram
ew open the iron door of the kiln,
nce immediately issued a gush of
ce light, that smote full upon the
nger's face and figure. To a careless
there appeared nothing very remark-
in his aspect, which was that of a
in a coarse, brown, country-made
of clothcs, tall and thin, with the
and heavy shoes of a wayfarer.
he advanced, he fixed his eyes—
ch were very bright—intently upon
brightness of the furnace, as if he
eld, or expected to behold, some ob-
worthy of note within it.

Good evening, stranger," said the
-burner; "whence come you, so late
he day?"

come from my search," answered
wayfarer; "for, at last, it is
hed."

Drunk!—or crazy!" muttered Bar-
to himself. "I shall have trouble
the fellow. The sooner I drive him
y, the better."

he little boy, all in a tremble, whis-
d to his father, and begged him to
the door of the kiln, so that there
t not be so much light; for that there
something in the man's face which
as afraid to look at, yet could not
away from. And, indeed, even the
-burner's dull and torpid sense be-
to be impressed by an indescribable
thing in that thin, rugged, thought-
visage, with the grizzled hair hang-
wildly about it, and those deeply-
en eyes, which gleamed like fires
in the entrance of a mysterious
rn. But, as he closed the door, the
nger turned towards him, and spoke

in a quiet, familiar way, that made
Bartram feel as if he were a sane and
sensible man, after all.

"Your task draws to an end, I see,"
said he. "This marble has already been
burning three days. A few hours more
will convert the stone to lime."

"Why, who are you?" exclaimed the
lime-burner. "You seem as well acquainted with my business as I am
myself."

"And well I may be," said the
stranger; "for I followed the same craft
many a long year, and here, too, on this
very spot. But you are a new-comer in
these parts. Did you never hear of
Ethan Brand?"

"The man that went in search of the
Unpardonable Sin?" asked Bartram,
with a laugh.

"The same," answered the stranger.
"He has found what he sought, and
therefore he comes back again."

"What! then you are Ethan Brand
himself?" cried the lime-burner, in
amazement. "I am a new-comer here,
as you say, and they call it eighteen
years since you left the foot of Graylock. But, I can tell you, the good folks
still talk about Ethan Brand, in the
village yonder, and what a strange
errand took him away from his lime-
kiln. Well, and so you have found the
Unpardonable Sin?"

"Even so!" said the stranger, calmly.

"If the question is a fair one," proceeded Bartram, "where might it be?"

Ethan Brand laid his finger on his
own heart.

"Here!" replied he.

And then, without mirth in his countenance, but as if moved by an involuntary recognition of the infinite absurdity
of seeking throughout the world for

what was the closest of all things to himself, and looking into every heart, save his own, for what was hidden in no other breast, he broke into a laugh of scorn. It was the same slow, heavy laugh, that had almost appalled the lime-burner when it heralded the wayfarer's approach.

The solitary mountain-side was made dismal by it. Laughter, when out of place, mistimed, or bursting forth from a disordered state of feeling, may be the most terrible modulation of the human voice. The laughter of one asleep, even if it be a little child,—the madman's laugh,—the wild, screaming laugh of a born idiot,—are sounds that we sometimes tremble to hear, and would always willingly forget. Poets have imagined no utterance of fiends or hobgoblins so fearfully appropriate as a laugh. And even the obtuse lime-burner felt his nerves shaken, as this strange man looked inward at his own heart, and burst into laughter that rolled away into the night, and was indistinctly reverberated among the hills.

"Joe," said he to his little son, "scamper down to the tavern in the village, and tell the jolly fellows there that Ethan Brand has come back, and that he has found the Unpardonable Sin!"

The boy darted away on his errand, to which Ethan Brand made no objection, nor seemed hardly to notice it. He sat on a log of wood, looking steadfastly at the iron door of the kiln. When the child was out of sight, and his swift and light footsteps ceased to be heard treading first on the fallen leaves, and then on the rocky mountain-path, the lime-burner began to regret his departure. He felt that the little fellow's presence

had been a barrier between his guest himself, and that he must now heart to heart, with a man who, o own confession, had committed the only crime for which Heaven afford no mercy. That crime, in indistinct blackness, seemed to shadow him. The lime-burner's sins rose up within him, and made memory riotous with a throng of shapes that asserted their kindred the Master Sin, whatever it migh which it was within the scope man's corrupted nature to conceive cherish. They were all of one fam they went to and fro between his b and Ethan Brand's, and carried greetings from one to the other.

Then Bartram remembered the st which had grown traditionary in r ence to this strange man, who had upon him like a shadow of the r and was making himself at home i old place, after so long absence tha dead people, dead and buried for y would have had more right to b home, in any familiar spot, than Ethan Brand, it was said, had conv with Satan himself in the lurid of this very kiln. The legend had matter of mirth heretofore, but lo grisly now. According to this tale fore Ethan Brand departed on search, he had been accustome evoke a fiend from the hot furna the lime-kiln, night after night, in to confer with him about the U donable Sin; the man and the fiend laboring to frame the image of mode of guilt which could neith atoned for nor forgiven. And, wit first gleam of light upon the mou top, the fiend crept in at the iron there to abide the intensest eleme

until again summoned forth to
e in the dreadful task of extending
's possible guilt beyond the scope
Ieaven's else infinite mercy.

hile the lime-burner was struggling
the horror of these thoughts,
n Brand rose from the log, and
; open the door of the kiln. The
n was in such accordance with the
in Bartram's mind, that he almost
cted to see the Evil One issue forth,
ot from the raging furnace.

Iold! hold!" cried he, with a tremu-
attempt to laugh; for he was
med of his fears, although they
mastered him. "Don't, for mercy's
bring out your devil now!"

Ian!" sternly replied Ethan Brand,
t need have I of the devil? I have
him behind me, on my track. It is
such half-way sinners as you that
usies himself. Fear not, because I
the door. I do but act by old cus-
and am going to trim your fire,
a lime-burner, as I was once."

stirred the vast coals, thrust in
wood, and bent forward to gaze
he hollow prison-house of the fire,
dless of the fierce glow that red-
l upon his face. The lime-burner sat
hing him, and half suspected his
ge guest of a purpose, if not to
a fiend, at least to plunge bodily
he flames, and thus vanish from the
of man. Ethan Brand, however,
quietly back, and closed the door
e kiln.

have looked," said he, "into many
man heart that was seven times
r with sinful passions than yonder
ce is with fire. But I found not
what I sought. No, not the Un-
nable Sin!"

'hat is the Unpardonable Sin?"

asked the lime-burner; and then he
shrank farther from his companion,
trembling lest his question should be
answered.

"It is a sin that grew within my own
breast," replied Ethan Brand, standing
erect, with a pride that distinguishes all
enthusiasts of his stamp. "A sin that
grew nowhere else! The sin of an intellect that triumphed over the sense
of brotherhood with man and reverence
for God, and sacrificed everything to its
own mighty claims! The only sin that
deserves a recompense of immortal
agony! Freely, were it to do again,
would I incur the guilt. Unshrinkingly
I accept the retribution!"

"The man's head is turned," muttered
the lime-burner to himself. "He may be
a sinner, like the rest of us,—nothing
more likely,—but, I'll be sworn, he is a
madman too."

Nevertheless he felt uncomfortable at
his situation, alone with Ethan Brand
on the wild mountain-side, and was right
glad to hear the rough murmur of
tongues, and the footsteps of what
seemed a pretty numerous party, stumbling over the stones and rustling
through the underbrush. Soon appeared
the whole lazy regiment that was wont
to infest the village tavern, comprehending three or four individuals who
had drunk flip beside the bar-room fire
through all the winters, and smoked
their pipes beneath the stoop through
all the summers, since Ethan Brand's
departure. Laughing boisterously, and
mingling all their voices together in un-
ceremonious talk, they now burst into
the moonshine and narrow streaks of
firelight that illuminated the open space
before the lime-kiln. Bartram set the
door ajar again, flooding the spot with

light, that the whole company might get a fair view of Ethan Brand, and he of them.

There, among other old acquaintances, was a once ubiquitous man, now almost extinct, but whom we were formerly sure to encounter at the hotel of every thriving village throughout the country. It was the stage-agent. The present specimen of the genus was a wilted and smoke-dried man, wrinkled and red-nosed, in a smartly-cut, brown, bob-tailed coat, with brass buttons, who, for a length of ·time unknown, had kept his desk and corner in the bar-room, and was still puffing what seemed to be the same cigar that he had lighted twenty years before. He had great fame as a dry joker, though, perhaps, less on account of any intrinsic humor than from a certain flavor of brandy-toddy and tobacco-smoke, which impregnated all his ideas and expressions, as well as his person. Another well-remembered though strangely-altered face was that of Lawyer Giles, as people still called him in courtesy; an elderly ragamuffin, in his soiled shirt-sleeves and tow-cloth trousers. This poor fellow had been an attorney, in what he called his better days, a sharp practitioner, and in great vogue among the village litigants; but flip, and sling, and toddy, and cock-tails, inbibed at all hours, morning, noon, and night, had caused him to slide from intellectual to various kinds and de-grees of bodily labor, till at last, to adopt his own phrase, he slid into a soap-vat. In other words, Giles was now a soap-boiler, in a small way. He had come to be but the fragment of a human being, a part of one foot having been chopped off by an axe, and an en-tire hand torn away by the devilish

grip of a steam-engine. Yet, though corporeal hand was gone, a spirit member remained; for, stretching fc the stump, Giles steadfastly averred t he felt an invisible thumb and fing with as vivid a sensation as before real ones were amputated. A main and miserable wretch he was; but nevertheless, whom the world could trample on, and had no right to sc either in this or any previous stage his misfortunes, since he had still k up the courage and spirit of a n asked nothing in charity, and with one hand—and that the left one—fo a stern battle against want and ho circumstances.

Among the throng, too, came ano personage, who, with certain points similarity to Lawyer Giles, had m more of difference. It was the vil doctor; a man of some fifty ye whom, at an earlier period of his we introduced as paying a professi visit to Ethan Brand during the lat supposed insanity. He was now a pu visaged, rude, and brutal, yet gentlemanly figure, with something ruined, and desperate in his talk, an all the details of his gesture and n ners. Brandy possessed this man lik evil spirit, and made him as surly savage as a wild beast, and as miser as a lost soul; but there was supp to be in him such wonderful skill, native gifts of healing, beyond which medical science could im that society caught hold of him, would not let him sink out of its re So, swaying to and fro upon his h and grumbling thick accents at the side, he visited all the sick-cham for miles about among the mou towns, and sometimes raised a d n, as it were, by miracle, or quite as en, no doubt, sent his patient to a ve that was dug many a year too n. The doctor had an everlasting e in his mouth, and, as somebody l, in allusion to his habit of swearing, was always alight with hell-fire.

hese three worthies pressed forward, greeted Ethan Brand each after his a fashion, earnestly inviting him to take of the contents of a certain k bottle, in which, as they averred, would find something far better th seeking for than the Unpardon- Sin. No mind, which has wrought lf by intense and solitary meditation a high state of enthusiasm, can en- e the kind of contact with low and ;ar modes of thought and feeling to ch Ethan Brand was now subjected. iade him doubt—and, strange to say, as a painful doubt—whether he had ed found the Unpardonable Sin, and id it within himself. The whole ques- on which he had exhausted life, and e than life, looked like a delusion.

Leave me," he said, bitterly, "ye e beasts, that have made yourselves shrivelling up your souls with fiery ors! I have done with you. Years years ago, I groped into your hearts, found nothing there for my pur- . Get ye gone!"

Why, you uncivil scoundrel," cried fierce doctor, "is that the way you ond to the kindness of your best ds? Then let me tell you the truth. have no more found the Unpar- ble Sin than yonder boy Joe has. are but a crazy fellow,—I told you venty years ago,—neither better nor e than a crazy fellow, and the fit panion of old Humphrey, here!"

e pointed to an old man, shabbily dressed, with long white hair, thin visage, and unsteady eyes. For some years past this aged person had been wandering about among the hills, inquiring of all travellers whom he met for his daughter. The girl, it seemed, had gone off with a company of circus-performers; and occasionally tidings of her came to the village, and fine stories were told of her glittering appearance as she rode on horse-back in the ring, or performed marvellous feats on the tight-rope.

The white-haired father now approached Ethan Brand, and gazed unsteadily into his face.

"They tell me you have been all over the earth," said he, wringing his hands with earnestness. "You must have seen my daughter, for she makes a grand figure in the world, and everybody goes to see her. Did she send any word to her old father, or say when she was coming back?"

Ethan Brand's eye quailed beneath the old man's. That daughter, from whom he so earnestly desired a word of greeting, was the Esther of our tale, the very girl whom, with such cold and remorseless purpose, Ethan Brand had made the subject of a psychological experiment, and wasted, absorbed, and perhaps annihilated her soul, in the process.

"Yes," murmured he, turning away from the hoary wanderer; "it is no delusion. There is an Unpardonable Sin!"

While these things were passing, a merry scene was going forward in the area of cheerful light, beside the spring and before the door of the hut. A number of the youth of the village, young men and girls, had hurried up the hill-side, impelled by curiosity to see Ethan

Brand, the hero of so many a legend familiar to their childhood. Finding nothing, however, very remarkable in his aspect,—nothing but a sun-burnt wayfarer, in plain garb and dusty shoes, who sat looking into the fire, as if he fancied pictures among the coals,—these young people speedily grew tired of observing him. As it happened, there was other amusement at hand. An old German Jew, travelling with a diorama on his back, was passing down the mountain-road towards the village just as the party turned aside from it, and, in hopes of eking out the profits of the day, the showman had kept them company to the lime-kiln.

"Come, old Dutchman," cried one of the young men, "let us see your pictures, if you can swear they are worth looking at!"

"O yes, Captain," answered the Jew, —whether as a matter of courtesy or craft, he styled everybody Captain,—"I shall show you, indeed, some very superb pictures!"

So, placing his box in a proper position, he invited the young men and girls to look through the glass orifices of the machine, and proceed to exhibit a series of the most outrageous scratchings and daubings, as specimens of the fine arts, that ever an itinerant showman had the face to impose upon his circle of spectators. The pictures were worn out, moreover, tattered, full of cracks and wrinkles, dingy with tobacco-smoke, and otherwise in a most pitiable condition. Some purported to be cities, public edifices, and ruined castles in Europe; others represented Napoleon's battles and Nelson's sea-fight; and in the midst of these would be seen a gigantic, brown, hairy hand,—which might have been

mistaken for the Hand of Des[t] though, in truth, it was only the s[h] man's,—pointing its forefinger to ous scenes of the conflict, while owner gave historical illustrat[i] When, with much merriment at abominable deficiency of merit, the hibition was concluded, the Ger bade little Joe put his head into box. Viewed through the magnif glasses, the boy's round, rosy v[i] assumed the strangest imaginable as of an immense Titanic child, the m grinning broadly, and the eyes and e other feature overflowing with fu the joke. Suddenly, however, that m face turned pale, and its expre[ss] changed to horror, for this easily pressed and excitable child had be[en] sensible that the eye of Ethan B[rand] was fixed upon him through the gla[ss]

"You make the little man to be af[raid] Captain," said the German Jew, ing up the dark and strong outlin his visage, from his stooping pos "But look again, and, by chance, I cause you to see somewhat that is fine, upon my word!"

Ethan Brand gazed into the bo[x] an instant, and then starting back lo fixedly at the German. What ha seen? Nothing apparently; for a cu youth, who had peeped in almo[st] the same moment, beheld only a v[a] space of canvas.

"I remember you now," mut[tered] Ethan Brand to the showman.

"Ah, Captain," whispered the J[ew] Nuremberg, with a dark smile, "I it to be a heavy matter in my box,—this Unpardonable Sin! By faith, Captain, it has wearied my s[houl] ders, this long day, to carry it ove mountain."

'Peace," answered Ethan Brand,
nly, "or get thee into the furnace
der!"

he Jew's exhibition had scarcely con-
ded, when a great, elderly dog,—who
med to be his own master, as no
son in the company laid claim to
,—saw fit to render himself the
ct of public notice. Hitherto, he
shown himself a very quiet, well-
osed old dog, going round from one
another, and, by way of being sole, offering his rough head to be
ed by any kindly hand that would
so much trouble. But now, all of
dden, this grave and venerable quad-
d, of his own mere motion, and
out the slightest suggestion from
ody else, began to run round after
ail, which, to heighten the absurdity
the proceeding, was a great deal
ter than it should have been. Never
seen such headlong eagerness in
uit of an object that could not
ibly be attained; never was heard
a tremendous outbreak of growling,
ling, barking, and snapping,—as if
end of the ridiculous brute's body
at deadly and most unforgivable
ty with the other. Faster and faster,
d about went the cur; and faster
still faster fled the unapproachable
ity of his tail; and louder and
er grew his yells of rage and anity; until, utterly exhausted, and as
from the goal as ever, the foolish
log ceased his performance as sud-
as he had begun it. The next mo-
, he was as mild, quiet, sensible, and
ctable in his deportment as when
rst scraped acquaintance with the
any.

may be supposed, the exhibition
greeted with universal laughter,
clapping of hands, and shouts of encore,
to which the canine performer responded
by wagging all that there was to wag
of his tail, but appeared totally unable
to repeat his very successful effort to
amuse the spectators.

Meanwhile, Ethan Brand had resumed his seat upon the log, and moved,
it might be, by a perception of some
remote analogy between his own case
and that of this self-pursuing cur, he
broke into the awful laugh, which, more
than any other token, expressed the
condition of his inward being. From
that moment, the merriment of the
party was at an end; they stood aghast,
dreading lest the inauspicious sound
should be reverberated around the horizon, and that mountain would thunder
it to mountain, and so the horror be
prolonged upon their ears. Then, whispering one to another that it was late,—
that the moon was almost down,—that
the August night was growing chill,—
they hurried homewards, leaving the
lime-burner and little Joe to deal as
they might with their unwelcome guest.
Save for these three human beings, the
open space on the hillside was a solitude,
set in a vast gloom of forest. Beyond
that darksome verge, the fire-light glimmered on the stately trunks and almost
black foliage of pines, intermixed with
the lighter verdure of sapling oaks,
maples, and poplars, while here and
there lay the gigantic corpses of dead
trees, decaying on the leaf-strewn soil.
And it seemed to little Joe—a timorous
and imaginative child—that the silent
forest was holding its breath, until some
fearful thing should happen.

Ethan Brand thrust more wood into
the fire, and closed the door of the kiln;
then looking over his shoulder at the

lime-burner and his son, he bade, rather than advised, them to retire to rest.

"For myself, I cannot sleep," said he. "I have matters that it concerns me to meditate upon. I will watch the fire, as I used to do in the old time."

"And call the devil out of the furnace to keep you company, I suppose," muttered Bartram, who had been making intimate acquaintance with the black bottle above mentioned. "But watch, if you like, and call as many devils as you like! For my part, I shall be all the better for a snooze. Come, Joe!"

As the boy followed his father into the hut, he looked back at the wayfarer, and the tears came into his eyes, for his tender spirit had an intuition of the bleak and terrible loneliness in which this man had enveloped himself.

When they had gone, Ethan Brand sat listening to the crackling of the kindled wood, and looking at the little spirts of fire that issued through the chinks of the door. These trifles, however, once so familiar, had but the slightest hold of his attention, while deep within his mind he was reviewing the gradual but marvellous change that had been wrought upon him by the search to which he had devoted himself. He remembered how the night dew had fallen upon him,—how the dark forest had whispered to him,—how the stars had gleamed upon him,—a simple and loving man, watching his fire in the years gone by, and ever musing as it burned. He remembered with what tenderness, with what love and sympathy for mankind, and what pity for human guilt and woe, he had first begun to contemplate those ideas which after-wards became the inspiration of his life; with what reverence he had then looked into the heart of man, view it as a temple originally divine, a however, desecrated, still to be h sacred by a brother; with what aw fear he had deprecated the success his pursuit, and prayed that the pardonable Sin might never be revea to him. Then ensued that vast intel tual development, which, in its progr disturbed the counterpoise between mind and heart. The Idea that sessed his life had operated as a me of education; it had gone on cultiva his powers to the highest point of wl they were susceptible; it had raised from the level of an unlettered lab to stand on a star-lit eminence, whi the philosophers of the earth, laden the lore of universities, might va strive to clamber after him. So m for the intellect! But where was heart? That, indeed, had withere had contracted,—had hardened,— perished! It had ceased to partake the universal throb. He had lost hold of the magnetic chain of huma He was no longer a brother-man, o ing the chambers or the dungeon our common nature by the key of sympathy, which gave him a righ share in all its secrets; he was no cold observer, looking on mankin the subject of his experiment, and length, converting man and woma be his puppets, and pulling the v that moved them to such degree crime as were demanded for his stu

Thus Ethan Brand became a fi He began to be so from the mo that his moral nature had ceased to the pace of improvement with his tellect. And now, as his highest and inevitable development,—as bright and gorgeous flower, and

icious fruit of his life's labor,—he
produced the Unpardonable Sin!
What more have I to seek? What
re to achieve?" said Ethan Brand to
iself. "My task is done, and well
.e!"

tarting from the log with a certain
rity in his gait, and ascending the
ock of earth that was raised against
stone circumference of the lime-kiln,
hus reached the top of the structure.
was a space of perhaps ten feet
oss, from edge to edge, presenting a
w of the upper surface of the im-
ise mass of broken marble with
ch the kiln was heaped. All these
imerable blocks and fragments of
ble were red-hot and vividly on fire,
ling up great spouts of blue flame,
ch quivered aloft and danced madly,
within a magic circle, and sank and
: again, with continual and multi-
nous activity. As the lonely man
t forward over this terrible body of
the blasting heat smote up against
person with a breath that, it might
supposed, would have scorched and
velled him up in a moment.

than Brand stood erect, and raised
rms on high. The blue flames played
i his face, and imparted the wild
ghastly light which alone could have
ed its expression; it was that of a
d on the verge of plunging into his
of intensest torment.

) Mother Earth," cried he, "who
no more my mother, and into whose
om this frame shall never be re-
ed! O mankind, whose brotherhood
ve cast off, and trampled thy great
t beneath my feet! O stars of
ven, that shone on me of old, as if
ght me onward and upward!—fare-
all, and forever. Come, deadly

element of Fire,—henceforth my familiar friend! Embrace me, as I do
thee!"

That night the sound of a fearful peal
of laughter rolled heavily through the
sleep of the lime-burner and his little
son; dim shapes of horror and anguish
haunted their dreams, and seemed still
present in the rude hovel, when they
opened their eyes to the daylight.

"Up, boy, up!" cried the lime-burner,
staring about him. "Thank Heaven, the
night is gone, at last; and rather than
pass such another, I would watch my
lime-kiln, wide awake, for a twelvemonth. This Ethan Brand, with his
humbug of an Unpardonable Sin, has
done me no such mighty favor, in taking
my place!"

He issued from the hut, followed by
little Joe, who kept fast hold of his
father's hand. The early sunshine was
already pouring its gold upon the moun-
tain-tops; and though the valleys were
still in shadow, they smiled cheerfully
in the promise of the bright day that
was hastening onward. The village, completely shut in by hills, which swelled
away gently about it, looked as if it had
rested peacefully in the hollow of the
great hand of Providence. Every dwelling was distinctly visible; the little
spires of the two churches pointed upwards, and caught a fore-glimmering of
brightness from the sun-gilt skies upon
their gilded weathercocks. The tavern
was astir, and the figure of the old,
smoke-dried stage-agent, cigar in mouth,
was seen beneath the stoop. Old Graylock was glorified with a golden cloud
upon his head. Scattered likewise over
the breasts of the surrounding mountains there were heaps of hoary mist, in
fantastic shapes, some of them far down

into the valley, others high up towards the summits, and still others, of the same family of midst or cloud, hovering in the gold radiance of the upper atmosphere. Stepping from one to another of the clouds that rested on the hills, and thence to the loftier brotherhood that sailed in air, it seemed almost as if a mortal man might thus ascend into the heavenly regions. Earth was so mingled with sky that it was a day-dream to look at it.

To supply that charm of the familiar and homely, which Nature so readily adopts into a scene like this, the stage-coach was rattling down the mountain-road, and the driver sounded his horn, while echo caught up the notes, and intertwined them into a rich and varied and elaborate harmony, of which the original performer could lay claim to little share. The great hills played a concert among themselves, each contributing a strain of airy sweetness.

Little Joe's face brightened at once.

"Dear father," cried he, skipping cheerily to and fro, "that strange man is gone, and the sky and the mountains all seem glad of it!"

"Yes," growled the lime-burner, with an oath, "but he has let the fire go down, and no thanks to him if hundred bushels of lime are not spoi If I catch the fellow hereabouts ag I shall feel like tossing him into furnace!"

With his long pole in his hand, ascended to the top of the kiln. A a moment's pause, he called to his

"Come up here, Joe!" said he.

So little Joe ran up the hillock, stood by his father's side. The ma was all burnt into perfect, snow-w lime. But on its surface, in the m of the circle,—snow-white too, thoroughly converted into lime,—la human skeleton, in the attitude o person who, after long toil, lies d to long repose. Within the ribs—str to say—was the shape of a hu heart.

"Was the fellow's heart made marble?" cried Bartram, in some plexity at this phenomenon. "At rate, it is burnt into what looks special good lime, and, taking all bones together, my kiln is half a bu the richer for him."

So saying, the rude lime-burner li his pole, and, letting it fall upon skeleton, the relics of Ethan Brand crumbled into fragments.

A BELL'S BIOGRAPHY

HEARKEN to our neighbor with the iron tongue! While I sit musing over my sheet of foolscap, he emphatically tells the hour, in tones loud enough for all the town to hear, though doubtless intended only as a gentle hint to myself, that I may begin his biography before the evening shall be further wasted. questionably, a personage in suc elevated position, and making so a noise in the world, has a fair c to the services of a biographer. E the representative and most illust member of that innumerable se characteristic feature is the ;ue, and whose sole business to ıor for the public good. If any of noisy brethren, in our tongue-ərned democracy, be envious of the riority which I have assigned him, have my free consent to hang them-es as high as he. And, for his his-, let not the reader apprehend an ty repetition of ding-dong-bell. He been the passive hero of wonderful situdes, with which I have chanced ecome acquainted, possibly from his mouth; while the careless multi-supposed him to be talking merely he time of the day, or calling them dinner or to church, or bidding vsy people go bedward, or the dead ıeir graves. Many a revolution has en his fate to go through, and in-ıbly with a prodigious uproar. And her or no he have told me his niscences, this at least is true, that more I study his deep-toned lan-e, the more sense and sentiment soul do I discover in it.

is bell—for we may as well drop quaint personification—is of antique ch manufacture, and the symbol e cross betokens that it was meant e suspended in the belfry of a ish place of worship. The old e hereabout have a tradition, that nsiderable part of the metal was ied by a brass cannon, captured in of the victories of Louis the Four-h over the Spaniards, and that a bon princess threw her golden fix into the molten mass. It is said, ise, that a bishop baptized and d the bell, and prayed that a nly influence might mingle with its . When all due ceremonies had performed, the Grand Monarque bestowed the gift—than which none could resound his beneficence more loudly—on the Jesuits, who were then converting the American Indians to the spiritual dominion of the Pope. So the bell,—our selfsame bell, whose familiar voice we may hear at all hours, in the streets,—this very bell sent forth its first-born accents from the tower of a log-built chapel, westward of Lake Champlain, and near the mighty stream of the Saint Lawrence. It was called Our Lady's Chapel of the Forest. The peal went forth as if to redeem and consecrate the heathen wilderness. The wolf growled at the sound, as he prowled stealthily through the underbrush; the grim bear turned his back, and stalked sullenly away; the startled doe leaped up, and led her fawn into a deeper solitude. The red men wondered what awful voice was speaking amid the wind that roared through the tree-tops; and following reverentially its summons, the dark-robed fathers blessed them, as they drew near the cross-crowned chapel. In a little time, there was a crucifix on every dusky bosom. The Indians knelt beneath the lowly roof, worshipping in the same forms that were observed under the vast dome of Saint Peter's, when the Pope performed high mass in the presence of kneeling princes. All the religious festivals, that awoke the chiming bells of lofty cathedrals, called forth a peal from Our Lady's Chapel of the Forest. Loudly rang the bell of the wilderness while the streets of Paris echoed with rejoicings for the birthday of the Bourbon, or whenever France had triumphed on some European battle-field. And the solemn woods were saddened with a melancholy knell, as often as the thick-strewn leaves were swept away from the virgin soil for the burial of an Indian chief.

Meantime, the bells of a hostile people and a hostile faith were ringing on Sabbaths and lecture-days, at Boston and other Puritan towns. Their echoes died away hundreds of miles southeastward of Our Lady's Chapel. But scouts had threaded the pathless desert that lay between, and, from behind the huge tree-trunks, perceived the Indians assembling at the summons of the bell. Some bore flaxen-haired scalps at their girdles, as if to lay those bloody trophies on Our Lady's altar. It was reported, and believed, all through England, that the Pope of Rome and the King of France had established this little chapel in the forest for the purpose of stirring up the red men to a crusade against the English settlers. The latter took energetic measures to secure their religion and their lives. On the eve of an especial fast of the Romish Church, while the bell tolled dismally, and the priests were chanting a doleful stave, a band of New England rangers rushed from the surrounding woods. Fierce shouts, and the report of musketry, pealed suddenly within the chapel. The ministering priests threw themselves before the altar, and were slain even on its steps. If, as antique traditions tell us, no grass will grow where the blood of martyrs has been shed, there should be a barren spot, to this very day, on the site of that desecrated altar.

While the blood was still plashing from step to step, the leader of the rangers seized a torch, and applied it to the drapery of the shrine. The flame and smoke arose, as from a burnt-sacrifice, at once illuminating and obscuring the whole interior of the chapel,

—now hiding the dead priests in a sa shroud, now revealing them and th slayers in one terrific glare. So already wished that the altar-sm could cover the deed from the sight Heaven. But one of the rangers—a m of sanctified aspect, though his ha were bloody—approached the captain

"Sir," said he, "our village meeti house lacks a bell, and hitherto we h been fain to summon the good people worship by beat of drum. Give me pray you, the bell of this popish cha for the sake of the godly Mr. Rog who doubtless hath remembered us the prayers of the congregation ε since we began our march. Who can what share of this night's good suc we owe to that holy man's wrest with the Lord?"

"Nay, then," answered the capt "if good Mr. Rogers hath holpen enterprise, it is right that he sh share the spoil. Take the bell and come, Deacon Lawson, if you will b the trouble of carrying it home. Hith it hath spoken nothing but papistry, that too in the French or Indian berish; but I warrant me, if Mr. Rc consecrate it anew, it will talk li good English and Protestant bell."

So Deacon Lawson and half a s of his townsmen took down the suspended it on a pole, and bore it ε on their sturdy shoulders, meanin carry it to the shore of Lake Champ and thence homeward by water. through the woods gleamed the fl of Our Lady's Chapel, flinging fant shadows from the clustered foliage, glancing on brooks that had n caught the sunlight. As the ra traversed the midnight forest, sta ing under their heavy burden,

gue of the bell gave many a tre-
ndous stroke,—clang, clang, clang!—
ost doleful sound, as if it were toll-
for the slaughter of the priests and
ruin of the chapel. Little dreamed
con Lawson and his townsmen that
was their own funeral knell. A war-
ty of Indians had heard the report
musketry, and seen the blaze of the
pel, and now were on the track of
rangers, summoned to vengeance by
bell's dismal murmurs. In the midst
a deep swamp they made a sudden
et on the retreating foe. Good Dea-
Lawson battled stoutly, but had his
l cloven by a tomahawk, and sank
the depths of the morass, with the
derous bell above him. And, for
y a year thereafter, our hero's voice
heard no more on earth, neither at
hour of worship, nor at festivals,
funerals.

nd is he still buried in that unknown
e? Scarcely so, dear reader. Hark!
plainly we hear him at this mo-
t, the spokesman of Time, proclaim-
that it is nine o'clock at night! We
therefore conclude that some happy
ce has restored him to upper air.

t there lay the bell, for many
t years; and the wonder is, that he
not lie silent there a century, or
aps a dozen centuries, till the world
ld have forgotten, not only his
e, but the voices of the whole
herhood of bells. How would the
accent of his iron tongue have
led his resurrectionists! But he was
fated to be a subject of discussion
g the antiquaries of far posterity.
the close of the Old French War,
rty of New England axe-men, who
ded the march of Colonel Brad-
t toward Lake Ontario, were build-

ing a bridge of logs through a swamp.
Plunging down a stake, one of these
pioneers felt it graze against some hard,
smooth substance. He called his comrades, and, by their united efforts, the
top of the bell was raised to the surface, a rope made fast to it, and thence
passed over the horizontal limb of a
tree. Heave-oh! up they hoisted their
prize, dripping with moisture, and festooned with verdant water-moss. As the
base of the bell emerged from the
swamp, the pioneers perceived that a
skeleton was clinging with its bony
fingers to the clapper, but immediately
relaxing its nerveless grasp, sank back
into the stagnant water. The bell then
gave forth a sullen clang. No wonder
that he was in haste to speak, after
holding his tongue for such a length of
time! The pioneers shoved the bell to
and fro, thus ringing a loud and heavy
peal, which echoed widely through the
forest, and reached the ears of Colonel
Bradstreet, and his three thousand men.
The soldiers paused on their march; a
feeling of religion, mingled with home-
tenderness, overpowered their rude
hearts; each seemed to hear the clangor
of the old church-bell, which had been
familiar to him from infancy, and had
tolled at the funerals of all his forefathers. By what magic had that holy
sound strayed over the wide-murmuring
ocean, and become audible amid the
clash of arms, the loud crashing of the
artillery over the rough wilderness-path,
and the melancholy roar of the wind
among the boughs?

The New-Englanders hid their prize
in a shadowy nook, betwixt a large gray
stone and the earthy roots of an overthrown tree; and when the campaign
was ended, they conveyed our friend to

Boston, and put him up at auction on the sidewalk of King Street. He was suspended, for the nonce, by a block and tackle, and being swung backward and forward, gave such loud and clear testimony to his own merits, that the auctioneer had no need to say a word. The highest bidder was a rich old representative from our town, who piously bestowed the bell on the meeting-house where he had been a worshipper for half a century. The good man had his reward. By a strange coincidence, the very first duty of the sexton, after the bell had been hoisted into the belfry, was to toll the funeral knell of the donor. Soon, however, those doleful echoes were drowned by a triumphant peal for the surrender of Quebec.

Ever since that period, our hero has occupied the same elevated station, and has put in his word on all matters of public importance, civil, military, or religious. On the day when Independence was first proclaimed in the street beneath, he uttered a peal which many deemed ominous and fearful, rather than triumphant. But he has told the same story these sixty years, and none mistake his meaning now. When Washington, in the fulness of his glory, rode through our flower-strewn streets, this was the tongue that bade the Father of his Country welcome! Again the same voice was heard, when La Fayette came to gather in his half-century's harvest of gratitude. Meantime, vast changes have been going on below. His voice, which once floated over a little provincial seaport, is now reverberated between brick edifices, and strikes the ear amid the buzz and tumult of a city. On the Sabbaths of olden time, the summons of the bell was obeyed by a pic-

turesque and varied throng; stately tlemen in purple velvet coats, broidered waistcoats, white wigs gold-laced hats, stepping with g courtesy beside ladies in flowered s gowns, and hoop-petticoats of maj circumference; while behind follow liveried slave or bondsman, bearing psalm-book, and a stove for his tress' feet. The commonalty, cla homely garb, gave precedence to betters at the door of the mee house, as if admitting that there distinctions between them, even in sight of God. Yet, as their coffins borne one after another through street, the bell has tolled a requiem all alike. What mattered it, wheth no there were a silver scutcheon o coffin-lid? "Open thy bosom, M Earth!" Thus spake the bell. "An of thy children is coming to his rest. Take him to thy bosom, an him slumber in peace." Thus spak bell, and Mother Earth received child. With the selfsame tones wil present generation be ushered to th braces of their mother; and M Earth will still receive her childre not thy tongue a-weary, mournful t of two centuries? O funeral bell! thou never be shattered with thine melancholy strokes? Yea, and a pet-call shall arouse the sleepers, thy heavy clang could awake no r

Again,—again, thy voice, remi me that I am wasting the "mid oil." In my lonely fantasy, I can s believe that other mortals have c the sound, or that it vibrates else than in my secret soul. But to hast thou spoken. Anxious men heard thee on their sleepless pi and bethought themselves anew

rrow's care. In a brief interval of
ʒefulness, the sons of toil have heard
e, and say, "Is so much of our quiet
nber spent?—is the morning so near
hand?" Crime has heard thee, and
tters, "Now is the very hour!" De-
ir answers thee, "Thus much of this
ry life is gone!" The young mother,
her bed of pain and ecstasy, has
nted thy echoing strokes, and dates
n them her first-born's share of life
and immortality. The bridegroom and
the bride have listened, and feel that
their night of rapture flits like a dream
away. Thine accents have fallen faintly
on the ear of the dying man, and warned
him that, ere thou speakest again, his
spirit shall have passed whither no voice
of time can ever reach. Alas for the
departing traveller, if thy voice—the
voice of fleeting time—have taught him
no lessons for Eternity!

SYLPH ETHEREGE

N a bright summer evening, two
ons stood among the shrubbery of a
ʃen, stealthily watching a young girl,
sat in the window-seat of a neigh-
ng mansion. One of these unseen
rvers, a gentleman, was youthful,
had an air of high breeding and
ʒement, and a face marked with in-
ʒct, though otherwise of unprepos-
ng aspect. His features wore even
minous, though somewhat mirthful
ʒssion, while he pointed his long
ʒinger at the girl, and seemed to
ʒd her as a creature completely with-
ʒe scope of his influence.

ʒhe charm works!" said he, in a
ʒ but emphatic whisper.

ʒo you know, Edward Hamilton,—
so you choose to be named,—do
know," said the lady beside him,
I have almost a mind to break the
at once? What if the lesson should
ʒ too severe! True, if my ward
ʒ be thus laughed out of her fan-
ʒ nonsense, she might be the better
ʒt through life. But then, she is
a delicate creature! And, besides,
are you not ruining your own chance,
by putting forward this shadow of a
rival?"

"But will he not vanish into thin air,
at my bidding?" rejoined Edward
Hamilton. "Let the charm work!"

The girl's slender and sylph-like
figure, tinged with radiance from the
sunset clouds, and overhung with the
rich drapery of the silken curtains, and
set within the deep frame of the window, was a perfect picture; or, rather,
it was like the original loveliness in a
painter's fancy, from which the most
finished picture is but an imperfect
copy. Though her occupation excited so
much interest in the two spectators, she
was merely gazing at a miniature which
she held in her hand, encased in white
satin and red morocco; nor did there
appear to be any other cause for the
smile of mockery and malice with which
Hamilton regarded her.

"The charm works!" muttered he
again. "Our pretty Sylvia's scorn will
have a dear retribution!"

At this moment the girl raised her

eyes, and, instead of the life-like semblance of the miniature, beheld the ill-omened shape of Edward Hamilton, who now stepped forth from his concealment in the shrubbery.

Sylvia Etherege was an orphan girl, who had spent her life, till within a few months past, under the guardianship, and in the secluded dwelling of an old bachelor uncle. While yet in her cradle, she had been the destined bride of a cousin, who was no less passive in the betrothal than herself. Their future union had been projected, as the means of uniting two rich estates, and was rendered highly expedient, if not indispensable, by the testamentary dispositions of the parents on both sides. Edgar Vaughan, the promised bridegroom, had been bred from infancy in Europe, and had never seen the beautiful girl whose heart he was to claim as his inheritance. But already, for several years, a correspondence had been kept up between the cousins, and had produced an intellectual intimacy, though it could but imperfectly acquaint them with each other's character.

Sylvia was shy, sensitive, and fanciful; and her guardian's secluded habits had shut her out from even so much of the world as is generally open to maidens of her age. She had been left to seek associates and friends for herself in the haunts of imagination, and to converse with them, sometimes in the language of dead poets, oftener in the poetry of her own mind. The companion whom she chiefly summoned up was the cousin with whose idea her earliest thoughts had been connected. She made a vision of Edgar Vaughan, and tinted it with stronger hues than a mere fancy-picture, yet graced it with

so many bright and delicate perfecti that her cousin could nowhere encountered so dangerous a rival. this shadow she cherished a roma fidelity. With its airy presence sit by her side, or gliding along her fav paths, the loneliness of her young was blissful; her heart was sati with love, while yet its virgin pu was untainted by the earthliness the touch of a real lover would left there. Edgar Vaughan seeme be conscious of her character; for his letters, he gave her a name was happily appropriate to the sensi ness of her disposition, the del peculiarity of her manners, and ethereal beauty both of her mind person. Instead of Sylvia, he callec Sylph,—with the prerogative of a cc and a lover,—his dear Sylph Ethere

When Sylvia was seventeen, guardian died, and she passed unde care of Mrs. Grosvenor, a lad wealth and fashion, and Sylvia's ne relative, though a distant one. an inmate of Mrs. Grosvenor's fa she still preserved somewhat of life-long habits of seclusion, and sh from a too familiar intercourse those around her. Still, too, she faithful to her cousin, or to the sh which bore his name.

The time drew near when Vaughan, whose education had completed by an extensive rang travel, was to revisit the soil o nativity. Edward Hamilton, a y gentleman, who had been Vaug companion, both in his studies and bles, had already recrossed the Atl bringing letters to Mrs. Grosveno Sylvia Etherege. These credentia sured him an earnest welcome,

ever, on Sylvia's part, was not fol-
ed by personal partiality, or even
regard that seemed due to her
sin's most intimate friend. As she
self could have assigned no cause
her repugnance, it might be termed
inctive. Hamilton's person, it is true,
the reverse of attractive, especially
n beheld for the first time. Yet, in
eyes of the most fastidious judges,
defect of natural grace was com-
sated by the polish of his manners,
by the intellect which so often
med through his dark features. Mrs.
svenor, with whom he immediately
me a prodigious favorite, exerted
elf to overcome Sylvia's dislike.
in this matter, her ward could
er be reasoned with nor persuaded.
presence of Edward Hamilton was
to render her cold, shy, and dis-
abstracting all the vivacity from
deportment, as if a cloud had come
ixt her and the sunshine.
e simplicity of Sylvia's demeanor
ered it easy for so keen an observer
Hamilton to detect her feelings.
never any slight circumstance made
sensible of them, a smile might be
to flit over the young man's sallow
e. None, that had once beheld this
e, were in any danger of forgetting
whenever they recalled to memory
eatures of Edward Hamilton, they
always duskily illuminated by this
ssion of mockery and malice.
a few weeks after Hamilton's ar-
he presented to Sylvia Etherege
iature of her cousin, which, as he
med her, would have been de-
d sooner, but was detained with
tion of his baggage. This was the
ture in the contemplation of which
eheld Sylvia so absorbed, at the

commencement of our story. Such, in
truth, was too often the habit of the
shy and musing girl. The beauty of the
pictured countenance was almost too
perfect to represent a human creature,
that had been born of a fallen and
world-worn race, and had lived to manhood amid ordinary troubles and enjoyments, and must become wrinkled
with age and care. It seemed too bright
for a thing formed of dust, and doomed
to crumble into dust again. Sylvia
feared that such a being would be too
refined and delicate to love a simple
girl like her. Yet, even while her spirit
drooped with that apprehension, the picture was but the masculine counterpart
of Sylph Etherege's sylph-like beauty.
There was that resemblance between her
own face and the miniature which is
said often to exist between lovers whom
Heaven has destined for each other, and
which, in this instance, might be owing
to the kindred blood of the two parties.
Sylvia felt, indeed, that there was something familiar in the countenance, so
like a friend did the eyes smile upon her,
and seem to imply a knowledge of her
thoughts. She could account for this
impression only by supposing that, in
some of her day-dreams, imagination
had conjured up the true similitude of
her distant and unseen lover.

But now could Sylvia give a brighter
semblance of reality to those day-
dreams. Clasping the miniature to her
heart, she could summon forth, from
that haunted cell of pure and blissful
fantasies, the life-like shadow, to roam
with her in the moonlight garden. Even
at noontide it sat with her in the arbor,
when the sunshine threw its broken
flakes of gold into the clustering shade.
The effect upon her mind was hardly

less powerful than if she had actually listened to, and reciprocated, the vows of Edgar Vaughan; for, though the illusion never quite deceived her, yet the remembrance was as distinct as of a remembered interview. Those heavenly eyes gazed forever into her soul, which drank at them as at a fountain, and was disquieted if reality threw a momentary cloud between. She heard the melody of a voice breathing sentiments with which her own chimed in like music. O, happy, yet hapless girl! Thus to create the being whom she loves, to endow him with all the attributes that were most fascinating to her heart, and then to flit with the airy creature into the realm of fantasy and moonlight, where dwelt his dreamy kindred! For her lover wiled Sylvia away from earth, which seemed strange, and dull, and darksome, and lured her to a country where her spirit roamed in peaceful rapture, deeming that it had found its home. Many, in their youth, have visited that land of dreams, and wandered so long in its enchanted groves, that, when banished thence, they feel like exiles everywhere.

The dark-browed Edward Hamilton, like the villain of a tale, would often glide through the romance wherein poor Sylvia walked. Sometimes, at the most blissful moment of her ecstasy, when the features of the miniature were pictured brightest in the air, they would suddenly change, and darken, and be transformed into his visage. And always, when such change occurred, the intrusive visage wore that peculiar smile with which Hamilton had glanced at Sylvia.

Before the close of summer, it was told Sylvia Etherege that Vaughan had arrived from France, and that she would meet him—would meet, for the first

time, the loved of years—that v evening. We will not tell how o and how earnestly she gazed upon miniature, thus endeavoring to pre herself for the approaching interv lest the throbbing of her timorous h should stifle the words of welco While the twilight grew deeper duskier, she sat with Mrs. Grosveno an inner apartment, lighted only by softened gleam from an alabaster la which was burning at a distance on centre-table of the drawing-room. N before had Sylph Etherege looked sylph-like. She had communed wit creature of imagination, till her loveliness seemed but the creation a delicate and dreamy fancy. E vibration of her spirit was visibl her frame, as she listened to the rat of wheels and the tramp upon the p ment, and deemed that even the br bore the sound of her lover's foots as if he trode upon the viewless Mrs. Grosvenor, too, while she wat the tremulous flow of Sylvia's feel was deeply moved; she looked une at the agitated girl, and was abou speak, when the opening of the s door arrested the words upon her li

Footsteps ascended the staircase, a confident and familiar tread, and one entered the drawing-room. From sofa where they sat, in the inner a ment, Mrs. Grosvenor and Sylvia not discern the visitor.

"Sylph!" cried a voice. "De Sylph! Where are you, sweet S Etherege? Here is your Edgar Vaugh

But instead of answering, or risi meet her lover,—who had greete by the sweet and fanciful name, w appropriate as it was to her chara was known only to him,—S

ped Mrs. Grosvenor's arm, while
whole frame shook with the throb-
; of her heart.

Who is it?" gasped she. "Who calls
Sylph?"

efore Mrs. Grosvenor could reply,
stranger entered the room, bearing
lamp in his hand. Approaching the
, he displayed to Sylvia the features
Edward Hamilton, illuminated by
evil smile, from which his face de-
d so marked an individuality.

s not the miniature an admirable
ess?" inquired he.

lvia shuddered, but had not power
urn away her white face from his
. The miniature, which she had
holding in her hand, fell down
 the floor, where Hamilton, or
han, set his foot upon it, and
ed the ivory counterfeit to frag-
s.

here, my sweet Sylph!" he ex-
ed. "It was I that created your
tom-lover, and now I annihilate
 Your dream is rudely broken.
e, Sylph Etherege, awake to truth!
the only Edgar Vaughan!"

e have gone too far, Edgar
han," said Mrs. Grosvenor, catch-
ylvia in her arms. The revengeful
, which Vaughan's wounded vanity
suggested, had been countenanced
his lady, in the hope of curing
a of her romantic notions, and
ciling her to the truths and reali-
f life. "Look at the poor child!"
ontinued. "I protest I tremble for
onsequences!"

deed, madam!" replied Vaughan,
ingly, as he threw the light of the
on Sylvia's closed eyes and marble
res. "Well, my conscience is clear.
but look into this delicate crea-

ture's heart; and with the pure fantasies
that I found there, I made what seemed
a man,—and the delusive shadow has
wiled her away to Shadow-land, and
vanished there! It is no new tale. Many
a sweet maid has shared the lot of poor
Sylph Etherege!"

"And now, Edgar Vaughan," said Mrs.
Grosvenor, as Sylvia's heart began
faintly to throb again, "now try, in
good earnest, to win back her love from
the phantom which you conjured up. If
you succeed, she will be the better, her
whole life long, for the lesson we have
given her."

Whether the result of the lesson corresponded with Mrs. Grosvenor's hopes,
may be gathered from the closing scene
of our story. It had been made known
to the fashionable world that Edgar
Vaughan had returned from France,
and, under the assumed name of Edward Hamilton, had won the affections
of the lovely girl to whom he had been
affianced in his boyhood. The nuptials
were to take place at an early date.
One evening, before the day of anticipated bliss arrived, Edgar Vaughan
entered Mrs. Grosvenor's drawing-room,
where he found that lady and Sylph
Etherege.

"Only that Sylvia makes no complaint," remarked Mrs. Grosvenor, "I
should apprehend that the town air is
ill-suited to her constitution. She was
always, indeed, a delicate creature; but
now she is a mere gossamer. Do but
look at her! Did you ever imagine anything so fragile?"

Vaughan was already attentively observing his mistress, who sat in a shadowy and moon-lighted recess of the
room, with her dreamy eyes fixed steadfastly upon his own. The bough of a

tree was waving before the window, and sometimes enveloped her in the gloom of its shadow, into which she seemed to vanish.

"Yes," he said, to Mrs. Grosvenor. "I can scarcely deem her 'of the earth, earthy.' No wonder that I call her Sylph! Methinks she will fade into the moonlight, which falls upon her through the window. Or, in the open air, she might flit away upon the breeze, like a wreath of mist!"

Sylvia's eyes grew brighter. She waved her hand to Edgar Vaughan, with a ges-ture of ethereal triumph.

"Farewell!" she said. "I will neit[her] fade into the moonlight, nor flit a[way] upon the breeze. Yet you cannot k[eep] me here!"

There was something in Sylvia's l[ook] and tones that startled Mrs. Grosve[nor] with a terrible apprehension. But as [she] was rushing towards the girl, Vaug[han] held her back.

"Stay!" cried he, with a strange s[mile] of mockery and anguish. "Can our s[weet] Sylph be going to heaven, to seek [the] original of the miniature?"

THE CANTERBURY PILGRIMS

THE summer moon, which shines in so many a tale, was beaming over a broad extent of uneven country. Some of its brightest rays were flung into a spring of water, where no traveller, toiling as the writer has, up the hilly road beside which it gushes, ever failed to quench his thirst. The work of neat hands and considerate art was visible about this blessed fountain. An open cistern, hewn and hollowed out of solid stone, was placed above the waters, which filled it to the brim, but, by some invisible outlet, were conveyed away without dripping down its sides. Though the basin had not room for another drop, and the continual gush of water made a tremor on the surface, there was a secret charm that forbade it to overflow. I remember, that when I had slaked my summer thirst, and sat panting by the cistern, it was my fanciful theory, that Nature could not afford to lavish so pure a liquid, as she does the waters of all meaner fountains.

While the moon was hanging al[most] perpendicularly over this spot, [two] figures appeared on the summit of [the] hill, and came with noiseless foots[teps] down towards the spring. They [were] then in the first freshness of youth; [nor] is there a wrinkle now on either of [their] brows, and yet they wore a str[ange] old-fashioned garb. One, a young [man] with ruddy cheeks, walked beneat[h the] canopy of a broad-brimmed gray [hat;] he seemed to have inherited his g[reat] grandsire's square-skirted coat, a[nd a] waistcoat that extended its immense [flaps] to his knees; his brown locks, also, [hung] down behind, in a mode unknow[n to] our times. By his side was a sweet y[oung] damsel, her fair features sheltered [by a] prim little bonnet, within which app[eared] the vestal muslin of a cap; her [ankle-] long-waisted gown, and indeed her [whole] attire, might have been worn by [some] rustic beauty who had faded half a[way]

y before. But that there was some-
g too warm and life-like in them, I
ld here have compared this couple
he ghosts of two young lovers, who
died long since in the glow of pas-
, and now were straying out of their
es, to renew the old vows, and
low forth the unforgotten kiss of
r earthly lips, beside the moonlit
ng.

Thee and I will rest here a moment,
iam," said the young man, as they
v near the stone cistern, "for there
o fear that the elders know what
have done; and this may be the last
: we shall ever taste this water."

hus speaking, with a little sadness
is face, which was also visible in
of his companion, he made her sit
n on a stone, and was about to place
self very close to her side; she,
ever, repelled him, though not
ndly.

Nay, Josiah," said she, giving him
mid push with her maiden hand,
e must sit farther off, on that
r stone, with the spring between us.
t would the sisters say, if thee were
t so close to me?"

But we are of the world's people
Miriam," answered Josiah.

he girl persisted in her prudery, nor
the youth, in fact, seem altogether
from a similar sort of shyness;
hey sat apart from each other,
g up the hill, where the moon-
discovered the tops of a group
uildings. While their attention was
occupied, a party of travellers, who
come wearily up the long ascent,
: a halt to refresh themselves at
spring. There were three men, a
an, and a little girl and boy. Their
: was mean, covered with the dust

of the summer's day, and damp with
the night-dew; they all looked woe-
begone, as if the cares and sorrows of
the world had made their steps heavier
as they climbed the hill; even the two
little children appeared older in evil
days than the young man and maiden
who had first approached the spring.

"Good-evening to you, young folks,"
was the salutation of the travellers;
and "Good-evening, friends," replied the
youth and damsel.

"Is that white building the Shaker
meeting-house?" asked one of the strangers. "And are those the red roofs of
the Shaker village?"

"Friend, it is the Shaker village," answered Josiah, after some hesitation.

The travellers, who, from the first,
had looked suspiciously at the garb of
these young people, now taxed them
with an intention which all the circumstances, indeed, rendered too obvious to
be mistaken.

"It is true, friends," replied the young
man, summoning up his courage. "Miriam and I have a gift to love each other,
and we are going among the world's
people, to live after their fashion. And
ye know that we do not transgress the
law of the land; and neither ye, nor
the elders themselves, have a right to
hinder us."

"Yet you think it expedient to depart without leave-taking," remarked
one of the travellers.

"Yea, ye-a," said Josiah, reluctantly,
"because father Job is a very awful
man to speak with; and being aged
himself, he has but little charity for
what he calls the iniquities of the flesh."

"Well," said the stranger, "we will
neither use force to bring you back to
the village, nor will we betray you to

the elders. But sit you here awhile, and when you have heard what we shall tell you of the world which we have left, and into which you are going, perhaps you will turn back with us of your own accord. What say you?" added he, turning to his companions. "We have travelled thus far without becoming known to each other. Shall we tell our stories, here by this pleasant spring, for our own pastime, and the benefit of these misguided young lovers?"

In accordance with this proposal, the whole party stationed themselves round the stone cistern; the two children, being very weary, fell asleep upon the damp earth, and the pretty Shaker girl, whose feelings were those of a nun or a Turkish lady, crept as close as possible to the female traveller, and as far as she well could from the unknown men. The same person who had hitherto been the chief spokesman now stood up, waving his hat in his hand, and suffered the moonlight to fall full upon his front.

"In me," said he, with a certain majesty of utterance, "in me, you behold a poet."

Though a lithographic print of this gentleman is extant, it may be well to notice that he was now nearly forty, a thin and stooping figure, in a black coat, out at elbows; notwithstanding the ill condition of his attire, there were about him several tokens of a peculiar sort of foppery, unworthy of a mature man, particularly in the arrangement of his hair, which was so disposed as to give all possible loftiness and breadth to his forehead. However, he had an intelligent eye, and, on the whole, a marked countenance.

"A poet!" repeated the young Shaker, a little puzzled how to understand s• a designation, seldom heard in the u• tarian community where he had sp• his life. "O, ay, Miriam, he mean• varse-maker, thee must know."

This remark jarred upon the susc• tible nerves of the poet; nor could • help wondering what strange fata• had put into this young man's mo• an epithet which ill-natured people • affirmed to be more proper to his m• than the one assumed by himself.

"True, I am a verse-maker," he • sumed, "but my verse is no more t• the material body into which I bre• the celestial soul of thought. Alas! • many a pang has it cost me, this s• insensibility to the ethereal essenc• poetry, with which you have here • tured me again, at the moment • I am to relinquish my profession • ever! O Fate! why hast thou wa• with Nature, turning all her hi• and more perfect gifts to the rui• me, their possessor? What is the • of song, when the world lacks the • of taste? How can I rejoice in • strength and delicacy of feeling, • they have but made great sorrows• of little ones? Have I dreaded s• like death, and yearned for fam• others pant for vital air, only to • myself in a middle state between • scurity and infamy? But I have m• venge! I could have given exist• to a thousand bright creations. I • them into my heart, and there let • putrefy! I shake off the dust of • feet against my countrymen! But • terity, tracing my footsteps up • weary hill, will cry shame upon• unworthy age that drove one o• fathers of American song to en• days in a Shaker village!"

During this harangue, the speaker gesticulated with great energy; and, as etry is the natural language of pasion, there appeared reason to apprehend his final explosion into an ode empore. The reader must understand t, for all these bitter words, he was kind, gentle, harmless, poor fellow ugh, whom Nature, tossing her ingredients together without looking at recipe, had sent into the world with much of one sort of brain, and dly any of another.

Friend," said the young Shaker, in the perplexity, "thee seemest to have with great troubles; and, doubtless, hould pity them, if—if I could but lerstand what they were."

Happy in your ignorance!" replied poet, with an air of sublime superiy. "To your coarser mind, perhaps, ay seem to speak of more important fs, when I add, what I had well forgotten, that I am out at elvs, and almost starved to death. At rate, you have the advice and exle of one individual to warn you k; for I am come hither, a disointed man, flinging aside the fragts of my hopes, and seeking shelter the calm retreat which you are so ious to leave."

I thank thee, friend," rejoined the th, "but I do not mean to be a t, nor, Heaven be praised! do I k Miriam ever made a varse in her So we need not fear thy disappoints. But, Miriam," he added, with concern, "thee knowest that the rs admit nobody that has not a to be useful. Now, what under the can they do with this poor varseer?"

Nay, Josiah, do not thee discourage the poor man," said the girl, in all simplicity and kindness. "Our hymns are very rough, and perhaps they may trust him to smooth them."

Without noticing this hint of professional employment, the poet turned away, and gave himself up to a sort of vague reverie, which he called thought. Sometimes he watched the moon, pouring a silvery liquid on the clouds, through which it slowly melted till they became all bright; then he saw the same sweet radiance dancing on the leafy trees which rustled as if to shake it off, or sleeping on the high tops of hills, or hovering down in distant valleys, like the material of unshaped dreams; lastly, he looked into the spring, and there the light was mingling with the water. In its crystal bosom, too, beholding all heaven reflected there, he found an emblem of a pure and tranquil breast. He listened to that most ethereal of all sounds, the song of crickets, coming in full choir upon the wind, and fancied that, if moonlight could be heard, it would sound just like that. Finally, he took a draught at the Shaker spring, and, as if it were the true Castalia, was forthwith moved to compose a lyric, a Farewell to his Harp, which he swore should be its closing strain, the last verse that an ungrateful world should have from him. This effusion, with two or three other little pieces, subsequently written, he took the first opportunity to send, by one of the Shaker brethren, to Concord, where they were published in the New Hampshire Patriot.

Meantime, another of the Canterbury pilgrims, one so different from the poet that the delicate fancy of the latter could hardly have conceived of him, began to relate his sad experience. He was a small man of quick and unquiet gestures, about fifty years old, with a narrow forehead, all wrinkled and drawn together. He held in his hand a pencil, and a card of some commission-merchant in foreign parts, on the back of which, for there was light enough to read or write by, he seemed ready to figure out a calculation.

"Young man," said he, abruptly, "what quantity of land do the Shakers own here, in Canterbury?"

"That is more than I can tell thee, friend," answered Josiah, "but it is a very rich establishment, and for a long way by the roadside thee may guess the land to be ours, by the neatness of the fences."

"And what may be the value of the whole," continued the stranger, "with all the buildings and improvements, pretty nearly, in round numbers?"

"O, a monstrous sum,—more than I can reckon," replied the young Shaker.

"Well, sir," said the pilgrim, "there was a day, and not very long ago, neither, when I stood at my counting-room window, and watched the signal-flags of three of my own ships entering the harbor, from the East Indies, from Liverpool, and from up the Straits; and I would not have given the invoice of the least of them for the title-deeds of this whole Shaker settlement. You stare. Perhaps, now, you won't believe that I could have put more value on a little piece of paper, no bigger than the palm of your hand, than all these solid acres of grain, grass, and pasture-land would sell for?"

"I won't dispute it, friend," answered Josiah, "but I know I had rather have fifty acres of this good land than whole sheet of thy paper."

"You may say so now," said ruined merchant, bitterly, "for my na would not be worth the paper I sho write it on. Of course, you must ha heard of my failure?"

And the stranger mentioned his nar which, however mighty it might ha been in the commercial world, young Shaker had never heard of am the Canterbury hills.

"Not heard of my failure!" exclaim the merchant, considerably piqu "Why, it was spoken of on 'Cha in London, and from Boston to N Orleans men trembled in their sho At all events, I did fail, and you me here on my road to the Sha village, where, doubtless (for the Sh ers are a shrewd sect), they will ha a due respect for my experience, give me the management of the tra part of the concern, in which case think I can pledge myself to dou their capital in four or five years. T back with me, young man; for tho you will never meet with my g luck, you can hardly escape my ba

"I will not turn back for this," plied Josiah, calmly, "any more t for the advice of the varse-maker, tween whom and thee, friend, I a sort of likeness, though I can't ju say where it lies. But Miriam an can earn our daily bread among world's people, as well as in the Sha village. And do we want anything m Miriam?"

"Nothing more, Josiah," said the quietly.

"Yea, Miriam, and daily bread some other little mouths, if God s them," observed the simple Shaker

Miriam did not reply, but looked down into the spring, where she entered the image of her own pretty face, blushing within the prim little cap net. The third pilgrim now took up the conversation. He was a sunburnt countryman, of tall frame and bony strength, on whose rude and manly face there appeared a darker, more sullen, obstinate despondency, than on those of either the poet or the merchant.

"Well, now, youngster," he began, "these folks have had their say, so I'll take my turn. My story will cut but a poor figure by the side of theirs; for I never supposed that I could have a right to meat and drink, and great praise besides, only for tagging rhymes together, as it seems this man does; nor ever tried to get the substance of hundreds into my own hands, like the other there. When I was about of your years, I married me a wife,—just such a neat and pretty young woman as Miriam, if that's her name,—and all I asked of Providence was an ordinary blessing on the sweat of my brow, so that we might be decent and comfortable, and have daily bread for ourselves, and for some other little mouths that soon had to feed. We had no great prospects before us; but I never wanted to be idle; and I thought it a matter of course that the Lord would help me, because I was willing to help myself."

"And didn't he help thee, friend?" demanded Josiah, with some eagerness.

"No," said the yeoman, sullenly; "for if you would not have seen me here. I have labored hard for years; and my means have been growing narrower, and my living poorer, and my heart colder and heavier, all the time; till at last I could bear it no longer. I set myself down to calculate whether I had best go on the Oregon expedition, or come here to the Shaker village; but I had not hope enough left in me to begin the world over again; and, to make my story short, here I am. And now, youngster, take my advice, and turn back; or else, some few years hence, you'll have to climb this hill, with as heavy a heart as mine."

This simple story had a strong effect on the young fugitives. The misfortunes of the poet and merchant had won little sympathy from their plain good sense and unworldly feelings, qualities which made them such unprejudiced and inflexible judges, that few men would have chosen to take the opinion of this youth and maiden as to the wisdom or folly of their pursuits. But here was one whose simple wishes had resembled their own, and who, after efforts which almost gave him a right to claim success from fate, had failed in accomplishing them.

"But thy wife, friend?" exclaimed the young man, "what became of the pretty girl, like Miriam? O, I am afraid she is dead!"

"Yea, poor man, she must be dead, —she and the children, too," sobbed Miriam.

The female pilgrim had been leaning over the spring, wherein latterly a tear or two might have been seen to fall, and form its little circle on the surface of the water. She now looked up, disclosing features still comely, but which had acquired an expression of fretfulness, in the same long course of evil fortune that had thrown a sullen gloom over the temper of the unprosperous yeoman.

"I am his wife," said she, a shade of irritability just perceptible in the sadness of her tone. "These poor little things, asleep on the ground, are two of our children. We had two more, but God has provided better for them than we could, by taking them to himself."

"And what would thee advise Josiah and me to do?" asked Miriam, this being the first question which she had put to either of the strangers.

" 'T is a thing almost against nature for a woman to try to part true lovers," answered the yeoman's wife, after a pause; "but I'll speak as truly to you as if these were my dying words. Though my husband told you some of our troubles, he didn't mention the greatest, and that which makes all the rest so hard to bear. If you and your sweetheart marry, you'll be kind and pleasant to each other for a year or two, and while that's the case, you never will repent; but, by and by, he'll grow gloomy, rough, and hard to please, and you'll be peevish, and full of little angry fits, and apt to be complaining by the fireside, when he comes to rest himself from his troubles out of doors; so your love will wear away by little and little, and leave you miserable at last. It has been so with us; and yet my husband and I were true lovers once; if ever two young folks were."

As she ceased, the yeoman and his wife exchanged a glance, in which there was more and warmer affection than they had supposed to have escaped the frost of a wintry fate, in either of their breasts. At that moment, when they stood on the utmost verge of married life, one word fitly spoken, or perhaps one peculiar look, had they had mu confidence enough to reciprocate might have renewed all their old f ings, and sent them back, resolved sustain each other amid the strug of the world. But the crisis passed, never came again. Just then, also, children, roused by their mother's vo looked up, and added their willing cents to the testimony borne by the Canterbury pilgrims against world from which they fled.

"We are tired and hungry!" c they. "Is it far to the Shaker villag

The Shaker youth and maiden loc mournfully into each other's eyes. T had but stepped across the thresh of their homes, when lo! the array of cares and sorrows that up to warn them back. The va narratives of the strangers had arrar themselves into a parable; they see not merely instances of woful fate had befallen others, but shadowy on of disappointed hope, and unava toil, domestic grief, and estranged fection, that would cloud the on path of these poor fugitives. But one instant's hesitation, they op their arms, and sealed their resolve as pure and fond an embrace as youthful love had hallowed.

"We will not go back," said "The world never can be dark t for we will always love one anoth

Then the Canterbury pilgrims up the hill, while the poet chant drear and desperate stanza of the well to his Harp, fitting music for melancholy band. They sought a where all former ties of natur society would be sundered, and al distinctions levelled, and a cold passionless security be substitute

rtal hope and fear, as in that other
ige of the world's weary outcasts,
grave. The lovers drank at the
Shaker spring, and then, with chastened
hopes, but more confiding affections,
went on to mingle in an untried life.

OLD NEWS

I. THE COLONIAL NEWSPAPER

ERE is a volume of what were once
spapers, each on a small half-sheet,
ow and time-stained, of a coarse
ic, and imprinted with a rude old
e. Their aspect conveys a singular
ression of antiquity, in a species
iterature which we are accustomed
onsider as connected only with the
ent moment. Ephemeral as they
e intended and supposed to be, they
e long outlived the printer in his
le subscription-list, and have proved
e durable, as to their physical ex-
nce, than most of the timber,
ks, and stone of the town where
were issued. These are but the
of their triumphs. The govern-
t, the interests, the opinions, in
t, all the moral circumstances that
e contemporary with their publi-
on, have passed away, and left no
er record of what they were than
be found in these frail leaves.
py are the editors of newspapers!
r productions excel all others in im-
iate popularity, and are certain to
ire another sort of value with the
e of time. They scatter their leaves
he wind, as the sibyl did, and pos-
y collects them, to be treasured up
ng the best materials of its wis-
. With hasty pens they write for
ortality.

It is pleasant to take one of these
little dingy half-sheets between the
thumb and finger, and picture forth the
personage who, above ninety years ago,
held it, wet from the press, and steam-
ing, before the fire. Many of the numbers bear the name of an old colonial
dignitary. There he sits, a major, a
member of the council, and a weighty
merchant, in his high-backed arm-chair,
wearing a solemn wig and grave attire,
such as befits his imposing gravity of
mien, and displaying but little finery,
except a huge pair of silver shoe-buckles,
curiously carved. Observe the awful
reverence of his visage, as he reads
His Majesty's most gracious speech;
and the deliberate wisdom with which
he ponders over some paragraph of
provincial politics, and the keener intelligence with which he glances at the
ship-news and commercial advertisements. Observe, and smile! He may
have been a wise man in his day; but,
to us, the wisdom of the politician appears like folly, because we can compare its prognostics with actual results;
and the old merchant seems to have
busied himself about vanities, because
we know that the expected ships have
been lost at sea, or mouldered at the
wharves; that his imported broadcloths
were long ago worn to tatters, and his
cargoes of wine quaffed to the lees; and
that the most precious leaves of his

ledger have become waste-paper. Yet his avocations were not so vain as our philosophic moralizing. In this world, we are the things of a moment, and are made to pursue momentary things, with here and there a thought that stretches mistily towards eternity, and perhaps may endure as long. All philosophy that would abstract mankind from the present is no more than words.

The first pages of most of these old papers are as soporific as a bed of poppies. Here we have an erudite clergyman, or perhaps a Cambridge professor, occupying several successive weeks with a criticism on Tate and Brady, as compared with the New England version of the Psalms. Of course, the preference is given to the native article. Here are doctors disagreeing about the treatment of a putrid fever then prevalent, and blackguarding each other with a characteristic virulence that renders the controversy not altogether unreadable. Here are President Wigglesworth and the Rev. Dr. Colman, endeavoring to raise a fund for the support of missionaries among the Indians of Massachusetts Bay. Easy would be the duties of such a mission now! Here—for there is nothing new under the sun—are frequent complaints of the disordered state of the currency, and the project of a bank with a capital of five hundred thousand pounds, secured on lands. Here are literary essays, from the Gentleman's Magazine; and squibs against the Pretender, from the London newspapers. And here, occasionally, are specimens of New England humor, laboriously light and lamentably mirthful, as if some very sober person, in his zeal to be merry, were dancing a jig to the tune of a funeral-psalm. All this is weari-

some, and we must turn the leaf.

There is a good deal of amuseme and some profit, in the perusal of th little items which characterize the m ners and circumstances of the count New England was then in a state comparably more picturesque than present, or than it has been within memory of man; there being, as only a narrow strip of civilization al the edge of a vast forest, peopled enough of its original race to contr the savage life with the old custc of another world. The white pop tion, also, was diversified by the in of all sorts of expatriated vagabor and by the continual importation bond-servants from Ireland and e where, so that there was a wild unsettled multitude, forming a str minority to the sober descendants the Puritans. Then, there were slaves, contributing their dark shade the picture of society. The conseque of all this was a great variety singularity of action and incident, m instances of which might be sele from these columns, where they told with a simplicity and quaint of style that bring the striking po into very strong relief. It is natura suppose, too, that these circumsta affected the body of the people, made their course of life generally regular than that of their descenda There is no evidence that the m standard was higher than now; or, deed, that morality was so well def as it has since become. There seen have been quite as many frauds robberies, in proportion to the nun of honest deeds; there were mure in hot-blood and in malice; and bl quarrels over liquor. Some of

hers also appear to have been yoked
unfaithful wives, if we may trust
: frequent notices of elopements from
l and board. The pillory, the whipping-
st, the prison, and the gallows, each
l their use in those old times; and,
short, as often as our imagination
es in the past, we find it a ruder
l rougher age than our own, with
·dly any perceptible advantages, and
ch that gave life a gloomier tinge.

n vain we endeavor to throw a
,ny and joyous air over our picture
this period; nothing passes before
fancy but a crowd of sad-visaged
·ple, moving duskily through a dull
y atmosphere. It is certain that win-
·rushed upon them with fiercer storms
·n now, blocking up the narrow for-
paths, and overwhelming the roads
·g the sea-coast with mountain snow-
·ts; so that weeks elapsed before the
·spaper could announce how many
·ellers had perished, or what wrecks
strewn the shore. The cold was
·e piercing then, and lingered further
· the spring, making the chimney-
·er a comfortable seat till long past
·y-day. By the number of such ac-
·nts on record, we might suppose
the thunder-stone, as they termed
·ell oftener and deadlier, on steeples,
·llings, and unsheltered wretches. In
, our fathers bore the brunt of more
·ng and pitiless elements than we.
·re were forebodings, also, of a more
ful tempest than those of the ele-
·ts. At two or three dates, we have
·ies of drums, trumpets, and all sorts
·martial music, passing athwart the
·night sky, accompanied with the
of cannon and rattle of musketry,
·hetic echoes of the sounds that
· soon to shake the land. Besides

these airy prognostics, there were rumors of French fleets on the coast, and
of the march of French and Indians
through the wilderness, along the borders of the settlements. The country
was saddened, moreover, with grievous
sickness. The small-pox raged in many
of the towns, and seems, though so familiar a scourge, to have been regarded
with as much affright as that which
drove the throng from Wall Street and
Broadway at the approach of a new
pestilence. There were autumnal fevers
too, and a contagious and destructive
throat-distemper,—diseases unwritten in
medical books. The dark superstition of
former days had not yet been so far
dispelled as not to heighten the gloom
of the present times. There is an advertisement, indeed, by a committee of
the Legislature, calling for information
as to the circumstances of sufferers in
the "late calamity of 1692," with a
view to reparation of their losses and
misfortunes. But the tenderness with
which, after above forty years, it was
thought expedient to allude to the witchcraft delusion, indicates a good deal
of lingering error, as well as the advance of more enlightened opinions. The
rigid hand of Puritanism might yet be
felt upon the reins of government, while
some of the ordinances intimate a dis-
orderly spirit on the part of the people.
The Suffolk justices, after a preamble
that great disturbances have been committed by persons entering town and
leaving it in coaches, chaises, calashes,
and other wheel-carriages, on the evening before the Sabbath, give notice that
a watch will hereafter be set at the
"fortification-gate," to prevent these
outrages. It is amusing to see Boston
assuming the aspect of a walled city,

guarded, probably, by a detachment of church-members, with a deacon at their head. Governor Belcher makes proclamation against certain "loose and dissolute people" who have been wont to stop passengers in the streets, on the 5th of November, "otherwise called Pope's Day," and levy contributions for the building of bonfires. In this instance, the populace are more puritanic than the magistrate.

The elaborate solemnities of funerals were in accordance with the sombre character of the times. In cases of ordinary death, the printer seldom fails to notice that the corpse was "very decently interred." But when some mightier mortal has yielded to his fate, the decease of the "worshipful" such-a-one is announced, with all his titles of deacon, justice, counsellor, and colonel; then follows an heraldic sketch of his honorable ancestors, and lastly an account of the black pomp of his funeral, and the liberal expenditure of scarfs, gloves, and mourning-rings. The burial train glides slowly before us, as we have seen it represented in the wood-cuts of that day, the coffin, and the bearers, and the lamentable friends, trailing their long black garments, while grim death, a most misshapen skeleton, with all kinds of doleful emblems, stalks hideously in front. There was a coach-maker at this period, one John Lucas, who seems to have gained the chief of his living by letting out a sable coach to funerals.

It would not be fair, however, to leave quite so dismal an impression on the reader's mind; nor should it be forgotten that happiness may walk soberly in dark attire, as well as dance lightsomely in a gala-dress. And this reminds us that there is an incidental notice of the "dancing-school near Orange-Tree," whence we may in that the saltatory art was occasiona practised, though perhaps chastened i a characteristic gravity of moveme This pastime was probably confined the aristocratic circle, of which royal governor was the centre. But are scandalized at the attempt of J athan Furness to introduce a m reprehensible amusement: he challen the whole country to match his bl gelding in a race for a hundred pour to be decided on Metonomy Common Chelsea Beach. Nothing as to the m ners of the times can be inferred fr this freak of an individual. There w no daily and continual opportunities being merry; but sometimes the pec rejoiced, in their own peculiar fashi oftener with a calm, religious sn than with a broad laugh, as when t feasted, like one great family, Thanksgiving time, or indulged a live mirth throughout the pleasant days Election-week. This latter was the t holiday-season of New England. M tary musters were too seriously imp tant in that warlike time to be clas among amusements; but they stirred and enlivened the public mind, and w occasions of solemn festival to the g ernor and great men of the provi at the expense of the field-officers. Revolution blotted a feast-day out our calendar; for the anniversary the king's birth appears to have b celebrated with most imposing pomp salutes from Castle William, a mili parade, a grand dinner at the to house, and a brilliant illumination in evening. There was nothing forced feigned in these testimonials of loy to George the Second. So long as t aded the re-establishment of a popish nasty, the people were fervent for house of Hanover: and, besides, immediate magistracy of the coun- was a barrier between the monarch the occasional discontents of the onies; the waves of faction some- es reached the governor's chair, but er swelled against the throne. Thus, il oppression was felt to proceed m the king's own hand, New England iced with her whole heart on his jesty's birthday.

but the slaves, we suspect, were the rriest part of the population, since was their gift to be merry in the st of circumstances; and they en- ed, comparatively, few hardships, er the domestic sway of our fathers. re seems to have been a great trade these human commodities. No ad- isements are more frequent than se of "a negro fellow, fit for almost household work"; "a negro woman, est, healthy, and capable"; "a young o wench, of many desirable quali- "; "a negro man, very fit for a tay- ' We know not in what this natural ess for a tailor consisted, unless it e some peculiarity of conformation enabled him to sit cross-legged. en the slaves of a family were in- veniently prolific,—it being not quite odox to drown the superfluous off- ng, like a litter of kittens,—notice promulgated of "a negro child to given away." Sometimes the slaves med the property of their own per- , and made their escape; among y such instances, the governor es a hue-and-cry after his negro . But, without venturing a word in nuation of the general system, we ess our opinion that Cæsar, Pom-

pey, Scipio, and all such great Roman namesakes, would have been better ad- vised had they stayed at home, fodder- ing the cattle, cleaning dishes,—in fine, performing their moderate share of the labors of life, without being harassed by its cares. The sable inmates of the mansion were not excluded from the domestic affections: in families in mid- dling rank, they had their places at the board; and when the circle closed round the evening hearth, its blaze glowed on their dark shining faces, in- termixed familiarly with their master's children. It must have contributed to reconcile them to their lot, that they saw white men and women imported from Europe as they had been from Africa, and sold, though only for a term of years, yet as actual slaves to the highest bidder. Slave labor being but a small part of the industry of the country, it did not change the char- acter of the people; the latter, on the contrary, modified and softened the in- stitution, making it a patriarchal, and almost a beautiful, peculiarity of the times.

Ah! We had forgotten the good old merchant, over whose shoulder we were peeping, while he read the newspaper. Let us now suppose him putting on his three-cornered gold-laced hat, grasping his cane, with a head inlaid of ebony and mother-of-pearl, and setting forth, through the crooked streets of Boston, on various errands, suggested by the advertisements of the day. Thus he communes with himself: I must be mindful, says he, to call at Captain Scut's, in Creek Lane, and examine his rich velvet, whether it be fit for my apparel on Election-day,—that I may wear a stately aspect in presence of the governor and my brethren of the council. I will look in also, at the shop of Michael Cario, the jeweller: he has silver buckles of a new fashion; and mine have lasted me some half-score years. My fair daughter Miriam shall have an apron of gold brocade, and a velvet mask,—though it would be a pity the wench should hide her comely visage; and also a French cap, from Robert Jenkins's, on the north side of the town-house. He hath beads, too, and ear-rings, and necklaces, of all sorts; these are but vanities,—nevertheless, they would please the silly maiden well. My dame desireth another female in the kitchen; wherefore, I must inspect the lot of Irish lasses, for sale by Samuel Waldo, aboard the schooner Endeavor; as also the likely negro wench, at Captain Bulfinch's. It were not amiss that I took my daughter Miriam to see the royal wax-work, near the town-dock, that she may learn to honor our most gracious King and Queen, and their royal progeny, even in their waxen images; not that I would approve of image-worship. The camel, too, that strange beast from Africa, with two great humps, to be seen near the common; methinks I would fain go thither, and see how the old patriarchs were wont to ride. I will tarry awhile in Queen Street, at the bookstore of my good friends Kneeland and Green, and purchase Doctor Colman's new sermon, and the volume of discourses by Mr. Henry Flynt; and look over the controversy on baptism, between the Reverend Peter Clarke and an unknown adversary; and see whether this George Whitefield be as great in print as he is famed to be in the pulpit. By that time, the auction will have commenced

at the Royal Exchange, in King Str Moreover, I must look to the disp of my last cargo of West India and muscovado sugar; and also the of choice Cheshire cheese, lest it g mouldy. It were well that I ordere cask of good English beer, at the lo end of Milk Street. Then am I to sp with certain dealers about the lot stout old Vidonia, rich Canary, Oporto wines, which I have now l in the cellar of the Old South meet house. But, a pipe or two of the Canary shall be reserved that it grow mellow in mine own wine-ce and gladden my heart when it be to droop with old age.

Provident old gentleman! But, he mindful of his sepulchre? Did bethink him to call at the work-s of Timothy Sheaffe, in Cold Lane, select such a gravestone as would please him? There wrought the whose handiwork, or that of his fel craftsmen, was ultimately in demand all the busy multitude who have le record of their earthly toil in these time-stained papers. And now, as turn over the volume, we seem to wandering among the mossy stones burial-ground.

II. THE OLD FRENCH WAR

At a period about twenty years sequent to that of our former ske we again attempt a delineation of s of the characteristics of life and ners in New England. Our text-book before, is a file of antique newspa The volume which serves us for a ing-desk is a folio of larger dimens than the one before described; and papers are generally printed on a w

et, sometimes with a supplemental
f of news and advertisements. They
ʼe a venerable appearance, being
rspread with the duskiness of more
n seventy years, and discolored, here
1 there, with the deeper stains of
1e liquid, as if the contents of a
e-glass had long since been splashed
n the pagc. Still, the old book con-
s an impression that, when the sep-
te numbers were flying about town,
the first day or two of their re-
ctive existences, they might have
n fit reading for very stylish
ple. Such newspapers could have
n issued nowhere but in a me-
ʼolis the centre, not only of pub-
and private affairs, but of fashion
gayety. Without any discredit to
.colonial press, these might have
1, and probably were, spread out
he tables of the British coffee-house,
King Street, for the perusal of the
ng of officers who then drank their
e at that celebrated establishment.
interest these military gentlemen,
e were bulletins of the war between
ssia and Austria; between England
France, on the old battle-plains of
1ders, and between the same antag-
ts in the newer fields of the East
es,—and in our own trackless woods,
re white men never trod until they
e to fight there. Or, the travelled
rican, the petit-maitre of the col-
s,—the ape of London foppery, as
newspaper was the semblance of
London journals,—he, with his gray
dered periwig, his embroidered coat,
ruffles, and glossy silk stockings,
en-clocked,—his buckles, of glitter-
paste, at knee-band and shoe-strap,
s scented handkerchief, and chapeau
ath his arm,—even such a dainty

figure need not have disdained to glance
at these old yellow pages, while they
were the mirror of passing times. For
his amusement, there were essays of
wit and humor, the light literature of
the day, which, for breadth and license,
might have proceeded from the pen of
Fielding or Smollett; while, in other
columns, he would delight his imagination with the enumerated items of all
sorts of finery, and with the rival advertisements of half a dozen peruke-
makers. In short, newer manners and
customs had almost entirely superseded
those of the Puritans, even in their own
city of refuge.

It was natural that, with the lapse
of time and increase of wealth and population, the peculiarities of the early
settlers should have waxed fainter and
fainter through the generations of their
descendants, who also had been alloyed
by a continual accession of emigrants
from many countries and of all characters. It tended to assimilate the colonial
manners to those of the mother country, that the commercial intercourse was
great, and that the merchants often
went thither in their own ships. Indeed,
almost every man of adequate fortune
felt a yearning desire, and even judged
it a filial duty, at least once in his life,
to visit the home of his ancestors.
They still called it their own home,
as if New England were to them, what
many of the old Puritans had considered
it, not a permanent abiding-place, but
merely a lodge in the wilderness, until
the trouble of the times should be
passed. The example of the royal governors must have had much influence
on the manners of the colonists; for
these rulers assumed a degree of state
and splendor which had never been

practised by their predecessors, who differed in nothing from republican chief-magistrates, under the old charter. The officers of the crown, the public characters in the interest of the administration, and the gentlemen of wealth and good descent, generally noted for their loyalty, would constitute a dignified circle, with the governor in the centre, bearing a very passable resemblance to a court. Their ideas, their habits, their code of courtesy, and their dress, would have all the fresh glitter of fashions immediately derived from the fountain-head, in England. To prevent their modes of life from becoming the standard with all who had the ability to imitate them, there was no longer an undue severity of religion, nor as yet any disaffection to British supremacy, nor democratic prejudices against pomp. Thus, while the colonies were attaining that strength which was soon to render them an independent republic, it might have been supposed that the wealthier classes were growing into an aristocracy, and ripening for hereditary rank, while the poor were to be stationary in their abasement, and the country, perhaps, to be a sister monarchy with England. Such, doubtless, were the plausible conjectures deduced from the superficial phenomena of our connection with a monarchical government, until the prospective nobility were levelled with the mob, by the mere gathering of winds that preceded the storm of the Revolution. The portents of that storm were not yet visible in the air. A true picture of society, therefore, would have the rich effect produced by distinctions of rank that seemed permanent, and by appropriate habits of splendor on the part of the gentry.

The people at large had been sor what changed in character, since period of our last sketch, by their gr exploit, the conquest of Louisburg. Af that event, the New-Englanders ne settled into precisely the same q race which all the world had imagi them to be. They had done a deed history, and were anxious to add n ones to the record. They had pro themselves powerful enough to influe the result of a war, and were then forth called upon, and willingly c sented, to join their strength agai the enemies of England; on those fie at least, where victory would redo to their peculiar advantage. And n in the heat of the Old French War, t might well be termed a martial peo Every man was a soldier, or the fat or brother of a soldier; and the wh land literally echoed with the roll the drum, either beating up for recr among the towns and villages, or st ing the march towards the fronti Besides the provincial troops, there w twenty-three British regiments in northern colonies. The country has ne known a period of such excitement warlike life, except during the Rev tion,—perhaps scarcely then; for was a lingering war, and this a stir and eventful one.

One would think that no very w derful talent was requisite for an his ical novel, when the rough and hur paragraphs of these newspapers can call the past so magically. We seen be waiting in the street for the arr of the post-rider—who is seldom n than twelve hours beyond his tim with letters, by way of Albany, f the various departments of the ar Or, we may fancy ourselves in the c

listeners, all with necks stretched out
vards an old gentleman in the centre,
o deliberately puts on his spectacles,
folds the wet newspaper, and gives
the details of the broken and contra-
tory reports, which have been flying
m mouth to mouth, ever since the
irier alighted at Secretary Oliver's
ce. Sometimes we have an account
the Indian skirmishes near Lake
orge, and how a ranging party of
vincials were so closely pursued, that
y drew away their arms, and eke
ir shoes, stockings, and breeches,
ely reaching the camp in their shirts,
ich also were terribly tattered by
bushes. Then, there is a journal of
siege of Fort Niagara, so minute
t it almost numbers the cannon-shot
bombs, and describes the effect of
latter missiles on the French com-
ndant's stone mansion, within the
ress. In the letters of the provincial
cers, it is amusing to observe how
ie of them endeavor to catch the
eless and jovial turn of old cam-
ners. One gentleman tells us that
holds a brimming glass in his hand,
nding to drink the health of his
respondent, unless a cannon-ball
uld dash the liquor from his lips;
he midst of his letter, he hears the
s of the French churches ringing, in
bec, and recollects that it is Sun-
; whereupon, like a good Protestant,
resolves to disturb the Catholic wor-
by a few thirty-two pound shot.
ile this wicked man of war was thus
king a jest of religion, his pious
her had probably put up a note, that
Sabbath-day, desiring the "prayers
the congregation for a son gone a
iering." We trust, however, that
re were some stout old worthies

who were not ashamed to do as their
fathers did, but went to prayer, with
their soldiers, before leading them to
battle; and doubtless fought none the
worse for that. If we had enlisted in
the Old French War, it should have
been under such a captain; for we love
to see a man keep the characteristics of
his country.*

These letters, and other intelligence
from the army, are pleasant and lively
reading, and stir up the mind like the
music of a drum and fife. It is less
agreeable to meet with the accounts
of women slain and scalped, and infants
dashed against trees, by the Indians on
the frontiers. It is a striking circumstance, that innumerable bears, driven
from the woods by the uproar of contending armies in their accustomed
haunts, broke into the settlements, and
committed great ravages among children, as well as sheep and swine. Some
of them prowled where bears had never
been for a century, penetrating within
a mile or two of Boston; a fact that
gives a strong and gloomy impression
of something very terrific going on in
the forest, since these savage beasts fled
townward to avoid it. But it is impossible to moralize about such trifles,
when every newspaper contains tales of
military enterprise, and often a huzza
for victory; as, for instance, the taking
of Ticonderoga, long a place of awe to

---

* The contemptuous jealousy of the British
army, from the general downwards, was very
galling to the provincial troops. In one of the
newspapers there is an admirable letter of a
New England man, copied from the London
Chronicle, defending the provincials with an
ability worthy of Franklin, and somewhat in
his style. The letter is remarkable, also, because
it takes up the cause of the whole range of
colonies, as if the writer looked upon them all
as constituting one country, and that his own.
Colonial patriotism had not hitherto been so
broad a sentiment.

the provincials, and one of the bloodiest spots in the present war. Nor is it unpleasant, among whole pages of exultation, to find a note of sorrow for the fall of some brave officer; it comes wailing in, like a funeral strain amidst a peal of triumph, itself triumphant too. Such was the lamentation over Wolfe. Somewhere, in this volume of newspapers, though we cannot now lay our finger upon the passage, we recollect a report, that General Wolfe was slain, not by the enemy, but by a shot from his own soldiers.

In the advertising columns, also, we are continually reminded that the country was in a state of war. Governor Pownall makes proclamation for the enlisting of soldiers, and directs the militia colonels to attend to the discipline of their regiments, and the selectmen of every town to replenish their stocks of ammunition. The magazine, by the way, was generally kept in the upper loft of the village meeting-house. The provincial captains are drumming up for soldiers, in every newspaper. Sir Jeffrey Amherst advertises for batteauxmen, to be employed on the lakes; and gives notice to the officers of seven British regiments, dispersed on the recruiting service, to rendezvous in Boston. Captain Hallowell, of the province ship-of-war King George, invites ablebodied seamen to serve his Majesty, for fifteen pounds, old tenor, per month. By the rewards offered, there would appear to have been frequent desertions from the New England forces; we applaud their wisdom, if not their valor or integrity. Cannon of all calibres, gunpowder and balls, firelocks, pistols, swords, and hangers, were common articles of merchandise. Daniel Jones,

at the sign of the hat and helmet, off to supply officers with scarlet bro cloth, gold lace for hats and waistco cockades, and other military foppe allowing credit until the pay-rolls s be made up. This advertisement gi us quite a gorgeous idea of a provin captain in full dress.

At the commencement of the c paign of 1759, the British general forms the farmers of New England t a regular market will be established Lake George, whither they are invi to bring provisions and refreshme of all sorts, for the use of the ar Hence, we may form a singular pict of petty traffic, far away from permanent settlements, among the which border that romantic lake, the solemn woods over-shadowing scene. Carcasses of bullocks and porkers are placed upright against huge trunks of the trees; fowls h from the lower branches, bob against the heads of those bene butter-firkins, great cheeses, and br loaves of household bread, baked distant ovens, are collected under t porary shelters of pine-boughs, gingerbread and pumpkin-pies, perh and other toothsome dainties. Ba of cider and spruce-beer are run freely into the wooden canteens of soldiers. Imagine such a scene, ben the dark forest canopy, with here there a few struggling sunbeams to sipate the gloom. See the shrewd men, haggling with their scarlet-co customers, abating somewhat in prices, but still dealing at monst profit; and then complete the pic with circumstances that bespeak war danger. A cannon shall be seen to its smoke from among the trees, ag

ie distant canoes on the lake; the
fickers shall pause, and seem to
rken, at intervals, as if they heard
 rattle of musketry or the shout
Indians; a scouting-party shall be
ven in, with two or three faint and
ody men among them. And, in spite
these disturbances, business goes on
kly in the market of the wilder-
s.

t must not be supposed that the
tial character of the times inter-
ted all pursuits except those con-
ed with war. On the contrary, there
ears to have been a general vigor
 vivacity diffused into the whole
id of colonial life. During the winter
1759, it was computed that about
ousand sled-loads of country produce
e daily brought into Boston mar-
It was a symptom of an irregular
 unquiet course of affairs, that in-
erable lotteries were projected, os-
ibly for the purpose of public im-
vements, such as roads and bridges.
iy females seized the opportunity
ngage in business as, among others,
a Quirk, who dealt in crockery and
ery, next door to Deacon Beauti-
's; Mary Jackson, who sold butter,
he Brazen-Head, in Cornhill; Abi-
Hiller, who taught ornamental work,
 the Orange-Tree, where also were
e seen the King and Queen, in wax-
:; Sarah Morehead, an instructor in
-painting, drawing, and japanning;
y Salmon, who shod horses, at the
h-end; Harriet Pain, at the Buck
 Glove, and Mrs. Henrietta Maria
e, at the Golden Fan, both fash-
ble milliners; Anna Adams, who ad-
ses Quebec and Garrick bonnets,
sian cloaks, and scarlet cardinals,
site the old brick meeting-house;

besides a lady at the head of a wine and
spirit establishment. Little did these
good dames expect to reappear before
the public, so long after they had made
their last courtesies behind the counter.
Our great-grandmothers were a stirring
sisterhood, and seem not to have been
utterly despised by the gentlemen at the
British coffee-house; at least, some gracious bachelor, there resident, gives public notice of his willingness to take a
wife, provided she be not above twenty-
three, and possess brown hair, regular
features, a brisk eye, and a fortune.
Now, this was a great condescension
towards the ladies of Massachusetts
Bay, in a threadbare lieutenant of foot.

Polite literature was beginning to
make its appearance. Few native works
were advertised, it is true, except sermons and treatises of controversial
divinity; nor were the English authors
of the day much known on this side
of the Atlantic. But catalogues were
frequently offered at auction or private
sale, comprising the standard English
books, history, essays, and poetry, of
Queen Anne's age, and the preceding
century. We see nothing in the nature
of a novel, unless it be "The Two
Mothers," price four coppers." There
was an American poet, however, of
whom Mr. Kettell has preserved no
specimen,—the author of "War, an
Heroic Poem"; he publishes by subscription, and threatens to prosecute his
patrons for not taking their books. We
have discovered a periodical, also, and
one that has a peculiar claim to be recorded here, since it bore the title of
"THE NEW ENGLAND MAGAZINE," a forgotten predecessor, for which we should
have a filial respect, and take its ex-
cellence on trust. The fine arts, too,

were budding into existence. At the "old glass and picture shop," in Cornhill, various maps, plates, and views are advertised, and among them a "Prospect of Boston," a copper-plate engraving of Quebec, and the effigies of all the New England ministers ever done in mezzotinto. All these must have been very salable articles. Other ornamental wares were to be found at the same shop; such as violins, flutes, hautboys, musical books, English and Dutch toys, and London babies. About this period, Mr. Dipper gives notice of a concert of vocal and instrumental music. There had already been an attempt at theatrical exhibitions.

There are tokens, in every newspaper, of a style of luxury and magnificence which we do not usually associate with our ideas of the times. When the property of a deceased person was to be sold, we find, among the household furniture, silk beds and hangings, damask table-cloths, Turkey carpets, pictures, pier-glasses, massive plate, and all things proper for a noble mansion. Wine was more generally drunk than now, though by no means to the neglect of ardent spirits. For the apparel of both sexes, the mercers and milliners imported good store of fine broadcloths, especially scarlet, crimson, and sky-blue, silks, satins, lawns, and velvets, gold brocade, and gold and silver lace, and silver tassels, and silver spangles, until Cornhill shone and sparkled with their merchandise. The gaudiest dress permissible by modern taste fades into a Quaker-like sobriety, compared with the deep, rich, glowing splendor of our ancestors. Such figures were almost too fine to go about town on foot; accordingly, carriages were so numerous as

to require a tax; and it is recorded t when Governor Bernard came to province, he was met between Ded and Boston, by a multitude of gei men in their coaches and chariots.

Take my arm, gentle reader, and c with me into some street, perhaps t den by your daily footsteps, but w now has such an aspect of half-fam strangeness, that you suspect you to be walking abroad in a dream. T there are some brick edifices which remember from childhood, and w your father and grandfather rem bered as well; but you are perpl by the absence of many that here only an hour or two since; still more amazing is the presenc whole rows of wooden and plast houses, projecting over the sidew and bearing iron figures on their fr which prove them to have stood the same sites above a century. W have your eyes been, that you n saw them before? Along the gh street—for, at length, you conclude all is unsubstantial, though it be so a mockery of an antique town,—a the ghostly street there are gh people too. Every gentleman has three-cornered hat, either on his or under his arm; and all wear wig infinite variety,—the Tie, the B dier, the Spencer, the Albemarle, Major, the Ramillies, the grave bottom, or the giddy Feather-top. at the elaborate lace ruffles, and square-skirted coat of gorgeous bedizened with silver and gold! way for the phantom-ladies, w hoops require such breadth of pas as they pace majestically along, in s gowns, blue, green, or yellow, brillia embroidered, and with small satin

nounting their powdered hair. Make
·; for the whole spectral show will
ish, if your earthly garments brush
nst their robes. Now that the scene
·rightest, and the whole street glit-
with imaginary sunshine,—now hark
he bells of the Old South and the
North, ringing out with a sudden
merry peal, while the cannon of
tle William thunder below the town,
those of the Diana frigate repeat
sound, and the Charlestown batteries
y with a nearer roar! You see the
wd toss up their hats, in visionary
You hear of illuminations and fire-
ks, and of bonfires, built on scaf-
s, raised several stories above the
ind, that are to blaze all night, in
g Street, and on Beacon Hill. And
· come the trumpets and kettle-
ns, and the tramping hoofs of the
ton troop of horse-guards, escorting
governor to King's Chapel, where
's to return solemn thanks for the
ender of Quebec. March on, thou
lowy troop! and vanish, ghostly
wd; and change again, old street!
those stirring times are gone.

pportunely for the conclusion of our
ch, a fire broke out, on the twentieth
March, 1760, at the Brazen-Head,
Cornhill, and consumed nearly four
Ired buildings. Similar disasters have
ays been epochs in the chronology
Boston. That of 1711 had hitherto
a termed the Great Fire, but now
gned its baleful dignity to one which
ever since retained it. Did we de-
to move the reader's sympathies
his subject, we would not be gran-
quent about the sea of billowy
e, the glowing and crumbling streets,
broad, black firmament of smoke,
the blast of wind that sprang up

with the conflagration and roared behind it. It would be more effective to
mark out a single family, at the moment when the flames caught upon an
angle of their dwelling: then would
ensue the removal of the bed-ridden
grandmother, the cradle with the sleeping infant, and, most dismal of all, the
dying man just at the extremity of a
lingering disease. Do but imagine the
confused agony of one thus awfully
disturbed in his last hour; his fearful
glance behind at the consuming fire,
raging after him, from house to house,
as its devoted victim; and, finally, the
almost eagerness with which he would
seize some calmer interval to die! The
Great Fire must have realized many
such a scene.

Doubtless posterity has acquired a
better city by the calamity of that
generation. None will be inclined to
lament it at this late day, except the
lover of antiquity, who would have been
glad to walk among those streets of
venerable houses, fancying the old inhabitants still there, that he might com-
mune with their shadows, and paint a
more vivid picture of their times.

III. THE OLD TORY

Again we take a leap of about twenty
years, and alight in the midst of the
Revolution. Indeed, having just closed
a volume of colonial newspapers, which
represented a period when monarchical
and aristocratic sentiments were at the
highest,—and now opening another volume printed in the same metropolis,
after such sentiments had long been
deemed a sin and shame,—we feel as
if the leap were more than figurative.
Our late course of reading has tinc-

tured us, for the moment, with antique prejudices; and we shrink from the strangely-contrasted times into which we emerge, like one of those immutable old Tories, who acknowledge no oppression in the Stamp-Act. It may be the most effective method of going through the present file of papers, to follow out this idea, and transform ourself, perchance, from a modern Tory, into such a sturdy King-man as once wore that pliable nickname.

Well, then, here we sit, an old, gray, withered, sour-visaged, threadbare sort of gentleman, erect enough, here in our solitude, but marked out by a depressed and distrustful mien abroad, as one conscious of a stigma upon his forehead, though for no crime. We were already in the decline of life when the first tremors of the earthquake that has convulsed the continent were felt. Our mind had grown too rigid to change any of its opinions, when the voice of the people demanded that all should be changed. We are an Episcopalian, and sat under the high-church doctrines of Doctor Caner; we have been a captain of the provincial forces, and love our king the better for the blood that we shed in his cause on the Plains of Abraham. Among all the refugees, there is not one more loyal to the backbone than we. Still we lingered behind when the British army evacuated Boston, sweeping in its train most of those with whom we held communion; the old, loyal gentlemen, the aristocracy of the colonies, the hereditary Englishman, imbued with more than native zeal and admiration for the glorious island and its monarch, because the far intervening ocean threw a dim reverence around them. When our brethren departed, we

could not tear our aged roots out of soil. We have remained, therefore, during to be outwardly a freeman, idolizing King George in secrecy silence,—one true old heart amongs host of enemies. We watch, with weary hope, for the moment when this turmoil shall subside, and the pious novelty that has distracted latter years, like a wild dream, place to the blessed quietude of re sway, with the king's name in ev ordinance, his prayer in the church, health at the board, and his love in people's heart. Meantime, our old finds little honor. Hustled have we b till driven from town-meetings; d water has been cast upon our ruffles a Whig chambermaid; John Hanco coachman seizes every opportunity bespatter us with mud; daily are hooted by the unbreeched rebel br and narrowly, once, did our gray h escape the ignominy of tar and feath Alas! only that we cannot bear to till the next royal governor comes o we would fain be in our quiet grave

Such an old man among new th are we who now hold at arm's length rebel newspaper of the day. The figure-head, for the thousandth t elicits a groan of spiteful lamentat Where are the united heart and cr the loyal emblem, that used to ha the sheet on which it was impresse our younger days? In its stead we a continental officer, with the Dec tion of Independence in one han drawn sword in the other, and abov head a scroll, bearing the motto, APPEAL TO HEAVEN." Then say we, a prospective triumph, let Heaven ju in its own good time! The materi the sheet attracts our scorn. It is a

cimen of rebel manufacture, thick
. coarse, like wrapping-paper, all
rspread with little knobs; and of
h a deep, dingy blue color, that we
e our spectacles thrice before we
distinguish a letter of the wretched
.t. Thus, in all points, the newspaper
type of the times, far more fit for
rough hands of a democratic mob,
1 for our own delicate, though bony
ers. Nay; we will not handle it with-
our gloves!

.lancing down the page, our eyes are
•ted everywhere by the offer of lands
.uction, for sale or to be leased, not
he rightful owners, but a rebel com-
:ee; notices of the town constable,
he is authorized to receive the taxes
such an estate, in default of which,
also is to be knocked down to the
est bidder; and notifications of
.plaints filed by the Attorney-gen-
against certain traitorous absentees,
of confiscations that are to ensue.
who are these traitors? Our own
friends; names as old, once as
ored, as any in the land where they
no longer to have a patrimony, nor
be remembered as good men who
e passed away. We are ashamed of
relinquishing our little property,
but comfort ourselves because we
keep our principles, without
ifying the rebels with our plunder.
der, indeed, they are seizing every-
re,—by the strong hand at sea, as
as by legal forms on shore. Here
prize-vessels for sale; no French
Spanish merchantmen, whose wealth
e birthright of British subjects, but
s of British oak, from Liverpool,
tol, and the Thames, laden with the
's own stores, for his army in New
k. And what a fleet of privateers—

pirates, say we—are fitting out for new
ravages, with rebellion in their very
names! The Free Yankee, the General
Green, the Saratoga, the Lafayette, and
the Grand Monarch! Yes, the Grand
Monarch; so is a French king styled,
by the sons of Englishmen. And here we
have an ordinance from the Court of
Versailles, with the Bourbon's own signature affixed, as if New England were
already a French province. Everything
is French,—French soldiers, French
sailors, French surgeons, and French
diseases too, I trow; besides French
dancing-masters and French milliners,
to debauch our daughters with French
fashions! Everything in America is
French, except the Canadas, the loyal
Canadas, which we helped to wrest from
France. And to that old French province
the Englishman of the colonies must go
to find his country!

O the misery of seeing the whole system of things changed in my old days,
when I would be loath to change even
a pair of buckles! The British coffee-
house, where oft we sat, brimful of wine
and loyalty, with the gallant gentlemen
of Amherst's army, when we wore a
red-coat too,—the British coffee-house,
forsooth, must now be styled the American, with a golden eagle instead of the
royal arms above the door. Even the
street it stands in is no longer King
Street! Nothing is the king's, except this
heavy heart in my old bosom. Wherever
I glance my eyes, they meet something
that pricks them like a needle. This
soap-maker, for instance, this Robert
Hewes, has conspired against my peace,
by notifying that his shop is situated
near Liberty Stump. But when will their
misnamed Liberty have its true emblem

in that Stump, hewn down by British steel.

Where shall we buy our next year's almanac? Not this of Weatherwise's, certainly; for it contains a likeness of George Washington, the upright rebel, whom we most hate, though reverentially, as a fallen angel, with his heavenly brightness undiminished, evincing pure fame in an unhallowed cause. And here is a new book for my evening's recreation,—a History of the War till the close of the year 1779, with the heads of thirteen distinguished officers, engraved on copperplate. A plague upon their heads! We desire not to see them till they grin at us from the balcony before the town-house, fixed on spikes as the heads of traitors. How bloody-minded the villains make a peaceable old man! What next? An Oration, on the Horrid Massacre of 1770. When that blood was shed,—the first that the British soldier ever drew from the bosoms of our countrymen,—we turned sick at heart, and do so still, as often as they make it reek anew from among the stones in King Street. The pool that we saw that night has swelled into a lake,— English blood and American,—no! all British, all blood of my brethren. And here come down tears. Shame on me, since half of them are shed for rebels! Who are not rebels now! Even the women art thrusting their white hands into the war, and come out in this very paper with proposals to form a society —the lady of George Washington at their head—for clothing the continental troops. They will strip off their stiff petticoats to cover the ragged rascals, and then enlist in the ranks themselves.

What have we here? Burgoyne's proclamation turned into Hudibrastic

rhyme! And here, some verses agai the king, in which the scribbler leave blank for the name of George, as if doggerel might yet exalt him to pillory. Such, after years of rebell is the heart's unconquerable rever for the Lord's anointed! In the n column, we have Scripture parodied i squib against his sacred Majesty. W would our Puritan great-grandsires h said to that? They never laughed God's word, though they cut off a ki head.

Yes; it was for us to prove how loyalty goes hand in hand with irreligi and all other vices come trooping in train. Now-a-days men commit robb and sacrilege for the mere luxury wickedness, as this advertisement te fies. Three hundred pounds reward the detection of the villains who st and destroyed the cushions and pu drapery of the Brattle Street and South churches. Was it a crime? I scarcely think our temples hallow since the king ceased to be prayed But it is not temples only that they r Here a man offers a thousand dollar a thousand dollars, in Continental ra —for the recovery of his stolen clo and other articles of clothing. Ho thieves are innumerable. Now is the when every beggar gets on horseba And is not the whole land like a beg on horseback riding post to the De Ha! here is a murder, too. A won slain at midnight, by an unkno ruffian, and found cold, stiff, and blo in her violated bed! Let the hue cry follow hard after the man in uniform of blue and buff who last w by that way. My life on it, he is blood-stained ravisher! These deser whom we see proclaimed in every

n,—proof that the banditti are as
e to their stars and stripes as to the
ly Red-cross,—they bring the crimes
a rebel camp into a soil well suited
them; the bosom of a people, with-
the heart that kept them virtuous,—
ir king!

Iere, flaunting down a whole column,
h official seal and signature, here
es a proclamation. By whose au-
rity? Ah! the United States,—these
teen little anarchies, assembled in
t one grand anarchy, their Congress.
l what the import? A general Fast.
Heaven! for once the traitorous
kheads have legislated wisely! Yea:
a misguided people kneel down in
cloth and ashes, from end to end,
n border to border, of their wasted
try. Well may they fast where there
o food, and cry aloud for whatever
nant of God's mercy their sins may
have exhausted. We too will fast,
at a rebel summons. Pray others
hey will, there shall be at least an
an kneeling for the righteous cause.
l, put down the rebels! God save the
!

eace to the good old Tory! One of
objects has been to exemplify, with-
softening a single prejudice proper
e character which they assumed, that
Americans who clung to the losing
in the Revolution were men greatly
e pitied, and often worthy of our
pathy. It would be difficult to say
se lot was most lamentable, that of
active Tories, who gave up their
monies for a pittance from the
sh pension-roll, and their native
for a cold reception in their mis-
d home, or the passive ones who
ined behind to endure the coldness
rmer friends, and the public oppro-
brium, as despised citizens, under a government which they abhorred. In justice to the old gentleman who has favored us with his discontented musings,
we must remark that the state of the
country, so far as can be gathered from
these papers, was of dismal augury for
the tendencies of democratic rule. It was
pardonable in the conservative of that
day to mistake the temporary evils of
a change for permanent diseases of the
system which that change was to establish. A revolution, or anything that interrupts social order, may afford opportunities for the individual display of
eminent virtues; but its effects are pernicious to general morality. Most people
are so constituted that they can be
virtuous only in a certain routine; and
an irregular course of public affairs de-
moralizes them. One great source of
disorder was the multitude of disbanded
troops, who were continually returning
home, after terms of service just long
enough to give them a distaste to peaceable occupations; neither citizens nor
soldiers, they were very liable to become
ruffians. Almost all our impressions in
regard to this period are unpleasant,
whether referring to the state of civil
society, or to the character of the contest, which, especially where native
Americans were opposed to each other,
was waged with the deadly hatred of
fraternal enemies. It is the beauty of
war, for men to commit mutual havoc
with undisturbed good humor.

The present volume of newspapers
contains fewer characteristic traits than
any which we have looked over. Except
for the peculiarities attendant on the
passing struggle, manners seem to have
taken a modern cast. Whatever antique
fashions lingered into the war of the

Revolution, or beyond it, they were not so strongly marked as to leave their traces in the public journals. Moreover, the old newspapers had an indescribable picturesqueness, not to be found in the later ones. Whether it be something in the literary execution, or the ancient print and paper, and the idea that those same musty pages have been handled by people once alive and bustling amid the

scenes there recorded, yet now in t[] graves beyond the memory of man[] it is, that in those elder volumes seem to find the life of a past preserved between the leaves, lik[] dry specimen of foliage. It is so diffi[] to discover what touches are really[] turesque, that we doubt whether attempts have produced any sim[] effect.

THE MAN OF ADAMANT

AN APOLOGUE

In the old times of religious gloom and intolerance lived Richard Digby, the gloomiest and most intolerant of a stern brotherhood. His plan of salvation was so narrow, that, like a plank in a tempestuous sea, it could avail no sinner but himself, who bestrode it triumphantly, and hurled anathemas against the wretches whom he saw struggling with the billows of eternal death. In his view of the matter, it was a most abominable crime,—as, indeed, it is a great folly,—for men to trust to their own strength, or even to grapple to any other fragment of the wreck, save this narrow plank, which, moreover, he took special care to keep out of their reach. In other words, as his creed was like no man's else, and being well pleased that Providence had intrusted him alone, of mortals, with the treasure of a true faith, Richard Digby determined to seclude himself to the sole and constant enjoyment of his happy fortune.

"And verily," thought he, "I deem it a chief condition of Heaven's mercy to

myself, that I hold no communion [] those abominable myriads which it [] cast off to perish. Peradventure, we[] to tarry longer in the tents of Ke[] the gracious boon would be revoked, I also be swallowed up in the delug[] wrath, or consumed in the storm of and br[]mstone, or involved in what[] new kind of ruin is ordained for horrible perversity of this generati[]

So Richard D[]gby took an axe, to [] space enough for a tabernacle in wilderness, and some few other ne[] saries, especially a sword and gun smite and slay any intruder upon hallowed seclusion; and plunged into dreariest depths of the forest. On verge, however, he paused a moment shake off the dust of his feet against village where he had dwelt, and to voke a curse on the meeting-ho[] which he regarded as a temple heathen idolatry. He felt a curios[] also, to see whether the fire and b[] stone would not rush down from Hea[] at once, now that the one righteous [] had provided for his own safety. But the sunshine continued to fall peacef[]

the cottages and fields, and the hus-
dmen labored and children played,
as there were many tokens of pres-
happiness, and nothing ominous of
peedy judgment, he turned away,
ewhat disappointed. The farther he
t, however, and the lonelier he felt
self, and the thicker the trees stood
ng his path, and the darker the
low overhead, so much the more did
nard Digby exult. He talked to him-
, as he strode onward; he read his
le to himself, as he sat beneath the
s; and, as the gloom of the forest
the blessed sky, I had almost added,
, at morning, noon, and eventide, he
red to himself. So congenial was this
le of life to his disposition, that he
n laughed to himself, but was dis-
sed when an echo tossed him back
long, loud roar.

n this manner, he journeyed onward
e days and two nights, and came, on
third evening, to the mouth of a
e, which, at first sight, reminded him
Elijah's cave at Horeb, though per-
, it more resembled Abraham's
lchral cave, at Machpelah. It en-
d into the heart of a rocky hill.
re was so dense a veil of tangled
ge about it, that none but a sworn
r of gloomy recesses would have
overed the low arch of its entrance,
ave dared to step within its vaulted
nber, where the burning eyes of a
her might encounter him. If Nature
nt this remote and dismal cavern for
use of man, it could only be to bury
s gloom the victims of a pestilence,
then to block up its mouth with
es, and avoid the spot forever after.
re was nothing bright nor cheerful
it, except a bubbling fountain,
e twenty paces off, at which Richard

Digby hardly threw away a glance. But
he thrust his head into the cave, shivered, and congratulated himself.

"The finger of Providence hath pointed
my way!" cried he, aloud, while the
tomb-like den returned a strange echo,
as if some one within were mocking him. "Here my soul will be at
peace; for the wicked will not find me.
Here I can read the Scriptures, and be
no more provoked with lying interpreta-
tions. Here I can offer up acceptable
prayers, because my voice will not be
mingled with the sinful supplications of
the multitude. Of a truth, the only way
to heaven leadeth through the narrow
entrance of this cave,—and I alone have
found it!"

In regard to this cave, it was observable that the roof, so far as the imperfect light permitted it to be seen, was
hung with substances resembling opaque
icicles; for the damps of unknown centuries, dripping down continually, had
become as hard as adamant; and wherever that moisture fell, it seemed to
possess the power of converting what it
bathed to stone. The fallen leaves and
sprigs of foliage, which the wind had
swept into the cave, and the little
feathery shrubs, rooted near the
threshold, were not wet with a natural
dew, but had been embalmed by this
wondrous process. And here I am put in
mind that Richard Digby, before he
withdrew himself from the world, was
supposed by skilful physicians to have
contracted a disease for which no
remedy was written in their medical
books. It was a deposition of calculous
particles within his heart, caused by an
obstructed circulation of the blood; and,
unless a miracle should be wrought for
him, there was danger that the malady

might act on the entire substance of the organ, and change his fleshy heart to stone. Many, indeed, affirmed that the process was already near its consummation. Richard Digby, however, could never be convinced that any such direful work was going on within him; nor when he saw the sprigs of marble foliage, did his heart even throb the quicker, at the similitude suggested by these once tender herbs. It may be that this same insensibility was a symptom of the disease.

Be that as it might, Richard Digby was well contented with his sepulchral cave. So dearly did he love this congenial spot, that instead of going a few paces to the bubbling spring for water, he allayed his thirst with now and then a drop of moisture from the roof, which, had it fallen anywhere but on his tongue, would have been congealed into a pebble. For a man predisposed to stoniness of the heart, this surely was unwholesome liquor. But there he dwelt, for three days more, eating herbs and roots, drinking his own destruction, sleeping, as it were, in a tomb, and awaking to the solitude of death, yet esteeming this horrible mode of life as hardly inferior to celestial bliss. Perhaps superior; for, above the sky, there would be angels to disturb him. At the close of the third day, he sat in the portal of his mansion reading the Bible aloud, because no other ear could profit by it, and reading it amiss, because the rays of the setting sun did not penetrate the dismal depth of shadow round about him, nor fall upon the sacred page. Suddenly, however, a faint gleam of light was thrown over the volume, and, raising his eyes, Richard Digby saw that a young woman stood before the mouth

of the cave, and that the sunbe[am] bathed her white garment, which [it] seemed to possess a radiance of its o[wn]

"Good evening, Richard," said [the] girl; "I have come from afar to [find] thee."

The slender grace and gentle lo[veli]ness of this young woman were at [once] recognized by Richard Digby. Her n[ame] was Mary Goffe. She had been a con[vert] to his preaching of the word in Engl[and] before he yielded himself to that [ex]clusive bigotry which now enfolded [him] with such an iron grasp that no o[ther] sentiment could reach his bosom. W[hen] he came a pilgrim to America, she [had] remained in her father's hall; but n[ow] as it appeared, had crossed the o[cean] after him, impelled by the same f[aith] that led other exiles hither, and [per]haps by love almost as holy. What [else] but faith and love united could [have] sustained so delicate a creature, wan[der]ing thus far into the forest, with [her] golden hair dishevelled by the bou[ghs] and her feet wounded by the tho[rns] Yet, weary and faint though she m[ust] have been, and affrighted at the dr[ear]ness of the cave, she looked on [the] lonely man with a mild and pitying [ex]pression, such as might beam from [an] angel's eyes towards an afflicted mo[rtal] But the recluse, frowning sternly [upon] her, and keeping his finger between [the] leaves of his half-closed Bible, moti[oned] her away with his hand.

"Off!" cried he. "I am sanctified, [and] thou art sinful. Away!"

"O Richard," said she, earnestly [I] have come this weary way becau[se I] heard that a grievous distemper [had] seized upon thy heart; and a [good] Physician had given me the ski[ll to] cure it. There is no other remedy

which I have brought thee. Turn
not away, therefore, nor refuse my
icine; for then must this dismal
be thy sepulchre."

way!" replied Richard Digby, still
a dark frown. "My heart is in bet-
ondition than thine own. Leave me,
ly one; for the sun is almost set;
when no light reaches the door of
ave, then is my prayer-time."

ow, great as was her need, Mary
did not plead with this stony-
ed man for shelter and protection,
isk anything whatever for her own
All her zeal was for his welfare.
ome back with me!" she exclaimed,
ing her hands,—"come back to thy
w-men; for they need thee, Rich-
ind thou hast tenfold need of them.
not in this evil den; for the air is
and the damps are fatal; nor will
that perish within it ever find the
to heaven. Hasten hence, I entreat
for thine own soul's sake; for
r the roof will fall upon thy head,
me other speedy destruction is at
"

erverse woman!" answered Richard
y, laughing aloud,—for he was
d to bitter mirth by her foolish
nence,—"I tell thee that the path
aven leadeth straight through this
w portal where I sit. And, more-
the destruction thou speakest of is
ied, not for this blessed cave, but
ll other habitations of mankind,
ghout the earth. Get thee hence
ily, that thou mayest have thy
!"

saying, he opened his Bible again,
xed his eyes intently on the page,
resolved to withdraw his thoughts
this child of sin and wrath, and to
no more of his holy breath upon

her. The shadow had now grown so
deep where he was sitting that he made
continual mistakes in what he read, converting all that was gracious and merciful to denunciations of vengeance and
unutterable woe on every created being
but himself. Mary Goffe, meanwhile,
was leaning against a tree, beside the
sepulchral cave, very sad, yet with
something heavenly and ethereal in her
unselfish sorrow. The light from the setting sun still glorified her form, and was
reflected a little way within the darksome den, discovering so terrible a
gloom that the maiden shuddered for its
self-doomed inhabitant. Espying the
bright fountain near at hand, she hastened thither, and scooped up a portion
of its water in a cup of birchen bark.
A few tears mingled with the draught,
and perhaps gave it all its efficacy. She
then returned to the mouth of the cave,
and knelt down at Richard Digby's feet.

"Richard," she said, with passionate
fervor, yet a gentleness in all her passion, "I pray thee, by thy hope of
heaven, and as thou wouldst not dwell
in this tomb forever, drink of this hallowed water, be it but a single drop!
Then, make room for me by thy side,
and let us read together one page of
that blessed volume,—and, lastly, kneel
down with me and pray! Do this, and
thy stony heart shall become softer
than a babe's, and all will be well."

But Richard Digby, in utter abhorrence of the proposal, cast the Bible at
his feet, and eyed her with such a fixed
and evil frown, that he looked less like
a living man than a marble statue,
wrought by some dark-imagined sculptor to express the most repulsive mood
that human features could assume. And,
as his look grew even devilish, so, with

an equal change, did Mary Goffe become more sad, more mild, more pitiful, more like a sorrowing angel. But the more heavenly she was the more hateful did she seem to Richard Digby, who at length raised his hand, and smote down the cup of hallowed water upon the threshold of the cave, thus rejecting the only medicine that could have cured his stony heart. A sweet perfume lingered in the air for a moment, and then was gone.

"Tempt me no more, accursed woman," exclaimed he, still with his marble frown, "lest I smite thee down also! What hast thou to do with my Bible?—what with my prayers?—what with my heaven?"

No sooner had he spoken these dreadful words, than Richard Digby's heart ceased to beat; while—so the legend says—the form of Mary Goffe melted into the last sunbeams, and returned from the sepulchral cave to heaven. For Mary Goffe had been buried in an English churchyard months before; and either it was her ghost that haunted the wild forest, or else a dreamlike spirit, typifying pure Religion.

About a century afterwards, when the trackless forest of Richard Digby's day had long been interspersed with settlements, the children of a neighboring farmer were playing at the foot of a hill. The trees, on account of the rude and broken surface of this acclivity, had never been felled, and were crowded so densely together as to hide all but a few rocky prominences, wherever their roots could grapple with the soil. A little boy and girl, to conceal themselves from their playmates, had crept into the deepest shade, where not only the darksome pines, but a thick veil of creeping plants, suspended from an overhan[g] rock, combined to make a twiligh[t] noonday, and almost a midnight a[t] other seasons. There the children [hid] themselves, and shouted, repeating [a] cry at intervals, till the whole part[y of] pursuers were drawn thither, and, [push-] ing aside the matted foliage, let [in a] doubtful glimpse of daylight. [But] scarcely was this accomplished, [when] the little group uttered a simultan[eous] shriek, and tumbled headlong dow[n the] hill, making the best of their way h[ome-] ward, without a second glance int[o the] gloomy recess. Their father, unab[le to] comprehend what had so startled t[hem,] took his axe, and, by felling one or [two] trees, and tearing away the cre[eping] plants, laid the mystery open to the [day.] He had discovered the entrance [of a] cave, closely resembling the mout[h of] a sepulchre, within which sat the [figure] of a man, whose gesture and att[itude] warned the father and children to [stand] back, while his visage wore a mos[t for-] bidding frown. This repulsive pers[onage] seemed to have been carved in the [same] gray stone that formed the walls [and] portal of the cave. On minuter in[spec-] tion, indeed, such blemishes wer[e ob-] served as made it doubtful wheth[er the] figure were really a statue, chisell[ed by] human art, and somewhat worn [and] defaced by the lapse of ages, or a [man] of Nature, who might have chos[en to] imitate, in stone, her usual handiw[ork of] flesh. Perhaps it was the least unre[ason-] able idea, suggested by this st[range] spectacle, that the moisture of the [cave] possessed a petrifying quality, [which] had thus awfully embalmed a h[uman] corpse.

There was something so fright[ful in] the aspect of this Man of Ada[mant] the farmer, the moment that he ˅ered from the fascination of his gaze, began to heap stones into the th of the cavern. His wife, who had ˄wed him to the hill, assisted her ˄and's efforts. The children, also, ap-˄ched as near as they durst, with ˄ little hands full of pebbles, and ˄them on the pile. Earth was then ˅n into the crevices, and the whole ˄c overlaid with sods. Thus all ˄s of the discovery were obliterated, ˄ng only a marvellous legend, which ˄wilder from one generation to an-˄, as the children told it to their ˄dchildren, and they to their pos-terity, till few believed that there had ever been a cavern or a statue where now they saw but a grassy patch on the shadowy hillside. Yet grown people avoid the spot, nor do children play there. Friendship, and Love, and Piety, all human and celestial sympathies, should keep aloof from that hidden cave; for there still sits, and, unless an earthquake crumble down the roof upon his head, shall sit forever, the shape of Richard Digby, in the attitude of re-pelling the whole race of mortals,—not from heaven,—but from the horrible loneliness of his dark, cold sepulchre!

THE HOUSE OF THE SEVEN GABLES

—

CHAPTER I

THE OLD PYNCHEON FAMILY

LF-WAY down a by-street of one
ur New England towns, stands a
wooden house, with seven acutely-
d gables, facing towards various
s of the compass, and a huge, clus-
chimney in the midst. The street
ncheon-street; the house is the old
heon-house; and an elm-tree, of
circumference, rooted before the
is familiar to every town-born
by the title of the Pyncheon-elm.
ny occasional visits to the town
said, I seldom fail to turn down
heon-street, for the sake of pass-
hrough the shadow of these two
uities,—the great elm-tree, and the
er-beaten edifice.

e aspect of the venerable mansion
always affected me like a human
enance, bearing the traces not
y of outward storm and sunshine,
xpressive, also, of the long lapse
rtal life, and accompanying vicissi-
that have passed within. Were
to be worthily recounted, they
d form a narrative of no small in-
and instruction, and possessing,
over, a certain remarkable unity,
might almost seem the result of
ic arrangement. But the story
d include a chain of events extend-
ver the better part of two cen-
, and, written out with reasonable
tude, would fill a bigger folio

volume, or a longer series of duodecimos, than could prudently be appropriated to the annals of all New England during a similar period. It consequently becomes imperative to make
short work with most of the traditionary
lore of which the old Pyncheon-house,
otherwise known as the House of the
Seven Gables, has been the theme. With
a brief sketch, therefore, of the circumstances amid which the foundation of
the house was laid, and a rapid glimpse
at its quaint exterior, as it grew black
in the prevalent east wind,—pointing,
too, here and there, at some spot of
more verdant mossiness on its roof and
walls,—we shall commence the real action of our tale at an epoch not very
remote from the present day. Still, there
will be a connection with the long past
—a reference to forgotten events and
personages, and to manners, feelings,
and opinions, almost or wholly obsolete
—which, if adequately translated to the
reader, would serve to illustrate how
much of old material goes to make up
the freshest novelty of human life.
Hence, too, might be drawn a weighty
lesson from the little-regarded truth,
that the act of the passing generation is
the germ which may and must produce
good or evil fruit, in a far distant time;
that, together with the seed of the
merely temporary crop, which mortals

term expediency, they inevitably sow the acorns of a more enduring growth, which may darkly overshadow their posterity.

The House of the Seven Gables, antique as it now looks, was not the first habitation erected by civilized man on precisely the same spot of ground. Pyncheon-street formerly bore the humbler appellation of Maule's-lane, from the name of the original occupant of the soil, before whose cottage-door it was a cow-path. A natural spring of soft and pleasant water—a rare treasure on the sea-girt peninsula, where the Puritan settlement was made—had early induced Matthew Maule to build a hut, shaggy with thatch, at this point, although somewhat too remote from what was then the centre of the village. In the growth of the town, however, after some thirty or forty years, the site covered by this rude hovel had become exceedingly desirable in the eyes of a prominent and powerful personage, who asserted plausible claims to the proprietorship of this, and a large adjacent tract of land, on the strength of a grant from the legislature. Colonel Pyncheon, the claimant, as we gather from whatever traits of him are preserved, was characterized by an iron energy of purpose. Matthew Maule, on the other hand, though an obscure man, was stubborn in the defence of what he considered his right; and, for several years, he succeeded in protecting the acre or two of earth, which, with his own toil, he had hewn out of the primeval forest, to be his garden-ground and homestead. No written record of this dispute is known to be in existence. Our acquaintance with the whole subject is derived chiefly from tradition. It would be bold,

therefore, and possibly unjust, to ture a decisive opinion as to its me although it appears to have been at a matter of doubt, whether Co. Pyncheon's claim were not un stretched, in order to make it cover small metes and bounds of Mat Maule. What greatly strengthens a suspicion is the fact that this troversy between two ill-matched ,tagonists—at a period, moreover, la as we may, when personal influence far more weight than now—rem; for years undecided, and came to a only with the death of the party cupying the disputed soil. The mo his death, too, affects the mind ferently, in our day, from what it century and a half ago. It was a c that blasted with strange horror humble name of the dweller in the tage, and made it seem almost a reli act to drive the plough over the area of his habitation, and obliterat place and memory from among m

Old Matthew Maule, in a word executed for the crime of witch He was one of the martyrs to terrible delusion, which should teac among its other morals, that th fluential classes, and those who upon themselves to be leaders o people, are fully liable to all the sionate error that has ever characte the maddest mob. Clergymen, ju statesmen,—the wisest, calmest, h persons of their day,—stood in the circle round about the gallows, lo to applaud the work of blood, late confess themselves miserably dec If any one part of their proceeding be said to deserve less blame tha other, it was the singular indiscri tion with which they persecuted

ely the poor and aged, as in former
cial massacres, but people of all
ts; their own equals, brethren, and
s. Amid the disorder of such various
, it is not strange that a man of
nsiderable note, like Maule, should
e trodden a martyr's path to the
of execution almost unremarked in
throng of his fellow-sufferers. But,
fter days, when the frenzy of that
ous epoch had subsided, it was re-
bered how loudly Colonel Pyncheon
joined in the general cry, to purge
and from witchcraft; nor did it fail
e whispered, that there was an inous acrimony in the zeal with which
had sought the condemnation of
hew Maule. It was well known that
victim had recognized the bitterness
ersonal enmity in his persecutor's
uct towards him, and that he de-
d himself hunted to death for his

At the moment of execution—with
halter about his neck, and while
nel Pyncheon sat on horseback,
ly gazing at the scene—Maule had
essed him from the scaffold, and
ed a prophecy, of which history,
ell as fireside tradition, has pre-
d the very words. "God," said the
: man, pointing his finger, with a
ly look, at the undismayed counte-
e of his enemy, "God will give him
to drink!"

er the reputed wizard's death, his
le homestead had fallen an easy
into Colonel Pyncheon's grasp.
it it was understood, however, that
olonel intended to erect a family
ion—spacious, ponderously framed
ken timber, and calculated to en-
for many generations of his pos-
—over the spot first covered by
og-built hut of Matthew Maule,

there was much shaking of the head
among the village gossips. Without absolutely expressing a doubt whether the
stalwart Puritan had acted as a man of
conscience and integrity, throughout the
proceedings which have been sketched,
they, nevertheless, hinted that he was
about to build his house over an unquiet
grave. His home would include the home
of the dead and buried wizard, and
would thus afford the ghost of the latter
a kind of privilege to haunt its new
apartments, and the chambers into which
future bridegrooms were to lead their
brides, and where children of the Pyncheon blood were to be born. The terror
and ugliness of Maule's crime, and the
wretchedness of his punishment, would
darken the freshly-plastered walls and
infect them early with the scent of an
old and melancholy house. Why, then,—
while so much of the soil around him
was bestrewn with the virgin forest-
leaves,—why should Colonel Pyncheon
prefer a site that had already been
accurst?

But the Puritan soldier and magistrate was not a man to be turned aside
from his well-considered scheme, either
by dread of the wizard's ghost, or by
flimsy sentimentalities of any kind,
however specious. Had he been told of
a bad air, it might have moved him
somewhat; but he was ready to encounter an evil spirit on his own ground.
Endowed with common sense, as massive and hard as blocks of granite, fastened together by stern rigidity of purpose, as with iron clamps, he followed
out his original design, probably without
so much as imagining an objection to it.
On the score of delicacy, or any scrupulousness which a finer sensibility might
have taught him, the colonel, like most

of his breed and generation, was impenetrable. He, therefore, dug his cellar, and laid the deep foundations of his mansion, on the square of earth whence Matthew Maule, forty years before, had first swept away the fallen leaves. It was a curious, and, as some people thought, an ominous fact, that, very soon after the workmen began their operations, the spring of water, above mentioned, entirely lost the deliciousness of its pristine quality. Whether its sources were disturbed by the depth of the new cellar, or whatever subtler cause might lurk at the bottom, it is certain that the water of Maule's Well, as it continued to be called, grew hard and brackish. Even such we find it now; and any old woman of the neighborhood will certify that it is productive of intestinal mischief to those who quench their thirst there.

The reader may deem it singular that the head carpenter of the new edifice was no other than the son of the very man from whose dead gripe the property of the soil had been wrested. Not improbably he was the best workman of his time; or, perhaps, the colonel thought it expedient, or was impelled by some better feeling, thus openly to cast aside all animosity against the race of his fallen antagonist. Nor was it out of keeping with the general coarseness and matter-of-fact character of the age, that the son should be willing to earn an honest penny, or, rather, a weighty amount of sterling pounds, from the purse of his father's deadly enemy. At all events, Thomas Maule became the architect of the House of the Seven Gables and performed his duty so faithfully that the timber frame-work, fastened by his hands, still holds together.

Thus the great house was b' Familiar as it stands in the writ recollection,—for it has been an ob of curiosity with him from boyh both as a specimen of the best stateliest architecture of a long-p epoch, and as the scene of events n full of human interest, perhaps, t those of a gray feudal castle,—fam as it stands, in its rusty old age, r therefore only the more difficult imagine the bright novelty with whic first caught the sunshine. The imp sion of its actual state, at this dist of a hundred and sixty years, dark inevitably, through the picture which would fain give of its appearance or morning when the Puritan magnate all the town to be his guests. A mony of consecration, festive as we religious, was now to be performe prayer and discourse from the Rev. Higginson, and the outpouring psalm from the general throat of community, was to be made accep to the grosser sense by ale, cider, and brandy, in copious effusion, an some authorities aver, by an ox, ro whole, or, at least, by the weight substance of an ox, in more manag joints and sirloins. The carcass deer, shot within twenty miles, had plied material for the vast circu ence of a pasty. A cod-fish, of pounds, caught in the bay, had dissolved into the rich liquid chowder. The chimney of the new h in short, belching forth its kit smoke, impregnated the whole air the scent of meats, fowls, and spicily concocted with odoriferous and onions in abundance. The smell of such festivity, making it to everybody's nostrils, was at on itation and an appetite.

Maule's-lane, or Pyncheon-street, as were now more decorous to call it, s thronged, at the appointed hour, with a congregation on its way to irch. All, as they approached, looked ward at the imposing edifice, which s henceforth to assume its rank ong the habitations of mankind. ere it rose, a little withdrawn from line of the street, but in pride, not desty. Its whole visible exterior was amented with quaint figures, con- ved in the grotesqueness of a gothic cy, and drawn or stamped in the tering plaster, composed of lime, bles, and bits of glass, with which wood-work of the walls was over- ead. On every side, the seven gables nted sharply towards the sky, and sented the aspect of a whole sister- d of edifices, breathing through the acles of one great chimney. The y lattices, with their small, diamond- ped panes, admitted the sunlight into hall and chamber, while, neverthe- , the second story, projecting far r the base, and itself retiring be- th the third, threw a shadow and ughtful gloom into the lower rooms. ved globes of wood were affixed un- the jutting stories. Little spiral rods iron beautified each of the seven xs. On the triangular portion of the le, that fronted next the street, was ial, put up that very morning, and which the sun was still marking the age of the first bright hour in a ory that was not destined to be all bright. All around were scattered ings, chips, shingles, and broken es of bricks; these, together with lately-turned earth, on which the s had not begun to grow, con-

tributed to the impression of strangeness and novelty proper to a house that had yet its place to make among men's daily interests.

The principal entrance, which had almost the breadth of a church-door, was in the angle between the two front gables, and was covered by an open porch, with benches beneath its shelter. Under this arched doorway, scraping their feet on the unworn threshold, now trod the clergymen, the elders, the magistrates, the deacons, and whatever of aristocracy there was in town or county. Thither, too, thronged the ple- beian classes, as freely as their betters, and in larger number. Just within the entrance, however, stood two serving- men, pointing some of the guests to the neighborhood of the kitchen, and usher- ing others into the statelier rooms,— hospitable alike to all, but still with a scrutinizing regard to the high or low degree of each. Velvet garments, som- bre but rich, stiffly-plaited ruffs and bands, embroidered gloves, venerable beards, the mien and countenance of authority, made it easy to distinguish the gentlemen of worship, at that period, from the tradesman, with his plodding air, or the laborer, in his leathern jerkin, stealing awe-stricken into the house which he had perhaps helped to build.

One inauspicious circumstance there was, which awakened a hardly-concealed displeasure in the breasts of a few of the more punctilious visitors. The founder of this stately mansion—a gen- tleman noted for the square and pon- derous courtesy of his demeanor—ought surely to have stood in his own hall, and to have offered the first welcome to so many eminent personages as here presented themselves in honor of his solemn festival. He was as yet invisible; the most favored of the guests had not beheld him. This sluggishness on Colonel Pyncheon's part became still more unaccountable, when the second dignitary of the province made his appearance, and found no more ceremonious a reception. The lieutenant-governor, although his visit was one of the anticipated glories of the day, had alighted from his horse, and assisted his lady from her side-saddle, and crossed the colonel's threshold, without other greeting than that of the principal domestic.

This person—a gray-headed man, of quiet and most respectful deportment—found it necessary to explain that his master still remained in his study, or private apartment; on entering which, an hour before, he had expressed a wish on no account to be disturbed.

"Do not you see, fellow," said the high sheriff of the county, taking the servant aside, "that this is no less a man than the lieutenant-governor? Summon Colonel Pyncheon at once! I know that he received letters from England, this morning; and, in the perusal and consideration of them, an hour may have passed away, without his noticing it. But he will be ill-pleased, I judge, if you suffer him to neglect the courtesy due to one of our chief rulers, and who may be said to represent King William, in the absence of the governor himself. Call your master instantly!"

"Nay, please your worship," answered the man, in much perplexity, but with a backwardness that strikingly indicated the hard and severe character of Colonel Pyncheon's domestic rule; "my master's orders were exceeding strict; and, as your worship knows, he permits of no discretion in the obedience of those who

owe him service. Let who list op yonder door; I dare not, though governor's own voice should bid do it!"

"Pooh, pooh, master high sheri cried the lieutenant-governor, who overheard the foregoing discussion, a felt himself high enough in station play a little with his dignity. "I take the matter into my own hands. is time that the good colonel came fo to greet his friends; else we shall apt to suspect that he has taken a too much of his Canary wine, in extreme deliberation which cask it w best to broach, in honor of the day! since he is so much behindhand, I give him a remembrancer myself!"

Accordingly, with such a tramp of ponderous riding-boots as might of self have been audible in the remo of the seven gables, he advanced to door, which the servant pointed out, made its new panels reëcho wit loud, free knock. Then, looking rou with a smile, to the spectators, he aw ed a response. As none came, howe he knocked again, but with the s unsatisfactory result as at first. now, being a trifle choleric in his t perament, the lieutenant-governor lifted the heavy hilt of his sword, wh with he so beat and banged upon door, that, as some of the bystan whispered, the racket might have turbed the dead. Be that as it migh seemed to produce no awakening e on Colonel Pyncheon. When the s subsided, the silence through the h was deep, dreary and oppressive, withstanding that the tongues of m of the guests had already been loos by a surreptitious cup or two of or spirits.

'Strange, forsooth!—very strange!"
ed the lieutenant-governor, whose
ile was changed to a frown. "But see-
that our host sets us the good ex-
ple of forgetting ceremony, I shall
wise throw it aside, and make free
intrude on his privacy!"

Ie tried the door, which yielded to
hand, and was flung wide open by
udden gust of wind that passed, as
h a loud sigh, from the outermost
tal, through all the passages and
rtments of the new house. It rustled
silken garments of the ladies, and
ed the long curls of the gentlemen's
s, and shook the window-hangings
the curtains of the bed-chambers;
sing everywhere a singular stir, which
was more like a hush. A shadow of
and half-fearful anticipation—no-
y knew wherefore, nor of what—
all at once fallen over the company.
hey thronged, however, to the now
n door, pressing the lieutenant-
ernor, in the eagerness of their curi-
y, into the room in advance of them.
he first glimpse, they beheld nothing
aordinary: a handsomely-furnished
n, of moderate size, somewhat dark-
1 by curtains; books arranged on
ves; a large map on the wall, and
wise a portrait of Colonel Pyncheon,
eath which sat the original colonel
self, in an oaken elbow-chair, with
n in his hand. Letters, parchments,
blank sheets of paper, were on the
e before him. He appeared to gaze
he curious crowd, in front of which
d the lieutenant-governor; and there
a frown on his dark and massive
atenance, as if sternly resentful of
boldness that had impelled them
his private retirement.

little boy—the colonel's grandchild,
and the only human being that ever
dared to be familiar with him—now
made his way among the guests, and ran
towards the seated figure; then pausing
half-way, he began to shriek with terror.
The company, tremulous as the leaves
of a tree, when all are shaking together,
drew nearer, and perceived that there
was an unnatural distortion in the fixed-
ness of Colonel Pyncheon's stare; that
there was blood on his ruff, and that
his hoary beard was saturated with it.
It was too late to give assistance. The
iron-hearted Puritan, the relentless persecutor, the grasping and strong-willed
man, was dead! Dead, in his new house!
There is a tradition, only worth alluding
to, as lending a tinge of superstitious
awe to a scene perhaps gloomy enough
without it, that a voice spoke loudly
among the guests, the tones of which
were like those of old Matthew Maule,
the executed wizard,—"God hath given
him blood to drink!"

Thus early had that one guest—the
only guest who is certain, at one time
or another, to find his way into every
human dwelling—thus early had Death
stepped across the threshold of the
House of the Seven Gables!

Colonel Pyncheon's sudden and mysterious end made a vast deal of noise
in its day. There were many rumors,
some of which have vaguely drifted
down to the present time, how that appearances indicated violence; that there
were the marks of fingers on his throat,
and the print of a bloody hand on his
plaited ruff; and that his peaked beard
was dishevelled, as if it had been fiercely
clutched and pulled. It was averred,
likewise, that the lattice-window, near
the colonel's chair, was open; and that
only a few minutes before the fatal oc

currence, the figure of a man had been seen clambering over the garden-fence, in the rear of the house. But it were folly to lay any stress on stories of this kind, which are sure to spring up around such an event as that now related, and which, as in the present case, sometimes prolong themselves for ages afterwards, like the toadstools that indicate where the fallen and buried trunk of a tree has long since mouldered into the earth. For our own part, we allow them just as little credence as to that other fable of the skeleton hand which the lieutenant-governor was said to have seen at the colonel's throat, but which vanished away, as he advanced further into the room. Certain it is, however, that there was a great consultation and dispute of doctors over the dead body. One—John Swinnerton by name—who appears to have been a man of eminence, upheld it, if we have rightly understood his terms of art, to be a case of apoplexy. His professional brethren, each for himself, adopted various hypotheses, more or less plausible, but all dressed out in a perplexing mystery of phrase, which, if it do not show a bewilderment of mind in these erudite physicians, certainly causes it in the unlearned peruser of their opinions. The coroner's jury sat upon the corpse, and, like sensible men, returned an unassailable verdict of "Sudden Death!"

It is indeed difficult to imagine that there could have been a serious suspicion of murder, or the slightest grounds for implicating any particular individual as the perpetrator. The rank, wealth, and eminent character of the deceased, must have insured the strictest scrutiny into every ambiguous circumstance. As none such is on record, it is safe to assume that none existed. T dition—which sometimes brings do truth that history has let slip, but oftener the wild babble of the ti such as was formerly spoken at the f side, and now congeals in newspaper tradition is responsible for all c trary averments. In Colonel Pynchec funeral sermon, which was printed, is still extant, the Rev. Mr. Higgin enumerates, among the many felici of his distinguished parishioner's eart career, the happy seasonableness of death. His duties all performed,— highest prosperity attained,—his and future generations fixed on a sta basis, and with a stately roof to she them, for centuries to come,—w other upward step remained for this g man to take, save the final step fi earth to the golden gate of heaven! pious clergyman surely would not h uttered words like these, had he in least suspected that the colonel been thrust into the other world the clutch of violence upon his thro

The family of Colonel Pyncheon the epoch of his death, seemed desti to as fortunate a permanence as anywise consist with the inherent stability of human affairs. It m fairly be anticipated that the prog of time would rather increase and r their prosperity, than wear away destroy it. For, not only had his and heir come into immediate en ment of a rich estate, but there w claim, through an Indian deed, firmed by a subsequent grant of General Court, to a vast and as yet explored and unmeasured tract eastern lands. These possessions— as such they might almost certainl reckoned—comprised the greater what is now known as Waldo County, the State of Maine, and were more ensive than many a dukedom, or n a reigning prince's territory, on ropean soil. When the pathless forest, t still covered this wild principality, uld give place—as it inevitably must, ugh perhaps not till ages hence—to golden fertility of human culture, it uld be the source of incalculable alth to the Pyncheon blood. Had the nel survived only a few weeks ger, it is probable that his great itical influence, and powerful con‑ tions, at home and abroad, would e consummated all that was neces‑ y to render the claim available. But, spite of good Mr. Higginson's con‑ ulatory eloquence, this appeared to the one thing which Colonel Pyn‑ on, provident and sagacious as he , had allowed to go at loose ends. So as the prospective territory was con‑ ed, he unquestionably died too soon.

son lacked not merely the father's nent position, but the talent and e of character to achieve it: he d, therefore, effect nothing by dint oolitical interest; and the bare jus‑ or legality of the claim was not so irent, after the colonel's decease, as ad been pronounced in his lifetime. e connecting link had slipped out of evidence, and could not anywhere be ad.

fforts, it is true, were made by the cheons, not only then, but at vari‑ periods for nearly a hundred years rwards, to obtain what they stub‑ ly persisted in deeming their right. in course of time, the territory was ly re‑granted to more favored in‑ duals, and partly cleared and oc‑ ed by actual settlers. These last, if they ever heard of the Pyncheon title, would have laughed at the idea of any man's asserting a right—on the strength of mouldy parchments, signed with the faded autographs of governors and legis‑ lators long dead and forgotten—to the lands which they or their fathers had wrested from the wild hand of nature, by their own sturdy toil. This impal‑ pable claim, therefore, resulted in noth‑ ing more solid than to cherish, from generation to generation, an absurd de‑ lusion of family importance, which all along characterized the Pyncheons. It caused the poorest member of the race to feel as if he inherited a kind of no‑ bility, and might yet come into the possession of princely wealth to support it. In the better specimens of the breed, this peculiarity threw an ideal grace over the hard material of human life, without stealing away any truly valuable quality. In the baser sort, its effect was to increase the liability to sluggishness and dependence, and induce the victim of a shadowy hope to remit all self‑ effort, while awaiting the realization of his dreams. Years and years after their claim had passed out of the public memory, the Pyncheons were accus‑ tomed to consult the colonel's ancient map, which had been projected while Waldo County was still an unbroken wilderness. Where the old land‑surveyor had put down woods, lakes, and rivers, they marked out the cleared spaces, and dotted the villages and towns, and cal‑ culated the progressively increasing value of the territory, as if there were yet a prospect of its ultimately forming a princedom for themselves.

In almost every generation, neverthe‑ less, there happened to be some one descendant of the family gifted with a portion of the hard, keen sense, and practical energy, that had so remarkably distinguished the original founder. His character, indeed, might be traced all the way down, as distinctly as if the colonel himself, a little diluted, had been gifted with a sort of intermittent immortality on earth. At two or three epochs, when the fortunes of the family were low, this representative of hereditary qualities had made his appearance, and caused the traditionary gossips of the town to whisper among themselves: —"Here is the old Pyncheon come again! Now the Seven Gables will be new-shingled!" From father to son, they clung to the ancestral house, with singular tenacity of home attachment. For various reasons, however, and from impressions often too vaguely founded to be put on paper, the writer cherishes the belief that many, if not most, of the successive proprietors of this estate, were troubled with doubts as to their moral right to hold it. Of their legal tenure there could be no question; but old Matthew Maule, it is to be feared, trode downward from his own age to a far later one, planting a heavy footstep, all the way, on the conscience of a Pyncheon. If so, we are left to dispose of the awful query, whether each inheritor of the property—conscious of wrong, and failing to rectify it—did not commit anew the great guilt of his ancestor, and incur all its original responsibilities. And supposing such to be the case, would it not be a far truer mode of expression to say, of the Pyncheon family, that they inherited a great misfortune, than the reverse?

We have already hinted, that it is not our purpose to trace down the history of the Pyncheon family, in its unbroken connection with the House of the Sev Gables; nor to show, as in a magic p ture, how the rustiness and infirmity age gathered over the venerable ho itself. As regards its interior life, large, dim looking-glass used to hang one of the rooms, and was fabled contain within its depths all the sha that had ever been reflected there,— old colonel himself, and his many scendants, some in the garb of anti babyhood, and others in the bloom feminine beauty or manly prime, or s dened with the wrinkles of frosty a Had we the secret of that mirror, would gladly sit down before it, transfer its revelations to our page. there was a story, for which it is diffi to conceive any foundation, that posterity of Matthew Maule had so connection with the mystery of the lo ing-glass, and that, by what appears have been a sort of mesmeric proc they could make its inner region alive with the departed Pyncheons; as they had shown themselves to world, nor in their better and hap hours, but as doing over again so deed of sin, or in the crisis of li bitterest sorrow. The popular imag tion, indeed, long kept itself busy the affair of the old Puritan Pynch and the wizard Maule; the curse, w the latter flung from his scaffold, remembered, with the very impor addition, that it had become a par the Pyncheon inheritance. If one of family did but gurgle in his throa bystander would be likely enough whisper, between jest and earnest,— has Maule's blood to drink!" The den death of a Pyncheon, about a dred years ago, with circumstances similar to what have been relate

colonel's exit, was held as giving
litional probability to the received
nion on this topic. It was considered,
reover, an ugly and ominous circum-
nce, that Colonel Pyncheon's picture
n obedience, it was said, to a pro-
on of his will—remained affixed to
wall of the room in which he
l. Those stern, immitigable features
med to symbolize an evil influence,
so darkly to mingle the shadow of
r presence with the sunshine of the
sing hour, that no good thoughts or
poses could ever spring up and blos-
there. To the thoughtful mind,
e will be no tinge of superstition in
t we figuratively express, by affirm-
that the ghost of a dead progenitor
erhaps as a portion of his own
ishment—is often doomed to become
Evil Genius of his family.

he Pyncheons, in brief, lived along,
the better part of two centuries,
perhaps less of outward vicissitude
has attended most other New Eng-
families, during the same period of
. Possessing very distinctive traits
heir own, they nevertheless took the
eral characteristics of the little com-
ity in which they dwelt; a town
d for its frugal, discreet, well-
red, and home-loving inhabitants,
well as for the somewhat confined
e of its sympathies; but in which,
t said, there are odder individuals,
now and then, stranger occurrences,
one meets with almost anywhere
. During the Revolution, the Pyn-
n of that epoch, adopting the royal
, became a refugee; but repented,
made his reappearance, just at the
t of time to preserve the House of
Seven Gables from confiscation. For
last seventy years, the most noted

event in the Pyncheon annals had been
likewise the heaviest calamity that ever
befell the race; no less than the violent
death—for so it was adjudged—of one
member of the family, by the criminal
act of another. Certain circumstances,
attending this fatal occurrence, had
brought the deed irresistibly home to a
nephew of the deceased Pyncheon. The
young man was tried and convicted of
the crime; but either the circumstantial
nature of the evidence, and possibly
some lurking doubt in the breast of the
executive, or, lastly,—an argument of
greater weight in a republic than it
could have been under a monarchy,—
the high respectability and political influence of the criminal's connections,
had availed to mitigate his doom from
death to perpetual imprisonment. This
sad affair had chanced about thirty years
before the action of our story commences. Latterly, there were rumors
(which few believed, and only one or
two felt greatly interested in) that this
long-buried man was likely, for some
reason or other, to be summoned forth
from his living tomb.

It is essential to say a few words respecting the victim of this now almost
forgotten murder. He was an old bachelor, and possessed a great wealth, in
addition to the house and real estate
which constituted what remained of the
ancient Pyncheon property. Being of
an eccentric and melancholy turn of
mind, and greatly given to rummaging
old records and hearkening to old traditions, he had brought himself, it is
averred, to the conclusion, that Matthew
Maule, the wizard, had been foully
wronged out of his homestead, if not out
of his life. Such being the case, and he,
the old bachelor, in possession of the

ill-gotten spoil—with the black stain of blood sunken deep into it, and still to be scented by conscientious nostrils—the question occurred, whether it were not imperative upon him, even at this late hour, to make restitution to Maule's posterity. To a man living so much in the past, and so little in the present, as the secluded and antiquarian old bachelor, a century and a half seemed not so vast a period as to obviate the propriety of substituting right for wrong. It was the belief of those who knew him best, that he would positively have taken the very singular step of giving up the House of the Seven Gables to the representative of Matthew Maule, but for the unspeakable tumult which a suspicion of the old gentleman's project awakened among his Pyncheon relatives. Their exertions had the effect of suspending his purpose; but it was feared that he would perform, after death, by the operation of his last will, what he had so hardly been prevented from doing, in his proper lifetime. But there is no one thing which men so rarely do, whatever the provocation or inducement, as to bequeath patrimonial property away from their own blood. They may love other individuals far better than their relatives,—they may ever cherish dislike, or positive hatred, to the latter; but yet, in view of death, the strong prejudice of propinquity revives, and impels the testator to send down his estate in the line marked out by custom so immemorial that it looks like nature. In all the Pyncheons, this feeling had the energy of disease. It was too powerful for the conscientious scruples of the old bachelor; at whose death, accordingly, the mansion-house, together with most of his other riches, passed into the possession of his n legal representative.

This was a nephew, the cousin of miserable young man who had b convicted of the uncle's murder. new heir, up to the period of his acc sion, was reckoned rather a dissipa youth, but had at once reformed, made himself an exceedingly respecta member of society. In fact, he sho more of the Pyncheon quality, and won higher eminence in the world, t any of his race, since the time of original Puritan. Applying himself earlier manhood to the study of the l and having a natural tendency towa office, he had attained, many years to a judicial situation in some infe court, which gave him for life the v desirable and imposing title of ju Later, he had engaged in politics, served a part of two terms in Congr besides making a considerable figur both branches of the state legislat Judge Pyncheon was unquestionably honor to his race. He had built him a country-seat within a few miles of native town, and there he spent s portions of his time as could be spa from public service in the display every grace and virtue—as a n paper phrased it, on the eve of an e tion—befitting the Christian, the g citizen, the horticulturalist, and gentleman.

There were few of the Pyncheons to sun themselves in the glow of judge's prosperity. In respect to nat increase, the breed had not thriven appeared rather to be dying out. only members of the family know be extant were, first, the judge him and a single surviving son, who now travelling in Europe; next,

ty years prisoner, already alluded
and a sister of the latter, who oc-
ied, in an extremely retired manner,
House of the Seven Gables, in which
had a life-estate by the will of the
bachelor. She was understood to be
tchedly poor, and seemed to make
her choice to remain so; inasmuch
her affluent cousin, the judge, had
eatedly offered her all the comforts
life, either in the old mansion or his
modern residence. The last and
ngest Pyncheon was a little country-
of seventeen, the daughter of an-
er of the judge's cousins, who had
ried a young woman of no family or
perty, and died early, and in poor
umstances. His widow had recently
en another husband.

s for Matthew Maule's posterity, it
supposed now to be extinct. For a
y long period after the witchcraft
sion, however, the Maules had con-
ed to inhabit the town where their
genitor had suffered so unjust a
th. To all appearance, they were a
t, honest, well-meaning race of
ple, cherishing no malice against in-
duals or the public, for the wrong
ch had been done them; or if, at
r own fireside, they transmitted,
n father to child, any hostile recol-
ion of the wizard's fate, and their
patrimony, it was never acted upon,
openly expressed. Nor would it have
singular had they ceased to re-
ber that the House of the Seven
les was resting its heavy frame-work
foundation that was rightfully their
. There is something so massive,
le, and almost irresistibly imposing,
he exterior presentment of estab-
d rank and great possessions, that
r very existence seems to give them

a right to exist; at least, so excellent
a counterfeit of right, that few poor
and humble men have moral force
enough to question it, even in their
secret minds. Such is the case now, after
so many ancient prejudices have been
overthrown; and it was far more so
in ante-revolutionary days, when the
aristocracy could venture to be proud,
and the low were content to be abased.
Thus the Maules, at all events, kept
their resentments within their own
breasts. They were generally poverty-
stricken; always plebeian and obscure;
working with unsuccessful diligence at
handicrafts; laboring on the wharves,
or following the sea, as sailors before
the mast; living here and there about
the town, in hired tenements, and coming finally to the almshouse, as the
natural home of their age. At last, after
creeping, as it were, for such a length
of time, along the utmost verge of the
opaque puddle of obscurity, they had
taken that downright plunge, which,
sooner or later, is the destiny of all
families, whether princely or plebeian.
For thirty years past, neither town-
record, nor gravestone, nor the direc-
tory, nor the knowledge or memory of
man, bore any trace of Matthew Maule's
descendants. His blood might possibly
exist elsewhere; here, where its lowly
current could be traced so far back,
it had ceased to keep an onward course.

So long as any of the race were to
be found, they had been marked out
from other men—not strikingly, nor as
with a sharp line, but with an effect
that was felt, rather than spoken of—
by an hereditary character of reserve.
Their companions, or those who endeavored to become such, grew conscious of a circle round about the

Maules, within the sanctity or the spell of which, in spite of an exterior of sufficient frankness and good-fellowship, it was impossible for any man to step. It was this indefinable peculiarity, perhaps, that, by insulating them from human aid, kept them always so unfortunate in life. It certainly operated to prolong, in their case, and to confirm to them, as their only inheritance, those feelings of repugnance and superstitious terror with which the people of the town, even after awakening from their frenzy, continued to regard the memory of the reputed witches. The mantle, or rather the ragged cloak, of old Matthew Maule, had fallen upon his children. They were half believed to inherit mysterious attributes; the family eye was said to possess strange power. Among other good-for-nothing properties and privileges, one was especially assigned them: of exercising an influence over people's dreams. The Pyncheons, if all stories were true, haughtily as they bore themselves in the noon-day streets of their native town, were no better than bond-servants to these plebeian Maules, on entering the topsy-turvy commonwealth of sleep. Modern psychology, it may be, will endeavor to reduce these alleged necromancies within a system, instead of rejecting them as altogether fabulous.

A descriptive paragraph or two, treating of the seven-gabled mansion in its more recent aspect, will bring this preliminary chapter to a close. The street in which it upreared its venerable peaks has long ceased to be a fashionable quarter of the town; so that, though the old edifice was surrounded by habitations of modern date, they were mostly small, built entirely of wood, and

typical of the most plodding uniform of common life. Doubtless, however, whole story of human existence be latent in each of them, but no picturesqueness, externally, that attract the imagination or sympathy seek it there. But as for the old str ture of our story, its white-oak fra and its boards, shingles and crumbl plaster, and even the huge, cluste chimney in the midst, seemed to c stitute only the least and meanest of its reality. So much of mankir varied experience had passed there so much had been suffered, and so thing, too, enjoyed,—that the very t bers were oozy, as with the moist of a heart. It was itself like a gr human heart, with a life of its o and full of rich and sombre remin cences.

The deep projection of the sec story gave the house such a medita look, that you could not pass it w out the idea that it had secrets to k and an eventful history to mora upon. In front, just on the edge of unpaved sidewalk, grew the Pynche elm, which, in reference to such t as one usually meets with, might be termed gigantic. It had been plan by a great-grandson of the first P cheon, and, though now fourscore y of age, or perhaps nearer a hundred, still in its strong and broad matur throwing its shadow from side to sid the street, overtopping the seven gab and sweeping the whole black roof its pendent foliage. It gave beauty the old edifice, and seemed to m it a part of nature. The street ha been widened about forty years the front gable was now precisely a line with it. On either side exten

uinous wooden fence, of open lattice-
rk, through which could be seen a
ssy yard, and, especially in the angles
the building, an enormous fertility
burdocks, with leaves, it is hardly
exaggeration to say, two or three
t long. Behind the house there ap-
red to be a garden, which undoubt-
y had once been extensive, but was
y infringed upon by other enclosures,
shut in by habitations and out-build-
s that stood on another street. It
uld be an omission, trifling, indeed,
unpardonable, were we to forget
green moss that had long since gath-
d over the projections of the win-
's, and on the slopes of the roof;
must we fail to direct the reader's
to a crop, not of weeds, but flower-
ibs, which were growing aloft in the
not a great way from the chimney,
he nook between two of the gables.
y were called Alice's Posies. The
dition was, that a certain Alice Pyn-
on had flung up the seeds, in sport,
that the dust of the street and the
ay of the roof gradually formed a
d of soil for them, out of which they
v, when Alice had long been in her
re. However the flowers might have
e there, it was both sad and sweet
observe how nature adopted to her-
this desolate, decaying, gusty, rusty
house of the Pyncheon family; and
the ever-returning summer did her
to gladden it with tender beauty,
grew melancholy in the effort.
here is one other feature, very es-
ial to be noticed, but which, we
tly fear, may damage any pictur-
ie and romantic impression which
have been willing to throw over our
ch of this respectable edifice. In
front gable, under the impending
brow of the second story, and contiguous to the street, was a shop-door, divided horizontally in the midst, and
with a window for its upper segment,
such as is often seen in dwellings of a
somewhat ancient date. This same shop-
door had been a subject of no slight
mortification to the present occupant
of the august Pyncheon-house, as well
as to some of her predecessors. The
matter is disagreeably delicate to handle; but, since the reader must needs
be let into the secret, he will please to
understand, that, about a century ago,
the head of the Pyncheons found himself involved in serious financial difficulties. The fellow (gentleman, as he
styled himself) can hardly have been
other than a spurious interloper; for,
instead of seeking office from the king
or the royal governor, or urging his
hereditary claim to eastern lands, he
bethought himself of no better avenue
to wealth than by cutting a shop-door
through the side of his ancestral residence. It was the custom of the time,
indeed, for merchants to store their
goods and transact business in their own
dwellings. But there was something pitifully small in this old Pyncheon's mode
of setting about his commercial operations; it was whispered, that, with his
own hands, all be-ruffled as they were,
he used to give change for a shilling,
and would turn a half-penny twice over,
to make sure that it was a good one.
Beyond all question, he had the blood
of a petty huckster in his veins, through
whatever channel it may have found
its way there.

Immediately on his death, the shop-
door had been locked, bolted, and
barred, and, down to the period of our
story, had probably never once been

opened. The old counter, shelves, and other fixtures of the little shop, remained just as he had left them. It used to be affirmed, that the dead shopkeeper, in a white wig, a faded velvet coat, an apron at his waist, and his ruffles carefully turned back from his wrist, might be seen through the chinks of the shutters, any night of the year, ransacking his till, or poring over t dingy pages of his day-brook. From t look of unutterable woe upon his fa it appeared to be his doom to spe eternity in a vain effort to make his counts balance.

And now—in a very humble way, will be seen—we proceed to open narrative.

CHAPTER II

THE LITTLE SHOP-WINDOW

It still lacked half an hour of sunrise, when Miss Hepzibah Pyncheon—we will not say awoke; it being doubtful whether the poor lady had so much as closed her eyes, during the brief night of midsummer—but, at all events, arose from her solitary pillow, and began what it would be mockery to term the adornment of her person. Far from us be the indecorum of assisting, even in imagination, at a maiden lady's toilet! Our story must therefore await Miss Hepzibah at the threshold of her chamber; only presuming, meanwhile, to note some of the heavy sighs that labored from her bosom, with little restraint as to their lugubrious depth and volume of sound, inasmuch as they could be audible to nobody, save a disembodied listener like ourself. The Old Maid was alone in the old house. Alone, except for a certain respectable and orderly young man, an artist in the daguerreotype line, who, for about three months back, had been a lodger in a remote gable,—quite a house by itself, indeed, —with locks, bolts, and oaken bars, on all the intervening doors. Inaudible, c sequently, were poor Miss Hepziba gusty sighs. Inaudible, the creak joints of her stiffened knees, as knelt down by the bedside. And inau ble, too, by mortal ear, but heard w all-comprehending love and pity in furthest heaven, that almost agony prayer—now whispered, now a gro now a struggling silence—wherewith besought the Divine assistance thro the day! Evidently, this is to be day of more than ordinary trial to M Hepzibah, who, for above a quarter a century gone by, has dwelt in st seclusion, taking no part in the busir of life, and just as little in its in course and pleasures. Not with s fervor prays the torpid recluse, look forward to the cold, sunless, stagn calm of a day that is to be like in merable yesterdays!

The maiden lady's devotions are c cluded. Will she now issue forth c the threshold of our story? Not by many moments. First, every dra in the tall, old-fashioned bureau is

opened; with difficulty, and with a
cession of spasmodic jerks; then,
must close again, with the same
:ety reluctance. There is a rustling
stiff silks; a tread of backward and
ward footsteps, to and fro, across
chamber. We suspect Miss Hep-
ah, moreover, of taking a step up-
:d into a chair, in order to give
dful regard to her appearance, on
sides, and at full length, in the oval,
gy-framed toilet-glass, that hangs
ve her table. Truly! well, indeed!
) would have thought it! Is all this
cious time to be lavished on the
tutinal repair and beautifying of an
rly person, who never goes abroad,
m nobody ever visits, and from
m, when she shall have done her
ost, it were the best charity to turn
's eyes another way?

Jow she is almost ready. Let us
lon her one other pause; for it is
n to the sole sentiment, or, we
nt better say—heightened and ren-
d intense, as it has been, by sor-
and seclusion—to the strong pas-
, of her life. We heard the turning
key in a small lock; she has opened
cret drawer of an escritoire, and is
ably looking at a certain miniature,
e in Malbone's most perfect style,
representing a face worthy of no
delicate a pencil. It was once our
l fortune to see this picture. It is
keness of a young man, in a silken
sing-gown of an old fashion, the soft
ness of which is well adapted to the
tenance of reverie, with its full,
er lips, and beautiful eyes, that seem
ndicate not so much capacity of
ght, as gentle and voluptuous emo-
Of the possessor of such features
shall have a right to ask nothing,

except that he would take the rude
world easily, and make himself happy
in it. Can it have been an early lover
of Miss Hepzibah? No; she never had
a lover—poor thing, how could she?—
nor ever knew, by her own experience,.
what love technically means. And yet,
her undying faith and trust, her fresh
remembrance, and continual devotedness
towards the original of that miniature,
have been the only substance for her
heart to feed upon.

She seems to have put aside the
miniature, and is standing again before
the toilet-glass. There are tears to be
wiped off. A few more footsteps to
and fro; and here, at last—with another pitiful sigh, like a gust of chill,
damp wind out of a long-closed vault,
the door of which has accidentally been
set ajar—here comes Miss Hepzibah
Pyncheon! Forth she steps into the
dusky, time-darkened passage; a tall
figure, clad in black silk, with a long
and shrunken waist, feeling her way
towards the stairs like a near-sighted
person, as in truth she is.

The sun, meanwhile, if not already
above the horizon, was ascending nearer
and nearer to its verge. A few clouds,
floating high upward, caught some of
the earliest light, and threw down its
golden gleam on the windows of all
the houses in the street, not forgetting
the House of the Seven Gables, which
—many such sunrises as it had witnessed—looked cheerfully at the present
one. The reflected radiance served to
show, pretty distinctly, the aspect and
arrangement of the room which Hepzibah entered, after descending the stairs.
It was a low-studded room, with a beam
across the ceiling, panelled with dark
wood, and having a large chimney-piece.

set round with pictured tiles, but now closed by an iron fire-board, through which ran the funnel of a modern stove. There was a carpet on the floor, orig- inally of rich texture, but so worn and faded, in these latter years, that its once brilliant figure had quite vanished into one indistinguishable hue. In the way of furniture, there were two tables: one, constructed with perplexing intri- cacy, and exhibiting as many feet as a centipede; the other, most delicately wrought, with four long and slender legs, so apparently frail that it was almost incredible what a length of time the ancient tea-table had stood upon them. Half a dozen chairs stood about the room, straight and stiff, and so in- geniously contrived for the discomfort of the human person that they were irksome even to sight, and conveyed the ugliest possible idea of the state of society to which they could have been adapted. One exception there was, how- ever, in a very antique elbow-chair, with a high back, carved elaborately in oak, and a roomy depth within its arms, that made up, by its spacious comprehensive- ness, for the lack of any of those artistic curves which abound in a modern chair.

As for ornamental articles of furni- ture, we recollect but two, if such they may be called. One was a map of the Pyncheon territory at the eastward, not engraved, but the handiwork of some skilful old draftsman, and grotesquely illuminated with pictures of Indians and wild beasts, among which was seen a lion; the natural history of the region being as little known as its geography, which was put down most fantastically awry. The other adornment was the portrait of old Colonel Pyncheon, at two-thirds length, representing the stern

features of a puritanic-looking pers age, in a skull cap, with a laced b and a grizzly beard; holding a B with one hand, and in the other up ing an iron sword-hilt. The latter ject, being more successfully depic by the artist, stood out in far gre prominence than the sacred volu Face to face with this picture, on en ing the apartment, Miss Hepzibah F cheon came to a pause; regardin with a singular scowl, a strange con tion of the brow, which, by people did not know her, would probably been interpreted as an expression bitter anger and ill-will. But it was such thing. She, in fact, felt a revere for the pictured visage of which on far-descended and time-stricken vi could be susceptible; and this forbid scowl was the innocent result of near-sightedness, and an effort so concentrate her powers of vision a substitute a firm outline of the ob instead of a vague one.

We must linger a moment on unfortunate expression of poor He bah's brow. Her scowl—as the wo or such part of it as sometimes ca a transitory glimpse of her at the dow, wickedly persisted in calling her scowl had done Miss Hepziba very ill office, in establishing her c acter as an ill-tempered old maid; does it appear improbable, that, by o gazing at herself in a dim looking-g and perpetually encountering her frown within its ghostly sphere, she been led to interpret the expressior most as unjustly as the world did. " miserably cross I look!" she must o have whispered to herself;—and mately have fancied herself so, t sense of inevitable doom. But her h

er frowned. It was naturally tender,
sitive, and full of little tremors and
pitations; all of which weaknesses
etained, while her visage was grow-
so perversely stern, and even fierce.
r had Hepzibah ever any hardihood,
ept what came from the very warm-
nook in her affections.

ll this time, however, we are loiter-
faint-heartedly on the threshold of
story. In very truth, we have an
incible reluctance to disclose what
ss Hepzibah Pyncheon was about to

t has already been observed, that,
the basement story of the gable
nting on the street, an unworthy
estor, nearly a century ago, had
ed up a shop. Ever since the old
tleman retired from trade, and fell
ep under his coffin-lid, not only the
p-door, but the inner arrangements,
been suffered to remain unchanged;
le the dust of ages gathered inch-
p over the shelves and counter, and
tly filled an old pair of scales, as
were of value enough to be weighed.
reasured itself up, too, in the half-
ned till, where there still lingered
ase sixpence, worth neither more
less than the hereditary pride which
here been put to shame. Such had
n the state and condition of the
e shop in old Hepzibah's childhood,
n she and her brother used to play
hide-and-seek in its forsaken pre-
ts. So it had remained, until within
w days past.

ut now, though the shop-window
still closely curtained from the
lic gaze, a remarkable change had
n place in its interior. The rich
heavy festoons of cobweb, which
ad cost a long ancestral succession

of spiders their life's labor to spin and
weave, had been carefully brushed away
from the ceiling. The counter, shelves,
and floor, had all been scoured, and
the latter was overstrewn with fresh
blue sand. The brown scales, too, had
evidently undergone rigid discipline, in
an unavailing effort to rub off the rust,
which, alas! had eaten through and
through their substance. Neither was the
little old shop any longer empty of
merchantable goods. A curious eye,
privileged to take an account of stock,
and investigate behind the counter,
would have discovered a barrel,—yea,
two or three barrels and half ditto,—
one containing flour, another apples,
and a third, perhaps, Indian meal. There
was likewise a square box of pine-wood,
full of soap in bars; also, another of
the same size, in which were tallow
candles, ten to the pound. A small stock
of brown sugar, some white beans and
split peas, and a few other commodities of low price, and such as are constantly in demand, made up the bulkier
portion of the merchandise. It might
have been taken for a ghostly or phantasmagoric reflection of the old shop
keeper Pyncheon's shabbily-provided
shelves, save that some of the articles
were of a description and outward form
which could hardly have been known
in his day. For instance, there was a
glass pickle-jar, filled with fragments
of Gibraltar rock; not, indeed, splinters
of the veritable stone foundation of
the famous fortress, but bits of delectable candy, neatly done up in white
paper. Jim Crow, moreover, was seen
executing his world-renowned dance, in
gingerbread. A party of leaden dragoons
were galloping along one of the shelves,
in equipments and uniform of modern

cut; and there were some sugar figures, with no strong resemblance to the humanity of any epoch, but less unsatisfactorily representing our own fashions than those of a hundred years ago. Another phenomenon, still more strikingly modern, was a package of lucifer matches, which, in old times, would have been thought actually to borrow their instantaneous flame from the nether fires of Tophet.

In short, to bring the matter at once to a point, it was incontrovertibly evident that somebody had taken the shop and fixtures of the long-retired and forgotten Mr. Pyncheon, and was about to renew the enterprise of that departed worthy, with a different set of customers. Who could this bold adventurer be? And, of all places in the world, why had he chosen the House of the Seven Gables as the scene of his commercial speculations?

We return to the elderly maiden. She at length withdrew her eyes from the dark countenance of the colonel's portrait, heaved a sigh,—indeed, her breast was a very cave of Æolus, that morning,—and stept across the room on tip-toe, as is the customary gait of elderly women. Passing through an intervening passage, she opened a door that communicated with the shop, just now so elaborately described. Owing to the projection of the upper story—and still more to the thick shadow of the Pyncheon-elm, which stood almost directly in front of the gable—the twilight, here, was still as much akin to night as morning. Another heavy sigh from Miss Hepzibah! After a moment's pause on the threshold, peering towards the window with her near-sighted scowl, as if frowning down some bitter enemy,

she suddenly projected herself into shop. The haste, and, as it were, galvanic impulse of the movement, w really quite startling.

Nervously—in a sort of frenzy, might almost say—she began to b herself in arranging some childr play-things, and other little wares, the shelves and at the shop-wind In the aspect of this dark-arrayed, p faced, lady-like old figure, there wa deeply tragic character, that contras irreconcilably with the ludicrous p ness of her employment. It seeme queer anomaly, that so gaunt and mal a personage should take a toy hand; a miracle, that the toy did vanish in her grasp; a miserably ab idea, that she should go on perple her stiff and sombre intellect with question how to tempt little boys her premises! Yet such is undoubt her object. Now she places a gin bread elephant against the window, with so tremulous a touch tha tumbles upon the floor, with the memberment of three legs and its tr it has ceased to be an elephant, has become a few bits of musty gin bread. There, again, she has ups tumbler of marbles, all of which different ways, and each indivi marble, devil-directed, into the difficult obscurity that it can Heaven help our poor old Hepzibah, forgive us for taking a ludicrous of her position! As her rigid and r frame goes down upon its hands knees, in quest of the absconding bles, we positively feel so much more inclined to shed tears of sympa from the very fact that we must n turn aside and laugh at her. For —and if we fail to impress it suit

on the reader, it is our own fault,
t that of the theme—here is one of
e truest points of melancholy interest
t occur in ordinary life. It was the
al throe of what called itself old
atility. A lady—who had fed herself
m childhood with the shadowy food
aristocratic reminiscences, and whose
igion it was that a lady's hand soils
elf irremediably by doing aught for
ead—this born lady, after sixty years
narrowing means, is fain to step
wn from her pedestal of imaginary
k. Poverty, treading closely at her
els for a life-time, has come up with
at last. She must earn her own
d, or starve! And we have stolen
on Miss Hepzibah Pyncheon, too ir-
erently, at the instant of time when
patrician lady is to be transformed
the plebeian woman.

n this republican country, amid the
tuating waves of our social life,
ebody is always at the drowning-
nt. The tragedy is enacted with as
tinual a repetition as that of a popu-
drama on a holiday; and, neverthe-
, is felt as deeply, perhaps, as when
hereditary noble sinks below his
er. More deeply; since, with us, rank
he grosser substance of wealth and
plendid establishment, and has no
itual existence after the death of
se, but dies hopelessly along with
m. And, therefore, since we have
n unfortunate enough to introduce
heroine at so inauspicious a junc-
e, we would entreat for a mood of
solemnity in the spectators of her
. Let us behold, in poor Hepzibah,
immemorial lady,—two hundred
rs old, on this side of the water,
thrice as many on the other,—with
antique portraits, pedigrees, coats

of arms, records and traditions, and her
claim, as joint heiress, to that princely
territory at the eastward, no longer a
wilderness, but a populous fertility,—
born, too, in Pyncheon-street, under the
Pyncheon-elm, and in the Pyncheon-
house, where she has spent all her days,
—reduced now, in that very house, to be
the hucksteress of a cent-shop!

This business of setting up a petty
shop is almost the only resource of
women, in circumstances at all similar
to those of our unfortunate recluse.
With her near-sightedness, and those
tremulous fingers of hers, at once inflexible and delicate, she could not be
a seamstress; although her sampler, of
fifty years gone-by, exhibited some of
the most recondite specimens of ornamental needle-work. A school for little
children had been often in her thoughts;
and, at one time, she had begun a
review of her early studies in the New
England primer, with a view to prepare
herself for the office of instructress. But
the love of children had never been
quickened in Hepzibah's heart, and was
now torpid, if not extinct; she watched
the little people of the neighborhood
from her chamber-window, and doubted
whether she could tolerate a more intimate acquaintance with them. Besides,
in our day, the very A B C has become a science, greatly too abstruse
to be any longer taught by pointing
a pin from letter to letter. A modern
child could teach old Hepzibah more
than old Hepzibah could teach the child.
So—with many a cold, deep heart-quake
at the idea of at last coming into sordid
contact with the world, from which she
had so long kept aloof, while every
added day of seclusion had rolled another stone against the cavern-door of

her hermitage—the poor thing bethought herself of the ancient shop-window, the rusty scales, and dusty till. She might have held back a little longer; but another circumstance, not yet hinted at, had somewhat hastened her decision. Her humble preparations, therefore, were duly made, and the enterprise was now to be commenced. Nor was she entitled to complain of any remarkable singularity in her fate; for, in the town of her nativity, we might point to several little shops of a similar description; some of them in houses as ancient as that of the seven gables; and one or two, it may be, where a decayed gentlewoman stands behind the counter, as grim an image of family pride as Miss Hepzibah Pyncheon herself.

It was overpoweringly ridiculous—we must honestly confess it—the deportment of the maiden lady while setting her shop in order for the public eye. She stole on tiptoe to the window, as cautiously as if she conceived some bloody-minded villain to be watching behind the elm-tree, with intent to take her life. Stretching out her long, lank arm, she put a paper of pearl-buttons, a Jew's-harp, or whatever the small article might be, in its destined place, and straightway vanished back into the dusk, as if the world need never hope for another glimpse of her. It might have been fancied, indeed, that she expected to minister to the wants of the community unseen, like a disembodied divinity, or enchantress, holding forth her bargains to the reverential and awe-stricken purchaser, in an invisible land. But Hepzibah had no such flattering dream. She was well aware that she must ultimately come forward, and stand revealed in her proper indi-

viduality; but, like other sensitive persons, she could not bear to be observed in the gradual process, and chose rather to flash forth on the world's astonished gaze at once.

The inevitable moment was not much longer to be delayed. The sunshine might now be seen stealing down the front of the opposite house, from the windows of which came a reflected gleam, struggling through the boughs of the elm-tree, and enlightening the interior of the shop more distinctly than heretofore. The town appeared to be waking up. A baker's cart had already rattled through the street, chasing away the latest vestige of night's sanctity with the jingle-jangle of its dissonant bells. A milkman was distributing the contents of his cans from door to door; and the harsh peal of a fisherman's conch-shell was heard far off around the corner. None of these tokens escaped Hepzibah's notice. The moment had arrived. To delay longer would only to lengthen out her misery. Nothing remained, except to take down the bar from the shop-door, leaving the entrance free—more than free—welcome, as if all were household friends—to every passer-by, whose eyes might be attracted by the commodities at the window. This last act Hepzibah now performed, letting the bar fall with what smote upon her excited nerves as a most astounding clatter. Then—as if the only barrier betwixt herself and the world had been thrown down, and a flood of evil consequences would come tumbling through the gap—she fled into the inner parlor, threw herself into the ancestral elbow-chair, and wept.

Our miserable old Hepzibah! It is a heavy annoyance to a writer, who

deavors to represent nature, its vari-
s attitudes and circumstances, in a
.sonably correct outline and true col-
.ng, that so much of the mean and
licrous should be hopelessly mixed
with the purest pathos which life
.ywhere supplies to him. What tragic
.nity, for example, can be wrought
.o a scene like this! How can we ele-
.e our history of retribution for the
. of long ago, when, as one of our
.st prominent figures, we are com-
.led to introduce—not a young and
.ely woman, nor even the stately re-
.ins of beauty, storm-shattered by
.iction—but a gaunt, sallow, rusty-
.nted maiden, in a long-waisted silk
.vn, and with the strange horror of
.urban on her head! Her visage is
. even ugly. It is redeemed from in-
.nificance only by the contraction of

her eyebrows into a near-sighted scowl.
And, finally, her great life-trial seems to
be, that, after sixty years of idleness,
she finds it convenient to earn comfortable bread by setting up a shop in a
small way. Nevertheless, if we look
through all the heroic fortunes of mankind, we shall find this same entanglement of something mean and trivial
with whatever is noblest in joy or sorrow. Life is made up of marble and
mud. And, without all the deeper trust
in a comprehensive sympathy above us,
we might hence be led to suspect the
insult of a sneer, as well as an immitigable frown, on the iron countenance
of fate. What is called poetic insight is
the gift of discerning, in this sphere
of strangely-mingled elements, the
beauty and the majesty which are compelled to assume a garb so sordid.

CHAPTER III

THE FIRST CUSTOMER

MISS HEPZIBAH PYNCHEON sat in the
.en elbow-chair, with her hands over
. face, giving way to that heavy
.vn-sinking of the heart which most
.sons have experienced, when the im-
. of hope itself seems ponderously
.ulded of lead, on the eve of an enter-
.se at once doubtful and momentous.
.: was suddenly startled by the tin-
.ng alarum—high, sharp, and irregular
.f a little bell. The maiden lady arose
.n her feet, as pale as a ghost at
.k-crow; for she was an enslaved
.rit, and this the talisman to which
. owed obedience. This little bell—

to speak in plainer terms—being fastened over the shop-door, was so contrived as to vibrate by means of a
steel spring, and thus convey notice to
the inner regions of the house, when
any customer should cross the threshold.
Its ugly and spiteful little din (heard
now for the first time, perhaps, since
Hepzibah's periwigged predecessor had
retired from trade) at once set every
nerve of her body in responsive and
tumultuous vibration. The crisis was
upon her! Her first customer was at the
door!

Without giving herself time for a

second thought, she rushed into the shop, pale, wild, desperate in gesture and expression, scowling portentously, and looking far better qualified to do fierce battle with a house-breaker than to stand smiling behind the counter, bartering small wares for a copper recompense. Any ordinary customer, indeed, would have turned his back and fled. And yet there was nothing fierce in Hepzibah's poor old heart; nor had she, at the moment, a single bitter thought against the world at large, or one individual man or woman. She wished them all well, but wished, too, that she herself were done with them, and in her quiet grave.

The applicant, by this time, stood within the doorway. Coming freshly, as he did, out of the morning light, he appeared to have brought some of its cheery influences into the shop along with him. It was a slender young man, not more than one or two and twenty years old, with rather a grave and thoughtful expression, for his years, but likewise a springy alacrity and vigor. These qualities were not only perceptible, physically, in his make and motions, but made themselves felt almost immediately in his character. A brown beard, not too silken in its texture, fringed his chin, but as yet without completely hiding it; he wore a short moustache, too, and his dark, high-featured countenance looked all the better for these natural ornaments. As for his dress, it was of the simplest kind; a summer sack of cheap and ordinary material, thin, checkered pantaloons, and a straw hat, by no means of the finest braid. Oak Hall might have supplied his entire equipment. He was chiefly marked as a gentleman—if such, indeed, he made any claim to be—the rather remarkable whiteness a nicety of his clean linen.

He met the scowl of old Hepzibah without apparent alarm, as having he tofore encountered it, and found harmless.

"So, my dear Miss Pyncheon," s the daguerreotypist,—for it was t sole other occupant of the seven-gab mansion,—"I am glad to see that y have not shrunk from your good p pose. I merely look in to offer best wishes, and to ask if I can as you any further in your preparatior

People in difficulty and distress, in any manner at odds with the wo can endure a vast amount of ha treatment, and perhaps be only stronger for it; whereas, they give at once before the simplest express of what they perceive to be gent sympathy. So it proved with poor H zibah; for, when she saw the yo man's smile,—looking so much brighter on a thoughtful face,— heard his kindly tone, she broke into a hysteric giggle, and then be to sob.

"Ah, Mr. Holgrave," cried she, soon as she could speak, "I never go through with it! Never, never, ne I wish I were dead, and in the family-tomb, with all my forefath With my father, and my mother, my sister! Yes, and with my brot who had far better find me there t here! The world is too chill and h —and I am too old, and too feeble, too holpless!"

"O, believe me, Miss Hepzibah," the young man, quietly, "these feel will not trouble you any longer, a you are once fairly in the midst

ır enterprise. They are unavoidable
this moment, standing, as you do,
the outer verge of your long seclu-
n, and peopling the world with ugly
pes, which you will soon find to be as
·eal as the giants and ogres of a
ld's story-book. I find nothing so sin-
ar in life, as that everything appears
lose its substance, the instant one
ually grapples with it. So it will be
h what you think so terrible."

'But I am a woman!" said Hepzibah,
eously. "I was going to say, a lady,
·ut I consider that as past."

Well; no matter if it be past!" an-
·red the artist, a strange gleam of
f-hidden sarcasm flashing through the
dliness of his manner. "Let it go!
ı are the better without it. I speak
ıkly, my dear Miss Pyncheon; for
we not friends? I look upon this
one of the fortunate days of your
. It ends an epoch, and begins one.
herto, the life-blood has been grad-
·y chilling in your veins, as you sat
·f, within your circle of gentility,
le the rest of the world was fight-
out its battle with one kind of
essity or another. Henceforth, you
at least have the sense of healthy
natural effort for a purpose, and of
ling your strength—be it great or
ll—to the united struggle of man-
l. This is success—all the success
. anybody meets with!"

It is natural enough, Mr. Holgrave,
you should have ideas like these,"
ined Hepzibah, drawing up her
t figure, with slightly offended dig-
. "You are a man, a young man,
brought up, I suppose, as almost
ybody is now-a-days, with a view
eeking your fortune. But I was born
dy and have always lived one; no

matter in what narrowness of means,
always a lady!"

"But I was not born a gentleman;
neither have I lived like one," said
Holgrave, slightly smiling; "so, my dear
madam, you will hardly expect me to
sympathize with sensibilities of this
kind; though, unless I deceive myself,
I have some imperfect comprehension
of them. These names of gentlemen and
lady had a meaning, in the past history
of the world, and conferred privileges,
desirable or otherwise, on those entitled
to bear them. In the present—and still
more in the future condition of society
—they imply, not privilege, but restric-
tion!"

"These are new notions," said the
old gentlewoman, shaking her head. "I
shall never understand them; neither do
I wish it."

"We will cease to speak of them,
then," replied the artist, with a friend-
lier smile than his last one, "and I
will leave you to feel whether it is not
better to be a true woman than a lady.
Do you really think, Miss Hepzibah,
that any lady of your family has ever
done a more heroic thing, since this
house was built, than you are performing in it to-day? Never; and if the
Pyncheons had always acted so nobly,
I doubt whether an old wizard Maule's
anathema, of which you told me once,
would have had much weight with Providence against them."

"Ah—no, no!" said Hepzibah, not
displeased at this allusion to the sombre
dignity of an inherited curse. "If old
Maule's ghost, or a descendant of his,
could see me behind the counter to-
day, he would call it the fulfilment of
his worst wishes. But I thank you for
your kindness, Mr. Holgrave, and will

do my utmost to be a good shop-keeper."

"Pray do," said Holgrave, "and let me have the pleasure of being your first customer. I am about taking a walk to the sea-shore, before going to my rooms, where I misuse Heaven's blessed sunshine, by tracing out human features, through its agency. A few of those biscuits, dipt in sea-water, will be just what I need for breakfast. What is the price of half a dozen?"

"Let me be a lady a moment longer," replied Hepzibah, with a manner of antique stateliness, to which a melancholy smile lent a kind of grace. She put the biscuits into his hand, but rejected the compensation. "A Pyncheon must not, at all events, under her forefathers' roof, receive money for a morsel of bread, from her only friend!"

Holgrave took his departure, leaving her, for the moment, with spirits not quite so much depressed. Soon, however, they had subsided nearly to their former dead level. With a beating heart, she listened to the footsteps of early passengers, which now began to be frequent along the street. Once or twice, they seemed to linger; these strangers, or neighbors, as the case might be, were looking at the display of toys and petty commodities in Hepzibah's shop-window. She was doubly tortured; in part, with a sense of overwhelming shame, that strange and unloving eyes should have the privilege of gazing, and partly because the idea occurred to her, with ridiculous importunity, that the window was not arranged so skilfully, nor nearly to so much advantage, as it might have been. It seemed as if the whole fortune or failure of her shop

might depend on the display of a diff[e]-ent set of articles, or substituting [a] fairer apple for one which appeared [to] be specked. So she made the chan[ge] and straightway fancied that everythi[ng] was spoiled by it; not recognizing t[hat] it was the nervousness of the junctu[re] and her own native squeamishness, [as] an old maid, that wrought all the see[m]-ing mischief.

Anon, there was an encounter, j[ust] at the door-step, betwixt two labori[ng] men, as their rough voices denoted th[em] to be. After some slight talk about th[eir] own affairs, one of them chanced [to] notice the shop-window, and direct[ed] the other's attention to it.

"See here!" cried he; "what do y[ou] think of this? Trade seems to be lo[ok]-ing up, in Pyncheon-street!"

"Well, well, this is a sight, to [be] sure!" exclaimed the other. "In t[he] old Pyncheon-house, and underneath [the] Pyncheon-elm! Who would have thou[ght] it? Old Maid Pyncheon is setting u[p] cent-shop!"

"Will she make it go, think y[ou,] Dixey?" said his friend. "I don't c[all] it a very good stand. There's anot[her] shop, just around the corner."

"Make it go!" cried Dixey, with [a] most contemptuous expression, as if [the] very idea were impossible to be c[on]-ceived. "Not a bit of it! Why, [her] face—I've seen it, for I dug her gar[den] for her, one year—her face is enou[gh] to frighten the Old Nick himself, if [he] had ever so great a mind to trade w[ith] her. People can't stand it, I tell y[ou!] She scowls dreadfully, reason or no[ne,] out of pure ugliness of temper!"

"Well, that's not so much matte[r,]" remarked the other man. "These so[ur-] tempered folks are mostly handy

siness, and know pretty well what
·y are about. But, as you say, I don't
nk she'll do much. This business of
:ping cent-shops is overdone, like all
·er kinds of trade, handicraft, and
lily labor. I know it, to my cost!
· wife kept a cent-shop three months,
l lost five dollars on her outlay!"

'Poor business!" responded Dixey, in
one as if he were shaking his head,
'poor business!"

·or some reason or other, not very
y to analyze, there had hardly been
bitter a pang, in all her previous
:ery about the matter, as what
illed Hepzibah's heart, on overhearing
above conversation. The testimony
regard to her scowl was frightfully
·ortant; it seemed to hold up her
·ge, wholly relieved from the false
·t of her self-partialities, and so hide-
: that she dared not look at it.

·he was absurdly hurt, moreover, by
slight and idle effect that her set-
· up shop—an event of such breath-
: interest to herself—appeared to
·e upon the public, of which these
· men were the nearest representa-
·s. A glance; a passing word or two;
·oarse laugh; and she was doubtless
·gotten, before they turned the cor-
·! They cared nothing for her dig-
·, and just as little for her degra-
·ion. Then, also, the augury of ill-
·cess, uttered from the sure wisdom
·experience, fell upon her half-dead
·e like a clod into a grave. The man's
·e had already tried the same experi-
·nt, and failed! How could the born
·y—the recluse of half a lifetime, ut-
·y unpractised in the world, at sixty
·rs of age—how could she ever dream
·succeeding, when the hard, vulgar,
·n, busy, hackneyed New England

woman, had lost five dollars on her
little outlay! Success presented itself
as an impossibility, and the hope of it
as a wild hallucination.

Some malevolent spirit, doing his utmost to drive Hepzibah mad, unrolled
before her imagination a kind of panorama, representing the great thoroughfare of a city, all astir with customers.
So many and so magnificent shops as
there were! Groceries, toy-shops, dry-
goods stores, with their immense panes
of plate-glass, their gorgeous fixtures,
their vast and complete assortments of
merchandise, in which fortunes had been
invested; and those noble mirrors at
the further end of each establishment,
doubling all this wealth by a brightly-
burnished vista of unrealities! On one
side of the street, this splendid bazaar,
with a multitude of perfumed and glossy
salesmen, smirking, smiling, bowing, and
measuring out the goods. On the other
the dusky old House of the Seven
Gables, with the antiquated shop-window under its projecting story, and
Hepzibah herself, in a gown of rusty
black silk, behind the counter, scowling
at the world as it went by! This mighty
contrast thrust itself forward, as a fair
expression of the odds against which
she was to begin her struggle for a
subsistence. Success? Preposterous! She
would never think of it again! The house
might just as well be buried in an
eternal fog, while all other houses had
the sunshine on them; for not a foot
would ever cross the threshold, nor a
hand so much as try the door!

But, at this instant, the shop-bell,
right over her head, tinkled as if it
were bewitched. The old gentlewoman's
heart seemed to be attached to the
same steel spring, for it went through

a series of sharp jerks, in unison with the sound. The door was thrust open, although no human form was perceptible on the other side of the half-window. Hepzibah, nevertheless, stood at a gaze, with her hands clasped, looking very much as if she had summoned up an evil spirit, and were afraid, yet resolved, to hazard the encounter.

"Heaven help me!" she groaned, mentally. "Now is my hour of need!"

The door, which moved with difficulty on its creaking and rusty hinges, being forced quite open, a square and sturdy little urchin became apparent, with cheeks as red as an apple. He was clad rather shabbily (but, as it seemed, more owing to his mother's carelessness than his father's poverty), in a blue apron, very wide and short trousers, shoes somewhat out at the toes, and a chip-hat, with the frizzles of his curly hair sticking through its crevices. A book and a small slate, under his arm, indicated that he was on his way to school. He stared at Hepzibah a moment, as an elder customer than himself would have been likely enough to do, not knowing what to make of the tragic attitude and queer scowl wherewith she regarded him.

"Well, child," said she, taking heart at sight of a personage to little formidable,—"well, my child, what did you wish for?"

"That Jim Crow, there, in the window," answered the urchin, holding out a cent, and pointing to the gingerbread figure that had attracted his notice, as he loitered along to school; "the one that has not a broken foot."

So Hepzibah put forth her lank arm, and taking the effigy from the shop-window, delivered it to her first c[us]tomer.

"No matter for the money," said s[he,] giving him a little push towards [the] door; for her old gentility was c[on]tumaciously squeamish at sight of [the] copper coin, and, besides, it seem[ed] such pitiful meanness to take the chi[ld's] pocket-money in exchange for a bit [of] stale gingerbread. "No matter for [the] cent. You are welcome to Jim Cro[w."]

The child, staring, with round ey[es] at this instance of liberality, wholly [un]precedented in his large experience [of] cent-shops, took the man of ging[er]bread, and quitted the premises. [No] sooner had he reached the sidew[alk] (little cannibal that he was!) than J[im] Crow's head was in his mouth. As [he] had not been careful to shut the do[or,] Hepzibah was at the pains of clos[ing] it after him, with a pettish ejaculat[ion] or two about the troublesomeness [of] young people, and particularly of sm[all] boys. She had just placed another rep[re]sentative of the renowned Jim C[row] at the window, when again the sh[op] bell tinkled clamorously, and again [the] door being thrust open, with its char[ac]teristic jerk and jar, disclosed the sa[me] sturdy little urchin who, precisely [two] minutes ago, had made his exit. [The] crumbs and discoloration of the c[an]nibal feast, as yet hardly consumma[ted,] were exceedingly visible about [his] mouth.

"What is it now, child?" asked [the] maiden lady, rather impatiently; "[did] you come back to shut the door?"

"No," answered the urchin, point[ing] to the figure that had just been [set] up; "I want that other Jim Crow."

"Well, here it is for you," said H[ep]zibah, reaching it down; but, re[cog]

ng that this pertinaceous customer
ild not quit her on any other terms,
long as she had a gingerbread figure
her shop, she partly drew back her
ended hand,—"Where is the cent?"
The little boy had the cent ready, but,
, a true-born Yankee, would have
ferred the better bargain to the
se. Looking somewhat chagrined, he
the coin into Hepzibah's hand, and
arted, sending the second Jim Crow
quest of the former one. The new
p-keeper dropped the first sordid
ilt of her commercial enterprise into
till. It was done! The sordid stain of
copper coin could never be washed
y from her palm. The little school-
, aided by the impish figure of the
ro dancer, had wrought an irrepar-
ruin. The structure of ancient aris-
acy had been demolished by him,
1 as if his childish gripe had torn
n the seven-gabled mansion! Now
Hepzibah turn the old Pyncheon
raits with their faces to the wall,
take the map of her eastern terri-
to kindle the kitchen fire, and blow
he flame with the empty breath of
ancestral traditions! What had she
o with ancestry? Nothing; no more
with posterity! No lady, now, but
ly Hepzibah Pyncheon, a forlorn
maid, and keeper of a cent-shop!
evertheless, even while she paraded
e ideas somewhat ostentatiously
ugh her mind, it is altogether sur-
ng what a calmness had come over
The anxiety and misgivings which
tormented her, whether asleep or
nelancholy day-dreams, ever since
project began to take an aspect
olidity, had now vanished quite
r. She felt the novelty of her posi-
indeed, but no longer with dis-

turbance or affright. Now and then,
there came a thrill of almost youthful
enjoyment. It was the invigorating
breath of a fresh outward atmosphere,
after the long torpor and monotonous
seclusion of her life. So wholesome is
effort! So miraculous the strength that
we do not know of! The healthiest glow
that Hepzibah had known for years had
come now, in the dreaded crisis, when,
for the first time, she had put forth
her hand to help herself. The little
circlet of the schoolboy's copper coin—
dim and lustreless though it was, with
the small services which it had been
doing, here and there about the world
—had proved a talisman, fragrant with
good, and deserving to be set in gold
and worn next her heart. It was as
potent, and perhaps endowed with the
same kind of efficacy, as a galvanic ring!
Hepzibah, at all events, was indebted
to its subtile operation, both in body
and spirit; so much the more, as it
inspired her with energy to get some
breakfast, at which, still the better to
keep up her courage, she allowed herself an extra spoonful in her infusion
of black tea.

Her introductory day of shop-keeping
did not run on, however, without many
and serious interruptions of this mood
of cheerful vigor. As a general rule,
Providence seldom vouchsafes to mortals any more than just that degree
of encouragement which suffices to keep
them at a reasonably full exertion of
their powers. In the case of our old
gentlewoman, after the excitement of
her new effort had subsided, the despondency of her whole life threatened,
ever and anon, to return. It was like
the heavy mass of clouds which we
may often see obscuring the sky, and

making a gray twilight everywhere, until, towards nightfall, it yields temporarily to a glimpse of sunshine. But, always, the envious cloud strives to gather again across the streak of celestial azure.

Customers came in, as the forenoon advanced, but rather slowly; in some cases, too, it must be owned, with little satisfaction either to themselves or Miss Hepzibah; nor, on the whole, with an aggregate of very rich emolument to the till. A little girl, sent by her mother to match a skein of cotton thread, of a peculiar hue, took one that the nearsighted old lady pronounced extremely like, but soon came running back, with a blunt and cross message, that it would not do, and, besides, was very rotten! Then, there was a pale, care-wrinkled woman, not old but haggard, and already with streaks of gray among her hair, like silver ribbons; one of those women, naturally delicate, whom you at once recognize as worn to death by a brute—probably a drunken brute—of a husband, and at least nine children. She wanted a few pounds of flour, and offered the money, which the decayed gentlewoman silently rejected, and gave the poor soul better measure than if she had taken it. Shortly afterwards, a man in a blue cotton frock, much soiled, came in and bought a pipe, filling the whole shop, meanwhile, with the hot odor of strong drink, not only exhaled in the torrid atmosphere of his breath, but oozing out of his entire system, like an inflammable gas. It was impressed on Hepzibah's mind that this was the husband of the care-wrinkled woman. He asked for a paper of tobacco; and as she had neglected to provide herself with the article, her brutal customer dashed down his newly-bou pipe, and left the shop, muttering so unintelligible words, which had the t and bitterness of a curse. Hereup Hepzibah threw up her eyes, unintionally scowling in the face of Pr dence!

No less than five persons, during forenoon, inquired for ginger-beer, root-beer, or any drink of a sin brewage, and, obtaining nothing of kind, went off in an exceedingly humor. Three of them left the open, and the other two pulled i spitefully in going out that the l bell played the very deuce with H zibah's nerves. A round, bustling, ruddy housewife of the neighbor burst breathlessly into the shop, fie demanding yeast; and when the gentlewoman, with her cold shynes manner, gave her hot customer to ur stand that she did not keep the art this very capable housewife took herself to administer a regular rebuk

"A cent-shop, and no yeast!" q she; "that will never do! Who heard of such a thing? Your loaf never rise, no more than mine wil day. You had better shut up sho once."

"Well," said Hepzibah, heaving a sigh, "perhaps I had!"

Several times, moreover, beside above instance, her ladylike sensibi were seriously infringed upon by familiar, if not rude tone, with v people addressed her. They evid considered themselves not merely equals, but her patrons and supe Now, Hepzibah had unconsciously tered herself with the idea that would be a gleam or halo, of some or other, about her person, which

re an obeisance to her sterling gen-
y, or, at least, a tacit recognition
t. On the other hand, nothing tor-
d her more intolerably than when
recognition was too prominently
essed. To one or two rather officious
rs of sympathy, her responses were
e short of acrimonious; and, we
et to say, Hepzibah was thrown into
ositively unchristian state of mind,
the suspicion that one of her cus-
ers was drawn to the shop not by
real need of the article which she
ended to seek, but by a wicked wish
stare at her. The vulgar creature
determined to see for herself what
of a figure a mildewed piece of
ocracy, after wasting all the bloom,
much of the decline of her life,
t from the world, would cut behind
unter. In this particular case, how-
mechanical and innocuous it might
other times, Hepzibah's contortion
ow served her in good stead.

never was so frightened in my
' said the curious customer, in de-
ing the incident to one of her
iintances. "She's a real old vixen,
my word of it! She says little,
e sure; but if you could only see
mischief in her eye!"

the whole, therefore, her new
ience led our decayed gentlewoman
ery disagreeable conclusions as to
emper and manners of what she
d the lower classes, whom hereto-
she had looked down upon with
itle and pitying complaisance, as
f occupying a sphere of unques-
ble superiority. But, unfortunately,

she had likewise to struggle against a
bitter emotion of a directly opposite
kind: a sentiment of virulence, we mean,
towards the idle aristocracy to which
it had so recently been her pride to
belong. When a lady, in a delicate
and costly summer garb, with a floating veil and gracefully-swaying gown,
and, altogether, an ethereal lightness
that made you look at her beautifully-
slippered feet, to see whether she trod
on the dust or floated in the air,—
when such a vision happened to pass
through this retired street, leaving it
tenderly and delusively fragrant with
her passage, as if a bouquet of tea-
roses had been borne along,—then,
again, it is to be feared, old Hepzibah's scowl could no longer vindicate
itself entirely on the plea of near-
sightedness.

"For what end," thought she, giving
vent to that feeling of hostility which
is the only real abasement of the poor,
in presence of the rich,—"for what
good end, in the wisdom of Providence,
does that woman live? Must the whole
world toil, that the palms of her hands
may be kept white and delicate?"

Then, ashamed and penitent, she hid
her face.

"May God forgive me!" said she.

Doubtless, God did forgive her. But,
taking the inward and outward history
of the first half-day into consideration,
Hepzibah began to fear that the shop
would prove her ruin in a moral and
religious point of view, without contributing very essentially towards even her
temporal welfare.

CHAPTER IV

A DAY BEHIND THE COUNTER

TOWARDS noon, Hepzibah saw an elderly gentleman, large and portly, and of remarkably dignified demeanor, passing slowly along, on the opposite side of the white and dusty street. On coming within the shadow of the Pyncheon-elm, he stopt, and (taking off his hat, meanwhile, to wipe the perspiration from his brow) seemed to scrutinize, with especial interest, the dilapidated and rusty-visaged House of the Seven Gables. He himself, in a very different style, was as well worth looking at as the house. No better model need be sought, nor could have been found, of a very high order of respectability, which, by some indescribable magic, not merely expressed itself in his looks and gestures, but even governed the fashion of his garments, and rendered them all proper and essential to the man. Without appearing to differ, in any tangible way, from other people's clothes, there was yet a wide and rich gravity about them, that must have been a characteristic of the wearer, since it could not be defined as pertaining either to the cut or material. His gold-headed cane, too,—a serviceable staff, of dark, polished wood,—had similar traits, and had it chosen to take a walk by itself, would have been recognized anywhere as a tolerably adequate representative of its master. This character—which showed itself so strikingly in everything about him, and the effect of which we seek to convey to the reader—went no deeper than his station, habits of life, and external circumstances. One perceived him to b personage of mark, influence, and thority; and, especially, you could just as certain that he was opulent if he had exhibited his bank acco or as if you had seen him touching twigs of the Pyncheon-elm, and Mi like, transmuting them to gold.

In his youth, he had probably b considered a handsome man; at present age, his brow was too hea his temples too bare, his remaining too gray, his eye too cold, his lips closely compressed, to bear any rela to mere personal beauty. He would made a good and massive portrait; ter now, perhaps, than at any prev period of his life, although his might grow positively harsh, in process of being fixed upon the can The artist would have found it d able to study his face, and prove capacity for varied expression; to da it with a frown,—to kindle it up a smile.

While the elderly gentleman s looking at the Pyncheon-house, both frown and the smile passed success over his countenance. His eyes r on the shop-window, and, putting a pair of gold-bowed spectacles, w he held in his hand, he minutely veyed Hepzibah's little arrangemer toys and commodities. At first it see not to please him,—nay, to cause exceeding displeasure,—and yet, very next moment, he smiled. Whil latter expression was yet on his he caught a glimpse of Hepzibah,

l involuntarily bent forward to the
dow; and then the smile changed
m acrid and disagreeable to the sun-
st complacency and benevolence. He
ved, with a happy mixture of dignity
l courteous kindliness, and pursued
way.

'There he is!" said Hepzibah to her-
′, gulping down a very bitter emo-
n, and, since she could not rid her-
: of it, trying to drive it back into
heart. "What does he think of it,
vonder? Does it please him? Ah!—
is looking back!"

The gentleman had paused in the
:et, and turned himself half about,
l with his eyes fixed on the shop-
dow. In fact, he wheeled wholly
nd, and commenced a step or two,
if designing to enter the shop; but,
it chanced, his purpose was antici-
:d by Hepzibah's first customer, the
e cannibal of Jim Crow, who, star-
up at the window, was irresistibly
acted by an elephant of gingerbread.
at a grand appetite had this small
nin!—two Jim Crows, immediately
r breakfast!—and now an elephant,
a preliminary whet before dinner!
the time this latter purchase was
pleted, the elderly gentleman had
med his way, and turned the street
ner.

Take it as you like, Cousin Jaf-
!" muttered the maiden lady, as
drew back, after cautiously thrust-
out her head, and looking up and
n the street. "Take it as you like!
l have seen my little shop-window!
l!—What have you to say?—is not
Pyncheon-house my own, while I'm
:?"

fter this incident, Hepzibah re-
:ed to the back parlor, where she

at first caught up a half-finished stocking, and began knitting at it with nervous and irregular jerks; but quickly
finding herself at odds with the stitches,
she threw it aside, and walked hurriedly
about the room. At length, she paused
before the portrait of the stern old
Puritan, her ancestor, and the founder
of the house. In one sense, this picture
had almost faded into the canvas, and
hidden itself behind the duskiness of
age; in another, she could not but fancy
that it had been growing more prominent, and strikingly expressive, ever
since her earliest familiarity with it,
as a child. For, while the physical outline and substance were darkening away
from the beholder's eye, the bold, hard,
and, at the same time, indirect character
of the man, seemed to be brought out
in a kind of spiritual relief. Such an
effect may occasionally be observed in
pictures of antique date. They acquire
a look which an artist (if he have anything like the complacency of artists
now-a-days) would never dream of presenting to a patron as his own characteristic expression, but which, nevertheless, we at once recognize as reflecting
the unlovely truth of a human soul.
In such cases, the painter's deep conception of his subject's inward traits has
wrought itself into the essence of the
picture, and is seen after the superficial
coloring has been rubbed off by time.

While gazing at the portrait, Hepzibah trembled under its eye. Her hereditary reverence made her afraid to judge
the character of the original so harshly
as a perception of the truth compelled
her to do. But still she gazed, because
the face of the picture enabled her—
at least, she fancied so—to read more
accurately, and to a greater depth, the

face which she had just seen in the street.

"This is the very man!" murmured she to herself. "Let Jaffrey Pyncheon smile as he will, there is that look beneath! Put on him a skull-cap, and a band, and a black cloak, and a Bible in one hand and a sword in the other, —then let Jaffrey smile as he might, —nobody would doubt that it was the old Pyncheon come again! He has proved himself the very man to build up a new house! Perhaps, too, to draw down a new curse!"

Thus did Hepzibah bewilder herself with these fantasies of the old time. She had dwelt too much alone, too long in the Pyncheon-house,—until her very brain was impregnated with the dry rot of its timbers. She needed a walk along the noon-day street, to keep her sane.

By the spell of contrast, another portrait rose up before her, painted with more daring flattery than any artist would have ventured upon, but yet so delicately touched that the likeness remained perfect. Malbone's miniature, though from the same original, was far inferior to Hepzibah's air-drawn picture, at which affection and sorrowful remembrance wrought together. Soft, mildly, and cheerfully contemplative, with full, red lips, just on the verge of a smile, which the eyes seemed to herald by a gentle kindling-up of their orbs! Feminine traits, moulded inseparably with those of the other sex! The miniature, likewise, had this last peculiarity; so that you inevitably thought of the original as resembling his mother, and she, a lovely and lovable woman, with perhaps some beautiful infirmity of character, that made it all the pleas-

anter to know, and easier to love ....

"Yes," thought Hepzibah, with g... of which it was only the more tolera... portion that welled up from her h... to her eyelids, "they persecuted ... mother in him! He never was a P... cheon!"

But here the shop-bell rang; it ... like a sound from a remote dista... —so far had Hepzibah descended ... the sepulchral depths of her rem... cences. On entering the shop, she fo... an old man there, a humble residen... Pyncheon-street, and whom, for a g... many years past, she had suffere... be a kind of familiar of the house... was an immemorial personage, ... seemed always to have had a w... head and wrinkles, and never to ... possessed but a single tooth, and ... a half-decayed one, in the front of... upper jaw. Well advanced as Hep... was, she could not remember w... Uncle Venner, as the neighbor... called him, had not gone up and ... the street, stooping a little and dra... his feet heavily over the grave... pavement. But still there was some... tough and vigorous about him, ... not only kept him in daily breath ... enabled him to fill a place which w... else have been vacant in the appar... crowded world. To go of errands, ... his slow and shuffling gait, which ... you doubt how he ever was to a... anywhere; to saw a small house... foot or two of fire-wood, or kno... pieces an old barrel, or split up a ... board, for kindling-stuff; in summ... dig the few yards of garden groun... pertaining to a low-rented tene... and share the produce of his labor ... halves; in winter, to shovel away... snow from the side-walk, or open

the wood-shed or along the clothes-
e; such were some of the essential
ces which Uncle Venner performed
ong at least a score of families.
thin that circle, he claimed the same
t of privilege, and probably felt as
ch warmth of interest, as a clergyman
s in the range of his parishioners.
t that he laid claim to the tithe pig;
, as an analogous mode of reverence,
went his rounds, every morning, to
her up the crumbs of the table and
rflowings of the dinner-pot, as food
a pig of his own.

n his younger days—for, after all,
re was a dim tradition that he had
n, not young, but younger—Uncle
ner was commonly regarded as
er deficient, than otherwise, in his
. In truth, he had virtually pleaded
ty to the charge, by scarcely aiming
uch success as other men seek, and
aking only that humble and modest
, in the intercourse of life, which
ngs to the alleged deficiency. But,
, in his extreme old age,—whether
ere that his long and hard experi-
had actually brightened him, or
his decaying judgment rendered him
capable of fairly measuring himself,
e venerable man made pretensions
o little wisdom, and really enjoyed
credit of it. There was likewise, at
s, a vein of something like poetry
im; it was the moss or wall-flower
is mind in its small dilapidation,
gave a charm to what might have
vulgar and common-place in his
er and middle life. Hepzibah had a
d for him, because his name was
nt in the town, and had formerly
respectable. It was a still better
n for awarding him a specie's of
iar reverence, that Uncle Venner

was himself the most ancient existence,
whether of man or thing, in Pyncheon-
street, except the House of the Seven
Gables, and perhaps the elm that overshadowed it.

This patriarch now presented himself
before Hepzibah, clad in an old blue
coat, which had a fashionable air, and
must have accrued to him from the cast-
off wardrobe of some dashing clerk. As
for his trousers, they were of tow-cloth,
very short in the legs, and bagging down
strangely in the rear, but yet having a
suitableness to his figure which his other
garment entirely lacked. His hat had
relation to no other part of his dress,
and but very little to the head that wore
it. Thus Uncle Venner was a miscellane-
ous old gentleman, partly himself,
but, in good measure, somebody else;
patched together, too, of different
epochs; an epitome of times and
fashions.

"So you have really begun trade,"
said he,—"really begun trade! Well, I'm
glad to see it. Young people should
never live idle in the world, nor old
ones neither, unless when the rheuma-
tize gets hold of them. It has given me
warning already; and in two or three
years longer, I shall think of putting
aside business, and retiring to my farm.
That's yonder—the great brick house,
you know—the workhouse, most folks
call it; but I mean to do my work first,
and go there to be idle and enjoy myself. And I'm glad to see you beginning
to do your work, Miss Hepzibah!"

"Thank you, Uncle Venner," said
Hepzibah, smiling; for she always felt
kindly towards the simple and talkative
old man. Had he been an old woman,
she might probably have repelled the
freedom which she now took in good

part. "It is time for me to begin work, indeed! Or, to speak the truth, I have just begun, when I ought to be giving it up."

"O, never say that, Miss Hepzibah," answered the old man. "You are a young woman yet. Why, I hardly thought myself younger than I am now, it seems so little while ago since I used to see you playing about the door of the old house, quite a small child! Oftener, though, you used to be sitting at the threshold, and looking gravely into the street; for you had always a grave kind of way with you,—a grown-up air, when you were only the height of my knee. It seems as if I saw you now; and your grandfather with his red cloak, and his white wig, and his cocked hat, and his cane, coming out of the house, and stepping so grandly up the street! Those old gentlemen that grew up before the Revolution used to put on grand airs. In my young days, the great man of the town was commonly called King; and his wife, not Queen to be sure, but Lady. Now-a-days, a man would not dare to be called King; and if he feels himself a little above common folks, he only stoops so much the lower to them. I met your cousin, the judge, ten minutes ago; and, in my old tow-cloth trousers, as you see, the judge raised his hat to me, I do believe! At any rate, the judge bowed and smiled!"

"Yes," said Hepzibah, with something bitter stealing unawares into her tone; "my cousin Jaffrey is thought to have a very pleasant smile!"

"And so he has!" replied Uncle Venner. "And that's rather remarkable in a Pyncheon; for, begging your pardon, Miss Hepzibah, they never had the name of being an easy and agreeable set of folks. There was no getting close them. But now, Miss Hepzibah, if old man may be bold to ask, why do Judge Pyncheon, with his great mea step forward, and tell his cousin to sh up her little shop at once? It's for yo credit to be doing something; but not for the judge's credit to let you!"

"We won't talk of this, if you plea Uncle Venner," said Hepzibah, colc "I ought to say, however, that if choose to earn bread for myself, it not Judge Pyncheon's fault. Neither he deserve the blame," added she, m kindly, remembering Uncle Venn privileges of age and humble familiar "if I should, by-and-by, find it c venient to retire with you to y farm."

"And it's no bad place, neither, t farm of mine!" cried the old m cheerily, as if there were someth positively delightful in the prosp "No bad place is the great brick fa house, especially for them that will a good many old cronies there, as be my case. I quite long to be am them, sometimes, of the winter eveni for it is but dull business for a lones elderly man, like me, to be nodding the hour together, with no company his air-tight stove. Summer or wi there's a great deal to be said in fa of my farm. And, take it in the tumn, what can be pleasanter thai spend a whole day on the sunny of a barn or a wood-pile, chatting somebody as old as one's self; or, haps, idling away the time with a nat born simpleton, who knows how t idle, because even our busy Yan never have found out how to put to any use? Upon my word, Miss H bah, I doubt whether I've ever bee

mfortable as I mean to be at my farm,
nich most folks call the workhouse.
ut you,—you're a young woman yet,—
u never need go there! Something still
tter will turn up for you. I'm sure
it!"

Hepzibah fancied that there was
mething peculiar in her venerable
end's look and tone; insomuch, that
e gazed into his face with considerable
rnestness, endeavoring to discover
at secret meaning, if any, might be
king there. Individuals whose affairs
ve reached an utterly desperate crisis
nost invariably keep themselves alive
h hopes, so much the more airily
gnificent, as they have the less of
id matter within their grasp, whereof
mould any judicious and moderate
pectation of good. Thus, all the while
pzibah was perfecting the scheme of
little shop, she had cherished an
acknowledged idea that some harle-
n trick of fortune would intervene
her favor. For example, an uncle—
o had sailed for India, fifty years
ore, and never been heard of since—
ght yet return, and adopt her to be
comfort of his very extreme and
repit age, and adorn her with pearls,
nonds, and oriental shawls and tur-
s, and make her the ultimate heiress
is unreckonable riches. Or the mem-
of parliament, now at the head of
English branch of the family,—with
ch the elder stock, on this side of
Atlantic, had held little or no inter-
rse for the last two centuries,—this
nent gentleman might invite Hep-
h to quit the ruinous House of the
en Gables, and come over to dwell
her kindred at Pyncheon Hall. But,
reasons the most imperative, she
d not yield to this request. It was

more probable, therefore, that the descendants of a Pyncheon who had emi-
grated to Virginia, in some past generation, and become a great planter there,—
hearing of Hepzibah's destitution, and
impelled by the splendid generosity of
character with which their Virginian
mixture must have enriched the New
England blood,—would send her a re-
mittance of a thousand dollars, with a
hint of repeating the favor, annually.
Or—and, surely, anything so undeniably
just could not be beyond the limits of
reasonable anticipation—the great claim
to the heritage of Waldo County might
finally be decided in favor of the Pyncheons; so that, instead of keeping a
cent-shop, Hepzibah would build a
palace, and look down from its highest
tower on hill, dale, forest, field, and
town, as her own share of the ancestral
territory.

These were some of the fantasies
which she had long dreamed about; and,
aided by these, Uncle Venner's casual
attempt at encouragement kindled a
strange festal glory in the poor, bare,
melancholy chambers of her brain, as
if that inner world were suddenly lighted
up with gas. But either he knew nothing
of her castles in the air—as how should
he?—or else her earnest scowl disturbed
his recollection, as it might a more
courageous man's. Instead of pursuing
any weightier topic, Uncle Venner
was pleased to favor Hepzibah with
some sage counsel in her shop-keeping
capacity.

"Give no credit!"—these were some
of his golden maxims,—"Never take
paper money! Look well to your change!
Ring the silver on the four-pound
weight! Shove back all English halfpence and base copper tokens, such as

are very plenty about town! At your leisure hours knit children's woollen socks and mittens! Brew your own yeast, and make your own ginger-beer!"

And while Hepzibah was doing her utmost to digest the hard little pellets of his already uttered wisdom, he gave vent to his final, and what he declared to be his all-important advice, as follows:—

"Put on a bright face for your customers, and smile pleasantly as you hand them what they ask for! A stale article, if you dip it in a good, warm, sunny smile, will go off better than a fresh one that you've scowled upon."

To this last apothegm poor Hepzibah responded with a sigh so deep and heavy that it almost rustled Uncle Venner quite away, like a withered leaf,—as he was,—before an autumnal gale. Recovering himself, however, he bent forward, and, with a good deal of feeling in his ancient visage, beckoned her nearer to him.

"When do you expect him home?" whispered he.

"Whom do you mean?" asked Hepzibah, turning pale.

"Ah! you don't love to talk about it," said Uncle Venner. "Well, well! we'll say no more, though there's word of it, all over town. I remember him, Miss Hepzibah, before he could run alone!"

During the remainder of the day, poor Hepzibah acquitted herself even less creditably, as a shopkeeper, than in her earlier efforts. She appeared to be walking in a dream; or, more truly, the vivid life and reality assumed by her emotions made all outward occurrences unsubstantial, like the teasing phantasms of a half-conscious slumber. She still responded, mechanically, to the frequent summons of the shop-bell, and, at demand of her customers, went pry with vague eyes about the shop, prof ing them one article after another, a thrusting aside—perversely, as most them supposed—the identical thing t asked for. There is sad confusion, deed, when the spirit thus flits away i the past, or into the more awful fut or, in any manner, steps across spaceless boundary betwixt its own gion and the actual world; where body remains to guide itself, as bes may, with little more than the me anism of animal life. It is like de without death's quiet privilege,— freedom from mortal care. Worst of when the actual duties are compri in such petty details as now vexed brooding soul of the old gentlewom As the animosity of fate would hav there was a great influx of custom the course of the afternoon. Hepzi blundered to and fro about her s place of business, committing the n unheard of errors: now stringing twelve, and now seven tallow-can instead of ten to the pound; sel ginger for Scotch snuff, pins for nee and needles for pins; misreckoning change, sometimes to the public d ment, and much oftener to her own; thus she went on, doing her utmos bring chaos back again, until, at close of the day's labor, to her i plicable astonishment, she found money-drawer almost destitute of After all her painful traffic, the w proceeds were perhaps half a dozen pers, and a questionable ninepe which ultimately proved to be co likewise.

At this price, or at whatever p she rejoiced that the day had rea

end. Never before had she had such
ense of the intolerable length of time
t creeps between dawn and sunset,
l of the miserable irksomeness of
'ing aught to do, and of the better
dom that it would be, to lie down
once, in sullen resignation, and let
, and its toils and vexations, trample
r one's prostrate body, as they may!
zibah's final operation was with the
e devourer of Jim Crow and the
hant, who now proposed to eat a
el. In her bewilderment, she offered
first a wooden dragoon, and next a
dful of marbles; neither of which
g adapted to his else omniverous
etite, she hastily held out her whole
aining stock of natural history in
'erbread, and huddled the small cus-
er out of the shop. She then muffled
bell in an unfinished stocking, and
up the oaken bar across the door.
uring the latter process, an omnibus
e to a standstill under the branches
he elm-tree. Hepzibah's heart was
er mouth. Remote and dusky, and
no sunshine on all the intervening
e,. was that region of the Past
ce her only guest might be expected
rrive! Was she to meet him now?
mebody, at all events, was passing
the furthest interior of the omni-
towards its entrance. A gentleman
ted; but it was only to offer his
l to a young girl, whose slender
e, nowise needing such assistance,
lightly descended the steps, and
e an airy little jump from the final
to the sidewalk. She rewarded her
lier with a smile, the cheery glow
hich was seen reflected on his own
as he reëntered the vehicle. The
then turned towards the House of
even Gables; to the door of which,

meanwhile,—not the shop-door, but the
antique portal,—the, omnibus-man had
carried a light trunk and a band-box.
First giving a sharp rap of the old iron
knocker, he left his passenger and her
luggage at the door-step, and departed.

"Who can it be?" thought Hepzibah,
who had been screwing her visual organs
into the acutest focus of which they
were capable. "The girl must have mistaken the house!"

She stole softly into the hall, and,
herself invisible, gazed through the dusty
side-lights of the portal at the young,
blooming, and very cheerful face, which
presented itself for admittance into the
gloomy old mansion. It was a face to
which almost any door would have
opened of its own accord.

The young girl, so fresh, so uncon-
ventional, and yet so orderly and
obedient to common rules, as you at
once recognized her to be, was widely in
contrast, at that moment, with everything about her. The sordid and ugly
luxuriance of gigantic weeds that grew
in the angle of the house, and the heavy
projection that overshadowed her, and
the time-worn frame-work of the door,
—none of these things belonged to her
sphere. But, even as a ray of sunshine,
fall into what dismal place it may, instantaneously creates for itself a propriety in being there, so did it seem
altogether fit that the girl should be
standing at the threshold. It was no less
evidently proper that the door should
swing open to admit her. The maiden
lady herself, sternly inhospitable in her
first purposes, soon began to feel that
the door ought to be shoved back, and
the rusty key be turned in the reluctant
lock.

"Can it be Phœbe?" questioned she

within herself. "It must be little Phœbe; for it can be nobody else,—and there is a look of her father about her, too! But what does she want here? And how like a country cousin, to come down upon a poor body in this way, without so much as a day's notice, or asking whether she would be welcome! Well; she must have a night's lodging, I suppose; and to-morrow the child shall go back to her mother!"

Phœbe, it must be understood, was that one little off-shoot of the Pyncheon race to whom we have already referred, as a native of a rural part of New England, where the old fashions and feelings of relationship are still partially kept up. In her own circle, it was re-garded as by no means improper for kinsfolk to visit one another, witho invitation, or preliminary and ceremo ous warning. Yet, in consideration Miss Hepzibah's recluse way of life letter had actually been written a despatched, conveying information Phœbe's projected visit. This epistle, three or four days past, had been in pocket of the penny-postman, who, ha pening to have no other business Pyncheon-street, had not yet made convenient to call at the House of Seven Gables.

"No!—she can stay only one nigh said Hepzibah, unbolting the door. Clifford were to find her here, it mi disturb him!"

CHAPTER V

MAY AND NOVEMBER

PHŒBE PYNCHEON slept, on the night of her arrival, in a chamber that looked down on the garden of the old house. It fronted towards the east, so that at a very seasonable hour a glow of crimson light came flooding through the window, and bathed the dingy ceiling and paper-hangings in its own hue. There were curtains to Phœbe's bed; a dark, antique canopy and ponderous festoons, of a stuff which had been rich, and even magnificent, in its time; but which now brooded over the girl like a cloud, making a night in that one corner, while elsewhere it was beginning to be day. The morning light, however, soon stole into the aperture at the foot of the bed, betwixt those faded curtains. Finding the new guest there,—with a bloom her cheeks like the morning's own, a gentle stir of departing slumber in limbs, as when an early breeze mo the foliage,—the dawn kissed her br It was the caress which a dewy mai —such as the dawn is, immortall gives to her sleeping sister, partly f the impulse of irresistible fondness, partly as a pretty hint that it is t now to unclose her eyes.

At the touch of those lips of li Phœbe quietly awoke, and, for a ment, did not recognize where she nor how those heavy curtains chan to be festooned around her. Noth indeed, was absolutely plain to her, cept that it was now early morning,

it, whatever might happen next, it
is proper, first of all, to get up and
say her prayers. She was the more inclined to devotion, from the grim aspect of the chamber and its furniture,
especially the tall, stiff chairs; one of
which stood close by her bedside, and
looked as if some old-fashioned personage had been sitting there all night,
and had vanished only just in season
to escape discovery.

When Phœbe was quite dressed, she
peeped out of the window, and saw a
rose-bush in the garden. Being a very
tall one, and of luxurious growth, it
had been propped up against the side of
the house, and was literally covered
with a rare and very beautiful species
of white rose. A large portion of them,
as the girl afterwards discovered, had
blight or mildew at their hearts; but,
viewed at a fair distance, the whole
rose-bush looked as if it had been
brought from Eden that very summer,
together with the mould in which it
grew. The truth was, nevertheless, that
it had been planted by Alice Pyncheon,
—she was Phœbe's great-great-grand-
aunt,—in soil which, reckoning only its
cultivation as a garden-plat, was now
unctuous with nearly two hundred years
of vegetable decay. Growing as they did,
however, out of the old earth, the
flowers still sent a fresh and sweet incense up to their Creator; nor could it
have been the less pure and acceptable,
because Phœbe's young breath mingled
with it, as the fragrance floated past the
window. Hastening down the creaking
and carpetless staircase, she found her
way into the garden, gathered some of
the most perfect of the roses, and
brought them to her chamber.

Little Phœbe was one of those persons who possess, as their exclusive
patrimony, the gift of practical arrangement. It is a kind of natural magic that
enables these favored ones to bring out
the hidden capabilities of things around
them; and particularly to give a look
of comfort and habitableness to any
place which, for however brief a period,
may happen to be their home. A wild
hut of underbrush, tossed together by
wayfarers through the primitive forest,
would acquire the home aspect by one
night's lodging of such a woman, and
would retain it long after her quiet
figure had disappeared into the surrounding shade. No less a portion of
such homely witchcraft was requisite,
to reclaim, as it were, Phœbe's waste,
cheerless, and dusky chamber, which
had been untenanted so long—except by
spiders, and mice, and rats, and ghosts—
that it was all overgrown with the desolation which watches to obliterate every
trace of man's happier hours. What was
precisely Phœbe's process, we find it
impossible to say. She appeared to have
no preliminary design, but gave a touch
here, and another there; brought some
articles of furniture to light, and dragged
others into the shadow; looped up or
let down a window-curtain; and, in the
course of half an hour, had fully succeeded in throwing a kindly and hospitable smile over the apartment. No
longer ago than the night before, it had
resembled nothing so much as the old
maid's heart; for there was neither sunshine nor household-fire in one nor the
other, and, save for ghosts and ghostly
reminiscences, not a guest, for many
years gone-by, had entered the heart or
the chamber.

· There was still another peculiarity of
this inscrutable charm. The bed-cham

ber, no doubt, was a chamber of very great and varied experience, as a scene of human life: the joy of bridal nights had throbbed itself away here; new immortals had first drawn earthly breath here; and here old people had died. But —whether it were the white roses, or whatever the subtile influence might be —a person of delicate instinct would have known, at once, that it was now a maiden's bed-chamber, and had been purified of all former evil and sorrow by her sweet breath and happy thoughts. Her dreams of the past night, being such cheerful ones, had exorcised the gloom, and now haunted the chamber in its stead.

After arranging matters to her satisfaction, Phœbe emerged from her chamber, with a purpose to descend again into the garden. Besides the rose-bush, she had observed several other species of flowers, growing there in a wilderness of neglect, and obstructing one another's development (as is often the parallel case in human society) by their uneducated entanglement and confusion. At the head of the stairs, however, she met Hepzibah, who, it being still early, invited her into a room which she would probably have called her boudoir, had her education embraced any such French phrase. It was strewn about with a few old books, and a work-basket, and a dusty writing-desk; and had, on one side, a large, black article of furniture, of very strange appearance, which the old gentlewoman told Phœbe was a harpsichord. It looked more like a coffin than anything else; and, indeed,— not having been played upon, or opened, for years,—there must have been a vast deal of dead music in it, stifled for want of air. Human finger was hardly

known to have touched its chords si the days of Alice Pyncheon, who learned the sweet accomplishment melody in Europe.

Hepzibah bade her young guest down, and, herself taking a chair n by, looked as earnestly at Phœbe's t little figure as if she expected to right into its springs and motive secr

"Cousin Phœbe," said she, at last really can't see my way clear to k you with me."

These words, however, had not inhospitable bluntness with which t may strike the reader; for the two r tives, in a talk before bedtime, arrived at a certain degree of mu understanding. Hepzibah knew eno to enable her to appreciate the circ stances (resulting from the second n riage of the girl's mother) which m it desirable for Phœbe to establish self in another home. Nor did she interpret Phœbe's character, and genial activity pervading it,—one of most valuable traits of the true N England woman,—which had impe her forth, as might be said, to seek fortune, but with a self-respecting pose to confer as much benefit as could anywise receive. As one of nearest kindred, she had naturally taken herself to Hepzibah, with no of forcing herself on her cousin's tection, but only for a visit of a v or two, which might be indefinitely tended, should it prove for the happi of both.

To Hepzibah's blunt observa therefore, Phœbe replied, as frankly, more cheerfully.

"Dear cousin, I cannot tell ho will be," said she. "But I really t we may suit one another much be n you suppose."

"You are a nice girl,—I see it
inly," continued Hepzibah; "and it is
any question as to that point which
kes me hesitate. But, Phœbe, this
use of mine is but a melancholy place
a young person to be in. It lets in
wind and rain, and the snow, too,
the garret and upper chambers, in
iter-time; but it never lets in the
shine! And as for myself, you see
at I am,—a dismal and lonesome old
man (for I begin to call myself old,
ebe), whose temper, I am afraid, is
e of the best, and whose spirits are
bad as can be. I cannot make your
pleasant, Cousin Phœbe, neither can
much as give you bread to eat."

You will find me a cheerful little
ly," answered Phœbe, smiling, and
with a kind and gentle dignity; "and
ean to earn my bread. You know I
e not been brought up a Pyncheon.
girl learns many things in a New
land village."

Ah! Phœbe," said Hepzibah, sighing,
ur knowledge would do but little for
here! And then it is a wretched
ight, that you should fling away your
ng days in a place like this. Those
eks would not be so rosy, after a
th or two. Look at my face!"—
, indeed, the contrast was very strik-
—"you see how pale I am! It is my
that the dust and continual decay
hese old houses are unwholesome for
lungs."

There is the garden,—the flowers to
aken care of," observed Phœbe. "I
ild keep myself healthy with exer-
in the open air."

And, after all, child," exclaimed
zibah, suddenly arising, as if to dis-
the subject, "it is not for me to

say who shall be a guest or inhabitant
of the old Pyncheon-house. Its master
is coming."

"Do you mean Judge Pyncheon?"
asked Phœbe, in surprise.

"Judge Pyncheon!" answered her
cousin, angrily. "He will hardly cross
the threshold while I live! No, no! But,
Phœbe, you shall see the face of him I
speak of."

She went in quest of the miniature
already described, and returned with
it in her hand. Giving it to Phœbe, she
watched her features narrowly, and with
a certain jealousy as to the mode in
which the girl would show herself
affected by the picture.

"How do you like the face?" asked
Hepzibah.

"It is handsome!—it is very beautiful!" said Phœbe, admiringly. "It is as
sweet a face as a man's can be, or ought
to be. It has something of a child's expression,—and yet not childish,—only,
one feels so very kindly towards him!
He ought never to suffer anything. One
would bear much for the sake of sparing
him toil or sorrow. Who is it, Cousin
Hepzibah?"

"Did you never hear," whispered her
cousin, bending towards her, "of Clifford
Pyncheon?"

"Never! I thought there were no
Pyncheons left, except yourself and our
cousin Jaffrey," answered Phœbe. "And
yet I seem to have heard the name of
Clifford Pyncheon. Yes!—from my
father, or my mother; but has he not
been a long while dead?"

"Well, well, child, perhaps he has!"
said Hepzibah, with a sad, hollow laugh;
"but, in old houses like this, you know,
dead people are very apt to come back
again! We shall see. And, Cousin Phœbe,

since, after all that I have said, your courage does not fail you, we will not part so soon. You are welcome, my child, for the present, to such a home as your kinswoman can offer you."

With this measured, but not exactly cold assurance of a hospitable purpose, Hepzibah kissed her cheek.

They now went below stairs, where Phœbe—not so much assuming the office as attracting it to herself, by the magnetism of innate fitness—took the most active part in preparing breakfast. The mistress of the house, meanwhile, as is usual with persons of her stiff and unmalleable cast, stood mostly aside; willing to lend her aid, yet conscious that her natural inaptitude would be likely to impede the business in hand. Phœbe, and the fire that boiled the teakettle, were equally bright, cheerful, and efficient, in their respective offices. Hepzibah gazed forth from her habitual sluggishness, the necessary result of long solitude, as from another sphere. She could not help being interested, however, and even amused, at the readiness with which her new inmate adapted herself to the circumstances, and brought the house, moreover, and all its rusty old appliances, into a suitableness for her purposes. Whatever she did, too, was done without conscious effort, and with frequent outbreaks of song, which were exceedingly pleasant to the ear. This natural tunefulness made Phœbe seem like a bird in a shadowy tree; or conveyed the idea that the stream of life warbled through her heart as a brook sometimes warbles through a pleasant little dell. It betokened the cheeriness of an active temperament, finding joy in its activity, and, therefore, rendering it beautiful; it

was a New England trait,—the ste old stuff of Puritanism, with a go thread in the web.

Hepzibah brought out some old silv spoons, with the family crest up them, and a China tea-set, painted ov with grotesque figures of man, bird, a beast, in as grotesque a landscape. The pictured people were odd humorists, a world of their own,—a world of viv brilliancy, so far as color went, a still unfaded, although the tea-pot a small cups were as ancient as the c tom itself of tea-drinking.

"Your great-great-great-great-gra mother had these cups, when she v married," said Hepzibah to Phœbe. "S was a Davenport, of a good family. Th were almost the first tea-cups ever se in the colony; and if one of them w to be broken, my heart would bre with it. But it is nonsense to speak about a brittle tea-cup, when I reme ber what my heart has gone thro without breaking."

The cups—not having been used, p haps, since Hepzibah's youth—had c tracted no small burthen of dust, wh Phœbe washed away with so much c and delicacy as to satisfy even the p prietor of this invaluable china.

"What a nice little housewife are!" exclaimed the latter, smiling, a at the same time, frowning so p digiously that the smile was sunsl under a thunder-cloud. "Do you other things as well? Are you as g at your book as you are at wasl tea-cups?"

"Not quite, I am afraid," said Phœ laughing at the form of Hepzib question. "But I was school-mistress the little children in our district, summer, and might have been so st

Ah! 'tis all very well!" observed the
iden lady, drawing herself up.—"But
se things must have come to you
h your mother's blood. I never knew
Pyncheon that had any turn for
m."

t is very queer, but not the less true,
t people are generally quite as vain,
even more so, of their deficiencies,
n of their available gifts; as was
zibah of this native inapplicability,
to speak, of the Pyncheons, to any
ful purpose. She regarded it as an
editary trait; and so, perhaps, it was,
, unfortunately, a morbid one, such
s often generated in families that re-
n long above the surface of society.
efore they left the breakfast-table,
shop-bell rang sharply, and Hepzibah
down the remnant of her final cup
tea, with a look of sallow despair
was truly piteous to behold. In
s of distasteful occupation, the sec-
day is generally worse than the
; we return to the rack with all the
ness of the preceding torture in our
s. At all events, Hepzibah had fully
sfied herself of the impossibility of
becoming wonted to this peevishly
reperous little bell. Ring as often
it might, the sound always smote
n her nervous system rudely and
lenly. And especially now, while,
her crested tea-spoons and antique
a, she was flattering herself with
s of gentility, she felt an unspeak-
disinclination to confront a cus-
er.

Do not trouble yourself, dear cous-
cried Phœbe, starting lightly up.
m shopkeeper to-day."

You, child!" exclaimed Hepzibah.
at can a little country-girl know of
matters?"

"O, I have done all the shopping for
the family, at our village store," said
Phœbe. "And I have had a table at a
fancy fair, and made better sales than
anybody. These things are not to be
learnt; they depend upon a knack, that
comes, I suppose," added she, smiling,
"with one's mother's blood. You shall
see that I am as nice a little saleswoman
as I am a housewife!"

The old gentlewoman stole behind
Phœbe, and peeped from the passage-
way into the shop, to note how she
would manage her undertaking. It was
a case of some intricacy. A very ancient
woman, in a white short gown, and a
green petticoat, with a string of gold
beads about her neck, and what looked
like a night-cap on her head, had brought
a quantity of yarn to barter for the
commodities of the shop. She was probably the very last person in town who
still kept the time-honored spinning-
wheel in constant revolution. It was
worth while to hear the croaking and
hollow tones of the old lady, and the
pleasant voice of Phœbe, mingling in
one twisted thread of talk; and still
better, to contrast their figures,—so
light and bloomy—so decrepit and
dusky,—with only the counter betwixt
them, in one sense, but more than three-
score years, in another. As for the bargain, it was wrinkled slyness and craft
pitted against native truth and sagacity.

"Was not that well done?" asked
Phœbe, laughing, when the customer
was gone.

"Nicely done, indeed, child!" answered Hepzibah. "I could not have
gone through with it nearly so well. As
you say, it must be a knack that belongs
to you on the mother's side."

It is a very genuine admiration, that

with which persons too shy or too awkward to take a due part in the bustling world regard the real actors in life's stirring scenes; so genuine, in fact, that the former are usually fain to make it palatable to their self-love, by assuming that these active and forcible qualities are incompatible with others, which they chose to deem higher and more important. Thus, Hepzibah was well content to acknowledge Phœbe's vastly superior gifts as a shopkeeper; she listened, with compliant ear, to her suggestion of various methods whereby the influx of trade might be increased, and rendered profitable, without a hazardous outlay of capital. She consented that the village maiden should manufacture yeast, both liquid and in cakes; and should brew a certain kind of beer, nectareous to the palate, and of rare stomachic virtues; and, moreover, should bake and exhibit for sale some little spice-cakes, which whosoever tasted would longingly desire to taste again. All such proofs of a ready mind, and skilful handiwork, were highly acceptable to the aristocratic hucksteress, so long as she could murmur to herself, with a grim smile, and a half-natural sigh, and a sentiment of mixed wonder, pity, and growing affection,—

"What a nice little body she is! If she could only be a lady, too!—but that's impossible! Phœbe is no Pyncheon. She takes everything from her mother."

As to Phœbe's not being a lady, or whether she were a lady or no, it was a point, perhaps, difficult to decide, but which could hardly have come up for judgment at all, in any fair and healthy mind. Out of New England, it would be impossible to meet with a person com-

bining so many ladylike attributes w[ith] so many others that form no necess[ary] (if compatible) part of the charact[er] She shocked no canon of taste; she w[as] admirably in keeping with herself, a[nd] never jarred against surrounding c[ir]cumstances. Her figure, to be sure[,] so small as to be almost childlike, a[nd] so elastic that motion seemed as e[asy] or easier to it than rest,—would har[dly] have suited one's idea of a count[ess] Neither did her face—with the bro[wn] ringlets on either side, and the sligh[t] piquant nose, and the wholesome bloo[m,] and the clear shade of tan, and the h[alf] a dozen freckles, friendly remembranc[es] of the April sun and breeze—precis[ely] give us a right to call her beautiful. [But] there was both lustre and depth in [her] eyes. She was very pretty; as grace[ful] as a bird, and graceful much in [the] same way; as pleasant about the ho[use] as a gleam of sunshine, falling on [the] floor through a shadow of twink[ling] leaves, or as a ray of firelight t[hat] dances on the wall, while evening [is] drawing nigh. Instead of discussing [her] claim to rank among ladies, it would [be] preferable to regard Phœbe as the [ex]ample of feminine grace and availab[ility] combined, in a state of society, if th[ere] were any such, where ladies did [not] exist. There it should be woman's o[ffice] to move in the midst of practical affa[irs,] and to gild them all, the very homeli[est] —were it even the scouring of pots [and] kettles,—with an atmosphere of lo[ve]ness and joy.

Such was the sphere of Phœbe. [To] find the born and educated lady, on [the] other hand, we need look no fur[ther] than Hepzibah, our forlorn old maid[, in] her rustling and rusty silks, with [her] deeply-cherished and ridiculous c[on] ousness of long descent, her shadowy ims to princely territory, and, in the y of accomplishment, her recollec- ns, it may be, of having formerly ummed on a harpsichord, and walked ninuet, and worked an antique tapes- -stitch on her sampler. It was a fair allel between new Plebeianism and Gentility.

It really seemed as if the battered age of the House of the Seven Gables, ck and heavy-browed as it still cer- nly looked, must have shown a kind cheerfulness glimmering through its sky windows, as Phœbe passed to and in the interior. Otherwise, it is im- ssible to explain how the people of neighborhood so soon became aware the girl's presence. There was a great of custom, setting steadily in, from ut ten o'clock until towards noon, elaxing, somewhat, at dinner-time, re-commencing in the afternoon, l, finally, dying away a half an hour so before the long day's sunset. One the staunchest patrons was little Ned ggins, the devourer of Jim Crow and elephant, who to-day had signalized omnivorous prowess by swallowing dromedaries and a locomotive. œbe laughed, as she summed up her regate of sales, upon the slate, while pzibah, first drawing on a pair of silk ves, reckoned over the sordid accu- lation of copper coin, not without er intermixed, that had jingled into till.

We must renew our stock, Cousin pzibah!" cried the little saleswoman. ie gingerbread figures are all gone, so are those Dutch wooden milk- ds, and most of our other playthings. ere has been constant inquiry for ap raisins, and a great cry for whis-

tles, and trumpets, and Jew's-harps; and at least a dozen little boys have asked for molasses-candy. And we must contrive to get a peck of russet apples, late in the season as it is. But, dear cousin, what an enormous heap of cop- per! Positively a copper mountain!"

"Well done! well done! well done!" quoth Uncle Venner, who had taken oc- casion to shuffle in and out of the shop several times, in the course of the day. "Here's a girl that will never end her days at my farm! Bless my eyes, what a brisk little soul!"

"Yes, Phœbe is a nice girl!" said Hepzibah, with a scowl of austere ap- probation. "But, Uncle Venner, you have known the family a great many years. Can you tell me whether there ever was a Pyncheon whom she takes after?"

"I don't believe there ever was," an- swered the venerable man. "At any rate, it never was my luck to see her like among them, nor, for that matter, any- where else. I've seen a great deal of the world, not only in people's kitchens and back-yards, but at the street-corners, and on the wharves, and in other places where my business calls me; and I'm free to say, Miss Hepzibah, that I never knew a human creature do her work so much like one of God's angels as this child Phœbe does!"

Uncle Venner's eulogium, if it appear rather too high-strained for the person and occasion, had, nevertheless, a sense in which it was both subtle and true. There was a spiritual quality in Phœbe's activity. The life of the long and busy day—spent in occupations that might so easily have taken a squalid and ugly aspect—had been made pleasant, and even lovely, by the spontaneous grace with which these homely duties seemed to bloom out of her character; so that labor, while she dealt with it, had the easy and flexible charm of play. Angels do not toil, but let their good works grow out of them; and so did Phœbe.

The two relatives—the young maid and the old one—found time, before nightfall, in the intervals of trade, to make rapid advances towards affection and confidence. A recluse, like Hepzibah, usually displays remarkable frankness, and at least temporary affability, on being absolutely cornered, and brought to the point of personal intercourse; like the angel whom Jacob wrestled with, she is ready to bless you, when once overcome.

The old gentlewoman took a dreary and proud satisfaction in leading Phœbe from room to room of the house, and recounting the traditions with which, as we may say, the walls were lugubriously frescoed. She showed the indentations made by the lieutenant-governor's sword-hilt in the door-panels of the apartment where old Colonel Pyncheon, a dead host, had received his affrighted visitors with an awful frown. The dusky terror of that frown, Hepzibah observed, was thought to be lingering ever since in the passage-way. She bade Phœbe step into one of the tall chairs and inspect the ancient map of the Pyncheon territory at the eastward. In a tract of land on which she laid her finger, there existed a silver mine, the locality of which was precisely pointed out in some memoranda of Colonel Pyncheon himself, but only to be made known when the family claim should be recognized by government. Thus it was for the interest of all New England that the Pyncheons should have justice done them.

She told, too, how that there was doubtedly an immense treasure of E[n]glish guineas hidden somewhere ab[out] the house, or in the cellar, or poss[ibly] in the garden.

"If you should happen to find [it], Phœbe," said Hepzibah, glancing a[side] at her, with a grim yet kindly smile, "[I] will tie up the shop-bell for good [and] all!"

"Yes, dear cousin," answered Phœ[be,] "but, in the meantime, I hear so[me]body ringing it!"

When the customer was gone, H[ep]zibah talked rather vaguely, and [at] great length, about a certain Alice P[yn]cheon, who had been exceedingly bea[uti]ful and accomplished in her lifetim[e,] hundred years ago. The fragrance [of] her rich and delightful character [still] lingered about the place where she [had] lived, as a dried rose-bud scents [a] drawer where it has withered [and] perished. This lovely Alice had met [with] some great and mysterious calam[ity,] and had grown thin and white, [and] gradually faded out of the world. [But] even now, she was supposed to ha[ve] the House of the Seven Gables, an[d] great many times,—especially when [one] of the Pyncheons was to die,—she [had] been heard playing sadly and beautif[ully] on the harpsichord. One of these tu[nes,] just as it had sounded from her spiri[tual] touch, had been written down by [an] amateur of music; it was so exquis[itely] mournful that nobody, to this [day,] could bear to hear it played, unless w[hen] a great sorrow had made them know [the] still profounder sweetness of it.

"Was it the same harpsichord [that] you showed me?" inquired Phœbe.

"The very same," said Hepzibah. [" It] was Alice Pyncheon's harpsichord. W[hen]

~as learning music, my father would
er let me open it. So, as I could
y play on my teacher's instrument, I
e forgotten all my music, long ago."
Leaving these antique themes, the old
y began to talk about the daguerreo-
ist, whom, as he seemed to be a well-
ining and orderly young man, and in
row circumstances, she had per-
ted to take up his residence in one
he seven gables. But, on seeing more
Mr. Holgrave, she hardly knew what
make of him. He had the strangest
panions imaginable: men with long
rds, and dressed in linen blouses,
other such new-fangled and ill-
ng garments; reformers, temperance
urers, and all manner of cross-look-
philanthropists; community-men
come-outers, as Hepzibah believed,
acknowledged no law, and ate no
d food, but lived on the scent of
er people's cookery, and turned up
r noses at the fare. As for the da-
rreotypist, she had read a paragraph
penny-paper, the other day, accus-
him of making a speech full of wild
disorganizing matter, at a meeting
his banditti-like associates. For her
part, she had reason to believe that

he practised animal magnetism, and, if
such things were in fashion now-a-days,
should be apt to suspect him of studying
the Black Art, up there in his lonesome
chamber.

"But, dear cousin," said Phœbe, "if
the young man is so dangerous, why do
you let him stay? If he does nothing
worse, he may set the house on fire!"

"Why, sometimes," answered Hepzibah, "I have seriously made it a question, whether I ought not to send him
away. But, with all his oddities, he is a
quiet kind of a person, and has such a
way of taking hold of one's mind, that,
without exactly liking him (for I don't
know enough of the young man), I
should be sorry to lose sight of him
entirely. A woman clings to slight acquaintances, when she lives so much
alone as I do."

"But if Mr. Holgrave is a lawless person!" remonstrated Phœbe, a part of
whose essence it was to keep within the
limits of law.

"O!" said Hepzibah, carelessly,—for,
formal as she was, still, in her life's
experience, she had gnashed her teeth
against human law,—"I suppose he has
a law of his own!"

CHAPTER

MAULE'S WELL

FTER an early tea, the little country-
strayed into the garden. The en-
ure had formerly been very exten-
, but was now contracted within
ll compass, and hemmed about,
ly by high wooden fences, and

partly by the out-buildings of houses
that stood on another street. In its
centre was a grass-plat, surrounding a
ruinous little structure, which showed
just enough of its original design to indicate that it had once been a summer-

house. A hop-vine, springing from last year's root, was beginning to clamber over it, but would be long in covering the roof with its green mantle. Three of the seven gables either fronted or looked side-ways, with a dark solemnity of aspect, down into the garden.

The black, rich soil had fed itself with the decay of a long period of time; such as fallen leaves, the petals of flowers, and the stalks and seed-vessels of vagrant and lawless plants, more useful after their death than ever while flaunting in the sun. The evil of these departed years would naturally have sprung up again, in such rank weeds (symbolic of the transmitted vices of society) as are always prone to root themselves about human dwellings. Phœbe saw, however, that their growth must have been checked by a degree of careful labor, bestowed daily and systematically on the garden. The white double rose-bush had evidently been propped up anew against the house, since the commencement of the season; and a pear-tree and three damson-trees, which, except a row of currant-bushes, constituted the only varieties of fruit, bore marks of the recent amputation of several superfluous or defective limbs. There were also a few species of antique and hereditary flowers, in no very flourishing condition, but scrupulously weeded; as if some person, either out of love or curiosity, had been anxious to bring them to such perfection as they were capable of attaining. The remainder of the garden presented a well-selected assortment of esculent vegetables, in a praiseworthy state of advancement. Summer squashes, almost in their golden blossom; cucumbers, now evincing a tendency to spread away from the main

stock, and ramble far and wide; two three rows of string-beans, and as ma more that were about to festoon the selves on poles; tomatoes, occupyin site so sheltered and sunny that plants were already gigantic, a promised an early and abundant harve

Phœbe wondered whose care and it could have been that had plant these vegetables, and kept the soil clean and orderly. Not, surely, her c sin Hepzibah's, who had no taste spirits for the lady-like employment cultivating flowers, and—with her cluse habits, and tendency to shel herself within the dismal shadow of house—would hardly have come for under the speck of open sky, to w and hoe among the fraternity of be and squashes.

It being her first day of complete trangement from rural objects, Pho found an unexpected charm in this li nook of grass, and foliage, and aris cratic flowers, and plebeian vegetab The eye of Heaven seemed to look do into it pleasantly, and with a pecul smile, as if glad to perceive that ture, elsewhere overwhelmed, and dri out of the dusty town, had here b able to retain a breathing-place. spot acquired a somewhat wilder gra and yet a very gentle one, from the f that a pair of robins had built th nest in the pear-tree, and were mak themselves exceedingly busy and ha in the dark intricacy of its boughs. B too,—strange to say,—had thought worth their while to come hither, p sibly from the range of hives bes some farm-house, miles away. H many aerial voyages might they h made, in quest of honey, or honey-lad betwixt dawn and sunset! Yet, late

now was, there still arose a pleasant
n out of one or two of the squash-
ssoms, in the depths of which these
·s were plying their golden labor.
ere was one other object in the gar-
ᵪ which nature might fairly claim as
 inalienable property, in spite of
ᵪtever man could do to render it his
ᵪ. This was a fountain, set round
ᵪh a rim of old, mossy stones, and
ᵪed, in its bed, with what appeared to
 a sort of Mosaic-work of variously
ᵪred pebbles. The play and slight
ᵪation of the water, in its upward
ᵪh, wrought magically with these
ᵪegated pebbles, and made a con-
ᵪally shifting apparition of quaint
ᵪres, vanishing too suddenly to be
ᵪnable. Thence, swelling over the rim
ᵪmoss-grown stones, the water stole
ᵪy under the fence, through what we
ᵪet to call a gutter, rather than a
ᵪnnel.

ᵪor must we forget to mention a hen-
ᵪp of very reverend antiquity that
ᵪd in the further corner of the gar-
ᵪ, not a great way from the fountain.
ᵪow contained only Chanticleer, his
ᵪ wives, and a solitary chicken. All
ᵪhem were pure specimens of a breed
ᵪch had been transmitted down as an
ᵪ-loom in the Pyncheon family, and
ᵪe said, while in their prime, to have
ᵪined almost the size of turkeys, and,
ᵪthe score of delicate flesh, to be fit
ᵪ a prince's table. In proof of the
ᵪhenticity of this legendary renown,
ᵪzibah could have exhibited the shell
ᵪa great egg, which an ostrich need
ᵪlly have been ashamed of. Be that
ᵪt might, the hens were now scarcely
ᵪer than pigeons, and had a queer,
ᵪy, withered aspect, and a gouty
ᵪl of movement, and a sleepy and

melancholy tone throughout all the
variations of their clucking and cackling.
It was evident that the race had degen-
erated, like many a noble race besides,
in consequence of too strict a watchfulness to keep it pure. These feathered
people had existed too long in their
distinct variety; a fact of which the
present representatives, judging by their
lugubrious deportment, seemed to be
aware. They kept themselves alive, unquestionably, and laid now and then an
egg, and hatched a chicken; not for any
pleasure of their own, but that the
world might not absolutely lose what
had once been so admirable a breed of
fowls. The distinguishing mark of the
hens was a crest of lamentably scanty
growth, in these latter days, but so
oddly and wickedly analogous to Hepzibah's turban, that Phœbe—to the
poignant distress of her conscience, but
inevitably—was led to fancy a general
resemblance betwixt these forlorn bipeds
and her respectable relative.

The girl ran into the house to get
some crumbs of bread, cold potatoes, and
other such scraps as were suitable to the
accommodating appetite of fowls. Returning, she gave a peculiar call, which
they seemed to recognize. The chicken
crept through the pales of the coop, and
ran, with some show of liveliness to
her feet; while Chanticleer and the
ladies of his household regarded her with
queer, sidelong glances, and then
croaked one to another, as if communicating their sage opinions of her
character. So wise, as well as antique,
was their aspect, as to give color to the
idea, not merely that they were the
descendants of a time-honored race, but
that they had existed, in their individual
capacity, ever since the House of the

Seven Gables was founded, and were somehow mixed up with its destiny. They were a species of tutelary sprite, or Banshee; although winged and feathered differently from most other guardian angels.

"Here, you odd little chicken!" said Phœbe; "here are some nice crumbs for you!"

The chicken, hereupon, though almost as venerable in appearance as its mother, —possessing, indeed, the whole antiquity of its progenitors, in miniature, —mustered vivacity enough to flutter upward and alight on Phœbe's shoulder.

"That little fowl pays you a high compliment!" said a voice behind Phœbe.

Turning quickly, she was surprised at sight of a young man, who had found access into the garden by a door opening out of another gable than that whence she had emerged. He had a hoe in his hand, and, while Phœbe was gone in quest of the crumbs, had begun to busy himself with drawing up fresh earth about the roots of the tomatoes.

"The chicken really treats you like an old acquaintance," continued he, in a quiet way, while a smile made his face pleasanter than Phœbe at first fancied it. "Those venerable personages in the coop, too, seem very affably disposed. You are lucky to be in their good graces so soon! They have known me much longer, but never honor me with any familiarity, though hardly a day passes without my bringing them food. Miss Hepzibah, I suppose, will interweave the fact with her other traditions, and set it down that the fowls know you to be a Pyncheon!"

"The secret is," said Phœbe, smiling, "that I have learned how to talk with hens and chickens."

"Ah! but these hens," answered young man,—"these hens of aristocr lineage would scorn to understand vulgar language of a barn-yard f I prefer to think,—and so would N Hepzibah,—that they recognize family tone. For you are a Pynched

"My name is Phœbe Pyncheon," the girl, with a manner of some rese: for she was aware that her new quaintance could be no othei than daguerreotypist, of whose lawless pensities the old maid had given h disagreeable idea. "I did not know my cousin Hepzibah's garden was u another person's care."

"Yes," said Holgrave, "I dig, and and weed, in this black old earth, the sake of refreshing myself with v little nature and simplicity may be in it, after men have so long sown reaped here. I turn up the earth by of pastime. My sober occupation far as I have any, is with a lighter terial. In short, I make pictures ou sunshine; and, not to be too n dazzled with my own trade, I have vailed with Miss Hepzibah to let lodge in one of these dusky gables. like a bandage over one's eyes, to c into it. But would you like to se specimen of my productions?"

"A daguerreotype likeness, do mean?" asked Phœbe, with less rese for, in spite of prejudice, her own yo fulness sprang forward to meet his don't much like pictures of that so they are so hard and stern; bes dodging away from the eye, and tr to escape altogether. They are consc of looking very unamiable, I supp and therefore hate to be seen."

"If you would permit me," said artist, looking at Phœbe, "I should

try whether the daguerreotype can
g out disagreeable traits on a per-
ly amiable face. But there certainly,
uth in what you have said. Most of
likenesses do look unamiable; but
very sufficient reason, I fancy, is,
use the originals are so. There is a
derful insight in Heaven's broad and
ple sunshine. While we give it credit
for depicting the merest surface,
ctually brings out the secret char-
r with a truth that no painter would
venture upon, even could he detect
There is, at least, no flattery in my
ible line of art. Now, here is a like-
which I have taken over and over
n, and still with no better result.
the original wears, to common eyes,
ery different expression. It would
ify me to have your judgment on
character."

e exhibited a daguerreotype minia-
, in a morocco case. Phœbe merely
ced at it and gave it back.

I know the face," she replied; "for
stern eye has been following me
it, all day. It is my Puritan ancestor,
hangs yonder in the parlor. To be
, you have found some way of
ving the portrait without its black
et cap and gray beard, and have
n him a modern coat and satin
at, instead of his cloak and band.
on't think him improved by your
ations."

You would have seen other differ-
s, had you looked a little longer,"
Holgrave, laughing, yet apparently
h struck. "I can assure you that
is a modern face, and one which
will very probably meet. Now, the
arkable point is, that the original
rs, to the world's eye,—and, for
it I know, to his most intimate

friends,—an exceedingly pleasant countenance, indicative of benevolence,
openness of heart, sunny good-humor,
and other praiseworthy qualities of that
cast. The sun, as you see, tells quite
another story, and will not be coaxed
out of it, after half a dozen patient attempts on my part. Here we have the
man, sly, subtle, hard, imperious, and,
withal, cold as ice. Look at that eye!
Would you like to be at its mercy? At
that mouth! Could it ever smile? And
yet, if you could only see the benign
smile of the original! It is so much the
more unfortunate, as he is a public
character of some eminence, and the
likeness was intended to be engraved."

"Well, I don't wish to see it any
more," observed Phœbe, turning away
her eyes. "It is certainly very like the
old portrait. But my cousin Hepzibah
has another picture,—a miniature. If
the original is still in the world, I think
he might defy the sun to make him look
stern and hard."

"You have seen that picture, then!"
exclaimed the artist, with an expression
of much interest. "I never did, but have
a great curiosity to do so. And you
judge favorably of the face?"

"There never was a sweeter one," said
Phœbe. "It is almost too soft and gentle
for a man's."

"Is there nothing wild in the eye?"
continued Holgrave, so earnestly that it
embarrassed Phœbe, as did also the
quiet freedom with which he presumed
on their so recent acquaintance. "Is
there nothing dark or sinister, anywhere? Could you not conceive the
original to have been guilty of a great
crime?"

"It is nonsense," said Phœbe, a little
impatiently, "for us to talk about a

picture which you have never seen. You mistake it for some other. A crime, indeed! Since you are a friend of my cousin Hepzibah's, you should ask her to show you the picture."

"It will suit my purpose still better to see the original," replied the daguerreotypist, coolly. "As to his character, we need not discuss its points; they have already been settled by a competent tribunal, or one which called itself competent. But, stay? Do not go yet, if you please! I have a proposition to make you."

Phœbe was on the point of retreating, but turned back, with some hesitation; for she did not exactly comprehend his manner, although, on better observation, its feature seemed rather to be lack of ceremony than any approach to offensive rudeness. There was an odd kind of authority, too, in what he now proceeded to say, rather as if the garden were his own than a place to which he was admitted merely by Hepzibah's courtesy.

"If agreeable to you," he observed, "it would give me pleasure to turn over these flowers, and those ancient and respectable fowls, to your care. Coming fresh from country air and occupations, you will soon feel the need of some such out-of-door employment. My own sphere does not so much lie among flowers. You can trim and tend them, therefore, as you please; and I will ask only the least trifle of a blossom, now and then, in exchange for all the good, honest kitchen-vegetables with which I propose to enrich Miss Hepzibah's table. So we will be fellow-laborers, somewhat on the community system."

Silently, and rather surprised at her own compliance, Phœbe accordingly be-took herself to weeding a flower-b but busied herself still more with cog tions respecting this young man, w whom she so unexpectedly found h self on terms approaching to familiar. She did not altogether like him. character perplexed the little count girl, as it might a more practised server; for, while the tone of his c versation had generally been play the impression left on her mind that of gravity, and, except as his yo modified it, almost sternness. She belled, as it were, against a certain m netic element in the artist's natu which he exercised towards her, possi without being conscious of it.

After a little while, the twilight, de ened by the shadows of the fruit-tre and the surrounding buildings, threw obscurity over the garden.

"There," said Holgrave, "it is t to give over work! That last strike the hoe has cut off a beanstalk. Go night, Miss Phœbe Pyncheon! bright day, if you will put one of th rose-buds in your hair, and come to rooms in Central-street, I will seize purest ray of sunshine, and make a ture of the flower and its wearer."

He retired towards his own solit gable, but turned his head, on reach the door, and called to Phœbe, wit tone which certainly had laughter ir yet which seemed to be more than in earnest.

"Be careful not to drink at Mau well!" said he. "Neither drink nor ba your face in it!"

"Maule's well!" answered Phœbe. that it with the rim of mossy sto I have no thought of drinking the but why not?"

"O," rejoined the daguerreotyp

cause, like an old lady's cup of tea,
s water bewitched!"

Ie vanished; and Phœbe, lingering
10ment, saw a glimmering light, and
1 the steady beam of a lamp, in a
1mber of the gable. On returning into
0zibah's department of the house,
found the low-studded parlor so dim
1 dusky that her eyes could not pene-
:e the interior. She was indistinctly
1re, however, that the gaunt figure
the old gentlewoman was sitting in
of the straight-back chairs, a little
1hdrawn from the window, the faint
1m of which showed the blanched
2ness of her cheek, turned sideway
ards a corner.

Shall I light a lamp, Cousin Hep-
1h?" she asked.

Do, if you please, my dear child,"
wered Hepzibah. "But put it on the
1e in the corner of the passage. My
3 are weak; and I can seldom bear
lamp-light on them."

Vhat an instrument is the human
:e! How wonderfully responsive to
ry emotion of the human soul! In
0zibah's tone, at that moment, there
a certain rich depth and moisture,
f the words, common-place as they
e, had been steeped in the warmth
her heart. Again, while lighting the
p in the kitchen, Phœbe fancied that
cousin spoke to her.

In a moment, cousin!" answered she.
"These matches just glimmer, and
0ut."

'ut, instead of a response from Hep-
h, she seemed to hear the murmur
1n unknown voice. It was strangely
3tinct, however, and less like articu-
words than an unshaped sound,
1 as would be the utterance of feel-
and sympathy, rather than of the

intellect. So vague was it, that its impression or echo in Phœbe's mind was
that of unreality. She concluded that she
must have mistaken some other sound
for that of the human voice; or else
that it was altogether in her fancy.

She set the lighted lamp in the passage, and again entered the parlor. Hepzibah's form, though its sable outline
mingled with the dusk, was now less
imperfectly visible. In the remoter parts
of the room, however, its walls being
so ill adapted to reflect light, there was
nearly the same obscurity as before.

"Cousin," said Phœbe, "did you speak
to me just now?"

"No, child!" replied Hepzibah.

Fewer words than before, but with
the same mysterious music in them!
Mellow, melancholy, yet not mournful,
the tone seemed to gush up out of the
deep well of Hepzibah's heart, all
steeped in its profoundest emotion.
There was a tremor in it, too, that—
as all strong feeling is electric—partly
communicated itself to Phœbe. The girl
sat silently for a moment. But soon, her
senses being very acute, she became
conscious of an irregular respiration in
an obscure corner of the room. Her
physical organization, moreover, being
at once delicate and healthy, gave her
a perception, operating with almost the
effect of a spiritual medium, that somebody was near at hand.

"My dear cousin," asked she, over-
coming an indefinable reluctance, "is
there not some one in the room with
us?"

"Phœbe, my dear little girl," said
Hepzibah, after a moment's pause, "you
were up betimes, and have been busy
all day. Pray go to bed; for I am sure
you must need rest. I will sit in the

parlor a while, and collect my thoughts. It has been my custom for more years, child, than you have lived!"

While thus dismissing her, the maiden lady stept forward, kissed Phœbe, and pressed her to her heart, which beat against the girl's bosom with a strong, high, and tumultuous swell. How came there to be so much love in this desolate old heart, that it could afford to well over this abundantly?

"Good-night, cousin," said Phœbe, strangely affected by Hepzibah's manner. "If you begin to love me, I am glad!"

She retired to her chamber, but not soon fall asleep, nor then very foundly. At some uncertain period the depths of night, and, as it w through the thin veil of a dream, was conscious of a footstep moun the stairs, heavily, but not with f and decision. The voice of Hepzi with a hush through it, was going along with the footsteps; and, ag responsive to her cousin's voice, Ph heard that strange, vague murr which might be likened to an indist shadow of human utterance.

CHAPTER VII

THE GUEST

WHEN Phœbe awoke,—which she did with the early twittering of the conjugal couple of robins in the pear-tree, —she heard movements below stairs, and, hastening down, found Hepzibah already in the kitchen. She stood by a window, holding a book in close contiguity to her nose, as if with the hope of gaining an olfactory acquaintance with its contents, since her imperfect vision made it not very easy to read them. If any volume could have manifested its essential wisdom in the mode suggested, it would certainly have been the one now in Hepzibah's hand; and the kitchen, in such an event, would forthwith have steamed with the fragrance of venison, turkeys, capons, larded partridges, puddings, cakes, and Christmas-pies, in all manner of elaborate mixture and concoction. It was a cook-

ery book, full of innumerable fashions of English dishes, and i trated with engravings, which re sented the arrangements of the tab such banquets as it might have befi a nobleman to give, in the great ha his castle. And, amid these rich potent devices of the culinary art one of which, probably, had been tes within the memory of any man's gr father), poor Hepzibah was seeking some nimble little titbit, which, what skill she had, and such mate as were at hand, she might toss up breakfast.

Soon, with a deep sigh, she put a the savory volume, and inquired Phœbe whether old Speckle, as called one of the hens, had laid an the preceding day. Phœbe ran to but returned without the expe

sure in her hand. At that instant,
ever, the blast of a fish-dealer's
ch was heard, announcing his ap-
ch along the street. With energetic
at the shop-window, Hepzibah sumed the man in, and made purchase
what he warranted as the finest
kerel in his cart, and as fat a one as
he felt with his finger so early in
season. Requesting Phœbe to roast
e coffee,—which she casually ob-
ed was the real Mocha, and so long
that each of the small berries
t to be worth its weight in gold,—
maiden lady heaped fuel into the
receptacle of the ancient fireplace
uch quantity as soon to drive the
ring dusk out of the kitchen. The
try-girl, willing to give her utmost
tance, proposed to make an In-
cake, after her mother's peculiar
od, of easy manufacture, and which
could vouch for as possessing a rich-
, and, if rightly prepared, a delicacy,
ualled by any other mode of break-
-cake. Hepzibah, gladly assenting,
itchen was soon the scene of savory
aration. Perchance, amid their
er element of smoke, which eddied
n from the ill-constructed chimney,
ghosts of departed cook-maids
ed wonderingly on, or peeped down
great breadth of the flue, despising
simplicity of the projected meal,
ineffectually pining to thrust their
owy hands into each inchoate dish.
half-starved rats, at any rate, stole
ly out of their hiding-places, and
n their hind-legs, snuffing the funny
osphere, and wistfully awaiting an
ortunity to nibble.
epzibah had no natural turn for
ery, and, to say the truth, had
y incurred her present meagreness,

by often choosing to go without her
dinner, rather than be attendant on the
rotation of the spit, or ebullition of the
pot. Her zeal over the fire, therefore,
was quite an heroic test of sentiment.
It was touching, and positively worthy
of tears (if Phœbe, the only spectator,
except the rats and ghosts aforesaid,
had not been better employed than in
shedding them), to see her rake out a
bed of fresh and glowing coals, and
proceed to broil the mackerel. Her
usually pale cheeks were all a-blaze with
heat and hurry. She watched the fish
with as much tender care and minuteness of attention as if,—we know not
how to express it otherwise,—as if her
own heart were on the gridiron, and
her immortal happiness were involved in
its being done precisely to a turn!

Life, within doors, has few pleasanter
prospects than a neatly-arranged and
well-provisioned breakfast-table. We
come to it freshly, in the dewy youth
of the day, and when our spiritual and
sensual elements are in better accord
than at a later period; so that the material delights of the morning meal are
capable of being fully enjoyed, without
any very grievous reproaches, whether
gastric or conscientious, for yielding
even a trifle over-much to the animal
department of our nature. The thoughts,
too, that run around the ring of familiar
guests, have a piquancy and mirthful-
ness, and oftentimes a vivid truth,
which more rarely find their way into
the elaborate intercourse of dinner. Hepzibah's small and ancient table, supported on its slender and graceful legs,
and covered with a cloth of the richest
damask, looked worthy to be the scene
and centre of one of the cheerfullest of
parties. The vapor of the broiled fish

arose like incense from the shrine of a barbarian idol, while the fragrance of the Mocha might have gratified the nostrils of a tutelary Lar, or whatever power has scope over a modern breakfast-table. Phœbe's Indian cakes were the sweetest offering of all,—in their hue befitting the rustic altars of the innocent and golden age,—or, so brightly yellow were they, resembling some of the bread which was changed to glistening gold, when Midas tried to eat it. The butter must not be forgotten,—butter which Phœbe herself had churned, in her own rural home, and brought it to her cousin as a propitiatory gift,— smelling of clover-blossoms, and diffusing the charm of pastoral scenery through the dark-panelled parlor. All this, with the quaint gorgeousness of the old China cups and saucers, and the crested spoons, and a silver cream-jug (Hepzibah's only other article of plate, and shaped like the rudest porringer), set out a board at which the stateliest of old Colonel Pyncheon's guests need not have scorned to take his place. But the Puritan's face scowled down out of the picture, as if nothing on the table pleased his appetite.

By way of contributing what grace she could, Phœbe gathered some roses and a few other flowers, possessing either scent or beauty, and arranged them in a glass pitcher, which, having long ago lost its handle, was so much the fitter for a flower-vase. The early sunshine—as fresh as that which peeped into Eve's bower, while she and Adam sat at breakfast there—came twinkling through the branches of the pear-tree, and fell quite across the table. All was now ready. There were chairs and plates for three. A chair and plate for Hepzi-

bah,—the same for Phœbe,—but w other guest did her cousin look f

Throughout this preparation, th had been a constant tremor in Hep bah's frame; an agitation so power that Phœbe could see the quivering her gaunt shadow, as thrown by fire-light on the kitchen wall, or the sunshine on the parlor floor. manifestations were so various, agreed so little with one another, t the girl knew not what to make of Sometimes it seemed an ecstasy of light and happiness. At such mome Hepzibah would fling out her arms enfold Phœbe in them, and kiss cheek as tenderly as ever her mot had; she appeared to do so by an evitable impulse, and as if her bos were oppressed with tenderness, which she must needs pour out a lit in order to gain breathing-room. next moment, without any visible ca for the change, her unwonted joy shr back, appalled as it were, and clot itself in mourning; or it ran and itself, so to speak, in the dungeon her heart, where it had long chained, while a cold, spectral sor took the place of the imprisoned that was afraid to be enfranchised sorrow as black as that was bright. often broke into a little, nervous, l teric laugh, more touching than tears could be; and forthwith, as i try which was the most touching gust of tears would follow, or perl the laughter and tears came both once, and surrounded our poor I zibah, in a moral sense, with a l of pale, dim rainbow. Towards Phc as we have said, she was affection —far tenderer than ever before, in t brief acquaintance, except for that

on the preceding night,—yet with
ontinually recurring pettishness and
ability. She would speak sharply to
; then, throwing aside all the
ched reserve of her ordinary man-
ask pardon, and the next instant
w the just-forgiven injury.

t last, when their mutual labor was
finished, she took Phœbe's hand in
own trembling one.

Bear with me, my dear child," she
d; "for truly my heart is full to
brim! Bear with me; for I love you,
be, though I speak so roughly!
k nothing of it, dearest child! By-
-by, I shall be kind, and only kind!"

My dearest cousin, cannot you tell
what has happened?" asked Phœbe,
a sunny and tearful sympathy.
at is it that moves you so?"

Hush! hush! He is coming!" whis-
d Hepzibah, hastily wiping her eyes.
him see you first, Phœbe; for you
young and rosy, and cannot help
ng a smile break out, whether or
He always liked bright faces! And
e is old, now, and the tears are
ly dry on it. He never could abide
s. There; draw the curtain a little,
hat the shadow may fall across his
of the table! But let there be a
l deal of sunshine, too; for he never
fond of gloom, as some people are.
has had but little sunshine in his
—poor Clifford,—and, oh, what a
k shadow! Poor, poor Clifford!"

hus murmuring, in an under tone,
speaking rather to her own heart
to Phœbe, the old gentlewoman
ed on tiptoe about the room, mak-
such arrangements as suggested
selves at the crisis.

eanwhile, there was a step in the
age-way, above stairs. Phœbe recognized it as the same which had passed
upward, as through her dream, in the
night-time. The approaching guest, whoever it might be, appeared to pause at
the head of the staircase; he paused
twice or thrice in the descent; he paused
again at the foot. Each time, the delay
seemed to be without purpose, but
rather from a forgetfulness of the purpose which had set him in motion, or
as if the person's feet came involuntarily to a stand-still, because the motive power was too feeble to sustain
his progress. Finally, he made a long
pause at the threshold of the parlor.
He took hold of the knob of the door;
then loosened his grasp, without opening it. Hepzibah, her hands convulsively
clasped, stood gazing at the entrance.

"Dear Cousin Hepzibah, pray don't
look so!" said Phœbe, trembling; for
her cousin's emotion, and this mysteri-
ously reluctant stop, made her feel as
if a ghost were coming into the room.
"You really frighten me! Is something
awful going to happen?"

"Hush!" whispered Hepzibah. "Be
cheerful! whatever may happen, be
nothing but cheerful!"

The final pause at the threshold
proved so long, that Hepzibah, unable
to endure the suspense, rushed forward,
threw open the door, and led in the
stranger by the hand. At the first glance,
Phœbe saw an elderly personage, in an
old-fashioned dressing-gown of faded
damask, and wearing his gray, or almost
white hair, of an unusual length. It quite
overshadowed his forehead, except when
he thrust it back, and stared vaguely
about the room. After a very brief inspection of his face, it was easy to
conceive that his footstep must necessarily be such an one as that which,

slowly, and with as indefinite an aim as a child's first journey across a floor, had just brought him hitherward. Yet there were no tokens that his physical strength might not have sufficed for a free and determined gait. It was the spirit of the man that could not walk. The expression of his countenance—while, not withstanding, it had the light of reason in it—seemed to waver, and glimmer, and nearly to die away, and feebly to recover itself again. It was like a flame which we see twinkling among half-extinguished embers; we gaze at it more intently than if it were a positive blaze, gushing vividly upward,—more intently, but with a certain impatience, as if it ought either to kindle itself into satisfactory splendor, or be at once extinguished.

For an instant after entering the room, the guest stood still, retaining Hepzibah's hand, instinctively, as a child does that of the grown person who guides it. He saw Phœbe, however, and caught an illumination from her youthful and pleasant aspect, which, indeed, threw a cheerfulness about the parlor, like the circle of reflected brilliancy around the glass vase of flowers that was standing in the sunshine. He made a salutation, or, to speak nearer the truth, an ill-defined, abortive attempt at courtesy. Imperfect as it was, however, it conveyed an idea, or, at least, gave a hint, of indescribable grace, such as no practiced art of external manners could have attained. It was too slight to seize upon, at the instant; yet, as recollected afterwards, seemed to transfigure the whole man.

"Dear Clifford," said Hepzibah, in the tone with which one soothes a wayward infant, "this is our cousin Phœbe,—little

Phœbe Pyncheon,—Arthur's only ch[ild], you know. She has come from [the] country to stay with us a while; [for] our old house has grown to be v[ery] lonely now."

"Phœbe? — Phœbe Pyncheon? Phœbe?" repeated the guest, wit[h a] strange, sluggish, ill-defined uttera[nce.] "Arthur's child! Ah, I forget! No m[at]ter! She is very welcome!"

"Come, dear Clifford, take this cha[ir,]" said Hepzibah, leading him to his pl[ace.] "Pray, Phœbe, lower the curtain a v[ery] little more. Now let us begin br[eak]fast."

The guest seated himself in the p[lace] assigned him, and looked stran[gely] around. He was evidently trying [to] grapple with the present scene, [and] bring it home to his mind with a m[ore] satisfactory distinctness. He desire[d to] be certain, at least, that he was h[ere,] in the low-studded, cross-beamed, oa[k-] panelled parlor, and not in some o[ther] spot, which had stereotyped itself [in] his senses. But the effort was too g[reat] to be sustained with more than a f[rag]mentary success. Continually, as [we] may express it, he faded away ou[t of] his place; or, in other words, his m[ind] and consciousness took their depar[ture,] leaving his wasted, gray, and melanc[holy] figure,—a substantial emptiness, a m[a]terial ghost,—to occupy his seat at t[able.] Again, after a blank moment, t[here] would be a flickering, taper-gleam i[n his] eye-balls. It betokened that his spir[itual] part had returned, and was doin[g its] best to kindle the heart's household [fire,] and light up intellectual lamps in [the] dark and ruinous mansion, where it [was] doomed to be a forlorn inhabitan[t.]

At one of these moments, of [less] torpid, yet still imperfect anima[tion,]

ebe became convinced of what she
at first rejected as too extravagant
startling an idea. She saw that the
son before her must have been the
inal of the beautiful miniature in
cousin Hepzibah's possession. In-
d, with a feminine eye for costume,
had at once identified the damask
ssing-gown, which enveloped him, as
same in figure, material, and fash-
with that so elaborately represented
he picture. This old, faded garment,
a all its pristine brilliancy extinct,
ned, in some indescribable way, to
islate the wearer's untold misfor-
e, and make it perceptible to the
older's eye. It was the better to be
erned, by the exterior type, how
n and old were the soul's more im-
iate garments; that form and coun-
nce, the beauty and grace of which
almost transcended the skill of the
t exquisite of artists. It could the
e adequately be known that the soul
he man must have suffered some
erable wrong, from its earthly ex-
ence. There he seemed to sit, with
iu veil of decay and ruin betwixt
and the world, but through which,
itting intervals, might be caught the
e expression, so refined, so softly
ginative, which Malbone—venturing
ppy touch, with suspended breath—
imparted to the miniature! There
been something so innately char-
ristic in this look, that all the dusky
s, and the burthen of unfit calam-
which had fallen upon him, did
suffice utterly to destroy it.
epzibah had now poured out a cup
eliciously fragrant coffee, and pre-
ed it to her guest. As his eyes met
he seemed bewildered and dis-
ed.

"Is this you, Hepzibah?" he murmured, sadly; then, more apart, and
perhaps unconscious that he was overheard, "How changed! how changed!
And is she angry with me? Why does
she bend her brow so?"

Poor Hepzibah! It was that wretched
scowl, which time, and her near-sightedness, and the fret of inward discomfort,
had rendered so habitual that any vehemence of mood invariably evoked it.
But, at the indistinct manner of his
words, her whole face grew tender, and
even lovely, with sorrowful affection;—
the harshness of her features disappeared, as it were, behind the warm and
misty glow.

"Angry!" she repeated; "angry with
you, Clifford!"

Her tone, as she uttered the exclamation, had a plaintive and really exquisite
melody thrilling through it, yet without
subduing a certain something which an
obtuse auditor might still have mistaken
for asperity. It was as if some trans-
cendent musician should draw a soul-
thrilling sweetness out of a cracked instrument, which makes its physical im-
perfection heard in the midst of ethereal
harmony—so deep was the sensibility
that found an organ in Hepzibah's
voice!

"There is nothing but love, here, Clifford," she added,—"nothing but love!
You are at home!"

The guest responded to her tone by
a smile, which did not half light up
his face. Feeble as it was, however,
and gone in a moment, it had a charm
of wonderful beauty. It was followed
by a coarser expression; or one that
had the effect of coarseness on the fine
mould and outline of his countenance,
because there was nothing intellectual

to temper it. It was a look of appetite. He ate food with what might almost be termed voracity; and seemed to forget himself, Hepzibah, the young girl, and everything else around him, in the sensual enjoyment which the bountifully spread table afforded. In his natural system, though high-wrought and delicately refined, a sensibility to the delights of the palate was probably inherent. It would have been kept in check, however, and even converted into an accomplishment, and one of the thousand modes of intellectual culture, had his more ethereal characteristics retained their vigor. But, as it existed now, the effect was painful, and made Phœbe droop her eyes.

In a little while the guest became sensible of the fragrance of the yet untasted coffee. He quaffed it eagerly. The subtle essence acted on him like a charmed draught, and caused the opaque substance of his animal being to grow transparent, or, at least, translucent; so that a spiritual gleam was transmitted through it, with a clearer lustre than hitherto.

"More, more!" he cried, with nervous haste in his utterance, as if anxious to retain his grasp of what sought to escape him. "This is what I need! Give me more!"

Under this delicate and powerful influence, he sat more erect, and looked out from his eyes with a glance that took note of what it rested on. It was not so much that his expression grew more intellectual; this, though it had its share, was not the most peculiar effect. Neither was what we call the moral nature so forcibly awakened as to present itself in remarkable prominence. But a certain fine temper of

being was now,—not brought out in relief, but changeably and imperfe betrayed,—of which it was the f tion to deal with all beautiful and joyable things. In a character whe should exist as the chief attribute would bestow on its possessor an quisite taste, and an enviable susc bility of happiness. Beauty would his life; his aspirations would all toward it; and, allowing his frame physical organs to be in consona his own developments would likewis beautiful. Such a man should have n ing to do with sorrow; nothing strife; nothing with the martyr which, in an infinite variety of sha awaits those who have the heart, will, and conscience, to fight a b with the world. To these heroic pers, such martyrdom is the ric meed in the world's gift. To the dividual before us, it could only a grief, intense in due proportion the severity of the infliction. He no right to be a martyr; and, bel ing him so fit to be happy, and feeble for all other purposes, a erous, strong, and noble spirit w methinks, have been ready to sac what little enjoyment it might planned for itself,—it would have down the hopes, so paltry in its re —if thereby the wintry blasts of rude sphere might come tempere such a man.

Not to speak it harshly or scornf it seemed Clifford's nature to be a arite. It was perceptible, even t in the dark old parlor, in the inevi polarity with which his eyes were tracted towards the quivering pla sunbeams through the shadowy fo It was seen in his appreciating n

he vase of flowers, the scent of
ch he inhaled with a zest almost
iliar to a physical organization so
ied that spiritual ingredients are
ilded in with it. It was betrayed in
unconscious smile with which he
rded Phœbe, whose fresh and maid-
figure was both sunshine and flow-
—their essence, in a prettier and
e agreeable mode of manifestation.

less evident was this love and
ssity for the Beautiful, in the inctive caution with which, even so
t, his eyes turned away from his
ess, and wandered to any quarter
er than come back. It was Hepzi-
s misfortune,—not Clifford's fault.
could he,—so yellow as she was,
vrinkled, so sad of mien, with that
uncouthness of a turban on her
, and that most perverse of scowls
orting her brow,—how could he love
aze at her? But, did he owe her
affection for so much as she had
tly given? He owed her nothing.
ature like Clifford's can contract
lebts of that kind. It is,—we say
ithout censure, nor in diminution
he claim which it indefeasibly pos-
s on beings of another mould,—
always selfish in its essence; and
must give it leave to be so, and
up our heroic and disinterested
upon it so much the more, with-
a recompense. Poor Hepzibah knew
truth, or, at least, acted on the in-
t of it. So long estranged from what
lovely, as Clifford had been, she
ced,—rejoiced, though with a pres-
sigh, and a secret purpose to shed
s in her own chamber,—that he had
ter objects now before his eyes
her aged and uncomely features.
y never possessed a charm; and if

they had, the canker of her grief for
him would long since have destroyed it.

The guest leaned back in his chair.
Mingled in his countenance with a
dreamy delight, there was a troubled
look of effort and unrest. He was seeking to make himself more fully sensible
of the scene around him; or, perhaps,
dreading it to be a dream, or a play
of imagination, was vexing the fair
moment with a struggle for some added
brilliancy and more durable illusion.

"How pleasant!—How delightful!" he
murmured, but not as if addressing
any one. "Will it last? How balmy the
atmosphere, through that open window!
An open window! How beautiful that
play of sunshine! Those flowers, how
very fragrant! That young girl's face,
how cheerful, how blooming!—a flower
with the dew on it, and sunbeams in the
dewdrops! Ah! this must be all a dream!
A dream! A dream! But it has quite
hidden the four stone walls!"

Then his face darkened, as if the
shadow of a cavern or a dungeon had
come over it; there was no more light
in its expression than might have come
through the iron grates of a prison window,—still lessening, too, as if he were
sinking further into the depths. Phœbe
(being of that quickness and activity
of temperament that she seldom long
refrained from taking a part, and generally a good one, in what was going
forward) now felt herself moved to
address the stranger.

"Here is a new kind of rose, which
I found this morning, in the garden,"
said she, choosing a small crimson one
from among the flowers in the vase.
"There will be but five or six on the
bush, this season. This is the most perfect of them all; not a speck of blight

or mildew in it. And how sweet it is!
—sweet like no other rose! One can
never forget that scent!"

"Ah!—let me see!—let me hold it!"
cried the guest, eagerly seizing the flower. which, by the spell peculiar to remembered odors, brought innumerable
associations along with the fragrance
that it exhaled. "Thank you! This has
gone me good. I remember how I used
to prize this flower—long ago, I suppose,
very long ago!—or was it only yesterday? It makes me feel young again!
Am I young? Either this remembrance
is singularly distinct, or this consciousness strangely dim! But how kind of
the fair young girl! Thank you! Thank
you!"

The favorable excitement derived
from this little crimson rose afforded
Clifford the brightest moment which he
enjoyed at the breakfast-table. It might
have lasted longer, but that his eyes
happened, soon afterwards, to rest on
the face of the old Puritan, who, out
of his dingy frame and lustreless canvas, was looking down on the scene
like a ghost, and a most ill-tempered
and ungenial one. The guest made an
impatient gesture of the hand, and addressed Hepzibah with what might
easily be recognized as the licensed irritability of a petted member of the
family.

"Hepzibah!—Hepzibah!" cried he,
with no little force and distinctness,
—"why do you keep that odious picture
on the wall? Yes, yes!—that is precisely
your taste! I have told you, a thousand
times, that it was the evil genius of
the house!—my evil genius particularly!
Take it down, at once!"

"Dear Clifford," said Hepzibah, sadly,
"you know it cannot be!"

"Then, at all events," continued
still speaking with some energy, "p
cover it with a crimson curtain, br
enough to hang in folds, and with
golden border and tassels. I cannot b
it! It must not stare me in the face

"Yes, dear Clifford, the picture s
be covered," said Hepzibah, soothin
"There is a crimson curtain in a tr
above stairs,—a little faded and mc
eaten, I'm afraid,—but Phœbe an
will do wonders with it."

"This very day, remember!" said
and then added, in a low, self-comm
ing voice,—"Why should we live in
dismal house at all? Why not go
the south of France?—to Italy?—Pa
Naples, Venice, Rome? Hepzibah
say, we have not the means. A d
idea, that!"

He smiled to himself, and threw
glance of fine sarcastic meaning towa
Hepzibah.

But the several moods of feel
faintly as they were marked, thro
which he had passed, occurring in
brief an interval of time, had evide
wearied the stranger. He was proba
accustomed to a sad monotony of
not so much flowing in a stream, h
ever sluggish, as stagnating in a
around his feet. A slumberous veil
fused itself over his countenance,
had an effect, morally speaking, on
naturally delicate and elegant out
like that which a brooding mist,
no sunshine in it, throws over the
tures of a landscape. He appeared
become grosser,—almost cloddish.
aught of interest or beauty—even ru
beauty—had heretofore been visibl
this man, the beholder might now b
to doubt it, and to accuse his own in
ination of deluding him with whate

ace had flickered over that visage, and
aatever exquisite lustre had gleamed in
ose filmy eyes.

Before he had quite sunken away,
wever, the sharp and peevish tinkle
the shop-bell made itself audible.
riking most disagreeably on Clifford's
ditory organs and the characteristic
asibility of his nerves, it caused him
start upright out of his chair.

"Good Heavens, Hepzibah! what hor-
le disturbance have we now in the
use?" cried he, wreaking his resent-
l impatience—as a matter of course,
d a custom of old—on the one person
the world that loved him. "I have
ver heard such a hateful clamor! Why
you permit it? In the name of all
sonance, what can it be?"

It was, very remarkable into what
ominent relief—even as if a dim pic-
e should leap suddenly from its can-
s—Clifford's character was thrown,
this apparently trifling annoyance.
e secret was, that an individual of his
aper can always be pricked more
ately through his sense of the beau-
ul and harmonious than through his
art. It is even possible—for similar
es have often happened—that if Clif-
d, in his foregoing life, had enjoyed
e means of cultivating his taste to
utmost perfectability, that subtle at-
oute might, before this period, have
npletely eaten out or filed away his
ections. Shall we venture to pro-
unce, therefore, that his long and
ck calamity may not have had a re-
eming drop of mercy at the bottom?
"Dear Clifford, I wish I could keep
e sound from your ears," said Hep-
ah, patiently, but reddening with a
nful suffusion of shame. "It is very
agreeable even to me. But, do you

know, Clifford, I have something to
tell you? This ugly noise,—pray run,
Phœbe, and see who is there!—this
naughty little tinkle is nothing but our
shop-bell!"

"Shop-bell!" repeated Clifford, with
a bewildered stare.

"Yes, our shop-bell," said Hepzibah,
a certain natural dignity, mingled with
deep emotion, now asserting itself in
her manner. "For you must know, dearest Clifford, that we are very poor.
And there was no other resource, but
either to accept assistance from a hand
that I would push aside (and so would
you!) were it to offer bread when we
were dying for it,—no help, save from
him, or else to earn our subsistence with
my own hands! Alone, I might have
been content to starve. But you were
to be given back to me! Do you think,
then, dear Clifford," added she, with
a wretched smile, "that I have brought
an irretrievable disgrace on the old
house, by opening a little shop in the
front gable? Our great-great-grandfather
did the same, when there was far less
need! Are you ashamed of me?"

"Shame! Disgrace! Do you speak
these words to me, Hepzibah?" said
Clifford,—not angrily, however; for
when a man's spirit has been thoroughly
crushed, he may be peevish at small
offences, but never resentful of great
ones. So he spoke with only a grieved
emotion. "It was not kind to say so,
Hepzibah! What shame can befall me
now?"

And then the unnerved man—he that
had been born for enjoyment, but had
met a doom so very wretched—burst
into a woman's passion of tears. It was
but of brief continuance, however; soon
leaving him in a quiescent, and, to judge

by his countenance, not an uncomfortable state. From this mood, too, he partially rallied, for an instant, and looked at Hepzibah with a smile, the keen, half-derisory purport of which was a puzzle to her.

"Are we so very poor, Hepzibah?" said he.

Finally, his chair being deep and softly cushioned, Clifford fell asleep. Hearing the more regular rise and fall of his breath—(which, however, even then, instead of being strong and full, had a feeble kind of tremor, corresponding with the lack of vigor in his character) —hearing these tokens of settled slum-ber, Hepzibah seized the opportu to peruse his face more attentively t she had yet dared to do. Her b melted away in tears; her profoun spirit sent forth a moaning voice, gentle, but inexpressibly sad. In depth of grief and pity, she felt there was no irreverence in gazin his altered, aged, faded, ruined f But no sooner was she a little relie than her conscience smote her for ing curiously at him, now that he so changed; and, turning hastily a Hepzibah let down the curtain over sunny window, and left Clifford to sl ber there.

CHAPTER VIII

THE PYNCHEON OF TO-DAY

PHŒBE, on entering the shop, beheld there the already familiar face of the little devourer—if we can reckon his mighty deeds aright—of Jim Crow, the elephant, the camel, the dromedaries, and the locomotive. Having expended his private fortune, on the two preceding days, in the purchase of the above unheard-of luxuries, the young gentleman's present errand was on the part of his mother, in quest of three eggs and half a pound of raisins. These articles Phœbe accordingly supplied, and, as a mark of gratitude for his previous patronage, and a slight super-added morsel after breakfast, put likewise into his hands a whale! The great fish, reversing his experience with the prophet of Nineveh, immediately began his progress down the same red pathway of fate, whither so varied a car had preceded him. This remark urchin, in truth, was the very emt of old Father Time, both in respec his all devouring appetite for men things, and because he, as well as T after engulfing thus much of crea looked almost as youthful as if he been just that moment made.

After partly closing the door, the turned back, and mumbled somethin Phœbe, which, as the whale was half disposed of, she could not perf understand.

"What did you say, my little fell asked she.

"Mother wants to know," repe Ned Higgins, more distinctly, "how Maid Pyncheon's brother does? I say he has got home."

My cousin Hepzibah's brother!" ex-
med Phœbe, surprised at this sud-
explanation of the relationship be-
en Hepzibah and her guest. "Her
:her! And where can he have been?"
'he little boy only put his thumb
is broad snub-nose, with that look
shrewdness which a child, spending
:h of his time in the street, so
i learns to throw over his features,
ever unintelligent in themselves.
n, as Phœbe continued to gaze at
, without answering his mother's
sage, he took his departure.

s the child went down the steps,
:ntleman ascended them, and made
entrance into the shop. It was the
ly, and, had it possessed the advan-
of a little more height, would have
i the stately figure of a man con-
rably in the decline of life, dressed
black suit of some thin stuff, re-
bling broadcloth as closely as pos-
:. A gold-headed cane, of rare orien-
wood, added materially to the high
ectability of his aspect, as did also
iite neckcloth of the utmost snowy
:y, and the conscientious polish of
>oots. His dark, square countenance,
its almost shaggy depth of eye-
's, was naturally impressive, and
d, perhaps, have been rather stern,
not the gentleman considerately
i upon himself to mitigate the harsh
t by a look of exceeding good-
or and benevolence. Owing, how-
to a somewhat massive accumula-
of animal substance about the
r region of his face, the look was,
aps, unctuous, rather than spiritual,
had, so to speak, a kind of fleshly
gence, not altogether so satisfactory
e doubtless intended it to be. A
ptible observer, at any rate, might

have regarded it as affording very little
evidence of the genuine benignity of
soul whereof it purported to be the
outward reflection. And if the observer
chanced to be ill-natured, as well as
acute and susceptible, he would probably suspect that the smile on the gentleman's face was a good deal akin
to the shine on his boots, and that each
must have cost him and his boot-black,
respectively, a good deal of hard labor
to bring out and preserve them.

As the stranger entered the little shop,
where the projection of the second story
and the thick foliage of the elm-tree,
as well as the commodities at the window, created a sort of gray medium,
his smile grew as intense as if he had
set his heart on counteracting the whole
gloom of the atmosphere (besides any
moral gloom pertaining to Hepzibah and
her inmates) by the unassisted light of
his countenance. On perceiving a young
rose-bud of a girl, instead of the gaunt
presence of the old maid, a look of surprise was manifest. He at first knit
his brows; then smiled with more unctuous benignity than ever.

"Ah, I see how it is!" said he, in
a deep voice,—a voice which, had it
come from the throat of an uncultivated man, would have been gruff, but,
by dint of careful training, was now
sufficiently agreeable,—"I was not aware
that Miss Hepzibah Pyncheon had commenced business under such favorable
auspices. You are her assistant, I suppose?"

"I certainly am," answered Phœbe,
and added, with a little air of ladylike
assumption (for, civil as the gentleman was, he evidently took her to be
a young person serving for wages), "I
am a cousin of Miss Hepzibah, on a

visit to her."

"Her cousin?—and from the country? Pray pardon me, then," said the gentleman, bowing and smiling, as Phœbe never had been bowed to nor smiled on before; "in that case, we must be better acquainted; for, unless I am sadly mistaken, you are my own little kinswoman likewise! Let me see,— Mary?—Dolly?—Phœbe? yes, Phœbe is the name! Is it possible that you are Phœbe Pyncheon, only child of my dear cousin and classmate, Arthur? Ah, I see your father now, about your mouth! Yes, yes! we must be better acquainted! I am your kinsman, my dear. Surely you must have heard of Judge Pyncheon?"

As Phœbe courtesied in reply, the judge bent forward, with the pardonable and even praiseworthy purpose—considering the nearness of blood, and the difference of age—of bestowing on his young relative a kiss of acknowledged kindred and natural affection. Unfortunately (without design, or only with such instinctive design as gives no account of itself to the intellect), Phœbe, just at the critical moment, drew back; so that her highly respectable kinsman, with his body bent over the counter, and his lips protruded, was betrayed into the rather absurd predicament of kissing the empty air. It was a modern parallel to the case of Ixion embracing a cloud, and was so much the more ridiculous, as the judge prided himself on eschewing all airy matter, and never mistaking a shadow for a substance. The truth was,—and it is Phœbe's only excuse,—that, although Judge Pyncheon's glowing benignity might not be absolutely unpleasant to the feminine beholder. with the width of a street,

or even an ordinary-sized room, in posed between, yet it became quite intense, when this dark, full-fed physi nomy (so roughly bearded, too, t no razor could ever make it smoo sought to bring itself into actual c tact with the object of its rega: The man, the sex, somehow or ot was entirely too prominent in the jud demonstrations of that sort. Phœ eyes sank, and, without knowing w she felt herself blushing deeply un his look. Yet she had been kissed fore, and without any particular sque: ishness, by perhaps half a dozen di ent cousins, younger, as well as ol than this dark-browed, grisly-bear white-neckclothed, and unctuously- nevolent judge! Then, why not by h

On raising her eyes, Phœbe startled by the change in Judge P cheon's face. It was quite as strik allowing for the difference of scale, that betwixt a landscape under a br sunshine and just before a thund storm; not that it had the passion intensity of the latter aspect, but ' cold, hard, immitigable, like a day-l brooding cloud.

"Dear me! what is to be done no thought the country-girl to herself. ' looks as if there were nothing softe him than a rock, nor milder than east wind! I meant no harm! Since h really my cousin, I would have let kiss me, if I could!"

Then, all at once, it struck Ph that this very Judge Pyncheon was original of the miniature which daguerreotypist had shown her in garden, and that the hard, stern, lentless look, now on his face, the same that the sun had so inflex persisted in bringing out. Was it, th

re, no momentary mood, but, how-
er skilfully concealed, the settled
mper of his life? And not merely so,
t was it hereditary in him, and trans-
itted down, as a precious heirloom,
m that bearded ancestor, in whose
ture both the expression, and, to a
gular degree, the features, of the
dern judge were shown as by a kind
prophecy. A deeper philosopher than
œbe might have found something
ry terrible in this idea. It implied
it the weaknesses and defects, the
d passions, the mean tendencies, and
moral diseases, which lead to crime,
handed down from one generation
another, by a far surer process of
nsmission than human law has been
e to establish, in respect to the
hes and honors which it seeks to
ail upon posterity.

But, as it happened, scarcely had
œbe's eyes rested again on the judge's
ntenance, than all its ugly sternness
ished; and she found herself quite
rpowered by the sultry, dog-day
it, as it were, of benevolence, which
s excellent man diffused out of his
at heart into the surrounding atmos-
ere;—very much like a serpent,
ich, as a preliminary to fascination,
said to fill the air with his peculiar
or.

"I like that, Cousin Phœbe!" cried
with an emphatic nod of approba-
n. "I like it much, my little cousin!
u are a good child, and know how
take care of yourself. A young girl
specially if she be a very pretty one
an never be too chary of her lips."

Indeed, sir," said Phœbe, trying to
gh the matter off, "I did not mean
be unkind."

Nevertheless, whether or no it were

entirely owing to the inauspicious commencement of their acquaintance, she
still acted under a certain reserve, which
was by no means customary to her
frank and genial nature. The fantasy
would not quit her, that the original
Puritan, of whom she had heard so
many sombre traditions,—the progenitor of the whole race of New England
Pyncheons, the founder of the House
of the Seven Gables, and who had died
so strangely in it,—had now stept into
the shop. In these days of off-hand
equipment, the matter was easily enough
arranged. On his arrival from the other
world, he had merely found it necessary to spend a quarter of an hour at
a barber's, who had trimmed down the
Puritan's full beard into a pair of grizzled whiskers; then, patronizing a ready-
made clothing establishment, he had
exchanged his velvet doublet and sable
cloak, with the richly-worked band under his chin, for a white collar and cra-
vat, coat, vest, and pantaloons; and
lastly, putting aside his steel-hilted
broadsword to take up a gold-headed
cane, the Colonel Pyncheon, of two
centuries ago, steps forward as the
judge, of the passing moment!

Of course, Phœbe was far too sensible
a girl to entertain this idea in any other
way than as a matter for a smile. Possibly, also, could the two personages
have stood together before her eye,
many points of difference would have
been perceptible, and perhaps only a
general resemblance. The long lapse of
intervening years, in a climate so unlike that which had fostered the ancestral Englishman, must inevitably have
wrought important changes in the physical system of his descendant. The
judge's volume of muscle could hardly

be the same as the colonel's; there was undoubtedly less beef in him. Though looked upon as a weighty man among his contemporaries, in respect of animal substance, and as favored with a remarkable degree of fundamental development, well adapting him for the judicial bench, we conceive that the modern Judge Pyncheon, if weighed in the same balance with his ancestor, would have required at least an old-fashioned fifty-six to keep the scale in equilibrio. Then the judge's face had lost the ruddy English hue, that showed its warmth through all the duskiness of the colonel's weather-beaten cheek, and had taken a sallow shade, the established complexion of his countrymen. If we mistake not, moreover, a certain quality of nervousness had become more or less manifest, even in so solid a specimen of Puritan descent as the gentleman now under discussion. As one of its effects, it bestowed on his countenance a quicker mobility than the old Englishman's had possessed, and keener vivacity, but at the expense of a sturdier something, on which these acute endowments seemed to act like dissolving acids. This process, for aught we know, may belong to the great system of human progress, which, with every ascending footstep, as it diminishes the necessity for animal force, may be destined gradually to spiritualize us, by refining away our grosser attributes of body. If so, Judge Pyncheon could endure a century or two more of such refinement, as well as most other men.

The similarity, intellectual and moral, between the judge and his ancestor, appears to have been at least as strong as the resemblance of mien and feature would afford reason to anticipate. In old Colonel Pyncheon's funeral d course, the clergyman absolutely canc ized his deceased parishioner, and op ing, as it were, a vista through the r of the church, and thence through firmament above, showed him seat harp in hand, among the crowned cho ters of the spiritual world. On his ton stone, too, the record is highly eulog tic; nor does history, so far as he ho a place upon its page, assail the c sistency and uprightness of his char ter. So also, as regards the Judge P cheon of to-day, neither clergyman, legal critic, nor inscriber of tomb-stor nor historian of general or local polit would venture a word against this e nent person's sincerity as a Christi or respectability as a man, or integ as a judge, or courage and faithfuln as the often-tried representative of political party. But, besides these c formal, and empty words of the ch that inscribes, the voice that speaks, the pen that writes, for the public and for distant time,—and which in tably lose much of their truth and fr dom by the fatal consciousness of doing,—there were traditions about ancestor, and private diurnal go about the judge, remarkably accord in their testimony. It is often instruc to take the woman's, the private domestic view of a public man; can anything be more curious than vast discrepancy between portraits tended for engraving, and the per sketches that pass from hand to h behind the original's back.

For example, tradition affirmed the Puritan had been greedy of wea the judge, too, with all the show liberal expenditure, was said to be close-fisted as if his gripe were of i

e ancestor had clothed himself in a
m assumption of kindliness, a rough
artiness of word and manner, which
st people took to be the genuine
rmth of nature, making its way
rough the thick and inflexible hide
a manly character. His descendant,
compliance with the requirements of
nicer age, had etherealized this rude
nevolence into that broad benignity of
ile, wherewith he shone like a noon-
y sun along the streets, or glowed
e a household fire in the drawing-
ms of his private acquaintance. The
ritan—if not belied by some singular
ries, murmured, even at this day,
der the narrator's breath—had fallen
o certain transgressions to which men
his great animal development, what-
r their faith or principles, must con-
ue liable, until they put off impurity,
ng with the gross earthly substance
t involves it. We must not stain our
e with any contemporary scandal
a similar purport, that may have
n whispered against the judge. The
itan, again, an autocrat in his own
sehold, had worn out three wives,
, merely by the remorseless weight
hardness of his character in the
jugal relation, had sent them, one
er another, broken-hearted, to their
ves. Here, the parallel, in some sort,
s. The judge had wedded but a
gle wife, and lost her in the third
fourth year of their marriage. There
a fable, however,—for such we
ose to consider it, though, not im-
sibly, typical of Judge Pyncheon's
ital deportment,—that the lady got
death-blow in the honey-moon, and
er smiled again, because her husband
pelled her to serve him with coffee,
ry morning, at his bedside, in token

of fealty to her liege-lord and master.

But it is too fruitful a subject, this
of hereditary resemblances,—the frequent recurrence of which, in a direct
line, is truly unaccountable, when we
consider how large an accumulation of
ancestry lies behind every man, at the
distance of one or two centuries. We
shall only add, therefore, that the Puritan—so, at least, says chimney-corner
tradition, which often preserves traits
of character with marvellous fidelity—
was bold, imperious, relentless, crafty;
laying his purposes deep, and following
them out with an inveteracy of pursuit
that knew neither rest nor conscience;
trampling on the weak, and, when essential to his ends, doing his utmost
to beat down the strong. Whether the
judge in any degree resembled him, the
further progress of our narrative may
show.

Scarcely any of the items in the
above-drawn parallel occurred to Phœbe,
whose country birth and residence, in
truth, had left her pitifully ignorant of
most of the family traditions, which
lingered, like cobwebs and incrustations
of smoke, about the rooms and chimney-
corners of the House of the Seven
Gables. Yet there was a circumstance,
very trifling in itself, which impressed
her with an odd degree of horror. She
had heard of the anathema flung by
Maule, the executed wizard, against
Colonel Pyncheon and his posterity,—
that God would give them blood to
drink,—and likewise of the popular notion, that this miraculous blood might
now and then be heard gurgling in their
throats. The latter scandal—as became a
person of sense, and, more especially, a
member of the Pyncheon family—
Phœbe had set down for the absurdity

which it unquestionably was. But ancient superstitions, after being steeped in human hearts, and embodied in human breath, and passing from lip to ear, in manifold repetition, through a series of generations, become imbued with an effect of homely truth. The smoke of the domestic hearth has scented them, through and through. By long transmission among household facts, they grow to look like them, and have such a familiar way of making themselves at home, that their influence is usually greater than we suspect. Thus it happened, that when Phœbe heard a certain noise in Judge Pyncheon's throat,—rather habitual with him, not altogether voluntary, yet indicative of nothing, unless it were a slight bronchial complaint, or, as some people hinted, an apoplectic symptom,—when the girl heard this queer and awkward ingurgitation (which the writer never did hear, and therefore cannot describe), she, very foolishly, started, and clasped her hands.

Of course, it was exceedingly ridiculous in Phœbe to be discomposed by such a trifle, and still more unpardonable to show her discomposure to the individual most concerned in it. But the incident chimed in so oddly with her previous fancies about the colonel and the judge, that, for the moment, it seemed quite to mingle their identity.

"What is the matter with you, young woman?" said Judge Pyncheon, giving her one of his harsh looks. "Are you afraid of anything?"

"O, nothing, sir,—nothing in the world!" answered Phœbe, with a little laugh of vexation at herself. "But perhaps you wish to speak with my cousin Hepzibah. Shall I call her?"

"Stay a moment, if you please," said the judge, again beaming sunshine o᾽ of his face. "You seem to be a litt᾽ nervous, this morning. The town a᾽ Cousin Phœbe, does not agree with yo᾽ good, wholesome country habits. Or, h᾽ anything happened to disturb you?—anything remarkable in Cousin Hep᾽ bah's family?—An arrival, eh? I thoug᾽ so! No wonder you are out of sor᾽ my little cousin. To be an inmate wi᾽ such a guest may well startle an inn᾽ cent young girl!"

"You quite puzzle me, sir," repli᾽ Phœbe, gazing inquiringly at the jud᾽ "There is no frightful guest in the hou᾽ but only a poor, gentle, child-like ma᾽ whom I believe to be Cousin Hepziba᾽ brother. I am afraid (but you, sir, w᾽ know better than I) that he is not qu᾽ in his sound senses; but so mild a᾽ quiet he seems to be, that a moth᾽ might trust her baby with him; and᾽ think he would play with the ba᾽ as if he were only a few years ol᾽ than itself. He startle me!—O, no ᾽ deed!"

"I rejoice to hear so favorable a᾽ so ingenuous an account of my cou᾽ Clifford," said the benevolent jud᾽ "Many years ago, when we were b᾽ and young men together, I had a gr᾽ affection for him, and still feel a ten᾽ interest in all his concerns. You s᾽ Cousin Phœbe, he appears to be we᾽ minded. Heaven grant him at le᾽ enough of intellect to repent of his p᾽ sins!"

"Nobody, I fancy," observed Phœ᾽ "can have fewer to repent of."

"And is it possible, my dear," joined the judge, with a commiserat᾽ look, "that you have never heard ᾽ Clifford Pyncheon?—that you kn᾽ nothing of his history? Well, it is

ight; and your mother has shown a
ery proper regard for the good name of
he family with which she connected
erself. Believe the best you can of this
nfortunate person, and hope the best!
t is a rule which Christians should al-
·ays follow, in their judgments of one
nother; and especially is it right and
vise among near relatives, whose char-
cters have necessarily a degree of mu-
ual dependence. But is Clifford in the
arlor? I will just step in and see."

"Perhaps, sir, I had better call my
ousin Hepzibah," said Phœbe; hardly
nowing, however, whether she ought to
bstruct the entrance of so affectionate
kinsman into the private regions of
e house. "Her brother seemed to be
ıst falling asleep, after breakfast; and
am sure she would not like him to
: disturbed. Pray, sir, let me give her
ıtice!"

But the judge showed a singular de-
rmination to enter unannounced; and
Phœbe, with the vivacity of a person
hose movements unconsciously answer
· her thoughts, had stepped towards
e door, he used little or no ceremony
putting her aside.

"No, no, Miss Phœbe!" said Judge
yncheon, in a voice as deep as a thun-
·r-growl, and with a frown as black
· the cloud whence it issues. "Stay
»u here! I know the house, and know
y cousin Hepzibah, and know her
other Clifford likewise!—nor need my
tle country cousin put herself to the
ouble of announcing me!"—in these
:ter words, by-the-by, there were
mptoms of a change from his sudden
.rshness into his previous benignity of
anner.—"I am at home here, Phœbe,
»u must recollect, and you are the
:anger. I will just step in, therefore,

and see for myself how Clifford is, and
assure him and Hepzibah of my kindly
feelings and best wishes. It is right, àt
this juncture, that they should both
hear from my own lips how much I
desire to serve them. Ha! here is Hepzibah herself!"

Such was the case. The vibrations of
the judge's voice had reached the old
gentlewoman in the parlor, where she
sat, with face averted, waiting on her
brother's slumber. She now issued forth,
as would appear, to defend the entrance, looking, we must needs say,
amazingly like the dragon which, in
fairy tales, is wont to be the guardian
over an enchanted beauty. The habitual
scowl of her brow was, undeniably, too
fierce, at this moment, to pass itself
off on the innocent score of near-sightedness; and it was bent on Judge
Pyncheon in a way that seemed to confound, if not alarm him, so inadequate-
ly had he estimated the moral force
of a deeply-grounded antipathy. She
made a repelling gesture with her hand,
and stood, a perfect picture of prohibi-
tion, at full length, in the dark frame
of the doorway. But we must betray
Hepzibah's secret, and confess that the
native timorousness of her character
even now developed itself, in a quick
tremor, which, to her own perception,
set each of her joints at variance with
its fellows.

Possibly, the judge was aware how
little true hardihood lay behind Hepzibah's formidable front. At any rate,
being a gentleman of steady nerves, he
soon recovered himself, and failed not
to approach his cousin with outstretched
hand; adopting the sensible precaution,
however, to cover his advance with a
smile, so broad and sultry, that, had it

been only half as warm as it looked, a trellis of grapes might at once have turned purple under its summer-like exposure. It may have been his purpose, indeed, to melt poor Hepzibah on the spot, as if she were a figure of yellow wax.

"Hepzibah, my beloved cousin, I am rejoiced!" exclaimed the judge, most emphatically. "Now, at length, you have something to live for. Yes, and all of us, let me say, your friends and kindred, have more to live for than we had yesterday. I have lost no time in hastening to offer any assistance in my power towards making Clifford comfortable. He belongs to us all. I know how much he requires,—how much he used to require,—with his delicate taste, and his love of the beautiful. Anything in my house,—pictures, books, wine, luxuries at the table,—he may command them all! It would afford me most heart-felt gratification to see him! Shall I step in, this moment?"

"No," replied Hepzibah, her voice quivering too painfully to allow of many words. "He cannot see visitors!"

"A visitor, my dear cousin!—do you call me so?" cried the judge, whose sensibility, it seems, was hurt by the coldness of the phrase. "Nay, then, let me be Clifford's host, and your own likewise. Come at once to my house. The country air, and all the conveniences— I may say luxuries—that I have gathered about me, will do wonders for him. And you and I, dear Hepzibah, will consult together, and watch together, and labor together, to make our dear Clifford happy. Come! why should we make more words about what is both a duty and a pleasure, on my part? Come to me at once!"

On hearing these so hospitable offe and such generous recognition of t claims of kindred, Phœbe felt ve much in the mood of running up Judge Pyncheon, and giving him, of h own accord, the kiss from which s had so recently shrunk away. It w quite otherwise with Hepzibah; t judge's smile seemed to operate on l acerbity of heart like sunshine up vinegar, making it ten times sourer th ever.

"Clifford," said she,—still too agitat to utter more than an abrupt senten —"Clifford has a home here!"

"May Heaven forgive you, Hep bah," said Judge Pyncheon,—reveren lifting his eyes towards that high co of equity to which he appealed,— you suffer any ancient prejudice animosity to weigh with you in t matter! I stand here, with an o heart, willing and anxious to rece yourself and Clifford into it. Do refuse my good offices,—my earn propositions for your welfare! They such, in all respects, as it behoo your nearest kinsman to make. It be a heavy responsibility, cousin, if confine your brother to this dismal ho and stifled air, when the delightful f dom of my country-seat is at his c mand."

"It would never suit Clifford," s Hepzibah, as briefly as before.

"Woman!" broke forth the ju giving way to his resentment, "wha the meaning of all this? Have you o resources? Nay, I suspected as mu Take care, Hepzibah, take care! C ford is on the brink of as blac ruin as ever befell him yet! But do I talk with you, woman as you Make way!—I must see Clifford!"

Hepzibah spread out her gaunt figure
ross the door, and seemed really to
:rease in bulk; looking the more ter-
•le, also, because there was so much
·ror and agitation in her heart. But
dge Pyncheon's evident purpose of
·cing a passage was interrupted by a
ice from the inner room; a weak,
mulous, wailing voice, indicating
pless alarm, with no more energy
self-defence than belongs to a fright-
:d infant.

'Hepzibah, Hepzibah!" cried the
ce; "go down on your knees to him!
ss his feet! Entreat him not to come
O, let him have mercy on me!
·rcy!—mercy!"

"or the instant, it appeared doubt-
whether it were not the judge's reso-
: purpose to set Hepzibah aside, and
o across the threshold into the par-
whence issued that broken and mis-
ble murmur of entreaty. It was not
/ that restrained him, for, at the
t sound of the enfeebled voice, a
fire kindled in his eyes, and he
de a quick pace forward, with some-
1g inexpressibly fierce and grim
kening forth, as it were, out of the
le man. To know Judge Pyncheon,
to see him at that moment. After
h a revelation, let him smile with
it sultriness he would, he could much
ner turn grapes purple, or pumpkins
ow, than melt the iron-branded im-
ssion out of the beholder's memory.
I it rendered his aspect not the less,
more frightful, that it seemed not
xpress wrath or hatred, but a cer-
hot fellness of purpose, which anni-
ted everything but itself.

'et, after all, are we not slandering
xcellent and amiable man? Look at
judge now! He is apparently conscious of having erred, in too energetically pressing his deeds of loving-kind-
ness on persons unable to appreciate
them. He will await their better mood,
and hold himself as ready to assist
them, then, as at this moment. As he
draws back from the door, an all-com-
prehensive benignity blazes from his
visage, indicating that he gathers Hepzibah, little Phœbe, and the invisible
Clifford, all three, together with the
whole world besides, into his immense
heart, and gives them a warm bath in
its flood of affection.

"You do me great wrong, dear Cousin
Hepzibah!" said he, first kindly offering her his hand, and then drawing on
his glove preparatory to departure.
"Very great wrong! But I forgive it,
and will study to make you think better of me. Of course, our poor Clifford
being in so unhappy a state of mind,
I cannot think of urging an interview
at present. But I shall watch over his
welfare, as if he were my own beloved
brother; nor do I at all despair, my
dear cousin, of constraining both him
and you to acknowledge your injustice.
When that shall happen, I desire no
other revenge than your acceptance of
the best offices in my power to do you."

With a bow to Hepzibah, and a degree of paternal benevolence in his
parting nod to Phœbe, the judge left
the shop, and went smiling along the
street. As is customary with the rich,
when they aim at the honors of a
republic, he apologized, as it were, to
the people, for his wealth, prosperity,
and elevated station, by a free and
hearty manner towards those who knew
him; putting off the more of his dignity,
in due proportion with the humbleness
of the man whom he saluted, and there-

by proving a haughty consciousness of his advantages as irrefragably as if he had marched forth preceded by a troop of lackeys to clear the way. On this particular forenoon, so excessive was the warmth of Judge Pyncheon's kindly aspect, that (such, at least, was the rumor about town) an extra passage of the water-carts was found essential, in order to lay the dust occasioned by so much extra sunshine!

No sooner had he disappeared than Hepzibah grew deadly white, and, staggering towards Phœbe, let her head fall on the young girl's shoulder.

"O, Phœbe!" murmured she, "that man has been the horror of my life! Shall I never, never have the courage, —will my voice never cease from trembling long enough to let me tell him what he is?"

"Is he so very wicked?" asked Phœbe. "Yet his offers were surely kind!"

"Do not speak of them,—he has a heart of iron!" rejoined Hepzibah. "Go, now, and talk to Clifford! Amuse and keep him quiet! It would disturb him wretchedly to see me so agitated as I am. There, go, dear child, and I will try to look after the shop."

Phœbe went, accordingly, but perplexed herself, meanwhile, with queries as to the purport of the scene which she had just witnessed, and also, wheth judges, clergymen, and other characte of that eminent stamp and respectab ity, could really, in any single instan be otherwise than just and upright me A doubt of this nature has a most d turbing influence, and, if shown to a fact, comes with fearful and startli effect, on minds of the trim, order and limit-loving class, in which we fi our little country-girl. Dispositions mo boldly speculative may derive a ste enjoyment from the discovery, sin there must be evil in the world, th a high man is as likely to grasp share of it as a low one. A wider sco of view, and a deeper insight, may s rank, dignity, and station, all prov illusory, so far as regards their clai to human reverence, and yet not f as if the universe were thereby tumbl headlong into chaos. But Phœbe, order to keep the universe in its place, was fain to smother, in so degree, her own intuitions as to Juc Pyncheon's character. And as for cousin's testimony in disparagement it, she concluded that Hepzibah's ju ment was embittered by one of th family feuds, which render hatred more deadly, by the dead and corrup love that they intermingle with its tive poison.

CHAPTER IX

CLIFFORD AND PHŒBE

TRULY was there something high, generous, and noble, in the native composition of our poor old Hepzibah! Or else,—and it was quite as proba the case,—she had been enriched poverty, developed by sorrow, eleva

the strong and solitary affection of
life, and thus endowed with hero-
, which never could have charac‐
zed her in what are called happier
umstances. Through dreary years,
zibah had looked forward—for the
t part despairingly, never with any
idence of hope, but always with the
ing that it was her brightest possi‐
y—to the very position in which
now found herself. In her own
ilf, she had asked nothing of Provi‐
ce, but the opportunity of devoting
elf to this brother, whom she had
oved,—so admired for what he was,
night have been,—and to whom she
kept her faith, alone of all the
ld, wholly, unfalteringly, at every
int, and throughout life. And here,
iis late decline, the lost one had
e back out of his long and strange
ortune, and was thrown on her sym‐
iy, as it seemed, not merely for the
d of his physical existence, but for
ything that should keep him mor‐
alive. She had responded to the
She had come forward,—our poor,
it Hepzibah, in her rusty silks, with
rigid joints, and the sad perversity
er scowl,—ready to do her utmost;
with affection enough, if that were
to do a hundred times as much!
re could be few more tearful sights,
id Heaven forgive us, if a smile in‐
on mingling with our conception of
-few sights with truer pathos in
i, than Hepzibah presented, on that
afternoon.

ow patiently did she endeavor to
) Clifford up in her great, warm
, and make it all the world to him,
hat he should retain no torturing
e of the coldness and dreariness
out! Her little efforts to amuse him!

How pitiful, yet magnanimous, they
were!

Remembering his early love of poetry
and fiction, she unlocked a bookcase,
and took down several books that had
been excellent reading in their day.
There was a volume of Pope, with the
Rape of the Lock in it, and another
of the Tatler, and an odd one of Dry‐
den's Miscellanies, all with tarnished
gilding on their covers, and thoughts
of tarnished brilliancy inside. They had
no success with Clifford. These, and all
such writers of society, whose new
works glow like the rich texture of
a just-woven carpet, must be content
to relinquish their charm, for every
reader, after an age or two, and could
hardly be supposed to retain any por‐
tion of it for a mind that had utterly
lost its estimate of modes and man‐
ners. Hepzibah then took up Rasselas,
and began to read of the Happy Valley,
with a vague idea that some secret
of a contented life had there been elab‐
orated, which might at least serve Clif‐
ford and herself for this one day. But
the Happy Valley had a cloud over
it. Hepzibah troubled her auditor, more‐
over, by innumerable sins of emphasis,
which he seemed to detect, without any
reference to the meaning; nor, in fact,
did he appear to take much note of
the sense of what she read, but evident‐
ly felt the tedium of the lecture, with‐
out harvesting its profit. His sister's
voice, too, naturally harsh, had, in the
course of her sorrowful lifetime, con‐
tracted a kind of croak, which, when
it once gets into the human throat, is
as ineradicable as sin. In both sexes,
occasionally, this lifelong croak, ac‐
companying each word of joy or sor‐
row, is one of the symptoms of a settled

melancholy; and wherever it occurs, the whole history of misfortune is conveyed in its slightest accent. The effect is as if the voice had been dyed black; or,—if we must use a more moderate simile,—this miserable croak, running through all the variations of the voice, is like a black silken thread, on which the crystal beads of speech are strung, and whence they take their hue. Such voices have put on mourning for dead hopes; and they ought to die and be buried along with them!

Discerning that Clifford was not gladdened by her efforts, Hepzibah searched about the house for the means of more exhilarating pastime. At one time, her eyes chanced to rest on Alice Pyncheon's harpsichord. It was a moment of great peril; for,—despite the traditionary awe that had gathered over this instrument of music, and the dirges which spiritual fingers were said to play on it,—the devoted sister had solemn thoughts of thrumming on its chords for Clifford's benefit, and accompanying the performance with her voice. Poor Clifford! Poor Hepzibah! Poor harpsichord! All three would have been miserable together. By some good agency, —possibly, by the unrecognized interposition of the long-buried Alice herself,—the threatening calamity was averted.

But the worst of all,—the hardest stroke of fate for Hepzibah to endure, and perhaps for Clifford too,—was his invincible distaste for her appearance. Her features, never the most agreeable, and now harsh with age and grief, and resentment against the world for his sake; her dress, and especially her turban; the queer and quaint manners, which had unconsciously grown upon

her in solitude;—such being the p[...] gentlewoman's outward characterist[...] it is no great marvel, although [...] mournfullest of pities, that the insti[...] tive lover of the Beautiful was [...] to turn away his eyes. There was [...] help for it. It would be the latest [...] pulse to die within him. In his [...] extremity, the expiring breath stea[...] faintly through Clifford's lips, he wo[...] doubtless press Hepzibah's hand, in [...] vent recognition of all her lavished l[...] and close his eyes,—but not so much [...] die, as to be constrained to look [...] longer on her face! Poor Hepzib[...] She took counsel with herself what m[...] be done, and thought of putting [...] bons on her turban; but, by the inst[...] rush of several guardian angels, [...] withheld from an experiment that c[...] hardly have proved less than fatal [...] the beloved object of her anxiety.

To be brief, besides Hepzibah's [...] advantages of person, there was an [...] couthness pervading all her deeds [...] clumsy something, that could but [...] adapt itself for use, and not at all [...] ornament. She was a grief to Cliff[...] and she knew it. In this extremity, [...] antiquated virgin turned to Phœbe. [...] grovelling jealousy was in her he[...] Had it pleased Heaven to crown [...] heroic fidelity of her life by making [...] personally the medium of Cliffo[...] happiness, it would have rewarded [...] for all the past, by a joy with no br[...] tints, indeed, but deep and true, [...] worth a thousand gayer ecstasies. [...] could not be. She therefore turned [...] Phœbe, and resigned the task into [...] young girl's hands. The latter too[...] up, cheerfully, as she did everyth[...] but with no sense of a mission to [...] form, and succeeding all the better [...]

t same simplicity.

3y the involuntary effect of a genial
.perament, Phœbe soon grew to be
olutely essential to the daily com-
:, if not the daily life, of her two
orn companions. The grime and
lidness of the House of the Seven
les seemed to have vanished, since
appearance there; the gnawing tooth
the dry-rot was stayed, among the
timbers of its skeleton frame; the
t had ceased to settle down so
sely, from the antique ceilings, upon
floors and furniture of the rooms
w;—or, at any rate, there was a
e wife, as light-footed as the breeze
sweeps a garden walk, gliding hither
thither, to brush it all away. The
lows of gloomy events, that haunted
else lonely and desolate apartments;
heavy, breathless scent which death
left in more than one of the bed-
mbers, ever since his visits of long
;—these were less powerful than the
fying influence scattered throughout
atmosphere of the household by the
sence of one youthful, fresh, and
roughly wholesome heart. There was
morbidness in Phœbe; if there had
1, the old Pyncheon-house was the
r locality to ripen it into incurable
ase. But now her spirit resembled,
its potency, a minute quantity of
r of rose in one of Hepzibah's huge,
-bound trunks, diffusing its fragrance
ugh the various articles of linen
wrought-lace, kerchiefs, caps, stock-
, folded dresses, gloves, and what-
: else was treasured there. As every
:le in the great trunk was the sweeter
the rose-scent, so did all the thoughts
emotions of Hepzibah and Clifford,
bre as they might seem, acquire a
:le attribute of happiness from

Phœbe's intermixture with them. Her
activity of body, intellect, and heart,
impelled her continually to perform the
ordinary little toils that offered themselves around her, and to think the
thought proper for the moment, and to
sympathize,—now with the twittering
gayety of the robins in the pear-tree,
and now to such a depth as she could
with Hepzibah's dark anxiety, or the
vague moan of her brother. This facile
adaptation was at once the symptom of
perfect health, and its best preserva-
tive.

A nature like Phœbe's has invariably
its due influence, but is seldom regarded
with due honor. Its spiritual force, however, may be partially estimated by the
fact of her having found a place for
herself, amid circumstances so stern as
those which surrounded the mistress of
the house; and also by the effect which
she produced on a character of so much
more mass than her own. For the gaunt,
bony frame and limbs of Hepzibah, as
compared with the tiny lightsomeness
of Phœbe's figure, were perhaps in some
fit proportion with the moral weight and
substance, respectively, of the woman
and the girl.

To the guest,—to Hepzibah's brother.
—or Cousin Clifford, as Phœbe now began to call him,—she was especially
necessary. Not that he could ever be
said to converse with her, or often
manifest, in any other very definite
mode, his sense of a charm in her
society. But, if she were a long while
absent, he became pettish and nervously restless, pacing the room to and
fro, with the uncertainty that characterized all his movements; or else would
sit broodingly in his great chair, resting his head on his hands, and evincing

life only by an electric sparkle of ill-humor, whenever Hepzibah endeavored to arouse him. Phœbe's presence, and the contiguity of her fresh life to his blighted one, was usually all that he required. Indeed, such was the native gush and play of her spirit, that she was seldom perfectly quiet and un-demonstrative, any more than a fountain ever ceases to dimple and warble with its flow. She possessed the gift of song, and that, too, so naturally, that you would as little think of inquiring whence she had caught it, or what master had taught her, as of asking the same questions about a bird, in whose small strain of music we recognize the voice of the Creator as distinctly as in the loudest accents of his thunder. So long as Phœbe sang, she might stray at her own will about the house. Clifford was content, whether the sweet, airy homeliness of her tones came down from the upper chambers, or along the passage-way from the shop, or was sprinkled through the foliage of the pear-tree, inward from the garden, with the twinkling sunbeams. He would sit quietly, with a gentle pleasure gleaming over his face, brighter now, and now a little dimmer, as the song happened to float near him, or was more remotely heard. It pleased him best, however, when she sat on a low foot-stool at his knee.

It is perhaps remarkable, considering her temperament, that Phœbe oftener chose a strain of pathos than of gayety. But the young and happy are not ill pleased to temper their life with a transparent shadow. The deepest pathos of Phœbe's voice and song, moreover, came sifted through the golden texture of a cheery spirit, and was somehow so

interfused with the quality thence [quired, that one's heart felt all] lighter for having wept at it. B[ut] mirth, in the sacred presence of misfortune, would have jarred ha[rshly] and irreverently with the solemn phony that rolled its undertone thr[ough] Hepzibah's and her brother's life. T[here]fore, it was well that Phœbe so [often] chose sad themes, and not amiss [that] they ceased to be so sad while she[was] singing them.

Becoming habituated to her [com]panionship, Clifford readily showed [himself] capable of imbibing pleasant tints [and] gleams of cheerful light from all [mat]ters his nature must originally [have] been. He grew youthful, while sh[e sat] by him. A beauty,—not precisely [seen] even in its utmost manifestation, [but] which a painter would have wa[ited] long to seize and fix upon his ca[nvas,] and, after all, in vain,—beauty, n[everthe]less, that was not a mere dr[eam,] would sometimes play upon and il[lumi]nate his face. It did more tha[n] illuminate; it transfigured him wit[h an] expression that could only be interp[reted] as the glow of an exquisite and h[appy] spirit. That gray hair, and those [fur]rows,—with their record of infinite [sor]row, so deeply written across his [brow] and so compressed, as with a [hard] effort to crowd in all the tale, tha[t the] whole inscription was made illegib[le,—] these, for the moment, vanished[. An] eye, at once tender and acute, [might] have beheld in the man some shad[ow of] what he was meant to be. Anon, a[s] came stealing, like a sad twilight, [anew] over his figure, you would have [been] tempted to hold an argument with[des]tiny, and affirm, that either this [mortal] should not have been made mort[al]

al existence should have been tem-
1 to his qualities. There seemed no
ssity for his having drawn breath,
1;—the world never wanted him;—
as he had breathed, it ought always
ave been the balmiest of summer
The same perplexity will invariably
.t us with regard to natures that
to feed exclusively upon the Beau-
, let their earthly fate be as lenient
may.

œbe, it is probable, had but a very
rfect comprehension of the char-
over which she had thrown so
ficent a spell. Nor was it necessary.
fire upon the hearth can gladden a
e semi-circle of faces round about
ut need not know the individuality
ne among them all. Indeed, there
something too fine and delicate in
ord's traits to be perfectly appre-
d by one whose sphere lay so much
e Actual as Phœbe's did. For Clif-
however, the reality, and sim-
y, and thorough homeliness, of the
nature, were as powerful a charm
ny that she possessed. Beauty, it
ue, and beauty almost perfect in
wn style, was indispensable. Had
e been coarse in feature, shaped
sily, of a harsh voice, and uncouthly
ered, she might have been rich
all good gifts, beneath this unfor-
te exterior, and still, so long as she
the guise of woman, she would
shocked Clifford, and depressed
by her lack of beauty. But nothing
beautiful—nothing prettier, at
—was ever made than Phœbe. And,
fore, to this man,—whose whole
and impalpable enjoyment of exce, heretofore, and until both his
and fancy died within him, had
a dream,—whose images of women

had more and more lost their warmth
and substance, and been frozen, like the
pictures of secluded artists, into the
chillest ideality,—to him, this little figure of the cheeriest household life was
just what he required to bring him back
into the breathing world. Persons who
have wandered, or been expelled, out of
the common track of things, even were
it for a better system, desire nothing so
much as to be led back. They shiver in
their loneliness, be it on a mountain-top
or in a dungeon. Now, Phœbe's presence made a home about her,—that very
sphere which the outcast, the prisoner,
the potentate,—the wretch beneath
mankind, the wretch aside from it, or
the wretch above it,—instinctively pines
after,—a home! She was real! Holding
her hand, you felt something; a tender
something; a substance, and a warm
one: and so long as you should feel its
grasp, soft as it was, you might be certain that your place was good in the
whole sympathetic chain of human nature. The world was no longer a delusion.

By looking a little further in this
direction, we might suggest an explanation of an often-suggested mystery. Why
are poets so apt to choose their mates,
not for any similarity of poetic endowment, but for qualities which might
make the happiness of the rudest handicraftsman as well as that of the ideal
craftsman of the spirit? Because, probably, at his highest elevation, the poet
needs no human intercourse; but he
finds it dreary to descend, and be a
stranger.

There was something very beautiful in
the relation that grew up between this
pair, so closely and constantly linked
together, yet with such a waste of

gloomy and mysterious years from his birth-day to hers. On Clifford's part, it was the feeling of a man naturally endowed with the liveliest sensibility to feminine influence, but who had never quaffed the cup of passionate love, and knew that it was now too late. He knew it, with the instinctive delicacy that had survived his intellectual decay. Thus, his sentiment for Phœbe, without being paternal, was not less chaste than if she had been his daughter. He was a man, it is true, and recognized her as a woman. She was his only representative of womankind. He took unfailing note of every charm that appertained to her sex, and saw the ripeness of her lips, and the virginal development of her bosom. All her little womanly ways, budding out of her like blossoms ou a young fruit-tree, had their effect on him, and sometimes caused his very heart to tingle with the keenest thrills of pleasure. At such moments,—for the effect was seldom more than momentary,—the half-torpid man would be full of harmonious life, as a long-silent harp is full of sound, when the musician's fingers sweep across it. But, after all, it seemed rather a perception, or a sympathy, than a sentiment belonging to himself as an individual. He read Phœbe, as he would a sweet and simple story; he listened to her, as if she were a verse of household poetry, which God, in requital of his bleak and dismal lot, had permitted some angel, that most pitied him, to warble through the house. She was not an actual fact for him, but the interpretation of all that he had lacked on earth, brought warmly home to his conception; so that this mere symbol, or lifelike picture, had almost the comfort of reality.

But we strive in vain to put the i into words. No adequate expression the beauty and profound pathos v which it impressed us is attainable. T being, made only for happiness, heretofore so miserably failing to happy,—his tendencies so hideo thwarted, that, some unknown time a the delicate springs of his charac never morally or intellectually str had given way, and he was now becile,—this poor, forlorn voyager f the Islands of the Blest, in a frail b on a tempestuous sea, had been fl by the last mountain-wave of his s wreck, into a quiet harbor. There, a lay more than half lifeless on strand, the fragrance of an earthly r bud had come to his nostrils, and odors will, had summoned up re iscences or visions of all the living breathing beauty amid which he sh have had his home. With his native ceptibility of happy influences, he hales the slight, ethereal rapture into soul, and expires!

And how did Phœbe regard Cliff The girl's was not one of those nat which are most attracted by wha strange and exceptional in human c acter. The path which would best h suited her was the well-worn track ordinary life; the companions in w she would most have delighted such as one encounters at every t The mystery which enveloped Cliff so far as it affected her at all, wa annoyance, rather than the piqu harm which many women might found in it. Still, her native kindli was brought strongly into play, not what was darkly picturesque in his ation, nor so much even, by the grace of his character, as by the sir eal of a heart so forlorn as his to one full of genuine sympathy as hers. ...e gave him an affectionate regard, ...ause he needed so much love, and ...med to have received so little. With ...eady tact, the result of ever-active ...l wholesome sensibility, she discerned ...at was good for him, and did it. ...atever was morbid in his mind and ...erience, she ignored; and thereby ...t their intercourse healthy, by the ...utious, but, as it were, heaven-di- ...ted freedom of her whole conduct. ...e sick in mind, and, perhaps, in body, rendered more darkly and hope- ...ly so, by the manifold reflection of ...ir disease, mirrored back from all ...rters, in the deportment of those ...ut them; they are compelled to in- ...e the poison of their own breath, in ...nite repetition. But Phœbe afforded ...poor patient a supply of purer air. ...impregnated it, too, not with a ...l flower scent,—for wildness was no ...t of hers,—but with the perfume of ...len-roses, pinks, and other blossoms ...much sweetness, which nature and ...l have consented together in making ...v, from summer to summer, and ...n century to century. Such a flower ...Phœbe, in her relation with Clifford, ...such the delight that he inhaled ...n her.

...'et, it must be said, her petals some- ...es drooped a little, in consequence of ...heavy atmosphere about her. She ...y more thoughtful than heretofore. ...king aside at Clifford's face, and see- ...he dim, unsatisfactory elegance, and ...intellect almost quenched, she would ...to inquire what had been his life. ...he always thus? Had this veil been ...him from his birth?—this veil, ...er which far more of his spirit was

hidden than revealed, and through which he so imperfectly discerned the actual world,—or was its gray texture woven of some dark calamity? Phœbe loved no riddles, and would have been glad to escape the perplexity of this one. Never- theless, there was so far a good result of her meditations on Clifford's char- acter, that, when her involuntary con- jectures, together with the tendency of every strange circumstance to tell its own story, had gradually taught her the fact, it had no terrible effect upon her. Let the world have done him what vast wrong it might, she knew Cousin Clif- ford too well—or fancied so—ever to shudder at the touch of his thin, deli- cate fingers.

Within a few days after the appear- ance of this remarkable inmate, the routine of life had established itself with a good deal of uniformity in the old house of our narrative. In the morn- ing, very shortly after breakfast, it was Clifford's custom to fall asleep in his chair; nor, unless accidentally disturbed, would he emerge from a dense cloud of slumber, or the thinner mists that flitted to and fro, until well towards noonday. These hours of drowsy head were the season of the old woman's attend- ance on her brother, while Phœbe took charge of the shop; an arrangement which the public speedily understood, and evinced their decided preference of the younger shopwoman by the multi- plicity of their calls during her admin- istration of affairs. Dinner over, Hepzi- bah took her knitting-work,—a long stocking of gray yarn, for her brother's winter-wear,—and with a sigh, and a scowl of affectionate farewell to Clifford, and a gesture enjoining watchfulness on Phœbe, went to take her seat behind the counter. It was now the young girl's turn to be the nurse,—the guardian, the playmate,—or whatever is the phrase,—of the gray-haired man.

———

CHAPTER X

THE PYNCHEON-GARDEN

CLIFFORD, except for Phœbe's more active instigation, would ordinarily have yielded to the torpor which had crept through all his modes of being, and which sluggishly counselled him to sit in his morning chair till even-tide. But the girl seldom failed to propose a removal to the garden, where Uncle Venner and the daguerrotypist had made such repairs on the roof of the ruinous arbor, or summer-house, that it was now a sufficient shelter from sunshine and casual showers. The hop-vine, too, had begun to grow luxuriantly over the sides of the little edifice, and made an interior of verdant seclusion, with innumerable peeps and glimpses into the wider solitude of the garden.

Here, sometimes, in this green playplace of flickering light, Phœbe read to Clifford. Her acquaintance, the artist, who appeared to have a literary turn, had supplied her with works of fiction, in pamphlet-form, and a few volumes of poetry, in altogether a different style and taste from those which Hepzibah selected for his amusement. Small thanks were due to the books, however, if the girl's readings were in any degree more successful than her elderly cousin's. Phœbe's voice had always a pretty music in it, and could either enliven Clifford by its sparkle and gayety of tone, or soothe him by a continued

flow of pebbly and brook-like cade But the fictions—in which the cou girl, unused to works of that na often became deeply absorbed—i ested her strange auditor very littl not at all. Pictures of life, scene passion or sentiment, wit, humor, pathos, were all thrown away, or v than thrown away, on Clifford; e because he lacked an experience which to test their truth, or becaus own griefs were a touch-stone of re that few feigned emotions could stand. When Phœbe broke into a pe merry laughter at what she read would now and then laugh for pathy, but oftener respond wit troubled, questioning look. If a tea maiden's sunshiny tear, over imagi woe—dropped upon some melanc page, Clifford either took it as a t of actual calamity, or else grew pee and angrily motioned her to close volume. And wisely, too! Is not world sad enough, in genuine ear without making a pastime of m sorrows?

With poetry, it was rather better delighted in the swell and subsiden the rhythm, and the happily-recu rhyme. Nor was Clifford incapab feeling the sentiment of poetry,— perhaps, where it was highest or est, but where it was most flitting

ereal. It was impossible to foretell
what exquisite verse the awakening
ll might lurk; but, on raising her
s from the page to Clifford's face,
ebe would be made aware, by the
t breaking through it, that a more
cate intelligence than her own had
ght a lambent flame from what she
d. One glow of this kind, however,
often the precursor of gloom for
ny hours afterward; because, when
glow left him, he seemed conscious
a missing sense and power, and
ed about for them, as if a blind man
uld go seeking his lost eyesight.
t pleased him more, and was better
his inward welfare, that Phœbe
uld talk, and make passing occur-
:es vivid to his mind by her accom-
ying description and remarks. The
of the garden offered topics enough
such discourse as suited Clifford
. He never failed to inquire what
ers had bloomed since yesterday.
feeling for flowers was very ex-
ite, and seemed not so much a taste
n emotion; he was fond of sitting
a one in his hand, intently observing
and looking from its petals into
be's face, as if the garden-flower
e the sister of the household-maiden.
merely was there a delight in the
er's perfume, or pleasure in its beau-
form, and the delicacy of bright-
of its hue; but Clifford's enjoyment
accompanied with a perception of
character, and individuality, that
e him love these blossoms of the
en, as if they were endowed with
iment and intelligence. This affec-
and sympathy for flowers is almost
usively a woman's trait. Men, if ened with it by nature, soon lose,
et, and learn to despise it, in their

contact with coarser things than flowers.
Clifford, too, had long forgotten it; but
found it again, now, as he slowly revived from the chill torpor of his life.

It is wonderful how many pleasant
incidents continually came to pass in
that secluded garden-spot, when once
Phœbe had set herself to look for them.
She had seen or heard a bee there, on
the first day of her acquaintance with
the place. And often,—almost continually, indeed,—since then, the bees kept
coming thither. Heaven knows why, or
by what pertinacious desire for far-
fetched sweets, when, no doubt, there
were broad clover-fields, and all kinds
of garden-growth, much nearer home
than this. Thither the bees came, however, and plunged into the squash-blos-
soms, as if there were no other squash-
vines within a long day's flight, or as
if the soil of Hepzibah's garden gave
its productions just the very quality
which these laborious little wizards
wanted, in order to impart the Hymet-
tus odor to their whole hive of New
England honey. When Clifford heard
their sunny, huzzing murmur, in the
heart of the great yellow blossoms, he
looked about him with a joyful sense
of warmth, and blue sky, and green
grass, and of God's free air in the whole
height from earth to heaven. After all,
there need be no question why the bees
came to that one green nook, in the
dusty town. God sent them thither, to
gladden our poor Clifford. They brought
the rich summer with them, in requital
of a little honey.

When the bean-vines began to flower
on the poles, there was one particular
variety which bore a vivid scarlet blossom. The daguerreotypist had found
these beans in a garret, over one of the

seven gables, treasured up in an old chest of drawers, by some horticultural Pyncheon of days gone by, who, doubtless, meant to sow them the next summer, but was himself first sown in Death's garden-ground. By way of testing whether there was still a living germ in such ancient seeds, Holgrave had planted some of them; and the result of his experiment was a splendid row of bean-vines, clambering, early, to the full height of the poles, and arraying them, from top to bottom, in a spiral profusion of red blossoms. And, ever since the unfolding of the first bud, a multitude of humming-birds had been attracted thither. At times, it seemed as if for every one of the hundred blossoms there was one of these tiniest fowls of the air; a thumb's bigness of burnished plumage, hovering and vibrating about the bean-poles. It was with indescribable interest, and even more than childish delight, that Clifford watched the humming-birds. He used to thrust his head softly out of the arbor, to see them the better; all the while, too, motioning Phœbe to be quiet, and snatching glimpses of the smile upon her face, so as to heap his enjoyment up the higher with her sympathy. He had not merely grown young;—he was a child again.

Hepzibah, whenever she happened to witness one of these fits of miniature enthusiasm, would shake her head, with a strange mingling of the mother and sister, and of pleasure and sadness, in her aspect. She said that it had always been thus with Clifford, when the humming-birds came,—always, from his babyhood,—and that his delight in them had been one of the earliest tokens by which he showed his love for beautiful

things. And it was a wonderful coin dence, the good lady thought, that t artist should have planted these scarl flowering beans—which the hummi birds sought far and wide, and wh had not grown in the Pyncheon-gar before for forty years—on the ve summer of Clifford's return.

Then would the tears stand in p Hepzibah's eyes, or overflow them w a too abundant gush, so that she v fain to betake herself into some corn lest Clifford should espy her agitati Indeed, all the enjoyments of this per were provocative of tears. Coming late as it did, it was a kind of Ind summer, with a mist in its balmiest s shine, and decay and death in its gau est delight. The more Clifford seemed taste the happiness of a child, sadder was the difference to be rec nized. With a mysterious and terri Past, which had annihilated his memo and a blank Future before him, he l only this visionary and impalpable N which, if you once look closely at it nothing. He himself, as was percept by many symptoms, lay darkly beh his pleasure, and knew it to be a ba play, which he was to toy and t with, instead of thoroughly believ Clifford saw, it may be, in the mirro his deeper consciousness, that he was example and representative of that g class of people whom an inexplic Providence is continually putting cross-purposes with the world; breal what seems its own promise in t nature; withholding their proper f and setting poison before them fo banquet; and thus,—when it might easily, as one would think, have l adjusted otherwise,—making their istence a strangeness, a solitude,

ment. All his life long, he had been
rning how to be wretched, as one
rns a foreign tongue; and now, with
lesson thoroughly at heart he could
h difficulty comprehend his little airy
piness. Frequently, there was a dim
dow of doubt in his eyes. "Take my
d, Phœbe," he would say, "and pinch
ard with your little fingers! Give me
ose, that I may press its thorns, and
ve myself awake, by the sharp touch
pain!" Evidently, he desired this
ck of a trifling anguish, in order to
ure himself, by that quality which he
t knew to be real, that the garden,
the seven weather-beaten gables,
Hepzibah's scowl and Phœbe's
le, were real, likewise. Without this
net in his flesh, he could have at-
uted no more substance to them
n to the empty confusion of imagi-
y scenes with which he had fed his
it, until even that poor sustenance
exhausted.

he author needs great faith in his
ler's sympathy; else he must hesi-
to give details so minute, and inci-
ts apparently so trifling, as are
ntial to make up the idea of this
en-life. It was the Eden of a thunder
ten Adam, who had fled for refuge
her out of the same dreary and
lous wilderness into which the origi-
Adam was expelled.

ne of the available means of amuse-
t, of which Phœbe made the most,
Clifford's behalf, was that feathered
ety, the hens, a breed of whom, as
have already said, was an immemo-
heirloom in the Pyncheon family. In
pliance with a whim of Clifford, as
roubled him to see them in confine-
t, they had been set at liberty, and
roamed at will about the garden;

doing some little mischief, but hindered
from escape by buildings, on three sides,
and the difficult peaks of a wooden
fence, on the other. They spent much
of their abundant leisure on the margin
of Maule's well, which was haunted by
a kind of snail, evidently a titbit to their
palates; and the brackish water itself,
however nauseous to the rest of the
world, was so greatly esteemed by these
fowls, that they might be seen tasting,
turning up their heads, and smacking
their bills, with precisely the air of
wine-bibbers round a probationary cask.
Their generally quiet, yet often brisk,
and constantly diversified talk, one to
another, or sometimes in soliloquy,—
as they scratched worms out of the rich,
black soil, or pecked at such plants as
suited their taste,—had such a domestic
tone, that it was almost a wonder why
you could not establish a regular interchange of ideas about household matters, human and gallinaceous. All hens
are well worth studying, for the
piquancy and rich variety of their manners; but by no possibility can there
have been other fowls of such odd appearance and deportment as these ancestral ones. They probably embodied
the traditionary peculiarities of their
whole line of progenitors, derived
through an unbroken succession of eggs;
or else this individual Chanticleer and
his two wives had grown to be humorists, and a little crack-brained withal,
on account of their solitary way of life,
and out of sympathy for Hepzibah, their
lady-patroness.

Queerly, indeed, they looked! Chanticleer himself, though stalking on two
stilt-like legs, with the dignity of interminable descent in all his gestures
was hardly bigger than an ordinary

partridge; his two wives were about the size of quails; and as for the one chicken, it looked small enough to be still in the egg, and, at the same time, sufficiently old, withered, wizened, and experienced, to have been the founder of the antiquated race. Instead of being the youngest of the family, it rather seemed to have aggregated into itself the ages, not only of these living specimens of the breed, but of all its forefathers and foremothers, whose united excellences and oddities were squeezed into its little body. Its mother evidently regarded it as the one chicken of the world, and as necessary, in fact, to the world's continuance, or, at any rate, to the equilibrium of the present system of affairs, whether in church or state. No lesser sense of the infant fowl's importance could have justified, even in a mother's eyes, the perseverance with which she watched over its safety, ruffling her small person to twice its proper size, and flying in everybody's face that so much as looked towards her hopeful progeny. No lower estimate could have vindicated the indefatigable zeal with which she scratched, and her unscrupulousness in digging up the choicest flower or vegetable, for the sake of the fat earth-worm at its root. Her nervous cluck, when the chicken happened to be hidden in the long grass or under the squash-leaves; her gentle croak of satisfaction, while sure of it beneath her wing; her note of ill-concealed fear and obstreperous defiance, when she saw her arch-enemy, a neighbor's cat, on the top of the high fence; —one or other of these sounds was to be heard at almost every moment of the day. By degrees, the observer came to feel nearly as much interest in this

chicken of illustrious race as the mot' hen did.

Phœbe, after getting well acquai with the old hen, was sometimes mitted to take the chicken in her h which was quite capable of grasping cubic inch or two of body. While curiously examined its hereditary ma —the peculiar speckle of its plum the funny tuft on its head, and a k on each of its legs,—the little biped she insisted, kept giving her a sagac wink. The daguerreotypist once v pered her that these marks betoken oddities of the Pyncheon family, that the chicken itself was a symbo the life of the old house, embodyin interpretation, likewise, although an intelligible one, as such clues gene are. It was a feathered riddle; a mys hatched out of an egg, and just as terious as if the egg had been addle

The second of Chanticleer's wives, ever since Phœbe's arrival, been in a state of heavy desponde caused, as it afterwards appeared her inability to lay an egg. One however, by her self-important gait side-way turn of her head, and the of her eye, as she pried into one an other nook of the garden,—croakir herself, all the while, with inexpres complacency,—it was made ev that this identical hen, much as kind under-valued her, carried s thing about her person, the wort which was not to be estimated eith gold or precious stones. Shortly there was a prodigious cackling gratulation of Chanticleer and al family, including the wizened chi who appeared to understand the m quite as well as did his sire, his mc or his aunt. That afternoon P.

id a diminutive egg,—not in the
lar nest—it was far too precious to
rusted there,—but cunningly hidden
er the currant-bushes, on some dry
ks of last year's grass. Hepzibah,
earning the fact, took possession of
egg and appropriated it to Clifford's
kfast, on account of a certain deli-
r of flavor, for which, as she af-
ed, these eggs had always been
ous. Thus unscrupulously did the
gentlewoman sacrifice the continu-
, perhaps, of an ancient feathered
, with no better end then to supply
brother with a dainty that hardly
l the bowl of a tea-spoon! It must
been in reference to this outrage
Chanticleer, the next day, accom-
ed by the bereaved mother of the
took his post in front of Phœbe and
ord, and delivered himself of a har-
e that might have proved as long as
wn pedigree, but for a fit of merri-
on Phœbe's part. Hereupon, the
ded fowl stalked away on his long
, and utterly withdrew his notice
Phœbe and the rest of human na-
until she made her peace with an
ing of spice-cake, which, next to
s, was the delicacy most in favor
his aristocratic taste.

e linger too long, no doubt, beside
paltry rivulet of life that flowed
igh the garden of the Pyncheon-
2. But we deem it pardonable to
d these mean incidents, and poor
nts, because they proved so greatly
fford's benefit. They had the earth-
in them, and contributed to give
health and substance. Some of his
pations wrought less desirably upon
He had a singular propensity, for
ple, to hang over Maule's well, and
at the constantly shifting phantas-

magoria of figures produced by the agitation of the water over the mosaic-
work of colored pebbles at the bottom.
He said that faces looked upward to
him there,—beautiful faces, arrayed in
betwitching smiles,—each momentary
face so fair and rosy, and every smile
so sunny, that he felt wronged at its
departure, until the same flitting witchcraft made a new one. But sometimes
he would suddenly cry out, "The dark
face gazes at me!" and be miserable the
whole day afterwards. Phœbe, when she
hung over the fountain by Clifford's
side, could see nothing of all this,—
neither the beauty nor the ugliness,—
but only the colored pebbles, looking as
if the gush of the water shook and dis-
arranged them. And the dark face, that
so troubled Clifford, was no more than
the shadow thrown from a branch of
one of the damson-trees, and breaking
the inner light of Maule's well. The
truth was, however, that his fancy—
reviving faster than his will and judgment, and always stronger than they—
created shapes of loveliness that were
symbolic of his native character, and
now and then a stern and dreadful
shape, that typified his fate.

On Sundays, after Phœbe had been at
church,—for the girl had a church-
going conscience, and would hardly have
been at ease had she missed either
prayer, singing, sermon, or benediction,
—after church-time, therefore, there
was, ordinarily, a sober little festival in
the garden. In addition to Clifford, Hepzibah and Phœbe, two guests made up
the company. One was the artist, Holgrave, who, in spite of his consociation
with reformers, and his other queer and
questionable traits, continued to hold an
elevated place in Hepzibah's regard. The

other, we are almost ashamed to say, was the venerable Uncle Venner, in a clean shirt, and a broadcloth coat, more respectable than his ordinary wear, inasmuch as it was neatly patched on each elbow, and might be called an entire garment, except for a slight inequality in the length of its skirts. Clifford, on several occasions, had seemed to enjoy the old man's intercourse, for the sake of his mellow, cheerful vein, which was like the sweet flavor of a frost-bitten apple, such as one picks up under the tree in December. A man at the very lowest point of the social scale was easier and more agreeable for the fallen gentleman to encounter than a person at any of the intermediate degrees; and, moreover, as Clifford's young manhood had been lost, he was fond of feeling himself comparatively youthful, now, in apposition with the patriarchal age of Uncle Venner. In fact, it was sometimes observable that Clifford half wilfully hid from himself the consciousness of being stricken in years, and cherished visions of an earthly future still before him; visions, however, too indistinctly drawn to be followed by disappointment—though, doubtless, by depression—when any casual incident or recollection made him sensible of the withered leaf.

So this oddly-composed little social party used to assemble under the ruinous arbor. Hepzibah—stately as ever, at heart, and yielding not an inch of her old gentility, but resting upon it so much the more, as justifying a princess-like condescension—exhibited a not ungraceful hospitality. She talked kindly to the vagrant artist, and took sage counsel—lady as she was—with the woodsawyer, the messenger of everybody's petty errands, the patched philosopher. A Uncle Venner, who had studied world at street-corners, and at ot posts equally well adapted for just servation, was as ready to give out wisdom as a town-pump to give wa

"Miss Hepzibah, ma'am," said once, after they had all been chee together, "I really enjoy these q little meetings, of a Sabbath afterno They are very much like what I ex to have, after I retire to my farm!"

"Uncle Venner," observed Clifford a drowsy, inward tone, "is always t ing about his farm. But I have a be scheme for him, by-and-by. We s see!"

"Ah, Mr. Clifford Pyncheon!" the man of patches, "you may sch for me as much as you please; but not going to give up this one schem my own, even if I never bring it re to pass. It does seem to me that make a wonderful mistake in trying heap up property upon property. had done so, I should feel as if Pr dence was not bound to take care me; and, at all events, the city woul be! I'm one of those people who th that infinity is big enough for us a and eternity long enough!"

"Why, so they are, Uncle Venn remarked Phœbe, after a pause; for had been trying to fathom the fundity and appositeness of this cluding apothegm. "But, for this s life of ours, one would like a house a moderate garden-spot of one's ov

"It appears to me," said the dag reotypist, smiling, "that Uncle Ve has the principles of Fourier at bottom of his wisdom; only they not quite so much distinctness, in mind, as in that of the systemati nchman."

'Come, Phœbe," said Hepzibah, "it is
e to bring the currants."

And then, while the yellow richness
the declining sunshine still fell into
open space of the garden, Phœbe
ught out a loaf of bread, and a
na-bowl of currants, freshly gath-
d from the bushes, and crushed with
ar. These, with water,—but not from
fountain of ill omen, close at hand,
onstituted all the entertainment.
anwhile, Holgrave took some pains
establish an intercourse with Clifford,
uated, it might seem, entirely by an
ulse of kindliness, in order that the
sent hour might be cheerfuller than
st which the poor recluse had spent,
was destined yet to spend. Neverthe-
, in the artist's deep, thoughtful, all-
ervant eyes, there was, now and
, an expression, not sinister, but
stionable; as if he had some other
rest in the scene than a stranger, a
thful and unconnected adventurer,
ht be supposed to have. With great
ility of outward mood, however, he
ied himself to the task of enliven-
the party; and with so much suc-
, that even dark-hued Hepzibah
w off one tint of melancholy, and
le what shift she could with the re-
ning portion. Phœbe said to herself,
How pleasant he can be!" As for
le Venner, as a mark of friendship
approbation, he readily consented
fford the young man his counte-
ce in the way of his profession,—
metaphorically, be it understood,
literally, by allowing a daguerreo-
of his face, so familiar to the town,
e exhibited at the entrance of Hol-
e's studio.

ifford, as the company partook of

their little banquet, grew to be the
gayest of them all. Either it was one of
those up-quivering flashes of the spirit,
to which minds in an abnormal state are
liable, or else the artist had subtly
touched some chord that made musical
vibration. Indeed, what with the pleasant summer evening, and the sympathy
of this little circle of not unkindly
souls, it was perhaps natural that a
character so susceptible as Clifford's
should become animated, and show itself readily responsive to what was said
around him. But he gave out his own
thoughts, likewise, with an airy and
fanciful glow; so that they glistened, as
it were, through the arbor, and made
their escape among the interstices of the
foliage. He had been as cheerful, no
doubt, while alone with Phœbe, but
never with such tokens of acute, although partial intelligence.

But, as the sunlight left the peaks of
the seven gables, so did the excitement
fade out of Clifford's eyes. He gazed
vaguely and mournfully about him, as
if he missed something precious, and
missed it the more drearily for not
knowing precisely what it was.

"I want my happiness!" at last he
murmured, hoarsely and indistinctly,
hardly shaping out the words. "Many,
many years, have I waited for it! It
is late! It is late! I want my happiness!"

Alas, poor Clifford! You are old, and
worn with troubles that ought never to
have befallen you. You are partly crazy,
and partly imbecile; a ruin, a failure, as
almost everybody is,—though some in
less degree, or less perceptibly, than
their fellows. Fate has no happiness in
store for you; unless your quiet home
in the old family residence with the

faithful Hepzibah, and your long summer afternoons with Phœbe, and these Sabbath festivals with Uncle Venner and the daguerreotypist, deserve to be called happiness! Why not? If not the thing itself, it is marvellously like it, and the more so for that ethereal a intangible quality which causes it all vanish, at too close an introspecti Take it, therefore, while you may! M mur not,—question not,—but make most of it!

CHAPTER XI

THE ARCHED WINDOW

FROM the inertness, or what we may term the vegetative character, of his ordinary mood, Clifford would perhaps have been content to spend one day after another, interminably,—or, at least, throughout the summer-time,—in just the kind of life described in the preceding pages. Fancying, however, that it might be for his benefit occasionally to diversify the scene, Phœbe sometimes suggested that he should look out upon the life of the street. For this purpose, they used to mount the staircase together, to the second story of the house, where, at the termination of a wide entry, there was an arched window of uncommonly large dimensions, shaded by a pair of curtains. It opened above the porch, where there had formerly been a balcony, the balustrade of which had long since gone to decay, and been removed. At this arched window, throwing it open, but keeping himself in comparative obscurity by means of the curtain, Clifford had an opportunity of witnessing such a portion of the great world's movement as might be supposed to roll through one of the retired streets of a not very populous city. But he and Phœbe made a sight as well worth seeing as any that the city could exhibit. pale, gray, childish, aged, melanch yet often simply cheerful, and so times delicately intelligent aspect Clifford, peering from behind the fa crimson of the curtain,—watching monotony of every-day occurrences a kind of inconsequential interest earnestness, and, at every petty t of his sensibility, turning for symp to the eyes of the bright young girl

If once he were fairly seated at window, even Pyncheon-street w hardly be so dull and lonely but t somewhere or other along its ext Clifford might discover matter to oc his eyes, and titillate, if not engross observation. Things familiar to youngest child that had begun its look at existence seemed strange to A cab; an omnibus, with its popu interior, dropping here and there a senger, and picking up another, and typifying that vast rolling vehicle, world, the end of whose journe everywhere and nowhere;—these jects he followed eagerly with his but forgot them, before the dust r by the horses and wheels had se along their track. As regarded nov

long which cabs and omnibuses were
be reckoned), his mind appeared to
e lost its proper gripe and retentive-
. Twice or thrice, for example, dur-
the sunny hours of the day, a water-
went along by the Pyncheon-house,
ing a broad wake of moistened
h, instead of the white dust that had
a at a lady's lightest footfall; it was
a summer shower, which the city
orities had caught and tamed, and
pelled it into the commonest routine
heir convenience. With the water-
Clifford could never grow familiar;
lways affected him with just the
e surprise as at first. His mind took
pparently sharp impression from it,
lost the recollection of this peram-
tory shower, before its next re-
arance, as completely as did the
t itself, along which the heat so
kly strewed the white dust again. It
the same with the railroad. Clifford
d hear the obstreperous howl of the
n-devil, and, by leaning a little way
the arched window, could catch a
pse of the trains of cars, flashing a
transit across the extremity of the
t. The idea of terrible energy, thus
ed upon him, was new at every re-
ence, and seemed to affect him as
greeably, and with almost as much
rise, the hundredth time as the first.
othing gives a sadder sense of decay
this loss or suspension of the
r to deal with unaccustomed things,
to keep up with the swiftness of the
ing moment. It can merely be a
ended animation; for, were the
r actually to perish, there would be
use of immortality. We are less
ghosts, for the time being, when-
this calamity befalls us.
fford was indeed the most invet-

erate of conservatives. All the antique
fashions of the street were dear to him;
even such as were characterized by a
rudeness that would naturally have an-
noyed his fastidious senses. He loved
the old rumbling and jolting carts, the
former track of which he still found in
his long-buried remembrance, as the observer of to-day finds the wheel-tracks
of ancient vehicles, in Herculaneum.
The butcher's cart, with its snowy
canopy, was an acceptable object; so
was the fish-cart, heralded by its horn;
so, likewise, was the countryman's cart
of vegetables, plodding from door to
door, with long pauses of the patient
horse, while his owner drove a trade
in turnips, carrots, summer-squashes,
string-beans, green peas, and new potatoes, with half the housewives of the
neighborhood. The baker's cart, with
the harsh music of its bells, had a
pleasant effect on Clifford, because, as
few things else did, it jingled the very
dissonance of yore. One afternoon, a
scissor-grinder chanced to set his wheel
a-going under the Pyncheon-elm, and
just in front of the arched window.
Children came running with their
mothers' scissors, or the carving-knife,
or the paternal razor, or anything else
that lacked an edge (except, indeed,
poor Clifford's wits), that the grinder
might apply the article to his magic
wheel, and give it back as good as new.
Round went the busily-revolving machinery, kept in motion by the scissor-
grinder's foot, and wore away the hard
steel against the hard stone, whence
issued an intense and spiteful prolonga-
tion of a hiss, as fierce as those emitted
by Satan and his compeers in Pande-
monium, though squeezed into smaller
compass. It was an ugly, little, venom-

ous serpent of a noise, as ever did petty violence to human ears. But Clifford listened with rapturous delight. The sound, however disagreeable, had very brisk life in it, and, together with the circle of curious children watching the revolutions of the wheel, appeared to give him a more vivid sense of active, bustling, and sunshiny existence, than he had attained in almost any other way. Nevertheless, its charm lay chiefly in the past; for the scissor-grinder's wheel had hissed in his childish ears.

He sometimes made doleful complaint that there were no stage-coaches, now-a-days. And he asked, in an injured tone, what had become of all those old square-top chaises, with wings sticking out on either side, that used to be drawn by a plough-horse, and driven by a farmer's wife and daughter, pedling whortleberries and blackberries, about the town. Their disappearance made him doubt, he said, whether the berries had not left off growing in the broad pastures, and along the shady country lanes.

But anything that appealed to the sense of beauty, in however humble a way, did not require to be recommended by these old associations. This was observable when one of those Italian boys (who are rather a modern feature of our streets) came along with his barrel-organ, and stopped under the wide and cool shadows of the elm. With his quick professional eye, he took note of the two faces watching him from the arched window, and, opening his instrument, began to scatter its melodies abroad. He had a monkey on his shoulder, dressed in a Highland plaid; and, to complete the sum of splendid attractions wherewith he presented himself to the public, there was a company of little

figures, whose sphere and habitation in the mahogany case of his organ, whose principle of life was the mu which the Italian made it his busi to grind out. In all their variety of oc pation,—the cobbler, the blacksm the soldier, the lady with her fan, toper with his bottle, the milk-maid ting by her cow,—this fortunate li society might truly be said to enjo harmonious existence, and to make literally a dance. The Italian turne crank; and, behold! every one of t small individuals started into the n curious vivacity. The cobbler wrou upon a shoe; the blacksmith hamm his iron; the soldier waved his glitte blade; the lady raised a tiny breeze her fan; the jolly toper swigged lu at his bottle; a scholar opened his b with eager thirst for knowledge, turned his head to and fro along page; the milk-maid energetic drained her cow; and a miser cou gold into his strong box;—all at same turning of a crank. Yes; moved by the self-same impulse, a l saluted his mistress on her lips! sibly, some cynic, at once merry bitter, had desired to signify, in pantomimic scene, that we mor whatever our business or amusemer however serious, however trifling,— dance to one identical tune, and, in of our ridiculous activity, bring not finally to pass. For the most remark aspect of the affair was, that, at cessation of the music, everybody petrified, at once, from the most travagant life into a dead to Neither was the cobbler's shoe finis nor the blacksmith's iron shaped nor was there a drop less of bran the toper's bottle, nor a drop mo

k in the milk-maid's pail, nor one
litional coin in the miser's strong-
x, nor was the scholar a page deeper
his book. All were precisely in the
ne condition as before they made
mselves so ridiculous by their haste
toil, to enjoy, to accumulate gold,
l to become wise. Saddest of all,
reover, the lover was none the hap-
r for the maiden's granted kiss! But,
her than swallow this last too acrid
redient, we reject the whole moral of
show.

The monkey, meanwhile, with a thick
curling out into preposterous pro-
ty from beneath his tartans, took his
tion at the Italian's feet. He turned
rinkled and abominable little visage
every passer-by, and to the circle of
dren that soon gathered round, and
Hepzibah's shop-door, and upward to
arched window, whence Phœbe and
ford were looking down. Every mont, also, he took off his Highland-
net, and performed a bow and
pe. Sometimes, moreover, he made
sonal application to individuals, hold-
out his small black palm, and other-
plainly signifying his excessive de-
for whatever filthy lucre might
pen to be in anybody's pocket. The
in and low, yet strangely man-like
ression of his wilted countenance;
prying and crafty glance, that
ved him ready to gripe at every
erable advantage; his enormous tail
enormous to be decently concealed
er his gabardine), and the deviltry
nature which it betokened:—take
monkey just as he was, in short,
you could desire no better image of
Mammon of copper-coin, symboliz-
the grossest form of the love of
ey. Neither was there any possibil-

ity of satisfying the covetous little devil.
Phœbe threw down a whole handful of
cents, which he picked up with joyless
eagerness, handed them over to the Italian for safe-keeping, and immediately
recommenced a series of pantomimic
petitions for more.

Doubtless, more than one New Eng-
lander—or, let him be of what country
he might, it is as likely to be the case—
passed by, and threw a look at the
monkey, and went on, without imagining how nearly his own moral condition
was here exemplified. Clifford, however,
was a being of another order. He had
taken childish delight in the music, and
smiled, too, at the figures which it set
in motion. But, after looking a while at
the long-tailed imp, he was so shocked
by his horrible ugliness, spiritual as well
as physical, that he actually began to
shed tears; a weakness which men of
merely delicate endowments, and destitute of the fiercer, deeper, and more
tragic power of laughter, can hardly
avoid, when the worst and meanest aspect of life happens to be presented to
them.

Pyncheon-street was sometimes en
livened by spectacles of more imposing
pretensions than the above, and which
brought the multitude along with them.
With a shivering repugnance at the idea
of personal contact with the world, a
powerful impulse still seized on Clifford,
whenever the rush and roar of the
human tide grew strongly audible to
him. This was made evident, one day,
when a political procession, with hundreds of flaunting banners, and drums,
fifes, clarions, and cymbals, reverberating between the rows of buildings,
marched all through town, and trailed
its length of trampling footsteps, and

most infrequent uproar, past the ordinarily quiet House of the Seven Gables. As a mere object of sight, nothing is more deficient in picturesque features than a procession, seen in its passage through narrow streets. The spectator feels it to be fool's play, when he can distinguish the tedious common-place of each man's visage, with the perspiration and weary self-importance on it, and the very cut of his pantaloons, and the stiffness or laxity of his shirt-collar, and the dust on the back of his black coat. In order to become majestic, it should be viewed from some vantage-point, as it rolls its slow and long array through the centre of a wide plain, or the stateliest public square of a city; for then, by its remoteness, it melts all the petty personalities, of which it is made up, into one broad mass of existence,—one great life,—one collected body of mankind, with a vast, homogeneous spirit animating it. But, on the other hand, if an impressible person, standing alone over the brink of one of these processions, should behold it, not in its atoms, but in its aggregate,—as a mighty river of life, massive in its tide, and black with mystery, and, out of its depths, calling to the kindred depth within him,—then the contiguity would add to the effect. It might so fascinate him that he would hardly be restrained from plunging into the surging stream of human sympathies.

So it proved with Clifford. He shuddered; he grew pale; he threw an appealing look at Hepzibah and Phœbe, who were with him at the window. They comprehended nothing of his emotions, and supposed him merely disturbed by the unaccustomed tumult. At last, with tremulous limbs, he started up, set his foot on the window-sill, and, in an instant more, would have been in unguarded balcony. As it was, the wh procession might have seen him, a w haggard figure, his gray locks floating the wind that waved their banners lonely being, estranged from his r but now feeling himself man again, virtue of the irrepressible instinct t possessed him. Had Clifford attained balcony, he would probably have lea into the street; but whether impe by the species of terror that someti urges its victim over the very preci which he shrinks from, or by a nat magnetism, tending towards the g centre of humanity, it were not eas decide. Both impulses might wrought on him at once.

But his companions, affrighted by gesture,—which was that of a hurried away, in spite of himsel seized Clifford's garment and held back. Hepzibah shrieked. Phœbe, whom all extravagance was a ho burst into sobs and tears.

"Clifford, Clifford! are you cra cried his sister.

"I hardly know, Hepzibah," said ford, drawing a long breath. "Fear n ing,—it is over now,—but had I t that plunge, and survived it, meth it would have made me another man

Possibly, in some sense, Clifford have been right. He needed a shock perhaps he required to take a deep, plunge into the ocean of human and to sink down and be covered b profoundness, and then to emerge bered, invigorated, restored to the v and to himself. Perhaps, again, he quired nothing less than the great remedy—death!

A similar yearning to renew

ken links of brotherhood with his
d sometimes showed itself in a milder
m; and once it was made beautiful
the religion that lay even deeper
n itself. In the incident now to be
tched, there was a touching recog-
on, on Clifford's part, of God's care
love towards him,—towards this
r, forsaken man, who, if any mortal
ld, might have been pardoned for
arding himself as thrown aside, for-
en, and left to be the sport of some
d, whose playfulness was an ecstasy
mischief.

t was the Sabbath morning; one of
se bright, calm Sabbaths, with its
hallowed atmosphere, when Heaven
ns to diffuse itself over the earth's
in a solemn smile, no less sweet
solemn. On such a Sabbath morn,
e we pure enough to be its medium,
should be conscious of the earth's
ral worship ascending through our
nes, on whatever spot of ground we
d. The church-bells, with various
s, but all in harmony, were calling
and responding to one another—"It
he Sabbath!—The Sabbath!—Yea;
Sabbath!"—and over the whole city
bells scattered the blessed sounds,
slowly, now with livelier joy, now
bell alone, now all the bells to-
er, crying earnestly—"It is the Sab-
!" and flinging their accents afar
to melt into the air, and pervade it
the holy word. The air, with God's
etest and tenderest sunshine in it,
meet for mankind to breathe into
r hearts, and send it forth again as
utterance of prayer.

lifford sat at the window, with Hep-
h, watching the neighbors as they
ped into the street. All of them,
ever unspiritual on other days, were

transfigured by the Sabbath influence;
so that their very garments—whether it
were an old man's decent coat, well
brushed for the thousandth time, or a
little boy's first sack and trousers,
finished yesterday by his mother's needle
—had somewhat of the quality of as-
cension-robes. Forth, likewise, from the
portal of the old house, stepped Phœbe,
putting up her small green sunshade,
and throwing upward a glance and smile
of parting kindness to the faces at the
arched window. In her aspect there was
a familiar gladness, and a holiness that
you could play with, and yet reverence
it as much as ever. She was like a
prayer, offered up in the homeliest
beauty of one's mother-tongue. Fresh
was Phœbe, moreover, and airy and
sweet in her apparel; as if nothing that
she wore—neither her gown, nor her
small straw bonnet, nor her little kerchief, any more than her snowy stockings—had ever been put on before; or,
if worn, were all the fresher for it, and
with a fragrance as if they had lain
among the rose-buds.

The girl waved her hand to Hepzibah
and Clifford, and went up the street; a
religion in herself, warm, simple, true,
with a substance that could walk on
earth, and a spirit that was capable of
heaven.

"Hepzibah," asked Clifford, after
watching Phœbe to the corner, "do you
never go to church?"

"No, Clifford!" she replied,—"not
these many, many years!"

"Were I to be there," he rejoined, "it
seems to me that I could pray once
more, when so many human souls were
praying all around me!"

She looked into Clifford's face, and
beheld there a soft, natural effusion; for

his heart gushed out, as it were, and ran over at his eyes, in delightful reverence for God, and kindly affection for his human brethren. The emotion communicated itself to Hepzibah. She yearned to take him by the hand, and go and kneel down, they two together,—both so long separate from the world, and, as she now recognized, scarcely friends with Him above,—to kneel down among the people, and be reconciled to God and man at once.

"Dear brother," said she, earnestly, "let us go! We belong nowhere. We have not a foot of space in any church to kneel upon; but let us go to some place of worship, even if we stand in the broad aisle. Poor and forsaken as we are, some pew-door will be opened to us!"

So Hepzibah and her brother made themselves ready,—as ready as they could, in the best of their old-fashioned garments, which had hung on pegs, or been laid away in trunks, so long that the dampness and mouldy smell of the past was on them,—made themselves ready, in their faded bettermost, to go to church. They descended the staircase together,—gaunt, sallow Hepzibah, and pale, emaciated, age-stricken Clifford! They pulled open the front door, and stepped across the threshold, and felt, both of them, as if they were standing in the presence of the whole world, and with mankind's great and terrible eye on them alone. The eye of their Father seemed to be withdrawn, and gave them no encouragement. The warm sunny air of the street made them shiver. Their hearts quaked within them, at the idea of taking one step further.

"It cannot be, Hepzibah!—it is too late," said Clifford, with deep sadness.—"We are ghosts! We have no right among human beings,—no right an[y]where, but in this old house, which [has] a curse on it, and which therefore [we] are doomed to haunt! And, besides," continued, with a fastidious sensibili[ty] inalienably characteristic of the m[an] "it would not be fit nor beautiful to [go] It is an ugly thought, that I should [be] frightful to my fellow-beings, and t[hat] children would cling to their mothe[r's] gowns, at sight of me!"

They shrank back into the dus[ky] passage-way, and closed the door. B[ut] going up the staircase again, they fou[nd] the whole interior of the house ten-f[old] more dismal, and the air closer a[nd] heavier, for the glimpse and breath [of] freedom which they had just snatch[ed] They could not flee; their jailer had [not] left the door ajar, in mockery, and sto[od] behind it, to watch them stealing o[ut] At the threshold, they felt his piti[less] gripe upon them. For, what other d[un]geon is so dark as one's own hea[rt] What jailer so inexorable as one's se[lf]

But it would be no fair picture [of] Clifford's state of mind, were we [to] represent him as continually or prev[ail]ingly wretched. On the contrary, th[ere] was no other man in the city, we [are] bold to affirm, of so much as half [his] years, who enjoyed so many lightso[me] and griefless moments as himself. [He] had no burthen of care upon him; th[ere] were none of those questions and c[on]tingencies with the future to be settl[ed] which wear away all other lives, [and] render them not worth having by [the] process of providing for their supp[ort] In this respect, he was a child,—a c[hild] for the whole term of his existence it long or short. Indeed, his life see[med] to be standing still at a period littl[e in] advance of childhood, and to cluste[r] reminiscences about that epoch; just after the torpor of a heavy blow, the sufferer's reviving consciousness goes back to a moment considerably behind the accident that stupefied him. He sometimes told Phœbe and Hepzibah his dreams, in which he invariably played the part of a child, or a very young man. So vivid were they, in his relation of them, that he once held a dispute with his sister as to the particular figure of a chintz morning-dress, which he had seen their mother wear, in the dream of the preceding night. Hepzibah, valuing herself on a woman's accuracy in such matters, held it to be slightly different from what Clifford described; but, producing the very gown from an old trunk, it proved to be identical with his remembrance of it. Had Clifford, every time that he emerged out of dreams so life-like, undergone the torture of transformation from a boy into an old and broken man, the daily recurrence of the shock would have been too much to bear. It would have caused an acute agony to thrill, from the morning twilight, all the day through, until bed-time; and even then would have mingled a dull, inscrutable pain, and pallid hue of misfortune, with the visionary bloom and adolescence of his slumber. But the nightly moonshine interwove itself with his morning mist, and enveloped him as in a robe, which he hugged about his person, and seldom let realities pierce through; he was not often quite awake, but slept open-eyed, and perhaps fancied himself most dreaming then.

Thus, lingering always so near his childhood, he had sympathies with children, and kept his heart the fresher thereby, like a reservoir into which rivulets were pouring, not far from the fountain-head. Though prevented, by a subtle sense of propriety, from desiring to associate with them, he loved few things better than to look out of the arched window, and see a little girl driving her hoop along the sidewalk, or schoolboys at a game of ball. Their voices, also, were very pleasant to him, heard at a distance, all swarming and intermingling together, as flies do in a sunny room.

Clifford would, doubtless, have been glad to share their sports. One afternoon, he was seized with an irresistible desire to blow soap-bubbles; an amusement, as Hepzibah told Phœbe apart, that had been a favorite one with her brother, when they were both children. Behold him, therefore, at the arched window, with an earthern pipe in his mouth! Behold him, with his gray hair, and a wan, unreal smile over his countenance, where still hovered a beautiful grace, which his worst enemy must have acknowledged to be spiritual and immortal, since it had survived so long! Behold him, scattering airy spheres abroad, from the window into the street! Little impalpable worlds were those soap-bubbles, with the big world depicted, in hues bright as imagination, or the nothing of their surface. It was curious to see how the passers-by regarded these brilliant fantasies, as they came floating down, and made the dull atmosphere imaginative about them. Some stopped to gaze, and, perhaps, carried a pleasant recollection of the bubbles onward as far as the street-corner; some looked angrily upward, as if poor Clifford wronged them, by setting an image of beauty afloat so near their dusty pathway. A great many put out their fingers or their walking-sticks, to touch, withal; and were perversely gratified, no doubt, when the bubble, with all its pictured earth and sky scene, vanished as if it had never been.

At length, just as an elderly gentleman of very dignified presence happened to be passing, a large bubble sailed majestically down, and burst right against his nose! He looked up,—at first with a stern, keen glance, which penetrated at once into the obscurity behind the arched window,—then with a smile, which might be conceived as diffusing a dog-day sultriness for the space of several yards about him.

"Aha, Cousin Clifford!" cried Judge Pyncheon. "What! still blowing soap bubbles!"

The tone seemed as if meant to kind and soothing, but yet had a terness of sarcasm in it. As for Cliffo an absolute palsy of fear came o him. Apart from any definite cause dread which his past experience m have given him, he felt that native original horror of the excellent ju which is proper to a weak, delicate apprehensive character, in the prese of massive strength. Strength is inc prehensible by weakness, and, theref the more terrible. There is no gre bugbear than a strong-willed relative the circle of his own connections.

CHAPTER XII

THE DAGUERREOTYPIST

It must not be supposed that the life of a personage naturally so active as Phœbe could be wholly confined within the precincts of the old Pyncheon-house. Clifford's demands upon her time were usually satisfied, in those long days, considerably earlier than sunset. Quiet as his daily existence seemed, it nevertheless drained all the resources by which he lived. It was not physical exercise that over-wearied him; for—except that he sometimes wrought a little with a hoe, or paced the garden-walk, or, in rainy weather, traversed a large, unoccupied room—it was his tendency to remain only too quiescent, as regarded any toil of the limbs and muscles. But, either there was a smouldering fire within him that consumed his vital energy, or the monotony that would dragged itself with benumbing e over a mind differently situated wa monotony to Clifford. Possibly, he in a state of second growth and covery, and was constantly assimila nutriment for his spirit and inte from sights, sounds, and events, w passed as a perfect void to persons r practised with the world. As all is tivity and vicissitude to the new of a child, so might it be, like to a mind that had undergone a of new creation, after its long-suspe life.

Be the cause what it might, Cli commonly retired to rest, thorou exhausted, while the sunbeams were melting through his window-curtain

e thrown with late lustre on the
mber wall. And while he thus slept
ly, as other children do, and dreamed
childhood, Phœbe was free to follow
own tastes for the remainder of the
and evening.

his was a freedom essential to the
lth even of a character so little sus-
tible of morbid influences as that of
ebe. The old house, as we have
ady said, had both the dry-rot and
damp-rot in its walls; it was not
d to breathe no other atmosphere
that. Hepzibah, though she had
valuable and redeeming traits, had
wn to be a kind of lunatic, by im-
oning herself so long in one place,
no other company than a single
es of ideas, and but one affection,
one bitter sense of wrong. Clif-
, the reader may perhaps imagine,
too inert to operate morally on
fellow-creatures, however intimate
exclusive their relations with him.
the sympathy or magnetism among
an beings is more subtle and
ersal than we think; it exists, in-
, among different classes of organ-
life, and vibrates from one to an-
r. A flower, for instance, as Phœbe
elf observed, always began to droop
er in Clifford's hand, or Hepzibah's,
in her own; and by the same law,
verting her whole daily life into a
er-fragrance for these two sickly
ts, the blooming girl must inevitably
p and fade much sooner than if
n on a younger and happier breast.
ess she had now and then indulged
brisk impulses, and breathed rural
in a suburban walk, or ocean-
zes along the shore,—had occa-
ally obeyed the impulse of nature, in
England girls, by attending a meta-

physical or philosophical lecture, or
viewing a seven-mile panorama, or listening to a concert,—had gone shopping
about the city, ransacking entire depôts
of splendid merchandise, and bringing
home a ribbon,—had employed, likewise,
a little time to read the Bible in her
chamber, and had stolen a little more to
think of her mother and her native
place,—unless for such moral medicines
as the above, we should soon have beheld our poor Phœbe grow thin, and
put on a bleached, unwholesome aspect,
and assume strange, shy ways, prophetic
of old-maidenhood and a cheerless
future.

Even as it was, a change grew visible;
a change partly to be regretted, although
whatever charm it infringed upon was
repaired by another, perhaps more
precious. She was not so constantly gay,
but had her moods of thought, which
Clifford, on the whole, liked better than
her former phase of unmingled cheerfulness; because now she understood him
better and more delicately, and sometimes even interpreted him to himself.
Her eyes looked larger, and darker, and
deeper; so deep, at some silent moments,
that they seemed like Artesian wells,
down, down, into the infinite. She was
less girlish than when we first beheld
her, alighting from the omnibus; less
girlish, but more a woman.

The only youthful mind with which
Phœbe had an opportunity of frequent
intercourse was that of the daguerreotypist. Inevitably, by the pressure of the
seclusion about them, they had been
brought into habits of some familiarity.
Had they met under different circumstances, neither of these young persons
would have been likely to bestow much
thought upon the other; unless, indeed,

their extreme dissimilarity should have proved a principle of mutual attraction. Both, it is true, were characters proper to New England life, and possessing a common ground, therefore, in their more external developments; but as unlike, in their respective interiors, as if their native climes had been at world-wide distance. During the early part of their acquaintance, Phœbe had held back rather more than was customary with her frank and simple manners from Holgrave's not very marked advances. Nor was she yet satisfied that she knew him well, although they almost daily met and talked together, in a kind, friendly, and what seemed to be a familiar way.

The artist, in a desultory manner, had imparted to Phœbe something of his history. Young as he was, and had his career terminated at the point already attained, there had been enough of incident to fill, very creditably, an auto-biographic volume. A romance on the plan of Gil Blas, adapted to American society and manners, would cease to be a romance. The experience of many individuals among us, who think it hardly worth the telling, would equal the vicissitudes of the Spaniard's earlier life; while their ultimate success, or the point whither they tend, may be incomparably higher than any that a novelist would imagine for his hero. Holgrave, as he told Phœbe, somewhat proudly, could not boast of his origin, unless being exceedingly humble, nor of his education, except that it had been the scantiest possible, and obtained by a few winter-months' attendance at a district school. Left early to his own guidance, he had begun to be self-dependent while yet a boy; and it was a

condition aptly suited to his natu force of will. Though now but twen two years old (lacking some mont which are years in such a life), he already been, first, a country schc master; next, a salesman in a coun store; and, either at the same time afterwards, the political editor of country newspaper. He had subsequen travelled New England and the Mid States, as a pedler, in the employm of a Connecticut manufactory of cologne-water and other essences. In episodical way, he had studied and pi tised dentistry, and with very flatter success, especially in many of factory-towns along our inland strea As a supernumerary official, of so kind or other, aboard a packet-ship, had visited Europe, and found mea before his return, to see Italy, and p of France and Germany. At a la period, he had spent some months i community of Fourierists. Still more cently, he had been a public lecturer Mesmerism, for which science (as assured Phœbe, and, indeed, satis torily proved, by putting Chanticl who happened to be scratching near to sleep) he had very remarka endowments.

His present phase, as a daguer typist, was of no more importance his own view, nor likely to be m permanent, than any of the prece ones. It had been taken up with careless alacrity of an adventurer, had his bread to earn. It would thrown aside as carelessly, wheneve should choose to earn his bread by s other equally digressive means. what was most remarkable, and, haps, showed a more than com poise in the young man, was the

t, amid all these personal vicissitudes, had never lost his identity. Home-
s as he had been,—continually chang-
his whereabout, and, therefore, re-
nsible neither to public opinion nor
individuals,—putting off one exterior,
l snatching up another, to be soon
tted for a third,—he had never vio-
d the innermost man, but had carried
conscience along with him. It was
ossible to know Holgrave, without
ognizing this to be the fact. Hepzi-
a had seen it. Phœbe soon saw it,
wise, and gave him the sort of confi-
ce which such a certainty inspires.
s was startled, however, and some-
es repelled,—not by any doubt of his
grity to whatever law he acknowl-
ed,—but by a sense that his law
ered from her own. He made her
asy, and seemed to unsettle every-
g around her, by his lack of rever-
e for what was fixed, unless, at a
ment's warning, it could establish its
t to hold its ground.

hen, moreover, she scarcely thought
affectionate in his nature. He was
calm and cool an observer. Phœbe
his eye, often; his heart, seldom,
never. He took a certain kind of inst in Hepzibah and her brother, and
ebe herself. He studied them atively, and allowed no slightest cir-
stance of their individualities to
pe him. He was ready to do them
tever good he might; but, after all,
never exactly made common cause
them, nor gave any reliable evi-
ce that he loved them better, in
portion as he knew them more. In
relations with them, he seemed to be
quest of mental food, not heart-
enance. Phœbe could not conceive
t interested him so much in her

friends and herself, intellectually, since
he cared nothing for them, or, comparatively, so little, as objects of human
affection.

Always, in his interviews with Phœbe,
the artist made especial inquiry as to
the welfare of Clifford, whom, except at
the Sunday festival, he seldom saw.

"Does he still seem happy?" he asked,
one day.

"As happy as a child," answered
Phœbe; "but—like a child, too—very
easily disturbed."

"How disturbed?" inquired Holgrave.
"By things without, or by thoughts
within?"

"I cannot see his thoughts! How
should I?" replied Phœbe, with simple
piquancy. "Very often, his humor
changes without any reason that can be
guessed at, just as a cloud comes over
the sun. Latterly, since I have begun to
know him better, I feel it to be not
quite right to look closely into his
moods. He has had such a great sorrow,
that his heart is made all solemn and
sacred by it. When he is cheerful,—
when the sun shines into his mind,—
then I venture to peep in, just as far as
the light reaches, but no further. It is
holy ground where the shadow falls!"

"How prettily you express this sentiment!" said the artist. "I can understand the feeling, without possessing it.
Had I your opportunities, no scruples
would prevent me from fathoming Clifford to the full depth of my plummet-
line!"

"How strange that you should wish
it!" remarked Phœbe, involuntarily.
"What is Cousin Clifford to you?"

"O, nothing,—of course, nothing!"
answered Holgrave, with a smile. "Only
this is such an odd and incomprehensible

world! The more I look at it, the more it puzzles me; and I begin to suspect that a man's bewilderment is the measure of his wisdom. Men and women, and children, too, are such strange creatures, that one never can be certain that he really knows them; nor ever guess what they have been, from what he sees them to be, now. Judge Pyncheon! Clifford! What a complex riddle—a complexity of complexities—do they present! It requires intuitive sympathy, like a young girl's, to solve it. A mere observer, like myself (who never have any intuitions, and am, at best, only subtile and acute), is pretty certain to go astray."

The artist now turned the conversation to themes less dark than that which they had touched upon. Phœbe and he were young together; nor had Holgrave, in his premature experience of life, wasted entirely that beautiful spirit of youth, which, gushing forth from one small heart and fancy, may diffuse itself over the universe, making it all as bright as on the first day of creation. Man's own youth is the world's youth; at least, he feels as if it were, and imagines that the earth's granite substance is something not yet hardened, and which he can mould into whatever shape he likes. So it was with Holgrave. He could talk sagely about the world's old age, but never actually believed what he said; he was a young man still, and therefore looked upon the world—that gray-bearded and wrinkled profligate, decrepit, without being venerable—as a tender stripling, capable of being improved into all that it ought to be, but scarcely yet had shown the remotest promise of becoming. He had that sense, or inward prophecy,—which a young

man had better never have been b than not to have, and a mature man better die at once than utterly to linquish,—that we are not doomed creep on forever in the old, bad w but that, this very now, there are harbingers abroad of a golden era, to accomplished in his own lifetime. seemed to Holgrave—as doubtless it seemed to the hopeful of every cent since the epoch of Adam's grandchild —that in this age, more than ever fore, the moss-grown and rotten Pas to be torn down, and lifeless instituti to be thrust out of the way, and t dead corpses buried, and everything begin anew.

As to the main point,—may we ne live to doubt it!—as to the better turies that are coming, the artist surely right. His error lay in suppo that this age, more than any past future one, is destined to see the tered garments of Antiquity exchan for a new suit, instead of gradually newing themselves by patchwork; applying his own little life-span as measure of an interminable achie ment; and, more than all, in fancy that it mattered anything to the g end in view, whether he himself sh contend for it or against it. Yet it well for him to think so. This thusiasm, infusing itself through calmness of his character, and thus ing an aspect of settled thought wisdom, would serve to keep his yo pure, and make his aspirations h And when, with the years settling d more weightily upon him, his early f should be modified by inevitable exp ence, it would be with no harsh sudden revolution of his sentiments. would still have faith in man's brigh

destiny, and perhaps love him all the
ter, as he should recognize his help-
ness in his own behalf; and the
ghty faith, with which he began life,
ld be well bartered for a far humbler
, at its close, in discerning that man's
t-directed effort accomplishes a kind
dream, while God is the sole worker
realities.

Holgrave had read very little, and
t little in passing through the
roughfare of life, where the mystic
guage of his books was necessarily
ed up with the babble of the multi-
e, so that both one and the other
e apt to lose any sense that might
e been properly their own. He con-
red himself a thinker, and was cer-
ly of a thoughtful turn, but, with
own path to discover, had perhaps
lly yet reached the point where an
cated man begins to think. The true
e of his character lay in that deep
sciousness of inward strength, which
le all his past vicissitudes seem
ely like a change of garments; in
enthusiasm, so quiet that he
cely knew of its existence, but which
e a warmth to everything that he
his hand on; in that personal am-
n, hidden—from his own as well as
er eyes—among his more generous
ulses, but in which lurked a certain
acy, that might solidify him from a
rist into the champion of some
ticable cause. Altogether, in his cul-
and want of culture,—in his crude,
, and misty philosophy, and the
tical experience that counteracted
c of its tendencies; in his mag-
mous zeal for man's welfare, and his
lessness of whatever the ages had
blished in man's behalf; in his faith,
in his infidelity; in what he had,

and in what he lacked,—the artist might
fitly enough stand forth as the representative of many compeers in his native
land.

His career it would be difficult to
prefigure. There appeared to be qualities
in Holgrave, such as, in a country where
everything is free to the hand that can
grasp it, could hardly fail to put some
of the world's prizes within his reach.
But these matters are delightfully uncertain. At almost every step in life, we
meet with young men of just about
Holgrave's age, for whom we anticipate
wonderful things, but of whom, even
after much and careful inquiry, we
never happen to hear another word. The
effervescence of youth and passion, and
the fresh gloss of the intellect and
imagination, endow them with a false
brilliancy, which makes fools of themselves and other people. Like certain
chintzes, calicoes, and ginghams, they
show finely in their first newness, but
cannot stand the sun and rain, and assume a very sober aspect after washing-
day.

But our business is with Holgrave as
we find him on this particular afternoon,
and in the arbor of the Pyncheon-
garden. In that point of view, it was a
pleasant sight to behold this young man,
with so much faith in himself, and so
fair an appearance of admirable powers,
—so little harmed, too, by the many
tests that had tried his metal,—it was
pleasant to see him in his kindly intercourse with Phœbe. Her thought had
scarcely done him justice, when it pronounced him cold; or, if so, he had
grown warmer now. Without such purpose on her part, and unconsciously on
his, she made the House of the Seven
Gables like a home to him, and the

garden a familiar precinct. With the insight on which he prided himself, he fancied that he could look through Phœbe, and all around her, and could read her off like a page of a child's story-book. But these transparent natures are often deceptive in their depth; those pebbles at the bottom of the fountain are further from us than we think. Thus the artist, whatever he might judge of Phœbe's capacity, was beguiled, by some silent charm of hers, to talk freely of what he dreamed of doing in the world. He poured himself out as to another self. Very possibly, he forgot Phœbe while he talked to her, and was moved only by the inevitable tendency of thought, when rendered sympathetic by enthusiasm and emotion, to flow into the first safe reservoir which it finds. But, had you peeped at them through the chinks of the garden-fence, the young man's earnestness and heightened color might have led you to suppose that he was making love to the young girl!

At length, something was said by Holgrave that made it apposite for Phœbe to inquire what had first brought him acquainted with her cousin Hepzibah, and why he now chose to lodge in the desolate old Pyncheon-house. Without directly answering her, he turned from the Future, which had heretofore been the theme of his discourse, and began to speak of the influences of the Past. One subject, indeed, is but the reverberation of the other.

"Shall we never, never get rid of this Past?" cried he, keeping up the earnest tone of his preceding conversation.—"It lies upon the Present like a giant's dead body! In fact, the case is just as if a young giant were compelled to waste all his strength in carrying about the cor of the old giant, his grandfather, v died a long while ago, and only needs be decently buried. Just think a r ment, and it will startle you to see w slaves we are to by-gone times,— Death, if we give the matter the ri word!"

"But I do not see it," observ Phœbe.

"For example, then," continued H grave; "a dead man, if he happen have made a will, disposes of wealth longer his own; or, if he die intestate is distributed in accordance with notions of men much longer dead th he. A dead man sits on all our judgme seats; and living judges do but sea out and repeat his decisions. We r in dead men's books! We laugh at de men's jokes, and cry at dead me pathos! We are sick of dead me diseases, physical and moral, and die the same remedies with which dead d tors killed their patients! We wors the living Deity according to dead me forms and creeds! Whatever we seek do, of our own free motion, a de man's icy hand obstructs us! Turn eyes to what point we may, a de man's white, immitigable face counters them, and freezes our v heart! And we must be dead oursel before we can begin to have our pro influence on our own world, which then be no longer our world, but world of another generation, with wh we shall have no shadow of a right interfere. I ought to have said, too, t we live in dead men's houses; as, instance, in this of the seven gables!

"And why not," said Phœbe, "so l as we can be comfortable in them?"

"But we shall live to see the day

ist," went on the artist, "when no
an shall build his house for posterity.
hy should he? He might just as rea-
nably order a durable suit of clothes,
leather, or gutta percha, or whatever
e lasts longest,—so that his great-
andchildren should have the benefit of
em, and cut precisely the same figure
the world that he himself does. If
ch generation were allowed and ex-
cted to build its own houses, that single
ange, comparatively unimportant in
elf, would imply almost every re-
m which society is now suffering for.
loubt whether even our public edifices
our capitols, state-houses, court-
uses, city-halls, and churches—ought
be built of such permanent materials
stone or brick. It were better that
ey should crumble to ruin, once
twenty years, or thereabouts, as
hint to the people to examine into
l reform the institutions which they
mbolize."

'How you hate everything old!" said
œbe, in dismay. "It makes me dizzy
think of such a shifting world!"

'I certainly love nothing mouldy,"
swered Holgrave. "Now, this old
ncheon-house! Is it a wholesome
ce to live in, with its black shingles,
l the green moss that shows how
np they are?—its dark, low-studded
ms?—its grime and sordidness, which
the crystallization on its walls of the
nan breath, that has been drawn and
aled here, in discontent and an-
sh? The house ought to be purified
h fire,—purified till only its ashes
nain!"

'Then why do you live in it?" asked
œbe, a little piqued.

'O, I am pursuing my studies here;
in books, however," replied Hol-

grave. "The house, in my view, is expressive of that odious and abominable
Past, with all its bad influences, against
which I have just been declaiming. I
dwell in it for a while, that I may know
the better how to hate it. By-the-by,
did you ever hear the story of Maule,
the wizard, and what happened between
him and your immeasurably great-
grandfather?"

"Yes indeed!" said Phœbe; "I heard
it long ago, from my father, and two
or three times from my cousin Hepzibah, in the month that I have been
here. She seems to think that all the
calamities of the Pyncheons began from
that quarrel with the wizard, as you call
him. And you, Mr. Holgrave, look as
if you thought so too! How singular,
that you should believe what is so very
absurd, when you reject many things
that are a great deal worthier of credit!"

"I do believe it," said the artist, seriously; "not as a superstition, however,
but as proved by unquestionable facts,
and as exemplifying a theory. Now, see;
—under those seven gables, at which we
now look up,—and which old Colonel
Pyncheon meant to be the house of his
descendants, in prosperity and happiness, down to an epoch far beyond the
present,—under that roof, through a
portion of three centuries, there has
been perpetual remorse of conscience, a
constantly defeated hope, strife amongst
kindred, various misery, a strange form
of death, dark suspicion, unspeakable
disgrace,—all, or most of which calamity, I have the means of tracing to
the old Puritan's inordinate desire to
plant and endow a family. To plant a
family! This idea is at the bottom of
most of the wrong and mischief which
men do. The truth is, that, once in every

half century, at longest, a family should be merged into the great, obscure mass of humanity, and forget all about its ancestors. Human blood, in order to keep its freshness, should run in hidden streams, as the water of an aqueduct is conveyed in subterranean pipes. In the family existence of these Pyncheons, for instance,—forgive me, Phœbe; but I cannot think of you as one of them,—in their brief New England pedigree, there has been time enough to infect them all with one kind of lunacy or another!"

"You speak very unceremoniously of my kindred," said Phœbe, debating with herself whether she ought to take offence.

"I speak true thoughts to a true mind!" answered Holgrave, with a vehemence which Phœbe had not before witnessed in him. "The truth is as I say! Furthermore, the original perpetrator and father of this mischief appears to have perpetuated himself, and still walks the street,—at least, his very image, in mind and body,—with the fairest prospect of transmitting to posterity as rich and as wretched an inheritance as he has received! Do you remember the daguerreotype, and its resemblance to the old portrait?"

"How strangely in earnest you are!" exclaimed Phœbe, looking at him with surprise and perplexity: half alarmed, and partly inclined to laugh. "You talk of the lunacy of the Pyncheons;—is it contagious?"

"I understand you!" said the art coloring and laughing. "I believe I a little mad. This subject has taken h of my mind with the strangest tena of clutch, since I have lodged in yo old gable. As one method of throw it off, I have put an incident of Pyncheon family history, with whic happen to be acquainted, into the fo of a legend, and mean to publish it i magazine."

"Do you write for the magazine inquired Phœbe.

"Is it possible you did not know i cried Holgrave.—"Well, such is liter fame! Yes, Miss Phœbe Pynche among the multitude of my marvell gifts, I have that of writing stori and my name has figured, I can ass you, on the covers of Graham a Godey, making as respectable an pearance, for aught I could see, as of the canonized bead-roll with wh it was associated. In the humorous li I am thought to have a very pretty v with me; and as for pathos, I am provocative of tears as an onion. shall I read you my story?"

"Yes, if it is not very long," s Phœbe,—and added, laughingly,—" very dull."

As this latter point was one wh the daguerreotypist could not decide himself, he forthwith produced his of manuscript, and, while the late s beams gilded the seven gables, began read.

CHAPTER XIII

ALICE PYNCHEON

THERE was a message brought, one
y, from the worshipful Gervayse Pyn-
eon to young Matthew Maule, the
rpenter, desiring his immediate pres-
ce at the House of the Seven Gables.
"And what does your master want
th me?" said the carpenter to Mr.
ncheon's black servant. "Does the
use need any repair? Well it may, by
s time; and no blame to my father
o built it, neither! I was reading the
l colonel's tombstone, no longer ago
n last Sabbath; and reckoning from
it date, the house has stood seven-
d-thirty years. No wonder if there
uld be a job to do on the roof."

"Don't know what massa wants," an-
ered Scipio. "The house is a berry
od house, and old Colonel Pyncheon
ink so too, I reckon;—else why the
l man haunt it so, and frighten a
or nigga, as he does?"

"Well, well, friend Scipio; let your
ister know that I'm coming," said
e carpenter, with a laugh. "For a fair,
rkman-like job, he'll find me his man.
id so the house is haunted, is it? It
ll take a tighter workman than I am
keep the spirits out of the seven
bles. Even if the colonel would be
it," he added, muttering to himself,
iy old grandfather, the wizard, will be
etty sure to stick to the Pyncheons,
long as their walls hold together."

"What's that you mutter to yourself,
atthew Maule?" asked Scipio. "And
iat for do you look so black at me?"

"No matter, darkey!" said the car-
nter. "Do you think nobody is to

look black but yourself? Go tell your
master I'm coming; and if you happen
to see Mistress Alice, his daughter, give
Matthew Maule's humble respects to
her. She has brought a fair face from
Italy,—fair, and gentle, and proud,—
has that same Alice Pyncheon!"

"He talk of Mistress Alice!" cried
Scipio, as he returned from his errand.
"The low carpenter-man! He no business so much as to look at her a great
way off!"

This young Matthew Maule, the carpenter, it must be observed, was a person little understood, and not very
generally liked, in the town where he
resided; not that anything could be
alleged against his integrity, or his skill
and diligence in the handicraft which
he exercised. The aversion (as it might
justly be called) with which many persons regarded him, was partly the result
of his own character and deportment,
and partly an inheritance.

He was the grandson of a former
Matthew Maule, one of the early settlers
of the town, and who had been a famous
and terrible wizard, in his day. This old
reprobate was one of the sufferers when
Cotton Mather and his brother ministers, and the learned judges, and other
wise men, and Sir William Phipps, the
sagacious governor, made such laudable
efforts to weaken the great enemy of
souls, by sending a multitude of his
adherents up the rocky pathway of
Gallows Hill. Since those days, no
doubt, it had grown to be suspected,
that, in consequence of an unfortunate

overdoing of a work praiseworthy in itself, the proceedings against the witches had proved far less acceptable to the Beneficent Father than to that very Arch Enemy whom they were intended to distress and utterly overwhelm. It is not the less certain, however, that awe and terror brooded over the memories of those who died for this horrible crime of witchcraft. Their graves, in the crevices of the rocks, were supposed to be incapable of retaining the occupants who had been so hastily thrust into them. Old Matthew Maule, especially, was known to have as little hesitation or difficulty in rising out of his grave as an ordinary man in getting out of bed, and was as often seen at midnight as living people at noonday. This pestilent wizard (in whom his just punishment seemed to have wrought no manner of amends) had an inveterate habit of haunting a certain mansion, styled the House of the Seven Gables, against the owner of which he pretended to hold an unsettled claim for ground-rent. The ghosts, it appears,—with the pertinacity which was one of his distinguishing characteristics while alive,—insisted that he was the rightful proprietor of the site upon which the house stood. His terms were, that either the aforesaid ground-rent, from the day when the cellar began to be dug, should be paid down, or the mansion itself given up; else he, the ghostly creditor, would have his finger in all the affairs of the Pyncheons, and make everything go wrong with them, though it should be a thousand years after his death. It was a wild story, perhaps, but seemed not altogether so incredible, to those who could remember what an inflexibly obstinate old fellow this wizard Maule had been.

Now, the wizard's grandson, young Matthew Maule of our story, popularly supposed to have inheri some of his ancestor's questiona traits. It is wonderful how many surdities were promulgated in referei to the young man. He was fabled, example, to have a strange power getting into people's dreams, and re, lating matters there according to own fancy, pretty much like the sta manager of a theatre. There was a gr deal of talk among the neighbors, p ticularly the petticoated ones, ab what they called the witchcraft Maule's eye. Some said that he co look into people's minds; others, th by the marvellous power of this e he could draw people into his own mi or send them, if he pleased, to errands to his grandfather, in the sp tual world; others, again, that it what is termed an Evil Eye, and p sessed the valuable faculty of blight corn, and drying children into mumm with the heart-burn. But, after all, w worked most to the young carpent disadvantage was, first, the reserve a sternness of his natural disposition, next, the fact of his not being a chur communicant, and the suspicion of holding heretical tenents in matters religion and polity.

After receiving Mr. Pyncheon's m sage, the carpenter merely tarried finish a small job, which he happe to have in hand, and then took his v towards the House of the Seven Gab This noted edifice, though its st might be getting a little out of fashi was still as respectable a family r dence as that of any gentleman in to The present owner, Gervayse Pynche was said to have contracted a dis

the house, in consequence of a shock
his sensibility, in early childhood,
m the sudden death of his grand-
her. In the very act of running to
nb Colonel Pyncheon's knee, the boy
d discovered the old Puritan to be a
pse! On arriving at manhood, Mr.
ncheon had visited England, where
married a lady of fortune, and had
sequently spent many years, partly
the mother country, and partly in
ious cities on the continent of
rope. During this period, the family
nsion had been consigned to the
rge of a kinsman, who was allowed
make it his home, for the time being,
consideration of keeping the premises
thorough repair. So faithfully had
s contract been fulfilled, that now,
the carpenter approached the house,
practised eye could detect nothing to
ticize in its condition. The peaks of
seven gables rose up sharply; the
ngled roof looked thoroughly water-
ht; and the glittering plaster-work
irely covered the exterior walls, and
rkled in the October sun, as if it had
n new only a week ago.

The house had that pleasant aspect
life which is like the cheery expres-
n of comfortable activity in the hu-
n countenance. You could see, at
e, that there was the stir of a large
nily within it. A huge load of oak-
od was passing through the gateway,
vards the out-buildings in the rear;
fat cook—or probably it might be
housekeeper—stood at the side-door,
gaining for some turkeys and poul-
, which a countryman had brought
sale. Now and then, a maid-servant,
tly dressed, and now the shining
le face of a slave, might be seen
tling across the windows, in the lower

part of the house. At an open window
of a room in the second story, hanging
over some pots of beautiful and delicate
flowers,—exotics, but which had never
known a more genial sunshine than that
of the New England autumn,—was the
figure of a young lady, an exotic, like
the flowers, and beautiful and delicate
as they. Her presence imparted an indescribable grace and faint witchery to
the whole edifice. In other respects, it
was a substantial, jolly-looking mansion,
and seemed fit to be the residence of a
patriarch, who might establish his own
head-quarters in the front gable, and
assign one of the remainder to each of
his six children; while the great chimney
in the centre should symbolize the old
fellow's hospitable heart, which kept
them all warm, and made a great whole
of the seven smaller ones.

There was a vertical sun-dial on the
front gable; and as the carpenter passed
beneath it, he looked up and noted the
hour.

"Three o'clock!" said he to himself.
"My father told me that dial was put
up only an hour before the old colonel's
death. How truly it has kept time these
seven-and-thirty years past! The shadow
creeps and creeps, and is always looking
over the shoulder of the sunshine!"

It might have befitted a craftsman,
like Matthew Maule, on being sent for
to a gentleman's house, to go to the
back-door, where servants and work-
people were usually admitted; or at
least to the side-entrance, where the better class of tradesmen made application.
But the carpenter had a great deal of
pride and stiffness in his nature; and, at
this moment, moreover, his heart was
bitter with the sense of hereditary
wrong, because he considered the great

Pyncheon-house to be standing on soil which should have been his own. On this very site, beside a spring of delicious water, his grandfather had felled the pine-trees and built a cottage, in which children had been born to him; and it was only from a dead man's stiffened fingers that Colonel Pyncheon had wrestled away the title-deeds. So young Maule went straight to the principal entrance, beneath a portal of carved oak, and gave such a peal of the iron knocker that you would have imagined the stern old wizard himself to be standing at the threshold.

Black Scipio answered the summons, in a prodigious hurry; but showed the whites of his eyes, in amazement, on beholding only the carpenter.

"Lord-a-mercy! what a great man he be, this carpenter fellow!" mumbled Scipio, down in his throat. "Anybody think he beat on the door with his biggest hammer!"

"Here I am!" said Maule, sternly. "Show me the way to your master's parlor!"

As he stept into the house, a note of sweet and melancholy music thrilled and vibrated along the passage-way, proceeding from one of the rooms above stairs. It was the harpsichord which Alice Pyncheon had brought with her from beyond the sea. The fair Alice bestowed most of her maiden leisure between flowers and music, although the former were apt to droop, and the melodies were often sad. She was of foreign education, and could not take kindly to the New England modes of life, in which nothing beautiful had ever been developed.

As Mr. Pyncheon had been impatiently awaiting Maule's arrival, black

Scipio, of course, lost no time in ushering the carpenter into his master's presence. The room in which this gentleman sat was a parlor of moderate size, looking out upon the garden of the house, and having its windows partly shadowed by the foliage of fruit-trees. It was Mr. Pyncheon's peculiar apartment, and was provided with furniture, in an elegant and costly style, principally from Paris, the floor (which was unusual, at the day) being covered with a carpet, so skilfully and richly wrought, that it seemed to glow as with living flowers. In one corner stood a marble woman, to whom her own beauty was the sole and sufficient garment. Some pictures, that looked old, and had a mellow tinge diffused through all their artful splendor—hung on the walls. Near the fireplace was a large and very beautiful cabinet of ebony, inlaid with ivory; a piece of antique furniture, which Mr. Pyncheon had bought in Venice, and which he used as the treasure-place for medals, ancient coins, and whatever small and valuable curiosities he had picked up, on his travels. Through this variety of decoration, however, the room showed its original characteristics; its low stud, its cross-beam, its chimney-piece, with the old-fashioned Dutch tiles; so that it was the emblem of a mind industriously stored with foreign ideas, and elaborated into artificial refinement, but neither larger, nor, in its proper self, more elegant, than before.

There were two objects that appeared rather out of place in this very handsomely furnished room. One was a large map, or surveyor's plan, of a tract of land, which looked as if it had been drawn a good many years ago, and was now dingy with smoke, and soiled, here

d there, with the touch of fingers. The
ᵣer was a portrait of a stern old man,
a Puritan garb, painted roughly, but
th a bold effect, and a remarkably
ong expression of character.

At a small table, before a fire of
ᵍglish sea-coal, sat Mr. Pyncheon,
ᵖping coffee, which had grown to be
very favorite beverage with him in
ance. He was a middle-aged and really
ndsome man, with a wig flowing down
on his shoulders; his coat was of blue
lvet, with lace on the borders and
the buttonholes; and the fire-light
stened on the spacious breadth of his
istcoat, which was flowered all over
th gold. On the entrance of Scipio,
ᵣering in the carpenter, Mr. Pyncheon
ᵣned partly round, but resumed his
ᵣmer position, and proceeded deliber-
ᵉly to finish his cup of coffee, without
mediate notice of the guest whom he
d summoned to his presence. It was
t that he intended any rudeness, or
ᵖroper neglect,—which, indeed, he
uld have blushed to be guilty of,—
t it never occurred to him that a per-
ı ın Maule's station had a claim on
courtesy, or would trouble himself
ᵒut it, one way or the other.

The carpenter, however, stepped at
ᶜe to the hearth, and turned himself
out, so as to look Mr. Pyncheon in
ᵉ face.

"You sent for me," said he. "Be
ᵃsed to explain your business, that I
ᵧy go back to my own affairs."

"Ah! excuse me," said Mr. Pyncheon,
ietly. "I did not mean to tax your
ᵉ without a recompense. Your name,
hink, is Maule,—Thomas or Matthew
ᵃule,—a son or grandson of the
ilder of this house?"

"Matthew Maule," replied the car-

penter,—"son of him who built the
house,—grandson of the rightful proprietor of the soil."

"I know the dispute to which you
allude," observed Mr. Pyncheon, with
undisturbed equanimity. "I am well
aware that my grandfather was compelled to resort to a suit at law, in order
to establish his claim to the foundation-
site of this edifice. We will not, if you
please, renew the discussion. The matter
was settled at the time, and by the competent authorities,—equitably, it is to
be presumed,—and, at all events, irrevocably. Yet, singularly enough, there
is an incidental reference to this very
subject in what I am now about to say
to you. And this same inveterate grudge,
—excuse me, I mean no offence,—this
irritability, which you have just shown,
is not entirely aside from the matter."

"If you can find anything for your
purpose, Mr. Pyncheon," said the carpenter, "in a man's natural resentment
for the wrongs done to his blood, you
are welcome to it!"

"I take you at your word, Goodman
Maule," said the owner of the seven
gables, with a smile, "and will proceed
to suggest a mode in which your hereditary resentments—justifiable, or otherwise—may have had a bearing on my
affairs. You have heard, I suppose, that
the Pyncheon family, ever since my
grandfather's days, have been prosecuting a still unsettled claim to a very
large extent of territory at the eastward?"

"Often," replied Maule,—and it is
said that a smile came over his face,—
"very often,—from my father!"

"This claim," continued Mr. Pyncheon, after pausing a moment, as if to
consider what the carpenter's smile

might mean, "appeared to be on the very verge of a settlement and full allowance, at the period of my grandfather's decease. It was well known, to those in his confidence, that he anticipated neither difficulty nor delay. Now, Colonel Pyncheon, I need hardly say, was a practical man, well acquainted with public and private business, and not at all the person to cherish ill-founded hopes, or to attempt the following out of an impracticable scheme. It is obvious to conclude, therefore, that he had grounds, not apparent to his heirs, for his confident anticipation of success in the matter of this eastern claim. In a word, I believe,—and my legal advisers coincide in the belief, which, moreover, is authorized, to a certain extent, by the family traditions,— that my grandfather was in possession of some deed, or other document, essential to this claim, but which has since disappeared."

"Very likely," said Matthew Maule, —and again, it is said, there was a dark smile on his face,—"but what can a poor carpenter have to do with the grand affairs of the Pyncheon family?"

"Perhaps nothing," returned Mr. Pyncheon,—"possibly, much!"

Here ensued a great many words between Matthew Maule and the proprietor of the seven gables, on the subject which the latter had thus broached. It seems (although Mr. Pyncheon had some hesitation in referring to stories so exceedingly absurd in their aspect) that the popular belief pointed to some mysterious connection and dependence, existing between the family of the Maules and these vast, unrealized possessions of the Pyncheons. It was an ordinary saying, that the old wizard,

hanged though he was, had obtained best end of the bargain, in his cont with Colonel Pyncheon; inasmuch as had got possession of the great east claim, in exchange for an acre or two garden-ground. A very aged woman, cently dead, had often used the me phorical expression, in her fireside t that miles and miles of the Pynch lands had been shovelled into Mau grave; which, by-the-by, was but a v shallow nook, between two rocks, n the summit of Gallows Hill. Again, wh the lawyers were making inquiry for missing document, it was a by-wo that it would never be found, unless the wizard's skeleton-hand. So m weight had the shrewd lawyers assign to these fables, that—(but Mr. P cheon did not see fit to inform the c penter of the fact)—they had secre caused the wizard's grave to be search Nothing was discovered, however, cept that, unaccountably, the right ha of the skeleton was gone.

Now what was unquestionably i portant, a portion of these popu rumors could be traced, though rat doubtfully and indistinctly, to cha words and obscure hints of the execu wizard's son, and the father of t present Matthew Maule. And here M Pyncheon could bring an item of own personal evidence into play. Tho but a child at the time, he either reme bered or fancied that Matthew's fat had had some job to perform, on day before, or possibly the very mo ing of the colonel's decease, in private room where he and the carpen were at this moment talking. Cert papers belonging to Colonel Pynche as his grandson distinctly recollect had been spread out on the table.

Matthew Maule understood the in-
uated suspicion.

"My father," he said,—but still there
s that dark smile, making a riddle
his countenance,—"my father was
honester man than the bloody old
onel! Not to get his rights back again
uld he have carried off one of those
ers!"

"I shall not bandy words with you,"
erved the foreign-bred Mr. Pyn-
on, with haughty composure. "Nor
l it become me to resent any rude-
s towards either my grandfather or
self. A gentleman, before seeking in-
course with a person of your station
l habits, will first consider whether
urgency of the end may compensate
the disagreeableness of the means.
does so, in the present instance."

Ie then renewed the conversation,
l made great pecuniary offers to the
penter, in case the latter should give
ormation leading to the discovery of
lost document, and the consequent
cess of the eastern claim. For a long
e Matthew Maule is said to have
ned a cold ear to these propositions,
last, however, with a strange kind of
gh, he inquired whether Mr. Pyn-
on would make over to him the old
ard's homestead-ground, together
h the House of the Seven Gables,
w standing on it, in requital of the
umentary evidence so urgently
uired.

The wild, chimney-corner legend
hich, without copying all its extrava-
ces, my narrative essentially follows)
e gives an account of some very
ange behavior on the part of Colonel
ncheon's portrait. This picture, it
st be understood, was supposed to
so intimately connected with the fate

of the house, and so magically built into
the walls, that, if once it should be removed, that very instant the whole
edifice would come thundering down in
a heap of dusty ruin. All through the
foregoing conversation between Mr.
Pyncheon and the carpenter, the portrait had been frowning, clenching its
fist, and giving many such proofs of excessive discomposure, but without attracting the notice of either of the two
colloquists. And finally at Matthew
Maule's audacious suggestion of a transfer of the seven-gabled structure, the
ghostly portrait is averred to have lost
all patience, and to have shown itself
on the point of descending bodily from
its frame. But such incredible incidents
are merely to be mentioned aside.

"Give up this house!" exclaimed Mr.
Pyncheon, in amazement at the proposal. "Were I to do so, my grandfather
would not rest quiet in his grave!"

"He never has, if all stories are true,"
remarked the carpenter composedly.
"But that matter concerns his grandson
more than it does Matthew Maule. I
have no other terms to propose."

Impossible as he at first thought it to
comply with Maule's conditions, still, on
a second glance, Mr. Pyncheon was of
opinion that they might at least be
made matter of discussion. He himself
had no personal attachment for the
house, nor any pleasant associations connected with his childish residence in it.
On the contrary, after seven-and-thirty
years, the presence of his dead grandfather seemed still to pervade it, as on
that morning when the affrighted boy
had beheld him, with so ghastly an
aspect, stiffening in his chair. His long
abode in foreign parts, moreover, and
familiarity with many of the castles and

ancestral halls of England, and the marble palaces of Italy, had caused him to look contemptuously at the House of the Seven Gables, whether in point of splendor or convenience. It was a mansion exceedingly inadequate to the style of living which it would be incumbent on Mr. Pyncheon to support, after realizing his territorial rights. His steward might deign to occupy it, but never, certainly, the great landed proprietor himself. In the event of success, indeed, it was his purpose to return to England; nor, to say the truth, would he recently have quitted that more congenial home, had not his own fortune, as well as his deceased wife's begun to give symptoms of exhaustion. The eastern claim once fairly settled, and put upon the firm basis of actual possession, Mr. Pyncheon's property— to be measured by miles, not acres— would be worth an earldom, and would reasonably entitle him to solicit, or enable him to purchase, that elevated dignity from the British monarch. Lord Pyncheon!—or the Earl of Waldo!— how could such a magnate be expected to contract his grandeur within the pitiful compass of seven shingled gables?

In short, on an enlarged view of the business, the carpenter's terms appeared so ridiculously easy, that Mr. Pyncheon could scarcely forbear laughing in his face. He was quite ashamed, after the foregoing reflections, to propose any diminution of so moderate a recompense for the immense service to be rendered.

"I consent to your proposition, Maule," cried he. "Put me in possession of the document essential to establish my rights, and the House of the Seven Gables is your own!'

According to some versions of the story, a regular contract to the abo effect was drawn up by a lawyer, a signed and sealed in the presence witnesses. Others say that Matth Maule was contented with a priv written agreement, in which Mr. P cheon pledged his honor and integri to the fulfilment of the terms concluc upon. The gentleman then ordered wi which he and the carpenter drank gether, in confirmation of their barga During the whole preceding discuss and subsequent formalities, the old Pu tan's portrait seems to have persis in its shadowy gestures of disapprov but without effect, except that, as M Pyncheon set down the emptied gla he thought he beheld his grandfat frown.

"This sherry is too potent a w for me; it has affected my brain ready," he observed, after a somewh startled look at the picture. "On retu ing to Europe, I shall confine mys to the more delicate vintages of It and France, the best of which will bear transportation."

"My Lord Pyncheon may drink wl wine he will, and wherever he please replied the carpenter, as if he had be privy to Mr. Pyncheon's ambitious pr ects. "But first, sir, if you desire tidi of this lost document, I must crave favor of a little talk with your daughter Alice."

"You are mad, Maule!" exclaim Mr. Pyncheon, haughtily; and now, last, there was anger mixed up w his pride. "What can my daughter ha to do with a business like this?"

Indeed, at this new demand on carpenter's part, the proprietor of seven gables was even more thund struck than at the cool proposition

render his house. There was, at least,
assignable motive for the first stipu-
on; there appeared to be none what-
r, for the last. Nevertheless, Matthew
ule sturdily insisted on the young
y being summoned, and even gave her
her to understand, in a mysterious
d of explanation,—which made the
tter considerably darker than it
ked before,—that the only chance of
quiring the requisite knowledge was
ough the clear, crystal medium of a
e and virgin intelligence, like that of
fair Alice. Not to encumber our
ry with Mr. Pyncheon's scruples,
ether of conscience, pride, or father-
affection, he at length ordered his
ghter to be called. He well knew that
was in her chamber, and engaged
no occupation that could not readily
laid aside; for, as it happened, ever
ce Alice's name had been spoken,
h her father and the carpenter had
rd the sad and sweet music of her
psichord, and the airier melancholy
her accompanying voice.

So Alice Pyncheon was summoned,
l appeared. A portrait of this young
y, painted by a Venetian artist, and
by her father in England, is said
have fallen into the hands of the
sent Duke of Devonshire, and to be
v preserved at Chatsworth; not on
ount of any associations with the
ginal, but for its value as a picture,
l the high character of beauty in the
ntenance. If ever there was a lady
n, and set apart from the world's
gar mass by a certain gentle and
d stateliness, it was this very Alice
ncheon. Yet there was the womanly
xture in her; the tenderness, or, at
st, the tender capabilities. For the
e of that redeeming quality, a man

of generous nature would have forgiven
all her pride, and have been content,
almost, to lie down in her path, and
let Alice set her slender foot upon his
heart. All that he would have required,
was simply the acknowledgment that
he was indeed a man, and a fellow-
being, moulded of the same elements
as she.

As Alice came into the room, her
eyes fell upon the carpenter, who was
standing near its centre, clad in a green
woollen jacket, a pair of loose breeches,
open at the knees, and with a long
pocket for his rule, the end of which
protruded; it was as proper a mark
of the artisan's calling, as Mr. Pyncheon's full-dress sword of that gentleman's aristocratic pretensions. A glow
of artistic approval brightened over
Alice Pyncheon's face; she was struck
with admiration—which she made no attempt to conceal—of the remarkable
comeliness, strength and energy, of
Maule's figure. But that admiring glance
(which most other men, perhaps, would
have cherished as a sweet recollection,
all through life) the carpenter never
forgave. It must have been the devil
himself that made Maule so subtile in
his perception.

"Does the girl look at me as if I
were a brute beast?" thought he, setting
his teeth. "She shall know whether I
have a human spirit; and the worse
for her, if it prove stronger than her
own!"

"My father, you sent for me," said
Alice, in her sweet and harp-like voice.
"But, if you have business with this
young man, pray let me go again. You
know I do not love this room, in spite
of that Claude, with which you try to
bring back sunny recollections."

"Stay a moment, young lady, if you please!" said Matthew Maule. "My business with your father is over. With yourself, it is now to begin!"

Alice looked towards her father, in surprise and inquiry.

"Yes, Alice," said Mr. Pyncheon, with some disturbance and confusion. "This young man—his name is Matthew Maule—professes, so far as I can understand him, to be able to discover, through your means, a certain paper or parchment, which was missing long before your birth. The importance of the document in question renders it advisable to neglect no possible, even if improbable, method of regaining it. You will therefore oblige me, my dear Alice, by answering this person's inquiries, and complying with his lawful and reasonable requests, so far as they may appear to have the aforesaid object in view. As I shall remain in the room, you need apprehend no rude nor unbecoming deportment, on the young man's part; and, at your slightest wish, of course, the investigation, or whatever we may call it, shall immediately be broken off."

"Mistress Alice Pyncheon," remarked Matthew Maule, with the utmost deference, but yet a half-hidden sarcasm in his look and tone, "will no doubt feel herself quite safe in her father's presence, and under his all-sufficient protection."

"I certainly shall entertain no manner of apprehension, with my father at hand," said Alice, with maidenly dignity. "Neither do I conceive that a lady, while true to herself, can have aught to fear, from whomsoever, or in any circumstances!"

Poor Alice! By what unhappy impulse did she thus put herself at once on terms of defiance against a stren which she could not estimate?

"Then, Mistress Alice," said Matt Maule, handing a chair,—gracef enough, for a craftsman,—"will it ple you only to sit down, and do me favor (though altogether beyond a p carpenter's deserts) to fix your eyes mine!"

Alice complied. She was very pro Setting aside all advantages of ra this fair girl deemed herself consci of a power,—combined of beauty, h unsullied purity, and the preserva force of womanhood,—that could m her sphere impenetrable, unless betra by treachery within. She instinctiv knew, it may be, that some sinister evil potency was now striving to p her barriers; nor would she decline contest. So Alice put woman's mi against man's might; a match not of equal, on the part of woman.

Her father, meanwhile, had tur away, and seemed absorbed in the c templation of a landscape by Cla where a shadowy and sun-streaked v penetrated so remotely into an anc wood, that it would have been no w der if his fancy had lost itself in picture's bewildering depths. But, truth, the picture was no more to h at that moment, than the blank v against which it hung. His mind haunted with the many and strange ta which he had heard, attributing m terious if not supernatural endowme to these Maules, as well the grands here present, as his two immediate cestors. Mr. Pyncheon's long reside abroad, and intercourse with men of and fashion,—courtiers, worldlings, free-thinkers, had done much tow obliterating the grim Puritan super

s, which no man of New England
h, at that early period, could entirely
pe. But, on the other hand, had not
whole community believed Maule's
ndfather to be a wizard? Had not
crime been proved? Had not the
ard died for it? Had he not be-
athed a legacy of hatred against the
cheons to this only grandson, who,
t appeared, was now about to exer-
a subtle influence over the daugh-
of his enemy's house? Might not
influence be the same that was
ed witchcraft?

'urning half around, he caught a
pse of Maule's figure in the looking-
s. At some paces from Alice, with
arms uplifted in the air, the car-
ter made a gesture, as if directing
nward a slow, ponderous, and invis-
weight upon the maiden.

Stay, Maule!" exclaimed Mr. Pyn-
on, stepping forward. "I forbid your
ceeding further!"

Pray, my dear father, do not inter-
t the young man," said Alice, with-
changing her position. "His efforts,
sure you, will prove very harmless."

Again Mr. Pyncheon turned his eyes
ards the Claude. It was then his
ghter's will, in opposition to his own,
t the experiment should be fully
d. Henceforth, therefore, he did but
sent, not urge it. And was it not for
sake, far more than for his own,
he desired its success? That lost
chment once restored, the beautiful
e Pyncheon, with the rich dowry
ch he could then bestow, might wed
English duke, or a German reigning-
ce instead of some New England
gyman or lawyer! At the thought,
ambitious father almost consented,
his heart, that, if the devil's power

were needed to the accomplishment of
this great object, Maule might evoke
him. Alice's own purity would be her
safeguard.

With his mind full of imaginary magnificence, Mr. Pyncheon heard a half-
uttered exclamation from his daughter.
It was very faint and low; so indistinct
that there seemed but half a will to
shape out the words, and too undefined
a purport to be intelligible. Yet it was
a call for help!—his conscience never
doubted it;—and, little more than a
whisper to his ear, it was a dismal
shriek, and long reëchoed so, in the
region round his heart! But, this time,
the father did not turn.

After a further interval, Maule spoke.
"Behold your daughter!" said he.

Mr. Pyncheon came hastily forward.
The carpenter was standing erect in
front of Alice's chair, and pointing his
finger towards the maiden with an expression of triumphant power, the limits
of which could not be defined, as, indeed, its scope stretched vaguely towards the unseen and the infinite. Alice
sat in an attitude of profound repose,
with the long brown lashes drooping
over her eyes.

"There she is!" said the carpenter.
"Speak to her!"

"Alice! My daughter!" exclaimed Mr.
Pyncheon. "My own Alice!"

She did not stir.

"Louder!" said Maule, smiling.

"Alice! Awake!" cried her father.
"It troubles me to see you thus!
Awake!"

He spoke loudly, with terror in his
voice, and close to that delicate ear,
which had always been so sensitive to
every discord. But the sound evidently
reached her not. It is indescribable wha

a sense of remote, dim, unattainable distance, betwixt himself and Alice, was impressed on the father by this impossibility of reaching her with his voice.

"Best touch her!" said Matthew Maule. "Shake the girl, and roughly too! My hands are hardened with too much use of axe, saw, and plane,—else I might help you!"

Mr. Pyncheon took her hand, and pressed it with the earnestness of startled emotion. He kissed her, with so great a heart-throb in the kiss, that he thought she must needs feel it. Then, in a gust of anger at her insensibility, he shook her maiden form, with a violence which, the next moment, it affrighted him to remember. He withdrew his encircling arms, and Alice—whose figure, though flexible, had been wholly impassive—relapsed into the same attitude as before these attempts to arouse her. Maule having shifted his position, her face was turned towards him, slightly, but with what seemed to be a reference of her very slumber to his guidance.

Then it was a strange sight to behold how the man of conventionalities shook the powder out of his periwig; how the reserved and stately gentleman forgot his dignity; how the gold-embroidered waistcoat flickered and glistened in the fire-light, with the convulsion of rage, terror, and sorrow, in the human heart that was beating under it.

"Villain!" cried Mr. Pyncheon, shaking his clenched fist at Maule. "You and the fiend together have robbed me of my daughter! Give her back, spawn of the old wizard, or you shall climb Gallows Hill in your grandfather's footsteps!"

"Softly, Mr. Pyncheon!" said the carpenter, with scornful compos[ure] "Softly, an' it please your worship, you will spoil those rich lace ruf[fles] at your wrists! Is it my crime if [I] have sold your daughter for the m[ere] hope of getting a sheet of yellow par[ch]ment into your clutch? There sits M[is]tress Alice, quietly asleep! Now [let] Matthew Maule try whether she be [as] proud as the carpenter found he[r] while since."

He spoke, and Alice responded, w[ith] a soft, subdued, inward acquiesence, [and] a bending of her form towards h[im] like the flame of a torch when it in[di]cates a gentle draft of air. He be[ck]oned with his hand, and, rising fr[om] her chair,—blindly, but undoubtin[g] as tending to her sure and inevita[ble] centre,—the proud Alice approac[hed] him. He waved her back, and, retr[eat]ing, Alice sank again into her seat.

"She is mine!" said Matthew Ma[ule]. "Mine, by the right of the strong[er] spirit!"

In the further progress of the lege[nd] there is a long, grotesque, and oc[ca]sionally awe-striking account of the [car]penter's incantations (if so they are [to] be called), with a view of discover[ing] the lost document. It appears to h[ave] been his object to convert the m[ind] of Alice into a kind of telescopic me[di]um, through which Mr. Pyncheon [and] himself might obtain a glimpse i[nto] the spiritual world. He succeeded, [ac]cordingly, in holding an imperfect s[ort] of intercourse, at one remove, with [the] departed personages, in whose cust[ody] the so much valued secret had b[een] carried beyond the precincts of ear[th]. During her trance, Alice described th[e] figures as being present to her spiritu[al]ized perception. One was an aged, [dig]

ed, stern-looking gentleman, clad, as
a solemn festival, in grave and costly
re, but with a great blood-stain on
richly-wrought band; the second, an
d man, meanly dressed, with a dark
l malign countenance, and a broken
ter about his neck; the third, a per-
not so advanced in life as the former
, but beyond the middle age, wear-
a coarse woollen tunic and leather
eches, and with a carpenter's rule
king out of his side-pocket. These
ee visionary characters possessed a
tual knowledge of the missing docu-
nt. One of them, in truth,—it was
with the blood-stain on his band,—
med, unless his gestures were misun-
stood, to hold the parchment in his
nediate keeping, but was prevented,
his two partners in the mystery,
m disburthening himself of the trust.
ally, when he showed a purpose of
uting forth his secret, loudly enough
be heard from his own sphere into
t of mortals, his companions strug-
d with him, and pressed their hands
r his mouth; and forthwith—
ether that he were choked by it, or
t the secret itself was of a crimson
e—there was a fresh flow of blood
on his band. Upon this, the two
anly-dressed figures mocked and
red at the much-abashed old digni-
y, and pointed their fingers at the
in.

At this juncture, Maule turned to Mr.
ncheon.

"It will never be allowed," said he.
he custody of this secret, that would
enrich his heirs, makes part of your
ndfather's retribution. He must choke
h it until it is no longer of any value.
d keep you the House of the Seven
bles! It is too dear-bought an inheri-

tance, and too heavy with the curse
upon it, to be shifted yet a while from
the colonel's posterity!"

Mr. Pyncheon tried to speak, but—
what with fear and passion—could make
only a gurgling murmur in his throat.
The carpenter smiled.

"Aha, worshipful sir!—so, you have
old Maule's blood to drink!" said he
jeeringly.

"Fiend in man's shape! why dost
thou keep dominion over my child?"
cried Mr. Pyncheon, when his choked
utterance could make way. "Give me
back my daughter! Then go thy ways;
and may we never meet again!"

"Your daughter!" said Matthew
Maule. "Why, she is fairly mine! Nevertheless, not to be too hard with fair
Mistress Alice, I will leave her in your
keeping; but I do not warrant you that
she shall never have occasion to remember Maule, the carpenter."

He waved his hands with an upward
motion; and, after a few repetitions of
similar gestures, the beautiful Alice Pyncheon awoke from her strange trance.
She awoke, without the slightest recollection of her visionary experience; but
as one losing herself in a momentary
reverie, and returning to the consciousness of actual life, in almost as brief
an interval as the down-sinking flame
of the hearth should quiver again up
the chimney. On recognizing Matthew
Maule, she assumed an air of somewhat cold but gentle dignity; the rather,
as there was a certain peculiar smile
on the carpenter's visage, that stirred
the native pride of the fair Alice. So
ended, for that time, the quest for the
lost title-deed of the Pyncheon territory
at the eastward; nor, though often subsequently renewed, has it ever yet be-

fallen a Pyncheon to set his eye upon that parchment.

But, alas for the beautiful, the gentle, yet too haughty Alice! A power, that she little dreamed of, had laid its grasp upon her maiden soul. A will, most unlike her own, constrained her to do its grotesque and fantastic bidding. Her father, as it proved, had martyred his poor child to an inordinate desire for measuring his land by miles, instead of acres. And, therefore, while Alice Pyncheon lived, she was Maule's slave, in a bondage more humiliating, a thousand fold, than that which binds its chain around the body. Seated by his humble fireside, Maule had but to wave his hand; and, wherever the proud lady chanced to be,—whether in her chamber, or entertaining her father's stately guests, or worshipping at church,—whatever her place or occupation, her spirit passed from beneath her own control, and bowed itself to Maule. "Alice, laugh!"—the carpenter, beside his hearth, would say; or perhaps intensely will it, without a spoken word. And, even were it prayer-time, or at a funeral, Alice must break into wild laughter. "Alice, be sad!"—and, at the instant, down would come her tears, quenching all the mirth of those around her, like sudden rain upon a bonfire. "Alice, dance!"—and dance she would, not in such court-like measures as she had learned abroad, but some high-paced jig, or hop-skip rigadoon, befitting the brisk lasses at a rustic merry-making. It seemed to be Maule's impulse not to ruin Alice, nor to visit her with any black or gigantic mischief, which would have crowned her sorrows with the grace of tragedy, but to wreak a low, ungenerous scorn upon her. Thus

all the dignity of life was lost. felt herself too much abased, and lor to change natures with some worm

One evening, at a bridal-party—not her own; for, so lost from control, she would have deemed it to marry)—poor Alice was becko forth by her unseen despot, and strained, in her gossamer white d and satin slippers, to hasten along street to the mean dwelling of a la ing-man. There was laughter and g cheer within; for Matthew Maule, night, was to wed the laborer's dau ter, and had summoned proud A Pyncheon to wait upon his bride. so she did; and when the twain v one, Alice awoke out of her enchai sleep. Yet, no longer proud,—hum and with a smile all steeped in sadn —she kissed Maule's wife, and went way. It was an inclement night; south-east wind drove the mingled s and rain into her thinly-shelte bosom; her satin slippers were through and through, as she trod muddy sidewalks. The next day, a c soon, a settled cough; anon, a he cheek, a wasted form, that sat be the harpsichord, and filled the ho with music! Music, in which a st of the heavenly choristers was echo O, joy! For Alice had borne her humiliation! O, greater joy! For A was penitent of her one earthly sin, proud no more!

The Pyncheons made a great fun for Alice. The kith and kin were th and the whole respectability of the t besides. But, last in the process came Matthew Maule, gnashing teeth, as if he would have bitten own heart in twain—the darkest wofullest man that ever walked bet

orpse! He meant to humble Alice
ot to kill her;—but he had taken
a woman's delicate soul into his rude
gripe, to play with,—and she was dead!

CHAPTER XIV

PHŒBE'S GOOD-BY

OLGRAVE, plunging into his tale with
energy and absorption natural to
oung author, had given a good deal
action to the parts capable of being
eloped and exemplified in that man-

He now observed that a certain
arkable drowsiness (wholly unlike
with which the reader possibly
s himself affected) had been flung
r the senses of his auditress. It was
effect, unquestionably, of the mys-
gesticulations by which he had
ght to bring bodily before Phœbe's
ception the figure of the memeriz-
carpenter. With the lids drooping
r her eyes,—now lifted, for an in-
it, and drawn down again, as with
en weights,—she leaned slightly to-
ds him, and seemed almost to regu-
her breath by his. Holgrave gazed
her, as he rolled up his manuscript,
recognized an incipient stage of that
ious psychological condition, which,
he had himself told Phœbe, he posed more than an ordinary faculty
producing. A veil was beginning to
muffled about her, in which she could
old only him, and live only in his
ughts and emotions. His glance, as
fastened it on the young girl, grew
oluntarily more concentrated; in his
tude there was the consciousness of
ver, investing his hardly mature fig-
with a dignity that did not belong

to its physical manifestation. It was
evident, that, with but one wave of
his hand, and a corresponding effort of
his will, he could complete his mastery
over Phœbe's yet free and virgin spirit:
he could establish an influence over this
good, pure, and simple child, as dangerous, and perhaps as disastrous, as that
which the carpenter of his legend had
acquired and exercised over the ill-fated
Alice.

To a disposition like Holgrave's at
once speculative and active, there is
no temptation so great as the opportunity of acquiring empire over the
human spirit; nor any idea more se-
ductive to a young man than to become
the arbiter of a young girl's destiny.
Let us, therefore,—whatever his defects
of nature and education, and in spite
of his scorn for creeds and institutions,
—concede to the daguerreotypist the
rare and high quality of reverence for
another's individuality. Let us allow
him integrity, also, forever after to be
confided in; since he forbade himself to
twine that one link more which might
have rendered his spell over Phœbe
indissoluble.

He made a slight gesture upward with
his hand.

"You really mortify me, my dear
Miss Phœbe!" he exclaimed, smiling
half-sarcastically at her. "My poor

story, it is but too evident, will never do for Godey or Graham! Only think of your falling asleep at what I hoped the newspaper critics would pronounce a most brilliant, powerful, imaginative, pathetic, and original winding up! Well, the manuscript must serve to light lamps with;—if, indeed, being so imbued with my gentle dulness, it is any longer capable of flame!"

"Me asleep! How can you say so?" answered Phœbe, as unconscious of the crisis through which she had passed as an infant of the precipice to the verge of which it has rolled. "No, no! I consider myself as having been very attentive; and, though I don't remember the incidents quite distinctly, yet I have an impression of a vast deal of trouble and calamity,—so, no doubt, the story will prove exceedingly attractive."

By this time, the sun had gone down, and was tinting the clouds towards the zenith with those bright hues which are not seen there until some time after sunset, and when the horizon has quite lost its richer brilliancy. The moon, too, which had long been climbing overhead, and unobtrusively melting its disk into the azure,—like an ambitious demagogue, who hides his aspiring purpose by assuming the prevalent hue of popular sentiment,—now began to shine out, broad and oval, in its middle pathway. These silvery beams were already powerful enough to change the character of the lingering daylight. They softened and embellished the aspect of the old house; although the shadows fell deeper into the angles of its many gables, and lay brooding under the projecting story, and within the half-open door. With the lapse of every moment,

the garden grew more picturesque; fruit-trees, shrubbery and flower-bush had a dark obscurity among them. common-place characteristics,—wh at noontide, it seemed to have take century of sordid life to accumul —were now transfigured by a. charm romance. A hundred mysterious ye were whispering among the leaves, wh ever the slight sea-breeze found its thither and stirred them. Through foliage that roofed the little summ house the moonlight flickered to fro, and fell silvery white on the d floor, the table and the circular ber with a continual shift and play, acc ing as the chinks and wayward crev among the twigs admitted or shut the glimmer.

So sweetly cool was the atmosph after all the feverish day, that the s mer eve might be fancied as sprinkl dews and liquid moonlight, with a d of icy temper in them, out of a sil vase. Here and there, a few drops this freshness were scattered on a man heart, and gave it youth ag and sympathy with the eternal youth nature. The artist chanced to be on whom the reviving influence It made him feel—what he someti almost forgot, thrust so early as had been into the rude struggle of m with man—how youthful he still was

"It seems to me," he observed, "t I never watched the coming of so be tiful an eve, and never felt anyth so very much like happiness as at moment. After all, what a good wo we live in! How good, and beautif How young it is, too, with noth really rotten or age-worn in it! T old house, for example, which so times has positively oppressed

ath with its smell of decaying tim-
! And this garden, where the black
ald always clings to my spade, as
 were a sexton, delving in a grave-
d! Could I keep the feeling that
y possesses me, the garden would
ry day be virgin soil, with the earth's
: freshness in the flavor of its beans
 squashes; and the house!—it would
like a bower in Eden, blossoming
a the earliest roses that God ever
le. Moonlight, and the sentiment in
a's heart responsive to it, are the
atest of renovators and reformers.
l all other reform and renovation,
uppose, will prove to be no better
a moonshine!"

I have been happier than I am now;
least, much gayer," said Phœbe,
aghtfully. "Yet I am sensible of a
at charm in this brightening moon-
t; and I love to watch how the day,
d as it is, lags away reluctantly,
 hates to be called yesterday so
a. I never cared much about moon-
t before. What is there, I wonder,
beautiful in it, to-night?"

And you have never felt it before?"
aired the artist, looking earnestly at
 girl, through the twilight.

Never," answered Phœbe; "and life
s not look the same, now that I
e felt it so. It seems as if I had
:ed at everything, hitherto, in broad
light, or else in the ruddy light of
aeerful fire, glimmering and dancing
augh a room. Ah, poor me!" she
ed, with a half-melancholy laugh.
shall never be so merry as before
new Cousin Hepzibah and poor
sin Clifford. I have grown a great
 older, in this little time. Older,
 I hope, wiser, and,—not exactly
ler,—but certainly, with not half so

much lightness in my spirits! I have
given them my sunshine, and have been
glad to give it; but, of course, I cannot
both give and keep it. They are welcome, notwithstanding!"

"You have lost nothing, Phœbe, worth
keeping, nor which it was possible to
keep," said Holgrave, after a pause.
"Our first youth is of no value; for
we are never conscious of it, until after
it is gone. But sometimes—always, I
suspect, unless one is exceedingly unfortunate—there comes a sense of
second youth, gushing out of the heart's
joy at being in love; or, possibly, it
may come to crown some other grand
festival in life, if any other such there
be. This bemoaning of one's self (as you
do now) over the first careless, shallow
gayety of youth departed, and this
profound happiness at youth regained,
—so much deeper and richer than that
we lost,—are essential to the soul's development. In some cases, the two states
come almost simultaneously, and mingle
the sadness and the rapture in one mysterious emotion."

"I hardly think I understand you,"
said Phœbe.

"No wonder," replied Holgrave, smiling; "for I have told you a secret
which I hardly began to know, before
I found myself giving it utterance. Remember it, however; and when the
truth becomes clear to you, then think
of this moonlight scene!"

"It is entirely moonlight now, except only a little flush of faint crimson,
upward from the west, between those
buildings," remarked Phœbe. "I must
go in. Cousin Hepzibah is not quick at
figures, and will give herself a head-
ache over the day's accounts, unless I
help her."

But Holgrave detained her a little longer.

"Miss Hepzibah tells me," observed he, "that you return to the country, in a few days."

"Yes, but only for a little while," answered Phœbe; "for I look upon this as my present home. I go to make a few arrangements, and to take a more deliberate leave of my mother and friends. It is pleasant to live where one is much desired, and very useful; and I think I may have the satisfaction of feeling myself so, here."

"You surely may, and more than you imagine," said the artist. "Whatever health, comfort and natural life, exists in the house, is embodied in your person. These blessings came along with you, and will vanish when you leave the threshold. Miss Hepzibah, by secluding herself from society, has lost all true relation with it, and is, in fact, dead; although she galvanizes herself into a semblance of life, and stands behind her counter, afflicting the world with a greatly-to-be-deprecated scowl. Your poor cousin Clifford is another dead and long-buried person, on whom the governor and council have wrought a necromantic miracle. I should not wonder if he were to crumble away, some morning, after you are gone, and nothing be seen of him more, except a heap of dust. Miss Hepzibah, at any rate, will lose what little flexibility she has. They both exist by you."

"I should be very sorry to think so," answered Phœbe, gravely. "But it is true that my small abilities were precisely what they needed; and I have a real interest in their welfare,—an odd kind of motherly sentiment,—which I wish you would not laugh at! And let me tell you frankly, Mr. Holgra[ve], I am sometimes puzzled to kn[ow] whether you wish them well or ill."

"Undoubtedly," said the daguerr[eo]typist, "I do feel an interest in [this] antiquated, poverty-stricken old maid[en] lady, and this degraded and shatte[red] gentleman,—this abortive lover of [the] beautiful. A kindly interest, too, h[elp]less old children that they are! [But] you have no conception what a dif[fer]ent kind of heart mine is from y[our] own. It is not my impulse, as rega[rds] these two individuals, either to b[less] or hinder; but to look on, to analy[ze] to explain matters to myself, and [to] comprehend the drama which, for [al]most two hundred years, has been dr[ag]ging its slow length over the gro[und] where you and I now tread. If perm[it]ted to witness the close, I doubt not [to] derive a moral satisfaction from it, [no] matters how they may. There is a c[on]viction within me that the end dr[aws] nigh. But, though Providence sent [me] hither to help, and sends me only [as] a privileged and meet spectator, I ple[dge] myself to lend these unfortunate be[ings] whatever aid I can!"

"I wish you would speak more pl[ain]ly," cried Phœbe, perplexed and [dis]pleased; "and, above all, that you wo[uld] feel more like a Christian and a hum[an] being! How is it possible to see pe[ople] in distress, without desiring, more t[han] anything else, to help and com[fort] them? You talk as if this old ho[use] were a theatre; and you seem to l[ook] at Hepzibah's and Clifford's mis[for]tunes, and those of generations be[fore] them, as a tragedy, such as I have s[een] acted in the hall of a country ho[use], only the present one appears to [be] played exclusively for your amusem[ent].

do not like this. To play costs the
reformers too much, and the audience
too cold-hearted."

"You are severe," said Holgrave,
impelled to recognize a degree of truth
this piquant sketch of his own mood.
"And then," continued Phœbe, "what
you mean by your conviction, which
you tell me of, that the end is drawing near? Do you know of any new
trouble hanging over my poor relatives?
so, tell me at once, and I will not
love them!"

"Forgive me, Phoebe!" said the
daguerreotypist, holding out his hand,
which the girl was constrained to
hold her own. "I am somewhat of a
mystic, it must be confessed. The tendency is in my blood, together with
a faculty of mesmerism, which might
have brought me to Gallows Hill, in the
good old times of witchcraft. Believe
me, if I were really aware of any secret,
disclosure of which would benefit
our friends,—who are my own friends,
likewise,—you should learn it before we
part. But I have no such knowledge."

"You hold something back!" said
Phœbe.

"Nothing,—no secrets but my own,"
answered Holgrave. "I can perceive,
indeed, that Judge Pyncheon still keeps
his eye on Clifford, in whose ruin he
had so large a share. His motives and
intentions, however, are a mystery to
me. He is a determined and relentless
man, with the genuine character of an
inquisitor; and had he any object to
gain by putting Clifford to the rack,
I verily believe that he would wrench
the joints from their sockets, in order
to accomplish it. But, so wealthy and
eminent as he is,—so powerful in his
own strength, and in the support of

society, on all sides,—what can Judge
Pyncheon have to hope or fear from
the imbecile, branded, half-torpid Clifford?"

"Yet," urged Phœbe, "you did speak
as if misfortune were impending!"

"O, that was because I am morbid!"
replied the artist. "My mind has a twist
aside, like almost everybody's mind, except your own. Moreover, it is so strange
to find myself an inmate of this old
Pyncheon-house, and sitting in this old
garden—(hark, how Maule's well is
murmuring!)—that, were it only for
this one circumstance, I cannot help
fancying that Destiny is arranging its
fifth act for a catastrophe."

"There!" cried Phœbe with renewed
vexation; for she was by nature as hostile to mystery as the sunshine to a
dark corner. "You puzzle me more than
ever!"

"Then let us part friends!" said Holgrave, pressing her hand. "Or, if not
friends, let us part before you entirely
hate me. You, who love everybody else
in the world!"

"Good-by, then," said Phœbe, frankly.
"I do not mean to be angry a great
while, and should be sorry to have you
think so. There has Cousin Hepzibah
been standing in the shadow of the
door-way, this quarter of an hour past!
She thinks I stay too long in the damp
garden. So, good-night, and good-by!"

On the second morning thereafter,
Phœbe might have been seen, in her
straw bonnet, with a shawl on one arm
and a little carpet-bag on the other,
bidding adieu to Hepzibah and Cousin
Clifford. She was to take a seat in the
next train of cars, which would trans-
port her to within half a dozen miles
of her country village.

The tears were in Phœbe's eyes; a smile, dewy with affectionate regret, was glimmering around her pleasant mouth. She wondered how it came to pass, that her life of a few weeks, here in this heavy-hearted old mansion, had taken such hold of her, and so melted into her associations, as now to seem a more important centre-point of remembrance than all which had gone before. How had Hepzibah—grim, silent, and irresponsive to her overflow of cordial sentiment—contrived to win so much love? And Clifford,—in his abortive decay, with the mystery of fearful crime upon him, and the close prison-atmosphere yet lurking in his breath,—how had he transformed himself into the simplest child, whom Phœbe felt bound to watch over, and be, as it were, the providence of his unconsidered hours! Everything, at that instant of farewell, stood out prominently to her view. Look where she would, lay her hand on what she might, the object responded to her consciousness, as if a moist human heart were in it.

She peeped from the window into the garden, and felt herself more regretful at leaving this spot of black earth, vitiated with such an age-long growth of weeds, than joyful at the idea of again scenting her pine-forests and fresh clover-fields. She called Chanticleer, his two wives, and the venerable chicken, and threw them some crumbs of bread from the breakfast-table. These being hastily gobbled up, the chicken spread its wings, and alighted close by Phœbe on the window-sill, where it looked gravely into her face and vented its emotions in a croak. Phœbe bade it be a good old chicken during her absence, and promised to bring it a little bag of buckwheat.

"Ah, Phœbe!" remarked Hepzib "you do not smile so naturally as w you came to us! Then the smile ch to shine out; now, you choose it sho It is well that you are going back, a little while, into your native air. Th has been too much weight on y spirits. The house is too gloomy lonesome; the shop is full of vexatio and as for me, I have no faculty making things look brighter than t are. Dear Clifford has been your o comfort!"

"Come hither, Phœbe," suddenly c her cousin Clifford, who had said v little, all the morning. "Close!—clos —and look me in the face!"

Phœbe put one of her small ha on each elbow of his chair, and lea her face towards him, so that he mi peruse it as carefully as he would. is probable that the latent emotions this parting hour had revived, in s degree, his bedimmed and enfeeb faculties. At any rate, Phœbe soon that, if not the profound insight o seer, yet a more than feminine delic of appreciation, was making her h the subject of its regard. A moment fore, she had known nothing which would have sought to hide. Now, a some secret were hinted to her consciousness through the medium another's perception, she was fain let her eyelids droop beneath Cliffo gaze. A blush, too,—the redder, beca she strove hard to keep it down ascended higher and higher, in a of fitful progress, until even her b was all suffused with it.

"It is enough, Phœbe," said Cliff with a melancholy smile. "When I saw you, you were the prettiest li

den in the world; and now you have
pened into beauty! Girlhood has
sed into womanhood; the bud is a
om! Go, now!—I feel lonelier than
id."

hœbe took leave of the desolate
ple, and passed through the shop,
nkling her eyelids to shake off a
-drop; for—considering how brief
absence was to be, and therefore
folly of being cast down about it
ne would not so far acknowledge her
s as to dry them with her handker-
f. On the doorstep, she met the
e urchin whose marvellous feats of
ronomy have been recorded in the
ier pages of our narrative. She took
n the window some specimen or
er of natural history,—her eyes being
dim with moisture to inform her
urately whether it was a rabbit or
ppopotamus,—put it into the child's
d, as a parting gift, and went her
. Old Uncle Venner was just com-
out of his door, with a wood-
se and saw on his shoulder; and,
ging along the street, he scrupled
to keep company with Phœbe, so
as their paths lay together; nor, in
e of his patched coat and rusty
ver, and the curious fashion of his
-cloth trousers, could she find it in
heart to outwalk him.

We shall miss you, next Sabbath
rnoon," observed the street philoso-
. "It is unaccountable how little
le it takes some folks to grow just
aatural to a man as his own breath;
, begging your pardon, Miss Phœbe
ugh there can be no offence in an
man's saying it), that's just what
ve grown to me! My years have

been a great many, and your life is
but just beginning; and yet, you are
somehow as familiar to me as if I had
found you at my mother's door, and
you had blossomed, like a running vine,
all along my pathway since. Come back
soon, or I shall be gone to my farm;
for I begin to find these wood-sawing
jobs a little too tough for my back-
ache."

"Very soon, Uncle Venner," replied
Phœbe.

"And let it be all the sooner, Phœbe,
for the sake of those poor souls yonder," continued her companion. "They
can never do without you, now,—never,
Phœbe, never!—no more than if one of
God's angels had been living with them,
and making their dismal house pleasant
and comfortable! Don't it seem to
you they'd be in a sad case, if, some
pleasant summer morning like this, the
angel should spread his wings, and fly
to the place he came from? Well, just
so they feel, now that you're going
home by the railroad! They can't bear
it, Miss Phœbe; so be sure to come
back!"

"I am no angel, Uncle Venner," said
Phœbe, smiling, as she offered him her
hand at the street-corner. "But, I suppose, people never feel so much like
angels as when they are doing what little
good they may. So I shall certainly
come back!"

Thus parted the old man and the
rosy girl; and Phœbe took the wings
of the morning, and was soon flitting
almost as rapidly away as if endowed
with the aerial locomotion of the angels
to whom Uncle Venner had so gracious-
ly compared her.

CHAPTER XV

THE SCOWL AND SMILE

SEVERAL days passed over the seven gables, heavily and drearily enough. In fact (not to attribute the whole gloom of sky and earth to the one inauspicious circumstance of Phœbe's departure), an easterly storm had set in, and indefatigably applied itself to the task of making the black roof and walls of the old house look more cheerless than ever before. Yet was the outside not half so cheerless as the interior. Poor Clifford was cut off, at once, from all his scanty resources of enjoyment. Phœbe was not there; nor did the sunshine fall upon the floor. The garden, with its muddy walks, and the chill, dripping foliage of its summerhouse, was an image to be shuddered at. Nothing flourished in the cold, moist, pitiless atmosphere, drifting with the brackish scud of sea-breezes, except the moss along the joints of the shingle-roof, and the great bunch of weeds, that had lately been suffering from drought, in the angle between the two front gables.

As for Hepzibah, she seemed not merely possessed with the east wind, but to be, in her very person, only another phase of this gray and sullen spell of weather; the east wind itself, grim and disconsolate, in a rusty black silk gown, and with a turban of cloud-wreaths on its head. The custom of the shop fell off because a story got abroad that she soured her small beer and other damageable commodities, by scowling on them. It is, perhaps, true that the public had something reasonably to complain of in her deportment;

but towards Clifford she was neith ill-tempered nor unkind, nor felt le warmth of heart than always, had been possible to make it reach hi The inutility of her best efforts, ho ever, palsied the poor old gentlewoma She could do little else than sit silent in a corner of the room, when the w pear-tree branches, sweeping across t small windows, created a noon-day du which Hepzibah unconsciously darken with her woe-begone aspect. It w no fault of Hepzibah's. Everything even the old chairs and tables, that h known what weather was for three four such lifetimes as her own—look as damp and chill as if the present we their worst experience. The picture the Puritan colonel shivered on t wall. The house itself shivered, fro every attic of its seven gables, do to the great kitchen fireplace, whi served all the better as an emblem the mansion's heart, because, thou built for warmth, it was now so co fortless and empty.

Hepzibah attempted to enliven m ters by a fire in the parlor. But t storm-demon kept watch above, a whenever a flame was kindled, dro the smoke back again, choking t chimney's sooty throat with its o breath. Nevertheless, during four da of this miserable storm, Clifford wra himself in an old cloak, and occupi his customary chair. On the morni of the fifth, when summoned to brea fast, he responded only by a broke hearted murmur, expressive of a termination not to leave his bed.

er made no attempt to change his
pose. In fact, entirely as she loved
, Hepzibah could hardly have borne
longer the wretched duty—so im-
cticable by her few and rigid facul-
s—of seeking pastime for a still sen-
ve, but ruined mind, critical and
tidious, without force or volition.
was, at least, something short of posi-
e despair, that, to-day, she might
shivering alone, and not suffer con-
ually a new grief, and unreasonable
g of remorse, at every fitful sigh of
fellow-sufferer.

But Clifford, it seemed, though he did
make his appearance below stairs,
, after all, bestirred himself in quest
amusement. In the course of the
enoon, Hepzibah heard a note of
sic, which (there being no other
eful contrivance in the House of the
en Gables) she knew must proceed
m Alice Pyncheon's harpsichord. She
s aware that Clifford, in his youth,
l possessed a cultivated taste for
sic, and a considerable degree of skill
ts practice. It was difficult, however,
conceive of his retaining an accom-
shment to which daily exercise is
essential, in the measure indicated
the sweet, airy, and delicate, though
st melancholy strain, that now stole
n her ear. Nor was it less marvel-
s that the long-silent instrument
uld be capable of so much melody.
pzibah involuntarily thought of the
stly harmonies, prelusive of death
the family, which were attributed to
legendary Alice. But it was, perhaps,
of of the agency of other than spir-
l fingers, that, after a few touches,
chords seemed to snap asunder with
ir own vibrations, and the music
sed.

But a harsher sound succeeded to the
mysterious notes; nor was the easterly
day fated to pass without an event
sufficient in itself to poison, for Hepzibah and Clifford, the balmiest air that
ever brought the humming-birds along
with it. The final echoes of Alice Pyncheon's performance (or Clifford's, if
his we must consider it) were driven
away by no less vulgar a dissonance
than the ringing of the shop-bell. A foot
was heard scraping itself on the threshold, and thence somewhat ponderously
stepping on the floor. Hepzibah delayed
a moment, while muffling herself in a
faded shawl, which had been her de-
fensive armor in a forty years' warfare
against the east wind. A characteristic
sound, however,—neither a cough nor
a hem, but a kind of rumbling and reverberating spasm in somebody's capacious depth of chest,—impelled her to
hurry forward, with that aspect of fierce
faint-heartedness so common to women
in cases of perilous emergency. Few of
her sex, on such occasions, have ever
looked so terrible as our poor scowling Hepzibah. But the visitor quietly
closed the shop-door behind him, stood
up his umbrella against the counter,
and turned a visage of composed benignity, to meet the alarm and anger which
his appearance had excited.

Hepzibah's presentiment had not deceived her. It was no other than Judge
Pyncheon, who, after in vain trying the
front door, had now effected his entrance
into the shop.

"How do you do, Cousin Hepzibah?
—and how does this most inclement
weather affect our poor Clifford?" began the judge; and wonderful it seemed,
indeed, that the easterly storm was not
put to shame, or, at any rate, a little

mollified, by the genial benevolence of his smile. "I could not rest without calling to ask, once more, whether I can in any manner promote his comfort, or your own."

"You can do nothing," said Hepzibah, controlling her agitation as well as she could. "I devote myself to Clifford. He has every comfort which his situation admits of."

"But, allow me to suggest, dear cousin," rejoined the judge, "you err, —in all affection and kindness, no doubt, and with the very best intentions,—but you do err, nevertheless, in keeping your brother so secluded. Why insulate him thus from all sympathy and kindness? Clifford, alas! has had too much of solitude. Now let him try society,—the society, that is to say, of kindred and old friends. Let me, for instance, but see Clifford; and I will answer for the good effect of the interview."

"You cannot see him," answered Hepzibah. "Clifford has kept his bed since yesterday."

"What! How! Is he ill?" exclaimed Judge Pyncheon, starting with what seemed to be angry alarm; for the very frown of the old Puritan darkened through the room as he spoke. "Nay, then, I must and will see him! What if he should die?"

"He is in no danger of death," said Hepzibah,—and added, with bitterness that she could repress no longer, "none; —unless he shall be persecuted to death, now, by the same man who long ago attempted it!"

"Cousin Hepzibah," said the judge, with an impressive earnestness of manner, which grew even to tearful pathos, as he proceeded, "is it possible that you do not perceive how unjust, how

unkind, how unchristian, is this c stant, this long-continued bittern against me, for a part which I constrained by duty and conscience, the force of law, and at my own pe to act? What did I do, in detrim to Clifford, which it was possible leave undone? How could you, his ter,—if, for your never-ending sorr as it has been for mine, you had kn what I did,—have shown greater ten ness? And do you think, cousin, t it has cost me no pang?—that it left no anguish in my bosom, from t day to this, amidst all the prospe with which Heaven has blessed me or that I do not now rejoice, whe is deemed consistent with the dues public justice and the welfare of soc that this dear kinsman, this early frie this nature so delicately and beautif constituted,—so unfortunate, let us p nounce him, and forbear to say, guilty,—that our own Clifford, in f should be given back to life, and possibilities of enjoyment? Ay, you li know me, Cousin Hepzibah! You li know this heart! It now throbs at thought of meeting him! There li not the human being (except yours —and you not more than I) who shed so many tears for Clifford's cal ity! You behold some of them n There is none who would so delight promote his happiness! Try me, He bah!—try me, cousin!—try the r whom you have treated as your ene and Clifford's!—try Jaffrey Pynche and you shall find him true, to heart's core!"

"In the name of Heaven," cried H zibah, provoked only to intenser in nation by this out-gush of the ine mable tenderness of a stern nature

n God's name, whom you insult, and
hose power I could almost question,
nce he hears you utter so many false
ords, without palsying your tongue,
-give over, I beseech you, this loath-
me pretense of affection for your vic-
n! You hate him! Say so, like a man!
ou cherish, at this moment, some black
urpose against him, in your heart!
peak it out, at once!—or, if you hope
to promote it better, hide it till you
n triumph in its success! But never
eak again of your love for my poor
other! I cannot bear it! It will drive
e beyond a woman's decency! It will
ive me mad! Forbear! Not another
rd! It will make me spurn you!"

For once, Hepzibah's wrath had given
r courage. She had spoken. But, after
, was this unconquerable distrust of
dge Pyncheon's integrity, and this
er denial, apparently, of his claim
stand in the ring of human sympa-
es,—were they founded in any just
rception of his character, or merely
e offspring of a woman's unreasonable
ejudice, deduced from nothing?

The judge, beyond all question, was
man of eminent respectability. The
urch acknowledged it; the state ac-
owledged it. It was denied by no-
dy. In all the very extensive sphere
those who knew him, whether in his
blic or private capacities, there was
an individual—except Hepzibah, and
ne lawless mystic, like the daguer-
otypist, and, possibly, a few political
ponents—who would have dreamed of
iously disputing his claim to a high
d honorable place in the world's re-
d. Nor (we must do him the further
tice to say) did Judge Pyncheon him-
, probably, entertain many or very
quent doubts, that his enviable repu-

tation accorded with his deserts. His
conscience, therefore, usually considered
the surest witness to a man's integrity,
—his conscience, unless it might be
for the little space of five minutes in
the twenty-four hours, or, now and
then, some black day in the whole year's
circle,—his conscience bore an accordant
testimony with the world's laudatory
voice. And yet, strong as this evidence
may seem to be, we should hesitate
to peril our own conscience on the as-
sertion, that the judge and the con-
senting world were right, and that poor
Hepzibah, with her solitary prejudice,
was wrong. Hidden from mankind,—
forgotten by himself, or buried so deeply under a sculptured and ornamented
pile of ostentatious deeds that his daily
life could take no note of it,—there may
have lurked some evil and unsightly
thing. Nay, we could almost venture
to say, further, that a daily guilt might
have been acted by him, continually renewed, and reddening forth afresh, like
the miraculous blood-stain of a murder, without his necessarily and at every
moment being aware of it.

Men of strong minds, great force
of character, and a hard texture of
the sensibilities, are very capable of
falling into mistakes of this kind. They
are ordinarily men to whom forms are
of paramount importance. Their field
of action lies among the external phenomena of life. They possess vast ability
in grasping, and arranging, and appro-
priating to themselves, the big, heavy,
solid unrealities, such as gold, landed
estate, offices of trust and emolument,
and public honors. With these materials,
and with deeds of goodly aspect, done
in the public eye, an individual of this
class builds up, as it were, a tall and

stately edifice, which, in the view of other people, and ultimately in his own view, is no other than the man's character, or the man himself. Behold, therefore, a palace! Its splendid halls, and suites of spacious apartments, are floored with a mosaic-work of costly marbles; its windows, the whole height of each room, admit the sunshine through the most transparent of plate-glass; its high cornices are gilded, and its ceilings gorgeously painted; and a lofty dome—through which, from the central pavement, you may gaze up to the sky, as with no obstructing medium between—surmounts the whole. With what fairer and nobler emblem could any man desire to shadow forth his character? Ah! but in some low and obscure nook,—some narrow closet on the ground-floor, shut, locked, and bolted, and the key flung away,—or beneath the marble pavement, in a stagnant water-puddle, with the richest pattern of mosaic-work above,—may lie a corpse, half decayed, and still decaying, and diffusing its death-scent all through the palace! The inhabitant will not be conscious of it, for it has long been his daily breath! Neither will the visitors, for they smell only the rich odors which the master sedulously scatters through the palace, and the incense which they bring, and delight to burn before him! Now and then, perchance, comes in a seer, before whose sadly-gifted eye the whole structure melts into thin air, leaving only the hidden nook, the bolted closet, with the cobwebs festooned over its forgotten door, or the deadly hole under the pavement, and the decaying corpse within. Here, then, we are to seek the true emblem of the man's character, and of the deed that gives

whatever reality it possesses to his li
And, beneath the show of a marb
palace, that pool of stagnant water, fo
with many impurities, and, perhap
tinged with blood,—that secret abor
ination, above which, possibly, he m.
say his prayers, without rememberi
it,—is this man's miserable soul!

To apply this train of remark som
what more closely to Judge Pynchec
—We might say (without in the lea
imputing crime to a personage of l
eminent respectability) that there w
enough of splendid rubbish in his li
to cover up and paralyze a more acti
and subtile conscience than the jud
was ever troubled with. The purity
his judicial character, while on t
bench; the faithfulness of his pub
service in subsequent capacities; his c
votedness to his party, and the rig
consistency with which he had adher
to its principles; or, at all events, ke
pace with its organized movements; l
remarkable zeal as president of a Bil
society; his unimpeachable integrity
treasurer of a widow's and orphar
fund; his benefits to horticulture,
producing two much-esteemed variet:
of the pear, and to agriculture, throu
the agency of the famous Pynchec
bull; the cleanliness of his moral c
portment, for a great many years pas
the severity with which he had frown
upon, and finally cast off, an expensi
and dissipated son, delaying forgiven
until within the final quarter of an hc
of the young man's life; his pray
at morning and eventide, and graces
meal-time; his efforts in furtherance
the temperance cause; his confining hi
self, since the last attack of the go
to five diurnal glasses of old sher
wine; the snowy whiteness of his lin

e polish of his boots, the handsome-
ess of his gold-headed cane, the square
ad roomy fashion of his coat, and the
neness of its material, and, in general,
he studied propriety of his dress and
quipment; the scrupulousness with
hich he paid public notice, in the
reet, by a bow, a lifting of the hat,
nod, or a motion of the hand, to all
ad sundry his acquaintances, rich or
por; the smile of broad benevolence
herewith he made it a point to gladden
e whole world;—what room could
ossibly be found for darker traits, in
portrait made up of lineaments like
ese? This proper face was what he
eheld in the looking-glass. This ad-
irably arranged life was what he was
nscious of, in the progress of every
ay. Then, might not he claim to be its
sult and sum, and say to himself and
e community,—"Behold Judge Pyn-
eon there"?

And, allowing that, many, many years
zo, in his early and reckless youth, he
ad committed some one wrong act,—
- that, even now, the inevitable force
circumstances should occasionally
ake him do one questionable deed,
nong a thousand praiseworthy, or, at
ast, blameless ones,—would you char-
terize the judge by that one necessary
ed, and that half-forgotten act, and
t it overshadow the fair aspect of a
letime? What is there so ponderous in
il, that a thumb's bigness of it should
tweigh the mass of things not evil
hich were heaped into the other scale!
his scale and balance system is a
vorite one with people of Judge Pyn-
eon's brotherhood. A hard, cold man,
us unfortunately situated, seldom or
ver looking inward, and resolutely
king his idea of himself from what

purports to be his image as reflected
in the mirror of public opinion, can
scarcely arrive at true self-knowledge,
except through loss of property and
reputation. Sickness will not always help
him to it; not always the death-hour!

But our affair now is with Judge
Pyncheon as he stood confronting the
fierce outbreak of Hepzibah's wrath.
Without premeditation, to her own surprise, and indeed terror, she had given
vent, for once, to the inveteracy of her
resentment, cherished against this kinsman for thirty years.

Thus far, the judge's countenance had
expressed mild forbearance,—grave and
almost gentle deprecation of his cousin's
unbecoming violence,—free and Chris-
tian-like forgiveness of the wrong inflicted by her words. But, when those
words were irrevocably spoken, his look
assumed sternness, the sense of power,
and immitigable resolve; and this with
so natural and imperceptible a change,
that it seemed as if the iron man had
stood there from the first, and the
meek man not at all. The effect was as
when the light vapory clouds, with their
soft coloring, suddenly vanish from the
stony brow of a precipitous mountain,
and leave there the frown which you
at once feel to be eternal. Hepzibah
almost adopted the insane belief that
it was her old Puritan ancestor, and not
the modern judge, on whom she had
just been wreaking the bitterness of her
heart. Never did a man show stronger
proof of the lineage attributed to him
than Judge Pyncheon, at this crisis, by
his unmistakable resemblance to the
picture in the inner room.

"Cousin Hepzibah," said he, very
calmly, "it is time to have done with
this."

"With all my heart!" answered she. "Then, why do you persecute us any longer? Leave poor Clifford and me in peace. Neither of us desires anything better!"

"It is my purpose to see Clifford before I leave this house," continued the judge. "Do not act like a mad-woman, Hepzibah! I am his only friend, and an all-powerful one. Has it never occurred to you,—are you so blind as not to have seen,—that, without not merely my consent, but my efforts, my representations, the exertion of my whole influence, political, official, personal, Clifford would never have been what you call free? Did you think his release a triumph over me? Not so, my good cousin; not so, by any means! The furthest possible from that! No; but it was the accomplishment of a purpose long entertained on my part. I set him free!"

"You!" answered Hepzibah. "I never will believe it! He owed his dungeon to you;—his freedom to God's providence!"

"I set him free!" reaffirmed Judge Pyncheon, with the calmest composure. "And I come hither now to decide whether he shall retain his freedom. It will depend upon himself. For this purpose, I must see him."

"Never!—it would drive him mad!" exclaimed Hepzibah, but with an irresoluteness sufficiently perceptible to the keen eye of the judge; for, without the slightest faith in his good intentions, she knew not whether there was most to dread in yielding or resistance. "And why should you wish to see this wretched, broken man, who retains hardly a fraction of his intellect, and will hide even that from an eye which

has no love in it?"

"He shall see love enough in mi if that be all!" said the judge, wi well-grounded confidence in the ben nity of his aspect. "But, Cousin He zibah, you confess a great deal, a very much to the purpose. Now, list and I will frankly explain my reaso for insisting on this interview. At t death, thirty years since, of our un Jaffrey, it was found,—I know n whether the circumstance ever attract much of your attention, among the sa der interests that clustered round th event,—but it was found that his visil estate, of every kind, fell far short any estimate ever made of it. He w supposed to be immensely rich. Nobo doubted that he stood among the weig iest men of his day. It was one of I eccentricities, however,—and not al gether a folly, neither,—to conceal t amount of his property by making d tant and foreign investments, perha under other names than his own, a by various means, familiar enough capitalists, but unnecessary here to specified. By Uncle Jaffrey's last w and testament, as you are aware, I entire property was bequeathed to n with the single exception of a life terest to yourself in this old fam mansion, and the strip of patrimon estate remaining attached to it."

"And do you seek to deprive us that?" asked Hepzibah, unable to strain her bitter contempt. "Is this ye price for ceasing to persecute poor Cl ford?"

"Certainly not, my dear cousin!" a swered the judge, smiling benevolent "On the contrary, as you must do the justice to own, I have constan expressed my readiness to double

eble your resources, whenever you
ould make up your mind to accept
y kindness of that nature at the hands
your kinsman. No, no! But here lies
e gist of the matter. Of my uncle's
questionably great estate, as I have
id, not the half—no, not one third, as
am fully convinced—was apparent
ter his death. Now, I have the best
ssible reasons for believing that your
other Clifford can give me a clue
the recovery of the remainder."

"Clifford!—Clifford know of any hid-
n wealth?—Clifford have it in his
wer to make you rich?" cried the old
ntlewoman, affected with a sense of
mething like ridicule, at the idea. "Im-
ssible! You deceive yourself! It is
ally a thing to laugh at!"

"It is as certain as that I stand here!"
id Judge Pyncheon, striking his gold-
aded cane on the floor, and at the
me time stamping his foot, as if to
press his conviction the more forcibly
the whole emphasis of his substan-
l person. "Clifford told me so him-
lf!"

"No, no!" exclaimed Hepzibah, in-
edulously. "You are dreaming, Cousin
ffrey!"

"I do not belong to the dreaming class
men," said the judge, quietly. "Some
nths before my uncle's death, Clif-
rd boasted to me of the possession
the secret of incalculable wealth.
s purpose was to taunt me, and excite
y curiosity. I know it well. But, from
pretty distinct recollection of the par-
ulars of our conversation, I am thor-
ghly convinced that there was truth
what he said. Clifford, at this mont, if he chooses,—and choose he
ust!—can inform me where to find
e schedule, the documents, the evi-

dences, in whatever shape they exist,
of the vast amount of Uncle Jaffrey's
missing property. He has the secret. His
boast was no idle word. It had a directness, an emphasis, a particularity, that
showed a back-bone of solid meaning
within the mystery of his expression."

"But what could have been Clifford's
object," asked Hepzibah, "in concealing
it so long?"

"It was one of the bad impulses of
our fallen nature," replied the judge,
turning up his eyes. "He looked upon
me as his enemy. He considered me as
the cause of his overwhelming disgrace,
his imminent peril of death, his irretrievable ruin. There was no great probability, therefore, of his volunteering information, out of his dungeon, that
should elevate me still higher on the
ladder of prosperity. But the moment
has now come when he must give up his
secret."

"And what if he should refuse?" inquired Hepzibah. "Or,—as I steadfastly
believe,—what if he has not knowledge
of this wealth?"

"My dear cousin," said Judge Pyncheon, with a quietude which he had
the power of making more formidable
than any violence, "since your brother's
return, I have taken the precaution (a
highly proper one in the near kinsman
and natural guardian of an individual so
situated) to have his deportment and
habits constantly and carefully over-
looked. Your neighbors have been eye-
witnesses to whatever has passed in the
garden. The butcher, the baker, the fish-
monger, some of the customers of your
shop, and many a prying old woman,
have told me several of the secrets of
your interior. A still larger circle—I
myself, among the rest—can testify to

his extravagances at the arched window. Thousands beheld him, a week or two ago, on the point of flinging himself thence into the street. From all this testimony, I am led to apprehend—reluctantly, and with deep grief—that Clifford's misfortunes have so affected his intellect, never very strong, that he cannot safely remain at large. The alternative, you must be aware,—and its adoption will depend entirely on the decision which I am now about to make, —the alternative is his confinement, probably for the remainder of his life, in a public asylum, for persons in his unfortunate state of mind."

"You cannot mean it!" shrieked Hepzibah.

"Should my cousin Clifford," continued Judge Pyncheon, wholly undisturbed, "from mere malice, and hatred of one whose interests ought naturally to be dear to him,—a mode of passion that, as often as any other, indicates mental disease,—should he refuse me the information so important to myself, and which he assuredly possesses, I shall consider it the one needed jot of evidence to satisfy my mind of his insanity. And, once sure of the course pointed out by conscience, you know me too well, Cousin Hepzibah, to entertain a doubt that I shall pursue it."

"O, Jaffrey—Cousin Jaffrey!" cried Hepzibah, mournfully, not passionately, "it is you that are diseased in mind, not Clifford! You have forgotten that a woman was your mother!—that you have had sisters, brothers, children of your own!—or that there ever was affection between man and man, or pity from one man to another, in this miserable world! Else, how could you have dreamed of this? You are not young, Cousin Jaffrey!—no, nor middle-aged,—but already an old man! The hair is white upon your head! How many years have you to live? Are you not rich enough for that little time? Shall you be hungry,—shall you lack clothes, or roof to shelter you,—between this point and the grave? No! but, with the half of what you now possess, you could revel in costly food and wines, and build a house twice as splendid as you now inhabit, and make a far greater show to the world,—and yet leave riches to your only son, to make him bless the hour of your death! Then, why should you do this cruel, cruel thing?—so mad a thing that I know not whether to call it wicked! Alas, Cousin Jaffray, this hard and grasping spirit has run in our blood these two hundred years! You are but doing over again, in another shape, what your ancestor before you did, and sending down to your posterity the curse inherited from him!"

"Talk sense, Hepzibah, for Heaven's sake!" exclaimed the judge, with the impatience natural to a reasonable man on hearing anything so utterly absurd as the above, in a discussion about matters of business. "I have told you my determination. I am not apt to change. Clifford must give up his secret, or take the consequences. And let him decide quickly; for I have several affairs to attend to, this morning, and an important dinner engagement with some political friends."

"Clifford has no secret!" answered Hepzibah. "And God will not let you do the thing you meditate!"

"We shall see," said the unmoved judge. "Meanwhile, choose whether you will summon Clifford, and allow this business to be amicably settled by

terview between two kinsmen, or drive
e to harsher measures, which I should
: most happy to feel myself justified in
voiding. The responsibility is alto-
ther on your part."

"You are stronger than I," said Hep-
bah, after a brief consideration; "and
ou have no pity in your strength!
lifford is not now insane; but the in-
rview which you insist upon may go
r to make him so. Nevertheless,
nowing you as I do, I believe it to be
y best course to allow you to judge
r yourself as to the improbability of
s possessing any valuable secret. I will
ll Clifford. Be merciful in your deal-
gs with him!—be far more merciful
an your heart bids you be!—for God
looking at you, Jaffrey Pyncheon!"

The judge followed his cousin from
.e shop, where the foregoing conversa-
on had passed, into the parlor, and
ing himself heavily into the great an-
stral chair. Many a former Pyncheon
d found repose in its capacious arms:
-rosy children, after their sports;
oung men, dreamy with love; grown
en, weary with cares; old men, bur-
ened with winters,—they had mused,
d slumbered, and departed to a yet
rofounder sleep. It had been a long
adition, though a doubtful one, that
is was the very chair, seated in which,
ie earliest of the judge's New England
refathers—he whose picture still hung
on the wall—had given a dead man's
lent and stern reception to the throng
distinguished guests. From that hour

of evil omen, until the present, it may
be,—though we know not the secret of
his heart,—but it may be that no
wearier and sadder man had ever sunk
into the chair than this same Judge
Pyncheon, whom we have just beheld
so immitigably hard and resolute.
Surely, it must have been at no slight
cost that he had thus fortified his soul
with iron. Such calmness is a mightier
effort than the violence of weaker men.
And there was yet a heavy task for him
to do. Was it a little matter,—a trifle to
be prepared for in a single moment, and
to be rested from in another moment,—
that he must now, after thirty years,
encounter a kinsman risen from a living
tomb, and wrench a secret from him,
or else consign him to a living tomb
again?

"Did you speak?" asked Hepzibah,
looking in from the threshold of the
parlor; for she imagined that the judge
had uttered some sound which she was
anxious to interpret as a relenting
impulse. "I thought you called me
back."

"No, no!" gruffly answered Judge
Pyncheon, with a harsh frown, while his
brow grew almost a black purple, in the
shadow of the room. "Why should I call
you back? Time flies! Bid Clifford come
to me!"

The judge had taken his watch from
his vest-pocket, and now held it in his
hand, measuring the interval which was
to ensue before the appearance of Clifford.

CHAPTER XVI

CLIFFORD'S CHAMBER

NEVER had the old house appeared so dismal to poor Hepzibah as when she departed on that wretched errand. There was a strange aspect in it. As she trode along the foot-worn passages, and opened one crazy door after another, and ascended the creaking staircase, she gazed wistfully and fearfully around. It would have been no marvel, to her excited mind, if, behind or beside her, there had been the rustle of dead people's garments, or pale visages awaiting her on the landing-place above. Her nerves were set all ajar by the scene of passion and terror through which she had just struggled. Her colloquy with Judge Pyncheon, who so perfectly represented the person and attributes of the founder of the family, had called back the dreary past. It weighed upon her heart. Whatever she had heard, from legendary aunts and grandmothers, concerning the good or evil fortunes of the Pyncheons,—stories which had heretofore been kept warm in her remembrance by the chimney-corner glow that was associated with them,—now recurred to her, sombre, ghastly, cold, like most passages of family history, when brooded over in melancholy mood. The whole seemed little else but a series of calamity, reproducing itself in successive generations, with one general hue, and varying in little, save the outline. But Hepzibah now felt as if the judge, and Clifford, and herself,—they three together,—were on the point of adding another incident to the annals of the house, with a bolder relief of wrong and

sorrow, which would cause it to sta[nd] out from all the rest. Thus it is that t[he] grief of the passing moment takes up[on] itself an individuality, and a charac[ter] of climax, which it is destined to lo[se] after a while, and to fade into the d[ark] gray tissue common to the grave or g[lad] events of many years ago. It is but [in] a moment, comparatively, that anyth[ing] looks strange or startling;—a truth t[hat] has the bitter and the sweet in it.

But Hepzibah could not rid herself [of] the sense of something unprecedented [in] that instant passing, and soon to be [ac]complished. Her nerves were in a sha[ke.] Instinctively she paused before [an] arched window, and looked out upon [the] street, in order to seize its permane[nt] objects with her mental grasp, and th[us] to steady herself from the reel a[nd] vibration which affected her more imm[e]diate sphere. It brought her up, as [I] may say, with a kind of shock, when s[he] beheld everything under the same [ap]pearance as the day before, and numb[er]less preceding days, except for the d[if]ference between sunshine and sul[len] storm. Her eyes travelled along [the] street, from door-step to door-step, n[ot]ing the wet sidewalks, with here a[nd] there a puddle in hollows that had be[en] imperceptible until filled with water. S[he] screwed her dim optics to their acut[est] point, in the hope of making out, w[ith] greater distinctness, a certain wind[ow,] where she half saw, half guessed, t[hat] a tailor's seamstress was sitting at [her] work. Hepzibah flung herself upon t[he] unknown woman's companionship, e[ven]

s far off. Then she was attracted by
haise rapidly passing, and watched its
ist and glistening top, and its splash-
wheels, until it had turned the cor-
, and refused to carry any further her
y trifling, because appalled and over-
rthened, mind. When the vehicle had
appeared, she allowed herself still an-
er loitering moment; for the patched
ure of good Uncle Venner was now
ible, coming slowly from the head of
street downward, with a rheumatic
p, because the east wind had got into
joints. Hepzibah wished that he
uld pass yet more slowly, and be-
end her shivering solitude a little
ger. Anything that would take her
of the grievous present, and inter-
se human beings betwixt herself and
at was nearest to her,—whatever
uld defer, for an instant, the inevita-
errand on which she was bound,—
such impediments were welcome.
xt to the lightest heart, the heaviest
apt to be most playful.

Hepzibah had little hardihood for her
n proper pain, and far less for what
must inflict on Clifford. Of so slight
nature, and so shattered by his pre-
us calamities, it could not well be
rt of utter ruin to bring him face to
e with the hard, relentless man, who
d been his evil destiny through life.
en had there been no bitter recollec-
ns, nor any hostile interest now at
ke between them, the mere natural
ugnance of the more sensitive system
the massive, weighty, and unimpress-
e one, must, in itself, have been dis-
rous to the former. It would be like
ging a porcelain vase, with already a
ck in it, against a granite column.
ver before had Hepzibah so ade-
ately estimated the powerful character of her cousin Jaffrey,—powerful by
intellect, energy of will, the long habit
of acting among men, and, as she believed, by his unscrupulous pursuit of
selfish ends through evil means. It did
but increase the difficulty, that Judge
Pyncheon was under a delusion as to the
secret which he supposed Clifford to
possess. Men of his strength of purpose, and customary sagacity, if they
chance to adopt a mistaken opinion in
practical matters, so wedge it and fasten
it among things known to be true, that
to wrench it out of their minds is
hardly less difficult than pulling up an
oak. Thus, as the judge required an impossibility of Clifford, the latter, as he
could not perform it, must needs perish.
For what, in the grasp of a man like
this, was to become of Clifford's soft,
poetic nature, that never should have
had a task more stubborn than to set a
life of beautiful enjoyment to the flow
and rhythm of musical cadences! Indeed, what had become of it already?
Broken! Blighted! All but annihilated!
Soon to be wholly so!

For a moment, the thought crossed
Hepzibah's mind, whether Clifford might
not really have such knowledge of their
deceased uncle's vanished estate as the
judge imputed to him. She remembered
some vague intimations, on her brother's
part, which—if the supposition were not
essentially preposterous—might have
been so interpreted. There had been
schemes of travel and residence abroad,
day-dreams of brilliant life at home,
and splendid castles in the air, which it
would have required boundless wealth to
build and realize. Had this wealth been
in her power, how gladly would Hepzibah have bestowed it all upon her iron-
hearted kinsman, to buy for Clifford the

freedom and seclusion of the desolate old house! But she believed that her brother's schemes were as destitute of actual substance and purpose as a child's pictures of its future life, while sitting in a little chair by its mother's knee. Clifford had none but shadowy gold at his command; and it was not the stuff to satisfy Judge Pyncheon!

Was there no help, in their extremity? It seemed strange that there should be none, with a city round about her. It would be so easy to throw up the window, and send forth a shriek, at the strange agony of which everybody would come hastening to the rescue, well understanding it to be the cry of a human soul, at some dreadful crisis! But how wild, how almost laughable, the fatality, —and yet how continually it comes to pass, thought Hepzibah, in this dull delirium of a world,—that whosoever, and with however kindly a purpose, should come to help, they would be sure to help the strongest side! Might and wrong combined, like iron magnetized, are endowed with irresistible attraction. There would be Judge Pyncheon,—a person eminent in the public view, of high station and great wealth, a philanthropist, a member of congress and of the church, and intimately associated with whatever else bestows good name, —so imposing, in these advantageous lights, that Hepzibah herself could hardly help shrinking from her own conclusions as to his hollow integrity. The judge, on one side! And who, on the other? The guilty Clifford! Once a byword! Now, an indistinctly-remembered ignominy!

Nevertheless, in spite of this perception that the judge would draw all human aid to his own behalf, Hepzibah

was so unaccustomed to act for hers that the least word of counsel wo have swayed her to any mode of act Little Phœbe Pyncheon would at o have lighted up the whole scene, if by any available suggestion, yet sim by the warm vivacity of her charac The idea of the artist occurred to H zibah. Young and unknown, m vagrant adventurer as he was, she been conscious of a force in Holgr which might well adapt him to be champion of a crisis. With this thou in her mind, she unbolted a door, c webbed and long disused, but which served as a former medium of c munication between her own part of house and the gable where the wan ing daguerreotypist had now establis his temporary home. He was not th A book, face downward, on the tabl roll of manuscript, a half-written sh a newspaper, some tools of his pres occupation, and several rejected guerreotypes, conveyed an impression if he were close at hand. But, at period of the day, as Hepzibah mi have anticipated, the artist was at public rooms. With an impulse of curiosity, that flickered among heavy thoughts, she looked at one the daguerreotypes, and beheld Ju Pyncheon frowning at her! Fate sta her in the face. She turned back fr her fruitless quest, with a heart-sink sense of disappointment. In all her ye of seclusion, she had never felt, as n what it was to be alone. It seemed a the house stood in a desert, or, by so spell, was made invisible to those v dwelt around, or passed beside it; that any mode of misfortune; misera accident, or crime, might happen in without the possibility of aid. In

f and wounded pride, Hepzibah had
at her life in divesting herself of
nds;—she had wilfully cast off the
port which God has ordained his
tures to need from one another;—

it was now her punishment, that
ford and herself would fall the easier
ims to their kindred enemy.

eturning to the arched window, she
ed her eyes,—scowling, poor, dim-
ted Hepzibah, in the face of
ven!—and strove hard to send up a
yer through the dense gray pavement
clouds. Those mists had gathered, as
o symbolize a great, brooding mass
uman trouble, doubt, confusion, and
l indifference, between earth and the
er regions. Her faith was too weak;
prayer too heavy to be thus uplifted.
fell back, a lump of lead, upon her
rt. It smote her with the wretched
viction that Providence intermeddled
in these petty wrongs of one indi-
ual to his fellow, nor had any balm
these little agonies of a solitary
; but shed its justice, and its mercy,
broad, sunlike sweep, over half the
verse at once. Its vastness made it
hing. But Hepzibah did not see that,
as there comes a warm sunbeam
every cottage window, so comes a
-beam of God's care and pity, for
ry separate need.

t last, finding no other pretext for
erring the torture that she was to
ict on Clifford,—her reluctance to
ch was the true cause of her loitering
he window, her search for the artist,
even her abortive prayer,—dread-
, also, to hear the stern voice of
ge Pyncheon from below stairs, chid-
her delay,—she crept slowly, a pale,
f-stricken figure, a dismal shape of
man, with almost torpid limbs, slowly

to her brother's door, and knocked!

There was no reply!

And how should there have been?
Her hand, tremulous with the shrinking
purpose which directed it, had smitten
so feebly against the door that the
sound could hardly have gone inward.
She knocked again. Still, no response!
Nor was it to be wondered at. She had
struck with the entire force of her
heart's vibration, communicating, by
some subtle magnetism, her own terror
to the summons. Clifford would turn his
face to the pillow, and cover his head
beneath the bed-clothes, like a startled
child at midnight. She knocked a third
time, three regular strokes, gentle, but
perfectly distinct, and with meaning in
them; for, modulate it with what cautious art we will, the hand cannot help
playing some tune of what we feel, upon
the senseless wood.

Clifford returned no answer.

"Clifford! dear brother!" said Hepzibah. "Shall I come in?"

A silence.

Two or three times, and more, Hepzibah repeated his name, without result;
still, thinking her brother's sleep un-
wontedly profound, she undid the door,
and entering, found the chamber vacant.
How could he have come forth, and
when, without her knowledge? Was it
possible that, in spite of the stormy day,
and worn out with the irksomeness
within doors, he had betaken himself to
his customary haunt in the garden, and
was now shivering under the cheerless
shelter of the summer-house? She
hastily threw up a window, thrust forth
her turbaned head and the half of her
gaunt figure, and searched the whole
garden through, as completely as her
dim vision would allow. She could see

the interior of the summer-house, and its circular seat, kept moist by the droppings of the roof. It had no occupant. Clifford was not thereabouts; unless, indeed, he had crept for concealment— (as, for a moment, Hepzibah fancied might be the case)—into a great wet mass of tangled and broad-leaved shadow, where the squash-vines were clambering tumultuously upon an old wooden frame-work, set casually aslant against the fence. This could not be, however; he was not there; for, while Hepzibah was looking, a strange grimalkin stole forth from the very spot, and picked his way across the garden. Twice he paused to snuff the air, and then anew directed his course towards the parlor-window. Whether it was only on account of the stealthy, prying manner common to the race, or that this cat seemed to have more than ordinary mischief in his thoughts, the old gentlewoman, in spite of her much perplexity, felt an impulse to drive the animal away, and accordingly flung down a window-stick. The cat stared up at her, like a detected thief or murderer, and, the next instant, took to flight. No other living creature was visible in the garden. Chanticleer and his family had either not left their roost, disheartened by the interminable rain, or had done the next wisest thing, by seasonably returning to it. Hepzibah closed the window.

But where was Clifford? Could it be, that, aware of the presence of his Evil Destiny, he had crept silently down the staircase, while the judge and Hepzibah stood talking in the shop, and had softly undone the fastenings of the outer door, and made his escape into the street? With that thought, she seemed to behold his gray, wrinkled, yet childlike aspect,

in the old-fashioned garments which s wore about the house; a figure such one sometimes imagines himself to with the world's eye upon him, in troubled dream. This figure of wretched brother would go wanderi through the city, attracting all eyes, a everybody's wonder and repugnan like a ghost, the more to be shudder at because visible at noontide. To inc the ridicule of the younger crowd, th knew him not,—the harsher scorn a indignation of a few old men, who mig recall his once familiar features! To the sport of boys, who, when old enou to run about the streets, have no mc reverence for what is beautiful and ho nor pity for what is sad,—no more ser of sacred misery, sanctifying the hum shape in which it embodies itself,—th if Satan were the father of them a Goaded by their taunts, their loud, sh cries, and cruel laughter,—insulted the filth of the public ways, which th would fling upon him,—or, as it mig well be, distracted by the mere strang ness of his situation, though nobo should afflict him with so much as thoughtless word,—what wonder if Cl ford were to break into some wild e travagance, which was certain to interpreted as lunacy? Thus Judge Py cheon's fiendish scheme would be rea accomplished to his hands!

Then Hepzibah reflected that t town was almost completely wate girdled. The wharves stretched out t wards the centre of the harbor, and, this inclement weather, were desert by the ordinary throng of merchan laborers, and sea-faring men; ea wharf a solitude, with the vesse moored stem and stern, along its mis length. Should her brother's aiml

tsteps stray thitherward, and he but
d, one moment, over the deep, black
e, would be not bethink himself that
e was the sure refuge within his
ch, and that, with a single step, or
slightest over-balance of his body,
might be forever beyond his kins-
n's gripe? O, the temptation! To
ke of his ponderous sorrow a secur-
! To sink, with its leaden weight
n him, and never rise again!

The horror of this last conception was
much for Hepzibah. Even Jaffrey
cheon must help her now! She has-
ed down the staircase, shrieking as
went.

"Clifford is gone!" she cried. "I can-
find my brother! Help, Jaffrey Pyn-
on! Some harm will happen to him!"
She throw open the parlor-door. But,
at with the shade of branches across
windows, and the smoke-blackened
ling, and the dark oak-panelling of
walls, there was hardly so much
light in the room that Hepzibah's
perfect sight could accurately dis-
guish the judge's figure. She was cer-
n, however, that she saw him sitting
the ancestral armchair, near the
tre of the floor, with his face some-
at averted, and looking towards a
dow. So firm and quiet is the ner-
s system of such men as Judge Pyn-
on, that he had perhaps stirred not
re than once since her departure, but,
the hard composure of his tempera-
nt, retained the position into which
ident had thrown him.

"I tell you, Jaffray," cried Hepzibah,
patiently, as she turned from the par-
-door to search other rooms, "my
ther is not in his chamber! You must
p me seek him!"

But Judge Pyncheon was not the man
to let himself be startled from an easy-
chair with haste ill-befitting either the
dignity of his character or his broad
personal basis, by the alarm of an
hysteric woman. Yet, considering his
own interest in the matter, he might
have bestirred himself with a little more
alacrity.

"Do you hear me, Jaffrey Pyncheon?"
screamed Hepzibah, as she again approached the parlor-door, after an ineffectual search elsewhere. "Clifford is
gone!"

At this instant, on the threshold of
the parlor, emerging from within, appeared Clifford himself. His face was
preternaturally pale; so deadly white,
indeed, that, through all the glimmering
indistinctness of the passage-way, Hepzibah could discern his features, as if a
light fell on them alone. Their vivid and
wild expression seemed likewise sufficient to illuminate them; it was an expression of scorn and mockery, coincid-
ing with the emotions indicated by his
gesture. As Clifford stood on the threshold, partly turning back, he pointed his
finger within the parlor, and shook it
slowly, as though he would have summoned, not Hepzibah alone, but the
whole world, to gaze at some object in-
conceivably ridiculous. This action, so
ill-timed and extravagant,—accompanied, too, with a look that showed
more like joy than any other kind of
excitement,—compelled Hepzibah to
dread that her stern kinsman's ominous
visit had driven her poor brother to
absolute insanity. Nor could she otherwise account for the judge's quiescent
mood than by supposing him craftily on
the watch, while Clifford developed these
symptoms of a distracted mind.

"Be quiet, Clifford!" whispered his

sister, raising her hand, to impress caution. "O, for Heaven's sake, be quiet!"

"Let him be quiet! What can he do better?" answered Clifford, with a still wilder gesture, pointing into the room which he had just quitted. "As for us, Hepzibah, we can dance now!—we can sing, laugh, play, do what we will! The weight is gone, Hepzibah! it is gone off this weary old world; and we may be as light-hearted as little Phœbe herself!"

And, in accordance with his words, he began to laugh, still pointing his finger at the object, invisible to Hepzibah, within the parlor. She was seized with a sudden intuition of some horrible thing. She thrust herself past Clifford, and disappeared into the room; but almost immediately returned, with a cry choking in her throat. Gazing at her brother, with an affrighted glance of inquiry, she beheld him all in a tremor and a quake, from head to foot, while, amid these commoted elements of passion or alarm, still flickered his gusty mirth.

"My God! what is to become of us?" gasped Hepzibah.

"Come!" said Clifford, in a tone of brief decision, most unlike what was usual with him. "We stay here too long! Let us leave the old house to our cousin Jaffrey! He will take good care of it!"

Hepzibah now noticed that Clifford had on a cloak,—a garment of long ago,—in which he had constantly muffled himself during these days of easterly storm. He beckoned with his hand, and intimated, so far as she could comprehend him, his purpose that they should go together from the house. There are chaotic, blind, or drunken moments, in the lives of persons who lack real force of character,—moments of test, in which courage would most assert

itself,—but where these individuals left to themselves, stagger aimle along, or follow implicitly whate guidance may befall them, even if i a child's. No matter how preposter or insane, a purpose is a God-send them. Hepzibah had reached this p Unaccustomed to action or respons ity,—full of horror at what she seen, and afraid to inquire, or almos imagine, how it had come to pas affrighted at the fatality which see to pursue her brother,—stupefied by dim, thick, stifling atmosphere of dr which filled the house as with a de smell, and obliterated all definitenes thought,—she yielded without a q tion, and on the instant, to the which Clifford expressed. For her she was like a person in a dream, w the will always sleeps. Clifford, ord rily so destitute of this faculty, found it in the tension of the crisi

"Why do you delay so?" cried sharply. "Put on your cloak and h or whatever it pleases you to wear! matter what;—you cannot look bea ful nor brilliant, my poor Hepzib Take your purse, with money in it, come along!"

Hepzibah obeyed these instructi as if nothing else were to be don thought of. She began to wonder, true, why she did not wake up, an what still more intolerable pitch of d trouble her spirit would struggle ou the maze, and make her conscious nothing of all this had actually pened. Of course, it was not real; such black, easterly day as this had begun to be; Judge Pyncheon had talked with her; Clifford had laughed, pointed, beckoned her a with him; but she had merely I

cted—as lonely sleepers often are—
a a great deal of unreasonable
ery, in a morning dream!

Now—now—I shall certainly awake!"
ught Hepzibah, as she went to and
making her little preparations. "I
bear it no longer! I must wake up
!"

ut it came not, that awakening mo-
it! It came not, even when, just
ore they left the house, Clifford stole
he parlor-door, and made a parting
isance to the sole occupant of the
n.

What an absurd figure the old fellow
now!" whispered he to Hepzibah.
st when he fancied he had me comely under his thumb! Come, come;
ke haste! or he will start up, like

Giant Despair in pursuit of Christian and Hopeful, and catch us yet!"

As they passed into the street, Clifford directed Hepzibah's attention to something on one of the posts of the front door. It was merely the initials of his own name, which, with somewhat of his characteristic grace about the forms of the letters, he had cut there, when a boy. The brother and sister departed, and left Judge Pyncheon sitting in the old home of his forefathers, all by himself; so heavy and lumpish that we can liken him to nothing better than a defunct nightmare, which had perished in the midst of its wickedness, and left its flabby corpse on the breast of the tormented one, to be gotten rid of as it might!

CHAPTER XVII

THE FLIGHT OF TWO OWLS

UMMER as it was, the east wind set
r Hepzibah's few remaining teeth
ttering in her head, as she and Clif-
l faced it, on their way up Pyncheon-
et, and towards the centre of the
n. Not merely was it the shiver
ch this pitiless blast brought to her
ne (although her feet and hands,
ecially, had never seemed so death-
old as now), but there was a moral
sation, mingling itself with the physi-
chill, and causing her to shake more
spirit than in body. The world's
ad, bleak atmosphere was all so
fortless! Such, indeed, is the im-
ssion which it makes on every new
enturer, even if he plunge into it

while the warmest tide of life is bubbling through his veins. What, then, must it have been to Hepzibah and Clifford,—so time-stricken as they were, yet so like children in their inexperience,—as they left the door-step, and passed from beneath the wide shelter of the Pyncheon-elm! They were wandering all abroad, on precisely such a pilgrimage as a child often meditates, to the world's end, with perhaps a sixpence and a biscuit in his pocket. In Hepzibah's mind, there was the wretched consciousness of being adrift. She had lost the faculty of self-guidance; but, in view of the difficulties around her, felt it hardly worth an effort to regain it, and was, moreover, incapable of making one.

As they proceeded on their strange expedition, she now and then cast a look sidelong at Clifford, and could not but observe that he was possessed and swayed by a powerful excitement. It was this, indeed, that gave him the control which he had at once, and so irresistibly, established over his movements. It not a little resembled the exhilaration of wine. Or, it might more fancifully be compared to a joyous piece of music, played with wild vivacity, but upon a disordered instrument. As the cracked jarring note might always be heard, and as it jarred loudest amid the loftiest exultation of the melody, so was there a continual quake through Clifford, causing him most to quiver while he wore a triumphant smile, and seemed almost under a necessity to skip in his gait.

They met few people abroad, even on passing from the retired neighborhood of the House of the Seven Gables into what was ordinarily the more thronged and busier portion of the town. Glistening sidewalks, with little pools of rain, here and there, along their unequal surface; umbrellas displayed ostentatiously in the shop-windows, as if the life of trade had concentred itself in that one article; wet leaves of the horse-chestnut or elm trees, torn off untimely by the blast, and scattered along the public way; an unsightly accumulation of mud in the middle of the street, which perversely grew the more unclean for its long and laborious washing;—these were the more definable points of a very sombre picture. In the way of movement, and human life, there was the hasty rattle of a cab or coach, its driver

protected by a water-proof cap over head and shoulders; the forlorn fig of an old man, who seemed to h crept out of some subterranean sev and was stooping along the kennel, poking the wet rubbish with a stick quest of rusty nails; a merchant or t at the door of the post-office, toget with an editor, and a miscellane politician, awaiting a dilatory mail few visages of retired sea-captains the window of an insurance office, lo ing out vacantly at the vacant str blaspheming at the weather, and frett at the dearth as well of public news local gossip. What a treasure-trove these venerable quidnuncs, could t have guessed the secret which Hepzi and Clifford were carrying along w them! But their two figures attrac hardly so much notice as that o young girl, who passed at the same stant, and happened to raise her s a trifle too high above her ankles. Ha been a sunny and cheerful day, t could hardly have gone through streets without making themselves noxious to remark. Now, probably, t were felt to be in keeping with the mal and bitter weather, and theref did not stand out in strong relief, a the sun were shining on them, melted into the gray gloom, and w forgotten as soon as gone.

Poor Hepzibah! Could she have derstood this fact, it would have brou her some little comfort; for, to all other troubles—strange to say!—th was added the womanish and maiden-like misery arising from a se of unseemliness in her attire. Thus, was fain to shrink deeper into hers as it were, as if in the hope of mak people suppose that here was only

ak and hood, threadbare and wofully
led, taking an airing in the midst of
storm, without any wearer!

As they went on, the feeling of in-
tinctness and unreality kept dimly
vering round about her, and so diffus-
itself into her system that one of her
nds was hardly palpable to the touch
the other. Any certainty would have
n preferable to this. She whispered to
self, again and again,—"Am I awake?
Am I awake?"—and sometimes ex-
ed her face to the chill spatter of the
d, for the sake of its rude assurance
t she was. Whether it was Clifford's
rpose, or only chance, had led them
ther, they now found themselves
sing beneath the arched entrance of
arge structure of gray stone. Within,
re was a spacious breadth, and an
y height from floor to roof, now par-
ly filled with smoke and steam,
ich eddied voluminously upward, and
med a mimic cloud-region over their
ds. A train of cars was just ready
a start; the locomotive was fretting
l fuming, like a steed impatient for
eadlong rush; and the bell rang out
hasty peal, so well expressing the
ef summons which life vouchsafes to
in its hurried career. Without ques-
n or delay,—with the irresistible de-
on, if not rather to be called reck-
ness, which had so strangely taken
session of him, and through him of
pzibah,—Clifford impelled her to-
ds the cars, and assisted her to enter.
signal was given; the engine puffed
th its short, quick breaths; the train
an its movement; and, along with a
dred other passengers, these two united travellers sped onward like the
d.

t last, therefore, and after so long

estrangement from everything that the
world acted or enjoyed, they had been
drawn into the great current of human
life, and were swept away by it, as by
the suction of fate itself.

Still haunted with the idea that not
one of the past incidents, inclusive of
Judge Pyncheon's visit, could be real,
the recluse of the seven gables murmured in her brother's ear,—

"Clifford! Clifford! Is not this a
dream?"

"A dream, Hepzibah!" repeated he,
almost laughing in her face. "On the
contrary, I have never been awake
before!"

Meanwhile, looking from the window,
they could see the world racing past
them. At one moment, they were rattling through a solitude; the next, a
village had grown up around them; a
few breaths more, and it had vanished,
as if swallowed by an earthquake. The
spires of meeting-houses seemed set
adrift from their foundations; the
broad-based hills glided away. Everything was unfixed from its age-long rest,
and moving at whirlwind speed in a
direction opposite to their own.

Within the car, there was the usual
interior life of the railroad, offering
little to the observation of other passengers, but full of novelty for this pair of
strangely enfranchised prisoners. It was
novelty enough, indeed, that there were
fifty human beings in close relation
with them, under one long and narrow
roof, and drawn onward by the same
mighty influence that had taken their
two selves into its grasp. It seemed
marvellous how all these people could
remain so quietly in their seats, while
so much noisy strength was at work in
their behalf. Some, with tickets in their

hats (long travellers these, before whom lay a hundred miles of railroad), had plunged into the English scenery and adventures of pamphlet novels, and were keeping company with dukes and earls. Others, whose briefer span forbade their devoting themselves to studies so abstruse, beguiled the little tedium of the way with penny-papers. A party of girls, and one young man, on opposite sides of the car, found huge amusement in a game of ball. They tossed it to and fro, with peals of laughter that might be measured by mile-lengths; for, faster than the nimble ball could fly, the merry players fled unconsciously along, leaving the trail of their mirth afar behind, and ending their game under another sky than had witnessed its commencement. Boys, with apples, cakes, candy, and rolls of variously tinctured lozenges,—merchandise that reminded Hepzibah of her deserted shop,—appeared at each momentary stopping-place, doing up their business in a hurry, or breaking it short off, lest the market should ravish them away with it. New people continually entered. Old acquaintances—for such they soon grew to be, in this rapid current of affairs—continually departed. Here and there, amid the rumble and the tumult, sat one asleep. Sleep; sport; business; graver or lighter study; and the common and inevitable movement onward! It was life itself!

Clifford's naturally poignant sympathies were all aroused. He caught the color of what was passing about him, and threw it back more vividly than he received it, but mixed, nevertheless, with a lurid and portentous hue. Hepzibah, on the other hand, felt herself more apart from human kind than even in the seclusion which she had just quitt

"You are not happy, Hepzibah!" s Clifford, apart, in a tone of reproa "You are thinking of that dismal house, and of Cousin Jaffrey,"—h came the quake through him,—"and Cousin Jaffrey sitting there, all by h self! Take my advice,—follow my ample,—and let such things slip as Here we are, in the world, Hepzibah in the midst of life!—in the throng our fellow-beings! Let you and I happy! As happy as that youth, those pretty girls, at their game ball!"

"Happy!" thought Hepzibah, bitte conscious, at the word, of her dull heavy heart, with the frozen pain in "Happy! He is mad already; and, i could once feel myself broad awake should go mad too!"

If a fixed idea be madness, she perhaps not remote from it. Fast far as they had rattled and clatte along the iron track, they might just well, as regarded Hepzibah's mer images, have been passing up and dc Pyncheon-street. With miles and m of varied scenery between, there was scene for her, save the seven old ga peaks, with their moss, and the tuft weeds in one of the angles, and shop-window, and a customer shak the door, and compelling the little to jingle fiercely, but without disturb Judge Pyncheon! This one old ho was everywhere! It transported great, lumbering bulk, with more t railroad speed, and set itself phlegm cally down on whatever spot she glan at. The quality of Hepzibah's mind too unmalleable to take new impressi so readily as Clifford's. He had a win nature; she was rather of the vegeta

d, and could hardly be kept long
e, if drawn up by the roots. Thus it
pened that the relation heretofore
ting between her brother and herself
changed. At home, she was his guard-
 here, Clifford had become hers,
 seemed to comprehend whatever be-
ged to their new position with a
ular rapidity of intelligence. He had
n startled into manhood and intellec-
l vigor; or, at least, into a condition
t resembled them, though it might
oth diseased and transitory.

he conductor now applied for their
ets; and Clifford, who had made
self the purse-bearer, put a bank-
e into his hand, as he had observed
ers do.

For the lady and yourself?" asked
conductor. "And how far?"

As far as that will carry us," said
ford. "It is no great matter. We are
ng for pleasure, merely!"

You choose a strange day for it,
" remarked a gimlet-eyed old gentle-
a, on the other side of the car, look-
at Clifford and his companion, as if
ous to make them out. "The best
nce of pleasure, in an easterly rain,
ke it, is in a man's own house, with
ice little fire in the chimney."

I cannot precisely agree with you,"
 Clifford, courteously bowing to the
 gentleman, and at once taking up
clue of conversation which the latter
 proffered. "It had just occurred to
 on the contrary, that this admirable
ention of the railroad—with the vast
 inevitable improvements to be
ked for, both as to speed and con-
ience—is destined to do away with
se stale ideas of home and fireside,
 substitute something better."

In the name of common sense,"
asked the old gentleman, rather testily,
"what can be better for a man than his
own parlor and chimney-corner?"

"These things have not the merit
which many good people attribute to
them," replied Clifford. "They may be
said, in few and pithy words, to have
ill-served a poor purpose. My impression is, that our wonderfully increased
and still increasing facilities of locomotion are destined to bring us round again
to the nomadic state. You are aware, my
dear sir,—you must have observed it, in
your own experience,—that all human
progress is in a circle; or, to use a more
accurate and beautiful figure, in an
ascending spiral curve. While we fancy
ourselves going straight forward, and attaining, at every step, an entirely new
position of affairs, we do actually return
to something long ago tried and abandoned, but which we now find etherealized,
refined, and perfected to its ideal.
The past is but a coarse and sensual
prophecy of the present and the future.
To apply this truth to the topic now under discussion.—In the early epochs of
our race, men dwelt in temporary huts,
or bowers of branches, as easily constructed as a bird's nest and which they
built,—if it should be called building,
when such sweet homes of a summer
solstice rather grew than were made
with hands,—which Nature, we will say,
assisted them to rear, where fruit
abounded, where fish and game were
plentiful, or, most especially, where the
sense of beauty was to be gratified by a
lovelier shade than elsewhere, and a
more exquisite arrangement of lake,
wood, and hill. This life possessed a
charm, which, ever since man quitted it,
has vanished from existence. And it
typified something better than itself. It

had its drawbacks; such as hunger and thirst, inclement weather, hot sunshine, and weary and foot-blistering marches over barren and ugly tracts, that lay between the sites desirable for their fertility and beauty. But, in our ascending spiral, we escape all this. These railroads—could but the whistle be made musical, and the rumble and the jar got rid of—are positively the greatest blessing that the ages have wrought out for us. They give us wings; they annihilate the toil and dust of pilgrimage; they spiritualize travel! Transition being so facile, what can be any man's inducement to tarry in one spot? Why, therefore, should he build a more cumbrous habitation than can readily be carried off with him? Why should he make himself a prisoner for life in brick, and stone, and old worm-eaten timber, when he may just as easily dwell, in one sense, nowhere,—in a better sense, wherever the fit and beautiful shall offer him a home?"

Clifford's countenance glowed, as he divulged this theory; a youthful character shone out from within, converting the wrinkles and pallid duskiness of age into an almost transparent mask. The merry girls let their ball drop upon the floor, and gazed at him. They said to themselves, perhaps, that, before his hair was gray and the crow's feet tracked his temples, this now decaying man must have stamped the impress of his features on many a woman's heart. But, alas! no woman's eye had seen his face while it was beautiful!

"I should scarcely call it an improved state of things," observed Clifford's new acquaintance, "to live everywhere and nowhere!"

"Would you not?" exclaimed Clifford, with singular energy. "It is as clear me as sunshine,—were there any in sky,—that the greatest possible stu bling-blocks in the path of human ha piness and improvement are these hea of bricks and stones, consolidated w mortar, or hewn timber, fastened gether with spike-nails, which men pa fully contrive for their own torme and call them house and home! T soul needs air; a wide sweep and f quent change of it. Morbid influenc in a thousand-fold variety, gather abe hearths, and pollute the life of hou holds. There is no such unwholeso atmosphere as that of an old home, r dered poisonous by one's defunct fo fathers and relatives. I speak of wha know. There is a certain house with my familiar recollection,—one of the peaked-gable (there are seven of the projecting-storied edifices, such as y occasionally see, in our elder towns, rusty, crazy, creaky, dry-rotted, dan rotted, dingy, dark, and miserable dungeon, with an arched window o the porch, and a little shop-door on c side, and a great, melancholy elm bef it! Now, sir, whenever my thoughts cur to this seven-gabled mansion—(fact is so very curious that I must ne mention it)—immediately I have vision or image of an elderly man, remarkably stern countenance, sitting an oaken elbow-chair, dead, stone-de with an ugly flow of blood upon shirt-bosom! Dead, but with open ey He taints the whole house, as I reme ber it. I could never flourish there, be happy, nor do nor enjoy what G meant me to do and enjoy!"

His face darkened, and seemed contract, and shrivel itself up, a wither into age.

"Never, sir!" he repeated. "I could
ver draw cheerful breath there!"

"I should think not," said the old
tleman, eyeing Clifford earnestly, and
her apprehensively. "I should conve not, sir, with that notion in your
d!"

'Surely not," continued Clifford;
d it were a relief to me if that house
ld be torn down, or burnt up, and so
earth be rid of it, and grass be sown
ndantly over its foundation. Not that
ould ever visit its site again! for, sir,
further I get away from it, the more
s the joy, the lightsome freshness,
heart-leap, the intellectual dance,
youth, in short,—yes, my youth, my
th!—the more does it come back to
. No longer ago than this morning, I
old. I remember looking in the
ss, and wondering at my own gray
r, and the wrinkles, many and deep,
t across my brow, and the furrows
vn my cheeks, and the prodigious
mpling of crow's feet about my
ples! It was too soon! I could not
r it! Age had no right to come! I
not lived! But now do I look old?
so, my aspect belies me strangely;
—a great weight being off my mind
feel in the very hey-dey of my
th, with the world and my best days
ore me!"

I trust you may find it so," said the
gentleman, who seemed rather em-
rassed, and desirous of avoiding the
ervation which Clifford's wild talk
w on them both. "You have my best
es for it."

For Heaven's sake, dear Clifford, be
t!" whispered his sister. "They
k you mad." ∕

Be quiet yourself, Hepzibah!" re-
ed her brother. "No matter what

they think! I am not mad. For the first
time in thirty years, my thoughts gush
up and find words ready for them. I
must talk, and I will!"

He turned again towards the old gentleman, and renewed the conversation.

"Yes, my dear sir," said he, "it is my
firm belief and hope, that these terms
of roof and hearth-stone, which have so
long been held to embody something
sacred, are soon to pass out of men's
daily use, and be forgotten. Just imagine, for a moment, how much of human
evil will crumble away, with this one
change! What we call real estate—the
solid ground to build a house on—is the
broad foundation on which nearly all
the guilt of this world rests. A man will
commit almost any wrong,—he will heap
up an immense pile of wickedness, as
hard as granite, and which will weigh
as heavily upon his soul, to eternal
ages,—only to build a great, gloomy,
dark-chambered mansion, for himself to
die in, and for his posterity to be miserable in. He lays his own dead corpse
beneath the underpinning, as one may
say, and hangs his frowning picture on
the wall, and, after thus converting himself into an evil destiny, expects his remotest great-grandchildren to be happy
there! I do not speak wildly. I have just
such a house in my mind's eye!"

"Then, sir," said the old gentleman,
getting anxious to drop the subject, "you
are not to blame for leaving it."

"Within the lifetime of the child already born," Clifford went on, "all this
will be done away. The world is growing
too ethereal and spiritual to bear these
enormities a great while longer. To me,
—though, for a considerable period of
time, I have lived chiefly in retirement,
and know less of such things than most

men,—even to me, the harbingers of a better era are unmistakable. Mesmerism, now! Will that effect nothing, think you, towards purging away the grossness out of human life?"

"All a humbug!" growled the old gentleman.

"These rapping spirits, that little Phœbe told us of, the other day," said Clifford,—"what are these but the messengers of the spiritual world, knocking at the door of substance? And it shall be flung wide open!"

"A humbug, again!" cried the old gentleman, growing more and more testy, at these glimpses of Clifford's metaphysics. "I should like to rap with a good stick on the empty pates of the dolts who circulate such nonsense!"

"Then there is electricity;—the demon, the angel, the mighty physical power, the all-pervading intelligence!" exclaimed Clifford. "Is that a humbug, too? Is it a fact—or have I dreamt it—that, by means of electricity, the world of matter has become a great nerve, vibrating thousands of miles in a breathless point of time? Rather, the round globe is a vast head, a brain, instinct with intelligence! Or, shall we say, it is itself a thought, nothing but thought, and no longer the substance which we deemed it!"

"If you mean the telegraph," said the old gentleman, glancing his eye toward its wire, alongside the rail-track, "it is an excellent thing;—that is, of course, if the speculators in cotton and politics don't get possession of it. A great thing, indeed, sir; particularly as regards the detection of bank-robbers and murderers."

"I don't quite like it, in that point of view," replied Clifford. "A bank-robber,

and what you call a murderer, likew has his rights, which men of enlighte humanity and conscience should reg in so much the more liberal spirit, cause the bulk of society is prone controvert their existence. An alm spiritual medium, like the electric t graph, should be consecrated to h deep, joyful, and holy missions. Lov day by day,—hour by hour, if so o moved to do it,—might send their he throbs from Maine to Florida, v some such words as these,—'I love forever!'—'My heart runs over v love!'—'I love you more than I can and, again, at the next message,—'I h lived an hour longer, and love you tv as much!' Or, when a good man has parted, his distant friend should be c scious of an electric thrill, as from world of happy spirits, telling hin 'Your dear friend is in bliss!' Or, tc absent husband, should come tid thus,—'An immortal being, of wl you are the father, has this mon come from God!'—and immediately little voice would seem to have reac so far, and to be echoing in heart. for these poor rogues, the bank-robt —who, after all, are about as hones nine people in ten, except that they regard certain formalities, and prefe transact business at midnight, ra than 'Change-hours,—and for t murderers, as you phrase it, who often excusable in the motives of t deed, and deserve to be ranked am public benefactors, if we consider its result,—for unfortunate individ like these, I really cannot applaud enlistment of an immaterial and mir lous power in the universal world-b at their heels!"

"You can't, hey?" cried the old

nan, with a hard look.
Positively, no!" answered Clifford.
puts them too miserably at disad-
tage. For example, sir, in a dark,
, cross-beamed, panelled room of an
house, let us suppose a dead man,
ing in an arm-chair, with a blood-
n on his shirt-bosom,—and let us
to our hypothesis another man, issu-
from the house, which he feels to be
r-filled with the dead man's presence,
nd let us lastly imagine him flee-
Heaven knows whither, at the
d of a hurricane, by railroad! Now,
if the fugitive alight in some distant
n, and find all the people babbling
ut that self-same dead man, whom
as fled so far to avoid the sight and
ight of, will you not allow that his
ural rights have been infringed? He
been deprived of his city of refuge,
, in my humble opinion, has suffered
ite wrong!"

You are a strange man, sir!" said
old gentleman, bringing his gimlet-
to a point on Clifford, as if de-
ined to bore right into him. "I
t see through you!"

No, I'll be bound you can't!" cried
ford, laughing. "And yet, my dear
I am as transparent as the water
Maule's well! But come, Hepzibah!
have flown far enough for once.
us alight, as the birds do, and perch
elves on the nearest twig, and con-
whither we shall fly next!"

ust then, as it happened, the train
hed a solitary way-station. Taking
ntage of the brief pause, Clifford
the car, and drew Hepzibah along
him. A moment afterwards, the
n—with all the life of its interior,
d which Clifford had made himself
conspicuous an object—was gliding
away in the distance, and rapidly lessening to a point, which, in another moment, vanished. The world had fled
away from these two wanderers. They
gazed drearily about them. At a little
distance stood a wooden church, black
with age, and in a dismal state of ruin
and decay, with broken windows, a
great rift through the main body of the
edifice, and a rafter dangling from the
top of the square tower. Further off was
a farm-house, in the old style, as
venerably black as the church, with a
roof sloping downward from the three-
story peak, to within a man's height of
the ground. It seemed uninhabited.
There were the relics of a wood-pile,
indeed, near the door, but with grass
sprouting up among the chips and scattered logs. The small rain-drops came
down aslant; the wind was not turbulent, but sullen, and full of chilly
moisture.

Clifford shivered from head to foot.
The wild effervescence of his mood—
which had so readily supplied thoughts,
fantasies, and a strange aptitude of
words, and impelled him to talk from
the mere necessity of giving vent to
this bubbling-up gush of ideas—had entirely subsided. A powerful excitement
had given him energy and vivacity. Its
operation over, he forthwith began to
sink.

"You must take the lead now, Hepzibah!" murmured he, with a torpid and
reluctant utterance. "Do with me as
you will!"

She knelt down upon the platform
where they were standing, and lifted
her clasped hands to the sky. The dull,
gray weight of clouds made it invisible;
but it was no hour for disbelief;—no

juncture this, to question that there was a sky above, and an Almighty Father looking down from it!

"O, God!"—ejaculated poor, gaunt Hepzibah,—then paused a moment consider what her prayer should be "O, God,—our Father,—are we not children? Have mercy on us!"

CHAPTER XVIII

GOVERNOR PYNCHEON

JUDGE PYNCHEON, while his two relatives have fled away with such ill-considered haste, still sits in the old parlor, keeping house, as the familiar phrase is, in the absence of its ordinary occupants. To him, and to the venerable House of the Seven Gables, does our story now betake itself, like an owl, bewildered in the daylight, and hastening back to his hollow tree.

The judge has not shifted his position for a long while now. He has not stirred hand or foot, nor withdrawn his eyes so much as a hair's breadth from their fixed gaze towards the corner of the room, since the footsteps of Hepzibah and Clifford creaked along the passage, and the outer door was closed cautiously behind their exit. He holds his watch in his left hand, but clutched in such a manner that you cannot see the dial-plate. How profound a fit of meditation! Or, supposing him asleep, how infantile a quietude of conscience, and what wholesome order in the gastric region, are betokened by slumber so entirely undisturbed with starts, cramp, twitches, muttered dream-talk, trumpet-blasts through the nasal organ, or any the slightest irregularity of breath! You must hold your own breath, to satisfy yourself whether he

breathes at all. It is quite inaudi You hear the ticking of his watch; breath you do not hear. A most refre ing slumber, doubtless! And yet, judge cannot be asleep. His eyes open! A veteran politician, such as would never fall asleep with wide-o eyes, lest some enemy or misch maker, taking him thus at unawa should peep through these windows i his consciousness, and make strange coveries among the reminiscences, p ects, hopes, apprehensions, weaknes and strong points, which he has here fore shared with nobody. A cauti man is proverbially said to sleep w one eye open. That may be wisd But not with both; for this were he lessness! No, no! Judge Pyncheon c not be asleep.

It is odd, however, that a gentler so burthened with engagements— noted, too, for punctuality—sho linger thus in an old lonely mans which he has never seemed very fonc visiting. The oaken chair, to be s may tempt him with its roomin It is, indeed, a spacious, and, allow for the rude age that fashioned it moderately easy seat, with capa enough, at all events, and offering restraint to the judge's breadth of be

bigger man might find ample accom-
dation in it. His ancestor, now pic-
ed upon the wall, with all his Eng-
1 beef about him, used hardly to
:sent a front extending from elbow
elbow of this chair, or a base that
uld cover its whole cushion. But there
: better chairs than this—mahogany,
ck-walnut, rosewood, spring-seated
1 damask-cushioned, with varied
pes, and innumerable artifices to
ke them easy, and obviate the irk-
neness of too tame an ease;—a score
such might be at Judge Pyncheon's
vice. Yes! in a score of drawing-
ms he would be more than welcome.
mma would advance to meet him,
h outstretched hand; the virgin
ughter, elderly as he has now got to
—an old widower, as he smilingly
cribes himself,—would shake up the
hion for the judge, and do her pretty
le utmost to make him comfortable.
r the judge is a prosperous man. He
rishes his schemes, moreover, like
er people, and reasonably brighter
n most others; or did so, at least,
he lay abed, this morning, in an
eeable half-drowse, planning the busi-
s of the day, and speculating on the
babilities of the next fifteen years.
th his firm health, and the little in-
d that age has made upon him, fifteen
rs or twenty—yes, or perhaps five-
-twenty!—are no more than he may
rly call his own. Five-and-twenty
rs for the enjoyment of his real
ate in town and country, his railroad,
k, and insurance shares, his United
tes stock,—his wealth, in short, how-
r invested, now in possession, or soon
be acquired; together with the public
ors that have fallen upon him, and
weightier ones that are yet to fall!

It is good! It is excellent! It is enough!

Still lingering in the old chair! If the judge has a little time to throw away, why does not he visit the insurance office, as is his frequent custom, and sit a while in one of their leathern-cushioned arm-chairs, listening to the gossip of the day, and dropping some deeply-designed chance-word, which will be certain to become the gossip of to-morrow! And have not the bank directors a meeting, at which it was the judge's purpose to be present, and his office to preside? Indeed they have; and the hour is noted on a card, which is, or ought to be, in Judge Pyncheon's right vest-pocket. Let him go thither, and loll at ease upon his money-bags! He has lounged long enough in the old chair!

This was to have been such a busy day! In the first place, the interview with Clifford. Half an hour, by the judge's reckoning, was to suffice for that; it would probably be less, but—taking into consideration that Hepzibah was first to be dealt with, and that these women are apt to make many words where a few would do much better it might be safest to allow half an hour. Half an hour? Why, judge, it is already two hours, by your own undeviatingly accurate chronometer! Glance your eye down at it, and see? Ah! he will not give himself the trouble either to bend his head, or elevate his hand, so as to bring the faithful time-keeper within his range of vision! Time, all at once, appears to have become a matter of no moment with the judge!

And has he forgotten all the other items of his memoranda? Clifford's affair arranged, he was to meet a State-street broker, who has undertaken to procure a heavy percentage, and the best of paper, for a few loose thousands which the judge happens to have by him, uninvested. The wrinkled note-shaver will have taken his railroad trip in vain. Half an hour later, in the street next to this, there was to be an auction of real estate, including a portion of the old Pyncheon property, originally belonging to Maule's garden-ground. It has been alienated from the Pyncheons these fourscore years; but the judge had kept it in his eye, and had set his heart on re-annexing it to the small demesne still left around the seven gables;—and now, during this odd fit of oblivion, the fatal hammer must have fallen, and transferred our ancient patrimony to some alien possessor! Possibly, indeed, the sale may have been postponed till fairer weather. If so, will the judge make it convenient to be present, and favor the auctioneer with his bid, on the proximate occasion?

The next affair was to buy a horse for his own driving. The one heretofore his favorite stumbled, this very morning, on the road to town, and must be at once discarded. Judge Pyncheon's neck is too precious to be risked on such a contingency as a stumbling steed. Should all the above business be seasonably got through with, he might attend the meeting of a charitable society; the very name of which, however, in the multiplicity of his benevolence, is quite forgotten; so that this engagement may pass unfulfilled, and no great harm done. And if he have time, amid the press of more urgent matters, he must take measures for the renewal of Mrs. Pyncheon's tombstone, which, the sexton tells him, has fallen on its marble face, and is cracked quite in twain. She was a praiseworthy woman enough, thin the judge, in spite of her nervousne and the tears that she was so oozy wi and her foolish behavior about coffee; and as she took her departure seasonably, he will not grudge the seco tombstone. It is better, at least, th if she had never needed any! The n item on his list was to give orders some fruit-trees, of a rare variety, to delivered at his country-seat, in the suing autumn. Yes, buy them, by means; and may the peaches be lusci in your mouth; Judge Pyncheon! Af this comes something more importa A committee of his political party b besought him for a hundred or two dollars, in addition to his previous d bursements, towards carrying on the campaign. The judge is a patriot; fate of the country is staked on November election; and besides, as v be shadowed forth in another paragra he has no trifling stake of his own, the same great game. He will do w the committee asks; nay, he will liberal beyond their expectations; th shall have a check for five hund dollars, and more anon, if it be need What next? A decayed widow, wh husband was Judge Pyncheon's ea friend, has laid her case of destitut before him, in a very moving letter. S and her fair daughter have scarc bread to eat. He partly intends to on her, to-day,—perhaps so—perh not,—accordingly as he may happen have leisure, and a small bank-note.

Another business, which, however, puts no great weight on—(it is w you know, to be heedful, but not o anxious, as respects one's perso health)—another business, then, was consult his family physician. Ab

lat, for Heaven's sake? Why, it is
her difficult to describe the symptoms.
mere dimness of sight and dizziness
brain, was it?—or a disagreeable
oking, or stifling, or gurgling, or bub-
ing, in the region of the thorax, as
e anatomists say?—or was it a pretty
vere throbbing and kicking of the
art, rather creditable to him than
herwise, as showing that the organ
d not been left out of the judge's
ysical contrivance? No matter what
was. The doctor, probably, would
ile at the statement of such trifles in
s professional ear; the judge would
aile, in his turn; and meeting one an-
her's eyes, they would enjoy a hearty
igh together! But a fig for medical
vice! The judge will never need it.
Pray, pray, Judge Pyncheon, look at
ur watch, now! What—not a glance!
is within ten minutes of the dinner-
ur! It surely cannot have slipped
ur memory that the dinner of to-day
to be the most important, in its con-
quences, of all the dinners you ever
e. Yes, precisely the most important;
hough, in the course of your some-
iat eminent career, you have been
iced high towards the head of the
ole, at splendid banquets, and have
ured out your festive eloquence to
rs yet echoing with Webster's mighty
gan-tones. No public dinner this, how-
er. It is merely a gathering of some
zen or so of friends from several dis-
cts of the state; men of distinguished
aracter and influence, assembling,
nost casually, at the house of a com-
on friend, likewise distinguished, who
ll make them welcome to a little bet-
r than his ordinary fare. Nothing in
e way of French cookery, but an ex-
llent dinner, nevertheless! Real turtle,

we understand, and salmon, tautog,
canvas-backs, pig, English mutton, good
roastbeef or dainties of that serious
kind, fit for substantial country gentlemen, as these honorable persons mostly
are. The delicacies of the season, in
short, and flavored by a brand of old
Madeira which has been the pride of
many seasons. It is the Juno brand; a
glorious wine, fragrant, and full of
gentle might; a bottled-up happiness,
put by for use; a golden liquid, worth
more than liquid gold; so rare and admirable, that veteran wine-bibbers count
it among their epochs to have tasted it!
It drives away the heart-ache, and sub-
stitutes no head-ache! Could the judge
but quaff a glass, it might enable him
to shake off the unaccountable lethargy
which—(for the ten intervening minutes,
and five to boot, are already past)—has
made him such a laggard at this momentous dinner. It would all but revive
a dead man! Would you like to sip it
now, Judge Pyncheon?

Alas, this dinner! Have you really
forgotten its true object? Then let us
whisper it, that you may start at once
out of the oaken chair, which really
seems to be enchanted, like the one in
Comus, or that in which Moll Pitcher
imprisoned your own grandfather. But
ambition is a talisman more powerful
than witchcraft. Start up, then, and
hurrying through the streets, burst in
upon the company, that they may begin
before the fish is spoiled! They wait for
you; and it is little for your interest
that they should wait. These gentlemen
—need you be told of it?—have assembled, not without purpose, from
every quarter of the state. They are
practised politicians, every man of them,
and skilled to adjust those preliminary

measures which steal from the people, without its knowledge, the power of choosing its own rulers. The popular voice, at the next gubernatorial election, though loud as thunder, will be really but an echo of what these gentlemen shall speak, under their breath, at your friend's festive board. They meet to decide upon their candidate. This little knot of subtle schemers will control the convention, and, through it, dictate to the party. And what worthier candidate, —more wise and learned, more noted for philanthropic liberality, truer to safe principles, tried oftener by public trusts, more spotless in private character, with a larger stake in the common welfare, and deeper grounded, by hereditary descent, in the faith and practice of the Puritans,—what man can be presented for the suffrage of the people, so eminently combining all these claims to the chief-rulership as Judge Pyncheon here before us?

Make haste, then! Do your part! The meed for which you have toiled, and fought, and climbed, and crept, is ready for your grasp! Be present at this dinner!—drink a glass or two of that noble wine!—make your pledges in as low a whisper as you will!—and you rise up from table virtually governor of the glorious old state! Governor Pyncheon, of Massachusetts!

And is there no potent and exhilarating cordial in a certainty like this? It has been the grand purpose of half your lifetime to obtain it. Now, when there needs little more than to signify your acceptance, why do you sit so lumpishly in your great-great-grandfather's oaken chair, as if preferring it to the gubernatorial one? We have all heard of King Log; but, in these jostling times, one

of that royal kindred will hardly win race for an elective chief-magistracy.

Well! it is absolutely too late for d ner? Turtle, salmon, tautog, woodco boiled turkey, South-Down mutton, roast beef, have vanished, or exist o in fragments, with lukewarm potato and gravies crusted over with cold The judge, had he done nothing el would have achieved wonders with knife and fork. It was he, you kne of whom it used to be said, in referen to his ogre-like appetite, that his Crea made him a great animal, but that dinner-hour made him a great bea Persons of his large sensual endowme must claim indulgence, at their feedi time. But, for once, the judge is entir too late for dinner! Too late, we fe even to join the party at their wi The guests are warm and merry; tl have given up the judge; and, conclu ing that the free-soilers have him, tl will fix upon another candidate. W our friend now to stalk in among the with that wide-open stare, at once w and stolid, his ungenial presence wo be apt to change their cheer. Neitl would it be seemly in Judge Pynche generally so scrupulous in his attire, show himself at a dinner-table with tl crimson stain upon his shirt-bosom. the-by, how came it there? It is an u sight, at any rate; and the wisest w for the judge is to button his c closely over his breast, and, taking horse and chaise from the livery-stal to make all speed to his own hou There, after a glass of brandy a water, and a mutton-chop, a beef-ste a broiled fowl, or some such hasty lit dinner and supper all in one, he had b ter spend the evening by the firesi He must toast his slippers a long wh

order to get rid of the chilliness
ich the air of this vile old house has
it curdling through his veins.

Up, therefore, Judge Pyncheon, up!
u have lost a day. But to-morrow will
here anon. Will you rise, betimes, and
ke the most of it? To-morrow! To-
rrow! To-morrow! We, that are
ve, may rise betimes to-morrow. As
: him that died to-day, his morrow
l be the resurrection morn.

Meanwhile the twilight is glooming
ward out of the corners of the room.
e shadows of the tall furniture grow
eper, and at first become more defi-
e; then, spreading wider, they lose
ir distinctness of outline in the dark
ty tide of oblivion, as it were, that
eps slowly over the various objects,
d the one human figure sitting in the
dst of them. The gloom has not ened from without; it has brooded here
day, and now, taking its own in-
table time, will possess itself of every-
ng. The judge's face, indeed, rigid,
d singularly white, refuses to melt
o this universal solvent. Fainter and
nter grows the light. It is as if an-
er double-handful of darkness had
en scattered through the air. Now it
no longer gray, but sable. There is
ll a faint appearance at the windows;
ther a glow, nor a gleam, nor a glim-
r,—any phrase of light would express
mething far brighter than this doubt-
. perception, or sense, rather, that
ere is a window there. Has it yet
nished? No!—yes!—not quite! And
ere is still the swarthy whiteness,—
shall venture to marry these ill-
eeing words,—the swarthy whiteness
Judge Pyncheon's face. The features
e all gone; there is only the paleness
them left. And how looks it now?

There is no window! There is no face!
An infinite, inscrutable blackness has
annihilated sight! Where is our universe? All crumbled away from us; and
we, adrift in chaos, may hearken to the
gusts of homeless wind, that go sighing
and murmuring about, in quest of what
was once a world!

Is there no other sound? One other,
and a fearful one. It is the ticking of
the judge's watch, which, ever since
Hepzibah left the room in search of
Clifford, he has been holding in his hand.
Be the cause what it may, this little,
quiet, never-ceasing throb of Time's
pulse, repeating its small strokes with
such busy regularity, in Judge Pyncheon's motionless hand, has an effect
of terror, which we do not find in any
other accompaniment of the scene.

But, listen! That puff of the breeze
was louder; it had a tone unlike the
dreary and sullen one which has bemoaned itself, and afflicted all mankind
with miserable sympathy, for five days
past. The wind has veered about! It
now comes boisterously from the north-
west, and, taking hold of the aged
frame-work of the seven gables, gives
it a shake, like a wrestler that would try
strength with his antagonist. Another
and another sturdy tussle with the
blast! The old house creaks again, and
makes a vociferous but somewhat unintelligible bellowing in its sooty throat—
(the big flue, we mean, of its wide chimney)—partly in complaint at the rude
wind, but rather, as befits their century
and a half of hostile intimacy, in tough
defiance. A rumbling kind of a bluster
roars behind the fireboard. A door has
slammed above-stairs. A window, perhaps, has been left open, or else is
driven in by an unruly gust. It is not

to be conceived, beforehand, what wonderful wind-instruments are these old timber mansions, and how haunted with the strangest noises, which immediately begin to sing, and sigh, and sob, and shriek,—and to smite with sledge-hammers, airy, but ponderous, in some distant chamber,—and to tread along the entries as with stately foot-steps, and rustle up and down the stair-case, as with silks miraculously stiff,—whenever the gale catches the house with a window open, and gets fairly into it! Would that we were not an attendant spirit here! It is too awful! This clamor of the wind through the lonely house; the judge's quietude, as he sits invisible; and that pertinacious ticking of his watch!

As regards Judge Pyncheon's invisibility, however, that matter will soon be remedied. The north-west wind has swept the sky clear. The window is distinctly seen. Through its panes, moreover, we dimly catch the sweep of the dark, clustering foliage, outside, fluttering with a constant irregularity of movement, and letting in a peep of starlight, now here, now there. Oftener than any other object, these glimpses illuminate the judge's face. But here comes more effectual light. Observe that silvery dance upon the upper branches of the pear-tree, and now a little lower, and now on the whole mass of boughs, while, through their shifting intricacies, the moonbeams fall aslant into the room. They play over the judge's figure, and show that he has not stirred throughout the hours of darkness. They follow the shadows, in changeful sport, across his unchanging features. They gleam upon his watch. His grasp conceals the dial-plate; but we know that the faithful

hands have met; for one of the cit clocks tells midnight.

A man of sturdy understanding, li Jaffrey Pyncheon, cares no more f twelve o'clock at night than for t corresponding hour of noon. Howev just the parallel drawn, in some of t preceding pages, between his Purit ancestors and himself, it fails in tl point. The Pyncheon of two centuri ago, in common with most of his co temporaries, professed his full belief spiritual ministrations, although recko ing them chiefly of a malignant cha acter. The Pyncheon of to-night, wl sits in yonder arm-chair, believes in 1 such nonsense. Such, at least, was l creed, some few hours since. His ha will not bristle, therefore, at the stori which—in times when chimney-corne had benches in them, where old peop sat poking into the ashes of the pa and raking out traditions like live co —used to be told about this very roo of his ancestral house. In fact, the tales are too absurd to bristle ev childhood's hair. What sense, meanin or moral, for example, such as ev ghost-stories should be susceptible c can be traced in the ridiculous legen that, at midnight, all the dead Py cheons are bound to assemble in th parlor? And, pray, for what? Why, see whether the portrait of their a cestor still keeps its place upon tl wall, in compliance with his testamei tary directions! Is it worth while come out of their graves for that?

We are tempted to make a little spo with the idea. Ghost-stories are hard to be treated seriously, any longer. Tl family-party of the defunct Pyncheor we presume, goes off in this wise.

First comes the ancestor himself,

black cloak, steeple-hat, and trunk-
eeches, girt about the waist with a
.thern belt, in which hangs his steel-
ted sword; he has a long staff in his
nd, such as gentlemen in advanced
e used to carry, as much for the
gnity of the thing as for the support
be derived from it. He looks up at
e portrait;—a thing of no substance,
zing at its own painted image! All is
fe. The picture is still there. The purse of his brain has been kept sacred
us long after the man himself . has
routed up in grave-yard grass. See!
lifts his ineffectual hand, and tries
e frame. All safe! But is that a smile?
is it not, rather, a frown of deadly
port, that darkens over the shadow
his features? The stout colonel is
ssatisfied! So decided is his look of
scontent as to impart additional dis-
ctness to his features; through which,
vertheless, the moonlight passes, and
ckers on the wall beyond. Something
s strangely vexed the ancestor! With
grim shake of the head, he turns
ray. Here come other Pyncheons, the
ole tribe, in their half a dozen genera-
ons, jostling and elbowing one another,
reach the picture. We behold aged
en and grandames, clergyman with
e Puritanic stiffness still in his garb
d mien, and a red-coated officer of the
d French war; and there comes the
op-keeping Pyncheon of a century
o, with the ruffles turned back from
s wrists; and there the periwigged and
ocaded gentleman of the artist's
gend, with the beautiful and pensive
ice, who brings no pride out of her
rgin grave. All try the picture-frame.
hat do these ghostly people seek? A
other lifts her child, that his little
nds may touch it! There is evidently

a mystery about the picture, that perplexes these poor Pyncheons, when they
ought to be at rest. In a corner, meanwhile, stands the figure of an elderly
man, in a leather jerkin and breeches,
with a carpenter's rule sticking out of
his side-pocket; he points his finger at
the bearded colonel and his descendants,
nodding, jeering, mocking, and finally
bursting into obstreperous, though inaudible laughter.

Indulging our fancy in this freak, we
have partly lost the power of restraint
and guidance. We distinguish an un-
looked-for figure in our visionary scene.
Among those ancestral people there is a
young man, dressed in the very fashion
of to-day; he wears a dark frock-coat,
almost destitute of skirts, gray pantaloons, gaiter boots of patent leather, and
has a finely-wrought gold chain across
his breast, and a little silver-headed
whalebone stick in his hand. Were
we to meet this figure at noon-
day, we should greet him as young
Jaffrey Pyncheon, the judge's only
surviving child, who has been spending the last two years in foreign
travel. If still in life, how comes his
shadow hither? If dead, what a misfortune! The old Pyncheon property,
together with the great estate acquired
by the young man's father, would devolve on whom? On poor, foolish Clifford, gaunt Hepzibah, and rustic little
Phœbe! But another and a greater marvel greets us! Can we believe our eyes?
A stout, elderly gentleman has made
his appearance; he has an aspect of
eminent respectability, wears a black
coat and pantaloons, of roomy width,
and might be pronounced scrupulously
neat in his attire, but for a broad crimson stain across his snowy neckcloth and

down his shirt-bosom. Is it the judge, or no? How can it be Judge Pyncheon? We discern his figure, as plainly as the flickering moonbeams can show us anything, still seated in the oaken chair! Be the apparition whose it may, it advances to the picture, seems to seize the frame, tries to peep behind it, and turns away, with a frown as black as the ancestral one.

The fantastic scene just hinted at must by no means be considered as forming an actual portion of our story. We were betrayed into this brief extravagance by the quiver of the moonbeams; they dance hand-in-hand with shadows, and are reflected in the looking-glass, which, you are aware, is always a kind of window or door-way into the spiritual world. We needed relief, moreover, from our too long and exclusive contemplation of that figure in the chair. This wild wind, too, has tossed our thoughts into strange confusion, but without tearing them away from their one determined centre. Yonder leaden judge sits immovably upon our soul. Will he never stir again? We shall go mad, unless he stirs! You may the better estimate his quietude by the fearlessness of a little mouse, which sits on its hind legs, in a streak of moonlight, close by Judge Pyncheon's foot, and seems to meditate a journey of exploration over this great black bulk. Ha! what has startled the nimble little mouse? It is the visage of Grimalkin, outside of the window, where he appears to have posted himself for a deliberate watch. This Grimalkin has a very ugly look. Is it a cat watching for a mouse, or the devil for a human soul? Would we could scare him from the window!

Thank Heaven, the night is well-nigh past! The moonbeams have no long so silvery a gleam, nor contrast strongly with the blackness of t shadows among which they fall. Th are paler, now; the shadows look gr not black. The boisterous wind hushed. What is the hour? Ah! t watch has at last ceased to tick; f the judge's forgetful fingers neglect to wind it up, as usual, at ten o'cloc being half an hour, or so, before ordinary bed-time;—and it has r down, for the first time in five yea But the great world-clock of Time st keeps its beat. The dreary night,—f oh, how dreary seems its haunted was behind us!—gives place to a fres transparent, cloudless morn. Blesse blessed radiance! The day-beam,—ev what little of it finds its way into t always dusky parlor—seems part of t universal benediction, annulling ev and rendering all goodness possible, a happiness attainable. Will Judge Py cheon now rise up from his chair? W he go forth, and receive the early su beams on his brow? Will he begin t new day,—which God has smiled upc and blessed, and given to mankind, will he begin it with better purpos than the many that have been spe amiss? Or are all the deep-laid schem of yesterday as stubborn in his hea and as busy in his brain, as ever?

In this latter case, there is much do. Will the judge still insist with He zibah on the interview with Cliffor Will he buy a safe, elderly gentlemar horse? Will he persuade the purchas of the old Pyncheon property to reli quish the bargain, in his favor? Will see his family physician, and obtain medicine that shall preserve him, to an honor and blessing to his race, un

utmost term of patriarchal lon-
rity? Will Judge Pyncheon, above all,
ke due apologies to that company
honorable friends, and satisfy them
t his absence from the festive board
s unavoidable, and so fully retrieve
iself in their good opinion that he
ll yet be Governor of Massachusetts?
d, all these great purposes accom-
shed, will he walk the streets again,
h that dog-day smile of elaborate
evolence, sultry enough to tempt
s to come and buzz in it? Or will he,
er the tomb-like seclusion of the past
and night, go forth a humbled and
entant man, sorrowful, gentle, seek-
no profit, shrinking from worldly
or, hardly daring to love God, but
d to love his fellow-man, and to do
what good he may? Will he bear
ut with him,—no odious grin of
gned benignity, insolent in its prece, and loathsome in its falsehood,—
t the tender sadness of a contrite
rt, broken, at last, beneath its own
ight of sin? For it is our belief, what-
er show of honor he may have piled
n it, that there was heavy sin at the
se of this man's being.

Rise up, Judge Pyncheon! The morn-
sunshine glimmers through the
iage, and, beautiful and holy as it is,
ns not to kindle up your face. Rise
, thou subtile, worldly, selfish, iron-

hearted hypocrite, and make thy choice
whether still to be subtile, worldly,
selfish, iron-hearted, and hypocritical,
or to tear these sins out of thy
nature, though they bring the life-blood
with them! The Avenger is upon thee!
Rise up, before it be too late!

What! Thou art not stirred by this
last appeal? No, not a jot! And there
we see a fly,—one of your common
house-flies, such as are always buzzing
on the window-pane,—which has smelt
out Governor Pyncheon, and alights,
now on his forehead, now on his chin,
and now, Heaven help us! is creeping
over the bridge of his nose, towards the
would-be chief-magistrate's wide-open
eyes! Canst thou not brush the fly
away? Art thou too sluggish? Thou
man, that hadst so many busy projects,
yesterday! Art thou too weak, that wast
so powerful? Not brush away a fly!
Nay, then, we give thee up!

And, hark! the shop-bell rings. After
hours like these latter ones, through
which we have borne our heavy tale, it
is good to be made sensible that there is
a living world, and that even this old,
lonely mansion retains some manner of
connection with it. We breathe more
freely, emerging from Judge Pyncheon's
presence into the street before the seven
gables

———

CHAPTER XIX

ALICE'S POSIES

Uncle Venner, trundling a wheel-
row, was the earliest person stirring
the neighborhood, the day after

the storm.

Pyncheon-street, in front of the
House of the Seven Gables, was a far

pleasanter scene than a by-lane, confined by shabby fences, and bordered with wooden dwellings of the meaner class, could reasonably be expected to present. Nature made sweet amends, that morning, for the five unkindly days which had preceded it. It would have been enough to live for, merely to look up at the wide benediction of the sky, or as much of it as was visible between the houses, genial once more with sunshine. Every object was agreeable, whether to be gazed at in the breadth, or examined more minutely. Such, for example, were the well-washed pebbles and gravel of the sidewalk; even the sky-reflecting pools in the centre of the street; and the grass, now freshly verdant, that crept along the base of the fences, on the other side of which, if one peeped over, was seen the multifarious growth of gardens. Vegetable productions, of whatever kind, seemed more than negatively happy, in the juicy warmth and abundance of their life. The Pyncheon-elm, throughout its great circumference, was all alive, and full of the morning sun and a sweetly-tempered little breeze, which lingered within this verdant sphere, and set a thousand leafy tongues a-whispering all at once. This aged tree appeared to have suffered nothing from the gale. It had kept its boughs unshattered, and its full complement of leaves; and the whole in perfect verdure, except a single branch, that, by the earlier change with which the elm-tree sometimes prophesies the autumn, had been transmuted to bright gold. It was like the golden branch, that gained Æneas and the Sybil admittance into Hades.

This one mystic branch hung down before the main entrance of the seven

gables, so nigh the ground that a passer-by might have stood on tip and plucked it off. Presented at door, it would have been a symbol his right to enter, and be made quainted with all the secrets of house. So little faith is due to exter appearance, that there was really an viting aspect over the venerable edifi conveying an idea that its history m be a decorous and happy one, and su as would be delightful for a fire-s tale. Its windows gleamed cheerfully the slanting sunlight. The lines a tufts of green moss, here and the seemed pledges of familiarity and sist hood with Nature; as if this hum dwelling-place, being of such old da had established its prescriptive ti among primeval oaks, and whate other objects, by virtue of their lo continuance, have acquired a graci right to be. A person of imaginat temperament, while passing by t house, would turn, once and again, a peruse it well:—its many peaks, c senting together in the clustered chi ney; the deep projection over basement-story; the arched window, i parting a look, if not of grandeur, yet antique gentility, to the broken por over which it opened; the luxuriance gigantic burdocks, near the threshold he would note all these characteristi and be conscious of something dee than he saw. He would conceive t mansion to have been the residence the stubborn old Puritan, Integrity, wl dying in some forgotten generation, l left a blessing in all its rooms a chambers, the efficacy of which was be seen in the religion, honesty, mod ate competence, or upright poverty a solid happiness, of his descendants, is day.

One object, above all others, would
ke root in the imaginative observer's
emory. It was the great tuft of
wers,—weeds, you would have called
em, only a week ago,—the tuft of
imson-spotted flowers, in the angle be-
een the two front gables. The old
ople used to give them the name of
ice's Posies, in remembrance of fair
ice Pyncheon, who was believed to
ve brought their seeds from Italy.
ey were flaunting in rich beauty and
ll of bloom, to-day, and seemed,
it were, a mystic expression that
mething within the house was con-
mmated.

It was but little after sunrise, when
cle Venner made his appearance,
aforesaid, impelling a wheelbarrow
ong the street. He was going his ma-
tinal rounds to collect cabbage-leaves,
rnip-tops, potato-skins, and the mis-
llaneous refuse of the dinner-pot,
hich the thrifty housewives of the
ighborhood were accustomed to put
ide, as fit only to feed a pig. Uncle
enner's pig was fed entirely, and kept
prime order, on these eleemosynary
ntributions; insomuch that the patched
ilosopher used to promise that, before
tiring to his farm, he would make a
ast of the portly grunter, and invite
l his neighbors to partake of the joints
d spare-ribs which they had helped to
tten. Miss Hepzibah Pyncheon's house-
eping had so greatly improved, since
ifford became a member of the family,
at her share of the banquet would
ve been no lean one; and Uncle
enner, accordingly, was a good deal
sappointed not to find the large
rthen-pan, full of fragmentary eat-
les, that ordinarily awaited his com-

ing, at the back door-step of the seven
gables.

"I never knew Miss Hepzibah so forgetful before," said the patriarch to
himself. "She must have had a dinner
yesterday,—no question of that! She
always has one, now-a-days. So where's
the pot-liquor and potato-skins, I ask?
Shall I knock, and see if she's stirring
yet? No, no,—'twon't do! If little
Phœbe was about the house, I should
not mind knocking; but Miss Hepzibah,
likely as not, would scowl down at me,
out of the window, and look cross, even
if she felt pleasantly. So I'll come back
at noon."

With these reflections, the old man
was shutting the gate of the little back-
yard. Creaking on its hinges, however,
like every other gate and door about
the premises, the sound reached the ears
of the occupant of the northern gable,
one of the windows of which had a side-
view towards the gate.

"Good-morning, Uncle Venner!" said
the daguerreotypist, leaning out of the
window. "Do you hear nobody stirring?"

"Not a soul," said the man of patches.
"But that's no wonder. 'Tis barely half
an hour past sunrise, yet. But I'm really
glad to see you, Mr. Holgrave! There's
a strange, lonesome look about this side
of the house; so that my heart misgave
me, somehow or other, and I felt as if
there was nobody alive in it. The front
of the house looks a good deal cheerier;
and Alice's Posies are blooming there
beautifully; and if I were a young man,
Mr. Holgrave, my sweetheart should
have one of these flowers in her bosom,
though I risked my neck climbing for it!
—Well! and did the wind keep you
awake last night?"

"It did, indeed!" answered the artist,

smiling. "If I were a believer in ghosts, —and I don't quite know whether I am or not,—I should have concluded that all the old Pyncheons were running riot in the lower rooms, especially in Miss Hepzibah's part of the house. But it is very quiet now."

"Yes, Miss Hepzibah will be apt to over-sleep herself, after being disturbed, all night, with the racket," said Uncle Venner. "But it would be odd, now, wouldn't it, if the judge had taken both his cousins into the country along with him? I saw him go into the shop yesterday."

"At what hour?" inquired Holgrave.

"O, along the forenoon," said the old man. "Well, well! I must go my rounds, and so must my wheelbarrow. But I'll be back here at dinner-time; for my pig likes a dinner as well as a breakfast. No meal-time, and no sort of victuals, ever seems to come amiss to my pig. Good-morning to you! And, Mr. Holgrave, if I were a young man, like you, I'd get one of Alice's Posies, and keep it in water till Phœbe comes back."

"I have heard," said the daguerreotypist, as he drew in his head, "that the water of Maule's well suits those flowers best."

Here the conversation ceased, and Uncle Venner went on his way. For half an hour longer, nothing disturbed the repose of the seven gables; nor was there any visitor, except a carrier-boy, who, as he passed the front door-step, threw down one of his newspapers; for Hepzibah, of late, had regularly taken it in. After a while, there came a fat woman, making prodigious speed, and stumbling as she ran up the steps of the shop-door. Her face glowed with fire-heat, and it being a pretty warm morning, she bubbled and hissed, as were, as if all a-fry with chimne warmth, and summer-warmth, and t warmth of her own corpulent veloci She tried the shop-door;—it was fa She tried it again, with so angry a that the bell tinkled angrily back at h

"The deuce take Old Maid Py cheon!" muttered the irascible hou wife. "Think of her pretending to set a cent-shop, and then lying abed noon! These are what she calls gent folk's airs, I suppose. But I'll eitl start her ladyship, or break the dc down!"

She shook it accordingly, and t bell, having a spiteful little temper its own, rang obstreperously, making remonstrances heard,—not, indeed, the ears for which they were intend —but by a good lady on the oppos side of the street. She opened her w dow, and addressed the impatie applicant.

"You'll find nobody there, M Gubbins."

"But I must and will find somebo here!" cried Mrs. Gubbins, inflicti another outrage on the bell. "I want half-pound of pork, to fry some fir rate flounders, for Mr. Gubbins's brea fast; and, lady or not, Old Maid Py cheon shall get up and serve with it!"

"But do hear reason, Mrs. Gubbins responded the lady opposite. "She, a her brother, too, have both gone to th cousin, Judge Pyncheon's, at his count seat. There's not a soul in the hou but that young daguerreotype-man, tl sleeps in the north gable. I saw Hepzibah and Clifford go away yest day; and a queer couple of ducks th were, paddling through the mud-pu es! They're gone, I'll assure you."

"And how do you know they're gone the judge's?" asked Mrs. Gubbins.

He's a rich man; and there's been a arrel between him and Hepzibah, this any a day, because he won't give her a ing. That's the main reason of her tting up a cent-shop."

"I know that well enough," said the ighbor. "But they're gone,—that's one ing certain. And who but a blood-lation, that couldn't help himself, I k you, would take in that awful-mpered old maid, and that dreadful ifford? That's it, you may be sure."

Mrs. Gubbins took her departure, still imming over with hot wrath against e absent Hepzibah. For another half ur, or, perhaps, considerably more, ere was almost as much quiet on the tside of the house as within. The n, however, made a pleasant, cheerful, nny sigh, responsive to the breeze that s elsewhere imperceptible; a swarm insects buzzed merrily under its ooping shadow, and became specks of ht, whenever they darted into the nshine; a locust sang, once or twice, some inscrutable seclusion of the tree; d a solitary little bird, with plumage pale gold, came and hovered about ice's Posies.

At last, our small acquaintance, Ned iggins, trudged up the street, on his ay to school; and happening, for the st time in a fortnight, to be the pos-ssor of a cent, he could by no means t past the shop-door of the seven bles. But it would not open. Again d again, however, and half a dozen her agains, with the inexorable per-acity of a child intent upon some ject important to itself, did he renew s efforts for admittance. He had,

doubtless, set his heart upon an elephant; or, possibly, with Hamlet, he meant to eat a crocodile. In response to his more violent attacks, the bell gave, now and then, a moderate tinkle, but could not be stirred into clamor by any exertion of the little fellow's childish and tiptoe strength. Holding by the door-handle, he peeped through a crevice of the curtain, and saw that the inner door, communicating with the passage towards the parlor, was closed.

"Miss 'Pyncheon!" screamed the child, rapping on the window-pane, "I want an elephant!"

There being no answer to several repetitions of the summons, Ned began to grow impatient; and his little pot of passion quickly boiling over, he picked up a stone, with a naughty purpose to fling it through the window; at the same time blubbering and sputtering with wrath. A man—one of two who happened to be passing by—caught the urchin's arm.

"What's the trouble, old gentleman?" he asked.

"I want old Hepzibah, or Phœbe, or any of them!" answered Ned, sobbing. "They won't open the door; and I can't get my elephant!"

"Go to school, you little scamp!" said the man. "There's another cent-shop round the corner. 'Tis very strange, Dixey," added he to his companion, "what's become of all these Pyncheons! Smith, the livery-stable keeper, tells me Judge Pyncheon put his horse up yesterday, to stand till after dinner, and has not taken him away yet. And one of the judge's hired men has been in, this morning, to make inquiry about him. He's a kind of person, they say, that seldom breaks his habits, or stays out o' nights."

"O, he'll turn up safe enough!" said Dixey. "And as for Old Maid Pyncheon, take my word for it, she has run in debt, and gone off from her creditors. I foretold, you remember, the first morning she set up shop, that her devilish scowl would frighten away customers. They couldn't stand it!"

"I never thought she'd make it go," remarked his friend. "This business of cent-shops is overdone among the women-folks. My wife tried it, and lost five dollars on her outlay!"

"Poor business!" said Dixey, shaking his head. "Poor business!"

In the course of the morning, there were various other attempts to open a communication with the supposed inhabitants of this silent and impenetrable mansion. The man of root-beer came, in his neatly-painted wagon, with a couple of dozen full bottles, to be exchanged for empty ones; the baker, with a lot of crackers which Hepzibah had ordered for her retail custom; the butcher, with a nice titbit which he fancied she would be eager to secure for Clifford. Had any observer of these proceedings been aware of the fearful secret hidden within the house, it would have affected him with a singular shape and modification of horror, to see the current of human life making this small eddy hereabouts;—whirling sticks, straws, and all such trifles, round and round, right over the black depth where a dead corpse lay unseen!

The butcher was so much in earnest with his sweetbread of lamb, or whatever the dainty might be, that he tried every accessible door of the seven gables, and at length came round again to the shop, where he or-

dinarily found admittance.

"It's a nice article, and I know t[he] old lady would jump at it," said he [to] himself. "She can't be gone away! [In] fifteen years that I have driven my ca[rt] through Pyncheon-street, I've nev[er] known her to be away from hom[e,] though often enough, to be sure, a m[an] might knock all day without bringi[ng] her to the door. But that was wh[en] she'd only herself to provide for."

Peeping through the same crevice [in] the curtain where, only a little wh[ile] before, the urchin of elephantine a[p]petite had peeped, the butcher behe[ld] the inner door, not closed, as the chi[ld] had seen it, but ajar, and almost wi[de] open. However it might have happene[d,] it was the fact. Through the passag[e]way there was a dark vista into t[he] lighter but still obscure interior of t[he] parlor. It appeared to the butcher th[at] he could pretty clearly discern wh[at] seemed to be the stalwart legs, clad [in] black pantaloons, of a man sitting [in] a large oaken chair, the back of whi[ch] concealed all the remainder of his figu[re.] This contemptuous tranquillity on t[he] part of an occupant of the house, [in] response to the butcher's indefatiga[ble] efforts to attract notice, so piqued t[he] man of flesh that he determined [to] withdraw.

"So," thought he, "there sits O[ld] Maid Pyncheon's bloody brother, wh[ile] I've been giving myself all this troubl[e!] Why, if a hog hadn't more manners, I['d] stick him! I call it demeaning a ma[n's] business to trade with such people; a[nd] from this time forth, if they want [a] sausage or an ounce of liver, they sha[ll] run after the cart for it!"

He tossed the titbit angrily into h[is] cart, and drove off in a pet.

Not a great while afterwards, there
is a sound of music turning the cor-
r, and approaching down the street,
th several intervals of silence, and
en a renewed and nearer outbreak of
isk melody. A mob of children was
en moving onward, or stopping, in
iison with the sound, which appeared
proceed from the centre of the
rong; so that they were loosely bound
gether by slender strains of harmony,
d drawn along captive; with ever
d anon an accession of some little
llow in an apron and straw-hat, caper-
g forth from door or gateway. Arriv-
g under the shadow of the Pyncheon-
n, it proved to be the Italian boy,
io, with his monkey and show of
ppets, had once before played his
rdy-gurdy beneath the arched window.
ie pleasant face of Phœbe—and
ubtless, too, the liberal recompense
iich she had flung him—still dwelt in
s remembrance. His expressive fea-
res kindled up, as he recognized the
ot where this trifling incident of his
ratic life had chanced. He entered the
glected yard (now wilder than ever,
th its growth of hogweed and bur-
ck), stationed himself on the door-
ep of the main entrance, and opening
s show-box, began to play. Each in-
vidual of the automatic community
rthwith set to work, according to his
her proper vocation: the monkey,
king off his Highland bonnet, bowed
d scraped to the bystanders most
sequiously, with ever an observant
e to pick up a stray cent; and the
ung foreigner himself, as he turned
e crank of his machine, glanced up-
rd to the arched window, expectant
a presence that would make his music
e livelier and sweeter. The throng of

children stood near; some on the sidewalk; some within the yard; two or
three establishing themselves on the
very door-step; and one squatting on
the threshold. Meanwhile, the locust
kept singing in the great old Pyncheon-
elm.

"I don't hear anybody in the house,"
said one of the children to another.
"The monkey won't pick up anything
here."

"There is somebody at home," affirmed the urchin on the threshold. "I
heard a step!"

Still the young Italian's eye turned
sidelong upward; and it really seemed
as if the touch of genuine, though slight
and almost playful emotion, communicated a juicier sweetness to the dry,
mechanical process of his minstrelsy.
These wanderers are readily responsive
to any natural kindness—be it no more
than a smile, or a word, itself not understood, but only a warmth in it—which
befalls them on the roadside of life.
They remember these things, because
they are the little enchantments which,
for the instant,—for the space that re-
flects a landscape in a soap-bubble,—
build up a home about them. Therefore,
the Italian boy would not be discour-
aged by the heavy silence with which
the old house seemed resolute to clog
the vivacity of his instrument. He persisted in his melodious appeals; he still
looked upward, trusting that his dark,
alien countenance would soon be
brightened by Phœbe's sunny aspect.
Neither could he be willing to depart
without again beholding Clifford, whose
sensibility, like Phœbe's smile, had
talked a kind of heart's language to the
foreigner. He repeated all his music,
over and over again, until his auditors

were getting weary. So were the little wooden people in his show-box, and the monkey most of all. There was no response, save the singing of the locust.

"No children live in this house," said a schoolboy, at last. "Nobody lives here but an old maid and an old man. You'll get nothing here! Why don't you go along?"

"You fool, you, why do you tell him?" whispered a shrewd little Yankee, caring nothing for the music, but a good deal for the cheap rate at which it was had. "Let him play as long as he likes! If there's nobody to pay him, that's his own look-out!"

Once more, however, the Italian ran over his round of melodies. To the common observer—who could understand nothing of the case, except the music and the sunshine on the hither side of the door—it might have been amusing to watch the pertinacity of the street-performer. Will he succeed at last? Will that stubborn door be suddenly flung open? Will a group of joyous children, the young ones of the house, come dancing, shouting, laughing, into the open air, and cluster round the show-box, looking with eager merriment at the puppets, and tossing each a copper for long-tailed Mammon, the monkey, to pick up?

But, to us, who know the inner heart of the seven gables, as well as its exterior face, there is a ghastly effect in this repetition of light popular tunes at its door-step. It would be an ugly business, indeed, if Judge Pyncheon (who would not have cared a fig for Paganini's fiddle, in his most harmonious mood) should make his appearance at the door, with a bloody shirt-bosom, and a grim frown on his swarthily-white

visage, and motion the foreign vagabo away! Was ever before such a grindi out of jigs and waltzes, where nobo was in the cue to dance? Yes, ve often. This contrast, or intermingling tragedy with mirth, happens dai hourly, momently. The gloomy a desolate old house, deserted of life, a with awful Death sitting sternly in solitude, was the emblem of many human heart, which, nevertheless, compelled to hear the trill and echo the world's gayety around it.

Before the conclusion of the Italia performance, a couple of men happen to be passing, on their way to dinner.

"I say, you young French fellow called out one of them,—"come aw from that door-step, and go somewh else with your nonsense! The Pynche family live there; and they are in gr trouble, just about this time. They do feel musical to-day. It is reported, over town, that Judge Pyncheon, w owns the house, has been murdere and the city marshal is going to lo into the matter. So be off with you, once!"

As the Italian shouldered his hurd gurdy, he saw on the door-step a ca which had been covered, all the mo ing, by the newspaper that the carr had flung upon it, but was now shuffl into sight. He picked it up, and perce ing something written in pencil, ga it to the man to read. In fact, it w an engraved card of Judge Pyncheon with certain pencilled memoranda the back, referring to various business which it had been his purpose to tra act during the preceding day. It form a prospective epitome of the day's h tory; only that affairs had not turn out altogether in accordance with t

rogramme. The card must have been
st from the judge's vest-pocket, in his
reliminary attempt to gain access by
he main entrance of the house. Though
ell-soaked with rain, it was still par-
ally legible.

"Look here, Dixey!" cried the man.
This has something to do with Judge
yncheon. See!—here's his name printed
n it; and here, I suppose, is some of
s hand-writing."

"Let's go to the city marshal with it!"
id Dixey. "It may give him just the
ue he wants. After all," whispered he
his companion's ear, "it would be no
onder if the judge has gone into that
oor, and never come out again! A
ertain cousin of his may have been at
s old tricks. And Old Maid Pyncheon,
aving got herself in debt by the cent-
op,—and the judge's pocket-book be-
g well filled,—and bad blood amongst
em already! Put all these things to-
ether, and see what they make!"

"Hush, hush!" whispered the other.
It seems like a sin to be the first to
peak of such a thing. But I think, with
ou, that we had better go to the city
arshal."

"Yes, yes!" said Dixey. "Well!—I
ways said there was something devilish
that woman's scowl!"

The men wheeled about, accordingly,
nd retraced their steps up the street.
he Italian, also, made the best of his
ay off, with a parting glance up at the
rched window. As for the children,
ey took to their heels, with one ac-
ord, and scampered as if some giant or
gre were in pursuit, until, at a good
stance from the house, they stopped
suddenly and simultaneously as they
d set out. Their susceptible nerves
ook an indefinite alarm from what they

had overheard. Looking back at the
grotesque peaks and shadowy angles of
the old mansion, they fancied a gloom
diffused about it, which no brightness of
the sunshine could dispel. An imaginary
Hepzibah scowled and shook her finger
at them, from several windows at the
same moment. An imaginary Clifford
—for (and it would have deeply wounded him to know it) he had always been
a horror to these small people—stood
behind the unreal Hepzibah, making
awful gestures, in a faded dressing-
gown. Children are even more apt, if
possible, than grown people, to catch
the contagion of a panic terror. For
the rest of the day, the more timid
went whole streets about, for the sake
of avoiding the seven gables; while the
bolder signalized their hardihood by
challenging their comrades to race past
the mansion at full speed.

It could not have been more than
half an hour after the disappearance of
the Italian boy, with his unseasonable
melodies, when a cab drove down the
street. It stopped beneath the Pyncheon-
elm; the cabman took a trunk, a
canvas-bag, and a band-box, from the
top of his vehicle, and deposited them
on the door-step of the old house; a
straw bonnet, and then the pretty figure
of a young girl, came into view from
the interior of the cab. It was Phœbe!
Though not altogether so blooming as
when she first tripped into our story,—
for, in the few intervening weeks, her
experiences had made her graver, more
womanly, and deeper-eyed, in token of
a heart that had begun to suspect its
depths,—still there was the quiet glow
of natural sunshine over her. Neither
had she forfeited her proper gift of
making things look real, rather than

fantastic, within her sphere. Yet we feel it to be a questionable venture, even for Phœbe, at this juncture, to cross the threshold of the seven gables. Is her healthful presence potent enough to chase away the crowd of pale, hideous, and sinful phantoms, that have gained admittance there since her departure? Or will she, likewise, fade, sicken, sadden, and grow into deformity, and be only another pallid phantom, to glide noiselessly up and down the stairs, and affright children, as she pauses at the window?

At least, we would gladly forewarn the unsuspecting girl that there is nothing in human shape or substance to receive her, unless it be the figure of Judge Pyncheon, who—wretched spectacle that he is, and frightful in our remembrance, since our night-long vigil with him!—still keeps his place in the oaken chair.

Phœbe first tried the shop-door. It did not yield to her hand; and the white curtain, drawn across the window which formed the upper section of the door, struck her quick perceptive faculty as something unusual. Without making another effort to enter here, she betook herself to the great portal, under the arched window. Finding it fastened, she knocked. A reverberation came from the emptiness within. She knocked again, and a third time; and, listening intently, fancied that the floor creaked, as if Hepzibah were coming, with her ordinary tiptoe movement, to admit her. But so dead a silence ensued upon this imaginary sound, that she began to question whether she might not have mistaken the house, familiar as she thought herself with its exterior.

Her notice was now attracted by a

child's voice, at some distance. It a[p]peared to call her name. Looking in t[he] direction whence it proceeded, Phœ[be] saw little Ned Higgins, a good way dow[n] the street, stamping, shaking his hea[d] violently, making deprecatory gestur[es] with both hands, and shouting to her [a] mouth-wide screech.

"No, no, Phœbe!" he screame[d.] "Don't you go in! There's somethi[ng] wicked there! Don't—don't—don't [go] in!"

But, as the little personage could n[ot] be induced to approach near enough [to] explain himself, Phœbe concluded th[at] he had been frightened, on some of h[is] visits to the shop, by her cousin Hep[zi]bah; for the good lady's manifestation[s,] in truth, ran about an equal chance [of] scaring children out of their wits, [or] compelling them to unseemly laughte[r.] Still, she felt the more, for this inciden[t,] how unaccountably silent and impen[e]trable the house had become. As h[er] next resort, Phœbe made her way int[o] the garden, where, on so warm an[d] bright a day as the present, she ha[d] little doubt of finding Clifford, and pe[r]haps Hepzibah also, idling away t[he] noontide in the shadow of the arbo[r.] Immediately on her entering the garde[n] gate, the family of hens half ran, ha[lf] flew, to meet her; while a strang[e] Grimalkin, which was prowling und[er] the parlor-window, took to his heel[s,] clambered hastily over the fence, an[d] vanished. The arbor was vacant, and i[ts] floor, table, and circular bench, we[re] still damp, and bestrewn with twigs, an[d] the disarray of the past storm. T[he] growth of the garden seemed to ha[ve] got quite out of bounds; the weeds ha[d] taken advantage of Phœbe's absen[ce] and the long-continued rain, to r[un]

npant over the flowers and kitchen-
getables. Maule's well had overflowed
 stone border, and made a pool of
rmidable breadth, in that corner of
e garden.

The impression of the whole scene
s that of a spot where no human foot
d left its print for many preceding
ys,—probably not since Phœbe's de-
rture,—for she saw a side-comb of
r own under the table of the arbor,
ere it must have fallen on the last
ernoon when she and Clifford sat
ere.

The girl knew that her two relatives
re capable of far greater oddities than
at of shutting themselves up in their
l house, as they appeared now to have
ne. Nevertheless, with indistinct mis-
ings of something amiss, and appre-
nsions to which she could not give

shape, she approached the door that
formed the customary communication
between the house and garden. It was
secured within, like the two which she
had already tried. She knocked, however; and immediately, as if the application had been expected, the door
was drawn open, by a considerable
exertion of some unseen person's
strength, not widely, but far enough to
afford her a side-long entrance. As Hepzibah, in order not to expose herself to
inspection from without, invariably
opened a door in this manner, Phœbe
necessarily concluded that it was her
cousin who now admitted her.

Without hesitation, therefore, she
stepped across the threshold, and had
no sooner entered than the door closed
behind her.

CHAPTER XX

THE FLOWER OF EDEN

PHŒBE, coming so suddenly from the
nny daylight, was altogether be-
nmed in such density of shadow as
ked in most of the passages of the
l house. She was not at first aware by
om she had been admitted. Before
r eyes had adapted themselves to the
scurity, a hand grasped her own, with
firm but gentle and warm pressure,
us imparting a welcome which caused
r heart to leap and thrill with an in-
finable shiver of enjoyment. She felt
rself drawn along, not towards the
rlor, but into a large and unoccupied
artment, which had formerly been the

grand reception-room of the seven
gables. The sunshine came freely into
all the uncurtained windows of this
room, and fell upon the dusty floor; so
that Phœbe now clearly saw—what, indeed, had been no secret, after the encounter of a warm hand with hers—
that it was not Hepzibah nor Clifford,
but Holgrave, to whom she owed her
reception. The subtle, intuitive communication, or, rather, the vague and
formless impression of something to be
told, had made her yield unresistingly
to his impulse. Without taking away her
hand, she looked eagerly in his face,

not quick to forebode evil, but unavoidably conscious that the state of the family had changed since her departure, and therefore anxious for an explanation.

The artist looked paler than ordinary; there was a thoughtful and severe contraction of his forehead, tracing a deep vertical line between the eyebrows. His smile, however, was full of genuine warmth, and had in it a joy, by far the most vivid expression that Phœbe had ever witnessed, shining out of the New England reserve with which Holgrave habitually masked whatever lay near his heart. It was the look wherewith a man, brooding alone over some fearful object, in a dreary forest or illimitable desert, would recognize the familiar aspect of his dearest friend, bringing up all the peaceful ideas that belong to home, and the gentle current of everyday affairs. And yet, as he felt the necessity of responding to her look of inquiry, the smile disappeared.

"I ought not to rejoice that you have come, Phœbe," said he. "We meet at a strange moment!"

"What has happened?" she exclaimed. "Why is the house so deserted? Where are Hepzibah and Clifford?"

"Gone! I cannot imagine where they are!" answered Holgrave. "We are alone in the house!"

"Hepzibah and Clifford gone?" cried Phœbe. "It is not possible! And why have you brought me into this room, instead of the parlor? Ah, something terrible has happened! I must run and see!"

"No, no, Phœbe!" said Holgrave, holding her back. "It is as I have told you. They are gone, and I know not whither. A terrible event has, indeed, happened, but not to them, nor, as I u doubtingly believe, through any agen of theirs. If I read your charact rightly, Phœbe," he continued, fixi his eyes on hers, with stern anxiety, i termixed with tenderness, "gentle as y are, and seeming to have your sphe among common things, you yet posse remarkable strength. You have wonde ful poise, and a faculty which, wh tested, will prove itself capable of dea ing with matters that fall far out of t ordinary rule."

"O, no, I am very weak!" repli Phœbe, trembling. "But tell me wh has happened!"

"You are strong!" persisted H grave. "You must be both strong a wise; for I am all astray, and need yo counsel. It may be you can suggest t one right thing to do!"

"Tell me!—tell me!" said Phœbe, in a tremble. "It oppresses,—it terrifi me,—this mystery! Anything else I c bear!"

The artist hesitated. Notwithstandi what he had just said, and most si cerely, in regard to the self-balanci power with which Phœbe impressed hi it still seemed almost wicked to bri the awful secret of yesterday to h knowledge. It was like dragging a hid ous shape of death into the cleanly a cheerful space before a household fir where it would present all the uglier a pect, amid the decorousness of ever thing about it. Yet it could not concealed from her; she must nee know it.

"Phœbe," said he, "do you rememb this?"

He put into her hand a daguerre type; the same that he had shown h at their first interview, in the garde

d which so strikingly brought out the
rd and relentless traits of the original.
"What has this to do with Hepzibah
d Clifford?" asked Phœbe, with im-
tient. surprise that Holgrave should so
fle with her, at such a moment. "It
Judge Pyncheon! You have shown it
me before!"

"But here is the same face, taken
thin this half-hour," said the artist,
esenting her with another miniature.
had just finished it, when I heard you
the door."

"This is death!" shuddered Phœbe,
rning very pale. "Judge Pyncheon
ad!"

"Such as there represented," said Hol-
ave, "he sits in the next room. The
lge is dead, and Clifford and Hepzibah
ve vanished! I know no more. All
yond is conjecture. On returning to
y solitary chamber, last evening, I
ticed no light, either in the parlor, or
epzibah's room, or Clifford's; no stir
r footstep about the house. This
orning there was the same death-like
iet. From my window, I overheard the
stimony of a neighbor, that your rela-
es were seen leaving the house, in the
dst of yesterday's storm. A rumor
ached me, too, of Judge Pyncheon be-
g missed. A feeling which I cannot
scribe—an indefinite sense of some
tastrophe, or consummation—impelled
e to make my way into this part of
e house, where I discovered what you
e. As a point of evidence that may be
ful to Clifford, and also as a me-
rial valuable to myself,—for, Phœbe,
re are hereditary reasons that con-
ct me strangely with that man's fate,
I used the means at my disposal to
serve this pictorial record of Judge
ncheon's death."

Even in her agitation, Phœbe could
not help remarking the calmness of Holgrave's demeanor. He appeared, it is
true, to feel the whole awfulness of the
judge's death, yet had received the fact
into his mind without any mixture of
surprise, but as an event pre-ordained,
happening inevitably, and so fitting itself into past occurrences that it could
almost have been prophesied.

"Why have you not thrown open the
doors, and called in witnesses?" inquired
she, with a painful shudder. "It is
terrible to be here alone!"

"But Clifford!" suggested the artist.
"Clifford and Hepzibah! We must consider what is best to be done in their
behalf. It is a wretched fatality, that
they should have disappeared! Their
flight will throw the worst coloring over
this event of which it is susceptible.
Yet how easy is the explanation, to
those who know them! Bewildered and
terror-stricken by the similarity of this
death to a former one, which was attended with such disastrous consequences to Clifford, they have had no
idea but of removing themselves from
the scene. How miserably unfortunate!
Had Hepzibah but shrieked aloud,—
had Clifford flung wide the door, and
proclaimed Judge Pyncheon's death —
it would have been, however awful in
itself, an event fruitful of good consequences to them. As I view it, it would
have gone far towards obliterating the
black stain on Clifford's character."

"And how," asked Phœbe, "could any
good come from what is so very
dreadful?"

"Because," said the artist, "if the
matter can be fairly considered, and
candidly interpreted, it must be evident
that Judge Pyncheon could not have

come unfairly to his end. This mode of death has been an idiosyncrasy with his family, for generations past; not often occurring, indeed, but, when it does occur, usually attacking individuals about the judge's time of life, and generally in the tension of some mental crisis, or, perhaps, in an excess of wrath. Old Maule's prophecy was probably founded on a knowledge of this physical predisposition in the Pyncheon race. Now, there is a minute and almost exact similarity in the appearances connected with the death that occurred yesterday and those recorded of the death of Clifford's uncle, thirty years ago. It is true, there was a certain arrangement of circumstances, unnecessary to be recounted, which made it possible,—nay, as men look at these things, probable, or even certain,—that old Jaffrey Pyncheon came to a violent death, and by Clifford's hands."

"Whence came those circumstances?" exclaimed Phœbe; "he being innocent, as we know him to be!"

"They were arranged," said Holgrave,—"at least, such has long been my conviction,—they were arranged, after the uncle's death, and before it was made public, by the man who sits in yonder parlor. His own death, so like that former one, yet attended with none of those suspicious circumstances, seems the stroke of God upon him, at once a punishment for his wickedness, and making plain the innocence of Clifford. But this flight,—it distorts everything! He may be in concealment, near at hand. Could we but bring him back before the discovery of the judge's death, the evil might be rectified."

"We must not hide this thing a moment longer!" said Phœbe. "It is dread-

ful to keep it so closely in our hea
Clifford is innocent. God will make
manifest! Let us throw open the do
and call all the neighborhood to see
truth!"

"You are right, Phœbe," rejoi
Holgrave. "Doubtless you are right."

Yet the artist did not feel the horr
which was proper to Phœbe's sweet
order-loving character, at thus find
herself at issue with society,
brought in contact with an event t
transcended ordinary rules. Neither
he in haste, like her, to betake hims
within the precincts of common life.
the contrary, he gathered a wild enj
ment,—as it were, a flower of stra
beauty, growing in a desolate spot,
blossoming in the wind,—such a flo
of momentary happiness he gathe
from his present position. It separa
Phœbe and himself from the world,
bound them to each other, by their
clusive knowledge of Judge Pyncheo
mysterious death, and the counsel wh
they were forced to hold respecting
The secret, so long as it should contir
such, kept them within the circle o
spell, a solitude in the midst of m
a remoteness as entire as that of
island in mid-ocean;—once divulged,
ocean would flow betwixt them, stand
on its widely-sundered shores. `Me
while, all the circumstances of th
situation seemed to draw them togeth
they were like two children who
hand in hand, pressing closely to
another's side, through a shad
haunted passage. The image of aw
Death, which filled the house, held th
united by his stiffened grasp.

These influences hastened the devel
ment of emotions that might not oth
wise have flowered so soon. Possib

deed, it had been Holgrave's purpose
let them die in their undeveloped
rms.

"Why do we delay so?" asked Phœbe.
This secret takes away my breath!
et us throw open the doors!"

"In all our lives, there can never
me another moment like this!" said
olgrave. "Phœbe, is it all terror?—
thing but terror? Are you conscious
no joy, as I am, that has made this
e only point of life worth living for?"

"It seems a sin," replied Phœbe,
embling, "to think of joy at such a
ne!"

"Could you but know, Phœbe, how it
is with me, the hour before you
me!" exclaimed the artist. "A dark,
ld, miserable hour! The presence of
nder dead man threw a great black
adow over everything; he made the
iverse, so far as my perception could
ich, a scene of guilt, and of retribu-
on more dreadful than the guilt. The
ıse of it took away my youth. I never
ped to feel young again! The world
oked strange, wild, evil, hostile;—my
st life, so lonesome and dreary; my
ture, a shapeless gloom, which I must
ould into gloomy shapes! But, Phœbe,
u crossed the threshold; and hope,
rmth and joy, came in with you! The
ick moment became at once a blissful
e. It must not pass without the
oken word. I love you!"

"How can you love a simple girl like
e?" asked Phœbe, compelled by his
rnestness to speak. "You have many,
ıny thoughts, with which I should try
vain to sympathize. And I,—I, too,—
ave tendencies with which you would
mpathize as little. That is less matter.
ıt I have not scope enough to make
u happy."

"You are my only possibility of
happiness!" answered Holgrave. "I have
no faith in it, except as you bestow it
on me!"

"And then—I am afraid!" continued
Phœbe, shrinking towards Holgrave,
even while she told him so frankly the
doubts with which he affected her. "You
will lead me out of my own quiet path.
You will make me strive to follow you,
where it is pathless. I cannot do so. It
is not my nature. I shall sink down and
perish!"

"Ah, Phœbe!" exclaimed Holgrave,
with almost a sigh, and a smile that was
burthened with thought. "It will be
far otherwise than as you forebode. The
world owes all its onward impulses to
men ill at ease. The happy man inevitably confines himself within ancient
limits. I have a presentiment that, hereafter, it will be my lot to set out trees,
to make fences,—perhaps, even, in due
time, to build a house for another
generation,—in a word, to conform myself to laws, and the peaceful practice of
society. Your poise will be more powerful than any oscillating tendency of
mine."

"I would not have it so!" said Phœbe,
earnestly.

"Do you love me?" asked Holgrave.
"If we love one another, the moment
has room for nothing more. Let us pause
upon it, and be satisfied. Do you love
me, Phœbe?"

"You look into my heart," said she,
letting her eyes drop. "You know I love
you!"

And it was in this hour, so full of
doubt and awe, that the one miracle was
wrought, without which every human
existence is a blank. The bliss, which
makes all things true, beautiful, and

holy, shone around this youth and maiden. They were conscious of nothing sad nor old. They transfigured the earth, and made it Eden again, and themselves the two first dwellers in it. The dead man, so close beside them, was forgotten. At such a crisis, there is no death; for immortality is revealed anew, and embraces everything in its hallowed atmosphere.

But how soon the heavy earth-dream settled down again!

"Hark!" whispered Phœbe. "Somebody is at the street door!"

"Now let us meet the world!" said Holgrave. "No doubt, the rumor of Judge Pyncheon's visit to this house, and the flight of Hepzibah and Clifford, is about to lead to the investigation of the premises. We have no way but to meet it. Let us open the door at once."

But, to their surprise, before they could reach the street door,—even before they quitted the room in which the foregoing interview had passed,—they heard footsteps in the further passage. The door, therefore, which they supposed to be securely locked,—which Holgrave, indeed, had seen to be so, and at which Phœbe had vainly tried to enter,—must have been opened from without. The sound of footsteps was not harsh, bold, decided, and intrusive, as the gait of strangers would naturally be, making authoritative entrance into a dwelling where they knew themselves unwelcome. It was feeble, as of persons either weak or weary; there was the mingled murmur of two voices, familiar to both the listeners.

"Can it be?" whispered Holgrave.

"It is they!" answered Phœbe. "Thank God!—thank God!"

And then, as if in sympathy with Phœbe's whispered ejaculation, they heard Hepzibah's voice, more distinctly,

"Thank God, my brother, we are home!"

"Well!—Yes!—thank God!" responded Clifford. "A dreary home, Hepzibah! But you have done well to bring me hither! Stay! That parlor-door is open. I cannot pass by it! Let me go and rest me in the arbor, where I used,—oh, very long ago, it seems to me, after what has befallen us,—where I used to be so happy with little Phœbe!"

But the house was not altogether so dreary as Clifford imagined it. They had not made many steps,—in truth, they were lingering in the entry, with the listlessness of an accomplished purpose, uncertain what to do next,—when Phœbe ran to meet them. On beholding her, Hepzibah burst into tears. With all her might, she had staggered onward beneath the burden of grief and responsibility, until now that it was safe to fling it down. Indeed, she had no energy to fling it down, but had ceased to uphold it, and suffered it to press her to the earth. Clifford appeared the stronger of the two.

"It is our own little Phœbe!—Ah! and Holgrave with her," exclaimed he, with a glance of keen and delicate insight, and a smile, beautiful, kind, but melancholy. "I thought of you both, as we came down the street, and beheld Alice's Posies in full bloom. And so the flower of Eden has bloomed, likewise in this old, darksome house, to-day!"

CHAPTER XXI

THE DEPARTURE

THE sudden death of so prominent a
ember of the social world as the
onorable Judge Jaffrey Pyncheon
eated a sensation (at least, in the
cles more immediately connected with
e deceased) which had hardly quite
bsided in a fortnight.

It may be remarked, however, that, of
the events which constitute a per-
n's biography, there is scarcely one—
ne, certainly, of anything like a simi-
importance—to which the world so
sily reconciles itself as to his death.
most other cases and contingencies,
e individual is present among us,
xed up with the daily revolution of
airs, and affording a definite point for
servation. At his decease, there is only
vacancy, and a momentary eddy,—
ry small, as compared with the ap-
rent magnitude of the ingurgitated
ject,—and a bubble or two, ascending
t of the black depth, and bursting at
e surface. As regarded Judge Pyn-
eon, it seemed probable, at first blush,
it the mode of his final departure
ght give him a larger and longer
sthumous vogue than ordinarily at-
nds the memory of a distinguished
in. But when it came to be under-
ood, on the highest professional au-
ority, that the event was a natural,
d—except for some unimportant par-
ulars, denoting a slight idiosyncrasy—
no means an unusual form of death,
public, with its customary alacrity,
oceeded to forget that he had ever
ed. In short, the honorable judge was
ginning to be a stale subject, before

half the county newspapers had found
time to put their columns in mourning,
and publish his exceedingly eulogistic
obituary.

Nevertheless, creeping darkly through
the places which this excellent person
had haunted in his lifetime, there was
a hidden stream of private talk, such as
it would have shocked all decency to
speak loudly at the street-corners. It
is very singular, how the fact of a man's
death often seems to give people a truer
idea of his character, whether for good
or evil, than they have ever possessed
while he was living and acting among
them. Death is so genuine a fact that it
excludes falsehood, or betrays its emptiness; it is a touchstone that proves the
gold, and dishonors the baser metal.
Could the departed, whoever he may be,
return in a week after his decease, he
would almost invariably find himself at
a higher or lower point than he had
formerly occupied, on the scale of public appreciation. But the talk, or scandal, to which we now allude, had reference to matters of no less old a date
than the supposed murder, thirty or
forty years ago, of the late Judge Pyncheon's uncle. The medical opinion, with
regard to his own recent and regretted
decease, had almost entirely obviated
the idea that a murder was committed,
in the former case. Yet, as the record
showed, there were circumstances irrefragably indicating that some person
had gained access to old Jaffrey Pyncheon's private apartments, at or near
the moment of his death. His desk and

private drawers, in a room contiguous to his bedchamber, had been ransacked; money and valuable articles were missing; there was a bloody hand-print on the old man's linen; and, by a powerfully welded chain of deductive evidence, the guilt of the robbery and apparent murder had been fixed on Clifford, then residing with his uncle in the House of the Seven Gables.

Whencesoever originating, there now arose a theory that undertook so to account for these circumstances as to exclude the idea of Clifford's agency. Many persons affirmed that the history and elucidation of the facts, long so mysterious, had been obtained by the daguerreotypist from one of those mesmerical seers, who, now-a-days, so strangely perplex the aspect of human affairs, and put everybody's natural vision to the blush, by the marvels which they see with their eyes shut.

According to this version of the story, Judge Pyncheon, exemplary as we have portrayed him in our narrative, was, in his youth, an apparently irreclaimable scapegrace. The brutish, the animal instincts, as is often the case, had been developed earlier than the intellectual qualities, and the force of character, for which he was afterwards remarkable. He had shown himself wild, dissipated, addicted to low pleasures, little short of ruffianly in his propensities, and recklessly expensive, with no other resources than the bounty of his uncle. This course of conduct had alienated the old bachelor's affection, once strongly fixed upon him. Now, it is averred,—but whether on authority available in a court of justice, we do not pretend to have investigated,—that the young man was tempted by the devil, one night, to search his uncl[e's] private drawers, to which he had uns[us]pected means of access. While th[us] criminally occupied, he was startled [by] the opening of the chamber-door. Th[ere] stood old Jaffrey Pyncheon, in his nig[ht] clothes! The surprise of such a d[is]covery, his agitation, alarm, and horr[or] brought on the crisis of a disorder which the old bachelor had an here[di]tary liability;—he seemed to choke w[ith] blood, and fell upon the floor, striki[ng] his temple a heavy blow against [the] corner of a table. What was to be do[ne?] The old man was surely dead! Assi[st]ance would come too late! What a m[is]fortune, indeed, should it come too so[on,] since his reviving consciousness wo[uld] bring the recollection of the ignomini[ous] offence which he had beheld his neph[ew] in the very act of committing!

.But he never did revive. With [the] cool hardihood that always pertained [to] him, the young man continued [his] search of the drawers, and found a w[ill] of recent date, in favor of Clifford[,] which he destroyed,—and an older o[ne] in his own favor, which he suffered [to] remain. But, before retiring, Jaffrey thought himself of the evidence, [by] these ransacked drawers, that some [one] had visited the chamber with sinis[ter] purposes. Suspicion, unless avert[ed,] might fix upon the real offender. In [the] very presence of the dead man, the[re]fore, he laid a scheme that should f[ix] himself at the expense of Clifford[, his] rival, for whose character he had once a contempt and a repugnance. [It] is not probable, be it said, that he ac[ted] with any set purpose of involving C[lif]ford in a charge of murder. Know[ing] that his uncle did not die by violen[ce,] it may not have occurred to him, in [the]

ry of the crisis, that such an in-
:nce might be drawn. But, when the
.ir took this darker aspect, Jaffrey's
vious steps had already pledged him
those which remained. So craftily
. he arranged the circumstances, that,
Clifford's trial, his cousin hardly
nd it necessary to swear to anything
e, but only to withhold the one de-
ve explanation, by refraining to state
it he had himself done and witnessed.
.hus Jaffrey Pyncheon's inward
ninality, as regarded Clifford, was,
:ed, black and damnable; while its
·e outward show and positive com-
sion was the smallest that could
sibly consist with so great a sin.
s is just the sort of guilt that a
1 of eminent respectability finds it
.est to dispose of. It was suffered to
e out of sight, or be reckoned a
ial matter, in the Honorable Judge
icheon's long subsequent survey of
own life. He shuffled it aside, among
forgotten and forgiven frailties of
youth, and seldom thought of it
in.

Ve leave the judge to his repose. He
ld not be styled fortunate, at the
r of death. Unknowingly, he was a
dless man, while striving to add
·e wealth to his only child's in-
:tance. Hardly a week after his de-
se, one of the Cunard steamers
ught intelligence of the death, by
lera, of Judge Pyncheon's son, just
the point of embarkation for his
ve land. By this misfortune, Clifford
ime rich; so did Hepzibah; so did
little village-maiden, and, through
that sworn foe of wealth and all
iner of conservatism,—the wild re-
ner,—Holgrave!

t was now far too late in Clifford's

life for the good opinion of society to
be worth the trouble and anguish of a
formal vindication. What he needed was
the love of a very few; not the admiration, or even the respect, of the
unknown many. The latter might probably have been won for him, had those
on whom the guardianship of his welfare had fallen deemed it advisable to
expose Clifford to a miserable resusci-
tation of past ideas, when the condition
of whatever comfort he might expect
lay in the calm of forgetfulness. After
such wrong as he had suffered, there is
no reparation. The pitiable mockery of
it, which the world might have been
ready enough to offer, coming so long
after the agony had done its utmost
work, would have been fit only to pro-
voke bitterer laughter than poor Clifford was ever capable of. It is a truth
(and it would be a very sad one, but for
the higher hopes which it suggests) that
no great mistake, whether acted or endured, in our mortal sphere, is ever
really set right. Time, the continual
vicissitude of circumstances, and the
invariable inopportunity of death, render it impossible. If, after long lapse
of years, the right seems to be in our
power, we find no niche to set it in.
The better remedy is for the sufferer
to pass on, and leave what he once
thought his irreparable ruin far behind
him.

The shock of Judge Pyncheon's death
had a permanently invigorating and
ultimately beneficial effect on Clifford.
That strong and ponderous man had
been Clifford's night-mare. There was
no free breath to be drawn, within the
sphere of so malevolent an influence.
The first effect of freedom, as we have
witnessed in Clifford's aimless flight, was

a tremulous exhilaration. Subsiding from it, he did not sink into his former intellectual apathy. He never, it is true, attained to nearly the full measure of what might have been his faculties. But he recovered enough of them partially to light up his character, to display some outline of the marvéllous grace that was abortive in it, and to make him the object of no less deep, although less melancholy interest than heretofore. He was evidently happy. Could we pause to give another picture of his daily life, with all the appliances now at command to gratify his instinct for the Beautiful, the garden scenes, that seemed so sweet to him, would look mean and trivial in comparison.

Very soon after their change of fortune, Clifford, Hepzibah, and little Phœbe, with the·approval of the artist, concluded to remove from the dismal old House of the Seven Gables, and take up their abode, for the present, at the elegant country-seat of the late Judge Pyncheon. Chanticleer and his family had already been transported thither, where the two hens had forthwith begun an indefatigable process of egg-laying, with an evident design, as a matter of duty and conscience, to continue their illustrious breed under better auspices than for a century past. On the day set for their departure, the principal personages of our story, including good Uncle Venner, were assembled in the parlor.

"The country-house is certainly a very fine one, so far as the plan goes," observed Holgrave, as the party were discussing their future arrangements. "But I wonder that the late judge—being so opulent, and with a reasonable prospect of transmitting his wealth to descendants of his own—should have felt the propriety of embodying excellent a piece of domestic architture in stone, rather than in wood. Th every generation of the family mig have altered the interior, to suit its o taste and convenience; while the terior, through the lapse of years, mig have been adding venerableness to original beauty, and thus giving th impression of permanence which I c sider essential to the happiness of a one moment."

"Why," cried Phœbe, gazing i the artist's face with infinite ama ment, "how wonderfully your ideas changed! A house of stone, indeed! is but two or three weeks ago, that y seemed to wish people to live in son thing as fragile and temporary as bird's nest!"

"Ah, Phœbe, I told you how it wo be!" said the artist, with a ha melancholy laugh. "You find me a c servative already! Little did I th ever to become one. It is especially pardonable in this dwelling of so mu hereditary misfortune, and under eye of yonder portrait of a model c servative, who, in that very charact rendered himself so long the evil dest of his race."

"That picture!" said Clifford, seem to shrink from its stern glance. "Wh ever I look at it, there is an old, drea recollection haunting me, but keep just beyond the grasp of my mi Wealth, it seems to say!—boundl wealth!—unimaginable wealth! I co fancy that, when I was a child, or youth, that portrait had spoken, a told me a rich secret, or had held fo its hand, with the written record hidden opulence. But those old matt

so dim with me, now-a-days! What
uld this dream have been?"

"Perhaps I can recall it," answered
Holgrave. "See! There are a hundred
ances to one, that no person, un-
quainted with the secret, would ever
ich this spring."

'A secret spring!" cried Clifford. "Ah,
emember now! I did discover it, one
nmer afternoon, when I was idling
d dreaming about the house, long,
g ago. But the mystery escapes me."
The artist put his finger on the con-
vance to which he had referred. In
mer days, the effect would probably
ve been to cause the picture to start
ward. But, in so long a period of
acealment, the machinery had been
en through with rust; so that, at
lgrave's pressure, the portrait, frame
d all, tumbled suddenly from its
sition, and lay face downward on the
or. A recess in the wall was thus
ught to light, in which lay an object
covered with a century's dust that it
ild not immediately be recognized as
olded sheet of parchment. Holgrave
ned it, and displayed an ancient
d, signed with the hieroglyphics of
eral Indian sagamores, and convey-
to Colonel Pyncheon and his heirs,
ever, a vast extent of territory at the
tward.

This is the very parchment the at-
apt to recover which cost the beauti-
Alice Pyncheon her happiness and
," said the artist, alluding to his
end. "It is what the Pyncheons
ght in vain, while it was valuable;
l now that they find the treasure, it
long been worthless."

'Poor Cousin Jaffrey! This is what
eived him," exclaimed Hepzibah.
hen they were young together, Clif-

ford probably made a kind of fairy-tale
of this discovery. He was always dreaming hither and thither about the house,
and lighting up its dark corners with
beautiful stories. And poor Jaffrey, who
took hold of everything as if it were
real, thought my brother had found out
his uncle's wealth. He died with this
delusion in his mind!"

"But," said Phœbe, apart to Holgrave, "how came you to know the
secret?"

"My dearest Phœbe," said Holgrave,
"how will it please you to assume the
name of Maule? As for the secret, it is
the only inheritance that has come down
to me from my ancestors. You should
have known sooner (only that I was
afraid of frightening you away) that,
in this long drama of wrong and retribution, I represent the old wizard, and am
probably as much of a wizard as ever
he was. The son of the executed
Matthew Maule, while building this
house, took the opportunity to construct
that recess, and hide away the Indian
deed, on which depended the immense
land-claim of the Pyncheons. Thus they
bartered their eastern territory for
Maule's garden-ground."

"And now," said Uncle Venner, "I
suppose their whole claim is not worth
one man's share in my farm yonder!"

"Uncle Venner," cried Phœbe, taking
the patched philosopher's hand, "you
must never talk any more about your
farm! You shall never go there, as long
as you live! There is a cottage in
our new garden,—the prettiest little
yellowish-brown cottage you ever saw;
and the sweetest-looking place, for it
looks just as if it were made of gingerbread,—and we are going to fit it up
and furnish it, on purpose for you. And

you shall do nothing but what you choose, and shall be as happy as the day is long, and shall keep Cousin Clifford in spirits with the wisdom and pleasantness which is always dropping from your lips!"

"Ah! my dear child," quoth good Uncle Venner, quite overcome, "if you were to speak to a young man as you do to an old one, his chance of keeping his heart another minute would not be worth one of the buttons on my waistcoat! And—soul alive!—that great sigh, which you made me heave, has burst off the very last of them! But never mind! It was the happiest sigh I ever did heave; and it seems as if I must have drawn in a gulp of heavenly breath, to make it with. Well, well, Miss Phœbe! They'll miss me in the gardens, hereabouts, and round by the back-doors; and Pyncheon-street, I'm afraid, will hardly look the same without old Uncle Venner, who remembers it with a mowing field on one side, and the garden of the seven gables on the other. But either I must go to your country-seat, or you must come to my farm—that's one of two things certain; and I leave you to choose which!"

"O, come with us, by all means, Uncle Venner!" said Clifford, who had a remarkable enjoyment of the old man's mellow, quiet, and simple spirit. "I want you always to be within five minutes' saunter of my chair. You are the only philosopher I ever knew of, whose wisdom has not a drop of bitter essence at the bottom!"

"Dear me!" cried Uncle Venner, beginning partly to realize what manner of man he was. "And yet folks used to set me down among the simple ones, in my younger days! But I suppose I am

like a Roxbury russet,—a great deal better, the longer I can be kept. Y and my words of wisdom, that you a Phœbe tell me of, are like the gol dandelions, which never grow in hot months, but may be seen glisten among the withered grass, and un the dry leaves, sometimes as late December. And you are welco friends, to my mess of dandelions there were twice as many!"

A plain, but handsome, dark-gr barouche had now drawn up in fr of the ruinous portal of the old mansi house. The party came forth, and (w the exception of good Uncle Venn who was to follow in a few days) ceeded to take their places. They w chatting and laughing very pleasa together; and—as proves to be often case, at moments when we ought palpitate with sensibility—Clifford Hepzibah bade a final farewell to abode of their forefathers, with har more emotion than if they had m it their arrangement to return thithe tea-time. Several children were dr to the spot by so unusual a specta as the barouche and pair of gray hor Recognizing little Ned Higgins am them, Hepzibah put her hand into pocket, and presented the urchin, earliest and staunchest customer, silver enough to people the Domda cavern of his interior with as var a procession of quadrupeds as pas into the ark.

Two men were passing, just as barouche drove off.

"Well, Dixey," said one of th "what do you think of this? My kept a cent-shop three months, and five dollars on her outlay. Old M Pyncheon has been in trade just a

long, and rides off in her carriage
h a couple of hundred thousand,—
koning her share, and Clifford's, and
œbe's,—and some say twice as much!
you choose to call it luck, it is all
ry well; but if we are to take it as the
l of Providence, why, I can't exactly
hom it!"

'Pretty good business!" quoth the
racious Dixey. "Pretty good business!"

Maule's well, all this time, though left
solitude, was throwing up a succes-
n of kaleidoscopic pictures, in which
gifted eye might have seen fore-
.dowed the coming fortunes of Hepzi-
a and Clifford, and the descendant of

the legendary wizard, and the village-
maiden, over whom he had thrown
love's web of sorcery. The Pyncheon-
elm, moreover, with what foliage the
September gale had spared to it, whispered unintelligible prophecies. And wise
Uncle Venner, passing slowly from the
ruinous porch, seemed to hear a strain
of music, and fancied that sweet Alice
Pyncheon—after witnessing these deeds,
this by-gone woe, and this present
happiness, of her kindred mortals—had
given one farewell touch of a spirit's joy
upon her harpsichord, as she floated
heavenward from the HOUSE OF THE
SEVEN GABLES!